Mind Dimensions
Books 0, 1, & 2

Dima Zales

♠ Mozaika Publications ♠

Copyright © 2015 Dima Zales
www.dimazales.com

Published by Mozaika Publications, an imprint of Mozaika LLC.
www.mozaikallc.com

Cover by Najla Qamber Designs
www.najlaqamberdesigns.com

e-ISBN:978-1-63142-079-5
Print ISBN:978-1-63142-080-1

MIND DIMENSIONS

The Thought Readers

Mind Dimensions: Book 1

DESCRIPTION

Everyone thinks I'm a genius.

Everyone is wrong.

Sure, I finished Harvard at eighteen and now make crazy money at a hedge fund. But that's not because I'm unusually smart or hardworking.

It's because I cheat.

You see, I have a unique ability. I can go outside time into my own personal version of reality—the place I call "the Quiet"—where I can explore my surroundings while the rest of the world stands still.

I thought I was the only one who could do this—until I met *her*.

My name is Darren, and this is how I learned that I'm a Reader.

CHAPTER ONE

Sometimes I think I'm crazy. I'm sitting at a casino table in Atlantic City, and everyone around me is motionless. I call this the *Quiet*, as though giving it a name makes it seem more real—as though giving it a name changes the fact that all the players around me are frozen like statues, and I'm walking among them, looking at the cards they've been dealt.

The problem with the theory of my being crazy is that when I 'unfreeze' the world, as I just have, the cards the players turn over are the same ones I just saw in the Quiet. If I were crazy, wouldn't these cards be different? Unless I'm so far gone that I'm imagining the cards on the table, too.

But then I also win. If that's a delusion—if the pile of chips on my side of the table is a delusion—then I might as well question everything. Maybe my name isn't even Darren.

No. I can't think that way. If I'm really that confused, I don't want to snap out of it—because if I do, I'll probably wake up in a mental hospital.

Besides, I love my life, crazy and all.

My shrink thinks the Quiet is an inventive way I describe the 'inner workings of my genius.' Now that sounds crazy to me. She also might want me, but that's beside the point. Suffice it to say, she's as far as it gets from my datable age range, which is currently right around twenty-four. Still young, still hot, but done with school and pretty much beyond the clubbing phase. I hate clubbing, almost as much as I hated studying. In any case, my shrink's explanation doesn't work, as it doesn't account for the way I know things even a genius wouldn't know—like the exact value and suit of the other players' cards.

I watch as the dealer begins a new round. Besides me, there are three players at the table: Grandma, the Cowboy, and the Professional, as I call them. I feel that now-almost-imperceptible fear that accompanies the phasing. That's what I call the process: phasing into the Quiet. Worrying about my sanity has always facilitated phasing; fear seems helpful in this process.

I phase in, and everything gets quiet. Hence the name for this state.

It's eerie to me, even now. Outside the Quiet, this casino is very loud: drunk people talking, slot machines, ringing of wins, music—the only place louder is a club or a concert. And yet, right at this moment, I could probably hear a pin drop. It's like I've gone deaf to the chaos that surrounds me.

Having so many frozen people around adds to the strangeness of it all. Here is a waitress stopped mid-step, carrying a tray with drinks. There is a woman about to pull a slot machine lever. At my own table, the dealer's hand is raised, the last card he dealt hanging unnaturally in midair. I walk up to him from the side of the table and reach for it. It's a king, meant for the Professional. Once I let the card go, it falls on the table rather than continuing to float as before—but I know full well that it will be back in the air, in the exact position it was when I grabbed it, when I phase out.

The Professional looks like someone who makes money playing poker, or at least the way I always imagined someone like that might look. Scruffy, shades on, a little sketchy-looking. He's been doing an excellent job with the poker face—basically not twitching a single muscle throughout the game. His face is so expressionless that I wonder if he might've gotten Botox to help maintain such a stony countenance. His hand is on the table, protectively covering the cards dealt to him.

I move his limp hand away. It feels normal. Well, in a manner of speaking. The hand is sweaty and hairy, so moving it aside is unpleasant and is admittedly an abnormal thing to do. The normal part is that the hand is warm, rather than cold. When I was a kid, I expected people to feel cold in the Quiet, like stone statues.

With the Professional's hand moved away, I pick up his cards. Combined with the king that was hanging in the air, he has a nice high pair. Good to know.

I walk over to Grandma. She's already holding her cards, and she has fanned them nicely for me. I'm able to avoid touching her wrinkled, spotted hands. This is a relief, as I've recently become conflicted about touching people—or, more specifically, women—in the Quiet. If I had to, I would rationalize touching Grandma's hand as harmless, or at least not creepy, but it's better to avoid it if possible.

In any case, she has a low pair. I feel bad for her. She's been losing a lot tonight. Her chips are dwindling. Her losses are due, at least partially, to the fact that she has a terrible poker face. Even before looking at her cards, I knew they wouldn't be good because I could tell she was disappointed as soon as her hand was dealt. I also caught a gleeful gleam in her eyes a few rounds ago when she had a winning three of a kind.

This whole game of poker is, to a large degree, an exercise in reading people—something I really want to get better at. At my job, I've been told I'm great at reading people. I'm not, though; I'm just good at using the Quiet to make it seem like I am. I do want to learn how to read people for real, though. It would be nice to know what everyone is thinking.

What I don't care that much about in this poker game is money. I do well enough financially to not have to depend on hitting it big gambling. I don't care if I win or lose, though quintupling my money back at the blackjack table was fun. This whole trip has been more about going gambling because I finally *can*, being twenty-one and all. I was never into fake IDs, so this is an actual milestone for me.

Leaving Grandma alone, I move on to the next player—the Cowboy. I can't resist taking off his straw hat and trying it on. I wonder if it's possible for me to get lice this way. Since I've never been able to bring back any inanimate objects from the Quiet, nor otherwise affect the real world in any lasting way, I figure I won't be able to get any living critters to come back with me either.

Dropping the hat, I look at his cards. He has a pair of aces—a better hand than the Professional. Maybe the Cowboy is a professional, too. He has a good poker face, as far as I can tell. It'll be interesting to watch those two in this round.

Next, I walk up to the deck and look at the top cards, memorizing them. I'm not leaving anything to chance.

When my task in the Quiet is complete, I walk back to myself. Oh, yes, did I mention that I see myself sitting there, frozen like the rest of them? That's the weirdest part. It's like having an out-of-body experience.

Approaching my frozen self, I look at him. I usually avoid doing this, as it's too unsettling. No amount of looking in the mirror—or seeing videos of yourself on YouTube—can prepare you for viewing your own three-dimensional body up close. It's not something anyone is meant to experience. Well, aside from identical twins, I guess.

It's hard to believe that this person is me. He looks more like some random guy. Well, maybe a bit better than that. I do find this guy interesting. He looks cool. He looks smart. I think women would probably consider him good-looking, though I know that's not a modest thing to think.

It's not like I'm an expert at gauging how attractive a guy is, but some things are common sense. I can tell when a dude is ugly, and this frozen me is not. I also know that generally, being good-looking requires a symmetrical face, and the statue of me has that. A strong jaw doesn't hurt either. Check. Having broad shoulders is a positive, and being tall really helps. All covered. I have blue eyes—that seems to be a plus. Girls have told me they like my eyes, though right now, on the frozen me, the eyes look creepy. Glassy. They look like the eyes of a lifeless wax figure.

Realizing that I'm dwelling on this subject way too long, I shake my head. I can just picture my shrink analyzing this moment. Who would imagine admiring themselves like this as part of their mental illness? I can just picture her scribbling down *Narcissist* and underlining it for emphasis.

Enough. I need to leave the Quiet. Raising my hand, I touch my frozen self on the forehead, and I hear noise again as I phase out.

Everything is back to normal.

The card that I looked at a moment ago—the king that I left on the table—is in the air again, and from there it follows the trajectory it was always meant to, landing near the Professional's hands. Grandma is still eyeing her fanned cards in disappointment, and the Cowboy has his hat on again, though I took it off him in the Quiet. Everything is exactly as it was.

On some level, my brain never ceases to be surprised at the discontinuity of the experience in the Quiet and outside it. As humans, we're hardwired to question reality when such things happen. When I was trying to outwit my shrink early on in my therapy, I once read an entire psychology textbook during our session. She, of course, didn't notice it, as I did it in the Quiet. The book talked about how babies as young as two months old are surprised if they see something out of the ordinary, like gravity appearing to work backwards. It's no wonder my brain has trouble adapting. Until I was ten, the world behaved normally, but everything has been weird since then, to put it mildly.

Glancing down, I realize I'm holding three of a kind. Next time, I'll look at my cards before phasing. If I have something this strong, I might take my chances and play fair.

The game unfolds predictably because I know everybody's cards. At the end, Grandma gets up. She's clearly lost enough money.

And that's when I see the girl for the first time.

She's hot. My friend Bert at work claims that I have a 'type,' but I reject that idea. I don't like to think of myself as shallow or predictable. But I might actually be a bit of both, because this girl fits Bert's description of my type to a T. And my reaction is extreme interest, to say the least.

Large blue eyes. Well-defined cheekbones on a slender face, with a hint of something exotic. Long, shapely legs, like those of a dancer. Dark wavy hair in a ponytail—a hairstyle that I like. And without bangs—even better. I hate bangs—not sure why girls do that to themselves. Though lack of bangs is not, strictly speaking, in Bert's description of my type, it probably should be.

I continue staring at her as she joins my table. With her high heels and tight skirt, she's overdressed for this place. Or maybe I'm underdressed in my jeans and t-shirt. Either way, I don't care. I have to try to talk to her.

I debate phasing into the Quiet and approaching her, so I can do something creepy like stare at her up close, or maybe even snoop in her pockets. Anything to help me when I talk to her.

I decide against it, which is probably the first time that's ever happened.

I know that my reasoning for breaking my usual habit is strange. If you can even call it reasoning. I picture the following chain of events: she agrees to date me, we go out for a while, we get serious, and because of the deep connection we have, I come clean about the Quiet. She learns I did something creepy and has a fit, then dumps me. It's ridiculous to think this, of course, considering that we haven't even spoken yet. Talk about jumping the gun. She might have an IQ below seventy, or the personality of a piece of wood. There can be twenty different reasons why I wouldn't want to date her. And besides, it's not all up to me. She might tell me to go fuck myself as soon as I try to talk to her.

Still, working at a hedge fund has taught me to hedge. As crazy as that reasoning is, I stick with my decision not to phase because I know it's the gentlemanly thing to do. In keeping with this unusually chivalrous me, I also decide not to cheat at this round of poker.

As the cards are dealt again, I reflect on how good it feels to have done the honorable thing—even without anyone knowing. Maybe I should try to respect people's privacy more often. *Yeah, right.* I have to be realistic. I wouldn't be where I am today if I'd followed that advice. In fact, if I made a habit of respecting people's privacy, I would lose my job within days—and with it, a lot of the comforts I've become accustomed to.

Copying the Professional's move, I cover my cards with my hand as soon as I receive them. I'm about to sneak a peek at what I was dealt when something unusual happens.

The world goes quiet, just like it does when I phase in . . . but I did nothing this time.

And at that moment, I see *her*—the girl sitting across the table from me, the girl I was just thinking about. She's standing next to me, pulling her hand away from mine. Or, strictly speaking, from my frozen self's hand—as I'm standing a little to the side looking at her.

She's also still sitting in front of me at the table, a frozen statue like all the others.

My mind goes into overdrive as my heartbeat jumps. I don't even consider the possibility of that second girl being a twin sister or something like that. I know it's her. She's doing what I did just a few minutes ago. She's walking in the Quiet. The world around us is frozen, but we are not.

A horrified look crosses her face as she realizes the same thing. Before I can react, she lunges across the table and touches her own forehead.

The world becomes normal again.

She stares at me from across the table, shocked, her eyes huge and her face pale. She rises to her feet. Without so much as a word, she turns and begins walking away, then breaks into a run a couple of seconds later.

Getting over my own shock, I get up and run after her. It's not exactly smooth. If she notices a guy she doesn't know running after her, dating will be the last thing on her mind. But I'm beyond that now. She's the only person I've met who can do what I do. She's proof that I'm not insane. She might have what I want most in the world.

She might have answers.

CHAPTER TWO

Running after someone in a casino is harder than I imagined, making me wish I'd downed fewer drinks. I dodge elbows and try not to trip over people's feet. I even debate phasing into the Quiet to get my bearings, but decide against it because the casino will still be just as crowded when I phase back out.

Just as I begin to close in on the girl, she turns the corner into a hall leading to the main lobby. I have to get there as quickly as I can, or she'll get away. My heart hammers in my chest as I fleetingly wonder what I'll say to her when I catch up. Before I get far with that thought, two guys in suits step directly into my path.

"Sir," one of the guys says, almost giving me a heart attack. Though I'd spotted them in my periphery, I was so focused on the girl that I hadn't truly registered their presence. The guy who just spoke to me is huge, a mountain in a suit. This can't be good.

"Whatever you guys are selling, I'm not interested," I say, hoping to bluff my way out of this. When they don't look convinced, I add pointedly, "I'm in a rush," and try to look beyond them to emphasize my haste. I hope I look confident, even though my palms are sweating like crazy and I'm panting from my run.

"I'm sorry, but I must insist that you come with us," says the second guy, moving in closer. Unlike his rotund monster of a partner, this guy is lean and extremely buff. They both look like bouncers. I guess they get suspicious when some idiot starts running through the casino. They're probably trained to assume theft or something else shady. Which, to be fair, does make sense.

"Gentlemen," I try again, keeping my voice even and polite, "with all due respect, I really am in a rush. Any way you can frisk me quickly or something? I'm trying to catch up with someone." I add that last part both to deflect suspicion of nefarious activity and because it's the truth.

"You really ought to come with us," the fatter one says, his jaw set stubbornly. They each keep one of their hands near their inner jacket pockets. Oh, great. Just my luck, they're armed.

Struggling to find a way to deal with this unexpected event, I channel the natural fear from my situation into phasing. Once I enter the Quiet, I find myself standing to the side of our not-so-friendly duo, with the world mute again. I immediately resume running, no longer caring about bumping into the immobile people blocking my way. It's not rude to shove them aside here, since they won't know any of this, nor feel anything when the world returns to normal.

When I get to the hall, the girl is already gone, so I move on to the lobby and methodically search for her. Seeing a girl with a ponytail near the elevator, I run over and grab her. As I turn her to get a look at her face, I wonder if my touch will also bring her into the Quiet. I'm pretty sure that's what happened before—she touched me and brought me in.

But nothing happens this time, and the face that looks at me is completely unfamiliar.

Damn it. I've got the wrong person.

My frustration turns to anger as I realize that I lost her because those idiots delayed me at the most critical moment. Fuming, I punch a nearby person with all my strength, needing to vent. As is always the case in the Quiet, the object of my aggression doesn't react in any way. Unfortunately, I don't really feel better either.

Before I decide on my next course of action, I think about what happened at the table. The girl somehow got me to phase into the Quiet, and she was already there. When she saw me, she freaked out and ran. Maybe, like me, this was the first time she's seen anyone 'alive' in there. Everyone reacts differently to strange events, and meeting another person after years of being solo in the Quiet definitely qualifies as strange.

Standing here thinking about it isn't going to get me any answers, so I decide to be thorough and take one more look at the lobby again.

No luck. The girl is nowhere to be found.

Next, I go outside and walk around the casino driveway, trying to see if I can spot her there. I even look inside a few idling cabs, but she's not there either.

Looking up at the flashy building towering over me, I consider searching every room in the hotel. There are at least a couple thousand of them. It would take me a long time, but it might be worth it. I have to find her and get some answers.

Although thoroughly searching a building that huge seems like a daunting task, it wouldn't be impossible—at least not for me. I don't get hungry, thirsty, or even tired in the Quiet. Never need to use the bathroom either. It's very handy for situations like these, when you need to give yourself extra time. I can theoretically search every room—provided I can figure out how to get in. Those electronic doors won't work in the Quiet, not even if I have the original key from the room's occupants. Technology doesn't usually function here; it's frozen along with everything else. Unless it's something mechanical and simple, like my wind-up watch, it won't work— and even my watch I have to wind every time I'm in the Quiet.

Weighing my options, I try to imagine having to use physical force to break into thousands of hotel doors. Since my iPhone is sadly another technology casualty of the Quiet, I wouldn't even be able to listen to some tunes to kill the time. Even for a cause this important, I'm not sure I want to go to those extremes.

Besides, if I do decide to search the building, now probably isn't the best time to do it. Even if I find her, I won't be able to go after her in the real world thanks to those idiot guards in my way. I need to get rid of them before determining what to do next.

Sighing, I slowly walk back to the hotel. When I enter the lobby, I scan it again, hoping that I somehow missed her the first time. I feel that same compulsion I get when I lose something around the house. When that happens, I always search the place from top to bottom and then start doing it again— looking in the same places I already checked, irrationally hoping that the third time will be the charm. Or maybe the fourth. I really need to stop doing that. As Einstein said, insanity is doing the same thing over and over again and expecting different results.

Finally admitting defeat, I approach the bouncers. I can spend forever in the Quiet, but when I get out, they'll still be here. There's no avoiding that.

Moving in close, I look in the pocket of the fatter guy to find out what I'm up against. According to his ID, his name is Nick Shifer, and he's with security. So I was right—he's a bouncer. His driver's license is also there, as well as a small family photo. I study both, in case I need the information later.

Next, I turn my attention to the pocket near which Nick's hand is hovering. Looks like I was right again: he has a gun. If I took this gun and shot Nick at close range, he would get a bloody wound and likely fall from the impact. He wouldn't scream, though, and he wouldn't clutch his chest. And when

I phase out, he would be whole again, with no signs of damage. It would be like nothing happened.

Don't ask me how I know what happens when you shoot someone in the Quiet. Or stab him. Or hit him with a baseball bat. Or whack him with a golf club. Or kick him in the balls. Or drop bricks on his head—or a TV. The only thing I can say is that I can unequivocally confirm that in a wide variety of cruel and unusual experiments, the subjects turn out to be unharmed once I phase out of the Quiet.

Okay, that's enough reminiscing. Right now, I have a problem to solve, and I need to be careful, with the guns being involved and all.

I smack my frozen self on the back of the head to phase out of the Quiet.

The world unfreezes, and I'm back with the bouncers in real time. I try to look calm, as though I haven't been running around like a crazy man looking for whoever this girl is—because for them, none of that has happened.

"Okay, Nick, I'll be happy to accompany you and resolve this misunderstanding," I say in my most compliant tone.

Nick's eyes widen at hearing his name. "How do you know me?"

"You read the file, Nick," his lean partner says, obviously unimpressed. "The kid is very clever."

The file? What the hell is he talking about? I've never been to this casino before. Oh, and I would love to know how being clever would help someone know the name of a complete stranger on a moment's notice. People always say stuff like that about me, even though it makes no sense. I debate phasing into the Quiet to learn the second guy's name as well, just to mess with them more, but I decide against it. It would be overkill. Instead I decide to mentally refer to the lean guy as Buff.

"Just come with me quietly, please," Buff says. He stands aside, so that he's able to walk behind me. Nick leads the way, muttering something about the impossibility of my knowing his name, no matter how smart I am. He's clearly brighter than Buff. I wonder what he would say if I told him where he lives and that he has two kids. Would he start a cult, or shoot me?

As we make the trek through the casino, I reflect on how knowing things I shouldn't has served me well over the years. It's kind of my thing, and it's gotten me far in life. Of course, it's possible that knowing things I shouldn't is also the reason they have a file on me. Maybe casinos keep records on people who seem to have a history of beating the odds, so to speak.

When we get to the office—a modest-sized room filled with cameras overlooking different parts of the casino—Buff's first question confirms that theory. "Do you know how much money you won today?" he asks, glaring at me.

I decide to play dumb. "I'm not sure."

"You're quite the statistical anomaly," Nick says. He's clearly proud of knowing such big words. "I want to show you something." He takes a remote from the desk, which has a bunch of folders scattered on its surface. With Nick's press of a button, one of the monitors begins showing footage of me playing at the blackjack table. Watching it, I realize that I did win too much.

In fact, I won just about every time.

Shit. Could I have been any more obvious? I didn't think I'd be watched this closely, but that was stupid of me. I should've taken a couple of hits even when I knew I would bust, just to hide my tracks.

"You're obviously counting cards," Nick states, giving me a hard stare. "There's no other explanation."

Actually, there is, but I'm not about to give it to him. "With eight decks?" I say instead, making my voice as incredulous as possible.

Nick picks up a file on the desk and leafs through it.

"Darren Wang Goldberg, graduated from Harvard with an MBA and a law degree at eighteen. Near-perfect SAT, LSAT, GMAT, and GRE scores. CFA, CPA, plus a bunch more acronyms." Nick chuckles as if amused at that last tidbit, but then his expression hardens as he continues. "The list goes on and on. If anyone could do it, it would be you."

I take a deep breath, trying to contain my annoyance. "Since you're so impressed with my bona fides, you should trust me when I tell you that no one can count cards with eight decks." I have no clue if that's actually true, but I do know casinos have been trying to stack the odds in the house's favor for ages now, and eight decks is too many cards to count even for a mathematical prodigy.

As if reading my mind, Buff says, "Yeah, well, even if you can't do it by yourself, you might be able to pull it off with partners."

Partners? Where did they get the idea that I have partners?

In response to my blank look, Nick hits the remote again, and I see a new recording. This time it's of the girl—of her winning at the blackjack table, then working a number of poker tables. Winning an impressive amount of cash, I might add.

"Another statistical anomaly," Nick says, looking at me intently. "A friend of yours?" He must've

25

worked as a detective before this gig, seeing as how he's pretty good at this interrogation thing. I guess my chasing her through the casino set off some red flags. My reaction was definitely not for the reasons he thinks, though.

"No," I say truthfully. "I've never seen her before in my life."

Nick's face tightens with anger. "You just played at the same poker table," he says, his voice growing in volume with every word. "Then you both started running away just as we were coming toward you. I suppose that's just a coincidence, huh? Do the two of you have someone on the inside? Who else is in on it?" He's full-on yelling at this point, spittle flying in every direction.

This fierce grilling is too much for me, and I phase into the Quiet to give myself a few moments to think.

Contrary to Nick's belief, the girl and I are definitely not partners. Yet it's obvious she was here doing the same thing I was, as the recordings clearly show her winning over and over. That means I didn't have a hallucination, and she really was in the Quiet somehow. She can do what I can. My heart beats faster with excitement as I realize again that I'm not the only one. This girl is like me—which means I really need to find her.

On a hunch, I approach the table and pick up the thickest folder I see.

And that's when I hit the biggest jackpot of the night.

Staring back at me from the file is her picture. Her real name, according to the file, is Mira Tsiolkovsky. She lives in Brooklyn, New York.

Her age shocks me. She's only eighteen. I thought she'd be in her mid-twenties—which would conveniently fit right within my datable age range. As I further investigate the information they've compiled on her, I find the reason I was fooled by her age: she intentionally tries to make herself look older to get into casinos. The folder lists a bunch of her aliases, all of which are banned from casinos. All are aged between twenty-one and twenty-five.

According to the folder, she does this cheating thing professionally. One section details her involvement in cheating both in casinos and underground gambling joints. Scary places by the sound of it, with links to organized crime.

She sounds reckless. I, on the other hand, am most decidedly not reckless. I use my strange ability to make money in the financial industry, which is much safer than what Mira does. Not to mention, the kind of money I bring in through legitimate channels makes the risks of cheating in casinos far outweigh the benefits—especially given what I'm learning today. Apparently casinos don't sit idly by while you take their money. They start files on you if they think you're likely to cheat them, and they blacklist you if you get too lucky. Seems unfair, but I guess it makes business sense.

Returning my attention to the file, I find little personal information beyond her name and address—just other casinos, games, and the amounts she's won under different aliases, plus pictures. She's good at changing her appearance; all the pictures feature women who look very different from one another. Impressive.

Having memorized as much of Mira's file as I can, I walk over to Nick and take my own file from his hands.

I'm relieved to find that there's not much to this folder. They have my name and address, which they must've gotten from the credit card I used to pay for drinks. They know that I work at a hedge fund and that I've never had problems with the law—all stuff easily found on the web. Same goes for Harvard and my other achievements. They probably just did a Google search on me once they knew my name.

Reading the file makes me feel better. They're not on to me or anything like that. They probably just saw me winning too much and decided to nip the situation in the bud. The best thing to do at this point is to placate them, so I can go home and digest all this. No need to search the hotel anymore. I have more than enough information about Mira now, and my friend Bert can help me fill in the rest of the puzzle.

Thus resolved, I walk back to myself. My frozen self's face looks scared, but I don't feel scared anymore because I now have a plan.

Taking a deep breath, I touch my frozen forehead again and phase out.

Nick is still yelling at me, so I tell him politely, "Sir, I'm sorry, but I don't know what or whom you're talking about. I was lucky, yes, but I didn't cheat." My voice quavers on that last bit. I might be overacting now, but I want to be convincing as a scared young man. "I'll be happy to leave the money and never come back to this casino again."

"You *are* going to leave the money, and you won't ever come back to this *city* again," corrects Buff.

"Fine, I won't. I was just here to have fun," I say in a steadier but still deferential voice, like I'm totally in awe of their authority. "I just turned twenty-one and it's Labor Day weekend, so I went gambling for the first time," I add. This should add an air of sincerity, because it's the truth. "I work at a hedge fund. I don't need to cheat for money."

Nick snorts. "Please. Guys like you cheat because you like the rush of being so much smarter than everyone else."

Despite his obvious contempt for me, I don't reply. Every remark I form in my head sounds snide. Instead I just continue groveling, saying that I know nothing, gradually becoming more and more polite. They keep asking me about Mira and about how I cheat, and I keep denying it. The conversation goes in circles for a while. I can tell they're getting as tired of it as I am—maybe more so.

Seeing an opening, I go in for the kill. "I need to know how much longer I'll be detained, sir," I tell Nick, "so that I can notify my family."

The implication is that people will wonder where I am if I don't show up soon. Also, my subtle use of the word 'detained' reminds them of the legality of their position—or more likely, the lack thereof.

Frowning, but apparently unwilling to give in, Nick says stubbornly, "You can leave as soon as you tell us something useful." There isn't much conviction in his voice, though, and I can tell that my question hit the mark. He's just saving face at this point.

Doggedly continuing the interrogation, he asks me the same questions again, to which I respond with the same answers. After a couple of minutes, Buff touches his shoulder. They exchange a look.

"Wait here," Buff says. They leave, presumably to have a quick discussion out of my earshot.

I wish I could listen in, but sadly it's not possible with the Quiet. Well, that's not entirely true. If I learned to read lips and phased in and out very quickly, I could probably piece together some of the conversation by looking at their frozen faces, over and over again. But that would be a long, tedious process. Plus, I don't need to do that. I can use logic to figure out the gist of what they're saying. I'm guessing it goes something like this: "The kid's too smart for us; we should let him go, get doughnuts, and swing by a strip club."

They return after a few minutes, and Buff tells me, "We're going to let you go, but we don't want to see you—or your girlfriend—here ever again." I can tell Nick isn't happy about having to abandon his questioning without getting the answers he wanted, but he doesn't voice any objections.

I suppress a relieved sigh. I half-thought they'd rough me up or something. It would've sucked, but it wouldn't have been unexpected—or perhaps even undeserved, given that I did cheat. But then again, they have no proof that I cheated. And they probably think I'm clever enough to cause legal problems—particularly given my law degree.

Of course, it's also possible that they know more about me than what's in the file. Maybe they've come across some info about my moms. Oh yeah, did I mention that I have two moms? Well, I do. Trust me, I know how strange that sounds. And before there's any temptation, I never want to hear another joke on the subject. I got enough of that in school. Even in college, people used to say shit sometimes. I usually made sure they regretted it, of course.

In any case, Lucy, who is my adoptive mom—but is nonetheless the most awesome mom ever—is a tough-as-nails detective. If these bozos laid a finger on me, she'd probably track them down and personally kick their asses with a baseball bat. She also has a team that reports to her, and they would likely chime in, too. And Sara, my biological mom—who is usually quite peace-loving—wouldn't stop her. Not in this case.

Nick and Buff are silent as they lead me out of their office and through the casino to the cab waiting area outside.

"If you come here again," Nick says as I get into an empty cab, "I'll break something of yours. Personally."

I nod and quickly close the door. All he had to do was ask me nicely like that. In retrospect, Atlantic City wasn't even that much fun.

I'm convinced I won't ever want to come back.

CHAPTER THREE

I start my post-Labor Day Tuesday morning feeling like a zombie. I couldn't fall asleep after the events at the casino, but I can't skip work today. I have an appointment with Bill.

Bill is my boss, and no one ever calls him that—except me, in my thoughts. His name is William Pierce. As in Pierce Capital Management. Even his wife calls him William—I've heard her do it. Most people call him Mr. Pierce, because they're uncomfortable calling him by his first name. So, yeah, Bill is among the few people I take seriously. Even if, in this case, I'd rather nap than meet with him.

I wish it were possible to sleep in the Quiet. Then I'd be all set. I'd phase in and snooze right under my desk without anyone noticing.

I achieve some semblance of clear thought after my first cup of coffee. I'm in my cubicle at this point. It's eight a.m. If you think that's early, you're wrong. I was actually the last to get into the office in my part of the floor. I don't care what those early risers think of my lateness, though. I can barely function as is.

Despite my achievements at the fund, I don't have an office. Bill has the only office in the company. It would be nice to have some privacy for slacking off, but otherwise, I'm content with my cube. As long as I can work in the field or from home most of the time—and as long as I get paid on par with people who typically have offices—the lack of my own office doesn't bother me.

My computer is on, and I'm looking at the list of coworkers on the company instant messenger. Aha—I see Bert's name come online. This is really early for him. As our best hacker, he gets to stroll in whenever he wants, and he knows it. Like me, he doesn't care what anyone else thinks about it. In fact, he probably cares even less than I do—and thus comes in even later. I initially thought we would talk after my meeting with Bill, but there's no time like the present, since Bert is in already.

"Stop by," I message him. "Need your unique skills."

"BRT," Bert replies. *Be right there.*

I've known Bert for years. Unlike me, he's a real prodigy. We were the only fourteen-year-olds in a Harvard *Introduction to Computer Science* course that year. He aced the course without having to phase into the Quiet and look up the answers in the textbook, the way I did in the middle of the exams. Nor did he pay a guy from Belarus to write his programing projects for him.

Bert is *the* computer guy at Pierce. He's probably the most capable coder in New York City. He always drops hints that he used to work for some intelligence agency as a contractor before I got him to join me here and make some real money.

"Darren," says Bert's slightly nasal voice, and I swivel my chair in response.

Picturing this guy as part of the CIA or FBI always puts a smile on my face. He's around five-four, and probably weighs less than a hundred pounds. Before we became friends, my nickname for Bert was Mini-Me.

"So, Albert, we should discuss that idea you gave me last week," I begin, jerking my chin toward one of our public meeting rooms.

"Yes, I would love to hear your report," Bert responds as we close the door. He always overacts this part.

As soon as we're alone, he drops the formal colleague act. "Dude, you fucking did it? You went to Vegas?"

"Well, not quite. I didn't feel like taking a five-hour flight—"

"So you opted for a two-hour cab ride to Atlantic City instead," Bert interrupts, grinning.

"Yes, exactly." I grin back, taking a sip of my coffee.

"Classic Darren. And then?"

"They banned me," I say triumphantly, like it's some huge accomplishment.

"Already?"

"Yeah. But not before I met this chick." I pause for dramatic effect. I know this is the part he's really waiting for. His own experience with girls thus far has been horrendous.

Sure enough, he's hooked. He wants to know every detail. I tell him a variation of what happened. Nothing about the Quiet, of course. I don't share that with anyone, except my shrink. I just tell Bert I won a lot. He loves that part, as he was the one who suggested I try going to a casino. This was after he and a bunch of our coworkers got slaughtered by me at a friendly card game.

He, like most at the fund, knows that I know things I shouldn't. He just doesn't know *how* I know them. He accepts it as a given, though. In a way, Bert is a little bit like me. He knows things he shouldn't, too. Only in his case, everyone knows the 'how.' The method behind Bert's omniscience is his ability to get into any computer system he wants.

That is precisely what I need from him now, so as soon I finish describing the mystery girl, I tell him, "I need your help."

His eyebrows rise, and I explain, "I need to learn more about her. Whatever you can find out would be helpful."

"What?" His excitement noticeably wanes. "No, Darren, I can't."

"You owe me," I remind him.

"Yeah, but this is cyber-crime." He looks stubborn, and I mentally sigh. If I had a dollar for every time Bert used that line . . . We both know he commits cyber-crime on a daily basis.

I decide to offer him a bribe. "I'll watch a card trick," I say, making a Herculean effort to inject some enthusiasm into my voice. Bert's attempts at card tricks are abysmal, but that doesn't deter him one bit.

"Oh," Bert responds casually. His poker face is shit, though. I know he's about to try to get more out of me, but it's not going to happen, and I tell him so.

"Fine, fine, text me those aliases you mentioned, the ones that 'fell into your lap,' and the address you 'got by chance,'" he says, giving in. "I'll see what I can do."

"Great, thanks." I grin at him again. "Now I have to go—I've got a meeting with Bill."

I can see him cringing when I call William that. I guess that's why I do it—to get a rise out of Bert.

"Hold on," he says, frowning.

I know what's coming, and I try not to look too impatient.

Bert is into magic. Only he isn't very good. He carries a deck of cards with him wherever he goes, and at any opportunity—real or imaginary—he whips the cards out and tries to do a card trick.

In my case, it's even worse. Because I showed off to him once, he thinks I'm into magic too, and that I only pretend I'm not. My tendency to win when playing cards only solidifies his conviction that I'm a closet magician.

As I promised him, I watch as he does his trick. I won't describe it. Suffice it to say, there are piles of cards on the conference room table, and I have to make choices and count and spell something while turning cards over.

"Great, good one, Bert," I lie as soon as my card is found. "Now I really have to go."

"Oh, come on," he cajoles. "Let me see your trick one more time."

I know it'll be faster for me to go along with him than to argue my way out of it. "Okay," I say, "you know the drill."

As Bert cuts the deck, I look away and phase into the Quiet.

As soon as the world freezes, I realize how much ambient noise the meeting room actually has. The lack of sound is refreshing. I feel it more keenly after being sleep-deprived. Partly because most of the 'feeling like crap' sensation dissipates when I'm in the Quiet, and partly because outside the Quiet, the sounds must've been exacerbating a minor headache that I only now realize is there.

Walking over to motionless Bert, I take the pile of cards in his hand and look at the card he cut to. Then I phase back out of the Quiet.

"Seven of hearts," I say without turning around. The sounds are back, and with them, the headache.

"Fuck," Bert says predictably. "We should go together. Get ourselves banned from Vegas next time."

"For that, I'll need a bigger favor." I wink at him and go back to my cubicle.

When I get to my desk, I see that it's time for my meeting. I quickly text Bert the information he needs to search for Mira and then head off to see Bill.

* * *

Bill's office looks as awesome as usual. It's the size of my Tribeca apartment. I've heard it said that he only has this huge office because that's what our clients expect to see when they visit. That he allegedly is egalitarian and would gladly sit in a cube with low walls, like the rest of us.

I'm not sure I buy that. The decorations are a little too meticulous to support that theory. Plus, he strikes me as a guy who likes his privacy.

One day I'll have an office too, unless I decide to retire first.

Bill looks like a natural-born leader. I can't put my finger on what attributes give this impression. Maybe it's his strong jaw, the wise warmth in his gaze, or the way he carries himself. Or maybe it's something else entirely. All I know is he looks like someone people would follow—and they do.

Bill earned major respect from me when he played a part in legalizing gay marriage in New York. My moms have dreamed of getting married for as long as I can remember, and anyone who helps make my moms happier is a good person in my book.

"Darren, please sit," he says, pulling his gaze from his monitor as I walk in.

"Hi William, how was your weekend?" I say. He's probably the only person in the office I bother doing the small-talk thing with. Even here, I ask mainly because I know Bill's answer will be blissfully brief. I don't care what my coworkers do in general, let alone on their weekends.

"Eventful," he says. "How about you?"

I try to beat his laconic response. "Interesting."

"Great." Like me, Bill doesn't seem interested in probing beyond that. "I have something for you. We're thinking about building a position in FBTI."

That's the ticker for Future Biotechnology and Innovation Corp; I've heard of them before. "Sure. We need a position in biotech," I say without blinking. In truth, I haven't bothered to look at our portfolio in a while. I just can't recall having biotech-related assignments recently—so I figure there can't be that many biotech stocks in there.

"Right," he says. "But this isn't just to diversify."

I nod, while trying to look my most serious and thoughtful. That's easier to do with Bill than with most other people. Sometimes I genuinely find what he says interesting.

"FBTI is going to unveil something three weeks from now," he explains. "The stock is up just based on speculation on the Street. It could be a nice short if FBTI disappoints—" he pauses for emphasis, "— but I personally have a hunch that things will go in the other direction."

"Well, to my knowledge, your hunches have never been wrong," I say. I know it sounds like I'm ass-kissing, but it's the truth.

"You know I never act on hunch alone," he says, doing this weird quirking thing he often does with his eyebrow. "In this case, maybe a hunch is understating things. I had some of FBTI's patents analyzed. Plenty of them are for very promising developments."

I'm convinced that I know where this is leading.

"Why don't you poke around?" he suggests, proving my conviction right. "Speak with them and see if the news is indeed bigger than what people are expecting. If that's the case, we need to start building the position."

"I'll do what I can," I say.

This generates a smile from Bill. "Was that humility? That would be a first," he says, seemingly amused. "I need you to do your usual magic. You're up for the challenge, right?"

"Of course. Whatever the news is, you'll know by the end of the week. I guarantee it." I don't add 'or your money back.' That would be too much. What if I get nothing? Bill is the type of person who would hold me to the claim.

"The sooner the better, but we definitely need it before the official news in three weeks," Bill says. "Now, if you'll excuse me."

Knowing that I'm dismissed, I leave him with his computer and go to my cube to make a few phone calls.

As soon as they hear the name Pierce, FBTI is happy to talk to me. I make an appointment with their CTO and am mentally planning the subway trip to their Manhattan office in SoHo when Bert pings me on Instant Messenger.

"Got it," the message says.

"Walk out with me?" I IM back.

He agrees, and we meet by the elevator.

"This chick is crazy," Bert says as I press the button for the lobby. "She leads a very strange life."

Outside his card tricks, Bert knows how to build suspense. I have to give him that. I don't rush him, or else this will take longer. So I just say, "Oh?"

"For starters, you're lucky you have me," he says, his voice brimming with excitement. "She's long gone from that address you found 'by chance.' From what I can puzzle out, that name—Mira—is her real one. Only that name disappeared from the face of the planet a little over a year ago. No electronic trail at all. Same thing with some of those aliases."

"Hmm," I say, giving him the encouragement I know he needs to keep going.

"Well, to get around that, I hacked into some Vegas casino databases, going on the assumption that she would play there as well as in Atlantic City, and sure enough, they had files on some of the other aliases that you mentioned. They also had additional names for her."

"Wow," is all I can say.

"Yeah," Bert agrees. "At first, only one led to any recently occupied address. She's clearly hiding. Anyway, that one alias, Alina something, had a membership at a gym on Kings Highway and Nostrand Avenue, in Brooklyn. Hacking into their system, I found out that the membership is still used sometimes. Once I had that, I set a radius around that gym. People don't usually go far to get workouts."

"Impressive," I say, and mean it. At times like this, I wonder if the business about him being a contractor for some intelligence agency is true after all.

"Anyway, at first there was nothing," he continues. "None of the aliases rent or own any apartments or condos nearby. But then I tried combining first names of some of these aliases with the last names of others." He pauses and looks at me—to get a pat on the back, I think.

"That's diabolical," I say, wishing he would get to the point already.

"Yes," he says, looking pleased. "I am, indeed . . . She, on the other hand, isn't very imaginative. One of the combinations worked. She's partial to the first name of Ilona. Combining Ilona with a last name of Derkovitch, from the Yulia Derkovitch alias, yielded the result I was looking for."

I nod, urging him on.

"Here's that address," he says, grinning as he hands me a piece of paper. Then he asks more seriously, "Are you really going there?"

That's an excellent question. If I do, she'll think I'm a crazy stalker. Well, I guess if you think about it,

I am kind of stalking her, but my motives are noble. Sort of.

"I don't know," I tell Bert. "I might swing by that gym and see if I can 'bump into her.'"

"I don't think that will work," he says. "According to their database, her visits are pretty sporadic."

"Great." I sigh. "In that case, yes, I guess I'll show up at her door."

"Okay. Now the usual fine print," Bert says, giving me an intense stare. "You didn't get this from me. Also, the name I found could be a complete coincidence, so it's within the realm of possibility that you might find someone else there."

"I take full responsibility for whatever may occur," I tell Bert solemnly. "We're even now."

"Okay. Good. There's just one other thing . . ."

"What?"

"Well, you might think this is crazy or paranoid, but—" he looks embarrassed, "—I think she might be a spy."

"What?" This catches me completely off-guard.

"Well, something else I should've said is that she's an immigrant. A Russian immigrant, in case you didn't get it from the unusual-sounding names. Came here with her family about a decade ago.

When combined with these aliases . . . You see how I would think along these lines, don't you?"

"Right, of course," I say, trying to keep a straight face. A spy? Bert sure loves his conspiracy theories. "Leave it with me," I say reassuringly. "If she's a spy, I'll deal with it. Now let me buy you a second breakfast and a cup of tea. After that, I'm off to SoHo to meet with FBTI."

CHAPTER FOUR

I make the trip to SoHo. The security guard at the FBTI building lets me in once he knows I have an appointment with Richard Stone, the CTO.

"Hi Richard, I'm Darren. We spoke on the phone." I introduce myself to a tall bald man when I'm seated comfortably in a guest chair in his office. The office is big, with a massive desk with lots of drawers, and a small bookshelf. There's even a plasma TV mounted on the wall. I take it all in, feeling a hint of office envy again.

"Please call me Dick," he says. I have to use every ounce of my willpower not to laugh. If I had a bald head, I'd definitely prefer Richard. In fact, I think I'd prefer to be called Richard over Dick regardless of how I looked.

"Okay, Dick. I'm interested in learning about what you guys are working on these days," I say, hoping I don't sound like I relish saying his nickname too much.

"I'm happy to discuss anything outside of our upcoming announcement," he says, his tone dickish enough to earn that moniker.

I show interest in the standard stuff he's prepared to say, and he goes on, telling me all the boring details he's allowed to share. He continues to talk, but I don't listen. Tuning people out was one of the first things I mastered in the corporate world. Without that, I wouldn't have survived a single meeting. Even now, I have to go into the Quiet from time to time to take a break, or I'd die from boredom. I'm not a patient guy.

Anyway, as Dick goes on, I surreptitiously look around. It's ironic that I'm doing exactly the opposite of what everyone thinks I do. People assume I ask pointed questions of these executives, and figure things out based on their reactions, body language, and who knows what else.

Being able to pick up on body cues and other nonverbal signals is something I want to learn at some point. I even gave it a try in Atlantic City. But in this case, as usual, I rely on something that depends far less on interpretive skills.

When I've endured enough bullshit from Dick, I try to invoke a frightened state of being so I can phase into the Quiet.

Simply thinking myself crazy is not that effective anymore. Picturing myself showing up like a dumbass at that Brooklyn address Bert gave me for Mira, on the other hand—that works like a charm.

I phase in, and Dick is finally, blissfully, quiet. He's frozen mid-sentence, and I realize, not for the first time, that I would have a huge edge if I were indeed able to read body cues. I recognize now that he's looking down, which I believe is a sign that someone's lying.

But no, instead of body language, I read literal language.

I begin with the papers on his desk. There's nothing special there.

Next, I roll his chair, with his frozen body in it, away from the desk. I love it when people in the Quiet are sitting in chairs with wheels. Makes this part of my job easier. In college, I realized I could get the contents of the final exams early by reaching into the professor's desk or bag in the Quiet. Moving the professors aside, though, had been a pain. Their chairs didn't have wheels like corporate office chairs do.

Thinking of those days in school makes me smile, because the things I learned in college are genuinely helpful to me now. This snooping in the Quiet—which is how I finished school so fast and with such good grades—is how I make a living now, and quite a good living at that. So, in some ways, my education really did prepare me for the workforce. Few people can say that.

With Dick and his chair out of the way, I turn my attention to his desk. In the bottom drawer, I hit the mother lode.

FBTI's big announcement will be about a device that will do something called 'transcranial magnetic stimulation.' I vaguely remember hearing about it. Before I delve deeper into the folder I found, I look at the bookshelf. Sure enough, on the shelf is something called *The Handbook of Transcranial Magnetic Stimulation*. It's funny. Now that I know what I'm looking for, I realize that aside from reading body language and cues like that, someone doing this 'for real' likely would've noticed this book on the shelf as a clue to what the announcement would be. In fact, the shelf contains a couple more books on this subject. Now that I think about it, I notice they have less dust on them than the other books on the shelf.

Sherlock Holmes would've been proud of my investigative method—only my method works backwards. He used the skill of deductive reasoning, putting the clues he observed together to develop a conclusion. I, however, find evidence to support my conclusion once I know what the answer is.

Returning to my quest for information about the upcoming announcement, I read the first textbook I noticed on the subject. Yes, when I have to—or want to—I can learn the more traditional way. Just because I cheated when it came to tests doesn't mean I didn't legitimately educate myself from time to time. In fact, I did so quite often. However, my education was about whatever I was interested in at the moment, not some cookie-cutter program. I cheated simply because I was being pragmatic. The main reason I was at Harvard was to get a piece of paper that would impress my would-be employers. I used the Quiet to attain the mundane requirements of my degree while genuinely learning about things important to me.

When I do decide to read, the Quiet gives me a huge edge. I never get drowsy, even if the material is a little dry. I don't need sleep in the Quiet, just like I'm not a slave to other bodily functions in there. To me, it feels like it took maybe an hour to finish the part of the book about the magnetic version of stimulation—and it was actually interesting in certain parts. I even skimmed a few other stimulation types, which seem invasive compared to TMS, as the book calls it. I didn't absorb it all, of course—that would require re-reading—but I feel sufficiently ready to tackle the rest of the folder I found in Dick's desk.

I catch myself writing the report to Bill in my head. In layman's terms, TMS is a way to directly stimulate the brain without drilling into the skull—which the other methods require. It uses a powerful magnetic field to do so—hence the 'Magnetic' in the name. It's been around for a while, but was only recently approved by the FDA for treating depression. In terms of harm—and this is not from the book but my own conjecture—it doesn't seem worse than getting an MRI.

It takes me only a brief run through the papers in the folder to realize that the FBTI announcement will exceed everyone's expectations. They have a way of constructing a TMS machine that is more precise than any before, while being affordable and easily customizable. Just for the treatment of depression alone, this device will make a significant impact. To top it off, the work can also lead to better MRI machines, which may open up a new market for FBTI.

Realizing I have enough information, I phase out.

Dick's voice is back. I listen to his closing spiel; then I thank him and go home.

I log in to work remotely, and write up my report in an email. I list all the reasons I think we should go long FBTI and my miscellaneous thoughts on why it would be a good investment.

I set the delivery of my email for late Friday evening. It's a trick I use sometimes to make it appear to my boss and coworkers that I work tirelessly, even on a Friday night, when most people go out or spend time with their families. I copy as many people as is reasonable and address it to Bill. Then I click send and verify that the email is waiting in my outbox. It'll sit there ready and waiting until it goes out Friday night.

Given how much money I'm about to make for Pierce Capital Management, I decide to take the rest of this week off.

CHAPTER FIVE

Showing up uninvited is not the only thing that makes me nervous about my plan to visit Mira. Another thing that worries me is the fact that the address in question happens to be in Brooklyn.

Why do people do that? Why live in the NYC boroughs? My moms are guilty of this as well—their choice, Staten Island, is even crazier. At least the subway goes to Brooklyn. Nothing goes to Staten Island, except the ferry and some express buses. It's even worse than New Jersey.

Still, I don't have a choice. Brooklyn is the location of the address, so off to Brooklyn I go. With deep reservations, I catch the Q train at City Hall and prepare for the epic journey.

As I sit on the subway, I read a book on my phone and occasionally look out the window. Whenever I do, I see graffiti on the walls of buildings facing the tracks. Why couldn't this girl live someplace more civilized, like the Upper East Side?

To my surprise, I get to my stop, Kings Highway, in less than an hour. From here, it's a short walk to my destination, according to my phone's GPS.

The neighborhood is . . . well, unlike the city. No tall buildings, and the signs on businesses are worn and tacky. Streets are a little dirtier than Manhattan, too.

The building is on East 14th Street, between Avenues R and S. This is the only aspect of Brooklyn I appreciate. Navigating streets named using sequential numbers and letters in alphabetical order is easy.

It's late in the afternoon, so the sun is out, but I still feel unsafe—as though I'm walking at night under an ominous-looking, ill-lit bridge in Central Park. My destination is across a narrow street from a park. I try to convince myself that if people let their children play in that park, it can't be *that* dangerous.

The building is old and gloomy, but at least it's not covered in graffiti. In fact, I realize I haven't seen any since I got off the train. Maybe my judgment of the neighborhood was too hasty.

Nah, probably not. It *is* Brooklyn.

The building has an intercom system. I gather my courage and ring the apartment door from downstairs.

Nothing.

I start pressing buttons randomly, trying to find someone who might let me in. After a minute, the intercom comes alive with a loud hiss and a barely recognizable, "Who's there?"

"UPS," I mumble. I'm not sure if it's the plausibility of my lie or someone just working on autopilot, but I get buzzed in.

Spotting an elevator, I press the up arrow, but nothing happens. No light comes on. No hint that anything is working.

I wait for a couple of minutes.

No luck.

I grudgingly decide to schlep to the fifth floor on foot. Looks like my assessment of the neighborhood was spot on after all.

The staircase has an unpleasant odor to it. I hope it's not urine, but my nose suggests it is. The noxious aroma on the second floor is diluted by the smells of boiled cabbage and fried garlic. There isn't a lot of light, and the marble steps seem slippery. Watching my step, I eventually make it to the fifth floor.

It's not until I'm actually staring at the door of 5E that I realize I don't have a good plan. Or any plan at all, really. I came this far, though, so I'm not about to turn around and go home now. I go ahead and ring the doorbell. Then I wait. And wait. And wait.

After a while, I hear some movement inside the apartment. Focusing, I watch the eyehole, the way I've seen people do in the movies.

Maybe it's my imagination, but I think a shadow comes across it. Someone might be looking at me.

Still no response.

I try knocking.

"Who is this?" says a male voice.

Shit. Who the hell is that? A husband? A boyfriend? Her father? Her pimp? Every scenario carries its own implications, and few promise anything good. None I can think of, actually.

"My name is Darren," I say, figuring that honesty is the best policy.

No answer.

"I'm a friend of Mira's," I add. And it's only when the words leave my mouth that I recall that she lives here under a different name. Ilona or something.

Before I can kick myself for the slip, the door swings open. A guy who appears to be a few years older than me stands there looking at me with tired, glassy eyes.

It takes a moment for me to notice one problem. No, make that one huge problem.

The guy is holding a gun.

A gun that looks bigger than his head.

The fear that slams my system is debilitating. I've never been threatened with a gun before. At least, not directly like this. Sure, the bouncers in Atlantic City had guns, but they weren't aiming them in my direction at point-blank range. I never imagined it would be this frightening.

I phase into the Quiet, almost involuntarily.

Now that I'm looking at my frozen self with a gun to his/my face, the panic is diluted. I'm still worried, though, since I am facing the gun in the real world.

I take a deep breath. I need to figure out my plan of action.

I look at the shooter.

He's tall, skinny. He's wearing glasses and a white coat with a red stain on it.

The white coat looks odd—and is that red spot blood, or something else? Questions race through my mind. Who is he? What is he doing in there that requires a gun? Is he cooking meth? It *is* Brooklyn after all.

At the same time, I can't shake the feeling that the guy does not look like an average street criminal. There is keen intelligence in his eyes. His uncombed hair and the pens and ruler in the pocket of his white coat paint a strange picture. He almost looks like a scientist—albeit on the mad side.

Of course, that does not rule out the drug angle. He could be like the character on that show about a teacher who cooks meth. Although, come to think of it, that same show made it clear that you don't do that in an apartment building. The smell is too strong to keep the operation hidden, or something like that.

Now that I've had some time to calm down in the Quiet, I get bolder. I begin to wonder if the gun is real. Or maybe I'm just hoping it's fake. Gathering my courage, I reach out to take it from the guy's hand.

When my fingers touch his, something strange happens. Or stranger, rather.

There are now two of him.

I look at the picture, and my jaw proverbially drops.

There is a second guy in the white coat, right there, and this one is moving. I'm so unaccustomed to the idea of people moving while I'm in the Quiet that I lose my ability to think, so I just stand there and gape at him.

The guy looks at me with an expression that's hard to read, a mixture of excitement and fear. As if I were a bear standing in the middle of a Brooklyn apartment building hall.

"Who are you?" he breathes, staring at me.

"I'm Darren," I repeat my earlier introduction, trying to conceal my shock.

"Are you a Reader, Darren?" the guy asks, recovering some of his composure. "Because if you're a Pusher, I will unload that gun in your face as soon as we Universe Split, or Astral Project, or Dimension Shift, or whatever it is you people call it. As soon as we're back to our bodies, you're dead, Pusher."

He has an unusual accent—Russian, I think. That reminds me of Bert's theory that Mira is a spy. Maybe he was right. Maybe she travels with a whole gang of Russian spies.

I only understand one thing about what the Russian guy is saying: he knows that I'm at his mercy when we get back. That means that he, like me, understands how the Quiet works.

The terms he's using sort of make sense to me. All except 'Reader' and 'Pusher.' I know that even if I were this 'Pusher,' I wouldn't want to admit it and get shot. He probably realizes that as well.

"I am sorry, I don't know what you're talking about," I admit. "I don't know what a Reader or a Pusher is."

"Right," the guy sneers. "And you're not aware of our bodies standing over there?"

"Well, yeah, of that I'm painfully aware—"

"Then you can't expect me to believe that you can Split, but not be one of us—or one of them." He says that last word with disgust.

Okay, so one thing is crystal clear: Reader is good, Pusher is bad. Now if only I could find out why.

"If I were a Pusher, would I just show up here like this?" I ask, hoping I can reason with him.

"You fuckers are clever and extremely manipulative," he says, looking me up and down. "You might be trying to use some kind of reverse psychology on me."

"To what end?"

"You want me dead, that's why, and you want my sister dead too," he says, his agitation growing with every word.

I make a mental note at the mention of 'sister,' but I don't have time to dwell on it. "Would showing up like this be the best way to kill you?" I try to reason again.

"Well, no. In fact, I've never heard of Pushers doing their dirty work themselves," he says, beginning to look uncertain. "They like to use regular people for that, like puppets."

I have no idea what he's referring to, so I continue my attempts at rational discourse. "So isn't it possible that I'm simply a guy searching for answers?" I suggest. "Someone who doesn't know what you're talking about?"

"No," he says after considering it for a moment. "I've never heard of untrained, unaffiliated people with the ability to Split. So why don't you tell me what you're doing here, outside my door."

"I can explain that part," I say hurriedly. "You see, I met a girl in Atlantic City. A girl who made me realize that I'm not crazy."

At the mention of Atlantic City, I have his full attention. "Describe her," he says, frowning.

I describe Mira, toning down her sex appeal.

"And she told you her name and where she lives?" he asks, clearly suspicious.

"Well, no," I admit. "I was detained by the casino when they thought we were working together to cheat the house. I learned a few of her aliases from them. After that, I got help from a friend who's a very good hacker."

There I go again, using honesty. I'm on a roll. I don't think I've ever said this many truthful statements in such a short time.

"A good hacker?" he asks, looking unexpectedly interested.

"Yes, the best," I reply, surprised. That's the completely wrong thing to focus on in this story, but as long as he's not angry and trigger-happy, I'll stick with the subject.

He looks me straight in the eyes for the first time. He seems uncomfortable with this. I can tell he doesn't do it often.

I hold his gaze.

"Here's the deal, Darren," he says, his eyes shifting away again after a second. "We're going to get back. I won't shoot you. Instead I will snap your picture. Then I'll text it to my sister."

"Okay," I say. I'll take a picture over a bullet any day.

"If you do anything to me before she gets here, she'll have proof that you were here," he elaborates.

"That makes sense," I lie. So far, there's very little of this that makes any sense at all. "Do whatever you think will help us resolve this misunderstanding."

"The only way to resolve it is to get proof that you're not a Pusher."

"Then let's get that proof," I say, hoping I'll get bonus points for my willingness to cooperate.

"Okay," he says, and I can tell that his mood is improving. "You must agree to submit to a test, then. Or a couple of tests, actually."

"Of course," I agree readily. Then, remembering the red stain on his coat, I ask warily, "Are they painful, these tests?"

"The tests are harmless. However, if it turns out that you're a Pusher, you better pray my sister isn't here at that point."

I swallow nervously as he continues, "I would just shoot you, you see. But Mira, she might make your death slow and very painful."

I rethink some of my fantasies about Mira. She's sounding less and less appealing. "Let's just do this," I say with resignation.

"Okay. Walk slowly to your body and touch it in such a way that I can clearly see it. Don't Split, or I will shoot you."

If 'Split' is what I think it is—as in phasing into the Quiet—then how would he be able to tell if I did do it? Though it seems unlikely, I decide not to push my luck. Not until I know the results of his tests.

"I'm ready," I say, and demonstratively touch my frozen self on the forehead.

CHAPTER SIX

The sounds are back. There are now only two of us.

He's less intent on shooting me—so I know I didn't just hallucinate our conversation.

As I watch, he reaches into a pocket under his white coat and takes out a phone. Then he snaps a picture of me and writes a text.

"You go first," he says.

I walk into the apartment, the gun pressed to my back, and gape at my surroundings, struck by what I'm seeing.

The place is a mess.

I'm not the kind of guy who thinks it's a girl's job to keep a place neat. But after a certain point, I am the kind of guy who thinks, 'what kind of slob is she?' I'm not sexist, though. I think the guy with the gun to my back is just as responsible for this mess as she is. An episode of that show about hoarders could be filmed here.

Pulling me from my thoughts, the guy makes me go into a room on the left.

It appears to be some kind of makeshift lab—if the lab had a small explosion of wires, empty frozen meal boxes, and scattered papers, that is.

"Sit," he says.

I comply.

He grabs a few cables off the floor, some kind of gizmo, and a laptop, all the while trying to keep the gun pointed at me. Whatever he's setting up is ready in a few minutes.

I realize that the cable things are electrodes. Still holding the gun, he applies them to my temples and a bunch of other places all over my head. I must look like a medusa.

"Okay," he tells me when it's ready. "Split, and then come back."

I'm still so much on edge that phasing into the Quiet is easy. Within an instant, I'm standing next to my frozen body, watching myself. I look ridiculous with all the electrodes.

I momentarily debate snooping through the apartment, but decide against it. Instead I phase back out, anxious to see what's coming next.

The first thing I hear is his laptop beeping.

"Okay," he says after a pause. "Right before you Split, you were at the very least showing an EEG consistent with a Reader."

"I know this is a good thing, but you don't sound too confident," I say. As soon as I say it, I regret it. Reader is good. Why would I say anything that might instill doubt? But I can't help it, because I also want to know more about myself. Getting answers was the whole crazy reason I came here in the first place—well, that, and to confirm I'm not alone.

He looks around the room, then finds a nook to put the gun in. I think this officially means he's warmed up to me.

"I've only tested myself extensively, and have run preliminary tests on my sister," he says, glancing at me again. "I have my father's notes, but I'm not confident this is conclusive. Aside from that, I have no idea if Pushers would have the same EEG results." He furrows his brows. "In fact, it's quite likely they might."

His trust is like a yo-yo. "Isn't there a better test you can do?" I say before he reaches for the gun again.

"There is," he says. "You can actually try to Read."

I keep any witty responses related to reading books to myself. "Will you at least tell me what Readers and Pushers are?" I ask instead.

"I can't believe you don't know." He squints at me suspiciously. "Haven't your parents told you anything?"

"No," I admit, frustrated. "I have no idea what you mean or what parents have to do with anything." I hate not knowing things, did I mention that?

He stares at me for a few moments, then sighs and walks up to me. "My name is Eugene," he says, extending his hand to me.

"Nice to meet you, Eugene." I shake his hand, relieved by this rather-civilized turn of events.

"Listen to me, Darren." His face softens a bit, his expression becoming almost kind. "If what you say is true, then I'll help you." He raises his hand to stop me from thanking him, which I was about to do. "But only if you turn out to be a Reader."

I have never wished to be part of a clique so badly in my life.

"How?" I ask.

"I'll teach you," he says. "But if it fails, if you can't Read, you have to promise to leave and never come back."

Wow, so now the rules have changed in my favor. I won't be killed, even if I'm this Pusher thing. Nice.

"We need to hurry," he adds. "My sister's on the way. If you're a Pusher, she won't care about your situation."

"Why?" I ask. In the list of pros and cons as to whether or not I should date Mira, the cons are definitely in the lead.

"Because Pushers had our parents killed," he says. The kind expression vanishes. "In front of her."

"Oh, I'm so sorry," I say, horrified. I had no idea Mira had gone through something so awful. Whoever these Pushers are, I can't blame her for hating them—not if they killed her family.

Eugene's face tightens at my platitude. "If you're a Pusher and she catches you here, you'll be sorry."

"Right, okay." I get that point now. "Let's find out quickly then."

"Put this on your fingers," Eugene says, and grabs another cable from the shelf.

I put the device on. It reminds me of a heart-rate monitor, the kind a nurse would use on you at a hospital.

Eugene starts something on his laptop and turns the computer toward me.

There's a program on the screen that seems to be tracking my heart rate, so my theory was probably right.

"That's a photoplethysmograph," he says. When he sees my blank stare, he adds, "How much do you know about biofeedback?"

"Not much," I admit. "But I do know it's when scientists use electrodes, similar to the ones you used on me before, to measure your brain patterns." I recall reading about it in the context of a new way to control video games in the future, with your mind— as nature clearly intended. Also to beat lie detectors, but that's a long story.

"Good. That's neurofeedback, which is a type of biofeedback," he explains. His voice takes on a professorial quality as he speaks. I can easily picture him teaching at some community college. Glasses, white coat, and all. "This is a simpler feedback." He points at my fingers. "It measures your heart-rate variability."

Another blank stare from me prompts him to explain further.

"Your heart rate can be a window into your internal emotional state. There is a specific state I need you to master. This device should expedite the training." He looks uncertain when he says 'should'—I'm guessing he hasn't done much of this expedited training before.

I don't care, though. From what I know of biofeedback, it's harmless. If it keeps Mira from shooting me, sign me up.

"Anyway, you can read up on the details later. For now, I need you to learn to keep this program in the green." He points to a part of the screen.

It's like a game, then. There's a big red-alert-looking button activated in the right-hand lower corner of the screen. Next to it are blue and green buttons.

"Sync your breath to this," he says, pointing at a little bar that goes up and down. "This is five-in and five-out breathing."

I breathe in sync to the bar for a few minutes. Whatever leftover fear I had evaporates; the technique is rather soothing.

"That's good," he says, pointing at the important lower corner. The red button is gone, and I'm now in the blue. I keep breathing. The green light eludes me.

I see the graph the software keeps of my heart-rate variability. It begins to look more and more even, almost like sine curves. I find it cool—even if I have no idea what that change means in terms of being able to Read.

The feeling this experience evokes is familiar, mainly because of the synchronous breathing. Lucy, my mom, taught me to do this as a meditation technique when I was a kid. She said it would help me focus. I think she secretly hoped it would reduce my hyperactivity. I loved the technique and still do it from time to time. It's something she told me she learned from one of her old friends on the force—a friend who passed away. You're supposed to think happy thoughts while doing the breathing, according to her teachings. Since I'm thinking of Lucy already, I remember fondly how she told me that she didn't know how to meditate just because she was Asian, which was what I used to think. It was the first lecture I received on cultural stereotypes, but definitely not the last. It's a pet peeve of both of my moms. They have a lot of pet peeves like that, actually.

Thus thinking happy thoughts, I try to ignore the bar, closing my eyes to do the meditation Lucy taught me. Every few seconds, I peek at the screen to see how I'm doing.

"That's it," Eugene says suddenly, startling me. When I open my eyes this time, I see the curves are even straighter, and the button is green.

"You did that much too easily," he says, giving me a suspicious look. "But no matter. Do it again, without looking at the screen at all."

He takes the laptop away, and I do my 'Lucy meditation.' In less than a minute, he looks at me with a more awed expression.

"That is amazing. I haven't heard of anyone reaching Coherence so quickly before on the first try," he says. "You're ready for the real test."

He gets up, gets the gun, and puts it in his lab coat pocket. Then, much to my surprise, he leads me out of the apartment.

I'm especially puzzled when he walks across the hall and rings the doorbell of the neighboring apartment.

The door opens, and a greasy-haired, redheaded young guy looks us over. His eyes are bloodshot and glassy.

Without warning, everything silences.

Eugene is pulling his hand away from my frozen self. He must've done that trick his sister pulled on me at the casino. He must've phased in and touched me, bringing me into the Quiet. It's creepy to think about—someone touching my frozen self the way I've touched so many others—but I guess I need to get used to the idea, since I'm no longer the only one who can do this.

Eugene approaches the guy and touches him on the forehead. I half-expect the guy to appear in the Quiet, too.

But no. There are only five of us: a frozen Eugene and me, the moving versions of us, and this guy, who's still a motionless statue.

I watch, confused, as Eugene just stands there, holding the guy's forehead. He looks so still that he begins to remind me of his frozen self.

Then he starts moving again. His hand is not on the guy's head anymore.

"Okay," he says, pointing at the guy. "Now you do the same thing. Place your hand on his skin."

I walk up to the guy and comply. His forehead is clammy, which is kind of disgusting.

"Okay, now close your eyes and get into that same Coherence state," Eugene instructs.

I close my eyes and start doing the meditation. And then it happens.

* * *

I'm so fucking stoned. That was some good shit Peter sold me. I've gotta get some more.

I feel great, but at the same time a part of myself wonders—why the hell did I smoke pot? My hedge fund does random urine tests on occasion. What if I get tested?

And then it hits me: *I* am not stoned. *We* are stoned. I, *Darren*, am not. But I, *Nick*, am.

We are Nick right now.

We are listening to "Comfortably Numb" by Pink Floyd, which is also how we feel.

I, Darren, tried pot before. I didn't like it nearly as much as I, Nick, like it right now.

We get a craving, but we're too lazy to get anything to eat.

The doorbell rings.

Wow.

Can that be a delivery? We don't recall ordering, but ordering something—pizza or Chinese—sounds like a great idea right about now. We reach for the phone when the doorbell rings again.

Oh yeah, the door.

Who's at the door? we wonder again, with a pang of paranoia this time.

I, Darren, finally get it: it's Eugene and me ringing the doorbell.

We get up, walk to the door, and open it after fumbling with the locks.

We're looking at Eugene, Mira's older brother, and some other dude, who I, Darren, recognize as myself. We wonder what the deal is.

* * *

Suddenly, I'm standing in the corridor, my hand no longer on Nick's forehead. I stare at Eugene, my mouth gaping and heart racing at the realization of what I just did.

"Eugene, did you want me to get inside this pothead's mind?" I manage to ask. "Is Reading 'Mind Reading'?"

Eugene smiles at me, then walks to his frozen self and touches his own temple, bringing us out of the Quiet. Then he makes some bullshit excuse to confused Nick for ringing the doorbell, and we walk back to Eugene's apartment.

"Tell me everything you just experienced," he says as soon as the door closes behind us.

I tell him. As I go on, his smile widens. He must've seen the same thing when he touched the guy. From his reaction, I guess this means I can Read, and since this apparently removes any suspicions he had about me, I also assume that Pushers can't Read. I think I'm starting to figure out at least a few pieces of the mystery.

This was the test—and incredibly, I passed.

CHAPTER SEVEN

What I did was not exactly how I imagined mind reading—not that mind reading is something I imagined much. The experience was like some kind of virtual reality, only more intense. It was like I was the pothead guy. I felt what he felt. Saw what he saw. I even had his memories, and they came and went as though they were mine.

But at the same time, I was also myself. An observer of sorts. I experienced two conflicted world views. On the one hand, I was Nick, feeling high, feeling numb, feeling dumb, but at the same time, I was myself, able to not lose my own consciousness. It was a strange merger.

I want to do it again—as soon as possible.

"Do you want tea?" Eugene asks, dragging me out of my thoughts, and I realize we somehow ended up at the kitchen table.

I look around the room. There are a bunch of beakers all over the place. Is he running some kind of chemistry experiment in here? A red stain on the counter, near an ampule with remains of that same red substance, matches the stain on Eugene's white coat. At least it's not blood, as I had originally thought.

"I will take your silence as a yes to tea." Eugene chuckles. "I'm sorry," he adds, joining me after setting the kettle on the stove. "The first time we Read is usually not as confusing as that. Nick's intoxicated state must've been an odd addition to an already strange experience."

"That's an understatement," I say, getting my bearings. "So how does this work?"

"Let's begin at the beginning," Eugene says. "Do you now know what a Reader is?"

"I guess. Someone who can do that?"

"Exactly." Eugene smiles.

"And what is a Pusher?"

His smile vanishes. "What Pushers do is horrible. An abomination. A crime against human nature.

They commit the ultimate rape." His voice deepens, filling with disgust. "They mind-rape. They take away a person's will."

"You mean they can hypnotize someone?" I ask, trying to make sense of it.

"No, Darren." He shakes his head. "Hypnosis is voluntary—if the whole thing exists at all. You can't make people do something they don't want to do under hypnosis." He stops at the sound of the kettle. "Pushers can make a person do anything they want," he clarifies as he gets up.

I don't know how to respond, so I just sit there, watching him pour us tea.

"I know it's a lot to process," Eugene says, placing the cup in front of me.

"You do have a gift for stating the obvious."

"You said you came here to get answers. I promised I would provide them. What do you want to know?" he says, and my heart begins to pound with excitement as I realize I'm about to finally learn more about myself.

"How does it work?" I ask before he changes his mind and decides to test me some more. "Why can we phase into the Quiet?"

"Phase into the Quiet? Is that what you call Splitting?" He chuckles when I nod. "Well, prepare to be disappointed. No one knows for sure why we can do it. I have some theories about it, though. I'll tell you my favorite one. How much do you know about quantum mechanics?"

"I'm no physicist, but I guess I know what a well-read layman should know."

"That might be enough. I'm no physicist myself. Physics was my dad's field, and really this is his theory. Have you ever heard of Hugh Everett III?"

"No." I've never heard of the first two either, but I don't say that to Eugene.

"It's not important, as long as you've heard of the multiple universes interpretation of quantum mechanics." He offers me sugar for my tea.

"I think I've heard of it," I say, shaking my head to decline the sugar. Eugene sits across from me at the table, his gaze intent on mine. "It's the alternative to the famous Copenhagen interpretation of quantum mechanics, right?"

"Yes. We're on the right track. Now, do you actually understand the Copenhagen interpretation?"

"Not really. It deals with particles deciding where to be upon observation with only a probability of being in a specific place—introducing randomness into the whole thing. Or something along those lines. Isn't it famous for no one understanding it?"

"Indeed. I doubt anyone really does. Even my dad didn't, which is why he said it was all BS. He would point out how the whole Schrödinger's cat paradox is the best example of the confusion." As he talks, Eugene gets more and more into the conversation. He doesn't touch his tea, completely immersed in the subject. "Schrödinger meant for the cat theory to illustrate the wrongness, or at least the weirdness of that interpretation, which is funny, given how famous the cat example became. Anyway, what's important is that Everett said there is no randomness. Every place a particle can be, it is, but in different universes. His theory is that there is nothing special about observing particles, or cats— that the reality is Schrödinger's cat is both alive and dead, a live cat in one universe and a dead one in another. No magic observation skills required. Do you follow?"

"Yes, I follow," I say. Amazingly enough, I actually do. "I had to read up on this when we wanted to invest in a firm that was announcing advances in quantum computing."

"Oh, good." Eugene looks relieved. "That might expedite my explanation considerably. I was afraid I would have to explain the double-slit experiment and all that to you. You've also heard of the idea that brains might use quantum computing in some way?"

"I have," I say, "but I've also read that it's unlikely."

"Because the temperatures are too high? And the effects are too short-lived?"

"Yeah. I think it was something along those lines."

"Well, my dad believed in it regardless, and so do I. No one really knows for sure, wouldn't you admit?" Eugene says.

I never really thought about it. It's not something that was ever important to me. "I guess so," I say slowly. "I read that there are definitely *some* quantum effects in the brain."

"Exactly." He takes a quick sip of tea and sets it aside again. I do the same. The tea is bitter and too hot, and I'm dying for Eugene to continue. "The unlikelihood that you mention is about whether consciousness is related to quantum effects. No one doubts that some kinds of quantum processes are going on in the brain. Since everything is made of subatomic particles, quantum effects happen everywhere. This theory just postulates that brains are leveraging these effects to their benefit. Kind of like plants do. Have you heard of that?"

"Yes, I have." He's talking about the quantum effects found in the process of photosynthesis. Mom—Sara—emailed me a bunch of articles about that. She's very helpful that way—sending me articles on anything she thinks I might be interested in. Or anything she's interested in, for that matter.

"Photosynthesis evolved over time because some creature achieved an advantage when using a quantum effect. In an analogous way, wouldn't a creature able to do any kind of cool quantum calculations get a huge survival advantage?" he asks.

"It would," I admit, fascinated.

"Good. So the theory is that what we can do is directly related to all this—that we find ourselves in another universe when we Split, and that a quantum event in our brains somehow makes us Split." He looks more and more like a mad scientist when he's excited, as he clearly is now.

"That's a big leap," I say doubtfully.

"Okay, then, let me go at it from another angle. Could brains have evolved an ability to do quick quantum computations? Say in cases of dire emergencies?"

"Yeah, I think that's possible." Evolution is something I know well, since Sara's PhD thesis dealt with it. I've known how the whole process works since second grade.

"Well, then let's assume, for the sake of this theory, that the brain has learned to leverage quantum effects for some specific purpose. And that as soon as the brain does that anywhere in nature, evolution will favor it. Even if the effect is tiny. As long as there's some advantage, the evolutionary change will spread."

"But that would mean many creatures, and all people, have the same ability we do," I say. I wonder if I have someone else who doesn't understand evolution on my hands.

"Right, exactly. You must've heard that some people in deeply stressful life-or-death situations experience time as though it's slowing down. That some even report leaving their bodies in near-death experiences."

"Yes, of course."

"Well, what if that's what it feels like for regular people to do this quantum computation, which is meant to save their lives or at least give their brains a chance to save them? You see, the theory asserts that this *does* happen and that all people have this 'near-death' quantum computation boost. All the anecdotal reports that mention strange things happening to people in dire circumstances confirm it. So far, the theory can be tied back to natural evolution."

"Okay," I say. "I think I follow thus far."

"Good." Eugene looks even more excited. "Now let's suppose that a long time ago, someone noticed this peculiarity—noticed how soldiers talk about seeing their lives pass before their eyes, or how Valkyries decide on the battlefield who lives and who dies . . . That person could've decided to do something really crazy, like start a cult—a cult that led to a strange eugenics program, breeding people who had longer and stronger experiences of a similar nature." He stands, tea forgotten, and begins to pace around the room as he talks. "Maybe they put them under stress to hear their stories. Then they might've had the ones with the most powerful experiences reproduce. Over a number of generations, that selective breeding could've produced people for whom this quantum computing under stress was much more pronounced—people who began to experience new things when that overly stressed state happened. Think about it, Darren." He stops and looks at me. "What if we're simply a branch of that line of humanity?"

This theory is unlike anything I expected to hear. It seems farfetched, but I have to admit it makes a weird sort of sense. There are parts that really fit my own experiences. Things that Eugene doesn't even know—like the fact that the first time I phased into the Quiet was when I fell off my bike while somersaulting in the air. It was exactly like the out-of-body experience he described. An experience I quickly discovered I could repeat whenever I was stressed.

"Does this theory explain Reading?" I ask.

"Sort of," he says. "The theory is that everyone's minds Split into different universes under some conditions. As Readers, we can just stay in those universes for a longer period of time, and we're able to take our whole consciousness with us." He draws in a deep breath. "The next part is somewhat fuzzy, I have to admit. If you touch a normal person who's unable to control the Split like we can, they're unaware of anything happening. However, if you touch a Reader or a Pusher—another person like us—while in that other universe, they get pulled in with you. Their whole being joins you, just like I joined you when you touched my hand earlier today. When you touch someone 'normal,' they just get pulled in a little bit—on more of a subconscious level. Just enough for us to do the Reading. Afterwards, they have no recollection of it other than a vague sense of déjà vu or a feeling that they missed something, but even those cases are extremely rare."

"Okay, now the theory sounds more wishy-washy," I tell him.

"It's the best I've got. My dad tried to study this question scientifically and paid the ultimate price."

I stare at Eugene blankly, and he clarifies, "Pushers killed him for his research."

"What? He was killed for trying to find these answers?" I can't hide my shock.

"Pushers don't like this process being studied," Eugene says bitterly. "Being the cowards that they are, they're afraid."

"Afraid of what?"

"Of 'normal' people learning to do what we do," Eugene says, and it's clear that he's not scared of that possibility.

CHAPTER EIGHT

I sip my tea quietly for a while. Eugene comes back to the table and sits down again, sipping from his own mug. My brain is on information overload. There are so many directions this conversation could go. I have so many questions. I've never met anyone who even knew the Quiet existed, let alone knew this much about it—other than Mira, of course, but chasing someone through a crowded casino doesn't technically qualify as 'meeting.'

"Are there other theories?" I ask after a few moments.

"Many," he says. "Another one I like is the computer simulation one. If you've seen *The Matrix*, it's relatively easy to explain. Only it doesn't answer as many things as the Quantum Universes explanation does. Like the fact that our abilities are hereditary."

I was initially curious about the computer simulation theory, but the heredity angle stops me dead in my tracks.

"Wait, does every Reader have to have Reader parents?" I ask. In hindsight, it's obvious from what he's said thus far, but I want it spelled out.

"Yes." He puts his now-empty teacup down. "Which reminds me. Who are your parents? How could you not have known that you're a Reader?"

"Hold on." I raise my hand. "Both parents must be Readers?"

"No." He looks upset for some reason. "Not both. Just one." It's obvious that this is a sensitive subject for Eugene.

Before I can question him about that, he continues, "I don't understand why your parents didn't tell you about this. I always thought this was an oral tradition, a story that every family who has the ability passes from generation to generation. Why didn't yours?"

"I'm not sure," I say slowly. Sara never told me anything. In fact, it was just the opposite. When I told my moms about falling off that bike and seeing the world from outside my body, they told me I must've hit my head. When I repeated the feat by jumping off a roof and told them of another out-of-body excursion, they got me my first therapist. That therapist eventually ended up referring me to my current shrink—who's the only person I've spoken to about this since then. Well, until I met Eugene, that is.

Eugene gives me a dubious look in response. "Really? Neither your mother nor your father ever mentioned it?"

"Well, I didn't know my father, so he's the more likely candidate, given that my mom never said anything," I say, thinking out loud. Based on the confusion on his face, Eugene isn't getting it. Why would he, though? My history isn't exactly common for your typical American family. "I was conceived through artificial insemination," I explain to him. "My father was a guy who contributed to a sperm bank in Israel. Could he have been one of us—a Reader?"

My genius father. What a joke. I rarely tell people this story. Having two moms can be awkward enough. The fact that Sara went shopping for good sperm to have a smart kid—that's just icing on the cake. But that's exactly what she did. She and Lucy went to Israel, found a high-IQ donor bank, and got one of them knocked up. I think they went overseas to make sure I would never, ever meet the father. Now you can see why I consider my shrink's job too easy. Whatever happens, blame the mother.

"What? No, that can't be," Eugene says, interrupting my ruminations. "It has to be your mother. Giving sperm like that is not something our people would do. It's forbidden."

"What do you mean?"

"We have rules," he says, and it's clear something about this upsets him again. "In the old days, all Readers were subject to arranged marriages—hence the whole selective breeding theory, you see. Today things are more liberal, but there are still a number of restrictions. For example, a Reader's choice of spouse, regardless of how powerful he or she is, is considered personal business now, but the expectation is that he or she be a Reader."

I file away the mention of 'powerful.' I'm curious how one can be more or less powerful when it comes to Reading, but I have other questions first. "Because of the selective breeding thing?" I ask, and Eugene nods.

"Right. It's about the blood. Having children with non-Readers gets you banned from the Reader community." He pauses before saying quietly, "That's what happened to my father."

Now I understand why this is a sensitive topic. "I see. So your mother wasn't a Reader? And that's forbidden?"

"Well, technically, marrying non-Readers and having children like me and Mira is no longer forbidden. You don't get executed for it, like in the old days. It *is* highly frowned upon, though, and the punishment for it is banishment. But that's not an issue in your case. What you're talking about—a Reader giving sperm—is forbidden to this day, as it can lead to mixing of the blood and is untraceable."

"Mixing? Untraceable?" I'm completely confused now.

"A Pusher mother might somehow get impregnated by Reader sperm," Eugene explains. "Readers consider that an abomination, and, according to what my dad told me, so do Pushers. They wouldn't give sperm either. The risk is admittedly infinitesimally small, since Pushers themselves wouldn't dare risk getting pregnant that way. Also, mixing aside, Readers like to keep tabs on everyone, even half-bloods like me, and sperm bank pregnancy would prevent them from keeping an account of the whole Reader family tree. Or at least it would require oversight of the whole process, which would be complicated."

That makes sense. But this leads to only one logical conclusion. Sara, my biological mother, must be a Reader. How could she keep this from me—her son? How could she pretend I was crazy?

"I'm sorry, Darren," Eugene says when I remain silent. "You must have even more questions than before."

"Yes. Your gift for understatement doesn't fail you," I tell him. "I have hundreds of questions. But you know what? You know what I really want to do?"

"You want to Read again?" he surmises.

He's spot on. "Can we?"

"Sure." He smiles. "Let's ring some doorbells."

CHAPTER NINE

I have to admit, I like Eugene. I'm glad I met him. It's refreshing to have another smart person to talk to, besides Bert.

It takes us a few minutes to choose our next 'volunteer,' a tall guy in his mid-twenties who lives a few doors down from Eugene and Mira.

"Hi Brad," Eugene says. "I ran out of salt as I was cooking. Mind if I borrow some?"

The guy looks confused. "Salt? Um, okay, sure. Let me see if I can get some." As he turns away, Eugene winks at me. As we agreed, I phase in and touch Eugene's forehead to bring him into the Quiet.

It works, as expected. We are in the Quiet, which I guess, given Eugene's favorite theory, might be another universe of some kind. I don't dwell on the many questions about this alternate reality, if that's what it is. I have something much more interesting to do. I walk up to Brad, touch his temple with my index finger, and close my eyes.

Then I do the breathing meditation.

* * *

What the fuck? Who runs out of salt? The thoughts running through our mind are less than flattering toward Eugene. And who's this other guy? His boyfriend? Wouldn't surprise us. We always suspected that Mira's geeky brother was gay.

I, Darren, realize that Brad knows both Eugene and Mira. And I know I only have seconds before I play his memory to the current moment, which Eugene told me would force me out of the guy's head. So I try to do something different. As Eugene instructed me earlier, I try to 'fall' deeper into Brad's mind.

I picture myself lighter than air. I visualize myself as a feather, slowly floating down into a calm lake on a windless day. I become a sense of lightness.

And then it happens.

We are in a movie theater. We are on a date. We look at the girl sitting next to us, and I, Darren, can't believe my eyes. We're sitting next to Mira. When we start making out with her, I, Darren, think that maybe I really have gone crazy. But no, there is a simpler explanation. I get it when I try falling deeper again.

We're standing in front of Mira's apartment door holding flowers. "These are for you," we say when she opens the door.

We feel pretty slick. The flowers are a means to an end. We want to get our hot neighbor into bed.

"Oh, how sweet," she says drily when she sees us. "Am I supposed to swoon now?" She then proceeds to tell us exactly what she thinks we're planning. I, Darren, realize that she must've done what I'm doing. She must've Read Brad's mind—or maybe she just used common sense. Why else does a guy give a girl flowers?

We're surprised at our neighbor's bluntness. Impressed, even. We admit that, yes, we want to sleep with her, but that she should still take the flowers. She does. Then she sets the ground rules. Nothing serious. She has no time for relationships, she says. A movie, dinner, and, if she thinks we're worth it afterwards, maybe she'll go to our place.

That's it. Just a one-time thing, unless the whole thing goes exceptionally well. In that unexpected eventuality, she might, maybe, initiate another encounter.

We agree. What sane guy wouldn't?

I, Darren, experience the dinner and the movie. It's awesome. All of it.

We get back to our—Brad's—apartment.

We're in the bedroom. We're kissing Mira. I, Darren, am jealous that an asshole like Brad gets to do this with Mira. That feeling doesn't last, though. We're immersed in the experience. Mira's perfect naked body. Her lips on ours. It's everything we ever hoped it would be.

Unfortunately, it's too much of everything we ever hoped it would be. I, Darren, can feel us— Brad—losing control. No amount of baseball stats will pull this guy back from the edge. Just like that, we have a problem. Apparently Mira is a little too good-looking, because before I, Darren, even realize what's going on, things happen somewhat . . . prematurely.

Mira's reaction to the situation is admirable. She's not mad, she insists. She says not to worry about it. Says she had a good time. She isn't fooling us, though. She leaves quickly and never speaks to us about this night, or anything else for that matter, again.

* * *

I'm back in my body in the Quiet, and the first thing I do is punch Brad in the face.

"What are you doing?" Eugene exclaims, looking at me like I'm crazy.

"Trust me," I say, resisting the urge to also kick the guy. What a loser. Not only did he sleep with Mira, he didn't even have the decency to be good at it. "He doesn't feel it. Right?"

"Well, yeah," Eugene admits. "At least I highly doubt he feels it. But it looks disrespectful."

It's almost too bad that Brad can't feel the punch. I debate punching him once we phase out, but decide against it. I mean, what possessed me? Mira isn't my girlfriend to be overprotective about. She might not even like me when we meet. One thing is clear, though. Without having said a word to her in real life, I like her.

It's shallow, I know. I'd like to say it's based on the fact that I liked talking to her as Brad at that dinner—which I did. But truthfully, I just want to see her body again. I have to kiss her again. It's weird. I wish I had been in someone else's mind for this, my second Reading. I wish it hadn't been Brad. I really need to find a boring person whose mind I can do this Reading thing with.

"Let's phase out," I tell Eugene, and without waiting for his answer, I touch my forehead.

The world comes back to life, and Brad brings us the stupid salt. Eugene thanks him, and we walk back toward Eugene's apartment.

"How was that?" Eugene asks on the way.

He has no idea this thing happened between his sister and his neighbor. I decide to respect whatever shred of privacy these two have, and at least not mention anything to Eugene.

"That was a good start," I say. "I think we should go outside and do some more."

"Eugene," a pleasant female voice says. A voice I just heard in Brad's memory. "Who the fuck is this?"

I look up and find myself staring down the barrel of a gun. Again.

CHAPTER TEN

Okay, I am officially sick of guns being pointed at me. Even guns pointed by a beautiful girl I just saw naked in someone's mind.

"Mira, put the gun down," Eugene says. "This is Darren. I just texted you his picture. You didn't get it?"

She frowns, still holding the gun trained on me. "No, I haven't checked my phone. Does your text explain how this creep stalked me all the way here from Atlantic City?"

"No, not exactly," Eugene admits. "But you have to cut the guy some slack. He tracked you down, but he has a good reason to be persistent. You're the first other Reader he's ever met."

I can tell that this knowledge surprises her. "How can I be the first Reader he's met?" she asks skeptically. "What about his parents? What about the other Readers from wherever his home is?"

"Manhattan," I supply helpfully. "And in regards to parents, I'll be having a very serious conversation with my mom about this very subject. For some reason, she didn't tell me anything about this. And I've never met my father, but Eugene convinced me that he couldn't have been a Reader because my mother got his sperm from a bank."

As I'm talking, Mira looks at me with more and more curiosity. "A sperm bank?" she repeats.

"Yes. My mom, she wanted a child, but couldn't bring herself to be with a guy, I guess." Thinking of my mom in this context is weird, at best.

"Why? Does she hate men?"

Did Mira just say that approvingly?

"She likes women," I say. "I have two mothers." I'm not sure why I added this last part. Usually you have to ask probing questions for a lot longer before I reveal such personal information.

To her credit, Mira hardly blinks at that. Instead she says with a frown, "If she got sperm from a bank, that would mean she voluntarily mated with a non-Reader. Why would she have done that? Surely she knew she'd get exiled, like our dad."

"That's a good point," Eugene says. "I can't believe I didn't see that when Darren first mentioned it to me."

"You say that like you're surprised I could make a good point," Mira says to her brother, but her tone is more teasing than sharp. "Don't forget, you wouldn't survive a day without me—the dumb, uneducated one."

Eugene ignores her statement. "Can we get out of this hallway?" he says. "I want to get something to eat."

Mira finally lowers the gun and puts it back in her purse. "Fine, I'll be right back." She goes into the apartment. I look at Eugene questioningly, but he just shrugs.

She's back momentarily. She changed from her heels and dress into jeans and sneakers. I wonder where she's been, so dressed up. She looks great in the simpler outfit, though, and I can't help thinking back to my experience in Brad's head.

As I'm sifting through the hot pictures in my mind, she tells Eugene, "Are you seriously going out like that?" She gestures toward his stained lab coat.

He mumbles something and disappears into the apartment as well. When he comes out, the lab coat is gone, and he's wearing a long-sleeved T-shirt that looks two sizes too big. Mira shoots him an exasperated look, but doesn't say anything else. Instead she walks over to the elevator and presses the button.

"I don't think that works," I say, remembering having to go up all those stairs.

"Trust me," she says. "It's just the first floor that doesn't work."

And she's right. The elevator comes, and we're able to exit on the second floor. From there, it's only a single flight of stairs to get out of the building.

"What exactly does it mean to be exiled?" I ask as we walk in the direction of the bigger street, Kings Highway, in search of a place to eat.

"It's complicated," Eugene says, looking at me. "Our dad was exiled from the community of Readers in St. Petersburg, Russia, and that was pretty bad. He couldn't visit his childhood friends and family. Readers in Russia, in general, are much more traditional, but it was especially bad almost thirty years ago, when I was born. It was terrible for him, he told us."

"But he did it for Mom," Mira adds.

"And for us. He left it all so he could have children with her." Eugene sounds proud of his father. "Thankfully, it's different here. In present-day America, especially the New York City area, the Readers' community is more open-minded. They recognize us as Readers—unofficially, at least."

"Yeah, just so they can make sure we don't openly use our skills," Mira says with a touch of bitterness.

"I think they have other ways to enforce that," Eugene says, glancing at his sister. "Besides, we all know how stupid it would be to reveal our existence to the rest of the world, half-bloods or not. No, they're genuinely less traditional here. At least now they are. But when you were born, Darren, things could've been worse." He gives me a sympathetic look.

"None of this explains why my mom didn't tell me about Readers, though," I say, still bothered by the thought of Sara hiding such important information from me.

"Maybe she was ashamed of being shunned," Mira suggests, shooting me a look that suggests she's not entirely over my stalking her. "Or she didn't want you to learn how to Split and Read. Maybe as you were growing up, she decided you wouldn't be able to keep the Readers' secret. No offense, but you don't look like the kind of guy who can keep your mouth shut."

"But she must've realized I'd discovered it. I as much as told her that as a kid," I say, refusing to rise to the bait. I have more important things to worry about than Mira's sharp tongue. I'm tempted to go to Staten Island right now, but I know it makes more sense to learn more from these two first, so I can ask my mom the right questions. Maybe then I'll be able to get answers and understand what happened.

"I'm sorry," Eugene says with a hint of pity.

"Oh, poor Darren, Mommy didn't tell him," Mira counters, her voice dripping with venom. "At least she's alive. Maybe that's why she is alive—because she knows how to keep a secret. She doesn't run around asking troublesome questions like our idiot father." As she says this, her hands ball into fists, and I see her blinking rapidly, as though to hide tears. She doesn't cry, though. Instead, she glares at her brother and says caustically, "The father whose steps you seem determined to follow, I might add."

"I thought you supported my research," Eugene says, clearly hurt.

She sighs and falls silent as we pass through a small crowd gathered in front of some yogurt place. "I'm sorry," she says in a more conciliatory tone when we're through. "I do support what you're doing. I support it to spite the fuckers who killed Dad—and because it could give us a way to make them pay for what they did. I just can't help thinking that all of this could've been avoided if he'd just researched something else. Alzheimer's, for example."

"I understand," Eugene says.

We walk in an uncomfortable silence for a few minutes. I feel like an intruder.

"No offense, Darren," Mira says as we stop at a traffic light. "It's a difficult subject."

"No problem," I say. "I can't even imagine how you feel."

We walk in a more companionable silence for another block or so.

"Are you leading us to that diner again?" Mira eventually asks, wrinkling her nose.

"Yes," Eugene says, a faint smile appearing on his lips.

Mira rolls her eyes. "That place is a real dump. How many cases of food poisoning does it take for you to realize it? Let's go to the sushi place on Coney Island. It's closer."

"Right, raw fish is the solution to health concerns," Eugene says, unsuccessfully trying to mimic Mira's very distinctive brand of sarcasm.

They fight about the place for the rest of the way. I'm not surprised at all when Mira gets her way. She seems like the kind of person who always does. I don't mind in this case, though. If choosing the place had been up for a vote, Mira would've had mine as soon as she mentioned food poisoning.

Listening to their bickering, I wonder how interesting it must be to have a sibling. Or frustrating. I mean, what would it be like to have a younger sister? Especially one who's as reckless as Mira? I shudder at the thought.

"Table for three," Eugene tells the waiter when we enter the place.

"Ilona?" A deep voice says, and Mira winces. "Ya tebya ne uznal." Or at least that's what it sounds like. It's coming from a tall, well-built guy with a tattoo in the shape of an anchor on his muscular forearm.

Mira walks over to him, hugs him, and kisses him on the cheek. They start talking out of earshot from us. Eugene crosses his arms and eyes the guy suspiciously.

"Can we get a table as far away as possible from that man?" he asks the waiter.

"I can put you in the privacy of one of our tatami rooms," the waiter offers.

"Thank you," I say, and slip a twenty into his hand. "Please make it the furthest one."

Mira heads back to us. She puts a finger to her lips when her back is to the guy.

We are quiet until we get to the tatami room.

"I will not discuss it," Mira says when we sit down.

Eugene glares at her. She doesn't even blink, opening her menu and pointedly ignoring her brother.

"I thought I told you not to do that anymore," Eugene says in a hushed tone. "I thought I told you not to deal with thugs. You won't find him—but you will get yourself killed. Or worse."

"Ot-yebis' Eugene," Mira says, her face getting flushed. Whatever she just said, Eugene takes a breath and stops talking.

The waiter comes, asking what we want to drink. Mira orders hot sake, showing the waiter what must be a fake ID. I stick with green tea, as does Eugene.

I'm dying of curiosity. Did I mention it's one of my few weaknesses?

It feels risky, but I can't help myself. I phase into the Quiet and watch the frozen faces of Mira and Eugene carefully.

They don't seem to be in the Quiet with me. If what Eugene said is true, pulling them in requires explicitly touching them. That's good. I don't plan to do that.

I walk out of the little alcove room the waiter gave us and go through the restaurant, searching for the guy Mira spoke to when we first arrived. His table is empty, with only dirty plates and a check lying there. Apparently he was on his way out when we entered.

I walk through the frozen patrons to the door. Outside, I spot my target. He hasn't gone far.

First, I look in his pockets. Anton Gorshkov, his New York driver's license tells me. Along with his age, height, and address on Brighton Beach. That doesn't tell me much. But I now have a new trick I've been itching to try again—the whole Reading thing.

I touch his forehead. I do the meditation. I realize as it starts that the process is a little quicker now.

* * *

We watch Ilona—whom I, Darren, know as Mira—walking toward us. We don't know the men she's with. We barely recognize her without the tight dress and heels she's usually wearing.

"Anton, kakimi sud'bami?" she says to us. It should've sounded like gibberish to me, Darren, but I gleefully realize that I understand exactly what she said. The approximate meaning is: "I'm surprised to see you here, Anton." And I'm aware of the full, subtle meaning of her words, which doesn't translate to English. In general, I understand every thought that goes through Anton's head. Apparently language doesn't seem to matter when it comes to Reading, which makes a weird kind of sense.

We shrug and say, "What are you doing here?"

"Decided to grab a bite to eat," Ilona/Mira responds in Russian.

"Who are the wimps with you?" we say. Again, the translation is approximate. The word for 'wimps' has a more insulting connotation in the original Russian.

"Math geeks," she answers. "I consult with them on how to improve my game."

We have a flashback to playing cards with Ilona. She's good. One of the best. We try to look at her companions, but she blocks our way.

"They work exclusively with me," she says. Then, seeing our stubborn look, she adds, "Viktor introduced us."

We now lose any inclination to look at the math geeks. Not when Viktor is involved. People who cross that guy lose their heads. Literally. There was a rumor that Viktor tapped Ilona, and perhaps it's true. We really don't want anything to do with him.

"It was good seeing you. Maybe I'll see you at this weekend's big game?" she says.

"I doubt it," we say. "I first need to collect some money."

I, Darren, try to go deeper.

Suddenly, it's late evening, and we're beating a guy in an alley. He's refused to get protection. Who does he think he is? Every Russian-owned business in this neighborhood pays protection money to Anton. Our fist aches, but we keep on pounding. No pain, no gain, we joke to ourselves. I, Darren, am horrified, but go deeper still.

Now we're sitting at a card game. We have a gambling 'hard on,' as we call it. I, Darren, can't believe my eyes.

In this dark room, filled with cigarette smoke and sketchy-looking characters whom we—Anton and me—find scary, there is Ilona. Or Mira, as I, Darren, remind myself.

She's wearing a tight dress, showing off her impressive cleavage.

We look at our cards. We have two pairs. We are golden. We bet to the limit.

She drops out. *Can she read our 'tells'?* we wonder, impressed.

The game moves forward.

Ilona wins the next round, calling one guy's bluff. We had no clue the fucker was bluffing. She deserves her reputation as a card prodigy.

As far as we know, she's never been accused of cheating. But we wonder how such a young, pretty thing can be this good without something up her sleeve. Then we chuckle at the realization that, in fact, she has no sleeves. With that strappy little dress, there's no fucking way she can be hiding cards.

Maybe someone at the table is cheating, and she's the partner? If that's the case, we'll keep our mouth shut. These men are not the kind of people you can accuse of cheating and live.

After seeing the game through, I, Darren, have had enough.

* * *

I am out of Anton's head. The experience of being someone else, even a lowlife like him, is beyond words. I'm going to do this over and over, until I get sick of it—which is probably never going to happen. It's so cool.

Right now, though, instead of enjoying the novelty of this experience, I'm wondering about Mira's sanity. I recall reading something about underground gambling and links to organized crime in her file in Atlantic City, but seeing it through this degenerate's eyes really put things in perspective for me.

Mira is nuts to be doing this. Why is she doing it? A Reader like her has to have a safer way to make money. Does she need something else in the criminal society? Eugene dropped a few hints about her looking for something or someone, but I still don't get it. A green monster in me wonders if she finds these men appealing. Anton did think of some scary guy who maybe had her protected or something like that.

Whatever the answers, I will not find them anytime soon. I have no intention of letting Mira know I learned any of this.

If she knew I snooped like this, it would kill whatever little trust she has in me—if she has any, that is.

CHAPTER ELEVEN

I re-enter the restaurant and find my way back to our little room. Then I touch myself on the forehead.

I'm back in my body. The sounds return.

"I must admit I love these places," I say, making small talk to cover any weirdness in my demeanor. "It's like a little piece of Japan in the middle of Brooklyn. This one isn't as hardcore as some I've seen. At least we're allowed to keep our shoes on."

Mira and Eugene comment on how some places in Brooklyn are more like that. Some do make you take your shoes off, and their servers wear kimonos.

I breathe easier. I officially got away with the little bit of snooping.

We all examine the menus.

"So, Darren, how long can you stay in the Mind Dimension?" Mira says nonchalantly, resuming the conversation.

"Mira," Eugene says, reddening as he looks up at his sister. "That's not very polite."

"Why is that not polite?" I ask, surprised. "Isn't Mind Dimension what she calls the place you guys 'Split' into? The place I call the Quiet?"

"The Quiet? How cute," Mira says, making me wonder if sarcasm is just the way she normally talks.

"Yes, Darren, that's what she's talking about," Eugene says, still looking embarrassed. "But what you don't know—and what Mira wants to take advantage of—is that this question is very personal in Reader society."

"Well, we're not in Reader society," Mira counters. "We're outcasts, so anything goes."

"Why is it such a big deal?" I ask, looking from brother to sister.

"In the Reader society proper, it's like asking someone how much money he's worth, or the size of his penis," Eugene explains as Mira chuckles derisively. "The time she asked you about is the measure of our power. It determines Reading Depth, for example, which is how far you can see into your target's memories. It also determines how long you can keep someone else in there. I'm surprised you even ask this, Darren. It seems self-evident how important this time is, since even without knowing about Reading Depth, there's the simple matter of longer subjective life experience."

"Of what?" I almost choke on my green tea. "What do you mean 'longer subjective life experience'?"

"You have got to be kidding me," Mira says, downing a shot of her hot sake. "Don't you know anything? I feel educated all of a sudden, and this is coming from a high school dropout."

I don't even question the dropout comment. I'm still on the life experience thing.

"You don't age while in the Mind Dimension," Eugene says. "So the longer you can stay there, the more you can experience."

"You don't age?" I can't believe I didn't think of it myself. If you don't eat or sleep, why am I surprised that you don't age?

"No, there's no aging that anyone's ever noticed," Eugene says. "And some of the Enlightened, the most powerful among us, can and do spend a long time in there."

I just sit there trying to readjust my whole world, which is becoming a common occurrence today.

When the waiter comes back, I order my usual Japanese favorite on autopilot. Eugene and Mira order as well.

"It's not that strange, if you think about it," Mira says when the waiter is out of earshot. "Time stands still there, or seems to."

"We don't know that," Eugene says. "It could also be that we're not there in a real, physical sense. Only our minds, or more specifically, our consciousness."

Mira rolls her eyes at him, but my mind is blown. "I was always bored when I spent too much time in there. I only used it when I was under some time crunch," I tell them, realizing all the opportunities I missed so far. "If I had only known . . . Are you saying that with every book I read in the physical world, I was literally wasting my life away—since I could've done it in the Quiet and not aged by those hours?"

"Yes," Mira says unkindly. "You were wasting your life away, as you are wasting ours right now."

She uses sarcasm so much that I've already become accustomed to it. It barely registers now. I'm more caught up in thinking about all the times I wasted hours of my life and the many millions of things I could've done in the Quiet. If only I had known that it would add more time to my life—or rather, not take time away from it. All this time, I thought I was just taking shortcuts.

"Well, I'm so glad I met you guys," I say finally. "Just knowing this one thing alone will literally change my life."

"Oh, and Reading wouldn't have?" Eugene winks.

I grin at him. "For that too, I'm forever in your debt and all that."

"Why don't you repay that debt a little by answering my question," Mira says, looking at me.

"Will you tell me yours if I tell you mine?" I joke.

"See how quickly his gratitude dissipates and turns into the usual tit for tat?" Mira says snarkily to Eugene.

I'm so flabbergasted by all the revelations that it barely registers that Mira just made a joke about tits.

"It's a deal," Eugene says, answering for his sister.

We pause our conversation when our food arrives. Eugene is served a three-roll special, Mira has a sushi bento box, and I have my sashimi deluxe. I'm a big fan of sushi—to me, it's like an edible work of art.

Returning to our discussion of how long I can stay in the Quiet, I say, "I can't give you an exact amount of time." Grabbing a piece of fatty salmon with my chopsticks, I explain, "As I said, I eventually get bored and phase out."

"But what's the longest you've ever been inside?" Eugene asks, adding a huge wad of wasabi into his tiny soy sauce bowl.

"A couple of days," I say. "I never really kept track of time."

Mira and Eugene exchange strange looks.

"You don't fall out of the Mind Dimension for a couple of days?" Mira says.

"What do you mean 'fall out'? I get bored and touch my skin to phase out. Is that what you mean?"

They exchange those looks again.

"No, Darren, she means fall out," Eugene says, looking at me like I'm some exotic animal. "When we reach our limit to being in that mode, what you call the Quiet, we involuntarily re-enter our bodies. For me, that happens after about fifteen minutes, which is considered pretty standard."

"I'm slightly above average for Readers, and practically a prodigy for a half-blood," Mira says, echoing his stare. "And my max time is a half hour. So you must see how this sounds to us. You're saying you can stay there for two entire days—or even longer, since you've never been pushed out."

"Right," I say, looking at them. "I never realized that was anything abnormal—well, more abnormal than going into the Quiet in the first place."

Eugene looks fascinated. "That would mean your mother had to have been extremely powerful. Almost at the Enlightened level, if you've never been forced out thus far."

"But if you get forced out, can't you just go right back in?" I say, confused.

"Are you messing with us?" Mira's eyes narrow.

"I think he really doesn't know," Eugene says. "Darren, once we get pushed out, we can't go right back in. The recuperation time is proportional to how long we can stay there, though it's not directly related. There's a strong inverse correlation between short recovery times and longer times in the Mind Dimension. So the elites get the best of both worlds: a short recovery time and a long time inside. How it all works in the brain is actually my area of research."

"Eugene, please, not the neuroscience again," Mira says with exasperation before turning her attention to me. "Darren, if you truly don't know about recuperation time, then your power must be off the charts. Only I didn't think a half-blood could have that much power." The look she gives me now is unsettling. I think I prefer disdain. This look is calculating, as though she's sizing me up.

"You have to let me study you," Eugene tells me. "So we can figure out some answers."

"Sure, I guess. It's the least I can do," I say uncertainly.

"Great. How about tomorrow?" Eugene looks excited.

"Hmm. Maybe the day after?"

He smiles. "Let me guess, you're going to spend a whole day going around Reading people's minds, aren't you?"

"Good guess," I say, smiling back.

"Okay. Thursday then," he says. He looks ecstatic at the prospect of putting more electrodes to my head.

"So, I can't Read another Reader's mind?" I ask as I eat a piece of pickled ginger. This is a question that's been bothering me for a bit.

"No. But I bet you wish you could," Mira answers, downing the last of her sushi.

"It's only possible to do that to someone before they learn to Split for the first time, when they're children," Eugene explains. "Once people have experienced the Split, they simply get pulled into your Mind Dimension with you if you try to Read them."

"And if you and I manage to Split at the same time?" I ask. "Would we see each other in there?"

"Now you're getting into very specific and rare stuff," Eugene says. "It's almost impossible to time it that perfectly. Dad and I managed it only once. Even if you did, you'll find that, no, you see the world still, as usual, but you don't encounter each other. The only way to have a joint experience is to pull someone in. If either of you touches the other, the other will get pulled in. Once that happens, you'll be using up the time of the person whose Mind Dimension you're in."

"Using up the time?" I ask, finishing the last bit of my sashimi. This was amazing fish, I realize belatedly.

"As you bring people with you, your time is shared with them. If I pull you in, together we would stay in my Mind Dimension for about seven or eight minutes—about half of my fifteen-minute total. Similarly, how deep you go into someone's memories is half your total time."

The Reading Depth thing gives me an idea. If what Eugene says is right, then I think I have a better gauge of my 'power' based on my Reading of Eugene and Mira's neighbor, Brad. That sci-fi flick that he and Mira watched at the theater left the big screen at least six months ago—which means that I can spend at least a year in the Quiet.

As blown away as I am by this realization, something prevents me from sharing this information with my new friends. They looked awestruck at the mention of two days. What would they say to a year? And how do I reconcile this and being a half-blood? How powerful is Sara, to give birth to someone like me?

"What's the maximum power a Reader can have?" I ask instead.

"That's something even people who are part of the regular Reader society probably don't know," Mira says. "And even if they did, they wouldn't share that information with us."

"There are legends, though," Eugene says. "Legends of the Enlightened, who were wise well beyond their years. It was as though they'd led whole extra lifetimes. Of course, some of these stories seem more like mythology than history."

Myth or not, the stories sound fascinating. Before I get a chance to think about them, however, I'm interrupted by the waiter who brings our check. I insist on paying despite a few feeble complaints from Eugene. It's part of my thank you to them, I say.

When we exit the restaurant, I tell them, "I wish we could talk for hours on end, but there's something I have to do now."

"You could pull us into the Mind Dimension and chat away; this way you wouldn't be late for your appointment," Mira says, giving me a sly look.

"Mira." Eugene sounds chiding again.

She must be breaking another Reader social rule I'm not aware of. Using someone for time, perhaps? It doesn't matter. I wouldn't mind doing what she's asking if I wasn't dying of curiosity. "It's not about being late," I explain apologetically. "It's about asking my mom some serious questions."

"Oh, in that case, good luck," Mira says, her voice sympathetic for the first time.

"Thanks. Do you guys know where I can rent a car around here?"

Going to Staten Island from Brooklyn, or from anywhere for that matter, is best to do by car. There's a ferry from downtown, but no thanks. That requires taking a bus afterwards. And the ferry is unpleasant enough by itself.

Though Eugene and Mira don't know about rentals, my trusty phone does. According to it, there's a rental place a couple of blocks away. Since it's on the way to their apartment, I get an armed escort to the place—Mira with her gun. I'm grateful for that, as I'm still not a fan of their neighborhood. On our short walk, we talk some more about Readers. Despite Mira's complaints, Eugene starts telling me about his research.

It sounds like he's trying to find neural correlates that accompany what Readers do. That discovery might lead to knowing how the process works. He thinks he knows approximately what goes on, all the way up to the Split. After that moment, things get complicated because technology is finicky in the Quiet, and the instruments remaining in the real world don't register anything—proving that no time passes in the real world after we phase in.

I only half-listen. It all sounds fascinating, but in my mind, I'm already having a conversation with Sara.

When we reach the rental place, I enter both Eugene's and Mira's phone numbers into my phone, and they get mine. We say our goodbyes. Eugene shakes my hand enthusiastically. "It was great to meet you, Darren."

"Likewise," I say. "It was great meeting you both."

Mira walks up to me, and gives me a hug and a kiss on the cheek. I stand there wondering if that means she likes me, or if it's just a Russian thing.

Whatever the reason for her actions, it was nice. I can still smell a hint of her perfume.

When they begin to head back, I turn to enter the car rental place. Before I do, I'm pulled into the Quiet again.

It's Mira.

"Darren," she says, "I want to thank you. I haven't seen Eugene this happy, this animated, for a long time."

"Don't mention it. I like your brother," I say, smiling. "I'm glad I had that effect on him."

"I also wanted to say that, as he *is* my brother, I, above all, don't want to see him hurt."

"That makes sense." I nod agreeably.

"Then we have an understanding," she says evenly. "If this whole thing is a lie, I'll be extremely upset." Her eyes gleam darkly. "To put it in other words, if you hurt my brother in any way, I will kill you."

She turns around and walks to her frozen body, which is standing a few feet away.

I don't get a hug this time around.

CHAPTER TWELVE

I'm driving the piece-of-shit car I picked up at the rental place. They didn't have anything nice, but at least this thing has Bluetooth, so I'm listening to Enigma's "T.N.T. for the Brain" from my phone on the car speakers. I raise the volume to the max.

In a confused stupor, trying to digest everything I've learned today, I follow my phone's GPS directions. I know I need the Belt Parkway and the Verrazano Bridge after that, but once I get on Staten Island, I typically get lost—usually only a few blocks from where my moms live.

I called ahead to make sure they were home, but mentioned nothing of what I want to discuss. I plan to ambush them with my questions. They deserve it. I love them dearly, but I've never been angrier with them than I am now—not even during my rebellious mid-teen years. I'm especially mad at Sara.

Alternative lifestyle aside, Sara and Lucy are living, breathing stereotypes of two similar, yet different, kinds of moms.

Take Sara, for instance. She's a Jewish mom to the core. Never mind that she's the most secular person you'll ever meet. Never mind that she married a non-Jew, which isn't kosher. She still regularly hints—and sometimes outright says—that since I've finished my degree from a good school (of course), I should meet a nice girl (meaning a Jewish girl) and settle down. At twenty-one. Right. And she has all the usual guilt-trip skills down to a T. For example, if I don't call for a couple of days, I get the whole 'you don't need to trouble yourself to call your own mother; it's not like I'm in any way important,' et cetera, et cetera. And then there's the weird stuff, like if I'm out late and make the mistake of mentioning it to her, she'll want me to text her when I get home. *Yeah.* Never mind that on other nights—when I don't talk to her—I might not come home at all, and she's fine with my lack of texting.

Lucy is no better. Well, in truth, Lucy is better now. She only expects a call from me once a week, not daily. But when I was growing up, she was worse than Sara. She must've read that book about being a Tiger Mom and tried to apply it literally, with probably the worst possible subject—me. In hindsight, I think I had ADHD when I was a kid. When it came to the violin lessons she tried to force me to take, I 'accidentally' broke a dozen of the stupid instruments to test her resolve. When I broke the last one (over another student's head), I was expelled, and that did it for musical initiatives. Then there were the ballet lessons. I was kicked out for beating up a girl, which was not true. I knew from a very early age that you don't hit girls. Another girl pushed the victim, but I, because of my reputation in the class, took the rap. Lucy also wanted me to learn her native Mandarin. I don't care if I mastered a little bit from her when I was a baby, or that I can string together a few sentences even to this day; that was just not going to happen. If I'd studied Mandarin for her, I would've had to take Yiddish lessons for Sarah, too. Oy vey.

So, finishing school early and going to Harvard was partially an attempt to make my mothers happy, but even more so a means to get away from their overzealous parenting techniques and experience some freedom in Boston. Not to mention that finishing college allowed me to get a job and my own place as soon as possible. Ever since I gained some distance, my love for my family has deepened greatly.

As I pull into their driveway, I see three cars outside. I recognize the extra car as Uncle Kyle's old Crown Victoria.

Great, he's here. That's the last thing I need.

"Hi Mom," I say when Sara opens the door. I've never really seen much of myself in her, which makes me wonder that much more now about who my father might have been. We both have blue eyes, and I could've inherited her height, I guess. At five foot seven, she's tall for a woman. She seems particularly tall when, like now, she's standing next to my other mom. Lucy is barely above five feet tall, but don't let her size deceive you. She's tough. Plus, she has a gun—and knows how to use it.

"Hi sweetie," Sara says, beaming at me.

"Hi Mom," I say again, this time looking at Lucy.

"Hi Kitten," Lucy says.

Hmm. Are they trying to embarrass me in front of Uncle Kyle?

"Hey Kyle," I say with a lot less enthusiasm as I walk in.

He smiles at me, a rarity from him, and we shake hands.

I have mixed feelings when it comes to Kyle. Even though I mentally call him uncle, he's not my blood relative. Sara was an only child. He's a detective who works with Lucy. As former partners, I guess he and Lucy are close—a camaraderie I don't pretend to understand, having never put my life in danger the way they have.

I imagine my moms decided to ask Kyle to come around when I was growing up so I'd have a male role model in my life. However, their choice for the task couldn't have been worse. As far back as I can remember, I've butted heads with Kyle. Pick an issue, and we're likely to be on opposite sides of it. Doctor-assisted suicide, the death penalty, cloning humans, you name it, and you can be sure we've had a shouting match over it. I like to think of myself as a free thinker, while Kyle clings to what was digested and fed to him by some form of authority, never stopping to question anything.

The biggest mystery to me is actually why someone so traditional even accepts my moms' relationship. My theory is that he has a mental disconnect. I imagine he tells himself that despite their marriage, they're just best friends who live together.

I also think he has a rather tragic crush on Lucy. He would call it brotherly love, but I've always been skeptical. Especially given his very professional, cold attitude toward Sara, a woman he's known for over twenty years. An attitude that was chilly all along, but grew downright frigid after the huge fight they had when he decided to discipline me with a belt when I was nine. I was clever enough to scream and cry like a banshee, and predictably, Sara had a major fit. She actually threw a vase in his face. I think he had to get stitches. After that, he only used words to discipline me, and his interactions with Sara became even more aloof.

Having said all that, after I stopped needing to deal with Kyle regularly, I began to feel more fondness for the bastard. I know he usually means well. He's the closest thing to a father figure I have, and he did come around a lot, generally with good intentions. He told me cool stories about back in the day when he and Lucy kicked ass and took names— stories Lucy never chose to share, for some reason. And I wouldn't be half as good a debater now if not for all that arguing with him. For better or for worse, he played a role in the person I've become, and that's an honor usually reserved for people you consider close.

"How's work?" Kyle asks. "Are we due for another financial meltdown anytime soon?"

Kyle isn't a fan of anyone in the financial industry. I can forgive that; few people are fans of them. Or should I say of us? Also, only a tiny portion of the population understands the difference between bankers and hedge fund analysts, or can tell any financial professional from another.

"Work is great," I respond. "I'm researching a biotech company that's going to use magnetic waves to manipulate human brains for therapy."

Lucy narrows her eyes at me. She knows I'm trying to start an argument again. But I have to hand it to Kyle: this time, he doesn't take the bait. Usually he would go into some Luddite bullshit about how frightening and unnatural what I just said sounds, how dangerous it is to mess with people's brains like that. But no, he doesn't say anything of the sort.

"I'm glad you're making a name for yourself at that company," he says instead. Is that an olive branch? "I was just on my way out, but I'll see you at Lucy's birthday party in a few weeks."

"Sure, Kyle," I say. "See you then."

He walks out, and Lucy walks out with him. He probably came to get her advice on a case. He does that to this day, despite not having been her partner for decades.

"When will you grow up?" Sara chides, smiling. "Why must you always push people's buttons?"

"Oh, that's rich, you defending Kyle." I roll my eyes.

"He's a good man," she says, shrugging.

"Whatever," I say, dismissing the subject with a single word. The last thing I'm interested in right now is an argument about Kyle. "We need to talk. You should actually sit down for this."

Alarm is written all over Sara's face. I'm not sure what she imagines I'm going to say, but she has a tendency to expect the worst.

"Should we wait for your mother?" she says. They both say that in reference to the other, and it's always funny to me. *Your mother.*

"Probably. It's nothing bad. I just have some important questions," I say. Despite everything, I feel guilty that I've worried her.

I notice that she pales at the mention of important questions.

"Are you hungry?" she asks, looking me up and down with concern. *Please, not the too-thin talk again.* If it weren't for Lucy intervening, my own lack of appetite, and my stubbornness, I would be the chubbiest son Sara could possibly raise. And the fatter I'd get, the happier Sara would be as a mom. She would be able to show me around and say 'see how fat he is, that's how much I love him.' I know she got that 'feeding is caring' attitude from

Grandma, who wouldn't rest until you were as big as a house.

The fact that Sara doesn't pursue the food topic now shows me how concerned she is. Is it some kind of guilt thing? Does she suspect what I'm about to ask?

"No, thanks, Mom. I just had some sushi," I say. "But I would love some coffee."

"Did you go out partying all night?" She appears even more worried now. "You look exhausted."

"I didn't sleep well last night, but I'm okay, Mom."

She shakes her head and goes into the kitchen. I follow. Their house is still unfamiliar. I preferred the cramped Manhattan apartment where I grew up, but my moms decided a few years back that it was time for the suburbs and home ownership. At least they have some of the same familiar furniture I remember from childhood, like the chair I'm now sitting in. And the heavy round kitchen table. And the cup, red with polka dots, that she hands to me. My cup.

"I smell coffee," Lucy says, coming back.

"I made you a cup, too," Sara says.

"You read my mind," Lucy responds, smiling.

I decide I'm not going to get a better segue than that. Is it literally true? Can Sara Read Lucy's mind?

"Mom," I say to Sara. "Is there something important you want to tell me about my heritage?"

I look at them both. They look shell-shocked.

"How did you figure it out?" Lucy asks, staring at me.

"I'm so sorry," Sara says guiltily.

The vehemence of their reaction confuses me, considering my relatively innocuous question. I haven't even gotten to the heavy stuff yet. But it seems like I'm onto something, so I just say nothing and try to look as blank as I can, since I'm not sure what we're talking about. I sense we're not exactly on the same page.

"We always meant to tell you," Sara continues, tears forming in her eyes. "But it never seemed like a good time."

"For the longest time, until you were in your mid-teens, we couldn't discuss it at all. Even among ourselves," Lucy adds. She isn't tearing up, but I can tell she's distraught. "We even tried reading books about it. But the books recommend saying it as early as possible, which we didn't do . . ."

"Saying what?" I ask, my voice rising. I'm reasonably certain I'm about to find out something other than what I came here to verify, since I'm not aware of any books about Reading.

Sara blinks at me through her tears. "I thought you knew . . . Isn't that what you want to talk about? I thought you used some modern DNA test to figure it out."

A wave of panic washes over me. I try not to phase. I want to hear this.

"I want to know what you're talking about," I say. "Right now."

I look at them in turn. Daring them to try to wiggle out of it. They know they have to spill the beans now.

"You were adopted, Darren," Lucy says quietly, looking at me.

"Yes," Sara whispers. "I'm not your biological mother." She starts to cry, something I've hated since I was a little kid. There's something wrong, weirdly scary, about seeing your mom cry. Except—and the full enormity of it dawns on me—she's not my birth mom.

She never has been.

CHAPTER THIRTEEN

How would anyone react in my shoes?

I don't know if it's seeing my moms so upset or the news itself, but I can't take the flood of emotion for long. I phase into the Quiet. Once the world around me is still, I pick up the coffee cup and throw it across the room. It shatters against the TV, coffee spilling everywhere. I get up, grab the empty chair next to the one where my frozen self is sitting, and hurl it across the room after the cup, yelling as loudly as I can. I stop myself from breaking more stuff, though; even though I know it will go back to normal after I phase out, it still feels like vandalism.

Then I take a couple of deep breaths, trying to pull myself together.

This explains things—things that Eugene and Mira told me about. Sara didn't lie to me. She never had my ability. She reacted to my descriptions of the Quiet as a normal person would. I should probably feel relieved. I feel anything but.

Why would they not tell me? After all, it's not like we haven't had conversations about being adopted. We had them all the time. Sort of. We talked about how Lucy didn't give birth to me, but loves me just as much as Sara who, allegedly, did. This would've been just more of the same.

I take more deep breaths. I sit on the floor and perform the meditation I have used four times already today.

I begin to feel better—well enough to continue talking, at least. I look at the shocked expression on my frozen face. I reach out and touch myself on the elbow. The gesture is intended to comfort the frozen me, which, once I do it, seems silly. The touch brings me out of the Quiet.

I take a deep breath more demonstratively in the real world. "If you're not my biological mother," I manage to say, "then who is?"

"Your parents' names were Mark and Margret," Lucy says. To my shock, she's crying too—

something I've almost never seen her do. A knot ties itself in the pit of my stomach as she continues, "Your uncle might've told you stories about Mark."

I'm almost ready to phase into the Quiet again. She said 'were.' I know what that means. And I have heard of Mark. He was the daredevil partner who worked with Lucy and Kyle.

"Tell me everything," I say through clenched teeth. I'm trying my best not to say something I'll regret later.

"Before you were born, we really did go to Israel, as we always told you," Sara begins, her voice shaking. "It's just that what happened there was different from what you know. Our friends Mark and Margret approached us with a crazy story, and an even crazier request."

She stops, looking at Lucy pleadingly.

"They said someone was out to kill them," says Lucy in a more even voice. "They said Margret was pregnant, and they wanted us to raise the child. To pretend it was our own." She gets calmer as she tells this, her tears stopping. "We always wanted a child. It seemed like a dream come true. They were the ones who came up with the whole sperm bank story. They said the danger they were in could spill into your life if anyone ever found out about the arrangement. I know it sounds like I'm making excuses for not telling you, but when they got killed, just as they moved back to New York to be near you . . ."

"Lucy and Mark were close," Sara jumps in, wiping away the moisture on her face. "Back then, they worked in the organized crime division together. Lucy and I just assumed the unit where they all worked had something to do with why Mark was killed, which is why I begged your mother to switch to another division." She looks at Lucy again, silently urging her to continue with the story.

"I investigated their deaths," Lucy says. "But I still, to this day, have no idea who killed them and why. The killer left no clues. The crime scene was the most thoroughly investigated one in my career—and nothing. All I know is that Margret was shot in the back in her own kitchen, and it looked like Mark was killed a few seconds later when he tried to attack the person who shot her. There were no signs of a break-in."

My mind's gone numb. How am I supposed to feel about something like this happening to the biological parents I never knew existed? Or about them giving me to their friends to raise, even though they knew they'd be putting Sara and Lucy in danger?

I can't take it anymore, so I phase into the Quiet again.

Once everything is still, I walk up to Sara, whose face is frozen in concern. I still love her, just as much as I did on my way here. This changes nothing. I've always loved Lucy the same as Sara, despite knowing we're not related by blood. As far as I can tell, this is no different.

I put my hand on Sara's forearm and try to get into the state of Coherence, as Eugene called it. I'm so worked up that it's much more difficult this time. I don't know how long it takes before I'm in Sara's memories.

* * *

We're excited Darren is going to visit.

I, Darren, feel ashamed somehow at the intensity of Sara's enthusiasm. If it makes her so happy, I should probably visit more often.

We're devastated at having the dreaded adoption conversation with Darren, after all these years. Our own little family secret. Before I, Darren, am naturally pushed out by getting to the present moment in Sara's memories, I decide to go deeper.

Picturing being lighter, trying to focus, I fall further in.

We're watching Darren pack for Harvard. We're beyond anxious. I, Darren, realize that I am not far enough and focus on going deeper.

We're on a date with Lucy. She's the coolest girl we have ever met. I, Darren, realize how creepy this thing I am doing can get, but I also know that I can't stop. I overshot my target memory mark and need to go back out of this depth, or in other words, fast-forward the memories. I, Darren, do what I tried before when I wanted to get deeper into someone's mind, only in reverse: I picture myself heavier. It works.

We've been obsessing about Israel for months. Our heritage must call us, as our mom Rose said. I, Darren, realize that Rose is Grandma and that I am close—and I jump a bit further this time by picturing myself heavier again.

We're in Israel. It's awesome. Even Lucy's initial grumpy 'there are almost no other Asians here' attitude gets turned around after spending a day at the beach.

We look around the beach. The view is breathtaking. I, Darren, make a note to visit this place someday.

"Hi guys," says a familiar male voice.

We're shocked to see the M&Ms, Mark and Margret, approach our chairs. So is Lucy, we bet. What could they possibly be doing here, in Israel? The last thing anyone expects when going overseas is to meet friends from New York.

I, Darren, see them, and Sara's surprise pales next to mine. It's not like they look exactly like me, Darren. But it's almost like some Photoshop genius took their facial features, mixed them up, added a few random ones, and got the familiar face that, I, Darren, see every day in the mirror.

"What are you doing here?" Lucy asks, looking concerned.

"We need to talk," Mark says. "But not here."

I, Darren, picture feeling heavy again, so I can jump forward a little more.

We're listening to the M&Ms' crazy tale.

"Who's after you? If you don't tell me, how am I supposed to help?" Lucy says in frustration after they're done. We feel the same way. We can't believe our friends are springing this on us and telling us next to nothing.

"Don't ask me that, Lucy. If I told you, I'd put you and, by extension, the unborn child in danger," Mark says. I, Darren, realize that his voice is deep, a lot like the voice I hear on my voicemail. My voice.

"But what about you?" we say, looking at Margret. "How will you be able to go through with this?"

Margret, who has been very quiet through this conversation, begins crying, and we feel like a jerk.

"Margie and I are both willing to do whatever it takes to make sure our child lives," Mark says for her. "Regardless of how much it hurts us to distance ourselves this way."

"So you won't come back to New York?" Lucy asks. That's our girl, always the detective, trying to put every piece together.

He shakes his head. "My resignation is already prepared. We'll stay in Israel until the baby is born, then come back to New York for the first year of the baby's life to help you guys, and then we'll move to California. We hope you can come visit us in California once the baby is older. Tell her—or him—that we're old friends." Mark's voice breaks.

"But this makes no sense," Lucy says, echoing our thoughts. "If you're going to quit and move anyway, the child should be safe enough—"

"No," Mark says. "Moving barely mitigates the risk. The people who want us dead can reach us anywhere. Please don't interrogate me, Lucy. Just think how wonderful it would be to have a child. Weren't you guys always planning to adopt?"

"We couldn't think of better people to trust with this," Margret says. "Please, help us."

We think she's trying to convince herself of her decision. We can't even imagine how she must be feeling.

"We'll pay for everything," Mark says, changing the subject.

We're in complete agreement with Lucy's objections to the money, but in the end, the M&Ms convince us to accept their extremely generous offer—money we didn't even know they had. We know what Mark's approximate salary range is, since he works with Lucy, and he can't be making that much more than she is. To someone with that salary, this kind of money is unheard of. Nor is it likely that Margret makes that much. We wonder if having so much money has something to do with the paranoid story of people coming after them.

I, Darren, however, don't think it's the money. Could it be the Pushers? After all, Pushers killed Mira and Eugene's family. Could they be behind killing mine? Learning more about Pushers becomes much more personal for me all of a sudden.

I, Darren, can't take any more of this unfolding tragedy. I might come back here someday, but I can't handle it right now. Still, like a masochist, I progress into the memories.

We're driving back from Margret and Mark's funeral. We haven't spoken most of the way. We have never seen Lucy this upset.

"Please talk to me, hon," we say, trying to break the heavy silence.

"I was the one who found the bodies," Lucy says, her voice unrecognizable. "And I did the most thorough sweep of the crime scene. And with all that, I have nothing. It's like a perfect, unsolvable crime from one of your detective stories. I can't take it. I owe it to Mark to find the fucker who did this . . ."

"Don't be so hard on yourself," we say. "You'll figure it out. If you can't, no one could."

"We should have moved," Lucy says.

She hits a weak spot—our own guilt. We wish we had told Mark and Margret not to come to New York for that first year, not if they were in that much danger. But we didn't tell them that. We could've offered to come to California for a year. Something. The biggest source of our guilt, though, is that we thought the M&Ms were crazy. We didn't delve deeper into their story because it led to the most miraculous result—Darren. But now that Mark and Margret are dead, they are vindicated. We don't think they were crazy anymore. We just feel horrible for doubting them and not preventing this disaster somehow.

I, Darren, officially can't take any more. I jump out of Sara's head.

* * *

I'm back in the Quiet, looking at Sara. Much of my anger has dissipated. How can I be angry after I just experienced how this woman feels about me? I feel a pang of guilt for having invaded my mother's privacy to get the truth, but it's over and done with now.

I walk toward myself and touch my elbow.

Though I'm out of the Quiet, Sara is still pretty much motionless, waiting for my reaction.

"I don't know what to say," I say truthfully.

"It's okay. It's a lot to process," Lucy says.

"You think?" I say unkindly, and immediately regret it when she winces.

"I'm sorry it took us so long to tell you," Sara says, looking guilty.

"Even today, you told me under duress," I say, unable to resist. I guess I still feel bitter about that— about being kept in the dark for so long.

"I guess that's true," Sara admits. "Like Lucy said, we had a hard time talking about this for years. Once you don't talk about something, it becomes this strange taboo. But if you didn't already know, what were you asking about before?" She gives me a puzzled look.

"Never mind that now," I say. No way am I ready to spout some crazy talk about being part of a secret group of people who can freeze time and get into the minds of others. I was only going to bring that up when I thought Sara was a Reader herself. "The most important thing is that what you told me doesn't change anything for me."

I know from just Reading her mind that this is what she most wants to hear. I mean it, too. Yes, I'm mad and confused now, but I know with time what I just said will be one hundred percent true. It will be as though this adoption conversation never happened.

For those words, I'm rewarded by the expressions of relief on their faces.

"If you don't mind, I want to go home right now. I need to digest all this," I tell them. This is riskier. I know they would rather I stay and hang out. But I really am beyond exhaustion at this point.

"Sure," Sara says, but I can tell she's disappointed.

"We're here to answer any questions you might have," Lucy says. Her expression is harder to read.

Lucy is right. I might have questions later. But for now, I kiss and hug them before getting out of there as quickly as I can.

The drive to Tribeca happens as if in a dream. I only become cognizant of the actual mechanics of it when I start wondering where to park. Parking in the city is a huge pain, and is the reason I don't own a car. I opt for one of the paid parking lots, despite having to pay something outrageous for it tomorrow. Right now, I don't care. Anything to get home.

Once I get to my apartment, all I have the energy to do is eat and shower. After that, I fall asleep as soon as my head hits the pillow.

CHAPTER FOURTEEN

It's amazing what a good night's sleep can do for the psyche. As I'm eating my morning oatmeal, I see the events and revelations of the prior day in a brand-new light. Even the adoption thing seems like something I can deal with.

I try to put myself in my moms' shoes. Let's say my friend Bert told me a strange secret. Let's further suppose he asked me not to tell it to anyone, and then died. Surely that would count as sort of like someone's dying wish. And as such, it would undoubtedly be hard to reveal the secret in those circumstances. Could that be part of the reason for my moms' lack of communication?

Now that I'm more rested, I also realize another aspect of my new situation: I might have some family I've never met. Grandmothers and grandfathers I didn't know existed. Maybe uncles and cousins. All of these new family members are probably out there in the mysterious Reader community. It's too bad Eugene and Mira are not part of said community. If they were, I would have a way of getting introduced to other Readers. Maybe I'd even meet my extended family and learn more about my heritage.

Also, now that I'm not so stressed, knowledge of my newfound skills begins to excite me. I mean, think of the possibilities. It reminds me of middle school, when I first mastered the Quiet. I'd had a ton of fun sneaking into the girl's locker room unnoticed, reading my first girlfriend's diary, spying on hot older women . . . Now that I think about it, there was definitely a pattern to my early use of the Quiet.

All those things, however, pale in comparison to what Reading will let me do. It's almost best that I only learned about it now, when I'm more mature and better able to use this power responsibly.

The choice for my first destination is easy.

Finishing breakfast, I get dressed. I grab a Blu-ray disk that I should've returned ages ago and go to the third floor of my building.

I only went out with Jenny a few times. She's not in any way special among my ex-girlfriends, except for one thing—proximity. She lives in my building, which naturally makes her my first stop. Now what was I saying about being mature enough to handle this responsibly?

Stopping in front of her apartment door, I ring the doorbell.

Jenny opens the door. "Darren?" she says, looking at me. I'm tempted to deny it, to say that I'm not Darren, but figure she's not in the mood for jokes.

"I found this movie I borrowed from you," I say instead. "I wanted to give it back."

"Oh. Okay, I guess. I'm just surprised to see you." She doesn't look just surprised, though—she looks angry. Or at least a little unnerved. Figuring there's no time like the present, I phase into the Quiet.

There had been a slight buzzing in the hallways of my apartment building, something I only realize now because it's gone. It's interesting how we ignore constant noises like that. I started becoming more cognizant of just how much we don't register about our surroundings when I first began phasing into the Quiet. So much happens around us that our conscious mind misses.

I touch Jenny's forehead. Though I had been conflicted about touching women in the Quiet, I decide that this is different. Or that Reading is worth it. It's easy to convince myself to let go of certain principles when they get in the way of something I really want.

I try to get into Coherence. It's even easier this time. As soon as I'm in, I do the lightness bit in order to jump deeper into her thoughts—otherwise all I'll see is her opening the door for me, which is boring.

* * *

We're at a club, making out with a girlfriend in order to get attention from the guys. Though this is not where I, Darren, intended to end up, I'm content to stay for a little while. I try to absorb every moment. We dance and grind with Judy, but it's all just for fun, a way to get attention. Eventually I, Darren, lose interest and try to go deeper.

We're getting ready to meet with Darren again. We're a little sad about our relationship with him. He used to be so hot—until he paid attention to us. At that point, his appeal dropped drastically. Why does that always happen to us?

No, we have to stop being our own worst critic. It could be Darren who's the problem, not us. When we saw him at that party in the penthouse, he seemed so confident and cocky, exactly what turns us on. But then he didn't ask us to go to his place that night, coming up with some lame coffee date instead. That's on him. Unless of course we start worrying about being a slut. We wish one day the inner critic would just shut the fuck up.

We pick the outfit for this evening very carefully. The new bra and panties should go a long way. I, Darren, think I recognize what day this is, so I jump further, to the part of her life I actually came here to witness.

Darren is standing without his shirt in our bedroom. He's in great shape. We hope we turn him on. As things progress, we worry a lot less about anything, instead focusing on what we're feeling as we give in to the purely physical part of ourselves.

When the experience is over, I, Darren, jump out.

* * *

I'm back in the Quiet. Okay, yeah. I wanted to experience what sex is like for a girl. And what better way to do so than to find out what it would be like to have sex with *me*? Not to mention, I'm not entirely sure how I'd feel about experiencing sex as a girl with a guy who's not me. There's no way I'm sharing this with my therapist. She'd have a field day with it.

Both Coherence and moving about in people's memories are getting easier for me already. This reminds me of when I first discovered being able to go into the Quiet.

Skills improve with experience. With the first few trips into the Quiet, it took being near death to activate the strange experience. A fall from a bike was only the first. There was also a fall off a roof into a sandbox, and a bunch of other stunts culminating in the time I fell into that manhole. Crazy, right? Who falls into a manhole? According to my moms, their childhood nickname for me was Taz, after the Tasmanian Devil from the cartoons. That's how much trouble I used to get into. But at least it gave me practice when it came to near-death experiences.

Then it started happening under less dire circumstances, like the time I got into a fight with our school bully, John. I still hate that guy. I momentarily contemplate finding him, Reading his mind, and messing with him. I decide against it for now. I would need to locate the prick, and that's too much of a bother at the moment.

Eventually, getting into the Quiet would happen when I did something as insignificant as watch a good horror movie. Progressively I got to where I am today, where any slight worry or nervousness can be harnessed for phasing in. I wonder what the path was like for Eugene and Mira. I'll have to remember to ask them.

Thinking of those two makes me wonder if I should stop messing around and go see them. No, I decide. Not yet. Not until I have some more Reading fun.

I look at Jenny. She's clutching the door, like she wants to close it as soon as possible. I feel a pang of guilt, and I phase out.

"Sorry if I intruded," I say. "I guess I should've left this by the door. I just figured, since we agreed to stay friends, it would be a good idea to bring this to you."

"Yeah, sure," she says. It doesn't take Reading to know she didn't actually want us to be friends when she said that. "It was nice of you to bring this back, and I'm glad you didn't just leave it by the door like some stranger."

"Okay, thanks. Sorry I bugged you. I'll see you around," I say. It's awkward, but I don't regret this. Jenny looks like she knows she's missing something, but since I'm sure there's no way she'll ever guess what just happened, I don't worry about it.

The door closes, and I'm ready for a drive around the city.

On a whim, I decide to go to the gym. There are plenty of people I can Read there. Plus, it would be nice to get a workout. I exercise mostly out of vanity, but at the same time, I do like to hear how good exercise is for your mind as well as your body. More bang for the buck.

Instead of my usual Tribeca location, I go to the Wall Street branch—I have a car, after all, so I figure I may as well use it. The Wall Street gym is classier.

By the time I get there, which isn't far, I curse the car idea. I would have gotten here much faster on foot, considering the traffic and the time it takes to find a parking spot. That's Manhattan for you. It's got some minuses.

I walk through the big revolving glass doors. This gym in general, and this location specifically, is very high end. Its membership price is ridiculous, but hey, I can afford it. It's nice and clean, which is a huge bonus for me. I might be a little OCD when it comes to cleanliness.

I wonder if it would make sense to exercise in the Quiet anymore. I used to do it on occasion when I was in a rush, but that was before I knew you don't age in there. Now that I know about the aging thing, it seems logical that muscles wouldn't grow bigger from any exercise performed in the Quiet. And growing muscles is really the only reason I do this.

Still, I'm not one hundred percent sure that it would be useless to exercise in the Quiet in general.

Certainly some skills stay with you. Just the other week, when I was convinced to play my first game of golf, I practiced in the Quiet so my game would be more impressive to my coworkers. The practice definitely helped, meaning some kind of muscle memory was retained. Another question for Eugene, I guess.

For now, I opt for a real-world workout.

I'm doing chest presses when I see a familiar face. We have a lot of celebrities at this gym, so I try to recall who this is. Then it hits me. Can that really be who I think it is? It's possible—his bank's headquarters are near here. If he did go to a gym open to the public, this would be the one he'd go to.

To make sure I'm right, I approach him.

"Excuse me, can you please spot me?" I ask, pointing at the bench I'm using.

"Sure," he says. "Do you need a lift?"

"I got it," I say, and I do. That's him. Jason Spades, the CEO. The man is a hero to us at the fund. His is the only bank that weathered the shit storm that befell most others—and he got a lot of the credit for it. From what I heard, his fame is well deserved.

"Thanks," I tell him when I'm done with my set.

He walks away, and on a whim, I phase into the Quiet. It's particularly easy in the gym—the heart is already racing, which to the brain must not be far from being frightened or otherwise excited.

It's very odd to see people holding heavy weights suspended in midair, though. It seems like their hands should fail any second.

I walk up to Jason Spades and touch his temple. It's time to flex my Reading muscles some more. I have to work on the meditation to get into the Coherence state for a moment. Next, I picture myself light as a feather. I'm hoping to enter his mind further than what seems to happen by default.

* * *

"Go to the gym today, take a day off, and do some gardening. You can't beat yourself up like this," our wife tells us at the breakfast table. "This kind of stress will give you a heart attack."

"You don't understand, babe. It's going to be the worst quarter results in the company history. Back in the day, CEOs jumped out of windows over this sort of thing," we say. We are grateful for her support, but we can't help feeling that she just doesn't get it. The enormity of it. Everything we've worked for is going to be ruined. No weekends, no vacations, endless sleepless nights—all for nothing.

We also think about the other thing, the thing we haven't even mentioned to her. How a trader was taking unauthorized risks and lost a big chunk of the bank's money. We're going to be held responsible by the investors for that, too. Combined with the quarter results, we'll look like an idiot—just like the rest of the bank CEOs. This is not the legacy we'd been hoping for.

I, Darren, decide I've had enough and jump out.

* * *

I'm speechless, torn between empathy and glee.

I do feel bad for Jason. It's painful to see legendary people like that fall. His disappointment is intense. His wife is getting him through it, though, and that's encouraging. Maybe there is something to the whole marriage thing after all. And he's probably wrong about his wife—I bet she understands what's about to come down. She probably just knows the right things to say to her husband. On a slightly more positive side, I'm glad he wasn't contemplating something insane, like blowing his brains out. I don't know what I'd do in that case. Would I try to stop him? Probably I would, though how to start that conversation without seeming like a lunatic is beyond me.

Anyway, I can't dwell on these depressing thoughts. Not when Jason's tragedy can be my get-rich-ridiculously-quick scheme.

I phase out, and on an impulse, I take out my phone. Did I mention I love smartphones? Anyway, I bring up my trading app. The bank's stock is the highest it's been in the past four years. Clearly nobody has any idea what's about to happen.

I have to act. I check on the price of put options. Those are basically contracts with someone assuring you they'll buy from you at an agreed-upon price within a given time period. It turns out that an option to sell at a lower price than where the stock is right now is dirt-cheap. That's because put options are like insurance, and in this case, people are betting the price will be steady or higher. I have thirty-two thousand dollars in cash in my trading account, and I use it all to buy the put options.

With some very conservative assumptions, if the stock drops even ten percent, I'll still be able to make a lot, either by selling the options or exercising them. If the stock completely tanks, like that of the 'too big to fail' banks during the crisis, I might end up making a cool million from the money I just invested. And, of course, I'll invest more of my money when I'm near a computer. There's only so much you can do on the phone. I think I might even put all of my savings into this, though I have to be careful. The SEC might wonder about me if I go overboard. Also, what if I Read someone else and get an even better tip? My money would be locked up for a few weeks. Though, I have to admit, it's hard to picture a better scenario.

And regarding the SEC, I wish I knew at what point someone shows up on their radar. Not that they'd have anything on me, even if they noticed my activity. They work on proof, unlike the casinos— proof like phone conversations or email records. Things they would not have in my case. Still, I don't want the bother of an investigation.

I can't believe Mira makes her money playing cards with criminals. This way is so much easier. I really hope she doesn't do it for money. If I find out that's the case, and offer Eugene and her some money, I wonder if they would accept. Somehow I think she might be too proud, but I ought to try. I'm feeling very generous right now. I've never had any trouble with money, even without the job at the fund, but now, with Reading, I see that I will quickly reach a new level of financial independence.

I'm so wired now, I have to go harder on myself during the rest of the workout. Lifting heavy weights seems to clear my mind. I'm not sure if that's a common experience or just me being weird. There's only one way to find out, so I Read a few minds to investigate. According to my informal gym-based study, other people also feel good after lifting weights. Good to know.

When I'm done with the gym and get in my car, I text Amy. She's an acquaintance from Harvard. That's another reason to go there, by the way—to make important connections that help you get jobs.

Networking is not why I want to meet with Amy today, however. I do it because she's crazy, in exactly the way I need.

She wants to do sushi, and after some back-and-forth, I give in. I guess I'll have sushi for the second day in a row. It's a good thing I like the stuff so much.

We meet at her favorite midtown place and catch up. She works at another fund, so it's easy to convince her this is just an impromptu networking session. Except I'm here for a different reason.

Amy is into extreme experiences of all sorts. In some ways, she's the opposite of me. For example, she's just bitten into Fugu sashimi. Fugu is that poisonous blowfish that the Japanese never allowed their emperor to eat. The fish contains tetrodotoxin, a neurotoxin fatal to humans and other creatures. If the chef messed up Amy's order, it could be deadly. Each fish has enough poison to kill around thirty people. And Amy's eating it like it's nothing. That's the sort of person she is. It's perfect for me, so I phase into the Quiet.

Amy is still, chopsticks carrying their potentially deadly load into her mouth. She isn't cringing or anything. I have to respect her for that.

I approach her and get into her mind, not bothering to rewind events.

* * *

We're chewing the Fugu. I, Amy, can't get enough of the stuff, while I, Darren, am severely disappointed. The flavor is much too subtle for me. It doesn't really taste like much of anything. Given the health risks, I would've expected this to taste like lobster multiplied by a hundred.

I go deeper.

We're flying in a plane. This is our first non-tandem jump, and we feel the adrenaline rush just getting on the plane. When it takes us to fifteen thousand feet, we get our first 'feargasm,' as we like to call it.

When we eventually make the jump, the feeling of free fall overwhelms us with its intensity. It's everything we thought it would be, and more.

Through it all, we don't forget the most important thing—and after sixty seconds of bliss that seem like a millisecond, we pull the cord to open the parachute.

We're already wondering what to do next. Maybe jump naked? Maybe under the influence of some substance?

The flight after the parachute opens gets boring, so I, Darren, seek something else.

We're snowboarding this time . . .

* * *

I get out of Amy's head eventually. Thanks to her, I'm able to cross off ninety percent of my bucket list. Through her eyes, I have surfed, bungee jumped, rock climbed, snowboarded, and even done BASE jumping with a wing suit.

I would never have done any of these things for real, particularly since yesterday I found out something that I'm still trying to wrap my head around: I can extend my subjective lifespan by just chilling in the Quiet. That means I have a lot more to lose than regular people.

I insist on paying for Amy's lunch. It's the least I can do to pay her back for the experiences I just gleaned through her eyes. I definitely got closer to understanding what drives her and other people like her to do these seemingly crazy things. Most of it was awesome—especially jumping out of that plane.

Of course, it wasn't awesome enough for me to risk my life. But now, thanks to Reading, I won't have to. I can just hang out with Amy again. I think I might be getting lunch with her more often now.

After I'm in the car again by myself, I, unbelievably, feel like I might've had enough Reading for today. I want to get together with my new Brooklyn friends a day early.

I text Eugene, and he excitedly invites me over.

Now the stupid car will finally come in handy.

CHAPTER FIFTEEN

I park in front of Eugene and Mira's building after an uneventful drive over. The spot is near a fire hydrant, but far enough away from it not to get a ticket. The nice thing about hydrant spots like this is that there's no one in front of the car. This makes parallel parking, a skill I haven't fully mastered, easier. No parking meters either, just a regular spot that's only a problem during Monday morning street cleanings. Impressive. I guess one nice perk of Brooklyn is being able to park like this on the street.

I make my way over to the building entrance. A friendly old lady holds the door for me. Apparently I don't look like a burglar to her, the way she just lets me walk right in. I'm glad, because this way I don't have to play with the intercom again.

Before the door closes behind me, I get that feeling again.

Someone's pulled me into the Quiet.

The door is frozen halfway between open and shut, the world is silent, and I'm standing next to frozen me and unfrozen Mira. I briefly wonder what part of my body she touched to get me to join her before I notice the wild look in her eyes and forget everything else.

"Mira, what's going on?"

"There isn't time," she says, running to the stairs. "Follow me."

I run after her, trying to make sense of it.

"They found me," she says over her shoulder. "They found us."

"Who found you?" I ask, finally catching up.

She doesn't answer; instead she stops dead in her tracks. There are men standing like statues on the staircase heading up to the first floor.

Finally coming out of whatever shock she's in, she goes through the pockets of a tall burly man wearing a leather jacket. Not finding whatever information she was looking for in his wallet, she touches his temple and appears to be concentrating in order to Read.

When she's done, she takes a gun from the man's inner pocket and shoots him. The sound of the shot, even with a silencer on the gun, nearly deafens me, and I put my hands up to my ears. She just keeps shooting, over and over. Then, when the gun begins to make clicking sounds, she uses the empty gun to beat the man's face into a bloody pulp. I've never seen anyone as angry, as out of control, as she is. Tears of frustration well up in her eyes, but none fall.

"Mira," I say gently. "You're not going to kill him that way. He'll still be alive when we phase out of the Quiet."

She goes on with her grisly attack until the gun slips from her fingers. She turns to me, the tears falling now. She brushes them away impatiently, clearly embarrassed that I've seen her lose control like this. "I know that—trust me, I know. It doesn't make a fucking bit of difference, anything I do to them. But I needed that." She takes a breath, pulling herself together. "And now we have to run."

"Wait," I say. "Can you please explain to me what's going on?"

"These fuckers' friends just kidnapped me," she says, pushing her way through the rest of the 'dead' man's three companions.

"What? How?"

"They're after Eugene," she says, running even faster up the stairs. "They're taking me hostage in case they don't find him at home. They want to use me to smoke him out. Only, he *is* home."

"What do they want with him?" I ask, confused. Eugene is one of the nicest people I've ever met. I just assumed this whole kidnaping business with Mira had something to do with her gambling adventures. The four men sure look like the same kind of guys as the one we ran into at the sushi restaurant yesterday. Why would they be after Eugene?

"I don't have time to explain, Darren," she says, and stops on the second floor. She turns to me and sizes me up, as though looking at me for the first time.

"Listen," she says, "I won't make it to the next floor, let alone the apartment. I'm about to fall out of the Mind Dimension—I can already feel myself slipping. Me running here was a desperate attempt. Even if I didn't pull you in, I wouldn't have made it. So, I need your help."

"Of course—what do you need?" I'm scared. I haven't seen Mira like this before. Sarcastic—yes; angry—a couple of times, sure. Even amused. But not vulnerable like this.

"You have to promise to save my brother."

"I will," I say, and it comes out very solemn. "But can you tell me what's going on?"

"Okay, pay attention. I might not have the time to repeat it. I need you to go into the Mind Dimension, the Quiet as you call it, as soon as my time's up. Once you're there, once you've stopped time for everyone around you, you have to come back up these stairs and go all the way to the apartment. Take one of their guns on the way—" she points at the men downstairs, "—and shoot the door lock to get into the apartment. Pull Eugene in to join you in your Mind Dimension. Tell him these guys are on their way up." She says it all in one breath, wiping her eyes and nose with her sleeve. It might be disgusting from anyone else, but somehow Mira makes even this display endearing. "If you pull this off, if you get him out of this fucking mess, I'll be forever in your debt."

"I'll do it, Mira," I say, beginning to think coherently. "I promise, I'll get him out of the building. I'm parked right outside. It shouldn't be a problem."

"Thank you," she says. The next moment, she's next to me. She hugs me, and I clumsily hug her back. I don't know how to act around a woman in such distress. I pat her back gently, hoping it makes her feel better.

Then she stands on her tiptoes and kisses me. The kiss is deep and desperate, her lips soft against mine. It's completely unexpected, but I return the kiss without a second thought, my mind in complete turmoil. So much for coherent thinking.

"Tell Eugene I'm sorry," she says, pulling away after a few moments. "Tell him this is my fault. I led them here. They picked me up at the gym, and I had some mail on me."

"The gym?" I say, a sick feeling in my stomach.

"Yes. I'm so fucking stupid. I took the mail out of the mailbox in the morning. They found it on me. Our address was on it," she says bitterly.

"Your gym is how my friend found you," I admit. "You used one of your older aliases there. I'm so sorry. I should've told you that."

"No, you didn't know the danger we're in. This is definitely on me. I should've asked you how you found me. And I should've changed gyms. We should've fucking moved a long time ago—"

"Where are you now, and more importantly, who are these people? You have to tell me before your time is up," I interrupt urgently.

"The men in this building are working with the ones who picked me up. I don't know for sure, but I think they're all involved with the people who killed our parents. The same Russian crew. The same Pusher is probably pulling their strings. Eugene can tell you more. I'm in the car where the friends of the assholes downstairs put me. At first they knocked me out somehow, maybe with chloroform or a shot. I don't remember. I don't have any bruises, so I doubt they hit me on the head. When I came to, about twenty or so minutes after, I Split and Read the driver. They gave our address to someone, which led to the group that came here. They work quickly; I didn't expect them to already be here. The ones holding me are going to this address in Sunset Park." She hands me a little piece of paper. I commit the address on the paper to memory. "After that, I Split again and ran here on foot. But it was too far. If I hadn't run into you—"

I phase out before she's able to finish her last sentence. Suddenly I'm standing downstairs again, next to the still-closing door.

Mira is gone.

As she instructed me, I instantly phase into the Quiet.

I run, even though rationally I know I have plenty of time. Unlike Mira, I can spend an insanely long time in the Quiet.

As I'm running, I digest the fact that after she pulled me in and her time ran out, I got pushed out. This is something I wondered about—what happens if you pull someone in, but then get out of the Quiet yourself. Looks like your guest in the Quiet is tied to you. If you get out, they get out.

My contemplation of the rules of this bizarre new world is interrupted by the people on the stairs. The guy in the leather jacket is back, standing there like nothing happened—which makes sense, since nothing actually has happened, at least not outside Mira's Quiet session. I take his gun as she suggested. I'm very tempted to Read them, but I decide to do the important part first.

I run up to the fifth floor. As I turn into their hallway, I see Eugene. He's wearing a ratty hoodie with dorky pajama pants underneath. I fleetingly wonder what happened to the white coat.

He's throwing out the garbage. I don't need to shoot the lock off their door after all.

I touch him, and in a moment he's staring at me, confused.

"Eugene, Mira is in trouble," I tell him instead of hello.

"What? What do you mean?" He looks alarmed.

"Please let me explain. She was just here, in the Quiet. She said she was kidnapped. She said they're after you."

"Who's after me?" He looks panicked now. "What are you talking about?"

"Come with me," I say, figuring a picture is worth a thousand words. "I'll tell you what she told me on the way down. You need to see them."

"See whom?" he asks, but follows me anyway. "Can you just explain?"

"There are some kind of mobsters who came here for you. I'm taking you to them," I say and pick up speed. "Mira said they're the same people who killed your parents. That some Pusher controls them. She said you would be able to explain this to me."

"And now they have her?" he asks from behind me, his voice low.

"Yes. She's in a car, being taken to a place in Sunset Park. I have the address," I say as we make our way to the four men on the stairs. "This is the problem," I say, pointing at them.

Eugene approaches the men. There is an unrecognizable, almost frightening expression on his face.

Without asking any more questions, he approaches the man wearing a blue tracksuit and touches the guy's temple. I decide to also indulge in Reading, since I'm waiting for Eugene anyway. I walk up to the guy in the leather jacket whose gun I didn't need.

* * *

We're driving to the address we were texted. We're happy we called shotgun, as Boris, Alex, and Dmitri are still bitching about having to share the backseat. Alex, who sits in the middle, apparently spreads his knees too wide for the others' comfort.

Haste was of the essence when we got the call, so we had to leave the restaurant, bill unpaid and food unfinished, and get into Sergey's car. Top priority and all that.

"Wait here," we tell Sergey—the driver—in Russian. I, Darren, understand this again, though the words sound foreign in my mind.

Next, we hand Sergey our phone with a picture of the target. If the target happens to waltz into the building behind us, Sergey is supposed to text us immediately.

I, Darren, am able to feel a more pronounced mental distance between myself and my host, whose name is Big Boris. I'm less lost in the experience, and I'm glad about that. I guess I'm getting better at this Reading business. His mind seems less of a mystery to me with this little bit of extra distance.

Encouraged, I try to focus on how he—or I, or we—got the idea to come to this building. Specifically, I'm looking for more details on this phone call he/I/we were recalling. All of a sudden, I'm there.

We're at the restaurant eating lamb shish kebab when we get a phone call. We look at the phone and see the number we memorized long ago, and the name 'Arkady' on the screen. A piece of meat gets stuck in our throat. It's the boss, and he always makes us nervous.

"Go to the location I'm going to text you immediately," he says, and we promptly agree.

We're not done with the meal, but we don't voice our annoyance to the boss. Not into the phone, and not even to the crew as we tell them what's what. We wouldn't dream of crossing Arkady; he's the craziest, toughest, most ruthless son of a bitch we've ever met.

I, Darren, repeat Arkady's phone number to myself over and over, so I can remember it in case it comes in handy later. Luckily, I'm very good when it comes to remembering numbers. Still, I need to write this down, along with the address where Mira is being kept, as soon as I can.

I realize that I managed to jump around Big Boris's mind without the usual feeling of lightness. Though with hindsight, I think I did feel light; it was simply on a subconscious level, like I was on a strange mental autopilot. I'll need to play around with this some more, this jumping about in people's minds, but now is not the time. I need to jump out of this mind and get Eugene out of this mess.

* * *

When I'm out of Big Boris's head, Eugene is staring at me.

"I couldn't find any confirmation that these men are the same people who killed Mom and Dad," he says.

"That's not the thing to focus on right now," I respond. "We have to get you out of this first. Then we have to rescue Mira."

"Sorry, you're right." He shakes his head like he's disgusted with himself. "There's no time to think about revenge—not that I'm in a position to do anything to them right now anyway. I'm not good at thinking under pressure."

"It's fine. But we have to be careful," I tell him, remembering what I just saw. "Their driver knows what you look like."

"I got that much out of Boris," he says, pointing at the short stocky guy in the tracksuit whose mind Eugene just Read. I internally chuckle, realizing the reason Big Boris needs the 'Big' distinction. He's the second Boris in the group.

"Walk with me," I say. "I want to show you where I'm parked."

As I lead Eugene to my car, I ask, "Is there a back exit from your building somewhere?"

"Not that I know of," he says, scratching his head as we stop in front of my parked car.

"How about a way to the roof?"

"That's through the sixth floor," he says, pushing his glasses further up his nose. "I think I can get there if I need to."

"Okay. Hopefully you won't have to. First, we need to try for the main door. They're walking up the stairs. It will take them time to get to your floor. I have an idea—follow me," I tell Eugene and head back to the building.

I run up the stairs, pushing the mobsters out of my way. Eugene follows. I pull the elevator door on the second floor. It's locked. I run to the third floor and do the same thing, getting the same result. The door on the fourth floor opens. So far, so good. I keep running, checking near the elevator doors on every floor until we get to the top, on the sixth.

"Okay, Eugene. Here's my plan: they think your elevator is broken. That gives you a good chance. As soon as I phase out and you're in the real world, press the elevator button. Since the elevator's on the fourth floor, it should get to you in plenty of time. No one is by the elevator on any of the other floors, so there's little risk of any slowdowns."

"Got it, Darren." He smiles for the first time since I've seen him today. "You know, I could've come up with this plan on my own. You're basically telling me to take the elevator down and walk out."

"Yeah, I guess I am. Also, pull up your hoodie and try to hunch as you walk out. Go straight to the car. That's where I'll be waiting, keeping it running," I say. This sounds doable, but I wouldn't want to be in Eugene's shoes right now. "If something goes wrong, run for the roof and text me. I'll phase into the Quiet and come talk to you. Can you phase in every few seconds and walk down to check on the bad guys' progress?"

"Yes," he says. "Since I'll only be spending a small fraction of my available time in each instance, I should be able to re-enter the Mind Dimension without waiting a long time in-between. Thank you."

"Thank me when this is over," I say and begin to walk down the stairs again. He continues to follow me.

"Darren," he says when we reach my frozen body in the lobby. "If something happens to me, promise you'll help Mira."

"I promise," I say. I have no idea how I'll do that, but it occurs to me that the last thing Mira made me promise was that I would save him if she didn't make it. Maybe it wouldn't be so bad having a sibling after all, the way these two look out for each other.

"Don't look guilty as you get out of the building," he says, looking in the direction where Sergey, the driver, is waiting for his comrades.

"Same to you," I say. "See you in a few minutes."

We shake hands.

I take a breath and touch my frozen self on the forehead. The sounds of the world come back.

CHAPTER SIXTEEN

I do my best to avoid looking suspicious, in case Sergey is watching me from the car. I pat my pockets, take out the car keys, and confidently walk back. The image I'm trying to project is: silly me, I forgot something in the car. I might not win an Oscar for my acting, but hopefully the performance will be enough to keep us off the Russians' radar.

As soon as I'm in the car, the first thing I do is fish out the pen I used to sign the receipt for this car rental and the receipt itself. On the back, I write the address and phone number I kept in my head.

Then I start the car.

I've never been this antsy. I stare at the car's digital clock, but it seems to have stopped. It feels like half an hour has passed when a single digit on the clock advances one minute.

The plan initially seemed simple enough—just wait for Eugene. I didn't expect the suspense to be this torturous. I take a deep breath and mentally count to thirty. It doesn't work.

There *is* something I can do, though, so I phase into the Quiet.

I'm in the backseat of the car. My frozen self is in the front. I've always wondered how the body I get in the Quiet decides where to show up. Of course, there is Eugene's mention of this possibly not being a real body. That still doesn't answer it completely. Whatever I inhabit now, who decided it should appear in the backseat? How did it get there? Why not show up, say, outside the car?

I open the door and get out. Now that he can't see me staring, I can get a better look at Sergey. He seems to be bored, so I assume I didn't raise his suspicions. Good. I also note the car he's driving is actually pretty nice—a Mercedes, no less. Apparently crime does pay.

I walk into the building. The goons are now approaching the second floor. It's scary how close they're getting to Eugene.

I run all the way up to the fifth floor.

Thankfully, I see Eugene opening the elevator door. This is it. The plan is working.

I go back to the car and phase out.

The noises are back, and the digital clock in the car is supposed to work normally; only it's still crawling. I wonder if using the Quiet messes with your time perception. I mean, how long can a few minutes last?

After what seems like another half hour of worry, but really is only three minutes according to the clock, I phase into the Quiet again. Eugene is still not out of the stupid elevator on the second floor.

I go back, phase out, wait ten seconds, and go back in. I repeat this a couple of times until I see the elevator door open. Yes! Finally.

Since I'm here anyway, I walk up to check on the mobsters. They're between the fourth and fifth floors. Satisfied, I go back to the car to phase out again.

Another few seconds, and I can't take it anymore. I phase into the Quiet yet again. Eugene is walking to the door in the lobby. His hoodie is pulled up all the way. His hunching is terribly fake, but as long as he doesn't look like himself, we should be out of this mess in a few seconds. I go back to the car and get out of the Quiet again, only to return a few seconds later.

Eugene is walking toward me. Sergey, the driver, is looking at him with too much concentration. Oh, no. I walk up to the car and touch Sergey's temple.

* * *

We're looking at a strange guy who just left the building in a very suspicious manner. He's trying to hide his face, so we can't see it, but we think he could be the target. Since we know we're here on Arkady's orders, we have to cover our ass. We take out our phone and text Big Boris about seeing something suspicious. Now it can't be said that we fucked up.

* * *

Done Reading the driver, I run back to the car and phase out. I swivel the steering wheel. My foot is on the gas. I shift the gear in the drive position. Then I phase into the Quiet again.

Eugene is a few steps away from the car. I walk up to him and touch his wrist. A moment later, another Eugene stands next to me, this one fully animated.

"I made it," he says on a big exhale, like he's been holding his breath this whole time.

"No. We're far from out of this. Sergey, the driver, just recognized you."

"Fuck. What do we do?"

"You'll jump into the car, and as soon as you close the door, I'll step on the gas. Buckle up as soon as you can—it might be a bumpy ride."

"Thank you again, Darren," he starts saying, and I wave dismissively.

"As I said before, thank me once we're out of this." Hurrying back to the car, I take a deep breath and phase out of the Quiet.

The next few actions happen in a blur. Eugene runs to the door and jumps into the car. As he closes the door, I stomp on the gas pedal, and we're at the first intersection in seconds.

As we pass the next intersection, I realize that I have no idea where I'm going, but it doesn't matter as long as it's away from that building. On a whim, I decide to keep going straight, and pump the gas again.

I'm going fifty miles per hour when I see the next light turning red a few feet away.

I'm forced to phase into the Quiet. This time, it's particularly eerie. I've never done this in a moving car before. The sounds of the engine, which was working overtime to get us moving faster, are gone. That's strange enough, but what's weirder is that the car itself is standing still. Everything in my brain tells me it should at least move a few extra feet according to the law of inertia, but it doesn't. It's as still as a rock.

I realize I should've done this phasing business at the last intersection. Or even the one before that. It's too late now, though, so I might as well get on with it.

This gives me a chance to check for any pursuers. I walk out of the car and look inside. Through the front window, I see expressions of sheer horror on both my own and Eugene's faces. I walk to Eugene's side and reach into the window. Touching his neck makes Eugene's Quiet incarnation show up in the back seat.

"Darren, what the fuck are you doing? You can't Split like this, in the middle of a car chase."

"Why not?"

"Well, for starters, when you get back, you increase the chance that you'll lose control of the car."

"We'll have to chance it—I'll be careful," I promise. "I had to do it because there was a red light at that intersection."

"Shit," Eugene says, following my gaze. Though here in the Quiet the light is actually dead, he doesn't doubt my powers of observation. And I'm sure he finally understands: the red light means we'll need to stop, and stopping is not a good idea when you've got a car full of very bad Russian dudes on your tail.

"Let's split up," I say. "I'll check out this intersection, and you go back and check on our new Russian friends."

"Okay," he says, turning around and running back toward his building.

I walk more leisurely to the intersection. Eugene has more distance to cover, and I want to give him a head start.

When I'm standing under the traffic light, I turn left and observe the road.

The closest car is about half a block away. I walk toward it. It's a small car, but that doesn't fill me with confidence. Small or not, if it T-bones us, it will hurt.

I open the car door. The speedometer is unreadable—another example of defunct electronics in the Quiet.

I Read the driver. Through his eyes, I learn that he's going thirty miles per hour. I also learn that he's late and is about to speed up. It's unclear what the final speed will be, but I believe he's about to give a noticeable push on the gas.

I make some quick estimates and decide that this guy will prevent me from turning right or going forward. I'll have to at least slow down at the intersection and make sure his car passes.

On the plus side, the car behind this one is a block away. Since I still have a little time while Eugene does his recon, I run to that car and learn its speed as well. It's also going thirty, but its driver isn't in a rush. He's the type of safe driver who slows down a little before getting to an intersection—which is rare, but admirable.

I walk back to my rental and spot Eugene running back. I have to say, I'm impressed with his speed.

"It's not good, Darren," he says when I'm within hearing distance. "They're in the lobby already, and Sergey's ready to pursue us."

"Damn it," I say, resisting the temptation to kick the car in frustration. "I have bad news, too. We have to actually stop on that light. At least to let this one reckless asshole through."

"Okay, but after that, if the path is clear, we need to go," he says urgently. "I Read them some more. They indeed have orders to kill me—and for running and causing them a headache, Big Boris has decided to make it slow if he gets the chance."

"Then it sounds like we don't really have a choice," I say, trying not to wonder what Big Boris would do with *me*. I'm not on the hit list, but I bet to him it would be guilt by association with equally dire consequences. "There's another car after the one that's the problem, but I think I can make it. Just tell me, should I turn right here or go straight? Do you have any idea where we're going?"

As I ask the last question, I realize that I should've brought it up much sooner.

"There's one place we can go," Eugene says. "Mira and I aren't welcome there. It's the community where Readers in Brooklyn live. It's a long shot, but I can't think of anyone else who could help. They're located on Sheepshead."

"And Sheepshead is where, exactly?" I'm forced to ask. My Brooklyn geography isn't very strong. All I know is the Brooklyn Bridge and, as of recently, Mira and Eugene's apartment.

"Go straight for a bit, then turn left on Avenue Y. It will be a wider street that we'll approach after a few more blocks. Once on it, we go straight, then right on Ocean Avenue. Straight from there until you hit the canal, after that you have to turn left . . ."

"All I got is that I'm going straight for now. Give me a heads up a block before we get where I need to turn."

"Okay," he says. "We should Split again shortly and see where they are at that point."

"Good plan," I say and approach the car.

"Careful," he reminds me.

I take a few breaths and prepare for getting back into driving. I even get into the car in the back, hoping it reduces the disorientation I might get somehow. I touch the back of my head, and the next moment I'm in the driver's seat of the car, my foot instinctively moving from the gas to the brake.

The braking is sudden, and my sushi lunch threatens to come back up. As soon as the car with the guy in a rush passes, I slam the gas again and go on red. The car behind the one that we let through is approaching, but we clear the intersection safely.

We get lucky on the next couple of streets—the lights are green. It's a miracle that we haven't killed a pedestrian. In Manhattan, we would've definitely killed someone by now. People there jaywalk left and right.

"Avenue Y is next," Eugene reminds me, though I actually saw this one coming—courtesy of alphabetically ordered street names. We just flew by W, and this one is X.

"It's yellow," I say, looking ahead. "It'll be red by the time we get there."

"Let's repeat what we did last time," he suggests, and I immediately agree.

I phase into the Quiet and pull Eugene in with me. We split up the same way we did the last time.

As I reach Avenue Y, I see that we're about to have a big problem.

There are too many cars here to safely repeat our earlier maneuver.

I Read the minds of the drivers who'll be closest to the intersection by the time we arrive. It seems like no one is in a rush, or plans to speed. But it doesn't matter—we still won't make it.

"They're already approaching Avenue T," Eugene says when he gets back.

That means they're five blocks away.

"How fast are they going?"

"They're insane—pushing a hundred miles an hour. You saw the Mercedes they're driving."

Our luck is just getting worse. My piece-of-shit rental would be pushing its limits if I tried going that fast, even if I was willing to risk it—which I'm not.

"Can we afford to wait for the light to change?" I ask.

"Not according to my calculations. We have to run the red light, and we have to turn right on the next street. We need to get off this main street so they can't easily catch up with us. It's my mistake. I should've had you turn and zigzag the streets earlier."

"I guess we'll need to phase out regularly and time the turn just right," I say doubtfully. It sounds like we don't have a choice.

The next minute is probably the most nerve-wracking of my life.

I phase in every second, check the intersection, and come back to the car. Over and over. It's hard to drive when you come back, and it's impossible to calculate this whole thing exactly. Still, I think—and Eugene verifies—that I can make the turn if I slow down just a tiny bit to let the Honda closest to us pass by.

The phasing out makes this process play out slowly, like a frame-by-frame sequence in a one-second-long movie stunt.

The Honda gently kisses our back bumper. Brakes screech all around us. I phase into the Quiet to learn what the other drivers will do in reaction to the chaos about to take place. Meanwhile, I also learn what they think of my maneuver, me, and all my ancestors. Out of the Quiet, they express their frustration with a deafening orchestra of honking. That cacophony of car horns and swearing is followed by a loud bang.

The Beemer we just cut off ended up getting rear-ended by an old station wagon. I feel a mixture of guilt and glee. Though no one is visibly hurt, the accident is my fault. On the flip side, however, this might actually slow down our pursuers.

I push the gas and turn the wheel to the right, getting off Avenue Y as Eugene recommended.

"I can't believe we made it," he says. "Now we need to go a roundabout way, and Split to check on our tail."

On Avenue Z, I turn again, and we reach Ocean Avenue uneventfully. The only issue is that we're unable to find our pursuers in the Quiet. At least, not by looking a few blocks behind. We take it as a good sign. We must have lost them.

"Now drive to Emmons Avenue and turn left," Eugene says. "You can't miss it."

He's right. I'm soon faced with the choice of either driving into some kind of canal or turning.

"It's not that far now," he says as we drive a few blocks down Emmons, following the water. I'm glad we're not being pursued at this point; this area is full of traffic.

"Make a left at that light," Eugene tells me. "We're almost there."

Before I get a chance to actually turn, however, the passenger-side mirror explodes.

CHAPTER SEVENTEEN

I phase in, and the noise of the busy street stops. I pull Eugene in with me. As we exit the car, we start looking around.

"Darren, look at this," Eugene says. He sounds more scared than I've heard him since we started this whole mess.

He stands a few feet to the right of the car and points at something in the air. When I take a closer look, my heartbeat spikes. It's a bullet. A bullet frozen in its path. A bullet that just missed the car. The sibling of the one that must have shattered that mirror.

"Someone's shooting at us," I say stupidly.

Eugene mumbles something incomprehensible in response.

Coming out of our shock, we frantically search the cars behind us. It doesn't take long to find the source of the bullets. Not surprisingly, it's our new friends.

How did they manage to get this close? How could I be so stupid—why hadn't I checked on them for so long? Why was I so convinced we'd lost them?

"Eugene, we need to get to wherever it is we're going. And we need to do it fast," I say.

"It's very close. If we turn now, we'll almost be there. Just a few more blocks."

"It might as well be miles if they shoot us."

I've never been shot at before, and I hate the feeling. I'm not ready to get shot. I haven't seen enough, done enough. I have my whole life ahead of me—plus all that extra time in the Quiet.

"Darren, snap out of it." I hear Eugene's voice. "Let's see if we can make this left turn."

Assessing the situation, we quickly realize that our chances of making this turn unscathed are very small. A Jaguar is coming toward us on the opposite side, driving at thirty-five miles per hour—and we'll likely crash into it if we take a sharp left turn. Still, we don't overthink it. A car crash with a seatbelt and an airbag beats getting shot. I think.

I walk to the car, take a calming breath, and phase out. As I'm pulling the wheel all the way to the left, I try my best not to phase into the Quiet out of fear.

With a loud screeching noise, my side of the car touches the Jaguar's bumper. The impact knocks the wind out of me, but the seatbelt holds me, and the airbag doesn't activate. Happy to have made it this far, I slam the gas pedal harder. The car makes all sorts of unhappy sounds, but at least we made it through that deadly looking turn relatively unscathed.

When we're midway through the block, I phase in and get Eugene to join me.

We look at our handiwork back at the beginning of the street. As a result of our crazy turn, the Jaguar hit the Camry in front of it. Its bumper is gone, and the once-beautiful car is pretty much totaled. I think the guy inside will have to be hospitalized—which I feel terrible about. Furthermore, the entire intersection is jammed with cars. Unless they plan to go through them, our trigger-happy friends can't pass.

Still, Eugene walks over to Read Sergey's mind, just in case.

"Darren, I'm such a fucking idiot," he says, slapping his hand to his forehead.

"What is it?"

"They know where we're going. Their boss texted them the address. That's how they caught up with us. I should've realized that if they're working with a Pusher, he or she would know the location of the Readers' community. That they would know we're likely to head that way."

"It's too late to blame yourself now," I tell him. "Let's just get there."

"I'm not sure we'll make it. Sergey plans to ram this car." He points at the tiny Smart Car that happens to be the smallest of those involved in the jam, and I realize that we have a problem. Our pursuers can go through the blocked intersection after all.

"We already have a little bit of a head start," I say, trying to summon optimism I don't feel. "We'll just have to make it."

"Okay," Eugene says. "From here, we can actually walk to our destination on foot before we get back into the real world. This way, you'll know the exact way there."

We take the walk. I realize we'll make it when we see the wall of the gated community that is our destination. Whether Sergey rams that car successfully or not, we can do this.

We're a mere three blocks from where we need to be.

When we get back to the car, I phase back out.

I push the little rental to its limits. I'm going eighty, the tires screeching as I make the next turn. I hear the loud bang behind us and know that Sergey followed through with his plan; the Smart Car is probably toast by now.

It's too late for our pursuers, though. We've reached the gate that separates us from our destination. I stop the car in the middle of the street and am about to phase into the Quiet when I'm pulled in instead by someone else.

"Eugene, you beat me to it," I say when everything goes still. Only when I look to my right, I don't see Eugene.

I see someone else—someone I've never met before.

CHAPTER EIGHTEEN

The guy is holding a huge military knife. Threateningly. I don't know what to make of it, since we're in the Quiet. I'm not sure what will happen to me if he uses the knife on me. Not that I care to find out. He doesn't look like someone who makes idle threats. I make a mental note to find out the risk of death in the Quiet. I know injuries don't stick. And yes, I cut myself to find out. Wouldn't anyone? My shrink thought it was 'interesting' that I cut myself in my delusional world—I recall her talking some nonsense about the physical pain helping me deal with some fictitious emotional one.

"I've seen that one before," the guy says, pointing the knife at frozen Eugene. "But who the fuck are you?"

I gape at him. I don't know what to make of his muscular build, short haircut, and military clothing. Is he some kind of Reader security guard?

"I'm only going to ask one more time," he says, and I realize I didn't respond to his question.

"My name is Darren," I say quickly. "I guess I'm a Reader."

"You guess?"

"Well, it's new information to me, so I'm not used to announcing it. Eugene and Mira are the first Readers I've ever met."

The guy's eyebrows lift, and he unexpectedly chuckles. "I've got news for you. If what you say is true, then today—right now—is the first time you've met a real Reader. Few of the people inside consider the Tsiolkovsky orphans that."

"You sound like you consider them Readers, though," I say on a hunch.

"No one gives a rat's ass what I think; I'm just a soldier. But I say if you can spend more than a second in the Mind Dimension and can Read a single thought, you're a Reader. I'm a simple person with simple definitions, I guess. Who cares how you got to be that way?"

"That makes sense," I say. "I'm sorry, I didn't catch your name."

"You didn't catch it because I didn't give it," the guy says, all traces of amusement gone. "It's Caleb. And knowing my name isn't going to help you, unless you have an explanation for what you and Eugene are doing here. This is private property."

"His sister Mira was just kidnapped. Eugene barely escaped getting killed. There are men coming after us as we speak," I try to explain. "Or at least they'll be here once we leave the Mind Dimension."

"How many?" he asks, coming to attention. The bit about Mira seems to have made an impression.

"There are five of them. They're driving a Mercedes; they could be here any second."

"What else should I know about them?" Caleb asks, his hand tightening on the knife.

"They're some kind of a Russian gang or something. Sergey, two Borises—"

"I don't give a shit what their names are," Caleb interrupts me. "If they're armed and heading this way, we won't be bonding on that level."

"Okay," I say. I have a bad feeling in the pit of my stomach.

"Stay here and don't move. Sam and I have sniper rifles pointed at your heads. If you so much as sneeze, we'll blow your brains out."

I don't have a clue who Sam is, but it doesn't look like Caleb's interested in answering questions right now. As I'm trying to come to grips with his threat, he leaves the car, and in a minute I'm forcefully phased out of the Quiet.

"Eugene, don't move," I say hurriedly. There's a red laser dot on his chest, as though someone has a gun pointed at him—which is apparently the case.

"Why?" he asks, confused.

I phase back into the Quiet instead of answering. I'm afraid of even talking while someone is pointing a sniper rifle at me. What if Caleb thinks my lips moving qualifies as movement and shoots? When I find myself in the backseat again with the world silent, I pull Eugene in.

"I just spoke to some scary-looking dude who's guarding this place. He pulled me in," I explain.

"Did whoever it was say they'll help?"

"Not exactly. He said not to move and that they have guns pointed at us." I swallow. "I saw a laser pointer on you."

"I see," Eugene says, surprisingly calmly. "We'll probably be okay. They'll most likely go Read our pursuers to verify you told them the truth."

"And on the off chance they don't?" I ask, though I can guess the answer.

"In that case, they'll let us resolve our differences with the people following us."

"Great. And we're supposed to just sit and wait?"

"I know I will. The Readers don't usually issue empty threats. If you were told not to move, don't move."

Annoyed with Eugene's ironclad logic, I phase out.

I sit without moving for about five seconds, until I realize that waiting next to Eugene's building earlier was child's play compared to this. I count twenty Mississippis before I phase in. The Mercedes is halfway between the corner where Sergey rammed that car and our current location. The fancy car is barely dented, but Reading Sergey's mind, it seems he doesn't agree with my assessment. He's furious about the damage to his car and determined to make us regret this chase, if he gets the chance. Reading the mind of his friend Big Boris, I get the feeling they'll have to get in line when it comes to doing evil things to us.

I walk back and phase out. I'm now back in the car, waiting for whatever it is that's about to happen.

After what seems like a couple of hours, I think I hear a car motor. As soon as I do, I also hear a gunshot.

I automatically phase in this time. My brain must've thought that shot was directed at me, and this is a near-death experience.

I get out of the car and look at my frozen self. No gunshot wounds. That's good. The only abnormalities about my frozen self are the humongous size of my pupils and the overly white shade of my face. The whole thing makes my frozen self look ghoulish. Eugene is even paler and is holding his head defensively. Like his hands can somehow protect him from a bullet.

I look around. The front end of the Mercedes is visible at the head of the street. I walk closer and realize its tires are in the process of blowing out. They must have been shot.

In a daze, I walk back and phase out.

The sound from the tires exploding reaches my ears now, followed by the screech of steel on pavement as the car continues to careen forward on the exposed rims. Another burst of shots are fired, and I phase into the Quiet again.

This time, just like the last, I didn't intend to phase in. It just happened under stress.

I get out of the car. My frozen self doesn't seem to have any blue in his eyes anymore, his irises swallowed up by the black of his pupils.

I walk to the Mercedes. When I look inside, I wish I hadn't.

I've never seen anything like this before. I mean, I've seen dead bodies in the Quiet, but not of people who were actually dead—or about to be dead—outside the Quiet. This is very different. Very real. These five people have bloody wounds in their chests, and their brains are blown out all over the car.

I feel my gag reflex kick in like I'm about to throw up, but nothing comes out. I'm not sure if it's even possible to puke in the Quiet; it's never happened to me before.

I feel bad about these men getting killed, which is a paradox, given that they were just shooting at me a few minutes ago. I think it has something to do with having Read their minds, like it bound us in some way. There's nothing I can do about it, though; they're gone now.

"Rest in peace," I mutter, walking back to my car. I morbidly wonder what I would experience if I Read one of them right now. Or more specifically, I wonder what I would feel if I catch someone at the right—or wrong—moment, and end up experiencing death firsthand?

I shake my head. I'm not doing that. Besides, I might experience that for myself when I get out of the Quiet; Eugene and I might be the next two targets Caleb shoots.

On the plus side, the Mercedes has no more tires at all. The added resistance should counteract inertia to prevent them from ramming into us—in theory. I'm no expert on blown-out tires.

I walk back to the car and phase out.

A few more shots fire in a blur, and the Mercedes moves a few more feet before it screeches to a stop on its rims. It didn't reach us by at least a hundred feet, but I still feel the need to swallow my heart back into my chest.

Things get suspiciously quiet for a few nerve-wracking seconds, and then the gate shutting us out of the community starts to open.

The guy I met before, Caleb, steps out, with a couple of other dudes who look pretty badass. One of them is toting a sniper rifle. I'm guessing that means he's Sam. He and this Caleb guy look like twins, with their stony, square-jawed faces and hard eyes. Sam is a bit taller, which makes him just short of enormous.

"Darren, Eugene, come with me," Caleb says curtly, and I see Sam shoot Eugene an unfriendly look.

"What about that?" Eugene says, gesturing at the car riddled with bullet holes. He's pointedly avoiding looking at Sam, which I find interesting.

"Both it and your ride will be taken care of. No one will ever find them, or those bodies, again," Caleb assures us.

I manage to feel grateful for having the foresight to say yes to the optional rental car insurance, which seems a bit shallow under the circumstances, even for me.

"Wait," I say, remembering the rental receipt. "I need to get the address where Mira's being kept. It's in the glove compartment."

Caleb walks to the rental and gets the paper I need.

"Here," he says, handing it over to me. "Now, no more delays. We need to have a chat."

And with that, under gunpoint, we enter the private Reader community of Sheepshead Bay.

CHAPTER NINETEEN

We're taken to some kind of ritzy clubhouse. It's in the middle of an impressive-looking housing community. A house here must cost millions. I didn't even know a place like this existed in Brooklyn—it's more like something you'd expect to see in Miami. Such a lavish compound sort of makes sense, though; Readers should be able to find a bunch of creative ways to make money given their abilities. Or, more accurately, our abilities. I need to get used to the idea that I'm a Reader, I remind myself, remembering the snafu with Caleb earlier.

Inside the clubhouse are an indoor pool, a large fancy restaurant, and a bar. Caleb takes us further in, into what looks like some kind of meeting room.

A dozen people of different ages are here, looking at us intently.

"That really is Eugene," says a hot blond woman who looks to be a few years older than Mira. "I can vouch for that."

"I knew that much," Caleb says, but finally lowers his weapon. "And this guy?"

"Never seen him before," she says, looking at me. I do my best to keep my eyes trained on her face, rather than her prominent cleavage. Being polite can be a chore sometimes.

"He learned about being a Reader yesterday," Eugene explains. Then he gives the blond woman a warm smile. "Hi Julia."

The woman smiles back at him, but her expression changes back to one of concern quickly. "Are you sure he's a Reader?" she says, sizing me up.

"Positive," Eugene says. "You know my family history with Pushers. It was the first thing I checked."

"You have to forgive me, but I must verify for myself," Julia says. "You can be too trusting, Eugene."

So these two somehow know each other. This must be what Eugene was talking about when he said things are less strict in modern New York than they were in Russia during his father's time. Despite being 'exiled,' Eugene and Mira are not completely cut off from other Readers.

"Bring in our bartender," Julia says to a short young guy to her left. He leaves and comes back with a young, extremely pretty woman a few moments later.

"Stacy, I just wanted to tell you about my new guest," Julia says, gesturing toward Eugene. "Put his drinks on my tab."

"Sure thing, Jules," the woman says. She probably expected something more meaningful, being summoned as she was. Stacy begins to walk away when I'm suddenly in the Quiet again, and the woman who knows Eugene—Julia—is standing next to me.

"Now, Darren, I want you to Read Stacy," she says. "Tell me something about her that no one else can know, and I'll know you're not a Pusher."

This reaffirms what I surmised earlier: Pushers can't Read at all. Otherwise, this test—and the test Eugene did when we first met—wouldn't make sense.

Without much ado, I walk up to Stacy and touch her temple.

* * *

We're walking into the room with Julia. *Oh shit, he's here*, we realize, looking at Caleb. Of all the times we've made a fool out of ourselves, the time we got drunk with Caleb is hardest to forget for some reason. Probably because he's a real man, unlike the rest of the guys here. It's mostly a bunch of rich mama's boys in this community. Well, except for Sam and the other guards.

I, Darren, try distancing myself from Stacy, the way I did in the now-dead Sergey's mind earlier. I latch on to her memory of something involving Caleb, and try to remember what happened. I also notice that the feeling of lightness coming over me is overwhelming this time. If I feel any lighter, I might actually start floating.

"Caleb, you can't drink that as shots. It's sacrilege," we say, watching our favorite customer down a shot of uber-expensive Louis the XIII Cognac like it's cheap vodka.

"How am I supposed to drink it?" he says, giving us a cocky smile. "Show me."

"Are you buying?" we say. "I can't afford a three-hundred-dollar shot."

"Sure," he says. "How much for the whole bottle?"

We grin at him. "You don't want to know. My suggestion would be to switch to good vodka."

"What's good?"

"Try this," we say, pouring a couple of shot glasses of Belvedere, the better of the two pricey vodkas they stock in this place.

We take a shot glass ourselves and cross arms with Caleb, planning to have our shot poured into his mouth, and hoping he does the reverse. "How about a toast?"

When we see the expression on his face, our heart sinks.

"I'm sorry, Stacy. I wasn't trying to hit on you," he says, gently pulling away.

Goddamn it. Not this again. What's wrong with the men in this fucking community? We know most others are probably just rich snobs, but Caleb is their security. What is his deal? And Sam's? It's like a girl can never get laid around here.

I, Darren, distance myself again. I feel a little gross. After all, I'm in the head of a girl who's clearly lusting after this guy. What's worse, from Reading her, I completely understood what it's like to want to take a guy home. I need to get out of Stacy's head, fast.

* * *

"Okay," I tell Julia when I'm out. "I think I have something to convince you. She wanted to sleep with him." I point at Caleb. I stress the word 'she' too much, and Julia smiles at my discomfort.

"You men and your homophobia," she says, walking over to Caleb.

In a moment, Caleb's double appears, the animated version of him looking at Julia curiously.

"He says that Stacy was interested in you," Julia tells him.

"That's his proof?" Caleb says, grinning from ear to ear. "That sounds more like an educated guess to me."

"Right, because every woman wants you?" Julia says sarcastically.

"You tell me."

"Not if you were the last man on the planet," Julia retorts sharply.

"Louis the XIII Cognac," I say, tired of their back-and-forth. "Three hundred dollars for a shot; vodka shots; turning the girl down. Any of that ring a bell?"

Caleb's face turns serious. "I do remember that now," he says, frowning at me. "But it doesn't make sense. It was months ago."

He stares at me intently, like he's seeing me for the first time. Julia is also staring. Then they exchange meaningful looks.

"Okay, Darren," Julia says, looking back at me. "You have to be one of us."

She walks toward herself and touches the frozen Julia's cheek.

The world comes to life again.

Julia looks from me to Eugene, then back to me, waiting for Stacy to leave the room. When the bartender is finally outside, the short guy who went to get her closes the door.

"Darren's one of us," Julia says. "I can vouch for that. He's not Pusher scum."

Everyone seems to relax. There had been tension up to this point, but that tension is gone now. They *really* dislike Pushers over here. Given what Pushers did to Eugene's family, and what I suspect they did to my own parents, I can't really blame them.

"That still doesn't explain what that half-blood degenerate is doing here," Sam—Caleb's annoying doppelganger—says. A few people nod their heads and murmur their agreement.

"Watch it, Sam. Eugene is my personal friend," Julia says, staring the guy down. Sam sneers, but keeps quiet. When Julia turns away, however, the look he gives Eugene is even more hostile than before.

"My sister has been taken," Eugene explains, ignoring Sam. "And I think Pushers are behind it."

This last statement gets everyone's attention, even the asshole Sam's.

"Why would Pushers be after Mira?" Caleb says, his eyes narrowing. It sounds like he knows her.

"They're not after her—they're after me," Eugene explains.

"Is this a continuation of that story you told me about your parents?" Julia asks.

Sam scoffs. "You mean that crazy conspiracy theory—"

"Shut it, Sam," Caleb cuts him off. "Let's get the facts without needless commentary."

I can tell Sam is dying to talk back, but decides not to. I guess that means Caleb outranks him or something.

"Please start from the beginning," Julia says to Eugene. "Tell everyone what you told me."

Looks like I was right earlier. There's definitely some kind of history between her and Eugene.

"I believe," Eugene says, giving Sam a hard look, "that my parents were killed because Pushers were trying to kill my father and me."

"Why would they want to do that?" Caleb asks.

"Because of my father's research. He was working on some things they would've found unnatural," Eugene says, and there's anger in his voice. "He was trying to figure out how Reading and Splitting into the Mind Dimension work in the brain."

The room grows tense again.

"That kind of research is forbidden," Sam says harshly, frowning.

"It's not forbidden," Julia corrects him. Like Caleb, she seems to have some authority around here. "As long as the research is never published and is only discussed with peers who are Readers themselves."

"My father was very discreet. Very few people knew what he was working on," Eugene confirms. "I believe something about his research made Pushers think that Readers would gain a big advantage if he succeeded."

"And would we?" an older woman asks. She's been quiet up until now, but from the way everyone looks at her, I can tell she's important.

"I'm not really sure," Eugene says. "I don't know the practical applications of what he was doing—but I imagine so. Any good science has real-world benefits."

"Eugene is more interested in theory, Mom," Julia tells the older woman. "He's above politics."

"So they're trying to kill you because you inherited the same research your dad was doing?" I decide to butt in.

Everyone looks at me with surprise. They probably assume I already know what's going on since I came with Eugene.

"Exactly," Eugene says. "When I used that first test on you to see if you were a Reader, I did it using the method Dad developed back in Russia. The fact that they tried to kill me today is extra evidence he was killed over his work. They missed killing me that day. I was shopping for groceries." He stops and takes a deep breath. "For those of you who don't know, my parents were murdered when their car exploded right in front of our house. My sister was coming back from school—she saw the whole thing."

Julia walks over to him and puts her hand on his shoulder. Her mother frowns, and Sam looks furious. I wonder if he has the hots for Julia, or just hates Eugene because he's a 'half-blood.'

"Was there any proof of his words in the minds of those men you killed outside?" Julia's mother asks.

"Kind of," says Caleb. "Sam and I checked them thoroughly. There were signs of Pusher activity in the mind of the driver. He drove their boss someplace, and the Pusher made him forget what he heard when the boss spoke to the Pusher on the phone. We couldn't get a visual on the Pusher, of course."

"The fact that there's a Pusher involved is good enough reason to help them as far as I'm concerned," Julia says.

"Right. The fact that his sister slutted around the Russian mob has nothing to do with her capture," Sam says, sneering again. I really don't like this guy. If he wasn't so big and scary-looking, I'd strongly consider punching him in the face.

"Mira was trying to find the people who killed our mother and father," Eugene says defensively. "I told her not to, but she wouldn't listen to me."

"Mira isn't someone who'd be easy to control," Caleb says, chuckling. Is that admiration I see on his face?

"Well, if you ask me, the simpler explanation for the kidnapping would be his sister's gambling debt," Sam says. "As to the original explosion, it's more likely that his father's 'friends' from Mother Russia had something to do with it. Isn't that more plausible than some crazy theory about Pushers?"

"I think the Pusher used the Russian mob for that very reason—so that the police would think the explosion had something to do with what my dad did in Russia," Eugene says, his face turning red with anger. "Only that's bullshit; Dad was the most honest and peaceful man I've ever met."

"Okay," Julia says. "We can debate this until the cows come home, and it won't solve anything. The only way to figure out what's really going on is to rescue Mira—which is what I think we should do."

"Julia, you need to consult your father on this," Julia's mom says, and Julia frowns at her.

"She's right," Sam says. "Jacob would never want to get involved in these exiles' business."

"Well, let's find out, why don't we?" Julia suggests, and walks over to a desk to get a laptop.

CHAPTER TWENTY

"What are you going to do?" Julia's mother asks.

"Skype with Dad, if that's what it takes," Julia responds, turning on the laptop.

As her video call is connecting, Julia motions for Eugene and me to come closer. We gather around the computer, and I see a middle-aged man with tired, beady eyes appear on the screen.

An expression of distaste crosses his stern face as he sees Eugene.

"Hello, Jacob, sir," Eugene says respectfully.

"Hi Dad," Julia says.

"Hello," I say politely.

"Who are you?" Jacob asks, staring at me.

"This is Darren, Dad," Julia says, "a new Reader we discovered."

"A new Reader?" he says, watching me intently. "You look familiar to me, kid. Who are your parents?"

"He doesn't know who they are," Eugene jumps in, and Jacob's face reddens at the sound of his voice. I'm glad Eugene volunteered this information because, as embarrassing as it is, I don't know the last names of my parents. Just their first names: Mark and Margret. I need to find out their last names when we're out of this mess. For all I know, I could have extended family in this very room.

"Everyone knows who their parents are," Jacob retorts, but he's not looking at Eugene. He's still boring into me with his beady eyes. "But we'll continue this conversation another time. For now, I'd like to know what this call is about," he says, turning his attention to Julia, "as well as what he—" he gestures at Eugene, "—is doing in our compound."

"Eugene needs our help, Dad," Julia explains. She then proceeds to tell her father a much smoother, more plausible version of the theory about Eugene's parents. She's good. She downplays the research Eugene and his dad worked on, which appears to be controversial in this community. She highlights the

Pusher involvement every chance she gets. "So I want to help them and learn more about this matter," she says in conclusion.

"Hell, no," her father says, catching me completely by surprise. "I thought I forbade you from ever consorting with that half-blood."

"This has nothing to do with my personal life; it's about standing up to the Pushers," Julia says, glaring at her father. Her face takes on a rebellious look, making me remember my own interactions with Uncle Kyle.

"My decision is final," Jacob says. "I want him out of the community. He should be grateful our security saved his life. If I had been at the compound, that would not—"

Before Jacob gets a chance to finish his last sentence, Julia closes the laptop with an angry bang.

This seems like as good a time as any for me to phase into the Quiet, and I do.

When everything is still again, I look around. Julia is clearly pissed. Her mother's expression is neutral. Though Sam is standing a bit to the side, he clearly heard the conversation because he looks grimly satisfied.

It's interesting to contemplate the fact that in this room, everyone could be doing what I'm doing right now, at any time. Are people watching me frozen as they do so? It's hard to imagine myself standing there, not moving, not thinking, as someone else goes about his or her business while I'm none the wiser.

Shelving these thoughts for later, I touch Eugene's forearm.

"What do we do now?" I ask him when he joins me in the Quiet. "That was a huge flop."

"I don't know what to say," Eugene says. "I didn't really have a clear plan."

"This Julia, how do you know her? She seems to be sympathetic."

"We had a class together in college. Then, for some reason, she agreed to date me." He smiles ruefully. "But when her father found out my status, he freaked out. He's very traditional."

"And this is supposed to be more open-minded than Russia?"

"That I'm alive is testament to that," Eugene says. "I thought we might have a chance at getting help here because Jacob hates Pushers more than anyone. Under normal circumstances, anyone even remotely in trouble with Pushers automatically becomes an 'enemy of his enemy' kind of friend."

"Except you," I say, looking at him.

"Right. I think my history with Julia hurt our chances. The problem is, this is Mira's life on the line, not mine."

"If you don't mind, I want to talk to Julia some more," I say, unwilling to give up.

"Go ahead," he says. He looks over at her, his face drawn. There's something in his eyes, in the way he watches her, that tells me he's far from over her. Then he shakes his head, looking away. "I'm not sure if it's going to help, though."

Instead of arguing, I walk over to her and pull her in.

"Darren." She smiles at me. "I was about to Split to talk to the two of you. It looks like you beat me to it."

"It's funny how that works," Eugene says. "I have this time-slicing algorithm I developed that simulates—"

"Eugene, I'm so sorry about my dad," Julia interrupts him gently. My guess is that she wanted to stop a science diatribe. I suspect it's not the first time she's done this. "Let's talk about what we can do for Mira, if you don't mind."

"After the conversation with your dad, I thought you wouldn't be able to do anything to help," Eugene responds, science forgotten as worry shadows his face again.

"I'm going with you," she says. "Together, we'll get her out of whatever trouble she's in."

"No," Eugene protests. "That would be too dangerous—"

"I'm doing this." She gives him a steely look. "I've had enough of people telling me what to do."

"No, Julia, I don't mean to tell you what to do." Eugene immediately backtracks. "I just worry about you, that's all . . ."

Her icy glare warms considerably, and she takes a step toward him.

"With all due respect," I interject, "how can you help us, Julia? This sounds like a job for someone like that." I point at motionless Caleb.

"I'm good at getting into places I shouldn't—picking locks, that kind of thing," Julia says, turning to look at me. "It's a skill that could come in handy in exactly the type of mission I imagine this will become. But you're right, we need Caleb or one of his people. We have to convince him to help without my dad's orders."

"How do we do that?" Eugene asks.

"Can we pay him?" I suggest. With the stock options I got at the gym, money will soon be easy to come by. Even easier than it usually has been for me.

"If you're talking about money, it won't work," Julia says. "But there are other forms of payment."

"What are you suggesting?" Eugene looks puzzled.

"Nothing sinister." Julia grins. "You see, your friend Darren seems to have impressed Caleb. Actually, he impressed both of us with his Reading Depth."

"Oh?" Eugene says, and I recall that this is a sensitive subject for these people. Something like asking about the size of someone's paycheck or his package were the analogies used, I think.

"What does my Reading Depth have to do with Caleb?" I ask.

"Caleb is obsessed with improving his fighting skills," Julia says. "He's already rumored to be the best fighter among the Readers. Still, he's always looking to get better."

"I'm not going to fight him, if that's what you're about to offer," I say, shuddering. I'm not a fan of violence, plus I'm not suicidal. The guy will probably kill me before I get a single punch in.

Julia laughs. If she weren't laughing at my expense, I would say her laugh was nice. In general, she's a very pretty girl. I can see why Eugene likes her, and I can tell that he truly does. I'm less clear why the reverse is true, but it must be, as I catch her giving him decidedly warm glances. It's weird—I always thought geeky types like Eugene didn't do well with women. Of course, this is based solely on my friend Bert, which isn't exactly a valid statistical sample.

"No, Darren, thank you for offering, but I'm not asking you to fight Caleb," she says, still having a hard time keeping a straight face. I'm insulted. How does she know I'm not secretly some Kung Fu master?

"You have an amazing Reading Depth," she continues. "You can offer to take him into the mind of some famous fighters. I suspect he would find the idea intriguing."

Eugene looks from me to her uncomfortably. "But—"

"Eugene, please, I'm trying to help save your sister," Julia interrupts, and Eugene falls silent, his expression smoothing out.

"Can someone actually do that? Bring another person into someone else's mind?" I ask, wondering what Eugene had been about to say. He'd seemed worried about something for a moment.

"Yes," she says, "absolutely. It depletes your power even faster than pulling someone in, but from what I saw, you won't have a problem with that."

"Why can't Caleb do this himself?" I ask. "Why can't he Read some fighter's mind on his own?"

"For all his fighting prowess, Caleb isn't very powerful when it comes to matters of the Mind Dimension," Julia explains. "He can't go back very far at all with his Reading, and he can't do it very often, which is exactly why such an opportunity might appeal to him."

I consider questioning her further to figure out what made Eugene uncomfortable, but then I decide against it. "Fine, I'll do it," I say instead. I can't see any other way to help Mira at the moment, and I find the idea of doing this fighter Reading thing rather intriguing. If Caleb is doing it to get better at fighting, does it mean that by joining him, I could get better, too? Or, more accurately, will I actually learn how to fight as a result of this?

"Great, Eugene, let's go so they can have some privacy," Julia says, grabbing his arm and pulling him back toward their frozen bodies.

"I don't know how to thank you for this, Darren," Eugene says on his way to his frozen body, and I shrug in response, still unsure what the big deal is.

As soon as they phase out, I walk up to Caleb and pull him in.

"Darren," he says with a smirk. "To what do I owe the honor of being pulled into your own personal Mind Dimension?"

"Julia said you might be able to help us, for a price," I begin, and Caleb laughs.

"Did she now? And what did Julia think would be my price?" His grin reminds me of a hungry shark.

"She said you like fighting, in all its forms," I say, hoping I don't sound crazy. "She said I can take you into the mind of a couple of fighters as payment."

"Interesting," he says, crossing his arms. "And did she say anything else?"

"No, just that."

"You really did just learn how to Read yesterday, didn't you, Darren?" he says, still grinning. "What Julia 'forgot' to mention to you is that very few Readers would agree to offer me this kind of deal."

"Why?" I ask, wondering if I'm about to learn the reason for Eugene's concern.

"Because it's considered a private, almost intimate experience to pull someone else into a Reading," Caleb says, his grin fading. "You get glimpses of the other Reader's mind, and vice versa."

"Oh." I try to keep my jaw from dropping. "What does that feel like?"

"I only did it once," he says, completely serious now. "But that time, it was incredible."

I stare at him for a moment, then shrug. "I don't care," I say. "To save Mira, I'll do it. I'll let you get inside the heads of a couple of people of your choice."

Caleb looks like a happy shark again. "We have a deal then," he says, smiling widely. "I'll let you know whose minds I choose."

Why do I feel like I did something reckless just now?

"Oh, don't make the long face," he says, apparently sensing my sudden unease. "I promise not to deplete your Depth. We both know you can go back very far, so getting to see a few fights shouldn't be a problem at all. We won't see how these men began their careers, only something fairly recent."

"Okay, sure." I decide to worry about it later.

"Good. Now pull Eugene and Julia back in."

I do as he says.

"Here's the plan, people," Caleb barks, taking control of the situation. "Eugene and Darren will leave, looking exceedingly disappointed. Julia, I'll meet you in the parking lot after I get the supplies I'm going to need. We'll pick you gentlemen up on Emmons Avenue."

"Who else is coming with us?" Julia asks. "Not Sam, I presume?"

"You presume correctly," Caleb says. "It will be just me."

"Just you?" Julia frowns.

"Oh, ye of little faith." Caleb smirks at her. "One of me is probably overkill for this mission."

"Yeah, yeah," she says. "I don't doubt your machismo, Caleb; I just want the girl to survive the rescue."

"She will," Caleb assures her. "You have my word on that."

"Okay, then let's get back to our real lives," Julia says.

"Hold up. Darren, there's something you should know," Caleb says, turning toward me. "I've known Mira for a while. She's a good kid. I was going to offer to help Eugene anyway—especially since I knew Julia would do something reckless, and Jacob would hold me liable for her actions regardless of my involvement. Not to mention, I like a good skirmish."

"So I didn't need to agree to this deal?" I say dryly, and he shakes his head.

"Nope. You didn't. But a deal is a deal." He winks at me. "I'm really looking forward to all this."

* * *

Leaving the community with apparent dejection, Eugene and I make our way to Emmons Avenue, to the exact place where we caused the last car crash. There are still bits of plastic and glass on the asphalt, but the broken cars have apparently been towed.

I'm deep in thought, trying to understand how I got involved in all this craziness.

"Darren, about taking Caleb into someone's mind," Eugene breaks the silence.

"He already told me; you see into each other's minds," I tell him.

"Oh, good. I'm surprised Caleb was so honest," Eugene says with relief. "Julia should've warned you. She can be kind of ruthless when it comes to getting what she wants."

Before I can reply, we're interrupted by a loud car honk. It's a Hummer—occupied by Caleb and Julia.

Of course Caleb drives a Hummer, I think as I get in.

"Give me that address, Darren. We have a damsel in distress," Caleb says.

I give him the address, and he sets his GPS to the location. With a roar, the Hummer is off, moving through the streets of Brooklyn like a tank.

CHAPTER TWENTY-ONE

W e park in a Costco lot in Sunset Park.

According to Google Maps, the place where they're keeping Mira is an industrial warehouse. What these guys are doing so far from Brighton Beach, none of us have a clue. Brighton Beach is where the Russian Mafia is supposed to be headquartered, according to Eugene. I hope that this actually plays to our advantage. If they do call for reinforcements, it's a twenty-minute drive without traffic, according to Julia's phone. Of course, that assumes the reinforcements are on Brighton Beach, and—this is a big one—that they're going to need reinforcements against the four of us.

Caleb jumps out of his seat and starts rummaging through the trunk of the Hummer.

"Are we shopping for supplies?" I ask, looking in the direction of the huge store. I'm only half-joking.

"I have everything I need," Julia says, hanging a messenger bag over her shoulder.

"They don't sell the type of stuff I need in Costco," Caleb responds, putting what has to be a rifle in a special carry case over his shoulder. "At least not in New York."

He puts on a vest with special pockets and straps the huge knife I saw previously to it, along with a couple of handguns.

"This is for you," Caleb says, handing me a gun.

The seriousness of the situation hits me again. We're going against armed criminals. Just the four of us. A scientist, a girl whose toughness I haven't fully determined yet, and, let's face it, a financial analyst. Caleb is the only person even remotely qualified for this rescue. Despite his unshakable confidence, the odds don't seem right to me.

Not to mention, the people holding Mira have an ace up their sleeve: a hostage.

All we have is our unusual skill set.

Caleb clearly has a plan, though. He leads us to an abandoned warehouse located a short distance from where we parked.

We walk up to the top floor, and Caleb methodically unzips his gun case and starts setting up. The gun is huge and looks very professional—complete with scope and silencer. I wonder if this is what he used to gun down our pursuers earlier. Eugene and Julia, who have been silent for some time, exchange impressed looks. Eugene seems grimly determined, while Julia looks thoughtful.

I gaze around the room we've found ourselves in. It's dusty and dark, despite large, floor-to-ceiling windows—probably because said windows are yellow and covered with grime. Caleb opens one of those windows, lies down on the floor, and aims the huge gun at the industrial warehouse across the street. Then he says curtly, "All right, Darren, pull us in."

I leverage my natural anxiety over what's about to happen and quickly phase into the Quiet. Then I touch everyone in turn, pulling them in.

Once we're all in, we walk down the stairs and cross the road. This part of Brooklyn is so abandoned that being in the Quiet doesn't seem like much of a change. At least not until we cross the road, and Caleb breaks the door with a series of kicks. Even in a scarcely populated area like this, such bold breaking and entering might've gotten us noticed and reported, if it took place in the real world.

"You know, I could've picked that lock," Julia says, looking at what's left of the door on the ground.

"You'll get your chance," Caleb tells her as he walks into the building.

We walk through the door and find ourselves in a large open space. There are a bunch of guys frozen in the process of walking around. They all have guns. Caleb walks between the guys and the windows, looking intently at the building we came from.

His plan is beginning to dawn on me.

He's figuring out how to shoot them from our location across the street. He's triangulating his shots; as soon as we phase back out, he'll shoot.

I'll have to remember to never piss off Caleb.

"Where's Mira?" Eugene asks after examining the hangar.

"Try Reading them," Caleb says without turning. "We need to figure that out, because once we get back to the real world, the information will be lost."

Right. Because you can't Read dead men. A chill skitters across my spine. Caleb is too calm about it. Too poised. His coldness makes me uneasy. I wonder if I, personally, am capable of killing. Even if it's an enemy. Even in self-defense. I don't know, and I hope I don't find out today.

For my Reading target, I choose a big guy near one of the columns. He must be on steroids or growth hormones—or both. Though he's my height, he must be at least two hundred pounds heavier than I am. Being that he's Russian, I wonder if he's trying to look like a bear. He's closer to a gorilla. I catch myself hoping that Caleb doesn't miss this specific dude with his rifle. We wouldn't want to face him in anything but a gunfight.

Putting my hand on his gigantic forehead, I jump in a few hours ago.

* * *

We see Mira playing cards with Vasiliy. There is one other guy in the room with her.

"Na huy ti s ney igrayesh?" we say. As usual I, Darren, marvel at understanding this. He, Lenya, was asking a question about why his idiot bro is playing cards with the hostage. Playing cards with a girl who is a renowned card cheat.

He, Lenya, is picturing what he would do with the hostage. We see images of Mira tied up and abused.

I, Darren, distance myself almost instantly and nearly puke—though this is not easy to do in my current position. Can you vomit mentally? This almost makes me want to jump out of this asshole's head, it's so sick. I also feel an instinctive need to protect Mira from ever coming near this guy. I feel dirty. The best way to describe the experience is it's as if I'm dreaming of being this scumbag. I am rethinking my earlier squeamishness toward killing.

I shouldn't jump out, however, as he's about to give me key information. I try to focus on what the guy's body is experiencing—an ache from yesterday's workout, soreness in the knuckles from punching someone, anything except those sick rape fantasies. This approach is flawed, though, because focusing on his body makes me realize he's getting turned on from these disgusting thoughts. Thankfully, before I'm forced out of his head from sheer horror, he refocuses on what he should be doing. And that is locking the door in front of him from the outside.

We lock the door, mentally praising Tolik, who is also in the room. At least he has his gun next to him, and isn't letting the bitch distract him. He also forbade untying her legs from the chair. Tolik will keep Vasiliy in check.

We walk out into the corridor and through a maze of concrete hallways until we reach the stairs. Then we go down to the main hall, where the rest of the guards are.

I, Darren, now know where Mira is being held.

I almost jump out, but I decide to try to go even deeper. I want to know who told this guy to lock the door from the outside. That's very specific. Whoever came up with that could've been trying to limit Mira's range of motion in the Quiet—and thus might be the Pusher fuck behind all this.

I jump further.

We're sitting in a banya. I, Darren, learn that a banya is a Russian spa—a bit like a sauna, but much hotter. Given how we, I mean he, feels when in there, it sounds like something I should check out.

I go further still, jumping around scenes from this goon's life.

Aha.

"Keep those doors closed," Piotr says. We look at Piotr and wonder who the fuck he is to be giving orders around here.

I, Darren, realize with disappointment that Piotr is another Russian I saw in the very room we're in now.

I jump out of Lenya's head.

* * *

"Darren, let's go," Caleb says as soon as I'm conscious of being myself again.

"Give me a minute," I respond. "I need to check that guy." I point at Piotr, sitting at a desk.

"Hurry," Caleb says.

I walk up to the guy. He looks a tiny bit more intelligent than the one whose mind I was in a moment ago. I place my hand on his forehead.

* * *

I'm in, but I don't know where to start. Intuitively I jump around scenes from this guy's life until I find it.

We're watching boxing on TV when another mind enters. Time stops; now there are more of us in his head.

I understand that the guy himself wouldn't have felt the Pusher enter his mind. Apparently people don't consciously notice either us or them when we do our thing. But I am very much aware of it. It's like a ghostly presence. And as I keep Reading, the Pusher begins to give instructions.

'Instructions' is a poor word for it, but I can't think of a better one. In reality, they're almost like experiences the Pusher inserts into the guy's mind. Like the reverse of Reading. The Pusher inserts experiences and reactions to them. How this will ensure the guy does what he's supposed to, I don't know, but it must work. To me, it feels a little bit like a very detailed story of what Piotr should experience when the time is right.

The experience in this case is pretty simple. 'Pick up the phone' is the first step. The Pusher seems to almost play out a fake memory for his target. Every detail of how it would be to pick up the phone is considered: which hand, the weight of the phone in his hand, and so on.

Next comes the instruction: 'Text all the trusted people with a request to meet at Tatyana Restaurant in an hour.'

Finally, Piotr is instructed to get up and go there himself.

After that, the Pusher's presence disappears. Based purely on the person's presence in this mind, I can't tell whether it was male or female. To my disappointment, whoever it was never came into physical contact with Piotr.

I Read Piotr's mind a little longer. I'm curious what he'll recall of the Pusher influence. As I expected, he remembers nothing. He arrives at the restaurant, slightly amused. *Isn't it strange how sometimes you drive someplace, but don't even remember the driving process?* he thinks.

It seems like the Pusher's influence has caused a mild memory lapse in the target's mind, but overall Piotr acts as though of his own volition. It's interesting to watch how he rationalizes his actions as happening of his own choosing and his memory lapse as one of those times when the conscious mind goes on autopilot and the subconscious takes over. The illusion of free will at its finest. It comes to me all over again how dangerous these Pushers are. Whatever they need done, all they need to do is plant the seed in someone's mind.

Mind-rape, Eugene called it. Now I understand why.

Knowing I won't get any more than this, I decide to jump out of Piotr's mind. People are waiting for me.

* * *

When I'm conscious again, Caleb is standing next to me looking like he's about to say something snide. I just head for the exit, explaining where Mira is as I move. The group follows.

"That's perfect," Caleb says when I finish my explanation. "If they're that far inside the building, they definitely won't hear my shots."

"Did any one of you Read a guy whose name was Arkady in there?" I ask. No one responds, so I assume they haven't.

We return to the room across the street, on the top floor near the window. Our frozen bodies are hunched near Caleb, who's lying on the floor with his eye to the scope of his rifle. I touch my forehead.

As soon as the phase-out process is complete, Caleb fires the first shot.

Then another.

Then another.

I lose count of the shots, as I'm more focused on plugging my ears. In the movies, silencers work much better than in real life. Despite the elongated device on the end of the barrel of Caleb's rifle, the noise is deafening in this room. I hope the area is abandoned enough that no one hears the shots—or if they do and call the cops, we're out of here before they arrive.

His shooting done, Caleb pushes off the floor to a standing position.

"Now things should go more smoothly in there," he says, picking up his gun. Wiping down his prints, he leaves the rifle behind and heads for the stairs.

We follow him all the way down to the ground level of the building we've just fired the shots from.

"Darren, take us into the Mind Dimension again," Caleb orders before we exit to the street. "We need to assess the situation."

"Okay, Sergeant," Julia says sarcastically. "Before we go running around again, can you please tell us the plan?"

"The plan will become clearer after we reconnoiter," Caleb says curtly. "The only thing I can tell you now is that with two armed guards in the room with Mira, stealth is of utmost importance. If I were them, I'd shoot the hostage as soon as I caught wind that some shit was going down."

Eugene looks pale, and a shudder runs through me. Without further ado, I phase into the Quiet once again and get everyone to join me.

We cross the street. I'm getting a sense of déjà vu. The door is locked again, which of course makes sense, but is no less annoying.

"Now you can practice picking the lock," Caleb says to Julia. "We want to be in as quickly as we can."

She goes inside her messenger bag and takes out what I assume are the instruments of a professional burglar. I wonder where she learned to do this. Her people seem too ritzy for thieving.

She struggles with the door for only a minute before we're in.

"Will you be able to do this faster when we actually get here?" Caleb asks.

"Yes. I can get it down to twenty seconds," she says.

We enter the hangar we inspected before. Though I'm not surprised by what I see, my gag reflex kicks in, and I barely hold back vomit.

They're all dead. Shot in the head, every single one of them. There's blood, lots of blood everywhere. Though it's my second time seeing a scene like this today, it's not in any way less disturbing.

Julia looks green too, making me feel a bit better about my own sorry state.

Caleb steps over the bodies in his way and just waltzes to the stairs. We gingerly follow, trying to keep our eyes off the dead people.

After a few flights of stairs, we reach a floor that appears to be the one we're searching for. We follow Caleb into the maze of corridors, which, according to

Lenya's—the disgusting gorilla's—memories, leads to the room where Mira is held.

There's a guy standing with his back to us at a bend in the corridor, looking toward the door. Another is standing by the door, looking at the hallway. This means there's no way for Mira to come out of the room, nor for us to turn the corner without one of these men raising an alarm. Not good.

"Okay," Caleb says. "We'll need to take these two guards out. Darren, Eugene, this one is yours," he says, pointing at the guy with his back toward us.

"Ours?" Eugene appears confused.

"You need to overpower him," Caleb explains with a sharp smile. "Silently, so the two guards with Mira don't hear us coming."

Caleb is enjoying this, I realize. Eugene must've acted arrogantly toward him in the past, or maybe Caleb is just a sadistic prick. Whatever the case, Caleb is clearly trying to shock the guy. Or is it my buttons he's trying to push?

"I can turn the corner and quickly grab the guy. When he can't move, you stab him," I propose, looking at Eugene.

"Good plan," Caleb says, glancing at me with approval. "I have some extra knives for you gentlemen."

Eugene doesn't seem as hesitant as I would expect at the prospect of stabbing someone. Have I misjudged him? After all, just because someone is a little geeky doesn't mean he can't be tough. Or score a hottie like Julia, I remind myself.

"What are *you* going to do?" Julia challenges Caleb.

"I'll take care of that one," Caleb responds, nodding toward the guy facing us.

"Wait—won't he shoot you as soon as you turn this corner?" Eugene asks. I know he's walking into some sort of smart-ass remark from Caleb.

Instead of answering, Caleb walks back into the hall leading to this turn. Then he pointedly turns the corner. In a blur of motion, the knife is in his hand; the next moment, after a lightning-fast throw, it's in the second guy's chest.

Show-off.

"Any more questions?" Caleb asks. No one responds. "In that case, Julia, see how fast and how quietly you can pick that lock."

Julia takes out her tools and does her thing. It takes her about a minute.

"That won't work," Caleb says when she's done. "But we'll get back to that in a moment."

Without waiting for an invitation, we all barge into the room.

The room still looks like I remember it. Or more accurately, how the now-dead Lenya—the gorilla—remembered it.

It was originally meant to be some kind of storage room. There are no windows, and the walls are painted a dull white color. In some places, the paint is chipping away.

Just like in the memory I obtained, there's a guy with a gun near him, though now he seems to be playing with his phone. It's a little odd, since his phone has a pink case. Just like before, there is Mira, tied to the chair, playing cards with another guard. Only unlike before, they're all frozen in the midst of their activities.

I walk up to Mira and touch her forehead.

As soon as she phases in, her eyes look like they're about to jump out of their sockets. She has an expression on her face I don't recognize. Then I get it—I've never seen her this genuinely happy to see me before. Her eyes scan the room, and she sees Eugene. Her face lights up.

"You did it," she says, turning toward me, and I hear the joy and disbelief in her voice. "You saved him. I don't know how I can thank you."

"I said I would," I say, trying not to think of all the ways I'd want Mira to express her gratitude. For the first time in my life, I understand the motivations of those hero types. For a fleeting moment, I feel like I really did something important. Something impressive. It's a great feeling.

"But what are you doing here?" she says, her expression changing as she fully registers the situation.

"What does it look like?" Caleb says. "We're rescuing you."

"In that case, why did you bring Eugene?" She looks at me like I'm an idiot, and all my heroic feelings deflate. Like I could've stopped a brother from trying to save his little sister?

"It's too dangerous," she says, turning toward Eugene. "You shouldn't have come." She looks from Caleb to Julia to me. Then at the corridor through the open door. "This is all of you?" she asks, her shoulders slumping.

"It's going to be enough," Caleb says.

She shakes her head. "This is going to be impossible." She doesn't wait for anyone to respond before she walks out of the room. She must not realize that we—well, Caleb—already took out the lion's share of her captors.

"As friendly as ever," Caleb says, giving me a wink. "Julia, go out and then lock and unlock this door again. Try to do it quicker and quieter this time."

We stay in the room to judge Julia's work. After the initial click of the lock, the rest of the stuff she does is pretty subtle, but still audible if you know what to listen for. She seems to finish faster this time.

Caleb waves at us to follow him and walks out of the room—to follow Mira, I presume.

"Do it ten more times," he says to Julia on the way out.

The three of us try to find Mira. We walk a couple of floors up. Everything seems abandoned. We find Mira on the seventh floor, punching the wall in frustration.

"What is it?" Eugene asks her.

"That fuck isn't here," she says, punching the wall again.

"Who?" Eugene says.

"The Pusher. The one behind all this. That chicken shit's not here. That was my main hope, the only silver lining to this. I thought he'd be overseeing the whole thing."

"I Read a mind earlier," I say. "The Pusher who influenced that mind was very careful to avoid revealing himself to his target."

"Then this is pointless. You guys should go back and wait. Maybe he'll show up eventually," she says.

"That's not happening," Caleb says, standing between her and the wall she's been punching. "Here is what *is* happening. You'll try to be as loud as possible as soon as you hear any funny sounds coming from outside your door. Talk loudly, ask questions—or even better, fall from your chair. That would distract them *and* get you out of harm's way."

"Yeah, yeah, don't try to teach a fish how to swim," she mutters. Then she takes a deep breath and glances at Eugene before turning her attention back to Caleb. "Look, even with those dead bodies I just saw downstairs, busting in here is going to be dangerous," she says in a more even tone. "Promise me that Eugene won't take part in this. They took me to smoke him out in the first place, so if you bring him, you'll be playing right into their hands."

"Yes, so he told us. We have a deal," Caleb says before Eugene starts protesting. "I won't force Eugene to come with us."

Mira gives him a disbelieving look, but seems a bit calmer as we make our way back to the room. I get the feeling that there's definite history between Mira and Caleb. I don't like it, not one bit. Though it can't be romantic, can it? He's a little too old for her, and he called her 'kid.' Maybe it's a bond between two kindred, sarcastic, pain-in-the-ass spirits?

When we rejoin her, Julia is still diligently practicing unlocking that lock.

Upon Caleb's request, she does a final run, which is extremely quick. She's way faster and much quieter than she was before. For the first time, I'm beginning to think we can pull this off.

"So what's the exact plan?" I ask.

"While Julia works on the door, Mira falls on the floor with her chair. Then I shoot these two," Caleb says, pointing his index finger in a gun motion at the two frozen guards.

"I'm not sure I can fall like that," Mira says, looking at her frozen self. Her hands are free, but her legs are duct-taped to her chair.

"We'll just have to practice that part as well," Caleb says, his eyes crinkling in the corners. I get the feeling he's going to enjoy this part, too.

"You want to tie me to a chair so I practice falling?" Mira says. She doesn't look happy.

"Exactly." Caleb grins. "See, Eugene, you're not the smartest one in the family."

Eugene and I free the frozen Mira from the chair and place her limp body gently in the corner of the room. I accidentally touch her exposed skin, but nothing happens. I guess once we pulled one Mira into the Quiet, touching her frozen self doesn't produce more Miras. It would have been kind of cool if it did.

Mira sits down in the chair and, muttering something in Russian under her breath, grudgingly allows us to tape up her legs with the duct tape her guards left lying around. She's now set up exactly as her frozen self was a few minutes ago.

She leans her body to the right, but the chair doesn't fall. She shakes it back and forth, and slowly, almost grudgingly, the chair falls over.

"Are you okay, sis?" Eugene asks her.

"Yes. Pick me up," she says, trying to push herself off the floor. Her position looks extremely uncomfortable.

"That was too slow," Caleb says. "Try again."

I get up and walk over to a dingy couch standing in the furthest corner of the room. I take the cushions from it, and lay them on either side of Mira. No point for this to hurt more than it already must.

"Thanks, Darren," she says before she begins shaking the chair again.

The cushions help, but it's clearly an unpleasant practice. She does it again and again over the course of about twenty minutes. We try to give tips—which are usually met with disdain.

Eventually Caleb decides she won't be able to improve further.

About five seconds to fall over is the best she can do.

"We need a different strategy to distract them," I say. "Besides falling, I think you should also start yelling. Scream 'mouse' or 'spider' at the critical moment and start waving your arms, acting like you're freaking out right before you fall."

Julia chuckles. Mira gives me a deadly glare. Caleb is about to say something, but Eugene shakes his head at him behind Mira's back. He must actually think it's a good idea.

"Just do it, sis," Eugene tells Mira. "It won't be the first time. Remember when you jumped on the table—"

"Don't say another fucking word," Mira interrupts him. "I'll do it."

And before her brother has a chance to say anything more, she quickly walks up to her own frozen body—which is now lying on the floor—and touches that version of herself on the cheek. That makes her phase out, and she's no longer in our company.

Only the Mira on the floor remains.

"But I was about to ask her to practice the new strategy," Caleb says with visible disappointment.

I can't help myself. I burst out laughing.

"This is a pretty serious situation, guys," Eugene says, but I can tell he's trying his best to suppress a smile. Despite the danger we're in—or maybe because of it—everyone finds the idea of Mira freaking out like that hilarious. Then again, Eugene implied that she's acted like this before. Maybe when she was little? It's hard to picture it now. I wish I could Read Eugene's or Mira's mind.

We exit the room. Caleb holds the door for everyone, making me wonder why he's being such a gentlemen all of a sudden. As soon as we're all out of the room, I find out.

He's decided to do a little practice on his own.

All I hear is a quiet rustling of clothing, and the next moment Caleb is holding two guns, one in each hand. Two shots fire at the same time. Two men in the room each have a bullet in their head.

I begin to feel even more confident about the success of this mission.

We walk back to our bodies and phase out.

"Any last words?" Caleb says to us all.

"I'm coming with you," Eugene says, his voice filled with determination.

"Of course," Caleb says. "I said I wouldn't force you. But if you volunteer, well, that's a different matter." He hands Eugene a knife. "You're in charge of stabbing the guy in the corridor, remember?"

I get a knife as well. *Great.* As though the gun I was given earlier wasn't bad enough.

We cross the street, for real now. The area is pretty dead, yet it seems infinitely more alive now than when we crossed this road in the Quiet—mainly because all the ambient noises of Brooklyn are back. With the increase in noise, my adrenaline levels go up as well.

Julia picks the lock on the front door in twenty seconds—just as she said she would. So far, so good. We walk through the hangar. My heart rate becomes a tiny bit calmer. This part isn't all that different from the version in the Quiet. The heavy walls block most of the sounds of the city. The dead men are just as frozen in death here as they were in the Quiet.

"Situation check," Caleb whispers when we're near the stairs.

I phase in, and pull everyone else in with me. We walk up the stairs until we get to the corridor and turn the corner again. In the few minutes it took us to walk across the street and through the hangar, the men have not moved; they stand in pretty much the same positions.

"Good," Caleb says. "We'll do another check, right before turning the corner. This will be my signal." He gives us a thumbs-up sign. Not the most imaginative signal, but it gets the point across.

We walk back and phase out. Now we finally get to make the trip up the stairs in the real world.

We all try to make our walk stealthy, but only Caleb succeeds. We get to the corner, and he does his thumbs-up sign. I phase in and pull them all in again. The men are still standing as they were.

"Are you ready?" Caleb says, looking from me to Eugene.

"Ready," I say.

"Let's get this over with," Eugene says.

I notice Caleb never asked to rehearse this part. I bet I know why: he realizes that if given enough information, Eugene might lose his nerve. Or maybe he thinks I'll lose mine.

We phase out. Everyone looks at me expectantly. I take a deep breath and turn the corner.

My heart is racing a hundred miles per hour, but I ignore it and grab the now-very-familiar Russian as soon as I turn the corner, placing my hand over his mouth to muffle his scream. I hold him as tightly as I can, but he struggles and I know there's very little time.

Out of the corner of my eye, I see Caleb make his move. I can't afford to pay attention to him, though.

I rotate my body, and Eugene is there with the knife. It's unclear if he jabs the guy with it, or if I push the guy onto the knife myself. However, it's quickly clear that it's done—the knife is there, in the man's stomach.

He makes a horrible grunting sound. My own stomach heaves, but I hang tight.

The grunt is echoed by the sounds of another wounded guard—the one Caleb must've thrown the knife at.

The guy I'm holding stops struggling, and I feel him going limp. I don't want to think about what that implies as I let him slide to the floor. Eugene looks pale as he steps back, dropping his knife on the ground.

Caleb is next to the guy by the door already and is holding the man's throat in a tight grip, blocking off air and preventing further sounds.

Julia begins to pick the lock on the door. I walk toward her and Caleb, trying to avoid looking at all the blood.

I hear faint screams inside the room. Mira must have started her performance.

Caleb eases the now-limp body to the floor.

I focus on the good things. The plan is going smoothly.

I try not to think of the gruesome parts.

Not surprisingly, there's a difference between stabbing people in the Quiet and seeing it done in real life. Blood flows. People actually die. The difference is huge. I can also actually throw up in the real world, an urge I fight with all my strength.

Julia is done with the door and looks at Eugene in triumph.

In a split second, her face changes—dread contorting her features. Her fright is contagious. Instantly I turn, so I can see what she sees.

Eugene is still standing next to the man he stabbed, but what he's not seeing, because he's looking away, is that the guy isn't dead, like we thought. He's lying on the floor and holding a gun aimed at us.

Before I can even digest the image in front of me, there is a shot.

It's the loudest thing I've ever heard. It's like my ears explode. Like the most intense thunder you could ever imagine.

Everything seems to slow, and then goes quiet. A very familiar kind of quiet. I realize that I phased in without consciously trying. Near-death experiences are becoming a habit today.

In the safety of the frozen world, I look around. There is a bloody circle on Julia's left shoulder. Her face is frozen in shock. Despite myself, I'm relieved. Though she's clearly been shot, even without being a doctor I know that shoulder wounds are rarely fatal. The real reason for my relief, however, is that my own frozen body is unscathed.

The biggest surprise is Caleb, who I thought was still in the process of laying the dead guard on the ground. In the time it took me to phase into the Quiet, he's already holding a gun. And the gun has smoke around its muzzle. He must've managed to take it out and shoot, almost as soon as the other shot was fired. Or maybe he saw it coming? Maybe he was phasing in every second, assessing the situation around us—something I now realize I should've been doing. Still, Caleb's speed is astounding.

The most incredible part is that I can actually see the bullet. It's a few inches away from the shooter's head.

With dread, I open the door into the room with Mira.

It's bad.

The guy who was playing cards with her is now standing. He's trying to get out of the way of his partner—the more suspicious guard, who's now pointing his gun down at Mira. She, with her chair, is lying on her side on the floor. She completed the difficult maneuver, as we'd planned. Only now it might be for nothing. The noise of the gunshots ruined everything.

I get closer to the suspicious guard and inspect the situation. The muscles in his wrist are taut. He looks like he's about to pull the trigger.

I refuse to accept this.

I touch his forehead.

* * *

We're still contemplating what to say in the text to the hostage's brother, whose number we located in the girl's pink phone, when we hear the shots outside the room.

Someone must be trying to free the hostage. Unbelievable. What idiot would even try something so stupid?

We know we need to follow orders, which were very explicit on this. Arkady made us repeat them. If any shit goes down, first order of business is to shoot the girl. After that, we must deal with whoever might've come after her. If we kill her brother, we get a big bonus.

We take the gun and aim. We're pressing the trigger.

* * *

I get out of his head. I have no doubt about it now. He's shooting. In his head, I felt my—or I should say *his*—finger squeeze the trigger. His brain already sent the instructions to his arm. In a second after I phase out, a shot will fire. A shot aimed directly at Mira.

If only he was just reaching for his gun. If only his partner would trip and fall to cover her somehow. If only the door was wide open already—I'm right behind it, ready to shoot.

I want to scream. I'm ready to kill. Only it's too late.

I can't just watch Mira die. I have to do something.

Not sure why, I approach the guard who was looming over Mira. The one who was playing cards with her before. Vasiliy, I remind myself.

I touch his forehead.

* * *

We're looking at the girl on the floor. We know what Tolik is about to do. We feel faint regret. We think it's a shame she'll be killed. We think it's a waste of a very nice female specimen.

I, Darren, realize that this one likes Mira in his own crude way. A way that's not altogether different from the way I like her. It makes this experience odd. It also seems to push me further with what I'm trying to do.

Without fully realizing what I'm doing, I focus on his regret. On the fact that he likes her. Even on his lust for her.

I picture it growing. I picture what regretting losing someone very close to me would be like and channel it into Vasiliy. I recall wanting to fuck Mira and channel those memories into him. I recall what losing my grandmother felt like, which has nothing to do with Mira, but seems useful, so I channel that into him, too. It feels like I'm pouring my essence into him. As if for a moment, we merge into the same person.

It feels like I'm achieving something, so I continue further, almost becoming my host.

I think of Tolik. He's my best friend. If I just get in the way of the gun, he'll never shoot. He'll stop, and then I can talk to him, explain why the girl must be spared. I picture us coming up with a scheme. We tell Arkady she's dead. Tolik gets full credit and a huge bonus. She and I disappear from NYC, maybe even from the US. I picture how grateful the girl will be when she realizes she owes her life to me.

I finally picture the simple action that can make it all come together. I need to fall on top of her. From where I'm standing, it will take less than a second to just fall down.

I will feel her body under my own. I'll be her strong protector. A real man. All I need to do now is show a little courage. And then, of course, Tolik will stop. He'll never shoot me. All he needs to see is that that she's important, and it will all be over . . .

* * *

As if in a trance, I feel almost pushed outside his head. I'm not sure what just happened.

I realize that in reality, there is only one thing I can do. I can open that door, and I can shoot Tolik. And hope I make it—hope I shoot him in time.

My brain screams at the impossibility of making the shot in time, so I try to hope that whatever I did inside Vasiliy's head will help.

I open the door. I push my frozen self out of the way and take his exact position. I close the door behind me.

Now, I try it in the Quiet. A test.

I open the door. My hand is steady. I shoot. His temple is red. It all takes no more than two seconds.

I'm ready. I take a breath and phase out.

I open the door for real this time. My hand is even steadier here than it was in the Quiet.

I hear the Russian's shot as I squeeze the trigger.

CHAPTER TWENTY-TWO

My own gun fires—but I don't hear it. I phase into the Quiet once more.

Tolik's head is frozen mid-explosion. Bits of his skull and brain are caught mid-flight toward the wall behind him. I killed him, but I don't even register that fact. Instead I focus on something else entirely— and what I see makes me feel like I'm about to burst with joy.

Vasiliy, the guy whose head I was in just a moment ago, is on top of Mira.

He took the bullet that was meant for her.

I roll him off her and see no signs of the bullet having traveled all the way through. It hit him in the right shoulder blade.

Mira is unharmed, other than some minor bruises due to falling with the chair. She hasn't been killed.

I know there is a possibility, however remote, that the bullet is still about to go through Vasiliy. I might've phased in at just the right fraction of a second to make the bullet freeze on its way out.

I run to my body and slam into myself, roughly grabbing whatever exposed skin comes my way.

I am in the real world again, hearing the sharp crack of the shot I just fired.

I rush into the room.

I ignore the sound of Tolik's body falling to the floor where I shot him. My entire focus is on Vasiliy, now crumpled on top of Mira.

He moans in pain.

She's quiet.

My heart sinks.

Tolik's shot must've reached her through Vasiliy's body.

Filled with panic, I roll him off her as fast as I can. His moans become screams at my rough treatment, but I barely notice his pain as I see Mira lying there, alive and unharmed.

Just as she was in the Quiet.

She's strangely silent, however, and I decide that she must be in shock. Feeling a tiny fraction calmer, I start cutting away the duct tape from her legs.

"You're a hero, Darren," Caleb says from the door. For the first time, I hear no sarcasm in his voice. "You should know I don't throw around compliments lightly."

"Help me untie her," I say, not knowing how to respond to that.

"Can't," he says curtly. "I need to bind Julia's shoulder."

I remember Julia's wound and I nod, continuing to work on the tape by myself. Mira still doesn't say a word. Her silence begins to worry me.

Finally, I succeed in cutting through the tape, and Mira slowly gets to her feet, still without speaking. Then, not looking at me, she walks to the gun that fell from Tolik's hand and picks it up.

She's going to finish Vasiliy off, I realize.

But instead of pointing the gun at the injured mobster, she points it at me.

I barely have a chance to register the tears gleaming in her eyes and the shaking of her hand before I instinctively phase into the Quiet.

Battling my shock and disbelief, I approach her and brush my fingers against her frozen cheek, determined to understand her strange behavior.

Instantly a moving Mira joins me in the Quiet. She wipes the tears from her eyes, looking around the room, and as her gaze lands on me, the expression on her face turns to fury. Stepping toward me, she slaps my face, the way wives do to cheating husbands in movies. Then she punches me in the stomach.

I'm stunned. What the hell is she doing?

"You fucking Pusher!" she says through clenched teeth. "Don't you ever come near me again!"

Before I can react, she turns around and touches her frozen self.

Numb, I look at my own self standing in front of her gun. His face looks more confused than it did on the day I first discovered being able to 'stop time.'

I now know what upset her so much.

I now understand what I did to Vasiliy.

Mira must've phased in after the shots went down. She must've Read Vasiliy. She must've seen the telltale signs of what happened in his mind.

Signs similar to what I saw earlier in Piotr's mind.

Signs of what I refused to really think about, until now.

I *made* Vasiliy protect her with his body.

I made him fall.

I overrode his free will.

I *pushed* him.

I'm what she hates most in the world.

A Pusher.

I touch my confused self on the forehead.

I am back in the real world, with Mira's gun in my face. It's shaking more than it did before.

Is this really how it's going to end? Is she going to kill me? I'm so numb that I just stand there, waiting for it.

But no. She slowly lowers the gun. Then, hurrying over to Tolik's dead body, she picks up her pink phone from the table next to him and runs out of the room.

Finally shaking off my strange numbness, I run after her.

"What the fuck was that?" Caleb yells after me, but I don't have time to explain.

I keep running after her, gaining speed, but she's fast. After chasing her down a couple of flights of stairs, I slow down and then stop. Even if I catch her, I have no idea what I'll say.

Feeling exhausted all of a sudden, I go back and rejoin Eugene and Caleb, who seem very confused.

Julia is bleeding, her face deathly pale, and Eugene is hovering next to her. His face is almost as pale as hers.

"What's going on?" Caleb asks, frowning at me.

"Don't ask," I say. "Please."

"Is Mira okay?" he persists.

"I think she is, yes," I answer wearily. "I mean, she's not hurt—physically, at least."

"Fine. Then help me," Caleb says. He gives Eugene the keys and tells us to get the car. Meanwhile, he picks Julia up like she weighs nothing, and starts down the stairs. Everything seems to happen in a haze.

Eugene and I get the car in silence. He looks back toward Caleb and Julia once, then looks around, probably hoping to spot Mira. She's nowhere to be seen, but we find the car in the Costco parking lot, where we left it. I drive to the curb, pull up, and Caleb carefully puts Julia in the back. Caleb reclaims the driver's seat, while I ride shotgun. Eugene gets in the back with Julia. I hear them talking quietly, but make out only her repeated insistence that she's fine.

In five minutes, we're parked at the Lutheran Medical Center. Caleb gets out as soon as the car's stopped. He leans in Julia's window. "You holding up okay?"

"Fine," she says. "Really. I'm okay." She doesn't look okay—she looks like she's about to pass out. Eugene doesn't look much better.

"I'll be right back," Caleb says. "Give me a minute."

As soon as he's gone, I hear the sound of Eugene's text alert go off. I don't know why, but the sound alone fills me with dread.

"Darren," Eugene says after a few seconds. "Mira just texted me. She's on her way here on foot. She says she wants you gone when she arrives."

I don't know what to say. "Okay. I'll go then."

"What happened?" Eugene asks, his face the very definition of confused.

"Talk to Mira," I say tiredly. "Please don't make me explain."

We share an uncomfortable silence. Through the haze surrounding me, I'm aware of Caleb returning a few minutes later with a wheelchair for Julia. How did he get one so quickly? Did he show his gun to someone in the hospital? Surely not, or security would be right behind him, I reason dazedly.

Caleb says something to Eugene and sends him on his way with Julia. Something about making sure she's okay and about being back once he drops 'the kid' at his house. He also suggests some bullshit cover story to explain the gunshot wound. I listen, but I'm mentally somewhere else.

When Eugene and Julia enter the hospital, Caleb starts the car.

"Are you okay, Darren?" Caleb asks me as he pulls out of the hospital parking lot.

"Yeah, sure," I say on autopilot. I'm far from okay, but he doesn't need to know that.

"All right then, I'll take you home. What's your address?"

I give it to him, and he puts it into his GPS.

"Okay, good. Now give me your number, too, and I'll get in touch with you soon. I've almost made up my mind about the first person whose fighting we'll experience."

"Great."

"You're in shock," Caleb says. "It happens sometimes after a battle. Even with the best of us."

I just nod. I don't care about his theories or approval. I don't care about anything. I don't want to think.

My phone rings. It's my mom Sara.

"Do you mind?" I ask Caleb. I think it's very rude to talk on a cell in front of someone.

"No worries," he replies, and I answer the call.

"Hello?" I say.

"Darren, I was beginning to worry," Sara says. This makes my stupor fade a little. Beginning to worry is Sara's default state. I don't believe the woman has ever called me when she was chill. Of course, if she thought I was in even a fraction of the trouble I've been in today, she would go to her second-favorite state—panic about me.

"I'm okay, Mom. I was just busy today." Understatement of the century.

"You aren't mad at us?" she asks, and I immediately realize I've been an ass. I should've called to reassure them about the adoption business from the day before.

"No. We're good, Mom," I say, forcing certainty into my voice. Better late than never, I always say.

She seems to believe me, and we move on to the usual 'how are you' chat that we have every day. The whole thing is surreal.

When I get off the phone, Caleb is just a few blocks from my place. We ride in a companionable silence the rest of the way.

"This is you," Caleb says when we get to my building.

"Thanks for the ride," I say, extending my hand to Caleb. "And for helping us out. That was some good shooting you did."

He shakes my hand firmly. "You're welcome. You weren't bad yourself, and I know these things. Get some sleep," he says, and I nod in agreement.

It's the best idea I've heard in a long time.

I get to my apartment, eat something, shower, and get into bed. Once there, I just sit for a moment, looking outside. It's still light out there, the sun only beginning to set. I don't care, though. I'm exhausted, so I lie down.

When I'm this tired, time seems to slow. It's like my head approaches the pillow in slow motion.

I think about everything that's happened to me today. I think about the things that are about to happen. In those couple of seconds it takes for my head to hit the pillow, I think of anything but the fact that Mira will hate me now. Anything but the biggest question of all.

What am I?

And then my head finally touches the pillow, and I'm out, falling asleep faster than I have in my entire life.

The Time Stopper

A Mind Dimensions Story

DESCRIPTION

I can stop time, but I can't change anything.

I can access memories, but not far enough.

My name is Mira, and my life is about finding the Russian mobster who killed my family.

Note: This is a short prequel from Mira's point of view. It takes place before Mira meets Darren. For optimal reading experience, we recommend that you read it before proceeding to *The Thought Pushers*, the continuation of Darren's story.

.

CHAPTER ONE

"It's so smoky in here; it's like someone set off a bomb."

As soon as I say the stupid line, I Split into the Mind Dimension, and time seems to stop.

Victor is squatting over his chair, about to sit down. If this was still the real world, his legs would hurt in a minute or so. As it is, he's as aware of his muscles as a wax statue would be. Shkillet, a guy at the poker table, is frozen in mid-stare at my body—a position I often find men in. The other players are similarly stuck at what they were doing when I Split. The strangest thing in the room is probably the thick cigar smoke that's no longer moving. It looks eerie, like frozen clouds on an alien world. I don't smell the smoke now, which is a relief. I also don't hear anything other than the sound of my high heels clicking on the floor as I walk around the room.

I look at these men, these dangerous men, and an inner voice tells me, "Mira, no sane woman would voluntarily be here. Not even to merely observe this poker game, let alone play with these savages." It's funny how this inner voice usually sounds like my mom.

"You're dead, Mom," I mentally reply to the inner voice. "And I'm here to find the fucker who killed you. Can't we have an imaginary conversation without all this nagging?"

The inner voice sneers—but that's me. Mom was too nice to sneer.

The Mind Dimension makes it safe for me to walk around the room and peek at my opponents' cards without them being the wiser. When I'm in the Mind Dimension, everything stops in a single moment. No matter what I do here in this alternate world, when I get back to my real body—the body that's still sitting at the table—I'll still be in the same situation as I was before I Split: still being stared at by Shkillet, and still having just said that line about the bomb.

When I first learned I could Split, I was a little girl, and I thought my soul was leaving my body. But that was back when I believed in such things as souls, and God, and goodness—words that are meaningless to me now. Back in those days, I also believed in silly things, like the fact that there is a purpose to life.

I don't any longer. Not since that day.

Since that day, I haven't believed in anything but myself. And sometimes—a lot of times—not even that. That little girl who believed in souls would certainly think I'm a stranger if she met me today.

And maybe, she would think I'm a monster.

Of course, that day did not just dispel my childish illusions. It also taught me more practical things, such as how impotent I am while in the Mind Dimension. How truly powerless. No matter how much I want to, I can't change anything in the real world. Like a ghost, I don't affect the world of the living. Maybe that's what I became that day—a ghost of my former self.

That day. Why does thinking about it always hurt the same way, no matter how much time passes? Why is it so vivid in my mind at a moment's notice?

For that matter, why does trying not to think about something bring that very thing into focus?

My mind flashes to that day as though I'm Reading other people, but it's as if I'm replaying my memories instead of someone else's.

I see myself walking home from school, my backpack heavy on my shoulders. I relive the excitement of seeing my dad's car in the driveway when I get home. He hasn't driven away yet, I think joyously, so I'll get a chance to say goodbye. That last line will be singed into my mind forever, but I don't know it yet.

And then I see the car explode.

I see it go up in flames.

I hear the most horrible sound.

Then . . . silence.

I open my eyes.

The fire is standing still.

The explosion had scared me so much that I automatically Split into the Mind Dimension, as sometimes happens under extreme stress.

Now in the Mind Dimension, I'm standing next to my other, frozen-in-time, self. She looks as terrified as I feel. I know that if I touch the exposed flesh on her/my body, I will leave the Mind Dimension—and the explosion will continue its destruction.

Leaving would've been a cowardly choice, a choice I didn't even think to make at the time. I would later regret that bravery—or rather, lack of imagination.

Instead of leaving the Mind Dimension, I run toward the car.

The flames are frozen. Unreal. As if they're made of red and yellow silk.

The full horror of the situation hits me only when I see the expression on Mom's face.

She looks white, or at least the parts of her face that aren't burned do. Her blue eyes are wide open, her irises almost black from her dilated pupils.

I open the car door and try to pull her out. In her body's rigid state, she's like a human-sized doll. As I'm straining under her weight, I know that this is futile. I've never been able to change anything in the real world by what I've done in the Mind Dimension. Still, I'm hoping that today will be different. That Mom will be out of the car in the real world simply because it matters so much to me.

Except the universe doesn't give a fuck what matters to me.

I quiet my mind and touch her face. I begin the Reading process, another brave action that will later haunt me. Like always, Reading her shows me the world through her eyes. I lose myself in her head. For that minute, *I* become *we*. The horror of my mom's last moments becomes mine—so it's me, too, who's beginning to realize we are about to burn alive.

Later, I will think about who caused the explosion and wonder if I can ever un-live it, but right now, I just leave her head and look into the car again.

Dad's face is free of burns. I will later hypothesize that the explosive was on the passenger side. His mouth is half-open in an expression of terror that contorts his whole face. I take all this in and am overcome with another idea that I will later regret.

I run to the side door and touch Dad's face through his open window, not really thinking about what I'm doing. Except I do know what I'm doing. I'm bringing him into the Mind Dimension. That's what touching another Reader does—and that's what Dad is, a Reader, like me and my brother.

Unlike Mom, who doesn't have our abilities.

As soon as I touch his skin, another Dad, a screaming Dad, shows up in the back of the car.

"Nyyyeeet!" He switches to Russian as he always does when he's stressed. Then he registers me and screams, "Mira, honey, no!" His accent is heavier than usual.

"It's okay, Dad," I soothe. "We're in the Mind Dimension."

"It's true. We are." He looks around, terror replaced with a different emotion on his face. A darker emotion that I can't exactly place. "Where is she?" he says after looking at the passenger's seat.

"I took her outside. I was hoping she'd stay outside."

Not saying anything, he gets out of the car and looks at Mom. "She's already burned."

"I know," I say thoughtlessly. "I Read her. She's in a lot of pain."

My dad looks like I flogged him with those words, but he quickly hides his reaction.

"In the real world, where are you standing, sweetie?" he says. "Tell me. Quickly."

"Over there . . ." I point. "Too far to help you."

"That's good." His shaking voice is filled with relief. "The blast shouldn't reach you there. But you still have to fall on the ground when you get back to your body and cover your ears for me. Promise me you'll do this. It's important."

"I promise, Dad." I'm beginning to understand what I have done to him. By pulling him out, I made sure that he could see himself dying in that car. That he could reflect on it. Dwell on it.

"I'm sorry." My voice also begins to shake. "I shouldn't have pulled you in."

"Don't say that." He smiles at me. It's one of the last smiles I'll have from him. "I'm glad I'll have a chance to . . . a chance to say good-bye."

I remember my thought right before I Split into the Mind Dimension and realize I had created something like an evil omen. A part of me knows that the idea is irrational, but I feel like I brought all of this on with that prophetic thought. *A chance to say goodbye.*

I squint as though I'm going to cry, but no tears come out.

"Don't." Dad reaches for me. "Let's spend the time we have left remembering the good times. Your Depth is only about a half hour—not enough time to spend on anything but happy memories."

He hugs me and tells me stories, determined to be with me for as long as I can stay, until I run out of Depth and become Inert—unable to go back into the Mind Dimension for a while. As I catch myself enjoying his stories and being with him, I hate myself more and more.

I'll later wonder what kind of bitch I was to extend such a moment for my father, but for now, I'm just happy to have him with me a little longer. For as long as I'm allowed.

"We're running out of time." Dad is trying his best to sound cheerful, but I know he's pretending. "You did the right thing," he says. "I'm really glad you pulled me out."

He's lying. Like my brother, Dad repeats lies to make them sound more convincing.

"To live even a few more minutes, to see you, is a treasure." His eyes look earnest, but I can see the truth. He isn't glad. He's terrified because he knows that as soon as my time runs out, he'll be taken out of the Mind Dimension and pulled back into his frozen body.

Into the explosion.

"There's nothing you can do for us now, Mira," he says. "Please take care of your brother; he's all you've got—"

I don't hear him finish that sentence because my time runs out. I will later grow to resent this limitation, my Depth. This finite amount of what-if time.

If only I could've stayed in the Mind Dimension forever. Then Dad and I could've talked forever. Or we could've explored that frozen-in-time world. Instead, I'm back in my body and the explosion is in my ears again, ears that feel like they might bleed. I fall on the ground, like I promised Dad I would. I welcome the pain of the fall because it numbs the pain from knowing that I don't have parents anymore.

With herculean effort, I pull my mind back to the present. To the poker table and the Russian thugs surrounding me. I really have to get it together. My Depth's being wasted as the seconds turn into minutes. If I run out of time, I'll be Inert for a while—which means no more Reading and having to play fair in this poker game, to boot.

I shake my head and try to focus, determined to forget Mom and Dad for the moment. I try to focus on something else.

Anything else.

To distract myself, I think of how strangely I experience emotions in the Mind Dimension. For example, if I cry there, because my face is dry once I get out, I don't feel as sad anymore. Sometimes things work the other way. I can be terrified when I get into the Mind Dimension, but once there, I'm much calmer. Probably because there I'm safe. So if I get any tears now, they would be gone when I'm back at that table. And tears should be falling down my face right now, but none come. Just like on that day. The worst one of my life—

I have to stop thinking about that day.

So I try to picture talking to my brother about emotions in and out of the Mind Dimension. He would want to study this phenomenon, as he—ever the scientist—would call it. It makes me feel somewhat better. Thinking of Eugene always helps take me out of the darkness, if only for a moment.

"I do take care of him. The poor bastard would've starved long ago without me, Dad." I'd say that to my father if I believed he was listening to me from Heaven. Of course, my father is not in Heaven or Hell—those are just constructs people make up to dull the pain of losing their loved ones. I know that, in reality, he's just gone, and nothing I say can reach him.

And that means I need to stop dwelling on what might've been and focus on the task at hand.

The fucker who put the explosive under my family's car might be in this very room right now.

I take a deep breath, finding comfort in anger and the violent fantasies of what I plan to do to him.

"It's time," I say out loud—though, of course, the frozen people can't hear it. "Let's see if any of you fuckers are thinking of explosions."

CHAPTER TWO

I'm hoping the guy I'm looking for, the guy who deals with bombs, will be primed by my words and think of setting up one specific explosion. I'll be the first to admit that this tactic is a long shot, but it's the only option I have since my Depth allows me to go back only a few minutes into their memories.

Not for the first time, I envy more powerful Readers. Those like the legendary Enlightened, the most powerful Readers of all, who have enough Depth to relive whole months, if not years, of someone's life. Someone like that would get the answer directly without any gimmicks, but I can't. There are no shortcuts for Readers like me. Given that Depth is spent at twice the speed when you

Read, I have to be careful about running out of my measly half hour.

Whatever Depth I spend on Reading is going to be worth it in this case, though. Trying to learn the truth is why I come to these games. Well, that and the money from the wins—but there are better ways to make money gambling than coming here. Safer ways.

My strategy for today is to spend only seconds of my Depth on people I think as unlikely candidates, leaving extra time—even if it's just a few minutes— for the others.

One such unlikely candidate is Shkillet, the guy who's staring at me in the real world.

Shkillet is not his real name, but a street alias. Probably has something to do with his too-thin pasty-looking face. He resembles one of those skeletons we had in science class before I dropped out of school. The Russian word for skeleton sounds a lot like the word *skillet*, only with a *yet* sound at the end. Shkillet's lisp could be the reason for the *sh* sound at the beginning.

Or I could be completely wrong. I was pretty young when we left the Motherland, and I do get some of these little ethnic things confused now and then—which drives my brother nuts.

I look at Shkillet's cards. He's not holding anything I need to worry about. But he is staring at me—the real-world me. In fact, if I drew a line from his pupils to that me, it would land directly on her/my boobs. Boobs that are nicely displayed in my red strapless dress, thanks to the Victoria's Secret pushup bra.

I intended that effect, but I'm still annoyed. Fucking men.

Stepping around him, I take off his shirt.

I know it seems weird that I'd undress someone, especially someone this unattractive, but I do have a purpose. I'm looking for tattoos. Over the course of my investigation, I've learned that a man's tattoos in the Russian criminal underworld reveal a lot about him. Well, only for the ones who've been in Russian prisons, but those are the ones I'm looking for. The most dangerous. The ones without souls.

Those who'd plant bombs on innocent families.

Shkillet is what I call skinny-fat. His body is gaunt with his ribcage sticking out, but at the same time, his stomach is flabby. I don't care about his looks, though. All that matters is that he has no tattoos. He does have a large birthmark, however, that reminds me of a Rorschach inkblot test. A counselor showed it to me during the one and only time I tried therapy. Most of her inkblots reminded me of people's brains blowing up—understandable, given the reason I went to see her in the first place—but this guy's birthmark looks like an exploding heart.

Okay, so Shkillet either hadn't been to prison back home or nobody bothered to put any ink on him while he was there. Either way, he's not likely to be a high-status criminal and thus probably isn't the person I'm looking for. Therefore, he's good for a measly five-second jump into his head.

I put my hand on his neck as though trying to measure his pulse. Where I touch people in the Mind Dimension never seems to matter, so I go for the least disgusting place. I clear my mind for Reading. The faster this part is, the more Depth I save. Eugene had figured out some techno-widgety new practice for me to improve how quickly I can do this, and I'm grateful for it with situations like this.

The feeling I get just before I'm about to Read someone comes over me, and I make sure I'm sent only a few moments back into his memories.

* * *

"It's so smoky in here; it's like someone set off a bomb," the girl says.

The sex bomb is talking about a real bomb, we think of replying, but decide against it. Not until we see how Victor responds. The guy's insane, and displeasing him is as easy as it is deadly.

This is why we realize that if we go through with our plan for the girl, we'll have to cut her throat afterwards. Had we just wanted to fuck her, then we could probably get away with leaving her alive afterwards—there are no rules against rape in this place. But we want her money, too, and that's why she'll have to die. Victor's underground casinos have only this one rule: retaliations due to game losses are forbidden. We shudder when we remember what had been done to the last guy who tried to pull some shit on a poker game winner. We'll have to ensure we're not caught.

We think about all the things we want to do to her before we kill her off, and get a painful hard-on. We imagine how we'd fill up that oh-so-fuckable pouty mouth of hers. We visualize grabbing those perfect titties, leaving marks, prying open those long legs . . . Our balls tighten in anticipation.

This is going to be even better than the last time. That whore from two days ago can't even begin to compare to this girl. Looks aside, that bitch hadn't even fought us, just meekly took it. The fight has become half the fun for us over the years. When they fight, and we finally bend them to our will, we feel the rush of power that's almost as fun as the sex itself. With this girl, it'll be even better because she's rumored to be feisty. The sarcastic remarks she's made throughout the game confirm it. So she'll likely fight, and fight well. We fantasize about her scratching our back with her perfectly manicured fingernails before we lock her wrists in a tight grip . . .

I, Mira, separate my own thinking from Shkillet's in horrified disgust. I need a shower. I need a dozen showers. I'm still in his head, but I can reflect on what I just learned without fully getting out. Separating my thinking this way allows me to spare my brain from getting more of the vile details of what he plans to do to me. Witnessing the memories of what he did to the poor girl he raped two days ago was terrible enough. And while I'm not clear if he killed her afterwards, I'm positive he's planning to kill me.

Given the circumstances, I dive a little deeper into his memories. I need to learn if he's armed and if there's anything else I need to know about.

We look at our cards. One fucking pair. Two more rounds like this, and we'll be completely broke. But not for long, we remind ourselves, feeling the weight of the ceramic knife in the holster in our boot.

It'll be best to do the deed swiftly. It has to happen here on the club premises before the bitch leaves and has the chance to get into her car.

Victor will be furious when they find the body. But he'd never suspect Shkillet. Getting no respect has some advantages—people underestimate us, and therefore, we can get away with anything.

I, Mira, separate again and think quickly. He managed to sneak a ceramic knife into this place. I guess the material didn't trigger the metal detector wands the bouncers pass over everyone's body upon entrance.

Damn it. This changes my strategy completely. I need to make sure to leave plenty of Depth to deal with this development. If one of these other men is the one I came here to find, it's his lucky day, because I'm skipping their vile heads.

Except Victor's. I've been waiting to meet him face-to-face for months because he's always seemed the most likely candidate, given what I've heard about him. There's no way I'm missing that chance now.

As I form a plan, I exit Shkillet's mind.

* * *

Still in the Mind Dimension, I approach Victor and unceremoniously rip the shirt from his body. As I do so, I note the pair of aces in front of him on the table.

And his tattoos.

Yeah, Victor's been in the Russian jail system—he's a *zek*, as these people call it. Russian tattoos fascinate me. Probably because Dad had one. He served time with a bunch of scientists for objecting to the nuclear arms race during the Cold War. His Reading skills saved his life, enabling him to get out of the prison camp after only a couple of months, but the hellish experience made him desperate to leave the Soviet Union. He waited years until he could, and by then, the Soviet Union was simply Russia. Still, as Dad liked to say about the new regime, "Nothing's changed—KGB still rules."

So now I try to memorize Victor's tattoos. I only recognize the meaning of the stars on his shoulders. *Vor v zakone.* Translated literally, it means 'a thief in law,' but the vernacular is a criminal authority of high caliber.

I examine him more. I've never seen this double-headed eagle tattoo before, though I think this is what the government symbol looked like back in the Czarist Russia. The Statue of Liberty super-imposed on the eagle also doesn't ring any bells. Perhaps Victor hates the Soviet Union and is reliving the pre-revolution glory days with this ink? Coupled with a symbol of America, maybe he's not so fond of communism, too? It's a theory that gains more credence when I realize that a lot of his prison images are anti-authority.

I also notice that Victor is ripped. How can I not? I am, after all, human. He's built like a swimmer, and his abs form a perfect six-pack.

Stop being a danger slut, Mira, I chide myself. *How can you even think about what he looks like after what was in Shkillet's head?*

Or, more importantly, given what I've heard about Victor. This tendency to drool over monsters is something I truly despise about myself.

So, to that end, I decide enough's enough. I need to give Victor a Reading and get the hell out. I'll be only half-empty of Depth, and that will have to be enough.

I put my arm on his chiseled chest, right on the serene face of Lady Liberty. Physical contact made, I concentrate.

I'm going back far enough to see what he did before he came into this room. With any luck, he might've been thinking of blowing up someone's car. If so, Shkillet won't be the only person I'll need to deal with . . .

* * *

We're inside Vera. She moans softly. With her bent over just the way we like, we have a nice view of her naked back. It's sinewy with muscle. In a perfect world, we like our woman to be a bit curvier, but there's something about her that we find attractive enough to overlook that fact. Our previous squeeze had nice love handles, but she, unfortunately, didn't appreciate our interest, instead opting to overdose while we were taking care of business. Women.

Besides the lack of curves on Vera, we also don't approve of the tattoo on her lower back. It's of Madonna holding the baby Jesus. When we fuck someone doggy-style, the last thing we need is a religious symbol staring us in the face, particularly since the tattoo artist made Madonna beautiful. Probably wanted to mess with the heads of everyone who'd ever fuck Vera in the future—which is a large number of people. Or, just as likely, the bitch arranged for the tattoo to have this effect herself.

As our thrusts deepen, she moans louder, and that brings us closer to the edge. In an effort to prolong the sensation, we direct our mind off the fucking and onto irrelevant things, like the dimples above her ass.

Unfortunately, they're actually a turn-on.

So then we try focusing on the little mole on her right shoulder blade. That works for a bit until we notice the way the sweat slicks her skin. Smooth, gleaming skin. Fuck. We lift our head to stare at the blank walls of the VIP room.

I, Mira, disassociate, albeit hesitantly. This is the first time I've ever caught a man fucking a woman, and it's . . . hot. It's nothing like Reading them while they fuck me. Of course, I'm not here on a hedonistic vacation. Each moment I spend watching this, a double moment is subtracted from my Depth—because that's how Reading works. Eugene explained that we share the time with the target. I guess that means that on some level, everyone can get into the Mind Dimension when touched, but non-Readers are pulled in only enough for us to Read them.

I fast-forward Victor's memories a few minutes into the future.

We're approaching the table and noticing the girl. She's the prodigy we've heard so much about, the only female *katala* we've ever met—though, to be fair, we met most of those card-shark shysters when doing our time in the all-male Gulag.

We look at her, this girl who's squeezed so many people dry at our establishment. She has the cheekbones and nose of Russian nobility. Someone in this girl's lineage must've survived the October Revolution back in 1917. Her features have a slight sharpness to them, along with an air of dignity. It's a contrast to the matreshka-like round face of someone like Vera, who looks like a common Russian farmer's daughter—and probably is.

With those big blue eyes, long eyelashes, and dark waves of hair, this girl reminds us of our daughter's latest pictures. Only Nadia looks much more innocent than this one, we think with a mixture of longing and pride. Keeping Nadia innocent is why we made the sacrifice of not being in her life all those years ago. She probably doesn't even know who we are, so there's no point dwelling on it. And even if she knows, she's in Russia, and we can't go back there.

"It's so smoky in here; it's like someone set off a bomb," the girl who reminds us of our daughter says.

That word—bomb—brings back flashbacks of that day in Chechnya when we lost two of our best comrades. Our heart rate increases, but then we calm down. The girl is just being a spoiled American princess. It happens to all the kids who arrive here. Her Majesty probably expected this illegal gambling club to enforce New York's non-smoking laws.

I, Mira, separate my mind from Victor's and feel a hint of disappointment. The fact that my words bring up his experience in Chechnya, which must've happened a long time ago, makes him unlikely to be the guy I'm looking for. Especially since he seems to have an aversion to explosions—almost a PTSD-type of reaction. It's not a certainty that he wasn't involved, of course, but it's enough for me to clear him. I'd crossed people off my list based on less credible evidence.

Thus decided, I exit his head.

* * *

I'm back in the silent room. I'm not going to Read the other players' minds. I'm going to conserve my Depth instead. I have two more things I have to do.

First, I take a look at the cards everyone else is holding. With the outcome of the next round in my head, I proceed to the second thing and run out of the room. Swiftly, I go through the dark corridor to the nearby bathroom. I check what I came here to check and confirm that it's still there—the thing that'll give me a chance when dealing with Shkillet. I'm a little calmer now and glad I took the time to explore this establishment in another Mind Dimension excursion; otherwise, I wouldn't have known about things hidden in nooks and crannies.

I run back to the room and approach my body. It's always strange seeing myself like that. Being able to examine myself from all angles used to magnify my teenage insecurities. Normal girls can drive themselves crazy with a mirror, but Readers have it much worse. I remember being depressed about the shape of the back of my ankles not long after my fifteenth birthday. Of course, since my parents' death, I haven't thought about shit like that ever again.

I prepare myself for exiting the Mind Dimension and reach out, placing my hand on my frozen self's face.

And just like that, I'm back in my body.

The sounds are back, and so is the smell of smoke. Victor completes the motion of sitting down in his chair. The dealer finishes dealing. Shkillet stops staring at me, and looks furtively at Victor to see if he would reply to my weird statement.

"What the fuck are you talking about?" says a bald guy who's smoking a cigar. "If someone brought a bomb in here, Victor would put that bomb into that yebanat's ass."

CHAPTER THREE

The next few rounds of poker proceed predictably, given that I know which cards everyone is holding, as well as the top cards of the deck. So obviously, I win every round I can. And as I win, I watch Victor's amusement grow. I'm not sure if it's my winning that he finds amusing or the men's reactions. They dare not give me any attitude, but when I sneak a look at Shkillet, I can tell he's barely hiding his anger. Today, out of spite, I've been winning more than I usually do, and two rounds ago, I called Shkillet's bluff—a bluff that would've probably worked if not for my Reading powers.

Since I don't have a lot of Depth left, I decide that now is the time for me to get out of here. Before I wear out my welcome, so to speak.

"Gentlemen." I stand up. "It's been a pleasure."

"Pleasure taking our money, you mean?" Victor, surprisingly, doesn't sound angry. More like he's teasing.

"Sure, that, and it's nice to finally put a face to the name . . . Victor." That might've come out too flirtatious, but hell, I'm too wired for finesse at the moment. As I start gathering my stuff, I see Shkillet begin to fidget. I can tell he's about to leave, too. He's determined to put that plan of his into motion.

I put my winnings into my purse and slowly walk out, trying not to look suspicious.

I know I should make a run for it once I'm in the hall instead of implementing my more dangerous idea of confronting him. But I don't. That would be like playing the last rounds of poker so Shkillet would win—something else I could've done, but didn't. He needs a lesson, and I'll enjoy giving it to him. Maybe with him, I'll finally get the chance to figure out if I'm capable of doing what must be done when the time comes. My brother doesn't think I'd take someone's life. He means it as a compliment, but that's not how I take it, and tonight, I'm betting my life that my brother is wrong.

I arrive at the bathroom door. Shkillet hasn't come out of the game room yet. I take out a pack of Marlboro Reds and a lighter from my purse. I don't really smoke, but pretending to smoke has come in handy at times. Being a girl with a cigarette in her hand is a good icebreaker when the room is full of men with lighters. So I'm a sort of social smoker, I guess. But unlike others, I hate every inhalation. Sometimes when I smoke, I can almost feel the stuff making my lungs and teeth yellow and gross.

As I put the disgusting thing in my mouth, the game room door opens. I light up, inhale, and try not to cough while glancing at the door. Shkillet's there, and we make fleeting eye contact before I exhale the smoke.

Bait set, I walk into the bathroom.

I close the flimsy door lock behind me, hang my purse on a little hook in an effort to free my hands, and run to the toilet as quickly as possible given the slippery floor and my high heels.

The toilet lid is opened, and I catch a glimpse of the disgusting stuff in the bowl when I throw my now-useless cigarette into it. God, would it have been that difficult to flush the shit? The sight and stench of it reminds me of a nightmare I had a few times about a dirty bathroom. And this reality might be worse than that nightmare if I don't hurry up.

I reach for the water tank just as I hear the lock on the door being picked.

Shit. He's faster than I thought he'd be. He must've run down that hall like a maniac.

I frantically lift the heavy tank cover . . . just as the door lock fails.

"What the hell?" Shkillet says in Russian as he steps inside and sees me standing there with the lid in my hands.

Good. Not what he was expecting. And I capitalize on that by throwing the lid at his head with all my strength.

He's not fast enough to duck.

As he staggers backward with a grunt, I turn and grab the gun in the plastic zipped bag from the tank. I'd found this weapon in one of my earlier excursions in the Mind Dimension. I'm ripping the bag open when someone's hands grab my left arm.

It's Shkillet.

His fingers are like pincers digging into my flesh.

I Split into the Mind Dimension to assess the situation.

The sounds of his panting are gone, and I observe us from my new vantage point.

One of his hands is on my arm, and the other is reaching into his boot for the ceramic knife he's hiding there. His eyebrow is split open—must be where the lid hit him. The blood running from that wound makes his face look ghoulish.

I examine the bag in my hands. I've almost opened it, but I'm not sure if I'll make it before he gets the knife out and uses it. But I can do something else if I aim right.

I look at my statue-like face that's paralyzed in fear. I'll try my best to be calmer when I get back into my head. Calmer and lethal.

Grabbing my hand, I jump out of the Mind Dimension and desperately will my muscles to act. As though in slow motion, my leg kicks backwards, aiming for his shin. My foot connects with something.

"Bitch!" He falls to his knees. I must've hurt his leg.

In the time I bought myself with the kick, I get the gun out. Whirling around, I see the knife already in his hand.

He swings, the knife swishing through the air an inch away from my leg.

Instinctively, I jump to the side, then slam the butt of the gun into his face. It connects with his nose with a disgusting crunch.

He looks stunned for a moment, and I do it again, swinging the heavy handle at his jaw this time.

He tries to grab me, so I hit the back of his head.

He crumples—his head landing right in that disgusting toilet.

Serves the fucker right. Now he'll drown.

I should gloat, but for some inexplicable reason, I get the urge to kick him away, to get his face out of that toilet. Do I actually want to save his life?

I take a closer look at him. His mouth and nose are above the water, so he won't drown in that muck.

Funny, but for someone who was just thinking of saving him, I feel a pang of disappointment. The practical side of me knows I can't let him live. So I take the gun safety off and aim the muzzle at the back of my would-be-rapist-and-murderer's head.

This is it.

Now I just have to pull the trigger.

Is my hand really shaking? What is wrong with me?

This man deserves to die. Maybe not as much as my parents' killer, but he does deserve it. And if I don't kill him, he'll likely come after me. So shooting him is self-defense. Or a pre-emptive strike, if I have to justify my actions.

And apparently I do—because I can't squeeze that trigger no matter how many reasons I come up with for doing so. Like: *he might be too chicken-shit to come after me.* Or: *this might be his first attempt at murder.* And even: *he might change his whole life around after this.* Yeah, right. I'm now grasping at straws to come up with excuses for myself, when the truth is that Eugene was right.

It's not easy to kill a person—even a bad person.

"Is someone in there?" someone says from the other side of the door.

Shit.

I rush to the door and open it a sliver.

"Hey there," I say to the guy at the door, who looks to be one of the bouncers. "I'm just powdering my nose, and I need to change after that. Can you please use the bathroom upstairs?"

The bouncer mumbles something derogatory about women but starts walking away. Taking no chances, I Split again and Read a second of the bouncer's mind. He's going upstairs—that's the good news. The bad news is that he's mentally cursing a specific woman, me, and not, say, women in general, or one of the few other possible women who visit this place, like Vera—Victor's fucktoy from the nearby VIP room.

I guess this makes my decision for me. I can't shoot Shkillet now. The bouncer will know that I was the one who killed him, even if I run as soon as I fire the shot. I'm not keen to find out how Victor would react to my murdering someone in his place.

I could, though, hold Shkillet's head under the water until he drowns. That way, no one would come running right away, and I could get away. Plus, the bouncer wouldn't necessarily think I'd done it—I'm sure he's seen more than one drunk in Shkillet's position.

The big question is whether I can actually do it . . . since I wasn't able to pull the trigger.

Damn it. I hate that Eugene is right, and today isn't going to be the day I finally prove my worth to myself.

I stuff the gun into my purse and walk through the place, paranoid all the way to the exit that someone's going to notice the size of my purse. Luckily, no one stops me. It makes sense, since the time to distrust someone is when he or she is on the way in, not out. Plus, what male bouncer is going to be staring at my purse instead of my cleavage?

Still, I'm only able to breathe normally when I get into my car and put the gun into the glove compartment. Even though I don't need it, I didn't want to leave it for Shkillet in case he regains consciousness and decides to come after me. I might not be a cold-blooded killer, but that doesn't make me stupid.

The drive back home happens in a post-adrenaline-rush haze, for which I'm thankful. I don't want to think about what just happened. I just want to get home and unwind.

When I arrive at the apartment I share with Eugene, I take my high heels off and tiptoe into my room, stepping over all the junk in the living room. Not for the first time, I promise myself to tidy up, but obviously, not tonight. Closing my bedroom door, I'm super-grateful that I didn't wake my brother. My earlier plan for a dozen showers forgotten, I get into bed and pass out.

My sleep is interrupted by a recurring nightmare—a skeleton trying to strangle me.

CHAPTER FOUR

"Mira, is that you?"

My brother has this annoying habit of talking to me when my mouth is full or when, like now, I'm under a cascade of blissfully warm water, trying to relax.

"No, Eugene, it's some fucking stranger using our shower!" I slam the sliding door for emphasis.

"Thanks for saying the F word—now I know it's you!" He bangs on the bathroom door. "Come to the kitchen when you're done."

I wish I'd slept instead of tossing and turning all night. Still, the little sleep that I had should keep me going, and this shower is doing wonders.

I put on jeans and a T-shirt and head to the kitchen. My curiosity is piqued because I smell food—an oddity because I don't think anyone is here besides Eugene. Which would mean that, whatever dish the smell is coming from, he would've had to cook it.

"Happy birthday to you," my brother sings when I enter. "Happy birthday to you—"

"Eugene, please stop. My ears are going to wilt." I use humor to cover up the fact that I completely forgot about my birthday. With everything that's happened, it was the last thing on my mind.

"I made pancakes." He puts a plate in front of me when I sit down at the table. "Eighteen. One for each year."

"Is that what those brownish ovals are?" I give him a questioning look. "And isn't it supposed to be a candle for each year, not pancakes?"

"Aha!" He winks and brings his hands out from behind his back. He's holding a cupcake with a lit candle. The strawberry vanilla cupcake from the local Italian bakery that I like. It's a miracle he didn't burn his clothes standing like that.

"Thank you." I take the pastry and place it on the table. "And thanks for wearing a clean lab coat on this special occasion."

"You're welcome." He's acting like he didn't hear my ribbing about the lab coat. "Make a wish."

A wish. All of a sudden, I feel an ache in my chest. None of my wishes are happy. None are normal. A normal girl would wish to meet a nice guy, someone who's fun and good-looking. But not me. I wish I could find my parents' killers and the person who sent them, and then find the will and fortitude to kill them.

"Is something the matter?" Eugene asks.

"No," I lie, smoothing out my frown. "It's silly."

"You wish they were here to say happy birthday?" he says softly, switching to Russian.

I nod. It seems pointless to put it into words. As pointless as wishing.

We share a silence during which I stab the first of my eighteen pancakes with my fork and take a bite.

A bite that I have to stop myself from spitting out.

"Eugene . . ." I try to swallow the soggy, half-cooked lump in my mouth. "These are awful."

Oh crap. As soon as I see the hurt look on his face, I realize I could've been more tactful. But seriously, these are the worst-tasting pancakes I've ever had.

"Sorry." He demonstratively puts a pancake into his own mouth and chews it. "I did what the algorithm said." His expression doesn't change; if he can taste the problem, he's not showing it.

"They're called recipes, not algorithms." I move the plate toward him. "And I'm sure it called for butter and salt, things that make food yummy—stuff that's clearly missing from these pancake-esque thingies."

"Potato, potahto ... Recipes are algorithms." He spears another pancake onto his fork. "And salt and butter are bad for you anyway."

"A lot of good stuff is bad for you." I reach for the cupcake he bought for me and place it on my plate. "And it's funny you brought up potatoes. Did you put that in these pancakes? Because there's this aftertaste—"

"I'm not an idiot, Mira," he says. "If I made potato pancakes, I would call them *draniki*. Do you remember how—"

He doesn't have to finish that question. Of course I remember Mom's draniki. A cross between pancakes and hash browns, they were the most delicious things ever—and a part of my childhood I'll never have again.

I interrupt him by demonstratively blowing out the candle and taking a bite of my cupcake, making that yumminess-signifying, "Mmmmmmm," as I do so.

Eugene smiles at first, but then his face goes dark, an expression so intense and unnatural for him that it frightens me. And considering he's looking over my shoulder, I'm really hoping it's not a huge-ass spider.

"What's that?" He points in that same direction.

"What's what?" Oh shit. Maybe it's one of those giant cockroaches that thrive in this building's garbage disposal system. Or their competitors, the rats.

"That." He stands up and peers at me. "The black-and-blue claw mark on your arm."

I look at my left bicep. Fuck. It seems that Shkillet left a bruise when he grabbed me yesterday.

"It's nothing." I tug my sleeve down—not that it does much good. "Don't worry about it."

"It's not nothing." An even darker look crosses his face. "How stupid do you think I am?"

"Do you really want me to answer that?" I take a bite of my cupcake and regret it immediately. I know where this is going, and the delicious cupcake begins to taste like cardboard.

"I heard you come in late last night." He sits back down slowly. "You were doing that again. You were consorting with those monsters."

"Calm down." I brush the cupcake crumbs from my fingers.

"How the hell am I supposed to calm down?" He plants his palms on the table, about to shove himself upright again—until I grab his arm. I can feel the tension in him as he yells, "You're coming home with fucking bruises, and you're telling me not to worry about it? It's my job to protect you, and you're on your way to getting yourself killed!"

"Lower your voice, please," I say through clenched teeth. "It's not your fucking job to protect me."

"How can you be so dumb—"

I've had enough. Grabbing the plate from the table, I hurl it toward the stove.

Eugene watches it shatter with utter shock, even though this isn't the first tantrum he's seen me throw in his lifetime. More like the hundredth in the past two years alone.

"Mira, I—" he begins.

"Shut up." I rise to my feet.

"Wait, Mirochka. Seriously, I'm sorry—"

I don't hear the rest because I storm into my bedroom and slam the door shut behind me. Then I crank up some music and begin throwing clothes into a bag: something casual, a gym outfit, and, on a whim, a nice dress I bought months ago after a spree of poker wins. I also throw in some shoes. I want to make sure I have what I need so I won't have to come back here today—because if I do, I'll have to deal with Eugene's sulking.

"I'm not mad," I say when I open the door again. "I just need to get out of the apartment."

"Don't go, Mirochka—"

"Thank you for the birthday wishes." I sling the bag over my shoulder. "I mean it. It was nice."

"You're welcome." He pinches the bridge of his nose. Eugene knows me well enough to know there's no salvaging this situation right now.

Still, I feel like the biggest asshole as I leave the house.

* * *

Yoga class helps a little. A pretty boy checking out my yoga-pants-clad butt helps a little more. After the gym, I head to my favorite sushi place. That and hot sake make me feel almost like a normal person.

Almost like my birthday is worth celebrating.

Determined to enjoy feeling normal for as long as possible, I take a lengthy walk on the Brighton Beach boardwalk. I try to stay focused on the nice weather, but my thoughts eventually turn to my investigation, as they always do these days.

They said my parents' death was a mob-on-mob hit. Eugene Read the detectives investigating the case, and learned that the police had cut short the investigation as soon as they learned of the Russian mob's involvement. But my dad was never in the Russian mob. He was a scientist, like Eugene. It didn't make any sense until Eugene told me something else that he saw in the mind of the detectives: signs of Pushing.

Pushers are the other side of the coin among people who can enter the Mind Dimension. They're like us—except they control people's minds, instead of reading them. And they hate us just as much as we hate them. It's not a huge surprise those evil fuckers are involved in this somehow, especially given Dad's research into our abilities.

As soon as I learned all this, I knew I had to take the investigation into my own hands. My brother honors our parents' memory by focusing on Dad's research, but I do it differently. I do it by trying to hunt down their murderers, and if it drives my brother crazy, so be it. I'm not a little girl anymore. In fact, as of today, I'm officially an adult—though I haven't felt like a child for a long time.

Determined to get back into my earlier birthday-enjoyment groove, I go to the movies. The one I choose is a romantic comedy, and I enjoy it immensely for the fiction that it is. Those writers make these things so light and fluffy, it's like a fairy tale. In real life—at least in my real life—people are self-destructive, violent liars who will cheat and steal if they can get away with it. Outside of the mob, they put on a façade of civility, but as a Reader, I know what hides behind their polite smiles. In the mob, they don't even try to hide it. The criminals are more honest, in a way. Then again, the depravity of some of the things I Read in Victor's club and other similar places is mind-boggling. I sometimes can't sleep for weeks after getting one of those 'snuff Reads'—

I shake my head. Man, I need to get back some positivity.

To do that, I grab some ice cream before leaving the movie theater. Nothing is more positive than ice cream.

Afterwards, I decide against getting dinner. Instead, I go into the theater bathroom to change into my killer dress, and while I'm at it, I put on some makeup and a pair of high heels. It's time to have some fun and go clubbing. Why the hell not? It's my fucking birthday.

* * *

"Are you Russian?" is what I think the guy tries to say to me over the pounding music of the dance club.

"Da," I yell, nodding to the beat.

"Can I buy you a drink?" he says in Russian. Or I assume that's what he says because I catch the Russian word for drink over the noise, and he also puts his hand to his mouth in that universal drinking gesture. Not to mention, he points at the bar.

I look the guy over. Tall, broad-shouldered, he looks like the kind of guy I would've liked if I'd remained normal. Since I'm trying to be normal tonight, I let him buy me a Grey Goose with Red Bull, my party-all-night drink.

I love these Russian-owned clubs, even if sometimes the owners are in the mob. The vodka selection is always topnotch, the DJs are great at mixing the tracks, the music they mix is more to my taste, and the bartenders never ask for ID. I have a fake one, of course, but I prefer not to be asked. What's more, here they never give you that I-know-that-ID-is-fake-but-hey-now-I'm-off-the-hook-little-girl look.

As I sip my drink, the guy introduces himself and gives me some compliments, but I only hear bits and pieces. Finally, I have to lean in and yell into his ear, "I can barely hear you!"

"Would you like to dance?" He leans down, yelling into my ear, and I can finally hear him.

"Absolutely." I'm about to add his name, but realize that I can't remember it. Talk about embarrassing. I can't ask him now. Of course, I can always Split and check his wallet for an ID, so maybe later I'll do that.

He's a great dancer, with a sense of rhythm that I haven't been lucky enough to run into before. And speaking of lucky, I've lucked out in that he's also just the right amount of grabby. Although, after a song or two, with the buzz from the drink starting to hit my brain, I decide that he's not grabby enough. I take his hands and stick them on my butt. He, smart guy that he is, gets the point, and from here on out, there's a lot more touching. He even goes for some ear-nibbling, which I approve of.

We dance like that for at least ten songs. My legs begin to ache, and my head is spinning. I feel great. I feel as if . . . well, as if it's my fucking birthday.

Another few songs, and I'm grinding against him. He clearly likes it—that or there's a flashlight in his pocket that I hadn't noticed before.

"Do you want to get out of here?" he asks me eventually.

"Sure." I give him one last grind—in case there's any misunderstanding as to where this night is headed. "Let's go to your place."

He's holding my hand as we start making our way through the crowd, and then, suddenly, he stops.

He's staring at the chest of a gargantuan bouncer.

"Leave," the bouncer growls. He must have sixty pounds' worth of lungs alone; I can hear him clearly over all the noise. "She stays."

"What's the problem?" the guy asks.

"You didn't hear me?" The bouncer starts rolling up his sleeves—never a good sign. In a Russian nightclub, could be a deadly sign.

"It's all right," I yell at my guy. "I know this man."

"You're with him?" His lips become a thin line. "Why didn't you tell me you were with someone?"

I shrug, taking his anger as a compliment. I'd love to tell him the truth, but whatever this shit with the bouncer is about, there's no reason to bring a civilian into it. Especially a guy who showed me a good time.

The guy walks away, shaking his head.

"Upstairs," the bouncer barks. "This way." He leads me up the stairs and points to a closed door with a tinted glass window in it. There's no way I can see what's waiting for me inside.

Damn. I shouldn't have left the gun in my car. Oh well, I think, and open the door.

"Hello," Victor says when the bouncer opens the door for me. "We need to talk."

Of all the clubs owned by shady people, I clearly chose the worst one.

And then I realize there's someone else in the room.

A man I didn't expect to see, let alone this soon.

Shkillet, his face black and blue with the injuries I inflicted, gives me a look that says, "You're dead now, bitch."

CHAPTER FIVE

"You have questionable taste in comrades, Victor." I'm not going to let either of them think they've thrown me. Never let them see you sweat—it's a motto I live by.

Shkillet's face reddens, and he reaches for his boot, but stops. "She's trying to disrespect you," he whispers to Victor, loudly enough that I can hear.

"When I want your opinion, Shkillet, I will provide it." Victor rises from his chair as Shkillet's red face turns white. "As for you, my lovely friend—" Victor inclines his head toward me, "—there's a very good reason why he's here."

"And that would be what? You need your toilets licked clean?" I stare at Shkillet, not backing down from the threat I see in his eyes.

"You whore." Shkillet's fingers twitch, likely itching to get to that knife. I know; I've felt that same hatred myself. Thankfully, he elects to spit on the ground instead of trying to skewer me.

"Spit on my floor again, and you'll be licking it off, Shkillet, understand? Also don't speak again until I say you can." If looks actually could kill, Victor's would've already murdered Shkillet ten times over. "Do I make myself clear?"

Shkillet nods, and I can tell it's killing him to do so.

Victor glares at him. "Say it."

Shkillet exhales. "I'll wait for you to ask me to speak, Victor." It sounds as if the words are being pulled from him.

"Now." Victor tugs his sleeves down. "As I was saying, there is a reason he's here, and it's because an accusation has been made."

"An accusation?" I try not to sound challenging—a task I, admittedly, have trouble with on occasion.

"Our comrade here told me some disturbing things about you." Victor leans against a table, arms crossed. "He claims that you work with the cops as a snitch, or worse, that you're a cop yourself."

"What?" I didn't expect that, and I don't have any clever, or even dumb, comebacks for him. "What are you talking about?"

"He said you'd deny it." Victor picks up a shot glass that's been standing on his desk and downs the contents in one gulp. "But his story is rather persuasive, so I figured we should talk."

This is bad. If Victor really believes this, I'm as good as dead. He wouldn't threaten a cop and let her live. Then again, if he truly believed I was a cop, given what I know of Victor, I would already be dead. I debate Splitting and Reading him to figure out what's what, but decide against it. After yesterday, my Depth is fairly low, even if some was recovered in the twenty-four hours that have passed. Still, if I overuse it, I'll go Inert and be unable to Split for many days.

"I'm not a cop." I start to fold my arms in front of my chest, realize it's a defensive gesture, and run my hands through my hair instead. "That's a ridiculous notion that only that syphilitic excuse for a brain could've come up with—"

"Suka." The Russian insult comes out of Shkillet with a snarl.

"I thought I told you to shut it." Victor points one threatening finger at Shkillet. "It's not that ridiculous, my dear. He says cops—your colleagues—did that to his face."

"Cops didn't do it. I did."

"I wasn't done." Now I'm the recipient of Victor's threatening finger. "What he said is just a piece of the puzzle, you see. After that last game yesterday, I asked around."

"And?" I ask, not liking where this is going.

"And you do have a tendency to . . . How should I put this delicately? To ask some odd questions during pillow talk."

Shkillet sneers, and I try not to blush. It's true that I've slept with a few gangsters. No one too monstrous, mind you, but definitely bad boys. I didn't do it just to get information, though. I was attracted to them—though I'm not sure if that makes it better or worse. Yeah, I did end up asking about explosion experts when a good moment presented itself, and if it just happened to be post-coitus . . . Well, that's when most men seem to let their guard down.

"I'm just interested in certain things." I shrug. "Maybe I'm looking for someone to do a job for me. To settle a score. That doesn't make me a cop."

Victor stares at me. I meet his gaze. I'm determined not to show any weakness. And right now, my knees are feeling pretty weak. I don't know what Victor has up his proverbial sleeve, and I don't know where he's going with this. I do much better when I have all the information.

"There's also the matter of your name. You claim it's Ilona, but we both know that you also go by Mira and Yulia and a bunch of others."

Crap. Where did he get that from? I thought I'd covered my tracks well. Changing my name was actually for my brother's sake, the going theory being that whoever killed Dad, if controlled by a Pusher, would want Eugene dead as well. But I can't exactly tell Victor that.

"I win large sums of money." I think really hard and really quickly, something I've learned to be good at. "Not just from you, but other legal venues as well. You can check with your people in Vegas. Given that, I think it's only natural for me to want to retain some anonymity."

"I can see that. To a point." Victor takes a big bottle of vodka and refills his shot glass. "But you must see how, bundled together, this doesn't look good."

"No, I don't agree." I shift my weight from one foot to another. "I'd make the worst, most conspicuous undercover cop in the history of undercover work. I mean, I'm usually the only woman at those games. I stick out like a sore thumb."

"She has a point there." Victor waves his shot glass in Shkillet's direction. "Even if I'd use a prettier metaphor to describe her."

"Why are you even listening to her?" Shkillet says in frustration. "She'll say anything to get out of here with her head still attached."

"Because something more is going on here." Victor downs the shot he's been holding. "And I find this one rather interesting."

"Then let me make her talk." Shkillet takes his knife out, his hands practically shaking with eagerness. "Two minutes, and she'll admit that she's a cop, just like I say she is."

"We'll talk about you sneaking a weapon into this establishment in a moment." Victor gives him a furious look. "First, I want to point something out to you. *I* ask the questions. I don't need your help. I'm a good judge of people, and I know she's hiding something. But I also think you're not telling everything."

"Oh, he's hiding things from you," I say, deciding to escalate matters.

"Is that so?" Victor raises his eyebrows, as if I can't possibly know what I'm talking about. "What would he dare hide?"

"The fact that it was me who fucked up his face, as I was trying to explain earlier," I say. "And that's just for starters."

"That's a lie." Shkillet's knuckles whiten around the hilt of his knife. "It was the cops."

"Also, he's hiding the fact that he's disrespected you." I ignore Shkillet's denial. "He's said things behind your back."

"Before you go further, my dear *Ilona*—" Victor holds up his hand, "—you should know that I won't treat a baseless accusation like that lightly."

"Baseless accusation, like calling me a cop?" I narrow my eyes at Victor. "How's this? He said he fucked your mistress. Though I think he actually raped her, because what woman in her right—"

"What the fuck are you talking about?" Shkillet growls, but shuts up when he looks at Victor.

I see why. Victor's face darkens, and it's scary to see, especially since it's most likely me, not Shkillet that he's angry at.

Without a word, Victor reaches into his desk, pulls out a gun, and places it on the desk with a loud clink of metal on glass. "I think you didn't understand me when I said I wouldn't take to this sort of shit lightly."

I nod. "I understood. But did he?" I point to Shkillet.

"You're a cop," Shkillet shouts. "And I sure as hell didn't go near Victor's lady."

"Oh really?" I say. "Then how would I know her name is Vera, if not from you?"

"You're a cop." Shkillet moves the knife from one hand to another, nervously.

"And how about the fact that she has a tattoo on her back of the Madonna holding the baby Jesus? The tattoo with a face you wanted to come all over?" I say. "Do I know that also because I'm a cop? Because you told my 'colleagues' that when they beat you up? How about the claim you made that she has a muscular back with dimples and a mole on her right shoulder? You're trying to say that it was some other fucking rapist who told people that?"

Victor's face is the most frightening thing I've seen in a long time. Shkillet sees it, he sees Victor reach for the gun, and he completely flips out, lunging at me with the knife.

Now I Split—no point in having leftover Depth if I'm dead.

In the Mind Dimension, I walk over to Shkillet so I can Read him to verify his intent. As I suspected, he knows he's a dead man and wants to make sure he takes me down with him.

Fuck. I overdid it with him. I didn't think he'd go for the kamikaze thing. At least he made me look honest, which means Victor will probably not only kill him, but do it slowly. Still, if Shkillet kills me first, his destiny will be only a small consolation for me.

I look at Victor. He's still angry, but confused, too. He didn't expect Shkillet to do what he did either. Like me, he probably didn't think the man had the balls for it.

I look at the path of Shkillet's body and the knife. I try my best to project it another foot, to where my frozen self is. I now know what I have to do.

Somewhat encouraged, I get out of the Mind Dimension.

As soon as my consciousness is back in my body, I begin to twist myself just the right way and step aside, hoping I didn't miscalculate.

Shkillet's knife swooshes through the air an inch from my neck.

I didn't miscalculate, thank God.

Shkillet comes to a dead stop, his beady eyes wide with shock. He can't believe I escaped his attack.

I see a blur of movement so I Split again.

Shit. He recovered too quickly. He's frozen in the process of making a wide swing at me. Unless I do something, he's going to disembowel me with that knife.

I look at Victor. In the few moments that have passed, he's grabbed the gun from his desk. But even if it's my opponent rather than me that Victor intends to shoot, it'll take too long for him to complete that movement, let alone aim the gun and fire it at Shkillet.

Besides, if he did that, there's no telling whether he'd shoot the wrong person—namely, me—given how close I'm standing to Shkillet. I decide against Reading Victor to see who he's going to aim that gun at. I have no Depth to waste on questions where the answer won't help the situation at hand. Instead, I Split back.

Even before my mind is back in my body, I begin mentally playing out a maneuver that I can best describe as a hula-hoop move. I try to do it over and over, to make sure it's the first and only thing that my body does when it gets the mind back. My body moves in the desired motion, but not fast enough, and I feel a burning pain in my side.

A pain that makes me involuntarily Split again.

Please, God, don't let me see myself dying. I turn to look at my frozen body in the Mind Dimension.

I'm in luck. Even though the hula-hoop move wasn't entirely successful, it did get me far enough out of the knife's path. Shkillet only grazed my side. And now he's off-balance.

I Split and get back to real time with a whirling kick to Shkillet's balls, a move I've done many times since starting my investigation. Nothing stops a man as quickly as a hit in that vulnerable place, and no man has ever deserved it more than Shkillet.

As my foot connects, Shkillet squeals loudly and grabs his damaged family jewels. Remembering Victor's unfinished vodka bottle, I grab it, determined to bring it down on Shkillet's head. But before I can, a shot rings out.

My heart feels like it's going to jump out of my ribcage as the room goes silent.

I automatically Split again and look around. My real body doesn't look like it's been shot. There's some more blood flowing from where Shkillet's knife grazed me, but that's it. When I glance at Victor's gun, I can't tell where he's pointing it because the air around the barrel is filled with smoke.

When I turn toward Shkillet, however, I see that the right side of his skull is flying away, with bits of blood and brain matter frozen in the air. So that's where Victor was aiming. And what's more, there's another bullet frozen midway on its trajectory toward Shkillet's chest.

Exhaling in relief, I decide to spend a few more precious moments of my Depth to Read Victor's intentions. If he's planning to shoot me, I want to know about it, even if there's not much I can do to stop him. Then again, maybe I'll throw that vodka bottle at him—get one last shot in before I go.

Inside Victor's head, I experience rage mixed with awe mixed with confusion. It's impossible to tell what he'll do for sure, so I leave the Mind Dimension and get ready to face whatever is in store for me.

Victor looks at Shkillet's bleeding body, then looks at me, the gun pointing at me for a brief, heart-pounding moment, but then he slowly lowers the weapon.

A bouncer rushes into the room. "What the fuck, boss? Your glass door is not that soundproof. If I heard it outside, anyone on the dance floor could've, too."

"We'll need some private cleaning in here." Victor puts his gun down on the table. "And as for the noise, tell the DJ to make up an excuse about a problem with his equipment. Also tell him to announce a half hour of open bar, starting now."

"Got it." The bouncer exhales and rolls his shoulders as he heads out the door. "That'll work, especially the second part."

"I'm not sure what just happened," Victor says when the bouncer leaves. "What you said about Vera was accurate, and only someone who's seen her naked would know those things. But something doesn't ring true because I have a hard time believing he'd dare." Victor waves toward what's left of Shkillet, and shakes his head. "Still, I did underestimate the little creep tonight. I ought to put on his tombstone: 'Shkillet, the underestimated.'"

"I'd make that 'Shkillet, the underestimated rapist.'" I give the dead body a shove with my foot.

"I don't know about that part." Victor extends his hand for the bottle I'm still holding.

"Believe what you want." I hand him the bottle. "Ask around. He was a rapist."

"But did he do that to Vera?" Victor frowns, pouring himself another shot. "That's what I have trouble with. Wouldn't she have told me?"

"She was probably ashamed. It happens a lot with rape victims. All I can say is, if he didn't, he sure lied about it. Just like he lied about me being a cop."

"And you're not?" Victor gulps down the shot. "You moved like some Spetsnaz soldier when he attacked you. It was—"

"I have good reflexes." I have to get his mind off what he thinks he saw. "That's all. It doesn't make me a cop."

"But it does make you an accessory to this." He points to Shkillet. "But here's what bothers me. If he lied and didn't fuck her, how'd he know what she had on her back?"

"Well, we can't ask him now." I shrug. "Maybe he was a peeping tom? That's not strange for a rapist."

"Perhaps." He gives me a suspicious stare. "Or maybe you are. Did you see me fuck her yesterday? Did you watch us and use the info to make it look like he disrespected me?"

"You wish. That's one of *your* voyeuristic fantasies. Besides, wouldn't you close the door and have some bouncer guard it if you were fucking?"

Victor sighs and rakes his fingers through his hair. "Talking to you is as frustrating as talking to Nadia. You're too good of a liar—probably helps you during poker."

I shrug and pretend not to know he's talking about his daughter.

"So." Victor exhales. "The fact that he attacked you could mean you're right. Maybe he knew that if he didn't attack you, his death would've been . . . slow."

"You give him too much credit. He's not that smart—only crazy." I twirl my finger next to my temple in a gesture for insanity.

Victor chuckles, but then he stops abruptly and stares at me.

Feeling like I'm under a magnifying glass, I can't help but notice the throbbing in my wound. The adrenaline rush has worn off, and it hurts like a son of a bitch.

"You're bleeding." He frowns.

"It's nothing." I don't want to give him the satisfaction of admitting to weakness. "But thanks for your concern."

"Listen, whatever-your-name-is, I want to continue this conversation someday."

Great. Just what I don't need. I think it, but don't verbalize it.

"In the meantime," he continues, "I'll spread the word that you're under my protection so you won't need to worry about the likes of Shkillet in the future."

I'm at a loss for words. I didn't expect him to say that. That's the third time I'm surprised today. I really should Read people more if I don't want these surprises, but it's tricky because of my limited Depth.

"Here's my card." He hands it to me as if this is a normal business deal. "Call me if you need anything."

I take the card. Then he walks to the door and lets his bouncers in.

"Take her to the hospital," Victor tells the big guy who brought me here earlier. "Put the bill on my tab." He looks at me after the bouncer nods. "I'll be seeing you later, Ilona."

Numb with shock, I let myself be herded through the club. There's no sign of the guy I'd danced with. Oh well. It's not like that would've been anything more than a one-night stand. I'm nothing if not realistic. There's no room in my life for a relationship.

* * *

Patched up and tired as a dog, I take a cab from the hospital to my car.

As I watch the streets whiz by, I have a million thoughts running through my head. They fight with one another, but the one that keeps getting my attention is that I have to get away. Away from Brooklyn, away from gangsters, away from all this shit. I need to let things settle here.

It's a smart idea, but what can I do? Where should I go?

Ideas pop up, then fizzle out. Should I visit Vegas again? No, I'd need a new set of IDs for that, since they're onto me big-time in that town. Monte Carlo is still out of reach; my fake papers aren't good enough for Europe.

As I get home and sneak into my room again, I realize that there is another place I could go. It's closer, and there's less heat for me there, even if it's not that far distance-wise.

By the time I get into bed, I'm on board with my new plan. I'll get a couple of nights of good sleep, get my stitches taken out, patch things up with Eugene, and then grab a bus to Atlantic City.

Has anyone been this excited about a trip to New Jersey before? I don't know, and I don't care. My world becomes all about the softness of my pillow as I fall into a blissful and much-deserved sleep.

The Thought Pushers

Mind Dimensions: Book 2

DESCRIPTION

What am I?

Who killed my family?

Why?

I need to get some answers before the Russian mob succeeds in killing *me*.

That is, if my own friends don't kill me first.

CHAPTER ONE

My phone makes the most annoying noises. Why did I put it next to the bed again?

I grudgingly struggle to wake up. The bothersome noises continue, so I grab the phone.

"Hello?" My voice is gravel-textured in my own ears. How long have I been asleep?

"Darren, it's Caleb. I'm waiting downstairs. Come on out."

The adrenaline rush hits me, and I phase into the Quiet. I'm lying on the left side of the bed near my other, frozen self. There's a pitiful, ultra-concerned look on his face. *My* face.

I reach for my wristwatch on the nightstand. It's 6:13 a.m.

The events of the prior days flash through my mind with startling clarity. The trip to Atlantic City, when I met Mira for the first time. Having my hacker friend Bert look her up. Meeting her and her brother Eugene in their Brooklyn apartment and learning that I'm a Reader. Mira getting kidnapped by the Russian mob, and our going to the Reader community for help. Caleb and Julia helping us. It all comes back to me, followed by the worst part.

I *Pushed* someone.

It's an action that no Reader should be able to do. Something that only Pushers, the people Readers hate, can do.

I took away someone's free will.

And now Caleb is here, at the crack of dawn.

Shit. My heartbeat jumps. Did Mira already rat me out? Maybe to the entire Reader community? And if she did, what does that mean for me? What do Readers do with Pushers? I remember Mira threatening to kill every Pusher she met. What happens if *I'm* one of those Pushers? If the other Readers found out I Pushed that guy to throw himself between Mira and that bullet, what would they do? Nothing good, I'm sure of it. But why would she reveal what I did? The only reason she's alive is because I made that guy take a bullet for her, and she has to know that.

Or could Caleb be here for some other reason? I do owe him a trip into someone's head, as weird as that sounds. Could he be here to collect? That would be preferable to the alternative of him knowing that I'm a Pusher.

If I'm even a Pusher, that is. Yesterday, I seemed to have proven that I'm a Reader. Proven it twice, to two different people. They were quite convinced of my Readerness. Does that mean Readers have no real understanding of what Pushers can or can't do, or does it mean something else entirely . . . perhaps that I'm neither a Reader nor a Pusher? Is there a third possibility? For all I know, there are other groups out there we haven't even heard of.

Or perhaps I'm both. A hybrid. Is it possible that one of my parents was a Reader, and the other was a Pusher? If so, I would be a product of blood mixing—something that Eugene seemed to think was a huge taboo. And he and Mira are half-bloods, so he's probably more open-minded about this issue than pure Readers. Does this mean that my very existence is against some stupid rules? That could explain why my biological parents were convinced someone wanted them dead.

It could explain why they were murdered.

I could sit here in the Quiet thinking for hours, but all the thinking in the world won't make Caleb leave. I need to figure out what he's doing here.

I get out of bed and walk naked toward the door. In the Quiet, no one can see me, so I don't worry about it.

I go down to the first floor wearing only my slippers and exit through the front door. There are actually a surprising number of people—motorists, pedestrians, even street people—frozen in that moment in time. They must be insane to be awake so early.

It takes me only moments to locate Caleb's car. It's parked precisely where he dropped me off yesterday. He seems to be a creature of habit.

He's holding his phone. It's kind of funny knowing I'm on the other end of that call. I examine the inside of the car carefully, looking for any clues as to why he might be here. I find nothing except two coffees in the cup holders. Is one for me? How thoughtful. I do find a gun in the glove compartment, but it doesn't really worry me. Caleb's the kind of guy who probably has guns hidden all over the place, just in case.

I don't go anywhere near Caleb himself—a touch could pull him into my Mind Dimension, as he calls the Quiet, and he'd know I was snooping. Not to mention the wisecracks he'd make about my being naked.

Disappointed that I couldn't get any extra information, I head back to my apartment. I touch my frozen self on the hand that's clutching the phone, and phase out of the Quiet.

"What's this about, Caleb? I just woke up." My voice still sounds hoarse, so I cough a few times, covering the phone speaker with my left hand.

"Come out, and we'll talk," he replies.

I'm not in the mood for a long debate. Knowing Caleb's capabilities, if he was here to do me harm, I probably would've woken up with his gun in my mouth.

"I'll be down in twenty minutes," I tell him.

"Make it ten," he says and hangs up.

Some people have no manners.

I quickly get up, brush my teeth, and get dressed. Then I whip up a green smoothie—my answer to breakfast on the run. Three frozen bananas, a big handful of cashews, a cup of spinach, and a cup of kale go into the blender. A few noisy seconds later, I'm on my way out with a giant cup in my hand. I often do this smoothie thing to save time on those few occasions when I actually go to the office.

Speaking of work, doesn't Caleb understand that normal people have jobs they need to be at on a Wednesday morning? I don't, but that's beside the point. I'm even more annoyed now. Then again, it's early, and this thing could potentially be over before the workday begins.

"You better have an important reason to get me out of bed this early." I open the door to Caleb's car.

"Good morning to you too, Darren." Ignoring my scowl, he starts the car as soon as I get in and pulls out. "Look, kid, I didn't want to wake up so fucking early, either, but Jacob took the red-eye, and he demanded to see you before your workday, so you're not inconvenienced too much. So here I am."

Jacob, the leader of the Reader community, wants to see me? Shit. Maybe Mira did tell everybody about my Pushing, and it got all the way to the top. Then again, Caleb doesn't seem overly hostile, so maybe I'm wrong.

As Caleb navigates a handful of streets, my nervousness over the possible reasons for Jacob's request is quickly superseded by the fear induced by Caleb's driving. I didn't blame him for driving like a maniac when we had to save Mira, but there's no reason to do so now.

"I don't need to be back for work, so please don't kill us," I say. Caleb ignores that statement, so I ask, "What does Jacob want?"

"What he wants is between you and him." Caleb honks at a guy who stopped at a red light, like that's a mistake or something. "I'm trying to make up for the time you took getting ready. We have an extra errand before I take you to Jacob." The light changes, and we surge ahead.

"What extra errand?" As I sip my drink, I realize he didn't make fun of it. Most people at least ask about it. In my experience, in mainstream America, pea-green morning drinks are looked on with either suspicion or ridicule.

"We're going to have some fun," he says in an apparent attempt to cheer me up. "A guy in Brooklyn is our first target."

"Our target?" I'm confused. "What are you talking about?"

"Our deal," he says, scowling at me. I really wish he'd keep his eyes on the road. "I thought of someone."

Our deal. Crap. I'd hoped he'd forget I promised to help him Read deeper into some fighter's memories than he can do on his own—something other Readers refuse to do for him. I was hoping to learn more about *why* they refuse, even though it's too late—I already agreed to do it in exchange for him helping save Mira.

"What can you tell me about this thing we're about to do?" I ask. All of a sudden, his driving isn't my biggest concern.

"Truth be told, not that much," he says contemplatively, looking at the road ahead. "When I did it before, it was with someone who's only a little more powerful than myself. The woman I did it with could only spend a day in the Mind Dimension. The length of time people can collectively spend in the Mind Dimension determines how strongly the minds Join, I believe."

"You believe?" Great. Any confidence I had in Caleb's understanding of this thing goes up in smoke. I wonder if he knows any more than I do.

"It's hard to describe, Darren. All I can say is, let's just agree to stay out of each other's heads."

That's when it hits me: he'll have access to my head. He'll have access to my thoughts in a way I still don't quite understand. If it's anything like Reading, he could theoretically find out what happened yesterday. He could find out I Pushed someone, if he doesn't know already. I have a feeling I'd be in deep trouble if that happened. More than anything, I want to ask him how he feels about Pushers, but that could just get him thinking about it, which could increase the odds of him snooping in my mind.

"The more I hear, the more I don't really want to do this, Caleb."

"Yeah, I'm a little hesitant myself," he says, and I begin to have hope. Then my hope is dashed as he adds, "But it's not like I get a chance like this every day. Who knows if I'll ever get another one like it. As for you—a deal's a deal."

"What do you mean, you might never get another chance like this? I'll totally do it some other day; you just caught me off-guard. I wasn't expecting you today. I'm not ready, psychologically. I'd like to give it a little thought before I just dive in." It sounds reasonable to me, but Caleb isn't sold.

"Oh, I'm not worried about collecting the debt you owe me." I can't tell if he's joking or threatening. "The chance I'm talking about has more to do with our target."

"Oh, and who's that? And why is it such a rare treat?" Curiosity starts to win out over dread, by a very slim margin.

"His name is Haim. I only found out he was in town when I pinged my contacts about capable people I could actually learn something from. He could leave at any time, given the nature of his work. That's why I want to get to him now."

I absorb this information as we get off the highway in what I think is one of the Heights parts of Brooklyn, an area known for Manhattan skyline views and old brownstone buildings.

Coincidently, we double-park next to one such home, a three-story brick townhouse. It's quaint if you like older architecture, which I don't. I can just imagine how musty it is inside.

The street, though, looks much cleaner than Mira's part of town. It's almost Manhattan-like. I can see why some of my coworkers choose to live here.

"Take us in," Caleb requests without turning off the ignition.

I comply and phase into the Quiet. The jitters from the ride make it easy; fear always helps me with the process. Instantly, the sounds of the engine disappear, and I find myself in the back seat.

I bring Caleb into the Quiet with me, and we make our way to the house in silence.

When we reach the locked door, Caleb breaks it with a few powerful kicks. His legs must be incredibly strong. Then he walks in like he owns the place, and I follow.

Surprisingly, it's nice inside—really nice. There's something exotic about the décor that I can't quite place.

On the first floor, there's a kitchen where we find a man and a woman sitting at a table, eating breakfast. Both are olive-skinned and dark-haired. The guy is fairly well built—which is expected, since Caleb said he's supposed to be some kind of a fighter.

"Him," Caleb says, pointing at the guy.

"How is this supposed to work?" I ask.

"You go about it just like you're going to Read him. Then, once I'm confident you're inside his head, I'll try to Read him at the same time. That's the best way to explain it. You'll feel a strange sensation—your instinct will be to reject whatever is happening. You'll have to fight that impulse. Instead, you'll need to allow me to share your Reading. If you don't, both of us will just end up Reading him separately, like the other isn't there."

"And then? What will it be like if this works?"

"That part is hard to describe. It's easier to just try it. Psychedelic is the best way I can explain it." He smirks—not a pretty sight.

Psychedelic is good, I guess. Some people pay to have that kind of experience. I was never one of them, but still.

"Okay, got it. And we stay out of each other's individual memories," I say, trying to sound nonchalant.

"Yeah, as much as we can, but it's a crapshoot. You'll see what I mean in a second. Good luck."

"Wait, how far into his memories should I go?" I ask, trying to postpone the inevitable.

"Don't go too deep. Your time will be split at least three ways when we do this. I promised not to squeeze your Depth dry, and I want to keep my word. Just try to go for the first violent memory you can. That kind of thing shouldn't be hard to locate when it comes to Haim." This last bit seems to amuse Caleb.

"Okay, fine. Let's do it," I say, placing my hand on Haim's wrist. I start getting into the Coherence state—the prerequisite for Reading. It comes to me almost instantly, despite the extra stress.

And then I'm inside Haim's mind.

CHAPTER TWO

"Haim, it's been so good having you around," Orit says to us in English. We take a sip of the tea she's prepared for us, trying not to burn our tongue, and reflect on how hanging out with our sister has been a highlight of the year.

"Now it's your turn," we say. "You have to visit me and Grandma in Israel."

Orit hesitates before she nods. Despite her agreement, we know she's not likely to come. We're not actually that upset about it; we're usually in too much danger to have little Orit around. But then again, we think she really ought to visit Israel at some point. Maybe she could find a husband there. Or finally learn a few words in Hebrew.

I, Darren, disassociate from Haim's immediate memory. I'm amazed yet again at the lack of language barriers when it comes to Reading. Haim's native tongue appears to be Hebrew, yet I understand his thoughts, just like I did with the Russians the other day. It seems to prove that thought is language-independent, unless something else explains this phenomenon.

I also reflect on how someone else's feelings become my own during Reading—for example, the olive-skinned woman at this table seemed very plain to me a moment ago, but inside Haim's head, everything is different. Her dark eyes and hair are just like our mother's—and the similarity is further highlighted by her caring nature . . .

I'm distracted from my rumination when I feel something new.

This *something* is hard to explain. Have you ever had a head rush from getting up too quickly or drinking too much? Multiply that lightheadedness a thousandfold, and you might get a glimpse of what this feels like.

All my instincts tell me I need to clear my head of this feeling. To get stability. To ground myself, which means I need to do the opposite—at least if I follow Caleb's instructions.

So I try to remain loopy. It's difficult, but my reward, if you can call it that, is a strengthening of this weird feeling. It now feels less like lightheadedness and more like free falling from a plane—a feeling I got to know recently from Reading my friend Amy's skydiving experience.

And then something completely different begins.

A feeling of unimaginable intensity overcomes me, a combination of overwhelming awe and wonder. There's a strange bliss to it, followed by a feeling of becoming something more than my own self—becoming a new being. It's both frightening and beautiful.

The sensation comes in waves of moments when I feel deep understanding of everything in the world, even the universe—or maybe even the multiverse— as though, all of a sudden, my intelligence has multiplied. That brief sensation of omniscience dissipates the next moment, and what I feel can best be described as cherishing something sacred, like standing in reverence next to a monument for fallen soldiers.

In the midst of all this, the knowledge dawns on me: I'm not alone. I'm part of something more elemental than myself. And then, I understand.

I'm not simply Darren, not anymore. I'm Caleb. And I'm Darren. Both at once. But not in the way

Reading allowed me to be other people. This is a much deeper connection. During Reading, I merely see the world through someone else's eyes. This Joint Reading experience is much more than that. I see the world through Caleb's eyes, but he also sees the world though *my* eyes. It almost blows my mind when I realize I can even see through his eyes how the world looks through mine, when filtered by his perception and biases.

I can tell he's trying not to get deep into my mind, and I try to reciprocate by focusing on not getting into his. As this is happening, the positive feelings I was experiencing thus far begin to turn dark. I sense something frightening in Caleb's mind. And the whole universe seems to be shouting one idea in our joint mind: *"We are staying out of each other's heads. We are staying out of each other's heads . . ."*

But before either one of us can actually follow this reasonable mantra, a barrage of memories is triggered, all at once.

On some level, I'm not sure how, I know that Caleb is seeing my most embarrassing and vivid memories. I don't know why it's happening; it could be because they shine so brightly in my mind, or it could be because he's curious about some of this stuff. Whatever the answer, he's reliving the time my moms talked to me about masturbating. If it were possible to turn red right now, I'd look like a tomato at the thought of sharing that particular memory. He's also reliving other things, like the time I first phased into the Quiet after my bike accident. The first time I had sex. The day I saw Mira in the Quiet and realized I wasn't alone.

On some level, I'm reliving all these memories at the same time. All at once, as though in a dream.

And then I realize something else is happening. With dread, I see a mental tsunami coming at me.

It's Caleb's memories.

CHAPTER THREE

Caleb, the device was found.

We read the text and are overwhelmed with relief.

"We?" a sarcastic voice in my head says. "It's me, kid, Caleb. This is my memory."

"'We' is how I experience it, Caleb," I snap back, hoping he can hear me. "You think I want to be here?"

"So get the fuck out."

"I would if I could."

"Try," Caleb thinks at me, but it's too late. I'm immersed back in Caleb's memory, which continues to unfold like a Reading session.

The text doesn't change our mission, we realize.

We're approaching the car, trying to get as close to it as possible before Splitting. It's a fine balance, this business of attacking someone who can also enter the Mind Dimension. It's a difficult art that we're still developing.

Typically, it's hard to catch someone unawares if he or she can Split. From childhood, those of us with the ability to enter the Mind Dimension learn to immediately scan the environment around us when we Split. Or at least the paranoid among us do.

The solution is very bold; few would have the balls to try it. The answer is to attack someone inside the Mind Dimension itself.

I, Darren, disassociate for a moment and think at Caleb, "Why attack someone in the Quiet? Nothing you do there has any effect in the real world."

"What did I tell you about getting out of my head?" He sounds angry, if it's possible to sound angry while thinking. "At the very least, stop the fucking commentary. For your information, when one of us dies in the Mind Dimension, it has an effect—a lasting effect. Trust me."

"But still, why not do your attack in the real world?" I ask.

"Look, kid, I'm not here to teach you anything. We're here for me, remember? But if it shuts you up, let me explain. One benefit of attacking someone in the Mind Dimension is that there's no possibility the person will see me until I pull him or her in. It's the ultimate stealth, and the reason for the development of this technique. Another huge advantage is that, in the Mind Dimension, a Pusher can't use random bystanders to aid himself—something that fucker would definitely try. But before going in and attacking people in the Mind Dimension, keep in mind that this technique has drawbacks. In a regular fight, I can leverage the Mind Dimension. It's a huge edge. I can Split and see where my frozen opponent is about to strike me. If the opponent isn't a Reader or a Pusher, I can Read him too, which gives me valuable information about my opponent's actions in the immediate future. Unfortunately, in this case, the opponent is a Pusher. All I can rely on is fighting prowess. This suits me just fine, since I'm confident in my abilities in that department. Still, I always strategize based on the assumption that my opponent is as good as, or better than, me—as unlikely as that is in practice."

"Wow, dude, that's way more than I ever wanted to know about the subject—and extremely arrogant, to boot," I think at him.

"You asked, asshole."

With no more commentary coming from Caleb, I get sucked back into his memory.

A car alarm blares in the distance. We decide that the location we're in now should work for our purposes: far enough that the Pusher couldn't have seen us coming, but not so far away that we can't fight when the moment arrives.

We Split, and the car alarm, along with other ambient noise, disappears.

Now that we're in battle mode, our need to kill the man in the car—the Pusher—is overwhelming. It overtakes our whole being. We rarely get a chance like this. A righteous, completely justified kill. No way will we face an attack of conscience over this. No, there won't be any lost sleep, or even an ounce of remorse this time. If anyone ever deserved to die, it's our current target.

This Pusher has been trying to damage the Readers' gated community for weeks now. He's responsible for the bomb that our men are disarming at this very moment.

So many Readers could have died. On our watch. This possibility is so unthinkable, we still can't fully wrap our head around it. And it was all avoided by mere chance, by a lucky discovery. We saw the telltale signs inside the mind of that electrician. We don't dwell on what would've happened if this had gone undiscovered. The only consolation is that we would've died along with the victims, given where the explosion was set to take place. We wouldn't have had to live with the shame of being Head of Security and allowing such a thing to occur.

Of course, the chicken-shit Pusher did none of the work himself. No. He mentally compelled the staff at the community instead.

Rage wells within us again when we focus on how these nice, regular people got their minds fucked with, simply because they happened to be contractors, plumbers, and gardeners working at the Reader community. We seethe at the injustice of it, at how they would've been blown up along with the Readers, collateral damage in the Pusher's eyes. We would never resort to such a maneuver. The idea of collateral damage is among the things that made us eventually leave Special Ops.

Our rage grows exponentially as we remember what Julia told us she gleaned while Reading Stacy, the bartender—what this slime did to her. The metaphorical rape of Stacy's mind, making her try to hurt the people she worked for, wasn't enough for him. The fucker took it a sick step further and made it literal. He decided to mix his unholy business with the abominable perversion of pleasure, making her do such twisted things . . .

We take a deep breath, trying to suppress our rage, which is beginning to overflow. Rage is not helpful in combat. At least not in the style of fighting we have cultivated. We need to be assessing, analyzing, and then acting. We know that historically, berserkers always died, albeit gloriously, on the battlefield. That's not our way. In fact, we practice something that can be said to be the opposite of blind fury. We call our style *Mindful Combat*. It requires a degree of tranquility. We take some more deep breaths. We mean for one person to die today, and he is in that car. We need to live on so we can hunt down and kill anyone else who's part of this crime, this conspiracy.

We're watching the man in the front window of his car. We're wary. We recognize people like ourselves, former military, and this guy's body language screams Special Ops. The way he parked away from any good sniping spot, the alert way he's sitting. All these clues point to elite training. But this guy is not from the Special Activities Division, our own background. We're pretty sure of that. He might've trained with the Recapture Tactics Team— though this asshole probably Pushed to get his way in, at least at the psych-profiling stage.

Taking a final deep breath, we shoot out the passenger window and punch the frozen Pusher in the face, knowing that the physical contact will bring him into our Mind Dimension. Killing him here is the goal. Doing it slowly, if possible, would be a bonus.

We prepare to shoot as soon as he materializes—but he doesn't. We're taken aback for a second. He should've materialized in the backseat, we think momentarily before a sharp pain in our right shoulder grabs our full attention.

Strangely, the Pusher seems to have materialized outside the car. We don't recall anyone ever becoming corporeal in the Mind Dimension this way. There's no time to wonder how it happened, or where he got the knife that's now lodged in our shoulder. With this injury, our whole world becomes focused on one thing only: survival.

The burn in our shoulder is excruciating, and just holding the gun in our right hand feels like torture. Doing our best to ignore the pain, we turn around and try to fire at the attacker. He anticipates the move, and with a twist, manages to get free. If not for our injury, there would be no way he'd get away with this, but as it is, a moment later our weapon clinks as it falls to the ground. His other hand reaches into his coat pocket.

It's time for a desperate maneuver.

We head-butt him—a move so dangerous that we normally discourage our people from using it.

The blow brings stars to our eyes, and a sense of disorientation, but it seems that the risk was worth it. The Pusher clutches his now-hopefully-broken nose. This is our moment.

Using our good left hand, we punch him in the nose—which he's clutching with his hands—and with the injured arm, we reach into his coat pocket.

We grab his gun, lift our right hand, and let it come down. Using the injured hand this way, with the gun as a makeshift club, hurts us less than a punch would have. The heavy gun handle lands on the same weak spot on the Pusher's nose.

He doesn't pull his hands away. The damage to his nose must be severe.

He tries to go for a low kick, hoping to hit our legs. We move out of the way of the attack, take the gun into our left hand, and take it off safety.

We shoot his left upper arm first. He makes a strange gargling sound.

We shoot his upper right arm next. This time, he screams.

We savor the fact that his pain must be excruciating.

A shot to each leg follows, and he falls to the ground, trying to get into some semblance of a defensive position.

Now the Mindful Combat part is over, and we can let the rage back in.

Still, we don't let the rage make us go too quickly. We kick and take a breath. Then kick again and again.

We're moving in a fog. Time seems to slow.

When our legs ache and we're satisfied with the amount of bone-crunching noises, we finally get tired of this game. After all, unless the Pusher dies of these injuries, he'll be good as new when he gets out. But that's not going to happen. We aim the gun at our opponent's head.

It's time to get to the point. It's time to begin killing this Pusher . . .

* * *

I, Darren, have to remind myself that this whole experience was just Caleb's horrific memory. I feel sick. But at the same time, I also feel surprisingly at ease with the memory. It's a very strange, contradictory combo.

"No shit," Caleb's voice intrudes. "We're part of the same mind for now, and my half of it is fine with it. How your half, the weak half feels, is irrelevant. You don't like it? Then get the fuck out."

I try, but I can't control it. Unbidden, another memory of Caleb's overtakes me.

* * *

We hear a loud noise and wake up. The alarm clock next to our bed is showing three a.m., meaning it's only been an hour since we went to bed. That's a single hour of sleep after hundreds of miles of running in the span of four days.

We're being dragged somewhere. The weariness dulls the panic a bit, but we know something bad is coming. And that's when the first punch lands. Then the second. Someone pushes us, and we slip on someone's blood and fall to the ground. After all that, they decide to beat the shit out of us?

We try to ignore the pain, making a valiant effort not to Split into the Mind Dimension. Such a reprieve would be cheating, and we want to feel like we earned our place here.

"Don't you want to quit?" a voice keeps saying, and we hear someone agree. That person's beating stops, but of course, he's out of the program. To us, there is no such option. We would give anything to stay in—lose anything, endure anything. We never quit. Ever.

Instead, we slowly begin to get up. A kick lands to our kidney, another to the small of our back, but rather than keeping us down, they have the reverse effect: they spur us into action. It feels like the world is pushing us down. We fight for every inch, every microsecond of progress we make, and we find ourselves standing on two feet once again.

The blows raining down on us from all around stop abruptly.

A large man steps forward.

"This one isn't just surviving—the bastard wants to fight. Look at his posture," he says, surprise mixed with approval in his voice.

We don't have the strength to answer. Instead, we strike at him with our right arm, instantly blocking his countermove.

The man's eyebrows go up. He didn't expect this much resistance.

Once in fight mode, muscle memory takes over, and we start the deadly dance of our personal fighting style. Even through our exhaustion, we feel a twinge of pride as a low snap kick penetrates the man's defenses. His right knee buckles at the impact; he falters, if only for an instant.

We become a flurry of fists, head, knees, and elbows.

The guy is already bleeding when someone yells, "Stop!"

We don't. More people enter the fight. The style we've developed can usually deal with multiple opponents, but not people of this caliber, and not when nearly dead from exhaustion. We contemplate the idea of Splitting to cope, but decide against it.

Fatalistically, we block the deadly barrage of their attacks, but eventually an opponent lands a perfectly executed round kick to the left side of our head, and the world goes dark.

* * *

I, Darren, get my bearings back.

"What the fuck was that?" I try to scream. Of course, I don't have a body, so the scream just goes into the ether that is our joint mind.

"Just some training," Caleb's thought comes to me in response. "You seriously need to focus. You're on the right track, seeking out the violence, but you're still in the wrong person's head: mine. Get back to Haim. Remember what we came here to do."

I try to remember. It feels like years ago when we came to Brooklyn Heights to Read this Israeli guy. And as I recall this, I realize that I'm still there with

Haim and Caleb, still conversing with Haim's/Caleb's/my sister Orit. The shock of becoming a double—no, triple—mind is still with me, but at least I can think on my own again.

"Hurry," Caleb hastens me. "We're about to fall into each other's memories again."

I don't want *that*, so I make a herculean effort to properly get back into Haim's head. I try the trick of feeling light. I picture myself as vapor in a fog, as weightless as a dandelion floret floating in a light morning breeze, and it seems to work.

As I get that now-familiar feeling of going deep into someone's mind, I try to zero in on and recall just a fraction of what I saw in Caleb's mind.

It seems to do the trick . . .

CHAPTER FOUR

The attacker in front of us leaves his midsection exposed for a moment; it's the last thing he'll do in this fight, we think as we unleash the burst.

"You did it, kid," Caleb's thought intrudes. "Finally, we're both in Haim's head."

"I got as much. You don't exactly think in Hebrew, do you?"

"Right. Now shut the fuck up and let me see this."

The 'burst' is what we mentally call this quick succession of punches to our opponent's solar plexus. We walk into our opponent as we strike, making the force of our punches that much more potent. We count twenty hits before he tries to block and stage a simultaneous counterattack.

Fleetingly impressed with his economy of movement, we grab his arm and use his own momentum to throw him off balance. He hits the ground, hard. Before he tries to pull us down with him, we kick his jaw—and feel the crunch of bone as the outer edge of our bare foot connects with his mandible. He stops moving.

He'll probably be fine. A couple of rib fractures and a broken jaw are a small price to pay for the opportunity to fight against us. Anyone who tried this outside our training module wouldn't learn a thing. They would die instead.

The training module is our response to the immense pressure from our friends at the Shayetet to teach our unique fighting style to their people. They know we've left Krav Maga, the martial art style of Israel, far behind. What we've developed transcends Krav Maga, transcends every fighting style we've ever encountered.

Fighting in these modules is a compromise. No death strikes, no aggressive groin assaults; no one dies in the training module. Such a compromise defeats much of the original intent, of course. This style was designed with a single purpose in mind: killing your opponent. Now much of our energy is wasted trying not to use the style as it was designed. Not killing our opponent feels unnatural, counter to everything we've spent our life working toward. A hollow imitation of what we envisioned. Much to our dismay, no one else seems to care about these nuances. They clamor for a school where civilians will learn this for their own amusement, refusing to understand that it's impossible to tame this training. This is not a sport for civilians; this is life or death. Anything less dishonors the work we have done, the lives taken in the evolution of our unique fighting style.

"Ha-mitnadev haba," we say in Hebrew, which, I, Darren, understand to mean 'next volunteer.'

We recognize the man who comes in: Moni Levine. He's a renowned Krav Maga teacher. They probably want him to learn from us in the hope that he can teach it afterwards. We hope that it works out somehow. We would welcome any opportunity to be left out of this futile teaching business.

I, Darren, disassociate as I have done during other Readings. This time is different, of course, since I still feel Caleb here. I feel his excitement. He clearly appreciates Haim's fighting style more than I do.

"*Don't distract*," Caleb's thought comes, and I let Haim's memory absorb me again.

"Azor, esh li maspik," Moni says after five minutes of brutal attacks. Not surprisingly, that means 'stop, I have had enough.'

We graciously tell him he did well and that he's welcome to return.

The next opponent enters. Then another. It must be ten or more in a row. None of them are a challenge. This is another part of the training that we hate. We fight almost robotically, letting our thoughts drift to the upcoming quick trip to the United States. We're concerned that this training module will make us develop deadly habits, like thinking idle thoughts during a fight . . .

I, Darren, disconnect again, only to have Caleb mentally convince me to find another recent memory of the same kind. So I do. It's nearly identical to the previous fight, but Caleb wants to experience it. And then another. And another.

We do this over and over, reliving at least a week—if not two or three—of non-stop fighting. It all starts to blur.

"I can't take this anymore," I think at Caleb eventually. The fatigue that I feel is not physical, but mental. Somehow that makes it more potent, inescapable. The human psyche isn't equipped to do what we're doing right now. I feel like I haven't slept in years, haven't rested in millennia. I'm forgetting

the time when I wasn't Haim. I can't recall a moment when I was *not* doing this accursed fighting.

"Fine," I get a response back. I feel a sudden, enormous sense of loss. It's as though the whole universe imploded.

After a few confusing moments, I understand. Caleb got out. I'm here by myself—no longer part of the joint-mind being.

Not willing to spend a millisecond longer than I have to in Haim's head, I instantly get out as well.

* * *

I'm back in Haim and Orit's kitchen in the Quiet. I look in shock at Haim, who's still frozen—with that wax-statue smile directed at his also-frozen sister. He doesn't look nearly as dangerous as I now know he is. In that, he's unlike Caleb, who always looks kind of dangerous with his badass manner and that gleam in his eye. And now that I've gotten a glimpse inside Caleb's fucked-up mind, I know that he's even more dangerous than he looks.

I try not to think too deeply about what I just experienced. It's too late, though; the violent images run through my mind, and I'm overwhelmed. It's not Haim's memories of the never-ending fight that do this to me. It's Caleb's. Those things he did to the Pusher are disturbingly fresh, replaying in my head over and over. I sit down at the breakfast table, in the empty chair next to Haim's sister, and try to take a few calming breaths. If I wasn't in the Quiet now, I think I would be sick.

"Are you okay, kid?" Caleb asks quietly.

"No," I answer honestly. "I'm far from okay."

"For what it's worth, I am never doing *that* again," he says, to my huge relief. "Your mind is too twisted."

"What? *Mine* is too twisted?" I say in outrage, weariness momentarily forgotten. The gall of this guy. I'm not the one who tortures and murders people. I'm not the one who took some kind of weird masochistic pleasure in brutal training. I didn't ask someone to Read a killer, so I could become an even better killer myself.

"You're one odd puppy." He smirks. "But it's not just that. I really hated that feeling in the beginning, when our minds Joined."

"I thought you'd done this before."

He looks serious for a change. "This was different from the other time I did this. Too strange. Way too deep. We didn't experience each other's memories to the same degree when I did it before. This time, it felt almost . . ." He looks away, like he's embarrassed to say the words out loud. "I don't know, like a religious experience. Sorry, kid. The whole thing was just way too deep for me."

Hmm, religious. That's an interesting way to look at it. I wouldn't have called it that, but now that he mentions it, I can see how the word makes sense. Not that I've ever experienced any kind of deep religious experiences myself, growing up under the care of two secular moms. I'd use the words *transcendental* or *trippy* to describe what happened.

"I'm in complete agreement," I say. "I never want to do it again, either." *Especially with a mind as screwed up as yours,* I think, but don't say it.

"And we won't speak of what we saw in there. That's just between us." He looks at me intently.

"Of course. That's understood," I say, a little too eagerly perhaps. I don't know the full catalogue of the things he saw from my past, but I have no doubt he got more than his share of embarrassing tidbits. Thankfully, he seems to have missed the memory I most wanted to hide—what happened yesterday. Otherwise, I might be suffering a fate similar to the Pusher in his memory. The thought fills me with dread.

"You must be capable of even more Mind Dimension Depth than I suspected," Caleb observes. "That Depth determines how far the minds intertwine during this experience. That must be why it was so intense."

I digest this information. If what he says is true, then this experience will be more potent with almost anyone else—Caleb's Depth is allegedly pretty shallow. I'll have to be careful if I ever try it again. Not that I'm planning on it.

"Are you okay to walk back?" he says, interrupting my thoughts.

"Yeah, I guess. I certainly don't see the point of sitting here," I say. "Did you at least learn Haim's fighting style? I'd hate to think we went through all that for nothing."

"Oh, in that sense, this was a huge success. It exceeded all my expectations. He's truly brilliant. Someday, I'm going to visit him in the real world, somehow get him to fight me, like he did with the people in his memory. That's only after I come up with some counters to his best moves, of course," Caleb says, chuckling.

"How does that work?" I wonder out loud. "Learning from Reading? Did I learn anything?"

"It'll help *me* more than you. A practical knowledge base plays an important role. In my case, I'm familiar with Krav Maga, Aikido, Keysi, kickboxing, and many other styles that were clearly influences on Haim's style. Thanks to that earlier knowledge, I'll be able to appropriate a lot of what we both experienced on a direct, conscious level. But for you, I have no clue. You should've learned something, but I don't know how much. And whether you can use whatever stuck in your mind in practice is a big gamble."

And before he even finishes speaking, he's standing next to me, aiming a punch at my face.

What I do next amazes me when I think of it later. I jump out of the chair and throw it at Caleb. Then, without conscious thought, my elbow stops his right hand mid-punch. My elbow hurts like hell, but the alternative would've been my face. What's even more amazing is that my left hand tries to hit him in mid-chest. I remember doing this as Haim. It's Haim's signature move, I think—this punch in the solar plexus.

Caleb takes the hit in the chest, seemingly only raising an eyebrow in response. This should've hurt, I think fleetingly. But then again, some people's abdominal musculature can reduce the impact of that hit. That little tidbit of knowledge comes to me from nowhere. I can't dwell on it too much because he throws a punch, which I manage to block, and then I see another flash of movement. Before I understand what's happening, a horrific pain explodes in my groin.

The world becomes pain. I can't breathe.

I fall to the floor, clutching my balls.

"Sorry about that," Caleb says. "You reacted so well, I thought I'd push you a little. I didn't think you'd manage to not block such an obvious, slow kick. A move that's a cornerstone of Haim's style. You had to have done it yourself, at least a thousand times back in his head."

He's smirking as he says that—the bastard.

If I had a gun in my hand, I would shoot him in his smug face. The pain is unlike any I've ever experienced. The kick might've been 'slow,' but it doesn't matter—it's such a sensitive area. I try to regain control of my breathing. "You. Literally. Busted. My. Balls," I manage to say with difficulty.

"You'll be as good as new when we get back to our bodies," he says, sounding utterly unapologetic.

"Fuck you." Even to my own ears, I sound like the sore loser in a schoolyard brawl.

"Here, lean on me as we walk out," he says, offering me his hand. I make him wait a couple of minutes, standing there in a strange hand-extended pose. When the pain subsides a little, I take the proffered hand.

Barely able to walk, I make my way out of Haim's sister's house. As soon as I'm standing next to my frozen self, I grab my elbow to phase out.

CHAPTER FIVE

The world comes back to life, the pain instantly gone. The sudden lack of agony feels like pleasure for a moment. It overtakes me as we start our mad drive deeper into Brooklyn.

Immersed in that bizarre lack-of-agony bliss, I'm thankful yet again for this particular property of phasing out: the fact that leaving the Quiet undoes any physical damage you receive while inside. However, I now know there's something irreparable that *can* happen to you in the Quiet.

Dying.

While I'm not yet sure how it works, I know Caleb was trying to kill that Pusher in the Quiet. His thoughts were clear on the matter—the Pusher was going to be erased from existence. Caleb had one-hundred-percent conviction of that.

I guess on some level I knew that death in the Quiet was a possibility, which is why I never tried to off myself there. A little cutting, sure, but I always avoided anything potentially fatal. I always had a feeling, an intuition, that if I died in the Quiet, it might spill over into reality.

"Am I getting the silent treatment the rest of the way?" Caleb says, pulling me from my morbid contemplation.

I realize that we've been driving in silence for a while. Caleb probably assumes I'm pissed about that below-the-belt hit of his. And I am, but it's a tiny part of my concerns at the moment.

"I'm just thinking about what happened. Why we saw the specific memories we did," I say, only half-lying.

"Someone told me once that you tend to find the memory your conscious—or sometimes subconscious—mind is dwelling on," he explains. He shrugs, like he's not sure whether that makes sense or not. "Seemed like a good enough explanation to me."

It makes sense. Caleb asked me to seek out violent fighting memories, and I saw his training. I had been wondering what Readers do to Pushers, and I got *that* memory. Now I just need to make sure my Pusher connection stays hidden. Caleb clearly didn't access that memory of mine, and I want to keep it that way. I'm more certain than ever that I don't want Readers to know anything about my secret.

"So that's why I saw all that violence in your head," I say. It's a calculated statement. I'm trying to cover up, since I just realized I could've given myself away by accessing that Pusher-related memory of his. If I can convince him that a Pusher being in the memory was just a coincidence and that violence was the real reason that moment in time popped up, he hopefully will never draw any other conclusion.

Caleb sighs at my statement. "That's not the only reason. When you get into my head, violence is what you'll find, no matter what your other interests are. There's not much else in there. You won't find two loving mommies, or puppies and rainbows."

Though he's trying to be sarcastic, I can't help but feel a twinge of pity. He sounds almost wistful. Is this cold-blooded killer wishing he had happier memories?

"Darren," he says as I ponder this. His tone is different now, harder to pin down. I'm not sure I like it. "There's something else we need to talk about."

My stomach twists. Does he know about my Pushing abilities after all?

"If Jacob asks you about Julia—which I don't think he will—say you don't know anything," he says, and I expel a relieved breath. I now understand the tone. It's worry, which sounds unnatural for Caleb. That's two unexpected emotions in a row. Did our being in each other's heads do something to him?

"Sure," I say, trying to sound like it's no big deal. "No problem. But why?"

"Since she's recovering, I don't see any need to worry her parents. Plus, she wouldn't want her father to know she helped Mira and got shot," he says curtly.

I get it now. It's not just Julia who doesn't want that. Caleb allowed his boss's daughter to get shot. I get the sense his ass is grass if Jacob finds out the truth.

"Your secret's safe with me," I say, possibly overacting a bit.

He doesn't respond, and silence falls again as we continue riding.

As we leave all the other cars behind in the mad rush to the Reader community, I think some more about what just happened. In theory, I should have some seriously impressive fighting skills for the first time in my life. And I don't mean simply being able to kick ass in a bar brawl either—what Haim did went way beyond kicking some dumb jock's butt. It's an exciting thought. If, by some misfortune, I get into a fight, I'll be able to hold my own. In theory, at least.

Recognizing the view outside, I realize we're passing by the canal—that small body of water on what Eugene called Sheepshead. We're on Emmons Avenue, the street where those mobsters were shooting at Eugene and me just yesterday. We're almost at the community, and I wonder again what Jacob wants.

When we leave the car in the parking lot, we're met by a dude I recall seeing the other day. The one who doesn't seem to like Eugene. Caleb's rude twin—and being ruder than Caleb is a challenge. I really dislike the look he gives me—kind of like a wolf eyeing a stray lamb.

"Sam, take Darren to meet Jacob and bring him back here when they're done," Caleb says.

Sam turns toward the lavish building without a word, walking briskly toward it. I follow him. The silence hangs over us the whole way.

Who knew Caleb would turn out to be the friendly one?

* * *

"Sam, you may go now," Jacob says dismissively after Sam leads me into the man's posh office.

"Darren, it's nice to meet you face to face," Jacob says as soon as Sam is gone. He shakes my hand firmly, giving me a reassuring smile.

"Nice to meet you too, Jacob." I try to return his friendliness and hope he doesn't notice how nervous I am.

He looks different in this face-to-face encounter than on Skype the other day. I guess Eugene brought out the worst in him. Today Jacob seems like a nice guy.

"I wanted to properly introduce myself." He sits down, gesturing for me to take the chair across from his desk. "We don't get new Readers every day."

"I see. There seemed to be an element of urgency for this specific visit." I try not to sound hostile as I take my seat. I also wonder if I should phase into the Quiet and take a look around the office. Given that he's aware of the Quiet, would Jacob leave anything informative lying around? Not likely, I determine, and decide against it.

"No true urgency, I assure you. More like satisfaction of my curiosity, and a proper response to a truly rare case. Your situation is very special. You said you didn't know you were a Reader until yesterday."

"I said it because it's true," I respond, a little too defensively. Modifying my tone, I continue, "I was adopted, you see."

"You have to forgive me if I sounded incredulous—I certainly didn't mean to imply deceit on your part. It's just such an unusual occurrence. Particularly the fact that you discovered on your own that you can Split. Did I get that part right?"

"Yes. It first happened to me as a child," I say. I tell him about the bike accident, about thinking I was about to die and the whole world freezing around me.

He asks more about my childhood, and I tell him a few stories. It's the friendliest interrogation technique I've ever encountered. The guy seems genuinely curious about me. And I have a weakness. Like most people, I like talking about myself. As I realize this, I proceed more carefully. I don't want to blurt out anything that can reveal my Pusher experience.

"The main thing I wanted to talk to you about today is discretion," Jacob says after I accept his offer of coffee, and he personally makes me a cup.

"Discretion?" I say, blowing on my coffee.

"We Readers have kept our existence a secret from other people since antiquity," he says, his voice becoming preachy and monotone. I get the feeling he's given this spiel many times before. "We have always firmly believed that if the public found out, they would do something terrible to us."

I recall both Mira and Eugene alluding to the Reader community having a non-disclosure stance when it comes to Reader powers. Remembering how Jacob reacted to Eugene on Skype, I decide not to go with 'I've heard this from Eugene before.' Instead, I say, "That's pretty dark."

"Yes," Jacob agrees. "But we can Read people's minds, as you now know, and that ability enables us to accurately assess human nature. Trust me when I say they would not take to us kindly at all. I wish it weren't so, but it's the truth."

"So what do you think would happen if our existence became common knowledge?" I ask, putting my suddenly chilled hands around the warm cup.

"We could become secret slaves to some government agency—and that would be the best case scenario." His jaw tightens. "The more likely possibility would be complete genocide."

Genocide? Wow, he doesn't pull his punches. "Does the prospect have to be so bleak?" I inquire, forcing myself to sip my coffee. I can't resist my tendency to play the devil's advocate. I haven't given this topic much thought after my friends mentioned it, but what Jacob says actually sounds plausible—which is why some pain-in-the-ass part of me questions it. My habit of questioning virtually everything drove my moms and my uncle nuts when I was growing up. "What about progress?" I say. "Surely in modern times, people wouldn't do something like that. It's not like we're that much different from anyone else."

"We're a different species." His tone sharpens.

"Well, strictly speaking, we're not." Even though I risk further eroding the positive tenor of our discussion, I can't help myself. "The ones you call half-bloods are proof of that."

And just like that, the conversation takes a bad turn. Jacob's face goes red. "You're not here to split hairs about semantics." He slaps his palm on the desk. "That so-called progress will just make our annihilation faster than we ever thought possible."

I stare at him, shocked into silence by his outburst. "I didn't mean to upset you," I say in a soothing tone after a moment.

He takes a deep breath and lets it out in an audible sigh. "I'm sorry. This is a sensitive issue for me."

"I understand," I say cautiously. I wonder if he's so touchy because Eugene, a half-blood, used to date his daughter. "You have to realize that I have a deep affinity for normal people—" I use my fingers to make air quotes around the word *normal*, "—since until recently, I assumed I was one. I didn't know Readers existed."

"Right, and that is probably a good reason for you to trust me. My people have had centuries to develop the best strategy for dealing with our situation—and it is *not* to let anyone know of our existence. That's why I thought it important to talk to you. You are new to this, and being young, you're by nature more idealistic, more naïve, than others. As a child, you didn't get the usual Reader upbringing. You didn't learn the horror stories of our turbulent past. Trust me, the danger to our people is real."

I realize now that I might've devil's-advocated my way into trouble. What if he thinks I can't keep their secret and decides to silence me for the good of the species?

"You make a good case, Jacob," I say solemnly. I pretend to think about it for a few seconds, hoping I'm not going overboard. "Upon reflection, I think you might be right about all this."

Pacified, he smiles. "Mostly everyone comes to that conclusion."

"I should tell you, though," I say carefully, "as a child, I might've inadvertently broken the rules that I intend to follow from now on. I tried telling people about being able to go into what you call the Mind Dimension. I don't think my attempts did Readers any harm, though. Everyone just thought I was nuts." I figure he can find this out anyway if he wants to—my moms' and my shrink's heads would be open books to any Reader—and by volunteering this information, I might be able to forestall any potential snooping. Not to mention, demonstrate my rule-abiding intentions.

As I'd hoped, Jacob shrugs, not looking overly concerned. "What's done is done. Like you said, it was dismissed; that's what matters most. It's not a crime when you don't know the rules. What's important is that you're discreet from now on. If you can mitigate some of your earlier slips, all the better. What's truly forbidden are demonstrations of Reader abilities with the intent to reveal our nature."

"Oh, I've never done that," I say. "If we're talking about Reading, I just didn't have a chance to show off that particular skill. Of course, I've abused going into the Quiet before. In either case, though, I never told—and wouldn't dream of telling—people about how any of this works, so I definitely have no plans to 'reveal our nature.'"

I do wonder if Readers approve of using powers the way I've been using them, for my personal financial gain. I'm not going to ask Jacob about it, though. If he said 'stop doing that,' I'd be out of a job. If it's forbidden, I'll stop when he explicitly asks me to. Better to ask forgiveness than permission, right?

"Good. That's what I thought," Jacob says, smiling again. "You seem like an intelligent young man."

"Thank you, Jacob. You don't need to worry. I work in a field in which confidentiality is important. Besides, I'm a very private person. And don't worry about the people I mentioned earlier, either—the ones who didn't believe me. I'll muddy the waters for them like you asked if it seems needed, but I highly doubt it will even be necessary," I say, meaning nearly every word.

"That's wonderful. Thank you for understanding."

A weight is lifted off my shoulders. I got worried for a second that my moms might be in trouble. Truth be told, they didn't for a moment believe my stories. If mitigation *is* needed, the place to start would be with my therapist. I've told her quite openly about the Quiet. Not that she believed me any more than my moms did. She thinks it's just a delusion. Still, I should probably show her that I doubt that delusion, now that, ironically, I know it's real.

This thought actually answers a question I've been pondering for a while—whether I should keep my standing appointment with my shrink tomorrow. Lately, I've been paying for my hour so I don't lose my weekly spot, but not actually going to therapy. But today, I've been feeling the urge to actually go. I can now conveniently tell myself that all I want from my shrink is to lie to her about no longer having visions of the world being stopped.

Yep, just going to go 'to mitigate,' and not to talk about anything that's bothering me—like the disturbing things I saw in Caleb's mind, for example. Or my guilt about Pushing that guy to kill himself. Or that I'm more adopted than I realized. Or even that I've met a girl—something my shrink has been nagging me about for ages, almost like a third mom. All that babbling about my feelings would imply that I'm sensitive or something—which I'm definitely not. Nope, this visit will be about this discretion business. But, because I'm there anyway, I might as well talk about some of these other issues with my shrink—the ones that aren't prohibited by the Reader code, at least. After all, that's what I pay her for.

"Now that we have the discretion issue squared away, there is another minor thing I wanted to ask you," Jacob says, distracting me from my musings about the upcoming therapy. "Does the name *Mark Robinson* mean anything to you?"

"No," I say, confused. "Should it?"

"No. Never mind. It doesn't matter." He gets up. "Sam will take you back now. I'm happy we're on the same page when it comes to keeping the Readers' existence secret."

He shakes my hand and walks me to Sam, who's waiting behind the door. Sam leads me back to Caleb, as silently as before.

CHAPTER SIX

"Where to?" Caleb asks me when we turn onto Emmons Avenue again.

"Can you please take me to Mira and Eugene's apartment?" I give him the address from my phone.

As we fly through the streets, something suddenly hits me. I *do* know the name Mark. That was the name of my biological father. Could that be the Mark Jacob meant?

If so, could Jacob have known my father?

When Jacob first saw me on Skype, he said I looked familiar. Did he say that because he saw my resemblance to this Mark person? Or is Mark

Robinson someone else entirely? After all, Mark is a pretty common name.

I realize I need to ask my moms about my biological father's last name.

"Here we are," Caleb says. He brakes suddenly, just about throwing me through the windshield. We're near the park across the street from Mira's building. "Do you want me to wait for you?"

"No, thanks. I'll just rent a car after this. But there is something I want to ask you," I say, unbuckling my seatbelt.

"What's that?" he asks. "You had a chance to chat on the way over, you know."

I ignore his annoyed tone. "What happens to people who display their Reader powers to the world? Jacob warned me to be discreet, but I forgot to ask him about the consequences. What if I slip up?"

"It's good that you didn't ask him that." Caleb furrows his brows. "But to answer your question, all I can say is nothing good would happen. This isn't a game, kid. It's deadly serious."

"Can you be more specific?" I'm irritated at being called a kid yet again.

"If Jacob told me someone had done that, and if there was proof, I'd probably put a bullet in that person. Is that specific enough?" Caleb says, giving me a level look. "It would never happen, though. No Reader has ever been that stupid, and I doubt you are either."

"But surely someone said something at some point," I persist. "Or else there wouldn't be these rules, right? Plus, there are ideas in regular people's minds that seem like they might've originated with us. Where else would the concept of psychics come from? Just think of the term *mind reading*. And now that I think about it, maybe that's also where the reincarnation myths originated, or even astral projection and remote viewing—"

"Don't forget Bigfoot," he says, looking pointedly at his car door. "Look, I'm no historian. Maybe back in the day, people blabbed, but they don't now. And I'm sure those that did back then were burned at the stake, tortured, or had something equally unpleasant done to them by the ancient Readers. Our ancestors were pretty hardcore in that regard. Back then, for example, you'd get killed for fucking someone other than your assigned mate. And they wouldn't kill just you—they'd kill the person you slept with. I think the reason no one ever does what you describe is that we all know this brutal history. Strictly speaking, no official has ever said, 'We don't do that to traitors anymore.' So I'm telling you the truth: I've never heard of any modern-day lapses. We've looked into a few psychics who talked about reading minds, but it always turned out to be some lowlife con artist trying to scam people out of money, not Readers doing something they shouldn't."

His eyes flash darkly when he mentions the psychics. I wonder what he did to them. I don't want to ask. I've had enough Caleb-related violence for one day.

"Okay, thanks. That explains it, I guess. Now, just one more thing I wanted to ask you," I say tentatively, unsure how to go about this.

He lifts his eyebrows in a silent question.

"Can I have a gun?" I say it quickly, deciding to just blurt it out. As I say the words, I can't help staring at his glove compartment.

"You mean *that* gun?" he says, following my gaze.

"Any gun will do." I'm happy he doesn't seem too pissed to learn I've been snooping. "That gun's a revolver. They have simple mechanisms that should function in the Quiet—I mean, the Mind Dimension."

"Most guns work in the Mind Dimension," he says. "Fine. Take it—quickly, before I change my mind."

I grab the gun and exit the car. I tuck the weapon into the waistband at the back of my pants, feeling very gangster all of a sudden.

"Take the coffee too," he says, handing me the cup. "It was for you. Good luck in there."

Before I get a chance to reply, he reaches over and shuts the passenger door, almost in my face. Then the car takes off, leaving a faint smell of burning rubber in its wake.

As he leaves, I remember another related question. What happens to the people to whom the hypothetically traitorous Reader tells the secret of our existence? I guess Caleb wouldn't know, since he's never dealt with anything like that. Or so he says. I can't imagine it would be anything good. All the more reason to dissuade the shrink of my earlier revelations. I don't want her to get hurt—she's done right by me, even though I think she's full of shit most of the time.

I walk over and sit down on a bench in the park to think things over while sipping the lukewarm coffee.

It's 7:28 a.m. Mira and Eugene are probably still sleeping, like most normal people. If I do what I'm planning, Mira might be upset for more reasons than just my Pushing yesterday. But then again, I doubt I can make things worse—and I have a feeling that the element of surprise will be to my advantage.

Convinced, I sit up and, using the above-average anxiety I'm feeling at the moment, phase into the Quiet. As the sounds of the street go away, I walk toward the building.

The gun helps when it comes to opening the downstairs door. It also works like a charm on the lock of the door to their apartment. My ears still ringing from the gunshot only I could hear, I gingerly enter the apartment, thinking that it's a good thing the damage will automatically be repaired when I phase back to normal.

I begin to question the sanity of my plan again as soon as I walk into what has to be Mira's bedroom.

Mira is asleep on a gray futon. Her room is much less messy than the apartment overall. So it seems like the mess I noticed the other day is more Eugene's fault.

I'm cognizant of a lacy bra and thong lying on the chair next to the bed. I didn't think this part of the idea through. I'm in luck, though. She's clearly not sleeping naked—the shoulder that's visible above the blanket is clothed in a pajama top.

As I stand there, I wonder what will happen when I pull her into the Quiet with me while she's sleeping. I was never able to fall asleep in the Quiet, which seems to imply that Mira will wake up as soon as she enters. I'm about to find out for sure.

I reach out, pull away a few stray strands of Mira's soft dark hair, and gently touch her temple. Then I take a calming breath, realizing the chips are about to fall where they may.

She appears in the Quiet as a second Mira on the same bed, but closer to the edge on my side. This Mira has her eyes open and stares at the ceiling for a moment. Then she turns and looks at her still-sleeping double.

"Please don't panic," I whisper softly.

Hearing me, Mira jackknifes to a sitting position on the bed. Swinging her feet down to the floor, she looks at me, obviously confused.

Dressed in polka-dot pajamas, without all the makeup and the femme-fatale clothing, she looks a lot more approachable than the last time I saw her. Like the proverbial girl next door. A little vulnerable, even. These illusions last for only a moment before I get the most seething look she's ever given me.

"What. The. Fuck," she says somewhat incoherently, and for the first time, I hear a slight Russian accent in her speech.

"I'm sorry to burst in on you like this," I say quickly. "But I really needed to talk to you. Will you please hear me out?"

She jumps up—eyeing her purse, which happens to be behind me.

My heart sinks as I realize she's looking for the gun I recall her carrying in that purse.

Before I can complete the thought about the gun, she's right next to me, throwing a punch. Without consciously planning it, I catch her small fist in my hand a millisecond before it connects with my face. Then I hold it for a few moments, looking into her eyes. She seems shocked at my quick reaction. As soon as she gets her wits back and starts struggling, I let go of her hand.

She tries to kick me in the shins next, and I step back, again without conscious thought.

She almost loses her balance when her leg doesn't connect with its intended target. Her frustration turns into anger, every expression clear on her face, and she runs for the door. I briefly regret my newfound fighting reflexes. Maybe if she'd hit me, it would've been cathartic for her. Maybe afterwards she would've been willing to listen. And I can't imagine her punches would've hurt me that much—given her slim frame and all. And I'm not being sexist here, by the way. Not exactly. If my tiny friend Bert had punched me, seeing as he can't weigh much more than Mira, I doubt I would've felt anything either.

I follow her and realize she's heading into what must be Eugene's bedroom. She must be thinking about pulling him into the Quiet with us. Or getting his gun. Or both.

I wait, letting her do what she wants. I feel fairly safe, figuring that if she didn't kill me yesterday, she's even less likely to do so today after a good night's sleep. Hopefully.

Eugene walks out, wearing only wrinkled tighty-whiteys and looking confused. I don't get a chance to smirk at his appearance because Mira—holding that gun of his—immediately follows him.

The most worrisome part of this is that her hand is steady. I didn't expect that at all. She looks much calmer than yesterday—much more ready to shoot me. How could I have misjudged the situation so horribly?

I hear the gun safety click off.

Is it possible to have a heart attack in the Quiet? If so, I might be flirting with that possibility, given how fast my heart is beating.

She's carefully aiming at my head.

I expect to see at least *some* doubt on her face, but she looks completely calm. Merciless. Her forearm tenses as though she's about to pull the trigger.

I put my hand in front of my face, like that could actually protect me.

"Mira, stop." Eugene puts himself between me and the barrel. "Think about what you're about to do. He can spend *months* in the Mind Dimension."

Either seeing her brother in the way or hearing his words causes her to hesitate.

I'm speechless. She really *was* about to kill me, and Eugene obviously thought so as well. As I take a calming breath, I try not to focus on this fact. The knowledge of what she was about to do stings badly. More than I would've imagined. Thinking about it now, I realize everything I'd convinced myself of was just wishful thinking. I was so sure she wouldn't hurt me. Now, as the hard reality hits, learning that she *would* kill me feels like a deep betrayal—even though it shouldn't.

And speaking of betrayal, Eugene's reasoning for why she shouldn't pull the trigger hurts nearly as much. It sounded like he only wants to spare me because of my power. Forget friendship. 'Don't kill him so we can use his abilities in the Quiet' is what he seems to have meant.

"It doesn't matter how long he can do it," Mira says. "What good is that to us?" Her voice sounds more uncertain, however, and her hand seems less steady.

"You know it can be huge," Eugene says. "We just struck at our enemies. They're bound to retaliate."

"How do you know he's not with them? And if he offered to help us, how could we trust him?" Mira lowers the gun, as though just realizing it's pointed at her brother's chest.

"Snap out of it, Mirochka. You always said that you judge people by their actions rather than their words." Eugene gives his sister an even look. "He saved me, and afterwards he saved you—risking his life in the process. Why don't you judge Darren by his actions?"

What I can see of her face from behind his back looks thoughtful. Eugene's reasoning is spot on. I couldn't have put it better myself. Now it's clear that she's trying to make up her mind. I wish it weren't such a tough decision.

"But he is one of *them*," she says finally. I see her wrestling with the temptation to raise the gun again, but she doesn't. "For all we know, he could've been trying to weasel his way into our confidence for some reason."

"It's unlikely, Mira, and you know it. He wouldn't have revealed his Pusher nature to save you, if that were the case," Eugene says.

"Maybe that was a slip," she says, sounding less and less certain.

"That doesn't make sense," Eugene says. "He did it intentionally; you saw him. Assuming the worst case—that he did have some agenda before yesterday—he *still* decided to save you. That would count for something if it were true. But I don't think things were ever that complicated. I think it's much more likely that he truly didn't know what he was . . . what he *is*."

"Yes, exactly," I finally jump in. "I didn't."

"Shut up," Mira says angrily. "You would say that regardless."

"Well," Eugene says thoughtfully, "maybe there's a way we can figure out if he's telling the truth."

"Oh?" Mira voices my own thought.

"Yeah. I've been pondering this very question last night, and I may have thought of a way." Eugene sounds progressively more excited.

"What way?" Mira asks, and the fact that there's hope in her voice gives *me* hope.

"A test," her brother says.

Mira's shoulders sag in dismay. "You tested him yesterday. You were confident he's a Reader after that."

"And he is," Eugene says defensively. "My test wasn't wrong."

"Fine, maybe Pushers can Read as well as fuck with people's minds," Mira says stubbornly.

"They can't Read," Eugene objects. "Father was certain of that. I remember him telling me about it, and I've gone over his notes. Plus, you saw Julia make the same assumptions as me, in front of a bunch of other members of that Reader community. If anyone knew Pushers could Read, they would've corrected Julia, but they didn't. No, Mira. He *is* a Reader. That usually would mean that he's not a Pusher. Only in this case, for some reason he is. Any way you slice it, he's a strange case—in terms of his growing up with no knowledge of Reading or Pushing, and now everything that he can do."

"Fine, so he's a strange case," Mira concedes. "It doesn't mean he's telling the truth about anything."

"Which is why there's another test I want him to take. It won't tell us everything, but it will tell us if he's being honest with us. See, using my equipment, I can set up a pretty good polygraph test." Eugene is beginning to sound almost giddy at the mention of equipment.

"A lie detector test?" Mira frowns.

"Exactly." Eugene beams at her. "Like what regular people use, only better, using my research and equipment. Ever since I learned that a Reader can't Read others of our kind, I've been trying to figure out how we can keep each other honest. This is the best idea I've had so far. I can re-purpose some of the neurofeedback and other biofeedback devices that—"

"But can't people beat those things?" Mira asks, interrupting him. I'm starting to feel like I'm not even in the room. "Will it be a hundred-percent accurate?"

"Nothing is that accurate. And I suppose he *could* beat it, but it's unlikely. People can learn to beat the standard tests, but even then they need to do all this research into the methods used, and then train themselves to modify their natural responses. None of which Darren's had time to do—especially since he doesn't even know the methods I'll be using. This is the first he's even heard about being tested, so he's had no time to prepare."

"Okay, Darren—if that's even your name." Mira stands up on tiptoe to look at me over Eugene's shoulder. "If you agree to submit to my brother's test, I'll listen to what you came here to say. And I might not shoot you afterwards."

"Sure," I say readily. "I'll take the test; I have nothing to hide."

That's pretty much the truth. With only one small caveat I don't mention: Eugene is wrong on many points when it comes to this whole plan. First, I actually do know a quite a bit about these kinds of tests. I'm one of those people who did the research into how to beat them. The theory of it isn't actually specific to the test being given, since they all relate to biorhythms. Regardless of what Eugene changed about his test, I'm sure it still works on the same principles. Principles that can be taken advantage of—if I choose to do so.

"Okay, great," Eugene says. "I'll get ready. You leave the Mind Dimension and come back here to our apartment." He walks into his bedroom—I assume to reach his frozen body and phase out. And hopefully put on some pants.

Mira lingers for a moment and gives me a hard-to-define look. "You better pass," she says, and without giving me a chance to respond, goes into her own bedroom.

CHAPTER SEVEN

In a strange stupor, I make my way back to my body on the bench and phase out.

The world comes alive, and I consider making a run for it rather than going back. If Eugene messes up his science, I could be in real trouble. Plus, from what I know of lie detection, it's not even an exact science. It's actually part scam, often meant to scare guilty people into confessing things they're trying to hide. That's the biggest secret I learned while researching this.

A polygraph test is certainly not something I'd trust with my life.

I *would* make a run for it, but I want Mira to stop looking at me the way she has been, like I'm some kind of a monster. Like I had something to do with her parents getting killed. Also, there is that practical matter—the reason I came here in the first place. This second element is what decides it for me.

I cross the road again, only in the real world this time.

Eugene buzzes me in and opens the door. He's now dressed in jeans and a T-shirt, and he informs me that the equipment is set up.

I try to make myself as comfortable as I can while he hooks me up to his laptop. I must look even more ridiculous than during the Reader test he gave me the other day. I have electrodes attached all over my head, presumably to measure my brain waves. I have a heartbeat monitor on my finger and a device that looks like a rubber band around my chest. I assume the latter is for detecting increased respiration. Another gadget seems to measure skin conductance—the measure of how sweaty you get. Finally, there are a few cables with purposes I don't understand. These make me nervous. I hope they're not meant to administer electric shock or something; that's what comes to my mind when I look at them.

Through all the setup, Eugene seems as excited as a kid at a birthday party.

After making what seems like a thousand adjustments, he finally seems satisfied. "I'm done," he yells, looking at the door.

Mira enters the room—carrying a gun, of course. She's swapped her PJs for skinny jeans and a low-cut tank top, a casual outfit for her. I can't believe I have the bandwidth to think *hot* about someone who wants to shoot me, but that's exactly what comes to mind when I look at Mira.

As she stares at me, her serious expression alters, and I see tiny crinkles form in the corners of her eyes. Great. She's amused at how ridiculous I look. I probably would be too, if I were in her shoes. I don't mind being mocked in this case; I'd sooner she laugh than point that gun at me. Maybe I should get myself a jester's hat so she doesn't feel the constant urge to shoot me.

She puts the gun down and sits crossed-legged on the floor, settling herself on top of a bunch of papers, cables, and other random stuff Eugene has lying around. I make sure *not* to look down her low-cut tank top—despite the fact that it would be possible. From what I've read, arousal can be misinterpreted as a sign of lying with these tests.

"Okay, Darren, what's two plus two?" Eugene asks.

Don't ask me why I bothered to learn how to beat the polygraph exam. Let's just say if my investing activities ever led to my having to take one, I wanted to be ready. Anyway, I know what this inane question is about. Eugene is establishing a baseline. His readings of my answers to the obviously true statements will later be compared to readings after I answer more important questions. So, if I wanted to cheat, I could make myself nervous as I answer this question. That wouldn't be difficult for someone like me, who's spent most of his life making himself nervous in order to phase into the Quiet.

But I decide against trying to cheat, also known as *using countermeasures.* First, I don't really have anything to hide, so why bother? Second, as unlikely as it sounds, Eugene could be right. The fact that he's using his own version of the test might mean there's some physical reaction he's monitoring that I might not have under control—some new principle I haven't read about. If that's the case, he may think I'm messing with the test. And messing with these tests is as good an indicator as any that you're hiding something. In our case, that's the last thing I want Mira to think. The whole point of this is to gain her trust.

"Please answer quickly," Eugene says, bringing me out of my thoughts. His expression is darkening, and I realize I already started my test on the wrong foot.

"I'm sorry," I say. "I'm a little nervous. I really want you guys to believe me."

"Fine. Take a deep breath," he says, looking at the monitor.

I do as he says, taking a couple of relaxing breaths.

"Good. Now, just answer what I ask you, when I ask you," Eugene says. "What's two plus six?"

"Eight," I answer quickly, letting him get a clean baseline.

"And what's your name?" Eugene keeps his eyes on his laptop.

"Darren," I say simply.

"Did you know that either I or Mira existed before you met her in Atlantic City the other day?"

"No."

"Did you save Mira yesterday?"

"Yes."

"Are you a Reader?"

"I'm not sure. I hope so."

"Are you a Pusher?"

"I'm not sure. I hope not."

"Did you know you might be a Pusher before yesterday?"

"No."

"Are you running a con game with us as targets?"

"No."

"Do you have a crush on my sister?"

"What?" I say, caught completely off-guard with this one. Then, realizing I'm messing up, I reluctantly admit, "Maybe. Well, yes. Not a crush, but—"

"Thank you," Eugene says with a smirk, his eyes leaving the screen for the first time during this barrage of questions. Then he turns toward his sister. "He's telling the truth."

I glance at Mira and catch a strange look on her face. Was she just blushing? That seems unlikely. I must be imagining things due to my embarrassment over being put on the spot like that. But I know why Eugene did it. He wanted to ask something that I would react to, so he can be sure his device detects lies when they happen. That last question was perfect for that. He's even more clever than I thought. *Asshole.*

"Okay, that's great. He's not lying." Mira turns away from me to look at her brother. "That still doesn't tell us what the fuck he is."

"You know he's not someone who means you any harm," Eugene says, his voice unexpectedly stern. "Shouldn't that be enough?"

This is the first time I hear that kind of tone in his voice. Mira looks taken aback too, so it must be a rare occurrence.

I decide to jump in. "Mira, I want to know what I am even more than you do. Eugene is right—I don't mean you any harm. The opposite, actually."

"Oh, shut up," she says dismissively. "The opposite. Right. You are so selfless. Please. I know your type. All you care about is yourself."

I look at Eugene for help. Eugene doesn't meet my eyes. I'm on my own.

Her lip curls. "You know I'm right. Quick, while you still have to tell the truth, why don't you tell us why you came? Was it to help us? Or was it to save your own skin?"

"Well," I say uncomfortably, "I guess under the circumstances I won't deny it. I came to ask you not to tell other Readers about what you saw me do."

"Exactly," she says, her voice dripping with disdain.

"You don't know what I know. You don't know how brutally Readers kill Pushers," I say, losing my patience. "It's not being selfish if I don't want to be murdered by Caleb or someone like him."

"And how would you know anything about Readers killing Pushers?" She gives me a suspicious look, making me realize I just goofed.

"I saw it in Caleb's mind, okay? He made me do that Joint Reading thing with him earlier today, and I saw through his eyes how he killed one of them." I realize I'm going back on my word to Caleb about not sharing what we saw in each other's minds, but I can't help it. I'm desperate to prove my case to Mira.

She doesn't have a comeback. She just looks at Eugene in shock.

"That was the truth," he says. "Now can we stop this foolishness? Darren is clearly not against us, so I'm going to unhook him. Meanwhile, Darren, I want to hear every little detail about the Joining."

As he gets me out of the cables, I tell them about my Joining with Caleb, omitting things that Caleb and I would consider too personal. I also swear both Mira and Eugene to secrecy, and hope that Caleb never finds out I divulged even the few details I shared.

"Unbelievable," Eugene says when I finish. "I would give my left pinkie to try that. I only did it one time, with Julia, but it was nothing like what you describe. Dad was right. This experience changes based on how powerful the participants are . . ."

As he speaks, Mira begins to glower at him. "No way," she interrupts. "I see where you're going with this, and the answer is *no*. I'll shoot him before I let you Join minds with him."

"What? Why?" Eugene says, clearly disappointed.

"Because even if he didn't know he was a Pusher before, he knows it now. Once he's inside your mind, he'll have you in his power." She turns to glare at me.

"Is that true?" Eugene asks me. He doesn't look scared; if anything, he looks excited. I guess the scientist in him is relishing all this.

"I have no idea," I say honestly. "I didn't realize that was a possibility until Mira suggested it just now. It was so confusing in there, I'm not sure if I would've been able to figure out how to do that, even if I wanted to try. Our minds were as one. I could've just as easily Pushed myself to do something while trying to influence him. And, of course, I wouldn't want to try it, especially with Caleb or you, Eugene. Him, because if it failed, he would kill me or worse. And you, because . . . well, I just wouldn't."

"There, you see, Mira? He wouldn't Push me," Eugene says. "And if I Join with him, that would beat any lie detector test when it comes to learning the truth."

"Do you even hear yourself?" She gives him an exasperated look. "Of course he says he wouldn't Push you. And besides, why are you trying to use truth-seeking as an excuse? Didn't your test just prove that he's telling the truth?"

Eugene says, "Well, yes—"

I'm beginning to get tired of their bickering. "I'm sorry to interrupt, Eugene," I say, "but this isn't necessary. I don't want to do any Joint Reading with you. The one time with Caleb was enough, trust me."

Mira gives me a grateful look. I guess I'm her ally in this. Eugene is doing a terrible job hiding his deep disappointment. I can't believe he still wants to do this, given what Mira just told him. If I thought someone could Push me under some circumstances, I'd avoid the said circumstances at all costs.

"It wouldn't be the same if you did it with *me*," he says pleadingly. "It wouldn't be like what you experienced with Caleb. This thing varies depending on participants' Depth and intellect. The higher those things are, the deeper the Joining. Also, the mind of the subject might make a difference. And possibly—"

"You're not helping your case with that," I say. "It was deep enough for me. I wouldn't want to make it deeper."

"Think about it," Eugene insists. "I think if we did it, you wouldn't regret it. You had a bad experience, so you're obviously going to be wary. I probably would be too, if I glimpsed something as frightening as Caleb's mind."

"Hey, that's not fair. Caleb saved me," Mira reminds him. "No need to get all high and mighty."

"So Caleb is a good guy, but me, who also saved you, you're ready to shoot," I say bitterly. "Did Eugene tell you why I did this crazy thing with Caleb to begin with? That it was actually payment to your precious Caleb for saving you?"

"Is that true?" she asks Eugene, giving me an odd look.

"Yes. I didn't get a chance to tell you." Eugene looks uncomfortable.

"I see," she says slowly. "Okay, Darren. Maybe I won't shoot you anytime soon. And I'm not a rat, so your secret is safe with me. Even if we don't really even know what that secret is. Are you happy now?"

"Yes. Thank you," I say, relieved. I'm okay with her attitude for now. It beats being shot or revealed as a potential Pusher.

"Great. Now that it's settled, can we get some breakfast?" Eugene gives us a big smile. "I'm starving."

Mira rolls her eyes. "How are you not much, much fatter?" she asks rhetorically before saying, "Sure. Let's go get something. I have some more questions for Darren, and we might as well kill two birds with one stone."

"I'm in," I say, though I'm not sure I want to answer any questions Mira is thinking of asking me. The green smoothie I had earlier was more of a snack, so a real breakfast sounds like a wonderful idea.

It takes them a few moments to put on shoes. One elevator ride and a flight of stairs later, we're walking through the lobby.

We approach the door. I feel chivalrous for some reason, so I hold open the glass door that leads outside the building. I'm doing it for Mira, of course, but Eugene benefits too.

"Thank you," Mira says, exiting after Eugene. "Where are we going to eat?"

"The diner?" Eugene suggests hopefully.

As I follow them, I have a sense of déjà vu. She's about to bring up the food poisoning story again. They'll fight. Then she'll get her way and choose the breakfast place she wants. I guess it's a thing with siblings; they have the same fights over and over, with the same results. Must be kind of nice.

Suddenly, there is a loud noise—a strange sound that scrapes at the inside of my ears.

I'm caught off-guard. Instinctively, I phase into the Quiet.

The argument between Mira and Eugene stops, their faces frozen. The sound also stops.

I turn around.

It's the glass door. It's shattering in a strange pattern. From a spot in the middle, the glass is flying out in small fragments. Farther out, the glass is falling in larger chunks.

Something struck that glass at high speed and with high force.

I feel cold as I rush into the building, fearing what I'll find there. It takes me less than a minute to discover the culprit.

It's a bullet.

A bullet is lying on the floor in the hallway.

I run outside and cross the street, frantically looking around. I see nothing, so I go through the park, straining my eyes as I scan the area. Finally, I spot something in the distance. I run toward it. As I get closer, I hope against all hope that it's just a large fly.

When I'm standing next to it, though, I know my hope is futile. The thing frozen in mid-air is what I feared it would be.

It's another bullet—flying at one of us.

CHAPTER EIGHT

I swivel my head from side to side, frantically trying to figure out where the shooter might be.

My brain almost subconsciously provides the solution for me as my legs take me where I need to go.

I run through the little park, almost tripping over frozen parents watching their frozen kids on the silent playground.

The shooter is sitting in a large van, holding a long rifle pointed in our direction.

The anger that I now feel is difficult to describe. I've never felt this enraged before.

This fucker just shot at me and my friends—and he's shooting at us through a park where little kids are playing.

Before this moment, I thought I would never consider Pushing anyone again. The reality of what I inadvertently did to that guy yesterday still horrifies me.

But now I feel ready to Push again—intentionally this time. It's the only option.

I approach the guy and grab him by the neck with all my strength. For a second, I forget why I'm here. I just relish choking him.

Then I give myself a mental shake. I don't know if Pushing works with corpses, so it's best if I don't continue with this. I loosen my grip and try to start the session.

I find it extremely difficult to get into the right state of mind while overcome with so many turbulent emotions. I must, however, so I concentrate.

I do synchronized breathing for a few moments, and begin to feel the necessary state of Coherence coming on. Suddenly, I'm in the shooter's vile head . . .

* * *

We're shooting at the target the second time and mentally cursing the boss in Russian. Why the fuck did he give this order on such a short notice?

The first miss is his fault. He didn't give us a chance to get our favorite rifle. The one with the scope that has been perfectly calibrated. Instead, we got this piece of shit.

We're not used to working like this. To not being a hundred-percent sure we're going to hit the target. It's unprofessional. The only silver lining is that, due to the urgency, we came here alone, so no one witnessed that embarrassing miss. Our marksman's reputation is unblemished.

I, Darren, disassociate from the Reading. This is yet another Russian mobster. He has been ordered to kill, and it's clear that he won't stop until that grim task is complete. But he doesn't know anything useful to me.

I begin my unsavory task. I try to repeat Pushing—the thing I did the other day.

I'm still unsure how I did what I did, so I rely on instinct and intuition.

I picture this fucker packing his rifle, closing the van door, and getting behind the wheel. I try to imagine hearing the van door close and feeling the ignition keys under my fingers. There is a huge urgency to get out of here. To be away. I visualize the switching of gears and the frantic clutching of the wheel, knuckles white, followed by the flooring of the gas pedal. I put my fear of that bullet into my vessel—his mind. I become fear. I channel it. There is only one escape from this fear, and that is to leave instantly and to go fast. As fast as humanly possible. No stopping, no slowing down, just a mad rush to safely, safety that's many miles away from here . . .

I do this thing for what feels like a half hour, battling a growing feeling of mental exhaustion mingled with disgust. When I finally can't take it for another second, I exit the guy's mind.

* * *

I run back through the park, shuddering when I pass by the bullet again.

I want to grab it, throw it on the ground, and stomp on it, but I resist the urge. It would be futile—nothing I can do to the bullet in the Quiet will change the fact that it will resume its potentially deadly path when I phase out.

Random thoughts enter my head. Should I have done the Pushing? Am I becoming the monster the Reader community is afraid of? The monster *I'm* afraid of?

Yes, I should've done it, I try to convince myself. It was necessary. If I didn't do something, the bullet that's still in the air would've been followed by more, until the shooter's job was done. Until he killed his target—one of us. Pushing was the only way I could think of to stop him. I didn't have a choice.

Besides, it's not like I'm going to cause his death, like the other time. Not that it was, strictly speaking, my fault yesterday—the second guard had been the one to actually pull the trigger. In this case, I think I merely caused the shooter to drive away. Admittedly, he will go fast, which has risks associated with it, but I didn't commit him to a definite fatal outcome.

I stop worrying about my actions when I find myself next to our frozen bodies again.

I look us over.

My frozen self's face looks scared, but knowing what I know now, the expression on his/my face is not scared enough.

Eugene just looks confused, not scared yet.

Mira is the only one of us who looks like she has it together. She looks focused and alert, ready to pounce into action, and her head is beginning to turn toward me.

No matter how much I stare at the three of us, I can't seem to make myself feel more confident in the idea I hatched up.

The plan is ridiculously simple. I will fall, and by doing so, I will try to get Mira to fall as well. She'll fall into Eugene. We should all go down like a stack of dominos—in theory, at least. And quickly, which is vital.

My hope is that the bullet will miss all of us if I do it right. This sort of tackling maneuver works for the Secret Service in the movies, so I figure it should work in real life. It *has* to work.

Not letting my brain come up with counterarguments for this plan, I focus on just going for it.

I reach out and touch my face. At the same time, before I'm even in my body, I put every ounce of my energy into willing my leg muscles to begin the movement that will cause me to spring in the right direction.

My whole world becomes the command I'm sending to my brain—the command for my leg muscles to act so I can fall.

My body seems to move before I even become aware that I've phased out of the Quiet. I feel my arms spread around Mira before they actually do so.

I only fully realize I'm out of the Quiet when I hear Mira's surprised yelp at the impact of my body falling on her.

I know I'm out because the street noises have returned. And then I feel the most unpleasant scraping sensation in my head. It's like a dental drill, but multiplied a hundredfold. It's quickly followed by intense pain. It's as though I just got hit on the head with a baseball bat—a baseball bat made of hot iron.

Everything is happening as though in slow motion. I feel like I'm going to phase back into the Quiet, but I manage to fight off the sensation.

In the next instant, I'm on top of Mira, who's on top of Eugene.

That part of my plan has worked.

They're both cursing, which means they're alive. Then I feel an explosion of pain in my head as I roll off the pile of bodies we formed.

I'm unable to get up. My head is pulsing with pain. It burns. It stings. It's horrible.

I bring my hand to the epicenter of the torment, and I feel warm liquid there.

In a moment of lucidity, I realize I've been shot. In the head.

"Darren, what the fuck—" Mira begins, but stops mid-sentence. "Oh, Darren, I am so sorry. Why are you bleeding? Did you hit your head when you fell? What happened?"

I feel her hands on my shoulder. She's turning me over.

"Eugene, please call 911," I try to say. "I think I've been shot."

"Zhenya, zvoni 911, bistrey!" she yells in Eugene's direction, and I don't know if she spoke in Russian, or if I'm losing my ability to comprehend English.

"Darren, look at me," she says to me gently. "You're going to be okay. I'm going to try to stop the bleeding."

I was right; that liquid I felt means I'm bleeding. This thought comes to me as though from a distance.

I hear the sound of ripping cloth, and in the next moment, I feel the pain intensify. She must've pressed the makeshift bandage to the wound. Some part of me realizes this must be an attempt to stop the bleeding.

I begin to reach for my head again, but she puts her hand on mine, preventing me from doing so. Her hand feels good, reassuring, so I just leave it there.

"Take deep breaths," Mira's voice says softly. "Yes, like that, slow and steady, this should help with the shock. How much does it hurt?"

I try to tell her it isn't so bad, but the words come out all jumbled.

"It doesn't matter, Darren, just talk to me," she says in a desperate, hushed tone. "Open your eyes, now."

I obey her command and open my eyes. At the same time, I lift my hand, the one that touched my head earlier, and take a look. My hand is covered in blood, and I can feel it streaming down my neck.

The world begins to spin, and then everything goes black.

CHAPTER NINE

I wake up.

How much did I drink last night?

My head hurts like hell.

I try to remember what happened. I'm not in my own bed, but lying down in some kind of bed in a moving vehicle. Ambulance?

I try to open my eyes, but the light strikes a hammer-blow of pain, so I close them again.

"Darren, I'm here," says a familiar soothing voice.

It's Mira's voice—and the reason I'm here comes back to me.

I was shot.

In the head.

That would explain this excruciating pain. I try to open my eyes, squinting cautiously.

"He's conscious," I hear Eugene say.

"That's good news," says an unfamiliar male voice.

"You're not a doctor to be saying what constitutes good or bad news." Mira's tone is sharp. "I want a doctor to see him right away."

"We're on the way to the hospital," the unfamiliar voice says defensively. He must be a paramedic, and the moving object I find myself in must be an ambulance, I realize.

"My head really hurts," I decide to complain. Talking makes the pain intensify, though, and the feeling I now have is like being carsick, only ten times worse.

"You got shot," Mira says gently. "Is there anyone I should call for you? Friends or family?"

There is care and concern in her voice. She sounds like she's actually worried about me and wants to help. She doesn't sound like the girl who was just about to shoot me herself not so long ago. The headache intensifies further when I try to think about this, so I stop. The idea of calling someone makes some sense, though.

"In my phone. Sara and Lucy are my family. Bert is my friend," I say, trying to reach for my pocket. Moving sends waves of nausea through my body. Am I dying? I wonder if that would end the pain.

"I got it," she says, putting one of her hands on mine and reaching into my pocket with her other hand.

Usually, I would have dirty thoughts in a situation like this—having Mira dig through my jeans this way—but I guess getting shot takes its toll. I feel like I might actually puke if the ambulance keeps on shaking the way it does, and I want Mira as far away from me as possible if that happens.

I take a few deep breaths and decide that maybe I woke up too soon. I think I need to rest for a few more minutes.

"What hospital are we going to?" Mira asks the paramedic as my thoughts grow progressively cloudier.

"Coney Island," I hear him respond as though in a dream, and then my mind goes blank again.

* * *

I wake up again. This time I know that I'm not in my own bed. I remember being shot. I also remember feeling sick in the ambulance, and I'm relieved that I'm feeling somewhat better. I even recall talking to someone. The reason for my feeling better is on the tip of my tongue, but it escapes me.

"When is the doctor going to see him again?" It's Mira's voice. "All he did was give him something for the pain."

Ah, that explains it. I recall telling someone I was in terrible pain. Or did I say something else? It's still a bit blurry, and the weightless feeling running through my body is not conducive to recall.

There's a trick I learned at the dentist's office. When a dentist asks me if I feel something during a procedure, I say that I do until I can't feel my face from all the Novocain. I must've automatically used this same technique when I spoke to the doctor in my woozy state, and he must've believed me and given me something pretty strong for the pain.

"The doctor will see him again after he gets the X-ray," says a different female voice. A nurse, I'm guessing.

"Okay, then when is he going for that X-ray?" Mira's voice rises. "Why is this taking so long?"

"Please calm down, miss. We're doing the best we can," says the nurse in a rehearsed monotone. "We have a lot of patients today and are very understaffed."

They have a back and forth, but I ignore it. Instead, I try to examine this feeling I'm experiencing from whatever is making me feel better. It's like a warm flow through my whole body. Like I'm hovering and floating in a warm bath at the same time.

Whatever they gave me for the pain must be really beginning to kick in.

"That bullet was meant for me," Eugene says after the person Mira was bugging about my care is gone.

"Yes. I hate to say it, but I told you so." Mira sounds angry. "When will you develop a sense of self-preservation?"

"You're right, of course," Eugene says morosely. "We should've slept at a hotel. I didn't think they would come after me again. Not this soon. I didn't even think the ones involved in your kidnapping bothered to share our address with anyone else—"

"Oh, spare me all the bullshit." Mira's tone is scathing. "I heard it yesterday, and now Darren is hurt because I listened to you. You just wanted to be near your precious equipment, as usual. That's all you think about."

With the nice feelings spreading though my body, I have a hard time following the conversation. But one thing I do get from it: Mira seems to care about me. At least she's upset that Eugene's lack of regard for her earlier concerns resulted in my injury. As I think this, the feelings of warmth in my body intensify. What drug did they give me? Maybe I should get a prescription.

"I really am sorry, Mirochka." Eugene sounds genuinely remorseful. "In the future, I will do what you say when it comes to paranoia."

She gets pissy about the word *paranoia*, and they argue some more, with occasional lapses into Russian. I feel myself slowly floating down from whatever cloud the pain medication had taken me to. Their sibling squabble is totally ruining my buzz.

"I can't believe Darren took the bullet for me," Eugene says at some point, and the comment catches my attention.

Truthfully, I can't believe it either. Well, strictly speaking, that was not my intent. I'd hoped to save everyone. But still. His remark makes me feel good, though some of that might still be the drug.

"He did," Mira responds thoughtfully.

They sit in silence for a bit, and I feel the buzz coming back, intensified. As it gets a hold on my body again, I feel decidedly drowsy and don't fight it. My consciousness flees, and I find myself going for a nice nap.

CHAPTER TEN

"Are you Bert?" I hear Mira's voice again as I wake up.

"Yes," Bert responds. "Thank you for calling me, Mira. Nice to meet you. How did Darren get hurt?"

I open my eyes.

"He—"

"Wait, I think he just opened his eyes," Bert cuts off Mira's explanation.

"Darren," she says, looking at me worriedly. "How are you feeling?"

I examine myself.

I'm hooked up to a monitor and have an IV in my arm, but the effects of the drug they gave me must've worn off. My head is throbbing again. But it doesn't seem to be as bad as before, which could be remnants of the medication, or a result of healing. I'm not sure which it is. The whole thing still feels a lot like a hangover, but at least the nausea has lessened, and having my eyes open doesn't make me feel like I have icepicks piercing my temples.

"Okay." I try to sound brave, but my voice comes out hoarse and pathetic-sounding. "Better."

"Here." Mira hands me a cup of water from the little table near my bed, and I drink it carefully.

"Where is Eugene?" I ask, looking around in confusion.

"He went to visit Julia," Mira says, and I detect a note of disapproval in her voice. Is she mad he left before seeing me recover, or does she just disapprove of him visiting Julia?

"How is she?" I ask.

"You're worried about Julia, now? She's doing better than *you*, I can assure you." Mira smiles. "She didn't get shot in the head."

"Oh, right," I say. "How am *I* doing?"

"I don't know," she says in frustration. "They took you to get X-rays of your head. Don't you remember?"

"No, I was kind of out of it," I say.

"Yeah, it must be the stuff they gave you for the pain. You looked quite loopy, drooling and mumbling something. In any case, that was a long time ago, and I haven't seen a doctor with the X-ray results, or even a nurse."

"Hmm," I say worriedly. "That sucks."

"Tell me about it." Mira frowns. "I'm thinking of getting you some food, and if they don't give you some attention by the time I'm done, I'm going to go around and try to talk some sense into these people."

The way she mentions talking to them sounds rather sinister. I wouldn't want her to piss off my doctor at this stage. But I really wish the X-ray results would arrive, so I could find out what's going on with me. Head trauma is nothing to sneeze at, especially for people who like to use their heads as much as I do. Also, I realize that Mira is planning to give this hospital's staff a hard time on my behalf, which is a strange idea.

"Bert, will you keep him company while I grab him something to eat?" Mira says, interrupting my train of thought.

"Of course," he says, getting that bashful look he always wears around girls.

"Do you want anything?" she asks him.

"No, thank you." He blushes.

"And you, Darren?" she says. "We never made it to that breakfast."

I consider the idea. Though my nausea has subsided a bit, I don't yet feel like eating. Or getting up. Or doing much besides talking. The IV they have in my arm feels a little itchy, and I wonder what will happen when I need to go to the bathroom. I'd better ask a medical professional when I get hold of one. On the plus side, I'm not wearing one of those goofy hospital gowns. Probably because they needed access only to my head. It still doesn't prevent me from looking ridiculous, of course. I can feel that my head is bandaged up like a mummy's, probably making me look like it's Halloween.

"No, I think I'll pass on the breakfast for now," I tell her. "I bet they're about to bring me some Jell-O, the hospital food of choice."

"I am going to get you one of those and a pudding of some kind," she says decisively. "If you haven't been told about the X-rays yet, what makes you think you can rely on these people for food?"

"Okay, Mira, thank you. I'll try the pudding if they have it," I say, looking at her in confusion. This caring side of Mira is odd and will take some getting used to. "Maybe something like apple sauce if they don't?"

"Okay, don't worry, I'll get you something," she says and turns to go.

As Mira is walking away, I notice Bert looking her up and down. For some reason, I'm annoyed at him for doing that. Then I mentally smack myself. Am I being jealous and protective of *Mira*?

"Dude," Bert says as soon as Mira is out of earshot. "Is that *the* Mira I looked up for you? Wow, I have to say, she is *so* your type. Why didn't you tell me you found her? And how did you get shot? And who's Eugene? And Julia? What the hell is going on?"

I sigh and concoct a story for Bert. I can't tell him anything about Readers or Pushers, so the story focuses on other things instead. I tell him that I stopped by Mira's house and that her brother and I ended up being friendly. It's almost what happened. Then I tell Bert how I learned about Mira and Eugene's parents being murdered by some unsavory Russian characters. I explain the murder by saying that their father had problems with someone back in the motherland—which could be true. I also say that Mira's quest for revenge backfired, and she got kidnapped as a result—which is false, but a much simpler explanation than the truth.

"You participated in a rescue? Is that how you got shot?" Bert says incredulously. "Are you crazy?"

"Actually, no," I say. "I was unscathed during that rescue. That was yesterday. This shot, obviously, happened today. I think it's safe to assume these thugs were from the same group as yesterday's kidnappers, though. They tried to kill her or her brother this time around, but missed and got me instead. I could actually use your help with this, Bert. There's someone I want to ask you to look up using your skills. Someone who might be giving orders in that organization."

"Yes, sure. I mean, they shot you, so it's the least I can do," Bert says. "Just never mention my name to those sorts of people."

I assure him that I'm not going to mention his name in the unlikely event that the gangsters and I have a friendly face-to-face chat. I then give him the name, Arkady, and the phone number I got the other day. I guess there is a silver lining to getting shot. I was out of favors with Bert when it comes to what he rightfully considers shady hacker activities, but he's not thinking about favors right now.

Seeing how willing he is to help, I decide to milk the situation a bit further.

"There are two more people I was hoping you could try to learn something about. These two are not Russian," I say.

"Who are they then?" he says to my dismay. I really hoped I could play the 'getting shot' card once more, and Bert would do this for me without further questions, but it sounds like I might have to go into this strange topic with him.

"They might be my parents," I say, and watch Bert's eyes go wide with surprise. "My biological parents."

I give him the story of how, *coincidentally*, I also found out that Sara is not my biological mother. I explain that it's a woman named Margret, whom I know very little about, and that my dad now also has a name—Mark. I also tell Bert that I plan to get my biological parents' last names from my moms when they arrive at the hospital.

"All right," he agrees when I'm done. "Text me their names as soon as you know. Also that mobster's number and name. In for a penny, in for a pound. But you've got to do something for me when you get better."

"I can promise to try," I say carefully. "What do you need?"

As I watch Bert's face, I begin cursing myself mentally for being greedy. When it was just the Russian guy I asked him to look into, he didn't need favors back. Whatever it is he's about to ask me, he's looking for the best way to say it—which, knowing Bert, means it will be something big.

"Can you ask Mira if she has friends she can introduce me to?" he finally says, his face turning red.

I blow out a relieved breath. I thought he was going to ask me to give him a kidney or something.

"I doubt she does, but I'll find out for you," I say, smiling. "If not, I will, in general, be on the lookout."

"Thanks," he says, shifting his weight uncomfortably.

I'm actually happy with this development. Bert finally found a workable approach to meeting women—asking me for help. It might work. I've always thought that Bert's biggest problem with women had been a lack of trying.

"I brought something for you," he says, reaching into his man-purse-looking shoulder bag in an obvious effort to change the subject.

He takes out a blue Gameboy 3DS and then a golden one.

This is our little guilty pleasure. When I'm in the office for the whole day, and when things are boring—which is often—we sneak away to a meeting room, sit with our backs toward the glass walls of the room, and play video games. To our coworkers, it might look like we're busy studying reports or reviewing financial statements.

This love of video games is what initially established our friendship back at Harvard. Well, that and the fact that we were both teens surrounded by adults.

Taking my hands from under the blanket that covers me, I use the incline function of my hospital bed. A few seconds later, I'm in a sitting position with a Gameboy in my hands. The IV in my hand feels a little funny, but manageable.

We load the devices and start playing a goofy fighting game Bert brought for this occasion.

"You're only slightly better than this game's AI," Bert says halfway into the first round. This is his version of trash talk.

I let it slide this time. There are so many things I can say. For example, I can point out that the character he chose to fight me with, Pikachu the Pokémon, is a yellow, goofy little creature that looks suspiciously like Bert himself. Or I could point out that he *should* be better at this game, given how much time he spends with games in general. However, that would be like saying he has no life, which is close to the truth for Bert. I wouldn't be so mean-spirited as to point that out, plus I don't want to piss him off until he gets me the information I need.

So, instead of saying anything, I try to go for a thrust with the sword of my own favorite character. I play as Link, the silent hero from my favorite game series of all time, the Legend of Zelda. The hit lands, and Bert goes quiet, clearly trying to concentrate on his comeback.

Soon I'm dodging thunderbolts as I catch Bert with my signature spin attack. The 3D of the screen begins to make the nausea come back, but I try to ignore it, determined to win.

"By the way, did I tell you that Jerry Buchmacker is dead?" Bert says, blatantly trying to divert my attention. Bert knows how much I hate to lose. I once threw a controller at his head back in college.

"What happened?" I say, knowing full well this is Bert's conspiracy-theory time. Even though we're playing, I have to indulge him to stay in his good graces. "And remind me who Jerry Buchmacker is, again."

"He was working on new artificial intelligence applications. Think self-driving cars, but in medicine."

"Oh yeah, I remember you talking about this guy when you consulted me about the company where he was the CTO. I told you it would be a good investment for Pierce's portfolio," I say, and start a new game, playing as the same character.

"Right, that one, and now he's dead. Another *suicide.*" Bert tries to make air quotes on the last word with the Gameboy in his hands. "I learned of what happened when Mr. Pierce asked me to find out if Jerry's death means we should liquidate the portfolio."

"Okay then, why is the guy *really* dead?" I say, mimicking his air quotes. I know full well where this is heading. I think I've heard this specific conspiracy theory before, and it's not as crazy as some other stuff Bert comes up with.

"It's the secret Neo-Luddite group again," he whispers, looking around as though they have ears in this hospital.

As I learned some time ago, a Luddite, as defined by Bert, is someone who's against any kind of progress. The Neo variety seem to be specifically against modern technological progress. From what I've gathered from my friend's admittedly biased description of them, they are a bunch of crazy people who would have humanity go back to living in caves if they could. The Unabomber was a flavor of one of these people, according to Bert.

This specific conspiracy theory states that there is a secret group that takes out talented scientists in critical fields, such as robotics, genetics, informatics, and nanotechnology. Their motive is to prevent the transformative changes these fields can bring.

I don't believe in this conspiracy, of course, but I do know there are people who fear progress and change. To them I say, "Go into the forest and try living for a day without sanitation, without your iPhone, without a gun to shoot wolves that want to eat you, and without antibiotics for the gangrene you might get from a simple cut. Then come back and tell me you still want to go back to the caveman days."

I certainly wouldn't.

"What makes you think this wasn't suicide?" I ask, even though I know I'm just encouraging Bert's craziness.

"Well, it's their MO," he says, and inside the game, gives me a particularly nasty punch.

"Right, of course," I say sarcastically, blocking the next kick and countering with a sword thrust.

Bert is clearly unhappy with my lack of faith in his theory, and the yellow creature on my screen throws my hero off the game platform as a manifestation of his grumpiness.

We go back and forth like this, with me playing the devil's advocate about the conspiracy and Bert kicking my ass in the game and stating more reasons for why the guy couldn't have committed suicide. A lot of it sounds rather persuasive, actually. There was no mention of depression in any of the files Bert got his hands on. There were long-term plans for vacations and conferences. Finally, and a clincher for Bert, the guy had a gorgeous girlfriend and had just proposed to her.

"What are you guys doing?" I hear Mira's incredulous voice from my left. It comes just as I'm about to deliver my theory of how the guy possibly killed himself as a weird manifestation of cold feet. Marriage can be a scary thing—at least as far as I'm concerned.

"Playing," I say defensively to Mira. I feel like I was just caught doing something obscene.

"Did the doctor say it was okay for you to play that stuff?" she says, frowning.

"I have no idea; the doctor hasn't come yet," I say. "But I doubt video game playing can be bad for you."

"That thing's 3D screen gives me, a person without head damage, a headache," she counters.

I can see what Bert is thinking without needing to do a Read. *Hot and into video games?*

I am impressed myself.

"So you have actually played before?" I ask.

"Of course." She narrows her eyes. "Why is that such a surprise?"

"No reason," I say swiftly.

"I'll tell you what. Before I go find the doctor, I'll play whichever one of you wins," she announces, crossing her arms. Our eyes nearly fall out of our sockets as the move pushes up her cleavage.

I can tell that Bert's and my thoughts converge on the same idea.

I have to win.

CHAPTER ELEVEN

I perform a combo attack, which consists of my best strategies. Bombs, boomerangs, sword thrusts—all go in desperation at the little Japanese creature on the screen in front of me.

The need to win is very strong, and I wonder if it's some primal part of my brain wanting me to be the victor in front of a female.

Whatever the reason, I throw all I have into this next attack.

It's futile, though. It seems like the prospect of playing with a real girl is a stronger motivator for Bert than for me. Plus, he's already better at this than I am.

He blocks my onslaught, and then, in mere moments, manages to wipe the game floor with my poor character.

He ignores the sour expression on my face as I hand him the Gameboy.

Mira and Bert begin the game, and Bert is practically beaming with excitement.

I try not to sulk while I eat the pudding and Jell-O Mira brought me.

"Is Eugene coming back?" I ask when I'm done with the food.

"Yes, he should actually be here soon," Mira says absentmindedly, not taking her eyes off the game screen. "I had him rent a car, in case they have my car's plates. I want us to give you a ride once you're discharged."

Their game is lasting an unbelievably long time—causing me to think in dismay that she might actually be better at it than I am. I probably would've lost to Bert already. Unless my sneaky friend is toying with her, trying to make this game last longer.

I look around for a doctor or at least a nurse. There are none in sight. My bed is one of a dozen such beds standing in a circle around the large room. It all looks very dreary and makes me want to check out of here as soon as physically possible. I hope the bullet hasn't done any serious damage to my head.

Most of the folks in here seem to be in a sadder situation than I am. There is a man all bandaged up like a mummy in the neighboring bed. Further down, there is an older person with an IV and a breathing machine. After a few seconds, I stop looking. In a hospital, you can easily see something you'll later regret. But then something catches my attention in the distance.

It's Sara, my more panicky mom.

"Guys, I need a favor," I say. "One of my moms is approaching, and I kind of want to have a private conversation when she gets here. Why don't you go look for that doctor together? Or just walk around?"

Bert chuckles. He knows my real concern. He knows Sara's tendency to say embarrassing stuff. I can picture a whole diatribe about her 'baby' in the hospital, or something even worse, like a nervous fit.

With a curse, Mira slams closed the Gameboy, signifying her defeat, and glances in the direction Sara is coming from.

"Hello, Mrs. Goldberg," Bert says, getting ready to leave.

"Hi Bert," my mom says. "And you must be Mira?"

"Hi, Mrs. Goldberg," Mira says uncomfortably.

"Please call me Sara," she says. "You too, Bert, how many times do I need to ask you?"

"Sorry, Sara," Bert says sheepishly.

"Nice to meet you, Sara." Mira attempts to smile at my mom. "Bert and I were just about to go look for a doctor, to see when Darren is getting his X-ray results."

"Thank you." Sara gives Mira an approving look. "That's very thoughtful. Let me know if they give you any attitude."

Great. I picture a scenario where Mira is arguing with my doctor, and then, after sufficiently pissing him off, she unleashes my mom on the poor guy. If disgruntled restaurant workers spit in your food, can you imagine what an upset doctor might do to you?

"If they give us any attitude, I will crush their servers," Bert says.

"Albert, you will do no such thing," my mom says sternly. "People could die."

"I'm sure Bert was kidding," I say, giving my friend a warning glare. He probably wasn't.

"I will keep him in line, no worries, Sara," Mira says with a smile.

"Good, thank you," Sara says, apparently satisfied.

As my friends give me the Gameboys and walk away, I realize with amazement how calmly my mom has been behaving. Was it Mira's attitude that calmed her so?

"Sweetie, what happened? You were shot. Does it hurt?" The barrage of questions begins as soon as Mira and Bert are out of the room, and I curse myself for the jinx. My amazement was clearly premature.

I go into a new variation of the story. In this one, Mira is a new friend who happens to live in a bad neighborhood. The shot was just a fluke, the result of being in the wrong place at the wrong time.

"I like Mira. She's smart and very pretty," my mom says when she stops her verbal version of hyperventilating. "And she clearly cares about you. But you should have her visit you in the city instead of the other way around. It'll be safer that way."

I now understand why the freak-out is not as bad as I expected. I think the fact that my mom found me with a girl—something she's been nagging me about for ages—trumps my getting shot in her twisted version of reality.

"Sure, Mom. It actually just so happens that Mira and her brother will be moving anyway," I say.

"Good." She pats my knee. "Let me know if you need suggestions for safe neighborhoods."

"Okay, Mom. Where's Lucy?" I say, trying to change the subject.

"Your mother will be here soon. She just texted me. Kyle dropped her off at the hospital entrance and is parking. She'll be here in a moment."

I'm actually a tiny bit worried about Lucy coming here. I hope she doesn't play detective with me. She sometimes can't help it.

I keep those concerns to myself, though, and say instead, "Okay. In the meantime, there's something I want to ask you . . ." I pause, thinking about it, and then I decide to just blurt it out. "What were the last names of my biological parents?"

Sara looks taken aback for a moment, but recovers quickly. "They were the Robinsons, and your biological mother's maiden name was Taylor," she answers readily.

The Robinsons. So Jacob was indeed asking about my father, Mark Robinson. Does that mean my father was a Reader? Maybe even part of that specific community? I make a mental note to try to learn more about this. Maybe I can find a reason to chat with Jacob again, or ask his daughter Julia about it when she recovers. Perhaps I can even talk to Caleb, as scary as that option sounds. Also, Mark worked with my mom Lucy and Uncle Kyle. I can try to pump them for information—though, of course, they don't know anything about Readers and Pushers.

I see Sara wave her hand at someone, and it takes me out of my thoughts.

Following her gaze, I see Lucy approaching.

"How are you, kiddo?" Lucy says when she gets to my bed. "What happened?"

I tell her the same story that I told Sara and how I don't yet know the details but that my friends are trying to get a doctor, or someone, to pay attention to us. As I talk, I can't tell if she's buying it. Lucy is like that; you don't know what's on her mind when she doesn't want you to. Must be a detective thing. However, as I learned over the years, the mere fact that she's hiding her expression signifies trouble.

"You guys catch up, and I'm going to go try to find Mira and Bert," Sara says and walks off without giving me a chance to respond. Did she pick up on Lucy's lack of expression also? The idea of her joining the doctor search is the very definition of overkill. If someone is not back here in a few minutes, I will be extremely surprised. Images of lionesses killing gazelles and bringing the bloody carcasses to their fluffy cubs spring to mind for some reason.

"Okay, now tell me what really happened," Lucy says as soon as Sara gets out of earshot.

My mom the detective. She's the reason I can usually lie so well. As a kid, I had to take my lying game to stellar levels in order to fool Lucy. I'm usually very smooth at it, but that's when I'm not worried about head wounds and don't have secret societies I have to keep quiet about.

"I didn't want to worry Sara," I say. "So I simplified things a bit, that's all."

"I gathered as much." A slight smile appears on Lucy's face. "Spill it."

"The short version is that some Russian mobsters want my friends dead. Before you ask, I truly have little idea as to why. Suffice it to say, these same people might've murdered their family first."

"What are your friends' names?" Lucy says calmly. She's acting as though I tell her about attempted assassinations all the time.

I give her Mira and Eugene's last name and everything I can recall about their parents.

"I'll look into it," she says, writing something in a small notebook.

She can actually find out quite a bit. She still knows people in the organized crime division, including my uncle Kyle, who's probably on his way up here as we speak. But it's doubtful she'll be able to help much. The Pusher who's behind all this, according to my new friends, would be beyond a regular detective's capabilities.

"Just information, Mom. Please don't go after anyone," I say and finally get a full smile out of her.

"You sound like your mother," she says. "You don't need to worry. I'm in the white collar division for a reason."

"Someone reported a gunshot wound?" an unfamiliar male voice says, and Lucy and I look up to see a stocky policeman approaching. Great. The staff at this hospital can't be bothered to get me my X-ray results, but they managed to file a report about my wound.

"It's all right, Officer," Lucy says, pulling out her badge and showing it to him. "I'm already on it."

The policeman immediately turns around and departs, muttering something under his breath about incompetent Coney Island nurses, and I suppress a chuckle. There are certainly benefits to having a detective for a mom.

"There you are." My uncle Kyle enters the room at that moment. "How's the injured soldier?"

Uncle Kyle is not my biological uncle, obviously. He's not even my adoptive uncle. He's Lucy's coworker. However, he's played the role of my uncle since I was little, and I'm used to thinking of him as such.

"Hi Kyle," I say, sitting up so I can shake his hand. It's our thing. We don't hug—we shake hands.

"Kyle, I'm glad you're here. I want to check on this doctor situation," Lucy says. "Please stay with him."

"Of course," Kyle says. "Give them hell."

And Lucy joins the doctor hunt, which I would find comical if it weren't for the fact that Mira is involved in it, too. Having Lucy there is literally bringing out the big guns—though I doubt she'll draw her weapon on the medical staff. At least not unless they really piss her off.

"I heard there is a girl involved in this shooting," Kyle says, winking at me. If there's one thing I always liked about Kyle, it's his lack of smotheringness. He doesn't ask me how I got shot. He probably isn't all that worried about me. And there is something refreshing about that.

This attitude of his has served me well over the years. There are tons of fun, albeit unsafe, things a boy wants to do but needs adult backing to actually do. For example, Kyle is the reason I know how to hold a gun. It's the result of a secret trip we took to a shooting range. To this day, my moms still think we went to the New York Aquarium and would probably still retroactively give Kyle a beating for taking me to a shooting range instead.

"Yes, there is a girl. If you stick around, you might meet her." For some reason, I'm hoping that he does. Since when do I care what Kyle thinks?

"I'll try," he says, smiling.

"I have something here that you might be interested in," I say, reaching for the Gameboys.

When I was little, Kyle was my go-to video game partner. For all his faults, I'm thankful for the hours he spent playing Mortal Kombat with me. Ripping his head off, literally—well, the head of his character at least, via the Fatality move in that game—is one of my favorite childhood memories.

"I haven't seen these before," he says. "Is there a way to make it less blurry?"

Kyle and his lack of technology know-how. I'm forced to teach him how to turn off the game's built-in glasses-free 3D effect. That's what he calls blurriness. It's a sacrilege to not see this game in 3D, but I'm not about to get into a verbal fight with him. A virtual game fight will have to suffice. Once the 3D is off, he chooses his character—Donkey Kong, who happens to be a tie-wearing giant gorilla. I myself go for the cartoony variation of Link, my usual princess-saving character.

As he did when I was a kid, Kyle plays cheap. He chooses a move that works and repeats it over and over. In this case, it creates the rather funny effect of a dancing gorilla.

As I'm about to execute a cunning plan of attack, Kyle's phone rings.

"I have to take that," he says, pausing the game.

He picks up the phone. As soon as whoever is on the other line starts talking, Kyle's expression turns somber, and he walks away from my bed. Must be detective business.

I make myself busy by exiting the fighting game and checking to see if I can get onto Wi-Fi in this place. That would let me buy more games if I'm bored, which I'm bound to be when everyone leaves. Assuming I need to stay here, which I hope I don't.

"I have to go," Kyle says when he comes back. He looks upset. "Something urgent has come up."

"Aren't you Lucy's ride?" I ask.

"Yes, but she'll have to cab it. This can't wait."

"See you later. Thanks for stopping by," I say, trying to hide my disappointment.

As he leaves, I realize that boredom might come sooner than I anticipated. Wi-Fi is a no-go, though at this point, given my experience with this hospital, I'm not surprised.

Luckily for me, the fighting game has a mode where you can fight the computer, so I start playing.

* * *

I'm in the middle of a particularly nasty fight when I realize my bed is moving.

I look back and see a woman in a white coat pushing it.

"Where am I going?" I ask. "And who are you?"

"The doctor wants to have a private conversation with you," says the woman in a monotone while continuing to push the bed. "I'm your nurse."

I try to process this information. Why would a doctor need to take me to a private room to talk? How bad is the news he wants to give me? Or did my family and friends cause such a ruckus that there is going to be a 'tell Darren off' session?

We don't end up going far. There is a little office room to the side of the large hall. The nurse closes the door and starts preparing some kind of medication.

"What are you doing?" I say, trying to sound calm. I'm afraid of needles, and the stuff she's prepping looks to be a shot.

"Just something for the pain," she says.

"I don't need anything," I say. "I'd rather have the pain I have now than the pinprick of a needle."

She approaches me, smiles, and takes the cable that goes from my IV to my hand. She unplugs it and connects it to the syringe she's holding.

"See, no shot," she says.

"I still don't want the shot until you tell me what's in it—"

Her pressing the syringe cuts me off.

My heart rate picks up.

Did she just give me a shot after I explicitly told her not to? Why would she do that?

Suddenly, a wave of warmth begins to spread though my body, causing some of my worries to dissipate.

No, something is not right. I force myself to think through the happy, comfortable feelings spreading through me. It's beginning to be difficult to care, but with a herculean effort, I make myself worry again.

Maybe she wants to steal your organs, I tell myself, trying to come up with the scariest scenario.

Time seems to slow down for a moment, and then the noises of the hospital disappear.

I find myself lying in bed next to my other self, and I'm overcome with momentary relief.

I made it. I phased into the Quiet.

My head is now completely clear of whatever she gave me, and I'm determined to figure out what the fuck just happened.

CHAPTER TWELVE

I get up and look at myself. My frozen self's pupils are tiny, like pinpricks. This must be the effect of whatever drug she gave me, as her own pupils are the normal black circle one would expect in a well-lit room.

Fleetingly, I note the bandage around my head; it looks as ridiculous as I thought, but that's not what I care about right this moment. I'd be willing to walk around Times Square bandaged up like a mummy, if that would help me get out of this predicament.

I notice that not only do I feel free from the drug she gave me, but the pain from my wound is also nonexistent, as is always the case in the Quiet.

I walk over to the woman and look through her pockets.

She has a real-looking hospital ID, which is a good sign. She's an RN named Betty March. That's encouraging to some degree—she knows about drugs and how to deliver them. But surely they aren't allowed to force something into someone's veins under these circumstances.

Time to do a little Reading, I decide, and touch her temple.

* * *

"Your boyfriend will be seen soon. Please go back and wait," we say to the girl who's been pestering the staff.

I, Darren, realize that this is a memory in which *we* just spoke with Mira. She's without Bert or my mother, which means this memory happened a while back. Whatever I'm looking for in Betty's memories—and I'm not yet sure what that is— happens later. I decide to experience every moment from here to the present to make sure I understand why she did what she did.

As the memories go by, I develop a healthy respect for the nursing profession. It's tough. Finally,

I get to what I think I need. She's in the ladies room at the time.

We're sitting on the toilet, and time stops. There are now more of us in Betty's head.

The feeling I have is the same as the one I had in the head of that Russian gangster, the one controlled by the mystery Pusher. I feel the presence of another mind—a spooky apparition that has no gender or identity. It's just a feeling that there's someone else here.

Like before, the Pusher starts giving instructions. This time, though, as I follow the instructions Betty is getting, I feel a chill overtake my disembodied mind.

'Walk up to Darren Wang Goldberg,' is accompanied by mental images of where my bed is located and what I look like, plus a desire to help a person in need.

'Take the patient to a private room,' is accompanied by mental images and instruction that the doctor wants to have a conversation with the patient. A conversation that is likely going to upset the rest of the people in the room.

'Administer 10mg of morphine by injection,' is accompanied by images of a patient suffering, doctor's orders, and a warning about a patient who's confused and who might resist the shot.

'Forget the injection,' is the next instruction, and it is accompanied by a feeling of blankness. Of emptiness. A Zen-like state of not thinking about anything at all and being at peace.

'Take the pillow, place it on the patient's face, and hold it there.' This macabre instruction is accompanied by a whole mental story. In this story, the person Betty is to smother has been begging her to do this for years. He's suffering terrible pain that even drugs can't make better. Incongruently, feelings of hatred for the patient are also introduced. The Pusher's instructions seem to say that this is the person who beat Betty and put her in the hospital, the monster who killed Betty's little boy.

Although somewhat in shock, I manage to think of how interesting it is to witness the way Pushing is supposed to work. I mean, when I tried it, I did it intuitively, using only a very basic example of this Pusher's work. This is much more subtle. Much more sick. If Betty does what she's instructed to do— and I have no doubt that she will—it will be proof that Pushers truly can make a person do anything they want. The justifications given don't even need to make complete sense. Just some hook into the person's mind is all that seems to be required. Just provide any rationale, and the victim does what you mentally force them to do.

Morbidly fascinated, I let the memory unfold. With precision, Betty carries out each instruction the Pusher has given her. As Betty performs each task, she seems to genuinely believe the instructions and the back stories the Pusher provided. When I asked her where she was taking me, she was convinced that I was going to speak to the doctor. She wasn't being deceitful at all. What I find particularly frightening is that each step of the way, she seems to have only a vague idea of what happened previously. It's a lot like a dream in which things seem to make sense, but don't upon awakening.

It's likely that by the time she starts killing my drugged, unconscious self with a pillow, she won't even recall the morphine shot she gave me.

The full implications of my position begin to dawn on me as I exit Betty's mind.

* * *

I'm back in the Quiet with the knowledge that the Pusher is trying to kill me—that maybe he has already killed me.

If that dose of morphine was too much, I might die of an overdose before the nurse even gets to me with the pillow. And if the injection doesn't kill me, the suffocation certainly will. I don't doubt that the

Pusher knows what he's doing, nor do I doubt that Betty is going to do as he instructed her.

Why is he trying to kill me? Is it because of my helping Eugene and Mira yesterday? That doesn't fully make sense to me. If anyone did something outstanding to save Mira, it was Caleb. Or did the Pusher think I was the brains of the operation? That's flattering, I guess, but completely wrong in this case.

I can't think about this too long, though. Not when I'm uncertain whether I can still save myself.

A dozen possibilities run through my mind. Can I Push the nurse myself and override what my nemesis just did? But what if she kills me anyway? Or changes tactics? Or does it even faster? I don't dare trust my life to something like that. Not unless I first put something more surefire into play.

Exiting the room, I look around.

Jackpot.

Just outside the room is a mountain of a man. An angry mountain named Frank, according to his name tag.

I touch his arm and focus.

* * *

This fucking hospital is like a zoo, we think angrily. No one has paid any attention to Lidia for hours. We have to find someone in charge and try to talk some sense into them.

I disassociate from Frank's thoughts. His plight is familiar. This place is definitely a dump. From what I gleaned in his mind, his wife needs attention much more than I do.

I feel a twinge of guilt over what I'm about to do. Frank might end up in trouble. Plus, I will be messing with his mind—and he's done nothing wrong.

But self-preservation wins over other scruples, and I try to replicate what I did earlier today.

'There is a woman in the other room who needs help. She's having a seizure and needs someone strong to hold her down until the doctors arrive. Otherwise, she might hurt herself or others. Perhaps helping her will get someone to want to do us a favor, and Lidia will get help faster. It's simple: just walk in, give the woman in there a huge bear hug, and don't let go. If she starts struggling too much, fall on the ground with her in your arms. Lie there until the doctors arrive to save her.'

I work different variations of the same scenario in Frank's mind. Compared to what I saw in nurse Betty's mind, a lot of my instructions are probably redundant. But now is not the time to try to perfect my Pushing technique. I need to cover all the bases.

Hopeful that the whole 'smothering me with a pillow' bit might now be avoided, I leave Frank's mind.

* * *

Next, I go searching for a doctor.

If I overdose from the shot the nurse gave me, a doctor might be able to save me. They do it to TV junkies all the time. Maybe I need an adrenaline shot to the heart, like in *Pulp Fiction*.

In general, I read that it's rather difficult to die in a hospital if you have doctors around. That's why people sign those 'do not resuscitate' papers. They don't want to be saved under certain conditions.

But first you have to *find* a doctor. I run around the floor in the Quiet, trying to stay within a short distance of the room where my unconscious self is.

I don't find a doctor, but there is a young woman whose ID states that she's a resident. I touch her earlobe and focus.

* * *

Twenty-two hours on the job. We drink the espresso-spiked latte, but it's now as effective as chamomile tea when it comes to holding on to some semblance of sanity.

I, Darren, disassociate from Jane's thoughts. I'm wary of entrusting her with the mission I have in mind, given how tired she is. That she's here in this condition and expected to treat patients borders on criminal negligence. I don't have much choice, though. She's the only person I can use in close proximity to the room where my physical body is.

First, I need to pillage her memories for a solution, to zero in on a memory of a specific topic. I did something like that once before, when I was searching for memories of my biological parents in Sara's mind.

I decide to try the same method, only being more intentional about it. The topic is morphine overdose. I try to feel light, as if I'm trying to get deeper into someone's memories. At the same time, I try to think of ODing patients.

"Jane, you will want to see this procedure," Dr. Mickler says as we're half-running after him.

"What's wrong with him?" we ask, looking at the thin, pale-looking guy on the table.

"Heroin," Dr. Mickler says.

I let the rescue scene unfold. There was no shot to the heart as in the movie. Instead, they used a drug called Narcan, which has a Naloxone Hydro-something as an active ingredient. It's very promising, as it saved the guy from that heroin overdose, and his vitals were very bad.

I scan more of Jane's memories, trying to find information about this drug. I learn that it will work for morphine just as well as it works for heroin.

I begin Pushing.

'Get Narcan. Go to a room.' I provide a mental picture of the path to the room.

'Don't get sidetracked when you see the nurse having an episode there. She's being held by the police. The key priority is to help the patient the nurse accidentally hurt. She gave him 10mg of morphine.'

I play out different ways the whole thing could unfold. When I feel like there's no other path for Jane but to save me, I reluctantly exit her mind.

* * *

I feel marginally better now that I've done something to fix the situation. I decide to get back to my body, phase out, resist falling asleep, wait a few moments, and then phase into the Quiet to see if my unwilling helpers are beginning their assigned work.

I walk back into the room, touch my frozen self's hand, and hear the noises of the hospital return.

CHAPTER THIRTEEN

I feel great. I'm not even all that concerned that Betty is about to try to kill me. The only thought I have is that it's no wonder people ruin their lives taking this morphine stuff. It's pretty awesome.

Somewhere I hear a door open. I'm only mildly interested.

I see Betty with a pillow in her hands. This reminds me that I'm supposed to remember something, but I'm distracted by this strange itch that I'm feeling on my arm. When I scratch the itch, it feels amazing.

Then Betty lowers the pillow on my face.

My respiration rate is slower than usual from the morphine; a memory surfaces, and through my opiate haze, I realize this pillow will make it even harder for me to breathe.

Phase into the Quiet, that's what I'm supposed to do. But it requires me to be scared, which is hard at the moment, even with the knowledge that I'm being suffocated.

Suddenly, the pillow is gone from my face.

I hear a thud, which is supposed to mean something to me.

I make my best attempt to phase into the Quiet, but I feel like I'm floating instead.

My lids feel heavy. Very heavy.

I close my eyes, hoping this will help me concentrate.

Maybe if I snooze just for a moment . . .

* * *

I'm wide awake and completely sober.

Every hint of pleasantness from the morphine is but a distant memory.

I'm feeling sick.

Something is in my arm, something that's hurting me, so I rip at it. There is a moment of pain and then relief.

I open my eyes and see that I'm holding the IV.

In front of me is Jane, the resident I Pushed, who looks surprised to be there.

She's holding the other end of the IV cable I just took out of my arm; attached to it is a syringe. I assume the drug, Narcan, is in it, which means my Pushing worked.

On the floor is Frank, the guy whom I used to tackle Betty, the nurse who just tried to kill me. She's cursing and trying to escape Frank, but he doesn't let go.

I'm overcome with a powerful wave of nausea and get sick onto the bed.

After all the pudding and my morning smoothie are gone from my system, I feel a tiny bit better. Well enough to unhook myself from the monitor, get up off the bed, and get away from the mess.

"You might want to help them," I tell Jane and quickly exit the room, heading back to where my bed was standing previously.

The whole gang—Mira, my moms, and Bert—are standing there. Their chat is interrupted by Sara, the first of them to see me. She begins waving.

I inhale deeply, smile, and wave back at them as I approach.

"Hello," I say, trying my best to ignore another wave of nausea. My intent is to make it seem like I'm feeling much better, or in other words, to lie.

"What are you doing up?" Sara says instead of a greeting. I guess, unlike me, she doesn't feel like it's been days since we saw each other.

"I needed to use the bathroom," I lie. "I'm feeling much better, having walked a bit."

"That's good. Movement is life," Sara says. She likes to dish out such pearls of wisdom from time to time. I'd normally tease her about it, but I'm in no mood right now.

"Where is your bed?" Mira says, her eyes narrowing.

She's sharp, this one. I should've probably talked to her in the Quiet first. She's not the one I'm trying to fool right now.

"I think they're changing the sheets," I say, having no idea of the plausibility of this statement.

"Well, you'll be happy to know that we spoke to the doctor," Sara says. "The bullet just grazed your head. The X-ray shows no fragments of the bullet and no skull fractures. Those couple of stitches are all the damage done. You hurt yourself worse that time you fell off the monkey bars."

"Or that time you fell off the shopping cart in Key Food," Lucy adds.

"Great," I say, interrupting the torrent of embarrassing incidents. "That means I can check out when I want, right?"

"The doctor promised he really would come by to see you after lunch. He said that if you want to check out at that point, he'll let you," Lucy says. "I'd make sure you're feeling one hundred percent before doing that."

Bert clears his throat. "Well, dude, I was just waiting to say good-bye. I have to go. Work, you know."

"Sure, thanks for stopping by." I pat him on the shoulder.

"We actually have to go also," Sara says, looking at Lucy. "Now that we know you're going to be okay. But you should eat something. According to your friend—" she nods her head toward Mira, "—all you've had is pudding and some Jell-O."

I can't believe my luck. I was just about to invent a way to get rid of them, but they're doing it for me.

"Sure, Mom, I'm actually going to head into the cafeteria right after you leave," I say. "Mira, do you want to go with me?"

"Of course," Mira says. "But there's a better option. My brother is almost here, so we can take you to a restaurant, get you some real food. Afterwards, we can have you back for that conversation with the doctor."

"Great," I say. "That works even better."

In reality, food is the last thing I want right now. I'm still feeling sick. What I do want is to be far away from this hellhole.

"Okay then," Sara says, giving me a hug. "Albert, let's walk out together. Let Mira and Darren decide where they're going to eat."

I think I catch her winking at Bert as she says that.

"Oh, Lucy, Kyle had to leave, so you don't have a ride," I say, remembering Kyle's quick departure.

"Right. He texted me. That's why I'm leaving now. I'm sharing a cab with your mother." She smiles and kisses my cheek.

"It was great to meet you, Lucy... Sara... Bert..." Mira gives each of my moms a hug, and Bert a kiss on the cheek. Must be a Russian thing.

"So where do you want to go to eat?" Mira says when they get out of earshot.

"I'm not actually hungry. I want us to get out of here quickly, though," I say, and start walking toward the exit.

"What's wrong?" Mira says, catching up with me.

"I'm feeling pretty sick—I just didn't want to worry my moms," I say. "I need fresh air."

"If you're sick, you should stay at the hospital," she counters, but I keep increasing my pace.

"There's something more going on," she says when I avoid the elevator. "You're taking the stairs on purpose. You don't want to run into your family and friend on the way out."

"You're right. Can I please explain when we get out of here? Otherwise, we might get delayed by hospital security or something worse," I say. "I got into a bit of trouble. I want to tell both you and Eugene about what happened. He would want to know."

"Okay," she says. "Let me check on him."

We walk the rest of the stairs in silence, Mira messing with her phone.

"Okay, he's parked near the south-side exit," she says. "It's this way."

I follow her.

"You know you're very lucky," she says out of nowhere.

"I am? Why?" Spotting Eugene's car, I head for it.

"Your family," she says. "It must be nice to have people who care about you so much."

"I guess," I say, shrugging. "Though it can sometimes be a nuisance."

"People never appreciate what they have." There's a bitter note in her voice, and I wince internally as I remember that her parents are dead. Shit. I didn't mean to be so insensitive. I rack my brain for something to say as we approach Eugene's car, a Camry, and get in.

"How are you?" Eugene says, giving me a concerned look.

"I'm fine. Just a scratch. Please start driving—I want to get out of here. There's something I need to tell you guys."

In the moments that follow, I describe the attempt on my life. When I get to the part about the Pusher, Mira orders Eugene to stop the car. He complies, pulling over to the side of the road as I continue with my tale.

I don't sugarcoat my Pushing, even though I know that I might be losing whatever pity-induced goodwill I might've had with Mira. I hope she appreciates my honesty, though. I hope she sees I had no real choice in the matter.

"That's pretty insane," Eugene says when I'm done. His eyes are wide with shock.

Mira doesn't say anything. Instead, she looks like she's concentrating.

"Darren's right about the Pusher," she says after a moment. "The fucker who killed our parents was there, at the hospital."

CHAPTER FOURTEEN

"What? How do you know that?" Eugene gives her a startled look.

"I Split to the Mind Dimension just now, of course," Mira replies. "Then I walked back to the hospital and Read the people there. I had to see if I could learn something more than Darren discovered about our enemy."

"And," Eugene prompts impatiently.

"And I didn't find any sign of the bastard. Only that tell-tale presence Darren described in the woman's mind." She looks upset as she says this.

"But how do you know it's the same Pusher?" Eugene asks.

"I just feel it. I can't explain it," she says curtly, and I know exactly what she means. There was almost a tone of voice to the Pushing instructions I glimpsed in the nurse's mind—the same tone that I heard in the Russian mobster's head the other day.

"What did the people I Pushed think about the whole ordeal?" I ask worriedly. "Are they going to call the police? Do you think I'll be wanted for questioning?"

"No. The resident and the visitor have amnesia, as does the nurse," Mira says, her expression now hard to read.

"Amnesia is a known side effect of Pushing," Eugene explains. "If you get someone to do something small, something they can justify to themselves, they can internalize the story the Pusher gives them or invent their own reasoning, creating an illusion of free will. But when it's something big, something they can't fathom doing by free will, the brain chooses to forget the incident altogether. It's a type of defense mechanism, I guess. They either don't remember what happened, or have only a vague recollection. My father thought it was akin to alcohol-induced amnesia."

I sort of understand. The alcohol amnesia thing happened to me once. I woke up next to Jen, this woman that I couldn't picture myself being interested in, beer goggles or not. Yet apparently we'd hooked up, and she told me a story that sounded like it happened to someone else.

"Right, so you're off the hook," Mira says to me. "I don't think anyone is going to be questioning you for that."

"Okay, good," I say, starting to feel cautiously optimistic. "Let's keep on driving. Start the car."

"What if he's still there?" Mira says, frowning. "Maybe we should go back."

"No, that's a terrible idea," Eugene says firmly.

"I agree," I say. "Being nearly killed twice in one day is plenty for me."

"You guys are such wimps," Mira says scornfully.

"I am not," Eugene objects. "We're blocks away from Brighton Beach, where the Russian mafia hangs out all the time—and the Pusher has used them in the past. He can Split, walk over, find a lackey, and make him come kill us. In fact, the hospital is so close that the Pusher can just call them on the phone. For all we know, they're already at the hospital by now. I'm all for vengeance, but if we get killed, we won't get any."

"Exactly," I say. "I'm too sick from the drugs and the head wound. I need to rest before I take another bullet for the greater good."

"Fine." Mira blows out an annoyed breath. "You're probably right. So what now?"

"I'm going to stay at a hotel," I say. "They now know my name, which means they might know where I live. I'm not taking any chances. In your case, it's even simpler. They do know where you live, so I suggest you follow my example."

"That's a good idea," Eugene says. "They are really after us, so it pays to be cautious. Needless to say, give a different name when you book your room."

"Right. And no going to the apartment to get shit, Eugene," Mira says, and I hear her also mumble something along the lines of 'a couple of pussies.'

"Wait, I just realized I forgot some stuff at the hospital," I say, patting my pockets.

"Are you looking for this?" Eugene says, getting a gun from the glove compartment.

"I was actually thinking of the Gameboys I left in that room, but that's also mine," I say. "Where'd you get it?"

"Mira got it out of your pants before the paramedics got to you," he says. "I've been holding on to it."

"Okay, thanks," I say, trying not to focus on the image of Mira getting something from my pants.

We don't talk much more on the way to the city, other than my asking Eugene to stop near a juice bar. A beet-carrot jumbo cup of juice is all I want today. I don't think I can keep anything more substantial down.

As I drink the juice, we make plans, which are very simple. Keep our heads low for a couple of days, and then regroup. Mira suggests we don't use credit cards for the time being, and we all stop by a bank to get cash.

I suggest a hotel that I know is halfway decent, but they refuse, preferring to stay in Brooklyn. I decide to go to that hotel anyway, having had enough of Brooklyn, and we agree to split up.

After that, I doze from the sugar high of my juice, only to be awakened later by the sudden stop of the car.

"This is you," Eugene says.

Looking out, I see the Tribeca Grand Hotel—my destination.

"Thank you," I say. "Thanks for the ride. And thank you, Mira, for looking out for me at the hospital. I really appreciate it."

She leans over her seat and gives me a peck on the lips.

I get out, my brain too overwhelmed with near-death experiences to puzzle out the meaning of Mira's little kiss.

Operating on autopilot, I get inside the hotel. It's nice, but its grandioseness is presently lost on me. I buy some Tylenol and water at the hotel kiosk, take four pills, and hope my liver doesn't fail. Then I request the biggest room they have available.

As they're setting everything up, I text Bert the names of my biological parents and the phone number of Arkady.

On the way to my room, I get some ice for my head. Then I get in, plop on the bed, order some Pay-Per-View, and mindlessly watch TV.

The Tylenol and the ice make the throbbing in my head subside a bit, and the exhaustion really hits me. It's still early, but I don't care. I'm going to go to sleep early yet again. If I keep this up, I might become one of those early-bird people.

As I get in bed, I set the alarm for eleven a.m. I know I'm being overly cautious, given the current time, but I do it anyway. My shrink appointment is during my lunch hour, and this time around, I'm determined to make it.

CHAPTER FIFTEEN

I become aware of some annoying noise. It's my phone alarm. *Why did I set it?* I wonder lazily, opening an eyelid.

Then I remember. I wanted to make it to my appointment. All of a sudden, the whole thing seems like a drag, and I try to go back to sleep. I rarely, if ever, keep my appointments with my shrink, so why rock the boat? It's not like I need to express my feelings and get in touch with my emotions. What possessed me to even think about going?

But as some of the ideas why I *should* see her begin buzzing in my head, sleep eludes me. After a few minutes of just lying there, I grudgingly get up.

I order room service and check my phone. I have five missed calls from Sara and one from Lucy, so I call both of them back.

Yes, I'm doing better. No, it doesn't hurt anymore—at least not much. Yes, Mira is a nice girl.

Done with my moms, I see an email from Bert.

I'm using an app Bert personally put on my phone. Allegedly, the email sent through this app is seriously encrypted, to the point where even the NSA might not be reading Bert's correspondence. He's paranoid like that. If you ask me, hiding so much might actually make the NSA more curious about you, but there is no way I can convince Bert of this. In any case, as I read, I see that this specific email is among those that I do need to stay private:

Dude,

The guy whose phone number you got is named Arkady Bogomolov. He's extremely dangerous. Not worth fucking with, trust me, even for someone as hot as Mira.

As for your parents, I'm surprised. I'm not finding much. Lucy has a case file on the murder, but don't tell her I know this. Glancing through it, I have to say, it seems very shady how they died. No clues as to who did it. Lucy clocked an unbelievable number of hours on that case without any luck, though you probably already know this. Anyway, I can get that case file for you if you swear to never talk to her about it. There was this OB-GYN, Dr. Greenspan, that your mom was going to, but his digital records don't go that far. I tried my phone con on them, but, get this, the physical records were stolen recently. Weird coincidence. I will keep digging, but don't expect too much. Sorry.

Bert.

I write my response:

Can you find out more about this Arkady character? Particularly, I want to know where he can be found in the near future. I just want to look at him from a distance, so don't get your panties in a bunch.

Yeah, and get me those files if you can. I don't want to ask Lucy for them. I won't tell her about the files, obviously, since I realize that you're much too pretty to go to jail.

When room service brings in my breakfast, I order a cab. The breakfast order turns out to be too small. I wolf everything down and still feel a bit hungry. I guess not eating much and throwing up the prior day is good for the appetite. I wouldn't be surprised if I lost a few pounds. There's no time to get more food, though, so I guess I'll have to make do. The shrink always has doughnuts at her office.

As I get dressed, I realize the biggest problem with staying in a hotel. All I have is my prior day's clothes, which have been through a lot. Thankfully, they're dark, so no blood or dirt shows. I will have to go shopping, but that can wait until after the appointment.

Leaving my room, I grab a cab and make my way to Midtown.

* * *

"Darren," the shrink says when I sit down on her comfy office chair. "I'm glad to finally see you here."

"It's good to see you too, Liz," I say, smiling. "Sorry it's been so long. Things have been hectic."

Her perfectly plucked eyebrows rise in surprise, and I can't blame her. I don't normally apologize for missing sessions—nor do I normally call her *Liz*. She asked me to call her that a while ago. Just Liz. Not Dr. Jackson or Miss Jackson. Not just Doctor. Not Ma'am or Madam. Not Mrs. Jackson or Mrs. or even Elizabeth. But, of course, I very rarely obliged in the past, so I can see how she might find it surprising that I didn't do the usual—which is to invent a new way to address her that she most likely would prefer I not use. Like Mrs. J, for instance.

She now knows things are different today. More serious.

"It's fine, Darren. I knew you would come visit me when you were ready for it—when you felt like you needed it. And as usual, this is a safe place, so please don't hesitate to share whatever is on your mind—whatever brought you here again."

"Thank you," I say. "I don't actually know where to begin."

"You're hurt," she observes, looking at the bandage on my head. "That might be a good place to start."

"Yeah, I got shot, actually. Came face to face with my mortality and all that. It was bad, but it's not exactly what I wanted to talk about today. At least not at first," I say as I shift in the chair. "If you don't mind."

This gets me another barely detectable expression of surprise. Her face is hard to read. I suspect she's had something done that interferes with showing emotion. Botox or something like that. Or she just developed that unreadable expression as part of her job. It's hard to say for sure.

"Of course, Darren. We can talk about whatever you want." She crosses her long, black-stocking-clad legs. "Start where you want to start."

I look her over while thinking of what to say next. She looks like the epitome of a MILF mixed with a bit of sexy librarian. The latter is due to the stylish spectacles she's wearing. She's slender, but with noticeable muscle definition on her exposed arms, particularly around her shoulders. She must be hitting the gym regularly, and it shows. Her long hair looks like it belongs to a woman in her twenties or teens. She always dresses in outfits that border on hot, but still pass for professional. I have no idea how old she is; it's not a gentlemanly thing to ask. All I know is that she already looked this way—awesome and middle-aged—when we first met almost a decade ago. She hasn't visibly aged since then.

As you'd expect, I used to have inappropriate thoughts about her in my early teens, but it was just a phase. Nowadays, I sometimes suspect that the tables might've turned, and it's not just because of the cougar-like vibes she gives off. It goes deeper. There are little things. Like, for example, when I talk, she seems to genuinely care about what I have to say. True, it could be just her doing her job. In fact, a good therapist *should* behave that way. But I find it hard to believe that the amount of attention and the heartfelt advice she gives me is merely her doing her professional duty. Her attention to me changed as I got older—or maybe I just started noticing it at that point. Then again, it could, of course, be wishful thinking and conceit on my part; it's beyond flattering to think a woman of this caliber wants me.

Oh, and besides the way she listens to me, there's also the fact that I think she's available. At least I've never heard her mention any family, and her desk lacks any pictures of children or a husband. Then again, these sessions are to talk about me, not her, so it's possible I just don't know about her personal life.

"Have you stopped time recently?" she asks, pulling me out of my jumbled thoughts. "You haven't talked about that for a long time, something I consider to be a good sign."

"Surprising you should mention that," I say, considering my next words carefully. She just opened the door to the issue of covering up my blabbing about the Quiet. "I think I made a huge breakthrough when it comes to that. Sorry it hasn't come up before in our sessions, but yeah, I don't believe that stuff anymore."

"Interesting," she says, but the expression on her face is anything but curiosity. She looks almost upset. Or, more specifically, she looks disappointed and perhaps a tiny bit worried. It's hard to tell with the Botox or whatever. "What brought this on so suddenly?" she asks, gazing at me.

"Not suddenly. It's been a while now. I guess I grew out of it. Isn't that the way of these things? Don't your other patients go into remission? Get cured? Shouldn't you pat yourself on the back?"

I find her reaction odd. She's acting like she doesn't believe me. Or doesn't want to believe me. Is it because she's afraid I'll stop visiting? After all, that was the reason for my getting into therapy when I was growing up—my so-called delusions. But doesn't she realize that that's not why I've been seeing her since I moved out of my moms' house? Then again, how would she know that? I don't even know why I'm still visiting her, or why I have this standing appointment that I so seldom keep, but pay for. My shrink tax, as I always jokingly think of it.

She gives me a penetrating stare. "I think something else is going on with you. Something like denial, perhaps? Maybe you met a young woman and want to seem sane for her? Whatever it is, I'm very curious to learn more about it. Some people think mental illness is like an infection: take the right antibiotic, and you can be cured. The truth is that there's no such thing as mental illness to begin with. Just different people with quirks and traits, some of them maladaptive. When it comes to these problematic features of the psyche, we usually have to treat them on an ongoing basis. There are few silver bullets in my profession. Catharsis is a myth of fiction. But then again, yours was always a special case. My biggest question is: if you're cured, what are you doing here?"

"That's unusually insightful," I say, impressed. "Almost creepy. I *have* met a woman that I'm interested in, but that's not why I say I'm cured. As to your last question, I'm not even sure why I'm here. I guess I have some new issues on my mind, and I feel most comfortable discussing them with you for some reason."

As I say it, I realize it's the truth. The irony of this doesn't escape me. I'm someone who has always been a huge skeptic about psychology as a treatment for anything. In fact, I always doubted it on a deeper level, going as far as to call it pseudo-science, though never to Liz's face. Of course, the fact that I came for therapy today doesn't prove the earlier me wrong. I just think I'm here more to talk to someone who's known me for a long time and who's acted like she cares about me. Here I can talk about things that I don't think my friends and family are equipped to help me with.

"I'm flattered that you feel like you can discuss things with me. Maybe a big change has occurred within you after all. And I'm very excited to hear about your relationship," she says, sounding sincere. If my meeting a girl makes her jealous on any level, she's extremely good at acting happy for me instead. So good that I concede that perhaps I was wrong about that whole business of her wanting to sleep with me. Then again, wanting to sleep with someone is not mutually exclusive with wishing him a happy love life. There are lots of Victoria's Secret models I wish I could sleep with, but if I learned that they had a great guy in their life, I would wish them luck. I think I would, anyway.

"Yes, the girl thing is interesting, but that's not exactly what I wanted to talk about either," I say. "At least not at first. It's this other thing. I did something to a man to save her when she was in big trouble. Mind you, I was morally justified, but the thing that happened to the man as a result was very bad, and now I'm feeling guilty."

Therapy has this effect on me. I say things there that magically put me in touch with my true feelings as soon as I say them, even if I didn't fully register those feelings until that moment. The skeptic in me would, of course, say that this doesn't justify the institution of psychotherapy. He would point out that I could've probably used a pet parrot instead of Liz to bounce words off of in this capacity. Regardless, it feels good to talk to her like that.

"Okay. If that's what you want to talk about." I notice she stops writing in her notebook and is looking at me with an unusual intensity. I rarely express feelings this way, and something about what I said must've resonated with her.

"I don't know if it is," I say. "There are other things that happened. I witnessed something terrible, and my life was in danger a few times. It's all difficult to deal with, especially when I can't discuss it with my family."

"I see." She gives me an encouraging look. "I can tell you have a lot going on. Just start at the beginning and tell me whatever you feel comfortable talking about. Start with this man you mentioned. What exactly did you do to him?"

"I sort of *persuaded* him to do something that ended up causing him great harm," I say. This is the closest approximation of the truth I'm able to come up with at this time. Even this, once I say it, I regret. It's risky. What if the Readers decide to Read my family and/or therapist for some reason? They might understand what sort of persuasion I'm talking about.

"You *guided* someone to hurt himself?" Liz says in a strange tone. She sounds almost excited. It's not the reaction I would've expected at all. "This is very important, Darren. Can you tell me as much as you can about this event?"

Something is off. My heart starts pounding in my chest, and I phase into the Quiet to give myself a moment to think. Liz's reaction is really odd. Now that she's frozen in that moment, I see her eyes gleaming with very non-shrink-like excitement. I've never seen her react this way, and I've told her some crazy shit over the years.

Is this some weird thing for her? Does she get off on stories of patients doing something shady? That doesn't make sense at all. Doesn't seem like her. However, there is something I can do to figure this out. I haven't done Reading for a while, and now is as good a time as any.

In fact, there is some poetic justice in getting inside the head of your therapist. It could be a lot of fun feeding her insights about herself that I glean from her mind. But most importantly, I can find out what's behind this strange reaction—as well as maybe settle the whole 'does she want me' debate once and for all.

I approach Liz and look for a place to touch her. Though I have phased into the Quiet in her presence many times before, I've never used the opportunity to do anything inappropriate, like touching her very temping cleavage area—and yes, I was tempted. I've never tried to analyze why I exercised this restraint. It just didn't feel right to do something like that. Not with a person whom I told about myself doing exactly this to girls at school back in the day—actions she told me not to worry about because they were just mild delusions, a slightly exaggerated version of a normal pubescent boy's fantasy.

I end up going for a light touch on her neck with the tips of my index and middle fingers. It's the sort of gesture I have seen doctors make when trying to get someone's pulse.

As my fingers touch her skin, I instantly pull my hand away, my heart rate picking up.

A second version of Liz is standing in the room, watching me pull my hand away from her frozen double. As the avalanche of confused thoughts hits me, some part of me is happy her neck was the part of her body I opted for. Otherwise, this would be not just the biggest surprise of my life, but also incredibly awkward.

"Thank you," Liz says, smiling. "I was about to do this to you myself. I now have very little doubt that you are sane . . . and probably one of us."

CHAPTER SIXTEEN

I'm so stunned that I find myself in that rare situation where I have nothing to say. I just look at her—the woman I thought I'd known all this time.

As it turns out, I didn't know her at all.

As moments pass, I begin to digest the severity of this deception. I recall all the conversations where I described the Quiet, and she acted like a shrink listening to a delusional patient. All the therapy meant to get me to stop imagining something that she clearly had always known was real. In a way, the anger I begin to feel is akin to the way I felt when I thought Sara had been a Reader but never told me—and sent me to a shrink, to boot. This is the shrink I eventually ended up with, and Liz's deception is worse than Sara's would've been had my mom turned out to be a Reader. Liz actually pretended to be fixing a problem she knew full well I didn't have.

"I know you must be confused and upset," she says, obviously reading my expression. "Before you make a final judgment, please allow me to explain."

I try to get my emotions under control. It's difficult. I have had a Reader in my life, all this time, and she allowed me to think I was crazy. When I feel like I won't shout obscenities at her, I say, "Why did you wait for years to reveal to me I wasn't the only one?"

She flinches for a second. I guess she's not used to my voice being so icy.

"I had many reasons for this deception, and my choices were pretty limited," she says, looking at me. "In the beginning, there was a chance that you might've been a rare, truly delusional case. This has happened before. Also, you were young enough when we met that you could've been making things up for attention. When you showed off your power to me, by knowing things in my books, I knew that you were sane and that you could do what you said. But you still could've been a Leacher—which would've been a big problem. You still might be, though I doubt it. I just didn't know what to do, so I waited. When you just told me about the way you protected your new friend, I was about to take things to the next level—"

"A Leacher? What are you talking about?" I stare at her, my head spinning.

"Before I say any more, I have to test you to be sure. I know you essentially admitted that you Guided someone, but I still have to do this."

"I did what?" I give her a confused look.

"You have to do the test first. I will not speak another word until after the test. Follow me," she says and walks out of the room.

I follow. What choice do I have? At least this time I'm not at gunpoint during the testing.

"Her," she says, pointing at the waiting room receptionist. "Make her walk into my office and say, 'Sorry, we're out of doughnuts.'"

Have you ever had a car accident? You know that feeling just before the accident, when you slam on the breaks with all your might? A situation where all you want to do is hit the pause button on the world? This is what I feel like right now.

I had been convinced that she was a fellow Reader, which would by itself have been odd. But now I begin to understand the enormity of this situation.

"What do you mean?" I say, wanting to hear it.

"Oh, come on, Darren. You're smarter than this. I think you know what to do," she says, smiling. "And you know what I'm talking about, even if you're not familiar with the terminology."

"Since it's a test, I want to be sure," I say. "What exactly do you want me to do with her?"

"Okay then. Do what you did to that man you mentioned. The one you Guided to do something that caused him harm in order to defend your new girlfriend. You had your hands on him after you 'stopped time,' didn't you? You willed him to do something, and then you saw that he actually did it? That's what you feel guilty about, isn't it? Just do that again—only this time no one will be hurt, and Camilla will just walk into the office and say that silly phrase. That's all. Then I can be sure that you're one of us." Liz's voice takes on the same gentle tone as when she gives me all sorts of mundane advice.

Except this time she's talking about Pushing, not how to best deal with stress. This can only mean that I'm right about my suspicions.

Liz is a Pusher, so the *us* she just mentioned is other Pushers. Liz wants me to prove I'm one of *them* by Pushing her receptionist.

My head feeling like it's about to explode, I walk up to the receptionist.

She's frozen in an unnatural position while starting a phone call. I gingerly place my finger on her right hand, the same hand that's pressing the number dial.

* * *

"Okay, Mr. Davenport, I will reschedule your appointment for two p.m., Monday of next week. Thanks for letting us know," we say and hang up.

I, Darren, separate my thoughts from Camilla's. I'm here for a reason, and I need to do what I came here to do.

I visualize getting up, opening the door, and saying 'I'm sorry, we're out of doughnuts.'

Just to be sure the whole thing makes sense in Camilla's head, I add a story around it:

'The patient Darren requested a doughnut. He explained how hungry he is and how difficult it is to go on with the session without the treat. However, he's diabetic and allowing him to take the doughnut from the box that's sitting on the desk would be a bad idea. So let's walk in and say, 'Sorry, we're out of doughnuts.' The box can be hidden when he gets out. And it's okay to interrupt the session for this reason.

In fact, it's critical to get this out of the patient's mind, so he can focus on the rest of the session.'

Hopeful that my Push will work, I exit Camilla's head.

CHAPTER SEVENTEEN

"Okay," I say. "Let's get out."

Without waiting for Liz's response, I walk back into the office and touch my forehead.

The ambient noises of the office come back. Liz is sitting in front of me, her arms crossed in anticipation.

There is a hesitant knock on the door.

Liz doesn't respond. I don't either.

Slowly, the door opens and Camilla walks in, looking extremely uncertain. I find it fascinating to watch this. On some level, this woman knows that interrupting the doctor with her patient is wrong, despite the rationalization I placed into her mind.

However, she's clearly unable to fight the compulsion.

"Sorry, we're out of doughnuts," she says, looking at me. Then she reddens and runs back out of the office.

"That's very good," Liz says, putting her hands on the handles of her chair. She was clearly tense the last few moments.

"Will I get some answers now?" I ask, figuring that's what I should say. "Am I one of you?"

I have a dilemma. I know more than I probably should. I decide not to show it. If she's a Pusher who assumes that I'm a Pusher too, then she would likely react negatively if she knew I was a Reader as well. She clearly isn't the Pusher who tried to kill me— whoever that is must know what I look like. Of course, it makes sense that the first Pusher I would meet face to face would not necessarily be the one who wants me dead. There are probably as many of them as Readers—not that I know how many Readers there actually are in the world. Still, I need to be careful: Liz could know that Pusher.

"Yes, you are one of us," she says. "We call ourselves Guides, for obvious reasons."

Guides. That's much nicer-sounding than Pushers. "Because we can force people to do what we want?"

"Force is a crude word for it, but yes—though I don't like to think of it that way. We don't force as much as provide guidance for people to wish to do what we intend. It's not all that different from making a thoroughly persuasive argument."

Yeah, right, I think, but don't say it. What argument could I have given someone to take a bullet for Mira? But then I realize that one could say that the Secret Service agents have been persuaded to do exactly that for the President.

"What are some of the other things you mentioned?" I resume my questioning. "What are Leachers? Why are they so dangerous? Why did you think I could be one?"

"Let's talk more privately," she says and looks like she's concentrating for a moment. The next instant, I'm standing in the middle of our chairs, looking at her touching my frozen self on the cheek. Was her touch a bit too gentle, almost sensual, or is that my imagination?

The room is silent again, which makes me realize that Pushers can also phase into the Quiet and pull others with them. Not a huge surprise, but I can't take anything for granted.

"Okay," she says after winding up her watch. I wonder if she's concerned about spending too much of her Depth, or whatever Pushers call it. "Leachers are a group of people who can also 'stop time,' which we call *Splitting*. Only instead of Guiding people, they do something disturbing and unnatural. They Leach people's minds of information—which is the ultimate violation of privacy. Make no mistake, this is not the harmless telepathy you might've seen in movies, where a mind reader gleans some surface thoughts. No, Leachers go much deeper. They can ferret out every secret, uncover every desire and forbidden fantasy. No memory is hidden, no interaction is sacred for them—they can access it all." Her nose wrinkles with barely concealed disgust as she adds, "And yes, they're very dangerous."

Given how void of emotion her face usually is, her disgust is that much more striking.

So, as I was beginning to suspect, Leachers are Readers. Leachers are considered an abomination by the Guides, just as Guides—Pushers—are considered a crime against nature by Readers. This isn't that surprising. Two groups who hate each other will always vilify one another.

Until now I had the Reader outlook, and I assumed Pushers were diabolically evil. After all, one of them killed Mira's parents, while another one, in Caleb's memories, wanted to blow up the Reader community. A Pusher also tried to kill me at the hospital. Or have me killed. That Pusher/Guide was likely the same one who killed Mira's parents. So in my short experience with them, Pushers don't have a good track record. But *I* can do what they do, and I'm certainly not a lost cause. Liz being one of them confuses things further. She's a good person. At least I thought so before I learned that the Liz I knew is not the real Liz.

I also realize something else. Clearly, Pushers/Guides can't Read/Leach the way I can— she's condemning the Reading ability, in fact. Nor did she expect a Reader to be able to pass that test with the secretary. All this adds up to something I already suspected: I *am* something different.

I decide I'm going to call Pushers *Guides* in my mind going forward, since it's a nicer term, with the exception of the fucker who's trying to kill me. He'll remain the Pusher.

"Why are Leachers so dangerous?" I ask, realizing that I've been quiet for too long.

"That's harder to explain without going into some history. I have to warn you, no real records of the time I'm going to tell you about exist. A lot of this is verbal tradition combined with hearsay and conjecture," she says and proceeds to tell me a story, a bit of which I already heard from Eugene. She doesn't talk about how phasing into the Quiet works or go into Eugene's Quantum Mechanics theory.

Instead, she tells me something that sounds like an origin myth.

As she explains it, Guides and Leachers started off from the same selectively bred branch of humanity. It all started, as these things sometimes do, with a crazy cult. There were people who began a strange eugenics program. It focused on breeding people who had one thing in common: they described the world slowing down when they were under extreme stress and having out-of-body experiences in near-death situations. This breeding, over many generations of arranged couples, led to a branch of humans that could bring about, at will, something like a near-death experience for variable lengths of time—only back then, they thought it was the spirit leaving the body. After this point, the breeding focused on extending that length of time in the spirit world—what I term the Quiet.

Almost a century later, two new aspects manifested among the people who, at that point, could spend some minutes in the spirit world. Some could Read, or Leach, as Liz put it, and some learned to Guide, or Push, as Readers would see it. The cult split into two groups. At first, they just lived apart, but soon, each group started to view the other as heretical. There was a leader on both sides, and Liz's version painted the Leacher leader as particularly evil and responsible for starting the war between the groups that would go on for ages.

Later in history, one Leacher was advising Alexander the Great, according to some accounts—or, according to others, Alexander himself was a Leacher. In any case, in the process of conquering the city of Thebes, he destroyed almost the entire Guide community of that time, along with six thousand regular people. And this was just the first of the genocides that Leachers tried to commit against Guides, according to Liz.

"Do you now see why I had to make sure you weren't a Leacher—as unlikely as that possibility was?" she says when she's done.

"No, not fully," I reply honestly. "I mean, what happened in history sounds really abhorrent, but are modern-day Leachers so bad? Plenty of countries and ethnic groups have dark histories in the past, but now they're mostly civilized. Just look at Europe. Why do you think Leachers still want to wipe us out?"

"Because they tried to wipe us out as recently as World War II," she says harshly. Then, moderating her tone, she adds, "Granted, that is now also history. Personally, I just don't trust them. They view everything as wrongs done to *them*, and they'll never forgive and forget. With their skewed perspective, they'll always want to get revenge. Of course, there are many among us who feel stronger about this issue than I do—and many who are more liberal and think bygones should be bygones. You'll probably meet both kinds, though most of my friends hold liberal views. This is Manhattan, after all." She smiles at that last tidbit.

"Okay," I say, though the idea of meeting more Guides seems of questionable safety. "So why did you think it unlikely that I was one of them? If one can Split, isn't there a fifty-fifty chance that the person is a Leacher?"

"Actually, the chance is more than fifty-fifty in Leachers' favor. There are more of them than of us—which is why I had to be extra careful. As to why I suspected you were one of us, well . . . you *look* like a Guide. Many of us have the look I'm talking about. It's a certain facial bone structure, a prominent nose—the look of a born leader, if you will. Of course, these things alone are not very reliable. A much bigger clue for me was the fact that you were adopted."

"Oh? How would that be a clue?"

"Leachers have strict taboos about breeding outside their little clique. They shun anyone born as a half-blood, as they call them. We're much more open about it. It was even encouraged to some degree in the past, when our numbers were particularly small."

"Really?" From what Eugene told me, a Reader's power is directly related to how long one can spend in the Quiet, and having children with non-Readers seems to reduce the latter ability. I wonder if it's the same for Guides, but I can't ask that without showing that I know too much.

Liz nods. "Yes, after one of the worst genocides, we were down to just a dozen or so individuals. If we hadn't become more open-minded, we would've had serious inbreeding problems. Even now, our genetic diversity is fairly low. Of course, back in the day, our stance on having kids outside the Guide community was the same as that of Leachers. And to this day, there are some people—we call them the Traditionalists—who want us to have assigned mates. Fortunately, they're a tiny minority and are usually ignored. The only downside, and the thing that scares the Traditionalists, is that children born of such mixed lineage usually have diminished Reach. So, theoretically, if we keep diluting our gene pool, we might lose the very thing that makes us different."

"What's Reach?" I ask, guessing that she gave me a segue into learning about the power variation that Readers value so much.

"It has to do with how long you can freeze time, which impacts how deeply and for how long you can Guide someone," she says, confirming my suspicions.

"Interesting. So how long can you freeze time and how does that affect your control over people?" I say, wondering if Guides have the same taboo when it comes to talking about this stuff.

"It's not a topic for polite conversation," she says, confirming my suspicion. "But if you agree to keep it confidential, I would be willing to share. You have, after all, shared your life with me all these years."

"Sure, I won't tell anybody," I say. "And your telling me this only begins to scratch the surface when it comes to making up for all this 'therapy.'"

"Fair enough," she says with a wry smile. "I can spend almost an hour in the Mind Dimension, which is what we call this place where we are right now. When I use my power to aid in therapy, I'm able to get my patients to change their undesirable behavior for as long as a week—but my Reach is much less than that. I'm just good at getting people on the right track with my suggestions, so they continue doing what I meant them to for a while. This works out nicely, since my patients usually see me once a week."

"You use Guiding for therapy?" I don't know why that surprises me, but it does.

"Of course, the ability can be—and has been—used to help people. I'm one of the few psychologists who can truly modify a patient's behavior. That's why people value my services so much, and why my fees are so high. Other doctors can only boast of being able to do this. My Guiding ability is invaluable when it comes to treating conditions like OCD and other disorders."

"But in my case, you couldn't use it because you thought there was a chance you could pull me into the Mind Dimension?"

"Right. Had I been sure that you were just a delusional patient, I would've helped you, after you were old enough."

"Old enough?"

"We don't Guide young children. It's one of the ancient taboos that we still follow in modern times. And it's a good thing. From what I know about developmental psychology, Guiding a child might leave adverse, long-term effects," she says.

"What about adults? Are there side effects to Guiding?" I wonder.

"It depends on the situation. The way I Guide my patients is completely harmless and improves their quality of life."

I think about all this. The taboo makes sense. I can see a number of creepy reasons someone might have a rule not to touch children, even in the Quiet. And especially in order to mind control them. The therapy she does is interesting, though. I picture using Guiding to stop someone from obsessive hand washing. It wouldn't be hard. The person would just think his OCD is going away rather than that he's being mind-controlled by his therapist. And would it be so wrong to do this? Probably not.

"You know," I say, looking at her, "I would've thought a Leacher's power would be more helpful to a therapist."

"Perhaps it would be, but I wouldn't know," Liz says with a shrug. "To me, some of the usefulness of talk therapy is in the talking itself. A Leacher wouldn't need to talk to the patients as much."

"I have to admit, you're making me feel better about this power. Upon first hearing about it, I thought it sounded a little creepy," I say, watching her face to see if she takes offense.

She doesn't. In fact, the corners of her mouth turn up in a smile. "Yes, I could see how it might seem that way. That's certainly how Leachers justify their hatred of us. Our ability seems unnatural if you don't think about it deeply. That's mostly due to the misconception we have about free will. Specifically, that it exists."

"Do Guides think free will is an illusion, then?" As soon as I ask the question, I realize I made a mistake. This is a philosophical discussion—and those, in my opinion, have as little place in polite conversation as money, politics, sex, and religion.

"I'm not sure if that's a group-wide view," Liz says. "I, personally, don't believe in free will. I've read studies that have convinced me of this. People concoct reasons, after the fact, for behavior that's outside of their control. A classic example of that is how a person's brain signals an arm to move before a person is conscious of deciding to move it."

"That doesn't fully make sense to me," I say. "I like to think that we can choose what happens to us. Otherwise, if it's all outside our control, people can get fatalistic."

She laughs, ending our debate. "You know, you'll feel right at home when I introduce you to my friends," she says, still smiling. "I can tell you're going to get along with some of them."

She wants to introduce me to her friends? That could be a problem.

"Actually, Liz, I'm not sure how eager I am to meet any Guides besides you," I say slowly. Pausing,

I look at her, and then decide to just say it. "You see, I think a Guide is trying to kill me."

CHAPTER EIGHTEEN

"What?" Liz's whole demeanor changes. "What are you talking about?"

I give her a carefully edited version of what happened to me at the hospital. I describe the attempt on my life, and lie that my mom—the detective—spoke to the nurse who tried to kill me. I say that the nurse reported blanking out during the whole ordeal, and that my mom, who is a seasoned investigator, seemed to believe her. This is as close as I dare get to the truth—which is that my friend, one of the 'evil Leachers,' read the nurse's mind and found out that the woman has amnesia.

"That is very strange," Liz says when I'm done. "It's true that if the nurse had been Guided to do something so out of character, she would've forgotten the event completely. But how do you know that she's not a Leacher agent just trying to make it look like one of us was after you? Or that it wasn't a strange coincidence?"

"Even if she was a Leacher, she wouldn't be able to lie to my mom any better than a regular person, I would imagine," I tell Liz. "And coincidence sounds like too much of a stretch to me. I mean, how often do people just forget something that they did, unless they're under the influence, or on drugs?"

"That does seem suspicious," she concedes. "But in any event, even if you're right, meeting the Guide community would be your best course of action. Trying to kill one of our own is not tolerated. If some Guide did try to harm you, he or she would face serious consequences."

"Oh? What exactly would happen to him?" I ask, intrigued.

"I'm not sure. We don't have much Guide-on-Guide crime. Back in the day, someone like that would've been sterilized or even killed. Now, I'm not sure. I know that we wouldn't let this person be taken into the regular judicial system. Not given what we can do. Most likely, this person would either face the Elders or receive vigilante-style justice from our community."

The Elders? I vaguely register the term, but I'm too interested in the topic at hand to ask her to explain. "So you're certain I would be safe?" I say instead.

She nods. "Even if someone wanted to kill you, I can't think of a safer place than where I want to take you," she says. "Not everyone will be there, only the more open-minded folks, who also happen to be my friends. And I'll introduce you to Thomas. He was in the Secret Service, so if anyone can protect you, it would be him."

Secret Service? It's funny that I thought about that agency just a few minutes earlier. "Unless this Thomas is the person trying to kill me," I say, half-jokingly. "Then I'll have brought myself to him on a silver platter."

"That's impossible," Liz says. "He was a patient of mine, like you, so I know what he's capable of. He wouldn't have any motive to try to kill you, in any case. If anything, he would find you a kindred soul. You were both adopted—" she says, then suddenly stops. "I'm sorry. I shouldn't have said that. Doctor-patient privilege and all that."

I think about this for a moment. It's not so much her certainty of my safety, but sheer curiosity on my end that helps me make the decision. If I accept Liz's invitation, I can meet more Guides. More people who can do what I do. I can learn things that I wouldn't be able to learn otherwise.

"Okay, I'll meet your friends," I say. "How do we arrange it?"

Liz smiles. "There's a party tonight, and now you're invited. Every one of them is going to be there." Then, glancing down at her watch, she says, "We best get back to our bodies. We've talked for quite a while, and I don't want to deplete my time."

Without giving me a chance to respond, she approaches her body and touches her frozen face, bringing us out of the Quiet.

I find myself back in that chair, looking at Liz and unsure what to say.

"Would you like to use up the rest of your hour? And do you plan to continue with your therapy?" she says, her therapist mask back on.

"I think I want to go now," I say after a moment of consideration. "As to the long-term therapy, can I get back to you on that?"

"Of course," she says. "It's entirely up to you. I have your contact information, and I'll get in touch with you about the party later today."

I leave Liz's office, chuckling slightly at the sight of the doughnut box in the trashcan. I bet Camilla threw out some perfectly good food to stay consistent with her earlier lie.

My head itches from the bandages, and I shudder at the thought of meeting new people while looking like this. On impulse, I make a decision to visit Doctor Searle across the hall from Liz's office.

"You have to make an appointment," the lazy-looking receptionist says, barely looking up from her computer. "We're booked through this month."

The conversation with Liz has altered some of my perceptions. I don't feel as much hesitation about Guiding people to do what I want. Somehow, it's better than Pushing them. It's semantics, I know, but it seems to work for me. Without any guilt, I phase into the Quiet and make the receptionist realize that the doctor will indeed see me now.

The good doctor needs a similar treatment. Without it, he failed to see why he, a dermatologist, should be dealing with gunshot wounds. After he's properly Guided, however, he gladly takes my bandages off, thus expanding his specialty. I even learn that my stitches will dissolve and disappear with time—so if all goes well, there will be no need to see another doctor. I'm healing quite nicely, all things considered. I just have to be careful when getting my next haircut.

The mirror in the doctor's bathroom improves my mood another notch. There's a small patch of shaved hair around the stitches, but nothing too obvious. If I brush my hair more to the side, you can barely see anything.

With that taken care of, I'm off to Saks Fifth Avenue.

If I'm going to a party, I need to get some clean clothes.

CHAPTER NINETEEN

Wearing my new getup, I return to the hotel. The leather jacket I bought for the occasion is a touch warm, but I should make a good impression on the Guides I meet.

My phone rings, and I see that it's Mira's number.

"Hi," I say, picking it up.

"Hi Darren." She sounds uncertain. "How are you feeling?"

"Much better today," I say, trying to sound both cheerful and sick at the same time. "Thank you for checking."

"That's good," she says, now sounding more sure of herself. "I'm happy to hear that."

Mira is checking on my wellbeing? It's both amazing and difficult to believe.

"So what are you up to?" she asks.

Suddenly, it hits me. She wants to see me. She's just being coy about it. But I already have plans, and I know that I can't bring her with me. Not to this party, not with her attitude toward Pushers.

"I think I'm going to try to take it easy tonight." I feel like an ass for lying, but I see no other choice. "I'll drink some chamomile tea and turn in early."

"Add honey and lemon to your tea," she suggests. "That's how my grandma cured almost any ill. Well, that and fatty chicken broth, but I don't recommend that one."

"Yep, I'll do the honey and lemon, thank you. I'd like to see you, though, as soon as I'm better—which should be after a good night's sleep. Would you like to have lunch with me tomorrow?"

"Yes, I think I would," she says softly and somewhat out of breath. Her voice sounds almost sensual. "Let's get in touch in the morning. Okay?"

"Okay, I'll call you. Thanks, Mira," I say, trying to sound more confident than I feel. "Say hello to Eugene for me. Bye."

"Bye," she says and hangs up.

Well, that was interesting. All of a sudden, I'm less excited about the party. If I hadn't agreed to go, I could've met up with Mira tonight. I bet catching her in this weird, pity-inspired 'let's not kill Darren today' mood would've been fruitful. By tomorrow, she might remember how she really feels about me.

The excitement about the party slowly comes back to me during my room-service meal as I speculate on the different ways the whole thing might go. I am all ready and psyched again by the · time I get a text from Liz.

Where are you now?

I text her my hotel address. I guess I trust Liz with my life at this point. Then again, if something goes awry, I can always switch hotels.

The limo will pick you up in ten minutes.

Now I'm impressed. My therapist definitely knows how to get attention. A limo to a party is seriously stylish.

I'm downstairs when I see the limo pull up. It's a black, high-end limo, not one of those new Hummer-types. It comes fully equipped, right down to a guy in a chauffeur hat who calls me *Sir* and opens the door for me.

On the way, the driver doesn't talk much, and I return the favor. I only have time to drink half of my glass of champagne before we arrive somewhere in the Meatpacking district. I don't recognize the place, but Liz is standing outside. She looks stunning. Her usual office attire is already sexy, but it pales compared to what she's wearing now. I have to make a concentrated effort to keep my eyes above her neck.

"I'm glad you came," she says. "Let me show you inside the place."

We go past the long line and the huge bouncers as though we're invisible. I have no idea if Liz just used her persuasive power, or if Guides own this club and Liz comes here so often that the bouncers recognize her. We also don't pay anything, even though places like this usually try to get you to pay a cover or buy bottle service to get in.

We go down half a flight of stairs and make our way into the most fancy club I've ever been in. I am not a fan of clubbing, but as a guy who has to carry on conversations with girls in their early twenties, I have to at least know the names of the more trendy clubs. However, this one I'm not familiar with— which is pretty suspicious. Can the Guides somehow *Guide* NYC denizens to keep their club a secret?

We walk onto a giant dance floor, and I follow Liz as she navigates through the crowd and toward a different set of stairs. As we make our way, I see some Hollywood stars on the dance floor, plus an heiress who's been in all the tabloids and at least one Victoria's Secret model. Actually, the model might be from Playboy—it's hard to tell them apart. The heiress might've also been in Playboy, come to think of it. As to why I know what's in Playboy—well, I subscribe. For the articles, of course.

Once we reach the stairs, we go down a floor and find ourselves in another large hall. Only here, things are much quieter. It's a cocktail party, and it's full of people dressed in suits and nice dresses. They walk around leisurely, holding champagne glasses, seemingly oblivious to the anarchy happening just above. I see the Mayor of New York City chatting with the Governor, and at least a dozen CEOs from Fortune 500 companies. What is this place?

Not our destination, it seems, as Liz leads me through this room. On the way, I see more prominent government and business leaders whose faces I recognize.

We walk down another flight of stairs. How deep does this place go? I didn't think New York building codes allowed so many things to be happening in the basement areas. Then again, given the people I just saw, whoever runs this place knows people who can bend the rules if needed.

The activity on this next floor is downright creepy. It's a masked ball. A bunch of people dressed in cocktail dresses and suits are wearing an assortment of medieval-looking masks. I half-expect to see an orgy or some kind of pagan ritual. Did these people see *Eyes Wide Shut* one too many times? To my disappointment, this isn't our destination either. Liz just waltzes right past the masked people.

This is when I realize something. Nobody seems to notice us. They act as though we're not here. Has someone Guided them to behave in this strange manner? That's the assumption I have to make.

This new floor features a room that's noticeably smaller than the others. A bunch of people I don't recognize are gathered in the center of the room, listening to someone sing. More people are sitting around on comfortable chairs and sofas located on the edges of the room. The place looks like a cross between a lounge and a country club.

To my surprise, I recognize the man singing in the middle of the room. He's a famous blind opera singer, whose name escapes me at the moment. He has dark bushy hair with some white strands around his face and a white beard. I notice he looks a little fatter than I remember him being.

"We're here," Liz whispers in my ear. "Let's wait for the end of the concert."

The opera singer is a genius. I am not a connoisseur, but I find the concert extremely moving. Possibly my mental state at the moment—alert anxiety—is a good fit for this sort of music.

When the singing is over and my hands are hurting from enthusiastic clapping, I look around the room. And this is when I get my first shock. There is a man looking intently at me—a man I recognize.

It's my boss, William Pierce—or Bill, as I call him in my head and behind his back.

He waves at me. When the clapping subsides, I make my way toward him. As I walk, I see him look down at his phone and then look up at me with a smile.

"I don't know what to say," I exclaim when I reach him. On instinct, I extend my hand for a handshake. It's not something I do in the office on a day-to-day basis; in fact, I can only recall shaking his hand twice—one time before and one time after my interview with him—but it just feels right for some reason. It's like we meet for the first time again.

He shakes my hand with a bemused expression. "Darren, what a pleasant surprise. It's an interesting coincidence that you're here now, given that I just received the most interesting email from you about the stock I asked you to research. The write-up is outstanding, as usual, and it's particularly impressive given that you managed to send the email while listening to the opera with me. Great multitasking. Particularly admirable given that Bert informed me recently that you'd been shot. Most diligent, even for you."

I am so busted.

"Okay, Bill, I fess up. I might've scheduled that email to go out at an opportune moment," I say, figuring the fact that my boss and I are both Guides changes our professional relationship anyway. And that does seem to be the case—he doesn't so much as blink at my familiar use of his first name.

"I figured that much. In fact, I've been onto this little practice of yours for a while. But so you know, I actually appreciate it—the people you copy on those emails believe that you really are working your ass off, and it sets a good example for them. Along with mitigating the impression they have of you as a slacker. Although I guess that's not the most important thing to talk about right now, given the circumstances."

"Yeah, I guess not," I say. "Did you suspect about me?"

"No. If I'd thought you were one of us, I would've brought you into our community a long time ago. Truth be told, I always thought you were one of the other guys. You're so good at knowing things that I thought you were Leaching the information from the

CEOs and other execs I asked you to talk to. Seems like I was wrong. Seems like you've come up with some ingenious ways to use the Mind Dimension."

"You thought I was a Leacher, and you still employed me?" I say, surprised. "I thought they were public enemy number one in Guide society."

"I'm not sure what Liz told you, but we're not so dogmatic in this group."

"Right. She said that you guys are quite open-minded. But there's a difference between being open-minded and hiring your enemy," I say, genuinely puzzled.

"Having Leachers investigate companies seems natural to me. They can cut through the bullshit and just read people's minds. Direct and effective. Seems like good business to me," he says, his eyes crinkling with mirth. "If I could ask someone for that skill in the job application, I would."

From the corner of my eye, I see a girl approaching us. She seems to have overheard the last thing Bill said, and instead of being shocked, she's nodding approvingly. This whole thing is a huge contrast to Mira's hatred for Pushers.

"So you're the new guy?" says the girl, handing me her tiny hand for a handshake. She's extremely short and petite. I'd guess she's under five feet, even with high heels.

Bill graciously introduces us. "Hillary, it turns out that I have known Darren for a number of years. He was right under my nose, so to speak."

"It figures," Hillary says, furrowing the eyebrows on her small face. "You've had one of us working at your hedge fund, and you didn't even notice. People are just cogs in that financial machine of yours, aren't they?"

Bill sighs. "Please, Hillary, can we have one conversation without your Occupy-Wall-Street rhetoric?"

"It's very nice to meet you, Hillary," I say in an effort to change the subject. "What do you do?"

"I'm an anthropologist. I'm also involved with a couple of charities," she says, turning her attention from Bill to look up at me. Her big blue eyes twinkle, and with the yellow cocktail dress she's wearing, she looks a bit like a doll.

"Right, and she has nothing to do with the spread of veganism in New York," Bill says. "Or with the bans on ape research."

Am I hearing what I'm hearing? Is Bill being playful? I never thought I would witness such a thing.

"I make a difference for the better," Hillary retorts. "I'm sorry that what I do is something someone like you wouldn't be able to understand.

Certainly, protecting the animals isn't profitable. That's your favorite word, isn't it? *Profit*. Or is it *bottom line*?"

"Bottom line is two words," Bill corrects her, grinning at the annoyed expression on her face.

He's clearly pushing her buttons, and she's falling for it. It's a very odd exchange. If I didn't know that Bill is happily married, I'd think he was flirting with Hillary. Flirting in a juvenile, pulling-the-girl's-ponytail style. Something I learned early on they do *not* appreciate. And speaking of his wife, is she one of us? I wonder, but I don't feel comfortable asking at the moment.

Bill's phone rings. He looks at it, then at us, and says, "I'm sorry—I have to take this." And with that, he walks to a corner of the room to get some privacy.

"So you guys don't get along?" I ask Hillary as soon as Bill leaves.

"I wouldn't go as far as to say that." Hillary shrugs. "William is just William, bourgeoisie personified."

Politeness would dictate for me to say something affirmative about Bill's inadequateness, but I don't want to. In a lot of ways, I admire the guy. He's on a very short list of people I've always looked up to and respected. In fact, seeing Bill at this party dispels all of my remaining doubts about the Guides. If he's a

Guide, that fact, more than any of Liz's reassurances, tells me that they're not all members of some evil cult. They're just a group like any other, with good and bad types in the usual distribution—with the Pusher hunting me being on the scumbag end of the spectrum. Returning my attention to Hillary, I say, "Since I work for him in that hedge fund, what you say about him could easily be applied to me."

"Somehow, I doubt it. You don't look like the type. Besides, you didn't know your nature. Now that you do, you might change your profession to something more meaningful." She gives me a hopeful smile.

I think she means this as a compliment, so I don't argue with her. I also wonder what I would do if money weren't a variable at all. I went to work for Bill because I wanted to work the least and make the most money doing it, not out of some burning passion for stock picking. Would I become a detective like my mom, perhaps? I think I'd consider that, especially if the job weren't so dangerous.

"So, anyway, Darren, tell me about yourself," Hillary says, bringing me out of my musings. Her earlier smile transfers to the corners of her eyes, and the last remnants of annoyance disappear from her face.

I tell her a little bit about my life. I assume she'd be interested in my being adopted and discovering phasing into the Quiet on my own, so I focus on those things.

As I tell the story, Hillary's little face continues to be highly animated. Though petite girls aren't my type—at least if Bert is to be believed—I think they have a unique cuteness about them. If I had a girlfriend like this, I'd mentally call her Nano, like that iPod Nano I had as a kid. Back then, as now, everything was becoming more and more portable, and a pocket-sized girlfriend like this is just the next logical step.

Size aside, something about Hillary looks familiar to me. I can't put my finger on it, though. I wonder how old she is. Twenty-four? Twenty-five? It wouldn't be gentlemanly to ask. She could easily be older than she looks; it's one of the benefits of being that size. As I focus on her features, I become certain that this is the first time we've met, and yet there's something nagging at my brain.

"So what was that thing Bill alluded to? The vegan thing?" I ask when I feel like I've shared enough of my life, and it's only courteous to learn a bit about her.

She grins. "Oh, he's blaming me for the rise of vegetarianism and veganism in New York. He thinks that just because I'm a vegan, I go around nudging people to follow in my footsteps."

"Wow. I'm still not used to thinking this way. Can you actually do that? Guide a meat-eater to go vegan?" I ask, impressed by the very idea of it.

"I can, and maybe I have strategically done that with the biggest trendsetters upon occasion," she admits. "But my humble efforts are not the sole reason why things are moving in that direction in New York—and other places, for that matter. People are just becoming more aware of the impact of their diet on the environment, of animal suffering associated with it all, and, of course, the one that matters to them most: their health. With the spread of books such as *The China Study*—"

"Hillary, we're trying to make a good impression here, and your propaganda will not help in that goal. I have to borrow Darren, if you don't mind," Liz says, startling me by appearing right next to me seemingly out of nowhere.

Hillary opens her mouth, looking like she's about to object. Before she can say anything, however, Liz grabs me by the elbow and drags me to the other side of the room.

CHAPTER TWENTY

"I didn't need to be saved. I was actually quite enjoying Hillary's company," I say to Liz as we walk away.

"Oh, good," Liz says with relief. "That girl can be insufferable. Still, I want you to meet Thomas right now. Then you'll be able to go back and finish your conversation."

We approach a sharply dressed guy who's about my height. He's a bit broader in the shoulders than I am, which is something I don't see often. He's also muscular. Not steroid-big like Caleb, but he clearly works out regularly, like I try to do.

"Thomas, I want you to meet Darren," Liz says, giving the guy a thorough kiss on the lips. The kiss part is really odd. Didn't she say earlier he was a patient of hers, like me? I catch myself before I get more bothered by it. It's not like I'm jealous. Okay, fine, maybe a tiny bit jealous. Thinking that a woman like Liz was interested in me had been a pleasant fantasy—and helpful for my self-esteem.

"It's great to meet you, Darren." Thomas shakes my hand with one of those excessively firm handshakes that I'm used to getting from men in finance.

As we shake hands, I realize that he seems to be part Asian. What makes this stand out is the fact that everyone else in this room is white. And now that I think about it, all the Readers I've met were also white. I guess it makes sense when you consider both of the groups' histories. After all, they—or *we*— began from a cult that did that whole selective breeding thing somewhere in Europe, according to what I've learned from Liz. Thomas's origins must be a bit different. It proves what Liz told me: that this group of Guides will welcome you regardless of your lineage, so long as you are somehow a Guide. I wonder if this means they would be okay with whatever I am. I'm not going to risk them finding out, of course, but their attitude does give me hope.

"Good to meet you too, Thomas," I say, realizing I'm staring at the guy.

He doesn't seem bothered by my staring at all. He's just standing there, looking at me, seemingly comfortable with the silence.

"So Liz told me that somebody's trying to kill you," he says casually after a moment. "She said that this person is one of us, a Guide."

"Yes, unfortunately, that's the case," I say, almost defensively. The way he emphasized the word *Guide* made it sound like he was skeptical.

"Can you tell me exactly what you told her?" he asks calmly. "Liz didn't give me many details because of the doctor-patient confidentiality."

"I'll leave you two to get acquainted," Liz startles me by saying, and walks away. I was so lost in my thoughts that I'd almost forgotten she was still there. I note Thomas following the sway of her hips with a very non-doctor-patient look and file it away as curious, but unimportant for the moment.

When he turns his attention back to me, I repeat the story I told Liz.

As I go through it, Thomas asks me a bunch of pointed questions. He's obviously familiar with the investigative process, perhaps from his Secret Service job. Had I not grown up telling lies to my mom Lucy, the detective, I might've been in trouble. As it is, I'm not sure if he completely believes me. My mom probably wouldn't have. Unlike her, though, he doesn't know my 'tells.' I hope.

"I find it hard to believe one of us would do such a thing," he says when I'm done explaining about the attempted killing. "But in any case, you did the right thing, getting a hotel room. I would also suggest ditching your phone and getting another one, and maybe getting out of town for a bit while I look into this."

"That's a good idea about the phone, Thomas," I say. "I should've thought of that. As far as getting out of town, my family is here, and so is my work. Where would I go?"

He shrugs. "Take a vacation. Visit friends or relatives you haven't seen in a while. Though, if you want to be completely safe, you should probably stay clear of your immediate family for the time being."

"I don't think I like that plan," I say, frowning. "I don't want to stay in hiding forever."

"Well, if you had more information—"

"I might be able to obtain it," I say, starting to feel hopeful. "I can't commit to anything, but if I did find out more, do you think you'd be able to help me deal with this person?" I know it's a lot to ask, but I could really use someone like Thomas on my side.

"Sure." He hands me a business card. "Here's my number. If you learn who this mystery Guide is, let me know immediately."

"I will, thanks," I say, and put his details into my phone. By habit, I call his number, so that he has mine. When the call connects, he looks at his phone and grunts approvingly.

"You know," he says, looking back at me. "If this whole thing is true and you figure out who this Guide is, he or she will try even harder to get rid of you."

"I don't think this person could be trying any harder," I say, meaning it to be a joke, but Thomas responds with a stony expression.

"The attempt on your life was very subtle," he says. "Our ability, if misused, can be much more harmful. If someone tried to kill you without subtlety, every member of that hospital staff would've tried to go for your throat. It wouldn't have been pretty."

I picture that with a shudder. He's probably right. The Pusher was being subtle because he knew there were Readers around, and he was trying to keep his or her identity a secret. Had secrecy not been part of it, things might've gotten truly ugly. Then again, I can do what the Pusher can—and I'm reasonably certain the Pusher doesn't know it.

"Do you think there is a chance this Guide might be in this room?" I ask, because I have to at least pose the question. I don't think it's Thomas, since Liz appears to trust him, but the other people in this room are still unknown to me—Bill excluded, of course.

"No, I doubt it," Thomas says. "I know everyone here, and I don't think any of them are capable of something like that. Not to mention, they would have no reason to be after you."

"Can you think of anyone who *would* have a reason to be after me?"

I expect Thomas to say no, but he looks thoughtful instead.

"Are both of your parents Guides?" he asks.

"I don't know. I'm still learning about them, but probably not both of them." This is as close as I dare get to the truth of my origins. "Why?"

"Well," he says slowly, "when I joined this group, I was warned about the Traditionalists. I was told they might go after me—which hasn't happened. So if you're not a pure Guide, they could be behind this. Though in your case, I'm not sure how they would know about your heritage."

"The Traditionalists?" I ask, confused. "Liz mentioned them before, but she didn't give me much detail. Why would they want to come after you?"

"They're extremists who have some archaic attitudes about purity of blood, and they're against marrying outside the Guide community, among other things," he says with distaste. "In a way, they're like those inbred Leachers. So you can see how I could be their target. You can tell I'm not 'pure' by just looking at my face."

"I see." I have a growing conviction that I'm not going to be a fan of these Traditionalists, even if they're not the ones trying to kill me.

"I wish I could tell you more about them and why they might target you, but I know very little. Like you, I didn't grow up with this stuff," Thomas says, and I remember Liz mentioning that he was also adopted. Despite his stoic demeanor, he must see us as kindred souls, given that our stories are so similar.

I want to hear about his background, but first, I need to find out more about these Traditionalists. "Is there anyone I could talk to about them?" I ask, and Thomas nods.

"You can try talking to Hillary," he says. "She knows more about this than most of us."

"All right, I will, thanks." I wonder why the tiny girl knows about this, but that's a topic I'll broach with her.

Thomas looks at me, falling back into his silent pattern, so I ask, "What did you mean when you said you didn't grow up with this stuff?" Since I'm not sure whether Liz meant to reveal his adopted status to me, I figure it's best to pretend complete ignorance. I don't want to get her in trouble.

He hesitates for a moment, but then he says, "Like you, I was adopted. My parents didn't tell me this until I was six years old." As he says this, I catch a glimmer of some emotion behind his expressionless mask.

"That's amazing," I say. "This is something we share. Well, almost. I guess the difference is that I always thought I had one biological parent, Sara. I assume you learned that both your parents were adoptive?"

"Yes," he says. "They told me a woman gave me to them. A woman they'd never met before or after the adoption. Someone whose identity I was never able to discover."

There seems to be a deep sadness to that part of the story. He clearly yearns to know more about his origins. I can relate, but I don't want to share my version of this story. Not if I have to reveal the names of my parents. So instead I say, "What about your abilities? Did you, like me, discover what you can do on your own?"

"Yes. It was during a car accident that I discovered that I was able to stop time—what everyone here calls Splitting into the Mind Dimension."

"For me, it was a bike accident," I say, smiling. "And I called it the Quiet."

Thomas returns my smile. "Did you also Guide someone on your own?" he asks. "I called it Hypnotizing."

"No. The first time I was able to do that deliberately was today, when Liz decided to test me to see if I'm a Guide," I say. "You discovered it on your own?"

"Yeah, it happened during a fight. I got into a lot of those as a kid," he says, his eyes getting a faraway, nostalgic look. "I stopped time to practice punching the bully I was fighting. As I was practice-hitting him in that mode, I also really willed him to trip. He was much bigger, and getting him on the ground was my only chance to walk away without some serious damage. Afterwards, he did trip. I, being a kid, wondered if that was because I'd willed it so hard. So the next time I got into a fight, I tried to repeat that trick. I did it during other fights until one day, I realized that I could do more than just make people fall over."

"Oh, I am so jealous," I say earnestly. "The fun I could've had if I'd discovered this as a kid."

"It only sounds fun in theory," he says seriously. "I thought I was completely insane."

"Ah, I was about to ask how it happened that you know Liz also."

"Well, before I was able to Guide people, I tried telling my parents about time stopping—"

"I did that too," I interrupt, excited.

"Right. So the result was probably the same too. They took me to see a psychiatrist," he says.

"Yep," I say, nodding my head.

"Did Liz tell you how in cases like ours, all roads lead to her?" he asks, glancing in her direction.

"No, she didn't. Are you saying I was led to Liz on purpose?"

Thomas smiles again. "This is how it works," he says. "She made herself known as an expert on the exact sort of 'delusional symptoms' someone like us might report. She wrote a few articles on the step-outside-the-world delusion, giving this phenomenon a psychobabble explanation, something about it being a way for some intelligent and slightly-too-introspective kids to cope with the world going too fast around them. So after a few doctors didn't know what to do with me, they referred me to her, the expert. The same thing happened to you, I bet."

"That's exactly what happened, yes."

"I think that happens to pretty much anyone in our situation in NYC—not that our situation is common, of course. Once I met Liz, and once I shared my Guiding experiences with her, she brought me into this world," he says, waving his hand in a gesture meant to encompass the whole room.

"Okay, I'm even more jealous now. Just to think, had I not avoided getting into fights, I would've discovered Guiding and joined this community much earlier in my life," I say.

"You don't want to have had my childhood." Thomas's face darkens. "Trust me, you wouldn't have wanted to join the Guides at that price."

"I'm sorry. I didn't mean to trivialize. I'm just saying it must've been cool to know what you are and that you weren't crazy. Besides, I bet eventually the bullies had to leave you alone."

"They did," he says curtly. I have a feeling some bullies of Thomas's past got a lot more than they bargained for. Good for him. Hell, if people stop trying to kill me for a few days, I'm tempted to make the time to find John, my own childhood nemesis. Now that I can Guide, he might get the urge to literally go fuck himself.

"It was nice to know I wasn't insane," Thomas says in a lighter tone when I remain silent. "I guess you had it tough in your own way. But hey, all's well that ends well, right?"

"Exactly," I say, happy that the topic is getting less sinister. I'm about to say more, but I notice Liz making her way back to us.

"Can you guys continue this later?" she says, sipping a pink drink. "I still need to introduce Darren to everyone, and since I have to leave early today, I'd like to get that task out of the way."

"Of course. I have to leave anyway," Thomas says.

"Okay, I'll give you a call, and maybe we can do coffee in a few days," I say.

"Sounds like a plan," he agrees with a smile.

"Okay, now that you have a man date, let's go," Liz says teasingly. Seeing my shrink joking and clearly buzzed is weird, to say the least.

As we walk away, she takes me by the arm and leads me around, introducing me to the people in the room.

I'm terrible with names, so I hope there isn't a quiz later, because I would fail it. I do notice a pattern, though. We all have some facial features in common, in the way Liz alluded to earlier. And whatever it is, I haven't noticed it with Readers. All these people seem rather interesting in their own ways, and I hope that with time, I'll get to know all of them.

What I also notice is that no one seems to be displaying any animosity toward me. So either my nemesis is an excellent actor, or the Pusher from the hospital isn't here.

The whole thing is beyond tiring. Maybe it's all that going-to-bed-early stuff from the last two days messing up my circadian rhythm, or maybe I'm still not fully recovered from my injury. Whatever it is, I'm beginning to get a serious craving for my bed back at the hotel.

Hillary is the last stop on this intro-tour. "See, I promised I'd give him back to you," Liz says to Hillary, smiling. "He's all yours to brainwash. Now, if you'll excuse me, I have some business to take care of."

"I heard you might know about something I find kind of interesting," I say to Hillary when Liz is gone.

"Sure, what is it?" she asks, grinning at me.

"I was hoping you could tell me about the Traditionalists," I say.

Her grin disappears without a trace. "You're new, Darren, so you don't know that this is a sensitive subject for me. But it is, and I'm sorry, but I don't want to talk about it," she says, her voice unusually harsh.

"Oh, I'm sorry. I didn't know that. Let's talk about something else." I feel like an oaf. Her face is so expressive that upsetting her just feels wrong. Like being mean to a little girl. It must be her petiteness messing with my brain.

"Do you want to get out of here?" she says consolingly. "I'm starving, and they never have anything edible."

I don't point out the large buffet filled to the brim with choice finger foods and consider this for a moment. I'm tired, but something about Hillary makes me want to get to know her better. I'm not sure what it is. It's almost as though there's some kind of connection between us.

"I'm game, but I have an errand to run on the way. Do you mind if I stop by the Apple store for a minute? They're open late, and I urgently need to get a new phone."

"No problem." She grins at me. "Let's go."

CHAPTER TWENTY-ONE

As we get out of the cab, I finish texting everyone my new phone number.

The place we end up is one that Hillary describes as a raw vegan restaurant. She swears it will be the best meal I've had in years, but as I look at the menu, I'm rather skeptical. As expected, they have many salads, but I'm surprised to find that they have other options as well.

"I guess I'll order coconut water for now," I say to the dreadlocked waiter who smells suspiciously like weed.

"That's an excellent choice, full of electrolytes. It's very good for you," Hillary says, smiling. "I'll have the same."

"I'll also get the spiral zucchini pasta with cashew-nut Alfredo sauce," I say hesitantly. This is the most promising-sounding dish on the menu, but that's not saying much.

"You should leave room for dessert. They're amazing here," Hillary says, ordering her own choice: a kale salad with honey-glazed pecans, plus guacamole with 'live chips'—whatever that is.

"So what did you think about our little community?" she says when the waiter leaves.

"They seem like good people," I answer honestly. "I can't wait to get to know everyone better."

"They are good people. I wish the rest of the Guides were more like them," she says, almost wistfully.

I figure she must be talking about the Traditionalists, but I don't press her, given her earlier reaction. Instead I say, "Yeah, I know what you're saying. Some Guide is trying to kill me."

"Kill you?" She looks stunned. "Why? How do they even know you exist?"

I share as much as I can for the umpteenth time today, telling her the same story I told Liz and Thomas. "So you see, someone is trying to kill me, but I have no idea how they know that I exist."

"Is that why you were asking about the Traditionalists?"

"Yeah, Thomas said it sounded like something they might do, and he said that you were the best person to ask about it," I say carefully.

"Then I guess you had a good reason to ask before. But I don't understand why they would want to hurt you. I mean, with Thomas, I can see it, but you . . ." She narrows her eyes, studying me intently.

"I don't know why he made that guess," I say, not wanting to raise the question of my heritage. "Maybe he was wrong."

"Maybe," she says. "I guess I can tell you what I know, in case it helps."

"That would be great."

She squares her shoulders. "Okay, to get a sense for the Traditionalists, try this thought experiment. Take the close-mindedness of any sort of extreme fundamentalist, add eugenics, dogma, fear of the unknown, and mix in an overwhelming, blind, and bigoted hatred of the Leachers."

"Okay. I'm picturing this and not liking the results."

"Well, that's just step one. Step two: now imagine growing up with people like that as parents," she says somberly.

I blink. "Oh, is that why—?"

"Yeah, that's why I was touchy earlier. But don't worry about it. You didn't know."

"Still, I'm sorry I upset you."

"It's okay. My folks are probably not even the worst of what's out there. Yes, they're obsessed with fear of exposure to regular people. And, yes, they're afraid of new technology or—more correctly—of progress of any kind. Oh, and if they had their way, life today would be like the good old days of yesteryear that I suspect never existed in the first place. All of those things are true, but even with all those things in mind, I don't think my parents would go as far as trying to Guide someone to kill anyone."

She stops talking and looks thoughtful. Is she wondering if she just told the truth? If her parents might be capable of murder in the name of their beliefs? I guess this topic is off the table for the time being.

Food and drinks arrive just in time to fill the silent moment we're having. She starts wolfing down her chips with the guacamole and offers me some.

"This is surprisingly good," I say, trying the chips. Apparently, they were made in a dehydrator, which slowly dried them without officially cooking them. That doesn't sound very 'raw' to me, but they taste a lot like corn chips, so I'm not going to complain. My own dish of the pseudo-spaghetti made from zucchini is also pretty good, though it has as much in common with the real thing as a hot dog with a real canine. I taste the drink too, like it, and tell Hillary, "This coconut water is different from the stuff I've gotten before."

"Of course, you probably got the one from the can," she says, and starts eating her salad. Her hands are so small that the fork looks big in them.

I wonder how Hillary and her friends would react to knowing the truth about me, so to test the waters, I ask, "The way you talked about the Traditionalists hating Leachers before, you made it sound like the rest of your community likes them."

"Compared to the Traditionalists, we're practically in love with them, sure," she says, spearing another bite of salad with her fork.

"Hmm, but I thought, at least from talking to Liz, that Leachers are to be avoided," I say, pushing the inquiry further. I hope she doesn't find the topic suspicious. I really want to find out how much danger I'd be in if my fellow Guides learned about my Reading abilities.

"I don't know about Liz, but I, personally, don't hate the Leachers. Not even a little bit," she says, giving me a guileless look. "In fact, I'm curious about them."

"Oh. And is that a common view?"

"No. Mine is probably a rare attitude. The rest of the group would consider me weird, even though they're pretty liberal. Even outside the Traditionalists, most Guides dislike Leachers with a passion."

"Is it because of the genocides?" I ask, remembering Liz's history lesson.

"Yeah, that's part of it. Bad history does that to groups. But there's more to it. It's widely believed that Leachers still, to this day, actively hate us—so disliking them back seems like a natural response," she says.

"But *you* don't," I clarify.

"Well, I wouldn't go as far as seeking them out. I agree that it's wise to avoid Leachers. Not because I believe they're evil, but because I think some of them may have the same 'us versus them' mentality that a lot of Guides do, even outside the Traditionalist clique."

"So we're supposed to dislike them because they hate us, and avoid them for the same reason. If they apply the same logic, isn't that a Catch-22?"

"You're a man after my own heart," Hillary says with a smile. "That's actually a pet peeve of mine, and I think you verbalized it perfectly. The entire human race has this tendency—the inclination to cling to their own group. This obsession with sub-dividing ourselves is responsible for practically every evil in the world. Everyone fails to see that the hatred between our people is just another example in a series of these meaningless feuds. They all start with people who are extremely alike, and then a tiny difference creeps in, and people separate along that difference, after which insanity ensues. Sooner or later, you get that 'we hate you because you hate us' deadlock, or worse."

"Wow, you really have given it some thought," I say, impressed.

"How could I not? It's so obvious. Take anything arbitrary, like skin color, income, politics, religion, nationality, or in this case, types of powers. You name it, and at some point, people find a way to separate over that arbitrary trait—and some become willing to kill over it. Once that thinking sets in, the groups start thinking of one another as less than human, which further justifies all manner of atrocities. The whole cycle is so pointless that I sometimes want to give up." She sighs. "But I don't. Instead, to quote a wise man, 'I try to be the change I'd like to see in the world.'"

"I wonder what Gandhi would've said about all this," I say, sipping my drink. "And, for what it's worth, I'm not racist, sexist, or any other *ist* myself.

In fact, since I didn't grow up with these stories about Leachers, I don't plan on hating them either. Like you, I'm curious about them, so I don't think you're weird at all."

"Thank you," she says, rewarding me with a wide, white-toothed grin. "You know, even though we just met, I feel like I know you already. Like I can trust you. But I don't know why. Is that strange?"

"No. I know what you mean," I say, and I do. It actually *is* strange. I'm drawn to this girl, but not in the way I'm usually drawn to pretty girls. It's more that I just like her.

She grins at me. "Good. I'm glad we're on the same page. And about your troubles . . . If you need help dealing with whoever's after you, I'd be glad to be of assistance."

I suppress a smile as I imagine her swinging her tiny fists in a fight. "Thank you, Hillary. I really appreciate the sentiment."

"But you don't think I can be of help," she guesses astutely. "Why? Because of my height?"

"No," I lie. "Because you seem so peaceful. I would've pegged you for a pacifist." I learned long ago that if a woman asks you a question pertaining to her size, you have to say whatever she wants to hear, and quickly. A special case of this rule is the dreaded 'does this make me look fat' question. The answer to that is always NO.

"You're right," Hillary says. "I'm not a violent person, but my Reach is probably the longest in our group." She flushes a bit as she says this last part, and I remember Liz telling me that this subject—the measure of a Guide's power—is considered impolite among them. I guess Hillary just told me the equivalent of her bra size or something along those lines.

"Your Reach?" I ask, looking at her. Liz explained the concept a bit, but I want to understand it better.

Hillary nods, her cheeks still pink. "Yes. Your Reach determines how much, how deeply, and for how long you can Guide a person. Mine is so great because all of my ancestors, including my parents and grandparents, adhered to the barbaric custom of breeding for this quality. In fact, had I been a good girl and mated with whomever I was told, my children might've grown up to become the Elders."

"Okay, brain overload," I say. "How can you Guide someone 'deeper'? And what are the Elders?"

"The quick version about Reach is this: let's say you Guide someone, and then let's presume I come along and I want to Guide them away from your course of action. Reach differences will determine my success."

"So even if I program someone, if you're more powerful than I am, you can reprogram them?"

"We never use such a derogatory term, but you got the gist of it, yes," she says. "And the Elders are those Guides who can spend lifetimes in the Mind Dimension. I don't know much about them. The rumors say that they live in the Mind Dimension together, each one taking a driver's seat pulling others into a weird community that, for all intents and purposes, exists outside time."

I stare at her, fascinated. "That's incredible."

"Yes, it is—although it freaks me out a bit. I find it difficult to imagine even talking to one of the Elders. Just think about it. In the time it takes you to blink, they can Split into the Mind Dimension, join their friends, and live a lifetime of experiences together. It boggles my mind, and I like my mind's equilibrium."

She's right. It's difficult to comprehend what she's describing. In a nutshell, it's life extension—and I find it beyond cool. I'd like to try living in the Quiet for a long time with a bunch of friends, or hopefully even with a girlfriend.

"So, anyway, back to Reach," Hillary says, pulling me out of my excited imaginings. "Mine is quite formidable, which means that if that Guide tries to use civilians to kill you, I could override his or her directive, provided I got involved in time."

"That would be amazing," I say, impressed. "I really appreciate it, Hillary. Here, let me get your phone number." I hand her my new phone. One of the 'Geniuses' at the Apple store transferred all my contacts, and it's as though I've had this phone for ages.

She inputs her number and hands it back to me. "I put my name there, but you can write in a nickname, like you seem to do with everyone else."

I take the phone back, vaguely embarrassed that she saw the nickname stuff. It's this thing I do. I come up with ridiculous nicknames for everyone, and then have fun with voice dial. Her nickname is going to be Tinker Bell. Imagining saying the words 'call Tinker Bell's cell phone' in a crowded bus is my kind of fun.

I look at the screen and see the words *Hillary Taylor* written there, along with the phone number. I decide that the nickname can be added later. For now, I dial her number, so that she has my contact info as well. It's when the phone is dialing that it hits me.

Taylor.

Sarah told me that my mom's maiden name was Margret *Taylor*.

No.

It can't be.

Can it?

It *is* a small community. How many namesakes can there be?

"Are you an only child, Hillary?" I ask, not fully thinking of the consequences of this line of questioning.

She looks stunned by my question. "Yes. No. Sort of. I had an older sister a long time ago, but she's dead. Why do you ask? And why do you look so shocked?"

Her sister.

Older . . . likely much older, given that Hillary looks to be only in her mid-twenties.

An older sister who's dead.

It has to be.

I can't believe it—but the resemblance is there.

With hindsight, that's what's been fascinating me about her face. We have the exact same shade of blue eyes. The same chin, similar cheekbones, and her nose is a miniature, feminine version of mine. Aside from the big height difference, we look like we could be related—and now I know why.

Because we are.

"I think you're my aunt, Hillary," I blurt out, unable to suppress my excitement.

CHAPTER TWENTY-TWO

The look on Hillary's face would be comical if it weren't for the fact that I'm feeling exactly like she looks.

"I found out today that my biological mother's name was Margret, and her last name was Taylor, like yours," I explain, my heart pounding with excitement.

She looks me over, and I see the dawning recognition on her face. She must've noted the resemblance also.

"But—" she starts, then swallows, staring at me. "This is such a shock. You have to forgive me."

"Yeah, I'm still kind of digesting it also."

"Margie had a child?"

"She must have," I say. "If I'm right, that is."

"But that can't be. Margie died more than twenty years ago. This has to be some kind of a mistake."

I just sit there and let her ruminate on it.

"You do look like her," she says after a pause. "And you look like our father . . . who's your grandfather, I guess. But how is this possible?"

"I'm not sure," I say, coming to a decision. "Before I tell you any more, you have to promise me that what I'm about to say will stay between us. Just us. Can you do that?"

I know it's dangerous telling someone the whole truth, but all my instincts say that I can trust Hillary. She was not anti-Leacher even before she knew we were blood relatives. So she could've been okay with my ability to Read even before this. I was thinking of telling her eventually, when I got to know her better. This just expedites the whole thing. I could've enumerated the pros and cons for trusting her all night long, but it all comes down to a simple matter of being able to judge people—and I judge her trustworthy.

"This is very strange, but I know I'll die of curiosity if you don't tell me whatever it is you know. So yes, I swear on my sister's grave that I will keep your secret," she says in a hurried whisper. "Tell me everything."

I tell her the whole story. I begin in Atlantic City, when I met Mira for the first time. I explain about how I learned to Read and then Guide, and how I discovered the truth about Liz. As I speak, Hillary listens with rapt attention, seemingly holding her breath in fascination.

"It all fits," she says when I'm done, and I see a growing sadness in her eyes. "You couldn't have known this, but your story fits exactly with what I know about my older sister."

"Is there anything you can tell me about my mother?" I ask. "I mean, your sister? I only recently learned of her existence."

Hillary nods. "I was little at the time, only about five or six," she begins, "but I know she was a rebellious teen."

I almost smile, listening. It must run in the family. I was definitely rebellious myself, and my moms would probably say I still am to some degree.

"She was not as bad as I later grew up to be," Hillary continues, "at least according to my parents. Still, they said she was pretty bad. She was also very powerful, and from what you just told me, she might've had more Reach than me."

"How do you figure that?" I ask, surprised.

"Don't you see it? Your adoptive moms, how they said they couldn't talk about your origins for years? How the subject almost became taboo?"

"Yeah . . ."

"That sounds like they were Guided not to talk about it by Margie," she says.

"But that's *years*." Now that I understand the concept of Reach better, I realize how extraordinary my birth mother's power must've been—and begin to feel better about Lucy and Sara keeping this important secret from me.

"Yes, amazing, I know. This Reach is exactly why my parents put extra pressure on her to marry and, more importantly, to *breed* with a person of their choosing—or rather that of the Elders' choosing." Hillary's jaw flexes, and her expression darkens with anger. "Margie not only refused that, but she ran off with a non-Guide lover. That he was actually a Leacher isn't something I knew, and I doubt our parents did either."

"So what happened after?" I say, my chest tightening.

"They disowned her," Hillary says through gritted teeth. "They tried to tell me I had no sister."

"That's horrible." I feel anger rising within me, too. What kind of parents would do that?

"Yes, it is," Hillary says furiously. "But I knew, of course, that I had a sister, and that she was my favorite person in the whole world. I've never forgiven my parents for that. Never."

Her blue eyes fill with moisture, and I have no idea what to do. I want to comfort her, but I don't know how. So I just put my hand on hers on the table and give it a reassuring squeeze.

"I'm sorry," she says, blinking rapidly to contain her tears. "As you can see, this is still very painful for me. But I shouldn't cry. This is a happy moment. Meeting you. Her son. My nephew."

"And to think, we almost ended up flirting with each other," I say in an effort to amuse her.

"Almost? Darren, darling, I've been flirting with you all evening," she says, a hint of a smile appearing on her features. "But I quickly saw that you weren't interested in me in that way, so I settled for making an awesome new friend."

The idea that my newfound aunt had been interested in me would've been funny, in a Jerry Springer sort of way, if it weren't for the fact that I had also been drawn to her. But she's right—the attraction hadn't been of the kind I feel for Mira. Still, I'm glad we found out the real situation before the night was over.

"So do I call you Aunty?" I ask, making another attempt to cheer her up.

It seems to work. She smiles, her infectious grin back in full force. I recognize this smile. On several occasions, I saw it on my own frozen face when I was in the Quiet. Would Liz say that our initial attraction, if that's what it was, was some kind of narcissism? Or would she bring up some Freudian crap to explain it? I'm not sure, nor do I know why I so often wonder what Liz would say.

"No way," Hillary says in response to my question. "No Aunty, please."

"Aunt Hillary, then?" I say, trying to sound innocent.

She rolls her eyes. "Please. I'm twenty-seven—way too young to be an aunt to someone your age."

"Fine, Hillary it is," I concede. We share a smile, and then I say, "So I have a grandmother and a grandfather? But they would hate me?"

"I'm afraid they likely would," she says. "If you're right about having a Leacher—or *Reader*—father. I should get used to saying this more PC term, I guess. I'm sorry, Darren, but as soon as I was old enough, I left Florida behind—mainly to get away from your grandparents."

"I see," I say, but I'm not overly upset. A few minutes ago, I didn't have an aunt, and now I do.

That my biological grandparents are assholes is something I can deal with. Maybe the ones on my father's side are better? Unlike Hillary, I have two sets of much less fucked-up grandparents from my adoptive moms.

"How much do you know about what happened to my mother?" I ask, wondering if Hillary can shed some light on my parents' murder.

"Not much," she replies. "I tried to find out what happened with Margret in New York. What I learned was all public information. She got married and was murdered with her husband shortly thereafter for some unknown reason." Hillary looks thoughtful for a moment. "You know, I just realized that if your father had really been a Reader, that could've been why they were killed."

I nod. "Right. I'm beginning to suspect the same thing."

"If so, it had to have been the Traditionalists," she says, and I see angry color blooming on her face. "Not the ones connected to my parents, but probably some other group. As crazy as my parents are, they wouldn't kill their own daughter. At least I hope not."

"That's a redeeming quality for sure," I say drily.

We sit there silently. She's deep in thought.

"It has to be the Traditionalists," she says again, as though she just had an epiphany. "Your existence goes against everything those fuckers stand for."

"You mean the whole mixing of the blood taboo?" I say, surprised by how detached I feel about the whole thing. It's as though we're talking about someone else, not me.

"Yes. In fact, I can hardly believe you even happened. That a child that's both us and them could even exist," she says wonderingly.

"Why not?" Readers seemed to believe such a thing possible, though highly undesirable.

"We have something like an urban myth that says that nature wouldn't allow such an abomination to even exist," she says, making a point to do air quotes around the word *abomination* and looking at me apologetically. "Mainly, this comes from these legends of Leachers raping Guide women. According to these myths, there have never been any children in such cases."

I raise my eyebrows. "You guys think the two groups are sexually incompatible?"

"Yes, but I take those stories with a big grain of salt. I believe that a lot of Leachers happen to be exactly like our Traditionalists in their attitude—the ancient Leachers, especially. This means they wouldn't have had sex with their enemy, under any circumstances, even to rape them."

"Yeah, given what I heard from my Reader friend Eugene, you might be right. He couldn't believe a Reader would ever donate to a sperm bank out of risk of this 'horrible' occurrence," I say, surprised by the bitterness in my voice. It sucks to think you're forbidden to exist.

"Exactly. Those ancient Leachers would've killed the prisoner women instead. I'm sure of it," she says. "All this just makes your existence that much more revolutionary."

"What's so revolutionary about it?"

"Oh, come on. Just think about it. What's the best way to mend centuries-old feuds?"

"I know the answer you're looking for is to intermarry, but I'm not sure it's that simple—"

"It is," she says confidently. "This was the reason why kings of warring nations sometimes married into each other's families. It's also why Americans—products of the melting pot—have forgotten many, if not all, of the prejudices of their European ancestors, who hated each other's guts."

My skepticism must be showing on my face because she continues, "I've thought about this a lot, Darren. There are examples all over the place—I'm an anthropologist, after all. If you have two groups who hate each other, you need to break the group identity that results in the whole 'us versus them' setup we talked about earlier. And what better way to break such identity than having children around that are representatives of both groups? Especially when they are as charming as you." She winks at me playfully.

"As flattered as I am to be the future and all that, allow me to play the devil's advocate for a moment and take your idea to its logical extreme. It wouldn't be just Readers and Guides who would need to intermarry. You're saying the human race should do so also?"

"Right," she says.

"But don't you think something would be lost if everyone assimilated into one giant human race? All those cute little cultural diversity things would go away, for example. Like ethnic foods, different languages, even ethnic music or mythologies." I'm not necessarily convinced that she's wrong, but I want to hear her counterpoints.

"I'm not sure you're right about that." She downs her glass of coconut water in a big gulp. "Certain things would stay. Take holidays such as Easter that stem from ancient pagan holidays. They're still around—colored eggs and the bunny and all. But even if we did lose some of this cultural heritage, it would be worth it if it meant world peace."

"But why stop at someone like me?" I ask. "That logic can be used to say that both Guides and Readers should intermarry with regular people."

"That's right," she says.

"But that would essentially wipe out our abilities. You'd get the same genocide sort of situation that Readers were trying to perpetrate on Guides—only in this case, it will be voluntary."

"That's not true. We'd have less divisiveness. And who said our abilities would go away? They might spread. In any case, once Guides and Readers accept you for what you are, I believe it will open a new dialogue between the groups."

"Or I would get killed to maintain the status quo." I'm no longer arguing for the sake of argument, but with a growing sense of peril.

"I won't let that happen," my aunt says seriously, and despite her size, she seems astonishingly formidable all of a sudden.

CHAPTER TWENTY-THREE

After Hillary and I spend half the night talking, I wake up late—but thankfully, not too late for lunch. I text Mira to confirm our plans, and she gives me the address where I'm to pick her up.

This time, when I go to a car rental agency, I get a much nicer car. I also wholeheartedly agree to buy the insurance, in case I end up in another high-speed chase with Russian mobsters.

After a frantic drive to make sure I'm not late, I park my shiny black Lexus near the lobby of Mira and Eugene's hotel.

Once I notify Mira of my arrival, I finally take a moment to check the emails on my phone. And there it is, the email from Bert I have been waiting for:

Dude,

I was able to find a good location where you can look at Arkady Bogomolov. It was an ingenious hack, if I do say so myself. I'll tell you all about it when I see you next. If I see you, that is, because this guy is bad news, and you best stay away from him. Your best course of action is to delete this email right now and go hang out with Mira.

Oh well, you have always been stubborn, so I guess you're still reading. The guy will be at a Russian banya called Mermaid. It's in Brooklyn, and the address is 3703 Mermaid Avenue. Hence the name, I take it. In their system, he's listed as getting a massage at 4:00 pm today. From a guy named Lyova—yuck.

Your mom's murder case files are attached.

You owe me.

Bert.

I quickly write a response:

Thanks, I owe you big.

Bert really outdid himself this time. I should take the time and figure out a way to help his girl troubles, as he requested. If the subject comes up, I will ask Mira if she has any girlfriends. I suspect she might not. There is something of a loner vibe about her. Also, the person for Bert would need to be pretty short, unless the girl wasn't into traditional gender binary.

Aware that I have little time, I quickly research the place Bert wrote about. As I learned from reading that gangster's mind the other day, *banya* is a kind of spa. I now confirm and expand on that memory online. Apparently, it's not the kind of place where girls get their manicures and pedicures. Instead, Russians go there to sit in extremely hot saunas and—I kid you not—to get spanked by brooms made out of birch tree branches. Yeah. It's essentially a public bathhouse with some weird S&M spin. Sign me up. Not.

This specific place is located not far from Coney Island Park, according to the map in the phone.

I guess I should tell Mira about this development. Maybe after we eat something, though—I'm starving. And, while I'm at it, I need to talk to her about meeting the Pusher community. This one is trickier. But then again, she'll be away from her gun, so it might be the perfect opportunity. Yes, she might freak—likely *will* freak—and I might ruin the date, if this is a date, but holding out on her might lead to an even bigger disaster.

And then I see her.

She walks out of the hotel lobby wearing tight Capri pants, sandals, and a strappy tank top. Her hair is done in a simple tight ponytail. This look is pretty casual, compared to her usual high heels, war-paint makeup, and skimpy cocktail dresses. I'm not sure what this dressing-down act means, but I think it's a good sign. After all, she usually dresses to kill when she's out looking for revenge.

I get out of the car and wave. She smiles and approaches. With a strange impulse of chivalry, I walk over and open the car door for her. She kisses me on my cheek—a surprise. Either based on my reaction to the smooch or because of my opening the door for her, I get rewarded with an even bigger smile and a thank-you.

"Where to?" I say when I get in.

"I'm in the mood for Russian food. Have you ever had any?"

"I had some blinis with caviar at the Russian Samovar place in the city, but that's kind of it," I say.

"That's an appetizer and isn't the kind of thing people eat every day. Not unless they're some kind of oil oligarchs," she explains. "But it's a decent example."

"Okay, that settles it. Can you direct me to a good place?" I say.

"Yeah. Take two lefts over there. We're going to this place called Winter Garden," she says, and I start driving.

A couple of turns later, I'm getting a bad feeling. "What part of Brooklyn is this place located in? It *is* in Brooklyn, right?"

"Yes. It's located where most good Russian food can be found. Brighton Beach," she says. "Have you ever been there?"

"No. But, Mira, isn't that the place where all the Russian Mafia hang out?" I try to sound nonchalant.

"A lot of people hang out there," she says dismissively.

"Right, but we're on their shoot-to-kill list," I say. "Other people are not."

"You're such a worrier." There is a hint of laughter in her voice. "Brighton Beach is a big place, and it's the middle of the day on a Saturday, with tons of people around. But if you're scared, we can get sushi."

"No, let's go to this Winter Garden place," I say, trying to sound confident. I don't point out that the last time we got shot at by those people, it was in the morning, or the fact that the bullets went right through a very public playground. I figure the odds are on our side, but even if not, I don't want to reinforce the idea that I am a 'worrier.'

"Great, turn onto Coney Island Avenue at that light. Yes, there." As I turn, she says, grinning, "I have been meaning to ask you, do you always drive this slowly?"

"What's the point of going fast when I see the light changing to red?" I say, realizing that she's beginning to talk and act like the Mira I'm more familiar with. It's oddly comforting and even fun in a way.

"You could've totally made that green," she says. "Next time, you should let me drive."

I picture her driving like Caleb, only worse, and make a solemn vow never to let her drive, unless it's an emergency. I also don't dignify her jibe with a response.

Her grin widens. "How is your head?" she asks when I stubbornly remain silent.

"Much better, thanks." With everything going on, I'd nearly forgotten about the wound. "Just a little itchy."

"That means it's healing."

"Cool. I hope that's the case. How was your day yesterday? How's your brother doing? Did he visit Julia again? How is she recovering?"

For the rest of the way to the restaurant, she tells me how boring it is at the hotel. How Eugene is impossible to be around when he doesn't have his 'science stuff' with him. He wants to run ideas by her, share epiphanies, and carry on conversations. Mira's only reprieve was his visits with Julia, who was let out of the hospital today. Now, Julia is apparently staying in the same hotel as Mira and Eugene until she's completely recovered—she doesn't want her family to know about her adventures.

"So Eugene is off your back, it seems," I say as we pull into a public parking lot. "He'll probably be busy with Julia from now on."

"Yeah, I guess," she says and makes a face before climbing out of the car.

"What's the problem?" I ask as I feed the parking meter.

"I'm not a fan of that relationship of his," she says as she walks toward a pathway that leads to a large wooden boardwalk. "Last time, Julia's father interfered with their relationship, and Zhenya was really hurt."

"Is Zhenya Eugene's nickname?"

"Yes, that's what I call him sometimes."

"What about you, do you have a nickname? I can suggest a few, like Mi—"

"No," she says. "Please don't. My name is already short."

She walks a few seconds in silence, and I wonder if I touched on a sensitive topic. Maybe her parents called her by a nickname, and this made her think of them?

"We're here," she says, bringing me out of my thoughts.

We're standing next to a place that has a sign that reads "Winter Garden." If no one tries to kill us during our meal, I'll have to admit that Mira made an excellent choice when picking this place. The tables are situated on a wooden boardwalk, with the beach and the ocean beyond it. The weather is beautiful, and the ocean breeze brings sounds of the surf and smells that I associate with vacation.

When we take our seats, I look at the menu.

"It's all in Russian," I complain.

"Think of it as a compliment," she says. "They must think you're Russian, though I personally have no idea why."

"That's okay. I don't want to be mistaken for a Russian. I don't have too high of an opinion of them after the last few days. Present company excluded, of course." I smile at her.

"Of course," she says sarcastically.

"In any case, I guess I'll have to behave like a tourist and ask for the English menu," I say, not looking forward to it.

"Or you can take a chance and let me order for you." She winks at me mischievously.

Did I mention how hot Mira looks when she's being intentionally mischievous?

"First you pick the place," I say, folding my left pinky finger. "Now you want to order for me?" I fold the ring finger. "Who's taking whom out?"

"Don't forget that I also wanted to drive." She chuckles and holds out her middle finger as though she wants to fold it in the same fashion. Except it looks more like she's flipping me off, and I suspect she's doing that on purpose.

My witty retort never comes because our waiter arrives and begins speaking in rapid-fire Russian.

Mira looks at me, and I nod, resigned.

Mira and the waiter have a long, incomprehensible discussion in Russian while I get distracted by a smell coming from somewhere. It's a nauseating aroma, and it takes me a few moments to realize that it's some idiot smoking a cigar.

The last time I saw people smoke in restaurants was in 2003. Did this guy not get the memo about the smoking ban? I guess he thinks the fact that we're outside is a loophole of some kind. If you ask me, it's an unthinkable breach of etiquette, and I'm tempted to tell the guy off.

I look the offender over. Okay, so perhaps I won't give him the stern lecture he deserves. He doesn't look like he'd get it. What he does look like is a mountain. Only mountains are peaceful and serene things, and this motherfucker looks extremely mean.

I contemplate forgetting about it, but I can't leave it alone. The smoke is going to ruin my meal. Deciding to take a different course of action, I phase into the Quiet.

The restaurant patrons freeze in place, and the ambient noises of people and the ocean surf disappear.

I savor the silence. It makes me realize that I haven't done this in a while. Not once today, in fact.

I approach the guy with the cigar.

Frozen in place, he looks a lot less intimidating. I reach out and grab his ear, like they used to do back in the day to spoiled children—or so Kyle told me.

Physical connection in place, I want to establish a mental one. The lack of recent practice shows. I need to consciously relax to go into his mind, but once I focus on my breathing, I'm in.

* * *

We're puffing on the Cuban cigar and wondering when Sveta will get here.

I quickly disassociate, not willing to smoke that monstrosity even in someone else's head. If it were possible to cough mentally, that's what I'd be doing right now.

I make a snap decision on how to proceed and instantly feel good about myself. I'm about to do this guy a great service—and help everyone around him.

I prepare to do the Guiding, which is a better term than Pushing for what I'm about to do.

'Smoking is bad.

If you keep it up, it will give you cancer.

Feel a strong desire to put out this cigar. Feel disgusted, appalled, and sick to your stomach.

Doesn't the cigar look like a turd?

Do you want to put shit in your mouth?

You will never smoke cigars, or cigarettes, ever again. You have the willpower to quit—for the rest of your life.'

To add to those indoctrinations, I try to channel my memory of the negative emotions I felt during anti-smoking ads. Some of those ads are so disgusting that I can't believe anyone can see them and go on smoking.

I'm convinced the guy will not be smoking for a long while.

For how long is an interesting question. According to Hillary, my biological mother made my adoptive parents avoid the topic of my origins for years. I suspect my Reach might be just as impressive. If I understand it correctly, Guiding Reach works a lot like Reading Depth. Both are based on another variable: the amount of time you can spend in the Quiet. I don't know the limits to my time in the Quiet, but I do know my Depth amazed Julia and others, and they didn't know the full Depth I was capable of. It would be reasonable to assume my Reach is equally long.

All that considered, I might've permanently cured the cigar smoker of his deadly addiction.

As I prepare to get out of his mind, I wonder how regular Guides do their Guiding. It must be very different for them. They don't get the experience of being inside the person's head the way I do. That's a Reader thing. For them, it must be more like blind touching and wishing. I'll have to ask Hillary more about it, maybe get some tips on how to Guide more effectively.

Realizing that I'm still inside the now-non-smoker's head, I focus and instantly get out.

* * *

My good deed done for the day, I walk over and Read the waiter, since I'm in the Quiet anyway. He thinks Mira is as hot as I do, but I can hardly blame him for that. The good news is that nothing Mira ordered for us thus far sounds life-threatening.

Satisfied, I phase out.

"Ee dva compota," I hear Mira say to the waiter with finality.

As the man leaves, I see my new non-smoker friend begin to cough with a funny look on his face. Then, staring at his cigar as though it's a cobra, he violently sticks the object of his distress into his water glass.

Success. I mentally pat myself on the back, but don't say anything to Mira. The last thing I want is to remind her of my Pushing abilities.

"Thank you for ordering," I tell Mira instead.

"See if you like the food, then thank me." She smiles. "Besides, you're paying, so I should thank you."

"Oh, good, you'll at least let me pay. That makes me feel like I *am* taking you out after all," I say, winking.

"Sure. I have to look out for your masculine pride and all that. You almost ran out of fingers counting your grievances," she says. "And of course, this has nothing to do with my being broke."

I consider this for a moment. "Don't you have all those gambling winnings?"

"Yeah, but I don't keep much of it."

"Where does it all go? Shoes?" I joke.

"Well, in fact, shoes do cost a pretty penny, but no. The bulk of our money ends up feeding my brother's research," she says, pursing her lips with displeasure.

"Oh, I didn't realize you support his research this much." In fact, I'd gotten the impression she disapproved of it. "What exactly does he study? I mean, I know it has something to do with how our powers work."

"I support his research mainly out of spite. Because I know it would piss off the fuckers who killed Mom and Dad." She glowers darkly. "And because I love my weirdo brother. As to what his research is all about, I wish I could tell you, but I don't really get it. When he starts talking about it, it's as though a part of my brain shuts off."

I chuckle at that, remembering how she always goes out of her way not to hear Eugene talk about his work.

A waiter comes back with drinks and says something to Mira in Russian.

"Try it," Mira says. "I think you'll like it."

I taste the liquid in my glass. It seems to be some kind of sweet fruit punch. "Yum."

"Yeah," she says knowingly. "That's Russian compote, made out of dried fruit. My grandmother used to make it all the time."

"It's a great start," I say.

"Good, the appetizers are coming too."

Sure enough, the waiter comes back with a tray.

"That's julienne, escargot, and you already tried blinis before," she says, pointing at the tray. "Give it a try."

I oblige, piling samples onto my plate.

"You know," I say when I'm done chewing. "This tastes a lot like French food."

"I'm not surprised," she says. "Czarist Russia's nobility had French chefs, and French cuisine is now part of Russian culture. Still, these dishes should be a little different."

The escargot, snails in butter and garlic, are outstanding. The julienne thing is a mushroom and cheese dish that reminds me of mushroom pizza, without the dough—meaning you can't go wrong with it. Blinis are very similar to the crepes I had before, only these come with red rather than black caviar.

"So far, it's awesome," I tell her, trying my best not to burn my tongue on the hot cheese of the julienne dish—which, so far, is my favorite.

"I'm glad." She sounds so proud that you'd think she cooked the food herself.

"I was wondering about something," I say as I blow on my food. "What are you planning to do after you get your revenge and all that?"

She gives me a vaguely surprised look, as though she's never been asked this before. "I plan to get my GED, since I never finished high school. After that, I'm going to enroll at Kingsborough College."

"Kingsborough? I've heard of it, but know very little about the place. Is it good? What do you want to study there?"

"Kingsborough is a community college. We locals call it 'The Harvard on the Bay.' It's probably not up to your high standards, but I can get my RN license after I get my Associate's degree and afterwards get a job."

"You want to be a nurse?" I ask, surprised. I wonder if she said the Harvard bit because she knows I graduated from there. Maybe she Googled me? I find the idea that she cared enough to do a search quite pleasant.

"I would make a good nurse," she says. "I'm not squeamish, and I don't faint at the sight of my own blood like some people." She gives me a pointed look.

"I didn't faint," I protest. "I lost consciousness because I was shot. That's completely different. I saw a ton of blood the other day, remember? No fainting."

"Methinks the gentleman doth protest too much . . ." She gives me a teasing smile. "I'm pretty sure you saw your own bloodied hand and fainted yesterday. But in any case, I think I would make a great nurse. My plan is to work in a neonatal unit, if I can. To deal with newborn babies." Her face softens as she says that last bit.

"Really?" I can't picture her working with babies. Being a kickass professional spy, maybe. But a nurse working with babies? It just boggles my mind.

She nods. "Yes, I like helping people. And I want to work in a place like that, a place where people learn the happiest news of their lives."

So she likes to help people. That's news to me. But something about that worries me a little. Could that urge of hers explain why she was so nice to me when

I was hurt? Was she only acting like that because that's how she would've treated any person in pain?

"I imagine it's not all unicorns and rainbows at the neonatal unit. Don't babies get sick?" I ask, picturing all the crying, and worried parents breathing down your neck. I don't know about other guys my age, but for me, crying babies are on par with scorpions and snakes.

"Of course. But I can Read them and figure out what hurts." She smiles again. "And then the doctors will be able to help them."

"You can Read a baby?" I don't know why that hadn't occurred to me before. If that's the case, then working with babies does sound like a uniquely helpful way to use Reading. Similar to what Liz does with her Guiding of OCD patients, but perhaps even cooler.

"Sure. You can Read many creatures," Mira says. "I used to Read my cat, Murzik, when he was alive."

"You could Read your cat?" Now I'm flabbergasted. "How was that? Do they have thoughts, like us?"

"Not thoughts, at least not my old lazy cat. But I was immersed in his experiences, which had something like thoughts in them, only fleeting. In that way, babies are similar. They feel more than think, and when you Read them, you can learn if something hurts or why they're unhappy."

"Wow. I'll have to try Reading some creature. And, I must say, yours sounds like an excellent plan. I hope you get your revenge soon, because this sounds much better than what you've been doing." As I say that last part, I realize I might've inadvertently criticized her.

"You don't say." Her voice drips with sarcasm. "Helping people is better than underground gambling with monsters?"

"Never mind," I say, sorry I blabbed too much. "Yes, obviously you'll be happier once you put that plan into motion. Besides, I assume your gambling days are over?"

"You assume?" she says, finishing her last crepe. "It's an interesting assumption. But I think we've spent enough time talking about me. Quid pro quo, Darren. What do *you* plan to do after you get out of this mess?"

"I'm going to take a vacation," I say without hesitation. "Go someplace warm, or maybe travel someplace interesting, like Europe. After that, I don't know. I already have a job at a hedge fund, but it's not the kind you described. It's not my passion or anything like that. It's just a means to make money."

"The horror," she says in mock shock. "Money is the root of all evil, don't you know?"

"Hey, I'm not complaining. It's just that you actually want to help people, and you've thought about a job that would make you happy. I haven't thought about that yet. I was thinking about being a detective the other day, but the paperwork and danger might be a drag. Not to mention the very thought of going back to school—"

"You can be a private detective," she suggests, interrupting. "You can do as much paperwork as you feel like doing—since it would be your own business. And, you can take only jobs that have the amount of danger you're comfortable with. Wives wondering about their philandering husbands, that sort of thing." There's only a little bit of mockery in her voice as she says the word *danger*.

I stare at her, struck by the idea. "You know, that could actually work. I could even use Reading to help me solve cases. I could be like one of those psychic detectives on TV. Only I'm afraid that taking on boring cases would defeat the original purpose of my enjoying the work."

She's about to respond, but the waiter comes again, with a bigger tray this time. He takes what's left of the appetizers, and we get our plates with the main course.

"That's called *chalahach*," she says.

"Really? It sure looks like lamb chop to me." I glance down at my plate. "A lamb chop with mashed potato and green beans. How very not exotic."

"Not exotic? This is a traditional dish from freaking Uzbekistan, or some other former Soviet republic. It's as exotic as it gets. And the way they make it here is amazing." She cuts off a piece and puts it in her mouth, closing her eyes in bliss as she begins to chew.

I try it and have to concur. "It's been sautéed in a different way than your usual lamb chop," I say.

"Exactly. Also make sure to use the sauce." She points at the red ketchup-like stuff in a saucer on my plate.

I follow her suggestion and admit, "It's even better with the sauce."

"Told you," she says, wolfing down her chop. "The sauce is Uzbek also. Or Tajik. I'm not sure."

For the remainder of the meal, we talk about why Russian food is so full of other cultures' cuisines, and I challenge her to come up with some original Russian dish. I also unsuccessfully try to think of a way to bring up my knowledge of Arkady's location without ruining our lunch.

"No dessert?" I say when the waiter brings us the check.

"I wanted to leave room for you to try something else," she replies as I pay the waiter with cash.

"Something else?" I say curiously, rising to my feet.

She gets up as well. "I wanted to get you a *pirozhok*, this meat-filled dough. It's definitely, positively a Russian food. They sell them all over the boardwalk."

"Great, more food, and the street variety to boot. I can't wait," I say, teasing.

Without saying a word, she goes into the indoor portion of our restaurant and comes back a minute later with a strange-looking pastry.

"This one is not street food. I assure you, it's safe," she says. "Try it."

The pastry tastes baked, not fried, and seems to be filled with something like apple preserves.

"I like it," I say. "But wasn't this supposed to have meat in it?"

"You wanted dessert, so I got you the apple variety. A pirozhok can have all kinds of fillings," she says and rattles off a weird list that includes eggs, cabbage, cherries, and—my favorite—mashed potatoes. Yes, Russians apparently eat starch filled with starch.

"Thank you, Mira," I say when I finish my pirozhok. "That was awesome."

"Don't mention it. Now let's walk it off by going toward Coney Island," she says. "I'm in the mood for a stroll."

"Okay. But now that we're done with our meal, there's something I wanted to talk to you about." I pause, and then at her expectant look, I say carefully, "I think you might get your revenge sooner than you thought."

CHAPTER TWENTY-FOUR

"You should've told me earlier," she says after I finish telling her the story about how I got Arkady's name out of the mobster's head and how my friend Bert found out about his whereabouts.

"I'm sorry. I didn't really get a chance before. Not with all the guns you kept pointing at me, and then getting shot and everything else."

"Fine," she says curtly. "We have to go to the banya. Now."

"But what about our walk? Besides, his massage is at four p.m., and it's two-thirty now," I say, already regretting that I told her.

"Listen, Darren, I'm sorry, but the walk will have to happen another day," she says. "Thank you for the lunch and for telling me this now, but I can't relax and enjoy myself, knowing about a lead like this. Plus, the guy is already there, I assure you. I know how a banya works."

We walk back to the car. I learn on the way that going to the banya is usually a full-day event and that our target is likely to want to get a couple of *parki*—the spankings with the birch brooms—before getting his massage.

I start driving, and she continues telling me what she knows of the Russian bathhouse culture. I'm beginning to feel that Russia is the one place I won't need to visit anytime soon. I suspect I have already learned and seen everything a tourist would have by just going on this one date— if this *is* a date—with Mira.

"Stop here," she says when, according to the GPS, we're a few blocks from the place.

I look around. The neighborhood looks a bit rundown and sketchy.

"We're going into the Mind Dimension," she says, clearly seeing the hesitation on my face. "So we're not really going to leave the car. Please Split and pull me in."

I do as she asks and phase in.

Immediately, I'm in the backseat looking at the back of my own head and that of Mira. I tap an exposed part of her shoulder, and in a moment, a livelier version of her is sitting next to me.

"Let's go," she says, and we make our way to the banya on foot.

We go inside, and I gape at the scene in front of me.

Picture Russian Mafia. Now picture them sitting with regular middle-aged Russian men and a small handful of women—all of them in their swimwear—at what looks like a mix between a cafeteria and a shower stall. Picture all that, and you'll begin to get an idea of what the inside of this Mermaid place looks like.

"Okay, which one is he?" Mira starts walking around. "They all look like a bunch of regulars."

"I say we Read people one by one until we find him or verify he isn't here yet. We can also look for the masseur," I say. "His name is Lyova."

"All right. You take the steam rooms, and I will do this area. The masseur is likely to arrive close to the appointment."

"You sound like you've been here before," I say, heading toward what must be the steam rooms.

"Of course," she says over her shoulder. "It's the best banya in Brooklyn."

I walk over and open the wooden door that leads to the steam room. The people here are even less covered than their counterparts in the lunchroom. They're also wearing pointy woolen hats that are supposed to protect their heads from overheating. If I hadn't read about this previously, I'd burst out laughing at the ridiculous sight. Completing the bizarre picture are two people lying on wooden shelves and getting the birch-branch spanking treatment.

I've never seen steam frozen in place before. It's weird. When my body touches it, it condenses into tiny drops of water on my skin. The room is not hot here in the Quiet, but I can tell that in the real world, this place is scorching. Everybody in here is covered with droplets of sweat.

I start Reading people, one after another. Two guys are programmers, another is an electrical engineer, and the majority are retired old men. No gagsters, no Arkady, no luck.

I leave this room and head over to a room that has a sign stating that it's a Turkish Spa. The glass entrance door is fogged up from thick steam. I'm going to come out wet if I go in there.

"Darren, over here!" I hear Mira call out from the table area, and I'm more than happy not to enter the room I was about to go into.

As I walk toward her, I see them. These guys stand out for a number of reasons. First, they are buffer and meaner-looking than the rest of the patrons. But the main reason I know we found what we're looking for is that I see the guy who tried to shoot me yesterday. He must've managed to handle the car safely, even after I Guided him to leave fast and to keep on driving. I guess I shouldn't be surprised, since I didn't command him to do anything truly suicidal.

He's sitting there, a shot of vodka held halfway to his mouth. Vodka in a steam room? Really? Someone has a strong cardiovascular system, or a death wish.

"That's the fucker who tried to shoot me," I tell Mira, pointing at the guy.

"Right, and that's the man we came here to Read." She gestures toward a particularly large specimen, who has tattoos of stars on his shoulders and a large silver cross hanging around his neck. His face is frozen in a scowl—probably his usual expression.

I approach and gingerly touch one of his meaty biceps. The muscle is so big, it looks like a strange tumor.

I focus momentarily, and I am in.

* * *

We're jumping into the cold water of the special pool by the steam room. There are ice cubes floating in it, we notice with satisfaction. Instead of the shock of cold water, our body just feels tingly, and the dip is extremely refreshing. The resulting pins-and-needles sensation on our skin, combined with the buzz from the vodka, almost makes us forget the unfortunate fact that we'll have to leave banya in a half hour and miss our massage, all because of that fucking phone call.

I, Darren, disassociate.

Something is odd about this mind. Something I've never come across before, but I can't quite put my finger on it.

I focus on the memories Arkady has about the phone call. I get vague images of it being from someone important, but someone outside the Russian organization.

Sounds a lot like our mystery Pusher, I decide.

Determined to investigate this, I almost instinctively feel lighter and rewind Arkady's memories to that point.

"On the Brooklyn Bridge?" we ask, confused. "Why the fuck would we meet there?"

"Because, I don't trust you, Mr. Bogomolov."

"That's a fucking joke, right? You don't trust me? Out of the two of us, I have far more reasons not to trust you, Mr. Esau, much more than the other way around," we say. "I'm still not convinced you're not setting some kind of a trap for me and my people."

"Well, you're just proving my point for me then. That's even more reason to meet in a public place, with lots of people around," says Esau. His voice sounds unnaturally deep. We're fairly sure he's using a voice scrambler.

"How will I find you?" we ask. "What do you look like?"

"I'll find you, so don't worry," says Esau.

"Oh, I'm not worried," we say. "But if you don't bring my money and the list, you should be worried. Very worried."

Images of the torture we would inflict on Esau in that scenario flash in front of our eyes.

"You will get the cash and the list," says Esau. Is that fear coming through the voice scrambler? "You're actually going to get two lists. One will contain more business for you."

Esau had ordered kills on and off from us for some time, but this is the first time he decided to put together a whole fucking list of people.

"We don't do bulk discounts," we say sarcastically. "This isn't fucking Costco."

"I wasn't asking for a discount. The list is merely a way to make sure I keep these pleasant conversations with you to a minimum. Your usual rate applies."

"Good," we say with satisfaction. "And if we're going to play this distrust game, then you better bring a downpayment for each name on this new list of yours."

"Of course, half the usual for each target," Esau says. "But, just as a heads up, since we're going to be bringing so much money with us, the memory card that contains the lists is encrypted. We're going to give it to you today, but will only provide the key to decrypt it once we're safely away from our meeting."

We're both impressed and annoyed. This last precaution might well have saved the man's life. Maybe. Depends on how well protected he'll be. The passcode can be gotten out of him if enough skill is applied in questioning. We haven't had anyone not talk before.

As if reading our mind, Esau says, "Furthermore, you should know that if something were to happen to me, I've made arrangements. The people on the list that you want, the ones in witness protection, will get a warning, and you wouldn't want that."

"Sounds like we have an understanding," we say, wondering if Esau is bluffing about these arrangements. Even if he is, we can't take the chance. Esau will survive today's meeting—which is fine with us. This way, we get more money down the line and can off him later. "I'll see you later today."

"Four-thirty, sharp," Esau says and hangs up.

We wonder if this could be a trap from the FBI or some other agency. Then we dismiss the thought. Those people wouldn't order hits. They go as far as using drugs and things like that, but assassinations are a line they wouldn't cross. Particularly the petty kinds of kills that this Esau guy had ordered—like the American kid Slava managed to screw up killing yesterday.

The American kid? I, Darren, take a mental step back, struck by the wording. Eugene is Russian, and at almost thirty years of age, he's not exactly a kid. If Arkady was thinking about him, wouldn't he call him a Russian guy or something along those lines? Unless . . .

Unless the shooting this morning wasn't directed at Eugene, like we all thought.

Suddenly, it all becomes clear. Of course. It was the Pusher. He tried to kill me, not once but twice—first via the shooter and then again in the hospital.

I'm the un-killed American kid in question.

Shit. Whoever this Pusher is, he's serious about eliminating me. Is it possible he had something to do with my parents' deaths? Or Mira's parents' deaths? Had he used this exact puppet—Arkady—to do it? I need to dig deeper into Arkady's head to find out.

I focus on going back a long time . . .

We spit out a tooth, but don't slow down. Instead, we execute our plan of attack on the Captain. A punch to the liver, another to his Adam's apple. The Captain has been teaching us Systema for the last couple of weeks. Learning the unit's secret martial art was one of the main reasons we joined this training. Well, that and curiosity. We wondered if this, of all things, will take away the boredom.

I, Darren, realize I'm too deep inside Arkady's past, so I try to go for more recent events.

The Chechen woman is shot in the neck. She falls, bleeding, convulsing, and trying to scream. We feel nothing, though we know that most people would feel pity at the sight. We vaguely understand the concept. We wonder if it's pity that compels us to think about how the woman was beautiful, and it's a shame we didn't get a chance to fuck her. No, that's more regret than pity. Pity is an emotion that still eludes us.

I'm still in too deep. Also, I finally understand what the strange thing about this mind is. The guy is a real-life, certifiable psychopath. He doesn't feel the usual range and intensity of emotions that other people do.

I decide I have to be careful about poking around in his head. His experiences make Caleb's disturbing memories seem like summer camp. The atrocities Arkady committed in Chechnya are there, in the back of our shared-for-the-moment mind, and I don't want to experience something like that. No amount of therapy with Liz would undo it.

So I mentally tiptoe around, trying to look at experiences that shed any light on the murders of the past. I'm drawing a blank, though, whenever I try to focus on anything having to do with my parents' murder. He must not have been involved in that.

I do come across many signs of the Pusher, though. And the explanation of why Arkady thinks he met Esau recently. The Pusher regularly makes Arkady forget things—like missions from this Esau. In fact, he often makes Arkady forget Esau's existence completely. To me, that means only one thing.

Esau and the Pusher are the same person.

I want to scream in excitement.

Unfortunately, it seems like the Pusher took obsessive precautions to never be seen by Arkady. Even when he Pushed Arkady, he probably walked over to him in the Quiet, rather than being physically in the room. This Esau identity must be the Pusher's way to control his pet Mafia goon by more conventional means—via the phone.

I look further into Arkady's memories.

We finish setting up the explosive device and get back into the car. As we sit there, we wonder why this Tsiolkovskiy guy needs to be eliminated in such a fancy manner. Bullet to the head would've been much cheaper and less risky. Every assassin knows that explosives can hurt the man who works with them. We've heard of this happening on many occasions. It's understandable for someone high-profile, but doing it to kill some Russian scientist? It doesn't make sense. But the client said he would pay double, claiming that Tsiolkovskiy might see it coming otherwise, so explosives it is.

I feel cold all over at my discovery. I can't even imagine what Mira will do when I tell her.

With a shudder, I get out of Arkady's head.

* * *

"Fuck," I say unimaginatively when I'm out and catch Mira's gaze.

"I take it you heard the phone conversation," Mira says. "We've got to hurry." She turns and starts to briskly walk away.

"Mira, wait." Catching up, I place my hand on her shoulder.

"What?" She gives me an annoyed look. "Didn't you Read the same information I did?"

"Yes, a Brooklyn Bridge meeting," I confirm. "But I learned something else, too. Something you might not have, given your Depth . . . "

Her face turns pale. "Tell me."

I take a deep breath. "He remembers planting a bomb under a car for a Russian scientist with the last name of Tsiolkovskiy. That had to have been your dad—"

Her reaction is so violent and sudden that I don't have time to say anything else. Grabbing a chair, she starts whacking Arkady's frozen body with it, over and over.

Then she puts the chair on the floor and sits down on it, propping her elbows on her knees and covering her eyes with her palms.

"Mira," I say softly, approaching her. "If you want, I can try to make him drown himself in that cold pool over there."

I don't know if I can actually do what I just said, both from a practical standpoint and from an ethical one. But trying it will certainly make more sense than beating up a man in the Quiet—an action that will have no impact in the real world.

"No, don't." Lowering her hands, she looks up, her eyes glittering brightly. "He's the key to the fucker who's pulling the strings."

I exhale, relieved she didn't take me up on my hasty offer. I might've balked at doing something *that* cold-blooded.

"So you want to go to the meeting at the Brooklyn Bridge?" I ask as she gets up from the chair.

"Yes. Once he brings us to the Pusher, I'll kill them both." Her voice is cold and sharp. "If we kill him now, the Pusher might get spooked."

"Okay, but—"

"Let's get back to the car. Let's not get into any particulars just yet," she says, striding toward the door.

I reluctantly follow her. As much as I want to catch this Pusher, I'm really not looking forward to confronting Arkady and his colleagues.

"Sorry about earlier," she says over her shoulder. "I just needed to vent."

"Of course, no worries," I say, and then we walk in silence for a few moments.

When we reach the car, I touch my neck through the open Lexus door, and the world comes back to life.

CHAPTER TWENTY-FIVE

"Please let me drive," Mira says as soon we're out of the Quiet.

Given her mental state, I decide to comply. Arguing with an angry Mira doesn't seem like a good idea to me. The girl definitely has a short fuse. Besides, I have some phone calls to make, given where we're heading.

As soon as she's behind the wheel, she floors the gas pedal, causing the Lexus to make a tire-screeching sound.

I take out my phone, happy to focus on something other than the streets of Brooklyn that are flashing by the car window much too fast.

"I'm calling Caleb," I tell Mira as I locate his number in my phone.

"That's a good idea," she says approvingly. "I was going to ask Julia to do this at the hotel, but this is even better. You two have a nice rapport."

"If Caleb and I have a nice rapport, I shudder to think how he treats people he dislikes," I say and dial the number on my screen.

The phone rings for a while. I wait.

Then it connects, but no one says anything on the other line.

"Hello?" I say carefully.

"Who? Oh, Darren." I hear Caleb's surprised tone. "Miss me already?"

"I can use your help, Caleb," I say, ignoring the jibe. "*We* can use your help."

"Oh, cutting right to the chase? I like it." Caleb sounds a bit less sarcastic. "What do you—the plural you—need?"

"Some of your unique help tonight," I say. "There's this—"

"Darren, let me stop you right there," Caleb interrupts. "I'm not in town. In fact, I'm out of state."

"Shit," I say.

"What's going on, Darren? Is it something serious?"

"Yes, it is, but I don't want to go into it right now," I say. "Not over the phone. I've got to think of something else."

"Are you in trouble? I can put you in touch with Sam or one of my other people."

"Sam the Asshole? You're kidding, right?"

"Sam's in charge in my absence, so he's the logical choice."

"No, thanks. I think we'll manage."

"Suit yourself—there's nothing I can do that Sam can't. The man is a machine. If I weren't the one with charisma, he'd be in charge," Caleb says, and I can't tell if he's joking or not.

"I appreciate that," I say. "And I may call you back about it, but I really think I'd rather work with someone I know."

Mira parks the car in the hotel parking lot, so I tell Caleb I have to get off the phone.

"Sure," he responds. "Let me know if you change your mind about Sam or if there's anything else you need."

"Well," I say as Mira exists the car, "I do have one quick question . . ."

"What is it, kid?"

"Do you know a guy named Mark Robinson?"

There is a moment of silence. Then: "Why do you ask? Where did you hear that name?"

"Jacob mentioned him," I say noncommittally.

"Hmm, that's odd. He's ancient history. One of our people who was murdered. A nasty affair. Do you know why Jacob mentioned him to you?"

"No," I say. Then, cognizant that Mira is about to come back and drag me out, I add quickly, "Thanks, Caleb. I'll call back later if we end up needing Sam."

"Okay." He hangs up, probably still wondering about my weird question. I guess he has no idea Mark had a son.

I phase into the Quiet and take a moment to digest what I just learned.

My father was a Reader. There is no doubt about that now. And my mother was a Guide. What I suspected ever since discovering my Guiding abilities has now been confirmed. And the theory of my parents being killed for their forbidden union is beginning to sound more plausible.

I phase back out and join Mira outside.

"So, judging by what I overheard, Caleb isn't available?" Mira says as she briskly walks toward her room. She's texting as she goes, and I assume she's communicating with Eugene.

"Yeah. Caleb offered the help of that Sam guy, but I wasn't sure about that idea."

"You did the right thing. Sam and I, we don't have good history," she says through clenched teeth.

"Oh?" I ask, hoping that this is not an ex-boyfriend or something along those lines.

"He beat up my brother," she says angrily. "It was on Jacob's orders, most likely, but still, there's no way we're going to deal with him."

"Shit. Sounds like we wouldn't want him involved, for sure. I've met the guy twice now, and I know he's a jackass. I just didn't realize to what extent."

We make our way to Mira's room and find Eugene waiting by the door. She lets us in, and we all grab seats around the room. Loveseat for Mira, an office chair for me, and Eugene sits on the bed.

"I think I should talk to Julia," Eugene says once we bring him up to speed on the whole situation. "If not Sam, she might know someone else who can help us."

"If you tell Julia about this, she'll most likely want to come," Mira says. "And I suspect you wouldn't want that."

"She wouldn't; she just got out of the hospital," Eugene says, but there is uncertainty in his voice.

"Even assuming that she would do the prudent thing and not join us, there is another problem with getting her involved," Mira says. "It might end up pulling her father, Jacob, into this, and I don't want to do that."

"Why?" I ask curiously.

"Because of his fear of exposure," Mira says. "This meeting is happening in a very public place—meaning that there's a chance that the confrontation with the Pusher could involve a lot of civilians."

"It's not like Jacob is this great humanitarian," Eugene chimes in. "It's just that, as you learned the other day, he's obsessed with keeping Reader existence hidden. He's a Purist."

"Exactly," Mira confirms. "The last thing we want is him stopping us from acting."

"But the three of us stand no chance," Eugene says, his shoulders sagging. "So we might want to risk talking to Julia.

"The two of us," Mira corrects. "There is no reason for Darren to join this. It's not his fight. And not Julia's either—so no Julia."

"I'm going to help you," I surprise myself by saying. "You forget that this Pusher tried to have me killed."

He also might've killed my parents, but I don't mention this. That might be a topic for later.

"Okay, but that's still just the three of us," Eugene says, looking at me gratefully.

The look Mira gives me is harder to read. She seems to be reevaluating me again. I'm reevaluating myself too. Mira just gave me a way out, and instead of taking it, I'm volunteering to join them. And dealing with the Pusher who tried to kill me is only a fraction of my motivation. The bigger part is staring expectantly at me with those beautiful blue eyes.

"There might not just be the three of us," I say, growing uncomfortable with Mira's intent stare. "But before I get into that, I need to ask you: what's a Purist? You said Jacob was one. What does that mean?"

"Purists are Readers who try to stick to archaic traditions, such as assigned mating," Eugene says bitterly. "Their biggest fears are things like exposure to the outside world and dilution of the Reader blood."

"The only good thing about them is that they want to exterminate Pushers," Mira says.

That one hurts. And doesn't bode well for what I'm building up the courage to tell them. It especially hurts because I no longer think of myself as *that* kind of Pusher. The Pusher she hates would hate her also if he's a Traditionalist. It's ironic how much these Purists sound like the Traditionalists Thomas and Hillary described. I almost regret we can't get Jacob involved. It would be a sort of poetic justice to let the two orthodoxies fight it out. They sound like they deserve each other.

"Mira," Eugene says uncomfortably, "you don't mean that. Darren is a perfect example of why thinking that way is wrong."

"It's okay, Eugene," I say graciously. "I kind of understand Mira's hatred for Pushers. I mean, I hate the guy who tried to kill me in the hospital. But it's also a fact that not all Pushers are the same. In fact, I think only a tiny minority are like that fucker."

"I didn't mean you, Darren." Mira drops her gaze, as if embarrassed. "You're something else entirely."

"And if I were as much a Pusher as you are a Reader, would you try to kill me again?" I say, deciding to put my cards on the table.

"You know that I wouldn't." She looks at me again. "In any case, you said you don't even know who or what you are."

The good news is that she isn't taking out a gun. Yet.

"Right, I didn't," I say carefully. "But I learned more about myself yesterday—and even more just a few minutes ago. Most importantly, I learned that

not all Pushers—or Guides, as they call themselves—
are the evil monsters you think they are. In fact, most
of them are regular people, just like me and you."

In the dead silence that follows, I tell Mira and
Eugene an abbreviated version of what happened
yesterday. About my shrink, about my aunt, about
Thomas.

"So these Pusher Traditionalists are like our
Purists?" Eugene says, staring at me.

"Yeah, and they sound just as fun too," I say.

"So it must've been one of *them* who killed Dad
because of his research," Eugene whispers.

"I'm not sure you should blame whole groups of
people, be it Pushers or Traditionalists among
them," I say cautiously. "It might be just one crazy
Pusher who took it upon himself to hire the Russian
mobster we Read . . ."

"So you yourself are really a Pusher?" Mira says,
clearly having a hard time digesting my story.

"I prefer Guide, but yeah, at least halfway, on my
mother's side, I am. I still don't know much about
my father, except I just confirmed that he was a
Reader."

"But that's forbidden," Eugene says, his eyes
widening.

"You're not one to judge," I say defensively. "Don't your people think half-bloods are forbidden, too?"

"It's different," he says uncertainly.

"Is it? Why couldn't you date Julia?" I say.

Eugene doesn't respond, and Mira seems to be trying to drill holes in me with her gaze.

"You lied when you said you were not feeling well when we spoke yesterday?" she finally says. To my surprise, that seems to upset her more than my being a Reader-Pusher hybrid. "You were actually going to a *party*?"

"I'm sorry I lied to you about that," I say to her honestly. "I just didn't think you'd like it if I told you the truth. 'Sorry, Mira—can't hang out, going to a Pusher party.'"

Eugene lets out a nervous chuckle and gets a furious look from his sister.

"And how do we know you're not lying right now, or haven't been lying to us all this time?" Mira says, turning to glare at me. "You lie so well when it suits you. How do we know this isn't some kind of a Pusher trick?"

"A trick to do what, exactly?" I'm getting tired of constantly being accused. "Hand you the Pusher who killed your parents?"

"He's right, Mira," Eugene says soothingly. "I don't see what possible nefarious Pusher purpose could be served by all this."

"Fine. Let's say I believe you." Mira's expression doesn't soften. "What does it change? What do I care if some Pushers think they're good and call themselves Guides? It doesn't change the fact that one of them should die today. It doesn't change our lack of plans. And no matter what you say about the few people you've met, the fact remains that they, like you, can fuck with people's minds—and that's wrong."

"It does change things because I have a plan in mind," I retort. "And Reading can also be said to be fucking with people's minds. I think a lot of people would rather be made to do something than have their deepest secrets stolen."

"Just like a Pusher to twist the truth," Mira says angrily. "Mind fucking is obviously—"

"Mira, please stop," Eugene interrupts forcefully. He's using that rare 'big brother knows best' tone of voice. "Let Darren tell us how we can deal with the situation at hand. We can exchange xenophobic drivel later."

"Fine," she says, folding her arms across her chest. "Do enlighten us, Darren."

"Okay," I say. "Thomas, the *Guide* from the Secret Service I mentioned earlier, offered to help me. Originally, it was in the context of what to do if I learned the identity of the person who tried to kill me at the hospital. Still, I'm sure he might be helpful in this situation, too."

"And you think you can trust him?" Eugene asks doubtfully. "You only met him yesterday."

"And he's a Pusher," Mira mutters under her breath.

"I think I can trust him, yes. If I didn't trust him, it would certainly be for reasons other than his being a *Guide*," I say, emphasizing the politically correct term. "The person I *really* trust is my aunt, but I don't want to involve her in this situation."

Mira gets a look of concentration on her face for a moment. "Fine. I just talked to Eugene, and he convinced me to give this insane idea a shot."

"You talked—" I begin, but then I understand. She phased into the Quiet and pulled her brother in for a private conversation again.

"I'm sorry about that, Darren," Eugene confirms my suspicion. "We had to think about such an unusual proposition. I vouched for you because I now see you as a friend. I hope I don't regret it."

"So you didn't want to trust me," I say, looking at Mira. Figures.

"If she didn't, she wouldn't," Eugene says. "Mira doesn't—"

"Shut up, Zhenya," Mira says, giving him an icy stare. "Don't you understand the concept of a *private* conversation?"

"Let me check to make sure Thomas even wants to help us," I say. "Otherwise, this is all pointless."

Since no one objects, I take out my phone and call Thomas.

"Thomas, this is Darren," I say as soon as he picks up. "You said to call you if I needed help with the Guide who's trying to kill me."

"I did. What's going on?" Thomas sounds instantly alert. "Did you learn his identity already?"

"Not exactly," I say, trying to get my thoughts organized. "But I do know where he'll be later today, and I want to confront him. I'm with some friends of mine, but it's only the three of us."

"Okay, hold your horses," Thomas says. "Start from the beginning."

"What I didn't tell you yesterday was that I had a clue I was investigating. A clue related to the connection this Guide seems to have to some Russian criminals. My friend and I found out that he'll meet the people he controls on the Brooklyn Bridge today," I say.

"I see." Thomas sounds calm, as though people call him up with this sort of convoluted story all the time. "Your friends, who are they?"

"Well, that part's complicated," I say, cursing myself for not telling him about my Reader connection the other day. "They're what you would call Leachers."

"What?" His tone sharpens. "How do you know Leachers? What are you doing in their company? Are you okay?"

"It's three-twenty already," Mira says from the couch. "We have to start preparing."

"Look, Thomas," I say, realizing that she's right. "This thing is happening at four-thirty, so we're quickly running out of time. I am okay. My friends can be trusted. I have a very good explanation for everything, but we really have to get moving. Can we meet in person and talk in the Mind Dimension? This way, no time will pass on the outside."

He's silent for a very long moment. "Listen, Darren . . . We just met, and this is a lot to take in and not a lot of time for me to make decisions."

"I know, and I would be cautious too if I were you." I'm cognizant of the fact that if I actually were him, I would've told me to go fuck myself. "There's something else you should know, something that might help you trust me. I learned at the party that

Hillary is my aunt. You can ask her about that. She knows the whole story."

Another silence.

"You know," he says finally, "I actually think I see it. There's a distinct familial resemblance. I just didn't realize it until you told me. That's incredible."

"Yeah, I know," I say. "Does that help? We're running out of time here, Thomas."

"Assuming I agree to help, then yes. It takes care of a big problem I was going to raise before you brought up the Leachers."

"What problem?"

"You said there'll be a bunch of Russian gangsters and at least one Guide. To make matters worse, this thing is happening on a public bridge. Do you understand what that adds up to?"

"No, I am not sure that I do," I say, confused. "Trouble?"

"You can say that again. It means that this Guide will have a lot of people he can potentially turn against us. We might not survive this encounter, and even if we do, there might be severe civilian casualties."

"Shit," I say, looking at Mira and Eugene in despair. I hadn't thought that part through.

"There is a solution, though," Thomas says. "I need to make a call. Where are we meeting?"

"Let's meet at the South Street Seaport. Behind the mall. The part that faces the bridge," I suggest. "It seems fitting, given the view and its proximity to the meeting."

"Okay. I'll bring some supplies," Thomas says. "Can you be there in an hour? That would leave us enough time to get to the bridge even if we have to walk."

"Yes," I say, looking at Mira and mentally cringing at the thought of the drive ahead. "We can probably get there even sooner."

"Okay. See you there," Thomas says and hangs up the phone.

I meet Mira and Eugene's expectant gazes. "I think he'll help," I say, trying to sound more confident than I feel.

"Well, we need to get to the bridge regardless," Mira says matter-of-factly. "So meeting this guy is not going to sidetrack us too much. So long as it's not some Pusher trap."

"If it is, it would have nothing to do with me," I say.

"I know," Mira says. "It's not you that I don't trust."

I almost say 'since when,' but I hold my tongue. "Mira, I'm a good judge of character. It's a part of what I do for a living," I say, deciding that bending the truth might help ease her anxiety. "I think Thomas is going to help. I really do."

"We don't have a lot of choices, Mira," Eugene adds. "We can't take them all on with just the three of us. At least this guy works in the Secret Service."

"I said meeting this guy is not going to sidetrack us," Mira says, getting up and walking to a night stand. "So stop selling me the car I already bought."

She takes a gun from inside the night dresser. "Zhenya, do you have yours?" she says as she stuffs it into the back of her pants.

"Yes, in my room." Her brother also gets up.

"Okay, go get it, and meet us downstairs," she says to Eugene in a commanding tone.

It looks like she's bossed him around before, because he rushes out of the room without hesitation or backtalk.

"What about you, Darren?" she says, her voice getting a bit softer.

"I have a gun in the glove compartment of the rental," I say. "But I hope I don't need to use it."

"We have to be ready for anything," Mira says and walks out of the room.

CHAPTER TWENTY-SIX

"You're going to kill us, Mira." Eugene is plastered against the passenger door as we run the second red light. We exited the Battery Tunnel just moments ago, but we've already flown though five blocks. "Seriously, we're not *that* pressed for time."

"We never should've taken that fucking tunnel," she says, swerving suddenly. I think she just scared a cab driver—and those guys have seen everything. I've always thought they were the ones driving like maniacs, but they've got nothing on Mira. Hell, even Caleb isn't as bad. But she's still eighteen, and thinks she's indestructible. I, by the way, never had that delusion. I'm only too aware of how destructible I am.

"There was traffic leading up to the bridges," Eugene mumbles, still defending the suggestion he made earlier to take the tunnel.

The constant bickering Eugene and Mira engage in makes Mira's horrible driving an even worse experience. They argue about how fast she should drive, which cars not to cut off, and the best route. Until now, I thought my moms were the worst people to be in a car with, but apparently I was wrong. Is this how all siblings behave, or am I just lucky to be in a car with a particularly bad example?

The rest of the trip lasts about three deep breaths, and then Mira swerves into a parking garage, tires screeching. I estimate that she enters it at about thirty miles per hour, but I could be lowballing it.

When I open the car door, there is a definite smell of burned tires.

As she hands the valet the keys, the expression on the guy's face is priceless. I give him a hundred-dollar bill to get him out of his stupor and instruct him to wait at least twenty minutes before parking the car. We might return right away if we decide to drive to the Brooklyn Bridge after our talk with Thomas.

We run from the garage to the meeting spot. Despite the tenseness of the situation, I notice the beautiful view. It's soothing to see the old ships anchored here at the Seaport, and it makes me wonder about the days when this was an active port. Near-death experiences seem to do that for me—they bring out my sentimental side.

It's a nice Saturday afternoon, and we're soon confronted with a crowd of people. They're mainly tourists, but there are some locals here as well. Mira makes way for us through the crowd, rudely elbowing everyone aside.

We're near the corner of the meeting spot, near the benches looking out onto the water, when the world goes silent. The crowds around us freeze, as do Mira and Eugene.

"Hello, nephew," says a familiar, high-pitched voice. "You should really return my calls."

Hillary is standing next to my frozen self, with her hand on the frozen self's cheek. Thomas is standing next to her.

"You called me?" I say, surprised to see her there.

"Yeah, like twenty times."

"Sorry I missed it. I was too busy keeping my lunch in my stomach. Mira's driving is insane." I'm finally getting rid of the strange shock that accompanies forced phasing. It's always spooky being in the Quiet in a crowded and noisy place like this. My brain expects people to start walking and talking, but they don't. Being pulled into this state without warning makes the disorientation worse.

"Which one is Mira?" Hillary examines a couple of pretty girls.

"Who's Mira?" Thomas peers at the crowd. "Is that one of the Leachers you mentioned?"

"I didn't fill him in yet," Hillary says. "You might want to tell him the full story."

Before I tackle the mystery of Hillary's presence, I do as she suggests and tell Thomas everything. I have to give Thomas his due. He doesn't freak out about having to deal with Readers, unlike my Russian friends' reaction to working with Guides. He also takes in stride the fact that I'm a weird hybrid of both groups. I suppose his upbringing—not being part of the Guide community from birth—can explain it. Still, bigotry is all too easy to adopt, so the fact that he seems to have an open mind on the matter only reinforces my positive impression of him.

"So which one is she?" Hillary says. "I'm going to die of curiosity."

"There," I say, pointing at Mira. "The one who's slicing through the crowd like an impolite knife through butter."

"Very pretty." Hillary smiles her approval. "But then I assumed she would be."

"Yeah." I shrug. "Can I bring her in? That guy with glasses is Eugene, her brother."

"Hold on," Thomas says. "Let's talk privately first."

"Okay," I say, "now that I've explained myself, why don't the two of you tell me why Hillary is here?"

"If you took my calls, you'd know my reason for being here." She gives me a determined look. "I'm joining this mission."

"What? No, you're not." I turn to Thomas. "Tell her it's not happening."

"You need me," Hillary insists, and Thomas nods.

She gives me a smug look. "See? And you're not in a position to tell me what to do."

"Of course not," I say quickly, not wanting to offend her. "That was not my intent. I just don't want you getting hurt, that's all."

"That would be sweet if it weren't insulting. Why am I more likely to get hurt than your girlfriend, for example?"

"I don't want her to be here, either. It's just that I can't stop Mira from going. She's a bit tougher than you . . ." I'm completely failing at finding a graceful exit out of my verbal mess.

"Uh oh, Darren. Are you saying Hillary isn't as tough because of her size? You're new to the community; otherwise, you'd know she doesn't like her size criticized." Thomas's tone is serious, but the corners of his eyes are crinkling with amusement.

"My size has nothing to do with anything," Hillary says, elbowing Thomas in the hip. "In this situation, I'm the one person you all need."

Thomas nods again. "Right. Remember that problem I told you about?" he says. "How the Guide can use everyone on that bridge against us?"

I look at Hillary, remembering what she told me about her Reach. "You think you can override anyone he controls?"

"The person we're going after could be a *she*, but yes," Hillary says. "I have the best chance of anyone I know."

"It's true," Thomas confirms. "You have to trust me, Darren. Hillary has a very good reason to be here. I wouldn't have brought her otherwise."

"And I wouldn't have come if he didn't drop your name, Darren," she says. "I'm still a bit hesitant, but I think my presence can actually help avoid any unnecessary violence."

"Now that we have established who should be here, it might be a good moment to point out who probably shouldn't," Thomas says, pointedly glancing at Mira and Eugene.

"We can't *not* take them. It's Mira's revenge," I say, my eyes lingering on Mira's face. "She's been doing nothing but dreaming about getting this person."

"You're just building the case against taking her. She sounds like she could be a liability," Thomas says. "She's likely to do something reckless and get herself or us in danger."

"I don't think we have much choice," I say. "She'll be there, no matter what we do. If we want to avoid violence, we better take her with us."

"Also, we might actually use them for my plan," Hillary says. "It's very crowded there, and they can help Darren with the Reading."

"Fine," Thomas says cautiously. "But I don't like it."

"Duly noted," Hillary says, winking at me. "We'll put that into the report, Mr. Secret Service."

"Pull them in," Thomas says, and I do.

In a moment, Eugene is staring at me, his jaw slack and his eyes wide. In contrast, Mira seems calm, and she's studying the new people inquisitively.

I make quick work of introductions.

"Hillary has a plan," I say. "Do you mind telling us what it is, Aunty?"

"I thought I told you not to call me that," she begins saying, and then cuts herself off. "Never mind. You're just like your mother in this. If I let it bother me, you'll just do it more often." She chuckles before turning to face Eugene and Mira. "I do have a plan," she says. "Why don't we walk over to those benches before I explain it? It might take a few minutes."

"Sure," Mira says, and makes us a path again, violently shoving frozen people aside. I guess this is her way of expressing her feelings about having to work with Pushers.

"She's feisty," Hillary whispers as we walk through a tunnel made of bodies left in Mira's wake.

"Tell me about it," I whisper back, making my voice as low as possible.

"Gorgeous ambience," Hillary says when we get to our destination. She's right; this place is famous for its awesome view of the Brooklyn Bridge.

"We didn't come here for sightseeing," Mira says testily. "Let's hear your plan, Pusher."

"First and foremost, young lady, you will not use that derogatory term on me." Hillary gives her a stern look. "I prefer *Guide*, if you must talk about my abilities at all."

"She didn't—" Eugene begins.

"I can speak for myself," Mira interrupts. "I'm sorry. I'll call you whatever you want if you'll just please hurry up."

"Sure," Hillary says. "Here's what I have in mind . . ."

And in the silence that follows, she walks us through her idea.

"That sounds as good as anything I could've thought of," says Thomas.

"Coming from you, I'll take that as a huge compliment." Hillary beams at him.

"I'm game," Mira says. "This should work."

"Me too," Eugene says.

"I guess I'm okay with it also," I say. "Sounds fairly safe."

"Exactly," Hillary says. "My main objective is that no one gets hurt."

I notice Mira's eyes gleam dangerously every time Hillary says something along those lines, but I keep quiet. There isn't much to be said.

We all walk with Hillary to where her body is. She's the one whose version of the Quiet we're all in.

"How are we going to get there?" I ask as Hillary is about to take us out of the Quiet.

"It's walkable," says Thomas. "But I'd rather drive there. If the plan goes south, we might need a ride nearby."

Everyone agrees, and Thomas convinces all of us that his car should be the one we take.

As soon as we get out of the Quiet, we walk to his car—a black minivan half a block away.

"How did you *not* get your car towed, parking there?" Eugene asks, impressed. "Or at least not get a ticket?"

"I have special plates," Thomas says, opening the side door. "I can park wherever I want."

Inside the car, behind the second seat, is a whole arsenal of weapons. No wonder Thomas wanted to take this car.

"I'm not touching a gun," Hillary says as soon as she sees Thomas's stockpile. "Don't even try to convince me."

"You're staying in the car anyway, so you should be okay." Thomas smirks. "Besides, I bet that if you needed a gun, you'd forget all about your pacifist principles. Just like if you were starving, you'd eat bacon. How about you guys? Can I interest you in a weapon, just in case?"

"I have my own," I say, tapping the back of my pants where I have the gun Caleb gave me.

"Same here." Mira mirrors my tap.

"Me too," Eugene echoes.

"Okay," Thomas says. "Then it's just me." He straps on a holster and puts a gun in it. He also puts a huge hunting knife in a scabbard on his belt.

"There's really no need for this," Hillary objects. "My plan doesn't require any guns."

"It's just for contingency," he says. "Now, everyone, please get in. We have to go."

"I call shotgun," I say and get into the front seat.

Mira, Eugene, and Hillary climb in the back.

"Buckle up," Thomas says and starts the car.

It takes us two or three minutes to get to the spot where the traffic is turning onto the Brooklyn Bridge.

"Here," Thomas says. "Darren, since you insisted, Split, now."

I find that the pre-plan jitters aid me in phasing.

That's part one of the plan.

I now need to pull everyone into the Quiet with me.

Originally, Hillary wanted to do this herself, saying she's the most logical choice as one with the most Reach. I insisted that it be me. I explained to her that I have previously spent hours in the Quiet, so the relatively short amount of time the plan requires should be a snap for me.

I'm not sure why I did it. Probably to show off in front of Mira. But there was a practical side to it, too. Hillary needs to worry about bigger, more important aspects of the plan.

I phase and end up outside the car. That's interesting. Usually, I would show up in the back seat. Because the seat is taken by my friends, however, it seems that my body chose to show up outside. I wonder how this works. The Pusher in Caleb's memory was able to control this process. Maybe I can figure out a way to do the same? Then I remind myself that maybe it's bad luck to want to be like that Pusher at a time like this. After all, Caleb killed him.

The cars around us are standing still. No honking or sounds of any kind. The silence seems foreboding all of a sudden.

Okay, I need to snap out of this funk. The plan is simple and easy. No danger.

To bring the rest of the crew into the Quiet with me, I touch them, one by one, through the car window.

"We walk from here," Thomas says when he shows up.

We cross in front of the frozen cars and walk away from the road. Right over on the other side is the pedestrian portion of the Brooklyn Bridge.

As expected on a nice Saturday afternoon, the place is extremely congested, but the plan allowed for this eventuality.

"As we agreed, I'll go ahead," says Thomas. "My job is to recognize the Guide. Otherwise, you risk pulling him into the Mind Dimension with us, and that wouldn't be smart."

"I'm still not sure about this part. It's actually one of the weaker points of the plan," Eugene says.

"How so?" Hillary says, looking up at him.

"How do you know that you'll recognize him?" Eugene says to Thomas.

"Well," Thomas says, "from what all of you have told me, it seems a near certainty that this Guide lives in New York. I mean, there's no way someone from out of town would be able to Guide so many people here and over such a length of time. And if he's indeed local, I will know him."

"I guess it could work," Eugene concedes, "if you have a good memory."

"There aren't that many of us," Hillary says. "Even I could do it, and I'm a bit of a recluse. Thomas is new, so he's recently been explicitly introduced to everyone by his girlfriend, who's our official social butterfly."

"Who's the girlfriend?" I ask, although I already suspect the answer.

"Liz, of course." Hillary smiles. "You didn't figure that out?"

"No, not really. The fact that he's her patient kind of threw me off," I say, hoping I don't piss off Thomas. Now that I think about it, I realize that the lack of significant-other pictures in Liz's office is explained by the semi-forbidden nature of her relationship with Thomas. Obviously, she wouldn't want to acknowledge him as her boyfriend in the work setting.

"Focus, people," Thomas interrupts. "I need your heads in the game. You can gossip later, when we're done with this."

"Yes, sir. Sorry, sir." Hillary salutes him.

Mira watches the whole exchange with a strange expression on her face. I wonder if her world just became more complicated. Before meeting these two, she'd thought all Pushers were evil, so everything was simple and clearcut. But now she's met her so-called enemies, and they—especially my aunt—probably don't fit Mira's evil-villain stereotype.

Thomas leaves, ignoring Hillary's mockery. As he moves a few feet away, he becomes difficult to see in the crowd. This place is much too packed to suit me.

"We have a lot of work to do," I say, looking over the crowd.

"Then let's start working instead of talking," Mira says and approaches a buff-looking guy to the right of us.

"She just skipped those four people," Hillary says, pointing at two elderly couples nearest us.

"Right, they're the Russian Mafia, for sure," I say, unable to resist a snarky tone. "I know you said we need to identify the mobsters in the crowd, particularly if any are trying to be stealthy, but I'm pretty sure they're all going to be much younger than these four."

This is the part of Hillary's plan that found good use for Mira and Eugene. They're supposed to help identify the gangsters in this crowd by Reading. I have my doubts about this being necessary, as I suspect mobsters won't be trying for stealth. I bet we'll find them hanging out together someplace. Still, since finding a use for Mira and Eugene meant they got to come along, I kept my mouth shut.

In any case, if any Russian gangsters are found in this way, Hillary will supply them with some special instructions. Then my aunt, Thomas, and I will instruct everyone else to leave the bridge as fast as humanly possible, but in an orderly fashion. This way, we'll clear the place of any innocent bystanders.

"It's ageism," Hillary says stubbornly, interrupting my thought process. "You're implying that people of a certain age are not capable of something that someone younger can do. And where do you draw the age line? Fifty? Sixty?"

"Hillary, we might end up spending a day in the Mind Dimension if we check every single one of these people," I say, trying to placate her. "Let's say, due to this profiling, you tell a mobster or two to evacuate the bridge by mistake. It won't be the end of the world."

"Fine," she says and approaches the elderly couples.

Because Hillary can do her thing by a simple touch, Mira, Eugene, and I leave all the unlikely candidates for her.

I get to my job, which combines Guiding uninvolved people to evacuate with the work Mira and Eugene are doing—since, like them, I can Read.

I approach the first candidate, a muscular guy, with a scar on his cheek. He, in theory, could be one of Arkady's men.

I touch his forearm and concentrate.

* * *

We worry about the white lies we put in our dating profile. Particularly those lies by omission.

Will she want to date a war vet? And if so, what about a vet who might actually have PTSD? Or do we have panic attacks? Would the difference even matter to her?

I disassociate with the conclusion that this one is not a mobster.

That established, I begin part two.

'The date is going to happen in Battery Park instead of here. It's a much longer walk and probably much less crowded. Text the date and change the venue. Walk off the bridge in an orderly fashion. Focus on not trampling anyone. When you begin to have the next PTSD episode or a panic attack, you'll feel relaxed, the anxiety will leave your body, and you'll begin to forget what caused this problem in the first place.'

Convinced the guy will leave the bridge and potentially have less of a PTSD problem, I exit his head.

* * *

One down, hundreds more to go. I take out a magic marker that I got from a pack Thomas had in his glove compartment, and put a big X on this guy's head. This way, Hillary will know he's been processed already. Eugene is putting a circle on his targets' heads to signify that they're clean and should be Guided to evacuate. Mira is using lipstick to draw her circles. In case it isn't obvious, the forehead marking was my idea.

I look around and see a guy with a shaved head. He looks more like an athlete, but it's feasible that he could be a mobster. He becomes my next target.

I quickly learn that the athlete is actually a plumber with a bodybuilding hobby. More importantly, though, he's not a criminal of any kind.

I am out of his head and ready to draw my X when I get approached by Thomas.

"I checked about a quarter of the bridge and didn't see anyone I recognize," he says. "How are things going back here?"

"Just look at the foreheads. These two big guys are clean," I say.

"Those four over there also," Eugene says, overhearing our conversation.

"That guy too," Mira adds from a few feet away. "And that woman."

Why she even checked a woman, I have no idea, but I don't say anything lest Hillary accuse me of sexism this time.

"I just took care of those elderly people and two children," Hillary says. "Even if we skip the unlikely targets, as Darren suggested, this will take a really long while. I didn't anticipate this many people being here."

"It's not like we're getting older or missing any appointments, with the time stopped and all," Eugene says.

"True, but this can be very tedious," I say. "We might need to get more selective in our choices. Rather than just younger, buffer men, why don't we focus on ones that have a criminal look to them also?"

"That's even worse profiling," Hillary says unhappily. "And it can lead to a lot more mobsters walking away. I'm not comfortable with that."

"I have an idea that can at least take care of the second problem," Thomas says. "We can add a compulsion for anyone remotely suspicious to give up their gun to the next police officer they see."

"That's clever," Hillary says, looking relieved. "People without guns simply won't comply. They won't have the context for the induction. So only the guilty will be impacted."

"Of course, some mobsters might not have a gun," I say. "And some innocent people might have a permit to carry a concealed weapon."

"What kind of criminals would they be without guns? But if they are, I say it's their lucky day—they get away free," Eugene says. "And the people who lawfully carry a concealed gun will end up showing their permit to the cops, get a breathalyzer test for doing something so wacky, and get let go. No harm, no foul."

"I agree," Mira says. "If we miss a few, it's not going to be that big of a deal."

"We still need a good number of mobsters to deal with the Guide. He might not be here alone," Thomas reminds us.

The plan is to have a bunch of Russian mobsters prohibit the Guide from leaving the bridge. Because Hillary is going to command them, in theory at least, the Guide we're targeting won't be able to override her because of her longer Reach. That's why she's so critical for this plan—and why I'm supposed to give any real mobster I find to her.

"I wouldn't worry about that," Mira says. "Most likely, the men we saw at that table in the banya are all here in one large group, and there will be plenty for that part of the plan."

"Okay, then that settles it," says Thomas. "I'll also take part in the evacuation now that we have a better way of doing it."

"Just mark up the people as you finish with them, like these guys have been doing, so we don't duplicate our efforts," Hillary says.

"Does anyone have anything to write with?" Thomas says.

"Here, use my eye shadow pencil," Mira says, handing him the strange writing instrument.

She uses way too much makeup, I decide. Especially since I know for a fact she looks amazing without it. I saw her first thing in the morning the other day, and she was drop-dead gorgeous. Unless she sleeps with makeup on. Can that be done?

"Put an X on the foreheads of everyone you Guided to evacuate," I remind Thomas as he takes Mira's pencil.

He walks off, saying nothing about the indignity of this marking. He had a problem with this part when we were talking about Hillary's plan. Indeed, he had an even bigger problem with my original idea for this—taking people's pants off, or just pushing them to the ground, like logs. This current system is actually a compromise.

I choose two new potentials. Both end up being civilians, and both get instructions to get off the bridge and give their concealed guns to the next police officer they see. Both get marked.

I fleetingly wonder how many non-mobster people who happen to have illegally concealed guns will end up getting into trouble today because of us. Oh well, that's their problem for carrying a gun without a permit.

I'm approaching my next target when I feel a delicate hand on my shoulder. "Darren, I wanted to speak to you," Mira says quietly when I turn to face her.

"What's up?" I ask, matching her volume.

"When we find the Pusher, the one responsible for my parents' death, I'm not going to follow the plan," she says, standing up on tiptoes to speak almost directly into my ear.

"Mira, please, this is a good plan. Don't do anything rash," I say, my heart beating faster—and not just because of her soft lips brushing sensually against my ear.

"I'm not an idiot," she whispers. "I'm going to wait until he's trapped first. But once he's trapped, instead of handing him over to the rest of the Pushers like Hillary wants, I'm going to kill him."

"I don't think that's a good idea," I say, confused as to why she's even telling me this. I'd wondered why Mira took that portion of the plan so calmly, given her desire for vengeance. Now I know. She never intended to go along with it. She wanted to double cross Hillary and Thomas.

"I'll need your help," she says. "I'll need you to lock the car after I run out, and slow them down in any way possible."

"No, Mira, I don't think I can do that," I say. "But how about this? As soon as we get back to reality, I'll Split and pull you in. Then we can talk about this. Okay? Promise you won't act until we talk?"

"Fine, we'll talk," she whispers. "But with or without your help, Arkady and the Pusher are not leaving this bridge alive."

And before I get a chance to respond, she walks away.

Thomas was right; we should've come without her. It's too late now, though. Maybe I can do something to stop her, like locking the car *before* she runs out. I can also phase out and warn Thomas and Hillary. But Mira trusted me, and I'm having a hard time picturing myself betraying her trust like that. Plus, there's a tiny part of me that agrees with her. My aunt is much too peaceful. Arkady's men repeatedly tried to kill me and my friends, and it was the Pusher who was pulling their strings. If those two die, I won't cry over them at all.

I walk further, avoiding a few people Thomas had marked, and head toward a small clearing in the crowd. Thanks to the clearing, I see Thomas in the distance.

And that's when I register the sight in front of me.

It's as Mira suspected.

All the Russian goons from the banya are standing in the middle of the Brooklyn Bridge. Only they're dressed now and very likely armed.

There's a clearing around them, probably because people were instinctively giving this group a wide berth. I don't blame the prudent pedestrians. I would've avoided these Russians myself.

Approaching them, I put circles on each forehead with an X underneath. A sort of skull and bones mark I came up with to signify the mobsters. None of them were otherwise marked, which means that Thomas isn't insane in his profiling. He rightfully realized these aren't innocent bystanders.

Now we need Hillary.

"Hillary," I yell, looking back. "Best come take a look at this. I think we're pretty much done with one part of the plan."

I see a tiny hand wave above the crowd for a moment. Did my aunt have to jump to make that happen? Or did Eugene lift her?

I decide to follow Thomas and tell him the news, because it doesn't seem like he heard me yell for Hillary.

As I head in his direction, I see Thomas.

He's touching someone.

Someone I recognize.

"Thomas, no! Stop!" I yell, hoping it's not too late.

But it is.

In a moment, we're going to have a new presence in the Quiet—someone who shouldn't be here at all.

CHAPTER TWENTY-SEVEN

I rudely push aside the people in my way, trying to get closer. As if getting closer is going to change anything.

Thomas's hand is resting on Jacob's shoulder, his fingers almost brushing against the man's neck.

Yes, Jacob—the leader of the Reader community. The man who gave me that 'no disclosure of powers' lecture the other day and mentioned the name of my father.

The last person I expected to see on this bridge.

I look closer and get another surprise. Next to Jacob is Sam, the guy Caleb mentioned as potentially helping us. A man Caleb called a machine. That

Jacob is with Sam makes sense. Sam is security, like Caleb. But the fact they're *here* makes no sense at all.

The world seems to slow, even in the Quiet—or maybe it's just my thoughts that speed up.

Did Caleb call in Sam despite my being against it? No, that wouldn't explain anything. I never told Caleb any details about this meeting. It has to be something else.

Did Eugene talk to Julia after all, and did she tell everything to her father? Eugene never left my sight, but maybe he did it in the Quiet? Would Eugene be so stupid? I can't imagine that he would be. There must be another explanation.

Then I wonder if the Readers might be after the same Pusher as us, for their own reasons, and they're here trying to get him too. This is a more plausible guess, but the coincidence of it would be too great. And why only Jacob and Sam? Why wouldn't they bring Caleb's whole team, plus the man himself?

And then I notice a briefcase in Jacob's hand.

A briefcase. The man on the phone was supposed to bring money for Arkady, and a briefcase seems like a good way to transport bundles of cash.

Can it be?

Is it possible that instead of a powerful Pusher, it had been Jacob—a Reader—on the phone?

That would explain why the mysterious puppet-master used the phone in the first place. True, it's easier to call people than walk over and touch them in the Quiet, but phone calls are easier to trace, and the mastermind in all this always seemed to be extra paranoid. And why waste money on a convoluted hit list if you can just make Arkady kill whomever you want for free?

If Jacob is the man on the phone, everything changes.

Thomas is within an inch of touching Jacob. I take out my gun, confused thoughts still buzzing in my head.

Could it have been Jacob who ordered me to be shot? Maybe he saw my resemblance to my father? He did mention on Skype that I looked familiar. If he knew whom my father married, it's not a big leap to assume that I'm a hybrid. And what could be worse than a hybrid to a Purist like Jacob? Not much, I imagine. Is it possible that Jacob had Caleb bring me to him in order to observe my reaction to the name *Mark Robinson*? With hindsight, it does make sense. There was no reason for Jacob to personally warn me against revealing my powers; Caleb or any other Reader could've done that.

As I think these thoughts, the fear that overtakes me is so intense, I half-expect to phase into the

Quiet—except I'm already there. So I don't phase; I just feel odd as the feeling intensifies. Phasing must provide me some relief in tense moments like these because I've never felt so much like jumping out of my skin before.

And then I see a second, not-frozen Jacob show up behind Thomas. This Jacob looks around him in confusion for only a moment. When he sees Thomas touching his frozen body, he seems to realize what happened. I can tell what he's thinking: someone pulled him into the Quiet.

Someone he doesn't recognize.

If Jacob's here for the reason I suspect, then he'll be scared now. He'll be feeling cornered.

For my part, the feeling is one of stunned immobility. I watch, in a trance-like state, as Jacob jumps back. He throws the briefcase he's been holding to the side, and begins to reach with the freed hand into the back of his pants.

When the briefcase hits the ground, it breaks open. Bundles of hundred-dollar bills spill onto the pavement.

There's no longer any doubt.

Jacob *is* the man on the phone—the paymaster for whom we laid this trap.

And that means Thomas is in danger, I realize instantly. We all are.

Metal flashes as Jacob removes his hand from the back of his pants. He's holding a gun now.

Why hasn't Thomas turned around already? I think in mute terror. Couldn't he hear the sound of the briefcase landing and splitting open? Or is he so focused on the Guiding that he's oblivious to his surroundings?

I raise my own gun and fire, aiming upwards.

It would've been better to shoot at Jacob perhaps, but I don't trust my marksmanship skills. Not with him so close to Thomas. Besides, I'd rather wound Jacob than kill him. That, unlike death, is reversible upon phasing out and would allow us to ask Jacob several pertinent questions.

The noise of my gun is deafening. It's like a roar of thunder, made stronger by the fact that my ears had adjusted to the almost absolute silence of the Quiet.

Thomas instantly turns around—which, of course, was my intent. There's no way he could've missed *that* terrible noise.

Everything that follows happens with astonishing speed.

Thomas turns and sees the man he just tried to Guide standing behind him, holding a gun. I would've expected Thomas to be confused, but instead, his reaction is lightning-fast.

With one swift motion, Thomas kicks the gun out of Jacob's hand. I wonder if my gunshot disoriented Jacob, causing him to become an easy target for that kick. Some Caleb-and-Haim-forged part of my mind also registers an extra detail about Thomas's maneuver.

It was a kickboxing move.

Almost immediately, Thomas punches the now-disarmed Jacob in the face.

That's a traditional boxing uppercut, the same fight-attuned part of my brain informs me.

Jacob staggers backwards. His movements seem to slow. That hit must've really taken his brain for a spin.

Thomas closes the distance between them in one powerful lunge and executes another punch. Boxing again, but this time mixed with something I can't even place.

Jacob staggers back again and falls. He looks drunk, like boxers do when they get that final knockout punch. Only he doesn't stay down. Instead, he begins crawling on the ground a little to the left of Thomas.

I see Thomas watching him. It's hard for me to tell if the expression on Thomas's face is disgust or pity, but what's clear is that he's not hurting Jacob for the moment. Maybe, like me, he wants him alive for questioning. Otherwise, it would be an easy thing for him to end the fight with just a single shot, or even a few well-placed kicks.

But then I understand what Jacob is trying to do.

"Kick him!" I try to scream at Thomas, but my voice is hoarse. Seeing that Thomas doesn't hear me, or doesn't understand what I'm saying, I raise my gun and point it at Jacob. At the last moment, I hesitate. I still don't trust my aim, and they're way too close to each other. So instead of shooting, I clear my throat, preparing to let out the loudest scream of my life. At the same time, Jacob speeds up his crawl, and his hand is by Sam's pant leg.

Jacob is about to pull Sam into the Quiet.

"Fucking shoot him, Thomas!" I scream, this time loudly. "Now!"

Thomas looks at me instead. I point at Jacob with an exaggerated gesture and slice the edge of my palm across my throat in the universal 'kill him' signal. Nodding, Thomas turns toward Jacob and raises his gun.

Only it's too late. Jacob rolls up Sam's jeans and grabs the big man's ankle.

"Watch out!" I yell at Thomas again. I also ready my own gun, determined to risk taking that shot if I have to. If Caleb is to be believed, Sam's a much more dangerous opponent than Jacob. He's on par with Caleb himself—and I've seen what Caleb can do. It's ironic that the man we almost asked for help is the very one we need help from.

I try to focus. I can't miss the moment Sam materializes in the Quiet. When he does, I'm taking my chances with my aim. There's no other choice.

Meanwhile, Thomas, after a brief hesitation, shoots Jacob in the chest. I'm startled by the noise, and also shocked by this turn, even though I was the one who suggested it. I hope that Thomas knows what Jacob just did, that he pulled in reinforcements. Is that why Thomas made that shot? Did he make a decision to keep his enemy's numbers controllable?

I'm still looking around for Sam, and so is Thomas.

And then another gunshot threatens to damage my eardrums. I look around and see, in absolute horror, that Thomas is clutching his chest. There is a circle of red spreading there.

No. This can't be happening. That's the only thought in my mind as Thomas makes a whimpering sound and slowly falls to his knees.

"No!" I hear a high-pitched voice echoing my thought from a foot away from me. It must be Hillary and the others, catching up with us. I have no time to check, however.

Now that Thomas is on his knees, I see where Sam materialized in the Quiet. He was directly behind Thomas from my vantage point. That's why I heard the shot, but didn't see the shooter.

The shooter who's now looking in my general direction and carefully aiming his gun.

I fire. The good news is that I at least don't shoot Thomas. He's still clutching his chest, but the fact that he's still upright, albeit on his knees, fills me with a sliver of hope. Maybe Sam's bullet went through his body without damaging any vital organs? Maybe it's just a flesh wound?

The bad news is that I clearly missed Sam, because he's standing unharmed.

Standing unharmed and firing his own gun— which is pointed at me.

Sam's gunshot is the scariest sound I have ever heard in my life. It seems to vibrate and fill my very being with dread. But as the feeling that my ears might bleed fades, I realize that I'm intact.

And then I see why.

Sam wasn't aiming at me. He was aiming at Thomas. I'm numb with disbelief as I watch Thomas falling to the ground, a pool of blood forming around his head.

The enormity of this loss is worsened by the knowledge that Thomas was the only one of us who would've stood a chance against Sam. And now Thomas is dead.

And we're fucked.

As I stand there, dazed, I see a gun appear from behind me. I recognize the slender long-fingered hands holding the weapon.

It's Mira's hands.

As I register this fact, she pulls the trigger.

At the same time, Sam does some military maneuver, where he rolls on the floor. I've seen this in movies, but never in the real life. Mira's shot must've missed him because I see Sam roll up to Thomas's dead body and turn it sideways, using our dead friend's body as a makeshift shield.

Sick with dread, I aim and take another shot. At the same time, two more shots get fired. It must be Eugene and Mira shooting at the same time, I realize vaguely.

"Darren, run!" Hillary yells, and I hear her acting on her suggestion.

"We should follow her." It's Eugene, sounding frantic.

I hear the sound of his departing feet, and then Mira yells, "We should cover them!" and fires another shot at Sam.

I glance back to see Mira backing away. I follow her example, shooting in the general direction of Sam as I begin to back away myself.

Sam peeks from his hiding place and fires another shot. I brace for the pain, but instead I hear an agonized shriek behind me.

From where Eugene and Hillary are.

Forgetting about creating the cover fire, I rush toward my friends. Mira does the same.

We see Eugene standing over Hillary, who's on the ground.

"She's alive," Eugene says quickly. "It's her leg. She's been shot in the knee."

He must be babbling in shock because it's obvious my aunt is alive. She's wailing like a banshee and clutching her leg.

In shock myself, I realize that I've kept my eyes off Sam for too long. I turn around—and see Sam standing much closer to us. Having abandoned his makeshift human shield, he's now in a half-kneeling position, using his knee to stabilize his gun while aiming at us.

Both Mira and I raise our guns in unison and fire. Sam's own shot echoes ours.

I brace for pain, but it doesn't come. Instead, I hear a thumping sound nearby. I again feel like I'm about to phase into the Quiet, only this time the feeling of frustration at it not happening is even more intense. Filled with terror, I look back. The pavement behind me is covered with blood.

And then I see its source.

It's Eugene. He's on the ground, convulsing, blood and brain matter seeping out from what's left of his head.

I feel sick, but I can't vomit. My brain feels woolen, my thoughts slow with stunned disbelief. Surely this is just a nightmare that I'll wake up screaming from. Eugene can't be dead. He can't be. It's only now that I realize how much I liked him. How I had begun to think of him as a friend. He can't be gone.

But I don't wake up in bed screaming. Instead, I turn and shoot again, over and over, trying to channel my hatred for Sam into every bullet.

The fucker seems unharmed, however. He's impossible to hit, with all the stupid rolling maneuvers that he does. I shoot again, but he rolls forward, doing something that looks almost like a somersault.

When he lands, I squeeze the trigger again, but my gun makes an empty clicking sound.

"Run, Darren!" Mira yells, taking a step forward. "You need to get out. Before he gets you too."

She takes careful aim and shoots. I hear a grunt and see Sam clutching his hand. Mira managed to hit his gun hand. I feel a wave of relief.

Emboldened by her success, Mira shoots again, but this time she misses. Sam does another one of those cursed rolls.

"Run, I said!" Mira screams, but I can't bring myself to move. Does she really expect me to leave her to fight Sam on her own? No fucking way.

And then it hits me. Maybe I do have to do what Mira says. If I get out in time, get back to my frozen self in the car, and phase us all out of the Quiet, I can at least save Hillary. No matter what damage Hillary received here in the Quiet, once she's pulled out of it, she'll be whole again. But what about Mira? If I leave her behind, she might be dead before I can get us all out.

"You run!" I yell at Mira. "I'll follow you."

Not waiting to see if she will follow my command, I frantically glance back at Sam. He's holding a knife now.

I know what I have to do. I have to attack him, to slow him down. As I think about this, I again experience that feeling. Like I'm about to phase into the Quiet. This time, though, it does something.

Time seems to slow down for me.

In this slow motion, I begin running toward him. As I run, I watch Sam's left hand grip the knife by the blade. His arm swings back, and then he lets the deadly projectile fly. In this same slow motion, I see the knife rotating in the air as it flies toward us. I try to brace myself—but then I see that the knife is not flying at me.

It's flying at Mira.

With an explosion of despair, I see the knife make the last deadly rotation as it strikes Mira's chest. It penetrates deeply, almost to the hilt, and I hear a scream of agony escape Mira's mouth.

Some irrational part of me wonders if I can run, phase us out before the knife does its deadly work, but then I remember the distance to the car and abandon that option. It's too far.

Mira's hands clutch the hilt of the knife, and a look of utter dread crosses her face. For the first time, I see her as the young and fragile woman that she is. Our eyes meet as she begins to cough up blood. Slowly, almost gracefully, she falls down. By the time she hits the ground, those deep blue eyes that are still staring into mine lose their focus.

She's dead.

No. I can't accept that—because if I do, I'll fall on the ground in grief. And I can't fall. Not now. Not after everything.

I feel my grief and terror transform into something else. A violent and uncontrollable fury.

I become wrath. I become rage.

A part of me registers Sam approaching, but instead of fear, I feel elation at what I'm about to do. The world becomes focused on a single point. On a single target.

A person. No, not a person—a thing, a piece of meat that I must destroy. A cancer that I must cut out.

A roar, like that of a wounded animal, leaves my throat.

I run at Sam.

He runs at me.

In a mixture of Haim's and Caleb's moves, I land blows to his stomach and face before he registers my intent. I kick his shin next, and Sam blocks it, but he misses the kick that goes for his balls. As my foot makes contact, he gasps and turns pale, but doesn't stop blocking and manages to deflect my jab at his solar plexus.

Recovering from my surprise attack, Sam attempts a punch of his own. I block his punch with my left forearm and slam my right fist into Sam's jaw with all my strength.

Excruciating pain explodes in my forearm and right fist, but it doesn't matter. All I can think about is the satisfying crunch his jaw just made. It's like music to my ears, and I want to hear more of his bones break. I want to hear it even if I need to break what's left of my own fingers in the process.

I feint with my right fist, and when Sam reacts to it, I try to hit his nose with my left elbow.

The pain in my arm is unbearable, but I ignore it, the elation of hearing the bone-crunching sound overriding everything else. His nose is bleeding now, likely broken.

He doesn't pause, though, and my moment of triumph is followed by an eruption of agony in my side. Air leaves my lungs with a whoosh, and I desperately try to regain my balance. Sam's knee connects with my ribs somehow, and I don't get a chance to stabilize myself. Not when Sam kicks my knee next, and I begin falling. As I fall, he manages to kick my flying body several times. I'm only able to block a few of the blows before I fall face down on the ground.

My body feels broken, and the metallic taste of blood is in my mouth. I try to spit it out, but I can't. My body doesn't obey me as kicks continue to rain down on me. I lose count of them, the pain blending together into an avalanche of suffering.

I don't know how I'm still conscious, but I suddenly become cognizant that he stopped. And before I have a chance to wonder why, I feel his hands grab my head, holding it in a viselike grip.

No, I scream in my mind as my head turns to the side with an impossibly loud crunch. There is an explosion of pain in my neck, followed by an awful numbness.

A numbness that engulfs my entire body.

In the horrifying absence of pain, I realize that I'm looking at Sam from a strange angle. This shouldn't be possible. I shouldn't be able to see him at all, since I'm lying on my stomach. And then I begin to understand.

I understand the numbness and the crunching noise.

I understand why I now feel like I'm choking.

My neck is broken. The spinal cord has snapped, and my head is twisted backwards. This is why the guillotine was considered a merciful death. When your head is separated from the body, there is no pain. You simply die. In seconds.

As my consciousness begins to slip, I stare at the sky, knowing it's the last thing I'll ever see.

CHAPTER TWENTY-EIGHT

Something smacks me in the face. The pain is a welcome surprise. That I can feel anything at all fills me with a sense of wonder.

I was never a believer in the afterlife, but I was apparently wrong. Something exists after death, or so it seems.

I open my eyes to even more confusion.

Why would there be an airbag in my face in the afterlife?

I'm suddenly fully alert.

Somehow, I'm back in Thomas's car. Next to me, I see Thomas himself. He's behind the wheel. He also has an airbag in his face, but he's moving.

He's alive.

"Ouch," I hear a high-pitched voice from the back.

Hillary's voice.

"You should've fucking let me drive." It's Mira's voice now. Sharp and annoyed, but unmistakably alive. The joy and relief that fills me is indescribable.

"Mira," I almost yell. "You're alive!"

"Why wouldn't she be?" Eugene's voice says from the back. "What the fuck happened after I was shot in the Mind Dimension?"

"Yeah, what happened?" Thomas echoes.

"You're alive too, Eugene! You're *all* alive. I can't believe it!" I'm hoping this isn't some hallucination or a trick of my dying brain. "I saw all three of you die. *I* died."

"Just the three of us?" Thomas asks. "So, Hillary, you didn't?"

"No," she says. "I was injured and bleeding, but when that monster killed Darren, I was still alive."

"Then we still stand a chance," Thomas says.

"Yes. In fact, the plan is almost unchanged," Hillary says. "Who were those men?"

"A leader of the Readers and his guard," I answer on autopilot as I try to process the fact that somehow we are all alive.

"What? How did one of us end up being one of them?" Hillary sounds almost as confused as I feel. "You know what, there's no time for that. I saw the mobsters with the marks Darren left on their heads. I can take control of them and then evacuate the rest of the people."

I manage to push away the airbag and look behind me.

Hillary has a look of concentration on her face.

"Okay, I just tried to take care of it," she says, her features returning to normal after a moment. "I hope it goes smoothly."

"What do you mean?" Mira and I say in unison.

"And how are we even alive?" I add, barely able to contain the turbulent mixture of emotions swirling inside me. "I thought we died—"

"Darren, when you get killed in the Mind Dimension, you don't die in the real world," Hillary says, looking at me. "We all feel like something bad is going to happen if we die in there, and it does—but it's not death. It's more of a major inconvenience."

"What? No, wait," I say, confused. "Yes, you do. You die, I'm sure of it. I—"

"No, you don't, as we obviously didn't," Mira says. "But we did lose something."

"Try to Split, Darren," Eugene says, looking at me. "Then you'll understand."

I do as he says. Phasing into the Quiet right now should be the easiest thing in the world. I've got all this residual fear and adrenaline stored up.

Only it doesn't happen. The frustrated feeling is familiar. It's exactly how I felt in those scary moments in the Quiet. It's like trying to phase and hitting a mental brick wall.

"The three of us are Inert now," Thomas explains as he gets his airbag situation under control. "We can't Split into the Mind Dimension."

It must be the overflow of emotion because the sense of loss I feel is intense. "We lost our powers?" I say in disbelief.

"Yes. For a while," Thomas says. "Not forever."

"So it's not permanent?" The wave of relief is nearly as powerful as my sense of loss a second ago.

"No, it's not. When you die in the Mind Dimension, it's a lot like using up your time, only the Inertness lasts much longer," Eugene explains.

"I've never run out of time in the Quiet before," I say, and I hear the note of unease in my voice. Logically, I know that temporarily losing my powers is in no way comparable to dying, but it still feels frightening. The Quiet has been my security blanket, a safety net I've used since childhood, and I feel its loss keenly.

"I understand, Darren." Hillary gives me a sympathetic look. "Like you, I've never run out of time, so I can't even imagine what that would be like. I'm so sorry it happened to you."

"He'll be fine. It'll come back," Thomas says. He doesn't seem overly concerned about his own loss of powers, but then again, his are more limited than mine or Hillary's.

As he speaks, something occurs to me. "So is this why you were so cavalier when you pointed that gun at me yesterday?" I ask, staring at Mira. That never made sense to me. Not after I saved her life the day before. "You weren't threatening to kill me. You were threatening to strip me of my power?"

"Right," she says. "Honestly, I was just bluffing. I wasn't really going to make you Inert. Not given what I knew about your insane Depth. I'm sorry about that whole incident. I wouldn't have done it if I'd known you were actually scared for your life." She pauses, then adds, "Most likely."

The puzzle pieces begin to fall into place. "So that's why Eugene said that weird shit about not shooting me because I can spend months in the Mind Dimension?"

"Yeah." Eugene nods. "It would've been a sacrilege to take away so much power. I couldn't let her do it. She can be cranky when she wakes up, so I didn't even realize she was bluffing."

I blow out a relieved breath. So it wasn't that Eugene wanted to use me, as I'd originally thought. He had been aware of the true cost of death in the Quiet all along and was simply trying to protect me.

Everything starts to make sense now. When Caleb said during our Joining that dying in the Quiet has a lasting effect, he didn't mean death; he meant the Pusher would be Inert. This also explains Caleb's slightly odd thought about it being time to 'begin' killing the Pusher. He must've meant that step one was making the man Inert. Without powers, it must be much easier to dispatch one of us outside the Quiet. And this is why Caleb tried to phase into the Quiet from not too far away. Once the Pusher was killed in the Quiet and therefore rendered Inert, Caleb, who still possessed his powers, would've made short work of him.

I'm still not solid on the details, but things are beginning to be clearer.

"How long will it take me to recover?" I ask.

"It varies for everyone," Eugene says.

"Wait," Thomas says, turning toward me. "Hold on a second. Is your 'Depth' the same thing we call

Reach? And if so, are you saying that yours is *months*? You never mentioned this, Darren."

I shrug, still thinking about my Inert state, but Hillary smiles proudly. "He is my nephew, after all."

"Is this why you didn't run when I asked you to?" Mira stares at me, her eyes shining. "You thought we were in mortal danger?"

"Well, yeah," I admit, somewhat embarrassed. "I couldn't just leave you there. Sam was right on our heels. I didn't realize you were trying to save my powers."

"I was actually trying to end her suffering," Mira explains, glancing at Hillary.

"Thank you," my aunt says.

There is a moment of silence as everyone seems to relive those terrifying moments.

"So what's with this car crash?" I ask finally. "How does that fit into everything?"

"That's my fault," Thomas says. "The shock of dying and then finding myself behind the wheel again was too much, so I rear-ended that guy."

"I took care of that driver," Hillary says. "He'll think he backed into a fire hydrant."

"You keep saying that you took care of things," Mira says. "But you're not explaining what you did or how you did it. What's happening on that bridge?"

"Oh, that. I Guided the mobsters to hold down your fellow Leachers—I mean, Jacob and Sam. The mobsters are probably moving in on them as we speak," Hillary explains.

"I still can't believe it," Eugene says through gritted teeth. "It's been Jacob all this time." In an uncharacteristic move for Eugene, he punches my seat in frustration. It doesn't hurt, so I don't say anything. I understand exactly how he feels.

"Wait, it just occurred to me. The name Jacob," Hillary says. "Didn't you say that the name of the person on the phone was Esau?"

"Yes," I say. "So?"

"Jacob and Esau were brothers in the Scripture. The guy practically gave you a hint as to who he is," Hillary says.

"So Jacob ordered that explosion," Mira says slowly, and I realize that this fact is only now beginning to dawn on her. "It was a Reader who ruined our lives, not a Pusher."

"Yes, it was Jacob using an alias of Esau," I confirm softly. "He ordered Arkady to use the explosives." Mira's entire world must be turning upside down. Pushers are not her enemies, while Readers, her own people, seem to be.

"I don't understand." Eugene sounds bewildered. "There was definitely a Pusher involved. He pops up in many of the gangsters' memories."

"There must be more to this," Hillary says. "After the police question everyone involved, we can access their files. Maybe something will turn up."

"What police?" Mira's voice gets soft. Dangerously soft. "What are you talking about?"

"I'm about to call them," Hillary explains. "That's the part of the plan that's now different. Easier, in fact. The gangsters should be able to hold those two Leachers down, and instead of us calling our Guide friends, I'll let the cops handle this. Guides are not equipped to deal with Leachers. They'll kill them, and I can't have that. Don't worry, though. Unlike Guides, Leachers can't get out of jail. Right?" she says, apparently missing the hard gleam in Mira's eyes.

"No fucking way—"

Mira's harsh words get interrupted by the sound of distant gunfire. One shot is followed by several in rapid succession.

Hillary turns pale.

Mira's head whips toward the bridge, and I see her coming to a swift decision. Before I can say anything, she springs into action. She opens the door, presses the door lock button, slams the door shut behind her, and begins running toward the bridge.

"Fuck!" Thomas fumbles with the lock. "I told you she'd be a liability."

I frantically unbuckle my seatbelt to go after her.

"Stop her," Thomas barks at Hillary as he finally unlocks the doors. "You're the only one who can."

"I can't," Hillary objects. "She's got a gun. She could shoot a civilian if I try to use them."

"This is not the time for pacifism." I don't see the expression on my aunt's face, but I hear Thomas curse and then say, "Fine. Improvise something. You there, hand me that rifle—"

I don't hear Eugene's response because I open the door and start running after Mira. Immediately, I'm reminded of the fact that I'm no longer in the Quiet. The cars around us are moving at full speed, and I almost get run over twice before I reach the sidewalk. When I hear screeching brakes, I attempt to phase in, but it's futile. I can't go into the Quiet.

I've been Inert less than five minutes, and I already hate it.

"I was barely able to control that last car, you know," a cab driver says cryptically from his window as I run past him. He's wearing a turban and speaking with a slight Indian accent. I'm pretty sure

I've never met him. "You're my blood relative, Darren, and I desperately want you to live. Please be careful."

My attention shifts from the strange cabby to the road I just crossed as I hear loud honking, followed by a thump. Glancing back, I see Eugene on the ground in front of a car. My heart skips a beat, but I don't stop.

I have to get to Mira.

As I get close to the bridge, I see a crowd of people rushing toward me. It must be Hillary's improvised Guided evacuation. Here and there, I notice familiar faces—people I'd Read and Guided myself.

At my approach, the crowd parts, leaving a wide path for me. It's odd, but it serves me, so I don't question it.

"Darren, hurry, she's almost there," says an old lady as I run onto the boardwalk-like portion of the bridge.

"It's me, Hillary, by the way," a little kid says as he runs by me. "Why do you look so shocked?"

Now I get it. The cabby, the old lady, the people giving me room to run, and now the kid. Hillary is Guiding these people to aid me, and she's giving me messages through them. I'd be very impressed if I weren't in such a panic.

Then I hear tires screech behind me again.

"A car almost hit Thomas. He's okay, though. Still running your way. Eugene is also okay; he just hurt his leg. He might not make it there in time," the buff guy with PTSD says as I pass by him.

Before I get a chance to feel reassured, there is a strange wail. At least a hundred people all around the bridge scream in unison like some hellish chorus, "No, Mira, don't!"

And then the people in front of me fall to the ground. What makes that move extra-spooky is that they do it simultaneously, like they were all stricken with some deadly poison at the exact same moment.

This gives me a clear view of what's about to happen—a view that explains why Hillary made them do that. She wouldn't give so many civilians bruises without good cause.

On the far end of the bridge, I see two large men fighting. Fighting to the death, by the looks of it.

One of them I recognize instantly. It's Arkady, the psychopath from the banya. He must be under Hillary's control. The other one is Sam.

The fury that gripped me earlier returns as I see Sam holding the same knife that he threw at Mira in the Quiet.

And then I register what Mira is doing.

This is what Hillary wanted me so desperately to see.

Mira is aiming her gun at the two fighting men.

In that instant, I also take in the rest of the scene. On the ground next to Sam and Arkady, two of Arkady's men are holding down Jacob. The rest of the mobsters, including the one who tried to shoot me the other day, are lying on the ground bleeding. Those must've been the shots we heard. The gangsters were probably shot trying to get Sam's and Jacob's guns away from them—and it looks like they succeeded.

"Mira, there is no need to kill anyone!" Arkady screams as he continues wrestling with Sam. Hillary must be speaking through his mouth as well.

Sam grunts and yells out in response, "Mira, stop him, and you and your brother will be welcomed with open arms in our community! This man is being controlled by a powerful Pusher. I need your help. Jacob needs your help. Shoot him! Now!"

"It's you I'm going to kill first, not him," Mira hisses, her aim unwavering. "And Jacob—I'm going to make him suffer." And with that, she squeezes the trigger.

At the deafening gunshot blast, Sam rapidly twists his body, and it's Arkady's head that explodes into little pieces instead of his own.

As I watch all this, I continue running.

Mira, unfazed by her miss, shoots at Sam. To my horror, Sam does the rolling thing he did in the Quiet. Only he does it even faster, avoiding Mira's bullet with uncanny precision. He seems to have started moving before Mira even squeezed the trigger. And then I understand: he can phase into the Quiet. He must be using that ability to anticipate Mira's movements.

Mira begins to back away toward me, still shooting in Sam's direction. Sam rolls again and stabs one of the Russians who are holding Jacob. There is a loud scream as his knife connects with the gangster's shoulder.

"Stop it, you insane Leacher! Stop or you'll be killed," the injured man screams, letting go of Jacob to clutch at his shoulder. Ignoring his words, Sam stabs the man again, this time in the heart.

"Okay, fine," the guy rasps out, blood bubbling up on his lips as he falls to the ground. "You leave us no choice."

That's Hillary talking, I remind myself again.

"Darren, move to the right!" yells a chorus of civilians who are lying on the ground around me. My aunt again. "Now!"

Without thinking, I jump to the right and immediately hear a gunshot. Glancing back, I see

Thomas standing a dozen yards away with a rifle in his hands. When I turn back to the scene ahead, I see Sam falling, with the top of his head blown into pieces.

"Now, you fucking stay down, Leacher," the other Russian who was holding Jacob says. I can't believe it's Hillary again. She sounds utterly cold. I guess if anyone could drive my pacifist aunt to bloodlust, Sam was the guy.

And then I realize she's not gloating at Sam being shot. She's talking to Jacob. He's managed to free himself from the Russian's hold and is reaching for the knife Sam dropped when he died.

"Mira, you're in Thomas's way," the Russian says. "Move, so he can take the shot."

I raise my own gun, but this time I'm somewhat reluctant to pull the trigger. If this were Sam, I would've shot him without a second thought. But this is Jacob. He knew my father. He can give me answers about my family.

Instead of moving as Hillary commanded, Mira is also raising her gun. She's apparently determined to kill Jacob on her own.

Taking aim, she squeezes the trigger.

Instead of a bang, there is a quiet click. Jacob is still standing there, unharmed.

Her gun is out of bullets.

Jacob blinks. He looks almost surprised to still be alive. Then he looks at the knife in his hand and, grabbing it by the blade, raises it over his shoulder.

I'm gripped by a horrible sense of déjà vu. He's raising the knife for a throw at Mira—just like Sam did in the Quiet.

This can't be happening again.

I won't let it.

Without thinking even a second longer, I shoot. The knife is still in Jacob's hand, so I fire again and again. Mindlessly. Furiously.

I don't stop squeezing the trigger until I'm out of bullets.

As the haze of rage clears from my mind, I see that the knife is no longer in Jacob's hand. It's on the ground, and so is the man himself, his chest covered with blood.

Numb, I stand there and stare at the man I killed, one thought foremost in my mind.

Mira is okay. That's all that matters.

"Let's go, Darren," the people lying around me chant in Hillary-Guided chorus. "It's time to go."

Shaking off my stupor, I begin to head back, only to realize that Mira is not with me. Instead of following me, she's walking to where Jacob's body is lying. Reaching him, she starts going through his pockets. Then she picks up another gun off the ground and shoots Jacob in the head.

I wonder if that means my own shots didn't kill him—and then I wonder why I care either way. He was about to kill Mira. How could I not shoot?

Her grisly task accomplished, Mira picks up the briefcase Jacob had been holding earlier—the one that flew open in the Quiet but is still intact here—and walks toward me.

"Let's get out of here," she says, her face pale and resolute.

I look at her without comprehension.

"It's over," she says gently. "Now we go." And looping her arm through mine, she starts pulling me away.

As we walk, the enormity of what just occurred dawns on me. Arkady, Sam, Jacob, the other Russian mobsters—they're all dead, and we were nearly killed ourselves. To say that I'm pushing the limits of my ability to cope with seeing Mira nearly die would be a massive understatement.

Lost in thought, I let her steer me toward Thomas, who's standing there waiting for us. Eugene is limping our way as well, looking extremely relieved to see Mira and everyone else intact.

"Good work," Thomas says to me as we approach. "I'm sorry that I couldn't take my own shot. She was in the way."

"Thanks," I mumble, feeling incredibly drained.

"You," Thomas says, looking at Mira and shaking his head. "You're the most reckless woman I've ever met."

She doesn't respond. For the first time since I've known her, she looks subdued. Serene, almost.

Thomas's black van, now with a broken bumper, is waiting by the curb as we head back to the road. Some guy I've never met is sitting behind the wheel.

"I don't know how to drive," Hillary explains from the back seat. "So I had this guy bring the car over."

"Thanks," Thomas says. "He can go now."

"Thank you, Robert," Hillary says to the driver. "Your car is where you left it. You can go."

The guy gets out and starts walking away, a blank look on his face.

"Well, don't just stand there." Hillary motions for us to get in. "It's over. Now let's get out of here."

Her words prompt everyone into action. Thomas gets behind the wheel, and we all get inside.

I look back as we drive away and see people still running away from Brooklyn Bridge.

CHAPTER TWENTY-NINE

As we drive uptown, I realize that I need to pull myself together. The drained feeling is overwhelming.

"I killed someone again," I finally say, speaking to no one in particular. "I really didn't want to."

"Don't feel bad about that," Mira says. "That fucker killed our parents. And possibly your parents, too. Besides, you just shot him. I'm the one who actually killed him."

So Jacob wasn't dead when Mira got there.

"I don't know if that helps," I say. "I knew him, you know. That makes it different, somehow."

"You should talk to Liz once everything settles down," Thomas recommends. "She can help."

Yes, talk to my therapist. That would be a good start. But I need something else right now. Something more immediate.

I need some information and some time to think things through.

"Can someone please tell me who the hell those men were?" Thomas inquires. "The people we just killed. What the hell was all that about? They were some of yours, obviously . . . Some Leachers, weren't they?"

"They were *Readers*," I say, emphasizing the proper term. I don't like double standards, and if Hillary and Thomas want to be called Guides rather than Pushers, they should return the favor. "The big bodyguard type you shot was one of their top security personnel, and the older, less-threatening-looking one that I killed—or Mira killed—was Jacob, that community's leader."

"Okay. But we came to get one of us—a rogue Guide," Thomas says patiently. "What happened? How did you guys get it so wrong?"

"Darren, do you want to play the detective?" Mira suggests. "Your guess is going to be as good as mine."

"Well," I say slowly, trying to think through the fog still filling my mind, "it sounds like Jacob killed your family because of your father's research. Because Jacob was a Purist, the research your father was doing might've been unacceptable to him." That's the only thing that makes sense to me, at least.

"What's a Purist, and what is this research?" Thomas asks.

"Purists sound a lot like the Reader version of Traditionalists," I explain, amazed to be the one who has the answers for once.

"And my brother's research is none of Pushers' business," Mira says before her brother can start going into an explanation.

"But what about the Guide we went to see in the first place?" Hillary says, confused. "You're saying there was no such Guide?"

"No," I say. "That's the weird part. Mira found signs of a Guide when she researched her parents' murder. And she wasn't the only one. I saw signs of a Guide when we were rescuing Mira the other day, and again when that nurse tried to kill me. That means that unequivocally, there's one involved. Maybe he was working with Jacob?"

"Working together?" Hillary says. "I doubt our Traditionalists would even talk to a Reader, let alone work with one."

"Same for our Purists," Eugene says.

"Be that as it may, evidence seems to suggest otherwise," I say. "In Arkady's mind, I saw the Pusher erasing Arkady's memories of Jacob sanctioning some hits. That would only make sense if they were working as a team."

"If they did team up, it would be a hypocrisy of unbelievable proportions," Hillary says. "Traditionalists are the very people who hate Readers the most, and I'm guessing the same applies to their Purist brethren."

"Purists hate you people with an almost religious fervor," Eugene confirms. "Working with a Pusher would be like making a deal with the devil for them."

"Maybe these two joined forces to fight an even bigger devil," I speculate. "A temporary alliance, perhaps? I mean, we saw today how powerful a team of Readers and Guides can be. Maybe they united for some common cause . . . like to kill *me*—the abomination."

"I don't know about that. After all, you didn't exist to them until recently," Eugene says. "Unless their union goes way back to your parents' time— which is possible, I suppose. But getting rid of my father's—and now my—research is a more likely motivation."

"So you mean I'm not done." Mira sounds more weary than angry. "You think there's another person, a Guide, who had something to do with our parents' death."

"I think I speak for everyone when I say you can call *that* person a Pusher, Mira," I say. "But my intuition tells me that Jacob is the one to blame for your parents' death. After all, he was the one who ordered the hit on them."

"You're more than done, Mirochka," Eugene chimes in. "You killed the people directly responsible for it. It's time to move on. Start to live your life again."

"He's right," I say. "Let Guides deal with that Traditionalist Pusher problem. Let *me* deal with it. Maybe it's as simple as ratting out this Pusher to his fellow Traditionalists. They might not approve of his allegiances. What do you think, Hillary?"

"That could work. Let me think about that," Hillary says pensively.

Mira just sits there quietly, her expression unreadable. I guess she has a lot to mull over. I sure hope she decides that her revenge is officially over. I want that for her. I want her to go to college and become a nurse working with babies, regardless of how uncharacteristic of her that plan seems.

What I don't say is that my own quest for revenge is definitely not over. Jacob and the Pusher knew about me somehow. They knew even before I was born. I'm certain of it. They must be the reason my parents went into hiding—the reason why they gave me to Sara and Lucy to raise.

It can't be a coincidence that right after I saw Jacob, I was shot at by his pet mobsters. Nor is it a coincidence that a half hour after that, the Pusher found me in the hospital and tried to kill me. One must have told the other about me. Jacob must've noticed that I look like my father and told the Pusher about it. It might also explain the OB-GYN records that Bert mentioned disappearing. Maybe this is the first time my parents' murderers realized my parents had a child. My birth mother's medical records could've helped them verify that.

"Darren, we should talk more about this," Thomas says, breaking into my thoughts. "As soon as the dust settles a bit."

"Sure," I say.

"There's one more thing," Mira says, reaching into her pocket. "Something that might help you, Darren. I found this."

She's holding a small black object in her outstretched hand.

"That's the flash drive Jacob brought," I say, understanding why she went through the dead man's pockets before she shot him.

"Yes. Except it's encrypted, remember?" Mira says.

"What's supposed to be on there?" Thomas asks.

"A list of targets the mob was supposed to kill for Jacob, and a list of witnesses that Arkady needed eliminated, I think," I say. "You know, with hindsight, I can see how a Reader could have an easier time getting a list of witnesses like that compared to a Guide."

"Indeed. With hindsight, a lot of things become obvious," Hillary says. "The trick is to see them beforehand."

"Give me the drive, and I'll get some people in the Service to try to crack it," Thomas offers.

"I'll give it to Darren," Mira says. "Whatever he decides to do with it is fine with me."

"I'll send you a copy," I say to Thomas. "But I have a friend who'll likely crack this thing faster than any of your experts."

The problem will be explaining to Bert why I'm having him crack this code. It might be tricky, but I'm sure I'll manage it.

"Okay, so now let's talk about what happened," Thomas says, looking at Hillary in the mirror. "Are we now fugitives from the law? How bad was it down there on the bridge?"

"Not too bad," my aunt says, sounding tired. "No one will remember any of us being there, for starters."

"That's good," Thomas says approvingly. "What about evidence? Did we leave any DNA on the scene?"

"I just twisted my ankle," Eugene says. "So no blood."

"Everyone else?" Thomas asks.

"I'm fine," I say. "Not a scratch."

"Same here," Mira echoes.

"And obviously, I never left the car in the real world," Hillary says. "Only in the Mind Dimension."

"Good. We might not go to jail after all." Thomas looks relieved. "Now give me your guns. I'll properly dispose of them."

We all place our guns in the back next to the rest of Thomas's artillery stash.

"Okay, I'll keep an eye on the police investigation," Thomas says when we're done. "It might have to wait until I regain my abilities, but if needed, I'll clean things up. Which brings me to the next bit of business. We all need to disappear for a while. Particularly those of us who are Inert."

"Disappear?" Eugene says nervously.

"Yes, get out of town," Thomas clarifies.

That's it, I realize. This is exactly what I need. A vacation. Some rest. Some time without being shot at.

"How do you guys feel about Miami?" I say, my mood lifting a little. "I sure could use some time in the sun, with an umbrella drink in my hand."

"I can't leave for a few days," Hillary says, "and Florida is far from my favorite place, but I might join you there in a bit."

"I'll pass. Liz and I will want to do our own getaway," Thomas says. "But Miami for all of you will work out perfectly. This way, you can tell your friends and family the truth—that you're taking a vacation. Darren, if you need help convincing your boss, Hillary and I can talk to him."

"No, it'll be fine. Bill knows that awesome resources like me can sometimes do strange things like this. He won't mind," I say dismissively. Then, turning toward Mira, I say, "What do you think? Will you join me? It'll be my treat, too."

"Oh, you forget." The tiniest of smiles appears on Mira's otherwise somber face. "I'm not broke anymore. It actually might be me taking you on vacation, not the other way around."

"What are you talking about?" Eugene gives his sister a puzzled look. "We *are* broke."

"This briefcase," she says, pointing at her feet. "It's filled with cash."

"Be careful with that." Thomas frowns, looking at Mira in the mirror. "That money can be traced to you if someone knows what he's doing."

"So we have a challenge, it seems. We'll need to spend all the money in Miami," Mira says. "And spend it as quickly as possible."

"I'm sure we can manage," I say drily. "We'll just have to drink a lot of champagne and get all-day spa treatments."

"The horror," Mira says, her smile widening. "I see a lot of expensive shoes in my future. All that time I'll have to waste shopping. Such a drag."

"If push comes to shove, you two can also go gambling," Eugene adds, getting into the spirit of it. "The money you win will be clean."

"That's a good way to launder money," Thomas says, chuckling. "Using a cash business like that."

"And it's only fitting," Hillary says, looking at me and Mira. "Given how these two met for the first time."

I take out my phone and do a little online searching.

"How's tomorrow for a flight?" I say. "Is that too soon?"

Mira shrugs. "Works for me."

"Sure," Eugene says. "But can we stop by our old apartment?"

"No," Mira and I say in unison.

"We don't know if Arkady ordered someone to watch the place and wait for you," I explain.

"Fine," Eugene says sadly. "Maybe some of that cash can go toward some new lab equipment."

"Maybe," Mira says. "Do they have stores that sell that type of stuff for cash?"

"I don't know." Eugene perks up a bit. "I'll have to look into it."

"I'm booking the tickets now," I say and begin navigating the airline's website.

"Okay, great," Thomas says. "That takes care of that. Now I need to know where to take everyone."

"Well, I see that you've been driving toward my place," Hillary says.

"Yeah, I assumed—"

"Good call," Hillary says, interrupting Thomas. "You assumed correctly. I'm going home."

"I'd like to go back to the hotel. Pick up a few things and talk to—" Eugene starts saying and stops abruptly.

"I'm sorry, Zhenya," Mira says softly. "You can't talk to her."

I look back and see Eugene's face turn pale.

He just connected the dots.

Without Reading, I can tell what Eugene is thinking right now. He was part of an operation that resulted in the death of Jacob—Julia's father. Whatever she is to him, it might be over now. He certainly can't see her any time soon. I have to say, I feel really sorry for him. Hell, I feel sorry for Julia also. She didn't seem to be best pals with her father, but I'm sure she'll be hurt when she learns what happened.

"If I may offer a piece of advice," Thomas says. "The three of you should get a brand-new hotel for the night."

We take his suggestion and use the remainder of the way to Hillary's place to decide on the hotel. We choose a nondescript one near the JFK airport. The logic is that a longer drive today will make our lives easier tomorrow when we fly out in the morning.

"Bye, Darren," Hillary says when the car stops. "Get in touch if you really meant it when you invited me to Miami."

"Of course I meant it," I say. "Join us when you can."

Blowing me an air kiss, Hillary leaves.

Thomas waits until she walks into her high-rise condo building and then starts driving.

The atmosphere in the car is that of complete exhaustion. It seems all of us have been through so much that we need to digest things in silence. I myself am so drained, I can't even think. Instead, I try to make my mind go blank and do the breathing meditation Sara taught me.

A meditation that I now realize she must've learned from my father, her colleague Mark Robinson.

As my breathing slows, I feel my eyes getting heavy, and I close them for a moment.

* * *

"Darren, wake up, we're here." Eugene's voice penetrates my drowsiness, and I realize I must've dozed off.

"I don't think we'll hear from each other for a while," Thomas says, clearing his throat as I unbuckle my seatbelt. "But when things settle down, I'd love to hang out with you."

"Sounds like a plan, Thomas," I say, opening the door. "Thanks for all you did for us today. I owe you."

"I, too, want to thank you," Mira says. "I'd be dead if it weren't for you."

Thomas looks as surprised as I feel. Mira sounds genuinely grateful. "You're welcome, Mira," he says, a bit uncomfortably.

We get out of the car, and Thomas pulls away with one last wave.

As we walk, I begin to feel more awake. Approaching the front desk at the hotel, I get three separate rooms for each of us.

We ride the elevator in silence.

"Yours is 505," I tell Eugene when we reach his door. "Yours is 504," I say to Mira. "And I'm in 503, right across the hall."

"Thank you, Darren," Eugene says.

"Sure, Zhenya," I say, winking as I use Mira's nickname for him.

Mira doesn't say anything, but as she takes the key from me, her fingers linger for a second, brushing against mine. Her touch is soft, sensual. Before I can say anything, though, she goes into her own room.

I follow suit, entering my room.

First order of business, I eat all the candy bars and peanuts from the minibar. I hadn't realized how starved I was until this moment.

Next, I take the longest shower of my life. As water streams over me, the tightness in my shoulders begins to fade. It's all going to be fine, I tell myself, feeling revived by the hot water.

As I towel off, I begin to feel a tinge of excitement for the trip to come. I love Miami—and Miami with Mira? That might be something else entirely.

My musings are interrupted by a knock on the door.

"Who is it?" I ask, wrapping the towel around my waist.

"It's me," Mira says behind the door. "I hope I'm not disturbing you."

"No," I say, opening the door and stepping back to let her in. "I was just taking a shower."

She comes into the room. Her hair is wet, and she's wearing a hotel bathrobe. She must've also just showered. Her face is clean and completely free of makeup, reminding me of the time I woke her up in her apartment in the Quiet.

As she looks me up and down, I realize that I'm wearing only the towel. I don't feel self-conscious at her stare, however. With all the time I invested in gym workouts, moments like this feel like payoff.

"I came to say thanks for saving my life," she says, lifting her eyes to meet my gaze. "And, well, for everything."

"Of course." I grin at her. "I hope that means you'll stop pulling a gun on me now."

"Yes, it does." She grins back. "If you're good, that is."

"Oh." I lift my eyebrows. "And what about if I'm bad?"

She steps closer, staring up at me. "If you're bad, then I'll find a way to deal with you," she whispers and stands up on tiptoe to give my earlobe a playful nibble.

I react instantly. This smallest of flirtatious gestures makes the towel around my hips begin to look like a tent.

All my earlier tiredness forgotten, I wrap my arms around Mira's back and lower my head to kiss her. The kiss is hungry, intense. It seems to last and last— all that near-death angst compacted into one moment.

When she pulls away to catch her breath, we're both panting and her hands are clinging to my shoulders.

"I came here to thank you," she murmurs, looking up at me, "and also to give your reward."

Stepping back, she unties the robe and lets it fall down to the floor.

The night that follows is easily the most rewarding of my life.

SNEAK PEEKS

Thank you for reading! If you would consider leaving a review, it would be greatly appreciated.

Darren's story continues in *The Enlightened (Mind Dimensions: Book 3)*, which is available at most major retailers.

Please sign up for my newsletter at www.dimazales.com to be notified when the next book comes out.

If you like audiobooks, please be sure to check out this series and our other books on Audible.com.

And now, please turn the page for sneak peeks into my other works.

EXCERPT FROM *THE SORCERY CODE*

Once a respected member of the Sorcerer Council and now an outcast, Blaise has spent the last year of his life working on a special magical object. The goal is to allow anyone to do magic, not just the sorcerer elite. The outcome of his quest is unlike anything he could've ever imagined—because, instead of an object, he creates Her.

She is Gala, and she is anything but inanimate. Born in the Spell Realm, she is beautiful and highly intelligent—and nobody knows what she's capable of. She will do anything to experience the world . . . even leave the man she is beginning to fall for.

Augusta, a powerful sorceress and Blaise's former fiancée, sees Blaise's deed as the ultimate hubris and Gala as an abomination that must be destroyed. In her quest to save the human race, Augusta will forge new alliances, becoming tangled in a web of intrigue that stretches further than any of them suspect. She may even have to turn to her new lover Barson, a ruthless warrior who might have an agenda of his own . . .

* * *

There was a naked woman on the floor of Blaise's study.

A beautiful naked woman.

Stunned, Blaise stared at the gorgeous creature who just appeared out of thin air. She was looking around with a bewildered expression on her face, apparently as shocked to be there as he was to be seeing her. Her wavy blond hair streamed down her back, partially covering a body that appeared to be perfection itself. Blaise tried not to think about that body and to focus on the situation instead.

A woman. A *She*, not an *It*. Blaise could hardly believe it. Could it be? Could this girl be the object?

She was sitting with her legs folded underneath her, propping herself up with one slim arm. There was something awkward about that pose, as though she didn't know what to do with her own limbs. In general, despite the curves that marked her a fully grown woman, there was a child-like innocence in the way she sat there, completely unselfconscious and totally unaware of her own appeal.

Clearing his throat, Blaise tried to think of what to say. In his wildest dreams, he couldn't have imagined this kind of outcome to the project that had consumed his entire life for the past several months.

Hearing the sound, she turned her head to look at him, and Blaise found himself staring into a pair of unusually clear blue eyes.

She blinked, then cocked her head to the side, studying him with visible curiosity. Blaise wondered what she was seeing. He hadn't seen the light of day in weeks, and he wouldn't be surprised if he looked like a mad sorcerer at this point. There was probably a week's worth of stubble covering his face, and he knew his dark hair was unbrushed and sticking out in every direction. If he'd known he would be facing a beautiful woman today, he would've done a grooming spell in the morning.

"Who am I?" she asked, startling Blaise. Her voice was soft and feminine, as alluring as the rest of her. "What is this place?"

"You don't know?" Blaise was glad he finally managed to string together a semi-coherent sentence. "You don't know who you are or where you are?"

She shook her head. "No."

Blaise swallowed. "I see."

"What am I?" she asked again, staring at him with those incredible eyes.

"Well," Blaise said slowly, "if you're not some cruel prankster or a figment of my imagination, then it's somewhat difficult to explain . . ."

She was watching his mouth as he spoke, and when he stopped, she looked up again, meeting his gaze. "It's strange," she said, "hearing words this way. These are the first real words I've heard."

Blaise felt a chill go down his spine. Getting up from his chair, he began to pace, trying to keep his eyes off her nude body. He had been expecting something to appear. A magical object, a thing. He just hadn't known what form that thing would take. A mirror, perhaps, or a lamp. Maybe even something as unusual as the Life Capture Sphere that sat on his desk like a large round diamond.

But a person? A female person at that?

To be fair, he had been trying to make the object intelligent, to ensure it would have the ability to comprehend human language and convert it into the code. Maybe he shouldn't be so surprised that the intelligence he invoked took on a human shape.

A beautiful, feminine, sensual shape.

Focus, Blaise, focus.

"Why are you walking like that?" She slowly got to her feet, her movements uncertain and strangely clumsy. "Should I be walking too? Is that how people talk to each other?"

Blaise stopped in front of her, doing his best to keep his eyes above her neck. "I'm sorry. I'm not accustomed to naked women in my study."

She ran her hands down her body, as though trying to feel it for the first time. Whatever her intent, Blaise found the gesture extremely erotic.

"Is something wrong with the way I look?" she asked. It was such a typical feminine concern that Blaise had to stifle a smile.

"Quite the opposite," he assured her. "You look unimaginably good." So good, in fact, that he was having trouble concentrating on anything but her delicate curves. She was of medium height, and so perfectly proportioned that she could've been used as a sculptor's template.

"Why do I look this way?" A small frown creased her smooth forehead. "What am I?" That last part seemed to be puzzling her the most.

Blaise took a deep breath, trying to calm his racing pulse. "I think I can try to venture a guess, but before I do, I want to give you some clothing. Please wait here—I'll be right back."

And without waiting for her answer, he hurried out of the room.

* * *

The Sorcery Code is currently available at most retailers. If you'd like to learn more, please visit my website at www.dimazales.com. You can also connect with me on Facebook, Twitter, and Goodreads.

EXCERPT FROM *CLOSE LIAISONS* BY ANNA ZAIRES

Note: *Close Liaisons* is Dima Zales's collaboration with Anna Zaires and is the first book in the internationally bestselling erotic sci-fi romance series, the Krinar Chronicles. It contains explicit sexual content and is not intended for readers under eighteen.

* * *

A dark and edgy romance that will appeal to fans of erotic and turbulent relationships . . .

In the near future, the Krinar rule the Earth. An advanced race from another galaxy, they are still a mystery to us—and we are completely at their mercy.

Shy and innocent, Mia Stalis is a college student in New York City who has led a very normal life. Like most people, she's never had any interactions with the invaders—until one fateful day in the park changes everything. Having caught Korum's eye, she must now contend with a powerful, dangerously seductive Krinar who wants to possess her and will stop at nothing to make her his own.

How far would you go to regain your freedom? How much would you sacrifice to help your people? What choice will you make when you begin to fall for your enemy?

* * *

The air was crisp and clear as Mia walked briskly down a winding path in Central Park. Signs of spring were everywhere, from tiny buds on still-bare trees to the proliferation of nannies out to enjoy the first warm day with their rambunctious charges.

It was strange how much everything had changed in the last few years, and yet how much remained the same. If anyone had asked Mia ten years ago how she thought life might be after an alien invasion, this would have been nowhere near her imaginings. *Independence Day, The War of the Worlds*—none of these were even close to the reality of encountering a more advanced civilization. There had been no fight, no resistance of any kind on government level— because *they* had not allowed it. In hindsight, it was clear how silly those movies had been. Nuclear weapons, satellites, fighter jets—these were little more than rocks and sticks to an ancient civilization that could cross the universe faster than the speed of light.

Spotting an empty bench near the lake, Mia gratefully headed for it, her shoulders feeling the strain of the backpack filled with her chunky twelve-year-old laptop and old-fashioned paper books. At twenty-one, she sometimes felt old, out of step with the fast-paced new world of razor-slim tablets and cell phones embedded in wristwatches. The pace of technological progress had not slowed since K-Day; if anything, many of the new gadgets had been influenced by what the Krinar had. Not that the Ks had shared any of their precious technology; as far as they were concerned, their little experiment had to continue uninterrupted.

Unzipping her bag, Mia took out her old Mac. The thing was heavy and slow, but it worked—and as a starving college student, Mia could not afford anything better. Logging on, she opened a blank Word document and prepared to start the torturous process of writing her Sociology paper.

Ten minutes and exactly zero words later, she stopped. Who was she kidding? If she really wanted to write the damn thing, she would've never come to the park. As tempting as it was to pretend that she could enjoy the fresh air and be productive at the same time, those two had never been compatible in her experience. A musty old library was a much better setting for anything requiring that kind of brainpower exertion.

Mentally kicking herself for her own laziness, Mia let out a sigh and started looking around instead. People-watching in New York never failed to amuse her.

The tableau was a familiar one, with the requisite homeless person occupying a nearby bench—thank God it wasn't the closest one to her, since he looked like he might smell very ripe—and two nannies chatting with each other in Spanish as they pushed their Bugaboos at a leisurely pace. A girl jogged on a path a little further ahead, her bright pink Reeboks contrasting nicely with her blue leggings. Mia's gaze followed the jogger as she rounded the corner, envying her athleticism. Her own hectic schedule allowed her little time to exercise, and she doubted she could keep up with the girl for even a mile at this point.

To the right, she could see the Bow Bridge over the lake. A man was leaning on the railing, looking out over the water. His face was turned away from Mia, so she could only see part of his profile. Nevertheless, something about him caught her attention.

She wasn't sure what it was. He was definitely tall and seemed well-built under the expensive-looking trench coat he was wearing, but that was only part of the story. Tall, good-looking men were common in model-infested New York City. No, it was something else. Perhaps it was the way he stood—very still, with no extra movements. His hair was dark and glossy under the bright afternoon sun, just long enough in the front to move slightly in the warm spring breeze.

He also stood alone.

That's it, Mia realized. The normally popular and picturesque bridge was completely deserted, except for the man who was standing on it. Everyone appeared to be giving it a wide berth for some unknown reason. In fact, with the exception of herself and her potentially aromatic homeless neighbor, the entire row of benches in the highly desirable waterfront location was empty.

As though sensing her gaze on him, the object of her attention slowly turned his head and looked directly at Mia. Before her conscious brain could even make the connection, she felt her blood turn to ice, leaving her paralyzed in place and helpless to do anything but stare at the predator who now seemed to be examining her with interest.

*　*　*

Breathe, Mia, breathe. Somewhere in the back of her mind, a small rational voice kept repeating those words. That same oddly objective part of her noted his symmetric face structure, with golden skin stretched tightly over high cheekbones and a firm jaw. Pictures and videos of Ks that she'd seen had hardly done them justice. Standing no more than thirty feet away, the creature was simply stunning.

As she continued staring at him, still frozen in place, he straightened and began walking toward her. Or rather stalking toward her, she thought stupidly, as his every movement reminded her of a jungle cat sinuously approaching a gazelle. All the while, his eyes never left hers. As he approached, she could make out individual yellow flecks in his light golden eyes and the thick long lashes surrounding them.

She watched in horrified disbelief as he sat down on her bench, less than two feet away from her, and smiled, showing white even teeth. No fangs, she noted with some functioning part of her brain. Not even a hint of them. That used to be another myth about them, like their supposed abhorrence of the sun.

"What's your name?" The creature practically purred the question at her. His voice was low and smooth, completely unaccented. His nostrils flared slightly, as though inhaling her scent.

"Um . . ." Mia swallowed nervously. "M-Mia."

"Mia," he repeated slowly, seemingly savoring her name. "Mia what?"

"Mia Stalis." Oh crap, why did he want to know her name? Why was he here, talking to her? In general, what was he doing in Central Park, so far away from any of the K Centers? *Breathe, Mia, breathe.*

"Relax, Mia Stalis." His smile got wider, exposing a dimple in his left cheek. A dimple? Ks had dimples? "Have you never encountered one of us before?"

"No, I haven't," Mia exhaled sharply, realizing that she was holding her breath. She was proud that her voice didn't sound as shaky as she felt. Should she ask? Did she want to know?

She gathered her courage. "What, um—" Another swallow. "What do you want from me?"

"For now, conversation." He looked like he was about to laugh at her, those gold eyes crinkling slightly at the corners.

Strangely, that pissed her off enough to take the edge off her fear. If there was anything Mia hated, it was being laughed at. With her short, skinny stature and a general lack of social skills that came from an awkward teenage phase involving every girl's nightmare of braces, frizzy hair, and glasses, Mia had more than enough experience being the butt of someone's joke.

She lifted her chin belligerently. "Okay, then, what is *your* name?"

"It's Korum."

"Just Korum?"

"We don't really have last names, not the way you do. My full name is much longer, but you wouldn't be able to pronounce it if I told you."

Okay, that was interesting. She now remembered reading something like that in *The New York Times*. So far, so good. Her legs had nearly stopped shaking, and her breathing was returning to normal. Maybe, just maybe, she would get out of this alive. This conversation business seemed safe enough, although the way he kept staring at her with those unblinking yellowish eyes was unnerving. She decided to keep him talking.

"What are you doing here, Korum?"

"I just told you, making conversation with you, Mia." His voice again held a hint of laughter.

Frustrated, Mia blew out her breath. "I meant, what are you doing here in Central Park? In New York City in general?"

He smiled again, cocking his head slightly to the side. "Maybe I'm hoping to meet a pretty curly-haired girl."

Okay, enough was enough. He was clearly toying with her. Now that she could think a little again, she realized that they were in the middle of Central Park, in full view of about a gazillion spectators. She surreptitiously glanced around to confirm that. Yep, sure enough, although people were obviously steering clear of her bench and its otherworldly occupant, there were a number of brave souls staring their way from further up the path. A couple were even cautiously filming them with their wristwatch cameras. If the K tried anything with her, it would be on YouTube in the blink of an eye, and he had to know it. Of course, he may or may not care about that.

Still, going on the assumption that since she'd never come across any videos of K assaults on college students in the middle of Central Park, she was relatively safe, Mia cautiously reached for her laptop and lifted it to stuff it back into her backpack.

"Let me help you with that, Mia—"

And before she could blink, she felt him take her heavy laptop from her suddenly boneless fingers, gently brushing against her knuckles in the process. A sensation similar to a mild electric shock shot through Mia at his touch, leaving her nerve endings tingling in its wake.

Reaching for her backpack, he carefully put away the laptop in a smooth, sinuous motion. "There you go, all better now."

Oh God, he had touched her. Maybe her theory about the safety of public locations was bogus. She felt her breathing speeding up again, and her heart rate was probably well into the anaerobic zone at this point.

"I have to go now . . . Bye!"

How she managed to squeeze out those words without hyperventilating, she would never know. Grabbing the strap of the backpack he'd just put down, she jumped to her feet, noting somewhere in the back of her mind that her earlier paralysis seemed to be gone.

"Bye, Mia. I will see you later." His softly mocking voice carried in the clear spring air as she took off, nearly running in her haste to get away.

* * *

If you'd like to find out more, please visit Anna's website at www.annazaires.com. *Close Liaisons* is currently available at most retailers.

ABOUT THE AUTHOR

Dima Zales is a *USA Today* bestselling science fiction and fantasy author residing in Palm Coast, Florida. Prior to becoming a writer, he worked in the software development industry in New York as both a programmer and an executive. From high-frequency trading software for big banks to mobile apps for popular magazines, Dima has done it all. In 2013, he left the software industry in order to concentrate on his writing career.

Dima holds a Master's degree in Computer Science from NYU and a dual undergraduate degree in Computer Science / Psychology from Brooklyn College. He also has a number of hobbies and interests, the most unusual of which might be professional-level mentalism. He simulates mind reading on stage and close-up, and has done shows for corporations, wealthy individuals, and friends.

He is also into healthy eating and fitness, so he should live long enough to finish all the book projects he starts. In fact, he very much hopes to catch the technological advancements that might let him live forever (biologically or otherwise). Aside from that, he also enjoys learning about current and future technologies that might enhance our lives, including artificial intelligence, biofeedback, brain-to-computer interfaces, and brain-enhancing implants.

In addition to writing The Sorcery Code series and Mind Dimensions series, Dima has collaborated on a number of romance novels with his wife, Anna Zaires. The Krinar Chronicles, an erotic science fiction series, is an international bestseller and has been recognized by the likes of Marie Claire and Woman's Day. If you like erotic romance with a unique plot, please feel free to check it out. Keep in mind, though, Anna Zaires's books are going to be much more explicit.

Anna Zaires is the love of his life and a huge inspiration in every aspect of his writing. She definitely adds her magic touch to anything Dima creates, and the books would not be the same without her. Dima's fans are strongly encouraged to learn more about Anna and her work at www.annazaires.com.

THE TWO
KINGS

BY

STEPHANIE HUDSON

The Two Kings
The Afterlife Saga #2
Copyright © 2020 Stephanie Hudson
Published by Hudson Indie Ink
www.hudsonindieink.com

The Two Kings/Stephanie Hudson – 2nd ed.
ISBN-13 - 978-1-913769-19-2

Dedication

I dedicate The Two Kings to the 96 LFC fans who lost their lives on that terrible day on the 15th of April 1989 in the Hillsborough disaster.
"You'll never walk alone"

Justice at last

All at once the crowd go silent,
Holding a breath in waiting,
So many Lives, so many Names,
All in the hands of debating.

There is no price for Justice,
There is only truth to remain,
To find it for the hearts that have suffered,
And every fan who feels the same.

A dream with heads held high,
A journey of heartache and pain,
A justice so utterly deserved,
A never fading memory we gain.

It's all about the hope we build,
And the mountain we all climb together,
In hopes to one day find,
A truth so deep it affects us forever.

Justice for the 96'
YNWA

WARNING

This book contains explicit sexual content, some graphic language and a highly addictive Alpha Male.

This book has been written by a UK Author with a mad sense of humour. Which means the following story contains a mixture of Northern English slang, dialect, regional colloquialisms and other quirky spellings that have been intentionally included to make the story and dialogue more realistic for modern-day characters.

Please note that for your convenience language translations have been added to optimise the readers enjoyment throughout the story.

Also meaning…

No Googling is required ;)

Also, please remember that this part of a 12 book saga, which means you are in for a long and rocky ride. So, put the kettle on, brew a cup, grab a stash of snacks and enjoy!

Thanks for reading x

CHAPTER ONE

HUNTED

Draven's eyes scanned over me checking that I wasn't going to go into shock from Vincent's outburst.

"I'm fine, you go," I managed to say but before I knew it Draven's hands were touching my face making me look into his incredible deep eyes. His gaze was edged with a concern he was most likely trying very hard to hide, no doubt to prevent me from panicking... Well, it wasn't bloody working!

"Keira, it will be alright, you don't have to worry." Was he joking? Of course I had reason to worry. I mean, I was being bloody hunted and images of me on a 'Wanted' poster in some supernatural tavern were filling my mind. But of course, instead of saying this I just nodded and pushed his hands from me.

"Go, I will be fine on my own and Takeshi needs you." I couldn't help but lower my face as I said this, not wanting him to see the pain in my eyes nor hear the worry in my voice. After all, my acting skills weren't ever going to win any awards. However, despite my best efforts he didn't look convinced, but he knew as well as I did that he needed to go. With that in mind he kissed my forehead and begrudgingly left with his brother to leave me with my own thoughts of dread.

1

I couldn't understand how, just hours after my own personal nightmare, we were having to deal with Draven's. It was like a cruel game of chance that we just couldn't win. We only wanted to be together, but it was like every force of Heaven and Hell was telling us no.

I decided to get up as I knew I would never sleep without Draven's warm touch on my skin. I went over to my bag, one which was still on the couch from the last few days I had spent here and grabbed the last pair of jeans and T-shirt that I had left. At least now it would be safe for me to go home and get some clean clothes, along with some other things that I might need soon. Then I stopped, thinking was I right? Would it be safe or was I forever to be in danger?

I had to stop myself before I lost my mind to all the dark places it wanted to go. I mean I couldn't live in fear forever and with Draven as my protector, what really was there to be frightened of?

Just as I had slipped into my clothes and tied my hair back there was a light tap on the door. Without waiting for a reply, Sophia came strolling in the room looking radiant as always, followed by Candra who had a plate full of food.

"Dominic thought you might need some company and also feeding," Sophia said as if I was some house pet that needed caring for. She then smirked as my face said it all. I rolled my eyes and watched Candra place the tray down knowing Draven was obviously worried I would be sat here freaking out on my own, so he had sent Sophia to check on me... Or should I say, more like *human sit me.*

"He worries too much," I said frowning but still the smell of hot chicken soup and crusty bread had me close to salivating. She just shrugged her shoulders and made herself comfortable on the couch opposite, folding her legs as though she was ready to start meditating.

"Well, at least you're looking better, you looked like Hell...and trust me, I'm well acquainted with the big man downstairs."

This she found hilarious, being her idea of a joke and I couldn't help but relax at the sound. Draven had been right to send Sophia.

There was just something about her that had you forgetting your worries and making you see the bigger picture. Or, should I say, no picture at all. Either way, it worked. She didn't seem as worried as Vincent or Draven, but who really knew her true feelings?

I sat in the big red velvet chair and rested the tray of food on my lap before diving in.

"I take it you were hungry?" She giggled as she watched me wolf my food down. I just nodded, not realising how hungry I was. I had finished nearly half of my feast before speaking.

"Sophia, I need to know... what's going on?" I asked, not knowing whether or not she was ever going to tell the truth. Her eyes widened and her face tensed for a moment before returning back to her usual relaxed state. She flicked a curly lock back over her shoulder before eyeing my face carefully.

"Keira, there is nothing that you should be worrying about. Dom will sort it out and make it right. This was something that he predicted would happen and he has taken precautions." She said all this in such a way that made me believe it had been rehearsed. It was so 'matter of fact' that I couldn't do anything but not trust her words. I had seen the panic on Vincent's face and then on Draven's too, so I knew this wasn't as clear cut as Sophia was making out. But I decided to play along and wait until I could get my answers from the one man I knew would give me what I wanted...after all, *I knew his weaknesses.*

"Okay then, answer me this...why is it nobody told me that Layla was being held prisoner right here under my nose?" I was determined that I would at least get that out of her.

"Oh no, I'm not falling for that trap again. These are things that only Dom can tell you, it's not my place." She held up her hands as though I had a large pistol in my possession and was about to mug her. But the only thing I needed from her was the truth, which just so happened to be the one thing this family had difficulty in disclosing.

I decided to admit defeat. I mean, Draven couldn't keep what was going on from me forever. I knew he didn't want me to worry, but not knowing was far worse than the truth...wasn't it?

"Keira, can I ask you something?" Sophia's voice was as soft as petals blowing in the breeze and she knew that with this seductive tone I would never be able to refuse her anything. But instead of showing just how willing I was to give Sophia anything she asked of me, I gave her my answer with a vague shrug of my shoulders.

"I guess I am just curious, but how does it work? I mean when you see us in our true form." She was edging forward in her chair and she eyed me as though ready to judge my response. This was something I didn't want to be talking about, but she was clearly waiting for my reply and I was obviously stalling for time.

"I'm not sure I understand what it is you want to know exactly," I said hoping that she would give up and drop this conversation. Of course, from the look on her face this wish wasn't likely to be granted any time soon.

"Well...can you see me now, you know... in my Demon form?" It was still hard to believe that such a beautiful creature as Sophia could ever be the powerful Demon she was. I still thought of her as this pretty little doll who captivated everyone around her. Of course, after seeing her lay a punch so hard on Draven's face that it sounded like bone-cracking, let's just say that it did shed a little Demon light her way.

I looked down at my now empty bowl and brushed the crumbs of bread off my top. It wasn't fair, they all had their secrets but the one thing they didn't understand about me, and they wanted a full explanation on how it all worked.

"To be honest, Sophia, even I don't fully understand how it works or why for that matter. But to answer your question, no, I can't see you in your Demon form, not at the moment." She sat there unmoved, but I could see the faint flicker of red in her eyes and normally this would have given me a reaction of my own but after tonight, I was starting to think I would never be the same again. After all the horrors I had seen in my life, including the most horrific kidnapping years ago, I thought I had experienced enough for one lifetime. However, I knew now that it had only been the beginning. This thought did make me shudder. What else exactly did fate have in store for this plain little Liverpudlian girl?

"I'm sorry, Keira, please forgive me. I sometimes forget that you are human. I can't imagine what it has been like for you to find out your world was not as you thought. You must love my brother very much." By the time she was finished I couldn't help the tears that fell down my cheeks and before I could look away in shame, Sophia was knelt at my feet leaning up to wipe the tears from my face.

"You are truly an amazing being, Keira, and never let anyone tell you any differently." She kissed both my cheeks before getting up off the floor and before I could thank her she was gone.

I curled up on the couch and waited until my tears ran dry. I couldn't help it and I knew I was being silly, but I think that without Draven's secure arms to keep me safe, I felt vulnerable from my own emotions. It was a mixture of relief and dread. I was happy that I had finally found closure to a nightmare that had been haunting me for years. Morgan was dead and you couldn't get more closure than that. But now I was in a world that I didn't fully understand, and I was way out of my league.

I got up and gave myself a mental shake, determined to bring myself back to reality. I knew why I was doing this so there was no reason to feel sorry for myself. I was alive and I still had the most important things in my life, my family and friends were all safe and I had Draven, that's all that mattered.

I looked down at my bare arms and ran my fingers over the scars of my past, knowing that for the first time, seeing them like this didn't bother me anymore. I had waited for so long to move on and get over hating myself for what I am, but now I knew my purpose. Because if I had never had this sight, then things with Draven would have gone quite differently.

He was my reason.

I went over to Draven's huge oak desk and searched for something I would look at for the last time. I found my case file and took out two pictures from many, before walking over to the double glass doors that led onto the balcony. I placed my warm hand in the middle and the glass responded as though it was alive, disappearing back into the wall. The cool air hit me, and my body reacted by covering my skin in goosebumps. I only had a t-shirt on and for once no gloves, so the feel of the night air on my scars was a feeling I was not used to. But for some reason it made me smile.

I walked over to the edge and noticed my blood was still on the floor in little droplets from where Draven had set me down before realising my feet were in such bad shape. I hoped the rain would come soon and wash it away as I didn't want Draven to have any reminder of what had happened earlier.

The wind had picked up now and I looked at the first picture. It was Morgan's mug shot. I had never seen a face so evil in all my life, not even after years of seeing humans one minute and then as Demons the next. I had never met anyone who emanated so much pure hatred. His twisted love for his sister had overtaken his senses and when he found she loved someone else, his love just ended up fuelling his rage, resulting in him killing them both in the most brutal of ways.

I don't know what it was that he saw when he looked at me... was it his sister incarnate or his guilt? Whatever it was, that twisted love was dead now and I doubt that his fate would have led him to the same place his sister was. She was now at peace.

I ripped up the face into as many pieces I could and threw them into the night, letting the wind take his face away from my nightmares once and for all. I then looked down at the last picture I held in my cold hands. This one was of me, broken and afraid. It was when I was in the hospital not long after they found me outside, where Morgan had dumped me to slowly bleed to death. This was actually the one thing Morgan had done with the last shred of humanity left in him.

I had cut my own wrists hoping he would believe the Demon that was torturing him had made me do it. It was my last hope of escape and my last chance to save my family. My dear family who he had talked about getting rid of like rubbish needing to be disposed of. I still thank God daily that it had worked and perfect smooth skin on my arms had been the only thing I had lost.

The picture was still painful to look at, bringing so many terrible memories back, but none as bad as when I saw my family's faces when seeing me for the first time. My mother had been crying so hard she couldn't breathe, my dad lashed out with an anger he couldn't control, and my sister couldn't even look at me, which had been the hardest response to take. Of course, I didn't blame her, as I would have probably been the same. But from there on I became a different person. I had been reborn into a hard shell of my former self and only my nightmares knew the truth…

I was afraid of the world, so I hid from it.

I was bitter at the world, so I was disgusted with it.

I hated the pity in judging eyes that watched with their silent stares. I was convinced that everyone around me was thinking, 'Oh dear, there goes the girl who tried to kill herself just to get away from living that nightmare.' But they were all wrong! I didn't want to die. I wanted to live damn it! But I knew one way or another this was my only chance at saving my family. After all, if Morgan hadn't done the right thing by taking me to hospital, then he wouldn't have needed to go after my family if I wasn't around any longer. But when everyone around you, even those closest to you, all believed you're as a suicidal case…well, then no matter what you do, you will always be classed and viewed in that same sad light.

I looked at my old self one last time before bringing the picture to my lips as I kissed that bitter, bruised me goodbye before ripping it the same way I had done with Morgan's and I let the wind take away my past forever. I fell to my knees and cried with happiness until my legs felt numb on my last cold night of being afraid.

I went back inside once the tears of my past had all dried up. I was close to freezing at this point and the only thing keeping me from realising earlier was my goal. I was hoping to find Draven back because not only was I bubbling over with a million questions, but I needed his touch again so badly. I felt like a junky needing another fix. It made me wonder if Draven had this effect on everyone or was it just me? Was it because I was so hopelessly in love with him, that it physically hurt when we were apart?

I decided the only way I was going to warm up without Draven was to take a hot shower. I was exhausted but I was fighting it as I wanted to wait for him to come back. I hadn't been in the bathroom since my nightmare when I first saw Sammael, but I knew I didn't have anything left to fear. Not when it came to that Demon, as I had witnessed Draven send him back to where he belonged.

I got undressed and let the steaming shower caress my skin, making my muscles ease and relax. I loved water and enjoyed it even more when it washed away my troubles along with cleansing my skin.

By the time I was finished my hair was squeaky clean and my fingertips looked like raisins, but I smelled great thanks to some luxurious bath products. Once I had dried myself off, I got dressed back into my clothes and went to sit on the couch hoping Draven wouldn't be long.

When I next awoke it was dark and I was still half asleep, but I was aware that I was being carried towards the bed. Strong arms gripped me tightly to a hard chest and I sighed taking in the tremendous scent. This was one of the things that always took my breath away with Draven. He always made my bones turn to jelly at just the smell of him. I still had my eyes closed as he laid me on the bed gently, but I felt the covers move back with one swift movement. His arms left my body leaving my skin feeling cold in their absence. He then pulled the covers back up over me.

I was waiting for him to get in next to me but he didn't move. I could still feel him lingering over me before a hand came to my face. I felt fingers softly trace my cheek, running up to move the hair that had fallen over one side of my face. Then, before his hands could leave me, I grabbed his wrist and pulled him to me. I lifted up my face to his before he could pull away. I didn't understand why he would want to pull away from me, but before I could think about it in depth my lips found his and everything stopped.

At first his lips wouldn't respond, and I was doing all the work but as soon as this thought hit me, his lips parted letting me in. His mouth was warm and so soft, but his kiss tasted different. However, my mind was still filled with an intoxication that I couldn't break from and this was where I found my drug of choice.

His hand held my face and just before his kiss grew more intense, he pulled back suddenly, causing me to open my eyes. I was about to protest and pull him back to me as my body was screaming to be touched. But then the faint moonlight touched the side of his face, making his perfect features light up like the Angel he was.

I gasped and bit down on my lip so hard I thought I would taste blood. Of course, it was a Draven, just not the one I was used to.

It wasn't Dominic... Oh no,

It was Vincent.

CHAPTER TWO

OOOPS

"Oh, no... Oh... I'm so, so... so sorry, I thought..." I couldn't continue as I was so ashamed of what I had just done but Vincent didn't move. I was screaming with embarrassment inside but on the outside, I couldn't even find the right words. I sat up, suddenly becoming wide awake and it felt as if my cheeks could barbecue steaks. I covered my face with my hands wishing I could take it back...what was Dominic going to say? Already I was referring to him as Dominic so as not to get the two confused again...well, you couldn't fault my logic!

I felt warm fingers find my hands and start to pull them slowly from my face.

"Keira, please don't hide yourself, it was not your fault, you were not to know it was me." He said this so sweetly I couldn't help but feel worse. I tried not to look at him, but now there was a glow of candlelight which helped to light up my guilty face. He remained bent down on one knee so that he could see me better.

"Look at me," he asked and unlike his brother, it didn't sound like a command. His hand found my chin and lifted my face so my eyes met his. They looked like blue crystals, full of emotion set in a handsome angelic face. His blonde hair was smoothed curls all pulled back from his face. It was the first time I had seen him looking so casual wearing a tight white t-shirt and jeans that fit him very well, too well in fact. It felt wrong thinking how sexy he looked in them. God, what was wrong with me? Well, at least I could say I was only human I thought on a thankfully contained snort.

"I am so sorry, Vincent," I said but he just smiled making my heart melt.

"There is nothing to be sorry about, Keira. But in the future, I think it best if Dom himself were the one to put you to bed." He was still smiling, and he playfully ruffled my hair before getting up. But then something made him stop to look at me one last time before leaving me alone with my shame. The way his gaze penetrated me, it made me blush seeing his soft eyes suddenly looking hungry for another kiss. Then he shook his head as though he was trying to get the memory of my lips out of his mind. He left the room swiftly, almost as though he had just taken flight, leaving the room in darkness once again.

"Goodnight Keira and...*sleep well,*" he echoed, his voice penetrating the walls before sounding further away and then fading into nothing but a bittersweet whisper. I threw my head down onto the pillow face first, grabbed the other pillow and sandwiched my head deep within the two, hoping I would wake and find it had all been a dream.

"Oh no, what have I done?" I mumbled into the pillow knowing that Dominic would know about this, he would find out one way or another. I wondered if Vincent would tell him. Oh God, Oh God...There was just one word that kept going around and around my mind....

SHIT!

I must have fallen asleep at some point, but I had no idea how it happened as after what I'd done last night I never thought I would sleep again! When I woke it was still dark, but I soon realised this was thanks to the bed's curtains that had been pulled around, encasing me in a material cage. I was lying on my front and my hair was loose, hanging down as I lifted my head up. I stretched out like a feline but froze when I felt my hands touch another body. I almost cringed as the memories of last night's mistake came flooding back to me.

I don't know why but my heart started pounding in my chest as I moved my nest of hair back to discover it was Draven (Dominic that was) lying next to me. Who else did I expect?

I looked at him and my eyes met perfection, only for once he was still asleep. It was the first time I had seen him like this, and I couldn't help but smile at being able to study his features at length. It's not as if I hadn't looked before, but I couldn't help the fact that being around Draven still had me in knots. Sometimes he was just so intimidating that I found myself looking away from his intense gaze. So it was nice to be able to stare freely without feeling embarrassed.

I tried to move closer to his face, which seemed to be lost in a peaceful state of sleep. His strong jaw moved slightly as I turned on my side to face him. There was enough light coming through the cracks in the curtains to show enough details. I had to resist the urge to stretch my arm out to touch his face, to brush a piece of his black hair from his olive skin. There was dark stubble covering his solid jawline and framing his perfect lips. I followed it up to his straight nose resting my eyes where his were still closed. He literally took my breath away. My dark Angel. His dark Demon.

I don't know how long I was staring at him, getting lost in his splendour but my bladder decided for me to get up and use the bathroom. I turned my head begrudgingly away from him and moved off the bed slowly so as not to wake him. His reactions were so lightning fast I couldn't help the little shriek that came from my lips as his strong hands gripped my waist, pulling my body to his as though I should never have been allowed to move in the first place.

My heart rate rocketed for two reasons: one being that I was scared about what his reaction would be at finding out what had happened last night and the other was the feel of his impressive erection pressing into my back as he spooned me. Ok, so it was more the second reason, but I couldn't help it, just the feel of him made the memories of the intense pleasure he caused me during sex was enough to get any girl's juices flowing. Hell, I thought I would find my release just thinking about it!

His huge arms were wound tightly around my torso and his head was above mine. But he hadn't woken, so grabbing onto me had just been an instinct and the thought made me smile to myself. I waited for his breathing to become steady again before I tried to move. Don't get me wrong, I could have stayed like this all morning, afternoon and night but my bladder was now swearing at me to go pee.

Getting free was no easy task, as every time I moved he just held me tighter. I managed to wiggle out of his hold and shimmy down, getting very embarrassed when the back of my head got closer to his... umm...Sergeant. I had to resist the urge to giggle at what I had christened his large manhood. I know I was being a prude, but the term penis was too much like sex education and the other words sounded too vulgar for something so perfect. So Sergeant it was, after all it was the one in charge most of the time, I thought with another cheeky smile

Once I got free, I slipped out of the curtain without letting in too much light and shuddered when my bare feet touched the slate tiled floor. I was still wearing what I had put on last night and when I lifted the t-shirt to my face, I was glad it still smelled fresh. This was thanks to the shower I'd had last night. When in the bathroom, I decided not only to use the toilet but to brush my teeth to get rid of morning breath and to wash my face. I brushed my tangled, messy hair and tied it back into a high ponytail. It was still wavy from being unable to dry it last night, so it made S shapes all the way down, curling up at the ends by my waist.

I really needed to get another hairdryer for when I was here. But wait... what was I saying? How did I know that Draven would still want me after last night? That thought was a painful one. I stared at myself in the gorgeous gilded mirror and my reflection didn't help my paranoia. My pale skin looked even paler than usual thanks to the cold chill in the air. My eyes looked almost as dark as the lashes that framed them and my lips were the only part of me that held any colour, like a red heart painted on a blank white canvas.

I shook off the feeling of dread and walked back into the room, only what faced me filled me with deeper dread, as Draven was now awake. The curtains had all been pushed back and Draven was still lying in the bed looking at me. The falling covers revealed muscle after muscle on his torso and that wasn't the only solid thing I could see. It was very evident that he was now most definitely wide awake, and his Sergeant looked like it could be used to bludgeon someone to death! The whole sight made me swallow hard. I could tell by his face that he didn't yet know the awful truth as he was smiling at me with a wide, cocky grin.

"What are you doing over there and dressed, may I ask?" His voice sent a shiver down my already cold back and I bit my lip at what the sound of that voice did to me. It was so rough and deep with lashings of authority to it. Oh yeah, he most definitely didn't know, either that or he damn well knew how to play it cool before erupting.

I stayed silent because I really didn't know how I was going to tell him. I walked over to him but stopped before I got to the bed and it didn't help when he started frowning as I paused to lean on his desk. I'd not felt like this since the time my neighbour's baby had thrown up on my homework and I had to try and explain it to my science teacher the next day. I'd received a hundred lines on reasons not to lie.

"Draven, we need to...talk." My voice didn't sound like my own and it didn't help that he wasn't taking me seriously because he was grinning as if it was funny. Well, he wouldn't be so amused in a minute and as someone very familiar at witnessing Draven's temper, this was not going to be pretty.

"Is that so?" he said as though he was mocking me, still with his confident grin that wouldn't leave his lips. He was propped up on his side with his hand holding his head up on his elbow and he looked like Adonis. He wasn't taking me seriously that much was clear. He then patted the bed as a gesture for me to join him, but I knew if I went over there then no will on earth would stop me making love to him before I could finish my disgraceful goal. But when I didn't move his smile disappeared and was replaced with another trademark frown. His eyes burned into mine, black and intense.

"If I didn't know any better I would say you look afraid of me, Keira. Is this true?" I couldn't do anything else but nod, not wanting to meet his dark gaze.

"Why in the world would you be frightened? Here..." He pointed to where he wanted me and then ordered,

"Come to me." I knew keeping Draven from what he wanted wasn't the best of ideas but I still couldn't move. I was rooted to the spot as though it was the safest place to be.

"I think I should stay here until you hear what I've got to say," I whispered without any backbone at all. He tilted his head to one side and commanded in a darker tone,

"Look at me." This left me feeling as if he was trying to burrow inside my head, making me do his will.

"Don't do that!" I said suddenly getting angry that he was trying to use his powers on me but he just laughed.

"Then obey me and come here." His face got soft and I couldn't help but trust his easy smile.

"I doubt you will still want that after I tell you what I've done...it's...well, it's something bad...like really bad... but it was a mistake and completely my fault!" I blurted out and he laughed again as though I was missing something.

"Poor Vincent, I doubt very much he feels the same way." He laughed again but this time I was sure it was at the sight of my mouth dropping open like a fish.

"What...? How...? You already know?" I asked dumbfounded.

"Of course, but you are not at fault," he said so matter of fact that I had to shake my head at him.

"You're not angry?"

"I might be a jealous fool over you Keira, but I do know the difference between an honest mistake and one not so innocent." He said this last part as if he remembered seeing Jack kissing me in his club.

"However..." he said drawing out the word before continuing.

"I will get angry if you don't give me what I want and you have kept me without your skin on mine for far too long, come here." He nodded next to him and I bit my lip, loving how demanding he was for my body. I walked over to the bed taking my time and watching his aggravation grow made me smile, giving me power.

He grabbed me before I had the chance to sit down and pulled my body so close to him. I could feel his passion for me press hard up against me in the most delicious way. Well, it looked like even Demon/Angel half breeds got morning wood.

His lips found mine before I could speak and his tongue parted my lips creating a fire in my lower belly. The intoxicating taste of his tongue on mine had something else in me burning very quickly. His hands ran up my back and into my hair. He pulled my hairband out gently, letting my hair flow down around us both. But before I could get too carried away, okay so too late for that, we still needed to talk about this. So, when his lips left mine and started to travel down to my neck, I took my opportunity to ask him,

"How did you know?" My voice was shaking with the pressure building between my legs with what his lips were doing to me.

"Vincent told me," he said as if it was obvious. He sat up and when I did the same, he shook his head telling me no. He gently pushed me back down as he expertly removed my clothes in silence. His eyes scanned every part of my now exposed skin and I saw his jaw twitch as he ground his teeth together. His hands gripped the top of my thighs and explored further up to my backside, once there he ground me into him further. I let out a moan as I felt it rub up against my weak spot.

"Draven, I think...uh…oh…mmm." I was stopped in my tracks as the feeling was getting more intense.

"You were saying?" he said into my neck, but I had lost my words and my mind for that matter. His hands were still pulling my body into him and moving me to his will. I felt like a bendy doll that just wanted to be played with.

We were soon on our sides facing each other and then he pulled me down to the right height. He was looking down at me with hunger in his eyes. His hands found the inside of my legs and he spread them apart so he could then enter me swiftly. The force made my back arch and I screamed out. His hands fought my body's reaction as I tried to pull up but his hands on my hips were stronger and pulled me back down onto his solid manhood, causing me to shriek out again.

The pleasure was clearly too much for me to take and I climaxed after only what seemed like seconds. But as he continued to thrust against me, he got even more aroused by the noises I was making. He growled at the sound of me screaming, which brought me mentally back to the bed that was getting a pounding. Flipping me fully onto my back, I felt his hands leave my hips in what was an almost bruising grip until they found what he was looking for. His hands covered my arms on his travels, moving them up over my head, using my wrists to restrain me. Once trapped to his liking, his mouth found my exposed nipple that looked to be straining to receive his hot mouth.

I looked down to see the deep purple ring around his black eyes as the Demon side was dominating his powerful body. He saw me looking down at him and this seemed to drive him into a supreme frenzy. His hands left my wrists and fisted into either side of the pillow under my head so that he could tear it apart. Ripping it in half caused spotless white feathers to rain down around us like angelic rain, landing on my equally white skin.

Then his arms wrapped around my body so tightly I could only just breathe as I knew what was coming next. For once he was the one to arch half his body upwards taking some of me with him, as it was time for both of us to climax in perfect sync. His neck went back, the tendons straining against his skin as his head looked at the canopy above. Then he released one last battle cry that turned into a growl as the war was won. The action reminded me of a wolf throwing his head up to howl at the moon.

Meanwhile, my head rolled back into the mass of feathers as I bit my lip to hold in the scream that found its way out anyway. When I had finished quivering, Draven's body collapsed on top of me, giving me a small amount of weight that was comforting. His head rested next to mine and I waited until his breathing calmed before speaking first.

"Well... that was... intense," I said smiling but he whipped his head up to look at me seriously.

"I didn't hurt you, did I?"

"No, no, of course not, what I meant was that it was intense, in a good way," I said smoothing out the line that had formed in between his eyebrows.

"Ah, well as long as you enjoyed it," he teased and then winked at me making me melt like butter on a hot crumpet.

"Umm... I don't think there would have been a woman alive or man, for that matter, who wouldn't have enjoyed that. That was bloody lovely." At this he let out a roar of laughter that made me jump.

"I have never had sex like this ever before so it means I sometimes lose control, which believe me is not something I am used to and with what you do to me, I have to be even more careful, as I have never experienced losing control around a human before... I forget how breakable you are." He had my hands in his, entwining his long, thick tanned fingers with my thin white ones. There was such a contrast in colour and size I let out a nervous giggle.

"Is that why you sometimes bite me?" I asked always being more than curious about that but he looked a bit ashamed.

"Yes," he said sternly before continuing.

"It is an impulse, like an animal instinct but with a human it seems to be more enhanced. The smell of your skin and the blood underneath, it is too much for me not to taste. But I have found I can contain it if I concentrate very hard." I was fascinated but I found myself wishing he didn't feel like it was a bad thing. During sex I had wanted him to bite me as it seemed to intensify the pleasure and now I had a better understanding about people who liked that sort of thing.

"So, the pillow got it instead," I remarked blushing. He lifted his eyes to look at me once, giving me a quirky smile before lowering them to one of my breasts where a single white feather had landed. He then got closer and blew on it making it tickle its way to my neck. I closed my eyes and sighed at the prickling it made on my skin. Then I flashed open my eyes and remembered what it was I wanted to tell him.

"I like it!" I blurted out but he just shook his head, knowing what I meant.

"I do, I don't know why but it just feels right when you bite me and of course there is the pleasure that follows." Now this had him raising an eyebrow and leaving the feather's journey.

"I think you are too good in giving in to my needs. I am selfish when it comes to getting what I want. I know this, but you have the power and right to tell me no, do you understand?" Oh I understood, but it still took me back on hearing it being spoken. He was saying that I was his equal and that he would, in fact, obey me if I so wished. Then, as if by nature, I had a flood of naughty thoughts whip through my mind all at once. Of course, he wanted to know what it was that had me smiling like an idiot but I just licked my lips before kissing him.

"So now tell me, is Vincent very angry with me?" I asked dreading the answer but judging from Draven's soft black eyes and a smile that made his face light up, then I guessed I was being paranoid again.

"Of course not, why would he be?"

"Because I kissed him," I said feeling the shame burn my cheeks.

"Yes, you did, but it was my fault. I should have been the one to put you to bed myself but instead I sent my brother to check on you. Granted, he got more than he bargained for, but I doubt very much that he minded. I can imagine he hasn't been able to stop thinking about it" He laughed at both a combination of his comment and my reaction to it.

"Oh don't say that!" I buried my head into the pillow that used to be in one piece only instead I got a face full of feathers. Draven fell on his back and pulled me on top of him so I couldn't hide. I rested my folded arms on his wide chest and looked down at him and again he was grinning.

"Well, I remember what our first kiss did to me. And after all, you were his first human kiss...poor bastard!" He laughed again making me shake with him, but I frowned hiding my smile and jabbed him in the side.

"You shouldn't say that!"

"Oh Keira, don't fret for he is fine. I am just teasing you but what can I say, I am half Demon," he said as he picked a feather gently from my hair. I made a growling noise that wouldn't have intimidated a mouse, making him smile and reward me with a full set of white teeth and for the first time I noticed his canines were larger than most humans. No wonder he had been able to bite me so easily.

His hands were tickling my sides and I couldn't help what came next. The worst thing in the world happened and I had no way to stop it in time.

I snorted.

His eyes widened at the new noise that just passed my lips and my hands flew to my mouth but of course, it was too late...it was out!

"And that was?" he asked mocking me as he couldn't contain his wicked bad-boy grin.

"I don't want to talk about it," I said getting defensive at my utter humiliation. I rolled off him, but he pinned me down and pulled the covers off me, leaving me exposed.

"Oh no you don't, I want to hear it again!" And then with surprisingly gentle fingers he tickled my defenceless naked skin until I was near to tears with laughter. Of course, the snorting came through like an uncontrollable little piggy, which made his roaring laughter boom harder and deeper. By the end of our little playing on the bed we were both trying to calm down enough to form actual sentences. Then it hit me, here I was having one of the best mornings of my life when there was still so many questions I needed answering.

"Oh my God... I can't believe I have been so self-centred! I haven't even asked you about Takeshi, is he alright?" Draven looked as though he found this endearing, but I just frowned. After all, he couldn't let me get away with everything, just passing it all off as cute.

"Don't scorn yourself and you are sweet for asking, but I think after everything you have endured you are entitled to a little distraction. Takeshi is fine now, he is resting. I gave him some of my energy to help him heal." He was smoothing my hair back from my face as he spoke.

"How did this happen to him?" I could tell he didn't want to tell me, but I raised my eyes to him before he could protest.

"Okay, I will tell you but Keira, I don't want you to obsess about something I will not allow to happen." I nodded to indicate he should continue.

"Lucius is trying to poison his mind so that his actions can't be seen for what he has planned. I don't know exactly what he is going to do but one thing is for sure, he knows about you." This made me shudder at the thought and Draven didn't miss my reaction as he pulled me closer to him, wrapping the covers around me like a secure cocoon making me feel like a caterpillar.

"But nothing will happen to you. He can't take you from me." This sounded very threatening and I couldn't imagine anyone being as crazy as to want to antagonise Draven. Well, apart from the obvious ones being Sammael and Morgan.

"But why does he even want me?" I asked bringing him back to my eyes which softened when they got there.

"Because, my lovely, you are mine and you are my only weakness. You are also a very breakable human as we both know so this puts the risks at a higher price. He will do anything to have you, to take you from me but he is not stupid and will not chance coming here himself. It just means that I will be a little more protective over you than I normally would." He said all this without too much emotion and I knew it was to spare me worry but because I had him figured, I worried anyway.

"Okay, next question, why the Hell didn't you tell me that you had Layla here imprisoned?" Ok, judging by his reaction to this question, I could add another crazy person to the list of 'Who would risk making Draven angry.' He did not look happy that I hadn't forgotten this small factor.

"We are not going to discuss this," he said flatly, but I was not going to yield that quickly.

"And why not? I think I have a right to know!"

"You do not yet know enough about our ways to understand."

He was trying to judge my response but whatever he saw in my face, it was not what he had hoped for. His face said as much.

"Understand what?" I shook my head at him but I had a feeling I was going to regret the truth.

"You will think our ways are barbaric and you won't look kindly on me for being the one who has to enforce such punishments. Is this something that you really want to know?" It wasn't so much a question but more a statement as he knew that I would not. I was torn between the two Dravens I knew. I remembered how cold he had first been to me and the sight of him fighting, ripping into those creatures they called Gorgon Leeches. How he wielded his two powerful swords that came from his Demon form, slicing into the body that Sammael had used as a vessel. It had been a truly frightening sight.

And of course, there was the other Draven who was with me now. The one who had taught me more about the pleasures my body could endure than anyone before him. I had felt more love and passion in these past few days than in my entire life. His soft voice telling me how perfect I was and how his eyes looked at me when he told me that he loved me. It was like two completely different people, but I couldn't help that I loved both of them to my very core.

"Okay, so I get the point but I don't exactly need details here." He was getting up and before I could protest he was leaning down to whisper in my ear.

"I have to do Demon/Angel man things." And he winked at me before leaving to use the bathroom. I couldn't believe how shocked I was just to see him doing something so human. I mean he was only using the bathroom for goodness sake, but I still couldn't believe it, even when I heard the toilet flush I found myself giggling. I got up, cleaned the evidence of our joining with some tissue and put my clothes on, still chuckling to myself before he came out. I wondered if he did the universal man thing by leaving the seat up. Ha!

When he came out he too was dressed and his hair was pushed back wet around his neck. The sight of him in designer jeans and a tight-fitting black vest made me need to sit down. His shoulders looked huge and it seemed every day he was taller. I was only five foot three so he was over a foot taller being I guessed, over six foot. I had never asked him, so I wasn't certain.

"How tall are you?" I asked thinking while I was pondering it, I might as well get all the facts. He looked at me with a curious smile and I knew he was wondering where the question had come from, but he obliged me anyway.

"I'm about six foot four, two hundred and forty pounds and I hate cucumbers, anything else you would like to know?" he asked and I could tell he was teasing me again.

"You hate cucumbers?" I said trying not to laugh at the thought. He came up to me as I was sat on the bed and put one hand on either side of my thighs, leaning into me smiling.

"I don't like the texture, but one thing I do like the texture of..." He was speaking over my mouth and the rest of his sentence was lost on my lips making it very clear what he was referring to. We were just about to do the naughty again when my phone started to vibrate, and I almost cursed out loud.

"Bloody technology!" I said instead, but Draven found my frustration funny and he jumped up quickly to retrieve my phone. Of course as soon as I saw who it was, this did make me swear.

"Oh bollocks!" I knew it wasn't ladylike but I couldn't help it.

"Keira, what's wrong?"

"Just reality," I said before flipping the phone open and saying begrudgingly,

"Hi, mum."

CHAPTER THREE

UNFORTUNATE FAMILY MEMBERS

"Hi honey, I've not caught you at a bad time have I? Only there was no answer at home." My mum's sweet voice made it difficult to lie so of course I ended up doing a lousy job of it.

"No mum, it's fine, is everything alright?" I noticed Draven had taken a seat and looked very amused at the dread on my face. The problem was that even though I was some distance from him, I knew he could still hear every word that was being said on both sides. Damn that Demon hearing!

"Yes, everything's fine sweetheart, I guess I just wanted to see if there's anything new with you."

"Umm, no not really, just plodding along, you know college and work and stuff." I was trying my best to sound casual but when I was faced with the most gorgeous, sexiest man alive staring at me and knowing every lie I made, oh and finding it hilarious at that, well let's just say it did make personal phone calls somewhat difficult.

"So, nothing new then?" My mum was being about as subtle as a bull at a tea party.

"Mum, is there something you wanted to ask?"

"Well, don't be angry with her, but Libby kind of hinted that you were courting?" Oh no, just when I thought it couldn't get any worse. I was going to murder my sister! When I didn't answer my mum cleared her throat down the phone.

"Keira?" My mum was getting impatient and I refused to look at Draven who, the last time I looked, was frowning.

"Umm…well yeah, mum…I'm sort of seeing someone," I said quietly but it didn't do me much good as when I looked up, Draven's unimpressed expression filled my view. He was quickly stood in front of me and mouthed the words 'sort of'.

"I mean yes, I am dating someone," I corrected and this brought the smile back to his lips making me roll my eyes.

"Well, that's nice Kazzy honey, me and your dad both think it's about time. But Libby mentioned that he's your boss." Oh boy, Libby was most definitely going to get an ear full from me when she got back. Better still, I thought, refusing to cook for a month would do the trick. But then poor Frank would be left to eat gruel and charcoal for the duration and that wouldn't be fair on him.

"Yeah mum, he owns the club but he's not my manager or anything like that, so it kind of doesn't count. In fact, we don't really see each other when I'm working, see I work downstairs and he…uh, well he is…um, not downstairs…" I was babbling on and on and for the first time I felt like kicking Draven in the shins as he stood there grinning at me like a mischievous child. I mouthed the words 'grow up' at him but this just added fuel to a naughty flame.

"Well, as long as it doesn't interfere with work, Kazzy, that's the important thing."

"No, it doesn't," I said trying to sound convincing but when you have the memory of Draven's hands all over your body when you were trying to work, it made it harder to lie.

"So what's he like? Libby said he's very handsome and that you were wearing makeup again, so I gather this means you must really like him." Bless my mum, but right now I just wanted my phone to blow up mission impossible style! But no doubt Draven would just use his powers to fix it again. He was definitely enjoying himself too much for this little call to end.

"I'm not wearing makeup again, Libby is exaggerating as usual. Jeez, I wore it once for Halloween."

"Don't get touchy, Kazzy, it's nothing to be ashamed of, you're just getting your life back on track and it's good to hear. We're happy for you, just remember to take it slow and don't let the fact that he's your boss and rich, intimidate you." She said the word 'rich' as if it was something fragile you shouldn't touch. I shook my head thinking sweet Jesus, could this get any worse? Of course the answer to that quickly followed.

"Oh, and don't forget to use protection, remember it's better to be baby safe than baby sorry." This had been my mum's motto since I turned seventeen. I just wanted to cry but from the looks of Draven he already was, with laughter that was! He was sat back down and I scowled at him. I waved my arm around at him to motion for him to leave but he just shook his head back at me, telling me a defiant no. So I mouthed the word 'fine' at him to indicate my anger.

"Mum, it's a bit soon for that." I was just thankful I didn't slip up and say 'too late' instead.

"Well, as long as you're careful when you do, that's all that counts." This of course was not the best time to panic about the fact that we hadn't actually been careful or even if we had to be for that matter. Could Demon/Angel half breeds even reproduce? Oh no, how could I have not thought about this sooner?!

"Anyway, what is the young man's name?" This made me laugh out loud. I just couldn't help it. For one, I didn't actually know how old Draven was, but I was pretty sure he was well past being called young man.

"His name's Drav...uh I mean... Dominic." At this Draven's eyes held something other than humour. They got soft and flashed a ring of purple flames, giving me the impression that he loved it when I called him by his first name.

"That's a nice name. Has he taken you anywhere fancy?" I couldn't help but smile when I saw Draven's face drop. Of course, we had been a bit preoccupied to go on an actual date, what with thinking Draven had kidnapped me, my psycho ex-art teacher after me and then there was stalker boy's Demon partner in crime, leading to me actually being kidnapped. So, to be honest, we just hadn't had the time. All in all, we'd had one hell of a week!

"Well, I have been a little busy and things are still fresh, we have only been dating a few days, mum. Anyway how's me dad?" I needed to get her off this subject. My mum wasn't old fashioned as such, but she still thought that a girl had to be wined and dined by a gentleman before she gave up the goods. Well, my goods had already been bought, stripped and spent, many times over and boy was Draven one hell of a buyer. Hell, he was a pro! But I wasn't about to disclose that bit of information to my mother.

"Oh he's fine, asleep on the couch as usual, I don't know why he bothers watching telly if it's just going to send him off to sleep." I could faintly hear some World War documentary in the background and it made me chuckle.

"Libby is back off their trip soon, isn't she?"

"Yeah, Sunday I think."

"I hope you haven't been scared all alone in that house by yourself, you know you can ring me and you know we have Skype now." Oh great, more lying.

"I ain't been scared, there's nowt to be scared of," I said and before I had thought about it, my Northern twang had shown itself in full force.

"Kazzy, use proper English, dear," she scolded. This had always frustrated my mother but considering she had married a Scouser (Someone from Liverpool) I was always surprised when she pulled us up on it. The sweetest thing about this was when Draven heard me sort of being told off by my mum, he came over and kissed the top of my head lightly. He mouthed the words 'I like it' and I couldn't help but smile.

"Libby also tells me that you have been painting again, I must say if this is down to this new guy you're now dating, I like him already." I could almost hear Draven smiling behind me as his arms wrapped around me.

"Yeah, I decided to take advantage of the amazing views around here, I'll send you one soon. Anyway, mum I'm going to have to go but..."

"Oh well, there was one other thing I wanted to tell you before you go." This was what I had been waiting for. I knew my mum well enough to know the hidden meaning behind the things she did and this time I knew that she had been stalling.

"What is it, mum?"

"Well, don't go off the handle, but someone's coming to visit you," she said trying to sound upbeat, as if that would help. I suddenly went solid in Draven's hold, knowing there was only one person who my mum knew I wouldn't be happy about seeing.

"Oh no, no, no…no way, mum! Not going to happen, not now, not ever!" I said in a stern voice that shocked Draven enough to drop his arms and face me. I was frowning so hard my cheeks ached.

"Catherine Kieran Williams, I didn't bring you up to have that attitude and family is important, you surprise me!" Ah, so now it was time for the guilt trip...parents!

"Mum please, I am just getting settled here and this is the last thing I need right now." Okay, so I know it was a cheap shot, going straight in for the guilt thing but trust me, when needs must!

"Keira, there would never be a right time for you to see your cousin in your book." Damn straight, I hated the bitch and a frozen Hell wouldn't even cut it!

"Does Libby know about this?"

"Not yet, but she won't say no, anyway it's only for a week or two." I thought I was going to choke on my own tongue.

"Anyway, I will let you know the details love, talk to you soon, bye, bye, kiss, kiss." And with that my mother put the phone down before I had chance to have the tantrum that I was very close to having.

"Arrrgggg...! SHIT, SHIT, DOUBLE SHIT!" I screamed out before I could contain it any longer and man did Draven looked more stunned than ever.

"Sorry about that but to say that I am pissed off right now would be a huge understatement!" I let my arms fly over my head like a drama queen. I had never been one for overacting but when it came to my cousin Hilary, no amount of overacting would ever be enough! She could give Margaret Thatcher a run for her money.

"I take it you don't like this person?" He was trying very hard to hide a grin and for a change he looked a bit worried about my reaction if he were to fail at concealing it.

"Is there a stronger word for hate?!" I said bitterly.

"I doubt you really mean that," he said as he followed me around the room as I was stomping around.

"I bloody do! Trust me on this one, she is pure evil." He might be almighty and powerful but when it came to keeping his face straight he failed miserably. His laughing didn't soften my features either.

"Draven!"

"I'm sorry, but it is hard to believe that such a cute and adorable creature could be so angry. You are too loveable to hate anything, Keira." He caught my face in his hands and made me look up into his face and when he kissed me, I inevitably turned to putty, although I like to think I did it begrudgingly.

"May I ask what it is exactly that you do not like about this Hellcat?" Umm... I liked that, Hellcat... it had a nice ring to it. Of course, it needed a few added words like...bitch, slut, skank, harlot, cow oh and man bollock eater!

"Everything!" At this he frowned as he wanted a serious answer. He didn't realise this was a serious answer.

"Just trust me on this one. She is beyond a handful and she seems to make it her mission in life to make me miserable at every opportunity. She will try and steal you away, that I will bet my life on!" This had him laughing again and I could sort of understand why, this to him must seem a very trivial thing to hate over.

"Well, she can try, but won't you feel satisfied when she doesn't succeed?" I had to admit, I liked the idea.

"She is very pretty, granted, but she would spread her legs for anything that has a pulse and wears underpants...oh, and having a shiny new car she will just class as a bonus. But she does seem to get whatever she wants and when she sees that I have you, she will go in for the kill". As soon as the last word was out of my mouth, he had picked me up and put me over his shoulder like a fireman. I let out a nervous giggle before he laid me gently on the bed. My legs dangled over the edge while he placed a hand on either side of my head. He came very close to my face before speaking,

"My sweet Keira, listen to me now when I say that I am yours, as you are mine, do you understand?" I nodded, as it was the only response I could give as I had lost all of my functions. The heavenly sight of his mouth had me hypnotized.

"So, we are not going to worry about this evil cousin, are we?" He was shaking his head and speaking in a way that had me agreeing to anything he wanted. He pushed himself against me when I didn't answer quickly enough, so instead I moaned at the feeling he was creating between my inner thighs.

"Good girl," he said before his lips curved up on one side into a wicked grin. We stayed like that for some time, kissing like teenagers before his strong arm held my back and pulled me up until my body was fully on the bed. He held all his body weight on his arms above me and lowered to kiss me again as if he was doing a press-up. Things were about to get heated for the second time this morning when there was a knock at the door. Draven growled at the disruption.

"LEAVE US!" He bellowed, but before they had chance to leave, I frowned at him and his dark eyes softened.

"Wait," he said before smiling at me. He got off me and went to open the door to Candra who had brought some food. I sat up and smelled the fresh bread and hot teapot. My stomach made noises as if it had food radar. He stood back and waited for her to place the tray on the table and before leaving she bowed her head to him saying,

"My Lord." Draven nodded in return but before she could leave, I quickly said,

"Thank you, Candra," and she turned looking shocked and then smiled gratefully before leaving. I got off the bed to tuck into a sticky croissant and some jam but more importantly a cup of tea which Draven had already poured for me.

"Thank you," I said taking it from him, but he just winked at me before pouring himself some juice. I still don't know why I kept getting shocked every time he did something so normal. I mean even Superman must take a leak and eat a cheeseburger once in a while...right?

"So, what would you like to do today?" Draven surprised me

with this question, and I had a feeling that the phone call with my mum had something to do with it.

"Umm... I don't know. What brought this on?" I asked after swallowing a mouthful of buttery pastry goodness.

"Well, I think your mother was right, I haven't gone about this the right way at all." He was smirking at the idea of dating a human, I could tell.

"To be fair, Draven, when have we had the time? When exactly were we supposed to go on this date? I mean before you kidnapped me and when you acted like you hated me or after, when we found out Morgan was coming for me?" I couldn't help but shake my head while laughing at the idea, but he didn't seem to find the funny side.

"Keira, I didn't kidnap you and I most certainly didn't hate you." I rolled my eyes again and refrained from making a sarcastic comment about that one.

"But I guess I get your point, which makes me wonder, what you would have said if I had asked you out on a date after our little car journey the second night you worked upstairs?" This question made me stop eating and look at him. Yep, he was being serious.

"Why, did…did you want to?" I swallowed hard while waiting for the answer.

"I was thinking about it, yes, but I had to fight with what was right and what I wanted. I am afraid my logic won over my heart that night. However, I still didn't want to leave you. It was my first experience at being worried about someone I loved and unfortunately it was not to be the last time I felt this way." I couldn't judge his facial expression this time, although I am usually good at it. But this time it was like a sadness he was trying to hide. I could tell he was worried about something, but I knew he would never tell me what.

"But I am still curious as to what your answer would have been?"

"That's a tough one because if I was listening to my heart, then I would have said yes, but the same as you, I would have gone with my logic and said no." At this he looked truly stunned and no wonder as with a man like Draven, you don't say no.

"Why would your logic tell you that?" I think my answer knocked his ego slightly because now he had come to sit next to me and was giving me a very intense stare.

"Because I knew there was something different about you and you did kind of scare me but come on, do you blame me? I mean, up until that point, you treated me like I was ...was..."

"Yes?" He raised a single brow, but I just looked down at my hands.

"Well, like I was some silly little plain and pale outsider that you needed to get out of your club quicker than cockroaches."

"Oh Keira, you can be so blind sometimes. You really don't look at yourself the way others do." He rested his big hand at the back of my neck before bringing his thumb round to put pressure on my chin, so I had no choice but to look up at him.

"I apologise for ever making you feel this way, but I needed you to stay away from me at the time. You don't know the endless nights I spent thinking…No, not just thinking, but fantasising about touching that soft pale skin of yours." At this he ran the back of his fingers up my bare arm with his other hand making me close my eyes, and my breath hitch at the sensations that assaulted me.

"Those times I am not proud of but now I have you I will do anything to keep you and that includes making you happy. So let's get back to that particular task, should we. What would you like to do today, my sweet beauty?" He leant his head down to catch my smile with his mouth and when he had finished, he licked his lips saying,

"Mmm sweet indeed, jam has never tasted so good." Then I went the colour of that jam, but this just seemed to excite him more.

"Okay, I have made my mind up, can I go home?" I said while he was kissing my neck though it made him stop and look back at me.

"You don't like being here?"

"No, no, it's not that, I love being here with you, but I guess I'm just ready for things to get back to normal."

"Keira, you belong to a Demon/Angel half breed who has to control the world's supernatural, I think you can kiss normality goodbye," he said laughing while he pushed his hair back with a pair of large hands. This was definitely a weak spot of mine, along with him mentioning that I belonged to him. I knew it was barbaric, possessive and even primal but for some reason it also just felt so very right. And well, it helped with him doing sexy ass things like pushing all his hair back. I just couldn't stop my heart from doing a backflip in my chest at the sight. It had me wondering what he would look like under an exotic waterfall, naked of course. Okay, that thought nearly had me panting!

"Well, as close to normal as you can get around me, plus I need to do stuff at home, human stuff and not to mention I have no clothes left."

"Now that is not what I call a problem, for if it was up to me, you would never wear clothes again. But then I would have to keep you hidden away for myself. I don't like it when you get leered at fully clothed as it is, so I can imagine others seeing you naked would send me into a blind rage." He wasn't joking. I remembered when I had heard the loud crash in the VIP area when Jack had kissed me and then the power to the entire club had gone out. Talk about blowing a fuse.

"Nevertheless, I still need to go home at some point, but I would like it very much if you came with me." I looked up at him giving him my best wide-eyed puppy look. Which I hoped made him melt in the same way one of his looks did to me.

"Of course I am coming with you, I'm not going to let you go alone." He said this as though it was such an obvious thing.

"Okey dokey, let's go, oh and by the way, I'm driving." I got up but he pulled me down onto his lap and kissed me before saying,

"Not a chance." But when I got up, I actually stamped my foot looking like a spoilt teenager. He got up and towered above me, only I wouldn't back down.

"Come on, I need to get my car back at some point and this way I have to give in to you next time." He gave me a huge grin that lit up his eyes and he rubbed his chin in an exaggerated gesture.

"Um...I like the sound of that, but you'd better remember this bargain, because have no doubt that I will collect, Keira." I felt almost giddy at the thought.

Minutes later we had made our way down a maze of stone passageways as Draven held my hand, leading me all the way. It didn't take us long to get outside and I was amazed at the door we went through. It was a hidden stone wall that moved when Draven touched it, causing it to slide to one side. It made me jump at the sound of stone grating heavily against stone.

It was in the same side of the house that held the metal door which led to the bins. I had used this door twice, once on my first night working in Club Afterlife and second when I had tried to escape from it. Draven had known I was in danger and that Morgan was after me, but I had tried to run from it all, including Draven. I had always wondered though just how he had got out to me so quickly that night. Well, now I knew the answer to that one. But thinking more about it, he did have wings and could have just jumped from the balcony above us, the one connected to the VIP.

When we got outside I was ready, already wearing extra layers as the weather had changed overnight, turning bitter cold. But I didn't mind so much as this way I got to see Draven in a black fitted leather jacket. The man made me feel warm down below at just the sight of him.

Oh my, my...

He caught me looking and he opened the door to my big blue truck with a confident half-smile.

"Thank you, kindly," I said while batting my eyelashes making him laugh.

"You are most welcome, my lady."

He suited being in my truck as he had such a rough side to him, especially when he had stubble framing the lower part of his face. I could imagine him chopping logs in half with one swing and with arms like his, this wasn't the only image I had of him. In most of my images I was entwined in those strong muscular arms. I started the engine, but because it was cold it didn't want to fire up first time. I stroked the dash and said,

"Come on big blue, time to wake up." Then she started after a few spluttering sounds, but I had a feeling this was down to Draven who had touched the ignition making God only knows what happen.

"You are so very sweet, you know that?" he said as I pulled the big Bronco round.

"Not so much, I can be naughty when provoked," I said giving him a wicked grin and a wink of my own.

"I wouldn't do that if I were you, not while you are driving and I am *very, very tempted.*" This was Draven's way of saying he was turned on, which of course was making me as horny as a teenager! I couldn't keep the smile off my face or the colour from my cheeks most of the drive home, but it was his fault. He wouldn't stop staring at me.

"You are a very careful driver, aren't you?"

"What you mean is slow...right?" His laugh said it all.

"Well, seeing as you're immortal and I am so very not, I think the speed limit is beneficial for both of us as I don't want to die young and you don't want me to die young, so it's a win, win situation." This was said in a light-hearted way, but it ended up having completely the opposite effect.

"I won't let you die, period!" His angry outburst was said in a way that made me shudder to think of anyone defying such a command. I decided to leave him to his thoughts as he looked out of the window for the first time. I mean, it's not like he could help it if something did happen to me. That was just the natural way of life. But nevertheless, I kept silent on the matter. I was a firm believer in 'it is better to have loved and lost, than never to have loved at all' and I was standing firmly by it.

The last few minutes of the drive were filled with the sights of the wilderness either side of the road and the sound of the engine. Draven didn't say another word. I think death was a sore conversation to have with him, but it was inevitable. So, at some point we would have to discuss it. Okay, granted not on our first date, that was kind of a depressing subject to bring up. Meaning now I was secretly scorning myself over it. I was trying to think of a way to bring him back so I did a very lame thing but hopefully one he would find more cute and endearing.

"Okay, I have one for you, why is six afraid of seven?" I asked hoping he wouldn't look at me as though I was totally nuts.

Ooops too late.

"I'm afraid I'm not following you." Jeez, hadn't he heard a joke before even one as lame as this?

"Nooo…" I said elongating the word whilst nudging him on the leg before continuing,

"…This is where you say, 'I don't know, Keira, why is six afraid of seven?' Yeah…" Okay, so this was painful but at least we were having a conversation again...*well sort of one.*

"Oh sorry, Keira please tell me, why is six afraid of seven?" Well, at least he was smiling again.

"Because seven ate nine!" I bit my lip waiting for his response and thankfully the car started to shake and fill with the sound of his laughter. He stopped just as we pulled up outside the house.

"That was adorable," he said taking my hands in his after I turned the key and cut the beast.

"Are you alright?" I asked cautiously.

"Yes I am. I am very, very happy and when I didn't know what it was to be this happy, how it feels I mean, well... it still takes me back but most of all, it makes me terrified at the thought of ever losing it….of ever losing you." His eyes glazed over making them look so deep you could have drowned in them. He brought my hands up to his mouth and kissed them over and over before saving his last kiss for my willing lips.

"Well, lucky for you I have never been this happy either and I ain't going anywhere!" Just as I finished this last word he was out of the car and round to my side opening my door and pulling me out into those solid arms I loved so much. He kicked the door shut and the sound made me jump but he just held me tighter to him.

"I just love that cute Northern English accent of yours but most of all..." he carried me to the porch steps before he continued with his sentence and placed me on the second step, so I was at the right height.

Then he leant in to kiss me but before he got there, he finished the sweetest sentiment just over my eager lips…

"I love you, my Keira."

CHAPTER FOUR

FIRST DATE

O k, this was the thing with having a ridiculously handsome boyfriend who'd had hundreds of years to perfect the art of kissing, you just couldn't help but feel a little self-conscious about your own ability. He seemed to enjoy it but I didn't know if the reason he kissed me so much was down to how good it was or the fact that he thought I needed the practice. Either way I wasn't complaining but I was kind of hoping for the first.

Once he had finished kissing me, he ran his thumb over my lips ever so slowly, but I still couldn't open my eyes. This was the other thing about Draven, he was, to say the least...*intense.* Those black, deep-set eyes would stare at me with no idea about what it did to me or maybe he did know and just relished the idea.

Draven was the type of man that if he wanted to stare freely at someone, then he would, without giving it much thought. Like the first night I saw him at the club. He was walking to the staircase that leads to the VIP when he saw me. He stopped right in front of my table and with a club full of people fascinated with his every move he stopped dead and stared at me as if he owned time. Like he could bend it to his will, keeping me trapped right there along with him. But unbelievably I had looked away first because as much as I loved Draven, he still kind of scared me.

Don't get me wrong, I know he would never hurt me, but I couldn't help feeling a fear at the immense power that lies beneath all that flawless skin of his.

I opened my eyes to see Draven smiling down at me.

"I hope my kiss wasn't sending you to sleep," he said knowing full well that was impossible.

"Quite the opposite actually," I said before going on tiptoes to kiss him on his nose and I laughed when he wrinkled it up. I turned on my heels and fished around for my keys in my jeans' pocket.

"I gather I don't have to invite you in like I would have to a Vampire?" I said giggling but he just frowned and said,

"You watch too many movies, Keira."

"Buffy, actually," I said as I threw my keys into the bowl by the door and started to wriggle out of my jacket. But Draven, being the ultimate old-fashioned gentleman, had already grabbed the shoulders and was peeling it off me. I had never had a guy take my coat off for me, which made me wonder in what era that had all started but more importantly, how old had Draven been when it happened?

"Buffy?" he asked breaking into my thoughts and revealing he really wasn't a TV watching kind of guy.

"Yeah, you know, Buffy the Vampire slayer, she kicks ass! Do you even watch telly?" He laughed at my question.

"I don't really get the time, but I am intrigued at how a human would destroy a Vampire, especially a woman." I was in the kitchen when he said this, and I was only glad that I wasn't handling a sharp implement.

"What? Wait a minute... Don't...don't tell me Vampires are real?" No way, he must be teasing me! No freakin' way!

"They are very real but not in the way history and myth portrays them. They are Demons that have been created by infected blood which genetically changes their Demon attributes. But they can have many weaknesses and young ones are fairly easy to kill." He said all this as though he had been giving a lecture on Demon kill zones.

"O...kay... that's a little hard to take." I was leaning over the sink when I felt Draven behind me.

"I'm sorry, but you did ask. Maybe next time I should try and sugar-coat it." I snorted and then replied,

"Uh yeah... I'm thinking vanilla frosted centre, pink icing, multi-coloured sprinkles and caramel glazed kind of sugar coating." Once again, he threw his head back and laughed, causing me to become momentarily hypnotised watching the muscles working in his neck with the movement.

I bit my lip and then turned back to the sink so that I wouldn't throw myself at him in my moment of weakness.

"I guess I shouldn't be surprised at anything anymore," I muttered before moving on,

"Would you like a drink?" I asked trying not to forget my manners even though the word Vampire still hung in the air like a cartoon bubble over my head. *My mum would be proud.*

"I am fine, thank you, my sweet." He said this in my ear, which sent sparks up and down my spine. Bloody Hell, but I was ready to strip naked and burn my clothes. Thankfully instead I filled the kettle and clicked it on. I got down a big mug that had my home team Liverpool FC on it and popped in a teabag.

"Did Frank inherit this house?" Draven asked and I was surprised at the question. Where did that come from?

"Umm, yeah he did."

"From his uncle?" Ok, how did he know that? I nodded and he could see the confusion on my face.

"I have been coming here for a long time, Keira, and I know the name of every individual who lives here. Why are you surprised?" He retrieved the carton of milk for me before I had time to turn.

"Thanks." I finished making my tea without answering him. I didn't know why I had been shocked, it's not like I was ever normal myself and now here I was with a supernatural boyfriend. I smiled when I said the word in my mind and Draven as usual didn't miss it.

"Seeing you smile just makes it even harder not to kiss you," he said taking my hot mug away and lifting me by the waist with one arm wrapped around me, pulling me up to reach his face.

"I take it you like kissing me?" I asked being brave after he had placed me back down and handed me my tea.

"Kissing you is like making love without getting naked," he said as if he meant every word.

"You're teasing me! I know…" I cleared my throat and whispered the rest,

"…I am not that good." I had been told once that I wasn't a great kisser because I never relaxed.

"Why would you ever think that?" He didn't look happy at my spoken thoughts. I walked into the living room and he followed, but when I sat down on the armchair, he shook his head and nodded at the space next to him. It wasn't that I didn't want to be close to him, but I didn't want him thinking that I was always so clingy. Thankfully I was wrong.

"I got told once that I don't relax enough to be a good kisser," I said shamefully and just shrugged my shoulders as if it was no big deal.

"Well, the boy was clearly a fool. It was a boy wasn't it?" he asked in earnest and I nearly choked on my tea.

"YES, of course it was!" I said laughing out loud.

"I was just checking, you might be inclined towards both sexes." He shrugged his shoulders like this was a common thing with his kind, which had me forming my next words,

"Do you like that sort of thing?" I lowered my eyes to stare at my tea while I went the colour of tomato soup.

"With you, no. I will not share you, Keira," he said firmly, watching me carefully before continuing,

"Kissing you makes it hard to stop, like taking a drug. I get lost in your taste and once I have had that taste, I become addicted. It is as if I can feel every fibre in your body speaking to me and the only way to communicate back is by using my lips on yours and my tongue to feel you…*to taste you.*" This came out like a sexual purr and I swallowed hard before licking my dry lips. He witnessed the motion and I could swear I heard a barely controlled groan come from deep within him. Well, I certainly hadn't had my kissing described like that before, that was pure Shakespeare.

"Thank you," I said shyly, but he tilted his head to one side and made me look at him.

"You do not need to thank me for explaining the truth about how I feel. Sex with you is very much the same feeling, only I use something else to communicate other than my tongue," he said in a bold, mischievous way and it was soon apparent that he was getting aroused by the topic. His hands started to find my skin and I had to concentrate on how to breathe. I hated the fact that I was going to have to stop it because there was a conversation that we really needed to have. I pulled his hands back from around me and pushed him away making him growl.

"Now stop that!" I said pulling my light brown eyebrows together in a frown.

"Then give in to me," he said in a hoarse voice, one that sounded desperate for his drug.

"First we kind of need to talk about something."

"Another worry?" he asked turning back to his smooth velvet voice of a man back in control.

"This is an important one and one we should have had sooner." I was going red just thinking about trying to form the words. Words I wished I didn't have to say.

"I should have mentioned this earlier, but we have made love six times now."

"Soon to be seven," he remarked confidently.

"Okay, here it is...I'm not exactly on the pill," I blurted out, but his reaction was the complete opposite to the one I had imagined. He was laughing at me.

"I gather this new worry is due to the 'Baby Safe' comment your mother made to you earlier." He couldn't keep his face straight, so I guessed that it wasn't something he was concerned about.

"So, I take it this is something we don't need to worry about?"

"You mean contraception?" Again, with the roaring laughter.

"I'm glad you find this so funny," I said sarcastically turning away from him.

"I don't mean to, but you have to see it from my side, I have never needed to have this conversation before. It's a real human moment for me." Well, when he put it like that I could kind of see his point.

"So Angels and Demons don't...reproduce?"

"We can but we are different than humans. We can control it." As soon as he said this my heart sank. Did he not have orgasms? I had been pretty sure that I could feel umm... stuff down below afterwards.

"How is that possible? I don't understand, how can you enjoy it if you don't...uhh...you know?" Again, he wasn't making this easy for me when he kept looking at me as if I was a child asking about the 'birds and bees' or 'where do babies come from?'

"I will explain." He playfully gripped my chin before continuing.

"When two of our kind have sex, it is not as intense as it is with a human, as I have recently learned first-hand. We can control every aspect of our bodies including whether or not the sperm is active." He was looking at me, waiting for me to ask questions about something I didn't understand but so far, in a weird way, I understood.

"So you mean dead or firing blanks?" I couldn't help but giggle as I noticed his male pride get a hammering, so he corrected me quickly.

"No. More like working to its full capacity."

"So how come being with a human is better?" I always thought he was just saying this part to make me feel better and less inadequate.

"The best way to explain is if you could imagine two powerful magnets that want to fight each other rather than mesh. Now take a magnet and a piece of metal, they are instantly attracted and drawn together."

"Okay... so I'm the metal in this picture...right?"

"I am not explaining this very well, am I? Being with another of my kind is not as fulfilling sexually because our powers are both strong, but when I am with you, imagine the intensity multiplied by thousands. Our senses are hypersensitive, so when it comes to you, every touch, every smell and every taste feels...*incredible.*" He leaned over my head and took in my scent, closing his eyes in what looked like bliss being discovered. I felt like a giant glass of wine being sampled.

"So, back to the baby part, doesn't that affect your...you know?" I was waving my hand around like the Queen of England waves from an open-top car.

"Orgasm? Climax?" he finished, making it clear he was enjoying himself with our little chat far too much.

"No, it doesn't affect the feeling you give me, but I have heard that when we do finally allow ourselves an active release the level of intensity is a dangerous thing. But I'm not an expert on these matters...First human remember?" He said this last part as he playfully poked me in the ribs making me close to snorting. I wanted to ask what he meant by 'dangerous' but held back, instead wondering if this was something he would ever want from me.

"But if that is something you wanted to do, then I could always go on the pill or we could use a Sergeant's jacket but I think extra-large would be in order cause...Oh...I mean..." I tripped over my words before I could think about what I was saying and I bit down on my lip. But it was too late, it was already out. He was close to tears with laughter and I was just close to tears.

"Why this is shocking, Miss Williams! Just when I thought I knew you well enough to judge what you would say next, you say something like that. You are so unpredictable, and I adore it. But may I ask is this term for protection a Northern thing or a Keira thing?" I couldn't speak and I was pretty close to biting all the skin from my lips.

"I will take the fact that you are trying to destroy those perfect lips of yours that it is in fact a Keira thing. I am most pleased," he said in triumph, but I had no idea why. I wasn't the only one who was unpredictable. He put his thumb to my lips to prevent me from biting them further, then he bent his head to kiss them, only when he got there, he bit them gently himself. I practically swooned.

"Mmm... I can now see why you do that, satisfying indeed." This made me smile and I had to first clear my throat to find my voice again.

"So, erm… back to the whole protection thing."

"I am afraid it wouldn't work like it does with human men. I am not being arrogant when I say they would be quite useless. But enough of this talk, I am hungry." He was above me before I even had time to blink. He grabbed my wrists and pulled me off the couch to him. He stared down at me and my neck arched right back to meet those hungry eyes.

"And my Sergeant orders his Private upstairs for drill training." My eyes widened in excitement and I couldn't help but giggle. The giggling however was promptly put on hold as his large palms felt their way down my sides finding my waist. There, he gripped me tightly before lifting me up and over his shoulder like he had done earlier. It was as if I weighed nothing at all and he sprinted up the stairs before I could count two steps, ending in my bedroom.

He slid me down, holding one hand behind my neck to lay me down gently. I tried to swallow down my lust a notch when I saw his purple eyes flash. I heard his shoes hit the floor before he joined me on the bed, but he just eyed me like a beast would do to its next feast. I felt the burning fever down below and the fear in my chest. He was like a man possessed...no, not a man...*A Demon.*

He started stripping the clothes off me as if he was trying very hard to resist the urge not to rip them apart. I was a bit relieved when he didn't as I was quickly running out of clothes. I sat up and pulled his vest from his chiselled torso and I noticed the denim stretching with the bulge that grew within it. He noticed my wide eyes at the sight, and he gave me one of his trademark bad boy grins. This was quite a surreal moment for me, given all the times I thought I had been dreaming about Draven visiting me in my room. Of course, all those times had been real and of course all those times I wanted him to be doing this to me now.

We were soon both naked and he seemed to be studying me in depth. The whole time I tried everything in my power to get the ball rolling as the embarrassment was getting too much for me to handle but he wanted his way with me. This was my torture.

"You make me nervous when you do that," I whispered nervously, which was crazy seeing as this was hardly our first time.

"Good, I love to watch you blush." His hands gripped tightly onto my hips and he pulled me down the bed to meet him. His fingers moved down my thighs and stopped when they reached under my knees. He held them in a strong grip, separating my legs and pulling them up around him so that he could easily enter me. I closed my eyes and braced myself for the feeling but screamed out anyway as I usually did, arching my back and taking even more of him into my willing body.

Would I ever get used to the immense pleasure it caused? As both our actions became more rapid the bed didn't agree with our activity and squeaked and creaked like a cow on an old rocking horse. Draven cursed in a few different languages and I couldn't help but find it a bit funny. I had never laughed during sex before, but it must have caused a tensed reaction down below because he gave me a look of surprise. Now I knew it was obviously a first for him also as I couldn't imagine anyone in their right mind laughing with Draven inside them.

Anyone but me that was.

"Are you laughing at me, young lady?" he said showing me his teeth when he grinned.

"No, Sir," I said giving him a cheeky smile which made his eyes soften like black velvet.

He pulled out of me making me let out a moan in disappointment, but he just mouthed the words 'trust me.' Then he got up and grabbed the end of my mattress with both hands. I was about to get up to make it easier but before I could open my mouth, he flung the mattress on the floor next to my window seat with me still lay upon it. I let out a gasp, but this just seemed to excite him further as the next thing I knew he was on top of me again and inside me. Then we continued with no further interruptions and my bed frame was happy again.

This time making love was more experimental as Draven kept changing positions, resulting in mind-blowing release after release and I was almost at the point of screaming out how I couldn't take much more. But before I could utter a word of protest, he changed something within me so that I could take it.

It was like giving me a clean slate and then he moved my body so that I had my back to him. We had never done it this way before and with the added bonus of the window seat it was a very comfortable position. I leant across it and his hands explored my back and ran up to my hair, grabbing handfuls of blonde waves before entering me again. I arched my back against him, and he moaned in response.

I loved the sound, so I did it over and over again, making it grow rough and more intense each time. This turned me on to an unbelievable level, so I matched his noises with my own until we both found euphoria at the same time. He let out the loudest moan I'd heard yet that quickly turned into a deafening roar to drown out my scream.

It was like entering Heaven.

He pulled my body backwards off the seat and I collapsed onto him as I still rode the floating cloud that had carried me to bliss. We both remained entwined in each other's arms like that for a while until he started to stroke my heated skin and brush back the damp hair off my forehead. Well, one thing was for sure, I wouldn't be putting on any weight any time soon not with that kind of daily workout. I smiled wickedly at the thought wondering what price people would pay to join Draven's gym.

My skin was still steaming, and Draven must have felt it too because he lifted the hair off my back and started to blow cool air over my shoulders. It felt amazing, like jumping into a cool swimming pool after sunbathing all day. He even made his skin cold to quicken the process.

"After that, I think you deserve an upgrade." I looked up at him, but I couldn't get a good view of his face, so I propped up to lean on his shoulder. He was grinning to himself.

"Oh really, so what will it be next?"

"Umm…I'm thinking Commander," I said and kissed him quickly on the cheek before getting up, but I didn't make it very far as he grabbed my hand and pulled me back down.

"Where are you going?" he asked, looking seriously not happy about me leaving and I couldn't help but giggle.

"Time for human girly things," I said using his earlier words back at him before getting up for the second time. I grabbed a purple fleece throw from the bottom of my bed and wrapped it around me. He groaned disapprovingly about me covering up, but I felt funny walking around naked.

"You make me want you all over again with that colour on your skin." He let out a sigh and I figured I'd mistaken the groan. I smiled and winked down at him before going to the bathroom. When I got there, I turned on the tap as I didn't want Draven hearing me pee. That was the beauty about being at Draven's home, his bathroom was bigger than my bedroom so even with supernatural powers I doubted he could hear. Well, I hoped not but maybe I was underestimating his abilities. Better if I just didn't think about it.

I finished my human activity and looked in the mirror to find I was no longer my pale self as I was glowing a very healthy colour. I brushed my hair with the spare brush I kept in one of the drawers and tied it up into a knot. I was going to have to take a shower as my hair was a train wreck, but my skin smelled of Draven, which was by far the nicest smell in the world. If I could somehow bottle it, I just knew I could make millions. I could call it something corny like 'Dark Rouge' or 'Demon Knight'...oh wait, but what about 'The Beast'. I giggled to myself and realised I had been doing a lot of laughing these days thanks to Draven. In fact, I couldn't remember a time when I had ever been this damn happy!

I walked back into the room to find the bed back to normal. Bless his gorgeous behind, he had made the bed. This shocked me as I didn't think a man like Draven would have ever needed to do this before. I wondered if this was the first time, like a bed-making virgin. However, he wasn't anywhere near the bed, he was once again dressed and stood on the other side of the room next to my desk. There he was studying my artwork and I felt my skin heat again. I wasn't the best artist in the world, not by a long shot, but I did it more for the pleasure it brought me than for the talent or lack of in my case.

He had in his hands the first painting that I had done since I was kidnapped by Morgan years ago. It was of the view next to the house of the surrounding mountains and lush waves of green forest that was in the masses. He was staring at it so intently that I don't think he noticed I was back in the room. But of course, I was wrong.

"You painted this?" he asked without looking at me and I walked over to him to look down at my mixture of greens and blues. I embarrassingly answered him,

"Yes, it isn't very good I know, but it's something I have always enjoyed doing." He turned to face me and looked at me with a serious expression. Then he gently placed two of his fingers over my lips.

"Keira, how can you say these things? Your work is beautiful, and your emotions show on the canvas, you were happy when you painted this, I can tell." He looked back at it as though he was proud, and I could feel my eyes welling up. I don't really know why I had this reaction, but if I were to guess I would put it down to my past.

It had been because of art that I had met Morgan in the first place as he had been my tutor (under false pretences). He had loved my art also, but I later found that even if I had swallowed a bucket of paint and then thrown up on the paper, he would have loved it. He was sick and twisted and the whole experience made me turn my back on my passion. Until, of course, I met Draven. Maybe this was why he liked this picture so much, maybe he knew it was down to him.

"Then I would like you to have it. But only if you want it of course... no pressure." He put his hand on the back of my neck and pulled my head into his chest, he kissed the top of it and said,

"I would be honoured. Thank you, Keira." He sounded so sincere and before I was reduced to blubbering, snotty tears, that is never an attractive sight on anyone, I said.

"You're welcome, but no selling it on eBay." He laughed and picked me up as if I had been a small child, swinging me around but as he did this my leg knocked a book to the floor. He put me down and started to pick it up but before I could grab it back, he had it open in front of him.

"No, don't!" But it was too late. My book of Demons was being folded back, page after page in his hands. He was shaking his head at all I had seen in the time I had moved here but one picture he came to made him tense with an emotion I didn't know. I looked down and remembered the dream it came from.

It was after Layla had stabbed me, my first night in Draven's bed, but I had forgotten the dream until it came back to me nights later. I'd been in Afterlife dancing with some old school friends of mine when I could see a pair of strange eyes watching me. At first, in the dream, I had thought they had belonged to Draven, but when I saw the body emerge from the shadows I realised it was a man I had never seen before.

He was very tall like Draven, with wide shoulders that looked built for swinging a warrior's axe. But that's where the similarities ended. Where Draven was olive-skinned and had dark features, hair and eyes, this guy was the complete opposite. He had blonde hair, tied back from his face but it was cut just above where his spine started. He had very pale skin which enhanced his startling dark eyes.

He had strong features, with a square jaw and hard mouth. He was stunning, but at the same time frightening as all Hell! It was mainly down to his sharp eyes and the way they followed me everywhere. Every movement my body made with the music, he matched with his gaze. It was both freezing and fiery. It was the look of a natural-born killer and he had just found his next victim, only something told me this creature liked to play first.

I remember trying to ignore him in my dream, but it was as if he was forcing himself into my brain, using my mind against me. My eyes weren't my own, so when I couldn't look away from him, I saw he was no longer in the distance. No, now he was right in front of me. I tried to run but my legs wouldn't work. I tried to lash out at him, but my arms wouldn't move. He had me paralysed and he looked down at me with sardonic satisfaction.

His hand came to my face and his skin felt like smooth marble with ice-cold fingers, leaving their mark in lines down my cheeks. Then the lights went out in the club and the room was plunged into a dark and deadly silence. I looked about the room but couldn't see anyone else. That's when the man in front of me spoke for the first time.

"They're all dead, little Keira girl." His voice was the deepest voice I had ever heard, and I would never forget the way my name sounded at that depth of evil. I looked down at my hands expecting not to see anything, but they were glowing deep red. At first, I thought my wrists had been slit again but then I realised it was from a reflection.

I had never felt a fear as strong before as I lifted my head to look back at him. It was like being a child again and knowing after a dream of something hiding under your bed, you just had to look. You had to check it was safe but braced yourself for the worst. You're breathing heavy with fear and with a scream just ready and waiting to be let out, one you knew was going to be needed. Well, that was that moment right now as my eyes slowly faced my nightmare.

What I found could only be described as how I imagined one of the Devil's minions to look like. There was a blood-red mist around his figure, but his body was blacked out. His face was in the deep shadows but his eyes glowed white making him look almost like the walking dead. Behind him were two massive bull's horns that came from his shoulder bones and attached to these were his wings hanging down like Demonic curtains.

It was as though a thousand bats had been killed and all their wings sewn together to make one huge set. They were worn and broken in places with holes nearer the edges. They then went down into points creating the ends, where finger-like claws looked deadly to the core. His hands were balled into fists by his sides and when he didn't touch me with them, I was about to turn and run.

"You can't run from me, little Keira girl. There is nowhere for you to hide. *Not now I know you.*" His voice wasn't coming from his lips but from every corner of the room, as though there was an army of him. I followed the whispers but couldn't make out anything, whipping my head back and to. I turned back towards him and found him leaning his face towards me causing me to take a frightened step back. Bloodstained lips curved into a sadistic smile showing me all his bloody teeth as though he had not long finished a human meal. His fangs started to grow past his lips and down his chin at the sight of my fear. A single droplet of blood dripped down his right fang, landing on the floor like it was made of glass as the tiny shatter echoed through the room.

"See you soon," he said and licked the top row of his teeth, cleaning the blood off with his tongue before clicking his fingers. This made all the lights in the club return and my terror sunk to new depths. He had illuminated the room for me to discover a blood bath. All my friends, everyone I ever knew, were now lying in broken heaps around us. Bloody, dismembered and tortured bodies that I could hardly make out individually. The walls and furniture ran red with blood as though a raging river of the life source had passed through, splashing up the sides in waves. Shattered heads that no longer had any faces stared back at me with empty eye sockets. Jaws hung broken and open in lifeless cries for help that hopelessly would never come.

I screamed uncontrollably which was what finally woke me up from my nightmare. I had got up after reliving the dream again to draw him from my memory, not really knowing who or what he was but I had to cast him out. Even now, I still got goosebumps from the picture. Sammael most certainly had nothing on this dude!

Draven was still gripping the book as if it was a small creature that needed to be contained.

"Draven, what's wrong?" My voice seemed to bring him back to the room, but his face was set in one of pure fury and hatred.

"Have you seen this man?" His voice was steel, cold and one I had rarely heard before.

"He was in a nightmare... why?" I was pretty sure I didn't want to know the answer to this, but it wouldn't be the first time I had received an answer I didn't like hearing. He dropped the book to the floor and turned to me to grab my shoulders. I looked up at him and hated the harsh, bitter face I found there.

"Because, Keira, the man in this picture is..." I swallowed hard, now knowing the truth before he even said it and understanding the shaking foundations of our combined fears.

I finished his sentence…

"Lucius."

CHAPTER FIVE

BODYGUARD TIME

It took a while for Draven to calm down from this new development and I tried to hide my worry for his sake. The only upside to all of this was at least I now had a face to put to the enemy. Draven had made some phone calls, but he spoke in a really ancient-sounding language so once again I was kept in the dark. I was trying to look busy until he had finished on the phone.

"Keira, I will have to leave you, but it won't be for long." I have to say the idea didn't have me doing backflips off the bed, but I guess this was proof there wasn't really much to fear.

"I am sending Ragnar over here to keep an eye on the house in my absence." Ok, so it looked as if I had spoken too soon.

"Great, Ragnar," I said before I could stop myself. He raised an eyebrow at me.

"Is there a problem I am not aware of?"

"No," I said sheepishly.

"He is exceedingly strong and one of my most loyal subjects."

"Yes, and your most loyal subject also hates me!" I said as if pointing out the obvious, but Draven just laughed. Well, at least this was making him find a better mood.

"Keira, he does not hate you. He is just not used to seeing humans around me, especially those who speak their mind so openly. Think back to the times he has seen you, once you came to my table to scorn me...yes?" Okay, so he had a tiny point there. His warm arms encased me in a secure hold before leaning down to my ear.

"I find this adorable, little Keira, but I can trust you to give him a chance, can't I? He is, after all, your new bodyguard." Oh, no way! Never going to happen! The new horror of having that fairy-tale giant counteracted the sound of Draven calling me 'little Keira' which tried to drag me back to the dream of Lucius. I think I was going to have to start wearing heels, giant ones that even hookers would shy away from...did they even make those? I shook away my daft thoughts and concentrated on the problem at hand.

"Draven, that's not going to happen, I don't need a bodyguard. Not when I have you," I said stubbornly then turned away leaving him trying to control his smile.

"Does that mean you are willing to move into my home and stay within those walls forever?" I turned back on my heel to face him to see that yes, that was a serious question.

"No, of course not, I still want to do my normal stuff, like work and college but come on, a bodyguard? Don't you think that's a wee bit over the top?" I could tell this was like flogging a dead horse. He wasn't going to budge on this.

"No, I do not and if I had my way you wouldn't be going back to college and as for the work thing, we will discuss it when I return. But Keira, understand if you want this 'normal life' you speak of, then there will be consequences and your protection comes first in my list of priorities." At this he sounded absolutely unmovable.

"Fine, but that's not going to look weird at all having some scary guy the size of a house following me everywhere I go. As if I can't get any weirder!" Okay, so I know I was sulking now, but for someone who just wanted to fade into the background having bloody Goliath hanging at my back wasn't part of my plans.

Draven made me look up at him and I winced when he looked hurt. I instantly felt guilty. I lowered my head feeling a bit ashamed of my behaviour. He put his hand under my chin and the slight pressure he applied gave me no choice other than to look up at him again.

"Keira, please don't make this any more difficult. I don't like leaving you as it is but if I have to do it then at least let me do so with a confidence that you will be safe. That's all I ask."

"I'm sorry, I guess I'm just grumpy because you're going that's all." I reached up on my tiptoes, but I still couldn't reach his lips, so he took the hint and leant down to me to meet me halfway.

"Now that reason I like," he said smiling.

Five minutes later Draven opened the door to find Ragnar filling the gap. The old wooden deck creaked angrily under his gigantic weight. His skin looked even more horrific in the daylight, like a worn leather mask that had been trapped inside a maiden torture device for days. He was much taller than Draven and as wide as the door frame. I gulped and Draven turned to me and took my hand giving it a squeeze to tell me it was alright.

Ragnar was wearing black trousers and a black t-shirt that looked as if it was crying out in pain from being stretched so tight. I hoped he wouldn't sneeze while he was here or that thing would rip clean off. His arms looked like tree trunks and the pure raw muscle was covered with bulging veins. His hands looked like spades that could have crushed my head like a grape.

"Keira, allow me to introduce you to Ragnar." I was trying to hide like a child behind Draven, but he pulled me to his side. I looked up at him and a nervous smile crept its way across my face.

"Hello...erm... would you like to come in?" I asked not forgetting my manners even in the face of a man who looked like he ate pro wrestlers for breakfast! He looked at me curiously and then back at Draven for his answer.

"Ragnar will stay outside." At this Ragnar nodded at his master, just like the loyal subject Draven had boasted about. Draven motioned for him to move and he left to walk the perimeter of the house. I noticed there was now a huge black Land Rover sat in my driveway. Well, I doubted Ragnar would have been comfortable in one of Draven's many sports cars.

"I won't be long." He kissed me long and hard, as though it was to be our last. Then he spoke to Ragnar before he left.

"Geyma austrvegr jenta og gi lifdagar ditt, lytte til andra" ("Guard the girl with your life, listen for others" in Part old Norse and Norwegian) He was just about to get in the car when he stopped. I was still in the doorway and couldn't understand what he was saying but he shouted back to Ragnar,

"Oh, and Ragnar, Ikke skirra austrvegr jenta, være hyggelig!" ("Do not scare the girl, be nice")

"Ja min herre" ("Yes, my Lord") He spoke for the first time and his voice matched his size. It was rough, like a person just recovering from having their tonsils out and being told to use sand as mouthwash. I watched as Draven got in the driver's side and drove off at a quicker speed than I would have liked, kicking up the gravel as he went.

The sky was clear over the house but there were darker clouds moving across the mountains that threatened the ground with rain. Ragnar gave me a nod before I went back inside to be properly alone for the first time since Monday and today was Thursday. I went to flick on the kettle and make a hot chocolate when I noticed the answering machine blinking. I pressed a button and a very polite voice told me I had forty-three messages. Forty-three! Wow Libby had been worried. I didn't have the time or the will to listen to them all, so I pressed the erase button.

I made two mugs of chocolate, as I thought it was only polite to make my 'against my will' guest a drink. I hadn't asked him but to tell the truth I was too scared to. I opened the door to find him standing guard by the frame. I just hoped we didn't have any visitors, it's not as if out here we got the Avon lady or anything but still I doubted Ragnar was going to look kindly on a postman. Maybe I would need to make a sign 'Beware of the Ragnar' or 'Warning, Demon Viking on patrol'.

"Hi, I... um...well, I made you a drink," I said and he cocked his large head to one side.

"Why?" he asked and I couldn't help but jump.

"Because I made myself one and it is cold out here. Plus, it's kind of what humans do," I said in a bit of a nervous whisper.

"They'd give men cups, like offering?" He sounded confused. He also didn't sound like he was used to speaking in English, but I understood it even with the strong Scandinavian accent.

"Guests usually get offered a drink...yes. Do you like chocolate?" I asked looking like a hobbit next to a muscle ripped Gandalf. He just shrugged his shoulders and I felt the wooden floor bounce from his slight movement. I just hoped he didn't go through it as I didn't know how I would explain that one. I passed him the mug and it looked like a thimble in his enormous hands. He looked at it as though it was going to do something more.

"It's nice...sweet," I said smiling at him. Like this he didn't seem so scary once you got used to the harsh features and colossal size. He placed it to his lips and I said quickly.

"It's hot!" But he smirked which added a nice glaze to his chestnut coloured eyes. He drank it all in one and my mouth must have dropped because he started laughing. At least I think it was laughter, either that or he was doing an impression of a bull grunting and getting ready to charge. He handed me back the mug which was still hot.

"Good?" I asked, determined to get more than a few words out of him, but he just nodded so I gave up. I moved to the open front door and he watched me carefully.

"I thanking you," he said and it looked as though he found it difficult thanking a human girl for anything.

"You're welcome. If you want anything else just let me know."

I had to admit that with my very own private Hercules standing guard I didn't worry about my new stalker. I could imagine getting hit by Ragnar would be like being hit by the Hulk.

I decided, once back inside, that while I was alone I would do a load of washing, take a shower and ring RJ to let her know I was still alive. I felt a bit bad that I had waited so long and after what had happened to Jack and Celina, I really wanted to make sure he was alright. Plus, this would be a conversation I really didn't want Draven to hear. When it came to me and Jack being friends, Draven didn't exactly approve that much was clear.

My mind continued to replay all that had happened over the last week as I got all the mundane human stuff out of the way. I jumped over the back of the couch and snuggled in ready for the whirlwind that was RJ.

"Hey RJ, its Kaz."

"Oh my God! What happened to you? Have you heard the rumours? People think the Dravens abducted you or something!" She sounded a little too happy about this idea. I wondered if she wasn't in fact the storyteller behind some of these rumours, but I just smiled at the idea, after all, what did I expect when befriending the town's biggest gossip.

"No, no, nothing like that. I just had some real personal stuff to deal with and the Dravens have kind of been helping me out with it." At least I could get away with saying that without lying.

"Like what? You know Jack has been really worried about you, he wanted to call the police!" She did sound concerned but also relieved, which was the sweet part of being best friends with my RJ.

"Some stuff from England, but it's all over now." For some reason saying it out loud made it seem even more real.

"Is Jack there?" I asked.

"No, but you have his cell number, right?"

"Yeah, I will give him a call. RJ, I kind of have something to tell you, something big but I don't want you to freak out ...okay?" I said, also asking myself if there was much point, as of course she was going to freak out. Hell, even I was still kind of freaking out.

"O…kaaay," she said slowly.

"You also have to promise me not to tell anyone and remember you're the only person that will know, so if I hear that the whole town knows tomorrow, then guess who I am pointing the finger at?" I reminded her.

"Okay, okay I get it, Jeez no need to go all 007 on me, deadly secret, pinkie seal and blood exchange! I promise." I didn't quite understand the other bits, but I decided to trust her anyway.

"Well…uh…I don't know really how to say this…"

"Jesus woman, just spill before the Arthritis kicks in will ya!" RJ said losing her patience.

"Me and Dominic Draven are sort of...well, we're kind of... *dating.*" I winced waiting for it fully expecting the outcome that sounded like she had been hit with a brick, given that she was now screaming.

"RJ...RJ? Focus honey." I tried but this just promoted a bellowing,

"OH MY GOD! OH...MY...FREAKING! NO WAY! That is some crazy shit! Tell me everything before I go insane with jealously and come around in a murderous rage." I laughed at the thought of RJ's face when she got here to kill me and met Ragnar by the door. So, instead of laughing at that thought I explained how Draven had helped me out with some issues with a stalker I'd had back in England and that's why I didn't like talking about my past. I didn't think telling her this would do any harm, well at least I hoped not. I carried on saying how Sophia wanted me to stay with them for a few days just to be sure he didn't come around looking for me.

"So how did it happen, you know you're one lucky bitch right?" I laughed and replied,

"Yeah, I know."

"So come on, spill it sister, how in holy moly batman did this happen?" I shook my head at my nutty friend and let out a sigh, wondering how I was going to get away with explaining this.

"I don't really know...it just kind of happened and I guess after spending some time together, something just clicked." Ok, this bit was a little vague but it sure was safer than telling her the insane truth. That I was born for him, even I couldn't get my head around that mountain of crazy.

"So, have you jumped his bones yet? Because I'm telling you now, it would not take me seconds to rip those..."

"Okay, okay, I got it." We both laughed.

"We're taking things slow." Just not those type of things, I added mentally. I was just glad I wasn't having to lie in person, not yet anyway.

"To Hell with slow! You will tell me though...right? I mean, when you do the dirty but beautiful deed." She sounded almost possessed.

"No, probably not, but I will tell you this, kissing him is like nothing I have ever felt before." I had to give her something.

"Then sex will be even better! I read an article about guys that are good kissers are almost always good in the sack." Amen to that! I could definitely agree with that assessment.

"Poor Jack, he was really smitten." This had me cringing with guilt.

"I really wanna talk to him, he has a right to hear it from me first, so hint, hint, don't go telling him."

"Not a soul, not until you give the word." This was the most serious I had ever heard her so I believed that she would keep her word. I smiled at the idea. This was going to be the hardest thing for RJ, so it made me respect her even more for it. RJ lived for gossip and when faced with the town's biggest story, she usually would have thought that it was her responsibility to tell the world. So, I understood how hard this was for her. If there was ever a need for a gothic news anchor, then they would have found gold dust in RJ.

"So, is he still your boss?" The questions went on like this for the next forty minutes. Everything from what he smelled like to what he ate for breakfast. The breakfast answer I had to make up because I just didn't know. All I had seen Draven eat was an apple. So of course, I said fruit.

"It figures, with a bod like that I would have guessed he was a health freak."

By the time she got off the phone it was dark outside and my stomach was growling at me after talking about food. I was going to order pizza but then remembered Ragnar out there and didn't think it fair to scare some poor pizza delivery guy half to death. That would most certainly get the townsfolk's tongues wagging.

I opened the fridge, but that didn't inspire much so I grabbed a frozen pizza from the freezer and turned the oven on high. I got the cheese out of the fridge and grated some more for extra topping. It was really tight in the cheese department, so I loaded her up. I put it on a tray and closed the door before ringing Jack's number.

"Keira! Are you alright? I have been so worried, did you get my messages?" He sounded upset that I hadn't called. Oh dear, here came the guilt.

"Hi, yeah I'm sorry I can explain, but I really don't want to do it over the phone." I told him.

"I will be right there."

"NO! I mean... no, that won't be a good idea. What if we meet up?" I said stumbling out the words before thinking about my extremely possessive boyfriend who very nearly hated Jack.

"When and where and I will be there?" Okay, this wasn't making it any easier with him being so noble and nice.

"How about that diner, the one with the funky food that looks like roadkill?" He laughed and I relaxed at the sound.

"Why, you got a death wish?" I shuddered at how well that statement mirrored the last few days.

"I will eat before I get there, can't die from warm coke, can you?" We both chuckled and chatted a while longer before arranging for an afternoon when he had some free periods. Of course, his lectures hadn't been affected by the fire, so he was still going to class. That reminded me that I needed to find out when my lessons were starting up again.

"Okay, I will see you tomorrow then."

"Yeah, I look forward to it, Kazzy," Jack said before hanging up. I smiled at the thought that at least now no one could be angry at me but the voice behind me told me that evidently, I could be oh so wrong.

"And just who will you being seeing tomorrow? Because I am pretty confident you weren't on the phone to me and that didn't sound like a female who is *so* looking forward to meeting you." Draven's deep voice filled the kitchen and it wasn't a happy voice at that. I turned to look, bracing myself for his cold stare and yep, there it was.

"Draven, I can explain," I said weakly, but he just gave me a stern frown and folded his arms across his wide chest, breathing heavy from trying to contain his anger.

"I sure hope so because I have only been gone a few hours and already you have another date lined up." Okay, so he was pissed but this was ridiculous.

"Don't shout!" I shouted.

"Draven, I was talking to Jack because he is my friend and he has been worried about me." If I thought back to how this sounded, I would have gone with something else, because this nearly sent him over the edge.

"Keira, this is not an advisable route to pursue," he warned me and my own anger grew deeper roots.

"And what does that mean?" I said now taking my own defensive stance and folding my arms.

"You are an intelligent girl, figure it out." He was acting like a very articulate child.

"Are you implying that I am not allowed to be friends with Jack?"

"Implying no, forbidding you, yes." I shook my head and rolled my eyes in disappointment.

"This is utterly outrageous, how can you be so...so...?"

"What?!" he snapped

"So bloody childish!" Great one Keira, this coming from the person who was close to stomping her foot in frustration. He didn't say anything to this but just looked astonished at the accusation. It actually made me wonder if he had ever heard this being said to him before...I almost giggled at the thought. What must it be like? All five foot and three inches of me telling all six foot four inches of pure muscle off like a spoilt child.

"Look, this is stupid and pointless. I am meeting Jack tomorrow...." At this he was about to interrupt and explode but I held my hand out to stop him.

"....to tell him that I just want to be friends and that I am in love with YOU!" At this he softened slightly, but not enough to get my blood down to its normal temperature.

"He deserves to know the truth and I ain't the type of girl to lead men on or let them go on thinking there is something more when there isn't. If you don't like it, then I'm sorry, but it's tough shit! This is who I am, and I am not going to change what I believe in, just because I'm with you!" By the end of this little speech I was breathing heavy and Draven looked as though he either wanted to make mad passionate love to me or knock my block off! I doubted anyone in his life had ever spoken like this to him and I couldn't help but be afraid and excited at the same time. Like jumping from a plane and being terrified of heights but letting the adrenaline rush take over your fear.

He looked as if he wanted to say something but instead, he was in front of me before I took my next breath. His lips crushed against mine forcing me back a step and the heat of the argument ended in my mouth. He pushed me further back onto the kitchen table and was pressing his need up against me, igniting my sweet spot.

"You drive me insane, you know that?" he hissed over my mouth and before I had time to protest his tongue parted my lips open for another passion-fuelled kiss. His entire being commanded the kiss to his erotic beat. My lips tried to keep up, but it was as if he couldn't get deep enough, couldn't taste enough and in return I failed to breathe. He angled my head with one large hand at the base of my neck and his other hand travelled a private journey down the base of my spine. I could almost feel my toes curling, Wizard of Oz style. Man, this Demon knew how to kiss, I say Demon 'cause there was nothing angelic about what this man was doing to my most intimate parts.

After the nicest make up kiss in history, I finally got back my breath. He pulled me up off the table and turned his head to smell the air where the scent of burning pizza filled the room.

"Oh, sodding hell, the pizza!" I got up and opened the oven door to a cloud of smoke. The smoke alarm went off and I grabbed a tea towel to wave in front of it. This must have looked odd to Draven because he reached up and grabbed the alarm, crushing it in a single motion until it made a pathetic dying sound before being replaced by silence. He made the window open without even going near it and he pushed the smoke out towards it in a gathered cloud. I stood staring, as though he was my own personal magician. I looked down at the plastic crumbs in his hand and his eyes followed.

"Too much?" he asked sheepishly before making the pieces fuse back together and even the battery acid that had escaped onto his hand flowed back into the casing. I couldn't tear my eyes off the sight. It was like watching the destruction of it in reverse. Once it was back together, he placed it back on the wall and fitted it into place. I looked at the tea towel in my hand thinking it could now retire. I laughed out loud at the thought of what Libby would have done if she had seen Draven doing this the next time she burnt something, which in her case was a daily occurrence.

"What's funny?" he asked light-heartedly.

"Just wondering if I will ever get used to seeing it?"

"Seeing what exactly?"

"The impossible." He grunted out a little laugh at my answer. I pulled out the black charcoal disc that once resembled something you could eat and broke it up to fit it in the bin.

"Well, there goes my dinner, looks like cheese on toast."

"That was pizza, right?"

"Hard to believe, I know." He looked so much happier now we had made up as he smiled back down at me.

"Then why don't you order one to be delivered?" he said passing me the phone and the takeout menu that was stuck to the fridge by a Union Jack magnet.

"Okay, but only if you help me eat it. So far all I have seen you eat is an apple. If I didn't know you were an Angel/ Demon, then I would think you have an eating disorder." He roared with laughter at my little joke and I loved that I could make him laugh so freely.

He let me pick the pizza and when it came, he wouldn't let me pay or get up to get it. I wondered what the delivery person thought when Draven answered the door. Well, at least Ragnar wasn't there to frisk him.

"You didn't have to pay for it," I said as he brought it into the living room.

"Keira, please don't say you have a problem with me buying you dinner, especially one that cost so little. It was, after all, my fault the first one burnt," he said taking the blame, which brought me no satisfaction.

"Okay, but the next one is on me." I took the box and put it on the coffee table ready to be devoured as I was starving.

"If you say so," he said in a mocking tone to add to his smirk.

"Do you ever get hungry?" I asked, as I grabbed a piece and

dangled the stringy cheese in my mouth before biting off the end. He watched me as if it was the first time he had seen me eat.

"Yes, but mainly for other things. I find watching you eat fascinating." I blushed like always.

"Why, because I'm a pig when it comes to food?" I said smiling because I just didn't care, I loved my food.

"No, not at all, I find you fascinating because I never knew watching someone eat could turn me on." Okay, now that I didn't expect.

"Don't be daft, how could you?" I said blushing.

"Quite simple, it makes me want to taste you," he said so matter of fact I was taken back. Then he leant over and grabbed a slice. Okay, so watching him eat it, I could actually see where he was coming from. This had never happened to me before, finding a guy sexy while biting into a pizza slice was a weird thing to get turned on about but it still happened. I was even more surprised when he ended up eating most of the pizza because after three slices, I was full. I put the box in the kitchen and grabbed a bottle of water out of the fridge.

I forgot to ask Draven if he wanted a drink, so I popped my head round to ask when I noticed he was looking at a picture of me and Libby when I was seventeen. It was one we'd had taken at Alton Towers, a theme park we went to for my birthday. I had shorter hair that looked way out of control and a little red vest with a short denim skirt. I looked so different to how I dressed now, and no doubt Draven was thinking the same thing. Well, it was summer and a very hot one at that. I got burnt on the shoulders that day and that night, when out with my friends, I was dancing like Michael Flatley doing Lord of the River dance.

"I hate that picture," I said as I tried to take it from his hands, but he just lifted it out of my reach, which wasn't hard. I was so short next to him that I knew there was no point even trying.

"Why? You look happy, was it a special day?"

"It was my birthday, I was seventeen," I said feeling my skin blush at the way I was dressed.

"I didn't think England had such good summers." So he did notice.

67

"We had a heatwave that year, plus I used to dress quite differently than I do now." I wasn't sure which Keira he preferred, the carefree young blonde who liked to show off her slim figure or the shy scared girl that stood next to him now, wearing black jogging bottoms and a grey long-sleeved top with thumb holes.

"I like that you saved your body for me, I do not think I would be happy for so many eyes seeing that flawless skin of yours in places that are for my eyes only. I like the way you dress now and that I am the only one who gets to unwrap you whenever I choose." He winked at me before placing the picture back.

"But I do have one question, why do you have metal teeth?" I laughed so hard tears formed.

"What? You do." I couldn't keep my face straight, he must have thought this looked more like a torture device. Then I stopped laughing as soon as I remembered what Sammael looked like when I had seen him in his Demon form. His lips had been sealed shut by thick metal pieces that looked like crude stitches. This had been his punishment and done to him by the Draven brothers.

"It was my brace, I had crooked teeth when my wisdom teeth started to come through."

"It looks barbaric, did it not hurt you?" Bless him for thinking about my pain.

"It just ached mostly, but sometimes the metal would stick in my gums. That I didn't like so much. But it was worth it." I said smiling showing him the result.

"I think I would have preferred you to have crooked teeth than go through pain," he said sincerely. I kissed him on the cheek for saying something so sweet.

"Okay, back to our date. Argument, check… make-up kiss, check…pizza, check… now moving swiftly on." He was smirking at my checklist thinking I was talking about sex.

"Draven! You've really never had a date before, have you? You don't fool around until the movie is on and the lights are off."

"Okay" He clicked his fingers confidently and the lights went out and the TV came on, amazingly on a movie channel. I giggled like I was back to being that seventeen-year-old girl.

I plopped down on the couch next to him with my back against his chest and picked up the remote. His arms went around me and I snuggled closer to him, loving every minute of the best date of my life.

"So what will it be, action, romance or horror?"

"Don't like comedies?" When he spoke, he blew air down my neck and my mind filled with his scent making it harder to find words to his question, especially when his large hand was moving up and down my neck.

"Yeah, sure I do, but I like being the one that makes you laugh...plus there is the whole snorting issue."

"Ah yes, I remember that adorable little noise you make." His hands then slid down to my weak spots and I started giggling. But I stopped him before I was in fits.

"Behave!" I warned.

"Never," he whispered seductively in my ear causing the word to be felt travelling down my spine.

"So, what is customary for a first date?"

"Well, it depends what the goal is. Horror usually gives the guy the chance to show how brave he is and protect the girl when she jumps at the scary bits, but I think you have already proved yourself in that department," I told him with a grin.

"Protecting you is my job, Keira." He leaned around to see my smile.

"One you get to do far more often than you would like." He just growled a little at my comment.

"Or there is action, this gives the girl chance to show she is cool with watching violence, which impresses the guy, but in this case I have seen enough action in the last few days to last me till the end of time," I added because this was so true, and Draven knew it too.

"I must agree with you there."

"So, then there is romance that gets you in the mood, but considering you get horny just watching me eat, then I don't think it's needed." He moved my hair from my neck and licked my skin, proving my last statement. I was momentarily hushed to silence and my teeth found comfort in my bottom lip.

"Okay, then I will choose...umm...mmm." I tried to sound

unfazed, but it wasn't convincing as I moaned when his licking turned into sucking. I let the remote slide out of my hands but before it could crash to the floor his hand left the front of my neck and caught it, before passing it back to me.

"You were saying?" he said over my skin and I could feel his lips turn up into a confident smile. I swallowed down the breath caught in my throat and tried to continue.

"That's not fair when you have such control over my functions like that." I shook my head and closed my eyes as I tried to focus on finding a movie.

"And you don't believe you have the same control over me? *Why do you think I find it so hard keeping my hands off you?"* He whispered this last part and I lowered my face to conceal a smile he could feel there.

"Okay, back to the movie...umm ah, here's one...Blade!" I thought I had chosen well until I heard the 'tut' behind me.

"More Vampires, Keira please tell me you don't have a thing for these vile creatures? I will never understand human obsession with the scum of the underworld." I turned to face him and in the glow of the flickering TV, he looked serious.

"I like Blade because he fights them. Okay, so he is one, but he still wants them destroyed. So, what is your beef with them?"

"Beef?" It was obvious he hadn't heard this expression.

"You know, why don't you like them or is hate a better word?"

"I don't want to discuss it," he said stubbornly but I frowned at him.

"Come on, just tell me...I think, all things considered, I can take it." Of course, I was soon proven wrong with the next words to leave Draven's lips,

"Lucius is the Vampire king."

CHAPTER SIX

VAMPIRES

I could now understand why Draven didn't want to talk about this with me. Not only had I had to accept that Vampires were actually real but now they had a freakin' King. Oh yeah and let's not forget that this was the very dude that was after me! This was really hitting the limits on my insanity meter.

"Okay, you're going to have to explain this all to me because otherwise I am left with all I know from movies and Bram Stoker." Draven made the TV go off and the lights come back on. Now making me wonder if we would ever just have a normal date that didn't include conversations that scared the living shit out of me. I sat facing him and folded my legs together ready for Draven's storytime.

"I should never have said anything. Being with me is already taking its toll." He traced a finger down the side of my face as if soothing out a worry line around my eye.

"And what is that supposed to mean?" I was a little hurt at this comment.

"It means that we have been together only but a few days and already I am telling you things that will only make your nightmares worse." He was trying to tread carefully around the subject, but I just guessed he was stalling for time.

"Draven! That is ridiculous. I have been going through this since I was seven years old and guess what...? You weren't around then, and I coped. I'm stronger than you think, please give me a little credit." This had him in the palm of my hand within seconds. I could tell my words had hit their intended mark.

"You are right. I forget how strong you are. I can't imagine what it must have been like for you to go through that on your own. I wish I had known of you sooner, I could have helped you."

"Things happen for a reason and I wouldn't change a thing...well, okay, being hunted by Demons might be one thing." I laughed but he frowned at my joke on the matter.

"Oh, come on, if I don't laugh, I will cry, so pick one." He didn't pick he just kissed me instead and obviously I complied.

"Anyway, you are stalling for time." He smiled over my lips and I couldn't contain my own.

"You know me well, Keira." I liked it when he said this giving me that warm tingling feeling deep inside.

"I have known Lucius since his beginning."

"Have you always been enemies?" I couldn't help but ask questions, but he only grinned at me, which told me he had been expecting me to do as much.

"No, we have not. For most of his years we were friends, we even fought side by side in battle but that is another story and one I am in no hurry to tell you." I gathered by his tone it was bad with no doubt lots of bloodshed.

"Is he as old as you?" He smirked at me. Draven had not yet told me how old he was, and this was one way to find out. I think he must be a little sensitive about his age.

"No, he is not. Why is it you are determined to know how old I am?"

"Because I find it fascinating and excuse me but weren't you the one who did everything in your power to find out all about me?" He just shrugged. HA! I had him there.

"Lucius has been around since the dawn of Christ and his rebirth was days after the crucifixion of Jesus," he told me.

"What!" I was almost lost for words. So that would make Draven older than Christ... *Holy shit!* I tried not to react, but he was staring at me, waiting for the slightest of reactions and he let out a low growl when he saw one.

"And when was that exactly?" I asked needing to hear him confirm this, making one of his eyebrows rise, but he just shook his head in submission.

"I think it was a Friday, April thirty-three AD. But I can't be certain as we didn't document dates the same back then as they do today," he said as if talking about something as mundane as the weather.

"Were you… *there?"* I felt kind of weird asking about it, but I was near brimming over with questions and I didn't want to be disrespectful.

"No, there was no need for us to witness his plans. And he was still a human then, well, of sorts. Powerful for a human, but as the son of one of the Gods, then it was to be expected." He was talking about it with little emotion which surprised me.

"What do you mean, there was no need? Couldn't you have prevented his death?"

"Yes, but this was not his wish, nor the wish of the Gods." He said this with such ease, I found it baffling.

"Okay, now I am confused, he wanted to die?" This was not the religious education I had learned back in school. I think my R.E teacher would have had one of her usual meltdowns listening to Draven talk about the crucifixion this way. Miss Brown used to keep a flask of coffee laced with whiskey in her top desk drawer. She used to swig from it when being bombarded with questions like 'Are there video games in Hell?' or 'Will I see my dog there with tyre marks on him from when he got run over?' Needless to say, she didn't last the year.

"It is not as it is written, though some humans still believe the truth. Do you really think a man as powerful as Him wouldn't know that one of his disciples was going to betray him?"

"You mean Judas, right? He sold out Jesus for thirty pieces of silver and revealed Jesus to the Romans, which is called the 'Judas kiss'." He looked quite impressed that I knew all this but come on, I was a history buff.

"Keira, for someone who is not very religious, you seem to

know your material. That is how the Bible tells it, yes, but the facts of man's whispered tales are never the best source in finding the truth. See, the faith that was being followed was dying out thanks to the Romans. Jesus knew that the memory of something great, outlives that of a great man. And sometimes it only takes one significant action to change the world forever. He made the sacrifice for that faith to live on indefinitely. Which it did, being now one of the world's oldest and most followed beliefs." It sure made sense, but what did I know?

"So, let me get this straight, you're saying that Jesus asked Judas to betray him?"

"Yes, that is what I am saying," he said calmly.

"But why? Why Judas and why go to all that trouble and pretence? Why not just hand himself over to the Romans?" I asked, totally intrigued.

"That's a lot of whys, Keira, even for you," he said laughing, but I just poked him in the ribs for making fun of me.

"I do not have all the answers, but know it became one of the greatest lessons of betrayal learnt for mankind that day and I know that the act itself created more of an impact this way. You see he needed a way for the Romans to be looked upon badly for their conquest and this turned out to be the ultimate sin. Judas was unfortunately caught in the crossfire. He did the deed before Jesus told the other disciples of his plans. So, when he kissed Jesus, this was the sign the Romans needed to arrest him. Judas was picked because of his well-known greed but through this act his sins were to be wiped clean in the eyes of God. He was actually known to be one of Jesus' most loyal disciples." I must have had my mouth open at this point because Draven playfully tapped my chin before carrying on.

"But after Jesus was crucified the other disciples hung Judas as a traitor. He was first left to burn in the sun for days. He was then made to eat the silver that turned out to be the price of his own life, along with their beloved Jesus'. Finally, before running short of air from choking, he was sliced open, allowing his guts to spill below his feet. Some say that the sky filled with another darkness, just like the crucifixion eclipse that happened on the ninth hour that

Jesus finally died." His hands found mine and he kissed them twice before looking up into my eyes to judge my reaction.

"Wow." I let out a sigh like I was deflating.

"So, I hate to ask the obvious, but what has any of this got to do with Lucius?"

"He was Judas, Keira," Draven said with what I could tell was controlled emotion. Me, on the other hand, well my mouth just dropped.

"Eh…come again?" I asked, needing to know that I'd just heard him right?

"I think I've found your limit," Draven stated.

"I think you're right," I said, thinking only one thing was needed right now and that something had a percentage on the bottle. I got up and went to the liquor cabinet in search of something strong.

"Are you alright?" Draven said looking a bit worried about the shaking bottle of Jack Daniels in my hand.

"I just need a human minute."

"Let me," he said taking the bottle from me and pushing me back down on the couch. He left me to my thoughts while he got the glasses and I hoped ice. It was such an emotional account of the most significant event in history. Emotional for me that was. Draven had told it with little conviction. I suppose as a human event, it didn't really affect him until Lucius came along. Which got me thinking, how did something like that even happen?

Draven was placing the glass in my hands and the ice made a cracking noise with the warm liquid that had been poured over it. He resumed his seat and placed the bottle on the table ready for seconds. He downed his back as though it had been apple juice.

"Do you ever get drunk?" I asked, bringing back the familiar roar of laughter that came from him when he found any one of my questions amusing.

"Not in the same way that you do, I get more relaxed, but that's about it."

"I like to sing when I am drunk and trust me nobody wants to hear that," I said taking a sip of the amber liquid. This had him laughing even harder.

"I think I would pay good money to witness that show," he informed me, making me nearly snort back,

"Then you would be asking for a refund real quick."

"I can imagine it would be highly amusing to see you intoxicated and well, I have never heard you sing before."

"And never will, not unless you like the sound of dying cats. You might be powerful, but nothing would save you from the pain of a shattered eardrum." He put both hands on my face and pulled me in for a kiss while he chuckled at my descriptions.

"I think you exaggerate immensely. Surely you cannot be that bad?" He really wasn't taking me seriously.

"Well, you're just going to have to trust me on this one 'cause you ain't ever going to witness it!" I told him firmly before taking another sip.

"You know, I just love it when you go all Northern like that, it is far beyond cute." I wrinkled my nose in disagreement.

"No, still cute," he said smirking.

"Anyway, let's get back to my questions. So, you said he is Judas or was or whatever, how is that even possible?" He frowned, not liking that we were back to this.

"Have you not had enough for one day?" I didn't answer. I just gave him a look which was pretty easy for him to interpret.

"Okay, but only if you promise one day to let me hear you sing?"

"Draven, you should be ashamed, that is blackmail!" But he just grinned like a bad boy and mouthed the word 'Demon' to me, looking sexy as sin while doing it.

"You can't pull that one every time! You don't see me doing something bad and then say, "well, I am a Cancerian"." I punched him when he started laughing and we ended up having a bit of a play fight on the couch. Well, more like I tried to reach his body parts and he kept restraining me. It was a big turn on, and I almost gave up my goal in order to have sex with him for the third time today. Wow, three times, that would be my record and one I would relish in achieving.

"Okay I give up, you win, my Goddess." I made a satisfied noise and grinned with it.

"Right, so explain, how is it possible for Lucius to be Judas?" He let out an exaggerated sigh before continuing.

"Well, the Gods in Heaven are not the only ones with plans. Judas renounced his faith with his last breath. He felt betrayed by Jesus, but he was wrong. Jesus tried to clear his name to his disciples in one of his last statements of the seven he gave before his death. But it was dictated wrong in the scriptures. His disciples thought he was just trying to prevent vengeance and didn't believe his words when he said, 'Truly Judas, I say to you, today you will be with me in Paradise.' But they left out the 'Judas' part for reasons of their own, mainly to justify murder. When this was found out by Judas it was too late, he could not change the fact that he turned his back on his faith and so he was not accepted into the paradise that Jesus spoke of. Instead, he was reborn by another God, one of the Netherworld."

"He became a child of the Devil?" Draven just nodded and I couldn't help but feel a small pain in my heart for how Lucius came to be.

"Then what happened?"

"Lucifer, who is father to most of the Demonic elders on this plane, needed a King to rule over the Vampir or Vampires as they're more commonly known. These Creatures have been around for thousands of years, but they were weak and unpredictable. They needed a leader, one stronger than them all, someone who could control them whilst making them evolve. Imagine these weak Demons like rodents suddenly becoming wild powerful cats. They mutated genetically so they became stronger, quicker and more methodical in their thinking. Lucius became their master and he is in all of the Demons that he turns."

"So it isn't humans that get turned?" I think he knew I was going to ask this because he tilted his head slightly.

"No, these rumours originated because years before medical science people weren't that great at distinguishing between death and someone who had just passed out for a time. As a result, a lot of people got buried alive and when the earth is wet and the graves shallow some of these unfortunate souls would claw their way out.

When rare cases like this happened, it would naturally be put down to their own myths of Vampires."

"Lucius is the only one who can change a Demon into something more and if they are partially gifted, then they are even more so when they are turned. He likes to collect powerful Vampires because he can control them." Draven turned serious and sounded almost respectful to his lost friend.

"So if I met a Vampire he wouldn't be able to change me or another Demon, am I right?" I asked what I thought was an important piece of information to know.

"Yes. Think about it, if they all had the power to change both humans and Demons then the world would soon be overrun. Considering they are immortal it would be very hard to stop them or to maintain control," he told me and again, this made perfect sense.

"So, what about the other rumours, you know, garlic, stakes to the heart, sunlight, silver and feeding on humans, that type of thing?"

"Garlic no, but sunlight and silver, yes. But sunlight is the only real weakness Lucius holds, although it cannot kill him it just weakens his abilities. He doesn't like these things because they are all a reminder of how he died as a human. So, his memories of them got transferred into each one he turns, therefore it can now sometimes be their weakness also."

"So, it can't kill them?" I asked.

"No, but they are no more difficult to kill than most of my kind. However, through Lucius' long life of rule, the more he turns, the more it makes him immune to his past fears. As for the myth of feeding on humans, I am afraid that part is true and not just for Vampires." I wasn't surprised. Not considering I hadn't been frightened when Draven had bitten me during certain breath-taking times. Meaning, I had already guessed as much.

"What about the spike to the heart thing?"

"Ah well, that is highly unlikely as it would have to be made by the same wood as the tree he was hung from and considering no one knows what type of tree it really was, then you would have to be extremely lucky. Plus, it wouldn't have to be in the heart, in theory anywhere would do it." Oh well, it was worth a try. I couldn't help but giggle at the conversation we were having. Draven didn't seem to mind. I think he was just glad I wasn't screaming or getting rip-roaring drunk to numb my fear. I put my strange behaviour down to a coping mechanism. Okay, so maybe good old Jack from the bottle was helping just a tad.

"So, they're not dead then?" Again, with another question.

"No, they have an immortal host like usual Demons but whereas most Angels and Demons outgrow their vessels, Vampires keep on to theirs because of the blood that regenerates them. The blood lust is down to wanting to be more powerful than the next. A lot of the times they feed on humans, but do not need to kill them. Many have been bitten, drank from and then healed. Most don't even remember. It is a very sexual act, and most prefer to have sex with the living. You do, however, get rogue Vampires that kill and trust me when I say I have had to deal with more than a few of those in my time." I could just picture him as a slayer but then he and Buffy popped in my head doing the bump and naughty, so I quickly pushed that far, far away.

"What are you thinking about?" he asked as I must have been staring at nothing. I usually did this when thinking hard about things.

"I guess I am still confused as to why he would want me." This changed Draven so quickly, it took me a moment to realise he wasn't still on the couch. His body was ridged and at first, I thought he had heard danger, like when you see a dog's ears go back when they know something's not right.

"That is quite enough for today. You do not need to be worrying about something that I will not allow to happen. And besides, this is supposed to be a date and I doubt it is customary to talk about so much death and destruction." I got up and put my arms around his neck, well tried to, but he got the hint and when I could interlock my fingers, he lifted his neck back up taking me with it. He held my waist and when he went to kiss me, I moved my head back causing him to let out a disapproving groan. I was teasing him, and he knew it from the big naughty grin that spread the width of my face. He tried again, but I moved and with his hands still holding my waist he couldn't do anything about it.

"You're enjoying this, aren't you?" he growled down at me.

"Maybe, but I take it you're not?" I loved teasing him.

"Cocky now, aren't we? What happened to that shy girl who used to flinch if I came too near or jumped if I touched her lightly? I think I must be spoiling you, Vixen," he said giving me a thoughtful half-smile and a new nickname. His eyes nearly closed from looking at me with such intense lust.

"Do you want to spoil me again?" I asked biting my lip.

"Always," he rumbled before lifting me up with his impressive arms and running with me up the stairs once again to my room. There he sat down on the window seat and I was on his lap where he kissed my neck still trying to reach my lips. I stayed firm, knowing that teasing him would be worth it in the end. See, I had a plan, I wanted to see what he would do when under my control, only giving in at the last minute. That was if I could last that long without kissing him first.

"Behave," I cautioned and he gripped me tighter. I moved to straddle him and felt his eagerness increase into a hard bulge. I pulled my top off, leaving me with just a plain black bra. I really needed to invest in some fancy underwear.

He cupped the material with me in it and gripped my breasts making me moan. He stood up and held me wrapped around him with one arm. With the other he unfastened his jeans and let his length breathe freely. He pulled down on my waistline and with a quick movement from each leg I was out of my black sweatpants quicker than it had taken me to put them on. He lifted me higher, before sitting back down so he could lower me fully onto him. This way was always going to be more intense as it breached deeper inside me making it harder to take, so when I screamed out, he lifted me off slightly, knowing this could be a problem.

"Hold on to my shoulders, sweetheart." His husky voice commanded, and I did as instructed. Then he started to control my movements using his hands on my hips to move me slow and steady. I thought that with me being on top it would put me in the driving seat but because of Draven's size it meant that I wasn't yet used to this position, as I had first thought. However, I was still in control, well, in one way at least. I still wouldn't let his lips touch mine and he looked like a man starved from his addiction. He was craving my lips, but I kept moving out of his way and he would growl and groan with agony at being withheld. However, it made my pleasure increase.

"Yield to me!" he commanded and I placed my lips near his ear to whisper,

"Not yet, big boy," I said slowly going for sexy sweet. So, in return he multiplied the storm that was happening in between my legs. I threw my head back and cried at the ceiling as he started to bite my neck but stopped himself before he could penetrate the skin.

"Do it!" I demanded and I could feel his gratified smile on my skin. I could tell he was happy he had regained back some control. He stood up suddenly and pulled me tighter into his groin. I screamed back as he used his length as punishment and his arms that held my waist gripped tighter still, not allowing me to leave his overpowering size. He walked over to my desk and sat me down, while keeping us securely connected.

There, he took back his control and forced me into a very powerful orgasm making me convulse in his arms uncontrollably. I could feel the energy grow inside me. The fire and ice fought each other under my skin. My blood raced around my body as if it was being pumped by two hearts, both Draven's and mine. His hand was supporting my neck as I jerked against him, clenching his length inside me as the sensations continued to crash through me. I felt sexually battered with just one orgasm but damn if I didn't want another! I could feel that he was close too, so I looked up at him and said,

"Kiss me, kiss me n..." He didn't even wait for the last word to leave my lips before he crushed his own to mine. He came quickly after that while still kissing me, crying out inside my mouth and I got my perverted wish when another battering to my senses hit me. He rested his forehead on mine, and I could see his smile. He lifted me over to my bed and lay me down before joining me.

"That was incredible, Keira. No one has ever teased me like

that before and well you discovered the outcome...it was just... just..." It wasn't often that you heard Draven lost for words, so this unfinished sentence was the biggest compliment I could have ever received.

"Ecstasy." I said before snuggling into my little nook situated under his neck and by his shoulder. He stroked my hair back and kissed the top of my head.

"Yes… yes it was. Sleep now, my little Vixen."

I didn't have any problems with that order as I was soon fast asleep and would have loved to say that I dreamt of Draven and I being together, but I didn't. Even though in life I belonged to him, this was no longer the case in my dreams. It seemed I had lost all control.

I belonged to someone else.

To another.

So, I dreamed of Lucius that night and in my dream…

I belonged to him.

CHAPTER SEVEN

LIFE INTERRUPTED

I woke to the lush feeling of a warm naked body next to me and I had to sigh, I was that happy. The body next to me shifted his weight and then I felt his breath by my ear.

"Good morning, my little Vixen." I loved it when he called me his. I rolled over to face him, to see he had clearly been wide awake now for some time. I stretched out and my bones made cracking noises at having to work again. For some odd reason Draven found this amusing.

"Morning," was all I said as I still felt quite shy in the morning. I still expected to wake up and find out it had all been an amazing dream. Of course, I was always thrilled beyond belief to find out it hadn't been. But mainly I was shy because I knew my hair would be a nest of knots and my breath strong enough to knock out large farm animals.

"You haven't been awake for hours staring at me again, have you?" I asked praying he hadn't, but his smile just confirmed my fears.

"If you owned a masterpiece, would you not spend a long time admiring it?" he said simply. I hid my head under the covers to hide my shame then felt the bed move when he started to laugh.

"Why are you hiding under there? Are you blushing again,

because you know that just enhances the picture of beauty." Oh please, let him stop before my cheeks exploded! He got frustrated when I didn't come out, so he made the covers float up to the ceiling using his hands to control them. I was still as naked as he was, and he laughed harder when my hands flew out to my private parts.

"Bring it down!" I shouted as it flattened against my ceiling.

"You will no longer use it to hide?" He raised an eye to me, and I nodded, making my quilt come waving down like a giant leaf, until landing first on my feet then gently to my shoulders.

"How do you do that?" I asked trying not to sound like a five-year-old.

"I use its energy to do my will," he said but when I frowned, he knew he would have to give me a bit more than that.

"Everything in this world and the next has energy, even though your eyes can't see, it is still there. Most of my kind can home in on some of these energies and once you get a feel for the right energy, you can use it, move it, break it and do anything you want with it."

"So, there are some things you can't...umm...home in on, is that right?" I pulled the covers under my arms and propped up on my elbow as I waited for his answer.

"No, there is nothing that I cannot home in on, but that is only because I have a more enhanced power than most. But don't forget I have to be stronger than the rest or there is very little point of me being here. My brother and sister are the same, they can find any energy, but they can't hold on to it for as long as I can." He said this more as a matter of fact than sounding arrogant.

"Is that what you did with the cabin?" This memory instantly squared his features into hard lines.

"It was," he answered shortly, clearly not liking where my questions were leading.

"So even things that big you can control?" I asked remembering the sight of the cabin that held me prisoner, being ripped apart by just Draven's thoughts.

"My rage helps increase my power, as it is fuelled by my Demon side which is stronger in all aspects of energy control."

"So, there are limits?" I asked wondering when he would stop the flow of answers as you could see it was coming soon.

"It takes a lot of our energy when we use our powers and we need a lot of rest after so much has been used. We need to regenerate the power that has been transferred." Now I knew why Draven had slept so much the night after the fight with Sammael, it must have worn him out and of course, there was the ripping apart of all those Gorgon Leeches to consider.

"Of course, feeding from humans helps." This also sounded very matter of fact and if I wasn't already getting my head around all this supernatural stuff, then running out of the door screaming would have surely followed.

"Okay, when you say feed, you do mean on their emotions...*yes?*" God, I hoped so. He had told me about this before and when I first found out, I went a little crazy. He explained how Angels and Demons both feed from human emotions to increase their energy. But some take it to the limit, keeping humans in extra happy or extra depressing states so they can keep absorbing whichever energy they preferred.

Draven had also told me how it wasn't always Demons that liked the negative energy and Angels that liked the positive. Angels can sometimes be bad and Demons sometimes good. One thing that he made clear though, was how no-one, not Demon, Angel or even Draven himself could feed from me.

"Yes, but of course, we do not eat humans, Keira, we are not animals." He sounded insulted but considering the conversation we had last night, could he really blame me? I may have thought this way, but I decided to keep my mouth shut on the matter.

"Umm... while you're in the answering mood, could I ask another question?"

"But of course." Ha, he wouldn't be so forthcoming when he heard it.

"It's about Lucius." There it was, the ultimate frown.

"Keira please, don't you think we have spoken enough on this matter?"

"Well, it is better for me to be prepared. I know you say he can't get me, but I would still like to be well informed just to be safe." Okay, this wasn't the only reason. After dreaming about him for the second time, I wanted to know if there was something more to his powers than other Demons had. Because usually when I had drawn what had haunted my dreams, it meant they couldn't come back. Like being locked out, but with Lucius this hadn't happened. I didn't want to tell Draven that I'd had another dream, especially not one where he had kissed me.

"What would you like to know?" he said, sighing in defeat.

"Well, I know it might be an obvious one but why isn't he still called Judas?"

"Because he was renamed by Lucifer when he was reborn into his new vessel. His name means Light, I think this was the Devil's idea of a joke, considering his body burnt in the sunlight," Draven said obviously seeing little humour in the fact himself.

"Uh, I think my joke about numbers was better," I said chuckling at how lame of a joke it was but hey, I had been telling it since I was six years old. This made him tickle me trying once again either to distract me or get me to snort. Both I thankfully resisted.

"So, he doesn't look the same, I mean as he once did?"

"No, his body was beyond healing," he said flatly.

"Okay... so does he have any special powers 'cause that would be useful to know?" He was growing more aggravated with every question I asked. So, I decided to add on a little extra to that question to butter him up.

"Because I find it hard to believe that anyone could be as powerful as you." It worked 'cause his frown was replaced with a knowing smile and he kissed me, but I kept my mouth shut (morning breath).

"Lucius is like most with his powers, although he is an extremely skilled fighter. But what makes him stand above the rest are his powers of manipulation. He can control any mind, Demon, Angel and of course humans are as easy to control as breathing."

"Not every human," I added knowing somewhat smugly that they couldn't control me.

"No, not every human." He repeated with a wink.

"Can he even control you?" I held my breath, but Draven's expression gave me the answer before he spoke.

"Yes. But the stronger the mind, the harder it is, usually he can control many minds at once but with stronger minds, like mine, Vincent and Sophia's, he can only control one at a time. This makes him more vulnerable when against numbers," Draven replied sternly.

"Has he ever tried to control you?" I knew I was stepping on thin ice, though I really was boiling over with questions, but I also knew he definitely had his limits.

"Yes, he did but only once and an act he was severely punished for, providing him with a day he won't be forgetting any time soon, of that I am certain." Okay, this was definitely the limit as he was scaring me with his intense gaze. But I had got the answers that I needed. Now I knew why Lucius was able to access my mind, unlike most. I can't say it was a happy, fuzzy thought to know, but definitely a helpful one.

Draven was still looking angry so I jumped on top of him and kissed him over everywhere my lips could reach. He liked this and his mood quickly changed, so we were soon thinking about other things we could be doing other than talking. But just before he could kiss me fully, I clamped my hand over my mouth.

"Oh no, you don't!" I grabbed the throw at the bottom of my bed and got up to wrap myself in it.

"Where are you going...oh wait... girlie human things again?" I nodded and said,

"Morning breath." And he laughed to himself as I walked to the bathroom. I also wanted to check on something else and was more than happy to discover I hadn't come on my period yet. I brushed my hair and plaited it, so it lay down my back. I also got rid of my bad breath and washed my face. I went back in and he hadn't moved an inch. The sight of him made me want to run over to him just to get there quicker. He was simply breath-taking.

The morning light from my window made his skin look like golden sand. His hair was wild around his neck and was as black as night. His shoulders looked huge and solid and I wondered how something so hard and powerful could be so soft to the touch. And I might add, very comfortable to sleep on.

When I was within reach, he didn't wait for me to climb back on top of him, he just grabbed me and put me there. The throw was on the floor and the covers only covered the lower parts of our bodies. I could tell he was happy in more ways than one. Oh yes very, very happy...ooh…um… Hello Commander Draven!

We were just kissing and fooling around, when all of a sudden, he stopped and held me tighter.

"Draven what is it?" His face was stone and his head whipped towards the door.

"There are other humans in the house." I froze as I heard footsteps on the stairs. Then it happened too quickly for me to react properly, my door opened and I screamed. Oh, and I wasn't the only one!

"ARRHHH...OH my god! Oh shit! I'm so sorry, I...I didn't think..."

"LIBBY!" I screamed as I fumbled for the sheets to cover us. Draven wasn't any help for laughing! Then it got worse as Frank burst into the room with a baseball bat in hand.

"What the...Oh Shit! Oh Man!" He turned around, covering his face with his hand and dragged Libby from the room as she was still apologising. Once they left, I could hear them both crack up. I was the only one in the house not laughing as the bed still vibrated from Draven's outburst.

"I CAN STILL HEAR YOU BOTH OUT THERE!" I shouted angrily, causing the giggling to cease and footsteps to be heard down the stairs.

I hit Draven on the chest, but it didn't have much of an impact like trying to break rocks with a jelly hammer!

"What's the use in having so many powers if you can't even prevent that from happening?" I dramatically pointed to the door. I was so embarrassed but thank God we weren't actually doing more than kissing. Okay we were both naked, but it could have been worse...not by much though.

"Do you want me to erase their memories?" he asked still being highly amused.

"You can do that?" I asked being hopeful, but Draven just smiled like he was teasing me.

"I can but I won't, this was far too funny to have missed, for anyone." And once again it set him off. I got up and got changed quicker than ever before. I didn't want to, but I knew I had to go down there first.

"Stay here," I warned and he nodded still with a thick smirk plastered on his handsome face.

"As you wish, Vixen," he said, sounding like a genie causing me to roll my eyes.

Libby and Frank were still giggling about it when I walked in the kitchen.

"Morning, Kaz," Libby said, as if it had never happened but it would have been more convincing without the bloody great big childish grin she wore plastered all over her face.

"Stop that!" I said but as soon as Frank went back outside to get their bags from the car, she came over to me and put her arms around me to whisper in my ear.

"My, my, what a lucky girl you are... oh my." She pulled back to reveal a huge smile. She, of course, was referring to the Godlike figure of a man lying upstairs in my bed. Damn straight I was lucky! I couldn't help but finally break down with laughter and lots of snorting. We were both in fits by the time Frank came back in.

Draven then made his appearance and was shaking Frank's hand in the hallway.

"Mr Draven, Sir... please don't worry about apologising, you're more than welcome here." Frank didn't sound right calling anyone 'sir' but he was obviously intimidated by Draven's reputation and Draven did send a lot of work his way. His men were hired for the downstairs security at the club.

"Please Frank, call me Dom and thank you for your hospitality, it was rude of us not to ask if I could stay the night." Oh come on, we weren't bloody teenagers!

"That's not a problem. Kazzy doesn't even need to ask," Frank said seeing me in the doorway and he came over to me to give me a bear hug, as it was Frank's way of saying 'hello' to me. He had always treated me like his little sister, and I loved it. But Draven looked frozen at the sight. He was ridged right until Frank put me down.

"Hey Kaz, you miss us?" he said laughing and ruffling my hair.

"Sure, just wish I'd known you were coming back early," I said through my teeth.

"Yeah, I bet you did!" he said before grabbing all the bags in one hand and running up the stairs with them. Libby came into view and I noticed she had pulled her hair down from the hairband that was holding it up. I had to stifle a giggle.

"Libs, you remember Dra... I mean Dominic, don't you?" Of course, she did, Draven is the most unforgettable man in existence. She came forward and shook his hand that he had extended first.

"Of course, hello Dominic, how are you?" she said politely.

"Very well thank you and I am sorry about you finding me in your home in such an inappropriate manner." Oh, Libby would be loving this, he sounded like Mr Darcy from Pride and Prejudice. She was a sucker for Colin Firth even if she had never read the book.

"It's fine, really, I guess I just never expected...well, you know. You're the first boyfriend of Kaz's that I have ever met." She was fishing for details now I could tell. I turned to her and gave her a stern eye, telling her in the only way sisters can understand nonverbally to shut it. Of course, she ignored it.

"Really, that surprises me," he said while giving me a look as if to say, 'We will be talking about this later.'

"Oh yeah, Kazzy rarely dated."

"Okay, enough of that, there is no need to go into details here," I snapped and they both laughed. Well, it didn't take my sister long to turn to the dark side. When she first heard I was going to be working at the club she was the first one to tell me things weren't right about the Dravens. Of course, she didn't know why, just rumours she had heard. She tried everything in her power to stop me from working there but now it seemed she was more than pleased about the outcome. Well, that certainly made two of us.

"Can I get you anything to drink?" she asked, putting on her posh voice the way my mother always did when she had company.

"No, thank you," he replied in his smooth velvet voice and I thought my sister's legs would give way.

"Are you sure? Kaz, tea's brewing." Of course, she didn't need to ask me. I usually couldn't function properly in the morning without a cup of tea and my sister knew this. Only from the looks of things, when she had first seen me this morning, it must have looked like I was functioning just fine.

"Ta. So how come you're home early?" I asked while we moved into the kitchen and Draven held out my seat for me before taking his own. Libby looked as though she had just swallowed a bug.

"Libs?" I said bringing her back around. Oh yes, she was definitely seeing Draven as Darcy.

"Uh…what did you say?"

"Back early?" I prompted again.

"Well, Frank got a call that there had been an accident with some of his Uncle's old property, so he has to meet with the insurance guys early tomorrow morning."

"What happened? I didn't know his uncle had more property." But from the way Draven stiffened in his chair, I was the only one in the room that didn't. It was only a very slight movement, but I seemed to be so deeply connected with him somehow, that no matter how small and insignificant I noticed these things.

"Oh yeah, he owned a cabin in the woods, but lightning struck it, can you believe it?" My heart nearly stopped. Now I knew why Draven was stiff in his chair. She was turning to look at me because I still hadn't given a response, so I asked the only thing that came to mind.

"When did lightning hit it?" I asked and she continued pouring the tea, but Draven looked at me and shook his head, telling me not to ask questions but it was too late for that.

"You're joking right, did you not see the storm on Wednesday night? It was awesome!" Oh yeah, I saw it alright, I was there seeing Draven bloody create it! My head started to drown in a pool of much-needed answers.

"Oh yeah, I…um… must have forgotten," I said through my teeth at Draven, but he just shrugged.

"So that was Frank's uncle's place?"

"Yeah, but Frank never really wanted it, it was almost a ruin. Frank's uncle lived there the year before he died. It was strange that he moved out there and no one in the family understood why." She placed the tea in front of me and I blew on the hot liquid. When Libby's back was turned Draven grabbed my mug quicker than my eyes could fully register, then he blew on it only to put back in front of me in another blink of an eye. I put it to my lips, and it was now the perfect temperature. Bless him. I mouthed the words 'thank you' but I think he was happier with the smile it brought to my face.

I went to open my mouth to ask something more, but Draven placed his hand on my arm and gave me a little squeeze, so I stopped myself. Libby called Frank to tell him his coffee was ready, and she took one of the other empty seats and smiled at both of us.

"Well Kaz, it is nice to see you looking so happy," she said and then nodded to my bare arm that Draven was still holding. Oh no, I had completely forgotten to put gloves on. To tell the truth, I had been getting used to the feeling without them thanks to Draven. I never thought it would be possible to forget my idea of a security blanket like my gloves but now I felt bad for Libby.

"Oh god Libs, I'm so sorry." I got up suddenly and Draven looked shocked at my reaction. I held my arms behind my back and excused myself to get some gloves. Libby and Draven both had the same facial expression...pity and God how I hated pity!

"Kaz, that's not what I meant!" She started to explain but I was out of the room as if it was on fire. I didn't mind Draven seeing my scars but anyone else seeing them had me in knots. I was hit with an overwhelming guilt. I never wanted these reminders but mainly I never wanted anyone else to be reminded of what we all went through. Frank met me on the stairs and I still had my arms behind my back. He was about to say something but saw why I was in a hurry and moved out of my way without the pitying face. Good old Frank.

I was soon making my way back downstairs, arms now covered, so I remained quiet the rest of the way down.

"I gather she has told you what happened to her?" Lib's voice sounded like controlled anger and it was the first time in a long time I had heard anyone talking about it. When it first happened, I would hear my family discussing it numerous times when they thought I was out of earshot. My Dad would be the worst, getting angry at everything and my Mum's tears would be the only sound to soften his attitude. This upset me more than the actual event.

Draven must have nodded because I didn't hear his response.

"Well, she must really trust you for her to have spoken about it. She doesn't talk to anyone about it, as in ever. I have to thank you, I have been worried about her for so long now, so to see her this happy, well, let's just say it has been a long time." I had tears in my eyes, and I couldn't help them. I loved my sister so much, but I thought that I had put on a good enough show to make them all think I was happy. Now I knew it had all been for nothing.

"She is an extraordinarily brave girl but also selfless. I believe these are the reasons for her silence. She thinks that she can deal with everything on her own, but she needs to realise that she has people around her who love her and want to help her." This was Draven's account of my reasoning behind why I was this way. He was spot on about the last part.

"Well, I am just happy that now she has you. I can tell you love her and have for some time now...am I right?" Libby was asking him, and I wanted to go down and stop the conversation but with tears still streaming down my face, I couldn't move.

"You are. I believe I fell in love with her the first time we met, although things were complicated back then. But I want you to know you never have to worry about her, I would never let anything like that happen to her again."

"Then I wish she could have met you years ago," she said and I could tell she was getting emotional about it. I heard her blow her nose. I felt a hole grow wider in my chest at the memories that I just wanted to be wiped clean. I hated that it still affected the people that I loved. I just wanted to be the one who had to deal with it, no-one else!

I got up, not caring about the noise and ran up the stairs with soaked cheeks. When I got into my room, I sat at the window seat and cried. I couldn't help but think about the contrast of feelings this window seat had endured in the past twelve hours. Just then I heard the door open and cringed as for the first time since being with Draven I just wanted to be left alone. I hated people feeling sorry for me and this was too much to handle. Draven had said I was brave, well this wasn't brave...this was pathetic! Crying because of feelings I didn't know how to deal with.

I didn't look at the door, but I knew it was Draven, I could feel him, like I was connected to his pulse. When I felt him getting closer, I turned away to hide my face and my raw watery eyes found the view outside my window, but for once the sight didn't make me smile.

"Keira, look at me." His voice was so soft it came out of him like a secret. When I didn't, he intervened by gripping my chin and gently turned me to face him. I hated people seeing me cry, showing them my weaknesses, making them feel awkward but with Draven it was different. I was torn between wanting him to comfort me and not wanting him to see me this way.

When I turned, he was knelt down by the seat, but he was still taller than me. His hand wiped away my tears and he held my cheek in his palm. His eyes were deep indigo like the midnight ocean thanks to a hint of purple breaking through with his own emotions. I bit my lip to try and stop the tears that continued, but just in time he pulled me into him and rested my face into his shoulder for me to sob. It was as though he felt my pain because without saying a word he made me feel what I needed the most,

He made me feel safe.

"I'm sorry, I just hate hearing my sister getting upset and I didn't know she still worried about me...not in that way," I said once I had finished crying and Draven just continued to smooth back my hair.

"Keira, please don't ever apologise for your emotions." He kissed my now salty cheeks and I smiled.

"Can I ask you something?" Draven asked me cautiously, so I nodded.

"Why have you never spoken about this to anyone but me?"

"I don't like pity and I don't like feeling as though he has won," I said honestly but Draven shook his head at me.

"Keira, you are amazing. You survived what that monster put you through but because of its aftermath you still torture yourself with unnecessary guilt. You don't want to talk about it because you don't want pity but with your refusal to discuss it, what are those who love you left to think? I know that you have dealt with it on your own and in your own way, but it is never healthy to carry so much emotional weight by yourself...you must understand that one day the weight will get too much for one pair of shoulders to cope with." I understood what he was saying. If I never spoke about it, how was anyone to know that I was coping? Maybe everyone thought that I just wasn't and then no matter what I did I would still get pity.

"You're right I need to face the truth instead of running from it. I wish someone had said it like that to me sooner," I said trying to match his smile. I hugged him and kissed him on the cheek for being so sweet.

"Right, now I am over my little meltdown." At this he frowned, but I continued anyway,

"You need to tell me what happened to Frank's Uncle." I wasn't surprised by his reaction,

He continued to frown.

CHAPTER EIGHT

EGO VEREOR DEMONS

I sat there and listened as Draven told me the horrors that infected Frank's uncle.

His name was George Miller and he was Frank's mother's oldest brother. From what I'd heard from Libby, he had been a well-liked man who always helped out with the community. He had been a fireman most of his life but took early retirement when his wife passed away with cancer. The death of his wife hit him hard, as it would with most, but it looked as though his family were kept in the dark about the true depth of his depression, because one day a hiker found his hanging corpse in his log cabin.

He hadn't spoken to his family in nine months. They put his suicide down to his desperation to be back with his wife. Frank had been the last person he had seen, two months prior to his death. He was also the last person he spoke to when he rang a week before he was found. He told Frank that he had left him everything, but his only wish was that the cabin and the land were never sold. He didn't care about the house which Frank had found the strangest thing of all as it had been in Frank's family for generations and his wife had adored the place.

Frank didn't understand at the time but just put it down to him sorting out his affairs. Libby told me that Frank had felt guilty ever since, thinking he could have maybe talked him out of it or got him some help. But when Frank spoke to him on the phone, he thought he sounded fine and like his usual self. Of course, he had been wrong.

The last time Frank saw him he had been with a woman who worked in the local library, but he never introduced her, and she never spoke a word to him. At the time Frank and Libby had been living with Frank's parents while they were house hunting for somewhere nearby. They had very nearly signed for a house, when Frank got the call about his uncle George.

Of course, this wasn't Draven's account of the events. No, this was all told to me by Libby not long after I first moved here. Draven knew Frank's uncle for very different reasons. George had started to actually get his life back together unbeknown to his family. He had an evening poker night with some of his old buddies from the fire department and he had finished restoring his cabin which he used for hunting. But one other passion of George's was to result in his death. He loved the written word but when he'd worked, he had very little time for it and with a house full of his late wife's romance novels he started taking weekly trips to the library. This was where he met the Ego Vereor Demon.

She was working as a Librarian and was instantly attracted to George because she could detect his grief. They soon became friends and started spending more time together. Draven suspected they also became intimate, which is another big no, no in the supernatural world. The only reason Draven was allowed to be with me was because I was different. I was classed as the 'Chosen One', but I was still in the dark as to the details on that one. All I knew was that I was sort of born for Draven, which was still a large pill to swallow and Draven wasn't giving me any water to help swallow it down with.

Her name was Yvonne Dubeck and Draven told me that she was called an Ego Vereor Everto, meaning 'Self Fear Demon' in Latin. She liked to feed from the negative emotions caused by paranoia. She would gradually gain the trust of these poor unsuspecting humans by befriending them and then little by little she would implant delusions of what people feared the most. In George's case it was Alien abductions.

He soon became obsessed that he had been abducted numerous times and was living in fear until his next abduction. In the end he became a recluse and lived in the woods like a hermit. The only person he would see was Yvonne as he never got abducted when she was around.

She would get stronger every second she was with him, but because he was a strong character, he would fight back getting better when not in her presence. Of course, she would not allow this to happen for long. In the end, she got the ultimate high when his paranoia got too much one day and he took his own life which unfortunately happened before Draven could intervene.

Draven had been too late to save George and Yvonne disappeared before her punishment could be inflicted. She was now on the wanted list or as Draven put it, she was now 'Marked' which I gathered was the equivalent to being on the America's topmost wanted list.

By the time Draven had finished I felt slightly sick at the thought. My heart ached for Frank's uncle and I couldn't help but shed a few tears during the story. It was just so sad to have first lost the women you love then be tricked by the next.

Trust really could be one of the deadliest of things mankind had to offer.

Draven assured me that George's soul would be reunited with his wife's, a bit like a safe passage to be favoured by his faith. As a rule, the Gods gave those who have been wronged by their kind special treatment. I tried to find out more, but Draven made a face like this was something I wouldn't want to know so this inevitably had me more confused than ever.

My phone vibrated as a message flashed up on my phone, but Draven was not happy about its sender.

"I do not understand why you can't just ring the boy and explain that your situation has changed." Draven was now sulking and even this was sexy.

"Because Jack is a friend and I would like to keep it that way. Besides, it would be rude to do it any other way and you need to get used to me seeing my friends," I said before reading his text message informing me that we were now meeting at two o'clock.

"Fine, but you know I don't share, Keira," he said sternly making me want to roll my eyes and explain how the 'Caveman boyfriend syndrome' really wasn't necessary.

"Well, in that case I will go and let you get ready for your date." This time I did actually roll my eyes.

"Come on! It's not a date, I am just meeting a friend and besides, you have your ex-girlfriend sat at your table every night!" This made him frown down at me.

"Keira, I have explained about Aurora. She means nothing." He had me looking back up at him to see the sincerity in that statement.

"And I have explained about Jack. And besides, you didn't tell me about Aurora, Sophia did." I reminded him but once again he just frowned.

"Anyway you don't have to go yet, it's not even twelve and I'm not meeting him until two."

"Where are you meeting him?" he said as sourly as anyone could.

"At a diner on fifth, why?" I asked cautiously.

"Because I need to know where to send Ragnar." This information granted him a groan of frustration.

"Oh no, Draven please you really don't..." He cut me off by kissing me and no will on earth could have me resisting.

"Keira, do not fret, no one will see him but you." Now I was the one frowning.

"And how is that going to work because I am pretty sure his stealth skills are limited thanks to his gigantic size?" He was laughing again, and this was probably due to the idea of Ragnar hiding away in bushes or behind trees.

"He has been given a power that will encase the minds of humans around him to simply pass him as if he was not there. He will not be seen, that I can promise you." He nodded slightly at this promise and I found it an endearing quality to add to many others.

"You did that for me?"

"But of course, why not? You didn't exactly hide your

displeasure in having a bodyguard." I gave him a huge grin and hugged him but my small arms wouldn't go all the way around, so I gripped onto his t-shirt. He liked this and held the back of my neck, which always sent tingly sparks down my spine.

"Thank you, but how will I see him?" I asked, thinking this was probably important, as let's just say, he was a big enough target for me to easily bump into.

"The power he has won't work on you, like most of my talents," he said as though he was both annoyed and proud that his powers hardly ever worked on my diverse mind. I hid my smirk in his t-shirt.

"Ah well, that's good to know. So, you don't have to go now," I said, but by the look on his face he had other commitments today and had to go anyway. I couldn't help thinking it was a kind of punishment because I was seeing Jack.

"I am afraid I do still have to go, but I will have Ragnar bring you back to me once you have finished with the bo...I mean Jack." He refrained from calling him 'Boy' as he saw my disapproving look. I hated it when he called him that, it was degrading but I think that was reason for it.

"It's alright, I will see you after work later," I said turning, knowing this caused another conflict between us. Draven didn't want me working at the club anymore, but I wasn't having any of it.

He let out a short laugh that sounded like a 'Hell No'.

"Keira, we have discussed this, you know my feelings on the matter." He was putting on his smooth velvet voice to try and bring me round to his way of thinking. Normally it would have worked, giving in to anything he asked of me but this time I remained strong. I sat down on my bed and folded my arms across my chest.

"Actually, we haven't. But this is not up for discussion, Draven. I am working at the club and downstairs not the VIP. Don't look at me like that! Would you prefer I find another place to work, one where you won't be able to keep an eye on me?" I challenged.

"I would prefer you didn't work, period." He was stood above me, moving my top off my shoulder so he could feel my skin there. I shuddered under his warm hands making me feel like he was creating sparks. This was a tactic to get what he wanted. He had learnt other ways to infiltrate my mind instead of using his powers.

"That isn't going to happen. So, tell me now, do I still have a job at your club, or should I start looking elsewhere?" He looked shocked that his power of persuasion wasn't working like he hoped. So, he upped his game. His hand moved up from my shoulder to my neck that just so happened to be a major weak spot of mine. He gripped the back of my neck with his full palm under my hair. He pulled upwards making me stand to face him and my heart rate doubled. He leant down to my ear but before he spoke, he kissed my neck, making me bite my bottom lip.

"Keira, listen to me, you do not want to work for me. You want to work with me...isn't that right? Forget this idea and join me at my table by my side, where you belong." His voice filled my mind like a white cloud of happy ideas, and I knew I was losing the fight quickly. It was like getting lightheaded on a hot day and staring at the sun for too long. I couldn't focus and every time I came close to finding my way back, he would touch me down my sides making it harder to breathe.

But his confidence was his downfall because when he thought he had me completely under his will he started to relax it, so I pushed as hard as I could making the fog fade and disperse into my clear mind once more. I opened my eyes and smiled up at him.

"Nope, sorry, didn't work!" And I couldn't help but laugh when I saw his face drop. He growled under his breath to show his displeasure at being beaten.

"Now stop that! You know you shouldn't be doing it anyway." I chastised.

"You will not listen to me on this matter, will you?" he said getting aggravated at my defiance.

"No, but I will meet you halfway, I will cut down my hours to three nights a week and work the hours you choose," I said making his face change from a displeased one to one of intrigue.

"You are very clever at getting what you want, aren't you?" he said raising an eyebrow at me, drawing out his sexiness to new levels.

"I learned from the master." I said winking at him and this had him showing his trademark bad-boy grin adding greatly to those levels once again.

"You did indeed. Right, while we are discussing compromise, I will allow you to work two nights a week downstairs of your choice but Saturday nights you will work upstairs in the VIP. And you will end each shift by joining me at my table. Is this acceptable?" he said in the most business-like manner I had ever heard from him yet. It made me realise how much of a ruthless businessman he must actually be.

"Alright, that sounds reasonable enough, but I will also be at the club with my friends once a week at least and you won't moan...right?"

"Moan?" he said seriously and I almost laughed.

"Yes YOU. Let's face it Draven, when it comes to me spending time with other people, we don't actually see eye to eye."

"And I suppose this little bargain means you will be spending time with friends that are also male?" God, he was so old fashioned, as if I was committing sin and adultery.

"Yes, I have male friends, just as you have female friends."

"Female council members, Keira, although I find it utterly adorable that you get jealous over me, I also know that it is completely unnecessary. You are the only one my eyes see." I couldn't help but blush when he said this.

I did get jealous but mainly over the amazing beauty, Aurora. She was Draven's ex-girlfriend and although when you're immortal and have been around for over one thousand years, those years are counted very differently. But twenty years for a couple to have been together is still a bloody long time in my book. Of course, it didn't help that she was the most beautiful creature alive and made starry nights and sunsets over the ocean look drab!

"Anyway, if I didn't know any better, I would say you were stalling for time to keep me here," he said before kissing me and I knew it was his way of a goodbye so for the first time I didn't enjoy it as much knowing this.

"Why do you have to go again?" I said after catching my breath. Ok, so I kind of lied about the whole not enjoying it comment. He laughed to himself as he clearly loved it when I was being this needy.

"I don't want to go but I do have some business that needs my attention. But Ragnar will bring you back to me," he said making me feel like a lost puppy being returned to his owner, that or a kicked ball over a neighbour's fence.

"It's okay I will just see you tonight after work. I should probably do some college work before I go back next week." The idea didn't have me dancing about the room with joy that was for sure. I had got so used to spending all my time with Draven that the thought of being apart made me feel a bit lost inside.

"I think you are smart enough." He playfully flicked my nose before continuing,

"So, I take it you have decided you are working Friday nights." I had chosen Fridays as it was always student night and very busy, which I liked because the hours went quicker, and the bands were good.

"If that is alright by my boss, then yes." He frowned when I called him boss but secretly, I think he liked it.

I walked him downstairs and Libby was sat on the couch with Frank, looking cosy.

"You two going out?" she asked like she was the mum in this picture.

"Dra...Dominic has to go back to work," I said and couldn't help but snigger a bit at the idea of Draven actually working. It was more like he just barked orders and they got obeyed. And I really needed to get used to calling him Dominic.

"Thank you for having me," he said this as if I'd had my friend to stay and his mum had told him to thank my mum, which in this case was Libby.

"Oh no problem, any time really. But before you go Frank and I were wondering if you would like to come over tomorrow night for dinner?" This was so sweet, and I was about to decline for him knowing this was a bit too soon for so much human company, when he shocked me.

"I would be delighted to, thank you but please, let me bring the wine." O...kay, this was going to be weird. I shot him a look as if to say 'really?' but he just smiled before agreeing on a time and saying goodbye. Once outside on the deck with the door closed behind us, I asked him if he was sure.

"Of course, why not? Is this not a customary gesture in humans?" He looked a bit hurt, so I backtracked.

"Uh, yeah... but I guess I didn't know if you would be comfortable that's all."

"Keira, I may have not spent a lot of time around humans, but I know how to behave around them and besides, if it all goes wrong, I can just blank their memories and replace them with more positive ones. Then they will have no other choice than to approve of me." I couldn't tell if he was joking or not but knowing Draven, then he would get his way no matter what.

"Well, I am pretty sure you're already in there but if you did want to seal the deal then maybe turn up in your Aston Martin and you will have Frank ready to sell his soul to you for one ride." He raised his eyebrows as if I had just given him an idea and I would be very surprised if he didn't turn up tomorrow night in the shiny beast.

"That's good to know. Ragnar is already on his way here and he will follow you to the diner and back, then later to the club, but remember, no one but you will see him. Oh and also, I thought you would want Libby to have forgotten what happened earlier so I altered her memory a little on the matter. She won't remember you getting upset." This was the most considerate act that anyone could have done for me, given my headstrong nature and hating anyone knowing my emotions. He knew how this affected me because his hand went to my cheek to lift my gaze to his.

"Your eyes look amazing in this light and when glazed by emotion they look deep enough to swim in. Mmm, truly stunning," he said stepping back to admire them and I automatically looked off to the side, returning back to my shy self. He had never mentioned anything about my eyes before but hearing it was a beautiful thing.

Before I had chance to look back fully, he was kissing me, softly at first then with more intensity. His arms wrapped around me like he never wanted to let me go.

"You are incredibly difficult to leave," he said once he had finished but by then my legs were like hot moulding clay.

It took two more kisses and an "I love you" before getting in his car and driving away, which made me feel cold as soon as he was out of sight. I saw Ragnar come around the side of the house and waved to which I received a nod in return. I went back into the house and Libby was ready to pounce.

"Right, tell me everything!" she said smiling and very nearly dragging my arm off when pulling me upstairs. But I was very willing as I was getting desperate to talk to somebody about it and if I couldn't be with him, then talking about him was the next best thing. We both jumped on the bed and folded our legs up like we used to do as kids. She looked so excited for me and I couldn't keep the silly grin off my face.

"You look so happy, Kazzy! I don't think I have ever seen you this happy," she said beaming, thanks heavily to pregnancy hormones.

"Well, I have never been in love before." At this she let out a high-pitched scream and clapped her hands together. I half expected Frank to come running up the stairs with a baseball bat again.

"So come on tell me, how did it all happen?"

"I don't really know but he sort of just confessed he liked me." Which was the truth, well kind of. I told her about how Sophia invited me to sit at their table after work and I ended up next to Draven. Ok, so this wasn't exactly the truth, but it was as close to it as I could get. I told her that after a few drinks I relaxed enough to start talking to him.

"It kind of happened really quickly from there on, but from what he told me he has had a thing for me for a while, which is really hard to believe." She screwed her face up as if she disagreed.

"No it isn't. He obviously has good taste and you could tell he felt something for you when he brought you home that night. But I do wonder what took him so long?" Well of course, I knew the answer to that one, but I wasn't about to disclose that to Libby. Could you imagine me saying 'Well see Libs, here's the thing, he is a Demon/ Angel half breed and is like the Mafia Godfather of the supernatural world we all live in.' I couldn't see it going down well somehow, so instead I just went with,

"I guess he was just being cautious."

"Well, he is most definitely not a snob, so I will be the first to admit I was wrong about him. I thought he would be surrounded by bimbo strippers that had massive fun bags, as Frank likes to call them."

"Fun bags?" I said laughing and shaking my head.

"Don't ask."

"It does restore my faith in human nature that money isn't everything though." This I also wanted to laugh at but managed to control my outburst. Firstly, Draven couldn't get any further from human if he tried and secondly, he wasn't the bimbo type. From the looks of Aurora he was more the blonde Goddess type, so I failed to see what he saw in me but happiness kept me from caring too much and I could deal with my low self-esteem later.

"So from what I gathered earlier, you have without a doubt hit all bases. So come on, dish the dirt, how was it?" This had me howling with laughter and I threw my head back on the pillow as more laughter was quickly followed with a blissful sigh.

"It is the most incredible, mind-blowing experience I have ever known. Simply put, it is like a taste of Heaven," I said, and she sighed at the thought.

"He looked um…fit," she said which is her way of saying well equipped.

"Err yeah." We giggled again.

I carried on talking about Draven for over an hour and only just had time for a quick shower ready to meet Jack. This thought wiped the constant smile from my face, as I knew I was about to hurt him and it was something I was ashamed of myself for letting it get out of hand. I had led him on when Draven had hurt me, and I used him in the worst way to get revenge. It was not a proud moment for me, and I was appalled at my actions. Well, now it was time to face the music and put things right, even if I needed to beg and grovel. I wasn't going to let it prevent me and Jack from being friends. I knew Draven didn't like it, but he would come around, wouldn't he?

I was ready for leaving with a fresh clean outfit that consisted of my usual jeans and long-sleeved top, with gloves underneath of course. I put my half-wet hair up in a messy twist and bits fell down at the sides. The only difference to my appearance was the happy new glow my skin had acquired.

I grabbed my long black jacket as it looked as if it might rain later and headed for the door. I shouted my goodbyes to Libs and Frank and opened the door to a very handsome face.

This was one I hadn't seen in years and one that would no doubt cause me even more problems in my overly complicated life, as it was now time for,

An ex from my past.

CHAPTER NINE

HELLO STRANGER

"Well hello, Keira, looking fine as always." Justin, Frank's brother, stood opposite me leaning casually against the door frame. His baby face features had grown into a strong looking expression and he was skinny no longer. It had been replaced with a wide chest and broad shoulders. He looked as if he had just jumped straight out of a surfing magazine with his long blonde dreadlocks tied back from his face by a piece of thin rope. He had surfer beads up both wrists and a fossilized shark's tooth tied around his neck with some black cord. He wore combat trousers and a t-shirt under a thin zip-up hooded sweater even though it was winter. And he looked fantastic, damn it!

"Justin, hey...what are you doing here?" I asked, trying not to sound as surprised as I was. I hadn't seen Justin since my sister's wedding and well, back then I'd had a bit of a crush on him. Ok, so maybe more than a crush, but he had been with a girlfriend at the time.

"Just here to see the big guy but I get you instead, which is far more of a bonus and may I say much easier on the eyes," he said looking me up and down in a show of appreciation. I felt the usual heat of my cheeks burning but tried to ignore it along with his obvious flirty looks. His lips formed a devilish grin at the sight while I opened the door wider and called to Frank.

"Are you staying for long?" I asked, secretly hoping not because knowing Draven's reaction to Justin's flirting, it would be like lighting a firework letting it go off in your hand and asking it nicely not to burn you.

"No, just passing through," he said casually before Frank came to the doorway.

"Ah, now look what the cat dragged in! You back from trekking the jungle?" Frank said this while grabbing his brother into a bear hug. Justin was trying to breathe and hit him on the back to be released.

"God Frank, what you trying to do, break my spine in two?" Justin took a swipe at him which he skilfully dodged. I moved out of the way to let them bond the way brothers did. I could never imagine going up to Libby after not seeing her for months and punching her. Oh yeah, she'd love that.

"So, how was Costa Rica? I thought you would have been on a diet of rice and beans, but you look like you have put some meat on those skinny bones, lad!"

"Yeah, well at least I'm still not a muscle head!" This was how it went on for the next few minutes as I was still trying to edge towards my car, until they spotted me.

"Where you off to, Kaz?" It hadn't taken Justin long to adopt my nickname.

"Oh, I'm meeting a friend." He looked a bit disappointed and Frank nudged him.

"Yeah, little Kaz here has been quite a hit with the guys in this town." I rolled my eyes at Frank, but he just laughed.

"I can see why," Justin said in a low voice I could still hear, making Frank chuckle louder.

"Don't even think about it, Romeo, she's taken." Frank tried to grab him into a headlock, but Justin moved quickly and was down by me in seconds, jumping off the porch steps. He looked down at me and I pulled at the cuff of my jacket nervously hoping I could just get outta here.

"So, who's the lucky guy?" I really didn't want to be talking about this now or ever and I was already running late for Jack.

"Oh, no one you know. Anyway, I must run, but it was great seeing you again."

"Oh, you'll be seeing me next weekend, that is if my big Bro don't mind letting me crash for a few days." He said this last part to Frank, and he looked happy enough that his brother was back. I, on the other hand, wasn't so sure Justin being back here was such a great thing.

"Sure, you know you can, but first you go and see Mum and Dad."

"Yeah, yeah, I was on my way there next." Justin rolled his eyes at me in a comic fashion and I smiled. Then he put his arms around me and pulled me to his now hard chest. I froze but he just hugged me to say goodbye. I swallowed hard which he must have heard because he laughed as I quickly unlocked my car door.

"Well, I guess I will see you next week then," I said while getting in my bronco and he watched me like a wolf would little red riding hood. I let out a nervous giggle before driving off. On the way to the diner I thought about how glad I was that Draven hadn't still been there when Justin had turned up. He didn't like Jack because he felt something for me but at least he behaved himself. But Justin, well he was just a big flirt and would do it in front of anyone, including Draven.

Oh yes, it was definitely better that Draven didn't know about Justin. Then it hit me enough to have me slapping my forehead. Ragnar had probably seen the whole bloody thing! Oh no! I couldn't see him which suggested I might have got away with it, but something told me this wasn't a likely outcome. Oh well, it was only a hug…right?

I got to the diner and checked the clock on the dash. I was only ten minutes late after some luck with traffic lights and a heavy foot on the accelerator. Jack was already inside and I waved as I passed the window. He had already secured a booth next to the window and soon the butterflies in my stomach turned to stinging wasps. I was dreading this, but I knew it was the right thing to do. Of course, it didn't help that he was grinning at the very sight of me. It was going to be like dumping a cardboard box of puppies in an alleyway.

He was wearing his usual ripped jeans and today's choice in t-shirt was a faded 'Rolling Stones' but the lips had cracked from years of washing. His hair was the same wild bronze with lighter bits at the front and it flopped around in every direction. His soft features and gorgeous honey eyes lit up as I came nearer.

"Here she is," he said, getting up and hugging me. I didn't tense up as I had done with Justin. I don't know what it was about Jack, but he was one of those guys that put you instantly at ease. He was tall and had a toned build because he spent a lot of hours hiking. We sat back down and I couldn't help but smile at the sight of him. Then it faded, as I realised that this might be the last time we were like this. That he might not want to be friends any longer. My heart sank.

"Hey Jack, I'm so, so sorry," I blurted out and at first, he looked shocked. I guess I'd needed to say it now for a long time that it was the first thing I wanted out of my lips. At least I had said it even if it was the last time he wanted to talk to me.

"What for?" He was making this even harder, especially when he wouldn't stop smiling at me like I was bloody wonderful.

"For everything! I have treated you all wrong, I should never have done that to such a good friend and then I gave you that letter and then I didn't call..." I was tumbling out my words like they were hot mouthfuls I had to get rid of.

"Keira, stop! You don't have to explain or apologise for anything. I am a big boy and knew what I was getting into." Oh God, this just made me feel even worse!

"What do you mean, getting into?" I asked feeling ashamed.

"Keira, I couldn't help the way I felt about you and I guess I still can't but I have known for some time that you didn't feel the same. That still didn't stop me though. I could tell that first night when you saw him that he was the only one you had feelings for... but Keira, that doesn't mean I blame you and I certainly don't want to stop being your friend." I had tears welling up and I hid my face behind my menu for a moment.

"I don't deserve such a good friend," I said looking down and reading nothing on the plastic in my hands. He pulled the menu from me and held my hands in his.

"Keira, I am lucky to have you as a friend. I won't lie and say I am thrilled that you and one of the Dravens are together but I am glad that you are with someone who obviously cares a great deal for you." This made me look up at him and his eyes showed such sincerity.

"How do you know that?"

"Keira, when you disappeared, he had everyone in the club spoken to. The band stopped and the lights on full. I saw the desperation in his face when I handed him that letter you wrote. I was stunned when he actually thanked me and even shook my hand," he said looking at the same hand as if seeing the memory on it.

"However, I wasn't surprised that he chose you. He is lucky to have you." This made me blush again as I wasn't great at receiving compliments, especially when I didn't think they were justified by how I had treated poor Jack.

"Keira, will you tell me something if I ask?" I knew this was coming and I told myself earlier that if he asked, I would trust him. He deserved that much from me, he deserved the truth. I nodded knowing this wasn't going to be an easy conversation to have.

"What happened to you that night?" His voice was soft and soothing. I knew this was him trying to make it easier for me. Then the waitress came over to us, giving me little more time to think about how I was going to start such a conversation. But the more I thought about it, the more I knew I had no other choice than to start at the gruelling beginning.

Jack ordered two sodas and I looked outside to find my watchdog on guard. I was about to wave but stopped myself before I looked nuts. After all, no one else could see him and this was proven when a couple walked past him and came into the diner. And trust me when I say, this was not a man you would just have walked past without a jaw-dropping moment!

I waited until the cokes came and the snotty waitress went back to refilling her salt pots. Bless Jack because he just sat patiently and waited for me to find the courage to start.

"Well, there really is no other way to put it, so here goes…I was kidnapped," I said but he looked like he was going to choke on the ice cube he'd been sucking on.

"Jack, are you ok?" I said handing him my napkin so he could dispose of the cube.

"I'm sorry, can you just run that through me again, please…you say you were…*kidnapped?"* He whispered that last word like it was a sin.

"Look, I think I need to explain my past before I explain that night. The thing is Jack, this is the most private thing I could tell anyone. I have been running from it for two years now and only my family knows the truth. It's the reason I came here and it's the reason I have lied," I said this expecting more of a reaction but no, so far so good.

"What kind of lies?" he asked in a non-judgmental tone.

"First, my real name is Catherine Keira Williams not Johnson and I am really twenty-three not twenty-one like everyone thinks." I let this sink in before carrying on. His face tried to remain unmoved, but I could see the shock in his eyes. Whatever he had expected, it hadn't been this. I continued to tell him about how and when I first met Morgan and what the result of that was. I tried to miss out the details, but Jack wanted to know, as many would. I answered his questions and saw how difficult it was for him to hear. He tensed his fists and gripped the table making it shake. He even ground his teeth whenever I got to a more disturbing part.

Once I had finished, I told him the second half but had to change it slightly to leave out all the supernatural stuff. I explained how he had tricked me into meeting him and luckily Draven found where he was keeping me before he could really hurt me. When I had finished, he leant back against the leather-backed booth and stared at his hands for a while before speaking. He then raised his eyes and I saw pure hate there for the very first time and it scared me when he said,

"I hope Draven killed the bastard!" This was so out of character that I shuddered. What could I say? Yes, he did, he stabbed him in the heart once but then he came back and killed himself? Nope I couldn't go with that. When he saw me struggle for an answer, he made it easy for me.

"You don't need to tell me, Keira, I think I can gather for myself what a man like Dominic Draven would do if someone tried to take something of his and Keira, I would agree with him. This Morgan clearly needed to be stopped and there is only one way I can think of to make that happen permanently," he said bitterly at the thought of me in the clutches of that mad man. He looked down at my gloves that were under my sleeves and shook his head at what they must be hiding.

"I don't think I have ever met anyone as brave as you. But I have to tell you, I never thought you tried to kill yourself. I always thought it must have been some kind of accident." This touched me more than he could ever know. I had not yet met anyone who thought this way. Everyone had thought I tried to commit suicide, even my family had thought that I had tried to end it all, but they had all been wrong. I just could never bring myself to tell them that they might have been next in Morgan's deluded, warped mind. I took his hand in mine and kissed it.

"Thank you. You don't know what it means to me to hear you say that. You are the first to have given me the benefit of the doubt. Everyone else just assumes…well, you know," I said looking down at my arms and I automatically pulled down on the material.

"I really appreciate you confiding in me and I will not say a word, but I guess you knew I wouldn't, otherwise you wouldn't have told me." I looked up to meet his face that had once again changed back to his usual happy go lucky self and he winked at me lightening my heart. He really was one of the greatest friends I had ever had.

"I don't deserve such a good friend," I said as I playfully flicked him with the end of my straw.

"Well, what can I say? I will just have to charge you later when your rich boyfriend opens you a bank account and buys you a Ferrari," he said laughing and I faked being hurt and flicked even more coke on him.

"Now pack that in!" I said before he could throw an ice cube my way. Jack then got up and went to the restroom and as I followed his tall frame walk away, I noticed a pair of eyes watching me. A pair of purple eyes.

Oh great! Draven had been watching my entire 'date' as he called it. I now swallowed hard knowing that I was going to be in for it later. I shook my head at him but the middle-aged trucker he was using, just mouthed the word 'No' at me while shaking his finger. When Jack got back, I decided to try and ignore him, and I carried on with Jack as if I hadn't noticed. Well, I was going to get an ear-bashing anyway so I might as well have a fun afternoon before Draven got hold of me. I mean what could he do, turn me over his knee? Now that thought had me squirming in my seat and a quick glance to the side provided me with a raised eyebrow from Trucker Draven. I quickly looked away.

"So Jack, it's my turn to ask something of a sensitive nature." He curved up one side of his mouth as if he had been waiting for me to ask.

"You want to know about Celina, don't you?" he said looking at me over his now refilled coke glass.

"Is it bad that the answer to the question is yes?"

"It's fine, well I mean it freaked the crap out of me when I saw her there but now, I guess I can finally move on. But I won't lie, it hit me hard." I couldn't help but feel sorry for him. All this time he had thought Draven had stolen his girlfriend away two years ago, he had even sort of believed that he might have killed her. Celina was Draven's assistant and had made me believe his fiancée at one point, but this had been a lie to keep me from feeling too strongly for him.

Of course, it hadn't worked but it still hurt like a gunshot wound to the heart. Celina, of course, was a Demon and had started a relationship with Jack years earlier. This was one of the biggest crimes a Demon or Angel could commit. So, when Draven saw her in his club with Jack, he put a stop to it. But instead of punishing her he allowed her to stay on this plane and work for him. Jack, of course, didn't know this and still doesn't, so I was curious as to what she told him that night he saw her up in the VIP area.

"She explained that she was actually engaged." My heart stopped for a moment but started again when he continued.

"She thought the guy had been unfaithful, but it was a misunderstanding. She ran away to her aunt's house and no one knew where she was to explain the truth. He works for Draven apparently, so when he saw her that night at the club, he took the opportunity to tell her what really happened. She didn't go into it and he wasn't there that night but when he works for Draven, she tags along." This story had been well thought out, but I gathered for a Demon lying wasn't a hard job to master and if it didn't work, they could just control the person's mind so they would believe what they were told. Which had me wondering if the reason he seemed to be taking this so well wasn't actually down to some mind manipulation? Whatever the reasons I was just glad he didn't seem to be hurting too much about it.

"I know what you're thinking, why not just tell me that, right?" he said and I just nodded, as I was pretty sure he wouldn't want to know what I was actually thinking!

"Well, she told me that her fiancé is a bit of a possessive type and she didn't want him finding out about me and doing me any harm. But when I helped Draven by giving him that letter, he agreed that he would not discuss our meeting with her fiancé." I was at a loss for words and knowing the truth about this wasn't making it any easier to pretend I didn't.

"So how do you feel now?" I asked cautiously.

"I guess I'm fine, now I know that is." Okay, I think he must definitely have received a little Demon therapy from the red-headed beauty Celina.

"Well, I'm glad something good came out of that night. Thank you for giving Draven that letter, you helped save my life," I said sincerely.

"I just wish I'd had the guts to do it sooner, but no offence, your boyfriend is one scary-ass dude!" I smirked and looked sideways to the trucker which Draven was currently using to listen in and I saw him grinning at this statement.

"Yeah, he can be," I said dryly at seeing the trucker's toothy smile as he obviously liked the idea that Jack was scared enough of Draven not to pursue me romantically. Then I laughed as the waitress eyed him warily, so he went back to sipping his coffee.

Thankfully, Jack thought I had laughed at his last comment so I said,

"Like I said yeah, he can be intimidating at times, but he means well, and he was extremely grateful for what you did," I said a bit louder than I needed to and the trucker snorted making the people next to him jump at his sudden outburst. Jack raised his eyes in disbelief.

"No, really," I said again.

"Well, no offence, Keira, but he was the last person I did it for." Okay, I was back to walking on thin ice now as I half expected the trucker to get up and throttle him because he swivelled in his stool and stared at us both with purple-tinted fury. I frowned at him giving him my sternest stare, trying in vain to will him to back down. Jack was turning to see who I was glaring at and I waited for disaster. My judging eyes were replaced by ones of dread and pleading. But just in time, Jack was faced with more of a creepy smile and it came across as that of a gay admirer, than the hate it had been. Jack sort of smiled back but quickly turned away clearly being freaked out.

"What was all that about?" he whispered behind his hand.

"Beats me," I said sucking on my straw and trying not to laugh at the memory of this big fat trucker smiling like a little girl dressed in her best, smiling at a boy she fancies. Well, if Draven wanted to play games then he definitely won with this move.

We continued to chat for a while longer until I noticed the time was getting on and I needed to get ready for work. Jack walked me out to my car after receiving an even creepier wink from his new trucker friend. Thankfully, we started laughing about it once we got outside. As I said goodbye, he leaned in to kiss me on the cheek when an almighty crash came from the dumpsters being turned upside down made us both jump.

"Holy shit, what the Hell was that?!" He was asking the right person as I had seen the whole thing, but I couldn't tell him that it had been my colossal bodyguard having a paddy at the sight of me being kissed goodbye. Jack couldn't see him, and I was thankful. Ragnar looked enraged and his skin looked inflamed as his anger intensified. I got in my car before Jack could finish his gesture.

I pulled away not caring how Ragnar got back. I felt like a prisoner having my every move watched. This wasn't protection, this was a dictatorship. Was I even in any danger? Or was this just an excuse for Draven to catch me doing things he didn't like? I know I was being irrational, but I just couldn't help being made to feel guilty for something that was obviously innocent.

By the time I got home, I was still gripping onto the wheel as if it was the enemy. We were going to have words tonight, that was for sure. I wondered would it always be like this? A constant up and down of agreeing and disagreeing. He was just going to have to get used to not getting his own way all of the time. I pulled up outside the house and Ragnar was there already, waiting for me. I sighed before cutting the engine and begrudgingly got out to deal with him and his face of thunder.

"Ragnar," I said nodding to him as I approached. He crossed a pair of stone pillar arms across his vast chest.

"You should learn your place and know not to anger your Master," he said in his usual hoarse, deep voice that had a strong accent but was amazingly in much better English. I got closer to him and crossed my own arms, but I doubted it had the same effect as he had. Nevertheless, I jutted out my chin and raised my head.

"He is NOT my Master, he is yours! I don't answer to anyone, do you understand?" I said this in my sternest voice, and I was amazed that it didn't shake in the face of this monster Viking. His reply was to just grunt at me which lifted up his shoulders as if he didn't believe me. This managed to enrage me further, but he just smiled to himself as though he knew the trouble I would be in later and moved to let me pass. I couldn't help it and knew it was childish but as I walked past him, I muttered 'Jerk' under my breath. But this just had him laughing heartily as he walked away to do his rounds of the house. I could still hear him once I was inside. Thankfully, Libby and Frank could not.

I tried to hide my frustration from them as I walked in the living room. Justin had gone but Frank and Libby were still talking about him.

"Oh hey Kaz, did you know Justin was here?" Libby asked, but before I could answer, Frank spoke for me.

"Oh yeah, I'll say." He sniggered.

"She was here to witness the boyish charms of my brother. I think he has a soft spot for you Kaz, because he wouldn't shut up about you after you left and wanted to know all about Dom. He also wanted me to ask you if you would take him to the club next weekend as he's coming back to stay for a few days?" Oh no! This was bad! I was about to protest but my helpful sister came to my aid.

"Yeah, sure she will." Did I say helpful?!

"Won't you?" she said giving me the eye as if to say, you bloody well will. So, with an internal wince I caved and nodded, knowing this was definitely going to come back and bite me in the ass and not in one of those nice, sexy ways!

I could just imagine Draven's opinion on this and the idea of having to tell him was making me forget Jack. Hell, he was a piece of cake to explain compared to Justin! If Draven thought me seeing Jack was bad, then this was going to be a disaster, titanic style. Jack was just minor league flirting but Justin, he was a big player and was definitely up there playing with the pros. The problem I faced was not controlling Justin, Oh no,

It was controlling Draven...

My Demon boyfriend.

CHAPTER TEN

NEVER A GOOD TIME

I was ready for work in record time and it was down to switching to autopilot. I was still frustrated with Draven's possessive behaviour, first with having Ragnar following me around for so-called 'safety' and then with Draven eavesdropping at the diner. But despite all this, my main frustration was the opposite to all these things. It was really down to how much I missed him when he wasn't around.

I was like a coffee junkie needed a caffeine fix and when I was without it, I was cranky. I would rather be around him disagreeing and arguing than not at all. I was still stewing over all these little factors when I was in my car driving towards Club Afterlife. It was strange, as though the closer I got to him the happier my body felt. I even turned on the radio and sang along to some cheesy music. I was halfway through Tina Turner's 'Simply the Best' when I arrived.

It was already starting to go dark when I got inside the club and as soon as I walked through the huge oak doors my body filled with a warm positive energy. One look upstairs and it took all my effort not to go running up the stairs into Draven's arms and say to hell with work! I wondered if he felt the same about me...could he sense that I was here?

The Club wasn't busy yet, but I knew that as soon as the band set up, then the club would flood with Goths, Emos and Rockers. We even had a few Cyber Goths. Now they were extreme but way cool in their outfits. With huge material hair and the biggest boots I had ever seen. Some wore coloured gas masks over their mouths, and I had no idea why but for someone dating a Demon, who was I to judge. At the moment the bar area only held a few early gothic birds with Mike and Helen working behind it. I hadn't seen them for what seemed like ages, but it had only been a week.

"Hey guys!" I said hoping for the same happy response.

"Well, look who's back, word had it you quit," Mike said in a friendly tone and my heart calmed after that. Helen waved before reloading the glasswasher.

"Yeah, I kind of did but no one else would have me, so here I am," I said half-joking and Mike smiled. This was a clear indication that none of them knew yet about my new relationship with their boss, along with mine.

"Well, it's good to have you back," Mike said but just then Cassie came from behind the backroom carrying some empty glasses and said,

"Speak for yourself." Well there went my happy vibe down the shitter!

Cassie had never liked me, and the feeling was most definitely mutual. She was a little slut and she didn't try to hide the fact. She hated me for two reasons, the first was that Mike took notice of me and the second was because I had been chosen to work in the VIP area. This had sealed the deal as she would have sold her soul to get up there. I smiled at her to show I was a bigger person than the Gothic Barbie lookalike that was now scowling at me. Mike rolled his eyes as he also wasn't her biggest fan, although you wouldn't have thought so to see Cassie throwing herself all over him like a wasp over a squashed grape. I think everyone felt sorry for him because of this but there was still a bet going as to when he would finally snap and tell her to make like Michael Jackson and "Beat it"!

The evening started to get busy when a band called 'The Shin Splints' started to play, but they were a little heavy for my taste. I was behind the bar serving the swarm of students when the worst thing possible happened. Ok, slight overstatement, but to a girl at work it was never a good time to get your period. I had to grab Helen and ask her for any girly supplies as I had stupidly forgotten to load up my bag. Lucky for me she always had some, so she informed me, making me feel like I had let down my side in the sisterhood.

I ran to the toilet to assess the damage and yep you guessed it, I had leaked. After some cleanup and lots of toilet roll, I was ready to go again until the worse bit about periods hit me…the pain! I usually didn't get bad periods but every once in a blue moon I would get a real doozy that would make me feel like I was giving birth to a baby elephant and tonight was the night for it. I could normally cope if I had pain killers to take, but I had none. Again, I had to ask Helen but on this she was no help. So, I soldiered on, only every now and again I had to stop for cramps.

"Keira, are you alright?" Mike asked as I was taking a minute by the sinks.

"Yeah, just cramps," I said as if I had spent the day running. Ha, me running, I hated to run!

"Kaz, I have five sisters and I know enough about girls to understand the signs. You get yourself off early, it's quietening down now and Jerry is fine with it." I wanted to laugh at this last part, of course Jerry would be fine with it, considering my new status with his boss, I think he would have given me his firstborn if I asked for it!

I nodded while already getting my bag and jacket from the hook in the back room. This was Jerry's office and also where we kept some of the spare bottles of spirits. Jerry was at his desk cashing up one of the tills.

"You off now?" he asked looking up. He was smiling until he saw my face then it dropped. I knew then that I was deathly pale.

"Umm…I hate to say this, but you don't look good, kid." He frowned and looked as though he was going to pick up the phone, but I knew who he'd call and I didn't want the fuss.

"I'm fine, just a bit of a headache but nothing an early night won't cure," I said making him think twice about the phone call idea.

"Yeah, that band was a bit far out tonight." Jerry liked his alternative music, but he was more of an old-fashioned lover of it than some of the new stuff and when tonight's band had mixed techno with screaming, it had all gotten too much for him.

"Well, Mr Draven wants you to go upstairs after your shift," he said trying to look busy and impartial. I nodded before leaving but my body not only hurt, it was now filled with dread. The last thing I wanted was an argument with Draven about today's disapproving Keira act. So, I did something very out of character. I walked out from around the bar and continued until I got to the double doors that led outside to the car park. I knew it was wrong and rude, but I just couldn't stand the rest of the evening pretending everything was fine, when all I wanted to do was curl up in bed and sleep through the pain. Why is it that if you don't take tablets straight away, then it doesn't ever seem to go or even fade? It just felt like a thorn bush was growing inside my uterus!

I saw my car in its usual parking space and got out my keys ready to stick in the lock. I looked around expecting to find Ragnar, but he was nowhere and suddenly I felt a bit vulnerable. This was getting ridiculous. I was getting dependant on having a bodyguard to feel safe. I took a moment to lean my head on the metal frame to cool my burning head before unlocking the door to the driver's side. It had taken me a while to get used to driving this side of the road and for ages I would go to the wrong side of the car which when I looked up, had happened again.

I was losing it again.

Then hands came out from behind me making me jump and scream out. They slammed the door shut before I could get in. I stared at the window, taking a deep breath when I knew it was Draven behind me and as soon as I inhaled in his perfect scent, I felt some of the pain ease. I wouldn't turn around to look at him, because I knew I would meet his temper. I felt him lean down to my ear and his lips touched my skin making me shudder.

"Why are you leaving me, Keira?" His voice was steady, as if he was using a lot of control not to get angry. I took in a deep breath and turned around to face him, hoping that the dim light from the few lamps around wouldn't show my sickly skin. I was expecting to find hard features but as soon as he saw me his eyes went wide, and his hand came to my face. He ran the back of two fingers down my cheek and then looked worried.

"You are very hot and also pale... are you unwell?" Oh great, now I had to lie to the Master of detection.

"I'm fine, it was just hot in there," I said looking down so he couldn't see my eyes lie. I was a dead giveaway when I looked people in the face.

"Then please tell me, why is it you think you can drive home in the passenger seat?" he said in a smug tone and one trying to hide the barest hint of humour.

"I said I am fine."

"Then answer my question, why were you leaving me?" he asked softly making his hand cold and putting it to my burning face. God it felt amazing. I closed my eyes and let his cold skin soothe me before answering him.

"Because I didn't want to argue with you," I said looking him up and down. God, now he looked hot! He was wearing a black pin-striped suit with a waistcoat but with no tie. His hair was styled back, and he had shaved the stubble off, making him look very smart and above all, utterly gorgeous. I bit my lip and tried to concentrate on keeping a steady rhythm in my chest. I expected this would make him angry, so when I saw him smiling at me, I was shocked and confused.

"And that's the reason you were going to go and say nothing?" His voice invaded my mind and I let it because every word out of that delicious mouth was making my pain fade. I felt a bit ashamed that this was what I was going to do and lowered my face without answering but he took my guilty face as confirmation. He bent his knees to look under where my face was hidden.

"I'm sorry," was all I could say, and he pulled me to him for an embrace. I let his strong arms hold me to him and I tried to swallow back the pain I had down below.

"Keira, there is no need for you to apologise. If you would like to leave then you are free to go, but I would like you to have protection at least," he said but I got the impression this was something he didn't want. So I quickly said,

"I don't want to leave you I just didn't want you to get angry at me for today." He frowned down at me, but I just rested my head on his chest because I didn't like it when he frowned.

"Why would I get angry at you? Just because I am used to getting my own way, it doesn't mean I will take it out on you when I don't." So this whole time I had been worrying for nothing! I was such a fool.

"Come back inside and join me, I have missed you." He whispered this last part before his lips were placed to mine for a very passionate kiss. While he devoured my taste, his hands felt for my skin, pulling up my black top at the sides. I could feel the cool night air hit my bare flesh and mixed with the heat from his hands it was like the two elements were fighting against one another. For one long blissful moment I forgot all about the pain.

When he had finished, he picked me up into his arms and walked around the side of the building out of sight from the front entrance. Thank God, because if he had walked back in the club with me like this I would have died with shame.

"Where are you taking me?" I asked, trying to look behind his huge shoulders that were blocking my view.

"Upstairs to the VIP," he said but I knew this wasn't going to be the conventional way. He looked down at me and smirked.

"Close your eyes," he said and he bent his knees slightly before launching us both upwards. Thankfully, this was as I closed my eyes. I felt us land and opened my eyes to find we were on the balcony outside the VIP area.

"Well, that was quicker," I said trying to pretend I hadn't been as terrified as I had. However, he just laughed heartily. He then placed me down gently before taking my hand in his and leading me through the glass doors. He looked happy so I didn't want to burst his bubble by telling him I really wasn't up for sitting at his table. But off we went anyway and as usual, we got every Demon/Angel eye in the place staring at us. Draven never cared about this and led me proudly to my seat. There we were met by the same council members who were always at his table.

Ragnar was standing guard as we approached and for the first time he acknowledged me and grinned after he nodded to Draven. I was shocked considering the last thing I had said to him was calling him a jerk.

They all stood when they saw their Lord of the Manor was back and with an empty seat by his side, he let me sit first. I had a feeling this was a big thing and the ultimate sign of respect.

I sat and in turn everyone nodded to me. Takeshi was back and had fully recovered from Lucius' mental attack. He wore his usual Japanese robe but this one was plain black apart from the purple Dragon that was embroidered on the back. Zagan was next to him and looked as scary as ever. I had never seen him in anything but his long black hood that hid most of his face. His long straight white-blonde hair hung down and I think he was Sophia's bodyguard or something, but I wasn't sure if there wasn't something more going on with them both as they seemed to flirt with each other a lot.

On the other side was Celina and of course the breath-taking Aurora. She was wearing a black dress that was cut across the chest showing a shameful amount of bust, even if she did have her hair down to cover it. I tried not to look but she caught my expression and smiled like an evil cat.

Draven's eyes didn't leave mine though, so I didn't care. Besides, I was in too much pain to worry. Sophia looked happy to see me but as soon as she saw my pale face, she knew something was wrong, but I just shook my head slightly to warn her not to say anything. I was lucky because Draven missed it while speaking with his brother.

Vincent had nodded to me and I think I blushed but didn't think it was visible from my sickly-looking skin. It had been the first time I had seen him since kissing him. I had said sorry that night, but when I got the next opportunity I should really say it again and again, and many times more.

Sophia kept eyeing me carefully, but she was true to my cause and kept quiet. But then a thought hit me. I wondered if she could get me some tablets or at least some more supplies because if I was staying the night, then I really needed more and really…as in really, really, didn't want to have to ask Draven for them. But how was I going to ask without Draven knowing?

"Keira, what would you like to drink?" Draven squeezed my hand bringing me back around from thinking of a way to talk to Sophia.

"Umm, just mineral water please," I replied and Draven looked concerned with my plain choice but when I didn't convey the reasons he allowed Loz, the waitress, to get my drink. I was caught between trying not to show my discomfort and answer the questions I was being asked. Then I decided I would try something new.

"Sophia…?" I tried to call out to her in my mind and concentrate on not shouting it out to everyone in the room instead.

"Sophia, can you hear me, in your head I mean?" I asked again and felt a bit stupid for trying but when she turned and looked at me I was hopeful. She winked when nobody was looking. Great! Well, this was a start. So I continued,

"Okay, right here goes… I am going to try something. Can you talk to me in my mind if I let you in?" I waited for a slight response and when Zagan stopped gazing at her she nodded the tiniest amount. So the next thing was for me to try and let her in but I wasn't quite sure how I even blocked them out to begin with. I let my mind wander and opened it up to my side where Sophia sat but this was beyond useless. So I tried another technique. I relaxed my mind and instead of pushing things out I let everything in, I opened up to the noises around me and listened for anything more. I could hear the hum of conversations behind me and the buzz of humans below. Then some glasses being put down, someone laughed behind us…Then it hit me I could hear Sophia saying over and over

"Hello…HELLO… can you hear me yet?" I had to try not to giggle but it was so funny because it was her voice, but it was in my head! It was so weird and amusing all at the same time.

"Okay, I can hear you, can you still hear me?"

"Yes, I can." I had to bite my lip to stop myself from smiling

but when my water was put in front of me, I had a reason to smile so I did, as I thanked Loz.

"This is so cool!" I said and she just raised her eyes at me before smiling.

"Okay, so what's wrong with you, because no offence but you look like shit?" She even sounded concerned in my mind and this was quite a surreal moment as I had never felt someone else's voice in my head before.

"It's the time of the month and I'm in pain, but don't tell Draven 'cause I don't want him to fuss and worry." She couldn't hide her frown but thankfully nobody was looking at us.

"Keira, he will find out sooner or later and my guessing is it will be the first. You need to explain you are not well and need to go to bed, you look exhausted."

"No, please don't say anything, not yet but I do need your help." She rolled her eyes and then looked down as if to say yes.

"Okay, I'll take that as you will help me. I need painkillers and umm...supplies." She sat there for a moment to think and Draven had noticed that I hadn't spoken to anyone for a few minutes. I felt his hand on my leg and I almost jumped.

"Are you alright?" His voice blew down onto me and because my mind was open it felt different, more powerful like the first time I had heard it. I closed my eyes for a moment and let it help my cramps. Then I closed my mind back up quickly before he figured it out.

"Yes, I'm fine." I gave him a smile that he didn't believe but thankfully, he didn't pursue it. Instead he took my hand and brought it to his lips to kiss. He then continued to hold it in front of him with mine engulfed in both of his hands which was such a sweet gesture I couldn't help my blush. I noticed Aurora's eyes bulge slightly at the gesture and I shamefully allowed myself a smug smile to creep across my lips. Meanwhile Sophia must have come up with something because she leant over to me and said,

"Oh Keira, you have to see this new dress of mine it is simply divine. It is made from Italian silk and has a cut across the... oh well, it would be better if I just showed you. Brother, you don't mind if I borrow Keira for a moment, do you?" It wasn't really a question but more of a statement as she had already stood and was taking my arm. Zagan stood also but she turned to him and a look was all it took for him to get the message.

"What are you up to, Sophia?" Draven said in an unhappy tone.

"Just girl stuff, which is none of your business," she said firmly enough to make Draven let go of my hand which he kissed again before doing so. Then I was quickly being dragged away by Sophia. She looked lovely in her coral halter neck dress that was made from a material that floated around her doll-like frame. It swayed as she walked, and it was cut short showing off her beautiful legs that looked like they belonged on a shaving advert.

She linked my arm in hers and walked me through the double doors that led into their vast home. As soon as the doors closed, I let out a moan and bent down to try and relieve the growing pain.

"Oh dear, you don't have much luck, do you?" Sophia rubbed my back and made large circles with her palm. I stayed like that for a minute before standing back up straight.

"Better?" was all she said, and I nodded.

"Thank you." She shrugged her shoulders and we carried on down the grand hallway. At the end was Draven's bedchamber and Sophia opened the door for me. Once inside I almost collapsed on the couch.

"I will be back with what you need, do you have a preference?" I told her what I needed, and she was out of the door before I could blink. I was finally glad be to be alone and in a horizontal position. I gripped at my stomach hoping this would somehow help but the pain just got worse because I couldn't relax. By the time Sophia came back I was close to agony. She had some clothes and bless her, some clean underwear.

"Right take these and then sort yourself out, but you had better be quick because it won't take long for my brother to get restless." I knew what she meant. When it came to me doing things without him, he was very suspicious. I swallowed the pills she gave me and went into the bathroom. Once I was finished having the quickest shower in history, I changed into the comfortable black gym pants and new underwear that still held a label and price tag…Wow $150 for a pair of knickers! That was insanity.

I walked back out expecting to see just Sophia, but I froze when I saw that Draven was now stood next to her with his arms folded. Sophia looked as though she was trying very hard not to giggle at my situation, but I just tried to act cool. Ok, so me and the word cool didn't really mesh well but it didn't mean I couldn't try.

"Why have you changed?" Draven was trying not to be demanding but it clearly took work. He was now looking even better as he had taken off his suit jacket and just had on a crisp white shirt under his waistcoat. His legs looked even longer in his well-pressed trousers and all I wanted to do was to expose what was underneath them.

"Well, I will leave you both. Keira, shopping tomorrow," she said and I now knew my price for asking her help, she was going to do the whole dress up the life-size human doll thing…again!

"Shopping?"

"Yeah you know, the places people go to buy clothes and stuff and from what I hear someone keeps ripping your clothes off, so it is only right that he should get you some new to replace the ones in pieces." She smiled and it was one of those pure bad to the bone grins that made me want to shudder. Draven shot her a look.

"Thank you, Sophia, you really don't understand the concept of prudence, do you?" he said in an unimpressed way.

"Glad I could help," she said before leaving. I was still processing what she had said and wanted to know how the hell she knew about my ripped clothes! I let out a sigh and walked over to the bed while Draven stood watching me as if I had just done the crazy chicken dance. I was just about to step up to the bed when I felt Draven's arms around me preventing me from going any further.

"Is there something wrong, what did Sophia show you?" Man can anyone say paranoia?!

"You're getting paranoid Draven, she just showed me this new dress and then asked me if I would go shopping with her tomorrow." The idea made me wince. I didn't love shopping and knowing that Sophia would make a big fuss over the whole expedition didn't help.

"And now?" he asked, running his hand down my back,

making it respond with pleasure. If it hadn't been bad timing, then I would have turned around and jumped on him. So it pained me to say,

"I'm just tired, that's all." As soon as I said this, he had me in his arms and placed me in bed as if the last few steps would have been too much. What he didn't realise was this just made me want him more.

"Then rest, so I can wear you out again." His lips curved into a sexy grin and he kissed me lightly before making the curtains around the bed move, encasing the frame in thick material. Of course, he didn't have to touch them to do this.

"Are you not joining me?" I said not being able to keep the disappointment from my voice. This obviously made him happy. He loved it when I was needy.

"Not yet but soon, now sleep," he ordered before pulling the last curtain across. Well, at least I had got away without him knowing why I was so tired. Maybe my acting skills were getting more convincing.

I lay there and let sleep take over the throbbing hurt in my belly knowing it wouldn't be long before Draven would want to know why I didn't want to make love to him and it pained me to know this was the first day we hadn't had sex. I guess I was subconsciously worried that he wouldn't feel the same about me. It wasn't like he was used to human women problems and this was a gross one. I was embarrassed beyond belief and this was one part about being human that I didn't want to share with my Demon Angel boyfriend.

Only a week.

CHAPTER ELEVEN

NO MORE EXCUSES

I knew I was dreaming but still it carried on. Normally with my dreams I would wake as soon as I realised what was happening but with this one it was bizarre and definitely different. Almost like someone was reaching out and giving me a taste of what I needed to see.

I was outside the Library in town, one that was closest to the campus. It was a sunny day and I could feel the heat on my skin causing my vision to turn blotchy when I looked up at the sun. I could almost hear and sense I was there for a reason, so I went inside. As soon as I thought it, I didn't even need to open any doors, I was right there by the information desk.

There I saw a man walk towards me and I knew it to be George, Frank's uncle. I don't know how I knew this, as I had never seen a picture of him but there he was, bounding his long legs this way. He was a man in his late sixties, but it was obvious that he kept himself in good shape as he hadn't lost his fireman's fitness. He had a full head of silver hair that caught the light in a shimmer as he walked past the tall windows of the library. As he got closer, I could see almond shaped eyes of smoky grey and he had laughter lines around strong features. This was clearly a man who had found lots of happiness in his life and those lines told his story.

I lifted my hand up and waved but even though he was staring in my direction he didn't react. It was as if I wasn't even here and when I looked down at myself and saw nothing, I knew why. I wasn't there to be seen. I was there to see.

I turned to face the woman behind the desk and knew it was Yvonne Dubeck, just as I had known it was George, only this time gaining a bitter taste in my mouth. It was a bit like being at a play and knowing who all the characters were without ever meeting the cast.

Yvonne Dubeck was a small framed, thin woman with half-moon glasses resting on her long beak like nose and she wore her hair pulled back into a tight bun. She was pale and her mousey coloured hair did nothing for the grey strands showing through. She wore a tight pencil skirt that looked hard to walk in and a plum coloured shirt with a thin bow attached around the neck in the same material. She wasn't much to look at, but something happened as soon as she caught sight of George.

Her eyes widened and started to glow around the edges for a split second. She looked excited and when he came to stand right in front of her she took off her glasses and her face softened, changing her appearance to one more striking. George couldn't find the words at first as her powers over him took effect. I could almost make out the negative energy she was extracting from him. She was stalling for more time with him as he asked where the World War Two books were. Of course, she offered to show him and off they walked.

I wanted to slap her away from him and somehow change the past, but it was useless, I was only there to observe. I tried to follow but couldn't move, so I shouted out in protest but that's when the scenery started to disintegrate. It was almost as if someone had put a match to a stretch of film that was playing out this horrifying start to the past. I closed my eyes tight and shook my head, wondering if in my sleep I was doing the same thing back in Draven's bed. This thought made me open them quickly, praying I would find myself back there. But even though I did find myself back on more familiar ground, it wasn't the safety I was looking for. I was back at Libby and Frank's house.

I was in my room and it was dark. I could just make out my long mirror but when I looked for my reflection to be staring back at me, there was nothing. I was stood by my desk which now was a set of old pine drawers. I noticed that my bed was missing and there was an old rocking chair in its place which was now in the den.

In the chair sat George with the lights off and he was looking into a telescope. I walked over to see what he was looking at and he didn't even stir as I approached. I looked up at a clear night sky covered in a blanket of stars. But this wasn't why I was there. I heard a noise that obviously George couldn't. It was a chanting I couldn't understand, but I knew who it came from. I walked over to the window still taking care that George couldn't feel me as I was now stood next to him. I looked down into the yard and directly below the window was Yvonne Dubeck, stood there no longer looking very plain.

She was naked except for a long black cloak around her shoulders with the hood raised. Her hair was down and wild, blowing around in the windy night's breeze. Her eyes glowed like the full moon above, white and pearly. Her nails grew impossibly long until they curled round back into her own hands. I felt revolted at the sight when they pierced the skin like razor-tipped arrows and she howled in pain or pleasure, I couldn't tell.

Blood spurted into the air from the contact and looked like a black fountain glistening under an evil moon. I felt as if I would soon lose my stomach contents but when I thought it couldn't get any worse, I felt the bile rise at the next stage of Yvonne's Demon phase. Her chanting increased in volume and each time the verbal drum would sound, I would see something else in her change. She moved her now looped nails together and as they interlocked, a symbol appeared like planets aligning. It was almost as if she was calling forth a greater power, sucking it in from the very earth and channelling it into the centre of her nails.

With each joint breath we took the power would grow brighter and stronger, increasing with every foreign word that passed her spit covered lips. She was now losing liquid out of every orifice and I wrinkled my nose as if I could scent the rancid smell of rotting flesh mixed with bleach. Her skin looked like plastic that was being stretched to the point before breaking, the blood behind bubbling just beyond the surface, giving her body a demonic glow.

Then something happened. The ball of energy had reached its sizable limit causing it to explode, making the room fill with a blinding light as though the house had created its own blue sun. George fell backwards off his chair and began to scramble his body backwards like a crab seeking safety into the corner of the room. As before, I couldn't move and wanted desperately to run to him to comfort the shaking man.

I looked up to a clicking noise, sounding as though a giant cricket was right outside. It started getting louder before showing its ugly self. It was Yvonne, who had now floated up to the window and with her hands raised up it made her head look bigger. Then the image kept changing from the truth, to what George was seeing. Where I could see Yvonne in her Demon form, he was watching himself about to be abducted by an Alien figure coming through the window.

He was screaming and when the clicking noise turned into a deafening high-pitched scream, he placed his frightened hands over his ears. I had terrified tears streaming down my face. Then the light disappeared, and it was obvious the feeding had begun. By this time George was in a state that was so beyond fear, he was no longer aware of anything else around him. Yvonne walked over to him and I saw first-hand a Demon feeding from a human.

It was like nothing I had ever seen before and my breath caught as a wave of fine blue mist flowed out of every pore in his body. It clearly didn't hurt as he wasn't even aware of what was happening. She placed a hand on him gently and it looked as though she had just had an orgasm. She let out a long shuddering moan and then touched her naked body with her hands that were now back to normal.

After that, the rest of her Demon side had retreated back to the depths of Hell and the harmless looking Librarian had returned. When she was finished, she kissed him on the head like you would when calming a whimpering child before turning to find me in her way at the window. I don't know how I had moved, but I knew it symbolised my need to stop her. This time she saw me as my body became whole again ready for the fight.

"Mmm... Electus, I bet you taste good." ("Chosen" in Latin) Her voice was like ice and I couldn't do anything but feel my skin prickle, feeling the aftermath from her feed. My skin wasn't the only thing in the room to grow cold. The moon came out filling the room with a natural blue light and I looked up to see the walls cracking as they had now turned to black ice. The floor was also being infested by this Demon and the freezing cold travelled up my legs after leaving the cracking floorboards.

I wanted to cry out, but nothing came. The Demon Yvonne got closer and the ice melted under her steps but refroze when she left each space. Her nails grew once more but unlike last time, they forged together at her middle finger into one long, flat blade. Before I knew what was happening, she rushed at me. I tried in vain to move but my legs were frozen to the floorboards below. Then it all happened in the blink of an eye, she plunged the blade into my gut making me bend over it and spit out blood over her naked body. I looked up to see her face change into that of Layla and I screamed out in both pain and cruel, unrelenting fear!

I shot upwards, gripping the pain in my lower stomach. It took me a while to realise I was back in bed with Draven. He had his arms wrapped tightly around me, but I couldn't hear what he was saying because there was still a ringing in my ears from the noise Yvonne had been making. I pushed it out of my head until my senses came back into focus. I was panting and Draven rubbed my back like Sophia had done earlier.

"That was a bad one," Draven said bringing me back even more to the room I was in. I nodded but then let out a moan as my period pains had come back with a vengeance. Draven noticed me grip at my stomach, so he whipped back the covers before I could stop him. The curtains flew back, and light-filled the room.

"No, don't!" I said through the pain, but he wasn't listening to me. He put his hand to the wet patch below me and lifted it to the light. My blood was on his hands…literally. I wanted to cry! I saw his face go pale before worry replaced it.

"Keira, what happened?!" he shouted, clearly worried and trying in vain to control his reaction.

"Oh no… no, no, no!" I said before burying my face in my hands. I could feel the tears wet my skin and then another almighty cramp brought me round.

"Keira, tell me?" His voice was now pleading.

"I'm fine, it's nothing…"

"Keira, you are bleeding it's not nothing! Now tell me…"

"I'm so sorry you had to see this." I interrupted feeling so embarrassed, it was worse than any pain my uterus was causing me.

"Keira, will you just…oh, now I see," he said as the bloody penny dropped, no pun intended. He relaxed instantly now he knew I was in no danger. He had already produced a cloth to wipe his hand clean before pulling me into him.

"Keira, do not be sorry, I just wished you would have told me. I knew something was wrong, but I never expected…"

"What? It to be so gross?!" I said bitterly,

"No! For it to be so, so… *human*," he finished softly before kissing me on my forehead.

"Do not be embarrassed, Keira, it is only natural. Are you in a lot of pain?" He was soothing back my hair off my wet face and when I jerked from the pain, he froze.

"I'll take that as a yes." He got up from the bed and even in this situation I still gasped at the sight of his amazing naked body on full view. He came back with some tablets and water. I took them and he knelt down to wipe the tears from my cheeks. I was about to apologise again but he put his finger to my lips.

"Ssshh don't do that," he said before kissing me, no doubt tasting the tears there.

"Right, well let's get you sorted," he said and was about to pick me up, but I protested.

"Please, I am so ashamed already, I can do it," I said getting up and making sure to hide my behind! He didn't like me getting up on my own but come on it was only a stupid period. I was about to look back at the mess I'd made of the sheets but before I could, Draven stopped me. Then a few seconds later he let me look. The sheets were clear and like brand new.

"You're too good to me, thank you," I said thinking that I had the most caring boyfriend in this world and the next. He really was so sweet with me, that it kind of made me want to cry again but thankfully I didn't. At least now I knew why I had been so sensitive lately.

"I fear I am not good enough, if I were then I would have noticed this sooner. Why didn't you tell me?" He looked hurt that I hadn't mentioned this to him, and I really didn't want to tell him why, but I couldn't see a way around it.

"Don't get mad, ok?" This made him raise his eyebrows with curiosity.

"I thought you wouldn't like me as much, you know, because we can't have sex." As soon as I said it, I felt a guilty lump form in my throat. Now he looked really hurt.

"Is that what you think of me, that sex is the only thing that I am attracted to?" He looked off to the side like the sight of me hurt before confirming it with,

"Oh, Keira, how could you?" He then moved away from me and I couldn't blame him, if it had been the other way around, I would have been beyond angry. God how stupid could I have been!

"You said you wouldn't get mad," I said quietly not knowing how else to fix this.

"Did I?" he asked sarcastically as we both knew he didn't.

"Look, I'm stupid and way too oversensitive and I let my insecurities get the better of me because of it, I know this, but I am also, so, so sorry." I was close to pleading.

"Sensitive, yes, but stupid no...Never!" He was coming back around, and I almost wanted to laugh as I realised I had never argued with anyone in the nude. I went up to him and raised his face up to mine as he was sat on the couch looking down.

"Please forgive me, I get oversensitive when it's the time of the...well, you know, and it plays on my insecurities. And when I still find it hard to fully understand what it is you see in me, all those insecurities get the better of me and make me say and think bad things." This was turning out to be the worst sorry in history but in a crazy way it seemed to be working. Until I added the icing to an already ruined cake and started trying to swallow over and over, as I knew what was coming next! Oh God, please No!

I ran from the room and nearly ripped the door off to get to the bathroom fast enough. There I threw up in the most expensive toilet I had ever used. I was saying a private prayer to God, asking for Draven not to hear me but of course I was too late. It was worse than him hearing me throw up, he was now seeing me throw up!

His hands came to my face and pulled back my hair as if he had read a manual on attending to sick girlfriends. Once he had it all, he held it tight with one hand and with his other he soothed my back.

"Please don't watch," I said before more came retching up. The pain was nothing compared to my new shame.

"Ssshh, don't talk." He wouldn't listen to me and he just stayed with me until I was finished and the contents of my stomach were cleared out. He handed me a tissue and I blew my nose and cleaned myself.

"Thank you, but I think I have it from here," I said looking down and he knew what I meant, so he gave me some privacy. Once I had finished sorting myself out and washing the trousers and underwear that had been given to me, I wrapped a towel around myself and went back out. Draven passed me some more comfy pants to put on and this time these were my own. He didn't say a word as he passed me some water and more tablets as the others didn't have much chance to work.

"Better?" he asked when I downed all the water to the last drop. I nodded before walking up to him and hugging him around the waist like he was a lifeline. He held me back and I felt him sigh.

"Did I say I was sorry?" I said again, hoping this would work but when I looked up, he didn't look very mad at me.

"Yes, you did and although it is nice, it is also unnecessary." He went to kiss me, and I turned my head. I had brushed my teeth like a woman possessed but I still didn't want him kissing me just in case.

"Although, when you do that, it doesn't help in the forgiving process," he said teasing me, but he knew why I did it. I held his hand and pulled him to the bed where he lifted me over the steps and into the bed like I was child that needed a boost. We snuggled down into bed and the lights morphed into a gentle glow. I knew this meant he wanted to talk.

"Are you still in pain?" He was obsessed whether or not I was still hurting, bless him.

"Not a lot," I lied.

"I wish I could take it away but unfortunately, I cannot heal what is not broken." This made sense as it was nature, so he kindly reminded me.

"But maybe I could still help." He lifted back the covers and lifted my top exposing my bare stomach.

"Hot or cold?" he asked, showing me his hand.

"Uh...hot?" He nodded and placed a very warm hand across my skin and pulled down my trousers exposing more of the area where I hurt. The heat helped more than I could have imagined. I relaxed back and let his warm tingling hand make my pain fade.

"Is this helping?" he asked after I was silent for a while.

"Oh yes, better than any painkiller," I said smiling to prove just how efficient it had been.

"Good," he said into my hair.

"You're like a hot water bottle without having to wait for the kettle to boil." He let out a deep and rough laugh and this brought a smile to my pale face.

"What did you dream about?" His question caught me off guard and I stiffened up in his hold. I knew I couldn't get away with passing it off as nothing, but I really didn't want him worrying anymore about me. Well, the one saving grace was at least I hadn't dreamt of Lucius. When I didn't answer he took my reaction for what it was and rested his lips at my ear.

"Tell me," he whispered but this made my stomach flutter and not from pain. His scent always did crazy things to my body and mind, making me want to surrender. I sighed and looked up at the

carved roof of the bed. Then I explained my dream to him but leaving out the details was hard to do when he kept asking questions. I could feel him grip the covers and heard a ripping sound when I told him of when she stabbed me.

"Draven! You promised you wouldn't overreact." He let go of the covers, making the material heal itself. When it was finished weaving itself back together you couldn't even tell where he had torn it. I looked round to face him and noticed he was deep in thought. I took a moment to study his features that were harder than I was used to. He was clearly not happy that I was being made to witness these things but come on, it had been far worse when I was seven. And then, of course, I didn't have my own delicious protector to wake up to, even if I had bled on his fancy bed.

"Were you frightened?" His voice was trying to stay neutral, but it sounded strained.

"Yes, but mostly I just wanted something big and pointed to whack her with! I wanted to help George." This brought him back to being my less serious Draven. He kissed my cheeks while he was still grinning to himself. It was probably the thought of me swinging a big sword like Zena the warrior princess but knowing my luck I would get it high above my head and then fall backwards with the weight.

"You would make a fierce enemy to have. I would not like to get on the wrong side of you." Ok, so now he was most definitely teasing me

"You have been on the wrong side of me and you survived."

"Barely," he mouthed over my skin before kissing me and he held my face in his unbreakable hold so I couldn't pull away. Of course, after about three seconds I didn't try to any longer. His hands moved around to my neck and down my back making my body cry out for more. Then my new situation must have dawned on him as his hands released me.

"How long does this last for?" he asked in a hoarse voice as he was clearly desperate to have my body in more than just an embrace.

"Umm, usually a week," I said in a hopeless tone. How would I last the night, let alone the week! Now this was painful.

"I could sleep at home if it would make things easier." I didn't really want to do this, but I didn't want to make this harder on him. But this wasn't the right thing to say as he let out a low growl and his face turned stern.

"Keira... do you think I only get pleasure from your body? It pains me to be away from you and this is not just down to what your body does to me," he scolded and I blushed but for once I hoped it turned my skin a healthier colour.

"It is your mind and heart that enslaved me, your body is just the bonus I get along with possessing you...and what a body it is." His hands ran up my sides making me inhale deeply. He wasn't the only one finding this excruciating.

"But if you..." He cut me off with another kiss and I was starting to think this was his favourite way of shutting me up.

"Enough of this talk of leaving me. You will not! Understand?" Ok, this was one order I was happy to comply with. I nodded, smiling at his domination over me and I kind of relished in it.

Once he was happy that the idea was firmly out of my mind, he pulled me closer to him after asking me if I was comfortable. I let my head rest on his chest while he played with my hair. The feeling was making my lids heavy and I yawned making him chuckle. He made the lights die and I knew that the sound of his strong heartbeat would soon have me fast asleep in the only place on earth I wanted to be. In his arms...

Forever.

CHAPTER TWELVE

A LONG WAIT

When I woke, I saw the morning light filter through the curtain cracks. I moved slightly and then realised Draven and I hadn't moved all night from the position we had fallen asleep in. I could tell he was still asleep because his breathing was steady and light.

I shifted slowly so I could see his face, but he was looking the other way. His arm was still securely around me as if he had tried to protect me from any more nightmares. I knew I needed to get up for obvious reasons, but that didn't mean I wanted to. I could have lazed there all day listening to his calm breathing.

I moved slowly trying to slide down under his hold, but his arm weighed a tonne. They were solid muscle, which rippled with unspeakable strength starting from his impressive shoulders to bulging biceps, down his corded forearms and then on to thick wrists and strong thick fingers that he had currently curled around my hip. Yep, one blow from that bad boy and you wouldn't be getting up again that was for sure!

I managed to scoot out without waking him and I gently put my warm feet to the cold slate floor. Once my skin was used to the shock, I got up and straightened my top that had twisted. I looked

145

back as I heard the bed shift but thankfully, he had just rolled over to his side. He was still asleep, so I tiptoed into the bathroom and after finishing my morning routine I walked further into the vast room.

At the end was a massive stone arch that was mirrored by a window letting in the morning flooding the room with light. Through the arch was a raised bath which had steps up into it like Draven's bed did. I walked closer and the bath was the biggest I had ever seen. Even bigger than Sophia's, which I had once been lucky enough to take a dip in. The cramps started telling me to ease the pain by taking a little innocent swim in it. I looked back at the door as though I was about to do something naughty but to Hell with it. I'm sure he wouldn't mind. So I bent over to where I thought the water came out but there was nothing. No tap, no spout, no hole...nothing.

I bent further in leaning over the rim, realising it was made from a block of carved stone. Then I had a thought. His shower was on a motion sensor so maybe this one was too. I waved my arm about, thinking how glad I was that I doing this alone as I felt like an idiot waving at a wall. But it worked. The stone wall to the side started to move and one block came out halfway causing the water to quickly start gushing from behind it. It poured into the stone pool below and I looked about for anything to add to the water. I noticed that there was a stone shelf hidden to one side and found glass bottles filled with luscious smells. I pulled the top off one and poured it in then bingo, the clear water started to create bubbles.

I stripped off my clothes and stepped in letting my hair down as I went. The temperature was perfect, and I sighed as the water devoured my skin. I dipped my head fully under and smiled as I came back up for air. I pushed the drips off my face and pushed my hair back. Then I stretched out and didn't once come into contact with the sides as you could have easily fitted ten people in there. I was about to close my eyes and rest my head back when I noticed the window.

I pulled myself over to the other side and an amazing view

opened up before me. The window was ceiling to floor and was as wide as the bath. The green sea of the mountains and national park painted the Earth's ground and a cloudless blue topaz filled the sky above. If I had the supplies before me, I would have painted it. I lay on my front and folded my arms to rest on the side so I could gaze out at this world's taste of perfection.

"Just beautiful," I whispered out loud before dipping my head back once more, only when I came back up, I was no longer alone.

"I must agree." Draven's voice sounded even more powerful as it echoed in the marble room. He was stood back, leaning on one of the stone pillars casually watching me and I could feel my skin burning from embarrassment. It was as though I had been caught with my hand in a cookie jar.

"Uh…how long have you been there?" I asked, dipping further under the water to hide my modesty. This action created a bad boy grin to break out on his lips.

"A while," he said knowing this would get more of a pink-cheeked reaction. Of course, when it did, his grin widened. He was dressed, unlike me and his long denim legs strolled over to the edge of the bath. I was still on the other side and he cocked his head back slightly to motion for me to come to him. When I didn't move, he frowned at my lack of co-operation.

"Come here," he ordered but again I wouldn't, and I knew teasing him wasn't a good idea seeing as I couldn't really give myself to him fully. But he replaced his frown with cunning eyes and wicked lips. Then he dipped one finger in the water swirling it around in circles and I jumped when it started to go cold.

"Okay, ok!" I said before giving in to him in record time. He sat on the steps next to the bath and dunked his arms in as I got nearer, pulling me the rest of the way. But not before he made the water turn back to its usual relaxing temperature.

"That was cruel!"

"I would call it more of a 'tactical decision'. And besides what can you expect when you look like this?" His mouth found my wet shoulder and he tasted the water off my skin. I closed my eyes with pleasure when his mouth moved closer to the curvature of my neck. Then I could no longer think when his hand expertly found the inside of my leg and moved it upwards, once there I let out a moan when he hit his mark. I quickly shifted before anything more happened and he groaned while my neck was still in his mouth.

"Draven, we can't, remember," I said barely legible. The feeling was burning the lower part of my body making me want him to take me so badly I couldn't breathe. His bite left my wet flesh and he looked up at me, although for a moment I thought he would do it anyway because his eyes were now his Demon purple. It was frightening. He stood up and I thought he was going to leave.

"Please don't go." This made him lose his Demon side and he smiled down at me.

"I am not going anywhere."

"Then what are you doing?" My question was quickly answered as he yanked off his t-shirt displaying a perfect male torso overflowing with muscles upon muscles. He continued getting naked and started to unbutton his jeans removing them from toned olive skin. This then made it even harder for me to control my burning urge to have him inside me.

"I am joining you of course, you're in my bath remember?" He added in a mischievous tone. I moved out of the way putting some safe distance between us. However, once he was in his hands searched for my ankles and when he found them, he pulled me into him. I quickly slid right into his body as if we were magnets and he held me in an iron hold so I wouldn't leave him again. I tried to worm my way out from him, but it was useless.

"Don't struggle," he whispered into my wet hair.

"But we can't do this," I said in vain.

"Keira, I just want to feel, nothing more. Let me feel you, all of you," he asked before he repositioned me so my back was against his chest and once there his expert fingers found me. I let out a moan and tensed in his arms. He moved very slowly and delicately over my bundle of nerves in a near maddening circular motion. He continued to move to his own rhythm and what a rhythm it was! My mind went cloudy and my breathing got heavy with each motion he made. He was just so skilled in the art, it was almost as if he could feel everything I felt and to increase the pleasure he would move it to how he also liked it.

"Do you want me to stop?" he asked in husky tones.

"No... please, ...oh please don't," I begged as I was close to ecstasy. I buried my head to the side into his chest and his other hand cupped my exposed, heaving breast before plucking at the hard nipple.

It felt as though my eyes were rolling back as the intensity increased and with every moan I let out I could feel his own pleasure increase behind me. His length was getting harder and bigger like a force of its own. So, I pressed back on it as I was still in between his legs with my back against his front.

I reached my arms up and around his neck, jutting my breast more firmly into his large palm. Once in this position I started to push back on him again and his fingers moved faster in return. He was kissing my neck and he licked up to my ear, before he turned it into nipping at my flesh. He took care not to bite too hard, but I could tell it was difficult for him. I bent my head to one side to allow him access but when he wouldn't do it, I lowered one hand from behind his back and found his manhood. It was actually the first time I had touched it and I quickly realised why it sometimes was hard to take. He was huge!

He groaned louder as my fingers gripped around his length and I got the reaction I wanted as he bit down into my flesh making me come instantly. I screamed out and jerked, causing the water to form little waves. He held me down and pulled me closer. My hand started to move quicker, harder and more determined as he sucked on my neck at the holes he had made there, each pull more demanding than the one before it. His release came quickly after and I felt the heat of it burst over my hand through the water.

We both seemed to jerk against each other in sync until our riding wave became a calm bob in the water. I looked down and saw little droplets of my blood from my neck disperse in the bathwater. Then he licked the puncture marks, sealing them closed. My body relaxed back into his and he held my head to him by encasing his hand at the column of the front of my neck until my breathing came back to its normal rhythm.

"Wow, that was… amazing," I said and then let out a satisfied sigh.

"Yes, I must agree and also a first," he said completely sated. I turned to look at him and when I saw him with wet hair, I wanted to do it all over again. I put my hands on his face and moved them back through his hair and down to his neck before kissing him. He was surprised by this gesture, as he didn't respond until my kiss got deeper and more intense. When I stopped, I didn't pull back from him. I just held my lips over his and licked the seam before finding his neck.

He seemed shocked by my enthusiasm, but he must have found it a massive turn on because he moaned letting out more air with his heavy breathing. Then out of nowhere his hands grabbed my wrists and he restrained them behind my back. I thought I had done something wrong until I saw his face. He had his eyes closed while he spoke.

"I don't think you should do that again while I can't have you fully. I was close to losing control and I don't think I could have stopped. But when we can, then what you just did would please me greatly." He said all this as if it was a strain and I smiled that I could do that to him. Man oh man, why did I have to be on!

"So, when you said this was a first, what did you mean?" I asked once I had given him a minute.

"I meant, I have never found pleasure this way, without sex that is." If his face hadn't been so serious, I would have laughed. No way!

"You mean…you never…you know?" I waved my hand around like this would help.

"Keira, use words, my love." He was mocking me as he actually knew what I meant but he just wanted to see me go red again. I was sure of it.

"What I mean is, you never found release without intercourse?" As soon as it was out Draven cracked up laughing to a point where he couldn't find words. I folded my arms across my chest and moved to the other side. He tried to control it, but he did a lousy job.

"Keira, come back here, I am sorry." He didn't look very sorry, so I shrugged and dipped my head back to get my hair wet ready for washing.

"I find it incredibly sexy when you do that" He was trying to butter me up, but I wasn't taking him on. I reached for the shampoo, but he got there first. When I tried to retrieve it, he simply held it higher above my head.

"Give it back," I ordered but he smiled down at me making me melt.

"Have you forgiven me?" he said making it impossible to stay mad at him.

"I don't know, say it again." I was now teasing him, but he obeyed by lowering the bottle and mouthing the words 'I'm sorry' over my lips.

We stayed in the bath for what seemed like ages as we started to play around splashing each other like teenagers and then he refused to let me wash my own hair. The problem with this of course was the feeling it created below. His large hands circling my head and neck was just heavenly and I tried very hard not to think of the bulge behind me that just never seemed to go down the entire time. Then it took me even longer to get out of the bath because he kept pulling me back in.

Finally, when I got out, he was there before me holding a big black fluffy towel to wrap me in. He rubbed me down before using the same towel on himself. He explained he did this as he liked the scent of me on his skin. I bit my lip at the compliment.

He handed me a black robe that was softer than anything I had ever felt before. I had no idea what material it was, but I just hoped it wasn't an animal. He allowed me time alone to change some things after yet another trip to his expensive toilet and when I went back into the bedroom there was food waiting for us, which made my stomach very happy.

We spent the morning together on the same couch, kissing, laughing, touching each other everywhere but managing to control ourselves enough not to go too far. He watched me eat all wide-eyed like a jungle cat. I never understood why he found this so fascinating. It made me feel a bit like a huge science project. He would bombard me with questions ranging on anything from my childhood to my favourite artists. Then it got more serious.

"And past boyfriends?" I gulped my tea. He had never wanted to know about this before.

"Why do you ask?" I was hoping he would reconsider his line of questioning. Of course, I'd be wrong.

"I am curious."

"About what, who I dated?" He just nodded and then added,

"Among other things." I loved the way he spoke, so fluid and precise but sometimes just sitting with him would transport me back to a time where he should be wearing a top hat and me a pretty bonnet. I cleared my throat to indicate I was ready for the first line of questions but the naughty grin on his face already told me what he was going to ask.

"How old were you when you lost your virginity?" It was so matter of fact that I laughed, making him frown. Well, it was his turn to be laughed at. If it had been me, I would have asked in a roundabout way, saying 'you know…the thing' or words like 'popped cherry' but there was none of that and Draven never minced his words. He was always straight to the point and sex was clearly no exception.

"I was seventeen," I said waiting for his reaction. He raised his eyebrows and it was clear he had not expected as much.

"What? Did you think I would have only lost it when I was twenty-one?" I had to laugh.

"No, don't forget Keira I have lived a long time and throughout history human girls have been a lot younger than that when they were taken."

"Taken?"

"Given." He corrected himself and then shrugged his shoulders, a gesture you hardly saw from Draven.

"Poor girls." My heart went out to them, young and frightened.

"It was expected Keira, they knew nothing of choice, not like today." He looked uncomfortable knowing this part of my past, but he continued to ask.

"Who was the boy?" This was Draven's way of degrading my former love partner no doubt.

"His name was Johnny Carlson and he was my first boyfriend."

"Did he... force himself upon you?" He had his hands balled into fists which he was trying to keep out of sight by his thighs.

"No, of course not! If anything, it was my idea." Now this shocked him.

"Why?"

"And why not? Teenage girls get strong sexual urges just as boys do. Plus, it was kind of fuelled by alcohol." This made him relax slightly.

"Can I ask, why are you asking questions you don't want to hear the answers to?" I asked getting up from the couch to stand over him.

"Because I want to know everything even if I can't change the past." He looked stern at the thought of not having that particular power.

"And what would you have changed exactly?" I smiled at the thought of meeting Draven years ago being so young and terrified, to the point it excited me.

"I would have been your first." Mmm, well I could have seen that going better than my first time...for starters I would have remembered it.

"And don't you think that would have been a bit weird considering the age difference." This made him roll his eyes at me.

"Keira, of course I would have waited for you to have come of age. I don't find anything attractive about an undeveloped body. I like my women to look like women." He quickly stood in front of me as he said this and began to run the back of his fingers over my curvy chest and then back up to my neck. I looked up at him feeling even smaller with bare feet.

"And do you like your women little?" I said smiling, thinking about Aurora who had legs longer than my entire body! Ok, a bit of an exaggeration there but you get my drift, she was bloody tall.

"Yes, most definitely," he purred before carrying on.

"Some of the most expensive and exquisite gifts on the planet come in small packages." This was sweet but come on, you never saw short models on the runway!

"Like what?" I challenged.

"Diamonds, for one." Ok, so he had me there. I shook my head at him.

"I can hardly be compared to a diamond, Draven."

"I agree, there is nothing on this planet I can compare you to, there is nothing as beautiful or breath-taking, but I would have very much liked to have given you the Hope Diamond, but alas it is no longer in my possession." I couldn't speak, it was a combination of things. Being that he thought me as being that beautiful or that he once owned the Hope Diamond!

"That is the one Marie Antoinette and Louis XVI owned, right? Only then it was called the French Blue." A proud smiled crossed his lips before laying them on mine.

"Clever girl, you are right and know your history well, which makes me wonder if your interest in the past is not due to more supernatural reasons." He liked the idea, I could tell.

"You mean for you?" I poked him in the ribs and he responded by tickling me back but when I tried to squirm away he grabbed my waist and flung me to the bed, pinning me down and proceeded to make me giggle with what his other hand was doing. We were both laughing and didn't hear when Sophia entered, or at least, I didn't.

"Well, that's a funny noise you're creating from Keira." Sophia of course was referring to my snorting like an excited pig.

"Thank you for knocking, Sophia," Draven said dryly.

"I did but you just couldn't hear it over the noise." Again, she meant my snorting. Draven lifted me up and we both walked over to the couch opposite Sophia. As always, she was perfection. Her silky mass of curls was twisted up loose allowing some to escape. She wore a beautiful halter neck fitted blue top with white trousers that had a high waistband but flared out onto open-toe sandals. She looked fit for a high-end ocean liner. I, on the other hand, looked like I had been clubbed over the head and dragged back to my cave. My hair was wild and wavy, and I was still in a robe.

"Did you both only just get up?" she asked with an evil grin, that she made look to cute.

"No, Keira and I shared a bath and I am trying to get her to stay in that robe all day but considering you're here, I know that won't last much longer," he said with feigned irritation. I on the other hand just did what I did best in these situations and blushed.

"You're right about that, 'cause I am not going shopping with her wearing that!" Oh no, she had been serious last night. I looked up at Draven with pleading eyes, but he just laughed.

"Oh no, you're not getting out of it, Keira my dear!" Sophia looked dead serious.

"Draven doesn't want me to go," I said bravely and Draven looked at me, then back at Sophia with folded arms. It would have been more convincing if he wasn't grinning like a bloody fool in love.

"I don't give a damn what Dominic wants! He has kept you to himself for too long, now it's my turn to have some fun with you." She made me sound like a doll being passed around. Who was next, Vincent....? Oops better not think that!

"Plus, you owe me, remember?" Oh no, she didn't just pull that card! Draven shot me a look and Sophia mouthed the word "busted" at me.

"Someone elaborate now." Draven's voice was cool and collected but I knew it wouldn't last.

"Sophia just helped get me some stuff last night, but that's it... isn't it Sophia?" I said this last part as a warning, one of course she didn't take.

"Is that so and how exactly did you keep this from me?" Oh, now he was intrigued.

"Ah now, my dear brother, but our little Keira here is very gifted and it seems has learnt some new tricks...but now, I am surprised she hasn't said anything." I decided to use this new gift right now.

"Great, brilliant, just...just freakin' peachy! Thanks a lot,

Sophia!" But this made it worse because she answered me out loud even though I was ready to let her in.

"You're welcome, darling." What the Beelzebub! Did she wake up the Hell side of bed this morning?! Draven shot her a look and then me. Oh dear, he was clearly waiting. He held out his palm and motioned for his question to be answered.

"Well, Keira here can talk to me without you hearing, she is using that big brain of hers and finds she can focus hard enough on letting me into her mind when she so chooses." I rolled my eyes like this wasn't that big a deal, but she carried on.

"She didn't want you knowing about her umm...unfortunate timing. But she was in pain and needed some supplies. I believe this was her only reasoning for trying to go home last night. But she didn't want to disappoint you, so instead she stayed and sought my help. It was very clever of her, was it not, brother?"

"It was indeed." Was all he said but his look said so many other things it was hard to pinpoint just one.

"I didn't tell you any of those things, how did you know I felt that way?" Draven was the one to answer, although the question was directed at his sister.

"When you open up your mind it gives way to your thoughts, not just the ones you choose for her to hear." He smiled at his sister as if he was proud of her deception. Great, well I will never be doing that again!

"Keira, show me." Oh shit! Now Draven wanted to see it first-hand and I had a feeling I was heading for a trap.

"No!" I said before folding my arms across my chest, giving evidence to the stubborn streak the Williams' name inherited.

"Oh, come on Keira, you even agreed that it was fun last night. Let's show him, you could even call him a rich arrogant fool and he would never know." She giggled as Draven growled at her.

"I said No!"

"Why not...Oh, she is stubborn isn't she?" Sophia stamped her foot and now I was the one laughing.

"She is indeed," Draven answered. Ok, this wasn't fair they were ganging up on me.

"Please Keira, do it for me, what is there to be afraid of?" His velvet voice was slowly winning me over, but I didn't let on.

"Because if I do, then you will be in my head and know everything and what if I can't get you back out? I want to keep my thoughts private, thank you very much!" Ok, so I did sound a bit whiny at this point, but peer pressure was never a welcomed thing.

"But what have you to hide from me?" Now he raised a single brow as if I was keeping secrets from him. Of course, there were a few, including the name Lucius.

"Nothing," I said a little too defensively.

"But you could block Sophia again."

"Yes, but you are stronger than her, you can almost access my mind already and I have to try very hard to resist, so if I do this, I might never find a way back again." Sophia huffed at this, not liking to hear how her brother's power was far greater.

"If that is the case, then show me via Sophia, talk to her and I will listen through her mind. When I hear your voice, I will be satisfied." I was failing fast and he knew it, so to seal the deal he ran his fingers down my cheek before whispering in my ear.

"Please, my love." And that was all it took to crack me.

"Fine! But know that I am not happy about being made to do this!" I said before lifting my knees up and getting comfortable. Draven didn't look as though he felt guilty for making me do this. He looked happy that he had won.

I relaxed my mind as I had done last night. I listened to the sounds around me trying to pinpoint one. I heard a door close in the distance and even some birds from an open window. I heard the clock pendulum rock its mundane motion, counting the seconds one, two, three and then my head filled with Sophia's smug voice.

"Good girl Keira, my brother will be pleased."

"Great, I am glad I could put on such a good freak show," I said unhappily but Draven's eyes lit up at his discovery.

"But look how happy you have made him, besides he would have asked me anyway and this way saves me a lecture." She even sounded sincere in my mind.

"So glad I could help," I said sarcastically and Draven laughed but stopped abruptly as though he had seen something he didn't like. His hand that held my arm tightened and his face became stern, giving me the feeling he was about to confirm the reason I didn't want to be doing this in the first place.

"Who is this boy, Justin?" The voice I had heard in my head filled me with dread, as it was no longer the sweet voice of Sophia's…oh no,

This voice belonged to Draven and now...

He had been granted access.

CHAPTER THIRTEEN

OH LORD... DRAVEN?

After that Sophia excused herself at Draven's request. This meant Draven wanted to talk to me about Justin without Sophia to witness our little discussion. Of course, I was still furious with him for deceiving me. Once we were alone, I got up and folded my arms.

"We are not talking about this!" I said as I grabbed my clothes from last night and went into the bathroom, but he was stood by the door before I could blink.

"Oh yes we are, my dear," he claimed but he didn't yet look as angry as I did, although I could imagine it wouldn't take long in coming.

"Alright, if we are going to talk about it, then first we are going to talk about you tricking me!" Ha! Now this made him look sheepish.

"Keira, please." He tipped his head, but I wouldn't give up that easily.

"Oh no, not this time! You forced me into something I didn't want to do and as a result you saw something that is going to make you paranoid. Explain how this is fair?" He was trying to think of something diplomatic to say but for once I had him stumped.

"I did not force you into anything." Oh, what a load of horse shit!

"No, you just used…what was it you called it…tactical decisions! It was a bloody guilt trip and you know it." I decided to get changed right in front of him and I did it while I was still having a go at him. He looked slightly amused by me dressing angrily.

"Answer me truthfully, if you can, did you know that would happen?" I had pulled my top on the wrong way round and he look down at it and nodded. Oh great, and when I was trying to make my point as well. I almost tore it off and put it back on the right way round.

"Okay, I will admit that I had an idea." I raised my eyebrows and sucked my lips in, and he thought twice about his last statement.

"Okay, ok…more than an idea." Now he looked guilty and it was about bloody time!

"You knew?" I said and he just nodded. I threw my hands up and made a 'GRRR' sound as I walked away. He was about to say something else, but I turned, knowing what it was.

"Oh no, don't you dare say it!"

"And what was I going to say exactly?" He leaned casually on his desk as he too had crossed the room. He looked smug.

"You were going to blame it on being half Demon," I said and his smug face was no longer. I had guessed right. Now I looked smug and we both couldn't help but laugh.

"Ha, you're laughing and therefore can't be angry any longer." In less than a blink he was before me capturing my face in his large hands and was now kissing me before I could protest. Ok, so not that I would have protested to having his lips on mine, but I could have put up a little resistance. When he finished he looked far too pleased with himself.

"And what are you looking so happy about?"

"I just survived my love's wrath for the first time. I feel almost human." He then winked at me and I knew it was just going to blow over and go down as one of our quickest disagreements yet.

"At the risk of angering you again, I would very much like it if you could oblige me and explain who this boy is. As from the embrace he gave you, I'm sure you could shed some light on the matter." He was trying to keep it light and cautious, so as not to bring up the fact that he had obtained this information under dishonourable terms.

"He is no one, just another friend or more like family as he is Frank's younger brother. He came to the house to see Frank as he's just returned back from travelling." I tried to make it as matter of fact as I could, but my voice wasn't as steady as it could have been. Thankfully, as soon as I had heard his voice in my head, I had blocked him out with all my might and that had been the end of his brief encounter with my thoughts. It could have been much, much worse, as he could have picked up on the fact that I have been hiding my dreams about Lucius.

"I think the boy has other ideas of friendship with you," he said in a stubborn tone.

"You got that from a hug? He's just a little…uh…touchy-feely, that's all. No hidden agenda." Ok, I knew this wasn't completely the truth, as he had made it a little too obvious that he liked me, but we did kind of have a thing once.

"Well, at least he is gone now," he said and I knew I should have used that opportunity to tell him about his stay next weekend, but I didn't. I just didn't want to worry him even more and if I was lucky, I could get away with him not finding out. I could just stay here for that weekend. But then I remembered how Frank had asked me to take Justin to the club one night. I think I was going to have to rethink this one.

Sophia didn't knock but just glided through the door without a care in the world.

"Are you ready?" she asked looking me up and down.

"I need to stop off and change first but then I'm good to go. I need to stop at the supermarket on the way back for tonight." Draven shot me a look.

"Oh no, I forgot I'm working," I said thinking I would have to call my sister and tell her it was off, but Draven smiled.

"Oh no you're not, we have made plans and I am not cancelling on your sister." He looked far too pleased about this.

"But…"

"No buts," he said firmly, and I knew on this he was concrete. So, I came up with a solution.

"Okay, but I work tomorrow night to make up for it." He was about to tell me 'No', but he thought twice about it when he saw my face, so he just sighed instead and then held up his hands in defeat.

"I think we should go in my car," I said to Sophia who was waiting with an amused expression. Draven let out a roar of laughter when he saw Sophia's face drop at my words.

"No way. I am not being seen dead in that thing!" I was hurt, but she didn't care on this matter because plain and simple, she was being spoilt.

"And what's wrong with my Bronco?" I asked crossing my arms.

"Keira, my dear, I might not be practical, but I am rich, and I do have standards to uphold. No offence." Ok, I had to admit I didn't think I would have seen her in my car but still, she shouldn't be so stuck up!

"Well, Draven goes in it," I said pleading my case one last time. But she just let out a snorted laugh, doing a far more ladylike job of it than I do.

"Yes well, he is a fool in love and clearly would do anything to keep you happy because have no illusions Keira, he would never have been seen dead in that thing you call a car before he met you."

"Alright, Sophia, that is enough, if she wants to drive, she will drive or she won't go at all," he said firmly but from the look on Sophia's face I was going to have to cave quicker than either of these two.

"It's fine, we will go in something ridiculously fast, with a shiny paint job," I said in defeat, but Sophia's smile told me that she had something else in mind.

"What?"

"Well, I was thinking…Limo." Oh no, this was getting worse by the second but now they laughed when my face dropped. I had only been in a Limo once and that was a Prom and it was filled with a load of drunken teenagers.

"That's a little over the top for shopping…don't you think?" She shook her head and again I gave up.

"Okay, but I need to get some food on the way back." They both looked shocked but what did they think, that I was getting the maid in to cook?

"What? I'm cooking tonight, Libby can't cook for toffee." They hadn't heard this expression before, and Sophia giggled.

"Are you sure?" Draven came up to me and I looked up at his bemused face.

"Yeah, I'm sure, I mean that girl burns everything. Once she…"

"No, I mean, do you not mind cooking tonight's meal?" Aww bless, he must be looking on this as a chore.

"No of course not, I cook most nights. Besides, I enjoy it and I'm quite good at it," I said being modest about something for the first time and Draven noticed it.

"Oh really?" he said as he kissed me, and Sophia just cleared her throat to indicate that she was still waiting.

"Okay, I'm ready," I said but it was a lie as all I wanted to do was stay there having him kissing me all day.

"Sophia, you remember what we talked about?" he said as he threw her something I didn't see. She caught it like it was part of her body she'd been missing, and she slid it into her pocket before I could make it out.

"No problem, leave it to me," she said winking at him and now I began to sweat.

"What are you up to?" I asked before she dragged me away from my happiness, which began with a D and ended in hot, sexy male. I could just make out him laughing as she pulled me out of the door.

There was a car waiting at the side of the building and it was like she said, a long black Limo. I really didn't want to turn up at home in this so I used the excuse that I needed my truck at home and that I would meet her there. She moaned a bit but agreed in the end.

I walked over to my blue beast and found Ragnar, my guardian, stood leaning against it. I sighed and hoped my car door wasn't dented from his immense bulk. I knew I wouldn't get away with driving back on my own. I couldn't believe how protective Draven was over me.

"Do you want me to drop you off somewhere?" I said sarcastically but he just grunted.

"Where you go, I must follow," he said not getting my humour. Ok, I was going to have to work on this. He got in the cab and I could almost hear the suspension cry out in pain. I tried to get it to start, but it was cold and didn't want to move like last time. And like last time I rubbed the dash and said,

"Come on baby, start for mamma," making Ragnar stare at me in disbelief.

"You speak to your car?" His question was serious, and I coughed back a laugh.

"Oh yeah, all the time. I don't have many friends." I looked across to him and he thought I was serious. I started the car and then turned to face him.

"Relax big guy, I'm joking but it worked, didn't it?" At this he finally laughed, making me jump. Would I ever get used to his version of a laugh? It was a cross between a deer's mating call and sandpaper being coughed up.

"You are a strange human girl." I couldn't tell if this was his idea of a good thing or bad, so I stayed silent. I swung the car around and made for the main road. I could tell he wasn't happy with my slow driving, but my motto was 'I preferred to get there later than dead' but considering he was immortal I doubted he would agree with me on this one. I was wracking my brain to try and bring up a conversation but come on, what did I have in common with a Viking Demon?

"I know it must be very boring for you to be babysitting me," I said, but he seemed not only surprised that I was speaking to him but also that I had sympathised with him at all.

"A different duty, yes. But I have been entrusted with guarding My Lord's most prized possession, so it is an honourable one." I let out a growl of my own.

"I'm not a Ming vase or the family crown jewels, and I am

most definitely not one of his possessions!" I said trying to get it through, but he remained unmoved by my outburst.

"Humans are too sensitive," he stated but I counteracted his statement with one of my own.

"And you? Were you not once human?" He turned towards me and I got a bit scared that I had gone too far.

"Yes I was, but I was a Warrior King and our women weren't outspoken. They knew their place well enough." He said this as a warning for me to behave for my Master, but I just chuckled as it was clearly far too late for that.

"Well, times have changed my large friend and I doubted even back then that Queens kept their mouths shut." I snapped back making my point. He didn't reply but he did at least look as though he was giving what I said some thought but then his thick lips curved on one side and his eyes moved sideways at me. I, however, was confused by his sudden amused behaviour but I was smart enough not to question it.

We pulled up outside my house and the Limo pulled up behind us. Thankfully, Libby and Frank were out. Ragnar walked over to the Limo and waited for me there. I made a motion at the blacked-out windows and one rolled down.

"I will be five minutes," I shouted to Sophia before running in the house to get ready. It didn't take long, but I remembered to grab my purse with my bank card and some cash, as I really did need to get some new clothes. I quickly changed my outfit to a fresh one and picked up my mobile phone that had been left to charge. And that was it, I was ready. I checked myself in the mirror and for a moment I didn't recognise the happy Keira staring back at me. It wasn't long ago that it had been a rare sight but these days I just couldn't stop smiling. Then the unbelievable hit me...

Draven really had fixed me.

The drive there was interesting, but this was more down to its passengers. Three Demons and a lip-biting human. If I wasn't already a little crazy this would have terrified the bee gees out of me. Oh great, now I had 'Staying Alive' in my head!

But let's face it, I wasn't exactly normal. If anything, I felt more comfortable than I would do with most humans. This was probably down to the fact that, all joking aside, I finally didn't actually feel that crazy anymore. Being around these Demons and Angels made every second of my life real. Every sight, every dream and every scary touch, I now felt that it had all pointed me to this strange family that I felt so much a part of, that it in itself scared me. I was terrified but for reasons opposite than what they should be.

I never wanted it to end.

Zagan sat in the front with the driver and Ragnar sat at the front of the Limo's long seats. He looked a little cramped, but I could imagine this he would be used to. I think he'd even look big in a Hummer! Sophia and I sat next to each other at the very back and I really didn't understand the need for this car for a simple shopping trip. But then we passed the turning to the mall I knew, so it made me speak for the first time.

"Uhh, did we just miss the turning?" Sophia laughed at me in response.

"Keira, did you really think we were going shopping in that tiny little mall? For a start they don't even have any designer stores."

"I don't buy my clothes from designer stores, remember, boring non-rich human here." She was laughing again, only this time she flicked her hair back.

"Well, you do now."

"Oh no, I'm not being dragged around some fancy store and spending a ridiculous amount of money on stuff I won't wear." She let out a moan, but I ignored it.

"Draven likes me the way I am, not because I come with diamonds, an expensive handbag and a five-hundred-dollar haircut." She was now pouting, and this might have worked around Draven but not me, although it was adorable. When I didn't budge, she spoke.

"Fine! We can go in your boring plain shops, but you have to at least come in some of mine."

"As long as you don't make me buy anything in them, then sure no problem." She was happy with this outcome. Well, this was a first, I had never had to get the rules straight before going on a shopping trip.

"What did Draven mean back there?" I asked once again breaking the silence. She tried to put on a blank expression, but it was hard when she really wanted to smile.

"I don't know what you mean."

"Oh, come off it! What did he throw you?"

"You will just have to wait and see." And that was all she would say on the matter.

I could tell we were heading into the city as I vaguely remembered coming back from the airport this way. The Limo got a lot of attention, especially when we got into more populated areas. People beeped their horns and waved as if we could have been celebrities. I was going bright red even though no-one could see me through the blacked-out windows.

"You don't like attention much do you?" Sophia asked, being a little surprised.

"What gives you that impression?" I said sarcastically but then I felt guilty afterwards so followed it by,

"Sorry, that was rude. I just get embarrassed when people watch me."

"Umm... but you don't mind Dom watching you?" She smirked and I laughed.

"I'm starting to get used to it, but it is still a little hard to take. I didn't like it before, you know, back when I thought he hated me." She turned to me in shock.

"You thought he hated you?" I wanted to say 'Well durr!' But I refrained.

"Yes of course, you do remember how he used to treat me, don't you?"

"Well, that's interesting. I guess I didn't see it because I just remember all the obsessing, he did over you and all the endless research. He wanted to know everything about you and without access to your mind, this frustrated him greatly. I remember when he came back one night from watching you sleep. He was in a rage because you had woken up and he realised he could no longer get away with being near you this way. It was the first time you started to really block him out. If I recall, he destroyed the dining room in the west wing, fireplace included." She was grinning at the memory and like this it was clear to see Sophia as a Demon not an Angel. She looked like an evil doll, one that could have ripped Chucky a new behind!

"It is still hard for us to accept that our powers do not work over you, but I can imagine no one finds it harder than Dom. This has most definitely never happened to him before." Again, she sounded smug with glee.

"Is he... very powerful?" I asked feeling nervous for the answer. She turned to face me and with serious eyes she scanned my face.

"Yes. He is the most powerful of our kind by far but after all he is the King." My reaction made her jump.

"WHAT?!" I screamed out and started shaking my head as though this had to be a dream…What the Hell…he was a king?! Was she shitting me?

"Yes, of course, but wait, how could it be that you didn't know? I would have thought it would have been obvious. You have heard him being regarded as My Lord, have you not?" She actually looked shocked.

"Yeah, but I just thought that was like a Lord of the manor type of thing but not like a…. like a…*well, like a bloody King!"* I hissed the word as if it had first been gargled in acid or something. It was just insane to think of him that way and even more crazy to think of him choosing me! Sophia laughed till there were tears in her beautiful eyes.

"Oh Keira, there is so much you still don't know but I am surprised this was not one of them. Oh dear, but you have gone pale, please don't tell me this is another thing you are going to overreact about? Dominic will not be pleased at me breaking you."

"I'm fine…I'm just…umm... a little overwhelmed with it, is all." I was still shaking my head and I noticed Ragnar smiling to himself. I guess my last statement to him about Queens not keeping their mouths shut had him thinking I believed I was one. Well, at least now he knew he'd been wrong. No wonder he was smirking.

"King?" I said again in disbelief.

"Yes, but not in the conventional sense. You have only history to gauge the ideas on, but it is not that way at all. His importance lies in the laws of our ways and how he chooses to enforce it. He is not your King, Keira, he is simply your other half and that is all you need to concern yourself with." Ha, well that was certainly easier to say than do.

"Okay, tell me something else that will take my mind off all this king stuff." This turned out to be another huge mistake.

"Okay, you really want to know what Dominic gave me earlier?" In hindsight I should have said no but of course in true Keira fashion I nodded, and she said something that made my pulse race with a near-blind panic of the experience I was about to endure…

"He gave me his credit card."

CHAPTER FOURTEEN

SHOPPING WITH A DEMON

S hopping with Sophia was a mix between shopping with an artist and a very spoilt child. She was a perfectionist in every aspect and eyed every item I picked up as though it was never good enough. Each shop I chose to go in was then followed by a very expensive designer store. Here, Sophia was in her element. She would get the different sections closed off just by showing a black bit of plastic which I presumed to be Draven's credit card. As soon as the assistants took one look at it, their eyes would bulge, and we would get star treatment. In one shop we went in, we even got champagne.

I looked so out of place that I felt like Julia Roberts out of Pretty Woman walking down Rodeo Drive. Okay, so I wasn't in a mini skirt and a crop top, but you get the picture. Next to Sophia it looked as though she had found a homeless person to spoil. She would try and get me to try on things that she picked out, but I would be adamant that spending over a thousand dollars on one item of clothing was just silly and pointless…well, for me anyway.

"And how much do you think one of Dom's suits cost?" She asked me when coming back out from behind the curtain in a gorgeous white summer dress which was backless showing off her silky skin.

"I don't even want to think about it," I said stubbornly before continuing,

"I like that one," nodding at the dress she wore but she was smiling at my response and no doubt to the first thing I said. It was true, I couldn't think about how much money he had. The thought made me feel queasy just like the word 'King' did. I couldn't help but think I was playing a game I just couldn't win. I was dating someone so far out of my depth that I sometimes felt as though I was going to drown in my insecurities. Every day I seemed to find out something else about him, that instead of making me relax, it was making me even more nervous to be around him. So, I did something very out of character when Sophia re-emerged.

"Sophia, where's the best place to get some sexy underwear?" Her eyes lit up and she clapped her hands.

"Now that's more like it!" She passed the dress to the assistant who already had arms full of outfits ready for her to try on.

"I won't try on the rest, but I will take them all," she said waving her clutch bag at the pile. The woman looked as though she would drop down and kiss her feet. After all the clothes were rung through the till and the women told Sophia the price, I gulped at the five-figure number. I coughed and the assistant shot me an evil glare. Sophia just thought it was funny as always. She handed over Draven's credit card and I noticed it was a black American Express card, the ones that don't have a limit...another gulp! Ok, so if I was trying so hard for my normal life and to be with Draven at the same time, then maybe a shopping trip with Sophia wasn't the best way to go. I found myself still shaking my head as we walked out of the store.

"What? Well, if you refuse to use it then I might as well." She smirked and I couldn't help but laugh with her. She was most definitely a Demon and the book 'The Devil Wears Prada' came to mind.

She didn't carry any shopping bags, oh no, not Sophia. Instead she would have someone from the store take them down to the limo for us. I was in awe at how the other half lived. Of course, the stores that I bought my clothes from didn't offer such a service and I wouldn't let Sophia ring up the driver to tell him to come and get them for me. She ended up calling me stubborn for most of the day, but I just laughed it off every time.

I was actually surprised to find that I was really enjoying myself and I did get quite a lot of things I needed. But now I was out of my league as Sophia linked my arm and pulled me into a Victoria's Secret shop.

Ragnar had followed my every move but whenever we went into a shop he stayed outside and this one was no exception. It was the first time I think I saw him blush…well, either that or he just had wind. I had to cough down a giggle.

She pulled me over to the really fancy stuff and now I was the one blushing. She picked up something that had more gaps than material. Then I spotted the most beautiful set and I was surprised with myself. I had always just stuck to plain white or black before and I hated red on me thinking it looked cheesy with my blonde hair, but this was different. It was black satin covered in blood-red roses and a vine that was made from black ribbon. It circled the corset and tied to the thong at either side. At the back it tied up with a thick red cord that crossed over so it could be pulled tighter. Everything matched including the suspender belt, stockings and amazingly the set included full-length satin gloves.

The design was called 'Temptress' and I didn't think it could get any more perfect. I bit my lips at the thought and Sophia waited beside me not saying a word but when I turned to her and asked what she thought, she just smiled and held up Draven's credit card.

In the end I bought the stuff with my own money, much to Sophia's dismay. I also bought some more underwear sets and some nice stuff to wear to bed, which were more of the comfort variety than sexual. I picked one set of pyjamas because the t-shirt had a pair of red lips with fangs protruding from them and underneath it said the words 'bite me'. I thought Draven would get a big kick out of these and if he didn't then, I most certainly would when I saw the classic Draven frown. Sophia thought it was funny anyway but no surprises there. After we had made our way around half of the shops my stomach started to cry out at me.

"You haven't let Dom pay for anything! My brother won't be happy." She looked serious but seeing as I didn't agree to any of it,

I could imagine that Draven would already know that I would be stubborn on the matter. Did he really think that Sophia would have been able to break me?

"Sophia, your brother knows I'm not the type of girl to just spend someone else's money Willy Nilly. But I wouldn't say no to lunch...will that make you happy?" She rolled her eyes at me and said,

"Well, it's a start. Come on, I know a place." Her face made me regret not picking the place first.

"Okay, but nowhere fancy...right, Sophia?" She winked at me and my dread doubled.

After a short Limo ride, we pulled up to a huge hotel with an all-glass front that reflected the cold but clear day. The doorman opened the Limo door and another in a red jacket opened the entrance. He did a double take at me and Sophia, making me giggle at what a pair we must have looked. Her beauty being absolutely flawless, and I must have looked like her personal beggar flagging behind. To make matters worse I tripped over my own feet and the guy had to steady me. When I thanked him, I was surprised when he winked at me. I rolled my eyes at myself as I felt my trademark blush creep along my cheeks and scuttled in after Sophia.

"Sophia, why have we come to a hotel?"

"Keira really, hotels do have restaurants and this one just happens to make the best Strawberry Daiquiri's in town." She walked straight past the queue and right up to the bar as if she owned the place. I followed like a red-faced sheep. Once there, she got served immediately and ordered me the same drink as her. I sat next to her with disbelief clear on my face. Then a very tall thin man dressed in a black suit approached with a lowered head. His gold name badge told me he was the hotel's Concierge and his name was Claude.

Claude looked at Sophia as though she was royalty, but I noticed he wouldn't make eye contact.

"Miss Draven, how kind it is of you to grace us with your presence. You look breath-taking as always." He was close to drooling and I couldn't help but clear my throat to fight my laugh.

He shot me a look as though he was going to have words with the doormen for letting in riff-raff.

"Miss Draven, is this person bothering you?" He asked Sophia and this time I did laugh, only I was the only one as she whipped round in her seat and gave him a heart-stopping look that stunned me to silence and had Claude almost cowering. She looked utterly insulted and for a moment I thought she was going to bend him over her knee and give him a good spanking. (And not in a nice naughty way.)

"How dare you, this is my very good friend, Keira, and if my brother were to hear of this grave insult to his future bride then I doubt he would look kindly on his investments within this hotel!" She sounded like a viper spitting out her disgust. This had him nearly grovelling at my feet in seconds and I was so embarrassed that I got up off the bar stool.

"My dear... I am so, so sorry, please forgive my ignorance and…." I cut him off quickly and said,

"It's fine, already forgotten about really…Sophia excuse me." I left when she nodded, and Claude was now singing his apologies to the unimpressed Sophia. I noticed the sign for the restrooms when I first walked in and I stomped off in that direction. Once I was inside, I let out a frustrated swear word and didn't realise there was someone already in there until she hurried out without washing her hands. Oh great! First, I looked like the homeless and now I'm an angry loon!

Ok, so he had insulted me but come on, it was an easy mistake, as I didn't exactly look like the type that would even be staying in this hotel, let alone a friend of the ridiculously rich Sophia, whose family were shareholders of the place. And what had been with the 'Bride to be' comment? I know they viewed me as being born for Draven but come on, we hadn't even been dating a week!

I calmed down for a few more minutes before going back out there and I hoped the rest of the guests had forgotten the little episode. If there was one thing I couldn't stand it was causing a scene and getting all the stares that went with it. I knew that the Dravens were used to this, but it didn't mean that I would ever be.

When back outside Claude was waiting for me and I swallowed a sigh.

"Miss Williams, please allow me to escort you to your table where Miss Draven is waiting." His thin features twitched at his discomfort at having to be in my company again. He must have thought that I would go running off to Draven and tell him what a nasty little snobby man he was to me. He was smiling, but I could see the tiny beads of sweat form while I followed him into the restaurant. I could almost hear his silent pleas to keep his job.

He pointed to the table with the best view and was about to leave after nodding to me when I stopped him.

"Thank you and you don't need to worry about earlier, I won't be mentioning this to Mr Draven." He looked surprised but ecstatic and I doubted very much he would be making the same mistake again.

"Thank you, and once again, I am extremely sorry for the offence I caused you." I shook my head and said it was fine again before going over to take my seat opposite Sophia.

"Have you finished wigging out?" Sophia asked grinning but I just folded my arms trying to be stern.

"That was a little over the top, don't you think?" She just shrugged her shoulders and picked up the menu.

"You think I was over the top, just wait until Dom finds out," she said smirking like she would indeed enjoy witnessing his reaction.

"Oh no, don't you dare. Draven doesn't need to hear about petty little mistakes. And anyway, what was with the whole 'future bride' thing?" This brought a smile to her face at just the very mention of it.

"Well, it is bound to happen...at some point anyway." I laughed at this and she shot me a look over her menu.

"Oh come on, we haven't even been dating a week! And considering how you guys regard time that must only be like minutes." I picked up my own menu and didn't recognise anything that sounded like food. I found myself wishing we had just gone to the food court and ordered a burger.

"Yes, but he has been waiting for you since the beginning of our time, so that kind of overrules that idea, don't you think?" she said using my own words against me but before I could reply she continued,

"Besides, what does time matter when love is involved?" she stated, so I decided to give up with a usual barely-there groan.

After giving her the silent treatment for all of a minute she gave me a coy smile before asking,

"Do you like your daiquiri?"

I sipped my cocktail and thought I might have to be alone with it, it was that delicious.

"Oh my, now this is damn good!" She smiled as if to say, 'told you so' and we both giggled when she ordered us two more.

"I won't tell Dominic about Claude insulting you." This shocked me and the only reason I could think of, was that Sophia was now getting used to my way of thinking.

"Thank you, but I really found it more funny than anything else, I mean come on, have you ever been seen with someone like me before or has your brother for that matter?" Her face gave her answer, which was an 'oh Hell no!'

"Which is why I can't help but think, if you had been sat here with Aurora, then that wouldn't have happened," I said this without thinking how Sophia would react, so when she banged down her glass I jumped, along with the other patrons.

"Keira! Don't be so, so…" She was trying to contain her frustration at me.

"So what?" I asked weakly

"So blind! I never liked Aurora and I couldn't have been happier when my brother finished it with her."

"Why?" Just then we were interrupted by a waiter and Sophia gave our order in what sounded like perfect French and then he promptly went away again.

"I ordered for you if that's alright?" I nodded thinking it was for the best seeing as I couldn't even read the menu and knowing my luck would have gotten something slimy and in a shell that should have been happily eating in a garden.

"Keira, there is something you should understand about Aurora. She maybe an Angel, but there is nothing Heavenly or pure about her. She is extremely self-absorbed and will only do good for her own gain. She has more Demon in her than I... that I can promise you." This shocked me enough for my jaw to drop. How could something so beautiful and radiant have a black heart? And if so, why had Draven been with her in the first place?

"So, why was he with her for so long?"

"I have said too much, forget I mentioned her." Oh no, there was no chance of that happening. I shook my head at her before saying,

"No way, come on, you can't start to tell me what I want to know and then stop. You know Draven won't tell me, so that only leaves you...please Sophia." I was close to pleading and could see my sad eyes reflected in her own.

"Fine, but I really need to learn how to say no to you!" she complained before continuing.

"You must understand, firstly my brother was very different before you entered his life and secondly, he is extremely used to getting what he wants. He had never known love until you, so you mustn't judge him on his past and for what he didn't know existed." When her serious eyes met mine, I knew it was going to be a hard version of Draven to take but I nodded my head anyway and prepared myself for the worst.

"He only used to see women as being there to pleasure his needs and very little more. Their beauty played an important part, yes, but he knew it never felt right. He spent his time forbidding himself to get close to anyone until Aurora came. Her beauty captivated him into believing she alone could satisfy his needs and for a while, I suppose she did. She sat at our table as a council member but never at his side, where she thought she belonged."

"Wait a minute, you mean no-one has ever sat next to him at that table other than you or Vincent?"

"That is correct." She smiled at my expression. I couldn't believe that something that had seemed, at the time, so innocent was such an immense gesture. I knew that it was probably down to my over-emotional state but I felt like crying (Thankfully though, I didn't).

"The idea of her becoming Queen consumed her, so after years of her persistence and Dom's denial, she took matters into her own hand." Sophia ordered another strawberry daiquiri, but I passed and ordered water instead.

"What did she do?" I was nearly on the edge of my seat and had to sit on my hands to squash the urge to shake the story out of her quicker.

"Well, as you know, Dom is very possessive and does not share what he considers belongs to him, although it was never an issue with other females." She laughed but I was being blonde.

"What do you mean by that?"

"Oh Keira, don't be naïve. Do I need to spell it out to you?" Then it hit me and soon had me hating this conversation.

"What? You mean Draven's been with more than one woman at a time?" Ok, now I felt even more out of his league and anymore conversations like this one and I would feel like I was on a different damn planet, I was that far from him!

"Keira, do not judge him, this is quite common among our kind, but you know he thinks very differently now he is with you." This still didn't help with the mental picture I had in my head of Draven surrounded by the most exotic creatures, all there to please his every need. Her words weren't taming my green-eyed monster in me that was for sure!

"Right," I said in a deflated tone, one she frowned at.

"Okay so, getting back to the story. Aurora, knowing his jealous nature, slept with another in his bed." My hands flew to my face in disgust. I mean, did she have a death wish? Sophia grinned at my reaction and looked delighted at what she was about to say next.

"I know what you're thinking, and we all held the same thoughts…what madness of love drives someone to do something so suicidal?" She looked sorry as soon as the words were out of her mouth because of course I could answer this one. Love drives us to do the most extreme actions.

"Sorry…I guess you can answer that one." I felt bad for her as she lowered her head, but I just leaned my gloved arm across the table and gave her hand a squeeze.

"Sophia its fine, but you're right, I can understand why love does make us do the craziest things but still, I would never be that suicidal!" I couldn't imagine the level of rage this would have put Draven in, having just seen a minuscule amount when kissing Jack. The thought made me shudder.

"What did he do?" I didn't want to ask but the darker side of me was burning to know.

"It may shock you as it did us all, but he did simply...nothing," she stated with only a quaint shrug of her delicate shoulders.

"WHAT?" I shouted this a bit too loud and the rest of the posh diners looked at me as though I had three heads. Sophia giggled before continuing.

"He did nothing, he just didn't care. He told the other Angel that he was welcome to her. After that she left the council and wasn't seen until years later when she eventually came back to plead for another chance. Dom allowed her to join his council but nothing more. He changed after the year she did that and none of us knew why...well, until now anyway."

"What do you mean changed?"

"I mean he lost his passion for pleasure. He became more withdrawn and didn't take many to his bed, if any. We all thought it was down to Aurora, but he would never talk about the reasons for his change. He started once again to do research into finding you, but it was not to happen that way."

"What do you mean?" I whispered, quickly biting my lip as I waited for the answer.

"You were always meant to find him. It was in the written Fates and you never challenge the Fates." I couldn't believe what she was telling me but if I thought that this was hard to take, then the next question I got answered threw me completely.

"Okay, so you said you thought it was Aurora that changed him but now you know it wasn't, so what did happen? Why that year?" She was once again laughing and then she took a slow drink before giving me my answer with a pair of devious lips hanging over her straw.

"Because my dear Keira..."

"It was the year you were born."

CHAPTER FIFTEEN

COOKING FOR A KING

After the bombshell Sophia dropped on me, I was quiet and deep in thought for the rest of our lunch. She didn't seem to mind only every now and again she would smile to herself when she saw my confused face. I mean, could this even be possible? Whenever Draven had mentioned about me being the Chosen One, I hadn't fully understood what it had meant but now…what did this prove? Had he felt my presence in the world as soon as I was born? I bit my lip at the thought. For some reason what Sophia had just told me, made everything more real…more terrifyingly real.

Once she had paid the bill and we were back in the Limo on our way home, she finally pulled me from my mental breakdown.

"Keira please, you look traumatised. Dom is going to be so angry with me!"

"I'm sorry, I guess I just never believed it until now. It's still hard to see why me," I said weakly and even Ragnar looked down at his feet. Sophia took my hand in hers and she looked at me with more love than from just a friend, this was from a sister.

"Then you are the only one. No one else doubts why. You are beautiful and in more ways than one. Aurora is beautiful, yes, but her soul is ugly and it seeps through to her skin. Your soul is pure, and it radiates off you in every way. In this she will never be able to compete. You are simply out of her league and of this she is painfully reminded every time she sees you sat by my brother's side." For the first time, hearing this, I couldn't help but feel sorry for her. It must be a hard pill to swallow.

"Poor girl," I said but Sophia couldn't contain her outburst. She laughed so hard it nearly brought on tears.

"Oh Keira, you are so funny! She does not deserve your pity. She is the creator of her own undoing. She knew about the prophecy and that one day you would come. She never really loved him anyway, it was the power she loved. There is no one in this world or the next, who she could love more than herself." I now knew why Sophia seemed to hate her so much. After all, wouldn't I be the same with Libby, if Frank had been the same way. One of the reasons I loved Frank so much wasn't how he treated me, it was how much he obviously adored my sister.

Ok, so now I was feeling slightly better and she could tell as now I was smiling to myself, so she added something more that sealed the deal on my mood.

"Anyway, you think she is beautiful, but she does have a team of girls who get her ready every night, but you drive my brother crazy without having to work at it! Why do you think it is that he won't allow you to come to my private room? He gets insanely jealous over you, far more than he ever did when he was with Aurora." I couldn't help the huge grin that split my lips and strangely, Ragnar started to relax more at the sight. He raised his head up and smiled to himself. It was an odd reaction for him to have but I just shrugged it off.

When we got closer to town, I decided it would be better for her to drop me off at home before I got my supplies for tonight's meal. I thought it was one thing going clothes shopping in a blacked stretch Limo, but to the supermarket…oh yeah, a tad much. Plus, I couldn't really see Sophia pushing a trolley around the frozen food section.

We pulled up outside the house and I thanked God that no one was home and I knew Libby and Frank must still be sorting out his uncle's insurance for the 'ruined' cabin. Ragnar grabbed all my bags even when I protested, and he was by my front door waiting before I could walk two steps. Then I remembered what I wanted to ask Sophia before she left. I turned around to find the window already down and she was sat there waiting.

"Yes?" she said, as though she knew there was something I was forgetting.

"How did you know?"

"I am finding it easier, the more I am with you, to read the signs. You wanted to ask something else about my brother?" I shook my head and smiled before asking the all-important question.

"What does your brother like to eat?" I don't know why but I found myself going red when I asked.

"Anything hot," she said, making me laugh at her answer.

"You mean spicy hot?"

"Use your imagination, honey! See you later." And with that the window went up with the same mischievous grin on her face that I was getting used to seeing. I found myself still smiling as I walked up the steps. Ragnar eyed me curiously and when I put my hands out to retrieve my bags, he just nodded for me to open the door. Well, he was well trained that was for sure I thought as he followed me in.

"You can just dump them there," I said but he cocked his head to one side reminding me of a dog that didn't understand a command. Then I felt guilty for thinking it.

"Dump?"

"Yeah, I mean you can just put them down over there." Ok, he must have thought I meant throwing them away... hehe, I giggled.

"Would you like a drink?" He actually smiled at me, but it fell away as quickly as it had appeared.

"No, I will be outside waiting." And with that he left to guard the house. I couldn't understand why one minute he was nice and then the next it was as if I was an annoying bug buzzing around that he wanted to swat. It seemed to be my time in life for not understanding men.

I grabbed all my bags and ran upstairs with them, but in true Keira style I tripped and landed on my knee.

"BUGGER!" I said out loud and then I heard Ragnar burst through the door and he was next to me in seconds.

"What is wrong?" he asked looking down at me, seeming very cramped in the narrow staircase to my attic room.

"Nothing, I just tripped." I was holding my knee, rubbing it knowing that it was going to leave a bruise. Then, I let out a shriek as I felt myself being picked up by the waist and carried into my bedroom. He plonked me down on the bed and I turned and looked up at the giant who was ducking his head to fit in my room.

"Umm... thanks?" I said feeling the heat rush to my cheeks. He frowned and then knelt down, but he was still higher than me. He lifted my leg up and it started to sting.

"Ouch!" I said but he just smirked at my baby-like behaviour.

"What are you doing?" I asked nervously when he started to lift my jeans up but he didn't answer me. He rolled them over my knee and, yes of course, it was bleeding. He put his face down closer to the cut and I pulled back making him growl.

"What are you doing?" I asked again, as he looked as if he was going to take a sip of my blood.

"I am going to heal it. My master will not be happy if he sees this, it will displease him...I will have displeased him."

"But this wasn't your fault, I'm clumsy that's all."

"Yes I know, he warned me of this, but you wouldn't have fallen if I had carried your bags up here." His eyes met mine and for once they weren't harsh or cold. I bit my lip at the feel of his massive hands which grabbed my leg back and pulled it closer to his face. He then took a few deep breaths making his massive chest expand and blew over it, causing it to instantly turn numb and icy.

He wouldn't allow my natural reaction to happen as I tried to pull away. It was impossible to move with his vice-like grip that had my leg locked. It felt like he was freezing my blood and the skin around the wound. I shivered as it started to run up my leg but then I felt him release me and after a few minutes of being under his control he spoke.

"It is finished you can open your eyes now," he informed me and I was surprised that I had indeed closed my eyes. I looked down and noticed the blood had, in fact, frozen and with the softest touch he casually brushed it away with calloused fingers. The red icy dust floated away to reveal unbroken skin underneath. I was amazed how quick it had healed but I was more shocked at how such a frightening giant could have been so gentle. I was touched and when he was about to stand, I put my hand on his shoulder.

"Thank you." He looked to his right where my hand was and then back at me. It seemed as if he wanted to say something more, but then shook his head and thought better of it. He lowered his head into a deep nod and then rose from his knees and left without saying another word. I looked down at my knee and touched the smooth skin for myself. Incredible, there wasn't even a mark!

After I pulled myself together, I got up to put my new clothes away and tidy my room a bit just in case we were spending the night here. I didn't want Draven thinking I was a slob, so I also changed the sheets and let the window open to let some fresh air in. That's when I saw him. Ragnar was below my window with his back to the house and he was staring out to the view of the national park's mountains. He had his arms folded and his head shook slightly before looking at his feet. I didn't know what was wrong with him, but I felt bad that it could be because of something I did. I was growing attached to my colossal protector and I didn't like seeing him in pain.

I had a quick cup of tea before ringing Libby to check we were still on for tonight. She sounded stressed out, but said it was fine and that they would be home in an hour. I reassured her again that I didn't mind cooking and I sat down to make a list while I finished my tea. I checked the cupboards for anything else we needed and added it to my list before grabbing my jacket. It had started to drizzle and I couldn't help but raise my head to it when I got outside. I didn't notice Ragnar next to me and when I opened my eyes, he was frowning at me.

"What? I like the rain" I said shrugging my shoulders before giving him a cheeky smile and walking over to my truck. I call it a truck because it was a huge Ford Bronco that I could have lived in. He followed, shaking his head as if I was crazy, which was becoming a habit of his.

I felt the truck sink down when Ragnar got in and I started the engine. When it started first time I smiled.

"What, no talking to it?" he asked not keeping the amused sarcasm out of his heavily accented voice.

"Nah, she's fine with rain, she just hates the cold."

"You are a different human," he stated as though he had just figured me out or was still trying to. I shrugged again as I pulled the car around and made for the main road.

"Don't you think I would have to be, all things considered?" Now, he was the one to shrug, only when I did it, it didn't make the car want to swerve. We carried on driving in silence for a while until it was starting to eat away at me so when I finally said something it came out sounding more like I was ranting.

"What's wrong with you? Is it because I called you a jerk because you know I'm sorry for that…don't you?" This made him turn to me in shock and I was glad that I had the road in front to keep my attention.

"You think that bothered me?"

"Didn't it?"

"No, you are a wilful human, so it is to be expected." Okay, so if this was the case then what was wrong with him?

"Well, if you hate protecting me so much then why don't you just ask Draven to get someone else?" He growled again and I jumped.

"You know there is no need to do that!" I snapped.

"I don't have a problem protecting you. It is a great honour for my Master to have chosen me," he said calmly.

"Then what is wrong? One minute you like me and the next you seem frustrated with me." I was determined to get to the bottom of it and if he was going to keep being my bodyguard then he needed to trust me.

"It is not you I am frustrated with." The way he said it answered my question, it wasn't me. It was him.

"Why?" I said softly but he just turned and looked thoughtfully out of his side window before answering.

"It is because you remind me of someone from my past." This stunned me into not asking more. It wasn't my place to pry into his past and more than ever I wished I hadn't pushed for it. So I tried my usual trick and told him a very lame joke.

"Okay, I have one for you, why is there no aspirin in the jungle?" He turned to face me as though I was having an episode.

"I do not understand the question, do you require medical attention?" Ok, what was it with Demons and jokes?

"It's a joke, so you say, 'I don't know, why are there no aspirin in the jungle?'" He didn't, he just nodded for me to continue.

"Because the parrots ate them all! ...get it? para-ceta-mol," I said repeating it slowly and then I could almost hear the cogs turning as he finally got it and the car started to shake under his laughter. Again, it sounded like a bull about to charge. I couldn't help but laugh along with him. He was still making grunting noises when I pulled into a parking space.

Once inside the store I started to wiz around the aisles as though it was a challenge and I only stopped when I couldn't find the aisle that held the dry herbs and spices. I found an assistant wearing a bright green top and patted him on the shoulder.

"Excuse me, can you show me where the herbs and spices are?" At first when he turned around, he had a kind face and was an older guy but then it quickly changed into something from my nightmares...

His eyes were the first part to change when a red ring appeared and started to bleed around the irises. With every fearful beat of my heart the blood in his eyes grew and like the tears that could no longer be contained they spilled over. I started to back up into some cans on the shelf but he just got closer. Then his face changed completely into the handsome, but terrifying, face of Lucius. I gasped, locking a breath in my throat that I could only hope wasn't my last.

"Can I help you, my Keira?" he said in a chilling voice that was followed by an even more chilling smile. His fangs hung over his curved lips and as a bloody tear fell down to his lips, his tongue quickly lashed out, taking in the taste of a single droplet. I closed my eyes and shook my head, trying in vain to release my mind from this nightmare.

"You're not real, you're not real!" I said over and over until his laughing stopped. I felt his hand on my arm and I let out a cry.

"Hey there, are you alright miss?" I opened my eyes to see the kind face of the old guy looking concerned. It took me a moment to pull myself together enough to form words.

"I…you…" I took a step back and took in as much air as I could to try and breathe through my panic. He's gone. It wasn't real. He's not here.

"Umm, yes sorry, I thought… I saw… something." I stammered out and before he could touch me again, I walked quickly away from him as he was still asking me what I needed. I kept feeling that I was going to be sick from the sight that wouldn't leave my infected mind. It was his voice, I could hear it over and over, 'My Keira' he had called me, as if I was his! I wiped away a stray tear as I continued around the store like I was lost. I leant over my trolley to get my breath, when I heard a familiar voice.

"Kazzy?" RJ's voice rang down the aisle and I looked up to see a bright pink head bobbing down towards me.

"RJ, hey!" I said, trying to sound my usual self.

"Hey, oh man, you look pale, well I mean, even paler than usual. You okay?" She did look concerned bless her and I felt like hugging her for the comfort she brought me.

"I'm fine, well you know, it's the time," I said rolling my eyes and then she started nodding the way girls always did. It was the one thing that united us all.

"Well, that sucks, especially having your boyfriend." She let out a naughty laugh and I couldn't help but join in.

"So, you back in college Monday?" she asked, as she followed me down the aisles.

"Yeah, but I have so much catching up to do. Oh, should I pick you up same time?"

"Yes please, I missed your car but of course I've missed you too." She nudged me and we both smiled. She continued to follow me around until I finished, and I was more than glad about it. She was like a Goth angel coming to my rescue and I wanted to kiss her for it. I lost track of time as we chatted but her funky spiked watch told me it was nearly six.

"Oh crap, I have to go but it was great catching up. Oh and RJ, I have someone I want you to meet next Saturday but I will explain more on Monday." This had her nearly running after me to find out, but I just waved and walked over to the cashier. I couldn't help but feel instantly safer when I saw Ragnar by my car and next time I wouldn't stop him from following me around the store. Not now I knew that not even grocery shopping was safe!

Ragnar could tell something was wrong as I didn't speak the whole way home. The only time words passed my lips was when I thanked him for carrying my bags into the kitchen. He looked as if he wanted to ask what was wrong but stopped himself. I tried to concentrate on other things but every now and again my mind would wander back to Lucius' face and I knew this was what he would want so, with that in mind, I clicked on the kettle ready for a cup of tea and went to work on tonight's meal.

By the time Libby and Frank came back the house smelled of herbs and spices as thanks to RJ, I had found them.

"Mmm... something sure smells good," Libby said as she parked herself down on the kitchen chair.

"How was it?" I asked but she just let out a sigh, which said it all.

"That bad?"

"Worse, I just want Frank to sell the place, but he won't because of the *promise he made to his uncle.*" She whispered this last part, as now Frank was walking through the door.

"Mmm Kazzy, that smells damn good, girl, what is it?" I smiled at him before saying,

"Well, it's a surprise but I hope you like spicy food 'cause it's a hot one." I smirked to myself wondering what Draven would make of it. Well Sophia had said he liked his food hot...ok, she didn't exactly specify that she meant his food, but considering sex was off the menu I gathered she was referring to what he liked to eat. I saw Libby's face and knew she wasn't as brave when it came to spices, so I added,

"Don't worry, I also made a mild one." At this she got up and kissed me before grabbing an open bottle of wine from the fridge and pouring me a big glass and I was more than grateful for it. She then poured herself a baby safe glass of OJ.

I told Libby about my shopping trip with Sophia and she was nearly in tears with laughter at my reconstruction of the day. She made me show her all I had bought and was impressed that some tops were actual colours rather than just shades. However, her eyes nearly popped out when I showed her my star buy. She ooo'd and ahhh'd over the satin material of the corset and asked me when I was planning on wearing it. I had given it a lot of thought when I bought it and knew that I would wear it for the first time we could make love again.

I decided that I would wear it under my work clothes and not tell him when my body was ready again but just surprise him. I would tell him that I was tired and hope he wouldn't follow me back to his room. Then I would wait for him to find me lying on his bed in some seductive pose and hope that I wouldn't be wearing it for much longer after that. I giggled to myself and Libby raised her eyebrows.

"Forget it, I don't want to know!" she said quickly before starting to laugh with me.

Everything was ready and because Libby loved it so much, I made my famous chocolate cake while the chicken had been marinating. Now the meal bubbled away and all that needed to be cooked was the rice. I didn't know why but I found myself playing nervously with my gloves waiting for the time to tick to eight. I missed him so much it was like a hole that only he could fill. Then I heard it and bit down on my bottom lip at the sound of the knock at the door. I ran to it like an excited child saying,

"It's ok, I've got it!" Libby just grinned at my enthusiasm to get to the door quicker than my legs could take me. I even skidded around the corner as my feet slid on the wooden floor. I steadied myself on the table by the door and took a deep breath before opening the door to the most handsome face I had ever seen…

My gorgeous boyfriend.

CHAPTER SIXTEEN

DINNER HUMAN STYLE!

Draven stood on my front porch like the world's most perfect date. His tall frame was clothed in a casual long-sleeved black cotton t-shirt, which showed his extensive amount of muscle underneath, thanks to the second skin effect. His long strong legs wore dark designer jeans that looked made for him and for all I knew they had been. He looked well-groomed with his hair back and his soft olive skin shaved.

I couldn't help the great big grin that was plastered on my face at the sight of those lush deep eyes that looked just as happy to see me. I bit my lip at the naughty thoughts that came running through my mind at just the sight of him and then it tripled the feeling when he winked at me. He was about to speak but I didn't let him, instead I just pulled his face down to mine and crushed my mouth to his for a very intense kiss, which by the end had me near panting.

"I take it you missed me?" he said over my lips before pulling away. I opened my eyes to find him smiling a confident smile. I just nodded and said,

"Maybe." This made him laugh.

"Oh really, only maybe?" He then placed his warm hand at the base of my back and pulled up my top to get to my skin, which he knew was a major weak spot (Along with everywhere else he touched) I let out a quiet moan and he laughed again.

"Mmm... I didn't think so," he said being cocky.

"That's not fair, Draven, and anyway, didn't you miss me?" I asked before putting my head down as I went all shy with the question I asked. His fingers found the underneath of my chin and pushed my face up to meet his black, serious eyes.

"Always," he said sincerely before picking me up by the waist to kiss me once more.

"Did you enjoy your shopping trip with my sister?" he asked once my feet came back in contact with the porch.

"It was interesting," I replied, trying to hold my features in place from giving away all that I had learnt.

"Sophia described it as both fun and frustrating, considering you were stubborn enough to use your own money." He was trying to hide his smile and be serious, but he was failing miserably.

"Oh come on, did you really think that I would have had a spending spree with your credit card? Surely you know me better than to go spending other people's money?" I folded my arms trying to look stern, but he just raised an eyebrow at me.

"Well, it was worth a try and besides, what is mine, is also now yours." This had me laughing and in turn him frowning. I shook my head at him, but he just mimicked me by shaking his head back. We both grinned at the same time. He unfolded my arms and wrapped them around his waist for a hug. I could feel him lean down and smell my hair before kissing it lightly.

"Did you buy anything nice?" As soon as he asked this, I went rigid under his hold and he didn't miss it. He moved me back so he could see my face which was turning different shades of pinks and reds.

"Why, what has Sophia said?" I would be having words with her if she had mentioned the underwear.

"Oh nothing really, just when I asked, she gave me a sly grin before saying it was interesting. This sparked my curiosity about what you had purchased." He could see me trying desperately to hide my half-smile by biting my lip.

"Keira, why do you have the look of a Nun who has been

thinking unclean thoughts?" His voice took on a very seductive tone and this made it hard to think clean thoughts when all I wanted to do was drag him into the woods and let him ravish me like a wild beast! Oh God, what was wrong with me? I blamed it on the two glasses of wine I had consumed. Only I knew it was really down to what his presence did to me.

"Well, I can be naughty sometimes." Yeah like now.

"Do you not like the idea of me being bad?" I continued, thinking God, what was wrong with me? I was being brave but with my head lowered, which I think he was getting more turned on about. I was about to walk back inside the house, but he grabbed my arm and pulled me back to face him. He moved my hair from my neck and whispered down in my ear that sent sparks down my back and continued right down to my most sensitive parts,

"May I remind you, I am half Demon and I know full well how attracted I am to your dark side, just as the Angel in me is addicted to the shy and good girl that stands before me now." He stayed at my neck and my heart nearly stopped as he placed his lips on the skin there. Both his hands came to encase the column of my throat and turn it to the side so he could get to it better, as his mouth opened, and I felt his teeth bite down to hold me still. A groan caught in my throat as I thought he would bite me but after I let the adrenaline kick up my pleasure to new limits, I had to come back down just as quickly. His teeth released me, and I felt his lips turn up into a knowing smile in place of his fangs. I swallowed hard and this made him laugh.

"Did I make my point?" he whispered before releasing his hold on me. It took me a moment to find my basic functions to respond and I really wanted to come back with something witty, but it doesn't really work when you're incoherent. Instead I caved into his control and just nodded like a frightened servant girl. Just then Libby appeared in the doorway and cleared her throat, bringing me back to my own mind. Damn he was getting better at finding new ways to control me!

"Umm Kazzy, I think the stuff needs stirring."

"Oh shit! You know I'm blaming you if it's burnt," I warned

but he just looked smug. I moved to walk back in when he held me back again by my waist and said,

"It will have been worth it." Then he let me go to save the dinner. He followed me in, and Libby was greeting him properly, the way our mother had taught us.

"Dominic, it is nice to see you again," she said putting on her posh voice, no scouse in sight! I giggled to myself while stirring the dinner which had started to stick slightly at the bottom of the pan. I turned the temperature down and Libby came walking in with two bottles of wine. I hadn't even seen Draven with anything in his hands but me. Libby mouthed the words "fancy" at me before putting them in the fridge. Draven followed behind and smelled the air.

"Mmm, smells good." I smiled at the compliment before giving him a wink.

"I have just got to cook the rice and then we're good to go," I said, just as Frank walked in from outside. He walked up to Draven and extended his hand.

"Dominic, how ya doing? I noticed the Aston outside. Man, now that sure is a nice car!" I hadn't even noticed the car he came in but now I was trying not to laugh. I knew he would bring it but what he said next did shock me.

"Well, if it's alright with Keira, then I thought you might like to take a drive before dinner." Frank looked like he was trying not to choke on his happiness.

"HOLY SHIT would I!" Draven laughed, especially when Libby hit him for being rude.

"Sorry babe, hey Kazzy you don't mind, do you?" He looked at me as though I held all his dreams in my hand and could crush them at any second.

"No, of course not, go and have sensible speed fun," I said and he came up to me and ruffled my hair.

"Thanks kiddo, we won't be long." I thought he was going to drag Draven's arm out after he came over to me and kissed me before leaving through the door with Frank. Me and Libby both went to the window and watched as two huge men acted like big kids. First Draven showed him the engine and you could almost hear Frank's enthusiasm as we both expected him to start jumping up and down. Then Draven slammed the hood and threw him the keys! None of us expected he would let Frank actually drive and from the look on his face, neither did Frank.

"Well, isn't that sweet of him. I have to say I'm impressed, Kaz, he's really making an effort and I think if he ever needed a kidney then Frank would be first in line. He has a friend for life now." I grinned at her before turning to boil the kettle. The grin was both down to my sister being impressed and the idea of Draven ever needing a kidney.

By the time they returned, Libby and I were chatting about them both and I had consumed another glass of wine while Libby stuck to her OJ. The door opened to the sound of Frank swearing about the power of the engine.

"Man, that is some serious shit you got there, I thought I was gonna lose her on that fuc...I mean... er tight corner." Draven was laughing at Libby's frowning face on catching her husband nearly saying the F-bomb. She got up and walked past him shaking her head.

"Babe! Aww come on baby, you should have seen me, it was awesome!" he said as he followed her out to set the table. Draven was still laughing as he came over to me.

"That was really good of you. I think you made his year, oh and you also have a friend for life," I said grinning, as I turned around to stir the rice that was very nearly done. I felt his hands on my shoulders and he leant down to whisper to me. He moved the stray hairs off my neck with his fingertips.

"I didn't just do it for Frank. I like to watch how you smile at other people's happiness, it makes your soul glow." I turned around to face him, smiling like a fool again and I pushed him lightly.

"Don't tease!" I said and he held up his hands and said,

"What me?" Before his cheeky grin fell on my happy lips. I wouldn't let him fully kiss me as I didn't want to get caught by my sister again.

"Now who is the tease?" He flicked me playfully on the nose and I frowned making him let out a rough laugh.

"Table's set, Dominic would you like to come through?" Libby said as she grabbed the wine.

"Sure," he said to Libby before she left to take the bottle to the table. He turned but then stopped to look over his shoulder at me like he had forgotten something.

"Oh and Keira, I am looking forward to a whole evening where you have to call me Dominic." Then he left to take his seat in the dining room, leaving me biting my lip as always. Dating him, I was surprised that I had any bottom lip left!

Libby came back to help me carry the bowls of food and when I walked through, I suppressed a giggle at the sight of the table laid out with her best china and silverware. I placed the bowls down and lifted the lids to release the smell of fiery spices. I pointed out the hot one and the mild one for Libby and me.

"Damn, that smells good," Frank stated as he dug in. Libby smacked his head lightly before saying,

"Frank! Guests first!" Frank rolled his eyes at Draven.

"Aww Libs, dudes don't care about that type of shi…stuff." He nodded to Draven for back up.

"It is fine, please." He held out his hand for Frank to continue. This made him turn to Libby and give her a smirk as though he had won a round. It was like watching a Punch and Judy show. Frank piled his plate and then we all dug in.

"Damn Kazzy, this is hot stuff! What do you call it?" Frank asked as he shovelled it down like it was going out of fashion. I said the answer trying not to laugh.

"Well, I call it…'Kazzy's Demon Chicken'!" As soon as I said it, all eyes were on Draven as he had erupted into raucous laughter and couldn't control it. Frank and Libby looked at each other as if he had lost it, so I added 'private joke' which was the truth. Once he had finished with his outburst, he leaned next to me and kissed me on the head before saying,

"It's delicious, sweetheart." Libby looked like her heart just melted at Draven's statement and mine did melt at Draven's statement.

Everyone had seconds and I loved to watch people enjoy my food. Libby rubbed her belly and said,

"Well, the babe's had enough, but thanks Kaz that was lovely."

"Yeah, cheers Kazzy, hot as Hell, but damn good!" Frank said as I took his empty plate from him before he started to lick it clean like a dog. Draven stood ready to help me, but I put my hand on his shoulder to stop him.

"It's fine, I've got it." But Libby got up to help me anyway and I knew this was more down to her wanting to gossip in the kitchen.

"Right, come on please tell me…what's wrong with him?" Libby asked as I opened the dishwasher.

"What do you mean?"

"Oh come on, there must be something wrong with him, otherwise we might have found the world's most perfect man and then we could sell his DNA for millions!" I laughed with her, but she was trying to be serious. I couldn't exactly say 'Well he is half Demon.'

"So, let's look at the evidence, he's kind, generous, rich, a perfect gentleman, utterly gorgeous to look at..." She was counting off his plus points on her fingers and had to swap hands to continue, there were so many.

"Oh yeah, and let's not forget according to you, an absolute sex God in the bedroom with a healthy amount of equipment! And saving the best for last…he clearly utterly and completely adores you!" She had me blushing and I was glad I was hiding my head as I loaded the dishes.

"Oh come on, please give me something!" I shook my head at the conversation we were having and let the door slam.

"Okay, so what's wrong with Frank?" I challenged.

"His feet reek!"

"Libby!" I shouted at her for being mean, ok, so I knew it was true and couldn't help but laugh.

"What? They do, and we're talking premium French cheese here. Oh, and he snores. So that's two things…your turn." I got the cake out to cut it in half and started to add the whipped cream to the middle. Libby passed me the strawberries out of the fridge.

"Well, there is one thing. He stares at me too much," I said quietly but she just laughed, not taking me seriously.

"Oh, poor you! Come on, that's not a fault, why would you mind that?"

"Well, you know I get all shy and besides, it's intimidating. He can be intense but mainly I don't understand why he does it." This made her smile turn serious.

"Oh Kaz, it's not hard to understand at all. You do remember all the attention you got in high school? Everyone fancied you but they weren't brave enough to ask you out."

"That's not true!" I was getting defensive now, but Libby wouldn't back down.

"Oh Kaz, open your eyes, you're beautiful and you never needed flashy, short clothes or loads of makeup to achieve that and sat in there is the proof! I mean, even now you have Justin drooling at the very sight of you. Frank said his brother was gutted to find out you're dating someone. Does Dominic know you're taking him to his club next weekend?"

"No and I need to talk to you about that."

"Oh no, you can't back out, do it for Frank and just palm him off with your friend RJ when you get there, but please just do it this one time, okay?" I would have loved to have said no but she knew my guilt would be on her side, so I just nodded.

"Okay, but I'm doing this for Frank," I said sternly wondering how the hell I was ever going to break it to Draven. The thought created butterflies in my food filled stomach.

"Anyway, getting back to Dominic, I'm just glad you have met someone who makes you so happy and he's lucky to have you, in my opinion."

"Thanks Libs and if I find out his feet smell, or he grinds his teeth in bed then you will be the first one to know." She hugged me and kissed my cheek from behind.

"That's all I ask," she said as I was still spreading the cream on the bottom layer of the cake. She watched me like a woman possessed as I heated the chocolate for drizzling. It soon became apparent what Libby's cravings were when she had Frank running out at stupid hours to get her bars upon bars of chocolate.

I added the sliced strawberries to the cream base before putting the top on. Then after putting it on a large plate, I poured on the runny, chocolate goodness and I thought Libby was going to pounce on me. I asked her to carry in the dessert plates for me as I thought it would be safer than giving her the cake, she might have run out of the house with it.

On my way there, I continued to think about the conversation and how glad I was that Draven didn't just walk in on it, when I froze and nearly dropped the cake. My heart started pounding in my chest and my palms started to instantly sweat!

I had forgotten the most important factor of dating a half Demon half Angel boyfriend...

Supernatural hearing!

CHAPTER SEVENTEEN

EMBARRASSING PAST

Libby looked at me as to why I had stopped dead in the hallway. What could I say? That Draven had most likely heard our entire conversation! Oh no, then it hit me, it wasn't only the stuff about Justin that he had heard. Well, one thing was for sure, if he didn't know what I thought about sex with him was like then he sure did now. In great detail!

I knew I had to move but I couldn't get my legs to work and Libby had given up waiting for me to come to my senses. I was staring down at the cake in my hands, wishing it would just self-combust so I didn't have to go back in there. Libby shouted my name impatiently and when I didn't answer, I heard her chair move along the wooden floor. Soon I found hands quickly taking the cake off me, only they didn't belong to Libby as I had first thought. They were Draven's and another thing I was forgetting about my unusual boyfriend was his ability to sense my thoughts when I was in meltdown mode.

"Keira, look at me." His voice was soft and gentle, but I knew once we were alone it wouldn't remain that way for long. I bravely did as I was asked and met a pair of dreamy dark eyes. He dipped his head closer to mine and I thought he was going to kiss me, he was so close.

"Come back to the table, we will discuss this later and don't worry, I'm not angry," he said before taking my hand and leading me back to the dining room.

"Kaz, what have you been doing?" Libby eyed me questionably and Draven came to my rescue, as I couldn't think quickly enough.

"She forgot a knife to cut the cake with, didn't you love?" he said softly and then produced a large kitchen knife from behind his back as he placed the cake down. I just bit my lip and took the knife from Draven with shaky hands. I was about to start cutting the pieces when my hand started to feel all warm and tingly.

It started to move without any control on my part and I knew Draven was worried that I wasn't up to the task of holding a sharp implement. My hand and his mind cut everyone a piece and as soon as I placed my own down in front of me, the knife was put down and I was once again in control of my own body parts. I felt Draven's hand squeeze my leg under the table and when I looked to my side, he was smiling at me. This made me relax enough to start up the conversation again. Only Libby beat me to it.

"So Dominic, I gather now you and Kazzy are dating, you will be staying in town longer than you usually do?" Libby asked as she devoured her baked dessert. Draven smiled at her question before answering it.

"Yes, I will be making my stay here more of the permanent kind. However, I will still need to leave for a few weeks at a time for business, but I will only leave when it is convenient for Keira to travel with me." Libby looked just as shocked as I did. He wanted to take me with him? I was almost giddy at the thought.

"Well, that will suit Kazzy alright, she's always loved to travel." She nodded for me to jump in, but I was still surprised at this new bit of information. We had never talked about his work before, let alone the idea of that work taking him from here.

When I first found out that the Dravens didn't come here for more than a few weeks at a time, I had just assumed that one day they'd leave here, and I would have to find a way to get over him. But then, of course, things changed when Draven and I had become an item. But still, we had never spoken about the future. So to find out that I would be expected to follow him around the world was an easy addition to our relationship. Libby, however, looked both happy for me but also gutted that I would be taken from her for weeks at a time.

"Can I ask what type of business you are involved in?" This was one thing Libby had always wanted to know but I still winced at her questioning.

"Libs! Come on, what's with the firing line?" I said, but Draven just put his hand on mine and smiled.

"Keira it is fine, I do not mind explaining my business. I deal in a lot of investments all around the world. These vary from anything to property, shares, nightclubs, casinos, hotels and even banks. My family have their hands in many different businesses, but mainly we provide the money behind new ventures, some pay off more than others, of course." He said this with such business efficiency that it made me want him to repeat it to me in the bedroom, while he was wearing one of his expensive suits. Hearing this wasn't just a first for my sister as I also didn't know until now what his business entailed. Now I knew it was a bit of ...well... everything.

"And you mentioned family, do your parents also deal in investments?" Her question was a perfectly normal one that was of course if his parents hadn't been a high-ranking Angel and Demon still living in Heaven and Hell. Oh dear. I bit my lip and took a huge gulp of my wine that finished it off. Draven picked up the bottle and refilled my glass, before doing the same for Frank and himself.

"No, I am afraid my parents are no longer with us. My brother and sister also share in our business but as the oldest, I am in control of the family's assets, which includes running the company. Most of which I can do from any country, with the occasional business trip." Ok, now it was getting hot in here. Why did he have to keep talking like that? Didn't he know it was just pushing my sex fantasies into overdrive. One of which was where I would be his naughty secretary doing overtime cleaning his desk. Oh but the possibilities were endless, I thought trying to hide a grin. And did he just say he was the oldest? I thought they were triplets. I quickly started to rack my brain as to whether or not I had told my sister that? Then his hand gripped the inside of my thigh and I felt strong fingers start to caress closer to my underwear.

I needed to focus, for starters this was most definitely not the time to be thinking about him ripping off more of my clothes, not at the dinner table with my pregnant sister and brother-in-law present. I tried to squirm away from his hand but suddenly, his grip tightened before the point of pain and only eased when I shifted back closer to him. My God, he was so demanding, which wasn't helping in keeping my sexual frustration in check.

"I am sorry to hear about your parents, Dominic and I'm sorry for my curiosity, Kaz hasn't really told us much about you, but I guess seeing as you have only been seeing each other a short time, then it's understandable."

"I really don't mind your questions, Libby. I understand that our family generates a lot of questions when we come here and no doubt small-town gossip follows, but there is nothing out of the ordinary with our reasons for being here." He said this with such ease that I choked on my mouthful of wine and started coughing at the burning in my throat. Draven started to pat me on the back and Libby passed me her water.

"Sorry, went down... the... wrong... way." I coughed out again, as it was like trying to swallow the lies that flowed so easily from his cunning lips. Oh man, now he was good, Hell he was a master at it and I suppose years of having to deceive humans helped. When I was drinking my water Draven eyed me as if to say 'that didn't help' but I just kept my eyes down.

"Sorry Dominic, you were saying?" Libby motioned for him to continue after my little episode.

"Just that the reasons behind the VIP not admitting locals is that my clients prefer to keep their privacy and business intact. Only Keira has been allowed to work up there and this was for two reasons, the first being she was not tainted by small-town gossip and knew what it meant to be discreet. And well, the second reason was more of a personal nature." He grinned to himself at being able to watch me freely when I first started to work there.

"Because you liked her?" Libby asked with a smirk plastered on her face.

"Libby!" I shouted, not liking being the main topic.

"Yes, because as soon as I saw her, I wanted to know her," Draven said this with honesty in his voice and Frank nudged Libby on the arm before contributing his feelings.

"I tried to tell them once, but neither would believe me. I knew when you brought her home that night, that there was more to it, but our little Kazzy here has never been one to admit when someone fancies her."

"Oh Frank, not you too, can we get off this subject please?" I said feeling my cheeks melting, but Draven was clearly amused with Frank's interpretation of the events.

"See!" Frank followed this by laughing and Libby frowned at him.

"Frank, you're embarrassing her."

"Na, she's a tough nut aren't you Kazzy? And one hell of a cook, I might add." This had me smiling, as it was one compliment that I liked to receive.

"Oh, I second that, but tell me, where did you learn how to cook?" Draven turned to me and I met his yummy eyes with confidence.

"Just at home experimenting and watching my mum as a kid, she loved to bake...hey Libs, do you remember her chocolate brownie cakes with the iced tops?" We both made 'mmm' noises and Frank rolled his eyes.

"Women and chocolate...do you understand it?" Frank asked Draven and he laughed before saying,

"It's all in the balance."

"Balance?" Frank repeated clearly confused.

"Well, women must be addicted to something as sweet as their natures." Libby and I both giggled like flirty teenagers and Frank just rolled his eyes.

"I must remember to tell my brother that one! I bet it's a big hit with the ladies." At this Draven released my leg and made fists under the table, which luckily, only I could see.

"Ah yes, Justin isn't it? Keira has mentioned him." This looked almost painful to watch as unbeknown to my sister and Frank, Draven was finding it hard to even say his name without straining and gritting his teeth.

"Yeah, he's just come back from travelling. He's a real free spirit kind of guy, which is code for he doesn't really know what he wants to do in life but he's a good kid."

"You say kid, but Frank, he's the same age as me," I said but instantly regretted anything from my mouth that sounded like I was defending him.

"Yeah, but I call you kid and besides, I'm going to be a daddy, so I have the right," he said as he rubbed his wife's belly and she rolled her eyes when he stuck his tongue out at me. Of course, I did it back but ruined its effect when I laughed and nearly snorted.

"You're both big kids," Libby stated before cutting herself some more cake.

"Congratulations, Keira told me you were expecting," Draven said making the proud parents beam.

"Thank you. I believe I made Keira late for work once when she found out the news, so she must have told you then." As soon as she said it Draven's face dropped slightly as this was the time when he had shouted at me for being late and he didn't know the reason for it. Well, not until now. I suppressed a smile at the memory.

"Yes," was all he said, and I knew he was probably feeling guilty having now found out my reason was a valid one. I had thought that maybe he had believed it was down to Jack, but this was something I could ask him when we were next alone, which I was both craving and dreading.

"So, your brother Justin, will he be visiting you again soon?"

"Oh yeah, didn't Kaz tell you? He's coming to stay next weekend and Kazzy offered to take him to Afterlife." Frank looked from me to Libby as if he had just put his foot in it, but of course I'd already done that moments ago in the kitchen.

"It must have slipped her mind," Draven said before giving me a chilling smile, one that made me gulp.

"Yeah, I was thinking I was going to introduce him to RJ," I said hoping this would cool things down, but it just made things worse.

"What the Goth with pink hair? Na, he's got a thing for

blondes." At this Draven was almost desperate to let out a growl, I could tell by the way his large fists were turning white under the strain. Libby shot Frank a look and shook her head slightly. At least she knew that this wasn't the best conversation to be having, so she thankfully changed the subject and asked who wanted coffee.

"Tea for me, please."

"Well durr, oh and don't worry Kaz, I wouldn't ask you to make it." Libby burst out laughing and Frank joined in as, of course, he had heard the story along with everyone else in my family! Draven looked as if he'd missed something and I frowned at them both.

"Oh sorry, you don't know why Kazzy hates coffee do you?" Libby had on her mischievous grin and I had to intervene quickly.

"Oh no, don't you dare! I mean it…Dra… I mean Dominic doesn't need to hear about childish stories." I warned her but this just made Draven even more curious. He cleared his throat before disagreeing with me.

"I beg to differ, I would love to hear stories about Keira as a child." Libby gave me a wink, but I just folded my arms and mouthed a big 'NO' at her.

"I'm sorry Kaz, but he's the guest." I grunted at this and just sat there looking extremely hacked off, but for Draven this just added to his amusement.

"Well, when Kaz was…umm how old?" Great, now she wanted my input.

"Eleven," I said grumpily.

"Yeah, that's right, she was eleven when my dad had some clients meeting him at the house. Our mother usually made tea and coffee whenever he'd have a meeting at home, but mum was called to the care home. See, our dad works in advertising and our mum works with the elderly. So when she got called away, Kazzy offered to help my dad by making the drinks. What she hadn't counted on was that they would all want coffee and she had never made it before. Dad told her that the filtered coffee was in the cupboard and it was in a jar with a red lid." She actually stopped to laugh, and I don't suppose my miserable face was helping.

"So she poured the whole jar in the bottom of the cafetière and added the water before putting on the top and letting it brew." Again, the word brew had her in fits, which I just rolled my eyes at.

"Yes, yes, get on with it, Libs," I said impatiently and this had them all laughing.

"Anyway, she got everything ready, sugar, cream, cups and then took in the tray. It was only when they all left, did Kazzy notice that no one had drunk their coffee as all the cups were still full. When she asked my dad why, he told her..."

"Because dear, nobody likes cream and sugar with a cup of gravy." At this Libby was crying with laughter and Frank had banged his fist on the table, before erupting with his usual hoarse grunting. Draven too found this all hysterical but instead of laughing at me, he pulled me into him and kissed the top of my head. I could feel his attempt at hiding his amusement, but the sound of his laughter had me joining in with them all.

"Why did you give them this to drink?" Draven asked through an outstretched grin.

"Because I thought it was the coffee, besides my dad's clients thought it was so funny, that it sealed the deal."

"Yes, I can imagine, very adorable indeed." Draven agreed and Libby tilted her head and mouthed an 'aww' at me when he wasn't looking her way.

"Yeah, well it wasn't as bad as the time Libby blew up the popcorn machine!" I giggled and Frank's eyes widened...he obviously hadn't yet heard this one. Now it was Libby's turn to get defensive.

"Catherine! Don't you dare!" Libby only ever called me by my first name when she was serious, but it sounded like the way my mum said it when I was in trouble.

"Oh, no way babe, you spilt her story, now I want to know yours." She frowned at her big husband but to no effect.

"Sorry Libs, but if the guest requests then I must deliver," I said in a smug tone.

"Frank lives here so that doesn't count!"

"Fine...Dominic please can you agree with me, that this is also one story you would very much like to hear." I asked in my sweetest tone and to seal the deal, I placed my hand on the inside of his thigh getting closer until I could just brush my fingers along his length. I smiled when I heard him suck in a sharp breath. He first had to clear his throat before speaking.

"I'm sorry, Libby, but forgive me for never being able to deny your sister anything." Libby raised her eyebrows first at Draven then at Frank.

"Traitors!" She commented but couldn't keep her face straight. I was smiling at my revenge and took a large swig of my wine before starting my story.

"Okay, so our parents had gone away for the weekend and left Libby in charge, as she is the oldest. She was told not to have anyone around, but Libby ignored the rules and invited her friends and before long there were about twenty people in the house. She decided to make popcorn when she was drunk, but because there was still un-popped corn in the bottom, she thought it would be a good idea to keep the machine on."

"I wasn't that drunk!" she added but I continued as if I hadn't heard her.

"So, when she forgot about it and the fire alarm started to go off, I was the one to find the flames. The popcorn machine was on fire and melting. Libby then came running in and opened a window before throwing it outside into our fishpond. The problem was one of our neighbours had heard the alarm and called the fire brigade! The next thing we knew we had to pile twenty drunken teens into a garage, clean up the evidence of a party and fish out the remains of the popcorn machine, all before the firemen piled in."

Frank clearly loved every minute of this story, so I purposely left out the bit where she had her boyfriend of the time to stay the night. In hopes she wouldn't mention me kissing a boy from my school who was two years older than me.

"So what happened? You ever get busted?" Frank asked Libby.

"No, I made Kaz burn some toast and blamed it on that but when mum and dad got back, they wanted to know why all the fish had died!" This once again made the house fill with the sound of laughter, but it died when she asked me the name of that boy I kissed.

"Thanks Libs! You know, I don't remember, you invited him! And what about that boyfriend of yours that you had to stay the night…eh?" I know it was cruel, but she had struck first. Frank being of the protective jealous type shot her a look and in turn she shot me one that translated into a 'thanks a lot!' at which I just shrugged my shoulders. Meanwhile, Draven had the same look as Frank, only directed at me.

"How old were you?" Draven asked me and I winced.

"Nearly fifteen." He frowned at my answer. I finished my wine letting the last drops gladly go to my head. Then I had a thought that would once again have me and Libby on the same page.

"Have you spoken to mum lately?" I asked and Libby looked like she had been caught stealing candy.

"Umm yeah, sorry about that, it kind of slipped out about you and Dominic, I take it she rang?" she said wincing at her own guilt.

"Oh yeah, she called alright! And I got the whole baby safe lecture, so cheers for that. But this wasn't the worst bit…oh no…, guess who's coming to stay?" My face must have said it all.

"No way, you're bloody shitting me!" It was rare for my sister to swear but where our cousin was concerned there wasn't enough swear words in the English language to cover it.

"I shit you not!" I said swearing myself, which was thanks to all the wine I had consumed. I think Draven could tell I was a little tipsy, so I decided to stop drinking the grape and move on to something safer or before he knew it I would start singing Dolly Parton's '9 to 5' and then I really would be doomed. I don't know what it was about that song, but it always seemed to be the one my drunken mind would favour.

"Okay, well that's not going to happen!" Libby stated and I could only wish it were true. If Draven and Frank both thought me and Libby were stubborn, then this was nothing compared to our mother. She was hands down the queen bee of stubbornness. Hell, she was the reason they invented the term, 'stubborn like a Williams'. Of course, this was only known in the family and not throughout Liverpool.

"Libs, I hate to break it to you, but I tried, mum won't budge," I said stating the obvious.

"We will see about that, wait until I speak to her." This sounded about as aggressive as a budgie singing the EastEnders theme tune to a little old lady! She looked at her watch and I could see her working out the time difference and when she got up, I knew she thought it best to deal with our mother herself. Even though I knew the outcome would still remain the same, there was nothing stopping me from dreaming otherwise.

"Good luck!" I said before she walked into the kitchen.

"What is it with you guys and this evil cousin?" Frank asked before getting up himself to take out the remaining dishes.

"Just wait and you will find out, because I can guarantee she will be here in a few weeks causing trouble and making everyone crazy…including you."

"You know me Kaz, Mr Laid Back."

"Yeah, you might be, but an unhappy wife equals an unhappy life." At this his face dropped, as now he understood my full meaning. Libby hated our cousin just as much as I did and from the sounds of the murmurs coming from the next room, she was making her full feelings known.

Frank left for the kitchen quickly and I would bet my life that he too was now praying for Libby to win over the iron will of our mother. I smiled to myself and then turned to look at Draven but for once, I found him looking away and in what seemed to be deep in thought. I knew what was coming and any minute now I would have to explain myself about Justin. I was about to speak and tell him I was sorry, but he turned to me abruptly,

"You are right, your mother cannot be swayed, and Libby is not pleased." He was about to say more when he stopped and smiled having heard something he liked.

"Now she is explaining the evening…do you want the verdict?" He leaned into me and my heart rate shot up a couple of notches. He moved the hair off my neck to get to my ear as usual.

"I think I have been accepted into the family." He sounded pleased and the kiss that followed made me think that maybe I wasn't in as much trouble as I had first thought. He pulled away and I knew the only reason was because Libby was now stomping back into the dining room.

"Well, you were right…the bitch arrives the week after next!" I sighed at the idea and Libby added even more shit to the pile.

"Oh, and she told mum to let you know that she can't wait until she gets here, as she really wants to..." She paused before continuing with a thought that would have me close to screaming...

"Meet your new boyfriend."

CHAPTER EIGHTEEN

SCREAMING IN THE NIGHT

The rest of the evening went by quickly but most importantly smoothly and thankfully with no more embarrassing stories about my past. It was getting late and it was only when a vibrating sound came from Draven's pocket, did I look at the clock. Of course, for a king of the supernatural world, I doubted eleven o'clock was past his bedtime.

It was strange to see Draven answer a mobile phone and it brought back memories of the first and last time I had seen it. Back then of course, I had been terrified of him but even then, my love had never faltered. It was a bizarre feeling to be obsessed with someone you both loved and feared. Now things were different. I had swapped fear for intimidated, but the obsession still remained as strong as the day it was first imprinted.

Draven stood and excused himself before continuing with his phone call. He spoke a language I couldn't understand, but if I were to guess it sounded from Asian descent.

"Well, that's me convinced, he's lovely," Libby whispered in vain as he could probably speak six different languages, listen to ten conversations while juggling cars and making a soufflé at the same time. Okay, scratch the soufflé part, but he could order

someone to make it while all this was going on. I giggled and Libby mistook its meaning.

"Pleased?"

"Yes and thank you for making him feel so welcome." I said this to both of them, but Frank just winked at me as if it was no trouble. Draven walked back in as he was placing his shiny black phone back in his pocket.

"I'm afraid I have just been informed that I have some business to attend to, so I must say goodnight, but I thank you both for your hospitality." My heart sank at the thought of spending the night alone. It's funny how all those years I coped, not knowing anything different, but now after less than a week of spending every night in his arms, I didn't know how I was going to face being without him.

"Keira, my driver is outside," he said, nodding to the door and I knew I had to say goodbye, but all I wanted to do was sit here and sulk. I wondered if it was actually business that was taking him away from me, or was I being punished for the 'Justin thing'?

He was shaking Frank's hand and then he gave Libby a kiss on the cheek as he thanked them again. I, on the other hand looked as though I was going to start sucking my thumb. I walked him to the door while Libby and Frank remained in the den to give us some privacy.

He took my jacket off the hook and started to hold it out for me.

"It's ok, I don't need it," I said thinking it was odd as I was only going to be out there for a short while unless he knew I would be clingy.

"Keira, it is cold out there tonight, look there's a frost." He was right, as when I opened the door, we were met by a sparkly blanket that covered the earth and was shimmering under the porch light.

"Yeah, but I won't keep you." He frowned at my reason.

"You do not want to come with me? I already told you, I will not be angry…"

"Wait, you want me to come?" His face softened as my mistake became clear. His hands took me by the waist and he pulled me into him roughly.

"Of course I want you to come with me, Keira, I never want to be apart from you, not even for one single night." My lips curved into a shy smile which made him let out a low groan at the sight. He loved it when I went all shy. He turned me around and slapped me lightly on my bottom which made me let out an excited scream.

"Right, go and get your jacket on before you freeze this perfect behind off," he said jokingly.

"Wait, I just need to grab some stuff and…" He stopped me and whispered into my hair.

"Keira, don't make a fuss but no you don't. Just go and tell your sister you're going, and I will wait for you in the car." I frowned but even though he couldn't see it as my back was to him, he still knew it was there as he laughed lightly before kissing the top of my head and letting me go.

I ran back inside wondering why he had said that I didn't need anything, but I pushed it to the back of my mind before it started to overload with worry. I quickly explained to Libby that I was going with him and that I would see her the next day. I also promised to make a Sunday dinner just to get out of there quicker.

I grabbed my jacket and ran out of the door to find a huge black Rolls Royce in the drive waiting for me. The man in a grey coat and black hat who was holding the door open was no stranger to me. He was the same driver who used to chauffeur me to and from work at the request of Draven. However, this car looked like a deadly creature under the moonlight, with its angry square grill that looked as if it would take a bite out of the Aston Martin that was behind it waiting to be driven by another of Draven's men. Its emblem gleamed silver and I was sure I remembered the winged figure was called the 'Spirit of Ecstasy'. Well, that sure was fitting. I don't think I could think of a better description and I wasn't just talking about the car. I stepped forward cautiously as though it wanted to eat me and only when I saw the figure of Ecstasy himself sat there waiting, did I hurry my feet. As soon as I ducked to get in I had Draven's hand held out to help me.

This car reminded me of two different forces fused together. The inside was the complete opposite to the outside. The inside was made with pure luxury in mind and the outside had you gulping at the sight. It was a bit like Draven. Half of him you would kill just to receive his soft touch and caress all over your willing body and the other half would kill you if you were crazy enough to go against it.

I ran my hand over the soft cream leather seat and thought it to be far too comfortable to be in a car. The back seats were more spacious than I expected and there was a clear screen between the driver and us. As always, Draven watched me like prey as I looked around at the walnut finish and cream carpets that also held footrests.

"You seem to like this car." Draven's voice was deep and smouldering, making me jump at the sound and when the doors locked before we pulled away, I swallowed hard. Like this it was easy to see him as a king. He sat back casually as if he'd known this level of luxury all his life and I felt like Oliver or Annie being taken under his wing.

I bit my lip at just how different our lives were and prayed to God for not only opposites to attract but for them to be able to withstand anything. I needed Draven and it pained me to know my need was far greater than his. It just had to be. Anything else just wasn't plausible. I mean, he could have anything he wanted, and I didn't know if I would ever understand why he would ever have wanted me. But I was left thanking God daily that he did.

"It's a beautiful car, it seems better than I remember, but why didn't you just drive the Aston back?" At this he cocked his head and smiled to himself.

"Because I like to have my hands free for other things…oh and it's an upgrade," he whispered into my hairline before tilting my chin upwards for a gentle kiss. We both sighed at the same time, when the sound of his phone vibrating brought our lips apart. I started to pull away but with supernatural speed his hands grabbed my body and pulled me into his for a demanding kiss.

"Only when I am ready to let you go, little one," he said in a hoarse voice, clearly thick with lust. Meanwhile, the phone became a background buzz soon forgotten as Draven's lips seared mine with burning need. I could tell he was fighting himself to keep control and if the deep frustrated growl was anything to go by then I would say that his rational mind had returned.

He let me go with a deep inhale and reached into his pocket to answer his phone.

"Speak!" he demanded in one of those 'I am your Lord and Master' tones. He listened for a moment before switching to another language to reply. I got the distinct impression he didn't want me to know what he was talking about.

I decided to ignore the call and I watched the night fly by in a black haze. Only when Draven's hand reached for mine as he moved closer to me, did I realise the phone had gone. I didn't turn my head to look at him but instead I rested it on his shoulder and snuggled closer before my insecurities got the better of me. He responded to this by stroking my cheek with his other hand.

"You must be tired." I didn't know whether he was asking me or talking to himself, but at the very sound of the word I could feel my eyes closing and getting heavy. The hum of the engine was creating a rhythm that my brain responded to by drifting off and shutting down. When Draven's hand started to make circles on my palm, I couldn't fight it any longer, so when his words whispered their usual command in a velvety tone, I was totally compliant.

"Sleep now." His words were the last thing I remembered.

I woke as I felt movement under my body and I soon realised I was being carried up some stairs. As soon as Draven felt me stir, he pulled my body closer to his and leant his head down.

"Ssshh, go back to sleep, my young beauty. You will be in our bed soon." The way he said 'our bed' made me smile under his jacket, which was pulled tightly around me. I could just hear a door open and the usual smell of old furniture filled my lungs. This room felt more like home to me than any other place on earth.

I felt him stop and the sound of the covers being pulled back made a whoosh sound in the air. I knew he was using his gifts, considering that his hands weren't free. He lowered me down and I could feel the heat escaping from my body as the distance between us grew.

I seemed to be in a semi-daze and didn't know whether this

was me dreaming as I started to feel the air on my skin where my clothes were being removed. His soft hands made sure to come into contact with skin with every inch of material that he pulled away from me. I bit my lip at the feeling his undressing did to me and the craving to have him take me was nearly uncontrollable. He lifted me slightly to pull the top over my head and then expertly removed my underwear. Then he ran his fingers gently over every curve and I inhaled deeply, taking in his scent.

He gently rolled me over so that I was lying on my front and he did the same motions down my back. His palm flattened on the base of my spine and he ran it up slowly till it reached the back of my neck.

He must have thought that I was in a deep sleep, as he started to whisper things to me in a different language before letting my hair loose. He gripped it with both his hands and twisted it. Then he placed it to one side so that he could kiss my neck and continue downwards, making my spine feel like sticky dough. Every touch felt like little electric pulses that lit up my nerves and senses like fireworks on New Year's Eve.

"My Lord, everything is ready…they…they are here and are awaiting your command." An unsure voice I didn't recognise spoke and when I shifted slightly from surprise his soft hands held me still.

"Ssshh… le sommeil mon pure" ("Sleep my pure one" in French). His voice acted like a warm blanket over my mind and I tried desperately to stay awake and focus on what was happening, but it was proving impossible.

"Tell my Council I will join them soon." His authoritative voice filled the night air making it such a contrast to how moments before he was talking so sweetly to me. He wasn't yet finished with me as his hands explored my skin and I knew that if I rolled over to fully announce I was awake his movements would stop, and he would leave. I wanted to ask him what it was that would soon take him away, but I was captivated by the immense bliss having his hands on my body created.

He smoothed back my hair so that he could see my face and the back of one finger traced my jawline. I couldn't help but bite my lip as he got closer to them and I heard him let out more air through his nose at his amusement. I felt his hands flatten on the bed either side of me and his body weight rested on them while he lowered his body closer to mine. His lips rested lightly on mine but for no more than seconds. Then he moved them to my ear and whispered,

"I love you, Keira."

And then with that, he was gone.

I don't know how long I slept, but when I awoke there was still the darkness that crept its way through the cracks of the curtains. I sat up and pulled the covers up to my neck as the night air was thick with an icy chill, one so cold that I could see my breath. In fact, the only thing that kept me warm was my blood that raced its way through my veins from fear. Fear caused by the realisation that I wasn't alone.

I sat deadly still as though my terror had me locked and frozen in time. I wanted to find the courage to move or speak but I could smell and feel that the air held another of my nightmares...

This was how I knew I wasn't alone.

I shifted when I heard a noise that sounded like nails scraping along a wooden floor and it was getting closer to the bed. I held my hands over my mouth to prevent a scream from escaping but my breathing under them was nearly as loud. Finally, I couldn't stand it any longer and I grabbed the curtain and yanked it back as fast as I could so I couldn't chicken out. They whipped back and I jumped at the noise they made.

I scanned the room but there was nothing but the sound of mocking laughter that seemed to come from every corner. The furniture hadn't moved but cast eerie long shadows on the floor. Some looked like twisted corpses dragging themselves closer, as if drawn to my fear. I shivered as the laughter faded into the night, creating an unnatural stillness to the silent space between me and the figure that was in hiding.

"Who...who's there?" I asked and my voice shook, sounding like my rib cage was being rattled.

"Are you afraid?" The confident voice asked, and the answer was confirmed when I recognised who it belonged to.

"No!" I lied bravely. Lucius' laughter echoed around the room as I didn't yet know where he was.

"If that is true, then come to me." His deep voice was commanding and had me nearly trembling. He was whispering 'Come to me' over and over until my ears followed it to the open glass doors onto the balcony. I started to move, and I didn't know why. Shouldn't I be running?

I grabbed the silk sheet that lay on the top of the thick covers and pulled it around my naked body as though it would provide me with some protection. It cocooned my cold skin with an icy layer and my feet found the steps around the bed.

My mind was screaming at me for what my body was doing. Why couldn't I control my actions? His whispering continued and when I was out of bed, I moved towards the balcony where his voice changed,

"Yes... yes...*further.*" His words consumed my thoughts and I was only there to do his will. My outer shell felt as though it was freezing all over but inside was pure Hellfire. My veins were molten lava and my heart was the cause of the eruption. I wanted to scream out to Draven but even though I still had my speech I couldn't use it.

I got to the open doors and saw the full moonlight up the marble floor giving it a bluish tinge. The balcony was empty, but I still continued further until the voice commanded differently. My hands went out to the metal railing for support and they turned wet when the frost that covered it melted under my warm palms. Then my fingers curled around it tightly as I felt his body so close to my own behind me. Hands found my shoulders and pushed away the silk that they found there. He moved my loose hair away to get to my bare neck and I counted my last minutes before he took me.

"Do you think I want to end your life, my little Keira girl?" His lips bent close to my ear as he said this and I started to tremble under his huge hands that still had hold of my neck on either side, encasing the entire length with icy solid fingers. I nodded and he moved my head to one side to the angle he wanted it. He traced his fingertips down from my ear to my bare shoulder blade.

"Something so pure should be enjoyed before death and you are too young before that event happens. However, I can still... *devour you!*" He gripped me roughly as he turned me into him so he could crush his mouth to mine. He tasted the blood there, as he bit down hard on my lips and sucked them before kissing me passionately and taking my body into his arms. I was locked in his half-naked frame and couldn't get free. The only veil between our bare bodies was the thin sheet of silk that felt as though it was slipping away into nothing.

My body wasn't the only thing locked, as my mind seemed to belong to him also. It was like being licked by flames and touched by ice. I had to concentrate, or I would never break free. I searched my own mind for his presence and when my head became hot and sticky, I found him hanging onto me like a black plague. I closed my eyes tight and pushed and pushed until I felt my limbs become my own again. First, I moved my fingers and they formed fists by my sides. My arms tensed and I pushed them out with all my strength hitting his solid chest.

I was surprised when he moved backwards, and I didn't know if it was down to me or the shock that I had overcome his power. I could now see his face for the first time, and it was hard, handsome and cold. His lightened skin only made his eyes all the more striking like bloody coloured crystals. He had an ethereal beauty, like a marble statue carved into perfect features for all time. Harsh lines of a chiselled face mirrored the clear-cut lines of a muscular body, with forearms tensing like tension wire on a bridge, as he flexed his fists in clear rage. His naked torso was clearly rippled without an inch of fat but, unlike Draven, he was of a slimmer build, swapping Draven's brute strength for stealth and speed.

His frown was soon replaced with a chilling smile and it only enhanced his terrifying face. I ran past him, back into the safety of the room only to be met by a blazing fire. I stopped dead at the sight of the flames that licked at the bed frame. The curtains had changed from their usual purple and gold material to a waving wall of red and orange. They moved like they were underwater and I stepped back until I once again felt cold marble under my feet. I heard the crackling of wood splitting under the immense heat and then, as I took even more steps backwards, the two trees either side of the door erupted into blue flames, along with the door frame. The glass started to pop and melt, making little deadly shards cover the floor when the doors gave up and shattered.

"You may be different to other humans, but you will never escape the hold I have on you!" I turned to face him and screamed at the sight of him in his Demon form. His body was black as if it had been burnt and flakes of ash fell to the ground beneath him. His huge horns that came from his shoulders held the start of his wings that were like half-bat and half-bird. They reached the floor and curled upwards with weapons situated on the multiple tips. Black claws grew longer and thicker from them at the sight of my fear. A smile crept its way across the unfamiliar Demonic face of Draven's enemy, that was now also my own.

"What do you want!?" I shouted at his laughter.

"So fiery for someone so small!" When he said this the flames flew out to the sides and started to melt the metal railing and what were once black roses, were now glowing red with heat.

"I will not have long to wait, and you will soon come to me." He sounded so sure of this, that I almost believed that I would do anything he commanded me to. He had a hold over me and we both knew it to be as strong as having the need to breathe. I was bound to him and I wanted desperately to cut the cord that connected us.

"NEVER!" I screamed, before falling to my knees and covering my head. I wanted to be saved by Draven. I wanted his hands to pull me from this nightmare and keep me safe. But he didn't come. There was no gentle caress, no soft words of love... only the sound of Lucius coming closer to take me.

"Draven...Draven!" I said his name over and over as my tears flowed freely down my cheeks.

"Years of waiting have taught the fool nothing of protecting what he loves the most and you, *my pure one*, will soon see what it means to be under my rule. Rest assured, no one will take you from me, not as I will soon be taking you from your foolish Lord!" His words were like venom that coursed its way around my body and infected it, making me shiver. I wanted to cry at the thought of being taken by the Devil's right hand from the man I loved. His threat scared me into never doubting that one day he would complete his goal and I would be at his mercy.

My head lifted to see that there was now only a small space which was not alight. He lifted his hand up and motioned for me to rise. I did as I was instructed, but as my eyes met the surrounding view, I noticed the flames weren't only confined to the balcony. Everything I had once thought to be the most beautiful scenery was now consumed by a red river of death. The burning trees were falling, as the sea of flames destroyed everything in its path. I knew none of this was real but when even my throat burned with inhaling the hot air and my nose filled with the smell of wood turning to ash, I still cried as though it was really happening. The balcony was crumbling away into the fiery abyss below and I felt as though I had been cast down to Hell itself.

It felt like the end of the world.

"Why are you doing this?" I asked hopelessly and as my hair fell down in front of my face, his hands were there to hold it back. He stood so close and my breath caught in my lungs making it hard to breathe. He gripped the bottom of my face and forced me to look up at him.

"Because I want you for myself." I closed my eyes tight and pushed him out of my head as I could feel his influence trying to tunnel its way back in.

"Never," I whispered fiercely making him laugh.

"You think I can be stopped?"

"Draven would never allow you to take me," I said lifting my head higher, believing in my words.

"Oh, but I have plans for your Dark Lord, ones that are breeding beneath his very nose and breathing life for a new future, *My future.* And it all begins tonight!" he said looking up to the sky as his wings expanded outwards making me flinch back.

"No!" I shouted at him then had to turn my face away at the evil I found before me. I felt him step up to me and gently raise my face to his. He forced me to look straight into the face of insanity that years of bitterness had created. Then he smiled at my fear and released my face, but his hand found my shaky one to lift to his lips to kiss it like a gentleman.

"You will not have long to wait until we meet again but for now, I will leave you with a gift." He nodded behind me and I turned while my hand was still locked in his. There, a flaming body emerged from the smoke-filled room and the screams could be heard across Hell's valley below. I could just make out the body of a young girl with long blonde hair and a small curved frame.

Her arms were bleeding from the deep cuts there and her naked legs were covered in melting flesh. The screams of agony pierced my ears and then I realised my own screams mirrored hers, as we were one and the same. My other self stood dying in front of me and I cried out to help her. She fell to her knees and I did the same. We looked like a mirror image of good versus evil, living and dying.

Lucius walked over to the burning me and picked her up into his bulging arms. His wings wrapped forward in a protective way and he started to walk back into the bedchamber. He looked back over his shoulder and said,

"Remember Keira…soon, *very, very soon.*" The flaming me in his arms started to scream once more and when I woke from this Hellish nightmare, I thought it was still my screaming that could be heard. It took me a moment to come to my own senses and not those under Lucius' control. But when I did finally calm, I came to realise that I could still hear the screams…

Only this time, they weren't mine.

CHAPTER NINETEEN

THE TEMPLE

The screams belonged to a girl, of that much I could be certain. The room was just as I had last seen it before the dream. It was only me that remained altered from the horrors I had witnessed. I inhaled, filling my lungs finally with the usual scent of the room I loved like home. There was no smell of burning oak, no flaking of the material under the flames that licked at them and most importantly the balcony was empty and intact.

However, my mental state was left fragile and frightened. I tried to shake off the feelings of dread and thankfully the full moon provided enough light for me to locate my clothes. I moved so slowly, as if I was half expecting something to jump out at me and the constant sound of someone's pain wasn't helping my nerves.

Once I was dressed, I wriggled my sockless feet into my trainers and moved towards the door I knew lead further into the fortress that was Draven's home. I opened it and the crack flooded the room with light, however this wasn't the only thing it let in. The sound was almost unbearable to hear, and it wasn't only the dream that had caused my distress. My memories of my own living nightmare came back at me like a wave of unsuspecting cruelty. This was what made my feet move from behind the safety of the door.

I knew that if I had been heard when Morgan had me locked away, then my horrific past may not have left me with such a deep scar. How I had wished for just one person to find me, to save me from his madness and my hopelessness. I had screamed and screamed until my throat was red raw and my lungs left empty. But no one came. No one ever heard my cries but the man responsible for them.

I knew that if ever I had heard the same, I would rather risk my life to help. I would rather put myself in danger than to live the rest of my years knowing that I had just walked on by. Not when I could have done something...*anything!* I just prayed that I saw Draven along the way, or at least someone that I knew could help.

I started down a long narrow corridor that I knew, as I had used it a few times, normally when being dragged away by Sophia. It consisted of stone arches that came down to blend with the soft stone walls. Luckily, there were light fittings attached and the flames, although needed, were also an unwanted reminder of the nightmare that Lucius had left me with his gift.

I pulled my zip-up sweater closer to my neck and even pulled the large floppy hood over my head, this way I felt more secure. It still didn't stop the shivers that convulsed my body, when the screaming stopped. I had to move faster! I had to get there and couldn't let my own fears prevent me from saving a life.

When I got to the end of the corridor, my knowledge of where I was ended. I knew if I turned right it would lead me to Sophia's room and I half considered it but when the screams got louder, I knew they were coming from the left. So with my mind set, I started walking down to opposite of where I knew. It seemed to be leading away from where people were or at least where they must have slept because it started to grow colder and not as well lit. I wished that I had a candle in my hand because I now feared that when I walked through the next door, darkness would greet me.

My hand made contact with the metal handle and I looked down only to realise I didn't have my gloves on. I found myself feeling even more vulnerable as I stepped through onto what felt like a balcony. The night air hit me for the first time tonight even though my mind wouldn't easily accept this truth as the dream had felt that real. I closed the door behind me as I knew I would soon be screaming myself if I allowed it to slam shut.

It didn't take me long to realise why the sight in front of me seemed so familiar. I had been here before, or so I thought. I was stood in a long corridor that was open to the night on one side. The balustrade was connected to large pillars that formed arches to the roof above. The walls held the same wrought iron lamps that lit when with movement, making me jump every time I heard the sound of flames igniting in their cages.

I had been here before, only then I was led to believe it all a dream. I looked over to see the massive courtyard far below and it looked as though a huge section of the house had been removed to fit in a Temple. The domed roof shone in the moonlight making it look like copper and I remember last time thinking the sculpture on top was a bird but now I knew better, as the figure of an Angel could easily be seen.

I was staring down at it from a different angle, as now I was on a different side of the house. I could just make out the side from where I had been that night. I remembered it so well when Draven had found me lost and scared in the darkness. At first, I didn't know it was him, only after he saved me from falling to my death did I soon come to realise who my Dark Saviour had been. This was yet another incident when his sister had been involved and tried to throw me into his path, but he had dealt with it in other ways. In other words, just another time that I was made to believe it had been all in my head.

I continued along the cold open hallway until I reached the door at the end and I thought how nice it would be if like last time, Draven was there waiting inside. It didn't take me long to find out my wish did not come true. Instead, it opened up into a cold landing and the only way left to go was down. The stone spiral staircase made my fear of heights rear its ugly head and a wave of nausea washed over me. My head spun at the sight of how far down it went and only when the screams started up again did it remind me why I was here. So, I swallowed hard before venturing down them into the unknown.

They seemed to go on forever and I found myself glad that they went down and not up, as my chest was already getting tight from my lack of fitness. I was at least glad that the moon was full and the sky clear, because there was no soft glow of any candles but there were lots of little slit windows that allowed the moon to shine through. The further I got, the more difficult it became as the stone wall was damp and the steps slippery. I lost my footing more times than I could count but thankfully I remained upright until finally, after what seemed like a small lifetime, I reached the bottom.

Now, of course, the screams could be heard even clearer and as soon as my foot hit the last step, I broke out into a run to get to the next door. The door was jammed but with a little persuasion, it creaked open with a deafening echo, allowing me access. Thankfully in the next part I found that I could breathe more easily, mainly due to the well-lit room and warm air. I could instantly tell that there would be people down here or why would there be lamps lit. The hum of voices also told me that life was in the distance.

The room I walked into looked like a shrine, with large holes carved out of the bare stone walls. Each hole was filled with what looked like artefacts and strange glowing orbs. One in particular reminded me very much of the one I had seen in my dreams on my very first night in my new home. It was purple and when I got closer it started to spin and pulsate in its place as though it was responding to my presence. I quickly took a step back not understanding the strange pull we seemed to have on each other.

Other holes held things that couldn't be explained without their owner present. What looked like wooden goblets and ancient coins were displayed along with a variety of other treasures. One of which included a large, plate-sized clay disc that was mounted and covered in symbols. I had no idea why these things were down here but if I was to dig out a guess, I would say that this would have been Draven's personal historical collection of sorts.

In the centre of the room I had to walk around a glass case containing a statue that held the top of a sword at an angle. It was being gripped tightly by a stone hand that obviously belonged to a woman. The top part was held high as if ready for a warrior to claim but the blade itself was cutting into the delicate stone fingers. It would have been a beautiful thing to behold if it wasn't for the constant black blood that ran down her arm in thin rivulets. It created a stark contrast as it travelled down a single thin white wrist and trickled over the expertly carved folds of her flowing sleeve. Each droplet was a continuous miniature river that streamed down to the floor, where it was captured by a black pool that was contained within the glass box.

It seemed so lifelike it was convincing to believe that if touched, flesh could be felt instead of what was probably cold marble. As I took in the whole sight, it appeared as if an Angel that had once been ripped from Heaven was trying to push up the very weapon that would save her, hoping for her saviour to be on the other side, ready and waiting. But whoa, where had that thought come from?

It seemed so bizarre a scene that it took my mind far from the reason I was there, and I didn't know how but I just knew that I would one day find out who this sword belonged to.

I dragged my eyes away from the twisted sight of the immense weapon imagining it to be just another part of Draven's collection and then I quickly started to wonder what he would think about me being here. Would he be mad that I was venturing into the unknown? Or would he see my quest as a noble one?

I quickly hurried past and onto the next part and although worried for the girl's life, I couldn't help but be intrigued at all the new things my eyes were laying witness to. This truly was another world.

Draven's world.

I knew this was one part of his life he tried desperately to keep separate from his human girlfriend and there was so much that I still didn't understand. It was only the love in my heart that made it all less important. To me he was just a man and most of all, the man I loved. I knew sometimes I doubted myself, but in this I was absolute. I knew deep down I had to be if I was ever to be allowed to stay with the man I had fallen in love with.

The next hallway was wide enough to get a bus down and the mouldings were breath-taking. Stone carved into artwork, pillars that looked like sandstone men holding up the ceilings with bulging muscles and endless strength. Huge arches cut off into smaller half-moons that were covered and framed with flowers that were gilded gold. The pillars also held gargoyles before they reached the elaborate ceiling and they were not weathered like the ones I was used to seeing.

No, these looked as though they could have been carved yesterday and this added to the fear they produced. I almost expected their eyes to start glowing and for them to growl as I went past. So of course, when the sound of stone moving above me could be heard I screamed, proving that no amount of preparing myself could have prevented my reaction.

I looked up but the grotesque creatures were still, only now with their heads turned towards me, looking down. This made me quicken my pace as now my heartbeat sounded in tune with the girl's screaming. It pounded in my chest and every step I made was then followed by the turning of a monstrous stone head.

"STOP IT!" I stopped and screamed out at them. I bravely stood, facing their judging looks as my anger got too much. I mean, what could they do to me? I didn't give it much thought as one by one they slowly turned to face the other way and I was amazed to see my little eruption had any effect on them.

By this time, I reached yet another door and before I went through it, I braced myself as I knew I'd come to the end of my journey. The screams could now be made out as words of help. A girl's voice was pleading to be freed and at least I knew I wasn't too late. I took a few deep breaths and walked through to face my mission.

Of course, I was wrong.

With a determined bravery I dug deep from my brain, I opened the next door and was mentally hit in the face when the screams ended with a deafening silence. This happened as soon as the first sole of my foot hit the ground in this next room. Well, I say room, but it was more the size of a bloody football stadium!

The floor was made up from a collection of broken tiles that made shapes and pictures I didn't understand the meaning of. There were lighter patches attacking darker ones, like clouds in a battle, merging into one sullen colour of grey. It actually looked like the floor was alive with energy and at first, I stepped back against the door that had now sealed behind me. I turned in a panic, but it was fruitless. I was locked inside what I soon discovered to be in fact a tomb.

So, with my fate now firmly sealed, I let my heaving chest calm before making my way into the centre where there stood the largest pillar I had ever seen in my life. It looked to be made to resemble the largest tree trunk in existence. Thoughts of the Jurassic age came to mind as that's how I imagined the Earth's green life to have been back then. Of course, being made of stone only made it look more like a fossil and the carved stone on stone vines worked their way up the great structure. I didn't know whether it was there for effect or was actually holding something mighty up above.

My eyes followed in awe as I reached the ceiling where it spread out like dead life finding home for the centuries. The vines continued along the ceiling as if once being a living force that at one time in history needed to suck at the air and now did so needlessly. I found myself looking up until my neck ached, in pure awe at the incredible structure.

I did this until I felt the dizzying effect infiltrate my brain, momentarily forgetting my situation. Unfortunately, when I did, I looked elsewhere to find the walls, floor to ceiling, covered with holes. It didn't take long for someone with half a brain cell to know what lay in these holes. They were the perfect size for a coffin to fit in widthways and I knew this was where the tombs of Draven's dead ultimately found rest. My mind raced with questions upon questions and I bit my lip as to what the answers could be. What exactly had I found down here, some supernatural morgue?

I knew one thing... Draven was not going to be happy!

I moved around the open space with my breath caught inside my chest, only to be released when absolutely necessary. I feared as though I may wake the dead with each footstep I took and given the size of the place, I had to take quite a few of them. When I finally crept across to the other side, I found that one wall was covered in the stone vines that seemed born from the fossilised tree that acted as a colossal pillar. They had snaked their way up, produced from the trunk in the middle and rained down this wall as if to guard something beneath and the shape very much resembled a gigantic door.

I knew I should turn back, but it was as if something powerful wanted me there, pushing me forward and watching it all play out from the side-lines. My fear was slowly being replaced with a need and a want so great I couldn't do anything to save myself from myself.

I felt my body react to my recklessness. My hairs stood on end thanks to the raised bumps on my skin. My heart rate doubled or even tripled as all my ears could make out was the beating drum that now played a doomed beat inside me. I tasted the acid that a nervous stomach produced and swallowed hard when I came only a foot away from the vine-covered wall. My body wasn't my own, being forced by a mind I only half controlled.

"Touch it'... 'yes'... 'touch it'... 'reach out." Whispers of the dead beckoned from each hole in the room that all held the same voice. I spun around half expecting to see thousands of decomposed bodies all stood there edging closer to me. I turned back to the vines and raised my hand causing a wave as they all hushed, waiting in turn for my mistake to play out like a Greek tragedy. My fingertips needed to touch the vines that polluted the wall, concealing a truth I needed to find. I only paused a second, but it was enough for the whisperers to urge me on one last time.

"Reach for us."

Then my skin came into contact with the cold stone that caused a startling reaction. The stone started to move under my fingertips as if I was finding a pulse on a resting corpse. It started to pulsate more violently before quickly producing thorns that pricked my palm and pierced it enough times over to extract my blood. My mind could faintly hear a chanting being whispered from behind but in the sight of a new fear of it now reacting to my blood, the noise became lost in a storm long passed by.

"Ouch!" I yanked my hand free and that wasn't the only thing the pain freed, as now my mind was completely my own again. I looked down at my hand and found there was a strange symbol that resembled the same birthmark I had under my hairline. It was more noticeable when I was a baby, when I had only thin wispy hair, but now it was completely covered under my thick blanket of blonde locks. It was an odd shape, like a thin quarter moon with its curve sitting inside a V on its side.

The blood had stopped escaping as I wiped it on my jeans, but it was still red and sore. I heard a noise and when I looked back up at the vines, they were now wide awake and alive with the new blood they had consumed. The part which had tasted my blood had turned a lush green colour and it grew thicker before retreating back beneath its stone brothers that lay behind it.

I staggered backwards quickly as the whole wall became alive with motion that reminded me of light grey snakes all slithering to get away. It all pulled back at once, as if my blood had been acid and the vines needed to get away from the infected area.

I don't think I had ever held the look of shock for so long. I gasped as the retreating vines revealed a huge wooden door that belonged at the end of a castle drawbridge. Well, that was just great... I had revealed a door, yes, but I would have to be the size of a two-storey building to open it!

Then, as if my thoughts held some greater meaning, the door started to split in the middle allowing an opening big enough for the giant from Jack and the Beanstalk to pass through. A blinding light poured out as though I was about to walk straight into Heaven itself. But then the sounds that escaped didn't sound like any Heaven I had ever envisioned. I raised my arm to offer some small protection against the strong beams, but the girl's screams had me throwing caution away and running into the bright unknown.

I ran until my eyes adjusted to the light that came from the end of the large tunnel I had been granted entrance to. My legs started to feel like jelly as it felt as though I had been running all night, but I didn't want to think about it now, I could rest later. Now I had to find her and considering her voice could now be heard crying little sobs, I knew the next place would be where I would finally find her.

I walked through a bright light that I thought came from the room but when the energy made my body tingle, I knew it had in some way acted as the door. I stepped through to the other side blinking to clear my now blurry vision. It was as if someone had taken a picture and the flash had me seeing nothing but black dots. When it cleared, I wanted to scream at what the next room held.

I was now quite clearly inside a prison.

The walls held heavy metal doors with only small barred windows in high pointed arches. The locks were strange and instead of holes for the keys to fit, they held little flat dishes that looked ready for a liquid to fill them. They were the weirdest looking locks I had ever seen. But these were all small factors compared to the banging and screeching sounds that my presence was causing.

"I smell human sweat upon flesh." One gargled voice spoke, and I shivered before nearly running back through the brightly lit portal.

"I smell a ripe fruit ready for plucking." Another voice spoke, only this one made my bones want to shake as its deep Demonic edge continued,

"One I would gladly tear apart, skin from flesh, flesh from bone!" I wanted to start screaming myself, but then the girl's sweet voice brought me round from my own Hellish experience and reminded me of her own.

"Help me, please." Her voice sounded strained from screaming and again the memories hit me harder than any of these monster's threats. I walked towards the door I thought the voice came from cautiously, knowing the other creatures did not think kindly of my interference or maybe they did, considering they seemed to be seeing me as more of a happy meal!

The doors went on and on, but the voice led me to her. I hesitated before going up to the door, remembering all the other mistakes I had not long ago made. But when she pleaded one last time, my senses left me being replaced by a rush of guilt and memories.

The metal door was cold, and I noticed a bluish light filtering through the window in the door. I thought this must be from a window inside the cell, but when I reached up on my tiptoes, I was wrong. The blue light came from the silhouette of a young slim girl who only wore a long white muslin gown. She had her back to me, and her black hair hung straight down her back like Black Beauty's tail. For a second I was like a deer caught in a car's headlights. I was frozen at the sight and the blue glow deepened a shade at my reaction to her.

"Are you human?" I asked the figure that still sobbed quietly.

"Yes, and I am very afraid, will you not help me?" Her voice floated over to me like a warm blanket of reassurance. How could such a velvet voice be immoral?

"What can I do, I don't know how to open the door?" She began to cry again, and I knew the sound well. It was my cry. The same hopeless cry I had once been unable to stop. I pulled on the door with every ounce of strength, but it was useless, I wasn't even making the metal rattle.

I pulled my body upwards to the window again, but now I saw something only the deepest, darkest corners of my mind knew about. The vision made me want to die from the pain it inflicted.

I looked through a watery vision at myself sat down on the floor by an inflated bed. I wore dirty clothes and my hair, knotted from weeks of neglect, fell in front of my face hiding my misery. I began to pull up my sleeves and feel the smooth skin there on my inner arms. I rattled my own body against the door at the vision.

"Stop it! Don't! Don't do it!" I cried out as the girl produced a small wooden box from behind her and when opened, the music that filled my mind with hate and revulsion played out. It was my very own private death song and I cried louder being now the one full of pleas.

"Please, don't do this!"

"*There is only one way to save those that I love.*" She whispered my own words, words that were supposed to be the goodbye of my past before continuing on with my repulsive actions. She then smashed the box to the floor and the mirror shattered into a life-changing weapon. She took the largest piece to her pale arm and drew the first red line across her skin, near to her elbow.

"STOP IT!" I screamed before looking away in my own disgust. It was like watching my own destruction being carried out in a dark, gothic play by a girl I didn't know. But I couldn't look away for long and the darkness of my own history compelled me to see it through as I had years ago.

I raised my head but now my scream was for a different reason. The black-haired beauty was now inches from my face and her features were covered only showing me the whites of her eyes through the black branches of her hair. Her hands weren't holding onto the bars like mine were, so she was either very tall or floating.

"You are the last hope, they come to kill me…stop them…stop them now!" As soon as she said it there were footsteps and voices that could be heard. I had to move if I was to help in any way. I would have to see who it was that held her here and more importantly, who wanted to kill her.

"I will be back, I will do what I can." Before I let my body fall down, I saw her lips mouth a word, something that seemed far too familiar than I would have liked, but at the same time my mind was coming up with a black wall. I got the feeling that she was trying to warn me against something or was it someone?

My hands hurt and my knuckles cracked from holding most of my weight for so long. I could hear the footsteps getting closer and panic set in as I searched desperately for a place to hide. My head whipped around for some dark corner, when I saw a pillar thick enough to hide behind. Once there, I could still hear her plea for me to help and tears filled my eyes at how hopeless a saviour I was. If only I knew where Draven was then he could help, he could stop all of this and one thing was for sure, people would surely get punished!

I tried to stay completely hidden but the need to look was far greater than the warnings that were ringing in my head. The pillar I was frozen behind was in the shadows, so when I peered round to see, I wasn't noticed. There stood three figures covered from head to foot in long purple robes which had a strip of gold symbols running down the middle like a racing stripe.

It looked like ancient scriptures, like hieroglyphics or Mayan text, but without being close enough I couldn't tell. The appearance of the men caused a reaction with the other inmates as shouts and bangs against their cells erupted. This was short-lived as with one blood-curdling command from the man in front, the room grew silent. He had spoken a language I had never heard and one that sounded as if it was very unlikely to have still been used today.

I watched as the taller one in the middle approached the door as the other two stood back to await the prisoner. I presumed the one in the middle to be the leader, as he seemed to order the others to be ready. He then raised his wrist to his mouth and to my disgust he bit down hard on his own flesh. I swallowed a disgusted lump at the sight of him taste his own blood before allowing it to drip onto the lock.

At least I now knew what the little dishes were there for as I heard the lock start to move and click open. I let my shoulders fall as I realised that I would never have been able to open them, as they required the blood of the supernatural.

I watched the leader lick his own wound like a dog, while he waited for the door to swing open. Once it did the innocent young girl came screaming out like a banshee showing her other side; her desperate one. However, the two guards were ready for her and caught her body as she tried to kick and scratch her way to freedom. I so wanted to run to her, but I knew I was next to useless up against these three. I felt the tears overflow down my cheeks as I watched them drag the screaming girl away down the corridor they had come from, the very corridor where I must now follow.

I tried to compose myself before I continued. I inhaled deeply and wiped my wet face with the back of my arm. Half of me wanted to run away and find a corner to curl up into until I was found. But I knew the half of me that willed me to do good in life would win. So, with my overbearing need to help a girl I didn't know, I stepped from behind my hiding place and followed the path to where hopefully death would not greet me.

My feet struggled over the deep cobbled floor and I was glad when I reached the narrow corridor so that I could steady myself on the walls. I continued down and the air felt tight and muggy. The damp walls made my hands slide from them as I felt my way along for support. Then, as I turned a corner, the light that had come from the prison could no longer be seen and plunged the tunnel into darkness.

I froze and leant on the wall until my breathing calmed. I

counted to ten before forcing my feet to move on. I had to use my other senses to find my way out of the darkness and I started to concentrate. My nose filled with the scent of wet stone and my touch only proved the reason.

But in the end, it was my ears that gave me hope as I started to hear the hum of chanting and then my eyes saw a gentle glow of candlelight work its way across the walls. The bright end told me I was near to where I would no doubt find the girl and who held her captive. I gulped the frightened lump, forcing it down my tight throat and moved into the next room.

Here my eyes came into contact with my destination…

The Temple.

CHAPTER TWENTY

IMPOSSIBLE REASONS

I walked closer inside where the brightly lit Temple hall hurt my eyes after becoming accustomed to the dark. I stood still, blinking frantically so as not to be taken by surprise, hoping that one of the pillars I hid behind was enough of a barrier from the droning voices that filled the room. My heart nearly stopped, and my blood froze from being so scared.

The chanting wasn't like anything I had ever heard. Not only was the language strange and very unnerving, but it seemed to be passing between Demonic lips. Its loud echoing felt as though it could crack the walls and destroy cities with only a few verses. I couldn't choke down the fear that kept rising back up my body like a growing illness. It kept getting louder and louder, which proved to be too much for my fragile human ears.

I could feel the marble floor beneath me vibrate and this was the only reason I hadn't yet crumpled to it like a frightened child. Nothing could compare to this moment. I had never experienced terror like it and I had never prayed so hard for it to be just another horrible dream. But as I felt the beads of sweat roll down my trembling face, I knew that no amount of hope in the world would make it so. My body shook so violently that I thought it would break into pieces.

Only when a great roar cut through the other voices, did it all go quiet. This finally made my senses return to me, along with my resolution. I decided to move further round, as I now knew I was still completely out of sight. I walked slowly to the next massive pillar which was like a masterpiece in its own right.

Painted blood red at the bottom, turning into flames of orange and gold as it curled upwards to the painted sky on the ceiling and dome. My eyes followed the story around the room that depicted a great war between Heaven and Hell. There were Angel warriors on horseback attacking winged Demons from a flaming sky. I sought out the next scene and had to narrow my eyes to make out the picture. There was a darker patch which at first, I thought was a falling dark cloud, descending on the Demons below. But then after staring at it in greater length I realised it was actually a wave of silver-tipped arrows, flying down ready to pierce their targets with deadly intent.

The painting was so skilled and accurate that I almost thought them real enough to touch. I shuddered at the idea that this could actually be based on a truth; an unknown war that humans were utterly oblivious to. The shiny floor looked like liquid and the reflection of the painted Heaven gave the marble a bluish tinge making it resemble a lagoon.

Finally, once I had finished looking around my magnificent surroundings, my eyes fell on the imposing figures that were stood around the room like a secret cult meeting. Each one was clothed in red robes that matched Hell's representation they stood by. My mind counted seventeen red bodies draped from head to foot in blood velvet then followed on as the next set of six bodies wore purple with thick gold symbols at the bottom.

This reminded me of a strange display of the signs of the zodiac combined with ancient runes. These weren't quite the same as the men who had taken the girl, but I soon came across them. My gaze rested at the top of the circle these robed beings had created by where they stood. At the top was a huge stone slab that acted like an altar and it too was covered in carved symbols that matched the robes.

I could feel my sweaty hands slip from the smooth cold marble that I tried to keep hold of. I was far too close now and knew this was very wrong, but my will to turn away wasn't half as strong as my will to stay. I bit down on my lip and rolled it back and to through my teeth. If I hadn't been here witnessing this cult-based nightmare, then I'm sure I would have felt the pain I was causing myself.

Instead I focused all my attention and energy onto the scene that was being played out in front of me like a sadistic opera. The group was clearly waiting for something, or more likely someone and I had a sick feeling it was the girl who I had made it my mission to save from her cruel fate.

I didn't have long to wait for the crescendo as a huge, tall cloaked figure walked out through what looked like a series of guards who bowed respectfully as their Master passed. He dominated the room and like a Mexican wave at a football game all the robed cult-followed suit and fell to their knees. They started the mind-numbing chant again, forcing me to place my shaky hands over my ears.

The deafening beat rattled my mind like thousands of war horses charging into battle and I could feel my courage getting beaten with every step. I looked on through a watery glaze and held on with shaky limbs. They all started to sway as the momentum increased into a powerful finish and as before a great roar projected off the domed roof and echoed about the room, creating a deadly silence that followed. I peered around again to see the leader of this demonic choir hold up his hands as he commanded the rest to stand once more.

His imposing figure wore an all-black robe that draped long over his face. It was decorated by one large gold symbol, positioned over his chest. It was the same circled symbol that mirrored the stone altar he stood in front of. It reminded me of the different moon cycles all intertwined around a circle with one prominent symbol in the centre. Then it hit me where I had seen that symbol before. I looked down at my palm and saw the half-moon with a V shape attached to it, only now on the altar and robe the V was upright.

The skin had dried blood around the edges, but the deep red

shape could easily be seen. It was unmistakable. The same symbol was not only on my hand, thanks to that strange vine entrance, but it was also on the back of my neck under my hairline. Hiding there like a dark secret waiting until this moment to make its reason known, a birthmark that sealed my fate and brought me here to find my true path. That thought terrified me far more than the Demons before me. I was in no way part of this sick and twisted cult! I wouldn't allow myself to think it. Then it suddenly hit me...

What if the man in black was Lucius?!

What if this had been his plan all along to get to me, first to control my dreams and then to play on my insecurities. Surely, if he'd had access to my mind then he would know my past. Then all that was left to do was to make me hear the girl's cries and I would come running. Just like he said, 'I will not have long to wait, and you will soon come to me'.

I started to shake yet again at the thought.

The man terrified me to my very core and to make it even worse, I was also a little bit fascinated with him. Lately, I had been trying to reject the idea and banish it from my mind like some law I was breaking. It felt against nature thinking about him but in some sick twisted way, I was drawn to him like bees to pollen. This forced me to be more afraid of myself and my own irresponsible actions. I didn't know what I would do when faced with the man who haunted and consumed my dreams but when I thought of him and his lips on mine, it made me quiver with both revulsion and a burning hunger.

I tried to put it all down to his powerful mind control and wished more than anything that I was strong enough to push him out and once again gain control over myself.

I started to look at the black figure a little closer and the size of his frame matched that of Lucius. He was tall, with squared shoulders but I couldn't see any of his features as most of his robe covered his body and face. My mind raced with thoughts and ways that he could have penetrated the fortress that was Draven's home. Then my hands flew to my mouth and the panic hit me. What if he had overpowered Draven somehow? It was the man himself who told me that Lucius was the only one who was equal to his power and being able to control the mind of anyone, including Draven, was sure to have an advantage.

Before I knew it, my face streamed with tears as the image of Draven being overpowered by Lucius got stronger in my mind. I was about to turn around and run away forgetting, or more like not even caring, about the girl who I had come here to rescue. Now my main concern was the man I loved and the overwhelming feeling that I had walked straight into a trap.

I turned my back to the pillar and could feel the beads of sweat from my back roll down and turn to ice as it came into contact with the marble. I shuddered as I leaned my body's weight against it for support while I thought a moment about what to do next. I needed to find Draven at all costs, but would I have enough nerve to even move from this spot?

The seconds that ticked by felt like a lifetime. Just when I had my mind set on getting out of this Hell, the Demonic voice of Lucius brought my attention to full alert and made my blood rush through my veins like a liquid inferno.

I turned to look back at the cloaked followers and realised they were all waiting for something to happen. Their heads all turned to one side of the hall to an opening that at first was invisible but only when a snow-white woman emerged could the entrance be seen. A bright light behind her just made her glow like a Heavenly entity, but when it faded back to where it came from, the features of an old woman could clearly be seen.

She had long white hair that flowed around her as though each individual strand was controlled by an unseen force. The long dress she wore did the same as it wrapped in and out of her tired-looking legs. The sleeves opened up into a V shape and the tips came down to the floor reminding me of Robin Hood's Maid Marion. Her face looked kind, despite its numerous wrinkles and her soft light eyes could even be seen from the other end of the hall, where I stood locked to the floor beneath me.

She reminded me of what Mother Earth would look like if she was in a human form. I felt connected to her through my love for all things pure and natural. This was how I knew this woman was most definitely an Angel. It was the same feeling I'd felt around

Vincent when I first saw him in his Angelic form. They had a pull towards them, and I could imagine that it was probably the same that evil people had towards Demons. Something in our genetic makeup was forged by the same hand. We were undoubtedly connected to these creatures and throughout history, even though our beliefs had never been proven, they had never faltered. Now, of course, I knew why.

Then Lucius held one hand out towards the old lady and motioned to take her hand, which the woman looked more than delighted with. She gracefully floated over to him and placed a frail, wrinkled hand in his. He bowed to her and led her to one side of the altar. My eyes remained locked as everyone now turned to the opposite side to where the old lady had entered.

Lucius let go of her hand and raised his other one before shouting out another dark command. I had never heard a Demon use another voice until now and after this, I never wanted to again! I could almost hear my own bones rattle thanks to the effect it had. It was the type of voice that great armies would have thrown down their arms and pledged an allegiance to a different ruler after just one battle cry. It was so loud, rough and deep it could have come from the Devil himself! It seemed to have different dimensions of evil to it and I had to bite down hard not to scream.

"Daiva!" ("Demon" in Ancient Persian) he shouted as he pointed one long velvet arm out to the guards who were bringing forth a screaming girl. She too was now dressed the same as the old woman and I noticed her old eyes flicker a brighter white before returning to their crystal blue colour. Whereas the screaming girl, who I had tried to save, had black tears rolling down her cheeks. It covered her beautiful face like deadly ink, and it dripped down her pure white dress, making the contrast even more startling.

He stretched out all four fingers together and retracted all again to his palm to motion the guards to bring her closer. She lifted up her tired head and saw herself moving towards him. She screamed louder and struggled even more against the two huge purple-robed men who had her by both arms. Swiftly though, Lucius stepped forward and struck the girl with the back of his hand. The impact across her face was strong enough to cause blood to spurt from her open mouth and hit the wall, which was at least fifteen feet away. This not only silenced her but made her body sway to an unconscious state.

I had opened my mouth to scream, but thankfully my shock and horror had stolen my voice, and nothing came out from my near bleeding, cracked lips. I pressed my nails into my palm, causing little half-moon indents that showed my frustration at having to watch helplessly. The girl's head was slumped forward and her dark velvet hair went to her knees. She was dragged the rest of the way to the altar and held opposite the gleaming old woman. Lucius touched the head of the girl and whispered something to make her re-awaken to her real nightmare. However, this time she had learnt her lesson and stood motionless at the mouth of Hell.

I fought frantically with every idea I had that entered my mind as each idea was as bad as the next. I needed to cause a diversion but even then, what could I do alone? I was outnumbered and most certainly out powered! I would not only be putting myself in danger of being captured, but it would no doubt be pointless as well. She would never have enough time to escape with all these monsters that stood around her. No, all I could do was watch on in horror and experience her end as though it was my own.

"Māha Arta" ("Moon Order" In Ancient Persian) Lucius spoke more words I didn't understand and looked up to the top of the domed roof as if waiting for something. None of us had to wait long for the dome to show a split in the middle and then part, moving back into the room showing us the night sky in its place. The vast black night was only filled by the fullest moon I had ever seen and was ringed with a blood-red outline that gave it the appearance of an evil sun.

The words passed his lips once more and the red ring glowed even brighter as if responding to his command. All of the robed figures were still looking up to it as if a God had emerged. Then abruptly Lucius seized the girl by the arm and turned her around into him, so her back was now against his hard chest. Her head tucked inches under his chin and with his other hand he held the bottom of her face and moved it up towards his lips. He mouthed words over her hair, and it seemed to send her into a trance, as she rolled up her eyes before closing her lids.

She started to sway but before she could hit the floor with her numb body he growled up to the moon and pushed her hard down onto the stone altar. He then grabbed a handful of her gown, tore it from her body with one quick motion and left her as naked as the day she was born. Her soft pale skin glistened under the moonlight and looked like milk rippling as it trembled in the night air.

What happened next came about so fast, I had to replay it in my head before reacting to it, like a time-lapse that had to be caught up with. He had produced a large ornate blade from behind his back and held it up to the moon as if to get it blessed before plunging it into the girl's body. Only the gold end that protruded from her heart could be seen and the sound of blood travelling up to her throat and out from her colourless lips could be heard.

The blood from underneath her flowed around the circles that covered the altar and soon all marble sides showed the life that had now left her, mirroring the night's deadly moon above.

Within seconds of comprehending what had just happened right before my eyes, I let out an almighty scream that pierced the night like the blade that had just pierced her delicate skin. This quickly had all the robed heads in the room turn to face me. Blind panic had me frozen in time and surprise had the others doing the same. For seconds shock was all that gripped at every being in the room but the sight of the black robe lifting his head towards me, had me soon moving into action.

My legs started to run towards the closest door that I could see, and my mind didn't stop to think what was through it and that it wasn't the same way I had come in. I turned my head just enough to see a long arm extend out towards me and hear him roar in a demonic voice,

"BRING HER TO ME!" But this had my body moving faster than ever before as it was beyond terrifying! I could hear all the footsteps behind me, but I didn't dare stop to look. I was waiting for hands to reach out and grab me but all the same, I kept my feet moving. I pushed my way through the heavy door and thanked God that it was unlocked. I jumped at the sound of it slamming behind me and only then did I realise I had to wipe my streaming eyes as I couldn't see properly for desperate tears. I told myself in my head to calm down or I would never find my way out. My body wanted to carry on, but my exhausted mind wanted to curl up in a corner and cry until there was nothing left.

I was in a strange room that had eight arched passageways which were situated in a long row going from one side of the room to the next. I knew I had to choose one as the sound of footsteps were getting closer. I closed my eyes, swallowed deep, and prayed I wasn't making a grave mistake when I took the one on the far left at the end.

It turned out to be through a narrow and wet corridor similar to the one that had lead me to the Temple but at least this one had some light. As I ran through the cobbled tunnel light ignited above me and I soon realised as the ceiling became inflamed, that this was the way the lamps were positioned. They extended up from the top of the wall into arches that joined the other side's lamp. Then when lit, they made the ceiling glow with fire.

This extreme heat in such a small space made me cough and beads of sweat soaked my face. I was thankful that it didn't go on for long as I could finally breathe more easily when fresher air hit me. I stumbled into the next room as I tripped on one of the larger cobbles that jutted out from the rest. I hit the floor with a thud and pain shot through my knees making me swear out in agony.

I scrambled to my feet, thinking about the bruises I would now have before scanning the room I was now stood in. The large oval room wasn't as grand as all the rest, in fact it looked a little dilapidated. The walls that were once richly decorated had long tears in the royal blue wallpaper, showing the deep red bricks underneath. This made the room look as though a savage beast had clawed away at it, trying to get to the flesh the paper concealed. What could have made those marks? But more importantly, what had I just walked into?!

Then I took a step closer seeing something that didn't just look like claw marks but something somebody had used their fingernails to write with. Then I fell back with a gasp, landing hard on my backside. There, staring at me from all around the room was the evidence that I had been right all along. Scratched, was the haunting name that had just made me a mouse in this game of chase…

'*LUCIUS,*'

That's when my mind finally put together the last remaining puzzle piece. I now remembered what it was the imprisoned girl had mouthed. It was a warning and it was also a name; the same that had spun a cruel web and decorated this room of desperation.

"*Lucius,*" I whispered before slapping a hand over my mouth to prevent it from ever saying his name again down in this Hellish place.

I could no longer hear the sound of being pursued and I didn't know whether or not that was a good sign. I examined the walls more closely and saw that the paper had what looked like old scriptures and huge fleur-de-lis in faded gold decorating what was left. It had been scratched all over the walls, some places with bloody fingernails still embedded. My eyes followed the cracked mouldings and broken furniture that was beyond repair, it too also held the same name crudely carved into the surfaces.

Doors with broken hinges were thrown around the room like scatter cushions. There were glass shards from shattered mirrors and lamps that once added to the décor. It looked like a grand bedchamber that someone had gone berserk in and this was the aftermath. As I walked further into the room, I found a large bed that had two legs missing so was laid to rest at an angle on its dais. Tattered curtains hung pathetically around the broken frame.

The mattress too was in one piece no longer, as it had clearly been ripped apart. There were no windows in this room, so the only light came from office type strip lighting that looked more out of place than me in Afterlife! It flickered and I could hear a faint buzzing as it tried to find the power to stay illuminated. This was by far the strangest room I had been in because, quite simply, it was the one most unlikely to have been here. It felt so out of place, like driving in the desert and then finding Las Vegas.

I found a door uncovered by a ripped tapestry and prayed that it was unlocked. I must have only been in there for mere minutes, but I had wasted enough time as it was, so I made my sore knees move into action and ran to the exit. Thankfully, the door was unlocked but once I was inside, I found myself wishing that maybe it hadn't.

For I was back in the prison.

It only took me a few seconds to realise that it wasn't the same one the girl had been held captive in. This one looked more serious, as the cells resembled one-man torture devices. They were caskets lined up against the wall like stone tombs and all that could be seen were a thin rectangle for their eyes to see through.

I was glad to find that no eyes could be seen looking back at me, but my blood ran cold as whispers started to come from behind the metal coffins. I couldn't make out any words as it was all being said in another language.

I moved to avoid them, giving them a wide berth as I made my way past. I was trying desperately not to lose it, but I could feel myself fading fast. All I wanted to do was hide away in a corner somewhere and cry myself into a sticky mess. This was most definitely my limit and I was so close to cracking that I needed a minute to calm my mind and focus on getting to Draven. He was the only reason I was still moving, and I knew if I had to crawl my way out of this Hell, that for him, I would keep going.

The wet stone walls made the air smell damp, but I was thankful that this room was at least cooler than the rest. My hair had started to cling to my neck which was irritating my skin, making me itch.

"ARRRH!" I screamed out at the sound of my name being whispered from around the corner. The room was in a sort of L shape with five large pillars running down the middle. The section I was in only had the small metal coffins along one wall but from what I was about to find out, that wasn't all this room had in store for me.

I bravely made my way around the wall, keeping far away from the one-man sized prisons, but as soon as I started to move, I realised they weren't empty. I shuddered back another cry as each thin rectangle now produced two orange glows and when they started to blink, it made me react to being watched. My hands flew to my mouth to keep my voice captive and as a result, I bit down into the skin on my hand to restrain it further. I didn't take my eyes off their's for a second, afraid that if I did, I would pay dearly for it. They moved with my body, following me as I went slowly out of sight.

Once around the corner it opened up into a bigger part of the room and this looked almost identical to the other prison, the one where I first saw the girl. There was however one startling difference. One wall, like the other, held heavy doors that lead into the separate cells. But on the opposite side was something I had never seen before and it looked as though made from the stuff nightmares were created from. All along the wall seemed to be alive with tortured souls trapped and begging to be set free. It almost looked like a giant womb spread over hundreds of people trying to claw their way out. Like a thick skin stretched out to near breaking point.

I stood motionless in the middle of two evils, waiting for the next safe move to come to me. I wondered if this was what Moses felt like when he parted the Red Sea, knowing that any moment either side of death could come crashing down on him and all that followed. I knew this was a completely illogical thing to be thinking and for one thing he had the Gods on his side! I knew perfectly well what I had on my side, both my sides for that matter and I doubted very much that they wanted to give me a big pat on the back and send me in the right direction!

I knew I had to move as I could now hear the voices from the Temple coming closer and I knew it wouldn't be long until they found me. What was worse? Talk about stuck between a rock and a hard place, this was more like walking a tightrope over a live volcano or going to Hell for a damn holiday.

I started to giggle nervously, and I think this was mainly down to the fact that I was slowly losing the plot and thought it was better to giggle than to cry and sob like a baby, I couldn't stop either. I counted three pillars and knew that if I was going to do this then I would have to do it one pillar at a time. I focused on the first pillar and started to move my feet.

The problem I faced was that the wall of souls started to respond even more by my movement. Hands tried to reach out and grab me. Faces would push even harder through the skin until features could almost be made out. Teeth snapped at me and looked as though they would soon bite their way through. As a result, I had a reaction of my own and moved further away, only nearer to the other wall. The one with all the cells.

They had barred windows that were lower than the ones in the other prison. Earlier to see into the girl's cell I had to pull myself up, but these you could easily see inside. This was a bad thing…

A very bad thing.

In the first cell I passed I could see a small man in the far corner just under his window. He was bent on his knees scratching away at the floor like someone possessed. He only had trousers on allowing the gruelling marks to be seen on his back. As he arched over it made the metal pins that stuck out from his skin stand out even more. There were two, one either side of each spine bone and it looked as though he had been stapled from the inside out. His hair was black and matted into clumps that hung down like dead rats.

The moon started to come out from behind a cloud and it cast first a shadow around the room before lighting it up. I gasped as I read the words that had been plastered around every available wall space. The words 'Come play with me' were written in blood that had seeped from beneath his broken fingernails. I swallowed back my disgust in the form of bile, when his face turned slowly to look at me.

His face looked withered with red cracks in his pale skin, but it was when he waved at me that it all became too much for a weak stomach that had been pushed to its limit. As soon as my eyes caught sight of the protruding bloody bones that were left of his fingers, I threw up outside his cell. He merely shrugged his shoulders before returning his pointed finger bones to scratch away at the only space left untouched, soon to be covered with his bloody ink. I had to steady myself on the pillar as I tried not to panic anymore. I concentrated on my breathing until it sounded somewhat semi-normal, before carrying on to the next pillar.

As I approached, I knew there was something better behind the next door as a feeling of utter calm and a warm tingle under my skin told me so. At least it made the tears cease to fall. Well, at least for the minute anyway. A bright light got stronger as I came closer. When inside the cell was visible, I had to blink a few times before my eyesight grew accustomed to the bright room as opposed to the dark and dingy ones I had been in for the last ten minutes. Inside there was an Angel sat on the top of what reminded me of a white step ladder. The room was painted white but was peeling away to reveal a grey stone wall underneath.

There were also strange white balls of different sizes around the floor that kept moving around the ladder. He kept his head down and his shoulders were slumped forward as if he had given up. He was wearing only white trousers that looked as though they were made from paper, but the strangest thing was his small white wings which came from his shoulder blades. The ends were tipped with a yellowish colour and the tops brushed against the wall.

I now realised that because of my fear, I had lost my barrier to keep the images of Angels and Demons in their true form out. This must have only happened since entering this area as back in the Temple they just all looked like crazy humans, which they clearly weren't!

"You shouldn't be here." A soft voice said and for the first time since being down this Hellhole, I actually felt comforted.

"I know… I'm lost," I stammered out.

"They're looking for you." Wow, he sure was great for pointing out the obvious, next he was going to tell me 'You're also a daft blond girl that just puked up because you just met Mr bloody bone fingers over there!'

"I know. Is there a way out of here?"

"You won't leave, not when he wants you." Ok, this guy had lost his appeal very quickly. The comfort thing had lasted about all of thirty seconds.

"Umm, thanks," I said sarcastically. I was about to move along but then his voice changed into a deep scratching, as if he was suffering with a throat infection.

"Don't let him get you or Draven will lose, Chosen One!" At the very mention of his name I flung myself against the door and shook the bars.

"Tell me, what have they done to Draven? Where is he? Is he

alright?" I hurried out my questions as if my mouth was on fire. But he just turned his body to face the other way and ignored me.

"Talk to me!" I shouted but he just raised his finger to his lips and said,

"Ssshh, *he will hear you.*" Then nothing more. I could feel another mental piece of string snap and I knew I would soon lose it altogether. I nearly ran to the other pillar as now the only thing in my mind was finding Draven!

The next cell door revealed a black room with only a small window for light, which was the size of a cereal box. This had bars crossing over casting diamond shapes over the room. Down under it was a black African woman sat with her feet crossed as though she was meditating. She was also clearly a Demon as there were two huge twisted horns coming from the side of her head just above the ears.

She was naked and had a full body with lots of curves and a pair of huge breasts, but I couldn't make out any other features as she was so dark-skinned and had her eyes closed. The horns mirrored along the floor stretching out their own terrorising shadows.

I was about to back away when out of the darkness I saw two white eyes without pupils. They stared straight at me and the whites of her teeth appeared. She then unfolded her arms and placed the palms on the floor outstretched in front of her. I watched in horror as the shadows took on a life of their own and came out towards me. They moved like snakes along the broken tiled floor and made their way up the door, coming closer still. I kept backing up but even when I could no longer see inside, I could still see the shadows reach up and out of the cell.

This made me momentarily forget about the gruesome wall behind me before it was too late. I backed up until I felt the writhing bodies but before I could react, a myriad of hands all reached out and grabbed a part of me. I squirmed and twisted to try and get free, but it was useless. Their grips tightened around my flesh and pinched my skin, making my eyes water.

"LET GO!" I screamed and I turned my head around even though there was a hand around my neck. I came face to face with one of the soul's heads and it looked as though it was smiling like some sadistic toy in a shopping bag. It snapped its teeth closer to my lips and the restraint on my neck prevented my head from moving away. I tried to pull away with harder force, but a pair of nails dug deep into my shoulder cutting the flesh there, making me cry out in pain and forcing me to remain still.

Hands then pinned my arms and legs and others gripped my waist. The ones which couldn't hold on to something just started stroking my trembling skin as if I was now a new pet. They pulled at my clothes to get closer to my warm body and my sweater came off my shoulders.

As the snapping teeth got closer, I closed my eyes to wait for the deadly impact. I knew pain well, but it never prepares you for the next round you face. I tensed my body, making it as hard as possible before the thing could take a chunk out of me. Thankfully, its breath was caught under the thin barrier, but the smell of hot sticky skin filled my nose instead of its foul breath. It was like being centimetres from the mouth of a shark, waiting for that precise moment to take you.

"Please don't!" I whimpered out one last time before its teeth came into contact with my face. Then a great roar filled the room making it stop in fear. It wasn't the only one, as my body finally stopped struggling under Demonic hands. I opened my eyes to see a large fanged mouth open just over my left cheek with what looked like a wired helmet piece poking at the strained surface. Thankfully it was frozen mid bite, thanks to the large pissed off figure that stood at the far end of the room.

The voice came again, barking another order out like the Hounds of Hell and slowly the hands and faces started to retract back into the wall. I moved away quickly, but one last hand that had its nails still embedded in my shoulder scratched my back taking some of my skin with it. My torn t-shirt showed four bloody lines where they had left their mark. I screamed at the pain that shot through me and when I heard a whooshing noise next to me, I turned to discover who my saviour had been.

"Ragnar!" I flung myself into his arms and fell onto his solid chest. I could feel the tears of relief rise up and it was only when he grabbed my arms to gently push me back, did I start to compose myself. Thankfully, he had allowed me some time before finding out what I was doing down here.

He looked down at me from his great height as if to give me the once over. He eyed my wounded shoulder and a low growl escaped his lips. He then punched his fist into the wall that had held me captive, causing a wave of agony rippling among the souls. The thick skin like substance bubbled in and out of tortured faces, like a stone thrown into a lake and Ragnar started to curse at it in a different language. Before it could stop showing its aftermath, Ragnar held me under my arm and started to pull me back the way I had come.

"What are you doing? We can't go that way!" I tried to protest but his grip tightened, making sure I was only going to go the way he wanted me to.

"You shouldn't be down here, what were you thinking?" He tried to control his anger, but this just enhanced my own.

"WHAT?! Do you know what I have been through?!" I tried to stop him from taking me the way I really didn't want to go, but against Ragnar it was probably like a fly bugging him.

"I can imagine" he said in a flat tone and glanced at my shoulder. I pulled my sweater over it and said in my defiant tone,

"It's fine!"

"How did you even get down here? My Lord will not be happy!" He just mentioned the magic words to bring me back from my tantrum.

"Draven…Is he alright? Where is he? Does he know that Lucius is here?" From the look on his face he most definitely *did not*. He was still pulling me around the room until we came to a door that I had not seen before. He stopped to look at me just before we went through it and the shock at what I had just said was evident.

"My Master is fine, of course, and what is this about Lucius?" He said this just as he pulled me through an opening in the rocks and we were both in darkness. I had no idea where he was taking me, but the trust I had in him made all my worries fade. It was like waking from a nightmare and finding someone on the other side to comfort you. The dark tunnel would have been the end of me if it wasn't for Ragnar's secure arms that led me through it with ease. It made me wonder if seeing in the dark was one of his Demon gifts. Of course, I didn't ask.

The dark didn't last long, thanks to Ragnar's long legs. The end of the tunnel was also the end of all the prisons, as now I found myself standing in the middle of an amazing circular room that was like a smaller temple.

This one was all white marble with a black and white diamond tiled floor. The walls were covered in black granite statues which sat on thrones of gold in their own little alcoves. Each one was different, and they all represented different forces. Wind and the Oceans both had great sapphires and pearls encrusted on their feet, while Fire and the Sun had rubies and amber, held in their hands. There were others like Earth, Night and the Moon all with various gems embedded amongst their figures.

The parts of the walls that weren't paying testament to these Godlike effigies were, in their own right, masterpieces. Covered with so many patterns and carvings you didn't know where to look. It was as though your eyes couldn't take in all the splendour they created. You just wanted to touch them. To run your fingers along the channels that formed integral art. The room was bright, as if the day's sun was getting at it somehow, but with no windows and the night not yet over I couldn't understand where it came from.

Ragnar realised I was no longer following like the good little sheep he expected of me and that I had stopped dead in the middle of the room. He rolled his eyes and raised his head before backtracking to me. I was still mesmerized by my surroundings, all jaw-dropping and wide-eyed when I felt his strong spade sized hand circle my arm and pull me in the right direction.

We crossed the room towards a set of oak doors that looked as though they belonged in an ancient church. The wrought iron fixtures creaked as the door was opened by two other men. A shocked gasp caught in my throat as I recognised the purple robes I had seen earlier. Ragnar felt me tense at the sight of them and looked down to meet my panicked face.

"Do not fear, they will not harm you." His voice was unusually

soft, and I never expected that a creature so big could even muster up a whisper. The effect it had made me calm enough to be led along through the doors into the next room. However, this relaxed state didn't last as long as intended because as soon as I saw the Temple I had fled from now opening up in front of me, I started to struggle.

"What are you doing? LET GO!" I was trying to dig my feet in, but Ragnar didn't even feel my resistance.

"Don't cause anymore more problems, young one!" His voice was stern, but his face looked guilty and now I knew why…

He wasn't here to help me…*He was here to catch me!*

He turned to face me, and his massive frame blocked out the view of the Temple at the end of the room. We were now stood in a wide arched room that was lit by crude twisted wood that flamed at the top and was making crackling and splintering noises. I could feel myself well up and his features softened through a watery vision.

"Why cry?" he asked me, but was he joking? I had been running from the Temple for what seemed like an eternity and now the man I trusted, or more like, who was trusted to keep me safe, was actually my enemy. Before I could answer his ridiculous question a voice behind him brought those tears to come crashing down my face.

"Bring her to me!" Ragnar moved to my side, allowing the sight of the powerful stance of Lucius, still dressed head to foot in his black robe with the long hood covering his deadly features. My head screamed for ideas, of on any way to escape, but it came up blank. I was faced with two colossal barriers in the form of powerful Demons. Ragnar, sensing I might try to run, had come up the back of me and when I took a frightened step back, I was met with his impenetrable chest. His two hands held me still, one on my shoulder (the one that wasn't still killing me) and one on my arm.

"How could YOU! How could you betray him?" I screamed out in anger at my once loyal bodyguard. Meanwhile, the black robe was coming closer and my heart sank further into the pit of misery that Ragnar held me securely over.

"My Lord." Ragnar's head nodded in respect, the way he would have once done towards Draven and at this I couldn't help shouting out,

"TRAITOR!" But Lucius started to shake his head before moving too fast for my eyes to see. A black whirl was all I could make out before blinking twice. Then, once my eyes had a moment to get back into focus, they were faced with the shadowed face looking down at me. Jesus, but Demons are fast!

His hand came up to my face and when I flinched away, he growled, making me shiver. He shook his head in what looked like disappointment and then delivered the final blow to my mental state, making me want to cry out at the cruel reality when he said...

"Oh Keira, why did you have to wake up?" The voice was smooth as silk, yet it cut through this nightmare like a fatal blow. The voice was masterful but with a loving touch and emotional concern. The voice was lost to me in a sea of questions.

The voice was none other than that of...

Dominic Draven.

CHAPTER TWENTY-ONE

A VIKING'S FIRST LIFE

I wanted to cry out at this cruel turn of events. It had been Draven all along. It had been Draven who had led that sick display in the Temple. One which had resulted in the murder and sacrifice of a young frightened girl. To say I was stunned didn't even touch on the boundaries to describe my mental state. I was, however, clear on one thing…

I was very close to a fully-fledged meltdown.

The minutes felt like hours before anyone said anything. I wasn't sure whether he was waiting for me to speak first or if he was just giving me time to process all that had happened. I found myself unable to look at him. All I could see was the black-cloaked image plunging a blade into a naked girl's body until it eventually went limp. This was the worst nightmare of all. Everything else that I had seen tonight had been a light summer breeze during a skip in the park compared to this.

I then became aware of being walked back into the statue room I had been in awe of before being forced back into the Temple by Ragnar. Well, as long as I was no longer the focus of all those cloaked figures all staring at the spectacle that had been me.

"Keira, look at me!" His voice cut through the silence like an impenetrable force and I had to suppress the urge to shudder. I finally made myself look from the floor where I had done all my thinking. He towered over me like an impending doom and I didn't know what I feared the most, losing the Draven I knew, or meeting the dangerous Draven that I knew he could be. But, as soon as I met his intense eyes, I knew I had nothing to fear but the temper that I had witnessed so many times before. It was like looking down the barrel of a smoking gun, the danger over but it could still leave a nasty burn once touched.

His powerful hands came to his head and removed his hood so that all his face could now be seen. His features told me he was less than happy, but concern was evident in his expression. He started to study me and found my cried-out eyes all puffy and red. My pale skin looked white with fright and my hair was now loose from where it had been pulled and tugged at from the Wall of Souls. So, in short, *I was a mess.*

His hand came to my face and for a minute I found peace with the feel of his gentle touch on my cold cheek. He traced my jawbone before getting to my bitten lips and his frown brought me back to my situation. I moved my face away from his hand and stepped back, once again into Ragnar's solid frame. This made all the muscles in Ragnar's chest tense as I could feel it ripple through my back. This wasn't the only reaction it caused as now Draven looked furious.

"Would you like to explain to me exactly what she is doing down here?!" His anger echoed off the Temple walls and it took me a minute to realise his question wasn't directed at me. Was he really going to blame Ragnar for this mess? My answer came in way of Ragnar's regretful voice.

"My Master…I do not know." It was the first time that I heard Ragnar sound anxious.

"You failed me! Find me the one who granted her access… NOW!" This was by far the most extreme I had seen Draven's temper get, as the solid stone walls seemed to vibrate enough so that stone dust fell down in various parts of the room. Ragnar just nodded and bowed before shouting his own command at some nearby guards. I watched as he walked from behind me towards them and it was only when I felt my own arm being taken hold of, did I turn and look to find Draven pulling me off to one side.

He swung me around so that he could back me against a stone statue of a warrior on horseback. I now stood at the base of the horse's legs and when I looked up, I saw the huge animal's head looming over me. My eye line begrudgingly came back down to meet Draven's cold dark stare, which had me soon wishing I was on the horse's back next to the warrior.

"Who brought you down here?" His question took me back.

"N..n…nobody." I stuttered out in a timid voice.

"Keira, do not try my patience, WHO?!" His shouting didn't help matters and it made me want to shout back, but for some reason I had lost all fight in me. I had resorted back to the same Keira that I was when I first met him. I had returned back to my pathetic way of being intimidated and controlled. I could feel him invading my mind for the answers and I knew that I would have to find the control that made me different from the rest. I swallowed hard and took a deep breath before answering his interrogation.

"Like I said, nobody brought me down here. I found my own way…*regrettably,"* I added bitterly, looking off to one side wishing to save myself his harsh features.

"You're lying! I warn you, Keira, do NOT lie to me!" He was getting more incensed with each word from my lips but I had to defend myself.

"Am I?!" I snapped back.

"I am going to give you one last chance." One eyebrow raised and he folded his arms but with his fists clenching as the seconds ticked by, I found myself looking over towards Ragnar for some comfort.

"There is no use looking at him for help, if he would have done his job properly, then this would have never happened!" He barked out.

"Don't blame him! He had nothing to do with any of this. And I am tired of trying to tell you that I came down here on my own!" At this his eyes flamed deep purple followed by a swift change into his Demon form.

The last time I had seen him like this was in a very different light, but to be on the receiving end of his rage made me want to cower to the floor. However, my dignity wouldn't allow me to react to such extremes. Instead, I just backed away until my body was flush against the cold stone. This, however, wasn't the only reason for the cold chill that travelled down my spine.

He looked as though he wanted to explode, but then a figure behind him came into view and his twisted face started to calm. He turned his head as the cloaked figure approached but his body still remained facing me, all tensed, ready to pounce.

"Dom, calm yourself. Why would she need to lie?" Vincent's voice had an instant effect, bringing his glowing body back down to his normal olive skin colour. This was when I realised that sometimes even without my gift, that if they wanted to, Angels and Demons could make you see their true forms. This I had never known until now and it answered some of my unasked questions. I watched wide-eyed as his human form returned and his anger subsided. I found myself mentally thanking Vincent and it was a thought he obviously heard as I watched him wink at me when Draven wasn't looking.

"Then explain to me, brother, how did she gain access through the Temple doors?" He didn't take his eyes off me while he addressed Vincent, but Vincent was the one person who wasn't intimidated by his brother's temper. If anything, he had been a witness to it more than anyone else.

"I am sure the answers will soon reveal themselves in time, but until then, why frighten the girl you love into telling you something she clearly doesn't know?" His words hit their mark and almost instantly his features softened into the Draven I knew. I stood deadly still like a caged bird, as I watched another figure emerge and even though cloaked from head to foot, I knew it to be Sophia. She didn't speak but now that we had a larger audience, Draven let out a sigh before barking his next command.

"Ragnar, take Keira back to my chamber, I will be there shortly." He turned his back to me, and this was when I finally found not only my voice, but also my own temper.

"NO! I am going home right now, and you can't stop me!" I stepped forward at this and I could almost hear everyone hold their breath as I made my millionth mistake of the night. He stopped dead and turned his head around slowly, adding to the dramatic effect.

"Oh, can't I?" he asked calmly, looking me squarely in the face, but I stood firm.

"N…no! I am not one of your desperate prisoners or one of your…your frightened servants that has to obey you! I'm my own damn person and I want to leave!" Everyone looked stunned and all I could hear was my own heart beating as though it was about to explode out of my chest and into Draven's arms.

He closed his eyes for a second, as though he was also living his own personal nightmare and for a minute, I thought he was going to let me have my way, but then he motioned for Ragnar to come closer.

"Very well, so be it. Ragnar take Miss Williams to my chamber even against her will if need be. *And by no means let her leave*. Do you understand?" This wasn't a question but more like a threat.

I was left dumbfounded! I couldn't find the words that I wanted to scream out at him. This was the first time he had ever referred to me using my last name and the coldness of it hit me like a sledgehammer. How dare he! This time he did walk away from me and only when Ragnar came behind me to edge me forward did I react.

"YOU CAN'T DO THIS!" I started to run after him, but Ragnar caught me before I even had a chance. I wanted to hit him, to pound my fists against his chest and make my palm come into contact with his arrogant face!

"Oh and Ragnar... do not dare to fail me again!" This was the last thing he ordered before walking back into the Temple.

"No, my Lord," Ragnar said through gritted teeth and it was the first sign that he was about as happy as I was with our situation. Ragnar seemed to take no pleasure in forcing me to go the way he wanted me to. I struggled and wriggled which was pointless against Ragnar's iron grasp. He directed me towards a door I hadn't yet been through and it made me wonder how big this honeycomb of endless ancient rooms and corridors really was?

We walked through into another room that looked more like a

massive cloakroom and this was the first time I had seen one full of actual cloaks. All of which were hanging down like lifeless bodies with their backs to us. They were all in order of colour and I guessed this was down to rank as I saw ones in red, purple and even white but there was none in black and I knew why. Draven was clearly the Master of this little Temple's cult and therefore black was meant only for the executioner.

As soon as the door closed behind us, Ragnar had obviously had quite enough of me making a fuss, so he whipped me round to face him and when I was expecting to see an angry face, I was shocked when I was met with one of hurt and regret.

"Please stop making this more difficult than it has to be. I take no pleasure in forcing you to do something you clearly do not want to do, but considering your regard for others, I will ask you to obey…just for once, make this easier for me." This had been the longest sentence I had heard him speak and it wasn't without its effect. I felt sorry for him. He didn't want to be my bodyguard any more than I wanted him to, but we were stuck with each other and through this mutual suffering, it seemed to bring us closer or at least on the same page. So, I just nodded my response and turned to walk by his side instead of in front with him gently pushing me.

"Thank you," he said quietly and this made my guilt start to show its nagging head.

"Why does he blame you?"

"I was ordered to watch over you and I failed." He spoke in a regrettable tone and my guilt tugged even more at my heartstrings.

"So, you were ordered to watch over me, even when I am here?" I asked as we walked down past row after row of hanging fabric.

"If you mean at the club, then yes, but down here then no… never, you were never supposed to find this place." I stopped and when he turned, he was faced with a very confused Keira.

"What do you mean?"

"No one of your kind has ever set foot down here before and it is utterly forbidden. Only the higher powers allow access to whom they choose, and humans are not worthy…sorry." He added the 'sorry' when he saw me frown at his lack of compassion for 'my kind' as he called us.

"So that is why Draven thinks somebody let me in?"

"That is the only explanation and that is why I want you to tell me who? It is the only way to reverse my actions." Okay, so he made a good case but it didn't change the fact that I still had nothing to tell him. If only I could make him believe me.

"Okay, I am going to tell you what happened and then maybe someone will finally believe me and then I have a chance at convincing Draven." Ragnar remained quiet as we walked through room after room until we finally came to not only the end of our journey but also the end of my story. At first, he didn't say a word he just looked deep in thought until his bushy eyebrows raised as if he had an idea.

"If that is the case, you can prove it."

"But h...?" Before I could finish, he grabbed my hands and examined them. This was when it finally sank in and I realised what he was looking for. The strange mark that was still left in my skin, thanks to the vine-covered door, for what I now knew to be the Temple doors. As soon as he found it, he dropped my hand as though I was going to infect him, then he staggered back a step and started muttering something in a different language. He was shaking his head as though he was seeing a ghost.

"What...? What is it?" I was getting even more frustrated with his strange behaviour.

"It must all be true...you are the one...the... no, never mind... it is not my place, but this does change things."

"Oh goodie, more cryptic clues, that's all I need!" I remarked sarcastically before walking back into Draven's chamber. It wasn't long ago when he was calling it our room but as it seemed, it sure didn't take long before Draven started shifting his weight around!

I walked back into the room and my heart sank at the sight. It was only a short while ago that I was wishing to see this room again more than anything else in the world. But now? Well, now it was cold and dead without the warm Draven I loved being here to welcome me. Instead, I had the temper filled Demon boyfriend to wait for and knowing I was soon to be in the firing line was not a thought that kept me all warm and fuzzy inside!

Ragnar made the lights illuminate the room and I half expected some horror to be there waiting for me. The past few hours had been some of the most traumatic I had ever experienced, and I was feeling mentally and physically exhausted. All I wanted to do was curl up into a ball on the bed and wake from this nightmare to find Draven's arms around me, reassuring me it was all a dream. Well, that wasn't necessarily true, I also wanted to grab my stuff and make a break for it but the chances of that happening were like Draven walking through the door full of apologies and a big bunch of flowers...

Never gonna happen!

Instead of the bed, I walked over to one of the lush, velvet armchairs and sat down like a deflating fairground balloon. Ragnar eyed me cautiously, fearing I would snap if he said or did the wrong thing.

Some things had been bugging me about Ragnar and I knew that I would never get another chance to find out about my Viking protector. So, I raised my chin and decided tonight was as good as any to add even more to my night of discovery.

"Is the reason your English is better because of me?" This was something I had noticed lately. The more time I had spent around him the easier his accent and wording seemed to get.

"Yes. My Master thought it better to improve my English while I would be spending more time around you. He thought it would be less challenging for you if you could understand me better. So, I relearned." He didn't seem as bothered with this request as I was. I couldn't believe the lengths that Draven thought it necessary to go to and for what? Making it easier for me to be protected? For me to be comfortable with it all? I was starting to understand why I was a thorn in Ragnar's side.

"Tell me something, you didn't want to be my bodyguard...*right?*"

"No, I did not," he said, not surprising me with his bluntness.

"Because you didn't like me?" His eyes met mine and for a

moment it was as if he was looking at someone else before answering me.

"I don't like humans." Wow, once again, blunt much!

"Why, you were human once?" I replied without trying to get my back up, but it was hard.

"I was, but once I was reborn, my view on mankind changed." He looked uncomfortable with where this conversation was going but if I was to bond with this Demon then I would first have to understand him.

"And what was it that changed that view?" This time it was he that was frowning but still, he continued.

"Because I saw how far man will go in search of power. In my culture we believed that the end of the Earth as we knew it, would find its peace in an ultimate battle between Gods and the forces of evil. Where, in which the old Gods would perish, and a new peace would come. This we called Götterdämmerung which means the 'Twilight of the Gods'."

"And this is your reason to hate us? Surely you can see, after all these years, that we have evolved?" At this statement he looked unconvinced and he just folded his tree-trunk arms, making the material on his black t-shirt almost tear with strain.

"Okay, I don't buy it…something else must have happened to you! You talk about the lengths man will go to in search of power but from what I have seen tonight, there must be the same ambitions in your kind, or Draven wouldn't need a prison-like that under his friggin' house!" At this I crossed my own arms, but I winced as the pain shot down my back thanks to what Demon fingernails had done.

"Remove your garment," he demanded nodding to my top.

"What!" I replied in horror.

"You need to be healed before he returns." He stepped towards where I was sitting, but I held up one hand to stop him.

"It's fine and looks worse than it is. Anyway, don't change the subject." I was being foolish, I knew, but I needed to feel the pain to be able to deal with Draven's temper. As though it would give me the anger I needed to challenge him on equal grounds. Besides, since the last time that Ragnar had healed me, I decided that it should only be left to Draven to touch me that way. Ragnar had clearly done quite enough for me already in the line of Draven's duty.

Ragnar just shrugged his indifferent shoulders, before walking back to one side of the door frame to lean upon. This door I couldn't keep my eyes off as I was still waiting for Draven's fury fuelled body to walk through at any moment.

"Am I not right? Why need that place if none of your kind craves more power, enough to break the rules and defy Draven?" I continued with my argument, but Ragnar seemed unmoved by my observation.

"There will always be those who feel the need to try and control a domination, which is not theirs to control."

"You're talking about Draven's domination aren't you, because he is…is King?" It was even harder to say it out loud than in my head. I was still trying to process all that I had seen tonight but to add the day's events as well… then it became a whole new ball game. I had witnessed Draven's rule first-hand tonight and I was terrified that I would forever see him in a different light. Would I still see him as Draven my boyfriend? Or Draven, the supernatural King of a secret world?

"There is a big difference in how your world and mine are controlled. Yours has appointed many men as leaders to gain power how they see fit. In my world, we have but one great leader, who is a direct bloodline to the Gods themselves, both beneath and above. His word is final and undisputed, but most of all, he does not exist purely to kill all those he cannot conquer, because he already conquers all. He has no need to start wars for power like man does. He has fought our wars to protect the balance in which he was born…that is what makes him a great leader. That is the difference." This was obviously something he was passionate about as it was the most animated I had yet seen him get.

"And throughout history, do you claim the same circumstances? Men back then were brutal in their quest for power, killing innocent people with little or no consequence and yet here you are trying to say we still operate with the same methods. Come now, you were a Viking were you not? You must see a difference?"

Again, he just shrugged his shoulders, which made me lose my cool.

"That isn't an answer!"

"I agree the methods of man have changed through the years, yes, but now instead of men to fight your wars, man has created the means to destroy not only their own race but every living thing on a planet. A planet which does not solely belong to them. Which is worse, an army that destroys a country or a single man that can destroy Earth by pressing a button?" Ok, so he had a bloody good point and one that was getting incredibly difficult to argue.

"You have a lot to learn, especially about our kind, but you are smart and strong-willed. This will help and is no doubt down to your gifts, but it does not mean you are always right, young human."

"I can imagine you would have sung a very different tune when you were human!" At this his face changed and I could almost see the memories of his human days fill his eyes with sorrow.

"When I was human my views were different, yes, but how I came to be what I am now is the reason they changed. My murder played a big part in that." I gulped at the word "murder" and sadness replaced my frustration.

"What happened to you?" I said in a low voice, full of concern for my unlikely friend. I waited for a facial feature to tell me he was uncomfortable with me asking but there was none. If anything, he just leaned back and looked casual on the door frame before starting his first life story as a human.

"My name is Ragnar Lodbrok and I was a Viking warrior who became King of Denmark and a large part of Sweden, but it was short lived."

"Because you were murdered for it?" The look on his face told me I guessed wrong.

"No, I was murdered because I chose a loved one over my throne, over the rule of my people and my need for power." I was stunned to silence, so he carried on his heart-breaking story.

"Before I became King, I had a family. My wife was also a warrior, we call them 'shieldmaidens' and that's how I met her. She became injured in battle and when the wounded were rounded up, one of my men discovered a woman lying in the dirt, dressed like a man." He took a minute to himself, as if he was seeing it all over again in his mind.

"I remembered seeing her fight and her skills on the battlefield impressed me enough to save her life, even though she had been fighting against me. Her name was Lathgertha and she bore me five strong sons and an even stronger daughter. She had the beauty of her mother and the wisdom of a great leader." He closed his eyes briefly, seeing his daughter behind closed lids, I imagined.

"She was my light, so she was rightly named Dalla, which means 'brilliance' in my old language of Norse. It was my love for the girl that was to become my end." I had tears welling up in my eyes and I hoped he couldn't see them from the other end of the room.

"Why, what happened to her?" I whispered my question.

"The English arrived on our lands and found Dalla and her mother by the river. We found the bodies but no ship in sight. My wife and daughter fought with the courage of an army, as my wife's body was among the fifteen dead. My daughter was nowhere to be found but after torturing the only survivors, I soon learned that she had been taken as a gift for an English ruler. King Aella of Northumbria was to take her into his bed before probably killing her." I gasped at the thought and Ragnar looking past it ignoring my sympathy.

"My sons were all around the world on their own conquests and knew nothing of this. So, against the better judgement of my advisors, I left my kingdom taking only two Knarrs and set out for your homeland." Oh great, not only was I human, I was also English, making it a double whammy in the eyes of Ragnar. No wonder he hated me!

I had given up trying to hide my tears as soon as he had mentioned the death of his wife. I could just picture it, the two Viking beauties fighting to save themselves and each other. Back to back, taking them down, one by one they fell, only it was all to be in vain. I wondered how many of them were there and how different this story would have been if they had given up and ran.

Would we even be having this conversation? Would he even be here?

"What happened when you got to England?"

"I took my small army and went to rescue my daughter, but I was too late. I found her lifeless body strung from a tree outside the gates. She had not met an honourable death by the hands of that tyrant, so in a rage, I ordered my men into a suicide mission and stormed the castle. We did not get far and in my uncontrollable wrath, I had lost my senses. My men died for nothing and I had been captured only to serve an even worse fate."

"What did they do to you?" I whispered before trying to sniff back yet even more tears.

"The King ordered me to be thrown into a pit of snakes, where they slowly bit me to death. Draven had followed my life with great interest because of my bloodline. I am a descendant of Odin, God of war, and the leader of souls. It was, therefore, natural for me to take my place by his side. My only request was for my revenge to be carried out by the hands of my sons."

"And was it?" I knew the answer as soon as I saw the sadistic smile creep upon his rough large lips.

"Yes, my sons fulfilled my wish and the wish of the Gods. Aella met his end by the mighty blood eagle."

"Does that mean he was eaten by birds?" I asked naively but when he laughed, I felt embarrassed.

"Well, what is it then?" I half snapped, not liking being laughed at when I had just shed tears for his story.

"I think you have experienced enough horror for one night," he told me unaffected by my exasperated tone, so I told him,

"I'm a big girl I think I can handle it." He rolled his eyes at my stubborn behaviour before giving in.

"Alright, but don't say I didn't warn you. This method of torture and execution is performed by cutting the ribs by the spine before breaking them. This is so they resemble blood-stained wings… and then of course we pull the lungs out before pouring salt into the wounds but usually the victim had died by this point." He said this so matter of fact that it chilled me to the bone. This just proved that my pig-headedness had nearly made me vomit! He must have seen me turn green and proved that even Demons love stating the obvious.

"I told you so," he said in a very satisfied tone. I gave him a fake smile that I added to a sarcastic look of disapproval.

"No wonder you hate me," I stated shamefully.

"I have never hated you." He tilted his head as if I had misread everything he had ever said to me.

"But you said…"

"I said I didn't like humans, but that was never the reason I didn't want to be your bodyguard."

"I don't understand, then why?" I shook my head as a natural reaction.

"Do you remember when I said you reminded me of someone?" I nodded as realisation took hold, making me look down at my feet as my face went red.

"My daughter had the same wilful spirit." He also looked down to find his own feet and for a moment we shared in the same awkward silence for reasons relating to the same.

This was named Dalla.

That was why he found it so hard being near me. I reminded him of the daughter that he had lost in the most awful way you can imagine and now he had to protect me. He was now forced to spend painful time around me. My guilt was unbearable.

"I will speak to Draven." I was sure once he knew the circumstances, Draven would relieve Ragnar from his duties concerning me.

"Why would you do that?" He looked confused.

"So that you don't have to protect me anymore." He was shaking his head as if I was missing something.

"He already knows my feelings," he told me softly.

"What!" I whispered in astonished horror.

"It was one of the reasons that I was chosen to guard you. He wanted me to form a connection, a bond so that I would guard you with my own life."

"But that's…That's cruel. To play on your history…with your loss." He shook his head before rubbing the back of his neck with a large red-skinned palm.

"Not cruel, it was smart, and I would have done the same." At this I reached my limit. I leant my head down into my hands and lost myself by counting up all the problems I had caused. I wanted to run away and try to make sense of all this craziness. I was human after all and knew that I would soon crack. I wondered just how long the conversation would take between me and Draven to go through everything that happened today. Tonight, had made me realise just how little I knew about the man that I loved.

I wanted to say more but I couldn't find any words of comfort for him, not any that I thought would make sense right then. I wanted to tell him that I was sorry. Sorry for everything, his loss, his lack of faith in humankind, but more than anything, I was sorry for all the trouble I had caused him.

But in the end, I didn't have time to say any of these things. Ragnar had straightened up at the sound of his King's footsteps coming closer. I held my breath and tried in vain to still my beating heart.

Draven marched into the middle of the room between me and Ragnar and it looked as though his temper hadn't yet subsided. And shamefully, if anything, this just ended up adding to his impressive beauty. He was a hard and handsome man painted on a rough canvas. The lower part of his face was covered in black stubble and his hair had been pulled back from his face in a black cord. This made his chiselled features all the more startling. He also still wore his black cloak, which made his dark eyes look as black as this horrible night. I couldn't take my eyes off him and his didn't leave mine. I was hoping to find love and compassion in them, but there was none.

He hid it well and I knew why.

This was the only way that Draven knew how to operate. He was going to try and frighten the answers out of me. But one thing he didn't count on was how well I knew his games. Because even though he clearly intimidated me, I was never truly frightened of him. I knew he would never hurt me, but I was wondering just how far he would take this interrogation of his.

He tactically removed his cloak with one flick of his wrist and then threw it toward Ragnar to take away. I had to catch my breath at the sight of his tanned naked torso that was ripple after ripple of solid muscle. Okay, so that intimidation level just went up a notch!

He knew what he was doing, as it looked as though he knew me well also. He only wore black fitted trousers with a black belt that had his family crest in brushed steel at the front.

"Did you find out who needs to be punished?" he asked Ragnar without looking at him and even though he couldn't see, Ragnar still bowed his head in respect.

"My Lord, she is telling the truth." At this Draven let out a growl and turned his head towards him, making Ragnar take a step back.

"LEAVE US! I will get to the bottom of this myself!" At this he turned his attention back to me, but Ragnar didn't leave, and Draven noticed.

"My Lord, if I may? She holds the mark to prove her story." He also found my eyes and I mentally thanked him, for at least one person was on my side.

"Is that so?" Draven was being an arrogant fool now and I felt like chucking a glass of water in his face and telling him to grow up...but I was no way brave enough, no matter how much foolishness still remained with me.

Draven nodded to the door as way of an order for Ragnar to leave but once again, he remained firm.

"You have more to say?"

"Yes, my Lord, I think you should pursue this after she has had some rest...I think she is too fragile for your questions...she is also hurt." At this Draven looked furious, turning to face him. I felt like running in between them both and protecting my loyal friend.

"Wohin?" ("Where?" in German) Draven growled out in another language that sounded like German.

"Schulter" (shoulder in German) Ragnar said and nodded towards my neck which made me pull my sweater closer over the four deep scratches that had been burning since they were made.

Once again at this, Draven growled a low groan of disapproval and it made me wish Ragnar would just leave to save himself.

"You are not under my rule to think for me! Incompetent fool! When I give an order, I expect it to be obeyed. NOW GO and obey me Ragnarök. I will deal with you later!" At this my smooth skin was replaced with bumps and I pulled my legs up underneath me closer to my body. Ragnar admitted defeat and left after his usual,

"Yes, my Lord."

Now was the part I was dreading, time to face the music, time to face the Demon for…

Draven and I were finally alone.

CHAPTER TWENTY-TWO

WHO WANTED A NORMAL LIFE ANYWAY?

I was determined not to be the one to break the silence first and thankfully I wasn't. After a small eternity of playing 'Who could stare the most' he finally looked away and my heart broke when it was in disappointment.

"Come here," was all he said in a controlled voice, but I still didn't move. This was Draven's way of dealing with things. But I knew it was due to his high ranking and now he was pulling that rank with me. He stood with his arms folded waiting for me to obey like all the rest did, but I just couldn't do it. This, however, he took the wrong way…

"If I didn't know any better, I would say you fear me… is this so?" He raised an eyebrow when I didn't answer him, so I folded my own arms and looked even more like a spoilt child before answering,

"No," was all I said before turning away from him, but not before I caught sight of a little smug smile form on his lips, which he quickly discarded.

"Good, then prove it. Come here." Again with the orders! If I had been in my right mind then I would have done as he'd asked, but I just couldn't think straight. I didn't have time or the comprehension for his dominance. I felt like I was drowning in a whirlwind of memories I didn't want. I saw him stood there like some cloaked God ready to control his armies. Ordering the destruction of anyone that got in his way!

NO…no! I wanted to scream out at myself for even thinking it. I was just so confused. My mind was like a box of puzzle pieces that had bits missing. I was trying to convince myself that what I had seen in Draven was a necessity, but there was still so much I didn't yet know. He was waiting for me to say something and I decided to play the only card I had. I just couldn't let him see how intimidated I was. I needed him to see that I was still his equal here and not just another servant to obey.

"I don't have to do what you command, Draven, especially when you refuse to let me go home," I said in a weak and unconvincing voice, which made his arms unfold as he walked over to his desk to lean upon it casually.

"I am not commanding you to do anything unreasonable, you are injured, and I want to fix it. As for the going home, that I will not allow because I need to get to the bottom of all that has happened tonight…*all that you have seen.*" He shook his head and rubbed his forehead with his fingers to express his feelings on the matter. He knew what I had seen, and this had been his worst nightmare. I had seen the truth.

"I'm fine." This was a lie, as I could still feel the blood that had trickled down my back, but I continued anyway,

"I don't need your help, all I needed was for you to believe me and the fact that you didn't, well…let's just say, it speaks volumes." This was also a lie as all I wanted was for him to scoop me up in his arms and comfort me. I had needed nothing but his help throughout my whole experience, but when the time came, he had destroyed that need by proving himself the enemy behind my fear. I still couldn't get out of my mind the thought of him killing that girl.

"Is that so? Well in that case, I will have you taken to the hospital immediately, considering how much I know you enjoy being in one," he replied sarcastically and I could feel the tears start to rise. As soon as he saw the hurt in my face, it looked as though he regretted it instantly.

"That was cruel," I said in a weak little voice to prove it, but he knew this already, after all, he had said it for that purpose.

"Yes…Yes it was…but I think I made my point. You are in pain and unless you enjoy the feeling, I suggest you come to me." He was right, I was in pain, but the pain of his coldness was far greater than any gash I had in my flesh.

"I think I will take the hospital, thank you," I replied bitterly, which made him laugh and not in a nice way.

"What? Injections, stitches, and bandages and above all, a doctor's questions?" He nodded to my covered arms as if to spell out my fears. I pulled my arms into my body as if to protect them in some way, which is where he found his answer.

"No, I thought not." He shook his head as if he was very tired of all of this and it made me do the same.

"I fear that my patience cannot take much more, so for what I am about to do, I apologise," he said making me frown.

"Apologise for what?!" I snapped back at his lack of compassion in his 'sorry'.

"For this!" Both his hands came out and I thought he was motioning for me to come towards him again. Of course, it was only when the armchair I sat in started to shoot forwards towards him, did I realise the reason behind it. It moved too quickly for me to get off as it travelled across the room and before I knew it, he was towering above me, getting exactly what he wanted…*total control.* He could see me calculating my next move and before I could escape from him, he had caught me by the waist.

"Oh, no you don't! Time to behave, my girl." He lifted me up and perched me on the desk before spreading my legs to step closer into me. This way I couldn't go anywhere and even when I tried to push him away, it felt like an impossible task. It took me back to when he had first kissed me, and I had tried to push him away. Of course, back then that had only been because of a guilty conscience, one that had been unjustified as he had me believe he was engaged to Celina.

Now, I was doing it for very different reasons and expressing myself was very much a part of that. I was trying to show my unwillingness but when his hands circled both my wrists and held them still, it was the end of that.

"Keira, be still!" he barked at me and finally I obeyed. He sighed in relief when I gave up and his eyes, for the first time, softened when they met mine. He let go of my wrists before finding my shoulder and when I cried out in pain, he froze.

I couldn't see his face as I had closed my eyes to help stop the tears, but I could feel his hands now gently removing my sweater. The feel of his touch on my bare skin had me coursing with a familiar feeling and I couldn't help wanting his lips to find mine. Talk about mixed emotions!

I finally opened my eyes, to find him frowning (No change there!) but he wasn't looking at me, he was examining my torn shoulder. He didn't ask like last time, instead he just grabbed a handful of material before tearing it from me. I was left with a torn t-shirt and a naked top half, exposing the damage. I saw him shake his head before saying,

"This isn't good." At which I wanted to reply 'well durr!' but I didn't think it would go down well, so I opted for silence.

"What did this to you?" he asked through gritted teeth and I could see he was trying hard to keep his anger under control.

"A wall of hands grabbed me." This made him swear out in another language and I wondered if I had just heard the F word in Latin?

"Draven, that isn't going to help." At this he rolled his eyes and decided not to respond. He lightly pushed my hair back and carefully pulled the bits that had stuck to the bloody mess, making me wince as he put the red clumps to the other side of my neck. Then he slipped down my bra strap which was in the way.

"Unfortunately, this is going to hurt, try to relax, ok?" Relax... Was he joking?

I knew what he was going to do, but I couldn't understand why it would hurt. He had done this to me twice before and it never hurt, it actually felt kind of nice. Like funny tingles lighting up my bloodstream.

"Ready?" he asked and when I nodded, I found out just what pain he was talking about. He placed his four fingers at my back and traced the cuts made in my skin. As he moved, he fused my skin back together and the burning felt like someone else was behind him pouring salt and vinegar into them. I closed my eyes once again, so that he couldn't see the pain in them, but I couldn't help the scream that came, making it more than evident at how this was feeling. Luckily, it didn't last long and by the time my breathing had got heavy, I was in his arms being held. His head was above mine and his hand holding on to the back of my head, keeping me close to his body.

"Shhh...I know it hurts but it's all over now. Just breathe... that's it... deep breaths for me." He was trying to calm me down and with each new breath I took, I was starting to feel better. All that was left was an itching where the new tissue had been formed or so I guessed. He could feel it too, so he manoeuvred my head so that I could look up.

"Better?" he asked and I opened my eyes at the sound of his voice, only when doing so, I wasn't faced with the human Draven, I was now looking at the purple energy that flowed through his veins. His huge wings looked blacker than they did all the other times and when looking at them this closeup, I could see that each feather coursed with the same energy. He took note where my eyes were staring, and I saw them ruffle slightly as if he was uncomfortable with being studied.

"Does it bother you, seeing me like this?" His deep purple eyes searched for the truth in my own and I wondered if my face had given me away. This had been the first time he had ever asked me anything like this before and you could hear the vulnerability in his question. Now making me wonder if Draven had ever felt vulnerable about anything before.

I felt sad that he thought it would have ever affected me. Even after everything that I had seen, this was one of the things that never bothered me. Surprised me, yes, but not in a negative way.

"No, it doesn't bother me, but what does is when you don't trust me," I told him.

"Here we go," he said in a condescending tone and then moved backwards to give me space. The air that was created by his wings turning quickly blew my hair back. I jumped down from the desk making him warn,

"Careful." But I ignored his remark and used the desk for support rather than a seat. I crossed my arms across my chest once again and it was only then when I noticed my near nakedness. I angrily pulled the rest of my top off and reached for my sweater from where Draven had thrown it, but before I could get there, he had it in his grasp and was handing it to me. I noticed the bloodstains inside it and let out a groan but when I tried to put it back on, he stopped me.

"Wait, let me clean it first." I was about to protest but he was already close to my body again and had produced a bowl of water with a soft wad of material. He was looking down at me again making my body start to yearn for his touch and when his hand rested on my good shoulder, I started to bite my lip at the feeling it created. His other hand was soaking the cloth in the water and I had little option to do anything but remain still. I watched him ring out the cloth with one strong fist before placing it on my skin, making me shiver.

"Cold?" he asked and I just nodded making him place a finger in the bowl and re-dampen the cloth before continuing cleaning my back. It was now warm.

"Thank you," I whispered and he looked happy to receive it. We remained silent until he was done and when his fingers left my now pink skin, I wanted to pull him back to me. But he stepped away once again and let me put the sweater back on without looking at me. I decided that if we were going to have this 'talk' then I couldn't keep staring at him in his other form.

I closed my eyes and listened to the noises around me until I heard something to pinpoint my thoughts on. I heard footsteps not far from the door and a bird cry out into the night. I wondered if it could be Ava and then realised that I hadn't seen her since that night by the cabin. This was all enough to change Draven back to his human form, as when I opened my eyes again, he was back.

"All normal again?" He had known what I had been doing and for some reason I felt guilty but when he laughed at my frowning face, I let it go.

"So, what now?" I said, just to fill the silence that he seemed content with.

"Why don't you tell me how this all started. What on this Earth's plane possessed you to find your way down to my Temple?" The hairs on my neck stood on end at the sound of the demanding Draven that had found his way crashing back.

"Oh, so you finally believe me now?"

"I might do, if you actually tell me what happened. But until then, I will try to reserve my judgement." Grrr! This made me so mad that I could have screamed at him, which is precisely what I did.

"What horse shit! Your judgement? I'm not some bloody servant of yours that is about to be punished for not serving drinks properly or that poor girl down there that you murdered!" This last part certainly got his attention alright, as I thought he would burst into flames with anger.

"You know nothing about that 'GIRL' you seem to think of as so innocent!" He was trying to control his temper by tensing his muscles and I could start to see his veins bulging along his arms.

"I know what I saw!" I snapped back.

"Oh, and what was that, me murdering an innocent human girl as some kind of sacrifice to the Devil himself?" He let out a roar like laugh that chilled me to the core.

"Don't mock me! Do you have any idea what I have been through tonight, you...you..."

"What?"

"Jack ass!" At this he let out a sigh, before holding the bridge of his nose between his thumb and forefinger.

"Is that why you thought I was Lucius?" he asked in a pained way.

"Yes. I didn't think it was possible for you to even be involved in something like that, let alone be in control of it." This must have hurt because he dropped his hand to his side and looked at me in disbelief.

"Right... Well, if that is the case, then why now are you so intent on believing me some leader of an evil cult that murders young girls, for what...pleasure?" he asked making a good point.

Could this all be something more? A part of his world I didn't understand just like the mountain of things left for me to learn. Either way, I still couldn't help but answer bitterly,

"And what else am I supposed to believe? I saw it all with my own eyes and until the bitter end I would never have thought it was you behind the blade." At this he was in front of my face in less than a second and he placed a finger over my mouth, before the gasp could escape it.

"Well, it was me behind the blade, Keira, but for good reasons, ones I fear you won't understand. And just to clarify, that 'girl' was anything but the good and pure human you so wrongly believe. She was, however, a very dangerous Angel." He let that thought stew in my mind for a while before continuing. He gave me space as the words 'Dangerous Angel' sank in.

God, but I was such a fool!

"But she…she was crying, she begged for me to save her…I…" I wasn't only saying this for Draven's sake. I needed to reassure myself with what happened.

"You were played, Keira. She used you! She wanted you to help her escape and if she had succeeded, she would have then killed you. I am just thankful she couldn't access your mind. Your gift, although extremely frustrating, does however keep you safe. Although, in this case, if my powers had worked on you like I had hoped, then you would still be in my bed, safely asleep and blissfully unaware of what happened tonight."

"You mean what you did," I corrected but again this didn't go down well and his reaction made him throw a chair across the room, turning it into mere splinters. I let out a scream, but he just shouted out.

"I MEAN WHAT I HAD TO DO!" As soon as he saw the fear in my eyes grow, he calmed, and his hand flew out to the remains of the chair. Now making it fuse back together so that it looked just like it did the day it was made.

"I'm sorry," he said with exasperation before continuing,

"I didn't mean to frighten you, but Keira you must understand, that what happened tonight was never anything I ever would have wanted you to lay witness to."

"Oh, and lying to me is so much healthier?"

"In this case, yes it would have been." He looked at my shoulder to make his point, but I just shrugged.

"So that is why I was so tired in the car, you were controlling me?" I guessed.

"Yes, and given the circumstances, was that so bad?" I knew the answer to this wasn't the one I would give. He was right in so many ways, but that didn't make it any less moral.

"What, taking away my free will...mmm let me think...Yes, I might find a problem with that! And anyway, if you knew what you would be doing tonight, then why even have me come with you? Why not let me stay at home, where there would be absolutely no chance of me finding that...that place?" I flung my arms up to emphasise my point.

"Keira, when will you understand it is simply not safe for me to leave you alone. A few hours, yes, but a whole night?" At this he shook his head as though he wouldn't even contemplate the idea.

"Well, it wasn't exactly safe me being here, now was it?" At this he growled, and I rolled my eyes at him.

"Yes, well if Ragnar had done his job like I ordered, then none of this would have happened." Now this got my blood boiling!

"Oh no, don't you dare blame him, this was my doing and mine alone. I will not have you scorning him any more than you already have done...he had his reasons for not standing outside my door all night!" At this Draven looked shocked at my concern for my new colossal friend.

"It wasn't long ago that you were singing a very different tune. Is there something I should know?" he asked looking furiously jealous.

"God, could you be any more paranoid...do you just think I am nothing but trouble?!" He now smirked at my reply and okay, so when I replayed that back in my mind, I now realised why he was finding it amusing. For one, he was counted as a King from the Gods and the other was that since he had first met me, I had been nothing but trouble! First, with my sicko stalker and now with Lucius after me, who could really blame him?

I knew right about now would have been the perfect time to tell him about my nightmares and that I seemed to have a new Demon vampire stalker and I'm pretty sure that later on I would regret not doing so, but I had my reasons…*I think.*

But let's face it, if Draven was like this over just one incident that didn't even include Lucius, then I couldn't bear to think how bad he would be if he knew just how many times I had been 'visited'. He would have me locked up in a bloody tower just to be safe. I would not only have Ragnar as my bodyguard but a whole bloody invisible fleet! An army outside my door to escort me to college every day. Okay, so it might come in handy in history class, considering most would have been around when major historical events were taking place. But I'm pretty sure that would still class as cheating and not research!

"What I meant was that I found out about his history. Draven, how could you do that to him?" Note to self, stop pissing off Demon boyfriend! At this he looked like he would soon turn purple again but when he closed his eyes to gain control, he wasn't the only one taking deep breaths.

"Listen to me carefully, Keira, as I will only say this once. What I order *my people* to do is *my* business and mine alone. If I choose to have one of my most faithful subjects take care of you when I cannot, then I would rather that a bond be formed as opposed to one of indifference!" he snapped after emphasising the fact that they were 'his people' not mine.

Because I was just the troublesome little human in this picture.
"But…"

"BUT NOTHING! I will not have this conversation with you, do you understand? There are more important issues to discuss than for you to be telling me how I should be conducting my business!" At this I finally gave in. Because what was left for me to say to this anger fuelled King? He was right anyway. What right did I have to tell him how to run his kingdom? He had saved my life and kept me safe by using his own judgement and here I was questioning that! *I was a fool.*

"I'm sorry, you're right, I shouldn't question your methods or stick my views into your business. Look, I should just go. You can have Ragnar take me back." I started to walk towards the door and away from him, mainly so that he couldn't see the tears that now rolled down my already salty cheeks.

I felt one hand being snatched in his hold before he pulled it back behind me, and with a small gentle tug, he turned me round to face him. I couldn't look at him and as a result my tears fell from my tired eyes, landing at his feet. His hand claimed my chin and lifted it up so that I couldn't continue to be a coward and had to face him. I met soft eyes, as the last shreds of temper melted away at seeing me cry.

"Oh, Keira," he whispered as both his hands came to my face to wipe all my tears away.

"I never wanted to put you through this. I never wanted what I am to affect you this way. You spoke of a normal life and now I realise that this is something I can never give you. It pains me to see that I am the cause of all of this." He lifted his tear-soaked hands to his face and looked down at them. He looked disgusted as he turned away from me and I was near to crying until I couldn't breathe in fear of what was to come. Was this the end? After all I had endured, after all we had been through…*it couldn't be!*

I couldn't allow it.

"What are…*are you saying?"* I spoke between sobs, but even at the sound he didn't look at me.

"I will have Ragnar take you home," was all he said and as a result I was close to crumbling to the floor.

"NO, no, no! You can't do this to me. I was stupid and I wasn't thinking! I see that now but please…you can't… you just can't!" I suddenly let my body fall to my knees and my devastated head followed. I cried even more when I felt his hand on my bowed head and I realised he was knelt on one knee in front of me.

"What Keira, tell me, what don't you want me to do?" His desperate voice asked with as much pain as my tears were made of.

"Leave… me…I don't want you to leave me!" And there we had it…I had finally broke. After a night from Hell I lost it. I had zero control left and Draven knew it as I started to cry it all out. He scooped me up into his arms and I buried my head into his chest, letting my tears invade his soft skin over hard muscle. I gripped my hands tightly around his neck and never wanted to let go. I didn't

know where he was taking me, but my tears wouldn't run dry at the possibility that it was going to be somewhere without him.

But then he spoke and in the end it was all my breaking heart needed to hear.

"Never! I would never leave you! Do you hear me! Not even until the day you no longer want me. Not even the day you stamp on my heart and set it on fire. Not until I hear you say that your love for me has been replaced with hate!" He pulled me to him tighter to prove this, before releasing me on the bed, but he didn't leave me. I felt his body get as close as he could to my own before making the covers devour our bodies in a blanket of secure warmth.

"Rest now, my love, for we can resolve this in the light of day." I didn't say another word as I rested my emotional body and intertwined it with the man I loved. And as if by hearing my thoughts the last thing I heard before crying myself to sleep, were the same thoughts from him…

"I love you."

CHAPTER TWENTY-THREE

CALM AFTER THE STORM

I wasn't sure if I had just had the worst night of witnessing nightmares in real life or whether it was just in my dreams. My thoughts felt as if they were covered in a deep morning fog and the heavier the clouds, the more I seemed to be lost in the darkness of my mind.

I could feel something comforting on my back. It was a circling motion, but when I turned around, I could see nothing there. I started searching for anything, listening, needing something that I couldn't place. I was walking through a misty white blanket of space. Then I heard it. My name was being spoken…no, not spoken, *but called.*

I began to walk without seeing. I was calling out, my lips producing no sound. I smiled when I finally recognised the voice and thanks to my reaction the voice got deeper, stronger and I knew he was nearby. Draven was searching for me also and the thought made me break out into a run. My legs pushed harder but after only minutes, his voice started to fade, and I pushed my body even farther. It was almost as if I was endlessly chasing him and although I was shouting out, my voice wouldn't follow my commands.

Finally, I stopped and stood breathless and breaking.

"Draven" His name finally escaped my lips and for the first time, I heard it being said. I hung my head down in disappointment at not getting a response. Then my heart flipped over as I felt a hand behind me on my shoulder and Draven's voice whispered in my ear,

"Wake up, Keira." It was smooth like drizzled cream over strawberries and this thought had me licking my rough lips. The feel of my tongue going over cracked skin made the fog start to clear and when I could see again, I knew exactly where I was. I was lying in Draven's bed sprawled out like a starfish. He was lucky his bed was enormous and could probably fit a baseball team in it or he would be teetering on the edge.

I shifted around and moaned as I usually do in the morning. My limbs felt like jelly, but thankfully my shoulder felt great. I now knew the reason I could feel a motion on my skin in my sleepy state. Draven was making circles with his fingertips over where I was hurt last night. It didn't take me long to realise I was naked, and my hair was loose and pushed to one side. Before looking at him, I raised my head and looked over the edge of the bed. I saw my clothes lying there in a heap where Draven had obviously discarded them. I felt him laugh next to me before speaking.

"You didn't need them." His voice was back to the usual 'self-confident' Draven I was used to, and when I looked round to face him, I saw not only what his voice told me, but that it was now calm waters again.

He was propped up on one elbow, staring at me. He looked as though he had been awake for hours, but he also looked bloody gorgeous! He could have rolled straight out of bed and done a photoshoot for the sexiest man of the year! This had me turning red as a boiled beetroot and fearing what my own appearance looked like. His hand went to my cheek and his lips followed but then after a frown he kissed my forehead lightly.

"I love it when you blush. However, these lips need work… Keira, what did you do to them last night?" His fingers went to the problem in question and he ran his thumb over them.

"I guess…" I had to clear my throat before continuing, as thanks to the crying mess I was last night, well it had left me sounding like I had swallowed not only a frog, but a toad, lily pad… and hell, any other pond life to go with it.

"I guess I gave them a rough time." He laughed and it sounded like a symphony to my ears.

"More like a massacre! Let me fix them." But before he could touch them again, I had moved away, making him growl. I remembered what it felt like last night and I thought after that, I would prefer to heal the normal way. He read my mind, of course.

"It won't hurt, not this time." When I didn't come back to him, he held one of his hands out as if he was offering a peace agreement.

"Trust me…*please.*" After asking me like that, I think I would have followed him off a cliff…oh no wait, we had already done that one. I was going to have to start thinking up new analogies, ones we couldn't possibly do together, ones like 'I would have gone naked parachuting with him' because let's face it why would he need a parachute, he did have wings. Okay, focus Keira.

I moved back into him and when he pushed me gently on my back, I closed my eyes. I felt him lean over me and when he placed his hand over my lips, I couldn't stop them from trembling.

"Trust me," he whispered again. Then when warmth started coming from his skin, they stopped trembling and instead, I was filled with a tingling that made them want to be kissed. It felt as though he was generating little lightning bolts from his fingertips, creating a storm on my lips and soon he could feel them smile under his hand. It only took seconds and as usual, when he was finished, he asked,

"Better?"

I nodded but still kept my eyes closed for the moment. Doing so as I replayed the horrible night's events back through my tired mind. I felt like Alice that had just fallen down the rabbit hole and had just woken up to find herself under the tree. What did she think? What did she do? Did she just get up and go home to carry on with her daily routine or did she have to go to therapy for the rest of her life? See, these are things they don't tell you in fairy tales…*the aftermath.*

Draven could obviously tell that I needed some time here, so he let me carry on with my mental whirlwind, without saying a word. However, this didn't mean that he didn't do anything and the feel of his touch on the side of my face was somewhat distracting. I wanted to put everything that had happened last night behind me so badly, that it felt tight in my chest with every breath I took. But I couldn't. I knew I could never just pretend it hadn't happened or even worse …that it didn't even matter. I needed explanations. I needed reasons, whys and hows. But my real fear was would Draven understand this need?

"Yes, he would." Draven's voice broke up my thoughts and now created new ones. He could hear my thoughts, because through the turmoil in my mind, he had gained access while my guard had been down. I opened my eyes to find him back in his original position, propped up on one elbow and staring intensely at me.

"I know you need answers, Keira. I was fully expecting to find you with a fragile mind and a worried heart this morning and I am fully prepared to explain everything you want to know. Last night, I regret not taking the advice of not only a servant, but of an old friend. Ragnar was right. He could see whereas I had been blind. He knew how fragile you were and was looking out for your best interests. I, on the other hand, just wanted answers and someone to blame for…well, it matters not what I wanted." He shook his head and took a deep breath before he looked back at me and said,

"But for my rash actions, I am greatly sorry. I realised in the end, but I fear it was too late. Will you ever forgive me?"

I listened in silence and with a blank expression, as I had never heard Draven not only sound so sorry but so sincere with it too. I was a bit blown away by it all, but it didn't take me long to follow with my answer.

"Shut up and kiss me, Draven" This he took as a good thing because the kiss was one of the most passionate I had ever experienced. Just when I thought it couldn't get any more intense…well, I found out being wrong sometimes was a very good thing indeed!

The fact that we couldn't follow it through with mind-blowing sex was a bit disappointing, but I didn't know whether this played a factor in how great the kiss was.

Draven had always excelled in the field of kissing, touching, taking my breath away…well, you get the picture. But this time his kiss made me feel like I was a teenager again. Heart pounding in my chest, insane new feelings you couldn't understand and unsurprisingly in between my legs.

His hands explored my face, neck, hair like he was on a quest of every feature my body held, until he finished by holding me so tight to his body that I felt as though we were one entity. He moved back to see my face and he was met by a very different Keira. I couldn't keep the daft grin off my lips and the sparkle out of my eyes. I was, to say the least, very, very happy again.

He moved his head back further to take in my full expression and his features turned into confusion.

"What is it?" he asked me in a comical little tone, and I guessed that I must have been staring at him as if we had only just met. As though this was a whole new side of Draven that I hadn't yet encountered. That of course being the sorry side.

"Nothing…it's nothing." I tried to pass it off as what I said it was and I decided to focus all my energy into rebuilding my mental wall. It didn't take me as long as usual, as something in me just seemed to click. I didn't need to strain my hearing on other noises or concentrate on what they were. Maybe I was growing stronger? The more I was around Draven, the more adaptable I became. Surely that crazy stuff I had witnessed last night should have sent me over the edge?

I could feel Draven waiting for me to speak, but I was too busy running through all the important questions I needed to ask him. This morning didn't change things just because his frowning face had been replaced by one of regret for his actions. I still needed to be in the know. He couldn't shut this all away as being his business, as he had done last night.

I moved a little further away from him and he shook his head slightly to show his disapproval. However, I didn't give in and neither did he make any attempt to pull me back. This time I was glad of it. I had to be stern. I had to get to the bottom of last night so that we could move on from it. I reached over the bed and grabbed my zip-up sweater to put on. Okay, so I was making a bit of a statement, but it felt like the only control I had, even if it was the most insignificant. I could feel his eyes searching for reasons in my actions, but I gave him none. Once comfortable and semi-dressed, I pulled the covers around my naked bottom half and sat up to face him.

"Okay, hit me with it," was all I needed to say to make him release a sigh. This had been the conversation he had been dreading and it was written all over his face. A line formed on his forehead and it was the first sign of his many years older than me that I had seen. (This excluding the fact that he was most probably thousands of years older) He hesitated, and it was quite obvious that he didn't know where to start.

"Okay, I'm going to make this easier for you by telling you what I know, and you can just fill in the gaps...Yeah?" He nodded and showed his palm by way of complying.

"So, I gather that phone call you got at my sister's was what, some kind of calling card to the Temple?"

"Of sorts, yes. But look Keira, I don't know how many details you are expecting to get from all this." He was trying to be stern, but I didn't back down.

"Oh, no you don't, you're not going to placate me with that! You're going to tell me what I want to know and answer my questions whether you like it or not." At this he raised his eyebrows to display his shock and I thought he was going to follow it by getting angry but when his brows smoothed, a smile played at the edge of his lips, displaying his amusement.

"Very well, but then can you promise you will try and understand my position, when I tell you things you are not going to like hearing?" This time I nodded, and he took my answer for what it was, a definite yes.

"When I received that call it was indeed to tell me that the Temple was awaiting me, and the girl made ready."

"You mean the dark-haired girl...that was in the cell, that you...?" I couldn't finish the words and say killed because it just wasn't the type of thing you would say to your boyfriend. Or at least any normal boyfriend, but there was nothing normal about Draven or about me for that matter. Usually couples argued about money or jealously, who does the washing up and what TV channel they're going to watch. But no, with me and Draven it was all about Demons, Angels, visions, dreams and evil stalkers! What I wouldn't give to just argue about something mundane, like him not picking up his dirty underwear off the floor.

"That *girl* has been one of our 'wanted' for some time indeed and trust me when I say for good reason." At this, his Demonic voice came through at the word 'girl' and I could hear him grind his teeth as he spoke of her.

"Tell me?" He shook his head at first, but he didn't outright tell me no, so I knew I had a little leeway.

"Draven, it's time to trust me." This got him alright.

"Okay, but I warn you, it will play on your pure heart and I fear I cannot stand to see you so upset, as you were last night," he confessed.

"You can't protect me from the truth, no matter how bad it is." He didn't respond to this but instead he showed me just how hard it was by rubbing his forehead with his fingertips in frustration.

"What do you mean by wanted…like being Marked, like when you told me about Yvonne Dubeck?" I asked, after he had been silent for a while and the sound of my voice brought him back to a conversation that he really didn't want to be having. He nodded first before explaining,

"Our legal system is not so different from yours. The only difference is that we are more likely to follow through with our punishments. These, of course, are very different. When one of my kind breaks the rules there are different steps that have to be taken. First comes the warning, where they are stripped of their powers for a time. This is depending on what rules have been broken, of course. But if the defendant hasn't been caught for this warning to be administered and they carry on their destructive ways, then they become part of the 'Wanted' or 'Marked' as I explained before."

He watched me shift my weight to get more comfortable and waited for me to finish. If anything, he looked happy for this little distraction and seemed content on waiting for me.

"What did she do?" This of course was the question he had feared. His hard face screamed out these feelings.

"She was a young soul, being that of only fifty-odd years. She was ill taught and had little to no guidance. These, however, are no excuses for her not to know the rules clearly. As I mentioned last night, she was an Angel but as you know, this does not automatically spell out clean soul." This I had remembered him telling me. The major misconception humans held was that Angels were always good and Demons always bad. This, however, was not the case and this story would no doubt prove this ancient fact to destroy the stone in which it was thought to be set.

"She was brought into her host with the good intention of lying low the first ten years, which is the first rule of being reborn. For those who are not used to the human world they are given a series of guidelines and are assigned a possession officer."

"Is that like a parole officer?" I asked naively and when he smiled, I felt my cheeks start to burn with embarrassment.

"Of sorts, yes, but they are more like guidance counsellors. They are there to guide them for the first years of their lives."

"Why aren't they called guidance counsellors then?" I know this question didn't really hit number one on the 'important things to know' scale but for him at least, it seemed to be nice little distraction. One side of his lips turned upwards, which he tried to hide with one hand which was resting over his chin. This was when I realised, I must have sounded like a child asking where babies come from.

"We call them possession officers because they possess new souls. They own them. It's a bit like being a parent. They are in control until they reach the right age and are safe to make it in the world alone."

"Did you have one?" At this he let out a series of raucous laughter that made the bed shake. When he finally composed himself, he took note of my frowning face and for once, he was the one biting his lip. He was trying very hard not to laugh again and I would have been laughing with him if it weren't at my expense.

"Sorry…it was actually a good question and as usual, unexpected. The answer is no, I did not have one." He was now just managing to compose a straight face when I asked him why not?

"Let's just say that Vincent, Sophia and I were kind of... umm...inbuilt with the knowledge of how it all worked...Anyway, where was I?" He pushed his thick black hair from his forehead, where it had fallen, thanks to his uncontrollable laughter. I instantly bit my lip at the sight. This was one of the hardest things about having such an amazingly handsome boyfriend, every time he did things like that, you found yourself wishing he would just shut up and undress you! I knew he had asked me a question, so I had to think back through the sexy haze that was Draven.

"Uhmm..." I gulped before answering,

"Possession Officer" I whispered, and he shot me a raised eyebrow look as if to say, 'What's wrong with you?' but he didn't ask, and I was glad for it. Instead he just gave me another half-smile before continuing.

"Okay, so back to my point. Her assigned officer was not very attentive to her studies and quit her after only a year. She wasn't even given a human name but after her escapades she was rightly dubbed Vetala. This was because her ways resembled that of the Demon from Hindu mythology. Vetala was believed to be an evil spirit that possessed the dead, made humans mad and killed children along with causing miscarriages." He took in my wince at hearing this and picked up my hand to kiss the palm before continuing,

"Of course, she was a rogue Demon that caused havoc in small villages, but the stories almost always outlive the souls that they have sprung from. In this case it looked like history was repeating itself and once again we intervened."

"Wait a minute...so you're telling me that... that tiny, young girl down there was a ...a child killer?" This brought his full attention back to my face and his hands stroked my cheeks affectionately before catching some escaping tears. He tilted his head to one side while giving me a wide-eyed look of concern. It reminded me of how my family looked at me after the incident with Morgan. After I had been kidnapped, my family never seemed to be able to look at me the same way again. Well, who could blame them? I certainly couldn't.

"Yes she was, along with other things. She became an expert in the art of manipulation. She liked to feed from the pain and suffering that would flow from the hopeless families that had lost loved ones. Parents who had lost the most dearest beings to their hearts. She was a monster and to the bitter end she tried to control you and make you set her free. First, she tried pity and when that failed, she showed you something that angers me to my very core. Keira, I'm sorry you had to be reminded of the pain you went through." Of course, he was referring to the vision she had made me see. She had played on my own living nightmare that Morgan had put me through. She knew my weaknesses and used them to her advantage.

"Wait, how did you know what she showed me?"

"When I finished her off, I saw through her eyes and scanned through her memories of her last encounters. When you screamed out, I knew what you had seen in the Temple, but I didn't know what you had seen before you got there. I hoped that you hadn't found her or more like she hadn't found you. But then when I saw her re-enactment of what you had gone through at the hands of that...*that sick f...!"* He paused before his Demon could fully continue roaring out his feelings for Morgan and closed his eyes tight as if trying to lock out a memory.

"I'm sorry, but as you can imagine, it affected me in a way you can't imagine." At this, I saw pain replace the anger in his eyes and they flashed from purple to two deep, black lagoons in the dead of night.

"How did she even know about my past?" I asked this more because I wanted to get him talking again, to try and get him past that image that no longer only haunted myself. He answered with just a name, one that I would have never expected to pass his sweet kissable lips.

"Layla."

"WHAT?! Are you serious? What the hell has she got to do with this?" I shrieked.

"Try to calm yourself and I will tell you, but you have to trust me, for she can't get to you." This wasn't as reassuring as it was supposed to be, I will tell you. I remained silent as a sign that he could carry on, but now I knew why this had been such a hard story for him to tell me.

"You remember me telling you that Layla escaped?"

"Well no actually, you didn't tell me, I found out, remember?" I said giving him one of those, 'See why you shouldn't lie' looks but he ignored it.

"Well, after she stabbed you, she went into hiding, or at least she tried to. My men found her, and I imprisoned her until she could face a trial. I needed to get to the bottom of her hate but before I could …umm, question her…" at this I butted in,

"You mean torture… *right?*" He rolled his eyes at me but seeing as I was so used to this by now, I let it go.

"Alright, yes I do, but the bitch deserved far worse. So, I will continue now that I haven't the need to spare you on the dark details. Yes, I was going to torture her and I would have enjoyed doing so, given what she tried to take from me and Keira, be warned, that if anyone else was to try again, then I would do what I feel is necessary, for my vengeance is dark and also deadly." From the bulging vein that pulsated through his tensed forearm and eyes that could now have you begging for mercy in seconds, I would be going against everything I ever believed in to deny this to be true. He was terrifying! I gently placed my hand on his stone-like shoulder and the feel of my skin on his, seemed to bring him back to my level of calm.

"I believe you," I whispered and he just nodded in response. I, however, made a mental note never to mention Layla's name ever again.

"I will continue." When I gave him a concerned look it was his turn to say,

"I'm fine, Keira." For once. I wanted to roll my eyes, only now realising how annoying it really was but I wasn't about to tell Draven this.

"I need to explain what the connection is between the two. See Layla, before working for me as a waitress, was a possession officer. The position didn't suit her and after a string of bad judgments and poor excuses for educated prodigies, she was renounced from her position and stripped of the powers she had been granted. This made her resentful. But she appealed to me for a softer sentence giving her the chance to rehabilitate. I gave her an opportunity by working for me in the club but with the chance of getting her old role back. She became impatient and frustrated, but I still don't know the full reasons behind her hate towards you." I shifted uncomfortably and played with the bottom of my sleeves as I usually did when hearing things that were hard to take.

"I quickly learned last night why it was Vetala who broke her out from the prison and when I saw it all through her eyes it started to make sense. Layla was Vetala's possession officer and although she left her, she considered her a mother figure and that she didn't leave her but freed her. Layla had formed a bond so strong that she must have called to Vetala for help before getting caught. How Vetala got her out I don't yet know but I do know that Layla betrayed her and pushed her into her own cell so that it would give her longer for the head start. By the time Vetala was discovered, Layla was long gone." Once again, he was tense at recalling all the events of Layla's deception.

"She played her prodigy like a fine-tuned instrument and let her play out your own dark symphony to you. Layla knew what she was doing when she told her about your past and I believe her last command was to get to you if she could." I was shaking my head by the time he had finished, but it got to a point where I was losing my not so cool persona and my cheeks were on fire with my own hatred.

The name Layla stuck in my throat like a piece of gum I knew I shouldn't swallow and the seven-year myth of it remaining in your gut became a good analogy for this sick reality. Would I ever get past this? The list of people who wanted me either dead or hurting was mounting at an impeccable rate.

"Wow! I mean, really… wow… I just don't get it! Why does everyone want to hurt me? See in my world I'm a nobody. I just go by unnoticed and stay quiet. I keep my business to myself and my past firmly locked behind closed doors. But in your world, I'm like this hunted possession that people want to hurt and hate! Why can't I have both…? Why can't I have you and be happy without having to sacrifice my sanity?" Ok, so I knew I was ranting on and being all self- pitying but come on…what else did I have to face? What was going to be next? And was I ever going to be ready for it?!

"I'm sorry Keira, but this is my fault. This is why I wanted to keep you from me and why I should still be trying to."

"NO! Don't you dare say that! I am in more danger without you and you know it. Besides, could you really just walk away from it all now, after what we have been through? Could you… walk away… from me?" My glazed eyes looked up to search for the same feelings as I had.

"No, I simply couldn't do that…not now, not ever! Not after experiencing you first hand. This skin to touch." He traced a thumb down my neck and it vibrated as my breathing got more intense.

"These lips to kiss." This short sentence ended over the lips in question and it did anything but calm my breathing. My heart rate went through the roof as he pulled on my leg making my body slide underneath him. He held all his weight over me as his kiss intensified. The feeling that coursed through my every nerve made every horror I had witnessed worth it ten times over. Being hunted meant nothing anymore as long as I had this feeling to hold on to.

His hands started to push up my sweater and the tingles shot up my side as though he was communicating with every hair follicle on my skin. I wasn't the only one breathing heavy and when I felt Draven's impressive erection rise, I knew I would have to find the senses to stop this bliss. I was still on and not that he would have minded a bit of mess, I certainly wasn't ready for that undignified step to be taken.

His tongue was creating magic in my mouth as it moved in its skilful dance. I waited for him to move to kissing my neck as he usually did, but when he got there I found myself arching into him and my head rolled back to give him greater access. I was losing control and knew if I didn't stop it all now I never would. Thankfully, when his hand found the inside of my thigh and the thought of the piece of string he would soon find there, it made me find my much needed sense, so I sat bolt upright.

"Hey!" he said in disapproval, and then his hands tried to reach out to pull me back down into the same position. When I shifted out of his grabbing hands he let out a low growl that rippled deep in his throat.

"Whoa, cool down there, cowboy. Painters and decorators are in, remember?" He let out an easy-going laugh at the analogy I'd used, before calming down his libido. He gave me a bad boy grin as he shifted back to the side of me and seeing him behave himself I relaxed my tensed muscles.

"See what you do to me?" He rubbed the back of his neck with his large palm and shook his head as if he was remembering what the feel of my lips on his did to his manhood. I thought this the reason because I too was still trying to control the commotion he caused to my nether regions. Raging river flooding the streets came to mind!

"Well, when I'm off then I can do that to you."

"When will that be again?" he asked in a hoarse voice that curled my toes.

"Friday...maybe Thursday, if we're lucky."

"If only I possessed the power to change time." At this I think he was only half-joking as when I looked over to him I couldn't help but see the covers had created a tent near his loins. I knew I had to get up as now I was dying for the bathroom but seeing as I didn't have anything on underneath, this was going to be like dangling the carrot. I pulled my sweater down as far as it would go but before I got up I couldn't help but pat his member and say, "down boy!" before jumping up quickly before he could react.

"HA! With you showing off those perfect little pink cheeks peeking out...not a chance!" I was glad I wasn't facing him as I went as red as rare steak and the feel of heat coming off my cheeks could quite easily have cooked one! I giggled as I walked into the bathroom and the change in my heart was so different to how I felt now, it was hard to keep up. One-minute life was throwing a curveball at me in the form of Lucius and then I was getting a home run when waking up next to Draven every morning. I felt almost giddy at the sound of Draven's voice that not only entered my ears but also seeped into my very soul.

The first thing I did was to go to his huge gilded mirror to examine the damage of last night's escapades. It was as bad as I had feared. My hair was loose but hung down in messy knots. My eyes were a dark blue, ringed with red circles that gave evidence of a night's crying. I had blotchy skin on my pale cheeks and it looked like I was suffering from a bad hangover or snotty cold.

I cringed at the sight and after first doing my morning routine I decided to splash some cold water on my face to calm my hypersensitive skin that I had put through Hell last night. I ducked my head and cupped my hands ready to capture the running water and when my hands were overflowing I threw the contents over my face.

I took a few heavy breaths before re-examining the tired face that belonged to me. I lifted my head expecting to see my stormy eyes judging my features but couldn't help the scream that erupted at what my vision found there.

A pair of blood-red eyes frozen in time. A heart-shaped pair of plump, hungry lips that overflowed with blood. Purple fuelled veins that spread out from the corner of my eyelashes over my cheeks, like an infection that was slowly being pumped through my bloodstream. As my mouth opened to scream once more, a pair of large white teeth gleamed in the morning sun.

I was faced with not the Keira I knew.

No. Now I was now faced with the Vampire Keira...

The one I didn't ever want to know!

CHAPTER TWENTY-FOUR

CHANGES

W as I dreaming?! I closed my eyes so tight until they hurt, and I was shaking my head, but none of these actions helped get the image from my memory. It was only when I felt the presence of someone behind me that I tried to force out the breath that had locked in my chest. It couldn't be him! Lucius may have dominated my dreams, but this was real wasn't it? This morning with Draven had happened?

I felt a hand come to my cheek and I let out a scream.

"Keira, what's wrong?" Draven's voice interrupted my fears and when I opened my eyes, I saw that it wasn't only my Demonic reflection there in his mirror, Draven's worried frown looked at me, but he couldn't see me the way I had seen myself. I had to try and find some words that would make sense but considering all I could see was my perfect Draven behind me, as opposed to my Vampire image that still remained.

Why couldn't he see me? Why did he not turn his head away in disgust? My eyes held no normal stormy blue in a pearly white frame. They had been replaced by a black iris in a pool of blood. My skin looked that of a diseased dead girl and my lips looked hungry for flesh. I looked further down to my bare neck which held two bloody spots where my life had been fed on. I closed my eyes again and told myself to wake up.

"Keira, look at me! What's wrong with you?" Draven's voice was shouting at me now. It was only when Draven started to shake me that I felt myself returning. I expected to close my eyes and once opened again, I would find that I was still in bed, but I wasn't. I was still in his bathroom in front of the fairy tale mirror that held the source of my new nightmare…this one staring at me and what I had become.

Then something happened. It was like a black veil that had been lifted from my face and cleared my senses. It took me a minute to realise that I was finally back! My face had returned to its usual mundane self and I let out a gust of air as though I hadn't been able to breathe in hours. I turned around into his tall body and sunk my head into his chest. He was waiting for an explanation, but he at least gave me a minute to think of one. His hand held the back of my head to him and I wrapped my arms around his waist, linking my fingers at the base of his back. He leant down his head to talk into my hair.

"Tell me little one, what did you see?" he whispered in such a way that I would have been a fool not to tell him the truth. I wanted to tell him everything that I had been keeping from him but when I played it out in my mind it didn't go as well as I had planned. I kept seeing his rage again and again like someone was showing it to me on a loop and although his anger wasn't focused on me, I would no doubt receive the brunt of it. He would hide me away from everything and everyone. I would never be able to live one minute of the day that wasn't completely controlled by Draven.

This would give him his last reason to lock me away to keep me safe. I couldn't do it! I had to win this battle myself. I had to make my own mistakes and follow them through. I mean, it was only his mental control over me that I had to fight and let's face it, if I could blank out Draven then how hard was Lucius going to be. I just needed to find his weakness. I needed to learn more about him to figure out the key to beating him.

Then something even stranger happened. My mind flipped suddenly, and I found myself wanting to tell Draven everything, to open up and have it all spill out like a downpour. It was the strangest feeling being so torn, like half of my mind wasn't my own...what the hell was wrong with me?!

Just as soon as these thoughts entered my mind and before my mouth could open, I was once again flipped around and thinking the opposite. I couldn't have Draven worrying even more than he should be. Deep down I knew I was making a huge mistake and knew I would pay for it at some point but for now, I set my mind on its current course and walked down its path.

"It was nothing...I just stubbed my toe and nearly fell, but I'm good now." I knew I wasn't putting on the best show of mental health and when he grabbed my arms and pushed me back so he could see my face, his however, said it all...utter disbelief.

"Keira, you screamed out, like you were terrified!"

"I guess I'm still a bit nervy that's all." He looked as though he wanted to say something more, but he could see that if he pushed the matter then it wouldn't have helped the situation. He would never know how thankful I was for this.

"Come, you need more sleep. You look exhausted." This was Draven's way of saying that I looked awful, I was sure. Actually he wasn't wrong. It was as though I'd needed to wake up for an explanation of the night's events. But now I knew it was all okay again, my body started to relax and the signs that it had been deprived of its usual eight hours sleep were starting to show. Of course, the only problem I had now was that I was terrified of what I might dream.

"No I shouldn't...if I do then I might not wake up until tonight and then I would miss out on the day. I have too much to do as it is." This made the hand that he had on my side tighten slightly.

"And that is?" This question I found a little insulting, considering I did have other things in my life that needed my attention. Ok, they weren't much but I still wanted to do well in college and get myself a degree, even if I had messed it up the first time. But still, better late than never...right?

I decided to keep my thoughts to myself, but it did make me turn my back to him and I walked back into the room without a word. Just the sight of his bed made me let out a yawn that was big enough for bats to have flown out of.

"That wouldn't happen if you slept." Draven's voice was behind me at my ear making me jump. My reaction made him rub the tops of my arms as though trying to reassure me that I was safe.

"I will have you know that I have lots of stuff to do," I said lamely but I could feel his smile before I could see it.

"Ah is that what this is…? Bruised pride I believe it is called. Let me rephrase my question, what I meant to say is, what is more important than much needed sleep for my beautiful vixen?" His tone was so easy and confident that I tried not to smile.

"Umm let me see…a ton of college work, cooking a Sunday roast, my job, friends…"

"Preparing to take out the human, Justin." Ok, this made me wince as I remembered we hadn't actually talked about Draven overhearing my conversation with Libby in the kitchen.

"Ah!" was all I could muster.

"Yes 'Ah' indeed." I turned to face him and could tell that this was one conversation I wouldn't be able to worm my way out of. I took a step back to look him in the face without straining my neck at his impressive height. It was only now that I realised he was fully clothed, wearing a long-sleeved, light blue cotton V-neck t-shirt. This was added to dark indigo jeans and black boots. My eyes traced his fine-tuned indents of muscle that could be seen through the material and when he folded his arms across that hard chest I couldn't help the gulping noise I made.

"Look, could we at least hold off this grilling until I put some clothes on?" I nodded to him and then motioned back to me. Of course, I was still only wearing a sweater that was barely covering my nether regions. Thankfully this worked in my favour as it brought a devilish smirk to his lips.

"I happen to like this look," he said as he tilted his head in order to get a better view. Then I saw a brief purple tinge flash in eyes that looked as though they wanted to devour me. I felt the heat invade my cheeks before turning away like a shy little girl. I looked about the floor for my jeans but came up empty, which had me wondering what he had done with my clothes last night?

"My side," was all he said and I suppressed a giggle at the idea of us already having our own sides in bed.

"You know, if you had let me grab some stuff last night then I would be searching through a bag right now, not to mention fresh clothes," I said as I walked around to his side finding my underwear and jeans, along with a pair of odd socks that I had put on yesterday. These weren't the only things that I noticed. On his side of the bed there appeared to be more room than I had first thought.

From the other side of the room it looked as if the bed was at the very end of the space, with his side very close to a stone wall. But now I was here I could see that there was even room for some more furniture. There was a bedside cabinet which was made from oak with wrought iron studs all down the legs. The cabinet held a burnt orange and red tiffany lamp that looked like a wilted flower that was melting down to the black metal base. I followed the stone wall along to find another tapestry hung there.

I wondered why I had never taken in these details before but then the answer came from behind me.

"It was a gift." He was referring to the old looking picture that ancient fingers had constructed God only knows how many years ago. The edge was a series of different symbols boxed round their own frames and inside the main picture consisted of a peaceful sunrise casting its warm glow over a sandstone kingdom. Little yellow homes topped with terracotta roofs that wound round and round the hills until they met up with a spectacular carved stone palace.

The palace itself was a work of art and reminded me of something right out of the Lord of the Rings novel. I couldn't help but reach my fingers out to touch the material, as if checking it was real. I could feel Draven behind me watching me as usual, which was what made me hesitate.

"Its fine sweetheart, go ahead," he whispered and I ran my fingers over the thousands of little bumps that made up one of the most beautiful pictures I had ever seen. I don't know what it was about it but it captured you into its world and held you there. It

made you want to see its own view from those windows and feel the heat on your skin from those powerful sunbeams.

"It's beautiful and…stunning." I wanted to ask him about it but before I formed words, he was making it disappear with one strong sweep of his arm. He had it gathered up and pushed it to one side like a curtain. I turned and looked up to ask him what he was doing but he just nodded back to the empty space which now wasn't so empty. The magical picture had gone but it had been replaced by a dark, mahogany door.

"Do you want to know why I told you not to bring anything?" I stared at him blankly before speculating.

"I thought you meant…well, you know, girly things which I found, thank you." I was referring to the box of supplies that had been left out for me to find in the bathroom, which I had been thankful for while completing my morning routine. He laughed lightly before shaking his head.

"That you can thank Sophia for but this…well, you can blame me, she was only doing what I asked, so please keep that in mind." I didn't see his face when he said this as he was opening the door for me to walk through first. He didn't give me much time to think about what it could be, because as soon as I walked in, I quickly discovered what it was he thought I might freak out at.

And he was right.

I took one step down into the biggest walk-in wardrobe I had ever seen. The ones on MTV cribs had nothing on this bad boy!

It was a huge room, almost double my own bedroom at home, and had every wall covered with hanging material. I couldn't tell but I think my mouth was gaping open. I looked to one side and it was obviously Draven's side as it had hundreds of suits hung in a specially designed closet that looked as if it rotated. There were lights above that made the colours stand out, not that there was much colour to speak of. Draven obviously preferred his black suits above any other but there was another section that held his more casual stuff, t-shirts, row upon row of jeans and then there was a whole other section with nothing but men's footwear.

There was a massive island in the middle that was suitable for Draven's height, but I just felt like a child next to it. It had frosted glass doors that fronted different sized drawers, which filled every space on all sides.

I heard him laugh behind me and before I could turn to him, he had turned my body to face the other side opposite his.

"This is your side," he said happily and I nearly lost my balance. Was he joking?! Of course, when I saw what he called my side I knew he wasn't. There was a wall full of clothes that looked all to be in my size. It was only when I looked closer that I noticed it was everything that I had seen yesterday. Tops I had picked up and put down because I refused to pay the store's prices, some I remembered hoping they would be on sale and I could get them later at a much lower cost. I even recall Sophia frowning at me when she would see me putting the clothes back.

I walked up to the endless amount of clothes and ran my hand along them. It was then that I would see some of Sophia's choices for me that she had seen in her expensive designer stores. Oh my God, there was even a dress there that had a price tag of six months wages!

"You...you can't. I can't let you do this," I stammered out but I had a feeling as soon as Draven heard it, that it wouldn't make much of a difference.

"And why not?" he asked unfazed by my refusal.

"Because, it's too much! I don't need all this...I can't pay you back for all this" This made him come up behind me and take me by the waist.

"You know I don't want you to pay me back, that's not why I did this. And besides, don't you think I owe you for all the clothes I have destroyed. This way at least I won't have to feel guilty." My mind was swimming with excuses and ways of saying no, but it was as though his voice was trying to smooth over these thoughts with ones of acceptance and approval. Of course, the added arousal his hands created on my sides did make my own thoughts harder to hear. And then he tipped it his way by speaking but a few words at my neck.

"Please, just let me do this for you." By the way he said this I knew I couldn't refuse him.

By the time I had finished showering it was lunchtime and I was starving. Draven had left me to conduct some business which I refrained from asking him about. After last night I thought it best to give myself a little breathing space between me and his 'Work'.

I had showered the last traces of the night's horrors away. However, I still couldn't bring myself to look at my image in the mirror. The thought of me changing again was just too much to bear. When Draven had been around I had used every ounce of willpower I had to push that vision from my mind but now I was alone, I just couldn't do it.

What the Hell was happening? Was this the power that Lucius had over me or was this part of his sick plan he had in store for me? I kept repeating over and over the part when Draven had first explained about Vampires. He had told me that Lucius couldn't change humans, only the supernatural. So why me?

Surely this was just a trick, a sick and twisted stunt to make my mind weak. I didn't feel any different, that was for sure. Okay, maybe a little stronger, but that had happened ever since I had been with Draven. I had put it down to the happiness I felt whenever he was near.

But more importantly, why, whenever I found enough mental power to think about telling Draven everything, was it quickly replaced with doubt and denial. I was fighting myself and it was so exhausting I felt like banging my head on the wall just in the hopes of finding some clarity.

I had hoped the shower would have worked in washing away all my fears but as I let the water flood my skin, I still felt his hands on me. I scrubbed and scrubbed my skin until red and blotchy but that didn't help the feeling that gnawed away at my brain. It was as if Lucius was right behind me mimicking my every move. When my hands were washing my hair, his fingers were running through every strand. When my palms soaped up my body there were his thoughts of desire looking down at me. Those icy eyes taking note of every curve, every mark years of living in this skin had made. I closed my eyes and tried to banish what the idea even did to me. Why was I getting aroused by the idea? I wanted to hate myself. I wanted to scream out 'what's wrong with me?'.

I felt as if I was in some way cheating on Draven. I wanted to put it all down to Lucius and his control but deep down I was just terrified that there was some substance behind it. I couldn't help myself feeling something more for this tortured soul that had been consumed by bitterness. His touch had been gentle, but I had to keep reminding myself that the motives behind them were deadly.

Now, of course, here I was with a towel wrapped around me looking at the vastness of colour which was my new wardrobe. Trying to pick from all of this I knew was the least of my problems but for some reason I was finding it next to excruciating. I mean, before I didn't feel that what I wore around Draven was that important, but now I felt like it was an issue. I started to question what he actually thought of my dress sense. Well, not that there was much sense to it...I mean comfort always played a big part.

I let out a big sigh and after standing there for nearly twenty minutes I decided I was being paranoid. When I started to filter through the clothes they were all items that I would have chosen for myself anyway, so that meant if he did have a problem with the way I dressed then wouldn't he have picked other stuff? New outfits that he hadn't seen me wear? But the more I looked, the more it just looked like a replica of the stuff I had at home.

In the end I just picked out a two-layered t-shirt that had long sleeves. It was black and light grey, which made my eyes appear a shade darker. This I matched with a tight pair of faded jeans that flared at the bottom. I then started to search around for underwear and socks before getting dressed in my new outfit, most of which had all the tags removed. I smiled at the thought of Draven not wanting me to know how much everything had cost. Well, at least he knew I wasn't with him for money.

I felt funny about going through his drawers but that was the only place left for them. I started at the top and almost screamed when I saw what was hidden there. It was completely filled with very expensive looking watches. One looked so full of diamonds that it would soon start bleeding them. I saw the name Piaget's Emperador Temple and bit my lip. There were other names like

Franck Muller Aeternitas that looked like it had more functions than a Swiss army knife. Another said Louis Moinet's Meteoris and this one looked as if it didn't only tell the time but also mapped the solar system!

There were other makes, some I even recognised but you would have needed to re-mortgage a house to purchased one. I gulped down the hard lump before moving on to the next drawer. Thankfully, this one just had men's underwear and socks, so this one I closed quickly so that I couldn't see any designer names. I dreaded to think how much he spent on his boxer briefs.

Lucky number three it was, and I hit the jackpot. I was a bit surprised when I saw it was very similar to the one I had at home. I half expected it to be full of red and black lace but when my favourite white cotton short briefs filled the space, I smiled. Of course, there were some other varieties but I grabbed the most comfortable ones as any of the others wouldn't be seen anyway, not until I was off and ready again for the naughty. The next drawer down held bras and the last one, socks. I took out what I needed and changed.

When I got back into 'Our' bedroom, as he kept calling it, there was food waiting for me. I sat down and helped myself to the plates full of sandwiches, cakes, fruit but most of all a pot of tea. I sighed with contentment as I filled my belly and sipped my warm mug of tea. It felt so good that it almost made me forget the last horrific twenty-four hours. I snuggled deeper into his velvet-covered couch and started to feel my eyes fall. I was still tired but I knew if I gave in and closed them I wouldn't wake again until the next day. Luckily, I heard the door open making me sit up, flashing my eyes wide open.

Draven entered and by the smirk he had playing at his lips, I knew he had seen me nearly nodding off. He took note of the empty plate and mug that I must have dropped on the floor. Unfortunately, it hadn't been empty and now there was a light brown liquid seeping from the rim.

"Sorry," I said as I picked it up and removed a napkin from the tray to clean the mess with.

"Why are you sorry?" he asked me in earnest and came over to me to stop my hands from rubbing at the rug that looked older than my family tree.

"Do you think you will ever get used to how clumsy I am?" I asked looking down feeling strangely nervous. He knelt down in front of me and gently removed the white napkin from my hands.

"I find it endearing," he said, before lifting my face up so that he could get to my lips easily. After another very intense kiss he got up and joined me on the couch, pulling my body into his.

"Now, I would like you to tell me why it is that a boy you classed as not having any interest in you is coming here to stay and commandeering you for an evening?" This question soon had me in knots and making a face like I was sucking on a sour gobstopper.

I knew I couldn't put it off any longer, but I really didn't know what to say. He had heard everything that me and Libby had spoken about in the kitchen, so now all that was left for me to do was explain why I felt compelled to entertain a guy that I had once had a crush on, who now evidently had a crush on me, to my Demon boyfriend who, let's face it, had jealousy issues. Boy...that was a toughie!

Oh yes…

This was going to be a long day.

CHAPTER TWENTY-FIVE

FINDING A BALANCE

The next week turned out to be a complete contrast to the previous week's events. That Sunday only needed for me to smooth things over with Draven about Justin's stay and he found the silver lining that at least he could keep an eye on him with us having our 'date' (as Draven had called it) at his night club. Of course, I didn't get this outcome without some extreme compromising. I had promised that I wouldn't be alone with him and I would invite all my friends. I also agreed to spend the night with Draven after I had driven Justin home. And again, of course, these were all very reasonable requests but when Draven had made his last request it had sounded more like a demand. And it was the one I was dreading the most.

"And of course, I must meet the boy." I remember his words and the venom behind the word 'boy'. I gulped at the sight of his stern black eyes glaring into the distance of the forest floor. At that moment, I was glad to have been on his balcony having this discussion because the heat generated from his expression alone was enough to boil blood.

Thankfully, my skin was comforted by the early afternoon breeze and I could think as clearly as the cloudless sky above me.

That was until Draven had let me continue with my endless questions about that night's events, then my mind overloaded on supernatural laws. Draven had started to explain who the old woman in white had been when the clear skies changed to stormy grey.

"Potnia is an old friend of mine and was waiting for the Blood Moon or Hunter's Moon, as it is also known," he explained as he took my hand and pulled me indoors away from the coming downpour.

"Blood moon?" I asked remembering the full moon ringed red shining down through the dome right before Draven had dealt out his version of justice. The memory made me shudder.

"It is when a crossing of souls is more likely to pass peacefully." He smiled at my frown and decided to elaborate.

"Potnia was over four hundred years old and needed a new vessel." Ok, so instead of frowning he found me scowling.

"Body, Keira, she needed a new body."

"What? So she is now walking around as that...girl, the child killer?!" I asked in disbelief.

"Yes, love, but don't fret. Her essence, her light, will change the vessel into something pure. We do not waste a good and young vessel." Well, at least they recycled I thought trying to get my head around all this and holding on to any silver lining I could find.

"So, what happened to the girl?" I asked in a whisper, as though it would somehow get into trouble if someone overheard.

"What do you think?" he whispered back with a wink which slightly unnerved me, considering the subject matter he was teasing me about. I just shrugged my shoulders not wanting to speculate. He grinned an evil smirk and thumbed towards the floor. The message rang loud and clear making me shiver. He laughed once before enveloping my body into his embrace. After that he wouldn't answer any more questions I had and even got a little irritated when I asked him about the room I had found with Lucius' name etched into the walls.

Instead, he decided a better technique would be distraction. So he picked me up and threw me over his shoulder before depositing me on the bed with a quick bounce before coving my body with his. There we fooled around with limits set in place for me but for Draven, I was all hands-on deck as I got to explore every inch of his delicious body. This was of course something that left me struggling to get my breath for the next two hours.

Thanks to Draven the nightmares of the night before were already becoming a distant memory that I was filing away with all the other bad crap I kept there. It was soon becoming an abyss in my mind…. an endless pit of dark phantoms that only found their way back to my active thoughts when I was asleep. Of course, the proverbial king of these nightmares had quickly stolen the black throne from Morgan and become the new jailer for this already scarred mind. His name of course was once Judas, the universal name used for betrayal. Now his new name, Lucius, was received from the Devil himself…

I really was starting to think that I had no luck!

I was now sat at my computer screen making my eyes water, I had been staring at it for so long without blinking. I rubbed my forehead as if trying to find a genie in there to help me with my report. I had so much college work to do I was feeling overwhelmed. I had caught up with English and had finished my Spanish revision but it was history that was my problem and in more ways than one.

The past had now replaced my fascination with millions of questions. These all based around one name…*Dominic Draven*. Every date, every major event and every catastrophe had me wondering where Draven had been in the world when it was all going on and how much of the world-changing events had really been down to rogue Demons and Angels. This was why I couldn't concentrate on the French revolution.

Halfway between wanting to poke myself in the eyes for an excuse not to work anymore and writing about the absolute monarchy that had ruled France for centuries collapsing in only three years, Libby thankfully walked into my room with a lifeline. A cup of tea.

"Oh the Lord be praised, you're a lifesaver!" Libby laughed at my outburst which had been a bit louder than I had intended.

"That bad is it?"

"You have no idea. Tell me again why I was persistent in going back to college?" I joked as I reached out to take the hot 'Simpsons' mug from her. I looked down and blew on its perfect mix of brewed tea and milk.

"Oh you know, education, job prospects, oh and don't forget, throwing a square hat in the air when you've finished."

"Mmm, my favourite part." Libby looked at me as if she still hadn't got used to seeing me in such a good mood these days. I had overheard her one night talking to Frank about it. She ended up in tears and I was just glad that now people had exchanged tears of sadness for ones of happiness. I had spent too long feeling guilty about all the problems I had caused. Well, at least now I was making up for it. Because now I had never been happier.

"You working tonight?" Libby asked as she pulled her coffee coloured sweater straight that was stretching thanks to the little bump showing.

"Yeah and I'm staying over so don't expect me home," I said with a wink as today was finally the day I had come off my period. She laughed and said,

"These days I never do." And although she had said it in a light-hearted way, I heard an underlying hint of regret. Alright, so the guilt thing hadn't left me completely. She had turned around and was making her way to leave when I had an idea.

"Hey Libs, I was meaning to ask, do you have any free time next week? 'Cause you know, I could use some help shopping." At this she whizzed around like someone had lit a rocket up her backside, only one that would make you smile 'cause she looked like a child did when they found out they were going to a theme park.

"Yeah, I would love to but wait, you only went shopping last week."

"Yeah, I know but it wasn't the same, you remember me telling you about the designer shops, right?" She laughed at the memory of my reconstruction of the famous shopping experience with Sophia.

"I would have loved to have seen you in Gucci." She laughed until tears glistened in her luscious, green eyes.

"Never going to happen… But hey, I wouldn't say no to the Gap."

We arranged a day that I was lesson free in the afternoon and giggled a little more over my day with Sophia, when this made me remember something vital that had almost slipped my mind. It was a promise I had made to myself about the day when I was no longer restricted to just heavy petting and intense kisses. I got up from my computer chair and walked over to my closet. I leant down and reached at the back for a stripy pink Victoria's Secret bag.

I pulled out its contents and Libby wolf-whistled. It was perfect and made me blush. She had always been able to do it since being taught by my dad when my mum wasn't around. The last time I had heard her exercise this talent was after a few too many at a family BBQ party.

The flames had set the fence alight and when the Fire service was called, they met their match in Libby, fuelled on too much Pinot Grigio. My embarrassed father had to apologise for his daughter's behaviour and sent her to bed. She was twenty-two at the time. I smirked at the thought then quickly replaced it with hot cheeks as I looked down at the mixture of satin and lace in my hands.

"Well now, won't somebody be having fun tonight?" she said before giggling her way out of my room. I sighed heavily, wondering how I was ever going to pull it off. My idea when buying it was to surprise Draven by wearing it under my uniform and going to bed early. There I would slip into the matching gloves and lie seductively on his bed waiting for my body to be discovered. Of course, now that the actual day had arrived, I was starting to get cold feet.

I arranged the corset on my bed with the matching items and stood back. I was trying to imagine his reaction to finding me in this perfect example of sexy, seductive underwear. I bit my lip at the thought.

I knew the last week had been particularly tough on him to keep his urges under control. A few times we had come close to crossing the messy line, but the thought of my embarrassment later was what gave me the power to stop. I still found it hard to believe that Draven was as infatuated with me as I was with him. He explained one night after an extreme kissing session how he felt.

"The obsession I have over you can't be explained in words and I fear there are no greater actions that can do my feelings justice. But when I say that I had never imagined happiness like this was obtainable for me, making this the one and only thing about human life that I envied, trust in these words. I had lost all hope believing that the Gods had created a soul mate that belonged to me, but now I have you here in my arms, I know it was worth all my lifetimes in waiting."

At this point I had difficulty in holding back the tears that materialized in the corners of my eyes and was just thankful the only light had been the low glow from the moon, which cast a bluish tint to the furnishings. It had been the sweetest thing anyone had ever said to me and I wished I could have responded with an equally beautiful response. But in the end knowing I couldn't find the words, I spoke with my lips. He smiled under my touch as he could feel my wet cheeks and there is where he found his feelings reciprocated.

Even though we hadn't made love that night it was still one of the most perfect nights of my life and one that will stay with me until the day the Gods decide to take me back. These thoughts were what changed my worried frown to an excited smile. I was going to go through with my plan and play the temptress for a night. After all, that was the name of the outfit and tonight I would do it justice.

I picked my mug back up and went back to the computer to try and retackle my own revolution. That was my rebellion with History. I looked down and saw even Homer Simpson was mocking me, with his speech bubble saying "Mmm... Donuts" making me think more about food than French royalists.

Draven had offered to help me, of course, but I felt that asking him about dates that were past too many lifetimes to comprehend does somewhat constitute as cheating. Not only that but I think his version of the past would contradict the written word, even though there was no doubt his account of events would be more reliable.

However, there was no getting around the fact that I still couldn't use any of it.

History is made up of a collective narrative of the dictation of the men and women that lived through those times, whether it is through words or codes or pictures and symbols. I don't think history would have been told in quite the same way if the world knew about how much Demons and Angels had to do with the outcome of how we live today. I could just imagine Mr Reed's face when reading my report that stated how Demons and Angels were responsible for the fall of world leaders because it wasn't beneficial to the Underworld's balance. It was almost worth doing to see his head spin 360 degrees.

It took me a while to get my head around the fact that one can't live without the other. We needed them as much as they needed us to survive. They fed from our emotions and we needed their protection from ourselves. Of course, this didn't mean that some of the world's problems hadn't slipped through the cracks. Bombs still exploded, wars still battled on and terrorists still held the upper hand in their fearless ambition to destroy the western world.

If I thought the world had its problems before knowing Draven, then I was sorely mistaken. However, I still couldn't decide which was worse, being blissfully unaware and putting my sightings of the other kind down to an overactive imagination or knowing the unbelievable truth had suddenly become believable. When I really thought about what I had learned and witnessed in just a few weeks, then any normal person would be in therapy for the rest of their days but no, not me, instead here I was thinking life had never been so sweet.

It didn't take me long to give up on history and concentrate on other things, getting ready for work being one of them…ok, ok, the only one.

After spending enough time in the bath to make the tips of my toes wrinkly, I decided to get out of the deeply scented water and dry my newly scrubbed, shaved skin. I then smoothed over some of Libby's fancy moisturizer until it felt fully soaked into every inch of my body's surface. I did this feeling almost giddy at the thought of what was to come. I found myself wondering what his reaction would be. Would he be expecting it or would he first just stand there in shock, before taking me in those solid arms of his.

We hadn't talked about my period again after the weekend, so I gathered he didn't want me to think of him as impatient but considering when we were together, we couldn't take our hands off each other I think his impatience was a bit obvious. So, tonight was a big deal. I wanted things to be perfect but as I had never done this type of thing before, I was still a bit nervous.

Back in my room I found my seductive outfit screaming out at me like some sex-fuelled beacon and I couldn't help but blush. I knew I would need help tightening the corset and the thought of asking Libby didn't help with my over sensitive reactions. After taking some time to put it all on and tying the ribbons to the thong, that was already starting to feel like cheese wire, I called down the stairs for my sister.

"Hey what's up…WOW! Holy shit, you look fantastic!" She then stuck her fingers in her mouth and wolf-whistled for the second time today. I rolled my eyes and turned around to show her the part that I was having a problem with and she started tugging like a woman possessed at the cord. I nearly lost balance a couple of times so she motioned for me to grab the desk for support. If I had known it was going to be like a mission to Mars getting me secure in this thing then I would have just opted for a bra. Once she had finished strapping me in, she stood back and said.

"Voila!"

"I'd say thanks if you hadn't broken most of my ribs already." I gave her a cheeky grin before going to look in the mirror. Thankfully, I had the foresight to put on my black trousers before Libby had come to my rescue so she didn't have to see my naked bottom. This, however, made me look like some kind of dominatrix!

"Go get 'em tiger!" Libby said before leaving me to continue getting ready for my big night. I frowned as I heard her making cat meows as she made her way downstairs.

I took one last look at myself as I reached for my black and grey striped top that I planned on wearing for work. I gulped as the corset under it had made my curves all that more…*well, curvy*. It had forced my body into a perfect figure of eight, making my assets seem all that more accessible. I tied my hair up into its damp twist and added a touch of mascara to my dark blue eyes that were already starting to show their doubts about tonight. Would I really go through with this?

"Yes…Yes, I will!" I said out loud as I grabbed my bag and made for the door.

Club Afterlife was buzzing with its usual Friday night energy as the band was playing their first set and the early signs of drunken Goths were starting to show. I had been working behind the bar for about an hour and already I was regretting not just changing into my sexy lingerie at the end of the night. The thong at least, because in my opinion these were only meant to be worn when there was a very high chance that they would be taken off again soon, like ten, twenty minutes tops.

I must have looked as if I had piles because I couldn't stop fidgeting with my behind. It was even more embarrassing when Mike even asked me if I was alright. Why I didn't just nod that I was fine I don't know but for some reason I had lost all rational functions and thought that saying 'bug bite' then motioning to my ass was a far better explanation. One word…*Idiot.*

I had to suppress the urge to smack myself on the forehead. Unfortunately, it didn't take me long to forget my shame and start fidgeting with the thong again. All I could think about was how thankful I was to be working tonight downstairs and out of the eye line of my watchful boyfriend. I had looked up a few times to see a figure standing there but considering that they could see much more of down here than we could up there, I could never be quite sure if it was him or one of his guards.

For a short time RJ and the gang had taken my mind off my unusual circumstances and for the first time tonight I forgot about the cheese wire in my ass. Jack displayed the same boyish charm that had you smiling at just the sight of him when coming to order drinks from the bar. When I helped him take them to our usual table he asked me to join them. I told them I would after my shift and didn't think Draven would mind me having one drink with my friends before going upstairs to join him. Plus, it would give me a chance to get some liquid courage down me before my time to do the dirty.

It was then that I saw something that couldn't have really been there. I was walking back to the bar when I saw someone staring at me in the crowd. His tall strong body stood out from the mass of jumping Goths around him. The band was playing their last song which was the one everyone knew. 'Stunned into Thunder' was the name of the song and it turned out to be quite fitting as now, there I was stunned to the very core as my feet refused to move.

The lights flashed in and out of darkness for effect and every time they came back up, my eyes would blink to find him still there staring at me, his intense eyes burrowing into mine. It felt as though I was standing there naked, with nothing to protect me from his luring smile. One fang exposed from deadly lips and he winked one serious eye at me, which struck me as more of a warning than anything that a wink generally implies.

"Lucius." The name escaped me in a whisper but as soon as I said it, the lights went off and when they illuminated again, the club was as it had been before the song ended. Lucius was gone. I shook my head and whispered,

"Couldn't be," as I walked behind the bar to finish my shift. The image of Lucius standing there in a long, black jacket that reached the floor and hair slicked back enhancing the hard features of his face, stayed with me until I heard my time was up.

"What did you say?" I asked in confusion as I could have sworn I heard it being said in the same voice that has started haunting my dreams.

"I just said time's up, you know, time to go enjoy life?" Mike gave me an odd look which was quickly turning to concern.

"Oh, yeah…life. Sorry, I guess I'm just tired."

"That Reed been working you too hard?" He smiled at me like I was some lost girl he had just found at the mall.

"Yeah, but that's nothing new," I replied before ordering a drink from him. I grabbed my bag from the back and found my drink ready and waiting for me to take over to my friends' table. As soon as I sat down, I felt better. I could quietly listen to everyone's stories about their week at college and RJ was never short of distracting conversation. She talked about what everyone was doing for Christmas vacation and how she wished that she had a family abroad to go to visit.

"So, how about you, Kaz, you going back to England for Chrimbo?"

"Umm, I don't quite know yet." I said half-heartedly, which she took for something other than nerves.

"Oh I get it, now you're with the God Draven, you don't want to lose sight of that fab bod of his! Hey, not that I blame you, if that was me, I wouldn't let him out of my sight for a second." At this point Jack punched her on the arm and gave her an evil look and for such a sweet guy, he really did dish out the dirties like a pro!

"Sorry Kaz, my sister is a little slow when it comes to stopping the nonsense from escaping from that shallow little head of hers... It's all the holes!"

"Hey! What'd I say?" I laughed at them while rolling my eyes and downing my drink.

"It's fine, but I'd better go. Oh before I do, are you guys all coming here tomorrow night?"

"Hell yeah, you did say that there was a hot surfer dude coming right?"

"I didn't say hot!" I said feeling the heat reach my cheeks which made Jack smile at me.

"Yeah, but that's how I know he's hot, because when I asked you on Monday you couldn't say yes when Sophia was around."

"So from that, you got hot?" I laughed as Chaz rolled his eyes at the rest of the group, making Lanie do her usual giggling fit.

"Nooo, but when you went the colour of my favourite jello then alarm bells rang," she said letting her pink hair cover half of her smug face.

"Whatever," I said lamely.

"Alright, we will see you tomorrow, go and tell wonder boy we all say hi." I couldn't stay angry at RJ, not when she made me smile so much. RJ and I had been an unlikely pair from the beginning but after everything I had been through in my past, she was a perfect friend. She drew attention to herself like bees to pollen and it kept me in the shadows where I was very happy to be.

When first moving here, she quickly became my ticket to a new life. My first friend who had welcomed me into her group, despite our differences. She knew there was something under the surface of my past and didn't buy my reasons for moving here for one second, but she never asked and for that I was more than thankful. Every now and again I would catch her looking at my covered scars and I could almost hear the question rattling around in her mind but again she never asked. And for RJ (Gossip queen extraordinaire) this must have been like torture.

This was how I knew she loved me. It was her never faltering ability to keep her mouth shut when it mattered the most. I suppose that is why I forgave all her little digs about Draven, not that there were many. But still, it must have been hard to see some new girl access the only thing that was completely out of bounds for this small town. Afterlife was like a drug and when the Dravens were around, that drug turned into full-blown obsession to fuel their new fix.

After saying my goodbyes, I made my way to the back staircase. Draven had told me that he liked to see me come up the main staircase, but I felt too exposed doing that, so I slipped past the crowd of drunken rockers to the door near the stage. This door had always been kind of hidden and it was only when I first went up to the VIP that I even knew it existed.

The two men that filled the doorway took only a slight look at me before they opened the door granting me access. I had used this door so many times you would have thought by now that I would at least get a smile, or some small indication that they recognised me. But no, I would always receive the same old cold stare from the both of them. This was what made me shiver as I climbed the stairs.

Once inside the VIP, I felt the warmth hit me like walking off a plane into a hot country. Every eye focused on me for a split second before returning to their strange companions. It had taken me a while to get used to the unusual characters that the VIP had to offer, but now I knew they were all Demons and Angels, well let's just say it didn't make it any easier but more enlightening.

As I walked around the tables, not being able to help the Marilyn Monroe swagger I had going on thanks to the steel bones in my corset, I noticed Rue, the blind waitress, give me a nod. It was only when I saw her palms turned slightly outwards did I realise how she spotted me. She had tattoos of eyes on her hands that did her seeing for her. I thought this was so cool when I found out, plus she had always been really nice to me even when some of the others had looked down at me for being human.

I winked my own hello back at her and walked around the front to the top table. My breath caught in my throat at the sight of Draven in his black suit. Everything was black, his shirt, tie and waistcoat. He was simply breath-taking like some modern-day Dark Knight.

He was looking very serious until his eyes met mine. The harsh glint he was portraying quickly left them and was replaced by a warm glow of fiery purple. He quickly stood and was around the front of the table in microseconds, making his body turn into a black blur. When his arms pulled my body into his, I let out a gasp at the surprise with him getting to me so fast. It was kind of like dating Superman in that way, and instead of the cape and spandex I got wings and an Armani suit. His hands tightened around my waist and his eyes searched out my lips.

"I've missed you, it was cruel to make me wait." His voice was deep and it rumbled out like a passionate man that had been starved of the touch he craved. I had no time to reply as his kiss drew me in like a spellbinding race. His lips covered mine with perfect precision and expert timing, making my toes want to curl up like the witch in the Wizard of Oz. Of course, the effect was similar to a house landing on me when he kissed me like that.

As you've already gathered, Draven had no problems displaying affection towards me in front of his Council, hell the whole VIP for that matter. But I, on the other, hand still couldn't help my burning cheeks from near exploding. When he finished tasting me, I looked down with embarrassment, which made him chuckle before raising my face back to his eye line. He smoothed his thumb across the blushed skin and smiled to himself.

"Mmm, keep blushing like that and I will stand here kissing you all night, my girl." This comment didn't help with the way my cheeks were melting like lava but again he found this amusing and laughed to himself as he pulled me behind him to his table. As always, his Council all stood for his approach and he sat me before taking his place next to me. There I was greeted by all except Aurora. No surprise there. She looked as dazzling as ever in her peacock coloured dress and hair glittering like the morning sun.

Sophia grabbed my arms and looked me up and down before giving me a cheeky wink. I had already seen her once today at college and told her my plans about tonight. This had made her clap her hands together in the middle of class, making everyone stop and stare like we were two morons that found the French revolution exciting. Reed had to swallow his tongue before committing the cardinal sin and asking Sophia to explain herself. If there was one thing you didn't do in this town it was to piss off a Draven.

I had my regular bottle of Corona waiting for me and when I felt Draven's hand start to feel up my leg, I couldn't help but start necking it.

"Whoa, easy there, rough night?" Draven teased as he knew full well that my night was completely uneventful. Ever since dating Draven my customers had all been super nice to me. I would even hear Jerry on the phone relaying my night back to Draven if anyone had caused me any trouble. I thought that this was sweet but massively OTT. I never said that I knew about these little check-ups, but I did find it funny whenever he asked me about my night.

"Just thirsty I guess," I said biting my lip at the bad liar I was.

"If I didn't know better, I would say you look nervous, my Keira." His velvet voice teased me, causing me to shrug my shoulders so that I didn't have to continue my lying. I sat quietly while the conversation continued on about how there was going to be some new guests coming to stay at the club. I put this down to the fact that the Dravens had stayed here much longer than usual and how normally they would have moved on to their next destination by now.

Draven explained that I might be seeing a few new faces soon as now that they were staying, his leaders were going to have to come to him to conduct their business. The business being the controlling of the rest of America's supernaturals. The way this worked was all down to the Angels and Demons that Draven put in charge of the different states. He was, after all, just one man (so to speak) and he couldn't deal with every supernatural on the planet. So the world was drawn up into sections which were all governed by district members of his council, a bit like police and politics.

I tried to follow the conversation, but I shifted, uncomfortable in my seat thanks to my squeezed rib cage that felt like it was sucking the air from my lungs. I twisted the bottle of Mexican beer round in my gloved hands and focused on the bubbling movement it was creating when Draven banged his fist down on the table in anger.

"NO, that is not good enough! I am their King and they will do as I order, there is no negotiating on this. For too many years they have lived in the shadows of the unknown and I will no longer stand for it. If they doubt the truth, then let them stand before me and speak it but I will NOT succumb to their wishes just because they forget how to Fuc…"

"Dom!" Sophia shouted at her brother, preventing him from saying the F word and this calmed him slightly. He was standing while making this speech and the entire room had been silenced by it.

"It will be handled, brother," Vincent said in a cool, controlled voice and I doubted there was another being alive that knew how to calm his brother's temper like he did. The very sound of his voice had Draven sitting once more.

"I have no doubt about that, brother," he said harshly and I noticed Aurora's eyes flicker with a burning passion at the sight of Draven's outburst, the sight made me feel sick in the pit of my stomach. Draven grabbed his claw-shaped shot glass in his anger and with the surface still aflame he emptied it of its glossy liquid.

This seemed to help with his rage and when he opened his eyes again, they turned to me.

"Forgive me, I hope I didn't scare you?"

"No, it's fine," I lied. Of course, I was scared of Draven when he was in a rage. I would have to be an idiot not to be. He knew I was lying but smiled at the effort I made all the same. He leaned into me and held my head with his big hands so that he could kiss me lightly on the top of my head. I felt my pulse race at just being closer to him and my bottom half felt the fire his touch created. I wanted him so badly I was close to exploding but the way the conversation continued I knew it would be a while yet. I almost felt like telling him that my body was fully accessible again and I was waiting for him to take full advantage of it right now but that would ruin my plan.

I decided to make the first move and after three drinks and an hour of debating Demon politics I got up from the table.

"I think I'll go to bed," I whispered and he was about to stand when I stopped him by laying my hand on his shoulder.

"It's alright, I will see you when you've finished." He nodded and took my hand, raising it to his lips to kiss it goodbye. Sophia got up as well and stated that she too was tired and would walk me back to Draven's room. On the way I asked her how I would know if Draven was coming back to the room before he saw me. I wanted to be prepared.

"I will get a message to him to knock before he comes in, that way you can get into position before he sees you."

"That will never work, can you imagine Draven knocking to get into his own room?" She laughed at the thought and admitted that no, she couldn't.

After a cheeky grin and a mischievous wink, she was gone, leaving me to enter Draven's bedchamber alone.

As usual, there was a drink waiting for me and after I downed the first glass of rosé wine I poured myself another. I let my bag slide to the floor before my clothes followed. I slipped each layer off as I let the wine slip down my throat to help with my nerves. Soon I had a pile around my feet and nothing covering my skin apart from my corseted bodice, stockings and thong with garter belt that were covering next to nothing. The set that was promiscuously called 'Temptress' was starting to work its magic by making me feel sexier than I ever had in my life.

I went into the bathroom with my bag to add the extra touches to the look I was trying to achieve. I let my hair down and ran my fingers through the still damp waves, creating volume. It hung down my back like a mane, curling around my curvy figure and moving with every heavy breath I took. I tried to control my shaking hands as I fished around in my bag for my black silk gloves that for once weren't fingerless.

I found them and replaced my usual ones, then found a small stick for my lips that Libby had lent me. It was the exact colour of the roses that were featured across my body like they were now a part of me. I smoothed it across my heart-shaped lips and broke my one rule about being blonde and wearing red lipstick. The high gloss made them look wet and inviting, so when they curled up into a smile I was surprised to find the whole look was starting to give me courage in my plans for seduction.

So, with my outfit in place I walked in my black stockinged feet back to lounge dramatically on the huge bed that was draped with luxurious black material which was a mix of velvet and satin. I almost laughed out loud when I saw how much I stood out against the gothic bedding. The blood-red roses almost came to life they looked so real amongst this perfect mix of rich, high-class theatrics. Then I remembered the matches I had brought with me.

I was normally used to Draven's click of the fingers and poof there would be the perfect setting for a perfect romantic evening but now I had to do things the mortal way. I decided to just light around the bed to create the focus to where I wanted most of the night's activities to happen and also if I were to light every candle in the room I would be there forever and a day, not to mention running out of matches.

Once that part was done I started to relax while I waited. I imagined Draven's strong hands searching my corset for access to my skin, would he undo the cord gently or would his demon side show through and tear his way through with impatience. My head rolled back at the sexual tension I was creating in my mind. I wanted him so badly and it wouldn't be long before he found the evidence of this for himself. I closed my eyes and retraced through the memories of his touch, the endless nights of passion fuelled by raw heat, passion and an unstoppable love that fused us together like one entity.

After hardly anytime at all my heart nearly stopped as I heard footsteps at the door. I expected for it to just open and see that tall frame silhouetted in the darkness but when I heard the door knock lightly, I was surprised. I smiled and mentally thanked Sophia as she must have delivered the message to her brother after we said our goodnights. I took a deep breath before trying to control my shaky voice, after all I needed to play the dominant one tonight and that would never work if I was stuttering.

I moved onto my side and cast my own shadows as I posed seductively, lifting one knee up and giving a full view of my new sexy look. I arranged my hair around one side and made sure my bulging cleavage was on full show. I licked my lips and said,

"Come in" in what I hoped was the sexiest voice that had passed through my lips in twenty-three years.

The door opened and there Draven stood, strong and solid but frozen in shock. He stepped further into the room, but it looked as if he had other ideas. He slowly moved his feet as if fighting with his own actions. I bit my lip as the idea that he might not like this new Keira that he was discovering in his room. I tried to banish that idea and after another deep breath, I had the guts to say,

"Won't you come closer?"

Again the figure was silent and I was starting to regret this pretty quickly as he had now stopped completely. I now wished I had taken the time to light all the candles so that I could see his features. His face was in complete darkness and I tried to narrow my eyes to make out if he was wearing his usual frown. I was about to speak but Draven beat me to it.

"Keira, I'm sorry, I didn't know you would be...but by the Gods..."

"Like what?" I asked before my mind had time to realise my mistake.

"So exquisite." The voice rumbled out like a starved man and it sent a shudder of mixed emotions to the core.

The voice of a man is a powerful thing when words like that are heard. The voice of a man's soul can seep through his lips, when words like that are spoken. And the voice of an Angel's heart was heard that night, for those words spoken belonged…

To the voice of Vincent.

CHAPTER TWENTY-SIX

MISTAKES AND A BED OF ROSES

I had frozen as if an ice queen had just cast a deadly spell. In my head a voice screamed out to cover myself up but in this case I wasn't the only one doing the wrong thing. Vincent still hadn't moved, although I was pretty sure it was wrong of him to be staring at me the way he still was. It was the first time I saw a flicker of the same power Draven held, run through his brother's body. I saw blue light emanate from his feet and as it travelled up his body it changed it to a darker shade reminding me of the day's sky turning into night.

He hadn't moved any closer, but I could almost hear the want in his bones begging him to work until they reached the bed's edge. Then the candles started to flicker making it the second time I had ever felt fear around Vincent. The first time of course, being in the car park where he caught me before his brother could follow in his footsteps to take me against my will.

After what seemed like a small forever, I forced some words from my trembling lips.

"Vincent...I...I am so sorry...I didn't know..." The words seemed to tumble out like a lost cause but whatever it sounded like it seemed to work because his response was a gentle,

"Ssshh, please don't do that." His smooth voice made my skin prickle and a weird vibration flashed down my naked neck. His glowing body faded back into the darkness now that he appeared to be calming whatever emotions had been running wild with his mind. Now that he was once again just a silhouette in the room, he decided he was going to move from the spot he had been glued to and finally my mind did the same and kicked into gear, covering myself up with the bed covers. By the time we came face to face, we were looking less risky about our situation. My skin was covered and his eyes didn't glow with the dangerous lust I had seen.

I bit my lip as if it would help prevent the situation from getting any worse… that being my big mouth. But this reaction made him smile and he knelt down to my level so he didn't look so threatening from the height of him towering above me. He wasn't much shorter than his brother, there being mere inches between them. His skin was paler than Draven's and the faint light from the now steady candles were casting a warm orange glow over his soft features. He was still smiling, and it looked as though he was trying very hard not to let his eyes linger anywhere else but on my face.

"You know, we really need to stop meeting like this," he joked and finally I could let air out of my mouth.

"I'm so sorry, I thought…."

"I know, Keira, you thought I was Dom," he said in a whisper before I could explain. At this I covered my shame-filled head in my hands.

"Oh God! Why does this keep happening? What is Draven going to say?" I know it was a little tactless, but it was all I could think about. I jumped slightly when I felt Vincent's cool skin come into contact with mine, but when his fingers started to pry my hands away, I relaxed when met with his sympathetic face.

"He's not going to find out, Keira, I think for everyone's sake this one should be kept between me and you. But I will tell you something…this is the last time I will be coming here to give you messages that Dom should be doing himself." It was the first sign of disapproval I had seen him direct at his brother before and it shocked me. It was as though he didn't think kindly on him for making me wait like this.

"He's not coming yet, is he?" I asked looking down to hide both my disappointment and relief.

"Not yet, no, he sent me here to tell you he had some business to deal with before joining you, only…"

"Only what?" I asked shamefully.

"Just that if he knew what you had planned, I think business would most certainly be delayed." He tried to hide a cheeky grin I didn't ever expect to see on Vincent's face. But the wink he followed it up with surprised me more. I laughed and its purpose became clear.

"I had a feeling he would never have knocked," I said more to myself than Vincent.

"And why would you have ever thought a man like my brother would have?" He laughed but when he saw my face, he could read his sister's name all over my thoughts.

"Ah, Sophia." He sighed and rolled his eyes.

"It wasn't all her fault, she just suggested that she could get a message to him to knock…you know…so I would know he was coming," I added quietly, which added to my shame.

"I see."

"You really won't tell him?" I asked hopefully.

"Oh trust me, the way Dom's temper is at the moment, it wouldn't be the smartest of things to do." He wasn't laughing anymore, and I shuddered at the words Dom and temper in the same sentence.

"Why, is he angry?"

"Yes he is, but trust me…" he motioned to my body with his hand and added,

"…this will help." This made my cheeks torch the blood beneath my skin. He shifted his weight and was standing again before I had time to blink. He was about to leave, but I grabbed his hand to hold him back. He looked down at the small, black satin fingers that had curled around his large palm.

"Thank you, Vincent."

"For what, exactly?" His eyes didn't dare look at mine, but his voice shook with leaked emotions.

"For being my...my friend," I whispered but as soon as the answer reached his ears his skin started to turn icy cold. I dropped my hand from his and tucked it under the covers to warm it back up. He turned from me but before he left, he corrected me.

"I'm much more than that, Angel." And with that bombshell, he was gone in a heartbeat.

I was left not only utterly embarrassed but also feeling a little guilty and I wasn't sure why. Was it my imagination or did Vincent seem to have a few deeper feelings swimming around in his mind? And even more confusing...were they really about me? I shook that idea out of my head quickly and put it all down to some hidden feelings about someone else. Maybe seeing me and Draven so happy together, made those emotions to finding his own happiness all that stronger.

I battled like this for about an hour and by the end didn't come up with any answers to Vincent's strange behaviour around me. In front of Draven he was as he had always been but when we were alone it was definitely different. More intense and I'm not just talking about all the accidents we kept having. Ever since that kiss we shared, I felt as if his eyes were following me everywhere. He would notice every move I made, and his senses would interpret every detail. If I frowned he would frown, if I smiled he would follow suit. I had put it all down to protecting what his brother loves but what if I was wrong? What if there was more to it?

In the end I must have fallen asleep because when I heard the sound of breathing above me I found myself in the dark. I had only opened my eyes a tiny degree, enough to add a figure to the breathing. I was acting asleep because I didn't know who it was that was stood above me like a statue of Rome. I was lying on my back with one arm above my head and the other resting lightly on my stomach.

I tried to keep my breathing light, like deep slumber would have induced but it was hard given the position I was in. I wasn't about to make the same mistake a third time and assume it was Draven that loomed deadly tranquil over me. If it had been Vincent

I wanted to pretend I was asleep but if it was Lucius then I knew I was still dreaming. Why were all the men in my life exceptionally tall and well built? Why couldn't we have all the baddies like little goblins, bumpy and disgusting and all the goodies tall and handsome? That would be helpful.

I felt my hair move away from my face but there was no hand that governed it. Then the bed covers followed and moved down my body exposing my rose-covered corset and matching thong. Then, what looked like a black hand rose above me and illuminated my body from the bluish sparks that ignited from under the shadowed skin. It moved over my figure, following every curve without contact. At this I heard a low growl that came from the chest of a supernatural. The covers kept disappearing to the bottom of the bed and soon I could feel the cold edge of the night on the thin material of my stockinged legs. They had stayed in place thanks to the suspender belt that attached on to the lace around my thighs.

The room was silent and I could hear the wild weather blowing nature to within an inch of its life outside. I didn't know what was worse, being out there and letting Mother Nature give me a sound lashing or in here without a clue as to who or what was taking in my sight like sleeping prey.

Then every nerve in my body lit up making me let out a moan in unspeakable pleasure. Fingertips had started to touch my ankle just after the blue light disappeared and then worked their way up with a fine art. It was like this hand was communicating with my blood making it ignite, fusing a connection with my vulnerable body and my even more vulnerable sex.

I bit down on my lip to hold in the moans that wanted to break free. I shifted under the fingers, but the lightest touch turned quickly into a secure hold on my inner thigh. Whoever it was didn't want to let me go. And deep down I didn't want them to, until Draven's face popped into my head and made my eyes flash open to face my stalker.

It was only when I was faced with the mixture of Angelic and Demonic glow of Draven's power that my heart flipped in both realisation and excitement. His eyes looked strained in a control he was trying not to lose and his other hand was balled into a fist by his side. The contrast to the gentle hand he touched me with and the other that was taking his frustration was blatantly obvious.

He was moving slowly as though he was trying hard not to get too carried away. One thing was clear, tonight was going to give me what I had been craving for, but I wasn't going to be in control as I had planned. His tensed muscles told me as much. He was now looking directly into my eyes, but he still hadn't spoken. It was as though he was drowning in my image before consuming my mind with his commanding voice. Soon he would do to me what he wanted to do and all the while giving me more pleasure than any normal human girl could take, I was sure.

He let his fist uncurl and his other hand left my leg so that he could pull my hands round to the front of me. I couldn't help it …

I spoke first.

"What…" I cleared my croaky whisper before continuing,

"What are you doing?" I asked but all I got was,

"Ssssh, be silent," with a shaking of his head. Then with a tight grip on my glove covered wrists and a sharp tug upwards, my body flung towards him as if I was the one with powers. I let out a gasp, but his lips caught it as my upper body was now securely in his concrete arms. He wrapped them around my waist and his fingers entwined in the tightly, tied cord at the back of my corset that concealed my breasts from him. I felt them about to pull it free, but he stopped himself, all the while devouring me in deep, sensual kisses.

He was trying to taste every inch of me as his mouth moved from mine to my neck and shoulders. He was still holding all my weight and one arm moved further around my back and up my spine to my neck, where his hand supported the top of my backbone as he bent it backwards. He grabbed a handful of my loose hair and pulled it downwards to encourage my movements, all the while never letting it hurt me.

His mouth played at the base of my ear before moving closer down to where my pulse was the fastest. There he didn't even bother to tease me with his teeth. No, he didn't have the will for that, proving as much when he bit down into my flesh making me cry out in a blissful pain that made me succumb to the pleasure growing in between my thighs.

I came suddenly with orgasmic results for the entire time that he remained sucking the essence out of me. I could feel the warmth of my blood seep out of the puncture wounds he had made but the two little streams didn't get far as he licked it back upwards, not wasting a single drop.

I was panting when he had finished tasting my blood and mixing it with his own as I was now very much a part of him, with our blood creating a new energy inside his veins. This idea made me smile in the dark, showing off the whites of my teeth, like a beacon to where my thoughts lay. After he noted the bliss in my eyes, he licked my small wounds again and I felt them start to fuse together, the skin replacing the stinging pain with an annoying itch. He touched it lightly with his thumb and after a few circular movements it was all as though it had never happened.

My body was still in its aftermath stages of a huge release, but Draven wasn't about to give me any time to recover. He raised me up further and took hold of me under the legs with one arm and the other held my upper body. He stood up straight and any other man's back would have strained with the awkward weight of carrying a body from leaning down. But Draven made me feel as though I weighed nothing more than a bag of leaves caught up in the wind. He walked towards the glass doors and I stiffened in his hold.

"Where are you taking me?" I whispered but he didn't answer. It was almost as if he was lost in his own world and I just hoped it was one where he didn't forget that I was a very breakable human that would no doubt catch my death if I went out into that stormy night. I gripped onto his suit jacket as he was still wearing what I had seen on him earlier, making me the only one who was the near naked one. This time he didn't need to touch the glass for it to respond and as it opened the cold hit me like a tidal wave of ice.

"Draven," I said in more of an urgent tone. But as soon as he took his first step outside, my mind was more concerned with the rippling vibrations erupting from under his skin. This close up, I could actually see the purple energy flowing through his veins as if

it had replaced his blood with light. Then I cried out with shock when I saw two huge dark wings emerge from his back making a ripping sound, as though they had cut their way from both his flesh and material.

The wind was fierce and whipped around our bodies like a lasso. My hair flew around like an abandoned flag and the rain started to pelt down as a warning to the ever-growing storm. I was about to beg him for shelter when I was silenced by a blank wall of feathers. His wings had shot forward creating a storm proof cocoon around me. He was covered up to the neck with the softest long feathers that any exotic bird would have been jealous of.

I couldn't help but reach out and touch them. I don't know why I was surprised to find them warm through my gloved fingers. I heard him groan a little and I wondered if it was a nice feeling to have them explored by human hands. I soon forgot about the wild night's weather and got lost in my heated little feather bubble. I could feel him taking me somewhere, but I didn't dare ask as it was evident that he wasn't in a talkative mood. The changes in his movements were the only indication that we were not just walking straight. I felt him climb stairs and jump long distances but all the time he kept me covered and safe.

I could have gone to sleep quite easily but excitement had me buzzing. Where was he taking me and more importantly, what was he going to do with me when we got there? Thankfully, my questions didn't plague me for too long as I felt him slow down and when his wings went back, I wasn't hit with the wind as I was expecting.

However, what did hit me was an incredible scent.

He was walking us into the most magnificent oasis of flowers. It was as though we had just broken into Heaven itself. I looked up at him to see him staring ahead with serious intent plastered on his face. I followed his eyes and saw a clearing in the middle of the treasures of the natural world.

I felt as if I was on drugs or at least how they always made out in movies. Flowers moved in a non-existent wind and the moon that should have been hidden behind stormy black clouds lit up the fantasy. We were outside I was sure, but I doubted even Draven was powerful enough to change the weather. There was no rain, no cold bitter chill, there was just calm life that reached up to the Heavens above. It was only when I followed the wall of life up that I realised we were in a glass dome and then it didn't take long before I could hear the rain lashing down against the glass. I loved that sound. The drops of water too heavy for its creators and leaving the clouds, like escaping souls trying desperately to get back to Earth.

His footsteps were in rhythm to the sound of the outside world and as it got angrier, he got calmer. I wanted to ask a million questions, but my eyes drank in this little hidden world instead of speaking of it. The smell of thousands of flowers all in bloom was intoxicating and I was getting drunk from their sweet perfumes. I wanted the sun to come out, so that I could soak in their dazzling colours, but the moon's light had to suffice.

The room was huge and only when we got to the centre did I see what was meant for us. The clearing was like an exotic red pool being that every inch of it was covered with deep red rose heads that matched my corset. There wasn't one thorn as he laid me down onto the softest bed in existence.

A bed of roses.

"A rose should be plucked among its sisters. It would be an insult against Mother Nature to deny her of your beauty." His deep voice echoed around the dome making it a mighty and unstoppable force. I shied away at his compliment, but he didn't allow this reaction for long.

"Look at me," he ordered, making my heart flip. I moved my eyes to his dark form and watched in amazement as his suit started to disintegrate. It was disappearing into the air like little particles of dust leaving an overwhelming body above me.

I took in every inch of his Godlike form, more like an oil painting from the world's greatest artists who had all joined force to capture his astounding mix of strength and beauty. He was the epitome of perfection.

Once naked, with only his wings behind him casting shadows, he came down to my level. There he studied me in great detail before his urges started to show. His hands gripped the material that concealed me, and I kept expecting to hear ripping noises. I was somewhat relieved when I didn't, as this was one outfit I wanted to keep safe or at least in one piece. Hell, and maybe framed by the looks of how this night would turn out!

"Turn around." I jumped at the sound of his Demon voice breaking through and I couldn't help but slowly obey. As I lowered myself back down on to my stomach I was shocked to see a bright light emerge from Draven's right arm. I looked to my right and saw a large blade of energy grow from his hand. I moved away but his left hand caught me and held me in place.

He leaned down to my ear and whispered,

"Trust me Keira, I won't hurt you." This was a little comforting but when I saw the blade coming closer to my back I couldn't help but flinch.

"Hold still and don't move." Ok, now I was panicking but closed my eyes tight as if that would somehow help. I felt his left hand on my side and the other one with the blade was coming nearer to my skin. Although I couldn't see it, I could feel the heat coming from this part of him. Then I felt my corset loosening at the bottom near the curvature of my behind.

The sound of the cord being cut could be heard over the storm that was my beating heart and when I felt the tighter part ping back I knew it was his way of freeing my body. It didn't take long before I could breathe easier and when he had finished, he motioned for me to turn back round to face him. I did so while still holding my corset in place, making his eyebrows rise.

His hands picked at the embroidered roses and worked their way down to undo the ribbons that were attached to my thong by hand. I was close to trembling in anticipation which was adding to the intensity of it all. And he knew it…Big time did he know it. He was getting some weird kick out of making me wait and when I opened my eyes, I saw him displaying an evil, dark grin.

"Tell me what you want?"

"You know," I replied in my shy way, but this wasn't good enough.

"Speak it!" he demanded louder and I had to close my eyes again so that I wasn't being controlled by his black gaze of desire.

"I want you…you to…to…"

"To what exactly? Say it, shout it!" He was working himself up until he would soon just take it anyway, so why not give him what he wanted. What we both wanted. I knew what he was doing, he was giving me a shred of control back…waiting until he heard the words, giving him the fire start!

He started to encourage the words as his hands moved to my sex, tracing a finger along the lines of my underwear. He then shifted his body down so that his face was inches away from my quivering need. Once there he moved his large hands round to cup my cheeks of my naked behind and when he pulled me up abruptly to bring the front of my thong to his face I wanted to shift away in embarrassment.

"Speak the words, Keira," he said softly taking a new approach. I tried to move again, not wanting to give in just yet but when he started to blow down on me, I felt like I was going to explode if he didn't kiss me down there.

"TAKE ME!" I screamed out and when he heard what he wanted, he flashed the whites of his fangs before replying with self-confidence oozing from every pore,

"As you wish." And then it happened…the first kiss to my most intimate place followed quickly by the greatest orgasm that I had ever experienced. It felt as though something inside of me had exploded and my reactions weren't controlled by any logical thoughts I possessed. It was wave upon wave of mind-blowing bliss and when my voice was dry from screaming, I had to move his head away to indicate that I couldn't physically take another second. After having his fill of the taste of me he released me and came back up to take his prize that he had waited for until I had had my fill.

"Now it's my turn," he whispered in my ear and then with a flash of movement he ripped away my corset and all other material covering my skin. He was like a man possessed, so much so his hands shook as if trying to contain the deep energy beneath him like a caged animal fighting its master to be freed. He covered my body in little bites that didn't pierce the skin but sent shivers down to my toes. His hands pulled me to him like I was never close

enough. Then, before he could enter me he asked me one last question.

"Do you belong to me?" It came out in a raspy breath and the purple eyes told me that I dare not speak anything but the truth.

"YesSSS!" As soon as the Y could be heard I screamed as he thrust himself into me with excessive force. Thanks to the moistness between my legs it slid in but the size, as always, still shocked me and was difficult to take. This was when I went into my own world of a seventh heaven. I thought that I would soon blackout as it was sending me into another world. Actually, the world I lived in could have been ending...skies falling, oceans flooding the land and Earth's core spilling out causing vast destruction and I wouldn't have known anything but the ecstasy he was inflicting!

Every movement he made caused a different pleasure, pain and sensation. He would move me around to his exotic dance and I became fixated on the pumping energy beneath his shadowy skin. His wings shook with the satisfaction he received and they twitched as his momentum built up until his release was near.

I couldn't have counted the amount of orgasms he gave me but by the time he was close I was a mere shell. I pushed myself to find my last moments of energy as I wanted his orgasm to be as powerful as all of mine were. I gripped his neck and pulled my body up into him. I locked my legs around his waist and joined into his rhythm before biting into his neck and then I added the catalyst.

"I belong to you...Take me now!" His head arched backwards, and his lower body drove forward for one last hard thrust. He released inside me and I in turn found my final raptures with the sound of his roars into the night. His fists grabbed handfuls of petals and crushed them into scented pulp. He was still coming, and his wings had stretched out behind him, tensing under the strain. I watched from underneath him in a bewildered state. It was the most pleasure I had ever seen him endure.

He collapsed on top of me but still managed to find the strength to hold his weight so as not to crush my smaller frame. He remained quiet, with only the panting beneath his chest. I could feel his heartbeat as though it was my own and for once I was the one to ask.

"Are you alright?" This made him realise that I was staring at him in awe and when he smiled it lit up my face along with his. It was the first time that Draven looked truly shattered after sex. This was surprisingly comforting. Usually it was just me.

His wings shook and ruffled as he stretched one more time before answering me, which reminded me of a bird getting comfortable before settling down for the night.

"Am I alright? Is that what you asked?" He was laughing at my question and I was left utterly confused with his outburst. He rolled over and pulled me on top of him making his wings come forward and wrap around me securely once again. The feathers tickled my naked body and made me let out a series of short little giggles.

"That's adorable," he said and before I could stop, he ruffled his feathers making them tickle me more.

"Oi! Behave!" I threatened but seeing as I was still laughing it didn't sound very convincing. He took my face in his hands and was about to kiss me but stopped before he reached my lips.

"You're incredible…that was...utterly incredible!" He spoke the words proudly, straining his neck to look up over his head as if confirming this to the Heavens.

Then he kissed me.

After one of the sweetest kisses he let me roll off him and to his side, where I nestled in my little nook under his arm and on his firm chest. I ran my fingers along the lines of his defined pecks, and he let out a satisfied sigh, which blew my wild hair out of my eyes. I found myself smiling as my mind was drifting towards a sleepy state. His arm pulled me close and his head flopped down to rest on mine. It didn't take long before sleep devoured us both in this bed of roses.

It turned out it wasn't only the first time that I had slept on a bed of roses but also…

Wrapped in the wings of an Angel.

CHAPTER TWENTY-SEVEN

THE SELF-ASSURED SURFER DUDE

I couldn't remember the last time I had slept as peacefully as I did that night. I woke with a feeling that a flame had been lit in my soul and the aftermath of last night would burn within me forever. Is that what was meant by the eternal flame? An everlasting love so powerful, so deep, that it became a part of you, as if it had in some way altered your DNA.

I felt stronger in an unnatural way and I knew that last night had been different in more ways than one. It was as if the reasons behind Draven's exhaustion after sex was down to him somehow passing over to me some of his power because when I looked over to him, he was still fast asleep. On the other hand I felt as though I could have climbed a mountain and still had time for a round of footie afterwards. My body tingled and my muscles felt brand new like after a full body massage.

The light was what woke me and I was now gazing at what it was reflecting off. Thousands of stunning flowers that made the glass dome seem like we were in the middle of a rainbow. The roses beneath us hadn't even lost their lustre after a night of being not only without water but also slept on. I looked to my left to see Draven peacefully breathing and adding to the beautiful sight, he was also still naked.

The light that was let in from the glass walls was making Draven's skin look like liquid gold that blanketed a broad muscular body. I couldn't help but start to touch his heated skin, starting at the shoulder blade. He was lying on his side, hiding his face from view and his night-black hair was chaotically hung around his cheek and neck. Like a night of sweating had made it stick to the lines of his face. Like this he looked kind of vulnerable, making me bite my lip at the thought.

My hand crept down further round to his chest and the lightness of his breathing made me wonder if he was in as deep of a sleep as I thought. I was soon answered when his hand shot up so fast and grabbed my wrist in a startled breath.

"Ahh" When he heard my voice, he relaxed his grip on my scarred arm and pulled it closer to kiss the white lines that decorated my pale skin. It was now that I realised I was as naked as he was and the light wasn't only making him look like a Mediterranean heartthrob but it was also showing my every imperfection. I wanted to shy away but the feeling of his lips brushing my skin was too hypnotic.

"Are you cold?" The question caught me off guard as I didn't feel cold but considering how he was now running his fingers over little pale bumps that covered my arms, then I guess my skin felt otherwise. He was leaving trails of warmth as his fingertips reached up to my face that he now had cupped in his palm.

"Because you know I can think of more than one way to warm up beautiful naked girls that I love."

"Have many of those do you?" I teased.

"Nope, only one but you'll be happy to know, I did find the cream of the crop." He quickly turned his body round to face me and in one quick movement he had my body disappearing underneath his massive frame as he towered above me. He shot me a bad boy grin before going in for the kill. His kisses started soft and gentle like being covered in butterflies, but it didn't take long before his Demon side started to devour me in the height of our morning passion.

He circled each hand around my wrist and raised them above my head so that he could pin me down.

"Speak to me," he asked in a raspy voice and I blushed at his request. It was silly the way I still got embarrassed around him even after all the nights we had shared but there was something about the sound of his voice that would always send sparks down my spine, like fireworks being lit by those supernatural hands of his. Finally, I gulped down my shame and spoke the words I knew he was waiting for. I raised my lips to his ear and whispered,

"Make love to me."

"It would eternally be my pleasure," was his sweet reply.

After a few hours of extreme morning exercise, we finally made it to his room and on the way back he explained to me what that place had been. Thankfully, I might add, I hadn't had to walk back in the nude because knowing my luck I would meet Vincent in the bloody hallway. No, he made some of my clothes appear, along with some of his own, so we didn't look too much like Adam and Eve on our way back from a roll in the hay in the Garden of Eden.

He explained how his sister's projects sometimes came in handy when trying to seduce his girlfriends. I had punched him playfully on the arm making him roar with a deep laughter.

"Don't joke about that!" I reprimanded him but he made it harder when he shot me a sexy sideways glance. We had walked through the numerous corridors hand in hand, as if we had been taking a morning stroll in a local park. He looked happier than he had last night and I wondered how last night would have really gone if he knew that he wasn't the only man to see me like that. I quickly pushed Vincent from my mind and on an impulse I squeezed Draven's hand tighter, making his eyebrows rise. God but he didn't miss a beat.

Back in his room he left to attend to some business while I had some breakfast and then a shower. The shower part I had been reluctant in doing as washing the scent of Draven from my body was not something I wanted to do. But then I would get a whiff of my pits and the part where I had been sweating was something I could live without. Maybe I could ask Draven to bottle his scent and make me soap from it.

After I was nicely wrapped in lush white fluffy towels, I walked back into the room to find it wasn't as empty as I had left it. A Draven of the shorter variety smiled sweetly at me and I shrieked in response to find Sophia sprawled out on the bed playing idly with the edge of one of the fringed pillows.

"You scared me half to death!" I screeched but I was met by a cool look of knowing.

"I doubt that, given the colour of your cheeks."

"Sorry?"

"The dead don't blush, Keira dear. Anyway, did you enjoy my pleasure dome?" The cool look of knowing turned quickly to smugness garnished with a slice of Demon. I decided to play dumb, evidently something I seemed to be good at.

"I'm sure that I don't know what you're talking about." It would have helped if I could look her in the eye when I lied but come on, that was never going to happen. She laughed making me turn from the opposite direction and when met by those amused dark eyes I just shrugged my shoulders.

"Oh come now, don't play coy with me sister, besides this bed hasn't been slept in and my rose petal floor has been crushed to a pulp."

"No it wasn't, it was fine this morning," I said in defence, but she had been expecting it and pointed at me, shouting,

"Ha, got ya!"

"Grow up would ya!" I said in a way that I would have to Libby but with Sophia, it was like having a naughty sister watching my every move.

"I do try," she replied sarcastically,

"But it's hard when you're immortal." I flashed her an un-amused eye roll but when it turned into a smile we both laughed. Draven was right, it was utterly useless trying to stay mad at Sophia. Like telling off a puppy for peeing in your favourite shoes and then resisting cuddling it when it started to cry for attention. Not that I was calling Sophia a dog, more like a tiger cub. Cute as a button but with one swipe could take your face off!

As graceful as a dancer from Swan Lake, Sophia dismounted the bed and followed me into my new dressing room. There she stood by watching as I scanned my wall full of clothes but every time I went to grab something, she made a sound that reminded me of the TV game show Family Fortunes, the noise they made when you got an answer wrong.

"Okay, my fashion muse, what would you have me wear?" I asked as I folded my arms and took a step back. She floated ahead of me and picked out a tight pair of stretch jeans in black and a charcoal grey tunic top with big bell-shaped sleeves and pretty light pink flowers around the bottom. It had a big roll neck and it looked warm and inviting. It was just a shame that it wasn't me.

"That's lovely but I doubt Draven would want me wearing something like that to meet Justin." She whipped her head around as though it was attached to an elastic band.

"You're meeting with Justin today?" She looked shocked with the idea and once again I found myself shrugging my shoulders.

"So what?" I said pulling out a pair of faded blue jeans down off the rack and grabbed a plain black T-shirt with long sleeves. I turned around to get some underwear out of the drawers and when I saw Sophia now sat on top of the large dresser island, it startled me. Her short dainty legs hung down like she was sat on a giant's doorstep.

"Sophia what are you…"

"I'm helping," she stated and her foot reached down for the lower drawer and pulled it open with the slightest flick of her ankle.

"Knickers?" She wore the cheekiest of grins and I couldn't help but laugh.

"What? That's what you call them in England isn't it?"

"Yeah, sometimes. So what was with the face… don't look at me like that, you know what I mean… when I mentioned Justin?"

"Nothing major, just answered a few questions for me, that's all." She jumped down and landed lightly on her feet like a cat on a tin roof…soundless and agile.

"Okay, so what's that supposed to mean?" She walked past me

and was leaving out of the door when she stopped and flung her perfect curls over one shoulder before answering me.

"Just that it explains why Dom was in such a foul mood last night, I guess he didn't want this day to arrive. After all, it's not every day a prince lets his princess go out on a date with a pauper. See you tonight, Keira dear." And with that she left making me want to throw something at the door behind her. In the end all I did was shout,

"IT ISN'T A DATE!"

After a quick change and a scribbled goodbye note to Draven, I grabbed the outfit that Sophia had picked out before running for the door. I was still stuffing it into my bag whilst half running down the corridor when I bumped into someone with a solid chest, which incidentally knocked me down.

"Ouch!" I said as my butt cheeks slapped on the cold stone floor.

"Keira!" Vincent's astonished voice filled the air and then quickly memories of us last night filled my mind. I started to mumble out words of apology, at least that's what I thought they were. I usually just started talking when I was nervous and while my mind was busy on other things, I was never sure what new trouble I was getting myself into with speaking.

He started to laugh as he helped me up and when my stocking feet slipped on the floor, he was fast as lightning catching me again. The feel of his arm tightly wound around my waist was like setting off a firecracker in my stomach. He leant down to my face and for a second my heart stopped. I thought he was going to kiss me. But if that was true then why was I closing my eyes instead of pushing him away.

"Are you steady?" he whispered and this seemed to break the spell. My eyes flew open and all I managed was a nod. It appeared he was quite reluctant to let me go but after too many seconds of silence his hand left my side. He looked down at my feet and another low laugh came from deep beneath his chest.

"Perhaps you should think about shoes, after all it is raining outside." Then it happened…I snorted out a laugh. If I didn't want to die of shame before, then now was a contender. His eyes widened making them look like crystal blue lakes that could have commanded the winter skies. His lips curved into an angelic smile at the new sound he had witnessed, and I bent down to pick up my shoes that had dropped from my bag. I kicked my feet into them just so I didn't have to look into his alluring eyes. It was powerful enough to feel them burning into my every move.

"You seem in a hurry."

"Umm, yeah, I guess. Just errands and stuff, my sister is a bit hopeless when it comes to cooking and she wanted me to cook today, while Justin's staying." As soon as the name was out of my mouth, I wanted to slip again and this time bash my head against the hundred-year-old stone floor.

"Ah, Justin. I must say, I haven't heard that name spoken in a faltering tone." Speaking like this you could tell he was Draven's brother alright. I couldn't help but say what I thought.

"Oh, not you too! God, what is it with the Dravens and paranoia. You all sound the same. Anyone would think I was running off to marry the bloody guy!" He was trying to hide his grin from my little outburst, but he was as lousy at it as his brother. At least with Sophia you knew where you stood.

"Is it not the right of a man to protect his woman, even from evils they cannot see?"

"Evil?" At this I laughed.

"Oh come on he's a family friend. What could he possibly want but friendship with his brother's, wife's sister…you don't understand." Okay, did that come out right? Why did I say that?

"Um yes… what do I know indeed? I'm sorry I pried… after all, I know nothing about a situation like that, being non-human and all." It was the first time I had seen him look hurt and his eyes turned to ice that looked ready to crack. He gave me a nod goodbye and turned but as he made his way down the hall he spoke one last time.

"Ragnar is waiting for you."

I wanted to smack myself on the side of the head for being so tactless. What was I thinking?

"Vincent I..." I started but it was too late, he was already gone. "How do they do that?" I muttered to myself.

On the drive home I didn't say one word to Ragnar until I pulled up the drive and cut the engine. Over the last week Ragnar and I had become unlikely friends but after Draven had not only apologized to him but also commended him on thinking solely of me that night in the Temple, we had created an understanding.

I realized the real reasons behind his reluctance to have me under his guard. I reminded him of the daughter he couldn't save. Draven on the other hand had made a ruthless decision making Ragnar my guardian and he knew that if he had these feeling that he would lay his life down to protect me. I hadn't been too pleased to hear this at the time but in Draven's eyes, he knew the best way to protect those that are dear to him.

"DAMN IT!" I shouted and hit the steering wheel with both palms. I had been stewing over what I had said to Vincent and what a complete idiot I had been. Ragnar looked over to me as if I had lost my mind but in my current state I didn't care and luckily, he didn't care enough to ask, or maybe he was just scared to. Ok, so not likely.

When I got indoors, I was just glad to hear that Justin wasn't there. He and Frank had gone on a boy's day out that consisted of fishing and drinking beer. I think it was more Frank's idea because the way Libby described it, Justin had been reluctant to leave the house this morning. He had asked about my whereabouts and when my sister had told him, he had looked...well... disappointed. This was all according to Libby, who loved nothing more than a good drama even when there's none to tell.

I decided to work some more on my report after hanging up the outfit Sophia had picked. I don't know why I had changed my mind but something in me had just snapped. They were all making a big fuss about me escorting Justin to the club, which was all it was ...escorting, NOT DATING! I said to myself over and over.

I decided that I would make an effort tonight, if not for Draven, then for myself. I knew deep down that I wasn't really angry at them, it was myself that I was upset with. I should have just nodded and kept my big mouth shut.

I tried to concentrate on my work but the lashing rain against my window was sending me into a daze. I was thinking about all that had happened in the past few weeks and how since Draven and I had become an item, my life really wasn't ever going to be the same again. I knew that sounded like a stupid statement but forgetting all the Demon and Angel stuff, this relationship was it for me. Draven would be the last man I would ever love or more like, would I be the last woman Draven would ever love? After all, he was going to outlive me.

"No Keira, don't do this!" I said out loud. I sat at my window seat trying desperately not to think about the real nightmares haunting me...my real fears. They weren't only the ones that wanted to hurt me, they were the ones that would indefinitely hurt me. Like Draven's face when I started to get older. Could he still love me then? And if so, we would have to hide away our love.

After a certain while no-one would be able to see us together. For one, Draven wouldn't age and two, I would just look like the sad granny that bagged herself a toyboy or worse, people would think I was his grandmother! Urgh gross! The thought had me near gagging. Thankfully, Libby had knocked on my door to save me from myself.

It didn't take too much to get my mind occupied on other things and after Libby had finished with telling me about every client at work and moved on to what morning sickness was like, I was very close to forgetting my other worries. I was, however, grateful to her for leaving this last part until I had fully finished the sandwich she had brought up for me.

The day passed too quickly and as the night approached, I was starting to dread the evening even more. RJ had called to check it was still on and that brought comfort to know that I wasn't going to be alone in this. The whole gang was meeting us and if I was lucky I could just palm Justin off with RJ, who let's face it, didn't exactly mind any male company. I started to get ready when I heard Frank and Justin come in and Frank's usual first question was about food…after Libby's health of course, which consisted of,

"How's my two babes doing?"

Frank had become obsessed with what Libby was now allowed to do and not do. The other day, I heard him telling her off because she was standing on the bed trying to change the quilt cover. He told her, as sternly as I had ever heard him that she was not allowed to do these type of things again until the baby was born. And that she now had two people he cared for to think about. Of course, my sister thought this was not only wonderful, as she hated doing laundry, but she quickly added anything else she hated doing to the 'no-can-do pile'. This quickly included dusting, cleaning bathrooms and ironing. Only what harm can come from standing over a board, moving one arm back and to I wasn't quite sure.

I quickly found myself stood in front of the mirror arguing with myself, as to whether Sophia's choice of outfits had been a good one. I was happy with the colours at least…or more like the lack of colours. Shades had always looked better on me. It wasn't the top that was the problem. No this was both comfortable and warm. It was the tight trousers that concerned me.

They hugged my skin like liquid tar, showing every curve on my bottom half. I tugged down the sweater tunic but unfortunately it didn't come down to my knees like I would have preferred. It passed my cheeks but only just. I made a loud tut and said,

"Ah, to Hell with it," before turning away from the mirror.

I had done my hair a little differently too, deciding I didn't want to look as though I was just there to do another shift. I twisted each side back into a low ponytail and let my waves hang loose. Only today they looked more like curls than waves due to it still being damp from this morning's shower. The shorter bits framed my oval face and I couldn't help but keep tucking them behind my ears. I had also added the slightest touch of mascara and clear lip gloss to 'enhance what was already there' in Libby's words.

I was now ready, but I hadn't yet seen Justin. It was strange to know there was another person staying in the house but it was only for one night and I would no doubt be staying at the club, so what did it matter. Justin was staying in one of the guest rooms on the floor below and I could hear footsteps directly below my room. I stayed up there for as long as I deemed acceptable beyond the point of being rude.

I grabbed my bag and phone before turning off my light to make my way downstairs but of course in true Keira fashion, I missed the last step onto the next landing and stumbled into the wall. I was just straightening up when I could feel myself being watched. I looked up to find Justin dripping wet, with only a towel covering his lower half. Oh my!

It seemed Justin had changed somewhat since Libby and Frank's wedding. Age had granted him with a well-toned body and sun-kissed skin. There were fine lines defining his washboard stomach and a trail of light blonde hair travelled down amongst where the towel was covering. I couldn't help scanning over his features with my cheeks ablaze.

His dreadlocks were different lengths but all looked like golden snakes following his every movement, like a master. Some had metal bands around with different symbols etched in the centres. There were also a few wooden beads here and there that matched the numerous beads tied around his wrists. There were other bracelets as well that cried out well-travelled surfer dude but right now it was hard to focus on anything with the grin he was now sending my way.

"Well, hello gorgeous, looking for me?" His tone shouted confidence but the wink he added at the end screamed cocky. I rolled my eyes making him laugh at me. He reached into the cupboard and grabbed another towel to hang around his neck, catching the drips that were clinging to his skin. That's when I noticed a huge deep scar that ran down one shoulder and disappeared into the underside of his arm. He noticed me staring but I looked away before I could judge his reaction.

"I'll meet you downstairs," I said in a shy voice as I made my way past but just as I came closer, he shook his head so that droplets of water flew around him like little fruit flies around grapes. They sprayed me and I giggled.

"Oi… Behave!" I warned in a less than threatening tone and then added a little punch on the arm. It instantly took me back to Draven earlier and the smile I wore, Justin misinterpreted. I was surprised to find his slender arms as solid as rock under weathered skin.

"I'll be down in a minute, just once I check I got all the trout out of my hair!" he joked as he watched me go down to the living room. There I found Frank still wearing his fishing gear, including a hat with tackle clung to the rim. His face was windswept red, and Justin was right, he smelled like fish. He started to tell me all about his day, just as Libby came in with two mugs of tea and one coffee for Frank (the non-tea drinker in the family).

"You look nice, is that new?" Libby nodded my way and I couldn't help but fumble out a semi lie. The last thing I wanted was to admit that Draven was now buying me clothes, let alone a whole new wardrobe.

"Bor…borrowed… from Sophia." She frowned as though she didn't believe me but I quickly switched the conversation around and asked her if she knew when B day was going to be. Of course, B day was code for 'Bitch day', in other words, when our dreaded cousin Hilary was going to be descending on us all like a plague. She pulled a face like it was sour milk she was drinking, and I was sure I saw a shiver crawl up her back.

"She enters our life and the misery begins next week."

"Be nice, honeybee," Frank said without dragging his eyes from the ice hockey game that was on replay.

"That was being nice, trust me, I could say far worse," she stated and I couldn't help but laugh at the sentiment that we both shared. There was a whole book on what I could say but more than half of it would have to be bleeped out.

She was the essence of evil and would make a perfect match for Lucius. The trouble that girl had landed me in over the years was of epic proportions and above all…unforgivable! Stealing boyfriends was only the tip of the iceberg but at spreading rumours, she was the titanic disaster.

She had once told an entire year of my school that the reason I had a large chest was due to an overdose of hormones I had to take because I was really born a boy, but my parents wanted another girl to save on buying me new clothes. Of course, this didn't help when I would borrow some of my sister clothes, adding fuel to the gossip fire.

By the time Justin came down, Libby and I were sat in the kitchen talking about who we would rather have staying at the house, these included Terminator, the evil doll Chucky, the Joker from Batman and Jason, hockey mask and all.

Justin cleared his throat to get our attention causing us to both turn at the same time. There our eyes met with him leaning casually in the door frame. For once he looked smart in a tight black shirt, even if the sleeves were rolled up to show strong-looking forearms, due to years of throwing a board around the sands of the earth, no doubt.

His wrists, as usual were covered in beads and leather ties but now with an added thick leather strap that was edged with a metal zip. His hair was different too, instead of hanging down around his face like vines from the jungle it was tied back and knotted with pieces of dreads. It was now that you could see his handsome face clearer and the sun-induced freckles added to his charm. His long legs carried him well in stonewashed jeans that had little tears at the knees and pockets.

"So, are you ready for our date?"

I grabbed the black leather boots Libby had lent me and tugged them on. I walked over to the door, realising they made me a little taller when opposite Justin but when I tried to pass him his arm blocked my way, leaning across the frame. I turned to him and said in a low voice,

"It's not a date." But his cocky smile told me he'd been expecting my response because before he let me pass he replied,

"Aww, don't kill the dream honey." Then he lowered his arm and followed me to the door where I was putting on my jacket. Libby had now joined Frank and perched herself on the arm of the chair her husband occupied.

"Have fun!" Frank said cheerfully, like we were off to the prom or something.

"Right kids, no candy after ten o'clock, no necking on the

couch and no scary movies, unless it's Jaws of course." Libby laughed and Frank sighed at his brother's humour, making me do the same until he added the next bit. This made my pulse quicken and Draven's angry face flash from my memories as Justin winked at his brother and said,

"Don't wait up!"

CHAPTER TWENTY-EIGHT

PISTOLS AT DAWN

All the way to the club I had been on edge and it wasn't only down to my passenger. I hadn't seen Ragnar outside and kept expecting him to pop up in my rear-view mirror. I knew I didn't have to worry about Justin seeing him because he was still invisible to everyone else, but I knew I wouldn't be able to help my reaction. Also, I was pretty sure Justin would class me as a mental case if I just screamed for no reason. Although, this idea did have its advantages, it might have stopped him flirting every time he opened his mouth.

Then I saw them...headlights with a strange red glow that Justin didn't seem to notice. They flashed once and I knew I was being followed but Justin didn't have a clue. The black car behind looked as huge and intimidating as its driver did and it had me gulping at the sight. And it didn't help that the closer we got to Afterlife, the more I kept thinking I was playing with fire and tonight I would see a Demon throw sparks.

"What you thinking about?" Justin was staring at me with confusion plastered across fine cheekbones. What should I say... 'Um, well actually I'm kind of hoping my boyfriend doesn't rip your head off and give it to his pet bird to play with.' In the end I said,

"Just college stuff." Which I could tell he didn't buy.

"So, will I get to meet my rival tonight, or will he let me have you all to myself?" He laughed lightly at the end, but I just growled and looked in my mirror tensely, praying that they could only see us and not hear us.

"You shouldn't joke...I'm taken and that means there's a no flirting rule," I said sternly but when I looked from the road to his face, I gathered I was just playing right into his hands by responding.

"Who said I was joking? Besides, I don't know how not to flirt...not with you anyway." I was expecting him to be wearing a cocky smile when he said this but the serious tone and glance out of the window, I wasn't expecting. Thankfully, the conversation turned to light-hearted tales of his expeditions around the world and I found myself hanging on his every word. I couldn't help myself. It was a mixture of the subject of travelling that was close to my heart and the fact that he was so damn charismatic.

He had just finished his story on helping baby turtles get to sea after just being hatched, when we pulled up outside the vast ivy-covered building that was both work and home to me. It made me wonder what my life would have been like without this place. If I had never come to Afterlife that night, never found a job here, what would have become of me? I would have probably been dating Jack and playing it safe by now and instead of worrying about a supernatural King's reaction, I would just have the usual mundane human reactions...shouting, pushing and maybe a fistfight to be broken up by security.

No, instead I had the image of Draven in his Demon form demanding power from Heaven and Hell, two large blades protruding from his hands all aglow and ready for action. A mighty roar into the night before striking his victim to the sound of my screaming. Yeah, something like that.

I took a deep breath and got out of my truck, slamming the door a little too hard for big blue. I couldn't help but say "sorry" out loud which made Justin chuckle.

"That's adorable."

"Shut up," I said playfully before hitting him on the arm, which he then placed around my shoulders and gave me a squeeze.

"Don't look so worried doll, just a bit of harmless fun… drinking, dancing…"

"Demons," I whispered under my breath.

"Sorry?"

"Oh, nothing," I said looking nervously around in case Ragnar was seeing him with his arm around me. The car behind had turned down the side of the building and out of sight but it didn't mean that no one was out there in the dark watching.

My heart started to sound like Dave Grohl playing the drums as the thought entered my head. I shrugged out of his hold and nodded to Jo and Cameron, the doormen. Of course, knowing Frank they knew Justin so instead of being stood out in the cold for another ten minutes chatting, I left him there and said I'd meet him at the bar.

Once inside, I felt that usual euphoria wash over me whenever I stepped through the doors. Like a magnetic pull or a drug that I didn't know I had swallowed as I entered. I had felt the same feeling the first night and it had remained that way ever since…the feeling that I belonged and the building knew it. I don't know why but every day it seemed to get stronger, especially since the Temple incident. Maybe it had acted like an amplifier.

The club was in full force and with bodies everywhere there wasn't an inch of space. Some looked clung together by the tight black clothes and matching pale faces, supporting heavy made-up eyes. When I first started I thought it was all very intimidating but now I knew what was upstairs, these lot looked like pet kittens playing under a tiger's cage.

I pushed my way past a couple that looked recently risen from the grave and with the evil stares I received they could have been zombies after my flesh. Who knows, in this place it could be possible for looks to kill, after all there was only one rule in Afterlife, no humans in the VIP…

So what exactly did that make me?

The bar wasn't as packed as everywhere else due to the band that was playing. It was a heavy gothic band with a girl as its lead singer. The soft sound from her lips then shocked me as she started to scream out the last few lines of what I assumed to be a chorus. Actually, the beat wasn't that bad and the crowd was enjoying themselves which freed up the bar. Mike was working and unfortunately Cassie the 'Goth Barbie' was collecting glasses. Jerry was also serving but Mike saw me first.

"Hey cutie, who gave you the night off? Ah, don't tell me, I think I can guess." He was smirking the whole time which told me he was pulling my leg.

"You know I don't work Saturdays, but what a shame your biggest fan does." I nodded to Cassie who was collecting only two glasses at a time.

"Thanks for reminding me, you've now destroyed an illusion I had been working on all night."

"So who was she this time...Jessica Biel or Jessica Alba?" He laughed at how well I knew him and just as he put my usual Corona with lime in front of me, he answered,

"Neither, smarty pants." I raised my eyebrows and put up a hand.

"Wait, don't tell me...I got this one...Umm... Sarah Michelle Gellar!" I could tell with his face I'd guessed right. Cassie was a grade-A pain in the ass who loved Mike and practically humped his leg whenever she got the chance, so I came up with the idea of blocking her out by pretending she was someone else. I doubted he actually did it but it was still something we joked about every time we saw each other.

"Hold on, here comes Buffy now."

"Actually, I preferred her in Cruel Intentions." He winked at me and just as she came up to the bar I whispered,

"Yeah, but that's only because she kisses a girl."

"Argh, gross! Who kissed a girl?" Cassie asked but not without the disgusted look my way. She probably thought I was a lesbian now and it would soon be around the club that I was cheating on Draven with some out of town Cyber chick.

The Dravens' prolonged stay was still generating an array of unusual tourists that travelled miles just for one night at Club Afterlife and maybe a glimpse of its famous Gothic millionaire.

Unfortunately, the drama and gossip of the town was still about me dating Draven. I think there was even one rumour the other day that I was pregnant and just saying it was his because I wanted his money. I had laughed until tears developed when RJ had told me. But I wasn't hurt by all these rumours. It came with the territory when dating the town's most influential man and besides, I knew the truth and that's all that mattered.

Of course, it caused a little friction at work to begin with but soon they just seemed to accept it was now a part of me and when I disappeared upstairs, it was as if I was forgotten about. On the shifts when I worked in the VIP, I would walk past without a word spoken to me, but on the shifts when I worked down here then it was as though nothing had changed. I was now two different people to everyone else but I was still the same person inside. It had bothered me in the beginning, that I couldn't have it both ways but I soon realised there was no other way it would work…it was them that had changed, not me.

"Oh my, oh my." Cassie was muttering to me which was odd in itself. Her killer instincts had kicked into overdrive and she was now fixated on Justin, who was walking this way.

"Move out of my way, my future husband just walked in and he's looking this way, oh and try not to speak, I don't want him running off." She budged me out of the way to stand in front of me. I wanted to laugh out loud but refrained. I didn't want to crush her dreams as soon as they had been created. Besides, this was going to be far too entertaining to watch.

Justin sure did attract attention even if he did look like a fish out of water. He was trying to look around for me and I had to wave behind Cassie's back. This was like giving a diabetic keys to the sweet shop because Cassie thought he was coming for her. He was now stood in front of us both trying to get to me.

"Hi, looking for someone 'cause my name's Cassie and I can be your someone." She flashed her white teeth under murderous red lips that were closer to hooker than hottie. She then added a girly hair flick, which ending up hitting me in the face with bleached blonde hair that even smelled like peroxide.

"Hey Cassie, I'm Justin and I've found who I'm looking for

thanks." He was trying to be polite but she didn't even flinch.

"Yeah, well why don't you tell her you've found me and let's me and you go party, I'm off in twenty minutes." At this he lost his gentlemanly patience and held her by the shoulders and moved her to the side to reveal an amused me behind which brought his smile back.

"Sorry kid, I play in the big leagues and I've found what I was looking for." He finished it with a wink at me, which sent Cassie over the edge. She went scarlet to the dark roots and huffed off shouting "dog" over her shoulder but Justin just replied with a "Woof, Woof" even though I think it was mainly aimed at me.

"Well, she was pleasant… Not!" he said before ordering a rum and coke.

"You just met the slut of Afterlife and survived, congrats," I said causing a warm smile to replace the cocky one.

We were only there a few minutes when a familiar pink head could be seen amongst the crowd. Boy, for such a little thing she couldn't half push her way through a room full of dancing bodies. She came bounding up to me so I met her halfway, where she gave me a huge hug, momentarily forgetting Justin.

She was wearing a ripped black tank top with net sleeves. This was matched with a pink tartan tutu skirt and tartan boots on top of fishnet tights that had seen better days. Her hair had grown out a bit, but the roots were now dyed red, so each pink spike now looked like it was bleeding into her skull.

"Nice hair," I commented and her eyes lit up with the compliment.

"You like? And who said red and pink clash. You look cute as usual but wait…what is this, doth my eyes deceive me?" She said this in a posh, old fashioned English accent (or at least tried to) before carrying on,

"Are you Keira, our innocent English rose, wearing the tightest black jeans I have ever seen?"

"No…so don't make me regret them…okay?" I said in a low voice and she just nodded, understanding my code.

"Mum's the word, old chap." She did it again and at this rate if she persisted to keep up the accent then I would have to teach her a few things, like for one not all English people sounded like Sherlock Holmes.

"So, what do we have here then, what did you bring me?" She motioned towards Justin with her netted hand and I turned to see him waiting for us. She giggled at the sight and as we walked over there, I heard her behind me saying,

"Yum, Yum."

"Justin, this is my very good friend RJ, RJ this is who I was telling you about." I thought I had introduced them properly, but I think Justin got the wrong idea.

"Keira, have you been telling people about me, you little minx?" He held a handout to RJ like something from a period drama on the BBC. I don't know why but Mr Wickham sprang to mind. He was being the perfect gentleman as we all chatted at the bar about what Justin had been up to the past few years.

"But if you're only a few years older than Keira, didn't you finish college?" SHIT! I hadn't thought about that, they all still thought I was twenty-one, not twenty-three. Of course, Justin knew what had happened to me as it would have been hard for Frank not to explain why he had to come over to England to console his wife. His family had been great in not disclosing this bit of information to anyone else and although Justin didn't know all the gruelling details, he still knew.

"Ah well... my parents didn't mind me taking some time out on account of being a free spirit and all. I'll go back, but only when I'm finished with travelling." He carried on but I was just thanking my lucky stars that Justin had been so cool with lying. If that had been me, I would have been busted Disney style and my big conk would have probably poked her eye out. But Justin was obviously a pro in this line of work.

By the end of his third story about helping out the locals, I think RJ was in love and ready to run away with him to become a world healing surfer, living in huts and mothering abandoned monkeys while making vegan meals for hungry locals.

"So do you like the band?" RJ was asking Justin, as I saw one of the friendliest faces on the planet coming towards us. Jack's messy hair flopped about in the crowd and a couple of girls dressed like vampire dolls drooled as he went past. His smile lit up my face as he approached and I couldn't help but laugh at his t-shirt that was black and the white lettering said, "Guns don't kill people, Zombies do" and the word Zombies was painted in fake dripping blood.

"Nice t-shirt," I said as he gave me a big bear hug.

"I wore it for you, knew you'd like it considering you work in a Gothic nightclub. Cute top, by the way." He gave me a great big grin that I expected most of the room could see. Meanwhile Justin had stopped listening to RJ and was staring at us. You could feel the heat from his glare and it made us both turn round at the same time.

"Oh, sorry dude, you must be Justin." Jack extended his hand and Justin slapped his own into it with an edge of aggression.

"And you? Sorry, Keira hasn't spoken about you." I blushed and felt like pulling out one of Justin's ribs and hitting him with it for being so rude.

"Oh, this is just my brother, Jack."

"Geez, thanks sis, that's real heartfelt." Jack hit a fist to his chest and joked about being the more mature one of the two. I quickly turned to RJ trying to disperse some of the tense atmosphere that was far too thick for me and asking,

"So, what's the band's name?"

"The Happy Yellow Stains, they're okay but the next band is called 'TCTF' and they rock." She then got Jack's attention and drank from an imaginary cup, her way of asking for a drink. He rolled his eyes at me and shouted for Mike who was trying to get away from Cassie at the time, so he seemed more than pleased about his reason for escape.

"What does 'TCTF' mean?" I asked when I really wanted to ask if it meant 'Tactless conversations to friends', but I swallowed that one and waited for my answer which was in no way what I was expecting.

"This Clown Tastes Funny."

"Sorry?" I thought she had just randomly told me something from a dream but no, that had been the answer. I hadn't heard anymore because a vibrating in my bag told me that I had a message. I fumbled in the side pocket and half answered Jack at the same time,

"Yes thanks," I said to the offer of a drink, but I noticed Justin had made it a point of ordering me one first and he slid the bottle my way. Jack just shrugged his shoulders and told Mike his order minus one Corona. I now had my phone in my palm and flipped it open to a message from an unknown number.

'Did you think it a wise choice to dress so sexy when surrounded by drooling boys, while your boyfriend looks on?'

OMG! Not only was he watching me but he was now texting me!

"Anyone I know? Or someone I wanna know?" RJ said trying to look at my phone which I was now clasping to my chest and turning rosy red.

"It's no one, just Libby." She wasn't convinced and laughed, saying,

"Yeah, right.", then she carried on talking to Justin. Next thing I knew my phone was vibrating in my sweaty hand making me nearly drop it.

'Nobody is it? Well, why don't you meet this nobody upstairs and we can discuss what colour your cheeks have blushed to?'

I couldn't help the smile that crept across my face like a deflowered maiden.

"Loverboy calling?" Justin said in a flat tone that had taken my smile to heart. Jack frowned but said nothing. And RJ nudged me and said,

"Bootie call."

I ignored them all and text back with a shaky hand.

'Is this who I think it is using modern technology to arrange a date? K xx'

I sent it and tried to listen to the conversation, but it was hard when I kept looking over my shoulder to where his shadow might be or for the phone to light up, letting me know I had a message back. I had been smart enough to put it on silent and vibrate. Sure enough seconds later it was glowing in my hand.

'Come to me and I'll show you what I can do without this phone in my hand. D xxx'

I gulped and bit down on my lip. I wanted to say goodbye and run for the stairs as quick as my legs could carry me, but I knew my guilt would be overwhelming, so I sent the text that I knew he wouldn't like…the one telling him no.

'I can't, not yet anyway but I promise I will see you later
Love K xxxx'

I really wanted to say 'See you in two shakes of a lamb's tail' but I knew I would be doing the wrong thing, so I flipped the phone shut and instead of sulking, I plastered on a smile and joined in with the conversation.

The others then arrived and Jack got Chaz's attention. We went over to sit in a booth. Justin made a beeline for me and ended up in between me and RJ. Jack then sat opposite me and gave me a smile that said, 'I feel your pain'. I mouthed a 'thank you' at him when no-one was looking. The night seemed to drag on and on, which made it near impossible to relax, knowing I still had hours until I could give in to what I really wanted to do.

"So where is the Prince of Darkness this evening?" Lanie asked as she snuggled up to Drew, who she had started dating not long after I had arrived here. Drew was RJ's best friend from childhood, so she'd had a few issues when she had found out and took a while to adjust but thankfully, she was now cool with it.

"Yeah, are we too beneath him to warrant an introduction?" Justin said spitefully and Jack's peaceful face turned deadly, but I butted in before anyone could say anything.

"Below the belt there Justin, he knows that I'm having a night with my friends and he doesn't want to intrude, that's all."

"Yeah and it's nice that he's been letting the bar give us all free drinks all night," Lanie said as she pushed her glasses back up her nose and looked to Drew for back up. But it was Jack who spoke up for him.

"Yes, he has and if I were you I would judge on what you know rather than on what you clearly don't!" Jack and Justin then had a staring match, which if I could've had money on, I would have picked Jack every time. His 'boy next door' charm had turned into something protectively lethal.

"Chill out Bro, he was just kidding around, weren't you Justin?" RJ came in and saved the day and when Justin didn't respond, she nudged him and gave him a look to back down.

"Sure, why not?" he said dipped in smugness. Okay, so Jack and Justin would never be sporting buddies but Justin didn't strike me as the type who shared his toys or conquests, which incidentally was what he classed me as. Not long after, I got up to use the bathroom and RJ came with me.

"Okay, so what was all that about?" she asked as soon as the other girls had left the bathroom. We both stood at the basins that were covered in expensive gold leaf and held up with twisted iron. The gilded mirror showed two very different friends having a discussion about two very different boys.

"I don't know what Justin's problem is, but it's not about Jack."

"Well durr, it's about Dominic Draven that's who! Oh, come on Keira, you can be so naïve sometimes. It obvious that Justin's got a major thing for you and the Dark Prince is in the way."

"I wish people would stop calling him that."

"Are you kidding, that's the shortened version, it's normally 'The Dark Prince of Hotness' but we shorten it out of respect." I couldn't help but laugh.

"Look, I know you will hate me for saying this but he kind of has a point, he has never come down to meet us…I mean, don't get me wrong, it's not like I'm expecting him to come down and kick it with us or anything but it would be nice to at least meet the guy." What could I say to that? If they only knew the truth, would they want to meet him then? I was about to answer when a noise from one of the cubicles startled us.

"Is someone…?" Just before RJ could finish, a girl emerged from behind a door and came to stand next to us. I knew instantly it was Draven. There was a flash of purple that RJ couldn't see, and my heart dropped. Had he heard everything? I started to replay our conversation over and over like a broken record that was now counted as evidence.

The girl finished washing her hands and I looked over to RJ who was putting on another layer of thick black lines under and above her eyes when something happened. The water that I had been running stopped…no that's not quite right, it hadn't just stopped but it froze.

It was as if this was a video being played and someone just hit the pause button. I looked to my right and RJ had frozen, still holding the eyeliner close to her lid. She was pulling a funny face like most girls do when trying to straighten their faces so that the makeup would somehow be applied better.

I then turned slowly to my left and found that only me and the girl were running in true time.

"Ah, crap!" I said making the girl laugh.

"Hi, Keira," the girl said sweetly, and I knew Draven was having far too much fun with my reaction.

"Hi," I said with an unimpressed edge to my voice and this just made the poor vessel Draven was using smile.

"If I was you, sweetheart, I would check my phone, you never know who wants… you…your attention." She corrected herself or was it he corrected himself?

"Draven you can't jus…" I started to object to him being here but by the time I turned back to face him, the girl was gone.

"Hey, are you ok?" RJ asked back in full swing of real-time and full of concern at my pale, confused face.

We finished in the bathroom and made our way through the crowd when I decided to hang back and check my phone…

'Don't keep me waiting Keira, or I will have to come and get you. See you soon. Dominic x'

GULP!

CHAPTER TWENTY-NINE

COMING TO GET ME

I was still in shock that he had gone to those lengths just to get my attention. RJ kept looking behind her making sure I hadn't got lost in the crowd. Bless her, she didn't know my half functioning state was due to just meeting my boyfriend in the girl's toilets in the form of a blue-haired nineteen-year-old girl with braces and furry boots.

I think that one would throw anyone off their game. I kept walking towards the booth but jumped when a hand came out of a bunch of dancing bodies which turned out to be my friends. The hand belonged to Justin, who was determined to make me stay and dance.

"Hey, there you are. I was looking for you." I was about to pull my arm away and walk back to the booth where Jack and Chaz were still chatting, but he gripped me tighter.

"Dance," he urged but I was still mad at him for being a jerk.

"Why, have you grown up in the past ten minutes?" I asked sarcastically.

"Look, I'm sorry about before, I was being a Jackass…forgive me?" He started to plead with hands together praying but when I didn't respond he made it worse by getting on his knees in front of everyone. This was causing a scene, so I grabbed his arm and pulled him up.

"*Okay, ok, but just one dance.*" I found myself whispering it, as if it would somehow help. I could tell he wanted to dance one on one, but I made it a group effort which thankfully RJ understood and got in between us as much as she could. I would have to remember to thank her later. Unfortunately though, it didn't last long enough to warrant thanks as she was quickly distracted by a tall Goth in army boots and a hacked off look. She went in for the kill and left me and Justin to dance with the couple, Lanie and Drew, who were currently making out.

"So, how did I do?" He leaned in to ask, sending over a whiff of aftershave mixed with saltwater that smelt so fresh you could have almost swam in it.

"Huh?" I said looking around only half-listening.

"You know… earlier, when I covered up my age."

"Oh that, yeah that was great…I'm mean really great. I guess I should have warned you that no one here really knows about me, well apart from Jack that is." His smile quickly turned sour at the mention of his new nemesis.

"Oh, that surprises me." He tried to play it cool, but I was having none of it.

"What's that supposed to mean?" I asked with a distinct protective tone that made my voice deeper.

"Just that he doesn't strike me as the type you could trust, but it could be his ulterior motive keeping him quiet." This actually made me stamp my foot and the look he gave me made me feel like I was an endearing spoilt little girl, which didn't help my mood.

"You don't know anything about him! And while we're on ulterior motives, what exactly are yours, why are you playing this game? I just don't understand."

"Isn't it obvious? I don't want to upset you, Keira, I really don't, but it's so frustrating being around you when all I want to do is…" He never got to finish his sentence because every person in the room was now staring at us making his words die away into the club's atmosphere. Even the music had ceased, making the only noise gasps from excited onlookers.

I turned to see RJ showing her tonsils as her mouth hung to her chin. She wasn't the only one sporting this look and finally I looked in the direction everyone else was fixated on, only to find myself doing the same thing. The only face that didn't match the rest of the room was Justin's… oh and a Demon's.

"Excuse me while I just steal my girlfriend away." Draven's powerful voice cut through the whispering room like a judge delivering his sentence. I found I had forgotten how to breathe, along with every other girl in the club. Justin looked like a little boy in the sandbox after being pushed down by the bigger kid. Meanwhile Draven barely even acknowledged his existence, which just made Justin's hate burn with an even brighter flame.

He didn't wait for his answer but instead took me gently by the arm and led me to the bar, along with every eye in the building. I don't know how but I knew Sophia was watching all this from above and giggling her little Demon heart out. He only looked back once to stare at the band, which quickly started back up again as though being secretly commanded to do so. This seemed to break the spell and once again everyone in the room began to dance to the new club beat.

Once we got to the bar Draven only had to nod at Mike to get him to move into action. Jerry quickly ran to his side and was about to take over, when Draven spoke.

"Mike, isn't it?" Mike, bless him, could only manage a jerky head bob in return. Jerry backed away, taking Draven's look as code and therefore letting Mike serve us.

"The lady would like a coke and I will have a Corona." He ordered the drinks with ease and perfect manners, not like I was used to seeing in the VIP. Don't get me wrong, he was never rude but there was always a clear-cut masterful tone with everything he ordered, although now he was acting like just another regular. Except he wasn't fooling anyone. Everyone in here knew who he was. You could see the gossip travelling around the club like a freight train.

Mike brought our drinks over, only mine had lost a bit on the way due to trembling hands which made a little tune from the ice tapping against the glass.

"Thank you. Now be sure to get one for yourself."

"Yes…Sir, Thank you…Mr Draven…Sir," he stammered out before moving to the other end of the bar to breathe.

"Cheers," Draven said tapping the side of my glass with the bottleneck. I had never seen him drink a bottle of beer before, so it looked a little foreign in his large hand. He wore an amused look, by which I could tell that he was enjoying my shock. He leaned into my ear and moved a stray piece of hair before whispering his thoughts, or more like mine.

"*You didn't think I would actually do it, did you?*" His cheeky smile made my heart flutter and I smiled with him.

"No, I didn't but I'm glad you did."

"Why, did you miss me on your date with the human boy?" he teased and I bit my lip.

"Firstly, you know it wasn't a date and secondly…I always miss you." At this he did something unthinkable in front all these people and I didn't know whether I wanted to cry out with shame or bliss. He had grabbed the back of my head with one palm and turned it aside to kiss me. The whole room seem to gasp at the same time making it sound like a surge. The kiss left me breathless.

"Ah, that's better. Now you'd better introduce me to your friends because the pink one is trying to refrain from running to the bar just to shake my hand." He turned just in time to look down at RJ, who looked close to hyperventilating.

"And you must be RJ?" His smooth tone had her instantly hypnotised into falling in deep and it took me back to the days when I had felt the same. It was like being pulled under the waters of a dark lagoon and knowing that you should try and swim to the surface but just don't want to…you just wanted to drown in him.

"Y…You know my…name?" she snorted out like she was meeting a celebrity.

"Keira has told me all about you and being one of her closest friends, I'm sorry I haven't met you sooner." Oh jeez, that did it, now she wanted his babies! For once she was speechless which was a monumental day in itself. That along with a Draven coming down to spend time with the common folk.

"Oh, that's alright, Keira had said how busy you were, and we all appreciate all that you do for our little town." I don't know why but her eyes kept fluttering like something was in them. Anyway, this had quickly become a change of tune as it wasn't long ago she was singing to Justin's little jealous beat. Now what? Had she joined cheerleader for the Dravens of Afterlife?

"Can I get you a drink?"

"That's very kind…thank you." Ok, this was getting weird now, like pod people had come and switched RJ with a quiet, polite, carbon copy just to try and impress Draven, their leader. Draven was clearly waiting to find out what form of liquid she wanted but she just stood there looking up like he was her new Gothic God.

"Bloody hell RJ, this is the part where you tell him what you want to drink," I said with a little overload on the attitude. I just couldn't help it, she was acting like someone I had never even met, a band groupie I could take but sister Rachael Jane, soon to join the church becoming the first Goth fairy nun…Oh no!

Draven looked down at me as if I was the one acting out of character, but I ignored him as what I had said seemed to have taken effect.

"Alright snappy McGee! What are you drinking then?" Hail Mary, she was back. I smiled and shook my coke in answer.

"Well, that's not much fun," she noted and had undeniably relaxed enough to drop the innocent act in front of Draven.

"No, but neither is getting wrapped around a tree…I'm driving remember."

"She wouldn't understand that, seeing as I'm the responsible one in the family," Jack said as he came up behind her, seeing us on his way to the bathroom. He laid two hands on either side of her shoulders as he spoke, and I was expecting there to be animosity in his tone, but he seemed his usual happy self even though he was now faced with Draven.

"Mr Draven," he said adding a nod in his direction, making me think tonight I had somehow entered the Twilight Zone. Ok, now it was official, Draven was extending his hand to him and saying,

"Please call me Dom, Jack," meaning I was in the Twilight zone. The kind where everyone is happy and getting along with one another. I was just about close to singing the Sound of Music, Julie Andrews's style when my bliss-filled cup smashed to the floor with the sight of Justin stomping his way over. I think Draven and Jack both frowned at the same time. I mean could this night get any weirder.

"So, this is the famous Dominic Draven then?" Justin spat out, making the cool exterior he was trying for look like a puddle of misery. It was funny then, that Jack was the one to react first and slapped him on the back while saying,

"Sure is buddy and Dom, this here is Justin, he's just such a swell guy," he said sarcastically before giving a respectful nod to Draven and walking off into the crowd. Meanwhile Justin looked like he was about to turn red from rage and start choking on his tongue.

"Well, we didn't think you were going to show up… did we Kazzy?" This wasn't helping my mental health I will tell you. No, in fact it was like wishing for an out-of-body experience just so that I could kick Justin in the shins to shut him up. What was even more surprising was that Draven seemed to be amused by the whole thing, not the eternal wrath I had been expecting.

"Ah, well that's surprising because Keira knows I always keep my word and I'm always watching over her." A little hint of the usual protective Draven burst through and Justin knew he had hit a nerve.

"A little paranoid aren't we…what's the matter? Worried someone will come and steal her away from you?"

"JUSTIN, that's enough!" I said giving him a severe scowl. But Draven merely laughed.

"I'd love to see them try for a start, but I think you missed the point. Being protective and being jealous are two very different things."

"Oh yeah, how's that then?" Justin baited.

"One is essential, the other is pointless. My protective side I welcome."

"And jealously, do you welcome that too?" It was like watching a tennis ball being flung back and to. RJ and I were in the middle, still looking from one to the other like mutes.

"No, I conquer it. Drink?" He turned abruptly to the bar and Justin foolishly looked smug as if he had won this round, but I knew differently. I was the only one who caught the purple glint of anger in Draven's eyes, that's why he had turned…to control the beast within, the beast that wanted to tear into Justin's vital organs!

"I will have a shot of something," piped up RJ and I was about to protest knowing how she gets when she has one too many, but Justin interrupted.

"I think I will join you. Draven, you game?"

"Always." The way he answered made me shiver with a hidden fear. It was the way he said it, like it was a game of life and death he was sporting. He was a chillingly lethal mix of perfect calm and Mt. Vesuvius and like the rest of Italy, nobody wants to be around when either erupted.

"So, what we having, big guy?" Justin asked with a distinctive lack of respect in the way he called him 'Big guy', as if it was meant as an insult.

"What about tequila?" I piped up trying to lighten the situation. It didn't work but it at least made Draven smile at me like I was sweet.

"I was thinking something a bit more…exotic." The smile he wore for me soon turned into one of cunning.

"Oooh, that sounds exciting." RJ clapped her hands together making the chunky metal rings clash.

"What do you have in mind?" she continued. Justin just rolled his eyes like he was bored of RJ drooling over Draven. Either that or he was jealous that he was no longer RJ's flavour of the month.

"You'll see," was all Draven offered before nodding in Jerry's direction. Thankfully for him he was at hand within a second knowing Draven was not a boss you kept waiting… for anything.

"Yes, Mr Draven, Sir."

"Jerry, can you bring me a bottle from the VIP reserve?" Jerry looked startled as if he would get caught out for saying yes. It made me wonder if he knew about the Dravens like I did. He looked terrified and let's face it, if you did know what they were, then you would be in your right mind to be scared shitless. It was a little different in my case, as I was already accustomed to their world even before I met the Dravens. Hell, maybe I was nuts, but the rest of humanity would not be so easily comforted by the idea that there were Demons and Angels feeding from their emotions.

"It's alright Jerry, proceed," he prompted, making Jerry scuttle off into the back room where he kept some of the bottles behind lock and key. It took me back to the night when I first stepped foot into the VIP. I had been given a crate of bottles to take up there and had been just as terrified as Jerry.

It didn't take him long to find the bottle Draven had asked for and I knew instantly what liquid the bottle held... Absinthe.

The bottle looked antique with a metal clasp at the top making it like a flask. The green liquid swirled around like a sea serpent trying to escape. RJ's eyes widened at the sight, but Justin just sighed.

"Absinthe, right? I had that same shit in Spain, supposed to make you lose your head, but it didn't even touch me," he boasted, but I was the only one that noticed the malicious grin flash across Draven's lips.

"Is that so? Then you should be just fine...right?" Draven taunted, looking over his shoulder at him. RJ couldn't help but giggle at the drama playing out. Meanwhile, I was ready for dropping the two egos and going home. Draven could be the bigger person here and let this all go but no, here he was pushing Justin into a game he would never win. For one Draven never got drunk and secondly, Justin was like a pit-bull with a bone, he would never back down and give it up.

Draven had acquired some glasses and flipped the clasp on the bottle top ready to pour. He gave it one last swirl before pouring out three, one a little less full for RJ. He slid it towards her saying,

"Ladies first."

"And who said chivalry was dead?" she said looking at me and I couldn't help but smile. It was surprising that a girl like RJ was a sucker for manners, given she was kind of rude to most people most of the time. However, Draven wasn't as pleasant with Justin and slid the glass down the bar which stopped right in front of him, making Draven seem like the luckiest son of a gun in the west.

I stood watching the three of them knock them back like it was water but as soon as the liquid touched the back of their throats the impulse to cough couldn't be helped. Of course, Draven remained silent, while the other two sounded like they smoked forty a day.

"Another?" Draven asked and, not waiting for their voices to return, he poured three more. I placed my hand over RJ's glass and gave him a warning look.

"Hey, I'm game," she protested and Draven gave me a wink she didn't catch. I hoped this meant that he would make hers a dummy drink so it wouldn't affect her.

"Yeah, me too, that's good stuff." Justin was trying too hard to sound convincing and Draven knew it.

"Okay, what do you say we make this a little more interesting?" he suggested and I just wanted to scream "grow up" to the both of them.

"What did you have in mind?" Justin showed just a hint of apprehension in his eyes making Draven's glint in return.

"RJ, do you want to see a little magic?" It was as if he was talking to a child and the size difference made it seem more plausible. Of course, she reacted like a child, clapping her hands again, something she always did when she was excited.

"Gonna pull a rabbit out of your sleeve, 'cause you know I've seen that one before?" Justin said adding an unimpressed expression to his slouched shoulders.

Draven ignored him and placed all three glasses in a row ready for his 'magic trick'.

"RJ, pick one." She looked at me and then back at him before pointing to the one in the middle. Draven smirked and said,

"Watch," he ordered slipping back to his masterful tone. He then leaned over and blew over the one at the end closest to himself making it begin the transformation. Three sets of wide-eyed humans, me included watched like puppets in the hands of a master.

A black cloud had emerged from deep within the emerald liquid making it turn into a black so dark it had a bluish tint. The amazing thing about the change was that it passed over the glass RJ had picked, keeping it lush bottle green colour that seem fresh in comparison to the destruction of the other two drinks. It was as though it floated through RJ's choice and hit its mark with the next, transforming it to a dark mist. Now we were all looking at two black drinks either side of one untouched.

"WOW! Now that was one hell of a trick. How in God's name did you do that?" RJ shouted and because I was at that moment taking a swig of my drink, I nearly choked on it. What she didn't realise in that question is how right on the money she had been. Draven knew of course the reason for my reaction, but he calmly just patted my back and carried on.

"Just a sleight of hand really, but please drink."

"Is it safe?" RJ asked a little timidly for the RJ character I knew, and I realised it was the first time I had seen her freaked.

"Yes, yours is no different but as for the other two, well I must warn you it can have some foul side effects if you plan on engaging in any dishonourable acts." He winked at RJ but scowled at Justin.

"Yeah right, just give it here Mr Hey Presto!" Justin reached across and downed it, trying his best not to make a gagging face with a coughing fit. RJ looked up at Draven and took note of his wicked smile at the sight of Justin, who had just downed every last drop. My stomach felt like a vat of acid had just been poured into it because I knew Draven and knew him well.

I recalled his words earlier and they swam around my head in their own little bubble making my brain ache.

'Keira knows I always keep my word,' he had said to Justin and now I wanted to repeat them, but I knew it was too late.

He had already drunk down his fate,

That's why Draven was smiling...

He had won.

CHAPTER THIRTY

DISHONOURABLE ACTS

Now, this was my dilemma. I was the one who had convinced Draven that Justin was not only to be trusted but he didn't hold any feelings for me but ones of friendship. This would all be fine and dandy if I still believed it to be the case but now, I was as sure of trouble brewing, as I was that the sun would rise tomorrow.

Draven had created this little game that would only benefit his needs. If Justin could only behave until I got him home it would work out being just a bad hangover for him in the morning. This would then provide Draven with his assurance of Justin's intentions, but this was Justin we were talking about. Oh, this was going to go terribly wrong and I would no doubt have to pick up the pieces. I just hoped they weren't body parts.

We all remained at the bar, each of us acting out the perfect example of ease and comfort, when not one of us was being himself or herself. RJ was trying her best to keep the conversation light and avoiding drama. (This was solely unlike her, I hasten to add) But at least she was doing better than me. I was nodding like a toy dog on a dashboard every time someone spoke. Of course, inside I was mentally punching myself for ever thinking this night was going to go well enough for me not to remember it for all the wrong reasons.

Justin kept up the bad boy "I don't give a shit who you are" persona but every now and again I could see a flash of the unknown when he looked deep into his enemy's eyes. Draven remained civil despite Justin's attitude but there was a definite undertone of the need to rip his head off as Draven flexed his muscles every time he spoke.

It was as if the very sound of Justin's voice was causing Draven's demon blood to flow faster. I knew this because without being able to control it I kept seeing his Demon form come to light. In the end, I had to try very hard not to keep making little gasps whenever it happened as the looks I received from both RJ and Justin were ones of worry mixed with a wary 'Is she nuts?' Then when I thought it couldn't get any worse, Justin said the unthinkable.

"Well, you know me and Keira go way back, isn't that right, Kazzy?" At this point I thought Draven would blow up because not only was Justin playing with fire with someone twice his size, he was playing with a man who could control that fire. Justin had come closer towards me and put his arm casually around my shoulders as he spoke. I just shrugged away and laughed nervously.

"Yeah, on account of Libby and Frank... you know, my sister?" I don't know who this last statement was aimed at because everyone I was looking at had sure as shit met my sister. I didn't know where to stand or to put my mouth for that matter. I ended up next to RJ trying not to look at Draven, who was glowing like Christmas.

"Of course, when I say way back, I mean we have history." Oh my God, was he trying to get himself killed! Draven looked as though he had somehow got even taller because he towered above Justin like he was getting smaller. I had to hand it to the surfer, he had the balls of a bull combined with the tact of a tidal wave and boy, he really knew how to make a bad situation worse.

"Is that so, then I think you had better elaborate, given the confused look on my girlfriend's face." Draven's voice came out in an eerie calm that went as deep as the Earth's mantle.

"Oh, I'm sure she remembers, it got pretty heated one night, but we never really gave it a go, on account of the distance thing but when Frank told me Kaz had moved here…well…"

"Well, then you just had to race back here as quickly as you could to see her again. That's very noble of you but tell me it must have been crushing for you to find her with another and no longer available for your taking." He raised his eyebrows making his eyes somehow appear deeper but before Justin could come back at him with another foolish comment Draven continued,

"Let me offer you some advice for the next conquest you have in mind. Never let oceans get in the way…A real man never would." Draven had finished his little speech with another shot finding home in the pit of an angry stomach.

"Excuse me, but I think I must have a say in these 'so-called' events." I said finding my angry voice and putting my timid one back behind lock and key.

"So-called? Oh Kazzy tell me you haven't forgotten your sister's wedding, I think she'd be disappointed to hear that?" Justin said in an over-exaggerated tone that made me want to smack that smirk off his handsome baby face!

"Yes, well, one night consisting of one kiss, when you had a girlfriend I might add, is hardly something I would call history! Besides after that day we became family so it's not even worth bringing up…"

"Family? I don't think…"

"No you don't, that's your problem! Now, I think it's time we went home before you make even more of a mountain out of a snowman!" I was really angry now and it didn't help when I saw Draven beaming at me as though I was the teacher who had told off a naughty bully. I was so tempted to just go and let these two battle it out and leave them but I would never forgive myself knowing what the outcome would be…. Draven 1- Justin 0, but with a shiny new coffin to sleep in. Plus, there was Frank to think about. I had made a promise and I was going to keep it, even if it killed me.

I turned to RJ and Draven, with close to steam coming out of my ears and they both knew it. But it was only RJ who had any sense to take my mood seriously, Draven on the other hand held a cocky smile curling up on one side and an arrogant glint to his black eyes.

"RJ, I will see you Monday, I'll pick you up at the usual time. Tell the rest I said bye." She nodded but I could tell the alcohol was starting to take effect because her eyes were glazed over as if she couldn't focus. She took this as her cue to leave first and with one last eye flutter at Draven and a scowl at bad boy Justin, she left to regroup.

"I will see you tomorrow, D," I said harshly but he looked unruffled by my lack of affection. I don't think he'd even registered that I called him 'D'. Something I had never done before, but I didn't want to call him Dominic and I wouldn't call him by his second name in front of Justin. No, that would be like filling up the tank and letting him go on all night and let's face it, the last thing Justin needed was any more fuel.

Draven didn't reply he just kept staring at Justin with this half-smile, as though he knew something the rest of the world didn't. Justin shifted his weight and found the ground with his eyes. I just rolled mine and said,

"Oh for Pete's sake!" as I walked past Draven but I didn't get far. His arm came out quicker than the breath from my lungs and in a moment the lights went out plunging the club into total darkness. I looked around after sounding my surprise and just as the rest of the club began to ask the obvious questions, Draven circled his arms around my waist before his hands pulled up my top to get to the skin on my back. I gasped again, only this time it finished inside his mouth that felt on fire. His kiss was passionate and full to the brim of want. I could hardly breathe in his crushing hold, but it didn't stop me from entwining my hands behind his neck.

After moments of bliss his lips left mine, giving me one last lick to my top lip before I opened my eyes. I expected to find the same darkness I had closed them to, but instead the room was lit even brighter and every eye seemed to be fixated on the two lovers at the bar. Justin could barely keep his mouth closed, let alone keep the utter disappointment from his face.

One look from Draven told me this had all been planned and he knew if no one could see us I would give it my all back. He had been right and that was what he wanted Justin to see. Mission accomplished! I was fuming inside but knew I couldn't show it in front of Justin. I was now sick to death of this game the two of them had me playing and for the first time since I'd met Draven, I didn't want to look at him!

Instead of saying goodbye again I just grabbed Justin's hand and dragged him to the front entrance leaving Draven at the bar. I didn't miss the evil wink and mouthed words, 'Good luck' that were directed at Justin as I pulled him past.

Once I was nearer the door, however angry I was I still couldn't help the little look over my shoulder to see if he was still staring at us. The answer was no. He was nowhere to be seen. He had just disappeared because there was no way he could have made it back through the crowd in that time. How did he get away like that with every eye in the room locked on his every move, I wondered?

Outside the cold air helped to clear my clouded mind but my anger stuck to me despite the weather. It had started to snow while we had been in the club and was quickly covering the ground with an icy blanket which would turn deadly soon enough. I had made the right choice leaving now as I didn't yet have snow chains on big blue.

I didn't look at Justin once as we snaked our way through the parked cars to get to my truck. Then Justin startled me making me turn around to his raucous laughter.

"What are you laughing at?" I asked not bothering to hide my hacked off tone.

"Just wondering if you make everyone who meets you this crazy?" That question hit me harder than I cared to admit, considering my past. After staring at him for longer than intended, I turned before he could see my eyes well up.

"Oh, no Keira, Jesus, I didn't mean it like that!" He ran over to me just as I took my next step. He gently put his hands on my shoulders to turn me round to face him.

"Look at me," he whispered and when I didn't, he placed the back of his hand under my chin.

"I'm sorry. I didn't mean to be an insensitive jerk."

"And back in there?" I nodded to the doors which we had just exited but he didn't look back.

"What I meant…what I mean is…"

"Justin, don't!" I stopped him knowing what was coming next. I didn't want to do this now. Hell, I didn't want to do this ever. The last conversation we had like this was a lifetime ago. I wasn't even the same person anymore. Back then, of course, I had been in his shoes. He had been the one with the girlfriend and he had been the one telling me it could never happen. Well, those words still rang true.

It could never happen.

"Why not, because you have some weird, possessive boyfriend who can buy you back?"

"Now that hurt," I said and pulled out of his hold.

"I didn't mean it the way you took it," he snapped back, making his hair coil around one shoulder. I stood hands on hips waiting.

"I meant it with concern. I'm worried about you. That guy in there isn't right, I don't know what it is, but I can't shake the feeling that he's…he's…"

"He's what?"

"Dangerous." He spoke the word as though he could somehow be overheard. I knew the truth and sure, sometimes it frightened me, but was it worse not knowing? What if that night had never happened and I just kept going through life working at the club, being obsessed with Draven, never to find out the truth…Would I be scared?

I didn't know what to say to him. Anything I said would end up being a lie, so I said the only thing that I knew would end this conversation... I spoke the truth.

"Justin, I love him." That looked as if I had broken him. He started to shake his head but once he saw the truth in my eyes, he stopped this motion. He let his shoulders drop and simply said,

"Okay."

"Come on, let's go home and raid the cupboards," I said light-heartedly pulling him back into the now. I automatically opened his side first before climbing into the driver's seat. Big blue was cold, and I had to give her a minute to start.

"All that money and he can't buy you a nice reliable car?" I hit him playful on the arm, just glad that he was getting back to his usual cocky self.

"I love this car so shut up before it hears you, or we will never get home."

"That's fine with me but I warn you, I get cold quickly, so you'll have to use your body heat to keep that from happening." He received another playful punch, which he caught. He held his hand over my wrist and I flinched at him being so close to my scars. He looked down and then smiled at my gloves before letting go.

"I never told anyone you know." His confession shocked me, but I couldn't respond.

"When it happened, I wanted to come and see you so badly, but I knew I couldn't. You didn't need that. You didn't need me to get involved. But I want you to know that I would have been there for you." He looked down at his tanned hands that were fiddling nervously with his belt end and it made me want to comfort him, but I couldn't move.

"I broke it off with Jessica that year because she didn't understand why I wouldn't tell her. She overheard my parents on the phone to Frank asking how you were and after that she wanted to know all the details. The stupid cow acted like it was gossip! After that I couldn't look at her. I don't know why I'm telling you this now, but I guess it's easier to express past regrets to the person you regret them with."

"Regrets?" I whispered out in a frosty breath.

"I always regretted saying no to you that night. I replayed it over and over on the plane ride home, knowing I had made the wrong choice. Your boyfriend was right in there, when he had said not to let oceans get in the way…A real man never would. I arrogantly thought that by coming back here you would be waiting with open arms to have me as your boyfriend. God how conceited am I?" At this I moved to cover his hand with mine. He was warmer than I was, and the cold touch of my fingers made him look up at me.

"I knew I never trusted that Jessica," I said making him laugh. I felt instantly better at the sound. Guilt was tearing into me, but I couldn't do anything about it. Anything I said would have been a lie to make him feel better, which I couldn't bring myself to do, knowing full well it would do more harm than good.

The rest of the way home he remained quiet and I didn't want to be the one to break into his thoughts first just so I could make myself feel better. I now wanted to take full responsibility for the way tonight had gone, but I knew deep down the reason I felt this guilt was down to him bringing up my past. I couldn't help the choices he had made and where he now stood because of them, but that didn't mean I wasn't sympathetic to them either. If anything, my mind was in more turmoil now than it had been in the club. Back then I only had Draven's actions to worry about, now it was my own actions that were the problem. What could I do to make everyone happy? I didn't want to be the cause of anyone's pain, let alone continue causing it.

Thankfully, autopilot had gotten us this far and it was only when we started to bump along the dirt gravel road that I realised we were home. I glanced towards Justin from the corner of my eye to find him still fixated on the side window. I cut the engine and sat for a minute before turning to say something.

"Justin, look I…" I stopped mid-sentence and my eyes fixated on what Justin had been looking at all this time. As soon as my brain registered what I was seeing my vision started to go foggy. Tears welled up until they became too heavy and overflowed down my cold cheeks.

"Who would do this?" Justin's voice cut through the nightmare, pulling me out of a frozen lake I was drowning in. I couldn't speak. I just kept repeating the words that were crudely plastered on my side window over and over.

I FOUND YOU
YOU CAN'T HIDE FROM ME
I'M COMING TO GET YOU
SEE YOU SOON

It looked as though it had been written on with red paint for effect. I still hadn't answered Justin. Instead, I just got out of the car and started to walk away. I couldn't handle it anymore. I had surely hit my limit and found my breaking point.

I didn't know where I was going but I soon found myself running. I just needed to get away from it all...Demons...Angels and especially Stalkers. I was terrified the price I was paying for Draven was turning into something far too deep for me to handle. I wanted to run to him and tell him everything, but every time the thought entered my head it was as though something else was pushing it back out again. Excuses that weren't my own kept clouding my resolution.

I got as far as the forest wall when Justin caught up with me, forcing me to stop and turn to look at him. Under the moonlight he bore a startling resemblance to an Angel, with his long dreads looking like roped gold and eyes pure of heart. He held me still but when I didn't respond to his words, he gave me a little shake.

"Keira, listen to me!" The panic in his voice mirrored the panic in my mind that felt like it would soon burst from me. I didn't know what to do! I couldn't tell him the truth...how could I? Who could I tell? Sophia? Vincent? NO! They would tell Draven and for these reasons my thoughts quickly shifted without result. What was wrong with me? Why couldn't I just tell him?

"Who did that? Was it him?" Justin looked furious now, but I was in shock. Did he know about Lucius?

"Who?" I asked in a shaky voice that crept up a notch.

"Who? That crazy ass boyfriend of yours, that's who! It's because he's jealous of us, isn't it? He's trying to frighten you, can't you see?" I was stunned. He thought Draven would do this... was he nuts?

"No, of course not!" I yelled at him for just thinking it, let alone confessing it.

"He's brainwashed you!"

"Justin please, you don't know him. He would never do this." I was pleading with him to believe me, but I knew his prejudice towards Draven wouldn't let himself trust in what I was saying.

"Then who did?"

"I don't know…maybe some sicko who knows about my past and gets his kicks scaring young girls." It was a long shot, but it was all I had to go with. I didn't really want to bring up my past for the second time tonight, but I was running out of options.

"And that's what you believe it is, because if you do then we should call the cops." Oh no, this was bad. What was I supposed to do now, call them and say what? 'Umm I think the Vampire King called Lucius is trying to kidnap me to get back at a Demon/ Angel half breed sent from Heaven and Hell…Oh and it just so happens he's my boyfriend!'… Uh, I don't think so somehow.

"Look Justin, you will just have to trust me here. I don't want to involve the police or anyone else for that matter. If it gets worse then I will do something about it but for now please, just be my friend." At this his anger finally subsided and I could just make out his eyes soften at my request. He still hadn't released me from his hold and after moments of praying for his trust in me, he finally gave me his answer.

"Come here," he said before pulling me in for an embrace. He wrapped his arms securely around me and I let my head rest on his shoulder. I was tired of fighting and being brave. I just wanted to feel another human emotion that was as weak and fragile as I was. I loved Draven with every breath in my body but right now…right at this moment, I just needed to feel equal. So, I shamefully allowed myself to be held and buried the immense guilt that was mounting up, deep and far away from this moment. I moved my arms and rested them on the lower part of his back while his were doing the same.

Then I couldn't help myself. I couldn't stop the tears from flowing once the first drop left my tired eyes. Soon I was sobbing. I was gasping for breath as I cried my heart out all on Justin's shirt. He moved one hand to the back of my head and stroked my hair giving me the much-needed comfort that I craved.

"Ssshh, you're alright, I've got you." It was these words that brought me back. He didn't have me, Draven did. I pulled back but Justin automatically tightened his grip around my waist. I didn't want to make it look obvious that I felt uncomfortable. I didn't want to hurt his feelings but on the other hand I didn't want him getting the wrong idea.

But it was too late. He raised his hand to wipe my salty cheeks dry but in doing so he brushed my lips with his thumb. I held my breath thinking of ways to stop this from happening. Sentences were spilling out of my mind but only one word made it past my lips.

"Please…" He took my plea for something else and moved his face closer to mine before I could stop what came next. The lips that met my own were soft but urgent. I tried to pull away, but his softness soon turned to hard pressure on my mouth. He held my neck with one hand and his other hand gripped at the material of my top, near my side. He was surprisingly strong, but my will was stronger. At the moment that he tried to force my mouth open I pushed all my weight forward like I was doing a rugby tackle, but it was only enough to move him enough to free my lips.

"NO!" I shouted making him frown in the dark and this quickly gave him a new edge as the bad boy act didn't seem too much like an act anymore. He tried again taking on a new rough approach but at this I saw red and pulled my arm back as far as it would go, before clenching my fingers into a fist and letting it fly.

"ARGGGHHH!" I knew I'd hit my mark even before I heard Justin bellow in pain. It had felt like my knuckles had crumbled like cookie crumbs. They started to throb instantly, but my anger was still keeping my adrenaline levels up for the real hurt to sink in fully.

"What did you do that for?!" He was angry but no way as angry as I was.

"Are you an idiot? I said NO, which guess what, in the world of crossing lines you just crossed a big one!" He was still nursing his jaw and a split lip that I had amazingly given him, when he decided to play the fool.

"I knew you wanted me to, you're just scared of being caught, but I am not afraid of your rich, pompous ass boyfriend…Not by a long shot!"

"Then you're a bigger fool than I took you for! You think I'm angry, just think yourself bloody lucky you only ended up with a split lip because I can guarantee you, if Draven had been here, you would have earned yourself a lot more than a bruised ego!" I raised my arms up in the air and turned my back on him walking away to think. I couldn't bear to think of what Draven would have done, but I knew one thing, I don't think all the will in the world would have stopped him from committing murder.

Justin just shook his head as if he was looking for the right words to say and I knew the argument was far from over. Or was it?

"I…I…" Justin spluttered out the words like he had them stuck in the back of his throat.

"What?" I said with my hands on my hips, but then it didn't take me long to realise something was wrong…so very wrong.

"I…I…I'm going be sick!" he said before bending over double and dropping to the floor.

"Justin!" I shouted before rushing back to his side.

It was as if his limbs had turned to mush but it didn't stop him from shaking. He was red hot to touch and I tried to soothe his back while he vomited into the undergrowth. His back would arch every time his body wanted to bring some more up but his stomach was quickly emptied, leaving him with nothing but bile to bring up. Finally, he stopped long enough to look at me, but it was as if he couldn't find me there in his sight. That's when I noticed the same black clouds that had been in those shots. Only now, they weren't in any drinks, oh no, now they were what covered both of Justin's eyes.

He put his hands out as if he was searching for something in the dark, but there was enough light from the porch lamp and moon to see clearly.

"Keira…Keira, where are you?"

That's when my heart froze.

Justin was now blind.

CHAPTER THIRTY-ONE

HEAVY IN MY ARMS

I was trying not to panic but every time I looked down and saw the picture of Justin shaking and grasping out at a world he could no longer see, then it was hard not to start screaming. I wanted to call out for help but what good would that do? This wasn't something doctors could help with and I was too ashamed to call for Frank. Justin had been my responsibility and I had let my PIG-HEADED boyfriend do this to him! And speaking of Demons, where was Ragnar all of a sudden? He hadn't left my side once since being 'assigned' to me but now he was nowhere to be seen.

That's when other worries entered my mind and the memory of the blood-red words started to burn back from my subconscious. What if we were both in greater danger? What if Draven hadn't done this to Justin? That was when I knew I had to move. I had to get us both inside as quickly as I could.

I grabbed Justin under his arm and tried to pull him up, but it was like dragging a sack of manikins around.

"Come on Justin, we have to get inside." He groaned, but my words must have taken some effect because he started to support himself to a degree. I hooked his arm around my neck to hold most of his weight, but my legs must have started to buckle because it gave him the extra strength to hold himself upright. I held onto his waistband for extra grip, which couldn't have been very comfortable for him but considering the circumstances, I think that having a mammoth wedgie was the least of his problems.

We staggered over to the steps when the porch light started to flicker.

"Justin, come on…we have to move faster, we're nearly there!" I couldn't keep the urgency out of my voice, and he knew it. He started to mount the steps two at a time and I fumbled around my pocket for the keys…Shit the KEYS! I had left them in the damn truck!

"Justin, you will have to wait here, I need to get the keys." I let him go and it was only then when I realised how much of my body weight he had been relying on, as he sacked it to the floor with a loud creaking thud.

He looked exhausted and I wished that I could somehow have transported some of my overdrive adrenaline into him.

I ran as fast as my legs could take me but just before I reached for the handle I stopped. My mind flooded with different scenarios. Could someone be watching me…waiting for a moment like this? I looked around nervously and found myself praying to see my giant guardian watching over me but instead my eyes met an eerie darkness, layered with a heavy haze of fog. I swallowed hard and opened the door which made me jump at the new sound. I was so on edge that my muscles ached from being tensed for so long.

My keys still dangled in the ignition and I kept telling myself not to look at my nightmare written on the opposite window but in the end I failed. The words were still there creating the need for my stomach to heave but somehow, they looked different, as if they were melting into new words. They followed an invisible path on the freezing glass and came to a stop when the very last drop formed the end of Draven's name.

TELL DRAVEN

I stared at my window, holding my breath in waiting. I don't know how I knew but I was certain this wasn't the end of the message. I wanted to prompt it on somehow, as if I wasn't just connecting to an inanimate object, but more like it had been possessed.

"Tell... Draven... what?" My voice shook like my body was reacting from the freezing weather, but I felt no cold. That's when it felt like the Heavens were the ones to answer me. With a flash of light the clouds opened and released their floods to the earth, drenching every inch of my clothing in seconds. I looked away from the window and up to the pouring sky, in hopes of some sort of sign. However, it was when I looked back at the window that I found my answer.

EVERYTHING!

The rain had washed most of the window clean but left bits that made up this word. Then I screamed as the window burst into a thousand pieces. It was like a firework going off and my car filled with tiny deadly shards. Thankfully, I was smart enough to cover my face, but one little piece must have slipped through because I felt a stinging to one side of my cheek. I could feel the warm blood trickle down my bitter cold skin and when I touched it there, I found a small shard embedded. I pulled it out and rubbed the blood away with my sleeve.

I felt as if time was standing still, like it does in the dream world. I was seeing things that weren't real. The rain from the sky was falling in slow motion, slow enough for me to catch individual droplets like falling tears. I had an image of Heaven crying and I was the only one who knew what was happening.

I don't know how long I stood there, motionless in my own living dreams but when the next thunderclap erupted, it brought me around enough to move. I grabbed the keys and looked at what remained of the window one last time. And one last time was all it took.

There, in the darkness, standing out like a beacon of Hell were two red glowing eyes staring back from the woods, watching this whole scene play out like a cat and mouse. I was the mouse. And being so, I ran as fast as any sane mouse would have done. I held onto the keys like a lifeline and flung myself at the door with heavy impact.

With the sound of my freaked state, Justin was encouraged to move as well and in the end all I had to do was drag him in the right direction and pull him through the door. I slammed the door shut, not caring about who I would wakeup but more concerned as to who I would be keeping out! I leant on the inside of the door and let my body slip down to the tiled floor. I joined Justin's side and let my head rest on his shoulder. He too was panting, and my head moved up and down with his anxiety.

"What was it? Why is this happening?" he whispered like the thing outside would still be there to hear us.

"I don't know why, but I will find out." What else could I say? Tell him that this could be the doings of badass Demons, rogue Angels, Vampires or even my boyfriend, the Supernatural King. What were next, Pixies, Elves and Goblins?! I didn't know if I could cope with anything else, I think at this point if I met Santa, I would have run screaming to the hills.

I needed to focus, but the only thing my mind wanted to do was panic. I wanted to curl up into a little ball and cry but something deep within me told me not to bother. I was strong enough for all of this. Like I was born to tame the horrors in my life and conquer them. So, with this in mind, I stood up and pulled Justin up with me.

He didn't ask questions, but he just complied and let me drag him up the stairs. He rested his arm around my shoulders and leaned in as much weight as I could stand, as we took each step at a time. Every now and again, we had to stop to both catch our breaths. When we got to his room I had to lean him fully against the door frame to get it open. It took me by surprise as it flung back and hit the wall, making the hinges rattle with the force. I was taken off balance and fell forward.

Justin knew we were outside his room and with one last burst of energy, pushed both of us in making us land on his bed. Now here I was lying under him, with both our chests rising in rhythm together. I shifted under his weight making him speak.

"Keira, wait." His voice was urgent, but both soft and sour.

I looked from the side and into his eyes that were starting to clear. Like the storm outside, the storm in his eyes was disappearing. The black clouds moved like smoke from his lids and dripped down his cheeks like mascara tears. I raised my hand to wipe them clear, but as soon as the black liquid touched my skin it started to tingle. It felt wrong, as though somehow what I was doing was not meant to be.

"I can see again… I can see you." He blinked, causing the rest of the blackness to drip away, leaving clear whites and crystal blues in its place. His hand came to my cheek and he gently wiped away the blood that had dried on my cheek. It was as if he didn't recognise the position we were still in, or if he did, he didn't want to change it. He moved his fingers over to my lips and he traced them with his thumb. I couldn't help the tremble that escaped them, but when he started to move his smile closer to them, I couldn't then stop the quiver.

"Justin, stop," I whispered as he lingered over my bitten lip before moving away to my ear. He was holding all his body above me like a muscular cage I couldn't move from. My quickened pulse was uncontrollable, and I had to bite down even harder on my lip to bring myself back. At any minute, I would have to tell Justin to stop again but in the end I didn't need to.

He reached my ear and simply said one word,

"Sorry."

And then with that, he rolled over to the side of me and passed out. I closed my eyes and allowed one single tear to fall before curling over and holding myself cradled for a moment, while I let the night's events sink in.

I don't know how long I lay there in a state of my own desolation, but when I sat up again, I was sure of what my next move would be. I left Justin alone once I had removed his shoes and covered him up with a bed blanket. I climbed the next set of stairs, being careful where each foot went, making sure not to wake Libby or Frank.

My room looked cold and forgotten. Neglected from endless nights with Draven, it hardly felt like my room at all anymore. I could almost see myself in the past still sat at the window seat waiting for another dream of Draven to come and find me. Back then, life didn't seem to be as worth living as it was now. I was just waiting in the shadows for a man I loved but didn't think existed the way he does now. But there was one thing I could say…life was, without a doubt, easier in those innocent days of being kept in the dark as to what Draven's world was really like. Would I change it knowing what I know now?

No I wouldn't, was the answer to that one.

And with this in mind I quickly changed into warmer, more practical clothes of jeans and a black long-sleeved top over my ever more secure gloves. I then pulled on a hooded sweater before doing the stupid thing and leaving the safety of my room. I knew what I should be doing was getting into my PJ's and collapsing my sorry state on my bed, but this I couldn't do. I needed answers. I needed to hear Draven tell me that he wasn't the one to cause tonight's disaster. And I just prayed I'd hear what I wanted to hear.

The worse part of this plan was knowing I was going to have to go back outside and face whatever it was that was out there. Hopefully, it would be gone by now and all I would have to do was get back to the club without another incident to push me over the mental edge. Luckily, the storm had calmed but it was still raining cats and dogs, so I grabbed a jacket that was hung up by the front door and slipped it on before braving the night.

I turned the key as if it was a grenade and held my breath as though death was going to be the one meeting me on the other side. So, when I opened the door, I couldn't help the sigh of relief that left my body.

I saw my truck sitting there like the finish line and after quickly locking the door, I ran through the rain so fast I was sure there would be a streamline behind me. I got to my truck and only when

I reached for the handle, did I realise how much I had been shaking the whole way. I couldn't grip it at first and closed my eyes in frustration. Seconds ticked by before I finally got a hold of myself and with a steadier hand opened the door.

I automatically went to brush the glass from my seat but found it strange when I felt nothing. I jumped in and slammed the door shut, when I noticed the window was still intact. How was that possible? Had I dreamt the whole thing? I found myself leaning over and feeling for any loose shards or even cracks, but there was nothing.

Halfway to Afterlife, I was still shaking my head in disbelief. I was now starting to feel as though I had lost it again. Was I really going crazy this time? As this thought entered my mind, I could no longer hold back the tears that mirrored the windscreen, which didn't exactly aid my driving.

The rain pelted against the glass faster than the wipers could cope and I knew that if this carried on, I would miss the turning. I decided to pull over and get a hold of myself for a minute.

I looked in my mirrors before stopping, which was when I saw that I was being followed. Lights loomed behind me like a warning glow and I knew that I couldn't stop now. I had to carry on and get there as fast as I could. I couldn't be sure I was being followed, but why would another car be out at this time and trying to match my speed? I didn't know, maybe I was just being paranoid, but I didn't want to take any chances after what I had seen tonight.

That's when I changed my plan and decided to pull over to wait. I indicated before coming to a stop on the side of the road. I wiped the condensation off the rear-view mirror with my sleeve, all the time not taking my eyes off the car behind. I held my breath and couldn't help shaking behind the wheel. It was only when the lights got closer, that I realised I'd been right. I had been followed.

The car came to a stop about fifteen feet behind me, but in the dark and in this weather, there was no telling what type of vehicle it was. I leant forward and my grip on the wheel tightened as I braced myself for my next move. I could just make out the driver's side door open and a figure emerged into the stormy night.

He was getting closer now and I waited until the very last

moment counting under my breath. One...two...three...and then I hit it! I pressed my foot to the floor, making the truck let out a screaming noise before it snaked its way back out onto the road. I gave the figure behind me one last look, before speeding my way onto the road that led to Afterlife. I couldn't stop the panicked breaths that fluttered out of my body and by the time I reached the parking lot outside I was a shaking mess. I needed to stop this before I had a panic attack, one I hadn't had in a long time.

Why was it that every damn time I saw something that reminded me of that twisted bastard, I could barely control myself? I remember my days at University when I would catch myself being followed and all those times were just another step Morgan took on the way to becoming dangerously obsessed.

"Get a hold of yourself!" I shouted and hit my fist onto the dashboard. The pain shot through my knuckles like it had done when I hit Justin, but it felt good and brought my mind round to safer thoughts. He was dead! He wasn't ever coming back to torture me, and nothing would ever be as bad as that in my life again. And I had to keep a hold of that thought and get through whatever life threw at me. Once you have experienced your own living Hell for months, anything after that should be a piece of cake. So with the mantra, 'He's dead' ringing in my mind, I calmed enough to get out of the car.

It was the first time I had seen the club closed and mine was the only car here. The place looked dark and eerie. In fact, it looked like the perfect place for the secrets it kept. My mind flashed back to the Temple and the horrors it housed there, making me shudder.

I looked around for any headlamps as I pulled the hood over my head to try and shield myself from the lashings of rain. Once I was sure I really was alone, I locked my truck and headed over to the main entrance. I ran, making the puddled floor splash back up my legs and soon my skin was covered in wet denim and goosebumps.

The main entrance had been transformed into an impenetrable force with huge iron gates that wouldn't have looked out of place on a castle door. They were as thick as my arms and had deadly looking spikes sticking out that no-one in their right mind would have chanced climbing. And what good it would have done them even if they did, as the next door was locked up and made of solid oak as thick as the stone walls that held them.

By this time, my fist was throbbing from hitting two hard surfaces all in one night. I looked down and even though it was dark I could still see the bruise that was forming under the moonlight. I touched the edges and winced when it hurt.

I rolled my eyes and muttered,

"Great, so what now?" Ok, so it didn't help my situation by talking to myself, but it did produce a thought. It took me back to my first day working in the club, back before the only things I knew about Draven was how damn sexy he was and how much I wanted him. Of course, that want quickly turned to need and that's when things got complicated.

I walked around the building to the right side. This was the side that was close to the cliff face of what was the biggest canyon in the national park. It was also the side where the huge, industrial bins were kept. I remembered my first day when I was taking out the "trash" as they say here. I not only nearly lost all eight fingers but also got locked out of the coded security door.

Unbeknown at the time, thanks to Draven, I had kept all my fingers intact. Back then his powers worked stronger on me than they did now and thanks to possessing part of my body for a short time, he helped me open the door. Since then it was as if he had left pieces of himself behind and till this day, I still remembered the code.

It was darker around the side as the trees blotted out the moon with a disturbing silhouette. They loomed over me like a cage and the rain hitting their leaves made a rustling that caused my imagination go into overdrive. Memories of the Gorgon Leeches Draven had fought by the cabin came seeping back and I could almost see their broken twisted bodies crawling from the forest, oozing black liquid and blood from their cracked limbs.

I was confusing the sound of the wind beating against nature with scratched nails along tree bark. This, unsurprisingly, made me move all the quicker and thankfully there was a light that flickered on when I reached the steps. The door was cold to touch and sent an icy chill down my spine. Thankfully the code was still the same and after I punched 1452 into the controls the door clicked and opened. I didn't hesitate. I walked into pleasant warm air but it was, for once, a silent empty space. The room looked bigger now minus all the bodies and when I accidentally knocked into a chair the noise echoed, bouncing off the tall arched ceilings. In that sense it reminded me of a church, and I couldn't help but laugh at the idea.

I looked up to the VIP but couldn't see anyone there. It was as silent as down here and now there was no need for security the doors and staircases were also empty. For the first time, the club looked defenceless. And for the second time, I entered the club using those stairs. These were the stairs that had started the obsession what seemed like a lifetime ago. I had watched Draven enter the club for the first time this year and stop to look at me sat in the booth closest to them. Then he disappeared up into the VIP room to never be seen down here again…that was until tonight.

The VIP was empty, but no surprises there. I moved into the centre and found myself in front of the top table and it looked odd to see Draven's chair empty. Then something hit me like a tidal wave I couldn't stop from crashing into me. My breath caught at the force of it and my vision blurred. I staggered back before I could regain control of myself.

I blinked back my fogged mind and focused on Draven's chair once more. There I saw myself sat curled up like a child crying. I held myself in a secure ball and my face was pressed close to the tall back, as if I was searching for a scent. I blinked again and the vision disappeared. What the hell was that? Was that even me? In the vision I had short dark hair and looked ill with misery. I didn't know what that was, but I knew one thing for sure…I would pray every night for it not to have been a glimpse of my future.

The huge double doors at the back were the ones that I had been through a hundred times, but it had never scared me before. Now, with no one around, it felt as though I was an intruder and in this place I was sure to get caught. What was I saying? This was like my second home for God's sake. What did I have to be frightened of really? Draven was behind these doors and Draven was precisely who I needed to have it out with right now. So, with that in mind, I pushed with all my might thinking that the doors would weigh a ton, but I was wrong.

As soon as I touched them, they opened automatically, so all my weight was thrown forward into the hallway. I landed on the floor in a heap and when I pulled my hood back that had covered my face, I found myself staring at some high stiletto heels that would have cost the same as my car.

"I forget how clumsy humans can be," said a satisfied voice that went through me, mainly because I knew whose voice it was. I got to my feet quickly to look my enemy in the face before giving her any more reasons to play with my emotions.

"Aurora?" was all I could say on being met with my boyfriend's ex, who clearly wanted to make a hood ornament out of my head.

She wore a long slinky dress that looked as though it was her second skin. It had a long slit up one leg exposing her stockings. It was a midnight blue colour which made her blonde hair look like it belonged to the sun's rays. She was astonishingly beautiful, which made it harder for me to swallow.

"I assume you're here to see Dominic?" I hated the way she said his name, like she owned it. Like she owned the rights to it, meanwhile I was still left calling him Draven as though he was still just my boss. All I could do was nod at her, which provoked a dark smile to wriggle its way across her red soaked lips.

"This way," she said and I had no other option than to follow her like a lost soul. We didn't say a word to each other along the different hallways we travelled. I couldn't recognise where we were, so it wasn't as if I could bail out now. Every time Aurora stepped into the warm glow of the wall lamps that flickered against our surroundings, she looked like a Goddess. She moved like she owned the place, swinging her perfect figure around with an air of grace and seduction. She would sweep the longer parts of her dress along with one hand like a bride on the way to see her groom. I wished I wasn't so jealous, but in the shadow of such perfection, it was a hard pill to swallow.

Finally, after an eternity of feeling like crap with my appearance, we had come to an end.

"He's in there but be warned, you may not like what you see." It would have been less convincing, if she hadn't been smiling at whatever warped thoughts she had to go along with this statement.

"And what is that supposed to mean?" I said not helping that my hands automatically went to my hips.

"Only the truth…enjoy." She opened the door for me to pass through, as though making sure that I would actually go inside. The door had been keeping in the sound of ethnic music, like sounds from an ancient east. There were a lot of people in this room and the noise of lots of conversations filled the incense smoked air.

I walked in to find familiar VIP faces, only they were different. They all looked happy, as if this was one big Demon/Angel party. It took my naive mind a moment to realise that it was indeed a party, but one of a very different variety. It was when I saw all the naked bodies that it clicked, I knew where I was.

I couldn't help but look, even though I didn't want to. There my eyes found groups all mingled together like human jigsaws. Only they weren't human and there was nothing humane about five men all sharing one girl. I winced for her, but when I saw that she wore an expression of ecstasy, I didn't feel sorry for her quite as much. She was lay amongst a bed of pillows and had five men I recognised, all from the same table at the club. Each one of them had a piece of her and was kissing each limb as if she was a Royal.

This theme continued throughout the room, only some corners were replaced with five girls all hung around one man. There were also some couples dotted here and there that were engaging in intercourse. And it didn't seem to matter where, chairs, tables, cushions and there was even a couple doing it on the bar where people sat around them as though there was nothing in the way of where to put their drinks.

Candles offered most of the light and in the side booths that were covered by bright pink and orange material the light made the bodies behind them seem like shadow puppets in some sexual show.

I stood dumbstruck for a moment and it seemed everyone was far too busy with each other to recognise me. I walked a bit further into the room, making sure not to get too close to their activities. I knew I had turned a very healthy shade of plum as I could feel my cheeks thawing out the rest of my cold body. I should have just turned around then as I knew Draven would never have been in here, as I had it on good knowledge that he never came to this room anymore. But, maybe I would see someone who would know where he was…someone not doing the dirty, I should add.

Ah yes, that would go down well, 'Excuse me for interrupting your orgasm but do you know where my boyfriend is?' Yeah, I'm sure that would go down well…*Not.*

I was nearing the middle which seemed to be the focus of the room. There, I noticed a girl dancing for entertainment. She wore a long flowing skirt that was low to the hips and looked as though staying there by the sheer power of magic. Her top half was nude with only a very large, gold necklace that covered her breasts. It spread out like a jewel-encrusted spider and barely even managed to cover her hard nipples.

The young girl was dark-skinned and like a gypsy, she had long black wavy hair that moved like a black river around a stream. She swayed her curvy hips to the music of instruments that were playing themselves in the corner. A large curtain covered half of the room and it was only when I walked around it that I found what it was concealing.

There, right in front of the dancing beauty, was an audience of great importance. The seats were made up completely of beds of rich crimson cushions. Gold bowls and pitchers were scattered around them, ready for the picking. It was as if I had stepped back in time and I half expected to see Jasmine and Aladdin to be sat there. That would have been better than what I did find.

Sophia was curled against Zagan, while he whispered in her ear, making her giggle. Vincent was also there with two beauties giving him every ounce of attention their bodies would allow. He was close to being covered completely by their legs alone. Even Celina and Takeshi were enjoying themselves in local company.

But this was not what made my stomach lurch and tie into knots in seconds.

No…This wasn't what made me want to cry out and run from the room with tear-filled eyes. No, it was none of these things, because there in the middle of it all was the King himself,

There in another woman's arms was…

Draven.

CHAPTER THIRTY-TWO

SOPHIA'S PLAY ROOM

I froze, lost to the unspeakable. I just couldn't believe what I was seeing. I had once again been having one of the worst nights of my life and here was my boyfriend in the arms of another, looking more than comfortable. I wanted to scream. I wanted to throw my arms up in the air and shout 'WHAT THE HELL!' But I didn't do any of these things. After staring for a full minute, I was finally noticed.

Sophia's eyes lifted from Zagan's neck and found mine that were still locked in shock. I saw her lips speak my name and knew that Draven would respond, but I didn't want to wait. I just wanted to run more than I ever had before and when I finally stopped running, I just wanted to cry until the end of time.

I felt so betrayed. Like a cold slap of reality had finally reached my cheeks, and the aftermath left a sickening metallic taste in my bitter mouth. I never even saw Draven's eyes move, but I knew they had found me. But by that time, I had turned and ran from this nauseating room that was known as Sophia's playroom. Well, I found nothing playful about it, considering it held my biggest fears…

Lies and betrayal.

Draven's lies. Draven's betrayal.

Part of me wanted to stay and wait for an explanation, to find out just how deep the lies ran, but I knew one look at him would open the flood gates to a never-ending misery. Every time I closed my eyes, I could see that exotic looking beauty draped across him as if she was stating her claim. I kept shaking my head as if this was some sort of nightmare that felt far too real for me to cope with. I was actually hoping to see Lucius so then it would have been confirmed, but when I heard my name being shouted and the sound of footsteps getting closer, I knew the horrible truth. I wasn't dreaming.

"Keira, damn it, wait!" It was Draven's voice sounding more and more irritated with every step I took further from him, but I knew my running was to be short-lived. I quickly felt him grab me, but I whirled around and pushed him back...*well at least tried to.*

"Just leave me alone!" I screamed out at him, but I couldn't look up at him when I said this. I turned back around, intending to storm off again but he had other ideas. He hadn't even moved an inch from my pushing him, which had been like me screaming at a brick wall and expecting it to come crashing down.

He grabbed me, this time by my shoulders and refused to let me go. I tried to struggle and worm my way out of his hold, but he held me like a bear.

"Keira, don't struggle... Stop it now!" He was shouting at me but this just added fuel to my jealous rage that was burning out of control.

"Draven, LET GO!"

"No, not until you listen to reason!" His voice made me want to shake with fear as his uncontrolled demon was coming through. His eyes started to glow purple and a vein pulsated in his jaw. I didn't know why, but in my head, I thought this would be a good time to make things worse and I wriggled my hands up to his chest and started pounding my fists against him as hard as I could.

This didn't hurt him, of course it didn't, but it sure did make him angrier. He was trying to control me and grabbed my wrists with lightning speed. Although he held me by my arms, my body had other ideas and I pulled back with all my weight, which seemed to add nothing at all.

"KEEP STILL, GIRL!" His voice now growled with a demonic frustration and it shocked me into doing as I was told.

"Is that it, do I have to scare you to get you to listen to me?" His eyes burned into me as though they were filled with purple lava ready to bubble over and burn me. I just swallowed and fear-filled tears started to swell up. He did soften slightly when he saw this, but when he saw the cut on my cheek from the glass shard earlier he saw red or more like purple again. His face went hard, and his hands tightened their grip, making it impossible to move any other way than how he wanted me.

"Fine, you have your wish." He then walked in front of me pulling me along like a child does a rag doll.

"Draven, let me go!" I shouted out as it seemed to be easier when I wasn't looking into his powerful eyes.

"NO! It's always the hard way with you, isn't it, Keira? You wouldn't just listen to me! No, instead I have you acting like a wild cat that can't be tamed." I didn't respond but I really wanted to say something that including scratching his damn eyes out!

He was taking me to his room, as now I was back in familiar territory. We only had one more corner to turn and we would be at his door. I had gradually started to relax under his hold and as a result he had loosened his grip. I knew if I wanted to make my move it would have to be now or once in that room he wouldn't let me leave until he saw fit. I had to act quickly, or he would home into my thoughts and put a stop to it before I even had chance to take a breath.

I counted to three and yanked my hand from his as hard as I could taking him off guard. I was already facing the right way, so all I had to do was sprint down the hall to the main doors.

"Oh no you don't, come here!" No surprises, I didn't get very far. I turned back as he spoke but by doing this I bumped right into his arms, as he was standing in front of me ready to catch me. He swept me up into his arms kicking and screaming to be let down, but then roughly pulled me into his body causing me to be still. He then kicked open his door making the hinges break and the wooden frame hang limply from the wall. As we passed through it, I could hear him say something under his breath and I watched the door heal itself before slamming shut and sealing me in.

He let go of me and I ran from him into a corner, panting like a small frightened animal. He, too, was breathing heavy and from what I knew about Draven, this was him trying to calm down. He had his back to me, and it gave me a chance to wipe the tears from my cheeks. I wasn't in the mood to let him see me crying and weak like the scared child I felt.

It was also the first time I noticed what he was wearing, as he had changed from earlier, before he had been wearing black trousers with a pinstriped shirt without a tie. Now he was more casual in a tight black t-shirt that looked stretched to the limit around his tensed arms. His shoulders looked huge and indestructible as though he had spent his life chopping wood and carrying tree trunks over his shoulders.

His torso went down into a V shape at the waist and his long legs were also hidden in black, not having changed his trousers from before. He looked frightening all in black and when I lost my nerve, I also lost my gift. The next thing I knew, two massive wings erupted from his back as though there was an angel inside of him trying to burst through his golden skin.

The wings took up a lot of space and seeing them inside a well-lit room, made me want to walk up to him and touch them. They were fascinating to watch. The way they moved with his body was so fluid and precise, as though the marriage between human and angel was so close to the thread, it was hard to believe they weren't one and the same. Not the way I was seeing him now anyway.

It had started with the wings but now the power had transformed his body into a Demonic host that flowed to every visible piece of him. Purple veins lit up his strong body, which had found a wall for both hands to rest against in frustration. He hung his head down and was muttering to himself in a different language that sounded pure evil.

"Sit down!" he ordered and when I pushed his buttons by saying no, he hit the wall making me jump.

"SIT DOWN!" he shouted, making me obey instantly. I placed

myself on the edge of the bed and held onto the bedpost with both arms hoping it would protect me from a Demon's wrath. The wall had crumbled under pressure in the shape of a fist. He turned his head and said with an eerie calm,

"Thank you."

He then turned his body and simply wiped the wall's stone dust from his knuckles that remained untouched and lifted a hand to the spot. The tiny particles scattered on the floor below all gathered in a little cloud and hovered its way back to the hole in the stone block. There they began to fuse back together and into the wall that was soon back to being whole again.

Seeing Draven get angry was one thing but seeing him in his true form getting angry was not something to ever forget. He seemed to get bigger with it and I wondered if the reason I could see him fighting that night in the forest was down to him increasing in size. He didn't speak again until he had calmed and with him having time to control his emotions was enough time for me to control mine.

I closed my eyes and placed a memory of the usual Draven in my mind. When I opened my eyes again, he was back and it was thankfully easier to breathe. He let out an exasperated sigh, making me stand once more. I didn't care if this set him off again, I wanted to be on equal grounds. I knew deep down that would never truly be, but the lie gave me more strength than the truth.

We were both now stood staring at each other, having some sort of Mexican stand-off. It felt as though we kept coming full circle, instead of ever moving forward. As though something wasn't right with us being together, some sort of imbalance the world was trying to correct. Why couldn't we just be together without other people getting in the way? Was I to blame with provoking the whole Justin thing? Was this my punishment?

"Tell me what you're thinking... please, it's driving me near to insanity." His desperation took me off guard. He came towards me slowly but stopped when I gestured for him to stop. At this he looked hurt.

"Why?" This was the only reaction to his question I could find, but this just made his features turn to a haughtiness I had never seen before, as if it was an obvious answer everyone knew but me. He looked for a second like he was going to answer me, but then thought better of it. Instead, he changed the subject and pointed to my face, bringing me back to the night's earlier horrors. The memory of Justin lying on the cold wet ground, blind and frightened sprang back into my mind, generating a spark of anger into my already watery eyes.

"What happened to you? Did he do this? If he did then...!" His fingers curled into fists, causing his knuckles to crack and turn white, making the blood from his hands to drain away and flow straight back to a fiery heart.

"You'll what? Blind him again? Torture him? Or will you just outright turn to a cold-blooded killer this time?"

"That BOY did this to himself, he had a choice!" The word boy was roared flashing his Demon at me to prove a point.

"Choice! What choice? 'Cause I doubt he would have poisoned himself!"

"I warned him what his actions would bring, but this would never have happened in the first place, if you would have done what I asked. But oh no, not my girlfriend, not my Keira, who always knows what is best!" For the first time, I was seeing Draven's mocking side and I didn't know whether to laugh or cry.

"I can take care of myself, Draven." I said stubbornly and somehow by standing up straighter and crossing my arms I was proving this.

"Ah yes, because that has been so well proven in the past." This was a cheap shot and he knew it. I could tell by the quick flash of guilt in his eyes that he tried to hide by looking down. His hair fell forward covering half of his face and after minutes of silence, he pushed it all back with both his hands and looked back up at me. He found me still shaking my head at him.

"So, you're blaming me for tonight, am I hearing that right?" I cocked my head to one side, trying to come across as confident but he didn't seem convinced. Of course, it didn't help when I was pulling down at my sleeves nervously, which he noticed.

"Partly yes... I tried to tell you of the boy's intentions but as usual, you would not hear of it. In the end I took matters into my own hands and decidedly knew how to protect what is mine."

"You're trying to justify nearly killing someone, just because they fancied your girlfriend?" I was expecting something more of a response than a simple shrug of the shoulders but no, that's all I got.

"The boy was in no danger, I take it the effects have worn off by now or you would be here accusing me of murder, not just an attempt, which it wasn't."

"Did it ever occur to you that I could handle it myself, without all your voodoo mumbo jumbo crap?"

"Voodoo?" He almost smiled but instead the corners of his mouth, although looking amused, did not quite make it to full humour mode.

"And how did you handle it may I ask...? And be warned Keira, if this has anything to do with that mark on your cheek, the boy will lose his head." This was a serious threat. One I didn't dare mock.

"I punched him," I said holding my head high and realising that my chin was jutting out I quickly lowered my head, which did make him smile. I soon understood this wasn't because he was amused with my behaviour, it was down to pride. I met his eyes and they were staring at the evidence of my bruised hand with a strange quirky grin, as if he was picturing me pulverising Justin's body into a bloody pulp.

"Let me see your hand," he ordered, but instead I just looked down and started to pull the cuff of my sleeve over my hand to hide it away. That's when I jumped and let out a surprised gasp at being touched. Draven had travelled across the room in a split second and was now pushing my sleeve back up my arm to inspect my hand further. He held my wrist firmly with one hand and the other soothed my purple knuckles with a warm touch that sent shivers up and down my spine.

For a moment everything stopped. Nothing mattered anymore while Draven was touching me. It was as though my world had paused and all that remained was me and the man who owned my heart, despite all the faults with our never-ending circumstances. I closed my eyes and sighed, letting the memories of tonight fade away into the abyss of my mind. His movements were as delicate as a butterfly's wings and his strength in the grip he still held around my wrist was fading too.

I saw the night in stages. First the night at the club when my heart fluttered at the sight of Draven unusually coming down to claim me. Then the terrible ordeal with Justin's kiss and what happened as a result of it. Then came the nightmarish eyes watching from afar, stalking in the night's rain through a mist of dark fears that still remained.

And finally being followed here, thus completing my crazy twisted evening. But then that wasn't it…there was still the worst to come. There had been Draven in the arms of another. That bitter cold slap was back and forced me to pull my hand free and open my eyes.

"How could you do that to me, Draven?" I said biting my lip in order to stop it from quivering with the tears that wanted to fall.

"And what did you see me do exactly?" I shook my head and turned away from him, putting a fist to my mouth to contain my pain.

"Stop playing games with my heart, Draven and tell me, who she is?" I lifted my head and turned to meet his gaze head-on in an attempt to be fearless. His face went tense before relaxing into a smirk that I wanted to slap off him.

"So you're jealous are you?" He looked triumphant and laughed bitterly, making me walk away from him which instantly caused my body to grow cold from the distance.

"What did you expect, of course I bloody am?!" I shouted without looking back.

"Good! Then you have some small shred of comprehension as to how I feel. Welcome to my world Keira, I can already see that you can't deal with it any better than I!" He wasn't laughing anymore and now it was his turn to fold his arms, but across his expansive chest it had more magnitude when he did it.

"I didn't do this for a game, Keira… I did this in hopes of a lesson learnt."

And so it was with these words that I realised I was the one to blame. I had unknowingly caused all of tonight's actions to go spiralling out of control. If I had just done what Draven had asked me to begin with, none of this would have happened. If, when I got that text message, I had just excused myself and walked up to the VIP area, then Draven wouldn't have felt as though he had to go to such lengths to prevent something he knew would happen.

I knew as well as Draven of Justin's affections for me, but I pushed it and pushed it, pretending it not to be true. I had been playing with fire from the moment I set foot into the club with another boy and I let Draven just stand there and watch. What had I been thinking?

"You planned it? You knew I would come back to the club and you sent Aurora to lead me into Sophia's playroom. You knew I was there watching didn't you?"

"I felt you as soon as you entered the building. I had everyone assembled in Sophia's room and let the party commence. I knew the added touch of having Aurora be your guide, would enhance my point." For the first time tonight he looked tired and relieved, as if he had given up the good fight and walked away with no prize in sight. He had achieved his goal, but without the slightest satisfaction.

"It was all an act?" I asked timidly.

"Of course it was! Keira, I needed to prove my point. I needed you to see, to feel, to taste the bitter sting of jealousy and fear that I was losing you to another. Do you understand?" I nodded and let a single tear roll down my cheek, which was filled with remorse and guilt.

"Why are you crying?" he asked softly, turning full circle to where we had started this conversation.

"Because I am ashamed of myself," I said, letting my emotions bubble up my throat and soon tears followed the invisible road on my cheeks. One tear stung my little cut thanks to the salty droplet running over to the side. I quickly looked down, letting them now find a home on the floor, when I felt strong hands wipe them free and gently push my face upwards to look at him.

"That makes two of us." Then like a child, I buried my head into his chest and flung my arms around him making him hold me, while I let all my emotions out onto the material that covered his solid chest. The feel of his hand smoothing the back of my head and down my neck soon calmed me.

Once he was assured this was so, his hands began to move down and remove my jacket. I didn't speak but just bit my lip with anticipation of being under his touch, skin to skin. He even smiled as to how many layers I had on, as he started to remove each item. Finally, he got down to the last pieces of material in his way and I let out a moan when his hands came into contact with my waist.

He held me under my top and lingered with his hands holding my hips and then, as if seeing a green light, he ran his hands up to my breasts taking my top with them. He kept moving until it freed my torso and then despatched it to the floor. He quickly did the same with my bra making me half-naked in his arms.

Now though, I felt it was my turn to shed some of his layers and with trembling hands I found the rim of his t-shirt. When I touched his skin he also let out a moan which was more animal than human. I lifted it up but could only reach so far. He smiled down at me when he had to take over by lifting it the rest of the way. I ran my hands across his chest and the lines of his defined stomach, causing him to find the small of my back and run his fingertips up my spine.

After a few soft journeys up and down my back, he then found my neck and more importantly my lips that were hungry to be tasted. He started to lean down but then stopped abruptly before reaching them. He looked towards the glass doors that led onto the balcony and his eyes hardened. I was about to ask what it was, but when he spoke foreign words that sounded like a demand, I thought otherwise.

Instead, I turned my head to look behind me, but before I could he wrapped his arms around my waist and lifted me to his lips. The kiss made me melt under a master's experience. I was now lost to the outside world and no longer cared what he had seen and what sounded like he had ordered away.

I no longer cared about Justin, Aurora or what had been stalking me that night. And most importantly, I no longer held an image of Draven in some other girl's hands because I was here...I was the now, and Draven made me feel as though I was the only one, as he picked me off the ground and carried me to the bed to make love to me like he owned every inch of me,

Which, of course…

He did.

CHAPTER THIRTY-THREE

TARNISHED PERFECTION

The next morning was the calm after the storm in more ways than one and the glass doors held picture proof. The sky was clear of all the dark and gloomy clouds that had filled it the day before. The day and night of rainfall seemed to have transformed the land into being even more of a lush green than usual. I couldn't help but smile at the sight, but I also think my contented mood was down to my night of incredible make-up sex, that had been eagerly provided by Draven. As the memories flooded back to me, an instant jolt of sexual hunger towards my lower regions made me giggle.

"And may I enquire what you find so amusing?" Even the sound of Draven's voice had my stomach flipping over. I tried to be cool but with the bloody great big grin plastered across my face, that was a hard task to accomplish. He was sat at his desk with his chair turned to the side to look at me. There were papers spread out in front of him, but from this distance I couldn't see what they were about.

I don't know how long he had been awake, but he was fully dressed and freshly showered. In the end the only answer I gave was a slight shrug of my shoulders, which in turn he mocked by doing the same. I was about to say something smart and ask if he

425

had recently checked the Kama Sutra out of the town's library after last night's wild sex escapades, but I was kyboshed by the ringing of my phone.

My clothes, as usual, were thrown around the room like shrapnel from a sex bomb. I didn't want to get out of bed naked and search for it, as in the light of day I was still kind of shy about showing him my body. Thankfully, I didn't need to as he had found it and made it to the bedside ready for me to take it…at a price. I tried to take the Abba singing phone from him, but he wanted something in return.

"Payment first," he said in a deep, smouldering voice that made me wish the phone would go to voicemail already and we could continue the payment in great depth. I kissed him on the nose instead, quickly remembering morning breath and grabbed the phone.

"Consider that a down payment," I said making him grin and then I answered the phone to a very flustered sister.

"Kazzy?"

"Yeah, of course it's me, you rang my number remember, what's up Libs?" She sounded both upset and furious and I was just praying that it wasn't aimed at me.

"Where have you been? Justin said that you brought him home last night, but then he didn't know where you went…so please tell me I'm just being paranoid and you're with Dominic." A guilty pang popped in my stomach at the sound of her worried tone and I knew I should have at least left a note or called first thing. Why didn't I think? Deep down I knew why…I had been so obsessed with having it out with Draven that nothing else seemed to matter at the time.

"I'm sorry, Libs, I should have left a note or rang but yeah, I'm at the club and I'm really…" I was about to say really sorry but she cut me off.

"Yes, yes I know you're sorry, but that's not important right now. I called because I need you to come home… like right now!" Ok, this panicked state had me really worried and Draven knew it because he took my other hand in his.

"What is it, is the baby ok?" I could feel panic start to set in that was until she snapped,

"No, no, nothing like that, I'm fine and so is the baby. It's something else that I can't handle alone."

"For God's sake Libs, you're freaking me out, just tell me!" Draven frowned when I mentioned God and I couldn't help but wonder what that look had meant?

"You're freaking out? I'm the one freaking out! Frank's had to go to the airport and I'm getting things ready here but I can't face her alone. I won't do it, Kazzy, I won't or I will end up committing murder and I can't have a jailbird baby!" I laughed at how dramatic my sister was being that was until the penny dropped just as I asked who he was going to pick up. I knew the answer and let out an angry growl of my own.

"NO, no, no, no, it can't be? She's early!"

"Tell me about it."

"I'll be back as soon as I can. I promise but is Justin still there? Maybe he could keep her occupied for a while." At the very mention of his name Draven looked as if he wanted to smash something up.

"Yeah, he's helping me to get things ready but he wants to split as soon as she arrives. He has met her before, remember the wedding." I recalled the event very well and when she hadn't succeeded then in getting him to give up the goods she had hated me even more to find that his attentions lay towards another member of the family, one she hated more than anyone!

"Right got it, I will be there soon, just hang on. Oh and Libs…" She paused and waited for me to carry on.

"If I'm not there when she arrives…"

"Yeah?"

"Stay away from sharp implements." Draven laughed at my warning and I hung up the phone.

"The cousin, I presume, has arrived."

"Oh yeah… the bitch has landed."

It took me longer to get ready than usual, thanks to while having a shower, Draven kept insisting that he could be of some assistance and made it difficult to do anything while being watched like a gazelle. He leaned all his body weight on one of the pillars and seemed content on watching me wash my hair. I tried to ignore him, but he was making it increasingly difficult when he kept making comments like,

"You missed a bit".

I think I would have enjoyed it more if memories of my cousin Hilary hadn't been playing in and out of my mind like a flicker book of misery and embarrassment. Draven knew I was preoccupied, and he would soon understand the full extent, when meeting her. I didn't know what he expected but I was certain on one factor, it was going to be a whole new kind of Hell on Earth than he was used to.

And it also took longer to change than usual and after standing there growing cold with just a towel around me, Draven couldn't stand it any longer.

"Keira, this isn't like you, you never usually care what people think about your appearance, so why are you fretting now?" I frowned and turned around to face him. He was standing close enough that I had to arch my neck up to see his expression clearly.

"I care what you think," I said, catching the hidden smile emerge.

"Ah, well I don't count as you know full well that I would find you most beautiful in any garment." I wanted to mock him about sounding his age in saying the word garment instead of the modern use of the word clothes. But instead I called his bluff.

"And if I walked in the club one night wearing a bin bag… that would be acceptable?"

"That depends," he said teasing me.

"On what exactly?"

"Whether or not the bag was used would be a factor, you may be a beauty in anything you wear but the smell I cannot account for and I'm not partial to the smell of human waste."

"Rubbish."

"Excuse me?" he asked, one eyebrow raised.

"I said rubbish, you know...you say tomato, I say tomato...let's call the whole thing off?" I started singing the song confidently until I got to the end and saw his expression. It was one of high amusement and I went bright red.

"You are so..."

"Don't say it!" I interrupted but he said it anyway,

"Adorable." I shuddered as I felt his lips on the sensitive skin near my collar bone. He licked where his kiss lay and made me giggle. We both laughed and I momentarily forgot about my cousin induced self-esteem issues. But it didn't take long and after Draven had finished kissing me, I was back to square one.

"Right, I know what to do but I warn you, you asked for this." I didn't even have chance to reply because he was gone and out of the room before I had turned back around. I was left miffed and confused.

The endless amount of clothes loomed before me and if they could have spoken, I was sure they would be all be pointing a limbless sleeve, laughing at me. Why was I finding this so hard? Why was Hilary the one person, besides Draven, who could influence my mood in such a way? I wanted to scream at myself for being so ridiculous but every time I went to pick something out, my hand would recoil, and I would be right back where I started.

I wasn't sure how long I had been stood there and I knew every minute that ticked by Libby would be going crazy. Finally, I heard the door open and when I turned, I was not only faced with one Draven but now two.

"See what I am faced with! She has been stood like this for half an hour just staring at her clothes. This is beyond my capability as a man, so I brought reinforcements." I wanted to laugh but the stern look on Sophia's face made me think it not wise. She took fashion very seriously and in her case she would class this as a code red world emergency.

"I see. You did the right thing, Dom, but now it's time for you to leave us, we have work to do." I couldn't help but gulp, and I shot Draven a panicked look, but with a smirk he crossed the room and kissed me.

"You left me no other choice, love," he whispered in my ear before leaving the room.

"It's not that bad...no really. I am just a bit indecisive this morning." She didn't buy it and with a lie told so badly, I wasn't surprised.

"So, this has nothing to do with the bitch that is showing up today then?" Okay, so she had me there, but what was it with this place, had some article gone out in the 'Demon/ Angel weekly'?

"It's okay, really. Jealously is a completely natural emotion and one that my kind usually finds great pleasure in feeding from. It's a shame really that we can't feed from you, with your mood I would be full up till New Year." I didn't laugh, unlike Sophia and I can imagine it was due to my hacked off expression that she found amusement in.

"I'm only kidding. Jeez, you are uptight this morning. No wonder my brother called me." She turned her attention to the clothes in front of her, with one hand running along the fabrics and the other rested on her shoulder as if she was posing for a photoshoot.

"So, what are we going for here? All out 'I'm better than you' sexy or seductively casual?" Umm none of the above. I didn't voice my thought, because she was already pulling clothes off the rack like a woman possessed.

"I dunno...I kind of just want to look...uhh..." I didn't know how to carry on without sounding pathetic, but it was clear she was waiting so I continued and said the words with my head hung down and my eyes finding the fleurs-de-lis that patterned the thick lush carpet.

"...like I deserve your brother." She emitted a small gasp at my confession.

"Oh Keira, anyone to doubt that is a fool and undeserving of your attention. This girl sounds like she needs some Demon ass-kicking therapy. Would her head look good mounted on a wall?" This made me laugh in a nervous 'God I hope she isn't serious' kind of way but I was soon feeling better. I could just picture Hilary's face when meeting Sophia for the first time...actually, it was the only thing I was looking forward to about her staying here.

By the time Sophia had finished, I felt like a giant Barbie doll. I was now stood looking at myself in the full-length mirror feeling a little red-faced. I had on a light grey sweater dress with a cowl neck and wide ribbing. It was so soft to the skin I couldn't stop playing with the sleeves. It was teamed up with a pair of tight, black leggings and black boots that added to my height. Sophia handed me a hooded coat with a stunning feminine charm. It was black also and tied at the waist with a belt in the same material. It fell to my knees with a slight flare, like a skirt and when I put it on it fit like it was made to measure.

"You look lovely, so much so my brother might buy me a TVR Cerbera." I gave her one of my 'you're so spoilt' looks but she just laughed.

"That's a car...*right?*"

"Keira, it's not just a car, it's so much more. The feeling you get when you reach speeds up to 240 miles per hour...it's like you're flying!"

"But you can already fly. And what is it with you and your brother with speed anyway?" I rolled my eyes, having only ever done the speed limit my entire life. Well, I wasn't so sure about what speed I was doing last night, but that had been different. Which brought me back to last night's horrors and why I hadn't yet told Draven about them? I couldn't understand it, every time something weird happened it was as though my mind would come up with its own ideas on how to deal with it and telling Draven wasn't even an option.

I had asked Draven after the wild untamed makeup sex, where Ragnar was last night. But was utterly taken back to find that he had been watching me all night. This had left me beyond confused and was just about to explain how I'd never seen him, when my mind crashed into a red light. I was at a blank and couldn't bring myself to speak about it. Why did this keep happening? What was wrong with me but more importantly, if Ragnar had been there last night, then why did everything go so horribly wrong?

The blood-red window message and the glowing eyes in the darkness, stalking me like some forest monster ready for its next feed but last of all, the car following me back to Afterlife?

Sophia's voice brought me back round to the now and the next set of horrors that awaited me...ones beginning with an H and ending in a great big Y me?

"My brother has a TVR Sagaris in purple, you know. Has he taken you in it yet?" My mind was everywhere and nowhere all at once. I could feel Sophia's mind trying to invade my thoughts. The feeling brought me round and I quickly shut myself off leaving her staring at me with a curious eye.

"Sorry, what was the question?" I blinked a few times and came back to the conversation.

"Keira, are you alright?" She knew something was wrong but thankfully I had something else to blame it on.

"Yeah sure, I mean I'm stressing 'cause of my cousin coming, but apart from that, I'm just dandy." I could tell she wasn't buying it and I wondered how much of my thoughts she had seen before I closed shop. I decided to distract her with another question.

"So I know you and Draven have loads of cars, but what about Vincent?"

"Ah, now Vincent prefers bikes but me... well...a helmet does nothing for a girl's hair." I laughed at her comment and hoped it was enough of a deterrent for her to drop her suspicious gaze. The last thing I wanted was her taking her anxious concerns to Draven.

Draven was waiting by his desk and I knew from the look that he had heard every word I had said. He stood up and was in front of me before I had time to blink. He took my hands in his and looked down at me with hurt in his dark eyes.

"How could anyone think that my Goddess could not be good enough? No, for it is I that is unworthy, Keira." I started to shake my head and was about to disagree with his last comment when his hand came to my face and his thumb held my lips shut. He then looked me up and down and finished with,

"You look enchanting as always." I blushed and his hand slipped back from my cheek and gripped my hair in a possessive hold before leaning down to my ear.

"The smell of your blood rushing to your cheeks drives me wild, take care Keira, or I will not let you go." I smiled shyly before I realised what he was saying.

"You're not coming with me?" I said this with puppy eyes and looked up at him.

"Now Keira, don't look at me like that, you know I can deny you nothing, but I have some things of importance to do before I can leave and I fear your sister cannot wait for you." I wanted to sulk, but I knew I would only be making him feel guilty for something he obviously couldn't help. Then I had an idea.

"Okay, but couldn't Sophia come with me instead?"

"I…" She was about to agree, but her brother spoke over her.

"Sophia is needed here," he said sternly and then shot her a look as if he was communicating something to her mind, something he didn't want me knowing. My sudden fears from earlier came back and I worried that he had heard more than our conversation in the dressing room. I only noticed her nod before leaving the room.

"Is everything alright?" I asked and my voice brought me back his attention. His dark eyes had been intense but softened when they turned my way.

"Yes, but of course. I am sorry I am letting you take on this Hellcat alone, but I will be along shortly…I promise." The promise he made ended on my lips and I sighed with delight. He placed one hand on the small of my back and the other held firm at my neck and then back into my hair. We started to get lost in each other's touch until the sound of Abba filled the air and I swore under my breath, which just so happened to still be in his mouth at the time.

"I would appreciate it if you refrain from cursing when I kiss you or you will start to give me a complex," he teased.

"That will be my sister then," I said with a groan.

"Then you'd better go before I get too carried away and tie you up." Mmm, that thought made me grin and also want to beg him to do just that.

"That's not a bad idea. Maybe you could answer it and tell her that." He smiled showing all his teeth and the gesture made his face light up in a way that made my knees go weak.

"Are you not going to answer that?" he asked with a knowing smirk.

"Nah, she will just think I'm driving."

"Umm… no, she won't," he said filled with confidence.

"And why not?"

"Because I have arranged for a car to take you home…don't look at me like that, Keira, it is simply so that I can pick you up later myself." I finished rolling my eyes and imagined the look on Hilary's face when Draven turned up in something little and sporty.

"Okay, but on one condition…" He raised one eyebrow and said,

"Which would be?" I replied easily with,

"*That you turn up in the Aston,*" to which he burst out laughing.

Out at the front of the building a car was waiting for me as Draven had said there would be. Ragnar was there waiting for me by a chauffeur-driven car, which I had no idea of the make. I had to admit I had missed the sight of my big bodyguard and a relief washed over me, knowing I had him with me once again. It looked as if he was trying to hide a smile as I grinned at him.

"So, you're back?" I asked as I stepped through the car door he was holding open for me. I also took notice that printed on the leather seats was the word 'Maybach'. I had never heard of this car make before but the luxury inside told me not only of its exclusivity and wealth, but also how fitting it was for royalty.

"I wasn't aware I was missing," he mocked in his heavily accented voice.

"Last night?" I prompted but I had to wait for his answer as he was nearly bending his body in two just to fit in the car. I waited to feel the cars suspension drop but when it didn't, I knew it was one well-built car, but I was still tempted to ask how much he weighed. He frowned at me for a moment but didn't answer. He looked as though he was deep in thought, as though looking for the answer himself. I decided to let it go quickly.

There were too many questions rolling round in my head to focus on just one idea. The rest of the way was travelled in silence, which didn't help my nerves thinking of finding my dreaded cousin at my destination. I fiddled nervously with the matching grey gloves Sophia had handed to me and then played with a loose strand of hair that Draven had tucked behind my ear before kissing me one last time, while saying his goodbyes.

I'd decided to wear my hair off my neck, and it was now securely twisted up and held by a heavy metal clip. I had noted tired eyes in the morning and thought of the bluish tint that had been there but when I had looked in the mirror in the dressing room they had gone. I put it down to the hot shower and blushing around Draven. To tell the truth, my skin had been amazing lately and I was starting to think happiness was the key. What else could it be? It wasn't only my skin either, it was everything. My hair was softer, my nails were shiny and strong, even my eyelashes looked thicker and longer.

Ragnar cleared his throat and it made me look up to the sight of my house coming into view. I sighed and noticed the curtain move. It must have been Libby watching out for me like a hawk. I let my shoulders slump down and suddenly my legs felt as if they were filled with liquid lead flowing freely through my veins. My body was reacting to the task at hand, given it didn't want to see her as much as my brain did.

Ragnar noticed the change in my body language and frowned. The car stopped and both the front door and car door opened simultaneously. That's when I saw Libby's desperate face first, followed closely by Justin's exhausted and no doubt crushed spirit. Hilary really did know how to grind the soul into one of utter misery!

Then there she was, all five feet and eight inches of fake smiles and cruel comments. She had changed her appearance, but that wasn't anything to be shocked at. She was always dyeing her hair, finding new fashion styles, but all were just as slutty as the next and what she wore now was no exception.

She was tall and very skinny, painfully so if you asked me. She had straight, platinum hair down past her shoulders that she styled into a flick at the sides. She had evil-looking green eyes that reminded me of a snarling cat. She had an oval face with small tight lips and always wore too much lipstick. Her short denim skirt barely covered her thighs, but I was surprised that she was even wearing tights with it. The hot pink halter neck top matched with the tiniest cardigan that didn't scream winter chic that was for sure, but the whole outfit reminded me of something a fifty-year-old cougar would wear.

I mustered all my mental strength and got out of the car, which was a mistake, but one I had no choice in committing.

"Kizzy Cat!" She squealed and squawked out the nickname I loathed. I tried to smile, but it felt so fake that it would fall off. She was running towards me and pushed my sister out of the way making her nearly lose her step. Luckily Frank was close by and helped steady her. It was one of the very few times I had seen pure hate in Frank's eyes, so finally one car ride had convinced him round to our way of thinking. Of course, having his pregnant wife nearly knocked to the floor was enough for Frank to scowl at anyone.

She reached me and gave me an insincere kiss on each cheek like she was continental, and I cringed when she combined it with phoney kissy noises. She took a step back and took one look at my clothes and then her eyes scanned the car that was behind me as if looking for someone. When she didn't find anyone else with me her 'fake love' soon died a quick death.

"Well, hasn't somebody found themselves a Sugar Daddy?" She smirked at the insult and I could almost hear her congratulating herself in her head. I just released a lacklustre laugh and looked back at the car. I saw Ragnar getting out and it took me a minute to realise that nobody else could see him. The car started to pull away and we all moved towards the house to give it more room to turn around. As I walked Hilary eyed me and then turned to face me at the steps.

"Well, you look better than I thought you would, and the extra weight is only to be expected…you know, all things considered after…" She stopped and then made a slitting wrist motion making an "Eeek" noise with it, which I didn't understand but I was too far gone in my fury I didn't care. The only noise I wanted to hear from the bitch was the sound of agony and restriction as a result of my hands around her throat!

She turned and went into the house and left everyone standing in disbelief staring at me, like I was a firework about to blow. Okay, okay, I had to get a hold of myself. I had to think logically. If I resorted to murder, then that wouldn't look good for my future and I couldn't imagine Draven visiting me in prison. Besides, what was I thinking?

I was forgetting the most important part about my relationship and how it could help me here…

After all, I was dating a half Demon!

CHAPTER THIRTY-FOUR

HEARTLESS HILARY

I finally managed to breathe and calm my actions down to just a growl in my throat. The rest looked at me like they were scared of what I was going to do next. I had heard the snarled displeasure of Ragnar behind me where he had obviously witnessed the whole thing. I turned my head to look back at him and had to shake my head slightly to control my mammoth protector from seeking revenge in the form of extreme violence and showing me first-hand what the 'Blood Eagle' looked like. I also didn't want to give way to the fact I was communicating with fresh air and let my family think their loved one was any crazier.

I walked up the steps past Frank and Justin and was about to walk past Libby when she caught my arm and stopped me. She was about to ask if I was okay, but I beat her to it.

"I'm fine," I said without any emotion in my voice. I hated Hilary with a passion and the idea that she hadn't changed a bit was not only upsetting but infuriating. I had been living with the spite and bitterness of that girl's personality for years and one of the bonuses about moving here was that I was finally rid of her. And now here I was, only being here for little over three months and she had already invaded. It was too much to bear.

I closed my eyes and mounted the remaining steps feeling like all hope was lost. I would have to try desperately to become one of those people who could ignore nasty folk and their degrading comments. But I had to admit, it was much harder than it sounded in my head. And I hated that it had taken her all of two minutes to insult me and for that insult to have struck me so deep this early on it only added substance to my growing dread.

I heard Justin asking Libby if our cousin realised that it was winter and she merely replied,

"Oh yeah, she knows."

The house was immaculate, and everything smelled of lavender and furniture polish. There at the club, I had been trying so hard with my appearance and here Libby had been doing the very same thing, only instead of her looks it was the pride of her home that had enforced such an effort to be made. I wondered why we both deemed it necessary to go to such lengths for someone we hated. She was clearly going to find fault with whatever we did.

I took off my jacket and instead of joining my cousin in the lounge, I diverted to the kitchen. I heard the front door shut and knew everyone else had gotten over their shock and was now putting on their fake happy voices. Libby was the second to escape and she joined me in the kitchen. I had clicked on the kettle but then decided tea just wasn't going to cut it, so opted for something stronger. I found an opened bottle of wine in the fridge and poured myself a glass…A very, very large glass.

"You've got the right idea… man, if I wasn't pregnant then I would have finished it off by now!" As soon as she said the words, I downed it and poured the rest of the bottle into my wine glass that really wasn't big enough for the job. I had to slurp at the edges so that the wine wouldn't spill. I didn't speak for fear of screaming like a mad man. I just kind of stood there, staring at nothing, waiting for this nightmare to end but every time I heard that screeching voice of hers, I just let out a shudder.

"I was kinda hoping you would turn up with Dominic, then that would have shut up that poisonous little mouth of hers! I can't believe she had the nerve to say that to you…I have a good mind to tell mum." I held up my hand and shook my head. It was like school all over again.

"What's the point Libs, she'll never believe it and even if she does, there's no use in upsetting her. Besides, her sister's little princess can do no wrong…remember?" Libby understood it all too well, as we had both had our fair share of the little Hellcat, as Draven had put it. Just then Frank came in and looked both scared and annoyed, I soon understood why. He feared his wife's unhappiness and hated the reasons behind it.

"Umm…I don't know how to say this but…."

"Just say it Frank." Libby snapped and then felt sorry for it, so smiled at her husband, as way of an apology.

"Hilary isn't happy with her room and wants one with a view."

"WHAT? Why that ungrateful little bitc…" Frank made a face like 'Shut up or she'll hear you' and Libby never finished her sentence, but I wasn't at a loss to know what the last part would have been.

"We don't have any rooms with a view available, the other spare room is full of stuff for the baby and…" Frank looked uncomfortable again and he shifted his weight, making the floorboards creak under the strain. For such a big guy he sure did look cute as a button when he did that.

"What is it, Frank?" Libby asked, not keeping the strain out of her voice.

"Well, she's got her eye on another room." His eyes looked up and we all followed as if we could see through the ceiling.

"She wants Keira's room," he said sheepishly.

"What…? No way, out of the question!" My sister defended my honour well, but I just wanted to give up and pray that I would last the duration.

"Its fine Libs, she can have it." I mean of course she wanted my room, she wanted everything I owned, so why not my room?

"No, she can't!" Libby was putting her foot down and Frank was torn between us two. He looked at me and then back at his wife and then back at me. He looked like somebody watching Wimbledon.

"Libs, really it's fine, I won't be spending the nights here anyway." At this Libby whipped her head around and scowled,

"Oh no, you're not bailing out on me, if I have to endure the cow, then so do you!"

"Libs chill. I just mean I won't be sleeping here, you can't deny me that, I do have a boyfriend and just because she's here it doesn't mean I'm going to give up every pleasure in my life." Libby's face softened at the remark.

"I know, I'm sorry, it's just that I don't want to be alone with her."

"And you won't, look I still have to go to college, and you'll be working in the day so that rules out the days…right?" She nodded and didn't look so deflated with the idea.

"And in the evenings I will take her to the club and she can amuse herself with the poor souls there. So, by the end of it, hopefully we will hardly see her." I didn't know who I was trying to kid, my sister or myself, but at least my little speech had worked on someone, because Frank's face lit up and Libby even smiled.

"Excuse me is someone going to tell me where I can unpack my stuff?" A voice came from above and there was nothing holy about it.

"Go tell her that I need to move some of my stuff first," I said to Frank and he walked out looking a bit happier than when he had first walked in.

"What a …"

"Yeah, I know, but if it makes life easier, then it's worth it," I said in a deflated tone. Just then Justin hurried into the kitchen looking like Steve McQueen out of the 'The Great Escape'. He closed the door behind him and leant back on it while letting out a relieved sigh. For the first time since being home, I wanted to laugh.

"Wow, that cousin of yours doesn't believe in playing hard to get. I feel violated. Never leave me alone with her again, I beg of you!" We both cracked up with laughter and soon Justin was smiling again. Seeing him like this had me wondering what he actually remembered about last night. Draven had told me that he would have no recollection about the night's events, but I needed to be sure. I would have to speak to him before he left.

"Seriously though, that girl is messed up! And she has major beef with you…what's that about, Kaz?" He nodded to me, but shock didn't take shape on my face.

"It's a long...oh so long, story." This statement made it clear that I didn't want to talk about it and nothing more was said.

"So, Justin, what did you think about Afterlife?" Libby asked trying to change the subject, unfortunately for me, it wasn't any better than the one we had been on.

"Yeah, it was cool, but man I must have been wasted 'cause I don't remember getting home last night. I hope I wasn't too much to handle?" Justin asked me and when Libby moved towards the sink Justin winked at me. Oh God, did this mean he remembered or was he just flirting with me? For once, I hoped it was the second.

I tried to put the nauseous feeling down to the wine going to my head and not that sick feeling I usually get when spending more than sixty seconds in Hilary's company. So that, combined with clearing out my stuff, didn't put me in the best of moods. Libby had wanted to help but I said that if she wanted to help at all then she would do her best by keeping our cousin at bay.

I was close to snapping and I almost wished for my old hopeless self to find her way back, because acting numb would have been a breeze. I didn't know what it was about Draven, but he brought out the fighter in me. He had found the part of me that had been locked away since the "Incident". Wow, it seemed like an age ago since I had referred to it like that. But the truth remained…

He had brought me back to life.

It didn't take long to stuff my clothes into a duffle bag that Frank had left out for me, nor did it bother me by sleeping in another room in the house. However, what did bother me more than anything else was the idea that she would be sleeping in a bed that Draven and I had shared. I was trying not to think about it, but every time I looked towards the bed and window seat, I could see us there making love and I didn't want Hilary infecting those precious memories.

I had emptied my wardrobe and drawers but the first thing I grabbed was my drawings. The last thing I wanted was Hilary finding my sketches of Demons and Angels. She already thought I was a freak, without knowing this side of me. The very thought had me shivering again.

I quickly moved into one of the rooms on the other side of the house where Libby had kept some of her gym equipment. Frank had carried the exercise bike and rowing machine down to the basement, so all that remained was a large inflated blue ball and a set of brightly coloured weights that were stacked in one corner.

I dropped my bags and sat on the bed with a sigh. It almost felt like the first day I had arrived here minus all the excitement. Libby tapped on my door and pulled me out of my sombre mood by offering to make me a cup of tea and a sandwich. My stomach rumbled at the thought of food.

"Oh, and Justin's heading off if you wanna say goodbye."

I needed to talk to him before he left, but the task left me with sweaty palms. What was he going to say? I stood up and pulled my sweater dress down loving how soft it felt on my skin. As I walked onto the landing, I heard Hilary in my room unpacking while on the phone to one of her 'few' friends.

"Seriously, you wouldn't recognise her, she's gone so fat!" She then giggled like someone on Nitrous oxide and I rolled my eyes, cursing under my breath as I knew she was referring to me. Maybe I had put on weight? No, I was not starting that again, last time I saw her it was my nose that she had me paranoid about. I just hoped she was using her own phone and own money to slag me off! Of course, when I reached the downstairs and saw the handset wasn't in its cradle, I knew this call was at the expense of Libby and Frank.

"You know she's on the phone to a friend up there and I know the girl works fast, but I can't imagine it's anyone in the US." I said drily and Libby looked furious, storming off upstairs calling her name, which left me and Justin in the kitchen alone.

"So, you've decided to escape?" I said lightheartedly and he smiled.

"You're free to come with me," he said with a seductive grin and I laughed nervously. I doubted that if he knew my secrets he would commit to such an offer.

"Me? Nah, I've always wanted to try out living in purgatory," I joked but given the circumstances it didn't seem that funny and although Justin laughed, I couldn't bring myself to follow him. Instead, I turned my attention to finishing the sandwich that Libby had started and proceeded to add mayo to one side when I stopped and thought about my cousin's comments. Damn her! I scraped the mayo off the knife into the jar and screwed the top back on. I could feel Justin's eyes on me and when I turned back around sandwich in hand he was smiling.

"Just remembered you don't like mayo?" he mocked and with a mouthful I nodded and said when only half-swallowed,

"Something like that."

He knew why, as he too had heard Hilary's comment outside. My pride had been butchered today and I was close to opening a tub of Ben and Jerry's from the freezer and devouring the whole lot alone in a dark room. God, why did I let that girl grate on me so much? Justin brought me out of my gluttony thoughts and asked me 'THE' question.

"Kaz, about last night…" I almost dropped my sandwich, but all I lost was a piece of lettuce. At least it gave me something to look at as I bent down to pick it up. He stopped me fidgeting after I'd put it in the bin and placed his hand on my arm.

"Keira, did something happen last night?" Oh shit! Was he starting to remember? He took a step closer to me and as I took a deep breath, my lungs filled with the scent of soap and seawater. How was it that he could still smell of the ocean when he was this far from it? I looked up and met his concerned expression.

"Did I…I, do something last night…? Did we do something?" I didn't know how to respond. Of course, it would have helped if I knew what it was exactly that he remembered, so I went with that.

"What do you remember?" He rubbed the back of his neck with his palm and looked lost in his thoughts, like he was trying to dig it out from somewhere deep in his memories. I just prayed he didn't find too much back there.

"It's weird…like having a dream and being convinced the next day that it was real. I remember being at the club and drinking at the bar."

"With me and Draven?"

"Draven?" he asked wondering no doubt why I had slipped up and called my boyfriend by his last name.

"Dominic," I corrected but when he looked at me as though he was drawing a blank I knew something was wrong.

"No it was just me and you… oh and then your friend with the mad hair turned up."

"RJ, you remember her but no one else?" That wasn't right, surely he should have remembered Draven being there and after all, it was before he had downed Draven's drugged shot.

"No, why, did he show up?" I didn't know how to answer.

"Umm…yeah, but you must have just missed him."

"What a shame," he said sarcastically and I hit him lightly in the stomach.

"Oi, be nice! Anything else?" I needed to get to the bottom of it all before he left.

"Well that's it really, after that it kinda goes all fuzzy but I have the strangest feeling that I…" I leant in expecting him to whisper but I think he took it the wrong way. He leant into me and gently moved my hair off my neck, sending shivers down my spine.

"What is it?" I whispered softly.

"That I kissed you and that I… liked it." His words rippled out of him, full of raw sexual emotion. Of course, just then Hilary decided to walk in and coughed to make herself known.

"Am I interrupting something?" she asked in a snooty voice and then I thought the best way to cover up the fact that it looked like we were doing something was to hug him. I slapped him on the back and then lifted my hand up to give him a high five. Thankfully, he followed my lead and slapped my hand, ending it with a ruffle of my hair.

"Catch ya later, sister-in-law!" I smiled at his efforts, but Hilary didn't look convinced. He walked back into the hall to grab his stuff and there Frank and Libby stood by the door, waiting to say their goodbyes. Hilary huffed at me as I walked past and I was sure I caught the words 'slut' whispered from her mouth, but I chose to ignore it as I knew it was said out of jealousy.

I found Frank giving Justin a bear hug and Libby quickly wiped a tear away thinking no one noticed. Since she had become pregnant, she had developed such a sensitive side she couldn't even watch a football game without crying for the losers. Poor Frank was scared to watch TV at all.

"Well, take care of yourself and my little nephew." Libby smiled and almost set off crying again.

"We don't know it's a boy," Libby said, and Frank mouthed the words "Jerk" at him making it obvious where he had got that idea from. Lucky for him, I was the only one that noticed it. Justin hit his brother on the back and then turned to wink at me. I smiled at him along with blushing and Hilary just received a nod, which made her storm off like a spoilt child. She sounded like she had bricks for shoes as she went storming off up the stairs.

"Something I said?" Justin joked before walking through the door and just as I was going to ask him if he needed a lift, I realised I didn't have my car, which had me wondering if that was the reason Draven had insisted on having a car take me home? In the end it didn't matter, because a beep from Frank's dad, who was now parked outside, told me that he was going home. Frank and Libby waved before going back into the house, but I still had unfinished business, so I ran down the steps calling his name. He turned looking happily surprised.

"Hold up a sec."

"What? Missed me already?" He was so damn cocky.

"I just wanted to know…to check…you're ok, right?" He looked confused and then smiled, lighting up his slightly freckled face.

"You worried about me?" He saw me frown so he continued without an answer.

"I'm fine, I know I should have the hangover from Hell but it's weird…like something I drank last night mustn't have agreed with me, but at the same time it did…does that make sense?" Oh yeah, it made sense alright.

"My only regret is towards you. I have a feeling that I didn't behave last night and if I offended you at all then I apologise." This had been the most sincere that I had seen Justin and for it I gave him a wink back myself. I had wanted to give him a hug, but the sight of Ragnar in the background staring with Hellfire in his eyes at Justin's back stopped me.

"Friends?" I asked and in the end he pulled me in for a hug anyway but at least this way it hadn't been me that had started it. The sound of a tree branch the thickness of my leg snapping behind us made him pull back and turn around.

"What was that?" The sight of a huge part of the tree that had been snapped back and split in three different places made him say,

"Man, you must have fat squirrels around here…what you feeding them, protein bars?" I laughed and waved to him and his dad before returning to the house. I watched the car go out of sight and before going inside I saw Ragnar staring at me, giving me a dirty look, so I did a very childish thing and stuck my tongue out at him before running into the house. I was still smiling to myself, when I walked into the living room.

"I don't know what you're smiling at? We still have to deal with that!" Libby said pointed to the ceiling.

"Let me handle it," I said as I left the room to go and talk to my cousin. I had a good mind to pick up Frank's baseball bat from under the stairs on the way but thought that was way too mafia. No, I was going to have to use my powers of persuasion and hell, maybe then if she didn't listen she could 'Say hello to my little friend!' I smiled at the thought, but my smile soon faded when I reached my…oh no, now it was her room. It was open so I knocked and walked in anyway, not waiting for a response.

"Kizzy Cat, what do you think?" The question was aimed at the changes to my room, as now she had moved everything to how she wanted it. My bed was sideways, the length against one wall and my desk had been stuffed in the corner, out of the way. She had even moved my rug and rolled it up to lean against the wall. She had also removed my purple blankets and pillows. She had dug out some yellow ones that were spare in the chest that was no longer at the bottom of my bed but pushed to the far wall. I wondered how she had the strength to do all of this.

"Umm yeah…it's great, I guess," I said unconvincingly.

"Well, I needed the room for my yoga. I can't function without an early start and exercise, you should try it sometime." Yeah like kick-boxing! I could just see myself doing a roundhouse kick to a certain somebody's head.

"Well, I do a lot of hiking," I lied when what I really wanted to say was 'Well lately I have being having loads of crazy wild sex, so don't have much energy for anything else' but I stupidly, took the high ground and refrained.

"Umm, yeah it shows." She looked me up and down and wrinkled her nose as if I smelled. Damn high ground!

"Yeah, well anyway, I wanted to invite you to the club tonight." I couldn't believe I even found the words, but they were out now and I couldn't take them back. My one consolation was that I was giving Libby some time out.

"Will that guy you've been kind of seeing be there?" I wanted to growl as a malevolent smile crossed her lips.

"My Boyfriend… well he does own the place," I said trying to get one back over her, but it didn't work, she just enlarged her smile and tapped a finger to her lips. I was getting impatient, so I put a hand to my hip and said,

"Well?"

"Yeah, I think it should be fun. In that case, I should have a shower now and shave my legs…you never know, I may get lucky!" This was her way of implying she could steal Draven from me, but I didn't bite.

"Let's hope so," I said before going to tell Libby the good news. For me, however, it was more like one of Shakespeare's tragedies. Well, at least I couldn't say my life was boring. I was trying to find other silver linings in having my cousin here, but that was the only one I could come up with so I rubbed my forehead as if I had a migraine on the way downstairs and found Libby in the kitchen.

"Is her majesty happy with her bedchamber?" Libby asked and I almost laughed, that was until I remembered I had to spend the entire evening with her.

"Yeah, she's moved it around and everything," I said in an overly whiney voice trying to mimic my lovely cousin, but Libby just looked even more furious, so to distract her I told her the good news.

"Well, you don't have to worry about her tonight."

"Why's that? You put arsenic in her tea?" I smiled at the idea.

"No, nothing that drastic, but you will be happy to know you have a Hilary free evening." Her eyes lit up and I could have sworn I even heard the baby shout a hallelujah!

"No way! You're the best...I love you ...I love you...I love you." She was dancing me around the kitchen, and I couldn't help but grin even though my doomed fate was lingering upstairs. Just then Frank came in wanting to know what all the commotion was about.

"Oh baby, the greatest news." His eyes lifted and he mirrored his wife's smile at once again seeing her so happy.

"We're on our own tonight honey!" As soon as she said it he let out a big,

"YES!" and give the air a victory arm pump out of excitement. Then, like kids, they high fived each other. I would have loved to have joined in, but at that point my dread doubled. I turned towards the window and the shiny sports car pulling up the drive confirmed my fears.

Now it was my time to introduce Draven to my boyfriend stealing cousin...

This was not going to go well.

CHAPTER THIRTY-FIVE

SEDUCING DRAVEN

I wanted to rush out of the front door and run into Draven's arms like something out of a movie, but I didn't want my insecurities to be on display. Draven would pick them up straight away and my mental barrier felt more like a ruin than a fortress. I was scared of what I might reveal. My thoughts were disrupted by a voice from above.

"Libby! Is there any reason the pipes make that noise, only I need a bath and…?" Hilary was calling down when she heard the car. At that point, I threw all caution to the wind and ran out of the front door. There I found Draven getting out of a sleek silver beast and looking as gorgeous as ever.

He wore dark jeans and a dark grey t-shirt, but the most amazing addition to this ensemble was the black leather biker jacket that fitted his every muscle, making his shoulders look mammoth and powerful. I couldn't help it when my steps faltered at the sight. I had to take a breath at the picture of the man before me. His hair was parted naturally and pushed back off his face curling slightly around his ears and neck, giving me a brilliant view of his incredible black eyes. He had a bit of stubble, giving him a roughness I adored, and when he saw me his eyes ignited with a passionate purple flame.

I bit my lip but couldn't wait any longer. I started back up again and ran straight for him, throwing my arms up and around his neck taking him off guard. It was difficult given the height difference, so he helped me by wrapping his arms around my waist and pulling me up to him. There I found eager lips and for a moment all my problems melted away in our kiss.

He didn't want to let me go and as far I was concerned, he could have me. I leaned down to his ear and he shuddered at my breath on his neck. I inhaled deeply and could have drowned in the mix of Draven's scent and leather.

"Take me away with you," I whispered and that's when he pulled my body back so that he could see my face.

"Keira, are you alright?" He was concerned and I mentally scorned myself for making him worry, so much for keeping a hold on my emotions.

He set me down as gentle as a rose on a lover's bed and gazed intensely into my eyes, as if searching out the answers from within. I closed my eyes and concentrated on guarding my thoughts of desolation, as I had already started to feel Draven's presence in my mind. I felt him trying to distract me by running his fingertips down my back and up to my neck. I could almost hear him frown and when I opened my eyes, I was proven right. Thankfully, that frown meant he hadn't accessed anything he had been hoping for.

"I'm fine, but I did miss you." These whispered, shy words made his frown soften and soon a smile replaced it.

"That's always good to know." I put my head down against his chest and held him around the waist giving him a much-needed hug. He knew there was something wrong, but I was just glad that he knew the right thing to do now was to just hold me tightly and say the words that made my heartbeat for him.

"Gods, but how I love you, Keira."

I could have stayed like this till the end of time, but when I heard the front door open, I knew our time was up.

"I hate to tell you this, but we seem to have an audience." He sounded amused and when I let out a sigh into the inside of his jacket, he laughed making his body faintly vibrate. I knew what I was going to face turning around, so breaking from Draven's hold was the very last thing I wanted to do. But it had to be done.

There in the doorway was my cousin leaning casually against the frame looking at her nails trying to seem unimpressed with our embrace. I grabbed Draven's hand and we both started walking towards her.

"Time to tame the Hellcat," Draven commented secretly, while we were still out of earshot. This had been perfect timing, as for once in front of my cousin I wasn't faking my smile.

"Well, well, what do we have here then? Where did she pick you up, from the tall, dark and handsome catalogue?" Okay, so there went my smile and really…how cheesy was that line.

"Dra…Dominic this is my cousin Hilary…Hilary this is my boyfriend, Dominic." I couldn't help the way I emphasised the word 'my' hoping she got the message, but to her that probably meant nothing but fair game.

"It's nice to meet you, Hilary," Draven said politely and for once I was wishing for his Demon side to be seen. That should do the trick.

"Oh, it's more than nice," she replied in a seductive tone, which sounded more like she was impersonating a man with a cold.

"Keira's told me so much about you." Yeah, like what a bitch you are, I wanted to add but had to swallow my insult.

"None of its true, I'm sure." She laughed and waved her hand about in a pathetic attempt at flirting.

"Hey, is that your car?" she asked, looking past me as though I didn't even exist.

"Yeah, she's one of Keira's favourites," he answered and then gave me a wink, which I'm happy to say Hilary didn't miss.

"Only one? Gosh, if that was me, I would favour them all, I'm sure." Hate her, Hate her! I repeated over and over in my head and by the look from Draven, I think he heard.

"Well, that one has special memories for us, it was the first time I drove Keira home…do you remember?" He turned to me and I'm sure my eyes glistened at the memory. I would never forget that night if I lived to be two hundred years old.

"Well, at least it was you driving or you might still be trying to get here…Kizzy Cat still drives like an old woman, no doubt." My hands formed fists by my side and when Draven actually laughed at her comment, I shot him a severe glare.

"There's nothing wrong with being careful," I stated but Hilary just laughed at me.

"I would rather live life on the edge any day. The thrill of a full-throttle speeding car and the excitement of danger is what gets my blood racing and…"

"I think my sister's waiting to say hi, Dra…Umm Dominic." I pulled at his arm before she could finish making me sound like a complete, boring geek. Draven soon got the message and opened the door for me. Unfortunately, he had kept it open for Hilary instead of slamming it in her face like she deserved.

"Oh, what a gentleman you are," she said, while fluffing her hair at him, making me roll my eyes at how shameful an act it all was. Draven's only response was a nod, but Hilary beamed at him as if he was Godly. If only she knew how true that was.

"Dominic, it's nice to see you again," Libby said as though she was the mother figure in all this. Well, if that was true then Frank was the big brother because he came up to him and slapped him on the back, like he was one of the guys.

"Dom, how ya doing my man?" Draven looked touched by such warmth in his welcome and he shook his hand.

"I'm very well, thank you, and I see you and your beautiful wife are both good." Libby couldn't keep the grin from her face and Frank beamed with pride at the sound of his wife being praised. Draven was truly gifted when it came to knowing exactly the right thing to say.

I grabbed my new hooded jacket from the coat stand and Hilary looked at me as if she wanted to rip my head off.

"What, you're going now and leaving me?" Oops, I had forgotten about tonight.

"Oh sorry, I forgot that Dominic and I have to go somewhere first but…I'm sure you could get a lift." At this her eyebrows shot forward and her lips formed an even thinner line.

"I could have a car come and pick you up," Draven suggested

and her hope was suddenly re-ignited. Libby saw my face drop and nudged Frank.

"That's alright Dom, I have to go into town later for Lib's chocolate baby fix, so I can just bring her with me and drop her off."

"Her? Who am I, the cat's mother? I think I would prefer…"

"So all's settled then, thanks Frank, you're the man!" I gave him a sisterly punch on the arm and pulled Draven back towards the door. I didn't need to look at Hilary to know I was getting 'I hate you' looks from behind.

"Good seeing you again, Dominic," my sister said but it was drowned out by Hilary saying,

"I look forward to seeing you later, Dominic." Draven heard the little growl that escaped from the back of my throat. For once he was the one trying to keep up with me as I was close to running to his car. He opened my door for me first and I saw him wave back to the house where Hilary was still watching. He got in the car just in time to hear me mocking my cousin.

"I look forward to seeing you later, Dominic," I repeated in a squeaky voice. Draven burst out laughing, which would normally have had me in stitches, but I was too far gone in my bad mood to find the humour. Instead, I crossed my arms tightly over my chest and took deep angry breaths. Why now? Why ever? Why couldn't the girl just leave me alone? It was clear neither of us liked one another, so why did she go out of her way to make my life a misery? I was so caught up in my own self-pity that I didn't realise we were far from the house and heading out of town.

"Where are we going?"

"You said we had to go somewhere, so that's where I'm taking you."

"What, to a place called 'Somewhere'?" I teased making him raise an eyebrow.

"Is that Keira humour I detect, but no, surely not…it couldn't be. My girlfriend is far too distracted by the unwanted visit of an evil cousin to be making jokes." I bit my lip to try and prevent the smile that was creeping across my mouth, but in the end, I failed and laughed anyway.

"Right that's it! Who are you and what have you done with my girlfriend?"

"Very funny, Draven."

"Ah it must be you, my fake Keira would never call me by my last name, she always calls me Dominic."

"What, like my cousin?" As soon as I said it, I regretted it.

"Ha! You're jealous!" he said with triumph and I cringed.

"Am not! Even though she was practically drooling over you!" Why was I just providing him with more proof that he was right?

"You know, I find it adorable when you get all possessive over me, but maybe now I can be forgiven for the same sentiments over certain human boys, who will of course remain nameless." He was right. What lengths would I go to, to keep Hilary's grubby little hands off my Draven?

"Maybe," I said sheepishly.

"So, are you going to tell me where we're going or not?" I asked changing the subject. He looked so damn sexy when he controlled the car the way he did. One hand on the wheel and the other changing through the gears as the machine demanded it. He wasn't one for doing the speed limit and along these empty roads he moved as if he and the car were one, gliding along as though they owned the road and commanded every bend to their will.

"I think not." He was smirking and a trademark bad-boy grin made my skin prickle at the thought of being touched by those strong hands that gripped the steering wheel, as if he was in a formula one. I had to look out of the window to hide my blushes at the thought of having sex in this car…Ok, well maybe not in the car but maybe on it, after all it wasn't the most spacious vehicle inside.

"What are you thinking about?" I think he must have caught my smile by my reflection in the window, because now he was staring at me.

"Nothing."

"Is that so, then why can't you look at me and why are you biting your lip, Keira?" Damn it, he was good!

"No reason." I tried to sound convincing but given I was one hell of a bad liar, I was fooling no one. He looked so bad, the way he leaned across to me with a look of seductive authority.

"Come here." I did as I was told and leaned over to meet him in the middle.

"We wouldn't be having improper thoughts now, would we, Keira?" I gulped and shook my head combining it with a feeble,

"Nn…no." That's when he gripped my leg with his free hand and worked it up to under my sweater dress.

"Really, let's change that then, should we?" Oh God, what this man did to me!

"Draven?" I replied quietly in response to what his touch was doing to me. I wanted to scream pull over and take me now! But I could no longer speak. I don't know which he controlled better, the car or me. My insides were on fire and as his fingers were gripped just below my sex, he was also making me crazy, waiting to be touched there. My head went back into the seat and I closed my eyes to release a moan before I could catch it back.

"And how about now…any dirty thoughts?" His teasing me just added to the excitement and I only just managed to shake my head to keep the playfulness going. This made his fingers edge further up my inner thigh, causing me to moan even louder.

"Umm, funny that, considering the reaction I'm receiving." Unfortunately we were approaching another corner making him need his free hand to change gear.

"Take over for me." At first, I thought he was referring to the car, but when he nodded down towards where his hand had been, I looked back at him in shock. I couldn't do that…*Not in front of him.*

"We're not shy, are we?" The corner had come and gone but he wouldn't touch me there, until I complied with his request.

"I can't…I…"

"Of course you can, just like this." He spoke so softly that it almost hypnotized me. He picked up my hand and placed it where his had been. Now with his hand on top of mine, he started moving our combined fingers to a rhythm that felt like a symphony. I was getting lost in the feeling of euphoria and every combined movement from us both and the machine we sat in, was sending me over the edge of ecstasy. Then my fingers were forced to cease their punishing circular motions in favour of a more direct approach. He moved them to brush over the most sensitive part and thanks to all the suspense I wanted to erupt as soon as pressure was applied. I cried out as it was nearing and my body thrust upwards, counteracting every move we made.

But then I realised it was no longer 'we' it was now only 'me'. I was pleasuring myself and Draven was watching with purple eyes. I wanted to stop from shame, but my body wouldn't let me. I was too far gone and lost in a madness that felt so right, it was insane.

I heard him groan and when I sneaked a look, he was clearly getting as much from watching this as I was from feeling it. His evidence was bulging out and trying to break free. I could barely understand how he was still driving, as most of his attention was focused on me and my wandering hands. I licked my lips and heard another groan ripple from him.

I continued to suck at my bottom lip as my pleasure was increasing and nearing its height. I felt it surge within me and with a few more precise movements of my fingers, I was there.

I arched my back and let out a gasp so animated, that I blocked out the sound of the engine's roar. Draven growled as my reflexes were causing me to vibrate, as the sensation of coming to my climax wasn't quite over. My body gave out one last jerk and then the aftermath started to settle. I was breathing heavy and I covered my face with my forearm to hide the shame that had set in.

"That was the most incredibly erotic thing I have ever witnessed, you are so damn beautiful…thank you." I could feel my cheeks burning and I had lost the feeling in my bottom lip, from being bitten to hell.

"Keira, look at me." He reached across and pulled my arm away from my blushed red face.

"I'm so embarrassed. I can't believe I did that in front of you."

"Well, I like to think that I helped."

"Helped… You were the cause! That was so sneaky!" He was having way too much fun with my disgraceful display of pleasure and couldn't keep from grinning.

"What can I say, I'm a man who knows what he wants and a man who always gets his way."

"Always?" I asked as I knew that wasn't true and wanted to pull him up on it.

"Okay, so most of the time." I gave him a look of disbelief and he continued,

"I got you, didn't I?"

"Yes, and if I recall, that didn't exactly go smoothly," I teased making him raise an eyebrow my way.

"The journey is half the fun, my dear, but the destination is worth the wait. More than anything, I wanted to make you mine as soon as I first saw you in the clearing that day, but I knew I had to move slowly or I would have frightened you off and yours was one mind I didn't want to control into loving me." He looked like he was replaying the memory back to himself and his eyes were brimming with sentiment.

"I hate to remind you, but when we met in the club you looked horrified that I was even in the VIP and you didn't try to hide your disapproval at Sophia's idea of me working up there." He looked away for a moment, so I couldn't make out his expression. I didn't know what that was about, but it concerned me…was he regretful?

"My actions back then were, I thought, in your best interest. After all, I didn't think the best place for the girl that was destined for me to love, was in a room full of my kind and I was right." He looked hurt, but it seemed to be aimed at himself and I couldn't understand why? I knew I should have let the conversation go, but I needed to know, I needed to reassure him that his feelings of self-loathing were unjust.

"But you weren't right…without the VIP… I…we…we wouldn't have got together." Finally, at this he smiled but it was one of a different kind, not one out of humour but far more calculating.

"Every night you were working I would watch you, I would sometimes catch your eyes searching me out, but I never gave in. I was battling with myself on what was right for you, but in the end, it was my lack of protecting you that changed things." His voice was so full of emotion that I wanted to comfort him, kiss him, tell him how I loved him even throughout his coldness to me. He was telling me things that, at the time, I longed to hear but was kept in the dark in the cruellest way.

"You mean Layla, don't you?" At the sound of her name his eyes turned hard and flashed with anger so deep it scared me.

"There you were so close to me and still, I couldn't prevent it. When I think she could have taken you from me forever, well then I knew I couldn't bear to have you living in harm's way, not because of me."

"That's when you decided to lie?" No matter how I tried, there was no getting away from the bitterness in my voice. When Draven had told me about his false engagement to Celina, one of his council members, I had wanted to die. I felt as though he had ripped my heart from me and he kept hold of it, until I found out the truth. He only nodded to this question, so I carried on.

"Then I was right, our relationship would have never happened if I hadn't worked there."

"Keira, do you really think I have that kind of strength and was going to let you get away from me that easily? I was biding my time. I was still trying to figure out who you really were and until then, I knew I wasn't going to risk your life because I was too impatient to make you mine. I have waited for you for too many lifetimes to comprehend, so I was not going to make any mistakes…well… that was the plan, but as we both know it didn't really work out that way."

"No? That surprises me, which part would you have changed, not our first kiss I hope?" I said trying to bring his mind back to sweeter memories. Thankfully, my efforts were rewarded with a warm smile.

"Actually, it was one of the moments I did regret." I looked hurt, so he quickly elaborated,

"Not the kiss, that was sensational and something I had yearned for every single time I saw you. But I never planned our first kiss would be on a rooftop in the middle of a storm, with you fearing me and I forcing you to listen to me despite your fear. What a fool I was to expect after what you were seeing in me, to stop and understand reasons that were unbelievable to you. It just proves how little I knew about the minds of humans, however you did surprise me."

"In what way?"

"You came back to me. The next morning you woke believing that night was real?" His question was answered with one look.

"I was never as astounded as I was that day. You, standing there with all your mighty wrath, demanding to speak to me like the little tough beauty you are and when you recalled the night in detail, I was stunned that you weren't afraid of me. If anything, you were there challenging me, if I could think it possible, I believe I fell in love with you even more that day. You were never supposed to remember that night and that's when I knew I no longer had any influence over your mind. I had to resort to using other means of keeping you from me until I was sure I could keep you out of danger."

"It was painful," I whispered shamefully.

"Oh believe me, it was more painful to watch and to know I was the cause just made it double the agony. I had never felt so many newly discovered emotions in such a short space of time. First to find that you harboured feelings about me that mirrored my own and then to fear that those feelings would die, due to my own actions…You know not what I suffered." I wanted to argue this, knowing what my own emptiness had been but I couldn't, not with seeing the hurt of the past still shadowed on his face.

"In the end, I came to realise that the only way to ensure your safety was to have you by my side, which worked to both our advantages. It also gave me the opportunity to make you mine… intimately." At this word, he seemed to let nicer memories seep through, and his hurt expression was replaced with one of fulfilment.

"Well, it all worked out for the best, we're together now and that's all that matters. However, we do still have one problem to get through."

"Keira, I will not let anyone harm you. Never again. Lucius will not get near you!" He gripped the steering wheel with anger, and I heard the leather cry out under his hands.

461

"That's not who I'm talking about," I said and he raised an eyebrow as way of asking me who.

"We still have my cousin to deal with." At this he let out a roaring laugh, causing the past tension to evaporate back to where it belonged, in the past.

We drove on for a while longer until I finally recognised where we were heading. But then we passed through the city towards its outskirts, giving me a nervous edge to everything my eyes took in. We passed business estates and a sports complex but when it seemed that we were continuing further still, I finally had to ask.

"Draven, where are we going?" He didn't answer me but thought a reassuring smile would satisfy my curiosity. I gave up and continued to look out of my window, but I could feel Draven's gaze on me as I did so.

We continued to head even further away from civilisation and when we turned onto what looked like a service road, I was left even more confused. Draven slowed down as a heavy guarded barrier was coming up. The barrier was only the start as it was positioned in front of some heavy iron gates that looked electrified.

I jumped at the sound of Draven's side window going down and an armed guard came over to inspect us. I don't know why, but my palms started to feel clammy. I had no idea what we were doing here but more than that, I didn't have any idea what those gates were guarding.

"Let's see your ID!" The man in the uniform said in a less than polite voice. Draven's hands tightened on the wheel and a serious growl was rising up his throat. The guard put his hand on his sidearm and backed up a step as if ready to engage in a hostile.

"Draven." I said his name as a warning to calm down, but he shot me a deadly look of composed anger. His eyes burned purple and when his hand went to open the door, I thought I would witness murder. Thankfully, my silent plea was answered in the form of another guard. He came running out of the office calling the other guard's name.

"Tony! Tony, don't man! Mr Draven sir, I'm so... so... sorry, he's new and doesn't know who you are yet." I couldn't see the men's faces as I was too low to the ground, but I didn't need to see him to recognise the panic in his voice. Draven didn't take kindly to being told what to do and I could tell it took all his energy to cool his temper and remain in the car.

"Very well, this time I will let the matter pass, BUT I expect his manners to improve or he will soon find himself on the unemployment list, do I make myself clear?"

"Yes Sir. Mr Draven, Sir." He nodded and walked back to the booth with Tony following like a naughty teenager. I could hear him asking who Draven was and with a tired tone he simply replied,

"He's your boss and owner of this place!" The guy cursed but I didn't quite catch all of it as Draven fired up the engine and revved the beast until it roared with perfect mix of engineering and raw power. The barrier went up and the gates opened, allowing us access to God only knows where.

"Okay... what the Hell was that all about?!" I was close to furious at how quickly Draven had flashed to killer in mere seconds. He wouldn't look at me which didn't help.

"Foolish mortals!" At this, I nearly choked on my own tongue. I had never heard him refer to humans as mortals before and for some reason the way he said it just made it sound degrading, insulting and pathetic.

"Excuse me, but you do remember that I'm one of those mere mortals don't you?" At this he finally looked at me. His face was a mixture of regret and disbelief.

"Yes, but you're not foolish." I crossed my arms and huffed at his weak argument.

"Who's the greater fool, the man who rises to the foolish behaviour of others or the man who acts foolish when faced with difficult situations?" My little speech had hit home and he smiled with a beam of respect in his dark eyes.

"You are right my reactions were just as foolish. You are a wise soul, my girl."

"Don't you mean 'my mortal'?" I asked giving in to his smiles and joining him.

"Umm…I guess, for the time being anyway." I let my jaw drop as we continued along the road towards a row of vast warehouses.

What did he mean by that and more importantly…

What the Hell did he have planned for me?

CHAPTER THIRTY-SIX

DRAVEN'S DISTRICT

I was about to ask, and he knew it that's why he spoke first.

"We're here." I knew from the sound of his voice that he wasn't going to tell me what he meant by me only being 'mortal' for now. So my only reaction consisted of a huff and crossing my arms across my chest once again, which caused Draven to find amusement and a soft laugh escaped from him.

We were approaching one of the largest warehouses on the east side and apart from a few people driving heavy plant vehicles it was pretty much deserted. There were huge yellow cranes and a lot of building equipment around, but no work was going on.

The place would have just seemed quite regular, if there had been busybodies going along in their daily routines. However, with it being so isolated it gave it an eeriness that caused my skin to prickle with goosebumps. I think Draven could sense my doubt, because he leaned across to me and gave my shoulder a light squeeze. It was only then that I realised he had stopped the car opposite a small access door to one of the warehouses situated further back than the rest and it looked nestled away in between two of the larger buildings.

"Why are we here?" I asked, without looking at him.

"I have some business to attend to here, but we shouldn't be too long." At this he opened his door and I was about to get out before I asked,

"Do you want me to stay in the car?" He answered me by exiting the car faster than my eyes could see and I jumped when my side door was opened. A hand reached in for me to take and I smiled at his old-fashioned manners.

"Of course not, why would I want that?" He cocked his questioning look to the side as I joined him. He closed my door behind me without touching it and I wondered if I would ever get used to witnessing his powers?

"Do you have a lot of business in construction?" I asked, trying to change the subject and I didn't know whether the wide grin was down to my efforts or the question I had asked.

"A few, yes, but don't let its outer appearance fool you. It's not what it seems."

"It never is with you," I commented as I walked towards the door, but he stopped me and pulled me back to him. He let go of my arm and folded his huge arms across his vast chest. My heart skipped a beat at the sight.

"Care to elaborate?"

"Well, Afterlife doesn't look like a nightclub from the outside, more like a centuries-old mansion."

"So you were only referring to my buildings, not me personally?" I shifted the weight from one foot to another and stared at my boots.

"Keira…" He dragged out my name like I was a naughty child.

"Well, come on Draven, when we first met, you weren't exactly nice to me!" At that he softened and unfolded his arms.

"And yet you still saw the good in me, I'm a lucky man indeed." At that I blushed, and I heard him groan. I looked up to see his eyes glowing purple and a look of intense desire transformed his features. He grabbed me and held me against him letting me feel his need for myself…a need that was growing very hard. I gulped as it pressed into me and he ran his chin over the top of my head.

"Do you know what you do to me when you blush like that?"

"I think I have an idea," I said, not being able to keep the teasing out of my voice. His hands found my back and with one hand resting on the small curve before my cheeks, the other started to trace my spine with his fingertips. I had to close my eyes as even more heat invaded my skin. He leaned his head towards my neck and started to brush the skin there lightly with his lips. That, combined with what his fingers were doing, was pushing me quietly over the edge.

"It makes me want to…" I felt him bite his own lip before continuing, as though he was trying to control himself or fight a greater urge.

"To?" I asked in a whisper, as though to prompt him further.

"…to bite you." I thought he would sink his teeth into me as he growled the words, but instead he licked and sucked my neck making my legs turn into jam.

"I think I should conduct my business another time." He started to pull me towards the car, but I pulled back and broke from his hold laughing.

"No, you can't do that! I'm not letting you come all this way to then just leave because of me." He gave me a bad boy grin and dipped his head to see me better.

"Are you telling me what to do, Keira?" He was teasing me, and I took a step back as he looked ready to pounce. Every step I took back, he took two more towards me.

"Because you have seen how I react to being told what to do," he said playfully, clearly loving every minute of this because his eyes were turning a brighter shade of purple, ringed with a distinct darker violet edge.

"I think you will live, you're a big boy." He looked down and replied.

"And getting bigger, so it seems." He raised his head and gave me a wink making me feel all gooey like a teenager again. We both laughed and he reached me with one last step and kissed my forehead.

"Umm, I think I could get used to being bossed around." I

looked up at him with raised brows. I knew that was never going happen. Draven wasn't a man to be spoken down to that was for sure.

"Well...as long as it's by you, that is," he added. I giggled and reached up on my tiptoes to kiss him. Thankfully, he met me halfway otherwise I would have had to have gone for kissing his neck instead, he was that freakin' tall. I most definitely looked even shorter around Draven, with him being over a foot taller than me.

After some intense kissing, he finally let me go and sighed at I knew not what.

"Fine, I'm convinced, but later you're all mine and then you can boss me about to your heart's content. I'm quite looking forward to being under your command." I rolled my eyes but couldn't hide my smirk at the idea.

"Come on," I said but he grabbed my gloved wrist to keep me from leaving his side.

"Wait." He pulled me back, so I was facing him and he rested both his large hands on my shoulders, making me once again feel tiny.

"I need you to do something for me." He ran his fingers up my neck and round to the hood on my jacket. I was about to ask him what he was doing but then he raised the large black hood over my head and pulled it down to cover half of my face. I think he caught the hurt look in my eyes before he covered them.

"Why, are you ashamed of me or something?" I knew as soon as I had said it that I shouldn't have, but I couldn't help it. At that he whipped it back down and anger flashed in his eyes.

"Why would you say that? Why would you even think it?!" he snapped.

"Then why?" I was trying to mask my guilt with anger, which I knew was foolish.

"Look, I would gladly want to relish in how proud I am to have you by my side and show what a rare beauty you behold, but it would be far too dangerous. Through those doors hold those that are not as loyal to me as the people you know in Afterlife."

"Then why even bring me here?" I couldn't understand, if it was so dangerous why he didn't he want me to wait in the car or bring me to this building in the first place.

"I wasn't ever intending on it, but when I arrived at your house I…I had a change of heart." He didn't want to be telling me this and I knew why.

"So, when you turned up, it was to tell me you were going to be late…wasn't it?" He rubbed the back of his neck with one hand in frustration.

"Yes, but when you ran into my arms and asked me to take you away, I wouldn't have left you for all the world." I bit my lip and swallowed my attitude.

"I'm sorry," I said as I reached out to his hand. He looked up at me with shock on his face.

"Why?"

"Because I didn't realise and because I shouldn't have thought you were ashamed of me." At this he just nodded.

"Please." He motioned to put my hood back up and I let him, knowing now the reasons. He was protecting me and didn't want anyone knowing my identity. As always, he was trying to keep me safe and I was being stubborn.

"You know, I didn't think it possible."

"What?" I asked looking up but only seeing his chest thanks to my low hood.

"That you could still look cute even when your face is covered." I'm not sure if he could see me smile but he reacted when I poked him in the ribs, not that he could feel much thanks to him being made of solid muscle.

"In that case, I will wear it up all the time." I felt him squeeze my sides and then kiss my head before saying,

"Don't you dare." I laughed and then felt him taking me by the elbow to lead me towards the door.

"Are you ready?" I didn't know why but there was something in his voice that put me on edge, and I found myself nervous enough to want to start scratching my scars. Of course, I was already biting my lip but it didn't seem enough somehow.

"You will be fine but stay close to me, ok?" He had obviously heard my worries but by saying this last part, he only ended up adding to my fears.

"And one last thing, try very hard to keep up your mental walls, there are things in here that I do not wish for you to...to truly see." A shiver crept up my spine and seemed to stay with me at the base of my neck. I was very close to running back to the car and finding my safety within its metal body, but I wanted Draven to think I was strong and fearless, not the frightened little girl I felt like. So, he engulfed my hand with his own and led me to the door.

I couldn't help but jump at the sound of his other hand banging a fist against the metal door. I couldn't see very much, but I was sure I felt him looking down at me and while we waited, he leaned down and whispered,

"You will be fine, my love," in the softest voice. Great! Here I was trying to appear brave and I was acting jumpy at the first hurdle. There was a gargled grunt from behind the door and a bang back.

"Piss off!" A deep grouse came from behind the banging.

"Nice welcome," I muttered and Draven growled and proceeded to pound his fist against the door causing a dent.

"Patefacio pro vestri vinco!" ("Open for your Master!" in Latin)

"Quod letalis?" ("And the mortal?") The voice sounded less angry now but still wary, so I wondered what they were talking about.

"Letalis est mei!" ("The mortal is mine") At this, the sound of metal scraping against metal could be heard and the door vibrated before opening. I couldn't help but hold my breath as the crack opening became wider and the beast from behind came into view.

My held breath was quickly followed by a gasp when I was soon faced with a massive Samoan, who looked as though he weighed at least 400lbs. He had a huge gut that meant it would have made it impossible for him to see his own feet, let alone other important parts of his anatomy.

He stood close to seven-foot-tall and would have made even Ragnar look small. I started my gaze at the bottom where I was surprised to see him wearing Jesus sandals and three-quarter length lightweight khaki trousers. My eyes followed up and found him wearing a black vest that had enough material to be a bedspread.

When I lifted my head enough to see his face my eyes looked so far back that my hood fell from my head. Mine weren't the only eyes to display shock. His skin was a honey brown colour but now thanks to extensive tribal tattoos that covered half of his face it was closer to black on one side.

The tattoos were one continuation from one that started on his shoulder and chest that curled up and attacked his face. It reminded me of waves that were made up of different intercut patterns and dots that were beautiful Samoan artwork in their own right. His eyes were the same honey colour that matched his skin tone and they glowed amber when they met my own.

"Lucifer's blood, Electus unus!" ("The Chosen One" in Latin) He stared at me as though I was some freak that sported two heads and cat's eyes! As soon as he made the mistake of speaking, Draven let go of me and grabbed the man's neck at record speed. He pinned him to the wall and soon the man's face turned a deep shade of scarlet. The swirls on his face started to move like cogs in a machine and I thought I was seeing things.

They also looked like they were writhing around in pain and they continued up into his shaved head and hair that he wore in a plaited Mohawk. I had stepped back and covered my mouth with my hands in shock. Draven was furious and his purple veins rippled through his neck as though they were trying to burst through the skin.

I couldn't see the rest of his body as he still had on his leather jacket, but I would bet good money that it would be the same everywhere else. A gurgling sound came from the man's throat like he was trying to speak. At this Draven just tightened his hold and cut off any sound.

"You will not repeat those words so long as you remain in this life and in exchange I will LET you remain in this life, with your head attached. Do I make myself clear, Ira?" Draven allowed him enough to nod and then released him, forcing him to carry his own body weight once again. His legs crumpled underneath him and he collapsed to the floor coughing and gasping for air to fill his lungs. Even though he had been choking moments earlier, he still managed to speak.

"Forgive my insolence Master, it shall not happen again." He bowed his head and I could see the tattoo move down from his head and wriggle nervously down his spine, which had transformed from cogs into an inky snake cowering out of sight.

Draven came back to me and without dropping his harsh expression he gently ran the back of his knuckles down the side of my face before raising my hood to conceal it once again. He then took my hand back in his vice-like grip and turned his head towards Ira the Samoan one last time.

"See that it doesn't or you will be seeing Lucifer once again and sooner than you may think!" His voice was like ice, cold and unforgiving, which was like hearing a different Draven altogether. Here he wasn't my Draven, soft and gentle. No, here he was the Master. Here he was the one in control and here...

He was a God.

I could feel the heat coming from his touch as he controlled my movements through the slightest turn of his hand. He was leading me through a low lit corridor which mostly offered a view of the rustic wooden floor that looked like it had seen better days centuries ago. Part of me wanted to pull back and tell him that I didn't want to go any further, but when he tightened his grip around my hand I knew it was his way of telling me that I had nothing to fear.

I was so torn between my doubts and the mental wave of reassurance that Draven was trying to inject into my mind, which left me feeling warm and tingling inside.

I knew we were nearing our destination when the hum of a deep baseline was beating through the next door and the vibrations found the soles of my feet. Draven opened the door and I jumped at the sound of metal grating against the ancient woodwork. The music and smell hit me all at once as it flooded the hallway, swirling up with the stench of stale alcohol combined with fresh sweat from a mass of dancing bodies.

The heavy rock music drowned out any other sound, including

that of my pounding heart. I was very aware that Draven was trying to get me to go into this room, but I held myself firm and rooted to the spot. I didn't want to face this place and although I couldn't see, I could damn well feel!

That was enough for me to be terrified because not one pair of feet that I could now see belonged to a human, at least not until I looked down at my own. I knew this for a fact. It was as if I could feel it vibrating from contaminated cells in my bloodstream.

"Come with me, Keira and trust me." Draven had leaned down to whisper and his words weren't the only comfort as his breath sent a security that seemed to cling to my skin and stay with me as an invisible force.

He left my hand for a second and placed his on the top of my head which he let slide down to the back and then rest on my neck, as he whispered,

"Good girl," into my ear. So I let myself be led through a crowd which, if they could, would have sucked the essence right out of me and fed from my ever-growing fear. It was never really explained why I was different from other humans or why they couldn't feed from my emotions and access my mind. Not that I was complaining, but I didn't quite buy this whole 'Chosen One' business that everyone seemed to be preaching.

As I watched the feet part, like Moses was coming in with his girlfriend in tow, I felt it wasn't only my own mental barrier that was keeping me from looking up and seeing these people for what they really were. Draven remained a constant presence in my mind keeping up his own walls of protection. I decided to tap into the feeling there and when I did I was amazed that I could for the first time detect some of Draven's thoughts.

Of course, as soon as I did I regretted it, as all I could feel was this overwhelming need to protect...But protect me from what? Why bring me here if he was so scared that something bad could happen to me? What was he not telling me?

It was amazing that, even though so many bodies were crammed into one space, they still found the room to let us pass without coming too near. I was so tempted to look up at Draven and see what it was he was doing to make this happen but knowing him I could imagine it only took one stern look and that was enough. I could hear some people mutter things as they backed away and some even bent over slightly because I could see as their knees suddenly came into view.

One woman even threw herself to the ground and started bowing like she was praying to Mecca. Of course, in her low strappy top, this didn't leave much to the imagination as her breasts kept protruding from the material every time she doubled over.

I found it fascinating as to why she would behave like this at just the sight of him. I would have to ask Draven when I had chance. It was almost as if she remembered him from another time. One lost to a faraway history where this amount of respect was not only expected but was demanded.

The place was bigger than I thought it was, as it was taking us a while to get through and it certainly wasn't down to the crowd. I turned back to look behind me just as a new song was being played with Draven still pulling me along. The death metal music that filled the air made the bodies join back up together after we had passed and all the feet were now jumping and moving at such speeds it was hard to tell where one pair started and the others ended.

I could tell we were getting closer to the stage area as the music was pounding in my ears, making them close to bleeding it was that loud. Luckily, Draven changed directions and soon I was able to hear more than screaming words in another language. However, whether the language was human or not was another question because it sounded more Demonic than anything else.

I had a feeling that this strange expedition was coming to an end as Draven's feelings were easing up on his worries and his grip on my hand had now loosened. I saw feet approach us and felt Draven's hand leave mine completely and take a new position from behind to rest on the small of my back.

"Wait." I let out a small gasp when I didn't actually hear the words being spoken but heard them being commanded in my head. I automatically did as I was told, because in a place like this I wouldn't be as stupid as to be my usual stubborn self. No, for once

I knew what was good for me and here I welcomed Draven's power.

To be perfectly honest with myself, it was in fact turning me on no-end. His demanding and possessive behaviour towards me was sending an uncontrollable need, one that was causing a pool to well in between my inner thighs. What was it with this man and the insatiable need he created in me? Even at times like this when I should be more concerned about making it out of this Demon pit with my sanity intact.

How much more could I take of the abnormal, before I finally hit my limit and was pushed too far over the edge to ever make my way back? The truth of the matter was I was no longer counting myself as part of the 'normal' world that others lived in and the fact that I was more than fine with it all was more than a little disconcerting.

"Is everything ready?" Draven's serious voice asked someone who had stopped in front of us and from the wide thick biker boots I was seeing I could tell it was a male.

"My Lord." I saw the man's feet move back as he offered more of his body on view and I knew this action was caused from him bowing in respect, as most of the others had done.

"Yes, Yes," Draven said impatiently and the man quickly straightened and carried on answering his 'Master'.

"Your usual retreat is ready and Leivic is waiting as you wished, my Lord." The man's voice didn't sound a confident one and the name Leivic sounded more like Lev…le…ich as he began to stutter in his nervousness. I couldn't help but feel sorry for him, as it was how I usually felt around my History lecturer Reed.

"Good." Draven's one clipped word compelled the man to bend once more in bowing before walking away backwards. He was also muttering something in a different language, but I imagined it was something in Draven's favour.

"Come, my Keira," he said sternly, but in a lighter tone than he had bestowed upon everyone else since being here. I was once again being led forward but this time with him by my side, instead of being pulled along like some lost little girl just been found by an officer taking me home.

Um...Home... that seemed like a million miles away and an age ago! Suddenly, I found myself with an overwhelming feeling of homesickness and a need to see English soil once more but no, instead of that, I was here in a Demon's secret club.

Only one thought came to mind...

Oh Lordy.

CHAPTER THIRTY-SEVEN

HISTORY AND HAREMS

We didn't have to go much further, but I knew I would have to pull my hood back to tackle the steps in front of me otherwise I would find myself finding the floor on a more intimate level. I was just about to move it back, when one arm wound around my waist like a band of steel and I felt myself being raised up. Draven was lifting me up the few steps as though I weighed no more than a kitten. I was about to start protesting at being carried at his side like a small child and say that enough was enough, but in the end, I didn't need to. I heard the whoosh of material being moved back and with two more steps I felt Draven stop next to me.

"Dom, my friend, how long has it been?" A laidback and gentle voice spoke, taking the tense fear from my situation. Before Draven answered him, he came to stand in front of me and raised his hands to lower my hood back. I looked warily up at him and saw that the short distance through the club had taken its toll on his features.

He looked tired and tense with worry. Little lines had formed around his eyes that matched the ones on his forehead from where he was still frowning. I knew it wasn't directed at me because as soon as I smiled up at him, he let his eyes turn back from their angry purple to their softer black. The lines disappeared and he even let himself smile before kissing my forehead. I loved the sight of Draven's eyes getting lost in my own and it took his friend to clear his throat to draw his attention back to his situation.

"Leivic!" Draven said his name as though he was one of his dearest friends and combined with the embrace, I suspected that here stood one of Draven's most valued companions. The two men were about the same height, but Leivic was of a slightly slimmer build. Both men were, of course, handsome, but where Draven's features were untouched by years of scars, Leivic's unfortunately weren't.

I couldn't help the tactless gasp that escaped my lips and both men turned around to look at me. I wished that I hadn't done it, but the shock of seeing such a handsome face butchered by whatever weapon had nearly split the man in two, had me displaying my shock freely.

The scar started at the top right side of his head and slashed across his face in a diagonal that left him with a line about half an inch thick of dead tissue that looked whiter than white against his tanned skin. It missed his silver-blue eyes and passed through his nose making it seem to bend further to one side. It cut through half of his lip that pulled it further down to the left and as I followed it, I noticed it went from his face and down his neck no doubt finishing on his shoulder. When I met his eyes again, I was left feeling ashamed of myself.

"And this must be the young flower that has captured my friend's stone heart and turned it into molten lava. I can see why Dom, she holds a rare beauty only equalled to the Gods, you are a lucky man, my friend." I must have blushed roses at this statement because both men were laughing heartily when they saw my reaction. I didn't know what to do at that moment, so I recalled my mother's words, 'When meeting new people always smile dear, hold out your hand and make eye contact,' which is precisely what I did.

"I'm pleased to meet you, Leivic," I said, having to clear my throat first. He took my hand as though it was made of fine china and lifted it to his scarred lips to kiss. Once seeing his kind eyes, it wasn't hard to see the handsome features that were damaged by his mighty scar. There was nothing but benevolence in his manner and his voice filled me with an ease.

"The pleasure is all mine I can assure you. I haven't seen my friend this happy since our battling days." The thought gave me shivers. 'Draven the Warrior' fit far too well for me not to get images flashing through my head of him fearlessly cutting through his victims as though nothing could stand in his way, a knife through butter came to mind.

"You honour us with your presence." He bowed to me and turned back to Draven, who looked full of pride at showing me to his beloved friend.

"Has she arrived?" Draven asked but Leivic just shook his head and laid a hand on his friend's shoulder.

"Have no fear, she will but while you wait you must relax. Come, everything has been prepared for you." It was the first time I started to take in my surroundings and noticed that this part of the club was private. Only a few people were back here and the only thing separating the rest of the club from this room was a wall of crimson curtains. They were thick but at the same time, transparent, like some magic window that kept distorting and rippling like water, but still allowing us to see out into the crowd.

I suspected that we could see out, but they couldn't see in. The people in this room were what consisted of the VIP and its servants. The raised space was lined with square booths that held large floor cushions which made up sunset coloured beds. Deep reds, vibrant pinks, golden yellows and burnt oranges filled the room with a Moroccan feel. Smoke coming from hookah pipes clung to the air and mixed with oil lamps smelling of different spices floated around me, tickling my nostrils.

Some of the booths had couples doing more than talking and I shamefully looked away from the naked body parts. Others were getting their entertainment from dancing beauties in long flowing skirts and jewelled tops that barely covered their breasts.

Although, while getting through the crowd the music had been deafening, here just behind the curtained wall it was only a mild humming. I was almost wishing for it to be just as loud once again because then the sounds of pleasure filled moans wouldn't have been making me turn scarlet.

I turned away from the sound, but not quick enough to avoid seeing the four naked bodies entwined together looking as though they were being filmed for a porn channel.

I heard Draven let out a guttural laugh and as I glanced up at him, I noted the amused look on his face, no doubt due to my uncomfortable reactions to this strange place. I was starting to understand that the world of the supernatural was even more sex driven than the human one, if that was possible.

"Come." Draven's voice was a husky command in my ear making the sexual tension between us close to snapping apart, whiplashing at my senses until his lips claimed mine. I thought this room would have me shying away from such feelings, but the tingling in between my legs had me facing the facts.

No matter where we were or what we were doing, one command in that sexy voice of his was all it took. He curled his fingers around the top of my arm and led me to our own private, cloaked booth. The square of vibrant colour was bigger than the rest and seemed more secure from prying eyes that were to be invading our every move. Sex entwined bodies stopped momentarily as we walked past, and one pair of eyes even peered over the nipple they were currently pleasuring.

Instead of moans of satisfaction, there were now murmurs of shock and disbelief. I suddenly felt more exposed than these naked people, as though I was walking myself through a dream or a nightmare, it was so surreal.

"Ignore them." I looked up to find that Draven's eyes were intently worried on my face and before I could utter a word, he swung me around so that I was hidden by his body. He then walked me backwards with a carefully placed hand steadying me at the small of my back. Taking one last step was all it took to make me fall backwards onto the bed of pillows. He grabbed my hand before I landed to lower me down gently and then turned back to speak to his friend.

"Give us a moment alone." His friend smiled at him and then cocked his head around Draven's large frame to give me a wink before departing. I couldn't help smiling at the expression on Leivic's face, like a mischievous little boy that knew his friend wanted to be naughty.

"Find something amusing?" Draven's voice brought me out of my daft grin that I was sporting.

"I like your friend." At this he raised one eyebrow and gave me a quizzical stare.

"What?" I said in defence, but this made him growl and I let out a little yelp as he grabbed me under my knees and pulled me under his body.

"Tough shit, you're mine!" At this his lips finally claimed mine and the curtained material floated around us, hiding away our heated bodies that were being overwhelmed with the sexual electricity we were producing.

I wanted to tell him no, wait, slowdown…anything to make him stop, so that I could clear my head, but the other part of me, my lust, wasn't agreeing with me. Don't get me wrong, it's not like I didn't want Draven doing this to me but here, surrounded by a room full of horny Demons and Angels all getting their kicks by watching us…uh, that would be a no.

I think he could tell what I was thinking because he seemed to be doing all the work. One hand was holding most of his weight above me, while the other was exploring my upper body and quickly unfastening my jacket to make exploring easier. He then abruptly stopped kissing my lips to look at me. I opened my eyes at the movement and found him frowning.

"Keira?" He said my name as if to prompt me into telling him what was wrong but even now, that frown of his sent butterflies cascading to my stomach. Like when you were a child and you had done something naughty in class and been sent to the Headmaster's office about it. It's the feeling when you're stood outside his door waiting to be reprimanded. It was like that when Draven looked at me the way he was doing now. Would I ever get used to the masterly figure as my equal? I surely hoped so.

"It's just…" was all I could manage in my shyest voice. This made his frown crumble and a soft smile replace it. He then let his body relax to the side of me and I wondered if his arm ached at all from holding all his weight on it for so long? It sure didn't seem like it. He ran soft fingers across my cheek and smiled at me.

"Keira, there is no need to be embarrassed. I wouldn't allow anyone to see us. I would never share you with anyone, which includes seeing you like this. Hell, if I could get away with hiding you away forever, for my eyes only, I would but I fear you would think it a little barbaric." I laughed.

"A little?" I mocked making him just shrug.

"If I had found you in a different time, I might have been able to get away with it, but now in these modern times I doubt harems would be acceptable." I could tell he was teasing me, but I still reacted the way he wanted me to. I let out a screech of disbelief and punched him on the arm that probably felt like I was gently lifting lint from his sleeve. He laughed and I tried to keep the anger on my face.

"Harem is it! Well, you're welcome to it, just don't expect me to be there lined up with the other desperate mistresses waiting for a turn at a royal roll in the sack!" I crossed my arms over my chest with a huff. I was fuming after I had finished my little speech and Draven knew why.

"Desperate?" he said raising an eyebrow with an amused look in his deep eyes. This time I was the one to just shrug my shoulders, not wanting to give him more fuel to play with.

"Royal roll in the…sack was it?" He was clearly enjoying himself and I rolled my eyes and made a move to get up, trying to put some distance between us. But his wandering hands that he hadn't removed from my body this entire conversation weren't having any of it.

I know I was acting a bit spoilt, but I couldn't help the green-eyed monster that was seeping its way into my brain's functions. I couldn't get the picture of beautiful women all lay around waiting to pleasure Draven out of my mind, like a visual poison running its course and Aurora was the very face injecting that burn through my veins.

I shifted and tried to sit up again, but Draven was quick and much stronger than I. His arm flashed across my body and forced me back down with little effort. He then moved his body on top of me and pinned my arms above my head.

"And where do you think you're going, little one?" He was still smiling, and I was still showing my anger, despite what being pinned down by the world's sexiest man was doing to my nether regions. I started to wriggle and when his erection pressed harder into me I stopped, realising what my movements were causing. My frown was quickly replaced with surprise and a bitten lip. He took note of what my teeth were doing to my lips and his eyes flashed purple with hunger.

"That looks tasty… here let me help you with that," and then he dived into my lips so quickly his words died on my skin. He took my bottom lip into his mouth and sucked it up before running his teeth over the inside making them quiver and turn hypersensitive.

He released my wrists but began desperately searching out the skin underneath my sweater dress. He growled when unconsciously my hips raised and met his groin in eager response. His reaction led him to lay more of his weight upon me and he forced his tongue into my mouth to claim even more of me. His kiss continued getting deeper until my chest heaved and I was soon panting for air. He felt my body arching and instantly calmed his responses. That was the first time I had seen Draven lose his control, if only for one second and it had me wondering what sex would be like if he ever did lose complete control?

I could see his jaw tense and his eyes close, as if he was fighting the Demon inside of him. His hands were shaking over my body and then they tensed into tight fists taking handfuls of my clothes into them. He looked as though he was close to losing his inner battle and would soon rip them to shreds. Part of me wished he would.

"Draven?" I asked nervously. My barely-there voice seemed to have a soothing effect as he released my clothes. He also began to breathe again, unlike before when he had been holding his breath for what seemed like the longest time. He opened his eyes which had now returned to their endless black pools of emotion. He could see that once again I was back to biting my lip and his lips curved into a devilish grin.

"I wouldn't do that again if I were you or I might not be able to control myself next time." I let my lip slip from my grip before he leaned down to kiss me again, this time gently as though he might break me.

"I take it I am forgiven?" he asked into my skin as he had moved to kissing me on my neck. When I started to shake my head, he pulled away from me making me instantly feel cold without his touch.

"No? Well, did I mention that in this Harem you would be the only one there to...how did you put it...roll in my royal sack?" Now he was mocking me.

"Did you ever have a Harem?" I asked but I couldn't help the emotional flush that flooded my cheeks. I wasn't sure I even wanted to know. Well, that's not entirely true. I did want to know but only if it was the answer that I wanted.

Of course it wasn't.

"Long ago, yes." He waited for my reaction and smiled an evil bad boy grin when he got it. I tried to look away, but he hooked a finger under my chin to force me to look back at him. He had one eyebrow raised and from the look of things he was enjoying every minute of my mental torture.

"You know the jealously you display towards me is intoxicating. It drives me crazy to know that your possessive nature towards me grants me my own. It gives me great comfort to know I do not stand alone in feeling like you belong to me and I to you." This statement couldn't help but make me smile, which in turn spread to his lips also.

"I have to admit, I do enjoy watching your reaction to jealousy," he said as he casually leaned his weight on one bent arm, as the other was preoccupied with running up and down my side. I decided to play him at his own game, although the saying 'playing with fire' came to mind, after all his temper was far worse than my own. It still didn't stop me though.

"So, I guess that night seeing me kissing Jac..." I didn't get any further with that memory as he covered my mouth with one strong hand quicker than my eyes could register.

"Do not remind me," he growled at me and his purple eyes flashed their discomfort at the subject. This was when I knew I had gone too far. He eased his hold and lowered his hand.

"It is not wise to let my mind return to that…that cruel night." He truly looked in pain, which shocked me. I mean, I remember the pain I had felt when seeing Celina kiss him. Did he feel the same that night when Jack had kissed me? It would seem so.

"Not so funny when you're on the receiving end, is it?" I asked smugly and this actually made him look sorry.

"Touché. You are right. I should not tease you on such matters, even if I do enjoy your reactions." He ran the back of his hand down my face before he continued,

"But you have to understand Keira, back then I did not love. I didn't give in to it, because it never fit. I always knew that one day I would find you and to fall in love with anyone but you, was something I wasn't capable of doing. But that doesn't mean I never gave in to the pleasures of the world. After all, I have lived more years where a Harem was not only acceptable, but it was expected of a…well, a being of my position." I think it was the first time I was seeing Draven uncomfortable talking about his past. The way he said the word 'being' was as though he didn't really know what to call himself was infectious and I would be lying if I didn't think this little insight was endearing.

I was about to tell him that he didn't have to explain as it was obvious he was uncomfortable but he held up a hand to stop me.

"No, I want to tell you, to explain who I was then and who I am now…because of you." He ran his thumb over my lip and down the column of my neck as he spoke, making me want to moan in pleasure.

"Back then I was hard and cold like a living statue that was here to represent Heaven and Hell combined. I have lived more years to count, but only now does it feel like I am alive. Like a rebirth. I never knew myself before I met you, I just thought I was the man who I had to be because of my responsibilities to a race I didn't respect. But after meeting you, I not only changed my view on love but on the truth of what I have really been placed here to defend." I couldn't help but raise my hand to his cheek and softly run my pale fingers against the flawless golden skin they felt there along his masculine jaw. His eyes flashed to mine and there was an emotion hidden there that I didn't yet have the knowledge to read. His voice brought me back from wondering too long.

"I started to see things I never knew existed. A certain compassion that humans can display freely to one another. Like Frank and the brotherly way he treats you, knowing you can depend on him for anything or the obvious love and worry on your sister's face that night when I brought you home in my arms. It started to fascinate me from my very first meeting with you. Almost as though you were honoured with the power of Heaven to wake me from my ignorance with the very first time I touched you."

I was close to tears by the time he had finished expressing his feelings and I was taken aback by everything that I had learned. Did I really do all that for him? Was I really the one who had changed him for the better? It was a nice thought, thinking I brought out the humanity in Draven that had never surfaced until now. Not to mention him saying he had never been in love before, now that was BIG!

With my fingers still to his face I cupped his cheek as I smiled up at him. I didn't know what to say, but when he met my gaze my eyes must have said it all. I loved him and I would love him until every fibre in my body was gone and had turned to dust, but even when my bones had joined the earth, the memory of our love would live on beyond the ages.

All of this I let out freely for him to find and when he grasped my fingers in his hand to hold them to his lips, I knew that he had heard me. He kissed my hand as if it was the most precious gift he owned.

"It is," he said startling me. I quickly put back up all my mental guards so as not to allow him too deeply into my mind. I still had secrets to keep but when I thought about them, I couldn't fully understand why? It was like someone had planted an automatic response to hide things. Images of something Draven might recognise or a voice he would sense controlling me. What was I doing? I needed to tell Draven everything. I needed to let him in...I...I need...What was wrong with me?

Why couldn't I? I raised my hands to my head to try and relieve the pressure pounding against my skull. Something was wrong, I knew that now. All this time...but how? It was like being here amplified it somehow, something was here that was doing these things to me.

"Keira? What's wrong?" I could hear the panic in Draven's voice, but it was being muffled by another. It was like trying to watch TV and talk to someone on the phone at the same time. I kept picking up bits of one and some of the other.

"Tell him you're fine," a voice hummed in my head. I shook myself as though that would somehow help. Then the next thing I knew I was opening my mouth and I heard myself saying,

"Everything is fine. I only have a slight headache." It was the strangest feeling, like an out-of-body experience.

"Good girl, now forget my voice and don't let him into your mind again." The voice sounded frustrated, as though he had lost some control and didn't understand why. I tried to focus on not losing it but it was quickly fading away into a far memory, the kind you never access often. Like a smell or a sound that pulls you back into the information of your past. I didn't fully understand what had just happened, but I knew one thing for sure, I was scared.

Draven looked less than happy with my answer but something in my face must have told him not to push it. By then I started to lose control over what it was I desperately needed to tell him. It was as though the last ten minutes were a dream but at the time you know exactly what is happening. One so real you can touch, taste and feel even the pain, but then after you wake, it slips away like the tide. Why couldn't I remember?

"Are you sure you're alright? You seem... distant?" he asked softly and of course he was right. I felt so far away, it felt as though I would never make it back home. I knew one thing for an absolute, something today had definitely changed. I knew something here was different, what exactly I couldn't say but it was there like a locked room in my mind and only I could find a way in. Now, of course, all I needed was to find the right key.

"Yes, I'm fine, sorry I was just thinking about stuff," I said after feeling his touch on my cheek.

"Anything I can help with?" If only, I thought pointlessly to myself. For one thing I didn't even know what it was that I needed help with.

"Well, maybe a kiss would help."

"Maybe? We'll just have to see about that 'maybe'." He pulled me into his arms and took my breath away into his mouth. It was dreamingly delightful.

It was only when a cough outside the fabric barrier caught our attention that I started to pull away. Draven, however, wouldn't allow that for long and pulled me back so that I was level with his face.

"I will not be dictated to!" he said urgently, as though a man starved of hunger, making him search out my lips like food.

"شما صبر کنید تا من آماده ام" ("You will wait until I am ready" In Persian) He spoke out angrily towards the vibrant curtain that concealed both us and the 'Intruder' before claiming me once more. I don't know how long his kiss lasted but I never wanted it to end. I never did. However, he finished it off by holding my face in both hands and then tilted it down so that his final kiss ended on my forehead.

"Inebriante." ("intoxicating" in Italian) he whispered and just before I could ask him what he meant, he let me go and spoke again.

"I have to go now, but I won't be long."

"Where are you going?" I asked, failing to keep the needy tone out of that question.

"I have to meet with someone. It's the reason I came here, but I will explain later." With that, he motioned his hand across and the material floated back without contact. Behind it a beautiful woman stood waiting, along with Leivic. As soon as Draven saw the woman, I could have sworn I'd seen him flinch. I was almost certain she was an Angel, as there was a Heavenly grace about her that had you looking at her in awe.

She was tall and slender, with a body displaying slight curves in just the right places. The dress she wore dipped so low you could see in between the two most noticeable curves and it looked as though she had glued the material to the sides to stop you from seeing her nipples. The stark white satin was almost glowing and had me squinting my eyes.

Her hair was a complete contrast making her look like a chessboard. Long straight midnight hair hung loose down her back like a cloak of silk. She had one side held back in a crystal-encrusted clasp that was in the shape of the zodiac sign for fire. I recognised it from when Libby had a brief fascination with fortune-telling and star signs.

Her skin was like her dress, spotless and flawless, the skin of a child that glowed along with every other part of her. However, her beautiful figure and perfect skin, was nothing in comparison to the pair of golden eyes that had depths a man could drown in. They were enchanting to witness, and I had no doubt Draven had been enchanted intimately. The thought had me close to tears.

"Hora." Draven nodded his head after saying her name in recognition. She smiled, displaying a set of pearly white teeth that would have been a dentist's wet dream. She bowed in respect, making me wish she hadn't as you could see right down her dress to her nakedness underneath. Well, I guess if you wore a dress that tight, you couldn't get away with underwear. I was almost smug when I saw Draven not looking. Oh yes, these two definitely had history.

"My Lord, it has been far too long, we must get acquainted once more." I wanted to get up and push her off those expensive-looking heels, Angel or not, I still wanted to kick her bony skeleton ass!

Draven looked back at me and obviously liked the brief look of rage on my face and thanks to conversations little past I knew why. He knew I was jealous. Hora followed his gaze to mine and what she saw there she didn't look worried. I mean why would she, I was a mere limpet in the shadow of the most exquisite coral.

"How rude of me, Hora this is my 'Electus' Keira, and Keira this is Hora, one of my loyal subjects." The way Draven said this sentence made my stomach fill with liquid desire. His voice smoothed over me like a warm blanket making me swoon. Luckily, I was still sitting down otherwise I would have looked like an idiot. It was the first time I had heard Draven introduce me as 'Electus', which I now knew meant "chosen" in Latin. Hora looked as if she had swallowed a bug and I suppressed the urge to laugh.

"Electus? Then the rumours are true for once. Congratulations, My Lord, you have found a rare treasure indeed. In that case, you should not keep the Oracle waiting any longer. I now understand her eagerness in speaking with you." After she said this all my misplaced ill will evaporated. Meanwhile Leivic had been silent but amused with me. His gaze had been locked with mine and was watching with great interest with thick arms folded across his chest. If he hadn't been smiling, he would have been quite terrifying to look at.

"Keira, I have to go but wait here for me to come back for you. Do not move...alright?" I nodded and he looked relieved.

"Good girl," he said before turning to an amused Leivic.

"Arkadaşım, bekçilik ve yakın kimse izin onu" ("My friend, keep watch and let no one near her" In Turkish). Leivic put a hand on Draven's shoulder and also replied in a language I didn't know.

"Hayatımda onu koruyacak" ("I will guard her with my life" In Turkish).

I would have loved to have known what they were saying, and my curiosity grew when they both turned to look at me before Draven left with Hora. I didn't actually receive a goodbye from Hora, but I did receive a respectful head bow. This definitely bumped her up to top billing of one of the nicer exes Draven had. The question of how many I would meet made me shiver. The amount of exes one could acquire over hundreds of years was staggering. One bitch named Aurora was enough for me thank you very much.

"Can I get you something to drink?" A deep accented voice brought me away from my darker thoughts of ex-girlfriends.

"Uh...ok, yes, thank you," I said suddenly shy without Draven by my side. I looked around nervously now I was unprotected and couldn't help but gasp at all the eyes staring my way. Leivic noticed my change and decided to intervene.

"Доста!" ("Enough" In Serbian) His booming voice made me jump and I wasn't the only one. All eyes had now taken their naked bodies back behind the curtains and we were left alone. He turned back to see my shocked face at his sudden outburst.

"I am sorry, did I frighten you?"

"N...no," I lied, and he smiled as he knew the truth. I couldn't help but wonder what he had said to make everyone leave us alone, so I couldn't help myself when I asked,

"Why is it your kind never stick to speaking just one language?" It's something I had always wanted to know, but never asked Draven about.

"Ah, for a human this must seem very odd." I nodded and thankfully he appeased my curiosity and enlightened me.

"You will not find all of us do this, just us oldies like me and Dom." He winked at me before continuing,

"It goes back to a time when streets were thick with spies and humans were somewhat wiser in their beliefs and trusting heavily in the supernatural. It made things complicated and more beneficial to speak in ways where only the old and the powerful could communicate openly. You see, as old as we are, comes with it the tedious amounts of experience and with that comes extensive knowledge. Languages are but one thing that we acquire over time. Of course, thanks to our endless days here, moving around the globe is inevitable when living in the human eye. So, as easy and natural as it is for you to speak English, it is the same for us in many different ways. It is now more habit than not I think." Ok, well with him putting it like that I could understand it a little better and might not find it so annoying now.

"You make my friend very happy. I have never seen him so." This turn in conversation made me smile.

"Thank you, but can I ask how long you have known him?" He raised an eyebrow at my question, making the scar on his face rise.

"Would you like me to tell you some stories about Dominic?" At this I nearly yelled out 'Oh God yes!' But thankfully I had the good sense not to. However, he could read the eagerness on my face, so I explained.

"He doesn't tell me much about his past." Leivic nodded at my statement with a coy smile.

"I understand... perhaps he does not wish to overwhelm you, but I see that you are an intelligent girl, I think you can handle it." He winked at me and I laughed. I was very much starting to like this friend of Draven's.

"Then let me enlighten you my dear, but first let me get you a drink to ease the shocking stories I have to tell."

I was so excited I could have danced around giving the naked Demons something really strange to watch.

I sat there with my legs folded, close to bouncing like a child waiting to hear the greatest stories of my life...

The stories of the man I love.

CHAPTER THIRTY-EIGHT

SACRIFICES

Leivic took a seat next to me and made himself comfortable among the pillows. He cast me a curious look as if he was still trying to figure out if I was real or not. I wanted to ask him what it was that he seemed to find so interesting, but my thoughts were interrupted by a waitress who had arrived with a tray of drinks in one hand and a large, ornate smoking pipe in another. He noted my raised eyebrow turn to scepticism and quickly added,

"It's for me," to which I responded with a nod.

"Thank you, Winnie," he said kindly and reached out to take the tray from her before setting it down on a little side table. All the while, I was thinking what an unusually tame name for a Demon and wondering if asking her where Pooh was wouldn't get me a killer look. Needless to say I refrained.

Once Winnie left, Leivic started to light the coal that was under the metal case on the top of the pipe. It was a metre high with a large glass vase at the bottom which held some form of liquid. I had seen these before in bars in Spain where you would find groups of people all sharing one. They came with multiple tubes with the mouthpieces on the end where they were smoked through. This one, however, was only meant for the one smoker.

Leivic had finished setting it up and started to suck on the end pulling the air through. He blew out a stream of smoke making the scent of the east cling to the surrounding air.

"I hope you don't mind?" he asked politely.

"Not at all." What was I going to say, 'Hell yeah, don't you care about your health?!' I don't think so somehow.

He passed me a drink of what looked like red wine and after a quick sip, it was confirmed. I didn't know why but I let out a sigh of relief. What did I think it would be...blood? He took another long suck from the pipe, causing a bubbling noise to emanate from the liquid at the bottom, before blowing it out from scarred lips.

It seemed to swim from his mouth and then took on a life of its own as it formed a smoke dragon in the air in front of me. It pranced along with its snaky tail following it as it opened its mouth. Leivic then blew out more smoke making little blue sparks in the shape of flames come from its mouth.

"That was seriously cool!" I said with a massive grin planted on my face. Leivic bowed his head to me and said,

"I'm glad you liked it but I fear such little effort deserved such an adorable reward." I turned to him shocked at his reply, asking what it was he meant.

"Sorry?"

"Your smile, I find it adorable. You are such an innocent soul yet you have witnessed so much horror in such a short life. However, you still remain pure and untainted by the cruelty of human life. That is a rarity indeed." I was both shaken and moved by his words. I must have shown my shock because he frowned.

"I have upset you...forgive me, I spend so little time around humans these days that I forget myself. One of my gifts is reading souls and I find it hard when I come across such a rare beauty in one, to not express my feelings." He paused to look at me sideways while pulling in another puff on his pipe. When he blew it out this time, it took me a while to make out the new smoky shape. Thankfully, just before its vapour was lost, I was pretty sure it was the same symbol I had received down in the temple from opening that door. It made me wonder what my new friend knew about it.

"You are strong though, unusually so for a breather and for this, Dom is a lucky man. There are not many who would be able to adapt so quickly with a blind faith like you have...Oh, but please don't get me wrong as I say so in paying you a compliment. You are truly destined for my dear friend indeed and I could not be happier for him. He is the one being in the world who deserves it the most I think."

I still didn't quite know what to say to this without brimming over with emotion. It had touched me that this man whom I had only just met thought so much of me. I felt blessed.

I was about to speak but as if knowing my thoughts, he held up his hand to stop me.

"Please, there is no need to thank me for words that are true. I speak them because it is fact and something you need to hear. Like my friend Dom, I never speak only to flatter." This made me smile, to know Draven wasn't the type of man to say what he didn't mean just for the sake of provoking a response. Although, saying things that would provoke a jealous response was a different matter.

"I would like to thank you all the same," I said feeling better.

I took a long sip of my drink, which helped me to relax a little at my current situation. I wondered how long I would be with Draven before places like this became the norm to me. If I thought my life was complicated before, then now it was off the charts crazy!

Leivic was silent during my thoughts, but when I heard the bubbling of liquid once again it pulled me away from the hectic track of my mind.

"So, how do you know Draven?" I asked before thinking about the question in my head. Man, I sounded dumb. I mean it wasn't as if they were college buddies for God's sake. I had to smile at this, thinking that at least with my last thought I was closer to the mark as no doubt the Gods most certainly had something to do with it.

Leivic on the other hand wore an amused smile that crept up on one side before he answered me.

"Well, there are very few of our kind who have not heard of their natural Master, but there are those certainly foolish enough not to obey him. I, however, count myself lucky enough to call him friend and I hold that title with great pride indeed." I couldn't help but smile at the affection in his voice when talking about the man I loved.

"I owe my life to Dominic and would give it undeniably in return. He saved me from my fate, which was far worse than my death." He watched as my eyes widened in horror. What could be worse than death…torture maybe?

"Would you like to hear my story?" I think he was checking that I was up to it and when I nodded, he looked pleased. It was almost as if he had been waiting to tell someone for so long that now he was jumping at the chance.

"I would," I answered, prompting another trademark bow from him and I found this all very endearing.

"First, I feel that I should tell you it is not a happy tale that I speak of, but one of great meaning and sacrifice." I nodded willing him to carry on and thankfully he did.

"You see, in my Demon form, for I am a Demon… did you know that?" he asked shooting me a look making his colossal scar twitch. I coughed out my answer.

"Um..m...no I didn't." I said trying to hide the shock of imagining such a nice, polite man as a scary Demon. I knew I was being naive again, but it was hard to dismiss what history had taught me over the years about who were the bad guys. I think Sunday school would have been quite a different lesson if the world knew the truth.

"I am what you would call a Reaper shifter." At this I couldn't help the sudden intake of air causing him to look hurt. I mean, what else was I supposed to do? Here I was having a very personal conversation with a...well...*with a bloody Reaper!* A Demonic merchant of death that's who!

"Please do not be frightened, I did not just take souls at a whim. I had contracts, just like anyone would."

"You don't do it anymore then?" I asked when he said the word 'Did' instead of 'do'.

"No, I gave up that right long ago. You see, I worked for Hell, gathering souls that were on my list, until one day there was one on my list I didn't want to take." His silver-blue eyes glazed over with the memory and I couldn't help but put my hand on his arm. I wanted to comfort him as it was obvious that this was not an easy story to tell. He smiled, making the scar across his face rise and fall. There were laughter lines around his eyes that creased at my gesture and he looked touched by my concern.

"Have you ever heard of the Goths?" I narrowed my eyes trying to understand what he meant then I looked around seeing many that were in this very club, but he started to shake his head.

"Forgive me, not the Goths you see today, all those lost people who dress in black and like to believe in our kind. I'm talking about an East Germanic tribe who played an important role in the history of the Roman Empire." When I was still at a loss, he winked at me.

"It is of no matter. I guess the second century is little taught in education today. Let's see...the Goth war was in 375, so that would put me in The Dniester about 365 AD." I could barely nod I was in that much shock. That would make the man I was speaking to now at over 1600 years old! Was that possible? How many lifetimes was that? Ok, so now I had a headache.

"Where is Dni...uh... what you said?" He laughed at me giving up on trying to say the right name and then said it again only slower...as if it would somehow help.

"Dniester is a river in Eastern Europe. The Dniester rises in Ukraine, near the city of Drohobych, close to the border with Poland and flows toward the Black Sea. That's where the tribe was situated at the time and being how I looked, I was being hunted."

"HUNTED! But why, did they know who you were?" I was horrified by the idea of Draven's friend being hunted like an animal, but I soon understood enough as the next words out of his mouth were the last ones I could have ever expected.

"I didn't exactly look human then. I was in my Demon form you see, which is a bear and..." I coughed out my disbelief, interrupting him.

"I'm sorry did you say a...*a bear?*"

"I did. I guess Draven hasn't explained much about our kind and our other forms has he?"

"I don't think Draven likes me knowing too much, which

makes it harder as most of the time I feel out of my depth not knowing, but I know Draven doesn't see it like that."

"I can understand it on both sides. If you were mine I would want to protect you from certain things. On the other hand, I can imagine you are brimming over with questions...it is after all, only human nature to be curious."

"You can say that again!" I said laughing at memories that took me back to how many questions I would ask Draven when I first found out about this other world. Hell, who was I kidding, I still did it on a daily basis.

"So where was I?"

"You were a bear," I said as though it was the most natural comment in the world.

"Yes, yes I was. I was hunting in the river at the time, but what I didn't realize was that I wasn't the only one. You see, in this tribe it was a sort of rite of passage for a boy to become a man, he had to kill a bear with nothing in his hand but a small hunting knife. I had my back to the boy and he crept up on me without making a sound." He took a moment to inhale another hit from his pipe but this time when he blew out his smoke, it started to give life to his story. One of my hands crept up to cover my mouth in quiet shock as he let the stream of smoke form a hand fisting a dagger held high. He continued on as he waved his hand through it making it disappear as if recoiling from his touch.

"I can imagine he grew up to be a great hunter, after all he had it in his bloodline as his father was not only the tribe's best tracker but their best warrior. He also had a daughter and her name was Siggwan. I believe it means 'to sing' in their native language." I knew, even without him saying so, that he was in love with the girl. I could see it in his eyes, his smile and mostly the way he said her name full of pride and the deepest meaning.

It was as if he could see her standing right in front of him. A hidden memory only he could access and then he turned his face as if to hide the secret smile he thought I didn't see. I couldn't help grinning behind my hand.

"That's what saved me from getting hurt. I heard her beautiful voice singing. I turned around in time to see her brother coming and managed to knock the knife from his hand without causing too much damage. Not that he could have killed me, but it would have still hurt. He ran off after that but not before finding his sister and taking out his anger on her. I found her later by the river washing the blood from her face."

"The bastard!" I said making him look at me in surprise. His raised eyebrow made me want to justify myself.

"I'm a strong believer that a man who hits a woman is nothing but a coward!" I said raising my chin, making him smile.

"And rightly so. I feel this way also which is why it hurt me to witness the damage his fists had caused." Once again, he took a minute to smoke and create a scene by blowing the magic through his scarred lips. This time the swirls were softer and formed the back of a girl on her knees facing the river. It was like watching a 3D black and white movie right in front of my face.

"I walked towards her and when she saw me, she didn't flinch…by the Gods but she didn't even look scared at the sight of this 1800lb, nine-foot Kodiak bear coming closer to her. She even smiled at me and I thought I had never seen anything as beautiful. She could stop my heart with that one smile."

"She must have been extremely brave," I noted before taking another sip of wine.

"She was fearless, more so than her brother was, that much was clear. She let me come next to her on the riverbed and then she turned to me and told me how she was glad her brother hadn't killed me. I wanted to thank her, but I couldn't change in front of her, so I decided to wait until nightfall."

"So, did you go back to find her?" I asked getting immersed in the story.

"I did find her again once I was human. I think you can guess what happened next. No doubt you can understand what type of love we shared?" He looked into my eyes and found his answer instantly.

"What happened?" At this question his eyes became intense for painful seconds before he had to look away from me, ripping his gaze away to look over his other shoulder. Then he took a shuddered breath into his pipe and blew out his answer. A roll of grey unfolded into what looked like an ancient book and a name slowly appeared.

In response I sucked in a quick breath willing the cruelty of it all not to be true but then he continued the horror with words, as if the smoky evidence wasn't enough.

"I received my next contract." My hands flew to cover my mouth as I shrieked.

"No! Oh God no."

"Yes, I am afraid so. When I refused to take her soul, I was merely informed that another would just replace me and take it anyway. So, I did the only thing I knew I could do." Pained lines circled his eyes like an evil frame.

"Wh...what did you do?" I whispered the question with a lump caught firmly in my throat, needing to know the end of his personal tragedy.

"I bargained." Those two words cut through me like his hand had cut through the smoke earlier and now I didn't know if I was brave enough to hear the end of this story as I once was. It turned out I wasn't given the choice as he carried on to the very bitter end.

"I traded her soul for mine. So simply put, I signed myself over to Hell's punishments so that she may live a full life and die with her soul intact. Of course, this meant a hundred lifetimes for me to rot in the pit...well, that was until Draven bargained for my life." The way he said the words 'my life' was as if he still couldn't quite believe this had happened, even after all this time. He turned his face to mine and now his pride was directed towards his friend and I myself also beamed with pride at what Draven had done. No wonder they were such close friends, Draven had saved him from the Devil only knows what.

I found I had tears in my eyes from his story and I could not begin to tell you how it touched me. Which reminded me of the saying, 'Is it really better to have loved and lost, or better to have never loved at all?' Before meeting Draven, I would have said to have never loved at all, but now? Well, now I knew I would rather have died after one kiss, than never have felt his touch, even if only for one fleeting, blissful moment in my lifetime.

"How did he get you out?" I found myself asking after seeing his next smoke figure was that of two male hands clasped together in a clear sign of brotherhood. Almost as if it was Draven's very hand pulling him from his unlawful sentence.

"A powerful being such as Draven needs very little in reason to get what he wants. I was just happy that I could return the favour."

"What? You saved his life?"

"Watch now, little Miss." This time instead of melancholy, a flicker of mischief came back to his silver-blue eyes with a quick spark of power shining through. He lifted the pipe to his lips once more and this time he took in a larger amount, making the liquid in the glass bubble furiously. He winked at me with his lips still around the tip before letting go and blowing out an endless long ribbon of white. With one hand slightly raised his fingertips twitched, making the escaping cloud take form.

My eyes widened as a small army of warriors grew from the smoke like dominos falling down in reverse. They each popped up one after the other until at the end there were two lone figures back to back in battle. I couldn't see what they were fighting but Draven's form was clear from the two swords that grew from his hands. This, of course, was a memory of him I wouldn't be forgetting anytime soon, thanks to my crazy ex stalker.

The other man fighting at his back was obviously Leivic and instead of the graceful moves of the sword, he swung around a huge battle axe the size of half his body.

"I wouldn't ever be so bold as to say I saved the life of his Highness but I most certainly can claim to have at least saved his body." He inhaled again to blow out the ending to this medieval, supernatural war that was taking place before my very eyes. I remained so deathly still, fearing that any sudden movements would cause the scene to just float away and slither back to Leivic's vault of memories.

The little smoke fight was as fast-paced as I expected with anything that included Draven in the picture. The two men whirled, bent and twisted their bodies, wielding their weapons this way and that, fighting invisible enemies with blurring speed. But just as the latest stream of smoke floated above the fight, a small cloud started to appear.

"What is that?" I let the question out through barely open lips still scared I would miss the brutal ending that left no doubt to what happened to my new friend.

"Abramelin." He hissed the name through a clenched jaw and just as I was about to ask him who he spoke of, the little cloud was suddenly turning darker and menacing. Then I quickly let out a squeak of surprise when a tiny lightning bolt erupted and travelled down towards the two figures still caught head-on in a smoky battle. At the last second, I watched as Leivic lifted his axe at just the right time to see something Draven could not reflected back from its surface.

I couldn't help but lean forward to try in vain to see what he saw but when his little head snapped up, I knew it was the fast-approaching deadly bolt racing from the sky. I could even see Leivic's tiny mouth shout the warning at the same time he moved to take Draven's place.

The lightning bolt quickly transformed from a jagged white zigzag into that of a deadly spear which missed Draven only thanks to him being pushed out of the way. I watched as his head looked up in time to see the spear strike down his friend, splitting the smoky image first in two before it evaporated for good.

Draven rose to his feet and with each step closer to where his friend's body would be his form too disappeared back to a time I didn't yet know. Tears fell from my chin as I only now realised how much the foggy reconstruction had gotten to me. It was only when Leivic spoke again that I realised I was still staring at the space where they had been.

"I don't think this scar would have suited him as it does me. I wear it well, do I not?" he asked me, laughing softly and giving me a playful nudge in the side. When I turned to him and he caught the first sight of my tears, his eyes turned a deeper shade of silver before ending up the colour of slate. He reached out and wiped away one of my tears with the back of a rough bent finger that had known hard labour at one time or another.

"What do you say, doesn't it suit me better?" He asked again and I couldn't help but smile back at him before swallowing the last of my emotional outburst. I cleared my throat and said,

"Oh, very handsome indeed…in a rough and manly way of course. Women love scars you know," I added, to which he responded with a wink in my direction.

"You have your own scars of the past I see." I gulped and looked down to my concealed arms, wondering how he knew?

"It is alright, I am sorry I brought it up, but you see we have something in common. We both have these scars as a reminder of the people we love. I sacrificed it for my friend, and for you?"

"For my family," I replied quietly and surprisingly honest for once.

"Do not be angry at Dom, for he did not tell me about your past. I was the one he asked to help find any information about you. When I learned about you, I was the one Dom sent to protect your sister and Frank at the time." I shot him a look of pure gratitude. Anyone who helped protect those I love earned my eternal respect and loyalty.

"Thank you, I…I don't know what to say." I lowered my head feeling doubtful I would ever be able to repay all these people who had helped me since Draven came into my life. Ragnar, Vincent, Sophia, Leivic and most of all Draven himself. And all this received by a person only used to doing everything herself. I wasn't used to having people to depend on. Don't get me wrong, my family were very supportive through my history with that evil, sick time. But since I'd had visions, I learned very quickly to keep my problems to myself or they would turn around to bite me in the ass, in the form of a mental hospital.

Now that was my true nightmare.

"You do not need to say anything, let alone thank me. I was more than happy to help and now, after meeting you I feel my friendship for Draven extends to his other self…to you, Keira. But on that note, I must leave you a moment, I will not be long, will you be alright?" I smiled at him before touching his hand that felt rough like sandpaper.

"Yes, of course, and thank you for telling me your story." At this he didn't answer but just kept staring at my hand on his, as though he had never felt a single touch for years. This made me feel conscious that maybe it was not the right thing to do, but as soon as the thought entered my mind, he lifted my hand to his lips and kissed my knuckles. He didn't say another word after that but nodded to me before he left.

I found myself only able to breathe after he had gone from my sight. I looked at my hand where his scarred lips had been and found it tingled slightly. I didn't know why but I was sure he had tasted me when his lips had parted slightly, and his tongue had lightly grazed me. I could still see the shiny mark of his kiss drying quickly. I know any normal person would have been freaked out by this, but I wasn't and found it oddly comforting. After all, he was half animal. Maybe this was just his way, like a cat or dog licking you when you stroke them.

I started to go over what I had just learned from Leivic and the more I learned about Demons and Angels, the more it seemed to make sense. They weren't that far apart from humans really and I wondered if that was what being on this 'plane' did to them. Did it make them more human?

Well, at least to some of them it did, and love seemed to be the key. It got me thinking what Draven was really like all his years before I came along? I had changed him, he had admitted as much. How was it he had put it earlier...? 'Back then I was hard and cold, like a living statue.' That's what he had said. Had I really made the blood flow back into his lifeless veins?

He certainly made out that I did. I found myself smiling to myself as I sipped my wine, only when my lips weren't feeling liquid on them did I noticed that my glass was empty. I don't know why but I really wanted another. I didn't usually like red wine, but there was something about this one that tasted a bit...addictive.

It was only when I was studying the glass that I noticed something weird-looking on the sides. It looked like crystallized particles that clung to the sides where the wine had once been filled. I lifted it to my nose but couldn't smell anything other than the rich aroma of fermented grapes.

I ran my finger on the inside collecting up the substance on my fingertip. Then I did a very silly thing before I could stop myself. I put the finger in my mouth and sucked it clean. The stuff felt like sugar grit but tasted bitter and as a result of my stupidity it was merely seconds before my head began to spin. I felt as though I was going to throw up but without the heaving process. I held my head in my hands as if this would help but it didn't and if anything, it felt as though it was the only thing keeping it on my body.

I felt my skin prickle as someone came near to me, but when I looked up there wasn't anyone there.

"You can hear my voice, young one." I sucked in a breath and curled my legs up to protect me as the voice that had haunted me earlier invaded my mind once again. It wasn't asking a question, but more like expressing an order. I looked around frantically for anyone I could tell but as soon as I thought it the voice boomed in my mind.

"NO, YOU WILL OBEY ME!" It screamed making my head vibrate in extreme pain. I let out a little moan and nodded at no-one to say I would comply. Anything just to stop the agony that rattled through me whenever it got angry.

"Good girl, now I want you to come to me, but I don't want you to let yourself be seen, do you understand?" I nodded again but wasn't sure if the voice would know my answer. Thankfully however it did, as I knew my sapped energy wouldn't have allowed for the power of speech.

"Good, but you have to stop crying or people will hear you." I hadn't been aware that I was crying but when I put my hands to my cheeks they were soaked with salty tears. My lips trembled as I tried to control the urge not to start sobbing. I wanted to be strong, but the voice started to get more urgent.

"Get ready to move when I tell you. I want you to stand up and slide out to your left and walk to the far wall. When you see the curtain move back, that will be your cue to leave." I shuddered at what I had to do next and inside I was screaming out which made it hurt all the more. I wished Leivic would come back to save me or even better, my dark knight Draven.

"That is not going to happen my dear, Draven is busy with the Witch and his friend has his hands full with another of my little diversions. So you see it is just you and me, now M...O...V...E!" He bellowed at me this time and my head pounded out every letter. The curtain flew back and I dipped out from within its protective shade. I saw the wall and my legs ran towards it without my help or control. Once there, I leaned against it panting in both physical weakness and being mentally scared out of my wits!

"Good, now I need you to follow the wall along until you find a black staircase, go down it and wait until I tell you otherwise." I did as I was told and found a staircase where the walls were painted black making it more like a tunnel of doom. There were little neon lights along the floor so that I could see enough to make it down each step. I continued on until the faintest light could be seen under a door.

I reached out for the handle when a pain so sharp and piercing hit me in the chest making me cry out and crumple to the floor. I was trying to catch my breath that was flowing out of me faster than I could take it back.

"NOT YET! I will tell you when to open the door!" I managed to get back to my feet and wipe my tears away angrily with my sleeve. I hated not being in control and this was the worst kind! At least, if this person had shown himself then there would be something I could channel my rage at. But for now, all the moment allowed me was an anger I felt towards myself for being so damn weak in this other world.

"On the contrary my dear, your mind is extremely hard to control and if it wasn't for the drugs I've been putting in your system, I would not be able to be controlling you now...Now get ready to move." I braced my hands on the door ready as instructed and now I could hear a heavy baseline had just started up. I wondered if this was what he had been waiting for...

And bingo, I had guessed right.

"NOW!" I narrowed my eyes at the throbbing pain I endured at his command and pushed the door open into the lower half of the club. When the first sights of people came into view, I let out an unheard scream. Every single person in the club was in their other form, making this the scariest place on earth and truly a room full of monsters!

Everyone was going into a frenzy for the band that was now playing and I guessed this had been what everyone had been waiting to see. I had never seen so many visions all at once unless controlled by a dream. The most I had seen together was four, back when I was twelve.

They had all been at a park, all huddled together like they were sharing a meal and when I got closer I hadn't been wrong. A boy had been injured by falling off his bike and they seemed as if they were just adults trying to help him. Only I saw the truth as they all sucked in a red glow from his body, making the little boy slump over more exhausted. Then I didn't know what they were doing to him but when I screamed out they all turned towards me and hissed. Of course, I'm not counting a swarm of Gorgon Leeches I had the displeasure in seeing.

I had told my mother that I had been sick, so that I could hide in my room for days, fearing they would find me. Now I knew they were feeding from the boy's pain. But here right now in time, now this was something different. It was as though they were feeding from each other and getting the ultimate high from it.

The room's low ceiling was hidden in a fog of energy and mangled bodies covered the floor. It was my idea of Hell, pure and simple Hell! So, I pulled my hood up as instructed and tried to make myself invisible. Every time a body got too close, I would sink away, terrified it would touch me.

Wings of all kinds could be seen well above the heads of Demons and Angels. Black and burnt red feathers all curled and pointed into deadly shards. Different materials, glass, wood and even plastic looked to have made up the most unusual ones. Fangs, claws, weapons of all kinds shone in the club's dim lighting. But the faces were what haunted me now. Contorted faces, with eyes where there shouldn't have been eyes, teeth where there shouldn't have been teeth and other added bits of skin that was stretched or loose over misshapen bone.

One girl had scales that flaked to the ground like snow when she danced. Others excreted liquid from other orifices that looked painful to watch. I gagged as one man's spit was dripping into another man's mouth and was being lapped up like liquid gold. The smell was another thing making me want to vomit. Acid bile and rotting flesh filled my nostrils, making me try even harder to breathe.

However, there weren't only Demons to be seen on the floor. Angels could be seen in bright glows that added more light in between the mass of figures. They had lighter coloured wings that always seemed bigger than those of the Demons.

They were undoubtedly beautiful creatures with skin of milky white or copper-gold that looked once fuelled by the absent sun. They were also going wild for the music and showed off more skin with every twist or jump they performed to the beat. Some even started to rip their clothes off so that naked parts could also show their excitement. I looked away not being able to take anymore, until I heard Demonic laughter in my head.

"What's wrong my dear, is the world you belong to a little less pleasing now you're far from your Master's bedchamber?" he mocked cruelly and I wanted to cry. It was somewhat true. I had been naive and now the world I found to be Draven's was even more tainted. There was no going back from this and I had no doubt this was what Draven had wanted to protect me from, but then why risk bringing me here in the first place?

"Stop!" the voice shouted making my eyes water and blur. I did as instructed and sank back to the wall behind me. Then I waited for what I recognised to be a diversion. Huge Angels were suddenly pushing their way through the crowd with ease and considering the crossed axes strapped to their backs, I could understand...these guys were seriously hardcore.

I watched them get to a group that had started to fight, only instead of the usual pushing and fist throwing I was used to working as a barmaid, these guys were tearing chunks out of each other! One guy got half his face caved in and parts of his flesh were flung into the crowd. One girl even jumped up to catch a piece as if claiming a trophy from a concert. I gagged down sick at the sight of her rubbing the flesh across her skin as if it was some kind of new beauty product, leaving bloody smears like markings on a commando.

The Angel sentinels had now disarmed the group fighting and unshielded their weapons. They were holding them out to the crowd as a warning, one aimed at the neck of the Demon that must have started the whole thing. He was an odd shape, with extremely long legs and a skinny waist but his upper half looked as solid as a tree trunk with arms that reached the floor and hands that curled up like iron spades.

The crowd was parting again and when I saw a scarred bear's head emerge, I couldn't help but scream at the sight of my new friend. The scream didn't go unnoticed as I was temporarily back in control and a voice screamed in my mind making me double over and hold my head in my hands as the torture ripped through me.

"MOVE NOW!" My legs started running to a door I could barely see through my tear-filled eyes and this wasn't only down to the pain. The memory of Leivic's true form was seriously frightening. He was indeed a bear, but one that had been severely tortured. It was like a bear had been set alight, skinned alive and then put back together again only to survive the whole ordeal.

He had no fur but just fleshy skin that had scarred into congealed groups. Like a melted plastic bottle, only skin coloured. And then there was the mighty scar that cut across his body from what looked as if it had nearly cut him in two. His eyes had turned into large black holes with a small white light that could be seen from deep within.

Those white lights had found my face when I had called out and now I could hear the urgency in my captor's voice.

We had been discovered and I just prayed it wasn't too late.

Too late to be saved.

CHAPTER THIRTY-NINE

DRAVEN'S WRATH

I got flung through the door and it took me a minute to realise that it wasn't down to mind control. Now there were actual hands aiding in my kidnapping as they pushed me backwards quickly into an opening. I squinted thanks to the sunshine that flooded my retinas and knew we were in a sort of alleyway at the side of the club. I looked up to see we were sandwiched between the two warehouses and we weren't alone.

"That didn't go to plan Agnomen, they now know we have the girl, we must hurry!" The Angel in front of me was talking to the one behind, who had hold of me. I looked to see that pure hatred filled the eyes of the Angel, as he glared deep into me. He was handsome, as all the rest were, but his evil mind did rear its ugly head in more than his actions alone.

His eyes were calculatingly cruel, almost as if he was going to enjoy watching me soon suffer. They were almost as white as the hot anger that also flashed through his hard expression and his hair was cut short, close to his skull. The blue fitted suit he wore didn't look cut out for fighting, but I could still see the muscles flexing under his jacket. The one major difference to this Angel was his wings or more like the lack of, as his were missing.

"You said the drug would last, Kokabiel, but she alerted them. I could no longer control her!" Again, the voice behind me spoke to a man standing in the shadows. He didn't want to come forward, as though he was hiding from me. And that name...where had I heard it before?

"She has been drinking it for days, I was not aware of her power to block us from her mind. I have still done what was asked of me!" A Demonic voice spoke from the shadows, one I hadn't heard before but seeing as I hadn't heard many, other than Draven's, then it could have been anyone. However, there was one thing now that I was almost certain of...

There was a traitor at Afterlife!

I wasn't given long to think about it as I was now being pushed forward into the street where Draven's car still sat. I wished more than ever that I was sat in there now, all safe and encased within its strong bodywork, but the fingertips digging into my arms when I tried to resist, brought me quickly back like whiplash.

"Do not make me hurt you girl, my master would not be pleased," he whispered down in my ear, making me flinch. A repulsed shiver crept up my spine from the memory of having him in my head.

"Galizur, bind her hands, that should stop her struggles." He then pushed my arms forward and the suited Angel named Galizur walked towards me with a sadistic grin plastered on his features.

"With pleasure." The words lashed out from behind that curled lip like venom and I shuddered as he touched me. He swiftly produced a pair of thick steel clamps like shackles, only engraved in symbols I didn't understand. His hands made quick work of fastening them on my wrists, making me wince at the feel of heavy metal banging against bone.

He ran his fingertip softly around one of the symbols and they ignited as if he had lit a match. The red flames sparked up and crackled as they licked at the air heating up the metal. Then the heated symbols started to glow crimson from the chain reaction his touch had caused.

"W...wh...what's happening?" I stammered out a plea as soon as the markings all began to move slowly around my wrists, making my skin tingle and burn. They didn't answer me as I watched the symbols pick up speed. The circling around the width of my wrist was taking flight in a blurring dance until I heard a hissing noise and I guess this signified that they were now locked securely.

As soon as they had me bound, they started to pull me roughly towards a black van that had its side door open ready. I knew that as soon as they had me in that van then that would be it for me, there would be no escape.

Game Over.

I started to panic inside because up until now I had still been waiting for Draven to come out and rescue me. But now my true predicament was hitting me, like a cold hard slap across the face. They were going to take me away from Draven. Away from my safety and away straight down the road that led to one Being I didn't ever want to meet...Lucius. These thoughts quickly catapulted me straight into Keira's personal panic mode!

In one last desperate act of survival, I started to pull all my weight backwards and tried to move in a twisting motion towards the ground. But it was all in vain as no matter how much I dug my feet in they just kept dragging my body closer. In my panic I could feel my breathing quickly accelerate to a point close to hyperventilating.

"LET ME GO!" I screamed out as it felt as though the last dregs of the drug were finally wearing off allowing me access to more of my own functions, but in doing so my oxygen was nearly spent.

"Well, look who found her fucking voice! Galizur, gag the bitch if you please." Galizur let go of my bound hands and pulled a bit of cloth from out of his pocket and started to twist it tightly but before he could get it around my mouth, I managed to scream out one last time.

"DRAVEN!" I used every last shred of breath in my lungs to call out his name and I was soon panting into the cloth tied like rope in my open mouth. I gagged and coughed, soon soaking the material in saliva. It seemed to be their turn to panic after my outburst because now instead of pulling and pushing me to the van

I had been lifted up under a strong arm and was being hurried towards the open door.

"Get her out of here, NOW! We don't have much time." After that I was thrown into the van and landed painfully on my side, knocking the wind out of me. I gripped with my hands and pushed with my feet to right myself, but all I got was a foot pressed on my ribs to keep me down. I looked on through blurry eyes as I saw the daylight disappearing when the van door slid home, sealing my fate in a steel cage.

I moaned at the sight and the foot on my chest applied more pressure to my bruised ribs. Then the sound of doors slamming on either side told me everyone was inside and when the engine started, I knew that was the end of my chances. I couldn't stop the overflow of heavy tears as I had lost all my hope and was giving in to the realization that I had been kidnapped for the third time in my life!

"WE'RE TOO LATE, LOOK!" One of my captors shouted just before a blood-curdling roar was heard that was so loud it made the van rattle and my ears pop. The foot released me and moved to the front window.

"Agnomen, you have failed. I will inform our Master of your incompetence." Galizur had been the one in the back with me and now his expensive black dress shoes weren't keeping me down, I could see everything that was happening. I shimmied up against the side of the van with my shoulder and saw Galizur in between the front seats blaming the one called Agnomen about what was happening now. What was happening, I didn't know but whatever it was had everyone terrified.

"You traitorous snake! I will have your head for this Galizur!" Agnomen spat out his words, but I still couldn't see what he looked like as he never looked back.

"I very much doubt that, but one thing I am certain...he will most definitely have YOURS!" He pointed forward and as all eyes followed they found Hell's fury in the Demonic form of their King...

Draven.

After that Galizur disappeared into a bright light, leaving a void I could finally see through.

"DRIVE DAMN YOU!" Agnomen screamed out, making the van wheels spin into life. Draven stood arms crossed, in the path of the accelerating van and didn't even flinch. The purple energy pumped through his veins like burning fuel and the flames licked at his skin, kissing each feather in his huge wingspan. They were out and double the width of the van that was heading his way. I wanted to shout 'get out of the way' but no words reached my lips in time.

Just as machine and body were to impact, Draven produced a large glowing blade from within his arm and moved gracefully to the side as the van went past. A purple fire engulfed his blade, one that was easily the length of me. I jumped at the sound it made as it sliced through one side, making a long jagged opening from the sliding door to the back end. It cut through the metal as though it was a razor to paper.

The van swerved to the side and turned back to right itself after the wheels had lifted off the ground. Draven was once again in the centre of the windscreen and mingled voices of panic drowned out the sound of the engine. Meanwhile, I had been flung about in the back, like a ship on stormy seas, hitting my head on the wheel arch. Soon I could feel the thin trickle of blood running down my cheek and the tangy taste of copper filled my mouth as it seeped through my lips.

This time Draven took long strides toward us and Agnomen opened his door and rolled out just as the van accelerated again. Coward!

Draven's sword went back into his body up his arm to its home. He then motioned with his hand towards the van causing the front of the vehicle to start flying through the air in pieces. The engine spluttered and then stopped just before it got to him. Another flick of his hand had the windscreen cracking and then in one large section it flew outwards and past Draven to smash on the ground behind him causing an eruption of glass.

The driver panicked at seeing this and started to scramble to get in the back with me. He was also an Angel, but with the terrified look on his face he looked more human than I did. There was no glow, no Angelic eyes of pearly white, just the look of a man who knew he was soon to die. In fact, the only reason I knew he was an Angel was the pair of wings on his back that were pinned to his body so that he could crawl through the seats. There were still bits coming out of the van like splinters from a woodcutter, flying through the air past Draven as he walked closer towards us. His eyes were erratic as though searching for me. He saw the Angel scurrying in the back and he nodded to something I couldn't see.

Then the earthquake started, or what I thought was an earthquake. The van started to rock and vibrate with some kind of impact I was yet to discover. The rip down the side of the door started to open further until a set of great Demonic claws could be seen. The razor-tipped hands hooked around the opening and started to peel away at the door, making me feel like a sardine in a can.

The door rolled back until a colossal Demonic bear stood in its opening. I didn't even notice it had started raining until I saw the water glistening from its scarred tissue making it all the more frightening. Leivic seemed to see me through his human eyes and for a moment I thought I saw regret in them. Maybe it was down to the utter fear he saw in mine which brought on instant guilt on my part. Whatever the feeling behind them it passed quickly as the Angel took our private moment to his advantage and grabbed the curved blade from his back. He began to come towards me, weapon in hand.

The action granted him another mighty roar that shattered the rest of the windows. Leivic seemed to let the anger surge through him and determined his actions from it. He reached out and wrapped a razor-tipped paw around the Angel's ankle just before he could reach me. I looked on in horror as the terrified eyes got further away from me as his body was dragged from the mangled van. I almost felt sorry for him until I saw the deadly looking blade slip from his fingers and quickly dropped that thought.

Leivic pulled the body out effortlessly and once clear, he threw him sideways toward the closest warehouse. He flew upwards like the wind that catches a paper bag and smashed into the building as though made of bricks. He then fell to the ground in a broken mess of feathers and bones. His mangled body started to crawl but to where I didn't know. One wing was dragging along behind him all broken and twisted. Blood pumped from the part it connected to his back, which was now open and oozing.

I soon realized why he was desperately trying to drag himself back this way...

Draven was coming.

That powerful physique, aflame with pure hate was walking this way and with me in his sights, he looked as though the power would rip him apart, bursting out and destroying everything with it. He got closer to the Angel that was still painfully pulling his slaughtered body an inch at a time across the watered ground. The Heavens were still pouring down, making the puddles around him turn into miniature rivers of blood.

Now I actually did feel sorry for him.

He turned his head up and was about to protest but Draven without even looking down speared him like a guillotine with one full-length sword that shot out of his arm so quickly, it caused my eyes to blur. The Angel twitched around the blade as its body was trapped to the wet, cemented road. He tried with one last attempt to move but with a swift twist of Draven's wrist, the blade turned inside his body and the Angel stopped moving. I wasn't sure if he had killed him as I didn't know if you could even kill Angels, but at a guess I would have said that he looked pretty dead to me. As soon as the movement was made and Draven withdrew his sword back into his arm, I turned my head away and closed my eyes, trying in vain to get the image of an execution out of my mind.

When I looked back Draven was by the torn doors of the van, next to Leivic who was about to help me out. Draven put a strong hand on the bear's arm and said in an aggravated stern voice,

"Leave her to me! Go and find the other one and bring him back to me...*alive.*" The word alive was said through gritted teeth and very little controlled Hell raised anger. His friend just nodded and withdrew his hand from Draven's grasp. Draven turned his face away from mine and said,

"Remember, I want him alive, Leivic...I need answers." I knew what that meant, and the word torture came to mind. Again, I closed my eyes to get the sight of Draven's idea of justice out of my head. I couldn't help but scream at the feel of someone touching my leg.

"Keira," was all he said, but it was soft enough to get me to look at him. He was right in front of me, so close I could feel his breath as he spoke. It was smooth and calming but I still flinched as he touched me.

He looked hurt but didn't stop as he put his arms around me and lifted me gently from the van. I had been huddled in the back with my knees up close to my chest, as though trying to protect myself. I must have looked like a small frightened child...Hell, who was I kidding, I felt like one!

He held me so close to his chest I could feel his heart pumping through my own body. Loud and strong, beating his anger around his Demon ignited blood so that the only thing on his mind was revenge. I wanted to touch his face, to soothe him some way, but I was scared. I didn't know of anything that would bring him down from this rage. His breathing was that of a man who was controlling something deep within him and the flex in his jaw every time he looked down at me, told me he was not happy about what he saw there. The bleeding from my head had stopped and now was nothing but a crusty red mark down my face. My eyes felt sore and puffy from many outbursts of sobbing and for some reason, I couldn't get my hands to stop shaking.

"It is the aftereffects of the drugs in your system, it will pass," he said quietly and I realized that he could hear my thoughts. No wonder, thanks to the drugs he could probably control me as well.

"Yes I could, but I wouldn't. Not even to make it so that you do not fear me. I wouldn't put you through that again," he said bitterly and I felt ashamed bringing on another overspill of tears. Here was the man I loved saving my life again and he could hear my fear of him, what must he think of me!

He put me down gently, checking I was steady on my feet before leaning me back against the side of his car. He lifted my head as though I would break if he applied too much pressure. I refused to meet his eyes being too ashamed of myself.

"Keira don't... Please look at me." He pleaded and on hearing his voice break, I did also. I looked up to find eyes full of pain and almost crumbled.

"I...I...I'm...so...rry." I managed to sob out broken words of shame, but he just shook his head and told me,

"Ssshh, be still." He then looked down at my bound hands. I had become so used to the feeling that I had forgotten the manacles they were still in. He raised them up to inspect the markings and he mouthed some words I couldn't hear. He then raised one of his own hands to his mouth and bit down hard enough to draw a stream of blood. I let out a little scream, but he didn't meet my eyes as if he had been prepared for my reaction.

He rubbed his bloody palms together so that both were fully covered and circled both my metal bound wrists. The fastening made the same hissing noise once they had finished spinning and unlocked, then falling from me but turning to dust before hitting the ground. He examined the skin underneath before being satisfied enough to let them go. One brief look at his now clean palms told me enough to know that the cuffs had absorbed his blood.

He then held me tightly by the waist to keep me up and he pinned me to the car with his hands leaning on either side of me. I could feel the tears roll off my chin to the ground and like a flash of light his hand caught one mid motion.

He opened his palm slowly to show me. It created purple sparks before disappearing into his own skin and then he raised the same hand to check my injuries. He moved my hair gently but little strands had dried and stuck to the blood. I couldn't help but wince when he pulled them which made him stop and growl.

"He will pay for this!" he growled as he let the rage flow back into him. This gave me the courage needed to raise my hand to his face and touch him cautiously. It was like stroking a lion that had been ready to pounce. However, the effect was different and instead of getting my hand ripped off, he turned his face into my palm and closed his eyes. He seemed to be breathing me in, as if taking the essence of me to help in calming him down.

Whatever it was doing, it seemed to be working as the flex in his jaw relaxed against me, the bulging vein at the side of his forehead disappeared and his heartbeat resumed its normal rhythm.

I just wanted us to get in his car and keep driving until we couldn't get any further away from this nightmare. I wanted him to take me away from this madness and wait for normality to take care of us both.

"That's not going to happen my love, normality can never exist in my world, it just isn't possible, and nor can it happen in yours...not...not when you belong to me," he said in a deep husky voice and pausing as though he found it hard to form the words I already knew to be true. I forced the tears back deep within myself and swallowed the bitterness at how unfair the whole situation was. How many times was my life going be faced with this type of thing and survive?

"I won't let them get you, I won't let them hurt you, do you hear me? I...I will keep you safe, I swear it!" He ripped himself away from me and clenched his hands into tight fists, causing the skin over his knuckles to turn a paler purple and then white. Hearing my thoughts were bringing back his anger and I mentally scolded myself.

"Dom!" Leivic was approaching and the cause of our situation was slapped back into view and it felt like a kick to the gut. He came from around the corner with a writhing Agnomen in tow and the last shreds of control crumbled around Draven as he let out a growl so bloodthirsty, you could taste the air change. It was now charged with a Demonic static so thick it was like trying to breathe while stood on the edge of a live volcano.

He turned his back to me and I closed my eyes at the feel of his folded wings brushing gently across my skin. I knew I wasn't going to want to see this and I wished I could have just kept them closed, curled into a protective ball and hide. But I knew I couldn't.

So I opened my eyes and saw the man I loved ignite into a raging fire fuelled by Hell itself and the sight had me once again gasping for air. His wings lost their soft feathery texture and were replaced by flickering purple flames licking angrily at the tips. Then they opened to their full wingspan, giving the dark grey skies a new light source.

"AGNOMEN!" Draven's Demonic voice said his name as if he

was at that moment the Devil's right-hand man. I hated hearing Demonic voices, but to hear it spoken from Draven's lips...well, that just made it closer to unbearable.

"Draven..." I said his name in one last attempt to keep him with me but he was too far gone now to hear my idea of reason. His only response was to turn his head slightly, looking over his massive shoulder to give me an order I knew better than to defy.

"Keira, get in the car now and don't watch this." At least his voice had turned back to normal to tell me this. At that moment the sound of the car unlocking made me jump. My nerves were shot to pieces and right now I was nothing more than a skin bag holding my bones in one piece.

I opened the door after trying to control my shaking hand and almost fell on weak knees into the seat. The door closed on its own and locked for extra measure. One of the two orders I had complied with, but there was no chance of me not watching what was about to happen. I had never known what was good for me and I wasn't about to change now. I knew full well what the consequences of my actions would be, but it didn't mean I cared!

No, I was going to see this nightmare through to the end, just as I had done with Morgan and how I would keep doing for the rest of my life even if it did bloody kill me! Why? Because it was my nature. Hell, but for all I knew it was even written into my DNA. And sometimes, no matter how we try, there is just no changing what we know could be a fatal flaw. There's no use fighting the inevitable.

So, with this in mind, I rubbed the last tears out of my eyes and sat there to watch as Draven walked over to the man Leivic was dragging on the ground. The side window was down slightly from where I had opened it earlier and I was glad because now I could add words to what my eyes would witness.

It had stopped raining now, but the black clouds threatened more. What was left was a sidewalk of dirty puddles and two bodies on the floor. One of which still hadn't moved.

Draven cracked his neck to one side before he grabbed hold of Agnomen and started dragging him closer to one of the larger puddles. I couldn't understand what he was doing but one look at

Draven told me that I was the only one. I could tell he had a plan and I wasn't sure if I noticed a dark madness creep upon those lips of his, that I loved invading my own.

"Tell me, bounty hunter, who holds your contract?" Draven pulled him up by the hair so that his face was just above the floor. That was when I had my first good look at the man behind my attempted kidnapping. I gagged down the bile rising in my throat at the sight of one of the most disgusting faces I had ever seen!

He had dirty, red hair that stood in one point at the back of his head which was currently in Draven's hand. His face looked as though made of chalk, hard and cracking around the edges. His lips were overflowing with blood and the corners split higher up his cheekbones, giving him a truly sadistic look. His nose was missing as if it had been chopped off with one swipe and all that was left was the two elongated holes and bone in the middle.

But believe me when I say that none of these were his worst features...oh no, it was all in his eyes. Or at least where his eyes should have been.

There, instead, were two gaping holes that were filled with moving darkness which bled outwards onto his face. It was only when I squinted my eyes that I noticed why it looked like the darkness beneath them was moving. I saw that they were in fact, made up from hundreds of big black flies that had all found a home there. Every time he winced in pain as Draven pulled him this way and that, one would fly away and retreat from the cruelty.

"Answer me!" Draven was losing his cool and with one hand still in his hair the other grabbed his neck and started to squeeze, releasing even more flies from hiding. He coughed out spilling even more blood to the ground, but no words would form.

"Your refusal to talk means signing your sentence to death, NOW TALK!"

"Tal...talk...ing...al...also...signs it!" he gritted out, just as Draven let go of his throat to allow him to speak. He dropped him to the floor and Agnomen's hands automatically went to his neck.

"This is your last chance, hunter. Now. Give. Me. That. Name!" Draven demanded, crossing his arms across his chest as he towered above the Demon at his feet. Like this the King in him could be easily seen. Power flooded his veins with every breath he took and with every breath I took, I knew I should not have been watching this.

"If I give you a name, you won't kill me?" This question was not received well, the evidence of that was found in Draven's dark laughter.

"You mistake me. Your refusal to talk only signs how your death will happen...for it will happen! You signed it with your pitiful life when you tried TO TAKE HER FROM ME!" He demonically screamed out this last part which made some of the glass windows on the warehouse shatter around us like deadly falling snow. Agnomen cowered closer to the ground seeking even the barest hint of shelter amongst the earthquake of his King's wrath.

"But your death, you can choose. Tell me what I need to know, and it will be swift. It is far more than you deserve. However, if you choose the other then be prepared to start praying to a God you do not worship. For nothing but he could save you the pain!" He did not give him long to decide. He walked over to one of the largest puddles, knelt down and placed his hand in the murky rainwater.

"IN nomine Patris, et Filii, et Spiritus Sancti. Emitte Spiritum tuum et creabuntur: et benedic hoc aquam manuum Dei Amen." ("In the name of the Father, and of the Son, and of the Holy Spirit. Send forth Thy Spirit and they shall be created and bless this water by God's hands. Amen. In Latin)

The words of perfect Latin flowed out of Draven with a pride I have never seen before. He circled his fingers through the water and it soon turned crystal clear then sealed itself with an icy top. Draven removed his hand just in time as the frost worked its way into the middle. He then got up from one knee and walked back to his prisoner.

Agnomen tried in vain to worm away but Draven was quickly above him once more and took hold of his head to drag him towards the frozen puddle of Holy Water. I watched on, wide-eyed and curious as to what he planned to do next. Agnomen saw his doom and started to twist and claw at the pavement. Before long, he was leaving thin trails of blood from fingers that were now missing nails and had filed down to the bone.

Draven soon dragged him to the spot, despite all his painful efforts and held his face above the icy glass that mirrored Agnomen's terrified face.

"You have chosen your fate...NOW FACE IT!" Draven shouted in anger before slamming his head downwards. The last of the flies came out at once in a black swarm, forcing his head backwards slightly but once they had all scattered, nothing was left to prevent this strange torture from being inflicted.

I watched on in horrified fascination as his head smashed through the ice and as soon as contact was made the water started to rise and bubble around him. He writhed around in pain, but Draven held his head firmly. His body was desperate to break loose and his sticky, folded wings tried to open. Draven simply reacted by holding the back of his head with one hand and gripping one wing with the other. He then yanked back taking the wing with his arm, ripping it straight from the Demon. More pain could be heard but Draven was unmoved and just threw the wing aside like a piece of trash.

I looked to the side, where Leivic was still stood but his face was contorted as if he could imagine the pain himself. I suddenly realized that this statement might be closer to the truth as he was once tortured in Hell.

Finally Draven pulled Agnomen's face out of the steaming water and let him drop back down just at the side of it. He was still alive, but it was obvious the amount of pain he was in. His face was actually now melting off, leaving a mixture of bloody bone and chalky tissue to drip to the cement in thick droplets, like crude gloss paint. Once again, I was gagging down bile.

"Now speak and I will end your misery!"

"YES...yes, yes any...thing...anything." It came out in a mangled mess of words due to the lack of lips that were now mostly on the floor. He didn't even have teeth, as now he was just a melting face full of deep empty bloody holes.

"I want a name, hunter." Draven barked out and this time he received his answer almost immediately.

"Gal...izur, Galizur was the one who hired me to get to the girl." Draven grabbed his head back so that he could stare into the deep pits of his eyes and said in a breathless fury,

"And who is Galizur contracted by?"

"Vampire...King... My Lord!" he spluttered out and Draven dropped him upon hearing words I could guess he already expected.

"Lucius!" Draven hissed turning his head to one side. Then the writhing body made a wheezing sound drawing Draven back to his victim.

"So, now I am your Lord. When your life hangs in my control of the balance, but by the Gods you are a fool, hunter! You know that if you had come to me with this information you would have been rewarded, but instead you turn your back on me and your faith and for what!? What price has Lucius put on her head?" When he didn't answer straight away, he received a prompting kick that sent him rolling up through the air and landing close to the car I was sat in.

"P...P...ower...Power of the spear. He has the spear of Longinus." Draven whipped his head round in disbelief.

"The Holy Spear," he said, shaking his head before continuing,

"The one you speak of is not in his possession. You have been deceived old, foolish Demon. Indeed, but you have!" He said this last part shaking his head as if sorry for a moment. Agnomen on hearing this started to shake his head saying,

"No... No, but it can't be." Over and over but Draven wasn't listening. He had ignited his body once more into purple fire and held his hands out to his sides. His wings shook and the energy started to ripple through his powerful chest and beat down his immense arms. It flowed down and out of his body through his wrists and hands. It kept seeping out from him until it formed two solid blades that touched the ground. These too were on fire as the flames curled around and hissed at the air that fuelled them.

He walked to a dry patch but the mangled van was in his way, so with what looked like very little effort he kicked the van and it slid to the other side of the road, creating track lines on the ground before coming to a stop by toppling over onto its side. The sound of the back-door glass smashing made me jump as little shards of it rained down on Draven's car roof.

He then started to scratch the ground with the tips of his blades causing little sparks to dance along the ground. It looked as if he was writing something or drawing some kind of pattern that was being scorched right into the cement.

Once finished, he motioned for Leivic to bring his prisoner to him and he did it without question. It was only when he bent down that his eyes burned into mine. He knew then that I had witnessed the whole thing. He closed them briefly as though sad at the idea. Then he opened them and shook his head at me before lifting Agnomen off the ground with one razor clawed paw. He carried him over to Draven and let him go on top of the marked ground.

Unbelievably, he was still muttering about Lucius still having the spear and Draven started to laugh as though he had finally lost it.

"As I said before, you are foolish to think I would ever allow something like that to fall in the hands of pure, power-driven madness." He leaned over him and flipped him face up so that he could get close to his face. He grabbed a handful of the jacket he was wearing and lifted him the last couple of inches.

"How do I know...?" Draven asked, wearing a sadistic grin that didn't fit those perfect lips.

"...Because you fool, *I have the Holy Spear!*" Draven snarled venomously and with that the Demon cried out as Draven let go. He flopped back down and continued to cry out cursing Lucius' name back to Hell.

"Don't worry, hunter, you will be seeing him soon enough!" And with that, Draven flew up in the air above him and turned full circle, letting the tips of his lengthy swords make the same circle on the ground around the symbol and its captured Demon.

Once each side met, the whole thing erupted into the deep, red flames of Hell itself and Draven came down from above with both his blades aimed at Agnomen's chest. The impact made him not only cry out but me also. It was horrific to watch but I couldn't stop. It was like the last hold over me was to see it through to the end with my once brief captor.

The two bodies were both now engulfed in the fire and only when the screaming stopped did the Heavens open again and flood the Earth with its waters. The flames died and Draven was left standing there alone, back to his human form. His wet hair hung down over his face as he continued to look at the spot Agnomen's body had disappeared through. I could just make out his lips moving through the rain-smeared glass. Then I watched in shock as he crossed himself and I soon realised what he was doing.

He had been praying.

Praying for dammed soul he had just sent back…

Back to be condemned.

CHAPTER FOURTY

MY PRETTY LITTLE BOUNTY HEAD

When Draven had finished, he looked up to find my face. I wanted to run out of this locked car and into his arms to comfort him. He looked so sad, so drained of energy that I touched the window. He turned to Leivic and was giving him instructions of some kind. I couldn't hear as the rain had picked up even more and the sound it made hitting the roof was deafening all other noises out.

The gap in the window was now allowing the water to spray inwards and soon my arm was wet through but I didn't care. Draven was pointing towards the mangled van and then back to the only body still lying on the ground. Then, when Leivic bowed his head in respect, Draven put his hand on one shoulder and shook his head. Leivic looked upset despite what looked like Draven's reassurance.

I felt so bad that I was the cause of so much destruction that I couldn't hold back the deep sob that broke free. I cried out with so much emotion that I was shaking. I covered my head in my hands, but it wouldn't stop my need to shake it back and forth, repeating silently, 'Why me?'' in my mind.

I should have been issued with a warning when I was born! Come too close and you will walk in my footsteps of the demolished road that I leave behind me. I know my mind was being dramatic, but I felt cursed. I felt consumed by a guilt I couldn't get away from. Almost as if I could feel a sticky layer of it clinging to my skin for me to carry around for the rest of my days.

But my biggest fear of all...

Would Draven simply get sick of dealing with it? Would he realise for himself first-hand just how it was, that some love was not worth losing your sanity over. I would have done anything for Draven's love but just how far would he go to keep mine?

I was still crying out into my palms when I felt a gentle hand on my shoulder. It was Draven's hand. I knew that as soon as he made contact with me. Like our blood was somehow connected, causing a reaction in me whenever he was near. He tried to pull me around to him, but I was resisting.

"Keira, please don't be frightened of me, I won't hurt you, my love." He spoke so softly as though anything above a whisper would have me cringing away like a frightened fawn. I pulled back with such force that it shocked him.

"I'm not frightened of you hurting me! I'm frightened of the hurt I cause you! Don't you see? Don't you see that it's me that causes this? All of this destruction is because of ME! I...can't...I can't...do this." That was all I could manage until I lost all control. I was sobbing until I couldn't breathe. Somehow, I was in Draven's arms and he was holding me so tight, as though he would never let me go. He was smoothing back my hair and whispering words in another language that were having a strange effect over me. It was these words that were seeping through my mind and making it cloudy. I tried to hold on to what little control I had left but it was exhausting.

"Let go, just let go." Draven whispered directly into my ear and it was hard not to obey. I wanted to get up and run away just for the space to think but when I started to struggle, Draven increased the pressure around me.

"Stop fighting me Keira, just let it all go." I lay my head into his shoulder and could feel the wet leather jacket slide on my cheek. I wanted to be free of all the guilty feelings I had weighing me down but what right did I have when others suffered.

One of his hands was moving up and down my back, making it harder not to close my eyes and let myself drift to another state of mind. He knew I was losing the battle and started speaking to me softly, dropping it back to a language I could understand.

"That's it, good girl. You're safe now, you're safe..." And this was the last thing I heard before the warmth of his words consumed me. I felt my body go limp and the feeling of being lifted before blackness filled my vision and sleep overwhelmed my senses.

———

I woke to the sound of voices that were irate. It was like when my parents used to argue but do it quietly so that 'the kids' wouldn't hear...of course we always did. They tried to keep it low but every now and again a word said sharply could be made out. My mind was still groggy, but those overwhelmed senses were slowly returning back to me. I didn't open my eyes, but I turned my head slowly to free my ear to hear better.

"You are wrong Sophia, what the girl needs is my protection and mine only!" That was most definitely Draven's voice and the added authoritative tone made it clear that he so wasn't happy.

"Yes, but keeping her locked away isn't the answer. She isn't some princess you can hide away in your tower! She needs to live her life, Dom." Sophia spoke carefully, but not careful enough. Draven's growl could be heard even if it came out deep and low.

"Dominic, Sophia is right. Don't let your love for the girl blind you into rash decisions. You can't just take her away against her will and we all know Keira enough by now to know that it will be against her will. She is almost as stubborn as you brother...but this you know." Vincent was trying to make Draven see sense and for a moment I took his silence as confirmation that it had sunk in. But I was wrong.

"She will do what is good for her. She may fight me on it but she will come around. I will take her somewhere safe so that no bounty hunter will find her. I will NOT allow what happened today to happen again! She was so close to breaking, so fragile that I fear the damage done is beyond repair." I could hear his breathing now coming close to panting in an effort to keep his temper in check before continuing.

"I am going to lose her if she keeps seeing this side of me...the fear in her eyes, by the Gods, brother..." At this I finally opened my eyes only to see Draven sat down with his head in his hands. I wanted to shout out to him, but I knew there was more for me to hear.

"Dom, the girl loves you and that fear you saw is one you mistake for a fear of loss. She will not leave you, if anything I think she fears you leaving her." Vincent must have gained a great deal of information from my mind, more than Draven had at any rate... either that or he was a Hell of a guesser.

"I never would, not unless it was to save her life. I tried to leave her alone in the beginning and look where that got me! I became a shell of myself and only when I have her do I become whole. You both know this. I can't let her go and I won't!" He was working himself up and it was almost as unbearable to hear as it was beautiful.

I couldn't stand to have Draven feeling so desperate, so lost in feelings that he wasn't alone in. I, too, felt as though I would lose him if my situation didn't get better. I almost wished that he could have taken me away...away from anyone who wanted to hurt me. Anyone who wanted to separate us. But I couldn't do it. His siblings were right, I still had a life of my own to live and I couldn't just walk away from it all...

Not again.

I had Libby and Frank. I had a little niece or nephew on the way that I didn't want to miss out on. No, I would have to stay and fight! I would have to rise up above it all and take each knock as it came. I would get back up and stand up for what I believed in. And hopefully, I would have Draven by my side to catch me if I failed and fell.

"What am I to do if I can't even protect her here in my home? They were so close to taking her. Far too close. If Leivic hadn't seen her leaving, then she might have been lost. It would have been too late!"

"What was she thinking, going outside by herself? Was she being controlled?" Sophia asked but Vincent was the one to answer her.

"Why don't you ask her yourself, I do believe she has been awake now for some time?" His voice held amusement and when I knew I had been busted, I opened my eyes fully to see everyone staring at me. I was on Draven's bed wrapped up in a warm blanket with my wet clothes now missing. They had been replaced by soft cotton pyjamas in navy blue. I had never seen them before, but they felt like they have been woven with a cloud. My hair had even been plaited to one side, I guess thanks to Sophia's nimble hands, which her smile told me I had guessed right.

Draven stood up and pushed the hair back that had fallen forward from looking down at his hands. Vincent was standing, lips amused and with arms folded, while Sophia stood in between them making her tiny frame look even smaller next to her brothers' larger ones. The staring silence was starting to make me feel uncomfortable, so I shifted in the bed into a sitting position. This was Draven's cue to step towards me.

"I think Keira and I need some time alone." I don't know why but the way he said this made me gulp. The other two quickly left without saying another word.

Draven came to the bedside very slowly, almost as though he was expecting me to scream at any sudden movements.

"It's alright. I'm not going to freak out." I tried to give him a genuine smile but I'm not sure it fully made it.

"I would not blame you if you did." He sounded as if his voice would crack, being pushed to breaking point. He knelt down on one of the steps next to the bed and leant forward so that our faces were level. It reminded me of how you would usually approach a frightened child.

"Well, I'm not going to. I think I did enough of that earlier." Draven didn't look convinced with my brave little act and was still waiting for me to crumble next to him.

"Keira." He said my name edged with doubt and riddled with worry.

"I'm fine," I said looking away from his intense glare that was trying to pry secrets from my soul.

"You are anything but. What you have seen...all you have witnessed...it is more than any of your kind can endure. So, to say that you are fine is not only doubtful, but also quite unbelievable." He placed his palm around my cheek to bring my face back to his view, but upon his touching me he found my damp skin there.

"Is this what you call fine?" I didn't answer his question but bit my lip instead. What did he want me to say? No, I wasn't bloody fine! I was just nearly kidnapped and then watched my boyfriend rip a van to pieces before turning on the people behind it all. Then to find that it was all down to a bounty on my head that wasn't just going to get old and make people forget about the whole thing! Umm no, I don't think I was fine, but it's not like I was about to give up on life for it all either.

"That's more like it. For a minute there you had me worried," Draven said, shocking me enough that my mouth opened to say,

"Excuse me?" I mean he had obviously just read my mind but since when was my internal freak out a good thing?

"Keira, understand me. If you hadn't been affected, then that would have made you numb and that worries me more than having you 'Freak out' as you put it. You know more than most than to bury deep feelings. Feelings, no matter how horrific, that's not the way to deal with them. You first have to face them before you can truly let them go or they will remain with you for an eternity and eat away at you until they've consumed every last piece of you"

"You sound like a man of experience from this type of thing?" I asked finding it hard to believe.

"Keira, I have many regrets in my long everlasting life. I have sent soul after soul back to where they will most certainly be condemned, over and over again until it soon became second nature to me but that does not mean I do not feel remorse. Of course, some deserve it more than most but if I felt nothing then who would I be? Where would be my balance? Good does not exist without the evil and right does not hold weight without knowing the wrong."

"So, what you're saying is to feel something, even pain, is

better than to feel nothing, even if the pain is spared?" I knew what he said made sense and I was taken back to the sight of Draven saying a prayer after sending Agnomen to face his eternal judgement.

"For a Being to feel nothing and live in this world with no emotions, well that would be a frightening thing indeed. Do you not agree?" I nodded in agreement.

"Keira, I want you to do something for me." Draven said this without any tones of authority, but it did not lack a certainty that he would get his way.

"What is it?" I asked nervously.

"I want you to come away with me. Somewhere I am sure to keep you safe." He asked me so seductively it was hard not to give in to him for anything he asked of me. But luckily, I knew Draven well and all of his tactics. I pulled away from him putting space between us.

"No, I am not running away!" He grabbed out to me to pull me back to him, but I moved quicker for once. This made him get on the bed to my level. Here, in one quick motion, he pulled me under him and held me trapped.

"You would not be running away, do not view it like that."

"Then how should I view it? It is what it is," I said stubbornly.

"It would be both of us going somewhere together, somewhere we could be alone. Secluded from everything and everyone who wants to take you away from me." He looked as though he was close to begging me, but I remained firm.

"So, we will both be running away?"

"Keira, I will not allow my pride to be my undoing. If that is what you want to see it as, then I will not stop you, but my love for you runs far deeper than my pride ever will!" he snapped getting angry, but I think it was mainly aimed at himself.

"I won't leave, Draven. Don't you understand that I did that once before and although it caused me to find you, I don't want me leaving here to be for the same reason," I pleaded, trying to break through his iron resolve.

"And that reason is?"

"Fear!" I couldn't help but shout the simple answer. It was

always for fear, it always had been. It can be labelled as a new start, fresh beginnings, even finding yourself, but all the while it was just down to plain and simple fear. A fear so strong it could change the course of your life. The first time it turned out to be for the better but next time? What the outcome could be wasn't worth exploring. As far as I was concerned, life with Draven couldn't get any better.

Okay, so maybe being with him and not being hunted would be good, but what was the guarantee that evil wouldn't just find us again. I couldn't leave Libby and the life growing inside of her. Frank and my new friends who accepted me, even though they all knew something about me wasn't quite right. That unbending faith in me that the ones I loved held in me was something I couldn't just walk away from. I had to stay, and I just hoped Draven would be the one to stay with me.

"Then let it be for love not fear." He tried one last time and held my face still when I started to shake my head.

"Are you saying that if I loved you, I would go with you?" This he didn't answer but he didn't need to.

"I could say the same. I could say 'If you loved me, then you would stay here with me, because you know how much it means to me.' But I don't need to do that because I know you love me, and I know you will stay with me...right here." He lowered his head in defeat. He let out a deep sigh, showing signs of his lost battle and his exhaustion from it.

"And if I took you by force? I take it you would never forgive me for that?" he asked bitterly.

"Draven!"

"I thought as much. Right, then an even more paranoid boyfriend it is then," he said while rolling off me and I knew he was acting spoilt from not getting his own way.

"There is no reason to overreact, Draven."

"You know it's a shame, I think you would have made such a sexy little prisoner," he teased and then before I could make a comeback he shut me up by kissing me so passionately that I forgot everything we had been talking about. We were starting to get carried away, which was fine by me, but Draven was starting to fight with himself.

He kept stopping and shaking his head, but then he would allow himself one more kiss and his control would go out of the window. His hands were searching out for my skin and as soon as he got there, we both moaned.

It was like a happy haze that enveloped my mind whenever Draven's skin came into contact with mine. He remained on top of me but felt his way down to hook one of my legs around his waist causing his need to press tightly against my own. We were now locked together and we both knew how to seal the union, but Draven kept hesitating, taking little stops to calm his breathing.

"Are you alright?" I asked after the third time this happened. He looked down at me with half shock and half guilt.

"Yes... no...I shouldn't be pushing you after all you've been through today, but Keira, I feel that if I don't take you now then my very skin will tear from my Demon!" This confession had the added effect of rippled muscles that tensed as his last shreds of control were fading away.

"Draven, I'm not as fragile as you think and if you don't make love to me right now, I will just have to continue on without you and we both know how much you like to watch." With that firmly planted in his mind, he let out an almighty roar and was soon kissing my neck in his answer.

He kissed the skin at the base of my throat gently but when his hand came up from my side and turned my face side onto the pillow, I knew what was coming. He held me still with one hand and the other hand caressed an area up from my shoulder.

"Such beautiful skin... like honey and milk." Draven's voice purred in my ear before leaning down to taste me.

"I like honey and milk," he said before his mouth sucked in my skin and he held it there, imprisoned in between his teeth. I could feel his canines extending but he was holding himself back. I had never felt this all the other times he had bitten me, but I put that down to the throws of passion. However, it seemed this time he was taking his sweet time.

The hand that had been holding my face to the side was now

venturing downwards. My top was pushed up to reveal my stomach and he seemed to take great pleasure in feeling his way down the length of my body until he reached the waistband of my cotton pyjama bottoms.

He still had my neck in his mouth, teasing and sucking it without actually biting it. I was so desperate for him to either touch me or bite me I was close to screaming for it. And boy did he know it, because as soon as the thoughts entered my mind, I could feel him smiling.

His fingers found the honey pot and spread my folds back to dip in further. I cried out at the contact and could feel my body soaking his fingers. Then he found my opening and applied a little pressure until his fingers teased just outside the entrance.

"Speak," he commanded and in true Draven style he wanted me to tell him what I wanted. I think he got off big time to hear me asking for it.

"It does, so be a good girl and give me what I want." His fingers teased even more, travelling to my clitoris making me squirm under his hands.

"Pll...eeeaaa...ssseee," I sighed out and this was his green light. He plunged his fingers inside me and bit into me at the same time making me find my orgasm instantly. In fact, I was still riding the waves of pleasure as he continued to suck the life source right out of me. This caused those waves to quickly turn tidal and I was screaming underneath him. I even bit into the pillow to try and contain myself but with his free hand he quickly tugged the pillow from beneath me, causing my screams to find to his ears again.

He seemed to love the sound as his sucking intensified and his erection grew stronger, pressing into me until my leg ached. Then I started to feel a little lightheaded and my body replaced the tensed muscles with sagging limbs. Draven let me go instantly and placed his hand over the two puncture marks in my neck which started to tingle. He remained there for longer than usual and when I was about to ask what he was doing he shook his head and said,

"Ssshh...relax little one" in his velvet voice. I did as I was told, closing my eyes and was soon finding my energy returning back to me as if Draven had just re-charged my batteries.

"I took too much from you and I need you strong for what I want to do to you," he said once he had finished at my neck and I opened my eyes to find him staring down intensely at me. I started to feel my cheeks burn as his eyes took in every curve and line of my face. He was studying me, that much was clear, and I wanted to turn away in my shyness which was strange considering what he just did to me.

He ran his fingers across my cheek and down to where his teeth had just had hold of me. I could still smell my sex on his hands, and I don't know why but it turned me on even more to know that part of me still remained on his skin.

"So beautiful, so innocent and utterly fragile. Purity at its highest existence." He looked as though he was saying this to himself as he kept his eyes down making his long thick lashes cast shadows under his eyes. Like this, his features looked so soft and young. Like this, he was a lover not a fighter and a man not a king.

His fingertips travelled down the hollow of my throat and kept on going until my top prevented it. This was when a naughty smile curved up on one side of Draven's lips. He looked as if an idea just entered his mind and before I had chance to ask, in one quick movement he rolled onto his back and pulled me with him.

I had a dizzy few seconds before I knew I was staring down at him and sat straddling his stomach with my knees either side of him. My hair fell to one side making the end of the plait tickle his upper arm. He didn't giggle like I would have, as I don't think a man like Draven ever would but instead he let out a deep, throaty laugh before moving it further up my neck.

"Did that tickle?" I asked mischievously.

"No, of course not, a man like me doesn't get ticklish," he said trying to be serious but doing a lousy job of it. I raised one eyebrow at him making him smirk.

"Really? Then I'm afraid I will need proof on the matter...just to be sure, you understand"

"But of course...be my guest," he said motioning with his hand up and down his body.

I cleared my throat before saying,

"Umm, I think I will need that removed before I conduct my

research." I nodded down to his clothed chest and he looked down at himself.

"I accept that, you may proceed," he said in over-exaggerated snobbery. I tried to hide my smile which must have been displayed as coy. He raised his arms to rest behind his head in the ultimate relaxed pose. I started at the bottom of his grey t-shirt that was already showing a line of skin before the waistband of his jeans. A little trail of dark hairs could be seen making their way down to join the other thicker region that surrounded his manhood.

"Oh, I think I'm going to enjoy this," I commented making him try very hard to hide a smug, 'the cat got the cream' look.

I decided that slow and extremely gentle was the way to go and as I gripped at the material ready to pull up, I purposely let the tips of my thumbs touch his sides as I pulled it upwards over his rippled stomach. Even then I could feel him shudder under my touch but when I looked up at his face it was still set in neutral. I was going to have to try harder.

He let me pull it up and over his head which now revealed his wide, naked chest. His solid muscles, even when relaxed, looked deadly strong. It had me wondering, if he could kick a van to one side being that strong on his lower half, then how much could he bench press with huge muscles like that!?

I thought I would go straight for the money and work at his sides, they were always a sure bet to get anyone squirming. I first used my fingertips and ran them upwards moving so slowly it all looked like slow motion. He flinched when I neared his underarm but still his face was set in stone.

"You're going to have to do better than that, my dear," he said being cocky, but I had to admit, it sure looked like he was loving all the attention. So I tried another tactic. I went back to the beginning and this time used my nails. I ran them up and down each time getting further up to his underarm. Each time I got closer, I could see him trying harder to resist the urge to laugh. I smiled at the sight of a victory that was so close to being mine.

"You're breaking, Draven," I warned but he just shook his head although I noticed he kept his mouth closed.

"Okay, you asked for it, time for hardball!" I squirmed further down his body and I heard him groan, only for a different reason. I shifted my body downwards so that my mouth was just over the skin on his sides. I looked up before doing anything to find his eyes closed and I wanted to laugh at the sight of him biting his lip.

I didn't touch him once but what I did do was far worse in tickling torture. I sucked in a lung full of air and blew it out over his skin so softly I felt his skin prickle up. I dragged myself up the length of him until I had reached the top but only found my disappointment when he hadn't made a sound. Damn him he was good!

Right this was it, my last play. I moved back down and this time I did make contact. I started to kiss his velvet golden skin, first over his stomach then down to his sides. I made sure to make them as light as humanly possible and as I made my way up I could feel his muscles flexing as the intensity of it all was becoming unbearable. I got closer to his arms, when I finally heard his noises of gargled laugher. I wasn't content with just winning. Oh no, I wanted to push him over the edge, so I climbed his body until my lips were above his. He was about to kiss me, but I pulled away and shook my head.

"My game, my rules so hold still and see if you can take this, big boy," I said making him smile at my aggressive tone. Whatever he thought, he did as he was told anyway.

"Close your eyes please."

"Please? I didn't think demanding and dominating girlfriends used words like please, little girl?" This made me growl at my little pet name and he laughed, which I caught by saying,

"Ha got ya!"

"Doesn't count, vixen." Now this pet name I didn't mind so much.

"Fine then...close your eyes and shut up, man slave!" I said trying to sound domineering but once again he laughed.

"That was adorable."

"Draven!" I warned making him comply.

"Right...sorry Mistress," he teased but I let it slide. I let him control his smile until both his mouth and eyes were closed and relaxed. Then with a fingertip I started to trace up his jawline to his lips. I began tracing the outside of them with such a gentle touch that I could tell he wanted to have me taste them. I then decided to use my nail and drag it across making them twitch. I got even closer and brushed my lips along, stopping to wet them with my tongue, this was his limit...only one of a different kind.

"Enough!" he shouted as hands came up making me jump when they grabbed the tops of my arms. He then pulled me roughly to his face and kissed me with a desperate need to have me. He held the back of my head and shifted his weight up so that he was sitting with me on his lap. He turned my head and deepened the kiss until every inch of my mouth was explored by his extremely experienced tongue.

Then he moved his hands down to grip my backside to lift me up. He shifted underneath me and I knew why as his steely length came forward. It must have been annoying him the way it was before. He grabbed my top and did the same thing that I had done to him not long before, only he did it with a lot less grace. My top flew over my head, only needing to break our kiss for less than a second.

We were now both topless in each other's arms and I held onto his shoulders as he explored my breasts. His palms kneaded them like dough and his fingers and thumbs caught my nipples between them making me squirm. Of course, every time I wriggled he would grow firmer until his erection pressed painfully against me. There wasn't enough room down there for all three of us.

"I want you!" he breathed in my mouth and the words would end in a deeper kiss.

"Yes...yes," I replied breathlessly wondering if it even made it past my lips.

Being at this point with Draven was like falling into a black hole. It was an endless state of want, no, not want but need, as though if he didn't take me soon I would never stop falling. I would never land. I would be forever somewhere in between belonging to myself and Draven. And I wanted to belong to him with every beat my heart made. I wanted him to take me, to be inside me so that we could merge our bodies, our souls and our everlasting love. It would all be one.

I don't remember feeling him removing the rest of our clothes but when I looked down there was ripped material in pieces all around us. I gathered that Draven couldn't wait either because after lifting me once more he hovered me over the length of him. I felt the tip wet and he moved it to mingle with my own wetness.

I wanted it so badly I could have shouted out to the Heavens, but I knew why he was waiting...I had my eyes closed. See, the thing with Draven was he was all about reactions, my reactions. He liked to experience mine as he made me his own, as he filled my body with more pleasure than I could take...he liked to watch. So I opened my eyes and stared into his.

"Good girl," he said before letting gravity take care of the rest. He shot up through me, making me scream at the extreme pressure having him fill me to the brim. He was big, no... not just big, but huge, there was no getting around that fact. I don't think it helped that I was small but somehow we just fit. I don't know how he didn't hurt me as much as he should, but his movements were gentle to start with, so that I could adjust to his size. And boy did I.

The rhythm picked up as Draven lost his gentle control. He did most of the work, holding my behind in a firm grip and moving me to his tempo. Of course, I didn't care what song it was, it was all amazing, reaching every last nerve ending that lived down there.

He seemed to know exactly the right moments when I was close to finding my release because he would pick up speed to drive me over the edge. He seemed to love the feel of my muscles constricting around him inside of me, because he would close his eyes and lift his face towards the ceiling.

Meanwhile, I was digging my nails into his back and screaming out in a pleasure so great, I could hardly stand it. I didn't know how many orgasms I could take, and every time Draven seemed more eager to push the limits.

He slowed down slightly to allow me time to regain my breath, but it was only seconds and then he would be forcing my body down on him once again with a furious energy. I was panting and every twinge of great pleasure had me gripping onto him once more. Then, this time he bent me back, so my breasts came forward and protruded from my chest. This gave him full access as he clamped his mouth around one nipple and began to suck.

I found this so fulfilling that it only took a few moments to make me cry out for mercy as I was coming yet again. He loved it but this time he couldn't stop. He carried on pumping and sucking so that I wasn't the only one finding my release. He held on to my back as he thrust up one last time then I felt the shuddering of him exploding inside me.

He cried out a growl and then bit down on my nipple like a wild beast, sucking the blood out from me which in turn caused me to experience an orgasm within an orgasm.

I came apart like never before and ended up collapsed on top of him...

That's when everything went dark.

CHAPTER FOURTY-ONE

CRUEL INTERRUPTIONS

I didn't know how I got to where I was, but it was beautiful. I was in a golden meadow that glistened in the sun's rays. Little daisies danced in the gentle breeze and when I looked down my skin was covered in a flowing white material that seemed alive. It snaked around my shoulders and worked its way down my naked body like it owned me. It was almost like invisible hands were behind the way it moved and when one side cupped my breast, I was convinced it was Draven's doing. Where was I?

"Draven!" I called out, but my voice echoed as though I was somewhere else. It bounced off walls that weren't there and came back to me. I tried again.

"Draven, where are you?" I cried out, but once again it didn't come from my mouth, it came from a memory I couldn't see. I held my hands up to my throat but found other hands already there waiting for me. They weren't my own. I turned quickly but found no face to blame.

I wished I could just relax into this dream world, but my uncertainty wouldn't let me. I started to feel cold and held my arms with my hands. I felt safer hugging myself but not safe enough. I started to feel a presence close by but not a soul, apart from mine, was in this golden circle. I looked around more closely trying to study my surroundings.

There was a dark forest that acted like bars of a cage edged around the sides that blocked any other view beyond. The trees seemed to sway from side to side as if they were caught in a secret storm I couldn't see. The white sheet had pulled in tighter forming itself around me like a second skin. It tingled under the sun and sparkled as though wet. I lifted the ends that skirted around my legs and held it to my face to find that it was wet. It smelled like blossoming lilies and felt as if it was made from their petals.

"Why am I here?" I asked out loud to no one but I was answered by a whisper that came flowing out from deep within the deadly looking forest.

"Because I want you." It wasn't a voice I recognised and made me shudder from the possessive tone in which it spoke.

"Am I dreaming?" I asked nervously, while holding myself.

"You are." The voice made me jump as this time it came from close behind my ear. I could feel a large body behind me and I instantly relaxed as I knew it to be Draven. I felt his large hands rest on my shoulders and his fingers curled up to hold my neck.

"Why am I here, if I'm asleep?"

"Because I can control your dreams." Once again, the answer blew across my neck from behind covering me in a calm haze. I felt my tightened muscles lose tension and I lowered my body slightly.

"Why would you want to?" I asked feeling like a child.

"You ask a lot of questions, don't you?" His deep voice held humour which I found strange. It felt different to how I imagined it would. I don't know why but something deep inside was trying to tell me something was wrong. Hands then tensed around my neck into a hold before a more urgent voice spoke.

"Don't listen. Just hear my voice, take it in and do as I say... yes...that's it... now, say yes to me." I was slipping away to somewhere I knew I would most certainly be lost. It felt as if I was drunk. I knew it was wrong whatever it was, but I couldn't stop myself from saying,

"Yes," Causing his hands to relax.

"Good. Do you like it here, Keira?" His hands ran down to my sides and because of it, my body started to sway. I was drifting further down and could only nod my answer.

"Would you like to stay here… here with me…*forever?*" It was such a seductive voice that there wasn't one fibre in my body that could have said no. I truly wanted to stay. I wanted these arms to remain around me until the end of time. Strong arms keeping me safe from everyone who wanted to hurt me.

My mind flashed back to Morgan and my prison; a concrete cell that was a basement in Hell. I saw myself being touched by un-welcomed hands as they roamed my body, invading my soul with venomous thoughts. I saw myself crying in my sleep as I pretended it to be in my dreams, but deep down I knew it was real. I knew it was happening, that's why I cried. After these visions stopped the arms that held me pulled me closer into a deep cage of muscle and bone.

"I would never let anyone hurt you…*Never!*" he said in anger and I had never believed in a voice with so much certainty before this moment…even if it was all a dream.

"Oh, Draven," I said softly, finding words one last time before I gave myself to this place forever.

"I'm sorry, my little Keira girl…but not even he can get to you here."

That's when I cried and crumpled to the floor despite the arms around me. My legs folded underneath me and I felt his body do the same. I cried out at him,

"NO…NO…PLEASE…NO!" I turned to face the man and without looking through fear, I pounded my fists against a huge chest of pale muscle.

"You can't take me! I want to go back…please… oh, please… let me go." I pleaded with the man in between sobs. He leant his head down to rest on mine and soothed back my hair that was flowing wildly in the wind. I looked up to see his blond hair doing the same, but the colour was darkened by the now stormy skies. It was like the Gods had turned angry and had taken away the sun as punishment.

He waited for me to calm and then whispered down into my ear.

"It is too late for that now...far too late. Even your dreams are not safe from me. You will be mine Keira...you will be mine and soon!" With that I finally looked up to find Lucius staring down at me with eyes filled with blood. Red tears ran down his cheeks and landed on my hair, making the contrast scream out. They weren't just filled with blood, but they looked as though made of the life source. His irises were flamed and licking out at the deep veined liquid that made every living thing possible.

His blood was on fire.

I screamed out and used every last shred of strength I had to pull my mind back to my own control. I thought of Draven and the love we had shared not long ago. I thought of the waves of pleasure he caused me to feel. Then I saw us both, locked in each other's bodies bound so tight we looked like one. Everything in sync, the way we moved, every breath, every scream. There was no greater force than ours making love and this was what brought me back. It was what freed me from my own dreams...

The very ones Lucius held in his hands.

I bolted up with a start and felt Draven shift quickly next to me.

"Keira, what's wrong?" His husky worried voice was still thick from sleep and my heart soared at the sound. I was just so happy to be back that I turned quickly and threw myself into him. He was caught off guard, but he held me securely as if he knew how much I needed it. He gave me a minute like this before asking me again.

"I'm fine, just a bad dream," I said knowing I should be telling him about it, but for some reason I couldn't let it out. Why did this keep happening? Why could I never speak about it? As soon as these thoughts entered my mind it started to shut down. I started losing the questions, like losing a thread on a knitted sweater. As if it was being pulled so quickly it started to disappear until there was nothing left to hold on to. Nothing left to keep me warm.

"Are you alright? Tell me about it, Keira." Draven pressed for an answer I couldn't give, so I lied.

"I can't really remember it now, let's just forget about it. How long was I asleep anyway?" I asked trying to dodge any more questions. Draven looked unconvinced but thankfully let it go anyway.

"Only a few hours, you passed out on me. I was worried I went too far." He looked like he did when he was guilty, but I smiled back at him.

"No, you didn't. You can never go too far." This was when his guilty look turned to one of steel. He frowned and pulled me close, holding my head the way Lucius had done in my dream. I tried not to shudder, but I couldn't help it, thankfully Draven took it for a chill and covered me up with the blanket.

"Keira, you still don't understand how much I hold back with you. If I ever totally lost control, I could hurt you and I would never allow myself to do that. I would never forgive myself!" He said the last part under his breath, but I heard it anyway. He held me protectively in the cocoon of his arms and I sighed at the idea of him holding back on me.

"How much do you hold back exactly?" I asked trying to look up at him, but he held me still preventing it.

"A lot. You are fragile Keira, much more so than my own kind." This hurt me. In fact, it cut into me like a blade. I pulled from his arms quickly startling him enough to let me.

"If I'm so bloody fragile then why be with me if you have to hold back? I mean, why not have one of your own kind to satisfy your real needs?" I know this was spiteful of me to say but I couldn't help what came out, it was as if it came from someone else. He pulled me roughly back to face him and I could see the anger and hurt mixed into one.

I almost whimpered out my sorry as soon as I saw his face. It was stone...emotional, cold stone. I knew I had gone too far, and I knew that I had truly hurt him with my words. He pulled away from me and got up out of bed without saying a word. I wanted him to shout at me, to shake me, Hell, anything but the cruel, cold hard silence that I had never received from Draven before.

"You had better get up and get dressed," he finally said and now I wished he hadn't.

"You want me to leave?" I asked in shock. Draven had never, ever before asked me to leave and I could feel the tears quickly start to form.

"Your cousin will be here soon, you shouldn't keep her waiting," he said without looking at me once. All the while I had watched him get dressed, keeping his eyes to the floor. Then he simply walked over to the door and opened it. However, before leaving completely he stopped with his hand on the handle and was about to look up to see the pain on my face only he didn't. Instead, he shook his head as if trying to get something out of there and left. He closed the door with a bit more force than what was needed, making me jump at the slam. Then I cried...again...for like the hundredth time that day.

I don't know how long I had been crying for, but it didn't feel enough. I wanted to get up and find him. I wanted to beg for forgiveness, tell him how stupid I was but I couldn't move. I was locked there and frozen in my misery.

Here I was, just had another dose of the best sex of my life and I had ruined it with only a few words... Grrr, I hated myself for it! I would never forget Draven's face. The face of someone hearing the cruellest words they had ever heard. On hearing them from the lips you kiss in passion. The same lips that smile upon seeing you. The very lips that told you they loved you.

How could I have done that? I wasn't a cruel person. If anything, I was usually the one that kept her feelings under tight grip but today what had happened? Of course, I had no one to blame but myself...my stupid, stupid self!

I carried on like that until the minutes ticked by but soon the sound of Abba was interrupting my mental scolding. I got up and didn't even care that I was stark naked. I felt numb so what did it matter? I found my phone inside my jacket pocket, which was hanging over a chair...which Draven had probably placed there.

"Hel..." I didn't even get chance to finish before a voice starting screeching at me.

"Where the Hell are you?" Hilary's voice boomed on the other end, making me wince.

"Uh...coming, where are you?" I asked trying to calm her down, but it didn't help and yet again I was stupid to believe otherwise.

"What do you mean 'Where am I?!' I'm at the Fucking club, that's where!" Her foul language wasn't a shock. I already knew there was about zero per cent ladylike manners in her.

"Right, well stay by the bar and I will meet you there. Give me ten minutes."

"Ten minutes! Get down here now or better still, send Dominic to keep me company," she said and I could hear her smirk replace the pissed off look she usually went for.

"Look, the longer I'm on the phone the longer I will be...so just..." That's when she hung up. Now, instead of wanting to cry I wanted to scream! I was close to giving up but instead I ran in the bathroom to get the quickest shower I could. I was almost crying again at the thought of washing away Draven's scent, but it couldn't be helped.

"Pull it together, Keira!" I scorned myself while washing with little care.

I kept my hair dry and once out of the shower tried to smooth it out as much as I could without the use of a hairbrush. I quickly dried myself to a degree but when pulling on a pair of clean jeans I realised I'd missed my leg, as I found getting them on without tugging was difficult. This was when Sophia came in.

She found me in a bra and bent over the arm of the chair pulling the waistband with frustration. I turned to see her walk in hoping it was Draven, when my hand slipped and smacked myself in the face, before rolling backwards off the seat landing on my back. I looked up finding her peering over the seat with an amused look.

"Wow, you even make getting dressed look dangerous," she mocked.

"It's a talent" I replied sarcastically. I got off the floor and grabbed the top I had picked off the armchair and pulled it on with embarrassment flooding my face. It was a long-sleeved black top with a faded peace sign on the front. I thought it a good choice and hoped Draven would find the deeper meaning. I then jumped up and down a few times to get the rest of my jeans over my bum.

"So, what did you say to my brother to put him into such a foul mood?" Oh great, now the Demon sister to contend with.

"Why, what did he say?" I asked sheepishly as I pulled my gloves up. I noticed her glance briefly at my scars before I hid them from sight.

"It's not what he said...it's more like what he just destroyed." I couldn't hide my shock and also couldn't help but ask,

"What did he just destroy?"

"Oh, only a priceless vase that was given to him as a gift from the Qianlong Emperor... who, I will mention, was the fifth emperor of the Qing dynasty in 1736. Let's put it another way, one like it sold at auction for about $80..."

"...Thousand!" I screamed interrupting her and close to praying I hadn't caused a temper that would cost so much.

"Oh no, not thousands, think bigger, think... millions," she said coolly and I fell back into the chair.

"80 million dollars...Oh God!" I held my head in my hands and it felt like it weighed a ton.

"Oh come on, it's not like you broke it...well, threw it across the room, smashing out the window and landing in the canyon below, but that's beside the point. Besides he will just fix it again. That is when he finds all the teeny tiny pieces, oh and when he's in a better mood of course. So, what happened?"

"It's all my fault, I said something really stupid!" I said, shaking my head but she just smiled at God only knows what.

"Come now, Keira, my brother is a big boy. Okay, granted he has anger issues, but he will not stay mad for long. After all he did send me in here to check you were alright." At this my head whipped up as though on a bungee.

"He did?" I asked full of hope. I mean he would have to care if he sent Sophia to check on me...wouldn't he?

"He did," she said repeating my words. At that, I stood up and grabbed my jacket as it was cooler now without Draven to warm me. It was always colder without him in the room.

"You never told me what you said?" Sophia asked me as she followed me down the hall. I only stopped to answer her before I opened the door that led out to the club.

"It doesn't matter but do me a favour?" She nodded and grabbed the door for me.

"Tell Draven that I'm sorry," I said and walked out into the crowded space that was the VIP. I knew what I must have looked like, eyes still red and puffy from a day's crying, hair un-brushed and wild. I still had little wet hair that clung to my neck and could feel the frizz trying to escape the clip I'd twisted it up into.

My clothes clung to my damp skin and felt uncomfortable as I walked. But I did walk. I walked on through the club doing an expert job of the walk of shame and with the look of someone trying to hide a pain that was as clear as vodka.

I carried on until his table came into view and the man himself. I noted he too had changed, and his look was haunting me. It was so harsh and cold, it was hard to believe it was the same man. His permanent frown forced his eyes smaller and fierce.

He was shooting back drinks with little care and one glass I saw him crush into a tiny crumpled piece that he threw aside. My gut hurt at the sight of his anger, knowing I was the cause was crushing. I almost wanted to go up there. Get down on my knees and beg but I couldn't, for one ...I was frightened. What if the outcome was to ask me to leave and this time not just his room but Afterlife?

Vincent saw me and his look was filled with pity. I didn't know whether it was for his brother's anguish or mine. Draven noticed his eyes and looked my way. For a second they softened at the sight. He noted the redness in my eyes and closed his own. But then when he opened them, all I saw was a purple flame engulf them.

It was as though he had just played the words I had said to him over again and all he found there was his hurt. Then he swiftly turned his face from mine and barked an order for another drink.

Everyone on the table looked too scared to speak but of course the only one smiling was Aurora.

I sighed and looked back down at a pair of feet that I made move towards the stairs. Of course, no will in the world could stop me from looking back before leaving. I found Draven staring at me but when I saw this, he knocked back his shot glass and threw it aside making it smash at Loz's feet. I looked away one last time and ran down the steps before the tears could start again.

Unfortunately, I found Hilary easily on account of what she was wearing. She had on skin-tight black leather pants that would have put Sandy from Grease to shame on the tightness level. She had matched this with a red leather halter top that laced up the front. She had pulled it on so tight that what little breasts she did have, were now closer to her chin. I think she had mistaken 'Gothic nightclub' for 'Whorehouse chic'.

I couldn't help but look at the door as means of escape. If only I could get away with running from everything. At the moment it was more my guilt I wanted to run from, but I knew that would follow me wherever I went, so really what was the point?

Hilary was standing at the bar and had her back end sticking out at an awkward angle. If this was to show off her body more, to me it just made her butt look weird. Don't get me wrong, I'm not usually a mean bitter person and very rarely bitchy, but where my cousin was concerned...well, let's just say it was fair game!

She hated me for some unknown reason that I couldn't care less about but years ago this unfounded hate would drive me insane wondering why. I had no idea what it was all based on, but one thing was for sure, I had become an expert living with it.

I had swallowed every insult, put up with every snide comment and had to accept just about every stupid and outrageous thing she did. Which, given her sexual tendencies, I was surprised the girl hadn't gotten into more trouble than she had. This was a girl without limits! Older men, younger men, married men and even a convicted man, so I'd heard. She had done it all... literally.

"About bloody time!" she said as I joined her. I didn't reply but just waved at Mike, ignoring her.

"Hey Kaz, just can't get enough of the place?" he joked and I laughed out one of those fake laughs that you reserve for hiding true feelings. No one ever suspects they're not sincere and it's better than just saying outright that you're not in the mood for jokes because you think your boyfriend hates you right now!

Mike looked to my right and waited for me to introduce my evil cousin and from the sounds of the clearing throat next to me, he wasn't the only one.

"Umm sorry, Mike, this is my cousin Hilary, Hilary this is Mike my work friend."

"Work friend?" He cocked his head to the side at my classification of our friendship.

"Well, we only see each other at work," I reminded him.

"Yes, why is that?" he asked making me smile for the first time in what seemed like hours. My smile was my answer and his flirting didn't go unnoticed.

"Hi, I'm Mike, your cousin's work friend," he said smiling, but Hilary was uninterested due to his interest in me.

"Charmed," she said as he took her hand to shake but her face spoke volumes, she was less than charmed. This was until she spotted another contender...the lovely Jack.

He came up behind me and gave me a hug. I turned into him and it felt good in his arms. I wanted to stay there and tell him all my problems. He was such a good friend, the type you could spill your life's woes to, and he would just sit there and listen. He wouldn't ever judge you. He wouldn't give you that 'I know how it feels crap'. No, simply put he became a strength that some people depended on forgetting what was troubling their mind free from the cage they built.

When did people even know how it felt? How could they when everyone experiences their feelings differently? Look at Hilary for example. She displayed her hate for me openly, but I kept mine hidden. Sometimes, people use pain and sadness to harbour it into something positive, while others hide it away and cry until they are empty. This was why I loved Jack. And this was why I had to keep him away from the venomous Hilary, before she infected him with her poisonous nature.

"Jack!" I said his name like it was a lifeline and he knew something was wrong when he saw my face looking up at him.

"Keira, are you alright?" The very question had me close to tears, but I closed my eyes to push them back. I nodded my head, keeping my eyes from finding his and turned back to find Hilary waiting.

"Sorry Jack, this is my cousin, Hilary," I said hating introducing her, but not having much choice in the matter. He turned his attention to my cousin, and she looked more than happy with her discovery. I mean, who could blame her, after all, apart from the Dravens, Jack was the most handsome guy in the club at any time.

With his tall, athletic build and bronze coloured hair that flopped in his toffee brown eyes that had flecks of gold. That soft-featured face that housed one of the greatest smiles I had ever seen. It was enough to melt any woman's heart...except mine that was.

It nearly did once, but my heart had already been captured by another. However, it was still flattering to know how Jack felt about plain old me. He was also one of the only people that knew my true past, which was special for other reasons. I could trust Jack, I knew that and it gave me a much needed comfort knowing I had that in a friend.

"Hi there, nice to meet you," he said and this time she gave him more of a reaction than she had done with poor Mike.

"Well, hello there. Keira didn't tell me she had a friend who works as a model," she said shamelessly flirting. Jack smiled and then she was lost. That smile was all it took for any female with a sexual urge the size of a salt pinch and Hilary had enough to make up a beach!

"Did they teach that English charm at your school?" Jack asked flirting back, causing Hilary to flutter her fake eyelashes at him.

"Oh no, I was just born with it," she replied winking, which almost made me want to gag! I cleared my throat and tried to put a spanner in the works before the engine went into overdrive.

"Umm Jack, is RJ here?"

"Oh Kizzy Cat, more handsome friends for me to meet?" she said putting on her nicest charm that I knew was as fake as the platinum hair on her head. A moment ago she was biting my head off, now I was back to Kizzy Cat.

"RJ is my sister and I think she's on her way with the rest of the gang," Jack said tearing his eyes away from Hilary and back to me.

"Designated driver tonight then?"

"You got it," he said and gave me an affectionate chin shake as if I was a child. Hilary looked like she wanted to scratch my eyes out because of it and this made me smile.

"But hey, can I get you lovely ladies a drink?" This was when Hilary barged in front of me and took her place next to Jack.

Jack bought us both a drink, but by the time the rest turned up I was already on my third while the other two were still on their first. I had quickly become the third wheel and if it hadn't been for Mike, I would have been stood there like a right sad sack.

They were flirting with each other like peacocks show their feathers to attract a mate. It wouldn't have surprised me if the humping would soon begin. Hilary would flick her hair back every now and again, which would land in my face. Jack would try and include me, but before I could answer, Hilary would interrupt as though the question had been aimed at her.

Thankfully, RJ's pink spikes came into view and I almost ran into her arms.

"Whoa there Sparky, where's the fire?" I gestured over my shoulder at the corrupt and the corrupted that were so close it looked as though they were sharing air.

"Ah, the dreaded cousin has landed then?" she said dryly.

"Please help me!" I pleaded.

"Lead the way, my young Padawan." I laughed at her Star Wars reference.

"Hilary, this is my sister, RJ," Jack said as he received an elbow in the side.

"Oh right, Keira mentioned you," Hilary said rudely making RJ turn an evil glare her way. If there was something you didn't do, it was piss off RJ!

"Hey," she said unimpressed and turned back to her brother.

"Yo bro, you wanna get me a drink or what?" she said clicking her black painted nails at him to get his attention away from Hilary.

"You know, I'm not your wallet, Rach!" He only ever called her this when he disapproved of something his sister did.

"Shut up, Jack! Anyway, I bought you the t-shirt you're wearing, so if it wasn't for me you would be half-naked by now...and this is the thanks I get...Sheesh, I don't know, kids today," she said to me with a smirk.

"Mmm, naked sounds good to me," Hilary said making Jack blush slightly before giving her a wink.

"Come on Hilary, I will show you to our usual spot." Thankfully RJ intervened and dragged her away leaving me and Jack at the bar. We needed to talk.

"Jack, I think I need to warn you about my cousin."

"Warn me? She seems really nice," he said smiling. Deluded but smiling.

"Yes seems so, but I know her, she's..." Before I could continue, he stopped me.

"Keira, if this is going to be a bitch session, I'll pass. I like to make my own judgments, if that's alright with you?" It was the first time Jack had ever snapped at me and I was gobsmacked. But I didn't give up.

"Look, I'm just trying to warn you that's all. She may seem nice but..."

"That's enough! Look, you might have some issues but the way I see it, here she is coming all this way to see you, and this is how you treat her, trying to warn your friends against her. Frankly, I'm surprised at you, I wouldn't have pegged you for the jealous type, Keira, but I guess what she says is true..."

"WHAT?!" I shouted making some of the other customers stare at me. Did I miss something?

"She doesn't know why you act this way towards her, but she can't help that you've always been jealous of her. I think it's sad that you make her feel this way, she clearly loves you." By this time, I knew my mouth was gaping open, but it couldn't be helped. All that came to mind was what I said,

"That BITCH!" I know it was tactless but after three Coronas, to Hell with tact! Jack looked at me as though he was really seeing me for the first time and he didn't like what he saw. He shook his head and left muttering something to himself. GREAT! BRILLIANT! This was just bloody marvellous! Now I was the bad guy.

One thing was for sure, this had been one shitter of a day and there was only one answer for it...

Lots and lots of tequila!

CHAPTER FOURTY-TWO

A LITTLE TOO MUCH FUEL

So that's what I did!

As the night went on, I drank lots. In fact, I drank more than lots. I drank until I got drunk and the pain of the day's events didn't bother me anymore. RJ had helped me in this. As it turned out she hated my evil cousin just about as much as I did. She had gotten pretty fed up of her stupid personality quicker than most. Sorry for the weak insult but when you're drunk it's hard to come up with more complex name-calling. I still had fun though.

It was just me and RJ at the bar, drinking and bitching about my horrid cousin. Soon I had forgotten all about stupid men in the world who hated me right now. Instead me and RJ solved all the world's problems and soon the answer became clear.

"MEN! Bloody men! They're all the sodding same!" I said not being able to help the full northern accent that came through whenever I was drunk. This made RJ giggle, which turned out to be her drunken trait.

"You know Draven's mad at me?" I said after swigging back my seventh Corona.

"Really… why?" she said swishing her rum and coke around in her short glass.

"Because I said something really stupid."

"Did you mean it?" she asked in earnest, which for drunken RJ was surprising.

"Mean what?" I said missing the conversation because I was concentrating on the ice swirling around in her glass...man, I needed to get a grip.

"You know, what you said that made him mad?"

"Yes…no...Oh, I don't know. Do you wanna know the worst thing about dating Draven?" This made her turn serious. She whipped her head around and tried to focus on my face, which looked more difficult than it sounded.

"I didn't think there could be anything bad about dating that God of a man," RJ said sighing, as if imagining it for herself. Of course, I laughed and said,

"Well yes, he is a God. King, God and supernatural wonder sex master but that's beside the point!" I'm thankful that when I said this, she didn't take it as literally as I had meant it or I could have more explaining to do and not just to RJ.

"Damn it! I knew the sex would be amazing, you lucky cow!"

"Yes, yes it is, oh my God, it's just mind-blowing but…" I said getting horny just thinking about it.

"But what? What else matters?" We giggled before I came back to what I was trying to say.

"Okay, so you were saying the worse thing is..." She held out her hand to prompt me back.

"It's being with someone who has the longest string of amazing looking girlfriends to contend with and when I say amazing, I really mean drop-dead gorgeous, Angels falling from the sky type of shit!" Another thing about my getting drunk was not only does my accent come through but I don't hold back quite as much on the swearing part. God, I was starting to sound like Hilary.

"Ouch! That's gotta hurt the ego!" RJ said, shaking her spikes.

"You have no idea. I met one of them today and I almost fell in love with her!" I said making her giggle again.

"Okay, this calls for another drink," she said standing up from the stool and nearly falling down it. My hand flashed out to steady her so quickly I surprised myself. I sure had good reactions for a drunken person and when did I get that strong?

"Wow, good reactions...like a cat...Kizzy cat... hehe." She sniggered and we both laughed again. After we had finished laughing stupidly, she got Mike's attention, who had clearly found the whole of our drunken display funny. He had a constant smirk every time he looked our way.

"Mike, my good fellow, could you please get me and my lovely pink-haired friend here a drink of your finest?" I said putting on the poshest English accent that I could in my state. He laughed as I waved at him like the Queen would do and RJ copied.

"Wish I could girls, but I have had my orders, no more alcohol."

"What! That's bullshit!" RJ said and I stopped her and said that wasn't the English way and showed her how it was done.

"Now, now my good man surely not, be a doll and replenish our drinks." Of course, this was followed by a hiccup, which made us all laugh.

"Sorry, no can do ladies, the order comes from above," he said and RJ leaned in and whispered,

"What, God?" Mike nearly wet himself he laughed so hard, then he nodded behind us to the VIP, making it time for me to drop the 'English charm'.

"What! That's bullshit!" I said copying RJ's initial reaction.

"Sorry, but it looks like your boyfriend doesn't like a drunken girlfriend in his club," he said smugly making us both frown.

"Oh dear, looks like he's still mad," RJ said finishing off her drink.

"Hey we're off, you coming?" Jack had come up to us and once he saw the state we were in, he frowned like the sight of us having legal fun was prohibited.

"Oh great, one drunken sister to contend with!" He glared at me as if this was all my fault and I glared back. No doubt Hilary had spread even more lies about me.

"Kizzy! You're drunk!?" Hilary said pretending to be horrified. Not long ago this girl was thrown out of college for smoking weed in class. I bet that story she'd missed when chatting to the gullible Jack.

"How will I get home now?" she said like some pathetic English damsel in need of a knight.

"Don't worry I will see you get home, even if others don't seem to care," Jack snapped at me. I was trying hard to come up with the greatest comeback of all comebacks but in the end, I just grunted like some strange fairy-tale troll. Jack rolled his eyes, while RJ leaned over into my ear and said,

"Good one."

They started to walk off and I shouted out to them.

"Wait...how do I get home?" I asked in a pleading voice that I hated to hear.

"Well, I can't take you. I'm at my limit as it is. Besides you should have thought of that before you got tanked up. My sympathies to Mr Draven," he said coldly before leaving with the others. RJ waved over Jack's shoulder, as now he was supporting most of her body weight.

"Great! Just fan...shitting...tastic!" I said out loud earning me some weird looks by depressed Goths. Ok, so this was unfair, not all Goths were depressed but Hell, I was bitter. In the space of a couple of hours, I had nearly been kidnapped, pissed off my boyfriend and lost my best friend to my arch-nemesis.

It was not a great start to anyone's week.

Of course, I knew what I had to do now. I had to face my own personal Demon, which just so happened to be my boyfriend as well.

I walked back to the bar and plonked myself down with a sigh. There was nothing else I could do, I had to go back up there or I would have nowhere else to stay. I considered waiting until everyone had gone and sleeping down here, but then I would just have looked like the coward I was.

I wasn't even sure Draven would let me stay? After all the times I had seen Draven angry, this was definitely the worst. I mean him shouting at me I could take, I could handle that but silence...That I wasn't used to from Draven. My guilt was overwhelming but now, being drunk just made it worse. Did he know that I was trollied? I sincerely hoped not.

"You okay?" Mike asked me quietly, as though to pull me from my sad state. I just shrugged my shoulders like a child and hopped off the seat.

"I guess I'd better go now but I will see you later, thanks Mike," I said before dragging myself over to the staircase I knew well. I weaved through the moving bodies that were making their way to the exit. Of course, it was closing time and I was the only one moving this way.

The band was getting their stuff ready to leave and I nearly fell over a guy's drum kit that was littered around the floor ready for packing away.

"Whoa there, easy girly," a man said, keeping me up straight. He wasn't much higher than me but his spiked Mohawk more than made up for it.

"Thanks," I said giving him a drunken goofy smile.

"No problem, cutie," he said winking at me. Bless him. At least he thought my behaviour was cute...hopefully, he wouldn't be the only one tonight, I thought as I reached the guarded door. Once again, the two guards who always manned this door stood, arms folded. Of course, as usual they didn't say anything to me which really got my back up.

"You know a hello, howdy, even a bloody head nod wouldn't go amiss!" I said throwing my hands up dramatically. They both frowned at me then looked at each other for the answer. Neither said a word which made me screech out,

"Grrrr, forget it guys!" I then pushed past them not caring about a reaction. It was one of the first times I got to open the door before they did. I stormed upstairs, panting all the way. I stopped at the closed door at the top before going in. It took me back to my first time and how nervous and unsure I'd been.

When I walked through my eyes quickly searched out Draven's table, but my heart dropped when I saw his space was empty. I didn't know why but the next person's space I went to was Aurora's. It was wrong of me. And I trusted Draven right? Then why did my heart plummet when I saw that she too was missing. I decided to walk around the back so that no one would see me. Everyone was far too busy to notice as I walked around with my hood drawn over my face. Of course, I didn't look so inconspicuous when I kept bumping into chairs.

"Sorry…eh, oops… my bad," I would mutter as I snaked in and out of the back tables. I turned my head to say another sorry for knocking some poor Demon's jacket off the back of his chair, making him mutter something back I couldn't understand. That's when I bumped into my first Draven of the night.

"Oh dear, my fault," I said before looking up swaying.

"Keira?" Vincent's kind face looked down at me now that my hood had fallen back.

"Oh, hey Vinnie," I said trying to act cool but considering I never called him that I wasn't fooling anyone. He tried to frown but couldn't keep the amusement off his face.

"Don't suppose you have seen your big angry bro around this shindig have ya?" I asked causing his apparent shock at hearing me speak like this deepen the colour of his eyes. He even laughed making me giggle.

"Come on happy, I think you need some air," he said taking my arm to steady myself.

"Ooh… air is good," I said happily before following my blonde shepherd. Once outside the cold air hit me, making me feel more lightheaded than before. I turned around and nearly lost my footing making Vincent reach out to steady me. We both turned around at the same time, making it so I was facing the night with my back to the door. He moved from holding my waist and decided holding my arm was safer.

"Feeling better?" he asked softly, which was nice to hear after being picked on all night...picked on, man, I sounded like a pouting child.

"I'm fine really and I know what you're thinking," I said trying not to let the hiccups free that I could feel brewing. He smiled at me and then crossed his arms over his chest...man alive he was sexy. No, what was I thinking...wrong Draven.

Wrong Draven!

"Oh really?" he asked dripping in smugness.

"Yes, you think I'm drunk, but I'm soo not," I said trying not to fall on the spot.

"Umm, that maybe more convincing without the hiccupping and swaying but whatever you say." He was teasing me, and it made me smile.

"I thought you were supposed to be the good one?" I mocked making him laugh.

"I'm not the one drunk," he replied.

"Ssshhh don't say that, Draven might hear you and then I will be in even more trouble!" I said holding my finger to my mouth to continue the 'Ssshhhing.'

"He already has," a voice said behind me making me jump, shriek and both my hands to fly up to cover my mouth. Vincent glanced over me and looked as though he wanted to burst out laughing. I think I would have kicked him if he had. I turned around to see my boyfriend stood there with his arms folded and as usual...*frowning*.

"Ah, shit!" I said making his frown deepen. This was enough for Vincent and he let out a series of raucous laughts.

"Thanks for the heads up, Vinnie boy!" I said making Draven's face flash a brief moment of amusement.

"Anytime, Keira my dear. Have fun you two!" he said as he walked past me but before he left, he whispered something in his brother's ear. Draven didn't respond but just closed his eyes momentarily and nodded once. Then we were left alone.

"Okay, come on, let's have it," I said motioning with my hands.

"Have what exactly, because I think you have had enough to drink?"

"Touché, pussy cat!" I don't know why I said this but Hell, who does when their drunk?

"Pussy cat?" One eyebrow rose at the question.

"Bloody Hell, Draven, it's just a saying, I'm not calling you a cat! Or a pussy for that matter...I think everyone on the planet knows you're hard, even those that haven't met you yet and..."

"...Hard?" he asked interrupting me and I stumbled mid-rant.

"Uh, yeah, Hard... like granite-hard, yeah that fits," I said thinking he would like this kind of analogy. I mean, didn't all men like this type of shit from their girlfriends? Although seeing his face right now, that analogy was more on the mark from the deadly look he was casting my way and not from his rock-hard frame. When he spoke, I finally knew why.

"You mean cold, unfeeling and emotionless…that type of hard?" Oh Lordy…Now he was definitely pissed!

"Eh…no?"

"No?" he mimicked again, confusing me even more.

"My bloody mouth! I don't mean you're hard, like mentally… wait this isn't coming out right…What I mean is…well, it's an English thing, I think…well anyway, it means you can handle yourself, which obviously you can being a…uh…well you being all demony and yeah…well, there you go, no pussy cat for you anymore" I didn't know what was going through my head but I'm pretty sure I meowed after saying this…Uh yeah, the look on Draven's face only confirmed my fears. Was that a smirk he was trying to hide?

"You're enjoying this aren't you?" I snapped, frowning at him.

"I must confess I find seeing this side of you entertaining, yes."

"Whatever! Anyway, I'm not drunk…more like tipsy." At this he snorted out his disbelief.

"Doubtful Keira, I have monitored how much you have had to drink, and I know your limits."

"Better than your own, no doubt," I said thinking what a good come back it was but then remembering this evening's argument and by the look on his face, it so wasn't!

"Umm, I didn't mean that…sorry," I added sheepishly.

"You know you have a dark and deadly tongue when you want to, but I never took you for being cruel" Ok, now that hurt!

"Oh my God! Draven, this is so stupid. If you really think I'm that bloody innocent than leave me now because I'm not! Look I'm not claiming to be bloody perfect…far from it quite clearly, but I don't want to be pers…umm… that word…"

"Persecuted?"

"Yeah that one, one of those every time I make a mistake. I am human after all!" I said finishing it with a hiccup. Apart from forgetting words and swaying, I think it was a pretty good speech.

"So, you're sorry?" he asked in truth.

"Oh jeez, get with the program. Of course I am for Christ's

sake, I have been all night!" His eyebrows knitted together and I frowned back at him, at least I think I did.

"Without the profanities, Keira."

"Oh shut up, you fool!" I shouted at him, getting angry that he wasn't big enough to accept my apology without making me jump through hoops! He looked dumbfounded at my outburst, but I didn't care.

"Me the fool? Ha, that is rich coming from you in your state!"

"Okay so I'm drunk, so bloody sue me!"

"I thought you were tipsy, which is it Keira?" He folded his arms again but looked as if he would be ready to catch me at any minute.

"See, there you go again...all foolish and such. Of course I'm drunk! But it's not like it's against the law...I'm a...ukup ...an adult." I said with a hiccup and trying to fold my own arms, but I wasn't sure I made it.

"It shows," he said dryly.

"I'm twenty...something and anyway in my land of home the limit is eighteen so I'm well old enough!" He looked as though he was trying very hard not to laugh at me which was making me mad.

"I'm not the law, Keira, you do as you please ...as always," he said softly but I could detect the coldness in this last part.

"Do you know something?" I asked opening my eyes wider at him.

"What?"

"This is...is…"

"Is?" He had to hold me steady as I got closer to him which made my mind lose its train of thought for a second.

"Bullshit! I'm sorry and that's that. If you refuse to accept that, then you need to...to…"

"To...?" Once again he was mocking me, but I noticed he had got closer to me and was holding me tighter on the arms.

"To grow up! Yes, you need to grow up. I mean you're a bloody half Demon and my stupid words hurt you. You know I didn't mean it and it's your fault anyway!" I had to stop because for some reason I couldn't manage talking and breathing at the same time.

"And how is this all my fault exactly?" He was letting his guard down because he was most definitely more amused than angry even though I was shouting at him.

"I can't help that you have so many beautiful women all lining up. A string of ex Goddess girlfriends, that all want to make ashtrays out of my head!" Ok, so now he was laughing at me and this made me push him.

"Stop it!"

"I would if it wasn't all so ridiculous," he said without letting me go...this was probably more for my own good as I would have no doubt landed on my butt.

"You're saying my feelings are ridiculous?"

"Yes and your state of inebriation just adds to it!" Ok, this time I did manage to pull away and after a wobble here and there I stayed on my feet at least.

"Steady," he said reaching out to me but didn't make contact.

"My feelings are not funny! Do you think I like feeling so inferior?"

"And how exactly do I make you feel inferior? Do I not give you everything? Do I not treat you well? Have I not given my heart to you and only you?" Okay, angry Draven again. Now it was his turn to be dramatic. When I didn't answer he carried on.

"I have given you parts of myself that I never knew I had to give. I will do anything for you, you know this and as you said, so delicately, that YES, I am in fact a Demon and yet your words cut me down like the Devil's touch. Does that not tell you something? Does that not scream out to you just how much I must care, love and adore you, if but only a few words do this to me? By the Gods, Keira, think woman!" Okay so now my rage had been replaced by tears of feeling very, very sorry for myself.

"Don't do that," he said calming down from his outburst.

"Do what?" I snuffled out while rubbing my runny nose on my sleeve.

"Keira, please don't cry." This somehow made me cry more and he reached out to hold me but I pulled back.

"I'm not crying! I have a cold," I said lamely and when he tilted his head it reminded me of all those times before. The times when people used to do that after the 'incident'. I would say 'I'm fine' and they would tilt their heads in disbelief.

"Come here, let me see."

"You can't see a cold, Draven," I stated lamely and he smiled down at me.

"I can, Supernatural remember? Come to me." He held out his hand for me to take but I remained stubborn.

"Did you really mean all that stuff?" I asked sniffing and rubbing my nose again.

"Yes I did. Those are my feelings, Keira, whether you wish to believe them or not. It is the truth and it pains me you have to ask...when will you trust me, Catherine?" He said my first name like it would get through to me making more of an impact...of course it worked, the jammy bastard!

"It's not you that I don't trust." At this he shook his head. He didn't understand me.

"It's me." He looked hurt at this and ran his hands through his hair, which was a clear sign he was frustrated by my answer.

"You're...you're not sure about your feelings for me?" It looked painful to ask.

"No, it's not that. I know how I feel, and I love you more than I have ever loved anyone before in my life. But I don't trust myself not to screw it all up!" There it was. It was out now for Draven to have to deal with and he looked pretty relieved if you asked me.

"Oh, Keira, my girl, you would have to do something pretty extreme to change the way I love you."

"Like?"

"Well, I wouldn't take kindly to you trying to kill me," he joked. Yeah, like I could, it would be like the moth against the flame.

"And cheating is a big no, no!" I said more for his benefit than mine, knowing I never would.

"NO! Absolutely not! No one should ever touch you. Keira, this is something I would never allow, you understand?" He looked furious at the idea and his purple eyes expressed it deeper.

"Well, that goes the same for you too, mister!" I said standing up to him and poking him in the chest. He looked shocked that even in his full Demon rage I would still stand up to him. His shock soon turned to delight and pride.

"I am not afraid of you," I said holding my chin high. He then grabbed quickly at the tops of my arms and pulled me close. I had to strain my head back to see his face.

"I would have it no other way, my little vixen!" he said down at me before crushing his lips to mine.

And with that kiss I felt the weight of the day and evening lift and fade away into the night. Well, as far as I was concerned the night could have it!

Because now Draven had forgiven me,

And it was about bloody time!

CHAPTER FOURTY-THREE

PASSAGEWAYS AND PERSUASION

I don't know how it happened, but when he had finished kissing me I was left feeling even more lightheaded and now also horny. I had to step back from him to clear my head, which was difficult considering I was feeling very drunk.

"Where are you going? Come back to me." He was being demanding again but in my stubborn mind I was calling the shots, which is what I decided to tell him.

"Excuse me Mr Demon King. I'm the one in control here and you just remember that please," I said flicking hair back that was already back. I wasn't what you called the smoothest drunk in the pub that was for sure!

Draven straightened up and looked as though he was trying not to laugh.

"I am sorry, my Princess, what would you wish me to do?" I smiled at the thought. I then crossed my arms and tapped my top lip, missing the first time and hitting my nose. This he laughed at, which earned him a look of warning.

"Forgive me, your Highness, for my insolence. It will not happen again." He then bowed gracefully, making out as though I was royalty. This prompted a series of giggles and snorts to erupt. I tried to compose myself and I coughed back another unwanted, but excited piggy noise.

"See that it doesn't. This is fun right?" I laughed out loud and he rolled his eyes at me before laughing again.

"If you say so, love."

"Hey! Less of the mocking and placating please. You're ruining my fun." I pouted my lips together making him stare at them like he wanted to bite me.

"I think I play the beast better than the servant so maybe we should play that game instead," he said, giving me a cocky smile that crooked up on one side.

"Oh no, this is my game and I won't be bullied. Besides, you're too used to getting your own way but not tonight, Mister!"

"Is that rightly so...Umm, then pray tell me, my royal Mistress, what would you have me do to please you?" His velvet voice dripped with seduction and left little bumps on my skin. I had to close my eyes as my belly filled with pure, liquid temptation.

When I took a deep breath to clear my head, I opened my eyes and screamed out. Draven had moved towards me so close that his face was now level with my own.

"Is something wrong, Vixen?" he asked, tilting his head and faking his concern as he could no doubt hear the heavy drumbeat of my erratic heartbeat from being so turned on. I loved the way he called me that. It made me feel as though I had a hold over him, plus the way he said it sounded sexy and raw.

I gulped before saying a shy,

"N..n..no," I backed up and every step I took he took another towards me. His dark eyes turned almost primal, like a hungry animal stalking its prey. I was getting ready for him to pounce and he knew it.

"Come now, Keira, I thought you didn't fear me." He was testing me, playing with me, like it was his game not mine. Of course, when my hands found the railing behind me, I knew I had nowhere else to go.

"Draven?"

"Yes, Keira." I closed my eyes to stop the world from spinning and his words were the cause.

"I think I need...need…" I was trying so hard to find words in the darkness and the black haze that was my mind.

"Yes, what is it you need?" And then that was it, I felt it coming!

It was horrible when you first realise it. Truly terrifying when you know what your body wants to do but you try to control it. It's like your body is working against what your mind tells it to do...or not to do in this case. I could even feel the exact moment all the colour drained from my face in a whoosh. Like my body needed the blood elsewhere. And then there it was, a nightmare situation coming out from deep within me and it had nowhere else to go but out and out and out…

It was coming.

"I need to...to be sick!" I shouted before turning around to throw up over the balcony. My stomach heaved out all the alcohol it had consumed over the last few hours. I felt Draven's hand rub my back and his other hand held my hair out of the projectile vomiting radius.

God how embarrassing!

"Ssshh, that's it get it all up and out of your system… good girl." I could do nothing but keep going until my stomach ached with the empty space. I looked down at the damage I had caused and couldn't see anything in the night, but it didn't stop me from hanging my head in shame.

"Have you finished?" Draven asked me softly and I could only nod as the humiliation wouldn't allow me to speak.

"Here, drink this." He handed me a glass of water, from where I didn't know, but I still took it gratefully. I consumed most of it in great gulps to wash away the taste of bile in my mouth.

"Easy," he warned as I started to down it. He took it from me before I had time to finish. Then without warning I was being lifted into his arms.

"What are you doing?" I asked as he lifted me higher to get a better grip.

"I'm taking you to our bed, my little drunken Princess." He said this like he owned me, which of course he did.

Meanwhile, I had never felt so mortified in all my life. I wanted to bury myself into a pillow and hide but I had to use Draven instead. I don't think he minded. I felt him look down at me as he walked with me to the edge of the balcony.

"Wait...you're not going to do what I think you are?" He stopped and looked down towards a smaller balcony below us that I had never noticed before. It was in complete darkness, so that might explain why it always remained unseen. It only looked big enough for one, with railings that curved round and tall like an iron cage meant for a giant bird...or a man with wings.

"This reminds me of the first time when you were in my arms... well, when you were awake anyway."

"And the first time?" I asked, shuddering but still unmoveable in his solid hold.

"Sophia's secret garden. One that I believe was made especially for your first appearance and what a sight I beheld upon discovering you. A beauty of the likes I had never seen before."

"The garden she created was breath-taking." I agreed thinking back to that day only to find myself remembering how breath-taking Draven was, not the greenery. I looked up when I heard Draven chuckle.

"Breath-taking is right, only I'm not talking about the flowers, sweetheart." I blushed at his compliment.

"I will never forget the way you felt in my arms whilst you slept. You fit so perfectly as you do now. As if you were made to have my arms holding you. If I had my way, I would carry you everywhere." I looked up to see him smiling to himself and I couldn't help mimicking it.

"That maybe so, but unless you want to see me chucking up again then I wouldn't jump down there." He laughed making me vibrate.

"That won't happen again, your body has settled now the poison has been removed. Trust me, you'll be fine," he said and before I could protest further, he squeezed me tightly to him and jumped. My breath caught in my chest and the feel of air flying up around my skin and hair had me gripping onto his clothes with fright.

I could feel my nails bite into the fabric, I held on so hard. I must have closed my eyes because it was black, and I could feel tears stream outwards from under my closed lids.

"You can open your eyes now," he whispered lowering his head so his soft amused voice could brush over me, giving me comfort.

I looked around to find we were on the little balcony and facing a black wooden door that looked impenetrable. I looked back up to see how far we had come and couldn't believe that this was the same route we had taken when Draven had taken me home for the very first time.

I had been so naïve. I mean, why had I never questioned this before? All the answers were right in front of me the whole time. I had just never asked myself the right questions.

"Persae Calorem" ('Persian Heat' in Latin)

The door opened after Draven spoke a few words I didn't understand, but I jumped slightly as it creaked loudly from the large iron hinges holding it in place. Draven sidestepped us in just as I was about to tell him that I was good to walk now.

"Please allow me this little pleasure," he said upon hearing my thoughts.

"You can read me?"

"It's a little easier when you're drunk. I find there are no walls at all to contend with. You're like an open book," he said in triumph.

"Oh goodie!" I said sarcastically.

"So you knew how guilty I have felt all night and yet you did nothing?" I asked frustrated.

"I must admit I was too angry with you to ease a guilt I wanted you to feel. I am sorry for it though," he said not sounding too sorry!

"Oh well, that's alright then." I said, again not keeping the sarcasm at bay. As we had this conversation, he had been walking me down a narrow hallway that only just fit the both of us. It was all stone with a solid arch above that was higher than it needed to be.

"Where are we?" I said, momentarily forgetting our conversation.

"My home is filled with secret passageways that only a handful of my people know. It allows me access to anywhere throughout my home so I can go by unseen."

"You mean free to spy?" I said noting the obvious which made him laugh.

"Clever girl… yes, to spy. I must know that the people in my Council can be trusted."

"That makes sense, as long as it's not used for other things," I said making a joke he didn't get.

"Care to elaborate on that?" he asked me in a teasing manner.

"Well, as long as there's no pleasure in what you see."

"Ah, the girls…forever the jealous Vixen you are. There is only one body I would spy on and I count myself lucky enough that I can stare at it freely without having to hide. Although, I can admit I have been known to watch you in the shower when you knew nothing about it."

"No you haven't!" I punched him lightly and he laughed again at me.

"Haven't I?"

"You're teasing me." I decided and he didn't answer but his bad-boy grin had me doubting in what I just said. I didn't get chance to check, however, because we had reached the end of the passageway. In front of us lay another black door which held no light underneath.

Draven's eyesight must have been that of an owl because I couldn't even see a handle or anything. It opened anyway and Draven motioned with the hand he held at my back. The whoosh of thick heavy material could be heard and then with the click of his fingers light erupted from lamps in the room. Except it wasn't a room at all, it was another hallway and this time one the size you would expect to see in a castle or stately home.

I had never been here before. I knew that much due to the different pictures the walls held. Great tapestries, the size of trucks, made the stone walls dance with brightly coloured thread that looked as if they were made yesterday. Even the smell of them was new and fresh and I could almost see the wealth of English ladies sat picking and plucking away on rainy days.

There were different themes as we moved along. On the floor

before we got to the stairs, were scenes of gardens and landscapes but as he climbed the stairs it quickly became more serious.

Battlegrounds where little fabric bodies lay dying on blood-soaked earth. Men in silver armour charged ahead with their spears held high and their swords at the ready. Horses with covered faces ran forth into an unknown death. I could almost hear the battle drums beat wildly against the skin of animals that were sacrificed to make them. It was only when Draven turned me away from them did I realise why...

He was reading my mind.

"Do not think of those times," he said shielding me from them as he took the last few steps quicker than the rest.

"Why not, history buff remember?" I said lightheartedly but obviously unconvincingly as well.

"There are some things that are not ever to be seen through the eyes that I love. It will pain me to see it again."

"Draven, they're just pictures," I whispered to him.

"No, Keira, they are not. They are my memories... memories from those that I have touched in the past and made an unfortunate connection to. So I buy these items they create as a means of escape from a haunting time they do not understand. Simply put, I take these memories back from them to free them." He sounded full of remorse at all the times he had done this. I didn't want to ask any more questions and from now on he didn't have to turn me away from these sights as I just didn't look.

Just how many wars had Draven seen? How many men killed in a battle they didn't start and all for a power that would not be their own? I shuddered again and Draven tightened his hold. He knew I was thinking about it but I couldn't stop feeling sorrow for all those poor souls I didn't know.

When Draven spoke about touching them I knew what it meant. It was when he possessed their minds. I suppose it was logical for some of their memories to be transferred during this time and I understood more than most the urge to get those images out. I had been doing that very thing most of my life. Was this what Draven wanted to shield me from, the pain of knowing? Was this how all those other people had found their release?

"I can hear so many questions running wild in your mind. I'm surprised you're not exhausted," he said, trying to get my mind off it all.

"There is still so much I don't know and sometimes my mind runs away with me."

"So I can see," he mocked playfully, but I could tell he was just happy that he had distracted me for the moment. To be fair, with Draven around that was never difficult to achieve.

For the moment we both remained silent as we continued on throughout his home and it seemed to be endless. Of course, from the outside it didn't seem half as big as it actually was. This was due to most of it being engulfed by the forest and cliff's edge. It was blanketed from outsiders and it was understandable why. For one it was a lot older than everyone presumed it to be. It would be pretty hard to understand how once an old monastery over a thousand years old ended up on the outskirts of a small New England town. Not when the place itself was only established in the sixteen hundreds.

I remember Draven telling me once that it was brought over here stone by stone because of the positioning and importance the land holds. Something about where the Temple lay was directly on top of a gateway to the other sides. Of course, I was fascinated by it all but the more questions I asked, the more disgruntled Draven became when talking about it.

I think he worried that my head might explode if told too much all at once. I couldn't really blame him as it must get very annoying and childlike to be asked so many questions about anything and everything. I mean it was like having my very own Supernatural Wikipedia man!

"And what is a Wikipedia man?" he asked me and I mentally slapped myself. I needed to put a stop to this mind-reading lark! It was becoming very frustrating and I was just thankful it didn't happen all the time.

"You really need to stop reading my mind!"

"Why? I'm thinking seriously about making you an alcoholic." He laughed at his own joke and I couldn't help but follow him. Draven was such a serious character by nature that it was always infectious to hear the sound of his laughter. And shockingly he was a pretty funny guy when he wanted to be.

"Hey, so that's why you let me drink all that I did, you wanted access to my mind?" I didn't think about it at the time but now it was clear. I mean if Draven knew about every drink I had, then why hadn't he stopped me earlier? Now it was obvious he had wanted me drunk all along, just enough so that I didn't have any mental walls to prevent him from hearing my guilt.

"You are your own person, Keira, you do as you please. I did not force you into drinking your bodyweight in Coronas and tequila shots."

"Umm, but you liked the outcome sure enough! And if that is the case, why did you stop me at all?" I folded my arms instead of clinging onto him.

"I must confess I did, but I knew if I didn't stop you when I did then we wouldn't be having this conversation now."

"And why is that?" I was a little miffed at the idea of him getting his own way at my expense.

"Because, my beauty, if you had drunk any more then I would be carrying a passed out Keira instead of a pissed off one." He tried to control his smirk but was doing a lousy job at it.

I made a noise that sounded like an 'Umph' as my only answer and by the looks of those perfect lips twitching in no doubt an attempt to hide his amusement, I gathered he thought himself victorious.

It wasn't until I looked away from him that I realised I knew where we were. It was the main hallway that led down to his room door that was now facing us. I had to smile at the sight of 'our' bedchamber, making me forget that I was a little mad at him.

"Home," I said under my breath, but of course he heard it because the next thing I knew he was lifting the whole of my body up to his face. I really don't know how he did it considering he had been holding me now for quite some time. Talk about superhuman powers or what!

He leant his head to my face and said tenderly,

"Yes, you are." His voice was laced with comforting pleasure as he said this. He walked us inside and placed me gently down on the couch as though I was made of fine china. Of course, I laughed out loud when he handed me a steaming, hot mug.

"I think you need this," he said smirking down at me. I looked down to see the thick dark liquid and one smell had me wrinkling my nose as the bitter aroma of coffee invaded my nostrils. Draven frowned at me.

"Keira, it will help sober you up." He tried to reason with me but there was nothing he could say to get me to drink the horrid liquid so many people loved.

"I think being sick helped with that, thanks. But I wouldn't say no to a nice cuppa?" He rolled his eyes at me.

"I thought that classified as a "Cuppa"" He tried to mimic my accent, but I don't think my mild Liverpudlian accent was his forte!

"Oh no, see a Cuppa means a cup of tea, I'm somewhat of an expert on this."

"Oh really, then please educate me so that I never make such a grave mistake again." He moved to sit next to me and instead of lounging out I moved my legs to give him room. I actually got excited about teaching him something, even if it was all just playful banter. I mean I knew I was drunk, but I hadn't completely lost all my marbles!

"Well ok, but you have to understand, 'we', as in the English people...well, let's just say, 'we' take drinking tea as a very serious business. See it can't be any old shit!" At this he laughed at me which I relished.

"But of course," he said as if obviously he was in agreement.

"See, some of the posher lot of us like something called 'Twinning's Breakfast Tea' but this is not your everyday stuff, more like the stuff you get out when you're rich Aunt comes to stay, and your mother wants to impress your father's sister." I explained all of this as if Draven understood which I very much doubted. I mean it's not like he had anyone in his family richer than himself. If anything, he was the rich Aunt!

"Okay, so I prefer something called PG tips which has a monkey and a comedian do the adverts or there's a brand called Tetley and they have little funny characters that I used to collect as a child with little teapots and..." I took one look at Draven's face to find him looking highly entertained at my drunken ramblings that I blushed before continuing,

"Anyway that's not important...where was I...Oh yeah, well either one brand is nice but you can't buy the stuff here, so I get my mum to send me a monthly supply... you still with me?" I asked raising my eyebrow and looking to the side. I knew I was babbling on a bit, so I wasn't surprised to find Draven sat there with one hand covering his grin. Like this, he reminded me of some sexy professor. With this thought I slapped my forehead as I remembered one vital bit of information...He could still bloody hear my thoughts!

"Should I purchase some glasses, tweed jacket and a schoolroom for this fantasy of yours?"

"Draven! You need to stop doing that! It's not fair to pry into my secret thoughts not when I can't hear yours anyway," I said pushing him, but he just grabbed my chin to pull me in for a fierce kiss which I stopped.

"Keira." He growled when I refused him.

"It's not wise to keep yourself from me," he warned but I had my reasons and considering I had not long ago puked up there wasn't a chance I was letting that kiss happen.

"You have to try and control yourself," I warned making him growl deeper in return.

"But I don't want to, in fact I want to strip you naked and bathe in your scent." On hearing this I shouted out in shock. Because, of course, he never actually spoke the words aloud, I had just heard them being said in his mind. He was actually letting me in.

"I heard you!"

"And did you like what you heard?" he asked like a true, cocky badass.

"Maybe. Okay yes, but I still want my cup of tea...besides this is cold now," I said handing him the mug I still had hold of.

"We can't have that now, can we?" He smirked as he reached across me and dipped his finger in the liquid. I watched over the brim like a child would have. I couldn't keep the grin from my lips when the liquid started to move around and around before turning a lighter shade of brown. Once he'd finished he pulled his finger out and popped into his mouth to suck it clean. I looked on as if it was the sexiest thing I had ever seen.

"Umm... I still have to say, I prefer coffee."

"That's because you're not English. Which makes me wonder what are you?"

"I'm a Demon/Angel half breed King of the supernatural world." He said it as though he had been doing every day of his life but then again I couldn't really see Draven saying this to himself every morning in front of the mirror. This thought once again had him laughing.

"I'm Persian, Keira," he then said proudly as if it was common knowledge.

"Oh...so no tea then?" I joked taking the first sip of my very own bee's nectar.

"So is that like the Prince of Persia?" I continued but he just stared back at me blankly.

"Sorry?" He obviously didn't understand the reference. Not a game fan clearly.

"It's a video game." Once again, he was frowning.

"There is a game people play, called this?"

"Yeah, we people play stuff like that. It was cool but I was hopeless...I kept dying, falling off walls and such, but my ex was really good at it." As soon as I mentioned an ex I realised my flaw. Note to self, never mention the exes and what's more, never, ever praise them! Draven's eyes flashed a deep purple and his frown made them look lost in the caves of rage.

"Oh come on, don't go all Demonic on me, it's not like you ever have to meet them like I do!"

"Lucky for them," he said coldly and when he saw my face, only then did he start to unclench his fists. We sat in silence for a while, until I finished my tea because in truth I didn't know what to say next. It seemed everything out of my mouth was just going to anger him or seem very childish in his ancient eyes.

"That's not true. I love to hear about what your life was like before I met you. It fascinates me to hear you speak. But feel free to leave out past lovers won't you."

"Deal. What do you want to know?" I said turning further to face him after placing my empty mug on the floor.

"What was your childhood like, was it a happy one?" I laughed at the thought of me as a child, all tomboy and scraped knees. Messy, wild, golden hair that grew more upwards than it did downwards. Dirty fingernails from digging worms in the garden and racing snails up my mum's clean windows.

Running into the wooded area near our house just after it rained because I loved the smell of wet earth and dripping leaves. Climbing trees and crying one day when my favourite one was ripped from the ground to make way for a new development of houses.

Making marble runs and our own board games out of crisp boxes, finished toilet rolls and sticky tape with my sister. Spending time with my best friend on the school wall talking about boys we fancied. Going to the school disco and having my first real kiss opposite the Maths room from a boy I fell hard for... Yes... apart from seeing Demons and Angels walking the Earth with me, yes it was a happy one indeed. Of course, I didn't need to voice my answer. I had just shown him everything by accessing my own memories.

"And yet seeing my kind never prevented you from finding such happiness. How is that?" He spoke so gently as he ran his fingers along my jawline and up the apple of my cheek.

"I don't know...I guess I just decided that it was better to live with it than not live at all."

"Good answer." He said this but he still looked sad for my early experiences with his kind.

"Do you wish you'd had a childhood?" I asked not meeting his eyes.

"It's hard to wish for something you don't fully understand. In my position, it was not practical to be a boy with power. Innocence is not a wise virtue to hold in my world. I had to be strong from the beginning just as I have to remain so now but..." He hooked my chin up so that he could see my eyes before he continued,

"But?" I asked shyly.

"But being here with you is like being the child I never had the chance to be. Here with you is my chance to feel a happiness I have never felt before. I have never had moments like this, Keira. I have never had someone to speak like this to. Stories to tell and to hear in return...It is all so new to me and yet I find that I could be happy to do it for all eternity and the rest of my days." I sucked in my bottom lip and held it with my teeth on hearing his wonderful words. His eyes followed the action and this time purple flashed in his eyes for a different reason.

"Oh trust me you would get tired of hearing my voice," I joked after a few seconds of squirming under Draven's intense gaze.

"That is impossible. I could listen to you until my ears bled. I especially like this new, no bounds Keira that speaks freely and with her adorable Northern English accent peeking through, thanks to a little... well, a lot of what is it usually called...liquid courage?"

"You just like that because you can hear my thoughts." Again, I was making him laugh.

"Yes well, there's that too. Have I told you lately how much I love you?" he said pulling me closer until my head tucked under his chin.

"Even when I throw up over your balcony and talk drunkenly about tea and video games?" I asked into the column of his corded neck.

"But of course. And what is it with that balcony that makes you want to throw up all the time?" He was making fun of me and it was working as my cheeks went cherry colour.

"Mmm, that blush of yours could warm any man's blood to boiling point." This wasn't an exaggeration as it didn't take long before I could feel his blood boiling for myself, down below that was. So much so that I had to shift myself to one side to give him more room down there.

"Can I ask you a question?" When I said this he lowered his head and kissed me on my forehead after smoothing some of my hair back.

"Anything."

"You might not like talking about it," I warned and this was when he moved further back to look at me.

"I will answer your questions even if I don't want to," he promised making me grin.

"It's about what happened to me today," I said, making his jaw tense at the subject. I think he was hoping that this afternoon was just going to evaporate into nothing and not have chance to make a full memory.

"One can only hope," he said bitterly before continuing,

"What is it you would like to know?"

"Well firstly...who was it that you went there to see?" I waited to see his response with eager eyes. I knew it was a woman from when Leivic said 'She is waiting for you'. I couldn't help the little twist of jealous curiosity that snaked in my belly.

"I was there to see a very good friend of mine, her name is Pythia." As soon as he said the name it pricked recognition from my brain. Where had I heard that name before?

"You like history, yes?" I nodded at his question as I was still searching my head for answers.

"Are you familiar with Greek mythology?" As soon as he said the words my mind clicked, and I found the answer.

"She's an Oracle!" I shouted a bit louder than what was needed.

"Actually she's The Oracle...as in, she's the only one."

"But I thought throughout history there has been many?" Even today some clairvoyants are sometimes considered to be the Oracles of our time.

"No, there is and only ever will be one. Pythia is the only direct communal link between the Gods from both sides. Greek mythology has her known as the Oracle of Delphi, where she was the High Priestess at the Temple of Apollo. There is some truth in this but it is only where she was found, not where she remained." He ran a single finger along my lips as he spoke and smiled when I shivered from the sensation.

"You see, it was believed back then that the Oracle changed from girl to girl but it was not true. Pythia just changed bodies every few years so that no one was ever sure it could be the real her. This still happens and it is imperative that it remains so. If she were to get into the wrong hands, then they would have a direct line into the Gods' plans. You can see how that would be bad?"

"So when she left Del..py?" I knew I said the place wrong when Draven grinned, but he didn't correct me, if anything he look like he enjoyed it better this way.

"She left behind a fake, who was believed for years after. I could not allow her to remain and besides, she did not want to. She had seen nothing of the world she knew so much about. She had only been allowed to stay within the Temple and the only people she would see were the priests and the Supplicants that underwent the arduous journey to consult the Oracle's Divine wisdom. She may have been this creature, but she was still just a girl as well."

"So you...?" I let the question hang for him to pick up on, which he did.

"So, I took her away to live how she desired as long as she was never discovered for what she really was. She calls upon me when she needs to tell me something and it is always on the seventh day of the month."

"Why?"

"Because the number seven plays an important part in my world. It is a Holy number for many of reasons...reasons, that I can't go into at this time."

"Cannot or will not?" I asked sceptically crossing my hands over my chest.

"Both," he admitted but he continued before I could protest,

"Keira, there are many things you will learn about my kind, even if these are things I do not wish for you to know, but at least let me tell you of them in my own time"

"Fair enough." I nodded knowing there wasn't much point arguing, as he would get his way whether I liked it or not. Of course, he growled at this thought of mine, but I didn't care, it didn't change the facts.

"Well, are you going to tell me?" I asked, proving my point, which he couldn't answer. Instead, he just shrugged his shoulders and we both let it go...*for now anyway.*

"What I want to know is why you needed to see her now, it isn't even the seventh?"

"That is why I had to go, I knew it must have been something very important for her to call to meet with me. It was not like her, but now I know why," he told me, somewhat begrudgingly.

"Are you going to tell me?" I said trying to prompt more from him.

"Keira..."

"I take that as a no then," I said not been able to keep the sulking tone from my voice.

"Let me put it this way, the last time I saw her we spoke about the same thing."

"And that was?"

"You," he said clearly as if it was all so obvious.

"Me? Why, did you tell her about me?" I asked shaking my head wondering what on earth they could be talking about me for.

"Actually, she was the one who told me about you." As soon as he said it, I don't know why, but I started to hold my breath. Why would she know anything about me unless the Gods had told her? And what would they have to tell her that would be so important to Draven? We had met without any help, so I didn't get it, which is what I said.

"I don't understand."

"Keira, how can you still doubt yourself and the importance of our union? Before today the last time I saw Pythia was over twenty-three years ago, on the seventh hour, on the seventh day, of the seventh month, 1987. So now you understand what it was that was so important for her to tell me."

"But...but that was..." I stammered out in utter disbelief, but Draven finished the sentence off for me. He cradled my face in his hands and looked at me as though I was his greatest gift received from above before saying the words I couldn't find...

"Yes...it was when you were born."

CHAPTER FOURTY-FOUR

LET SLEEPING DOGS DIE

That night my dreams were filled with strange images of an Oracle I had never met and a prophecy I didn't understand. For most of it I was in a Temple, but not the one I had seen before. Somehow I knew this Temple was in Europe but I wasn't exact on where.

It was all made from the purest of white marble and in my mind, it kept flashing in between the old and new. One minute the great structure would be degrading flakes of old stone and weathered floors. And then it would flashback to its glory days of radiant light and gleaming pillars of fine craftsmanship.

I seemed to be the focus of the room as all eyes were on me. There were faces here I didn't yet recognize, but somewhere deep down I knew them. It was a bit like when someone you know tells you so much about a friend so that when you meet this person you feel like you instantly know them. Well, it was like that, only with a Temple full of people. They all lined the pillars and looked on with anxious faces.

As though everyone there knew my fate but me.

I continued my assessment of the people looking on with a clear mix of desperation and fear. It was only when I looked down at myself did I really understand these looks fully. I was barefooted and lines of blood trickled down them, creating deep crimson footprints behind me. I wasn't in pain as I probably should have been, but can you really feel pain in a dream?

It looked as if I had just walked in and interrupted a battle. Everyone seemed to be wearing combat gear, black and oh, so ready for action. It was like good vs evil and the only thing that separated them was me walking in the middle of the room causing them to part and take each side of the Temple.

I was dressed in a white gown that floated around my skin as though I was underwater. It was so thin and wispy that I almost felt naked. Of course, this stark white material that covered my skin was the perfect contrast to show the deep red liquid, pumping steadily from my heart. I had been stabbed there, that much was clear as now there was a long deep slice that led down past my breasts. It looked as though I had woken in the middle of having heart surgery and decided on going for a stroll.

It was a weird sensation looking down at oneself in this state. I kept thinking that surely I should be dying not walking towards an altar at the other end of the room. I should have felt weak and fallen to the floor to let the last of my life drain from me, but I felt strong. I felt as though my blood was leaving me but being replaced by something else...something unearthly... something that felt as though sent by the Gods.

It was only as I got closer did I notice myself standing to one side trying to push herself through the crowd of supernatural warriors. I was in my own dream looking on in horror. I was screaming something to myself in a blind panic.

I was dressed in pyjamas and my hair plaited to one side, messy, as if I had just woken up from a nightmare. Then I kept flashing in and out of each of my other-selves. One minute I was the nightmare Keira and then I was left watching the other me walk towards a brightly lit altar where I knew certain death awaited me.

"Don't go there, RUN, RUN!" I was screaming out at myself, but when my head simply turned back to look at me, I merely shook my head to indicate a firm 'No'.

Then I was back to the bloody Keira shaking my head and mouthing the words,

"No, it will be alright." I wanted to go over and comfort myself. I looked so frightened and so utterly breakable. Draven was right... I was fragile. I looked so frail like that but not now. I wasn't fragile like this, I felt strong. Invincible. Godly.

I whispered a goodbye and started off as fast as I could into a lightening run. I could just hear one last scream from my other self as I ran into the altar and collided with the brightest flash of light, almost as if a meteor had just impacted where I stood.

That's when I woke up and found I was dressed like the Keira in my dream, the frightened one. I had wet cheeks from tears I didn't remember crying. I had a scratchy throat from screaming words I didn't shout out in the real world. But most of all I was heartbroken from watching myself die.

What a horrible dream and most disappointing of all was that Draven wasn't there at my greatest time of need. He hadn't been there in my dream and he wasn't here now either. I was in my own bed at home and it took me a moment to realize why. Draven had driven me home in the early hours of the morning and stayed with me until I fell asleep in my new room.

Now he was gone, and my heart ached for him as the morning sun flooded my room that wasn't yet familiar to me. After a few seconds of getting my bearings, I whipped back the covers and looked at my chest. What I was expecting to find exactly I didn't know but there wasn't a gaping hole like there had been in my dream. There was no sliced flesh and bloody feet. No flowing white gown and no strong buzz of energy raging through my veins.

I was still shaking my head when I heard a knock at my door. Libby didn't wait for me to say, 'come in', she never did. She was dressed for work but instead of her usual power suit, she had on a loose white shirt that allowed more room for her growing bump. Her cheeks were glowing, and the sight of her happy mood told me two things, One...she had enjoyed her night away from the She-Devil. And Two...she hadn't yet had the pleasure of her company this morning.

"So, how did it go last night?" She plonked herself down on my bed and handed me the mug that she held in both hands. This time instead of Homer Simpson, it was a Liverpool LFC mug with the words 'You'll Never Walk Alone' below the team's crest of a Liver Bird.

"Thanks," I said taking the mug of tea and my first sip of the morning. I didn't smoke but I would imagine that this was my equivalent of having my first cigarette of the day.

"So?" she prompted, "What happened?"

"She met Jack, that's what happened," I said deflating. Libby just raised her eyes at me and smiled, obviously missing the bigger picture. Her next words confirmed it.

"But that's a good thing...right? I mean, it gets her out of our hair and gets her focus off Dominic, so drinks all round...or not." She added this last bit when she saw the misery on my face.

"Don't get me wrong, I'm glad she didn't spend the night chasing after Dra...Dominic but I don't want that at the expense of Jack's feelings. Besides, I don't think he is as good a friend as I first thought. Not after hearing all about me from our delightful cousin," I said bitterly and Libby covered her mouth in a dramatic shock.

"Why, what did she say?"

"I'm not completely sure, but I can guess. It's what she does, Libby. She plays the victim and I'm left to play the bad guy. You should have seen his reaction to me after just one evening of her lies. Anyway, I've decided I don't care. I mean, if he really was my friend, he wouldn't have believed such bullshit from someone he'd only just met!"

"Didn't you warn them about her?"

"A little, well mainly RJ but I didn't want to go around slagging off my relation to my still new friends. They still don't know about me...about my past and I don't know how long I can keep that part of my past a secret. Jack is the only one who knows." Libby put her hand on my arm and nodded at my problem. For the first time in a long time, I didn't feel so strange talking about this kind of stuff and Libby could tell.

"You don't have to tell anyone anything you don't want to.

They will still be your friends and I hate to bring this up but aren't you worried about your biggest threat here?"

"I don't under..."

"Hilary...she knows everything too, remember. Not that I think you have anything to be ashamed of, but I understand why you don't want people knowing, what with small-town gossip and all. But are you not worried that the girl who hates you most in the world will take an opportunity like this and try and ruin everything for you?" Libby looked scared for me, but I just shrugged my shoulders.

"She wouldn't go that far. Look, I know she hates me for reasons I am resigned to the fact that I will never figure out, but I don't imagine she would ever go that far!" She raised an eyebrow to indicate she clearly did.

"Trust me on this," I said as I tried to get up but as soon as my legs touched the floorboards I had to sit back down. My head started to spin thanks to a Corona induced hangover.

"Rough night?" my sister asked as she noted my head in my hands.

"Uh...something like that. I drank way too much last night and I'm not sure if I won't be an alcoholic by the time we get rid of Hilary." I only half-joked. But then I remembered last night how easy it was for Draven to read me. Well, at least he didn't read anything I had been hiding and I wondered if this was because I hadn't thought about it once last night? Well, whatever the reason, my problems remained clear, one, why the Hell couldn't I just tell him what had been going on and two... bloody Hilary!

"Well, at least one of us can drink. Right, well I'm off to work now, but will I see you after college?" She stood up, whereas I couldn't at the moment and looked down at me waiting for an answer.

"Yeah, but not for long, I've got work tonight so at least that should mean Hilary won't be around here either." I sounded tired every time I even said her name.

"Okay chuck, I will see ya later. And try not to put up with too much shit from her and don't worry about Jack, he will see her for what she is soon enough...they always do."

"Yeah, but I don't want him to get hurt."

"Sounds like to me like he deserves a good kick up the ass to wake him up," she said as she walked to the door.

"Libby!" I scolded, but she just smiled and blamed the hormones before leaving me alone in the house with someone I wanted to staple things too.

I got up and the first thing I did was go in search of pills to numb the pain from not only my hangover. While I was in the kitchen the other pain in my life walked in. She was dressed in a pink tracksuit that had stars on her bony backside. The hooded top was one of those that only covered half of her torso, but she matched it with a skimpy pineapple top.

"Man, I just love exercising in the morning!" she said overly energetic.

"I prefer sex," I said under my breath.

"Excuse me?" she asked snootily.

"Oh nothing...Juice?" I asked holding it out to her, making her wrinkle her nose.

"I only drink organic, freshly squeezed and no offence, but you don't look like the type to buy that."

"None taken," I said, wondering if that was supposed to be an insult or not, because I wasn't sure it was that lame.

"So, what are we doing today?" she asked me, casually leaning back on the fridge. I found myself staring at it just hoping the door would slam into her.

"Sorry...what do you mean by we because I have college?" I shook my head, but she just smiled, reminding me of the Grinch at Christmas.

"Perfect!" She then clapped her hands together and left the kitchen, leaving me both worried and confused by that comment. I ran out after her and found her halfway up the stairs.

"What do mean perfect? Do you have plans?"

"Of course, but I have to get ready and need a shower if I'm going to scrunch my hair...it has a natural wave you know..." I didn't give two bird shits about her so-called wavy hair but what I did need to know about was her so-called plans.

"Well, I need to get ready for college now."

"Yes, I know you do, 'cause I'm not going to be seen dead with you wearing your hair like that!" She was still climbing the stairs to the third floor and I was still following until we reached the top.

"What do you mean 'with me'?" She stopped outside my old room and opened the door before answering me.

"I'm coming with you, of course! It's a great chance to meet Jack again and besides, you didn't expect me to hang around in this rickety old house all day, did you?" I couldn't answer her in my mental breakdown, and she smiled at what she knew she did to me.

I would have preferred her to have just punched me in the gut and get it over with 'cause any physical pain was better than the mental pain I was going to get constantly with her around. I was still standing there dumbstruck when she walked into my room and turned around to say one last thing.

"Oh and Keira...My room remember!" And with that, she slammed the door in my face making me close my eyes against the air that hit me.

"Brilliant!" I said as I got in my room to change. I knew there was no chance at a shower now as she would purposely use all of the hot water. Thankfully, I'd had a wash and stuff before I went downstairs but my hair still looked a state from a night of tossing and turning. Of course, the weather didn't help as I soon discovered when we got outside.

Thankfully, I had my car here now as Draven had it driven back to me this morning. We had decided it was better if I had woken up here because I needed to go to college, and I didn't want my sister to have to deal with our cousin alone. In the end it wouldn't have mattered because she didn't even have to see her, unlike my own funfest this morning.

We were on the way to college when Hilary started to moan...again.

"My god Kizzy Cat, you still drive like an old woman. I'm surprised you even make any lectures. Do you ever get pulled over for going too slow?"

"No I don't, do you ever get pulled over for going too fast?" I asked knowing full well that she didn't have her license anymore because she had too many points for speeding.

"I bet Dominic never lets you drive." She laughed to herself and avoided my question.

"He does actually!" I said fighting the urge to stick my tongue out at her after saying it. However, she didn't take much notice of my responses to her insults. No, she was more preoccupied with applying a fresh layer of pink lipstick that in my mind made them look more like she had just spent the night sucking her thumb! Did I sound bitter? That might be because my cousin free day had quickly turned into Nightmare college…first lecture, 'how to avoid bitchy cousins like you would a zombie'.

"You do know that you can't sit in my classes with me, don't you?" I was still trying to put her off, even though we were nearly there. I would have been gladly late for all of my lectures if it would free me from her company.

"Well durr! Do you think I want to spend my time sat listening to American toffs talking a load of shit I don't care about…I mean, it's obvious you don't do beauty at this school of yours!"

"Gee thanks!" I said making her laugh at me, not with me.

"Then what are you going to do?"

"Oh, didn't I tell you…I meeting up with Jack and he's going to show me around and stuff. Then he's taking me to this bar he likes." She noticed my face drop and a dark, satisfied smile wriggled its way across her lips. Then I smiled at the one thought of Hilary's day not being picture-perfect.

"Let me guess, is it called 'Willy's One Eyed Joe' by any chance?" Now I couldn't keep the smirk from my face.

"Oh, so you've been there?" It wasn't really a question as she knew the answer, more like her prompting me for more information.

"Yeah, a few times with the gang after lectures. You'll have fun…it's just your kind of place," I said knowing she would hate every minute of the dilapidated building that called itself a social meeting place. It had two regulars that looked glued to their seats and to look at, you just knew when they finally did move from 'their' seats, the stool cushions would be indented with their distinct ass impressions.

We didn't speak again until I parked my truck in its usual spot.

I had been trying to work out what I wanted to say most of the way there, but I knew that it was going to be a pointless exercise trying to reason with this destructive girl. Even now, to look at her you wouldn't really be putting her down to be the biggest bitch in Britain and now currently the US.

Today she had tried to tone down her slut look and went for a pair of tight, skinny jeans that made her thin legs look like matchsticks and matched it with a white T-shirt that said 'I love Yoga' on the front and then on the back had a winked eye with the words 'It makes me flexible' underneath. Even naïve little me could read in between the lines to its seductive inner meaning.

"Look Hilary, I need to say something." I tried to make my voice sound serious but when it croaked, I realized that it was never going to happen the way I wanted it to. But I still needed to try and seeing Jack's new red Toyota parked two spaces away made me follow it through.

"Jack's a really good friend of mine and with you leaving soon, I can't help but think it's not a good idea to...you know...do anything". At this she laughed and turned to look at me fully for the first time this journey. That's when I fully understood my mistake. I had just made this game even more tempting to play.

"Kizzy, Kizzy, Kizzy, are you jealous?"

"NO!" I shouted a little too defensively.

"Really...'cause you know Jack told me how you two nearly hooked up, but you just used him to get to Dominic. I'm just so glad you haven't spoiled him for me. It's no fun when they're vulnerable, but thankfully he got over you quickly enough, his words, not mine. Actually, I think his exact words were 'Used and abused' and imagine his shock when finding out this wasn't the first time." By the time she had finished, I was close to jumping on her and clawing her eyes out, but I was frozen.

"Don't worry about old Jackie boy. I will take good care of him...I think he'll make a good fuck don't you?" She opened the door as she could see him coming over, but she didn't close it behind her until she finished driving in the last nail in the coffin with her spiteful speech.

"Oh wait, you wouldn't know would you, seeing as you never

really got that far!" And then she slammed the door leaving me red-faced and close to tears, I was that angry. I therefore, couldn't help the rage-filled scream that erupted making Jack turn to face me in concern. I grabbed my bag and wrenched open the door. I then slammed the door making Jack jump at my behaviour. I stormed up past them and when Jack grabbed my arm to stop me, I yanked it free.

"Just leave me alone!" I snapped at him making his usually soft features turn cold. I pulled my bag strap back over my shoulder and half jogged to my first class. I knew I wasn't being fair, but I couldn't stop thinking about what Hilary had said to me. I knew Jack wouldn't have said most of the things she said but he must have said something. Could I be sure that Jack was the friend I always thought he had been? Now, I wasn't so sure. Man, I hated her so much it made my head hurt!

"Hey Kaz, where's the fire?" I turned before I went through the door to see RJ's pink hair next to me. She looked like I felt. Her eyes were deep-set in sleepless bags and no amount of makeup would cover up the same hangover we shared.

"Just trying to get away from the new couple," I said and nodded to Jack and Hilary who were walking hand in hand. She rolled her eyes and walked with me inside, obviously wanting to get away from them as much as I did.

"I tried to tell him about her poisonous ways, but he wouldn't listen. Did you know she has already infected him into believing a load of bullship about you?"

"Bull...ship?" I couldn't help but ask.

"Ah, I'm trying this new thing out for my mom. She wants me to curb on the bad language as my sister has started swearing, saying she gets it from me! So I have replaced a few words like fudge instead of fuc..."

"Yeah, Yeah, I get it!" We both laughed and thanks to RJ, it was a nice little diversion to make me forget the 'Hellcat beast' and the beauty, Jack'! I didn't want to talk about it anymore, especially since my first class was with the dreaded Reedinator! RJ walked me, bless her and it reminded me of my first week here. I don't know what I would have done if it hadn't been for meeting RJ.

In there I found Sophia in our usual seats, filing nails she didn't need to file.

"What's up, home bird?" she said trying on a street vibe. I was laughing once again.

"Meh, well, let's just say I've been better but what's with 'in the ghetto hood' talk?"

"I knew you needed cheering up," she said as I took my seat.

"I'm down with that!" I replied trying for the same accent, but if you're British and not from Essex, it's quite hard to do.

"So, I gather the bitch is still a thorn in your peachy behind?" I groaned my answer.

"I understand and I see only one solution to this girl."

"What's that...violent crimes?" I only half-joked.

"Nope, just some good old Demon intervention, I think it's time I met this cousin of yours."

I could say only one thing to that,

"Fudge, yeah!"

CHAPTER FOURTY-FIVE

THANK THE DEVIL FOR DEMONS

My history class didn't go quickly enough, but at least I had Sophia there with me to help keep my sanity in check. I had to submit my assignment and held my breath as I made my way down the steps to Reed's desk. Sophia hadn't ever handed in anything but just made him think she had. She offered the same service for me, but I declined.

"I have this crazy idea of passing this class by handing in actual work," I had said before getting ready to leave.

"You're right...that is just so crazy!" she mocked and I couldn't help shaking my head in laughter. Sophia was one of those people who was so infectious to be around, that it was hard to remember any problems I had. She had a way of making them fade into the 'not important' part of your brain. That's where Hilary was right now...way back there, where my mind just said, 'why do we give a shit?'

"Keira, you're smiling at yourself again." For this she received a little flick on the arm making her giggle. We walked down to the front and I watched in amazement as she handed him a newspaper making him think it was her assignment. But of course, the newspaper deserved an A star, even though it really was a lousy paper. The biggest stories were about the Dravens themselves but considering no one really knew anything about them, there really wasn't that much printed holding their name.

I remember reading the paper and scanning it for any details on them but they were mainly only mentioned when they donated to a charity or paid for any new construction the town benefited from.

I handed my paper over and Reed looked over it as if he wanted to pee on it, before even reading the first line. I gulped as those beady eyes found mine and then returned to his laptop without saying a word.

"Did you see that, the way he looked at my work like he knew it would be rubbish or something? *Could you read his mind...he's going to fail me right?"* I whispered to Sophia as I trailed behind like a blubbering fool.

"Don't be paranoid, Keira. He was actually looking forward to reading it." I frowned utterly unconvinced.

"What? It's true. Anyway, forget about Reed, we have bigger fish to scare."

"It's fry...bigger fish to fry." I corrected but she just looked at me from the side and gave me a confident smile.

"Not today it isn't," she said in a way that displayed the true nature of what she was. I was close to feeling sorry for what she had in store for my cousin...well, almost!

We were soon outside, and I found myself glad that my cousin was nowhere to be seen, that was until my phone started up and Abba filled the courtyard we were sat in. When I saw it wasn't a number I recognized, my heart sank.

"Hello?"

"Kizzy Cat, where are you?" Hilary's voice grated on me even when she was putting on the nicey, nicey act. That's how I knew she was still with Jack. I explained where and I heard her repeating it over to the blind, deaf and dumb dude in question.

"We will be there in five. Jack has been called into work so you have to take me home now." I knew she was still trying to sound fake in front of Jack, but even he must have heard the cheek in that demand.

"Well I still..." And that's when she hung up leaving me to finish that sentence with only Sophia as my audience.

"…have classes," I finished weakly.

"She hung up, didn't she? You know I don't think I'm going to like this girl." Sophia looked half delighted and half furious at the idea.

"Good, because given how fast my cousin works, pretty soon she will have sucked everyone I know into her twisted lies and God only knows what they will think about me then?"

"I gather you're referring to her most recent work?" Sophia nodded past me and I turned to see Hilary and Jack both walking arms locked, in the distance.

"How'd ya guess?" I asked sarcastically.

"Oh, I don't know, maybe the fact that I can smell the hate for you, coming off her like cheap perfume." I turned my eyes to hers to find them glowing with the same hate. I suddenly felt wary about introducing my cousin to my Demon friend but before I knew it, Hilary's voice was making my skin crawl and grating on my last nerve.

"There you are, you're so hard to spot in a crowd, being so short and all." She would have carried on but the sight of Sophia had her stopping dead in her tracks. Sophia was, as always, in her designer wear that screamed money.

She was also one of the most beautiful creatures the world had to offer and when coming face to face with her for the first time, she often took your breath away. This is what happened now and I couldn't help but smile. Hilary had always been a jealous person by nature. Never being satisfied with what she already had but trying to take or crush what those around her had!

No one seemed to be saying anything, so I decided to intervene.

"Guys, this is Sophia," I said trying not to look at Jack but finding it hard when he seemed to be searching out my eyes. I didn't understand why, but I got the distinct impression that he wanted to talk with me. Whatever the case, I didn't fold. I was still too hurt and felt far too betrayed to give in now. If he wanted to believe Hilary's lies over what our friendship meant, then that was just fine and dandy!

"And this must be Hilary, nice to meet you. Of course, I feel like I already know you, with everything Keira has told me about you." Sophia said this with a sharp tone of knowing in her voice and I don't think Hilary missed it. She just stared blankly at her as if still in a state of uncertainty. Surprisingly, it was Jack that broke the tension.

"Hi Sophia, I'm Jack, I've seen you around but don't think we have ever been introduced properly," he said being his usual ultra-friendly self.

"Hi Jack, of course I have heard a lot about you too. You're one of Keira's very best friends, aren't you? She's always saying what a truly great and trusting friend you are, which is rare these days, is it not?"

"I guess," he said with one emotion running quite clear...guilt. Was it possible that with one sentence Sophia had gotten through to him? Well, with the way Jack looked at me now would suggest the answer to that question was a yes. It was as though he had just been reminded of our friendship and felt my feelings of betrayal for himself. I looked away and gave Sophia a warning look which only made her smile.

"So, how do you two know each other then, 'cause no offence, but you don't look like you would have much in common?" Hilary had found her voice and unfortunately the shock of Sophia's beauty hadn't curbed her wonderful way with words.

She looked back at me with my baggy jeans and overly large jacket that made me look as though I had dressed for an expedition. Her eyes floated back to Sophia's delicate little frame that was dressed in winter chic. A designer red, fitted coat and black leggings that disappeared into fur-trimmed boots. Looking at us both side by side then she was right, we looked like unlikely looking friends indeed.

"My brother Dominic is in love with your cousin," she said as simple as pie. I coughed out a word not even I knew, and Hilary looked as if she had swallowed a bug. Meanwhile, Jack looked hurt and turned his head to one side as if trying to hide a reaction already seen.

"Your brother is Dominic Draven, Keira's boyfriend?" Hilary asked as if to clarify the connection.

"Yes, but that's not why we're friends, it's only how we met," Sophia said, clarifying herself.

"Well Kizzy Cat, I have to give it to you, you certainly work quickly with the locals. If I didn't know any better, I would say that the Dravens consider you part of the family." Hilary said this as an insult but one disguised as a compliment.

"We do indeed. But wait, where are my manners, you should come up to the VIP tonight after Keira's finished work, to meet us all... properly." The way Sophia said this last word sent a shiver along my spine. It sounded more like a promise of some kind.

"WHAT?!" I shouted by mistake, making everyone, including people not in this conversation stop and stare at me. I decided to try this diplomatically instead of screaming blue murder.

"Do you think that's a good idea, I mean, you know how your brother likes to keep his business private?" I gritted out the word 'Private' and was mentally pleading with her, but she ignored me and looked at Hilary more closely.

"Nonsense, she is after all family and I'm sure Dominic would like to meet her properly this time." I almost growled at her.

"Sorry Sophia, I'm sure Kizzy is just trying to keep Dominic all to herself, she was always a bit selfish when it comes to the many men in her life... there's been quite a few." Hilary finished this by laughing at herself but it was at my expense. I could feel my lip curl and only hoped I didn't let out the growl I could feel brewing.

"Fine, well it looks like I'm outnumbered on this one," I said not being able to keep the spoilt tone from seeping into my words. Sophia didn't even look sorry, which made me think she was planning something. Actually the only one that looked sorry for me was Jack, which got me thinking that Sophia's cutting manner had indeed made him think twice about being so quick to trust someone he barely knew.

We all said our goodbyes but while Hilary was giving Jack a more thorough bye I took Sophia to the side out of earshot.

"What's the big idea here?! I mean, I'm all for knocking her down a peg or two but even I think a room full of 'energy-sucking' Demons and Angels is a bit much!" Sophia just smiled like I would imagine a cat to do when walking the fence and winding up the neighbour's dog. It was both evil and cute at the same time.

"Why Keira, my dear, don't you trust me?" She added this little innocent act by fluttering her eyes at me.

"You forget, Sophia, that I know what you're capable of and remember your relentless schemes when trying to get me and Draven together."

"And it all worked out well, did it not?" Well, I had to give her that. In truth, she had ended up playing a massive part in our 'union'. However, I didn't tell her this, but she took my silence in her favour all the same.

"Great, well tonight should be a breeze then!" I said sarcastically, but she just laughed and gave me a wink before fake coughing which drew me to my cousin's unimpressed face.

"So, are we going or not?" she asked looking down at me as if I was some bloody chauffeur of hers, one that she just caught without wearing their hat or making a wrong turn, well she wished! I was close to saying 'To Hell with it' and making her walk home, 4-inch heels or not!

Ok, so I didn't, no instead I said goodbye to everyone and started walking off in the direction of my truck, after muttering,

"Let's go, Miss Daisy." I didn't wait for Hilary but with her long legs it didn't take her long to catch up and I soon heard the clopping of her heels behind me, reminding me of being chased by a horse.

We got in the truck and drove home in silence. It made me wish that everyone who had been suckered into Hilary's nicey, nicey act would just witness for themselves just how vindictive and cold she could really be.

By the time we got home, I was close to screaming in frustration from the tense ride. I noticed my knuckles were still white from gripping the steering wheel so hard and they remained the same when I was gripping the handle of my mug of tea. I kept trying to tell myself that it would soon be over. Only a week of this crap and then I could relax again, well as much as I could with a bounty on my head.

Hilary had gone to start getting ready for tonight which I was dreading. The reasons were wholly selfish I admit, as the idea of Hilary spending anytime in the VIP was only burning a brighter rage inside me. Not only did I not want her anywhere near my boyfriend, but I also wanted to keep my secret life intact. It was like being a superhero in a sense and I know that may sound egotistical, but it was like living a double life.

Downstairs I was just like everyone else, but once I crossed that invisible barrier, I became one of them. I became a part of their world and the idea that Hilary would soon to be fortunate enough to walk into my Heaven was infuriating. I felt so bitter I couldn't taste my tea. I couldn't taste the sandwich I had made myself and I couldn't swallow the idea that this evening was going to happen whether I liked it or not! I even found myself picking up the phone a few times to call Draven and tell him, plead with him, about how much I objected to tonight. But thankfully my pride stopped me.

Of course, none of this helped when the She-Devil herself came and interrupted my sombre thoughts.

"What time do you go to work?" she asked, as she danced in the room like she owned the state. Man, I hated her. I hated what she did to my life every time she was around. It was like she went out of her way to try and destroy any ounce of happiness I found. Of course, the only blessing about the 'Incident' was that she left me alone without adding to my misery. But of course, she didn't need to try and damage an already damaged situation, which just so happened to be the last shreds of my life at the time.

"Six-thirty," I said without keeping the depressed tone from my voice. It didn't help when I saw her basking in her own glory. I was stupid really, what I should be doing was playing her at her own game. Smile that fake smile to hide my distaste at having her so close to me. Laugh that fake laugh at the unfunny things she said and totally hide the fact that I hated the idea of her joining the VIP club. Her crush on Jack was one thing but this…well, if she got her fake nails into any of the Dravens I don't think I could prevent murder. Ok, time to try and play this a different way.

"Are you excited?" I asked making her turn to me in shock and I had to suppress a coy smile.

"Uh, I guess," she replied in a softer tone I wasn't used to.

"It will be nice having someone else there as proof it's not as scary as it's made out," I said trying to sound casual, but I had to turn round to hide a smile I had no control of. I opened the fridge and broke off a few squares of chocolate.

"What do you mean by that?" Ok, now she looked a bit more concerned as her eyebrows knitted together and a hand automatically went to her hip.

"Oh, it's just with all the small-town gossip Afterlife generates, there's bound to be a few horror stories, but none are true I can assure you."

"Like what?" She genuinely looked interested and I think this was the first actual conversation we had had together in years. Like this, it took me back to better times when we were younger and before Hilary's vendetta against me was born.

"Oh, you know… just stuff like how when some people have gone up there in the past and never been seen again, that type of thing…oh but you will have to ask Jack on the details...he knows all the best gory stories." I could now see the faint flicker of both doubt and fear mix through her eyes. I should have stopped there and hoped it was enough to put her off but my mental relapse of personality wouldn't let me.

"But I doubt any of its true. I mean yeah, there are some weird people up there, but they all seem nice to me. And I don't think Dominic would allow anything to happen in his club, he's had people kicked out before for drugs and stuff." She just nodded and I could see her mind doing ten to the dozen.

"Is that how you got with Dominic, by serving him?" It was an innocent enough question but as ever, coming from Hilary's lips it quickly turned into an insult. However, I swallowed it like all the rest and answered her.

"Sort of, but I was never allowed to serve his table directly. We kind of got to be friends first and then he just asked me out." Ok, so that was completely made up but what could I tell her...the truth? Umm no, I don't think that would have gone down well at all.

"Well, I guess in a small town, the pickings are limited," she said as she had soon lost interest, but it didn't prevent her from jabbing at me one last time. With that she left the kitchen and I didn't see her again until we had to leave for the club, where no doubt another nightmare was to begin.

At least in this one…

I didn't have my own demons to contend with.

CHAPTER FOURTY-SIX

VIP DEJA VU

We didn't really speak on the way to the club and a few insults about my slow driving hardly constituted as conversation. I looked to my right and found Hilary twisting a tassel of her scarf round in her fingers. It looked like she was nervous. Maybe some of what I had said earlier had sunk in.

The drive felt like my first time going to the club, it was that long-winded. I put this down to the uncomfortable situation and a mind full of anxious worries. What was going to happen tonight? I had no clue and just kept asking myself the same question over and over...what was Sophia up to?

This was the one question rolling around in my mind like waves in an unsettled sea. It was only when I heard an agitated voice that I was brought back from auto-pilot to realise what Hilary was saying.

"You're going to miss the turn!" Her words registered just in time for me to slow down and make the turn onto the private road that led to Afterlife.

It was dark out and the night was full of snow-filled clouds in a sky we couldn't see. Well, that was according to the weather channel anyway. But you could almost taste it in the air and when it was cold enough to see your breath, then the chances were when it did come down, it was going to stick. Even Hilary was wearing warmer clothes, although I wasn't sure what was underneath that long jacket of hers. For all I knew it could be a bikini.

Thankfully, when we got inside it was confirmed she wasn't naked but it sure came close. She wore a little black lace dress with a corseted top that flared out at the skirt. The red netting could be seen around the edges and was what gave the skirt body, sticking out like a tutu. She matched this slutty look with the highest heels in the form of knee-high boots.

Her makeup looked like something she had stolen from a vampire movie, with black eyes, pale skin and blood-red lips. Her hair hung down in loose curls that looked like they had started to drop out of style, even though you could smell the hairspray radiating from her head a mile away.

I couldn't help but look down at my plain self and was glad to see I was only wearing black trousers and a black shirt that wrapped around and tied at the back. I added a tiny bit of colour in the form of a purple tie with white piping that RJ had given me once. She explained that now she was a full out Goth and no longer a tamer Emo, she had given me a bag of ties to wear for work. This was only the second time I had worn one as the first was when Layla had attacked me. Of course, the memory sent shivers up and down my spine and it didn't have anything to do with Layla. No, it was down to Draven touching me the way he had done that night… Our first real intimate contact.

I think Hilary took my little moment as one of jealousy, as she looked pretty pleased with herself. I was tempted to tell her the only time I had ever dressed like that was at Halloween, but I thought better. The last thing I wanted was to prompt her in any way.

At this time, it wasn't hard to get to the other side of the club as it only really started to get busy when the band was due to start, and they weren't even here yet. However, I had to stop her before she walked up the main staircase.

"What are you doing?" she asked me, looking down at my hand that still gripped her arm. It was as if she would get burned by my touching her and she yanked her arm away and glared at me. I ignored it all and explained.

"We don't go that way." I motioned towards the guarded door and she frowned.

"Not me, I want to make an entrance!" And with that she went up the steps alone and fearless. One thing I did envy was her confidence. I mean, she had it oozing from every pore and you could tell that by everything she did. I turned around and was still shaking my head when I got to the door.

"Evening."

The new sound made me flinch back. Was it me or did the guards just speak to me? I looked up at their faces and realised it was true, they had just spoken. It had been both deep and heavily accented. Eastern European I think. And for once they didn't look so fierce. Wait, was that what I thought it was…

Oh wow, I even received a smile…well sort of one. It was kind of crooked to one side, but he added it with kinder eyes and the other one even winked at me. I ended up laughing out my,

"Hello." I then walked past with them both looking amused and it didn't take me long to realise why. Last night! Last night I had been drunk and had a go at the both of them for never saying 'Hello' to me. Oh dear, me and my big drunken mouth!

Of course, by the time I got to the VIP, I was blushing like a priest in the lingerie section of Marks and Sparks! I walked through the back tables again like I had done last night, and my eyes scanned through all the bodies to get to the man I was looking for. I found his chair empty and this night was starting to mirror the one before. Well, at least I wasn't inebriated. However, unlike the night before, an extra guest sat at their table in the form of my arch-nemesis Hilary.

She was smiling and fake laughing, which meant she wasn't quite getting the Demon welcome I was hoping for. I was too deep in my melancholy to watch where I was going and like last night I walked into someone. Two strong hands came out to steady me and the feel of them holding me tightly had me trying to remember to exhale.

"A beauty blushing and falling into my arms, must be my lucky night after all," Draven's voice mused and the sound of his velvet tone had me close to swooning. Of course, it also had me blushing more and when he saw this, I swore I heard him groan.

His hands flattened to my skin and he moved them up my sides making every bit of my flesh bump up with tingles, even under the thick material of my jacket.

"Come with me I want you, Keira." His voice was deep and guttural which indicated his 'Want' in abundance. I swallowed hard and tried to focus on simple functions, but in the arms of a God, who could?

"I can't, I've got to work and my boss might see." I teased but by the way he tightened his hold on me, he meant business. I gulped again and kept my eyes down watching his chest rise and fall with heavy breathing. He was wearing a full navy suit with waistcoat and white shirt with a red tie that made him look like he'd just walked off a photoshoot for the world's sexiest man title.

Draven had a wide frame, thick with more muscles to count but in his suits it always made him look slimmer and more powerful in a different way. He screamed authority with every thread he wore, and he was definitely one man that wore the suit not the suit-wearing the man.

"Your BOSS does see you and if you don't come with him now he will just take you and I think those perfect rose cheeks of yours will explode with shame at the sight of me throwing you over my shoulder and having my way." His eyes burned into me and started to search down the length of me like he was going to devour me where I stood. Ok, so I was gulping hard again.

"You wouldn't," I said in whispered desperation but the look on his face told me I was wrong.

"Wouldn't I? Are you willing to take that chance, little one?" He looked down at me and I shyly looked down to my feet at the sound of the pet names he was giving me. I think I preferred "Vixen" to "Little one" But I had to admit, it did sound endearing.

When I didn't respond he bent over and in one swift movement he put my waist to his shoulder and tightened his arm around my legs to hoist me up and over before I could say boo to a goose! I squealed out a little scream, but he just laughed heartily in return.

"Draven! Put me down!" I said as sternly as I could while being turned on and embarrassed at the same time.

"Umm, I don't think so I like the view and besides, it puts you at the best height for..." I was about to ask what when I felt his teeth on my bum cheek closest to his face and I squealed again.

"DRAVEN!" I shouted but once again he just laughed off my reprimand. Meanwhile, everyone in the VIP was witnessing this and some laughed at the sight. Draven was simply unaffected by their stares and even sounded somewhat proud of the sight at having a squirming girlfriend in his arms like a fireman.

I couldn't help but feel heat burn under my skin as the whole of the upstairs continued to watch our every move. I noticed new faces that I had never seen before and realised most of the old faces I had become accustomed to were no longer sat at their usual tables. I was, however, happy to see my cousin's face turn a strange shade of scarlet along with another blonde at the table...Aurora.

I smiled.

Ok, so being over Draven's shoulder did have quite a few advantages, the most obvious being the way he made me feel in my nether regions but also seeing my rivals red with rage was somewhat satisfying!

We stopped and I turned around to see him place two fingertips to the glass and it opened to let the cold night air in. Thankfully, I still had my jacket on, but it still took my breath away and in this temperature you could see it leaving me.

He must have felt me shiver because he squeezed me tighter before lowering me to the ground and spinning me around so that my back turned. I soon found myself situated between the stone wall and pinned by one hot horny male.

I braced myself for the cold to penetrate my jacket as he walked me backwards but he placed a palm against it before backing me up completely. His eyes concentrated for a split second and then stepped into me closing the space between us and pressed himself up against me, now making me feel the immense heat from both sides. He still had his palm out to the wall and soon his other joined in blocking me in. Not that I minded, but it was once again making it difficult for me to remember how to breathe.

"Was that for me?" I asked shyly, still not being able to look up at him.

"I do not like it when you are cold and this is the only private place I can have you alone, unless of course you will agree to come back to our bedchamber with me?" he said raising one eyebrow.

"No, Draven, I'm here to work remember?" I said more sternly giving my shyness a back burner. He laughed making me cross my arms, which wasn't easy in the small space he gave me.

"And you are willing to leave me to your cousin's devices alone, unprotected and without your body to comfort me?" Now I was the one laughing at his raised eyebrow that looked sexy as Hell when he did it.

"I think you will survive. Besides, you can thank your sister for that! I don't know what she was thinking." His evil grin told me he did.

"Come on, out with it," I said, making him raise his eyes in surprise.

"I do believe you have developed the talent of reading me too well. I will have to watch myself around you." His velvet voice teased.

"I also have an inbuilt stalling detector and guess what, Draven...it's buzzing." He laughed again and his hands came up to hold my face. He leant down and claimed my lips with his.

He deepened the kiss when I tried to move and with that I couldn't resist. I was soon getting lost in his mouth and the way he moved us both had me so close to saying 'oh, to Hell with work, let's go, big boy!'

His hands started to move from my neck and find the zip to my jacket. I could barely hear the sound of my jacket being opened to reveal my body over my heavy breathing. Bloody Hell, I wanted him and when I felt his smile in the kiss I knew he had heard that part in my mind.

I soon wasn't the only one breaking our locked lips as I let out a gasp at the feel of my body lifting. He had grabbed my legs so quickly I barely felt him move. He had pulled them apart and stepped his body in their place, then he wrapped them around his waist so that his body held all my weight. I was pinned to the wall and his arousal became clear. He slid his hands up my shoulders and down my arms to pull the sides of my jacket away revealing my heaving chest.

He suddenly stopped what he was doing to stare down at me, quickly making me self-conscious.

"Is something wrong?" I asked now getting worried at his frozen hands and hidden expression. His features were in shadow, but it was easy to spot his smile as his perfect white teeth flashed.

"Wrong? Why would you ask that? That word should never be allowed to be used when you are around." He sounded half amused and half deadly serious, which was such a contrast, it was confusing.

"Then why have you stopped?"

"I stop to admire my Vixen. I never thought a woman dressed more like a man could turn me on to the point of embarrassment." I frowned and shook my head to disagree but with one hand resting on my behind to hold me up the other was free to pull at the tip of my tie. He was right. I guess I was dressed more like him than myself, minus the jacket of course.

"I remember the night you first wore a tie, in fact I kept it. Not being able to keep all of you, I decided I had to take a part of you to remember." I closed my eyes at the memory he spoke of and for the second time this night I was reminiscing.

The feel of his fingertips running down my neck made me arch my head backwards to give him further access. The shirt I wore was a cross over so it didn't reach my neck and the tie I wore low so the knot rested between my curves. Curves he was now trying to explore.

"I want to take you inside and make you mine completely. Will you let me do this?" he asked, which was a first.

He started kissing my neck as if to seal the deal, but I had to remain in control. I wanted to hold on to the small amount of power I had and decided no matter how horny I was I would show some restraint. I wanted Hilary to see that I did work in the VIP and not just spend all my time being felt up by Draven. So, with all the will I had, I said the words my body completely disagreed with.

"No, I can't, Draven... I have to work." It came out like the lie it was. My skin wanted his touch. I was craving for it to the point that if he merely said the word 'sex' then I would find my release. However, my words didn't seem to register as he continued to taste me anyway he could. It felt so good to be under his hands after the day I'd had. But every time I was about to cave and let him have his way with me, I saw Hilary's face pop in my head and knew I would never hear the end of it if I left with Draven.

So, with one last effort, I reached up to push at Draven's chest. At first, he didn't feel it so I tried a different approach. I concentrated on letting some of my barriers down and shouted out in my head,

"STOP!" This made him react. I could see the shock in his eyes as he let me go and let my body glide down until my feet were touching the ground.

"I'm sorry, I'm not sure it was meant to be heard as a shout. I just know that if I left now without working, I wouldn't ever hear the end of it with Hilary." It all came out in a mumble, but he seemed to understand me. I think maybe he was getting used to my many quirks.

"And you care, why exactly?" he said seriously, now being the one to fold his arms. He didn't look very happy with me and I felt like chuckling at how spoilt he was being. So, instead of giving him an answer he wouldn't understand, I just raised myself on my tiptoes and put my hands on his face.

"I love you, Draven, but don't be spoilt." And then I finished with pulling his face down so that I could kiss his nose, however, I only just managed to reach his chin. He was still frowning but it had softened him a little. I tried to turn and move out from his stance but when one arm flashed out like it was spring-loaded, I stopped dead and sighed.

"Draven, be reasonable," I said turning to meet his gaze. I could feel it burning into me so I might as well look to complete the total lack of co-operation. I was shocked, however, when I saw him grinning in a smug, self-congratulating way. I frowned.

"What?" I asked trying not to bite my lip at the sight of a smile that drove me wild.

"Oh, nothing." He shrugged and when I let out a little growl he laughed before elaborating.

"Just a thought that you didn't bank on, but I however, well… let's just say it's going to make for an interesting night." He made a clicking noise with his tongue and winked at me making my heart flutter. He played the 'bad boy' only too well and it made me want to crumble at the sight.

This time he turned to leave, and I doubted my arm stopping him was going to be as effective. So, I grabbed his suit jacket instead, making him stop to look down at me with eyes so deep, I nearly lost myself in them.

"And what is that supposed to mean exactly?" I couldn't keep the negative tone out of my question, just like he couldn't keep the arrogant smile from touching the corners of his perfect lips. He then reached for my hand that was still clutching at his collar and uncurled my fingers from the material. He lifted my now free hand to his arrogant smile and kissed it like a perfect gentleman would. His eyes found me over my knuckles and they flashed deep purple at his own thoughts.

"See you soon, Keira…I'm looking forward to an evening when my favourite person is the topic of conversation." My mouth dropped open and inhaled cold air quickly making him laugh as he turned away.

"NO wait! I have changed my mind, I think we should go." The words tumbled out in panic and he turned only his head as the rest of his beautiful body faced towards the frosted glass. He had one eyebrow raised and again looked too sexy for words. Breathe Keira, just breathe, I reminded myself.

"Relax my love, they're only stories." He turned fully now and trailed one fingertip along my jawline and down to the hollow of my throat. I couldn't help but close my eyes at the touch.

"…Keira stories," he whispered and my eyes flashed open but were met with the empty space where Draven once stood. He had disappeared without making a sound. I couldn't help the chill that snaked up my back now my heat source was gone. I looked down to do my jacket back up but it was already zipped shut. How did that happen? Man, oh man, he was good!

I swallowed the huge lump that was named Hilary down my dry throat and stood, not knowing quite what to do next. This was bad...very, very bad.

I took a few deep breaths and when that still didn't seem enough to make me walk back through the doors, I took a few more. I could just imagine Draven smirking at my cowardly behaviour as no doubt he still knew I was out here. Maybe if I waited long enough, he would come out and get me.

No, then she would win, and I would feel like a failure. I mean, this was war, right? Then it was time to fight fire with fire and this time I wasn't going to be the one burnt...oh no, this time I wasn't going to play by any rules. To Hell with the rules of conduct and to Hell with the rules of right and wrong. What was fair or not, I just didn't care anymore. This was going to be the night that Hilary would see a different Keira.

This was the night that Hilary would see the side that plays with Demons and has Angels on her side! Oh yes, this time it would be, oh so different! Ok, so my badass attitude was fooling no one, especially me. But Hell, at least it had made me open the doors and come in from the balcony.

I tried not to look at the table that was currently entertaining my own personal nightmare. Freddy's razor hands and Jason's hockey mask had nothing on the sight of Hilary flirting with my boyfriend. So I didn't look. I refused to look. I walked over to the bar and was met by Karmun.

"Hey Chica, how's my favourite human?" He gave me a smile that instantly put me at ease and made me forget my justifiable worries.

"I have been better, Karmun," I replied bitterly and for the first time I allowed myself to look over to his table. I saw Draven laughing and I didn't know whether it was something Hilary had just said or that he had overheard my comment. I hoped for the latter and knew full well that his superior hearing was up to it.

I walked behind the bar and into the back room that no-one but me used. There I took off my jacket and laid it across the back of one of the only chairs in this tiny little space. There wasn't much room for furniture but there was a small desk that held nothing more than dust. I walked over to the mirror I usually gave myself the once over in before I started my shift. It took me back to the days that my heart beat faster and my stomach held nothing but knots at the idea of seeing Draven. Of course, my body still reacted like that but now I was with him, it didn't ever last all night like it used to.

I twisted a loose strand back up into its place and straightened my tie, not being able to keep the grin off my face. The recent memory of Draven tugging at it on the balcony at least gave me some more colour to my very pale face. I looked up from my tie and let out a gasp at what I was seeing.

The mirror no longer held my image but was now milky white and steamy. I shuddered at another memory and almost screamed as words started to form in the picture of mist. Again, I was taken back to a point in my past, only this time it was that night Justin kissed me and what horrors followed with the writing in my truck window. It was the same and yet it felt different at the same time.

It was as if someone was trapped inside the mirror world and writing messages to communicate words they could not say. Of course, as soon as the words started to become readable, I let out my held breath and my shoulder muscles relaxed.

You look beautiful my love.
Remember not to work too hard or you will have your boss to
answer to.
See you soon Vixen
D x

I don't know how he managed to write perfect script in vapour covered glass, but he did. It wasn't fair that even like this his writing made mine look like the scribbles of a child in comparison.

I ended up walking out of there giggling to myself and biting my bottom lip in between the little snorting noises I was making. Karmun eyed me curiously but remained silent on the matter. This was a small factor compared to my other audience, who even though was across the room, still reduced my breathing to feel heavy. I could still feel his eyes taking in my reaction to his private message.

I managed the rest of the night without giving in to my natural impulses and looking his way. I don't know how, but I could almost taste his displeasure at this and felt as though I had paid him back for earlier.

Now who was the one being smug? However, it didn't last long as my mind kept twisting into whys, wants and whats? Why had my cousin been asked here? How I wanted her to leave and most importantly, what was it that she was telling the man I loved?

My cousin's presence wasn't the only difference in tonight's shift as I wasn't allowed to waitress tonight. Well, to be exact there wasn't much I was allowed to do. Karmun soon informed me that due to Draven's new guests, he didn't think it wise for me (as a human) to be serving them quite so soon. He wanted them to get 'used' to my being here.

I had sulked for a few minutes and then gave up trying. I mean, he may be my boyfriend, but he was also my boss. So instead, I was to help Karmun behind the bar. It didn't take long for me to feel more in the way than help. Not with me keep having to ask him questions on where things were and what drinks go in what glasses. It wasn't exactly like any bar I had ever worked behind before. For one, I had no idea how he knew which drinks were being ordered?

"I'm being more of a hindrance than a help," I said to him half an hour into my shift and bumping into him for the fifth time in three minutes. He just laughed and smoothed out his silken hair with both hands.

Karmun had lush coffee-coloured skin and large almond-shaped golden eyes that looked like honey. His black, long hair hung perfectly past his shoulders and never once seemed to get in the way of his job. Mine, no doubt would have been caught in everything if down and drinking from glasses to find meter long hair curled in it was not an appealing thought. This was just one of the many reasons that I almost always kept it up and firmly out of the way. Unless, of course, I was with Draven, then I never seemed to have a choice in the matter as it was obvious how he preferred it to be.

He soon shrugged off my worries and gave me a reassuring smile.

"You're too kind to me you know?" I said quietly as he poured drinks into exquisite looking silver goblets.

"Oh Keira, what a sensitive soul you are. Actually, it's nice to have the company again," he said this and I could have sworn I saw a hint of sadness in his eyes. One he was trying to hide.

"Again? Were there two of you behind here?" I asked, although I could tell it made him uncomfortable to speak of. He looked as if he wasn't going to answer at first, but when the silence got too much, he answered me.

"Yes, before you came. Do you remember when you first came up to the VIP?" He asked me and I made a gurgled noise as my answer. Did I ever remember! How on earth could I ever forget?! That was the night that changed my life forever...you don't forget things like that easily.

"Well, do you remember when I told you we were short-staffed due to..." He looked as though he couldn't finish so I finished for him.

"...Compromising circumstances." This had been a term he had used on my first meeting with him and I had thought it odd back then to use that explanation of someone either quitting or getting sacked. I couldn't ignore the flinch I saw his body display as I repeated his own words.

"You have a good memory, Keira. Yes me and Constantine made a...a good pair." He looked so full of pain that I couldn't help it when I placed a hand on his arm.

"I'm sorry," I whispered, and this brought his eyes out of his own personal moment of pain and they flew back to mine. He then slowly looked down and stared at my hand touching his. I didn't know whether I had gone too far by my comforting gesture, but when he smiled, I no longer felt threatened. I still removed my hand in case it was in fact unwelcome.

"Why are you sorry?" he asked in earnest and I wondered at the answer. I mean I didn't know the details. So I answered as honestly as I could.

"I can see that this Constantine must have been a dear friend to you," I said without meeting his eyes, that didn't look natural being so serious.

"He was...is more than a friend to me." This time the way he said 'is' had me looking up and I couldn't help but take a step back at the sight of his anger. Karmun was all air and summer breezes but like this all trace of calm was gone and in its place was the darkest of storms. When he noted my response the deep creases in his face smoothed and his eyes widened from the hardened slits they were.

Then, it was as if we had never had this conversation. He gave himself a laugh and a shake before continuing with the night ahead. I may have only been human, but it didn't stop me from knowing his light-hearted mood was touched with a fake coating that hid something painful that he tried to bury deep within him.

I knew from that moment, I would never look at him in the same way. I would never forget those honey eyes close to spilling over with a devastating emotion of loss. I knew those eyes. I knew that look and I knew that pain. Only where his was for another, mine had been for the loss of myself.

Staring at yourself in the mirror for hours, searching for a face you once knew, was what made time flash by in the years that followed my living death. After what happened with Morgan, I felt the strongest part of me die and it was only the heart of another that brought me back to life.

With these thoughts in mind, I turned without thinking towards the one who held my heart so close to his own it made one unbelievably powerful creation.

Draven was sat back, all ease and power radiating from him like glowing embers. It made me inhale more air than needed and the slight noise I made was enough for him to hear and turn his head. His reaction caused mine to bite my lip. He grinned at me and then motioned for me to come to him. His hand extended and his fingers pulled as though he had me hooked.

I was embarrassed at such a command being made in front of

everyone so freely and I lowered my head letting the shorter parts of my hair fall forward covering my shame. I did manage, without looking at him, to shake my head indicating a 'no', before turning away from him. I could hear his laughter from here. This caused my cheeks to turn a deeper shade, which I hid with my hair. When I did finally glance back, I saw him lean into his sister to whisper to her, all the while a super confident smile lay upon his lips like it would never go away.

"He wants me to tell you that you have finished for the night," Karmun said bringing me back to the fact I wasn't alone.

"Uh, no I'm not, I work till ten and it's only..." I was interrupted before finding out the time.

"He's the Mast...boss, Keira, not me and you finish whenever he wishes it." He tried to say this without emotion, but I could detect the bitterness in the way he was about to say "Master", but instead he chose the word boss. I was now caught between stubbornness and curiousness. I didn't want to give in so easily but then again, I didn't know what tainted stories my cousin was telling everyone on Draven's Council. I bet Aurora was just loving it! That thought made me shudder. It was also the reason my stubbornness won.

"I don't care what Draven says!" I said a little louder than what was necessary for only Karmun to hear. He looked shocked at my lack of co-operation and a little impressed, I think.

"I am here to work and so far I have done little of that, so please give me a job I can do that makes me think I am worthy of being paid." He smiled at me now, making me do the same, but his smile soon became directed behind me. At first I expected to see Draven as I turned but then I had to smile when I saw he had sent his reinforcement. So this was what he had being whispering...sneaky Demon!

"Hello Keira, are you ready to come and play with us?" Sophia asked me sweetly rocking back and to on her heels. She looked like a little ballerina from a trinket box and the image of that I quickly wiped from my memory and started to rub my gloved arms self-consciously.

Sophia noticed my reaction, but of course she did. She was like her brothers, always watching and analysing everything I did. It was an annoying family trait. As if everyone was waiting for the first signs of a meltdown, I knew wasn't going to happen. At least this was what I suspected anyway.

"I was just telling Karmun how my time isn't up yet so he should give me another job to do...maybe stocking up or something." They both laughed at the idea of this.

"What?" I asked them both frowning.

"I doubt Dom would be pleased to see you doing heavy labour, Keira," She said in composed amusement.

"Draven doesn't want me doing anything! Working full stop!" I ranted, but she took little seriousness in my words.

"Oh Keira, come now, what exactly do you see wrong in my sentence. my brother is now getting persecuted for what... being too thoughtful?" She was trying not to smile at knowing guilt was my biggest weakness.

"I...I...that's not what I meant, I just..." I was close to chewing my bottom lip off at a statement that sounded reasonable enough, that it was hard to argue against. Not that I still didn't want to and with the added look of victory in her face made it all that much harder not to. Of course, instead of thinking of a good response I just let out a defeated breath and rolled my eyes.

"Fine, but I'm not happy about it!" My shoulders slumped as light came to her features.

"Really Keira, anyone would think we were trying to get you to walk over hot coals and dance naked whilst killing bunnies!"

"You do realise my cousin is sat over there, right?" I said sarcastically making her laugh.

"Which reminds me, why on earth would you do this to me?" I asked her, pleading a cause that was far too late...unless they were willing to kick her out.

"Look, I know you are angry at me about having her here but despite being little 'Miss Naughty Demon' this one was not me. This one was an order and one you will have to take up with someone else." Sophia tried not to laugh as my mouth dropped open and I could only imagine what a simpleton I looked.

"What? Draven?" She only nodded at my outburst and I felt my gut twist into a hard ball of rage. Why? Why, why and more whys? I now knew the reason behind his evil grin earlier. It wasn't at his sister's request at all, it was at his. Well, this changed things. My night's frustration was quickly turning to a lethal weapon I was about to let loose in Draven's direction.

Oh yes, my shift had now finished but my work for the night was definitely not over!

Not by a long shot.

CHAPTER FOURTY-SEVEN

KEIRA STORIES

I turned to Karmun before leaving with Sophia and said one word.

"Drink." The word came out ruder than I had meant it to, but instead of being offended Karmun found amusement in my order. I guess Draven was rubbing off on me. I had a shot of tequila in front of me before I could blink.

Everyone who knew me here knew my drinking preference and it wasn't hard to realise which one of the two I needed the most right now. Hell, Karmun even knew I didn't need the salt or lime. No, I already had a sour taste in my mouth that didn't need adding to.

"Come on, let's get this shit over with," I said to Sophia in passing. I knew without looking at her the shock that I would have found considering I didn't usually curse like that. I'm not even sure she had ever heard it from me before now. I could feel her giggling beside me and had no doubt she was loving every minute of this, being a Demon and all.

For once, I couldn't get to Draven's table quick enough and he watched me with curious eyes. I could see he wasn't taking my evil glare seriously, if anything he looked more excited by this than worried.

By the time I got to my usual chair, I was starting to think one shot wasn't nearly enough. Draven stood and the rest followed, all except Hilary but no surprises there.

"Hello, beautiful," he said with a voice so deep and full of meaning. He leant down to brush his lips to mine and skimmed a finger down my cheek lightly. Of course, all my built-up rage dispersed at his gentle touch and was being replaced by rose coloured cheeks.

I sat down, looking the exact opposite of my cousin, which was like having ice and fire in the same room and putting bets on which one would win. I liked to think I was the fire, considering I had Draven's direct heat next to me. Also Hilary wasn't trying to conceal her icy glare that was burrowing its way into my forehead.

It almost caused me physical pain to try and understand why? Why so much hate and why so much energy to go on hating someone for so long? It must have been exhausting for her. For years I had never found my answers, but it wasn't through lack of trying.

And then it hit me! This was why Draven had Sophia invite her. This was the reason behind one evening of discomfort. He wanted to know as much as I did, he just would never admit it. He could read her mind and know, given the right questions, he would discover the truth behind the hate. It was genius really! Ok, so now I wasn't so angry at Draven but still, I wasn't exactly looking forward to this.

I gave myself a mental shake, before joining in with whatever conversation was occurring before my arrival. Of course, it didn't go unnoticed that the sound of my cousin's voice was already grating on me. I could feel his hand squeeze mine in reassurance to the fact.

"I have to say, Kizzy Cat, I'm surprised you can even call this a job...you must have too much fun." I could hear the inner meaning to this comment like a cat scratching at a chalkboard.

I knew her tactics and her mind games better than most, so it didn't surprise me that although her tone sounded friendly it was laced with vindictiveness.

"Well, this was a quiet night for me, but I wouldn't usually have a family member here and I really didn't want to miss out." I felt as though I was going against everything Holy saying this but considering my lying was that bad, I doubted anyone believed my words anyway. She smirked at me and turned to answer a question, I didn't quite hear asked from Takeshi.

"You're going to have to do better at lying than that, my love." Draven purred in my ear making my lids close at the scent that floated its way down the side of my face. I heard him laugh quietly to himself and thought it down to being able to hear my heart rate kick up a notch.

"Thanks," I whispered sarcastically, making him laugh out louder this time. Of course, this caused everyone to stop and look at us.

"So, what have I missed?" I asked, hoping for an insight into the evenings 'interesting night' as Draven put it on the balcony. Of course, as soon as Hilary opened her mouth, I found myself regretting it.

"Oh, Dominic's been learning all your dirty little secrets but don't worry, I saved the best ones until you were here." This time everyone laughed but me.

"I bet that made for a boring conversation, as there's not much to tell in that department," I commented but from the looks of Hilary she didn't agree.

"Really, you don't think so? I guess I must have a better memory than you." She challenged and Draven felt me tense next to him.

"I'm not afraid of you." I snarled not caring for the serious turn this was taking. Everyone else looked as though they were watching a game of tennis, back and to, trying to keep score. Well, I knew who Aurora was cheerleading for.

"Maybe that's your mistake, after all I have known you a long-time cousin and know full well what you're capable of," she answered like I would have, and it made me think she had heard these exact words from me once upon a time.

"Likewise," I replied sealing the tension you could have sliced with a blade. I don't know why but being here like this with

Draven at my side and my enemy sat opposite taunting me, a new me came out...

The fighter in me.

She started laughing and waving her hand around like an embarrassing memory had just hit her. It hadn't, it was just her next move in this chess game of real life.

"Well, I had just finished telling them how you used to come home from school and wet yourself because you thought there were monsters in the toilet." She said like this was enough to knock a couple of pawns off the board. I laughed myself showing her up.

"Yes, I was good at hiding the truth as a child. It was in fact because being bullied at the age of seven and avoiding a head dunking was something no parent wants to hear." At this I had turned her story back on herself making her the bad guy she was.

I took note of Draven's growl under his breath, everyone but Hilary heard it, and all flinched at the sound. I felt his hand on my leg tighten reassuringly.

Of course, this reason had been true but so had the other one. For at that time to me, monsters had existed as they do now. This was one story that would not give her the upper hand and make the others in alliance to her little charade. Amazingly, even Aurora looked a bit dissatisfied at the turn the game took but no surprises, my cousin wasn't finished with me yet. Oh no, she was just warming up.

"Oh Keira that's awful, I wish Dom had been there at your school. I bet he would have frightened them off for you and kicked their ass!" Sophia said kindly and the image she planted made me grin. How much simpler my life would have been back then if Draven had been in it to protect me.

But the sad fact remained that this could never have happened as Draven had never had the chance to be a boy. But the thought of us being the same age and being childhood sweethearts was a nice dream to see. It made me look up at him and he gave me a bad boy grin before winking at me.

"I have a pretty good idea what I would have done," he said making me shudder at the image he was now planting in my mind.

I have seen scary Draven too many times to ever forget how powerful a sight it truly was. I was so close to asking him to do a private showing for my cousin to see but grinned to myself knowing he wouldn't.

Pity, I thought as I reached for my bottle of Corona that had been waiting for me.

"Do you remember Simon, dear Kizzy Cat?" I coughed out my mouthful, nearly wearing my drink than consuming it! She wouldn't…Surely not! She couldn't really be ready to go that far. Draven noted my reaction with a worried frown. Of course, this would happen, any mention of another man's name was bound to kill my strongest pawn. Ah, to Hell with pawns, she had gone straight for my Queen and had her sights once again on my King!

"That is not a story Hilary, that's a private and personal matter. One I do NOT want to be discussed!" I said in a way that proved I was taking pages from Draven's book in ordering people. Of course, I remained calm which added to its desired effect.

"Oh Kizzy, come on, it was what…seven maybe eight years ago. I remember my mum telling me about it. She didn't think your parents would ever forgive you!" She laughed again but now all questioning eyes were on me, including Draven's.

I wanted to lunge over the table and claw at her face. I wanted to maim, I wanted to hurt, and I wanted to destroy! This time she had really gone too far, and I wanted her to pay. This now wasn't just the fighter coming out of me, this was the Demon.

"That's enough Hilary, you go too far," I said still remaining an eerie calm that was wearing thin. Icy thin, that was soon to crack.

"Apparently it was you that went too far and with a married man, I believe…what was he, twice your age at the time, about sixteen years older?"

"SHUT UP!" I screamed out at her as I stood in my rage burning her with my stare. My ice had broken and left me with deadly shards that my mind wanted to throw her way. I was shaking I was so angry but in the middle of my own turmoil I hadn't seen that I wasn't the only one having a meltdown. I didn't give it much thought as I was facing my cousin in a standoff that would surely this time end in broken bones.

"Right, that's it bitch! I have had it with your shit! Outside...NOW!" I was waiting for her to take me up on the offer, but she just leant back, crossed her legs and held her hands up as if she was innocent.

"Kizzy, what did I do wrong? Surely Dominic knows about your past...lovers?" She just kept digging my grave getting carried away with the way she was trying to bury me.

"Right, that's it!" I turned and was about to go around to her side when Draven reacted.

"Enough!" he shouted and a heated hand whipped out and shackled my wrist. I gasped at the sight of Draven towering above me, face frozen in pure rage. He clicked his fingers and I turned back to Hilary in time to see her eyes roll back and her head smack the table as she passed out. At least, I gather she had passed out and Draven hadn't just outright killed her... either way I'm sure I would forgive him.

He still had hold of me, as if he was preventing me from running off and this was when realisation hit me. That was exactly what he was doing, he was undoubtedly angry, and it wasn't just at my cousin. I gulped as I could feel his temper mounting up like Mount St Helens. I tried to pull away, but he pulled me back and leaned down to whisper one word.

"Stay." The way he said the word made little bumps wriggle across my skin.

"Zagan, take the girl home and get her out of my sight!" he ordered with a tension in his voice that made me more than a little wary. Meanwhile, Zagan had gone to Hilary's side in a second and scooped her leggy body up in one swift motion. I didn't want to look at Draven, but I found I couldn't look away. His features were stone. His jaw set in a way that made me want to cringe back, but his vice grip was going to make that impossible.

Zagan was walking to the back staircase when Draven spoke again.

"Wait," he then nodded to his brother once, communicating without words. He then let go of my wrist and left my side to go over to Zagan and his burden. I was about to leave also not wanting to wait around for Draven's wrath, but something caught me.

It was Vincent.

He wasn't as forceful as his brother and entwined his hand in mine and gently pulled me to sit back down next to him, which was in Draven's chair. I felt as if I was breaking some unspoken rule by doing so, but it was only my own reaction that confirmed this was not the case.

Vincent didn't let go of my hand and I noted that it was cooler than his brother's was and also a little smoother. It was as I would have imagined flexible marble to be.

I watched Draven stand close to Hilary and that's when I noticed that it wasn't only the attention of his Council that lay witness to this night's spectacle. Every eye was watching, flitting between their Master and his girlfriend.

"Hilary, can you hear me?" It came out as another order not a question.

"Yes," she said as though talking in her sleep. It was a peaceful voice and one I remembered from before she had changed into the hateful bitch she was today. It took me back to when we were actually friends. When we used to laugh and play together and there was nothing but a strong family bond between us. Really, what went wrong?

"I want you to give me a name." His voice was smooth and hypnotic, like all those times he used to make me sleep and control my mind into thinking he wasn't really there.

"Draven, don't do this," I pleaded quietly but when he shot me a look I backed down, knowing it was fruitless.

"A name?" she repeated like a drugged hospital patient.

"Yes, the name of the man you spoke of, Keira's past...lover." He said this like it caused him physical pain. The word 'lover' coming out in what could only be classed as utter disgust.

I wanted to crawl away from the rest of the night. To hide the shame that had too quickly replaced the anger I felt. And as if sensing this Vincent let go of my hand and rested it on my shoulder, ready no doubt for me to try anything his brother would frown upon. It was silly feeling like a prisoner amongst my own boyfriend's family but given the type of family Draven had I suppose it was as natural to them as breathing. I looked to my other side in hopes of finding Sophia on my side, but from the harsh expression reflected in her eyes I found nothing but the shadow of Draven there.

"Simon...Simon Carter," Hilary said unconsciously acting out as Draven's puppet. I didn't like my cousin, that was no secret, but it was not a nice thing to witness Draven's control over us mere humans, no matter who his victim was.

"Good girl, now sleep and forget this night." He patted her on the head like you would a sleeping child and she drooped more into Zagan's hold. My emotions were mixing into one and making it difficult to feel anything concrete. One minute I feared what Draven's reaction would be and then I would be too angry to feel that fear.

Of course, there were the others...shame, embarrassment, guilt, hurt and cold. That last one was more down to Vincent's presence and the chill he sent down me with not only his touch but his stare into what seemed like empty space. I don't know what he saw there but it was as though he was searching out for some hidden answers from a source I couldn't see.

Before I knew it, my cousin was out of sight and Draven was coming back to my side. I guess it would be too much to hope this night would just carry on as if this had never happened. I soon got my answer.

"Come with me, Keira, now!" Draven's demand filled me with a dread so deep it felt like I would never be able to crawl out of it! Vincent released me but the cold pit in my stomach didn't. Draven had retaken possession of me, and I found myself being more pulled than guided to the back doors leading into his home.

"Draven please, this is silly...I..." I stopped that sentence when I saw just how un-silly this was by his expression alone. That look would have stopped armies in their tracks and made them think twice about landmass and extended power.

He looked back at the looming hallway and continued towards the end which felt more like my end. It seemed like an age of silent footsteps, until we got to his door. Before I could protest, the door opened and he zoomed round to the back of me, gripping my waist and controlling me onward. I had nothing to back up on but his indestructible body which was moving forward like a pressing wall behind me.

Now anger was building up inside me like a firecracker ready to explode in the palm of my hand. It made me storm inside instead of backing away and only when I heard the door slam did I face him.

"This is ridiculous, Draven, you can't behave this way when you hear something you don't like!" I shouted at him letting the firecracker go, so to this he let off his own rocket.

He drove his tensed arm and fist down into the black velvet couch, making me scream as he broke it in two. It splintered up in every direction, making it look like an animal had just clawed its way through it.

Draven hadn't spoken a word, not even made a sound. I was so shocked at the sight of his outburst that my mouth hung open and only then did this seem to calm him slightly. He straightened his body and closed his eyes as if trying very hard to control himself better. I smartly decided to stay silent.

"Did...did he...he force you?" He said each word slowly and from the looks of things, painfully.

"What? I..." I was trying to process his question when he spoke again, only in a more forceful tone.

"Did he RAPE you?" he shouted out making me want to suddenly cry.

"I...I..." was all I seemed to manage but Draven was losing the battle within him to stay even this level of calm.

"Yes or No, Keira?!" He gritted out the question between clenched teeth.

"N...No!" I said spluttering out the word as now I was crying. The sight of tears flowing down my flustered cheeks made his hard exterior soften slightly.

"You'd better not be lying to me, Keira. I will find out and he will die for ever touching you." His threat was so real, a sob broke from me, however he still didn't move.

"I...I'm not...not lying." I spoke in between trying to breathe and cry at the same time. He could see my pain and there he also saw the truth. He let out a breath I don't know how long he had been holding, as it seemed he hadn't been breathing this whole time. I could see his figure start to move towards me through blurred eyes, but I moved back a step.

"Don't!" I cried making him halt. I blinked making my flooded eyes overflow and clear my vision for a moment. Now, I could see a different pain in his face… one I had put there. Instead of coming any closer, he folded him arms and waited.

"I need you to explain." His voice was now less strained, but it was still guttural.

"Explain what?!" I shouted, waving my arms at him. He didn't react in anger and I soon realised it was never me that he had been angry at. It had been someone named Simon.

"Forget it! I'm so out of here, Draven!" I stomped toward the other door, but I heard it lock without him moving.

"You're not going anywhere until you tell me what I want to know."

"The Hell I'm not! You can't do this! You can't just act like this! I'm your girlfriend, Draven, not some bloody little girl you can control into doing what you order. You can't hold me captive with this bullshit macho, I'm the man King, so you will do what I say, crap!" I was panting like a wild animal and digging my nails into my fisted palms, just to stop from hitting out.

"Are you finished?" he asked calmly but this just made it worse and with a growl I turned to punch the door. I didn't make contact with wood or stone or anything but flesh. Draven had caught my fist in his hand and prevented a few broken knuckles, maybe even a wrist and some fingers.

"I'm really going to have to teach you how to punch without hurting yourself, that was all wrong," he said without humour. I yanked my hand out from his and he let me.

"Arrhh!" I made this frustrated noise as I walked back away from him towards the glass doors.

"You're not leaving Keira, so deal with it!" He was losing his patience, but I no longer cared.

"I need air, Draven, or do you think me capable of jumping off, sprouting wings and escaping?" I snapped back. The doors opened letting in the cold night air that licked at the thin material of my shirt. I wished I still had my jacket on but my anger and stupid pride wouldn't let me say 'Umm scrap that, I think arguing inside is better.'

I walked to the edge and took in deep breaths trying to calm myself down. I was so tired of coming back to this type of problem with Draven. It was like being on a constant rollercoaster of never-ending ups and downs. I didn't know from one day to the next what was going to happen to knock me and Draven back to this destructive path we were walking down.

I wanted to scream out...Why?! What's wrong with me that I don't get to have happy ever after? Why don't I deserve good old fashioned normal for once? Just one evening when I don't almost die, get kidnapped or see monsters every corner I turn. Why don't I get to hold on to the Draven I love without seeing the Demon in him at any bump in the road? I answered my own question...

Because, Keira, he was a Demon… Is a Demon.

I shook myself and added on to that distinction. He was also an Angel. A bright star in my life that I couldn't live without, even if I tried. Like living without the only light in the darkness of my past. He was my reason for breathing and now I knew I had to take the good with the bad, just like everyone else in the world did.

Perfect didn't exist and if it did, without the bad you wouldn't recognise the good. It would make it irrelevant. It would be nothing, but dust and sand combined in an endless desert. Could you separate the two? Tell them apart. The answer was no, and you wouldn't even try.

I loved Draven and there was no force great enough to get me to change that, not even the Gods themselves could get me to say otherwise. So this...this, right now meant nothing but another glitch. A thorn in my side that Draven himself would no doubt remove. So I decided that I would tell him about how stupid this all was.

I would tell him about a man that I had some teenage infatuation with that ended in me shamefully kissing an older man at sixteen and near throwing myself at his mercy. How I had ended broken-hearted as he stopped things before they became a crime and him declaring his love for his wife.

How my teenage dream of me being his wife was crushed leaving me with only the memory of one stolen kiss. How I had run away from home believing I would never find another love like it and how I would remain alone until he was with me. I was sixteen and the next time I learnt about what love really was, was when I was twenty-three. It was when I found my home, my heart's home.

When I met my Dominic Draven.

I jumped at the feel of something being put over me. It was a thick, lush, warm blanket that Draven had put around my shivering body. He wrapped it around me as if I needed protection against the elements. It was only then that I realised it had been snowing and I was wet along with cold. I wondered why he had waited this long, normally Draven would have...

"I had to wait. I had to let you...finish." He spoke in my ear causing a warm sensation on my neck. I shuddered when his fingers started to trace the skin there and his fingertips circled in my hair.

"I had to hear the rest of it. I needed to see for myself. To see if this...this man had hurt you in any way. You understand that I could never allow such a man to live if he had. I needed to know from your own thoughts that he hadn't touched you in that way...in my way. I would have killed him, Keira and my reasons would have been final and just." He spoke so softly, it was hard to think clearly, to really comprehend he was talking about murder.

"No!" I protested but he moved a hand to the back of my head and smoothed down my wet hair. He remained out of sight, but his other arm wrapped across my front pulling me back forcefully to his hard body, holding me captive.

"Yes, Keira!" I shuddered at his possessive voice that spoke of how I was his and never would belong to another.

"No-one who has hurt you will live in the same world you do. I would never allow it. But seeing as there was very little harm done, only for a sensitive teenage mind to have suffered, then no harm will come to him." His hand snaked up my torso, still feeling like a band of iron holding me to him. I quickly sucked in a breath when a hand curled one breast and squeezed as if to emphasise his point of ownership.

"I can imagine turning you away, even at the tender age of sixteen was punishment enough. A strong character he must have been." I tried to turn around to look at him, but he held me still so that I couldn't move from him. I knew now why he needed me upset. He wanted access to a fragile mind. He wanted to see the truth and only my thoughts would have portrayed such. But he had seen lots more. He had received a direct window into my soul, into my heart and every feeling it held locked there.

"Yes and dare I say it was very enlightening." His voice almost shook, barrelling over with emotion. He kissed my head and then moved down to my neck to suck in my flesh, at the same time running a thumb over my hard nipple making me shiver.

I could feel the drops of snow that had melted on his heated skin roll down onto my own. I closed my eyes and felt myself slowly turned around to face him.

"Keira, open your eyes," he whispered as a plea, no longer an order left in his body. I looked up sluggishly to find his face painted with so many emotions. Pain, focus, guilt, relief but most of all...love. He cupped my face in his hands and pulled our faces closer together.

"Can you ever forgive me?" he whispered above my lips.

"Ye..." I didn't get to finish the word over his lips but buried inside his kiss.

He moulded our bodies together and kissed me with every passion lit fibre in his body. I felt a whoosh of air as his other form burst from his outer self, all the while never leaving my lips. He gripped onto me so tightly as if he would die if he ever let me go. Like both our lives hung in the balance and the only thing stopping the end was this very kiss, a perfect act of love that stopped time. Our time, no one else's… just ours.

His wings came out and rushed forward covering us in a dark feathery cocoon, making the only light the warm purple glow that both our skins now wore. Mine was reflecting from the raw supernatural energy that pumped around him and bit my lip at the sight. I shuddered again making him hold me closer and his hands spread out on both the top and bottom of my spine. He needed me as I needed him and in both our minds we were one.

"Forever," he breathed freeing me to take my own breath.

"Forever," I repeated not only his word but also the same feeling that was bursting out from me like his Demon side. And then it dawned on me, like a knife had sliced into my heart and started cutting me down like the wound I was left within my dream.

Was that what it all meant? The light at the end… my heart missing because Draven still had hold of it? Still had hold of what I was leaving behind. My end. My death.

Because of course, I didn't have forever...

But he did.

CHAPTER FOURTY-EIGHT

FEARING FOREVER

"Kaz come on, be reasonable, Mum and Dad will be crushed." My sister was stood cradling her growing bump in her hands and with the mothering glow lighting her features it was hard to tell her no... *again*.

"I can't Libs, I'm sorry but it's only one Christmas," I repeated again feeling like a broken record.

"You're wrong, look Kaz, I don't want to upset you but think about it." She tilted her head as though I was missing something majorly important. I rolled my eyes as a natural reaction to a conversation we had been having for days.

"I know you're pregnant, but jeez, it's not like I'm missing the kid's first Christmas." When she started shaking her head, I finally figured that wasn't what she meant.

"Keira, come on now, it's not like I'm expecting that to be the reason. This has to do with you." I had wondered how long it would take her to drop my nickname and go in for a more serious tone.

"I don't..."

"Keira, I really don't want to say it, but I see I have no other choice. It will be our first Christmas when we're all together...you know, like really there..." She was finding it so hard not to push me, but I finally got to the inner core of why this was so important for everyone.

It was the first time in years my parents would see me... the old me, that they thought they had lost...well, more like taken from them. She was right, this was important. After all, I don't think I really remember the last Christmas where I wasn't faking smiles and making comments I didn't feel. Back then I had been numb. I had been a shell and a broken soul left bleeding on the inside.

"You mean not like the zombie Keira Christmas?" I said trying to lift her worried frown. Thankfully, she laughed and I wasn't left feeling as guilty.

"Okay, I get it, but Libs this is going to be really hard. I mean Dra, Dominic is very overprotective." I winced as I said this as though my mind was mocking me saying 'Yeah right and the rest!'

"Well, he could come as well. I mean it's not as though he couldn't afford the airfare." Well, she was right there. He did have his own private jet for starters. I decided not to tell her that part. The fact of the matter was that Draven would be fine in small one dinner circumstances but spending a week with my family wasn't something I could imagine happening. Not only that, but I wasn't raving about the idea of putting my family in danger. After all, I was still being hunted.

"Look, I will speak to him, but I can't make any promises...okay?" She nodded but her smile told me that she thought this was so a done deal!

I left the kitchen to find Hilary behind the door. I could tell by her smirk that she had heard every word. I decided not to stick around and ran up the stairs to my new room. I only tripped once, which was unusual for me these days. I don't know why but ever since I had been with Draven, I had become a little less clumsy and more coordinated. I wondered why that was exactly?

The week after the VIP incident thankfully went by without a hitch. Unfortunately for me, I wasn't allowed to bring the matter up with Hilary about her behaviour at the club, because thanks to Draven's mind control, she was left thinking it was a quiet night. The fact that I had to swallow my hate for that heinous act was easier said than done. I couldn't even pretend anymore.

Libby had noticed the change, but I couldn't even tell her about it. So, as far as she was concerned, she was left thinking I had just lost all will when it came to my cousin. The fact that she had decided to stay until the beginning of December didn't help matters. As it turned out, me and my sister had both been deceived and deluded thinking it was only ever going to be just a week.

Once in my room, I had time to think about the whole Christmas problem. Either way I looked at it I was going to be hurting someone. If I didn't go then I knew my Mum would be crushed. My dad, I think would understand but he would feel disappointment for my Mother's sensitive nature. Libby wouldn't let me get away with not going. And no doubt there would be waterworks to contend with thanks to a bunch of baby hormones that made crying at anything her new sport. But all of these options seemed better than the alternative. Telling Draven was not a thing I would look forward to that was for sure. I can imagine the 'NO' word would get used a lot.

I tried to look at things objectively, weighing up the pros and cons, but the deeper I looked the more I hated to admit things to myself...I was scared. I know it was an irrational response, but I had grown so used to my new life here I was scared of going back to my past, even if I was only revisiting.

Stupid as it was, I feared that I would be opening up old wounds by going back, while here it didn't even feel like I'd ever bled. Here was new. Here was safe. Here was Draven. Okay, so maybe it would be alright if he was with me. I mean he could play human for a week, couldn't he? Thankfully, the sound of Abba singing pulled me from my mental breakdown before a headache set in.

"What's up ma' Bitch!" RJ's 'I'm from the hood' greeting made me giggle. I just hoped...no, no, scrap that more like prayed, that her next image change didn't include gun tattoos, rap music and sayings like 'Bust a cap in your ass'.

"Hey, RJ what you up to?"

"Not a whole lot which is why you're going to help me," she said sweetly, telling me instantly that this might not be something I would want to do. I loved RJ but sweet was not in her genetic makeup.

"Okay, hit me with it," I pushed.

"I need you to come on a private mission with me 'cause if I don't get out of the house now my Mum is going to make me babysit the brat and unless locking kids in cupboards is acceptable babysitting conduct, then I severely suggest we go shopping or God forbid even hiking! Anything just to get me out of this house in the next couple of minutes!" I was nearly in tears with laughter by the time she had finished her little rant and after some more over-exaggerated comment about her younger sister and friends, we arranged for her to meet me here. She turned up in record time.

I ran down and was met by not one Thomas but two. Jack had also come with his sister. I gathered neither wanted to spend a Sunday babysitting. Jack nodded to me with his lips held firm in a thin line. We still hadn't spoken thanks to my cousin. God only knew the lies he had been told and it hurt me more than I let on that he had chosen her side over mine. I guess I had to admit it to myself sometime, that we weren't as good friends as I once thought. I shook myself from any more of those thoughts before I started getting upset 'cause honestly, I missed him.

Hilary came down the stairs behind me and nearly knocked me out of the way to get to Jack.

"Excuse me!" she huffed as she squeezed past me as if I had been a bus standing in her way.

"You're excused," I said bitterly and walked towards RJ trying to ignore Jack's glare.

"Come on RJ, let's go before we miss the movie," I said doing a vague impression of my happy self.

"Oh a movie, which one?" Hilary squealed as she hung onto Jack's arm as if he was a prize doll.

"I don't know what it's called, the one where robots kill astronauts," I said hoping that alone would put her off.

"Oh, I saw the trailer for that one but it's not out yet in the UK. What do you say Jack, are you game?" He looked down at me and then back at Hilary's pleading eyes. Which pleading eyes would he choose? Please say no, please say no. I repeated hoping somehow it would enter his brain...

It didn't.

"Sure, why not. Killer robots sounds like a good way to spend a Sunday, very typical Sunday thing," Jack joked and I was the only one not left smiling.

"Well, that's great then! Isn't that great RJ?" I said shooting her a look to say it was anything but!

"Err...yeeeah," she said drawing out the word and looking at me like I had gone a little crazy too.

"Right then, well let's all go together," I said again wondering when it was my brain was going to shut down and stop talking.

"Right, off we go then," I was still saying as we all piled into Jack's new car. I was still muttering stupid obvious comments like this until Jack said something that made my brain click into panic mode.

"Hey, I know this sounds kind of like a bad cop movie, but I think we're being followed." Jack's eyes kept wandering back to the rear-view mirror with masked worry. Mine weren't even trying to hide it as it was just there plain to see. I felt my throat starting to get tighter and my mind went into warp speed at all the different possibilities. The best one of course would be that it was nobody but knowing that this was me we were talking about, it was probably the Supernatural's best assassin!

I kept looking behind us and seeing the black beast in the form of a four-wheel-drive behind us getting closer had me fidgeting nervously in my seat. However, it seemed that Jack and I were the only ones taking any notice. Then we all screamed.

I thought I was going to see my heart in my lap as I looked down to check when it burst from my chest! Thankfully, I was in one piece... for now at least.

"Jeez Kizzy, are you going to answer that!" My cousin snapped impatiently. I didn't miss the look Jack gave her and I couldn't help but smile a little. It was like the tiniest beacon of hope that he wasn't entirely lost to me. I was trying to retrieve my phone and lifting myself up to dig deeper into my jeans pocket when I noticed Jack's gaze in the mirror. He looked at me as though he was trying to communicate something secret to me, but I was at a loss to know what. Instead I just frowned and tried to concentrate on shutting up Abba before my cousin decided to comment again.

"Hello?" I said unsure of the number and its caller.

"Keira." A voice I knew better than any other sound on Earth sounded strained in my ear.

"What's wrong?" Was the question that first escaped my lips as Draven never rang me and I knew if he ever did, it wouldn't be just for a quick chat. No, it would be important.

"Would you like to explain to me why it is that you are in a vehicle with that boy?" His question was thick with disapproval and filled my mind with a different kind of worry. However, the only question that I thought to ask was a tactless one.

"How did you...?"

"You are being followed, Keira," he said as though utterly obvious. Ah... that would be Ragnar then.

"So..." he prompted as I went silent.

"Sooo... I'm off to watch a movie with RJ, Hilary and Jack," I said making sure he understood the way I said Jack to emphasize that he wasn't the only one and this was so not a date! Although, it was nice to know he still got jealous. Childish I know but what could I say, I just couldn't help myself.

"A movie," he breathed out in relief and I smiled, earning a hateful look in the mirror from Hilary. My smile deepened.

"Yes, something about killer robots in space so it should be very educational." I giggled at my own joke and Draven laughed his deep throaty laugh making my legs turn to jelly.

"Well now, that does sound terrifying, but pray tell me, who will you be sitting next to for moral support?" Although his voice was teasing, I could tell he was desperate to hear it would be RJ, my cousin, a female stranger, or even a bloody nun, minister, or leader of the Gay parade, basically anyone but Jack! I laughed again.

"Female." I answered not wanting to say any names out loud. I could now hear him grinning.

"So, I will see you later D...Dominic." I nearly always slipped up on saying his name and whenever I did manage to say it, it never felt right coming from me. However, he didn't seem to think as I did.

"I have never loved the sound of my name before I heard it said from your sweet lips." I knew I was now blushing because RJ had rolled her eyes at me. However, it didn't last long as my cousin decided now was the time to open her big gob!

"Oh Kizzy, I forgot to ask you, did I give you those plane tickets home your Mum gave me...oops are you still on the phone? Never mind, we'll talk about our trip home for Christmas later." Only three words came to mind at precisely that moment. 'What a Bitch!' I screamed in my head but it was soon drowned out by the profound growl that came from the other end of the phone. Ok, so now I was in trouble and Hilary knew it! Hell, she had planned it, executed it, counted on it and accomplished it.

When she had been standing behind the kitchen door this morning, I now knew what she had been listening to and as a result, where I had three words, Draven now only had one.

"Explain." His voice was dry and devoid of the sweet sentiments he had spoken not long ago, which made me gulp. It took me a few moments to try and figure out how exactly to deal with this. So I decided the best option was to play it down...way, way down.

"Oh, it's nothing really," I said in a flighty way.

"Kizzy, I don't think your Mum would be too pleased to hear you calling a family Christmas together nothing, she would be crushed!" Hilary said enlightening us all to her feelings that were completely false. She didn't care two craps about my mother's feelings, what she did care about, what she in fact lived for, was making my life as miserable as possible and at this moment she was doing one heck of a job at it!

"Keira." Draven said my name as a warning.

"Look, I'll explain later," I whispered gently, trying to get him to calm down.

"You mean you haven't told him, yet you've known for weeks!" At that point I had lost my patience with my destructive cousin and I couldn't stop my reflex motion in kicking the back of her chair... hard.

"Ouch...excuse me!" she moaned.

"Oh sorry there, did that hurt?" I asked feeling both childish and triumphant at the same time.

"No, it didn't," Hilary huffed and crossed her arms looking like the victim here and I couldn't help but mutter 'Pity' under my breath which only Draven heard.

"It is indeed such a pity that you didn't explain these plans of yours to me sooner! I will let you go now, but Keira, you and I are going to have a little chat... very soon." Draven sounded utterly hacked off and in some ways I couldn't blame him. I mean, I'd had so many opportunities to tell him but every time I chickened out. He even asked me once what I usually did at Christmas.

It was one of those blissful mornings when we lay in bed together, entwined limbs and softly spoken words. He had asked me questions about my childhood and about holidays I'd had, places in the world I had seen and where I would like to go. All these had been easy to answer but when the conversation turned to my weeks off college, I had known all along that everyone but Draven expected me to be going home to England for the holidays.

"I will see you later then," I said deflated and for once, not looking forward to that later. I don't think he actually said goodbye but only repeated "Later" then hung up. The car was filled with an awkward silence, which I was perfectly happy enduring given the mood I was now in.

"I guess he wasn't happy about hearing that news," RJ stated the obvious and I had to drag my glare away from the back of Hilary's head to respond.

"Something like that," I muttered.

"Well, it wasn't my fault! You should be more honest with your boyfriends, shouldn't she Jack?" Hilary really didn't have a limit on the 'bitchometer', no it just kept getting higher and higher until one day, my guess was that someone would just outright murder her and her meter would be no more. I was still holding out for that day. Ok, so I wasn't really. I wouldn't actually want someone to kill my cousin, but I could settle for a damn good ass-kicking!

Jack didn't respond and I was more than thankful for that. RJ made me smile as she rolled her eyes at my cousin's statement and started talking about something my cousin couldn't contribute to, which was the dreamy drummer from the band Acid Criminals. RJ continued on about how they were coming back to town and were playing at Afterlife once again, but I just found myself nodding and "Oooing" and "Ahhing" at the right times.

This was all my fragile mind would allow. There wasn't much room for anything else besides the screaming inside my head that half wanted me to lash out at Hilary with a stiletto heel in hand or repeatedly keep slapping myself on the side of the head!

I didn't know who to blame the most...I mean, I knew who I wanted to blame but I couldn't. It had been my responsibility to tell Draven sooner rather than later and with only a week until I was supposed to leave, I knew that I was cutting it fine.

I guess deep down I didn't want to admit it to myself. I didn't want to leave Draven, but I was torn between what I wanted and what I should want. I should want to go back home and be a family for Christmas. I should want a little space from all the craziness my life had been enduring since I met Draven. All these things I should want, but I didn't.

As all I wanted for Christmas was Draven.

My Draven.

New Mistakes, Old Moves

To everyone in the theatre I must have seemed like the toughest girl in existence. I had sat through two hours of evil robots ripping the limbs of humans and mutilation so great that it sent a few people running from the movie with their hands held firmly over their mouths.

I hadn't even flinched. Of course, when you live a life seeing some of the most gruesome beings that walk the Earth along the same path as you, then it was very difficult to get squeamish at movie blood and special effects. The real thing was so very different. The smell, the sound and of course the sight your eyes absorb is an everlasting and unforgettable one.

However, these were none of the reasons why I hadn't reacted to the scenes on screen. No, the reasons all started with the letter D. The sound of disappointment in his voice was such a regular occurrence in my case, it made me wonder if I could do anything right in his world. Well, I was soon to find out because when coming out of the cinema, the first sight I saw was a shiny, sleek-looking black Ferrari.

I was no car freak but even I could tell that there was a Hell of a lot of zeros parked on the sidewalk and so could everyone else for that matter. Everyone coming out of the theatre was now struck down and staring at the black car like a space ship had just landed and I went bright red...Ferrari red.

"Oh... My... God!" Hilary said very slowly.

"You lucky bitch!" RJ said elegantly and Jack...

Well, Jack just whistled.

I watched on in horror as people started taking out their phones and snapping pictures. Some even rang their friends to tell them about the car they were seeing. Words like 'Ferrari Enzo', 'Over two hundred miles an hour' and 'Carbon fibre' filled the air.

There was even one guy surrounded with a group of friends all listening to him reel off stats and figures, as if he was Ferrari obsessed. But the one figure that everyone started whistling at was the price tag,

"A cool million dollars easy," he said while fishing around his bag for what was to be a digital camera.

As much as I loved seeing Draven, this was one moment when I just wanted to walk away. The windows were tinted as black as the body but that soon wasn't going to be enough to conceal the car's owner. The driver's side door open upwards giving the car the appearance of having wings...which just so happened to be very fitting for Draven's character.

He unfolded his body in a surprisingly graceful way considering his size. The little crowd gasped, and it now gave something for the girls to gawk at in awe.

He straightened his frame to reveal grey denim-covered legs, a tight black t-shirt underneath the world's sexiest jacket. It was maroon coloured leather that fitted him like liquid skin. It moulded to his perfect structure in the style of a biker's jacket.

Rounded at the neck was a thin collar that curved down with the zip that was off to one side. The whole jacket was framed with tan coloured piping and the sight of his arms made me try to swallow down the feelings that his body was causing to my own. I had an insane urge to walk over to him and start licking at his skin like a cat.

The leather strained over his biceps and just before the crease in his elbow was a thick line of piped maroon leather that went the other way round his arm like a band. The material went low down his arms and flared out at his wrists thanks to the zips that were loose at his forearms.

Holy mother of God, did he look sexy! I was close to hyperventilating, along with every other female that was also having improper thoughts about my boyfriend. But most striking of all was the face. Set in a honey-coloured stone of flawless skin was the deepest, darkest eyes anyone had ever witnessed.

A strong jaw flexed when our eyes met, and I knew he was angry. Draven did broody better than anyone on the planet and now was no exception. I knew this was coming and that was quite evident considering I had sat unnerved for two hours of body mutilation without wincing. Killer Robots from space had nothing on Draven's wrath!

Draven only took a few steps before he reached us as with his long muscular legs a few strides was all it took. As habit, one look from the owner of the prestigious nightclub Afterlife, the crowd dispersed and avoided his unhappy gaze. I wished I could have joined them. Meanwhile, Hilary had pushed in front of RJ so that she was next in line for when his look returned.

"Dominic, what a surprise, Kizzy Cat didn't say you were meeting us." The nickname I loathed made its way past her lips having an effect on me like barbed wire across my skin. I couldn't help my scowl, which Draven didn't miss. He never did.

"I am here to pick up Keira, We have a date...don't we?" After emphasizing my correct name, he made it very clear this was an order not a request, which I had no choice but agreeing to. I first had to clear my throat before answering.

"Umm, Ye...yes, I guess we do." I couldn't help speaking unsurely and this softened Draven's features slightly.

"Oh well, I guess you want to get as many dates in before she leaves you." Hilary's acid tongue whipped out and I wanted to growl but Draven beat me to it. Everyone looked shocked and Jack took a cautious step closer to me. Draven didn't like this one little bit.

I decided to try and defuse the situation before a real-life reconstruction of the movie we just saw was to happen. I took a step closer to Draven and looked up at him with big sloppy eyes that hopefully resembled a puppy. I just hoped he liked puppies.

"Hilary, you know I haven't yet decided anything about Christmas, I told you that earlier." Although I was speaking to my cousin, this was really aimed at Draven. I didn't really give two hoots about what my cousin thought, but Hell if she was going to use me to get closer to my man then I would do the same.

"And remember you saying that it would be nice if my parents were to finally meet my boyfriend and how Christmas would be the ideal opportunity?" I said smoothly which was amazing considering what a bad liar I was. Of course Draven would know this was lies, but the others didn't.

"Hey RJ, we gotta get going if we're going to meet the rest of the gang, but hey, Kaz, we will probably catch you later at the club," Jack commented while edging his sister away who hadn't yet spoken a word. She was still staring at Draven like a starving wolf would to a giant T-bone.

"That's cool, I will see you later, but is it alright to give Hilary a lift home?" I said.

"It's ok, why doesn't Dominic give me a ride and you go with Jack?" Hilary said shamelessly flicking her hair back and I wasn't the only one who looked utterly shocked. I turned to Jack and saw his face had numerous more lines, which looked out of place on Jack's 'happy go lucky' features.

He was looking at Hilary as though he was seeing her for the first time and he didn't like what he saw there. I couldn't help but feel for him, I mean there was a small part of me that wanted to scream out 'I told you so', but I was not the type that would have ever followed through with that impulse. It just made me hate her even more! She could hurt me all she wanted. Hell, I was close to being immune, but not Jack. Not my friend.

I was fuming but in the end it was Draven who cut her down into pieces and finally put her in her place. He leant into her and lowered his head slightly to get to her ear. I was next to him, so I heard every sharp edge to his words.

"It is only Keira that I want, and I will take her now. I suggest you leave, while you still have the kindness of others who are prepared to put up with you. I doubt your degrading act will hold much longer!" She had been holding her breath in the hopes of something else a close proximity could mean, but she was oh so wrong. I couldn't help but try and hide the biggest grin I had ever felt brewing.

For the first time since we were young children, Hilary looked like she wanted to cry and for the first time I couldn't find any sympathy for the emotion. She deserved far worse and I think way down, on some deeply buried level, she knew it too. She huffed once and turned away to follow Jack and his sister to his truck. I couldn't help but notice an action that looked as if she was wiping a tear from her face, which stopped me smiling.

"Keira, get in the car please." Draven's cool tone was direct and precise. It made me shudder. I turned around to realize he was no longer next to me but by the car door waiting. I was torn between giving in or making a run for it.

"I wouldn't even try...so, if you please." He finished by nodding to the low bucket seat.

"Fine!" I snapped, surrendering as I stormed over to the curb. I felt like I was bending over to such a degree that I was about to sit on the floor. It was the lowest car I had ever been in and no doubt the most expensive. I think if Draven ever sold his car collection, he could have bought Brazil with the funds received.

I jumped at the sound of the door slamming home and thought he had closed it with a little too much force for such an expensive car. I watched as he walked slowly around to the driver's side which reminded me of home as it was on the UK side. He slid into the seat that was positioned further back than my own, allowing for his impressive leg length. He didn't just start up the beast and let us go roaring off like I thought he would. He just sat there and lowered his head as though he was trying to find the best way of dealing with this.

"Draven I..."

"Do you want to leave me?" he blurted out as if he could no longer contain it. Almost like the idea of that question was burning a hole in his chest and he had to, no more like... needed to, stop the pain it caused. It was the first time I had ever seen Draven seem desperate.

"NO! I don't want to leave you!" I said forcefully. His head whipped round to look at me and once he read the truthfulness in my eyes his shoulders relaxed. It was only then that I took notice of the rest of his body. His hands had fisted around the steering wheel and the leather around his arms groaned under the strain. These all eased as he studied my face.

"Right...right," he said twice to himself before starting the car that started to vibrate around me in anticipation.

"Then you will not leave," he said as if it was final, and the conversation was now over, which it so wasn't.

"Draven you can't just say that, I..."

"And why not?! You do not want to leave me and therefore you are not going anywhere," he said in a fairly controlled manner.

"I have other commitments, I can't just..."

"You can and you WILL, that is final Keira!" He interrupted again and it was starting to get on my last nerve. This time he didn't wait for a response and pulled the car out with the speed and manoeuvring of a formula one driver. It did briefly make me wonder if he owned one of those as well.

"We are going to talk about this," I said trying to keep calm but with the speed he was doing I kind of felt as though I was having an argument on a rollercoaster.

"No, we are not!" he said simply and I felt as if I was being told off by a parent.

"Fine!" I said folding my arms like the child I felt. He took this entirely the wrong way.

"I am glad you see things my way for once, it is for the best."

"Draven, you mistake me, I said fine because if we are not going to discuss it then I will end up leaving and you will not know why, but that will be through your doing, not mine!" I barked at him causing his reactions to filter through to the Ferrari.

He sped up before applying the brakes and turning the wheel so that the car screeched across the road and snapped around facing the other way. I screamed out, which he ignored, and my hands flew out to brace myself on the dash and window as we continued spinning. It was like watching life in slow motion and I wondered if this was what happened to people in car accidents.

Did they have that moment when they waited for impact or did it just happen in the seconds time gave us? I found myself waiting for something, but I wasn't sure what. All I knew was when I opened my eyes that the car was now on the other side and we were hammering it down the empty road.

"Draven, pull over," I said surprisingly calm.

"What?"

"Pull over NOW!" I shouted giving calm the boot! I was glad that he didn't argue. We carried on until the road widened for us to pull over but even in those few minutes I hadn't regained any cool. He stopped the car and after undoing my seatbelt I tried to find the handle...unsuccessfully.

"Where the Hell is this bloody thing?" I waved my hands around in frustration as I lost the last shred of sanity. The door opened without being touched. I nearly fell out in my haste and my legs wobbled like jelly thanks to Draven's stunt driving. I used the car to steady myself until I ran out of frame and then I started walking. Okay, more like stomping.

"Keira! Keira stop!" Draven shouted after me, but he seemed to have his hands around me in the nanoseconds before his words hit me. I turned around and pushed him as hard as I could. Of course, it didn't cause his body to react to the pressure, but he did stop him trying to touch me.

"You Idiot! How dare you scare me like that! I will never get in the car with you ever again if that is how you are going to drive! Do you understand me?" I was screaming at him and if anyone were to drive past and see this, I had no doubt that it would probably find its way onto the front page of the town's newspaper.

Draven looked guilty as Hell for scaring me and when he tried to touch me again, I moved back.

"Don't!" I threw at him. He looked hurt but damn it, he deserved it!

"Keira, I am sorry for scaring you, but you have to know, no harm would have come to you."

"Oh right, Mr. Immortal! Look, you may be indestructible but I am not, so let's try and remember this fact alright, because the next time you want to drive like you're in a drag race I will be happy to stand on the side-lines and watch and survive. You get me?"

"You are so angry," he stated like this was some sort of shock.

"You're Goddamn right I am angry!" He frowned at my reference to God but I just said his name in warning and his brows smoothed.

"I understand and once again, I am sorry," he said in earnest and he tilted his head to catch my eyes that he found watering. I couldn't help it, I wasn't exactly crying but I was on the verge. I hated confrontation, but when I was this angry, I found it difficult to come back down from boiling point. My fists clenched and I gathered this was something we had in common.

"Would you like to hit me?" he asked me with no humour in his voice. He was serious? I looked up at him and he nodded towards my clenched fists.

"What? No!" I said.

"You look like you do. It's alright I don't mind, besides it may make you feel better. I could show you how, without hurting yourself." He was deadly serious and I almost burst out laughing.

"Draven, I'm not going to hit you."

"You hit me once before, remember?" He now had the slightest of smirks and I knew why.

"Yes and if I remember correctly we had sex soon after." Now he wore a full badass smile. He also took a step closer towards me making my heart rate hitch up a notch.

"A perk on my part, but just so you know, I am willing to sacrifice myself to the cause at any given moment, I can assure you." I bit my lip at the image he projected into my mind.

"I will let you beat me down, if you will only forgive me. It was an inexcusable mistake on my part and one that will not happen again." A man like Draven was not the type to make a habit of apologizing, so when it happened you didn't take it lightly. Besides, who could not respond to such an apology?

I looked down, which he didn't like. He hooked a finger under my chin and applied a little pressure to make me look back up at him. His head was tilted again, and his eyes penetrated mine like a fire was burning behind them. Of course, there was a burning, deep and full of emotions too hot to touch. They started to glow purple at the sight of me yielding. I was about to say something before he got carried away, but he didn't let me. He took my head in his hands and angled me to lock his lips with mine.

His kiss didn't start off soft and then deepen, no, this time he kissed me with such a fever-induced hunger that it took my breath away. His hands left my face and encircled my body so that he could lift me to his height. I was thankful because given the height difference my neck would have suffered from it. It was only when he knew my need for oxygen was growing did he let me go, rather reluctantly I might add.

"Am I forgiven?" he asked over my lips with his eyes closed.

"Yes," I whispered and although I couldn't see, I could feel his smile spread over mine.

"Then come, my little one," he said in a husky voice that was still thick with lust. He took my hand that seemed tiny encased in his and pulled me around so that I was facing the car. I decided at that moment that there was no point. I pulled back making him stop. He turned to face me and his look was full of questions he was about to ask but I just held up my hand.

"Look Draven, there's no point me coming with you if you're not going to listen to me. I am telling you that although I do not want to leave you, I will still have to go." He was about to argue and add words to his shaking head but I beat him to it. I came right up close to him and placed my hands on his chest. He started breathing hard.

"Dominic," I whispered his name making it sound right for once. He looked down at me, eyes full of an emotion I couldn't grasp.

"I never want to leave you, but I would not be the person you love if I didn't think of others before myself. It would hurt my family if I didn't go and I can't do that...not even for you." I held my breath after saying this last part and I could no longer look into his eyes, so they found my feet before carrying on,

"I have hurt them enough to last more than one lifetime and I will not add more guilt to my soul." I was speaking so quietly that anyone else would not have heard me. I also had tears rolling down my cheeks that I didn't want him to see.

"Catherine, look at me." The sound of my first name always made me shudder. As though he was seeing a different me standing here, one I was always trying to hide. I looked off to the side instead of braving his eyes. It was not enough for him. He decided that he would take the steps to change this. He got down on his knees so I was at his level.

I was in shock and I showed it. A man like Draven also does NOT get down on his knees for anyone! Well, evidently now he did.

"Draven don't." I tried to get him to get back up, but he shook his head. If anyone had been driving past now it would look like he was proposing to me and that would have made the front page for sure!

"I now understand why I must let you...let you go." He looked as though it actually caused him physical pain to say those words. I felt a hopelessness seep within me that no matter what choices I made in life, I kept making the wrong ones. No matter what I did I would have to hurt someone, but it felt like I would be hurting myself more than anyone. It was a strange feeling but it was almost like someone was telling me in the back of my mind that I was making the wrong decision. Maybe I was, but there was nothing I could do about it.

I let myself crumble down to his level which he let out a little moan about but before he could protest further I wrapped my arms around his neck and hugged onto him so tightly I could have been classed as a limpet. I kissed his neck twice and told him the three most important words in life.

"I love you." He groaned in response and kissed me back. The next thing I knew was that he had lifted us both to a standing position only my feet weren't exactly touching the ground. I giggled as he swung me around and my legs dangled in the air like a small child sat on a big chair.

"You're so little," he said teasingly as he set me back down.

"And you're a big oaf!" I said as my come back, which was received by raucous laughter. We walked back to the car and when I hesitated to get in he spoke in a guilty voice,

"It's alright, I won't go too fast."

My answer was given by getting in the car and soon we were making our way to Afterlife at a speed that only just broke the law. It looked as though it was causing Draven a great deal of concentration to maintain this speed and I had to suppress a satisfied smile. I could see by the natural road signs that we were near the turning for Afterlife. There was always a double twisted tree that had split in the middle and wound back together like brothers. This was my sign that we were near.

"There was something I wanted to ask you."

"You know that you can ask me anything." I smiled at his answer and thought if I wanted Draven to dress up in a furry loincloth and swing from trees like Tarzan, he would draw the line. I found myself biting my lip to stop from laughing.

"Is this 'something' funny?" he asked smiling as well.

"No, but I just had a funny thought. Ok, so I was going to ask you something about me leaving."

"Was?" He raised an eyebrow, an action that always made my heart flutter. It was so hard having a conversation with someone so unbelievably handsome it was hard enough to even concentrate on forming words in your brain let alone saying them.

"Well, I say was because that was before we...more like you, freaked out."

"Keira, I did not 'freak out' as you put it."

"Oh, you so did, but that's beside the point," I said poking at him only instead of getting a soft fleshy bit it was just solid muscle. Come to think of it, I don't think Draven had any soft and fleshy bits!

"The point then, my dear?" he prompted and turned around to face me. It was now that I realized we had stopped and were outside the secret wall that led to his garage/car museum.

"I want you to come with me." There, I had said it and now I could feel myself wincing ready for his answer.

"But of course," he answered as easily as that. I was shocked that I even shook my head slightly.

"Of course?" I repeated.

"Yes, Keira. Do you really think that I would let you go alone? I will buy the house next door if need be." He wasn't joking.

"I don't think that Mr. and Mrs. Sutton would be happy about selling, all their cats are buried in the garden and John worked forever on that vegetable patch."

"Keira, what are you talking about?"

"Prize turnips," I giggled making him see that I was teasing him again.

"You crazy human." He called me, trying to hide his smile. He turned back forward and lifted his hand to the stone wall. I had seen it a few times but I still jumped at the sight and sound of it moving back and sliding over. There it left a hole the size of a dumper truck and as we drove in slowly, I always felt as if I was entering the Bat Cave. Draven would have made an excellent Batman although in Demon form, he would be classed more as a birdman than bat and if you ask me birdman doesn't quite have the same ring to it.

"So, you're coming with me, even if you have to play 'Crazy Human' for a few weeks?" I asked getting excited about the idea. He whipped his head around so quickly, on any normal person it would have snapped off.

"You want me to spend it with you and your family?" O...k, what did he think I wanted him to do?

"Uh...yes? That's if you want to?" I was getting worried now. Maybe he didn't want to spend any more time around humans than he had to. After all, before he met me, he wasn't exactly our biggest fan.

"Of course, but I didn't think you would want me to...well, to invade on that part of your life." He was surprised that I wanted him to be a part of my family, how crazy was that!

"Well, I can't say it will be the life of luxury you're used to and my Mum won't let us sleep together, not until we're married that is..." Oh shit, I went too far... much too far with the speaking, Keira!

I bit down on my lip just below the point of it bursting open. I can't believe I had said the 'M' word around him! I felt like smacking my forehead, but I think this would have given away my view of marriage a little too much. I mean I could only just get my head around being Draven's girlfriend but...wife!

And then it struck me like an arrow to the heart at how that could never be.

Never, never be, all thanks to one little word...

Immortal.

CHAPTER FOURTY-NINE

HOBBIES

"Married?" he enquired, obviously amused thinking about it. His face had brightened, and his eyes were wider than I had ever seen them before.

"I didn't mean that! I just was explaining the rules," I hurried out.

"You said and I quote, 'Not until we're married'. So I think that constitutes as evidence of something you have been thinking about." He was so bloody smug!

"No I haven't," I said stubbornly making him laugh at me before saying,

"Yeah right," as he got out of the car and came around to my side to open my door.

"Stop smiling Draven, it does nothing for your badass image!" I said congratulating myself on what a great comeback that was. I took the hand he held just because I knew there was no way of getting out of this car gracefully without it. He tugged a little too hard not knowing his own strength or maybe he did because he caught me in his arms as I was flung towards his chest.

"No, but it does wonders for my Angel side," he said in the ear he was now nuzzling. His hand pressed on the small of my back and pulled my body even closer into his own, while his other hand ran up and rested on holding the back of my neck. My spine felt as though it had run off and left me. I was putty in his oh so capable hands.

"It is nice to know what you think about," he whispered in the sexiest voice imaginable and once again I was trying to think about how to breathe without panting. He was kissing up my neck and I soon found myself wedged between his solid body and carbon fibre. Luckily Ferraris seemed to be smooth and rounded enough not to dig in anywhere uncomfortable and I believed the marketing department for Ferrari didn't use this as enough of a selling point.

I mean, surely if men bought one of these they certainly knew they were going to get laid, so maybe they should roll with that. Sex on this car would not disappoint, but I could imagine Draven as a partner would even make a VW Beetle look sexy.

"You're thinking about my car," Draven said shocking my mind into shut down, fearful of what he could find there.

"You're projecting your thoughts, Keira, it's not hard to hear when you're shouting in your mind. Of course, I have no objection to listening to your sexual fantasies and with you being my first passion and collecting cars my second, I think combining the two would prove not only to be an incredible experience but also the limit on my frayed control. YOU drive me insane." He finished his evaluation by pushing me hard against the car and kissing me until my toes curled. His hands came up to remove my jacket and under my top, making me gasp as he took hold of my breasts in each strong hand, filling his palms with my bra covered mounds. He was breathing hard and he wasn't the only one finding there wasn't enough oxygen to fill our lungs.

"I want you now, Keira. I want to strip you naked and take you up against this machine, but I WILL lose control and I cannot allow that to happen." He was fighting with himself I could tell. His eyes were closed, and he had spoken through gritted teeth. He then released my breasts and took a new position.

He now had hold of the car either side of my head and when I shifted against him, accidentally... on purpose, I pressed against his need, I heard the sound of metal crunching, making me flinch. I turned my head slowly and saw there were now two hand-shaped dents in the car's roof thanks to Draven's pressure. The thought about how that could have been my head made me realize he hadn't been exaggerating about losing control.

"Draven, you hurt the car!" I shouted jokingly. This made him open his eyes and the purple flames started to fade. He raised an eyebrow and gave me a smug smile.

"I thought you didn't like this car."

"Not when it's at 'kill me' speeds but I do otherwise. Plus it's very comfortable for kissing against." He laughed but when his eyes flashed a brilliant, deep purple flame I knew he was thinking about something a little more than just kissing.

He placed his hands over the dents and soon the sound of the roof popping told me he had fixed it.

"See, all better and healed. Although, I don't think the car would have survived much more than me kissing you and I do like this car. It was given to me by Enzo's son, Piero Lardi Ferrari."

"Really? Is he like the owner or something?" I asked feeling completely out of my depth.

"No, he only owns ten per cent of the company." When I frowned he continued,

"He's his son from a mistress and was only made acceptable as his legal heir after the death of his wife. See that Ferrari there?" He pointed to a sleek red car that was a masterpiece in its own right. It was higher up than the rest and after following him, weaving in and out of all the parked vehicles he owned, I could see it better as it was up on a dais. Even I knew what car this was as it was such an icon.

"It's a Ferrari F40," I said making Draven's head incline towards me. He held a strange look, I think it was somewhere between pride and impressed.

"It is indeed and one of my most prized possessions. I was the first to buy one and it was presented to me by Enzo himself. It was the last car to be commissioned by him before his death and he knew that being 90 years old, it would be his last but he was proud to know at the time it was the fastest street-legal production car ever to be made."

"It figures," I said sarcastically and Draven laughed.

"What's that one over there?" I pointed to a little silver car that didn't have a roof and was numbered 130 at the front, side and back. The car had tartan on the seating and two red stripes at the rear of its wheel arch. Of course, to me it was just a nice kind of cute looking old car but what did grasp my interest was that, unlike any other car here, it was in a very large glass box with frosted symbols etched all around the base. I walked around and was about to touch the glass when a hand shot out and shackled my wrist.

"Don't!" Draven's warning was enough to make me retract my hand.

"Why, what's wrong, it's just a car...isn't it?"

Draven looked uncertain for a moment and then tried to replace it with a fake smile.

"It is." And that was all he said on the matter.

"Why did you name it Little Bastard?" I asked referring to the black writing at the back of the car which was situated under 'Porsche'.

"I didn't, his first owner did." Draven looked a bit disgusted which I didn't understand but as he was pulling me away, I quickly understood how this was one car he was not proud of owning. I had a million questions flooding my mind but the only question I asked was,

"His? I thought people usually associate cars as female?"

"I guess they do but with that car they would be wrong. It is most definitely male." He was not comfortable talking about this so I decided to let it go. Maybe I would ask Sophia some time.

"I suppose it's nice you have a hobby," I said lamely not knowing what else to say.

"Well, could you see me playing golf?" He joked and I burst out laughing. That was the last thing I could see him doing.

"Definitely not. But what was your hobby before cars were invented?" I asked feeling cocky which didn't last long when I got my answer.

"I also collect weapons," he said like it was collecting stamps.

"Of course, you do," I mumbled causing him to shoot me a smirk from the side. He then playfully tugged on my jacket and when I looked up he was now full out grinning.

"And what about you?" He looked genuinely interested.

"Me? Oh the same. You wanna see my axe collection, I bet it will beat yours any day." At this he burst out laughing and the sound filled my heart. I loved to hear him laugh.

"What a fierce little warrior you would have made," he said as he led me up a back staircase I'd been up a few times before.

"Are you mocking me?" I ran up a few steps ahead of him so that we were at the same height. He stopped as I poked at his chest and he folded his arms which always made him look twice as large as usual.

"I wouldn't dare, you frighten me too much," he said trying not to smirk again but doing a lousy job of it.

"I should think so and don't you forget it, Mister." I poked him in the nose this time, making him squint which was so funny to watch.

"Mister is it now...? Right, you asked for it!" I started backing up as he began stalking me, with my hands held up as if I was surrendering.

"Now, Draven behave, no playing on the stairs." I was starting to laugh and panic at the same time. He kept coming closer like I was his prey and the second I took my eyes off him I knew he would get me and win.

"It's too late for that, Keira." His eyes flashed once, twice and I decided to take my chance and turned just before he lunged for me. Of course I lost and when he grabbed me at the waist I half screamed and giggled like a little girl.

"Got ya!" he said as he scooped me up into his arms and ran the rest of the way up the stairs to the landing. Once at the top he threw me up in the air like I was a feather pillow and caught me before I hit the floor.

"Draven!" I squealed.

"Yes, my love?" he said calmly.

"You can put me down now, you cheated." He stopped walking.

"Cheated! How did I cheat?" he asked pretending that I had insulted him.

"You used powers I don't have and that's classed as cheating,"

I stated but he just grunted a laugh and continued down the hallway.

"Oh trust me, you have powers greater than mine, vixen." He didn't explain more, nor did he put me down. I was starting to think that Draven liked any excuse so that he could carry me, and I would never understand why.

"So you were telling me about your hobbies, your real ones?"

"Oh, well they're a bit lame compared to yours," I said shyly.

"Nothing you do could be lame," he said sweetly and when I didn't answer him, he gave me a little jiggle to get me to tell him.

"Okay, well... I used to collect postcards."

"You're right, that is lame," he teased.

"Oi, don't be mean." I tugged on his ear and his head went down but when I let go he kissed me and finished with an 'Oww' on my lips, it made me giggle, again.

"I am sorry and I was teasing you, it is not lame, it is sweet and endearing."

"Well, it's not that sweet and endearing as you didn't let me finish. I also collected rude and funny postcards." I stuck my chin out as if this was something to be proud of.

"Oh, you dark horse you!"

"I bet you collect horses too," I said as it was easy to imagine Draven upon horseback, in tight pants and riding boots...yum, yum, yum.

"I have many horses, yes, and most do tend to be dark." He was such a tease but I loved it when we were like this, all playful and relaxed.

"Show off!"

"Yes, yes I am," he said as though this was common knowledge. Of course, after today's Ferrari incident there was no getting around that image statement.

We were soon at his door, but I seemed to be the only one surprised when it opened with Sophia standing there waiting for us.

"Has Keira lost the use of her legs now?" Sophia asked frowning like I was some accident-prone fool...oh wait, almost forgot, *yes I was.*

"No, my little sister, she hasn't, I just enjoy carrying her," he said more seriously than I expected.

"Like a doll?" Sophia said with hands-on-hips as if this wasn't acceptable behaviour. He didn't answer right away, instead he let my legs slide down and then he smoothed my hair back from my face and kissed my forehead before saying,

"She is my doll, my beautiful porcelain doll that I want to play with, so please leave us." I bit my lip making Draven growl under his breath. My cheeks screamed out fuchsia pink at how embarrassed I was, but Sophia just huffed and folded her arms.

"And when do I get time to play with her, I hardly ever get to spend time with her now?" She was sulking and here we were so overwhelmed with the need to make love, if she didn't leave now, I was afraid we would do it in front of her!

"Sophia." Draven said her name as a warning, but she wasn't afraid like everyone else would have been.

"Dominic." She reflected back in the same tone. Draven growled again. At this rate I was willing to bet he was part animal as well as all the other stuff.

"Look, dear brother, there is a reason I am here, and it is to tell you that your other guests have started to arrive. So put down your dolly and leave her to me." She was playing of course...at least I really hoped so because in my experience with Sophia, if there was one thing she loved to do more than argue, that was to give this life-size doll a makeover.

"Dracu'!" (F**k in Romanian) Draven shouted and I froze.

"Now was there any need for that, really Dom?" His sister was acting shocked, but I could see the excitement in her features. She was a Demon after all. I bet she was just loving the drama.

"If I asked you not to work tonight, would you obey?"

"Obey?" I repeated the word he knew I hated hearing. I mean, if he wanted me to do something, then he sure was going about it the wrong way!

"Of course, I don't mean obey, more like... listen," he said in a softer tone and I knew he was trying new tactics.

"I will meet you halfway and work downstairs instead, alright?" He nodded and looked relieved, which made me wonder what type of guests he had turning up that had him glad I wasn't around. I doubted they were super friendly out of town family members that was for sure!

"Thank you. I will come to get you when all is well. Sophia will see you downstairs when you are ready." Of course, I would need a babysitter to make sure I obeyed, I thought bitterly. He read my expression.

"It is for both my peace of mind and your security," he said, while running the back of his hand down my cheek. I only raised my face once to show that I understood but he knew I didn't like it. I thought I could at least be trusted to make my way downstairs without hitting trouble.

"Good girl, have I told you today how I love you?" He looked down at me waiting for my smile and he didn't have to wait long. When I looked around, I noted Sophia in the background sticking her fingers down her throat pretending to barf. Draven's head snapped round to glare at his sister.

"Excuse me, Romeo, but I believe they're waiting," she said after clearing her throat.

"Let them wait!" he roared, showing his full authority on the matter. It made my skin heat up and tingle at the sight. Then he turned around and took me in his arms to kiss me like he never wanted to stop. I don't even know how long Sophia had to stand there and wait but by the time he released me I was panting and bright red from shame that someone had been witnessing it. He didn't care though. It was as if he felt it was the most natural thing in the world for him to express how he felt about me in front of his siblings... and everyone else for that matter. I loved that he never acted ashamed of me or tried to hide the fact that we were together.

"Later, my Vixen," he said by way of goodbye and I was sure he said this to get to see even more colour invade my cheeks. His smile told me I was right. I felt hot and flustered until he left the room which instantly made me feel the opposite...

Cold and lost without him.

CHAPTER FIFTY

FIGHTING DEMONS AND ALMOST KISSING ANGELS

Sophia waited with me like a good little girlfriend sitter until it was time for my shift. I had taken a shower and got ready under the watchful eye of my fashion muse and when I emerged from the bathroom wearing faded, light blue jeans and a long-sleeved, black stretchy top she just shook her head.

"What?"

"Why you insist on wearing shades rather than actual colours is beyond me. Black makes you look very pale," she said with the knowledge that she was definitely more experienced in this department.

"I am pale," was my only reply. I walked over to the couch that Draven had broken not long ago but the next morning I had made him fix it because that couch had good memories for me. Very nice memories indeed.

"You're smiling to yourself again, Keira." Sophia would have an idea what I was smiling about I was sure of it. I didn't say a word, but I did stick out my tongue at her like I was five. She loved it!

I then grabbed my long fingerless gloves off the back of the couch where I had put them before getting in the shower. I tried not to notice the way Sophia always eyed my scars as I pulled my sleeves up to put my gloves on.

It was a mixture of pity, which I hated, and admiration to what I had been through. Draven had no doubt told his siblings about my tragic little story because he shared everything with them. Hell, Vincent had even witnessed it himself when he tuned into my memories once. It was back when they needed to know what Morgan was up to and finding out that he had teamed up with some heavyweight Demon big wig named Sammael.

Sophia was sat on the desk looking at her nails, acting bored by the time I was ready. She saw me reach for the door and jumped as lightly as a cat to the floor to accompany me. We were walking silently down the hallway when I remembered a question I wanted to ask her.

"What's with that car in the glass box?"

"Has Dom told you about it?" she asked with a bemused look on her delicate features.

"Umm...not exactly." She raised her eyebrows at me.

"Well alright, No he hasn't, but I was kinda hoping you would." I gave her a pleading look I was used to working on Draven.

"Sorry, but no dice. Ha, don't look at me like that. Anyway, why do you want to know so badly?"

"Because he won't tell me," I answered honestly.

"Well, that makes sense." She didn't elaborate. I soon realized she wasn't going to spill the dirt on the car's history, so I gave up. Maybe I would Google it later and see what I'd come up with.

We parted at the door of the staircase I usually took to get up to the VIP. Of course, my two favourite doormen were there ready to greet me.

"Evening," they both said at not only the same time but also in the same tone. I had to suppress a giggle.

The club wasn't yet full but for a town that had very little on the entertainment side, it usually got quite busy for a Sunday night. The band had started to set up and I knew by the time they were ready to play their first song the dance floor would be packed. It was like the calm before the storm and I noticed Mike at the bar stocking up ready for that storm.

We had offers on at the moment for cocktails and Mike had been showing me how to make the most popular ones. The Woo Woo was a big hit, along with Sex on the Beach. If I were to pick one, the Long Island Iced Tea was the winner, but that was down to the alcohol content not that it had any form of tea in it! Two of those and I would be wearing my knickers on my head and singing Dolly Parton with a hairbrush microphone!

That's what I had been doing, making cocktails not dancing naked, when the "Gang" walked in with the added addition of Hilary the 'Evil Queen Bitch Bee.' Well, at least that little drilling from Draven had tainted that permanent smirk she always wore. I would have to remind myself to thank him later for that.

"Kaz, hey can we talk?" Jack's desperate voice broke my thoughts. He had wedged himself in between two people I was serving but given his size they didn't want to argue. Jack wasn't small, in fact he was at least six foot and had wide shoulders and a physique that backed up his love of rock climbing and hiking. He was wearing a black t-shirt that said "Clowns are the lowest form of wit" in white writing across the chest. I had to smile. I knew for a fact RJ had bought this for him as she knew he hated clowns with a passion. The film 'IT' was not on his top ten greatest films list!

His hand leant in and took mine which caused a few people to stare at me like my head had just done a three-sixty and I had puked green stuff.

"Uh yeah, sure, but it will have to be later though," I said not being able to help the blush that tinted my cheeks. He winked at me and let go of my hand to move with the others. Hilary had watched the whole thing with an even greater hatred burning in her eyes. I couldn't help but notice how Jack avoided her gaze and took a wide birth of where she was stood. Was I missing something? Trouble in the pits of Hell by any chance? I couldn't really say "paradise" as that word didn't mix with Hilary.

The rest of the night I spent wondering what Jack wanted to tell me so badly and also having this nagging feeling that something horrible was going to happen when I found out. The night was in full swing when Mike came up to me after doing a round of collecting glasses.

"Hey Kaz, I think you should know there's some commotion coming from your friends' usual booth. Your cousin looks a little wasted and there's a lot of shouting." Oh great! Hello something horrible.

"Okay, I will deal with it. Will you be alright if I leave you for a little bit?"

"Yeah, no worries, the bar's calmed down now, you go and good luck." Wishing me good luck told me that he wasn't exaggerating the situation. Here we go again I thought, as I made my way through the thick crowd of headbanging Goths. It was only when I got closer to our usual booth that I could hear what was being said. Of course, when I heard my name I stopped. I decided to hear this out and I ducked out of sight and stood by the staircase hidden, so that I could hear the rest of it.

"My God, you have all been suckered in by her little innocent act! Did you seriously all really think she just had some sort of pathetic cold-blooded disease?"

"What are you talking about?" Lanie asked quietly and I was surprised it wasn't from RJ.

"Hilary don't!" This was Jack's warning but why would she listen to him at the crucial point of trying to ruin me. I was in two minds to stop this, but I found I didn't care anymore. I just had to know how far she would go to kill me off.

"I'm talking about the long sleeves, those horrible gloves she never takes off and about her trying to hide what she did!" She was almost laughing, like it felt so good to be the one to spill all my life's dark little secrets. At that moment I felt sorry for her and how sad it all was.

"Hilary, she told us it was bad circulation and we don't need to know any more than that!" RJ said and I wanted to hug her for it. Hilary was losing her audience, but I don't think she even cared anymore. She wanted the glory of it, even if the reaction would not be to the full extent.

"Don't be naive. Isn't it obvious to you all, she... tried... to...

kill... herself!" She said each word slowly for that extra bit of drama.

Most of them gasped...all except Jack.

"Shut the fuck up!" Jack shouted out and it was always an odd thing to hear Jack getting angry, like it was going against nature.

"Oh, fuck off, Jack! Of course, you're going to believe all her lies, you're still in love with the silly cow. What did she tell you, some sappy little story about her being kidnapped...oh please...I thought you were smarter than that! She is a manipulating little bitch who tried to kill herself after a man who didn't love her had sex with her and left!" My mouth dropped at this point and I felt bile start to rise from my belly.

"No!" Jack said still defending me.

"Yes! A poor teacher who got his life ruined because she couldn't take rejection, so she came up with this idea that he kidnapped her and raped her. Of course, he gets to spend the rest of his days rotting in jail thanks to a girl you all call friend!" And there it was, my life in her eyes...suddenly I didn't feel so sorry for her, oh no, now I just wanted to rip her head off!

I stepped into view just as Jack was fighting my corner, the rest saw me, but Jack still had his back to me.

"That's not true, you spiteful bitch! I was told what really happened and it was proven to be true!" Bless him, but he'd obviously done his research, it was of course all over the internet...if you knew where to look that was.

Any other time this news would have mortified me but right now it seemed it was in my favour. Hilary hadn't been expecting that I had told anyone, let alone they would have found out the truth themselves. Considering all options she was looking pretty stumped for someone that had been so confident just seconds ago.

It was at this moment that Hilary looked past Jack and spotted me. The rage must have shown on my face because for a moment she looked frightened. Jack noticed her reaction and turned to face me. He was red-faced and pissed off as Hell but when he saw my face it turned quickly to one emotion.

God, I hated pity.

That's when I didn't say anything. I just let action take over. I walked past Jack calmly and stood motionless in front of my cousin looking at her with God only knows what expression. I was feeling so many emotions it was hard to pinpoint just one.

"What, what are you going to do, bitch?!" she spat out down at me with her arms held out. I wiped the spray very calmly from my face before reacting. I turned my body back which must have looked to everyone that I was turning to leave...which there was no way in Hell I was!

I pulled my fisted hand back making sure my thumb was tucked over my fingers, my arm held back like a slingshot ready to fire. I remember seeing her sniggering face as I turned back, quickly turn to shock before my fist came in to contact with her face. I could feel her nose crumple beneath my knuckles and then her body fell backwards and crashed to the floor.

"That, you bitter bitch!" I shouted down at her. She covered her nose with her hands, and it wasn't long before I noticed the blood pumping from between her fingers. I looked at my hand that was still fisted and yep, it too had blood on it.

"You broke my nose, you whore!" she shouted back with a gargle as some of the blood must have been dripping into her mouth. I wrinkled my nose at her in disgust and shook my head.

"You're pathetic! You really are. I have had to put up with your shit for far too long, so count yourself lucky I didn't break more than your Goddamn nose!" I fumed at her as she tried to get back up.

"You see, this is what she does! This is the real her! She's a destructive little parasite that craves attention!" Man, what did she want me to do...kill her! She had regained her legs and was waving her hands to make her point. This just made more blood flow freely from a nasty gash I had given her on the bridge of her nose.

"You won't ever stop, will you? You won't until you take everything from me, fine if that's what it takes!" I had lost all control now and I yanked up my sleeves and was ripping my gloves down my arms. I heard every single person staring at me gasp at the sight of my butchered arms. I threw my gloves at her and she flinched at them like they would sting her. It was the first time she had seen the result of my past and I think it caused her pain to see… to really see.

"Right, well this is what you wanted, isn't it! You wanted to see me humiliated then we might as well go all the way! Come on Hilary, join in, add your part of the story, tell them how I did this to myself to DIE! Oh no, we can't let them know the truth, that I did this to save myself from a mad man who was not only going to kill me but also my family! THIS IS WHAT YOU WANTED, ISN'T IT?" I was screaming now and thankfully my friends had circled us to hide us both from view of the club.

"SAY IT!" I screamed in her face when she didn't respond.

"Y...yes," she whispered like a frightened child. She was also now crying and couldn't stop looking at my arms. Well, if it was hitting home it didn't register, I was too far gone for that.

"WHAT?" I held my hand up to my ear and turned my head.

"Come on, Hilary, WE CAN'T FUCKING HEAR YOU!" I roared.

"YES!" she shouted back and that was when I lost all control. I launched myself at her like a bear. I think Leivic would have been proud.

My mind was a red mist of twisted pain that made no sense of anything, no action my body made was coming from reason. We were on the ground and I had hold of fists full of her hair that I was pulling back. She wasn't exactly defenceless, and she fought back with everything she had. I felt the contact her knee made in my face and felt my lip burst against my teeth. But the strange thing was is that it wasn't pain I was feeling, no… it was pure, raw adrenaline.

Her hand was on my face and as someone was trying to part us her nail scratched down my cheek and neck. I was like a possessed wild cat and I bent over double trying to get free from somebody's strong arms wrapped around me to get back at her.

"LET ME GO!" I screamed at my back, but I still couldn't see who it was, although I assumed it was Jack, but man he was strong. I looked up to see the damage I had done to Hilary's face and I was glad to report it looked worse than mine felt.

She had blood covering the lower half of her face and a nasty red lump under one eye. Her hair was stuck up on one side and her top was torn at the shoulder, there was also a scratch there that I didn't even remember doing. It was only then that I noticed Jack had her in a locked hold at the wrists that were crossed over her torso. Ok, so if Jack was holding her then who was holding me?

"Stop struggling, Keira, and I will let you go." Vincent's cool calm voice floated down my neck making me shiver. There was something about Vincent that made you realize very quickly he had an 'I might be calm but don't fuck with me' type voice. I relaxed in his arms and in turn, he relaxed his.

"This is over between us, Hilary, do you understand? No more!" I said turning to walk off, but she wasn't satisfied with the beating we'd both just had.

"The Hell it is bitch! I won't be happy until I have taken everything from you, like you have done to me, including me fucking your rich ass boyfriend!" I actually laughed before I ran back to her and hit her one last time, which knocked her for ten. She was out cold in Jack's arms and I felt absolutely no remorse. Vincent grabbed my arms back just in case I decided to take it a step too far, although I think I'd already done that.

"Enough!" he shouted at me and I nodded in agreement. Jack bent slightly to hold all her weight as she had slumped backwards.

"Can you take care of her?" Vincent asked Jack taking full control of the matter and for once I was just glad it was an Angel watching my back, seeing as he was blessed with more patience than either of his siblings.

"Yes, but who are you?" Jack was watching the position of Vincent's hands with wary interest. I think his look prompted his grip to tighten in a protective reflex.

"She is safe with me. I am Vincent Draven." He announced this in a way that matched his brother's authority head-on. It sounded strange and out of character for Vincent to act so coldly, but I guessed he didn't like being questioned by a mere mortal boy.

I also wondered if he knew me and Jack kind of had history of sorts and if this was the reason for his distaste. I also found it strange to think of him as a Draven. To me he had always been

Vincent or the more playful Vinnie when I was drunk! Either way it was weird to hear it said aloud.

I pulled myself out of my absurd thinking and noticed how all of my friends were sort of frozen in shock at seeing him for the first time. RJ looked as though she was about to throw herself down in front of him as a self-sacrificing 'wannabe' virgin. Everyone else just looked scared of us both. I suppose for such a shy girl they hadn't expected me to turn into a demented lunatic, 'one flew over the cuckoo's nest' style.

Any other time and I would have turned scarlet and fled from the room. I wasn't one for centre of attention at the best of times but right now, right at this second, I just didn't give a damn. Everyone was waiting for me to speak, I knew that, but I didn't want to explain and from what everyone had just witnessed, I knew I certainly didn't have to justify my actions. So I said the only thing that came to mind.

"Jack, can you take her home?" I asked quietly and he agreed by way of a sympathetic look.

"Thanks," I muttered as I then let Vincent walk me away. It was as though he knew I'd had enough, but he still had hold of the top of my arm like he was scared if he let me go I would go back there and kill her. My voice was devoid of emotion which wasn't like me, but I was tired. I was tired of feeling a shame I didn't deserve and a fault that wasn't my own. But most of all, a guilt that just wasn't warranted. I was just very, very tired.

"You can let go now," I said in an exasperated voice.

"I don't think so, I tried that before and now someone's unconscious." His voice could only be described as controlled calm.

"Yes, but the right person," I pointed out, cocking my head to the side out of habit. He didn't reply to that one, instead he just directed me to the door that led to the VIP. I really didn't want Draven to see me like this and it made me wonder if he knew anything about what had happened. But more importantly, if he knew then why was Vincent down here?

I didn't ask but that was mostly because we were right next to the stage so hearing any answer he gave me was just not going to happen. The doormen eyed me as if it was the first time they had ever seen me. I suppose I wasn't looking too hot right now.

Once through the solid wooden door the music changed to a background hum and Vincent's hand dropped from holding my arm to smooth its way down the length to take my hand in his. I held my breath all the way down.

He was now walking in front of me with our bodies linked by entwined fingers. I was led upstairs but when faced with the two doors in front of me I knew which one I wanted to take. Thankfully, he knew it too. One led into the VIP area and the other onto a long outside corridor which bypassed the VIP to get into the home part of the nightclub.

"You don't want to go in there, do you?" Vincent stopped before opening door number one.

"Not yet, no," I answered simply.

"I can feel that. Come with me." He turned around me brushing against my body and I followed his movements because he still had my hand tightly encased in his. I don't know why but it was only at this moment I realized that my sleeves were still pushed up my arms and my gloves weren't concealing them like they usually were.

This was when my shame actually hit me. I knew the numbness wouldn't last long and when it finally came, it would slam into me like the sea does a body falling from the clifftop. How could I face anyone again?

"Are you in pain?" Vincent's soft voice broke through my personal desolation and when I looked up from the scars I'd only just focused on, I realized we were outside of sorts. I was stood on the open hallway and the winter air hit me making me shiver. I was sure Vincent asked me something about pain and I looked up to find him stood very close, looking down at me with an odd expression.

"Yes...No, I…" Was that even an answer I had given him? I wasn't sure.

"I can feel your pain, Keira, but I don't know that it's only physical." I thought about that for a moment. He could feel me? I also took this moment to assess myself. I flexed my hands and my right one hurt when doing so. A sharp pain across my knuckles penetrated to the bone but I didn't need any guessing as to why that was.

I must have sucked in air because Vincent noted my movements and the sound of pain I had expressed. He took my right hand in his and examined it with a great deal of care. He frowned and before I could ask, the hallway illuminated from the moonlit glow to a warm, flaming orange. The wrought iron lamps on the walls were aflame from just a nod of his head. I almost gasped at how beautiful he was. Like a living statue of the Archangel Michael.

He reminded me of a fountain I had seen once in Paris as a child. The statue stood at the top of the fountain in the Place Saint-Michel. The Boulevard Saint-Michel is one of the two major streets in the Latin Quarter of Paris. This was as far as I remembered from one of my many educational trips my parents took us on. Our family vacations always had some historical learning factor to play, not that I minded of course but Libby did tend to get a bit bored.

"Keira, what are you staring at?" he asked me softly and yep, I was staring at him as though he was some ancient oil painting created by the masters of his time. I looked down quickly and muttered a barely audible,

"Nothing."

"I think you have cracked a knuckle, but I can't be sure, bend it this way." He was holding my hand like a breakable antique and he moved my fingers individually, when I felt the pain in my middle finger I yelped, and he groaned.

"Dom is not going to be happy about this, what were you thinking?" He accused me and I yanked my hand from his despite the pain in doing so.

"I have pride, Vincent, just like any other!" I snapped at him without daring to meet his crystal blue eyes.

"Was it worth it?" he asked me, keeping his voice so neutral it was close to being without feeling.

"Without a doubt!" I answered honestly. Damn right it had been worth it!

"It still affects you greatly, doesn't it?" It wasn't really a question, more of a statement that I wanted to play dumb too.

"I don't know what you're talking about," I said moving away from him but as I started to walk the other way, I was blocked by a pale arm coated in solid ripples of muscle. They tensed under the flames that cast shadows along the stone wall his palm was pressed against.

"I think you do, and I think you're afraid when you no longer need to be." This time I did face him, as if to prove him wrong about that fear. In his face I found my lies. Because, he was right, I was afraid.

"Your brother can't protect me from everything."

"I...We can and we will." He looked as though he had wanted to say something else but stopped himself. I started to shake my head and without thinking, rubbed my arms that were still on show.

"You can't protect me from myself... no one can." At this, a single tear rolled down my cheek and stung my skin as it touched on the scratch my cousin had given me. Vincent took a deep breath and took hold of my hands that had started to scratch away at my scars. He moved them away and replaced them with long pale fingers that touched each scarred line as gentle as a butterfly.

"You have to let go of your past, Keira. These scars you hold onto are only skin deep, they do not connect to your heart or your soul. These scars do not define you, *you define them*. They do not represent death and destruction as you think but they represent life, the very life you chose to want to live...So... make it worth it." He said this last part leaning his head down so he could look deep into my eyes, holding me prisoner. His voice was like someone wrapping a warm blanket around me, when I was standing in the snow. I was still looking down at my feet and when I saw my hair blowing around my waist I realized Hilary must have pulled it down earlier.

I felt Vincent's finger curl under my chin and raise my face up to his. He was stood so close now that he was mere inches away. Our chests rose and fell in sync with each other as our eyes met. When his hands came up to hold my face, my breath hitched. My God, he made me nervous.

"No tears," he whispered, and he smoothed his thumbs under my eyes and down my cheeks to take the tears away.

"What are we going to do with you, my girl?" he said smiling down at me. Vincent wasn't as tall as his brother, but he was still a whole head above me. Actually there wasn't anything about the two brothers that was remotely similar. Vincent looked like the Angel he was. Pale luminous skin that was framed with a halo of golden blonde short curls that looked almost childlike. His features were strong like a white knight, with high cheekbones and a long straight nose. His chin wasn't as square as his brother's which gave him more of an oval face. And the most striking aspect were those lips, being a dark contrast to his face with a natural red pigment tinting them, reminding me of an apple you just wanted to bite into.

"I guess I'm a mess," I admitted.

"Don't worry, it takes more than a bruised eye and a few scratches to keep the beauty from touching you, but I can't account for my brother's reactions at seeing you less than perfect, he is..." He let out an exasperated sigh before carrying on,

"...very possessive when it comes to what belongs to him." This was said in a confusingly sad way which I didn't understand. Of course, I blushed at the compliment.

"Blushing won't help, my dear," he said in a very sultry way that made me shudder.

"Are you cold?" Before I could even answer he pulled me into his arms and started rubbing my back that quickly created warmth from his actions.

"I'm ok," I said timidly at being held so close.

"I'm going to have to heal you...is that alright?" He pulled me back a little to judge my expression but still kept me held to him.

"I thought that was against the rules?" I asked.

"Deep wounds need our essence. Sometimes our blood can heal them, but superficial wounds can be healed by just the right touch." He had moved me, so my back was flush against the wall and speaking while examining the damage. His fingers stroked the column of my neck before his other hand joined it by holding the whole length of my neck steady. He could feel me gulp down my anxiety at being held by the throat, so he cocked his head and winked at me.

"Relax, I won't hurt you, sweetheart." His words invaded my mind like a black cloud coating all my fears in the darkness so that I couldn't see them, couldn't feel them. I decided to close my eyes to add to the effect.

"Just breathe, beautiful." I could hear the smile in his comfort. So I did as I was told. I took a deep breath and relaxed as I exhaled it. That's when I felt it. The tingling cool air that began to caress the skin on my neck. I could feel his fingers grip my top and pull it to one side to reveal more of the mark that Hilary had left there.

His head leaned in so close until his lips hung over the mark, almost as if he was about to take a bite right out of me. I felt the cool air come from him and enter my pores, reminding me of the time that Ragnar had healed the cut on my knee from my fall on the stairs. If anyone were to walk in on us now it would look as if Vincent was trying to give me a love bite.

It didn't take long until my neck went a little numb and Vincent let go of his hold. I opened my eyes to find him now casually brushing off the dried blood from my skin. It felt like someone had just sprayed me with liquid nitrogen.

"Was it good for you?" He laughed at himself, making me follow suit. I couldn't help but smile at his kindness and warmth.

"Behave!" I said, as one of the most unserious warnings possible but it made him laugh harder.

"Around you, that will be difficult." I couldn't believe how openly he was flirting with me.

"I thought there was only one bad boy in the family," I teased.

"You thought wrong." He winked again and his eyes flashed a bright blue that was startling to witness. It was like I was watching the waves of the ocean through his eyes.

"Let's see what we can do about this lip of yours." I couldn't help but take a step back, but I quickly found I had nowhere to go. I couldn't help my reaction. I mean, having Vincent so close to my neck was one thing, but my lips! My mind kept going back to that night when we had kissed, and my heart thundered in my chest.

"I think it will be fine," I said quickly causing a trademark

Draven brother bad boy grin to invade his lips...ok, so I take it back, they obviously did have a few things in common.

"Normally, I would agree with you, but considering how much you bite your lip when nervous I don't think it would last the night. And from what I have gathered for myself, I do believe my brother is fond of those lips of yours." Ok, so now I was beetroot red.

"You shouldn't be flirting with me," I bravely said and he raised one blonde, amused eyebrow at me.

"Me flirting? I am shocked you think this. I was merely stating facts, that's all. Besides...Angels don't flirt." He was now teasing me and I tried not to smile at his playfulness.

"Oh no? I guess they don't bullshit either." I was now sporting a full-on smirk after that comeback and he was trying very hard not to do the same.

"But of course not... that wouldn't be very angelic of me now would it? Of course, my father is a Demon, so I am bound to have a streak or two." He winked again and took a deciding step closer.

"Now stop stalling and let's fix you up before Dom gets anxious about your whereabouts." He sounded both seriously demanding and vivacious at the same time. Whichever he meant, I did as I was told.

"Close your eyes," he ordered gently and as soon as I did his palm covered my left eye which I gathered was the bruised one. He didn't apply much pressure, but I could feel the heat building, making little beads of sweat form on my forehead.

It was stranger than the sensation had been on my neck, like some deep heat therapy was being used. Then I noticed his head had moved very close to mine as I could feel his breath on my cheek. This time we weren't inches away but millimetres. One small action from either of us and we would be touching.

I started to see red spots behind my eyes and as if I had told him so, the feeling of heat stopped, and his hand moved away allowing my skin to breathe in the cool night air again. He might have moved his hand away, but his lips were now directly over my own and I was terrified if I moved even one tiny muscle, there would be contact. The tension of our situation was building like a tightly wound mechanical toy and any second one of us would let go and allow its inbuilt reaction to be released.

"Don't move. Hold very still for a moment as this might feel strange." Strange! This whole night couldn't get any stranger! Here I was after just beating the crap out of my cousin, outside on a magically lit hallway with my boyfriend's brother, who was so close to kissing me, it felt strangely right amongst a night full of so wrong.

NO! I couldn't think like that, what was I thinking? It was just from the effect of all this craziness in the air, that's all, nothing to it!

I was still mentally scolding myself when I felt the same cold air hit my lips with the force that felt like the pressure of his lips. I flinched when it happened, and Vincent's hands whipped out faster than my action and grabbed the tops of my arms to hold me still.

His lips hung over mine like a tempting well to a dying man who just wanted to drown in its cool liquid. I could smell them and almost taste the air that passed over them. It was sweet like honey and cold like an ice cube had just been held to my mouth to suck. I even had to resist the urge to do so. Minutes seemed frozen and it felt as though I was lost in a labyrinth of time.

"There, all better... although a little flustered." I opened my eyes to find a safer distance between us and Vincent's features could only be described as cocky.

"Uh um...I...uh...thanks," I said reverting back to shy, safe Keira.

"Oh you're more than welcome. It was an honour to almost kiss you, one I doubt I will forget as soon as I know I should do." He looked away to the sky when he spoke and just before I could say anything that might comfort the regret in his voice, he turned to me suddenly and took my hand.

"Come, I need to get you back to my brother. I can feel him waiting and his impatience is growing." I didn't doubt that for a second knowing Draven. However, I still wanted to say something to Vincent, but I didn't know how, so instead I showed him.

I pulled back on his arm, making him stop and look at me. I didn't give him chance to protest. I threw myself into him and wrapped my arms around his body which made his every muscle tense. I didn't care, I just wanted to explain, but this was the only way that felt right. I then lifted myself up on my tiptoes and put my lips to his cheek to kiss him lightly. Once there I whispered in his ear...

"Thank you, Vincent, it was great for me."

CHAPTER FIFTY-ONE

ALL FOR THE HEALING

Vincent and I didn't say another word to each other as he escorted me back into the VIP. The first thing I noticed was Draven pacing like a wild animal, back and forth by the balcony. We walked round to meet him, and I started to see all the unfamiliar faces that made up Draven's guests. I don't know why, maybe because I wasn't yet used to them, but they all seemed a lot scarier than the last lot.

One table we passed looked like they wanted to first play with me and then devour me. A girl with bright orange hair even licked her cherry lips as I went by making me shudder.

Draven spotted us immediately and the harsh eyes and tense jaw told me he had really been waiting. He stormed towards us, now wearing a very power inducing black suit. Everything on him was black apart from a very deep purple tie that brought out the purple now in his eyes. He was not happy.

"Where have you been?!" At first I thought he was asking me, but he was looking over my head, which wasn't hard given my lack of height. His gaze burned into his brother's, who stood calmly behind me.

"Calm yourself, Dom, she is fine. She just got herself into some trouble," Vincent said in the most lucid way possible. I wanted to shout back 'Traitor' to him, but I doubt the timing would have been right.

"Tell me!" was all he said but his words sounded as if they had been skimmed through acid first.

"It was nothing," I spoke up, feeling as this was about me, I might as well have some say on the matter. He glowered down at me, but he didn't reply, instead he raised a finger to my lips and shook his head. This was all the warning I needed. When Draven was this far gone it was sometimes best to let the beast calm down before pulling on its tail.

"She got into an altercation with her cousin." He was choosing his words very decidedly, which I appreciated.

"I will kill the bitch!" Draven shouted, shocking me enough to make my mouth form an unattractive "O". He turned as if he was about to do it right then when Vincent's hand shot out and restrained him back.

"Keira attacked her, Dom," Vincent said, as though he was trying hard not to smile. I'm glad to report he achieved it because I don't think I could have stopped myself sticking my tongue out at him. Draven stopped dead and Vincent's hand dropped now he knew his brother wasn't about to run off to kill a 'not so' innocent human girl.

"She what?" Draven sounded as though the wind had been knocked out of him.

"I went down to get Keira as you asked and found her on top of her cousin, pounding her fists into her head and trying to rip out her hair." Vincent said this like reciting poetry. Personally, I don't think it was as bad as he made out. I mean, for starters I had only been trying to rip out a handful not the whole lot. But I guess tomato, tomato!

"Was she hurt?" he asked seriously as he now started scanning my face and body for injury.

"Excuse me...I'm right here!" I said getting inpatient. Draven growled down at me and I rolled my eyes once and shut up.

"She received a scratch down her neck, a bruised eye and a cut lip." Ok, so now it was like he was reading off an inventory. Draven made me jump by placing his hands on my neck and turning me this way and that to see for himself. He traced where every mark had been as though it was still visible, which I knew it wasn't.

"You healed her yourself?" Draven's cold question frightened me. Would he be angry?

"Yes, she was in pain and I didn't think you would want her walking in here like that." This was one Hell of an interrogation.

"Your actions were right. Although I would want to heal her myself, that would not have been practical at this time. You did well, brother. I would not have been pleased if anyone else had touched her." Draven was speaking as though the reason for this conversation wasn't stood next to him. I felt like slipping out from them both and making my escape.

"Well, if you two will excuse me, I think I will get a drink." I was about to slide out from the Draven sandwich I was currently in when Draven's hand gripped my waist in a very primal way.

"Stay!" was all he needed to say or more like growl in this case.

"Okey, dokey," I replied quietly as he slid me back in place.

"And what of the cousin?" he inquired.

"Bloody, bruised and beaten. She fought well, brother." Oh jeez wasn't I just the star pupil? It felt as though I was in some weird, supernatural parent-teacher conference.

Draven looked down at me and took my hand in his.

"Good girl, I am proud of you," he said before squeezing my hand, that was my right hand that had the 'maybe' broken knuckle. I yelped in pain and Draven snarled letting go of the pressure but not my hand. He lifted it to examine.

"Ah yes, well, I meant to tell you about that. Naturally, she hurt her fist in the beating process and that I could not heal...without..." He didn't need to finish, evidently Draven got it.

"Yes, I understand. I would not have permitted that. I will fix it myself," he stated in his usual masterful manner. Vincent made his move to leave, but Draven spoke again putting full weight into his next command.

"Give me your hand, brother." Draven asked Vincent who looked as though he had expected what was about to happen. I was being moved to stand by Draven's side while Vincent stepped forward to place his hand in Draven's. They both closed their eyes and I could just make out the faint flickering under their lids, almost as if they were watching something.

I was waiting for a reaction I could never predict but he did startle me again when something he saw made a rumble ripple its way up through his chest. I was moving backwards slowly trying to get away from whatever it was, but his hand snapped out and stopped me without even opening his eyes. It was as if he could feel every move I made.

Although I was breathing hard and scared of his next reaction, the hand that held on to my wrist started to sooth his thumb around in circles to put me at ease. Then he spoke but I didn't know what.

"Vous êtes le seul homme qui j'ai confiance pour toucher son de cette manière sans avoir besoin de vous tuer à cause de cela » ("You are the only man I trust to touch her this way without the need to kill you because of it." In French)

Draven's words, even though in perfect French tongue had been icy cold, even I could tell that without knowing the meaning behind them. If I was a betting woman, I would put money on the fact that Draven had just seen all that Vincent had, including him healing me. One thought...oh shit!

Draven let go of his hand and instead of hitting him like it looked he wanted to do, he shocked me and grabbed him behind the neck and pulled his forehead closer to touch his own.

"Frater", ("My brother" In Latin) he whispered, and Vincent repeated the word. It was such a touching moment that I found my eyes tearing at the sight of such a strong unbreakable bond. This action was the very translation of the word Brother. A love that didn't need words to describe, it was just enough, singled and defined by its purity. It made me realize just how much strength the word Brother had. Brother at arms, Brotherhoods and Blood Brothers all had the same thing in common...they all represent men as comrades.

My feelings must have been giving off signals as bright as Las Vegas because when I looked up they were both looking down at me with odd expressions painted on their handsome faces.

"What?" I said burning red.

"Viena veida" Vincent said ("One of a kind" In Latvian)

"Yes, she is." Draven said beaming with a pride I didn't know the cause of.

"Hello, right here remember!" I said getting fed up of the mixture of languages I would never understand and the conversation that was going on above my short head!

"Oh I know. I would never forget that, my little one." Vincent smirked at my given pet name and I scowled making them both laugh.

"I will leave you alone a moment," his brother said bowing his head slightly to us both, a sign of deep respect. Draven then took my wrist in his oversized hand making me feel like the doll his sister joked about me being earlier.

I felt so breakable in his grip that I should have been scared by it not turned on as I was. He gently led me to the balcony and took off his suit jacket before letting the doors open even though I was touching them. He eased the soft fabric over my shoulders and then led me through the doors into the cold, late November night.

"Are you alright?" he asked me without looking at my face. He was still behind me holding my shoulders from where he had placed the jacket.

"I'm fi..."

"Please don't say fine. Not to me Keira, trust me enough not to placate me with 'fine'." He interrupted before I could say the word that he knew was not true.

"What do you want to hear me say, Draven?" I said regretting how snappy it sounded.

"I want to hear you say how you actually feel and not what you know I want to hear." Well, he was being honest maybe I could be too.

"You're not going to like it," I reminded him before committing to anything.

"I'm a big boy," he mocked impatiently.

"Yes a very angry big boy." He waved his hand around dismissing this notion without words.

"Alright, but don't get mad, ok?" He nodded keeping his lips in a firm line.

"I feel guilty, I hate myself for what I did and I'm ashamed for what everyone saw. I don't know if I can face any of my friends again now they know the truth about my past and I don't want the pity that comes with it. I HATE pity! And now they have something to pity me for, I can't stand it. I want to bury myself in a hole and never come out. It's…it's like when I found out you knew all about my past and how I wanted to hide that from you forever and if there was any way I could take the information back, then that would be one of my three wishes!" I was almost left breathless by the time I had finished my little explosion of feelings. I mean can anyone say information overkill.

Draven was left looking astounded at my outburst and now I found myself adding to my long list of regrets. He was trying to search for the words to comfort me, but from a bombshell of emotions like that he had too many options to choose. I doubted he knew where to start. Hell, even I didn't!

"I don't think you express your feelings to me enough. You obviously feel an overwhelming need to shut everyone out where your problems are concerned, myself included, but what I don't understand is, why?"

"Why?" I repeated stupidly.

"Yes, Why? Why is it you feel the need to keep all these feelings locked away in a place where I am supposed to hold the key? You make me feel quite useless and that is not a feeling I am accustomed to. I only want to help you but I can only do that when you let me."

"But you do help me. You help me by just being with me. I don't feel like this all the time, Draven. Most of the time I am blissfully happy and that is thanks to you. I guess I should have been more prepared that this was coming. My cousin's hatred for me knows no boundaries." I was stood facing him, hugging myself taking little steps back every time he took a step towards me. I didn't want his touch because I knew with it I wouldn't be able to carry on this conversation.

"Where do you think her hate stems from?" I was surprised by his question...didn't he know?

"I thought you were the mind-reading expert, you tell me." I shrugged my shoulders and let them slump back down with a sigh. He turned away for a moment so I couldn't see his face and I didn't know if this was a deliberate act or not. Was he hiding something?

He still had his back to me giving me a fantastic view. His wide back looked huge thanks to the black waistcoat that pulled tight across his muscles and then there was his perfect behind that looked like you could bounce nickels off it. I was close to drooling by the time he spoke.

"I think her hate goes back to a time when her father left but that was all I got from her. Her mind is too far gone and consumed by a pain and rage even she is confused. If she does not know her own mind, then neither can I. I cannot read what she can't see, but I have tried." This was not a shocking revelation. I knew Draven would have tried to find a reason for her behaviour and I was only sorry that he didn't find one.

"Do you still have that file on my past?" I asked, making him turn back to me in surprise.

"Yes, but I don't understand...*why?*"

"Because I think I might need it to get answers." Draven just lowered his head as acceptance. He didn't like it, but he wasn't going to argue.

"Let me see that hand." He beckoned me to him with his hand and I found myself moving without thinking. I gave him what he wanted and placed my injured hand in his. He held me with such care it was surprising how gentle such a warrior could be. Then I winced.

"The knuckle is broken. See how it is sunken in. The knuckle is the end part of the metacarpal bone, here." He showed me on my other hand and continued to explain it to me in detail. It was like having a consultation with a real doctor and I had to admit I was impressed.

"Since when did you go to medical school?" I mocked laughing, which made him flash me a brilliant white smile that would have made any dentist fall in love.

"I have always studied medicine, even in its infancy."

"Are you like...qualified?" I asked wondering if a game of doctors and nurses would ever happen. He raised an eyebrow at my giggle.

"I have my doctorate if that is what you mean." I couldn't help it, my mouth actually fell open.

"Are you really surprised, Keira? I am an educated man, who has had a lot of time on his hands and have not spent all of it fighting battles and waging wars like you may think." He looked a little offended as he said this.

"Hey, I didn't say that but come on, this coming from the man who said himself that he collects weapons as a hobby, so cut me some slack. I didn't know you also collected degrees!" I finished sarcastically, crossing my arms. Draven now looked amused and it was becoming increasingly difficult to keep up...was he happy? Was he mad? Was I crazy?

"I suppose there is still a lot we need to learn about each other. I know of your love for the arts but did you know about my own passion for the same subject?" This was difficult to imagine for all the wrong reasons. I knew that I was stereotyping Draven in a sense, but it was hard to picture him sat reading Finnegan's Wake by candlelight and going to art galleries on his days off to admire Andy Warhol's Campbell's Soup Can or Claude Monet's the Lily pond.

"Now I do," I said looking down at my hand that was once more trapped in his. He decided to change the subject.

"This might sting a little," he said and when I reacted by trying to move my hand from his he merely tightened his grip. Before I could utter a word of protest, he lifted it to his mouth and bit down on me hard enough for me to shriek in pain.

"Draven, what are you...!" I was struggling to get free when he just looked up at me over my hand with piercing, dark eyes. He watched mine widen in horror at the sight of him latched onto me like...well, like a Vampire.

I could feel his teeth retract from my flesh, but his lips stayed enclosed around the holes they had just made. He then seemed quite happy continuing to suck the blood from me, making the act strangely erotic. He had bitten me just below the knuckle closest to my thumb on the soft fleshy part and I couldn't help but release a moan.

He started walking my body backwards and pushed me up against the wall to restrain me from struggling further. Once my back was flush against the stone, he let his blood-soaked lips leave my skin. It wasn't hurting anymore and after the initial shock the only pain had been his teeth popping into my flesh. He licked my blood from his lips as though the taste was a fine cognac he had just experienced.

"Mmm, utterly divine…even your blood is honey-sweet. Now hold still for me." He'd closed his eyes and then flashed them open when speaking the command. I just nodded my frightened head. He let one finger trail down my cheek.

"Don't look so scared, little one, I won't bite you again…well, not tonight anyway." He finished by winking at me before plunging those same fangs into his own hand without taking his eyes from mine. It made me scream.

"Ssshh now," he soothed, after releasing himself. I looked down and saw a large tear across his palm the full length, as if he had just given himself another lifeline. His flesh looked like it had been torn with a jagged edge as it made a zigzag where he had pulled his teeth along it. I flinched and wrinkled my nose showing my distaste.

"Doesn't it hurt?" I asked, now being the one to cradle his large hand in both of my own. I watched in sick fascination as his blood pooled in his palm before overflowing onto my finger and dripping to the floor. Was I expecting his blood to somehow be different? His grin brought me back to the question I asked.

"I do not feel pain like you do. It is more awareness than anything else." Oh, well kudos to you I thought sarcastically.

"Close your eyes, this will feel…odd." I did as I was told almost immediately as Draven placed his open wound on top of mine. I was struck by five different sensations all within minutes of each other and each one stealing the breath from out of me. I tensed every muscle I had as the first wave shook me…it was pain. It shocked me as if I was being burned from the inside out. It was like flames had ignited in my bones and was licking at the inside of my skin.

"Keira, please sweetheart, try to relax." His voice sounded strained and I realised he was gripping my hand against my force to remove it.

Thankfully the pain died very quickly and gave way to other feelings in its stead. The burning was diminished by a freezing cold that seem to spread like icy tentacles up my arm. It didn't hurt but it wasn't what I would call pleasant.

The next wave after the chill to course through my body could only be described as energy. It replaced the cold tremors and turned it into an energy that was filling me up, racing through my veins like morphine. It made me feel strong, so strong that I had to fight the urge to tense my bicep and test it. I wanted to plough my fist into something but then I almost laughed out loud as that was what had got me into this position in the first place...since when I had I become so violent?

With my thoughts running riot, I must have been reacting because Draven had tightened his grip just before the point of it being painfully broken.

"Try not to struggle, my girl," he said and though the words were kind they came through as firm and determined. Was I making this hard on him? I decided to relax or at least try to. Of course, when the energy travelled up my arm and seemed to disappear in my heart, I let out a sigh. I wanted it back, that strength it gave me almost like a taste of a drug so rare I didn't know whether I would ever feel it again.

Then I realised that it wasn't the first time I had felt its presence. When I thought about it, it was actually a common occurrence. I thought about the aftermath of every time we had sex and yes there it was, only a diluted variation.

I wondered if Draven knew about this. This energy he seemed to transfer into me and this immense power of his that he would force into me. One that made me feel a little stronger before collapsing into an ecstasy induced slumber.

That was what was kind of happening now, the feeling you get when you know you don't have long before you erupt into the most blissful abyss of an orgasm. I don't know how it happened. It came out from somewhere deep within me that was like a creature lurking in my belly waiting to show itself in all its ferocity. One minute I was feeling like Supergirl and the next my legs were quivering with the need to sink to my knees and curl up and convulse.

And then BAM, the last stage hit me, and I did just that! I came so violently, I lost my legs and let my body give way to gravity. Of course, Sir Isaac Newton didn't account for the Dravens of the world to be there to defy it. He caught me in his arms and was gently lowering me to the ground instead of letting me fall and no doubt injuring me further. Although, after that last bit of the experience it would have been worth a bump to the head!

Not surprisingly I was panting. I could now completely understand why he hadn't wanted Vincent to do that to me. Not only did my hand feel fine but as a result my body felt like someone had injected me with sunshine. I felt fantastic!

Draven still had his arms around me as I seemed to be in a crouching position by the wall. I sure was glad no-one at that moment decided to get some fresh air, or they would have encountered more than they bargained for.

"Are you alright?" Draven's voice hummed in my ear causing the last exotic shudder to come racing up my spine. I jerked in his arms making him pull me tighter into his frame. I could only nod at his question. I think he could tell I wasn't in the right frame of mind to form words just yet, so he just smoothed back my hair and held his lips to the back of my head. His other hand held my face under his chin and he only relaxed when our breathing was in sync. I pulled back to look at him.

"Did you know that would happen?" I asked.

"I did," he said unquestionably.

"Right, well next time you do that I think we should be on a bed," I said full of lightheaded humour.

"Next time?" He raised a perfectly shaped eyebrow before continuing,

"Tell me Keira, are you planning on joining a fight club any time soon or are you just referring to your utter lack of self-preservation and inability to take care of yourself?" He was jesting with me I know but I acted insulted.

"Let me get this right...you're saying you don't think I can take care of myself?" I said putting my hands on hips after he had helped me up, an action that didn't help my case.

"If the shoe fits," he said looking blasé with a smidgen of amusement.

"Well, I have made it this far and I'm still in one piece." Now I was smiling because I knew what his comeback would be.

"Ah yes, thanks to a few patch ups by yours truly." His eyes lit up at the challenge giving off little sparks of purple. That was the thing with Draven's eyes. Real strong emotions brought out their true colour. Of course, when he was turned on they were at their brightest.

"Well, that's nothing, just like having an MOT in my case. Besides I don't have health insurance and I don't have the money to pay for the health care here, so I guess you're good for some things." I couldn't help but laugh at his expression. Shock mixed with the need for a cunning come back played with his perfect features.

"Oh, is that all I'm good for?" He grinned at me making me bite my bottom lip.

"Umm...I guess you're a good kisser," I teased again making him growl.

"Oh and the sex isn't bad." I continued trying so hard not to laugh it almost hurt. His growl got deeper, and I could see the playful beast in him come to the surface.

"You know, I will have to punish you for all those statements you just made," he said stalking towards me and pinning me to the wall for a very different reason this time. His arms looked tense, like they wanted to rip their way through the black material that encased them. He held each hand flat against the wall behind either side of my head and ducked his head to my level but could only reach as far as my forehead. I couldn't help but gulp with the intimidation he was projecting.

"Oh... that's ok, because I don't think you're very good at that either," I mocked laughing nervously but I was soon shut up by the slap I received to my backside.

"AHH!" I shrieked out in surprise.

"Hey!" I said looking up to see his evil grin and cocky eyes. It hadn't really hurt but just shocked me. If truth be told it actually felt quite nice, in a sexual way. Not too hard but firm enough to be told who was in control. Pain morphing into pleasure.

"You were saying?" he said as if he had won a round and was back in the control he was used to having.

"Haven't you ever heard about Karma?"

"Yes and I believe you just received it, although my guess is that you enjoyed it so maybe it doesn't count, or maybe you just need an increased dose," he replied dropping his hand by his side and pulling it back as if ready to do it again. I pushed my bum against the wall and held it with both hands saying,

"Don't you dare!" At this he roared with laughter, throwing his head back as it came thick and fast. Then like lightning he had both my back cheeks in two hands and raised me up, so I slid up the wall to his level.

"I will have my way with you!" he said with his voice guttural and thick with lust.

"Not now you won't," I said being smug, although I wished that he could. My want was burning a hole inside me the size of Texas!

"And why is that, my Vixen?" he asked, spoken like a true lover.

"Because Draven, that Karma I just spoke of has come around to bite you in the ass." I put my hands on either side of his face and turned it to whisper the last part in his ear...

"Because you have guests."

CHAPTER FIFTY-TWO

NEW PEOPLE BRING NEW HATE

He groaned unhappily and I laughed in his locked embrace. His hands still had their firm hold on my cheeks and his need to have me was pressing deep.

"You think being King would mean I could do what I want, when I WANT!" He bellowed this last part towards the door, and it was one of my first glimpses seeing Draven being spoilt. I couldn't help it...I laughed again.

"And may I enquire what it is you find so amusing?" He sounded pissed off but one look at my smiling face and it was hard for him to stay that way.

"You're acting like someone is about to take your favourite toy away and send you to your room without supper," I said through half bursts of giggles. He gave me a grumble and a dark look before easing into a half-smile.

"You are my favourite toy, my doll, and I do not ever want to let you go."

"But you must," I said with a sigh.

"Must I?" He raised an eyebrow, one of Draven's regular expressions that made my toes curl.

"Well, like I said, you do have guests." His hands inadvertently held on to me tighter, making me groan from the desire that shot through me with the action.

"Make more noises like that and I never will," he warned in my ear and then began kissing my neck to prove his point. I loved how Draven never wanted to leave me. I got such a thrill from the hold I had over him. This was my power and although compared to Draven's, it was at the lower end of the scale, it was still there, and it was still mighty. Or so his growing erection told me!

He worked his way around from my neck and kissed me deep and intense. As if he was on an expedition to discover every last bit of my mouth. He didn't have his hands free as they were still holding me up from behind, but I could tell where they wanted to be. I, on the other hand, wrapped my arms up and around his neck, this being easier, as now we were at the same height.

I ran my fingers through his hair, which I knew drove him crazy. I grabbed handfuls and tugged slightly at my impatience to have more of him, Hell, I wanted every last bit of him. All there was to give.

He moaned in my mouth as he fought with himself to keep control. What was I doing? I knew we needed to be back inside but this game was just too damn good to give up playing. It was a bit like taunting a wild beast through the bars of a cage, any minute now they would rip through the steel like hot claws through butter and I wouldn't be able to hold him back.

Most of me didn't want to. I would have given anything to shut down that part of me that was screaming reason. I knew I was keeping Draven from something important and I knew I would have loved to have continued to be selfish but that wasn't who I was. So very reluctantly, I let go of his soft, midnight black hair and tried to put an end to his raging desires... and mine. No surprises he released a low growl.

"What it is you do to me? You burn my soul and set alight my veins, only to douse them out in the seas of your reason. If only I had your will, I would be the strongest being alive." This last bit of his declaration sounded bitter. He let me slide down the length of him and the strain in his suit pants looked almost painful. If only he knew how painful it was for me to see it and to know it would be hours before I could embrace it with my own body of want.

"Well, if you think for one second this is easy for me, then you don't know me at all," I said in a hoarse whisper.

"Good to know," he replied with a grin before adding,

"Very well then, if I must then I must."

"I'll be waiting," I said raising my eyes as though I was some helpless little puppy he was about to leave. Ok, so I wasn't making this very easy on him. He looked down at me and traced the line of my jaw with a featherlight touch.

"What did I ever do to deserve such beauty in my life, I will never know but I will be thankful of it for the rest of my days," he said with closed eyes and I looked down at the compliment, flushed and embarrassed.

"You will get used to it one day and see the beauty in yourself, as I do but for now, I will content myself with the delectable rose blush that blooms in place of its pride." He was smiling and I was turning from rose to a less poetic beetroot. Now he was laughing at the changes in colour, obviously enjoying my responses with a little too much enthusiasm. I pushed him lightly and then in a playful manner gave him a coy smile.

"Draven, I do believe you are stalling."

"Guilty as charged but given the inducement, do you blame me?" He winked and I giggled like a schoolgirl. He was such a flirt. No flirt wasn't the right word. It wasn't a strong enough word, more like sexually dangerous and downright sinful.

"Right time to go and play host, Draven."

"Are you not coming? I could escort you back to our bedchamber," he said innocently enough that anyone who didn't know him would have thought these words from a choir boy.

"Oh no, I'm not falling for that one! Put me and you in the same room as a bed and we're bound to fall into it," I remarked confidently.

"Or be pushed," he teased making me smile.

"Besides, I think I'll stay out here a little longer, I need the air." He knew my full meaning behind it and laughed heartily.

"Me and you both. Very well, I will go but do not stay out here for too much longer, it is cold." I nodded and started to remove his jacket, but he shook his head.

"No please keep it. I want to know at least part of me is wrapped around you." He leant down placing the tips of his fingers under my chin and kissed me lightly on the lips as if not daring to go any deeper in case he lost all control.

"When you have finished here, please go straight to our room, many of my new guests do not know of you yet and need to be warned. Will you wait for me?" I nodded making him drop his hold under my chin.

"Good girl. Till later then." One more quick kiss and he was gone.

I stood on the balcony trying to catch my breath in the cold night. It was so peaceful despite the evening's events. I tried to process everything that had happened and although it was easier to deal with guilt and regret, I found it hard to fully feel those emotions freely. I was glad that I was strong enough not to care for once in my life. I was glad that I had stood up for what I believed in, no matter what the consequences.

Well, at least one thing was for sure, Jack was no longer fooled, and I had a feeling he would make those feelings known to me soon enough. I could almost see the sorrow pouring out of his eyes as he stood holding my limp cousin in his arms. It also looked as though he would have liked to have swapped places with Vincent and be the one holding me. Of course, all of this meant that sooner or later I was going to have to have it out with my cousin and when it happened, I would just have to pray for control. I couldn't let myself get like that again.

I took a deep breath and felt better when the icy air shocked my body. The night was so crisp and clear, my breath looked like smoke. I shuddered and pulled Draven's jacket closer around my body breathing in his scent. I could have passed out taking in so much. It was like nothing I had ever encountered before. So distinct, so manly, I could have bathed in it and found sexual release from it alone.

I wasn't sure how long I stood out there, going over and over in my mind the different possibilities tonight had caused. But when I'd had too much of persecuting myself to the point of purgatory, I decided enough was enough. I turned on my heels and made my way back inside.

The doors opened to a buzzing nightlife of such an array of characters that my eyes were like saucers taking everything in. Some so normal looking they could have been people waiting at the bus stop to get home from work. Others looked as if they had just walked off a monster movie set! Although I wasn't allowing myself to see their true nature, (as I think I would have been scared shitless) they were still frightening in their own right. Mostly down to the eyes and the clothes they wore.

On one table, they were all wearing long black jackets, like highway robbers from the Wild West. Although they were without the cowboy hats, they still managed to keep hold of the leather pointed toed boots that were tipped with silver. All five of them had beards only in different styles. Some plaited, others twisted into two points. One had his so long that it rested on the table next to his drink. It was quite ironic seeing as none of them had even one single hair on their smooth, bald heads.

Another table was made up of all women, which up until now had been unusual for the VIP. They were utterly and stomach wrenchingly beautiful. They all wore very dressy evening gowns that made the VIP seem as though it had turned into a cruise liner for the evening.

Almost every female had their best dress on, I was sure. Suddenly I felt like running back onto the balcony and dealing with the cold for the night. It would have been easier than standing there feeling like the pauper amongst kings and queens. I looked down at myself and almost felt so plain that I would disappear at any moment.

Thankfully, I had taken Draven's jacket off before walking in here or it would have looked as if I had stolen it from someone. Despite being massive on me, it was obviously something I would never have been able to afford. After all I was still just a waitress. Draven's fortune didn't affect me in the slightest. I wasn't with him for money and the fact that I wouldn't let him buy me anything was more fun because I got to see his aggravated expression.

I had it folded over my arm and decided to leave it at the bar in case he needed it for any reason. Karmun seemed to have his hands full and I was in two minds whether or not to give him a hand. He had multiple trays all lined up ready to be picked up by the constant stream of waitresses coming to collect. There seemed to be a few more additions for tonight, and I felt left out. I mean, I understood that Draven wanted me to be safe, but what would happen...another Layla incident? I didn't think so.

"Hey honey, I didn't know you were still here?" I don't know why but he sounded both shocked and strained when he said this. It was odd coming from him. I put it down to the extra stress of the night. It wasn't usually this busy up here which made me realise that downstairs was very quiet in comparison, which was usually the other way around. I turned around briefly and noticed the lights downstairs were out and there wasn't a body in sight. At that moment, an unwelcome shudder crept up my spine like spiders crawling under my skin and skipping along my spine. I shook my head, but the fear didn't leave me as realisation hit...

I was now the only human left.

"Yeah, still here but hey you look like you could use a hand, let me..."

"NO...! Umm sorry, sorry...but you know what my Lord said, you were not to work up here tonight and I would not like to make him unhappy. Besides it's calming now, you go..." He looked around nervously and he seemed very twitchy, as if Draven was watching him or something. I shrugged it off and decided to give up. At least he knew I had offered.

"Okay, well could you get his jacket back to him, I think I'm going to call it a night." At this mundane news he seemed to relax more, and he even managed a smile at me.

"Yeah sure, no problem. Have a good sleep, won't you?" he said, like he wasn't only talking to me...weird. Again, I put it down to his stressful situation.

"Uh yeah...will do, see ya," I replied warily.

I turned around and lost my footing which brought me

screaming back to the first time I had ever set foot in the VIP and like that night I fell into a Demon.

My foot kind of crumpled underneath my ankle forcing all my body weight to one side. Unfortunately for me, that was the side of one of Draven's guests who was walking past. I crashed into him and put my hands out to stop myself from falling further, only in doing so they gripped onto a body I had never seen before.

I was just righting myself when my body was suddenly flung backwards in a violent, swift movement of an arm whipping out and catching me in the ribcage. It momentarily knocked the wind from me and left me gasping. I had ungracefully landed on my butt and was wondering if it would leave a nasty bruise when a booming voice came from above me.

"How dare you touch me, you vile human bitch! Someone should teach you manners you disgusting parasite...GO and fuck off!" A man in a pin-striped suit was now dusting himself off as if I had infected him with my human girly germs!

I couldn't believe he had just spoken to me like that! How dare he? The audacity of the man! I didn't give a shit whether he was a Demon or not, I wanted to claw at his shiny, expensive blue suit and rip it to shreds with my bare hands.

Everyone was now staring, and I was scowling so hard it was hurting my face. I'd had just about enough of this night and being put down by people! I got up despite all the warning glares I received but then I stopped and really looked around... wait a minute...those glares weren't directed at me after all. No, they were directed at him. And soon, I knew why...

I turned to see the scariest sight any human eyes could witness. Draven stood by his chair and had witnessed everything. Then without any warning, an almighty roar ripped out from him in a bloodcurdling way that made my knees shake. Silence rode the room like a plague-infested wave among every person there.

It was at the end of the most horrific sound ever known to man, one that was enough to make your ears want to bleed, that Draven crashed his fists down onto the table and split it clean in two. Bottles, glasses and anything that was using the surface went cascading down into the middle to meet the rest of the destruction.

I didn't really have time to take in the fear that no doubt was held in every person's eyes just like mine. This was because in the seconds all this happened it only took a second more before the suited man was being held up in the air by his throat, with Draven's hand firmly enclosed around it.

Draven stood so tall before me it was as if he had grown even bigger in the height of his rage. The suited man was left dangling and gasping for air as Draven's hand grew tighter to cut off the noise. For a second I thought he had killed him without another thought.

"HOW DARE YOU TOUCH HER!" He roared and then erupted into his full Demon side. There was no purple glow, just the burning red hot flames of raw hate powered energy. I had only seen this side of him once before and that was when Morgan had me firmly in his grasp. Of course, I remembered how that ended but would he really go that far again?

"Mmmyyyy...L...L...Lord" He was trying desperately to speak but Draven's hand was acting as though it had a mind of its own. It was enjoying causing the pain and it squeezed again, only this time it caused the dangling man's eyes to haemorrhage. I thought I was going to be sick at the sight. Blood was actually dripping down his face.

"I WILL KILL YOU!" Draven had lost so much of the man I loved I didn't know who it was I was looking at. Was he really in there somewhere? Somewhere deep down like he was being held captive there until the beast was finished. His wings were now just feathered flames that fanned out and licked at the air around them.

"I...I...I...di..didn't...k..k..kkknnnnoooww" He screamed out in pain using the last shred of breath he had left.

"THEN YOU WILL BE PUNISHED FOR YOUR IGNORANCE!" His Demon voice took over and made it near impossible to detect anything I knew from memory. That's when the man started to die, and this was when I couldn't take any more.

"NO!" I screamed, causing everyone in the club to gasp at the same time. Draven's head turned around without even giving an inch to allow the man some breath. I mean, yeah, I had hated him only minutes ago, but nobody deserved to die because of the incident and I most certainly didn't want it on my head!

Draven's look made me want to literally cry with fear. It was so lost in the pit of damnation that I couldn't tell if he could actually see me! I don't know how I managed to carry on but somewhere I found the bravery that even I was shocked at finding.

"Draven please...I am begging you, please...please just let him go." I had an odd kind of aching in my voice that took me back to the first time I had heard it. It was my pleading for life. It was something I vowed I would never do again in front of another human being...But I was no longer dealing with human beings, now was I?

"Did you hear that, DOG! The girl is begging for your life! The very girl you shoved to the ground like nothing but shit beneath your shoe. And here she stands, at the mouth of Hell, begging me to save your pathetic soul when you have done NOTHING to earn such pity! WHAT HAVE YOU TO SAY!" He lost it again and I had to raise my trembling hands to cover my ears that couldn't take anymore.

The man was just gargling and spurting to try and form words but with Draven's unwavering strength there wasn't a chance. Just how much could he take? I knew one thing for sure, if he'd been human, he would have been dead the second his feet were off the ground. It had already looked as if Draven had broken his neck in several places. Bone was jutting out at two different angles and every time he tried to speak, it bobbed up and down painfully.

"SPEAK!" Draven barked out the order as his last thread of patience had snapped. I knew it wouldn't be long until it would be too late, and I would never look at Draven the same way ever again.

"Draven stop this! He can't speak for God's sake!" I yelled at him with floods of tears streaming down my face. At the mention of God everyone gasped and Draven's eyes flashed round to seek mine once more. They looked like the pits of Hell lived there, like a portal straight to the gates were right past those eyes.

"I AM GOD'S RULING HERE!" He said first to me and then to the rest of the room that were witnessing this side of their

Master. I held my head in my hands and let out a series of sobs mixed with words like 'Please' and 'Let go' making something in my actions enough to get through to my Draven. I heard a thud before me and when I lifted my head, I was now faced with the broken man in a pile at my feet. I couldn't help but flinch back.

"BEG!" One command came past his lips that I could not imagine kissing again. Would I ever make it past this point...? Far, far past the point of no return? I responded by shaking my head, but the words wouldn't surface through my shaky tears.

"BEG the 'Chosen One' for your life!" Draven's voice cut through me as though I was being split in two. I didn't think I would ever be pieced back together after this. At the name 'Chosen One' everyone took a step back from me like I held some horrible disease. They all sucked in air that wasn't needed and their eyes all turned Demonic like someone had just flipped a switch... that someone was Draven.

Most looked terrified of me, one girl even dropped the glass she had been holding. I jumped at the sound of it smashing into tiny pieces on this cold stone floor that I just wanted to swallow me whole. Demonic and Angelic eyes all burned into me, bright and unwavering. I thought about them in the night, in this darkness my mind was swimming in, and their eyes were all I could see.

"No...no, no, no," I repeated over and over, but it was as if no-one was hearing me. I wondered if I was even saying the words or just screaming them in my head.

"Pl...please...for..for...forgive mmme." The man was crawling towards me, hands outstretched as though trying to touch me, to hang on to me like his last shred of hope at survival. I cried for him and stepped back. Then he yelped in pain as Draven placed his foot on his back to stop him moving. I could hear the sickening sound of bones cracking as he applied greater pressure.

"Don't touch her!" he warned and instantly the man's hands retracted to cradle his body.

"Please, oh please STOP THIS!" I shouted at him, wondering if my words could penetrate such a Demonic soul that consumed him.

"He does not deserve to live after such an insult to his Master.

However, I will let him breathe but be warned, this is through the mercy of MY Chosen One, not through my rule and wrath. You owe your life to this human, Gastian, but you have my word you will not go unpunished!" I closed my eyes at the sound of his judgement and another overflow of salty tears followed their brothers and sisters.

The man had now collapsed, a new stream of blood flowing freely from his mouth that was the only indication he gave that he was still alive...your body doesn't pump blood when you die, I told myself.

"Take him away! As I have been his judge, I will be his punishment, for it will be by my hands only." He was addressing the room now and turning around so that every eye was in his view, making many flinch back and I didn't blame them.

"Let this be a warning to you all and let it travel to unattended ears. If anyone is to touch this girl, to look at her wrong or even breathe too hard in her direction, they will stand before me and be judged. An injunction with my law, your judge will also be your executioner! Heed my words, the girl belongs to ME!" He had his arms straight out at his sides at 90-degree angles, as if he was challenging anyone to step forward and test his authority as their King. This was all I could bear. I felt like a ghost of myself looking in on the craziness of my life and shaking my head at how this had happened. How had I grown to accept this? When did I learn how to live half a life?!

I let out one last cry and while Draven's back was to me, as he addressed his people...I turned and...

I ran.

I somehow made my legs work, even though they didn't want to, I forced them. I used every ounce of mental strength I had left and poured it all into moving. Moving as far away from Draven as I could get. I managed to push past the people in my way and thanks to Draven's new law no one dared to try and stop me. I reached the staircase and launched down it with a speed that shocked me. It was like running in a dream, one moment you don't think you're even moving but the next you feel as though flying, bending time to your will.

As soon as I was sure that my feet were at the bottom I ran for the only exit I was sure wouldn't stop me. Getting through the empty club was like running on an empty playing field. In my crazed state I could even smell wet, dew-covered grass.

I cornered the bar, taking in briefly its cold dark state now that it wasn't infested with warm bodies...warm human bodies! That was why I was running. It was such a need to be with my own kind it felt like I would self-combust if I didn't breathe Afterlife free air and speak to another human soul. I felt as though I was drowning in there and all I needed was to be free and breathe. Like that man being held by Draven's hand, had also been squeezing the life out of me...

The 'me' out of me.

I almost jumped over the bar just to make it all happen quicker. The door was in view and the exit sign glowed above me and in my state of mind I was reading it as something different...It said 'Home'.

I pushed on the bar that would release me from this supernatural torment. For the first time since stepping foot in Afterlife, I couldn't help but cry as I said goodbye. For now I knew that I never wanted to set foot in there ever again. But would I? Would I, if the man I loved came back to me?

I was outside by the time I thought about the Draven I had lost back there, and the fresh snow covered the ground like a comforting blanket had been laid to protect the Earth from the harsh elements. Of course, sensibly the snow was classed as one of those harsh elements but right now, I just wanted to fall and let it cover me too.

So that is what I did. One minute I was running, the next I was falling blissfully to my knees that impacted with soft and fuzzy snow. It sprayed upwards around me and I let out an almighty cry as I had reached my limit. I lowered my head and sobbed uncontrollably until I was gasping for air to fill my lungs. The cold sharp pains of the icy air actually helped soothe the pain in my heart.

The dull ache of when my heartbeat so feverish only an hour

ago for my Draven. Was this it...? Was this the end of all my happiness? The answer came behind me.

"No, it isn't!"

Draven's voice broke into the night like some thief that could steal the stars...

Stars I wanted to pray to.

CHAPTER FIFTY-THREE

COLD HARD FEAR

"Keira, please get up." His voice was back to the way I remembered it which seemed an age ago. It wasn't a command, but it was him pleading. I started to shake my head. I still couldn't speak yet, as I knew one word and the dam would crack, opening the floodgates for me to drown in my misery.

I had my back to him, hunched over in the snow with my head still cradled in my arms. My hair was still loose and hanging past my waist, the ends getting wet in the snow and curling up as if they hated the cold.

"Please, my Love, it's cold, you'll freeze!" He sounded desperate, hurting and in pain. I looked down at my hands and saw how white they were. My skin was almost translucent, reflecting off the white sheet beneath me. I felt like part of it, as if it was sucking my essence within its freezing depths, becoming captured in its brutal purity. God knows at that point I wanted to. At least freezing was better than feeling!

"I can't," I whispered but I knew he would hear me. Then I felt him, like the sun rising behind me. It almost burned.

"DON'T TOUCH ME!" I screamed. The sound of a bird or some other animal moving through the surrounding forest made me realise how loud my scream had been. His hands left me as if I had stabbed him with my invisible sharp edges.

"Keira?" His voice was pleading...begging. That word. That terrible word that now had new meaning for me. It added to a pain that had stayed with me from the very first day that Morgan had taken me. This made me very, very angry!

I got up quicker than I thought possible for my unsteady legs. I spun round to face him and my foot sunk deeper in the snow's layers.

"NO! How dare you! How could you? HOW COULD YOU!?" I screamed at him and pushed him so hard I felt pain in my arms. It didn't matter, would anything I do hurt this man!

He didn't put up any attempt to stop me. No, he just stood there and took it with a deep regret coating his eyes. Thankfully, he was back to being Draven or I don't think even in my rage I would have had the courage to do this to the flaming Demon Draven that had sizzled out for now. It was starting to feel like this was a daily routine. Get up, see friends, argue with Draven and scream at him. Get ready for work, see friends, beat up my cousin, get thrown to the ground by an ignorant Demon and watch as Draven tried to kill him. Then yell at Draven some more. Even by my standards, that was one Hell of a day!

"Fight back! What's wrong with you? Scream at me, command me, order me to stop oh, mighty King! Aren't you afraid of anything, Draven?!" I was seething to a point I could only see him through a misted red blur.

"Are you finished?" he asked calmly which broke me down to a level I didn't think there was. I pulled my hand back and slapped him on the face so hard it did finally leave its mark. His cheek blazed red which helped me ignore the stinging whip his face left across my palm.

His head was still held down to one side and his eyes didn't look at me. A deep pain scarred them from their beauty, and they had never looked blacker and colder as they did at this point. His hair had fallen forward and covered his forehead and the side of his face I had slapped. The contrast of his red skin and his jet-black hair was startling.

I was waiting for a reaction, but I was left disappointed because he gave me nothing. He straightened his face and looked down at me as though waiting for the next round of crazy I had to deliver.

"Fine, I guess if that does nothing to your frozen heart then let's see if this will...Goodbye Draven!" I said, with tears streaming down my cheeks. I turned and started to walk the other way not waiting to see if it had affected him the way I wanted it to. I didn't get far.

"NO! You will not leave me! You cannot, do you understand?" He was standing in front of me again now and I didn't even see his body move. It was like he had transported.

"Watch me!" I snapped back. At this he restrained me. He held the tops of my arms in two solid vices.

"Stop this!" he shouted but those were my words! The very words I had begged for that life he cared nothing for. And I had been the one hurt by it!

"BEG!" I said almost spitting the word at him. At this it seemed to sink in.

"Come on, Draven! What wrong? When it's on the other foot it isn't as gratifying is it!"

"You think ANY of that was gratifying!" He was seriously pissed now and for some reason I felt better for it. Anything was better than having Draven just stand there and take it like he was stone... cold, hard, unbreathing stone.

"Well, did you stop once, just once...for one tiny second in that flaming head of yours to think about how it made ME FEEL? DID YOU?" He actually winced as though I'd branded him with a red hot poker.

"Wait, now let me answer that one for you...NO!" I stomped.

"He hurt you, he threw you to the ground, I saw it and I reacted like anyone in my position would." He spoke the words like a true King.

"You really believe that don't you?" His features set in granite and he folded his arms across his chest before answering.

"Yes."

"Then you really are an idiot! Think back to my face, Draven...this face!" I pointed at my face and walked him backwards because I kept pushing forward and he had nowhere else to go.

"This face, that was covered in tears as it is now. My pleading face that was begging, BEGGING, Draven! Begging you to stop, begging you not to let me witness what you were doing, what you wanted to do, what you DID! Do you know when the last time I begged, Draven? DO YOU? Let me take you back to my Hell!"

"No! No, I ask of you, Keira, please don't do this!" He lowered his head like this was the most painful thing he had ever heard but I kept going, there was no stopping me now.

"One name, Draven, MORGAN!" I screamed the name at him like wielding a weapon making him roar in rage. He then shocked me when he bent over double and looked like he was trying not to erupt again. I didn't care...I just didn't care, so I carried on.

"I begged him, every DAMN DAY! I begged him to let me go or let me die, just anything so that I could have control back over my life. A control I begged for so that I didn't belong to him anymore. I had to nearly die to get free and when I made it out of there with my life I vowed never to beg ever, ever, ever again!"

"No." he whispered in his agony, but I was too lost to see it for what it truly was. So I cruelly carried on...

"Tonight I broke that promise because of you. I was terrified, Draven, and it wasn't because of what had happened, it was because of you. I was terrified of you!" This was the straw that broke him. Draven finally got it! And he looked like he wanted to die because of it.

He fell to the ground just as I had and covered his face with his hands as though he was trying to prevent it from caving in. I stood back and watched in horror at what I had done. I had gone too far. I know I had wanted to hurt him, but this?

I had gone way too far.

"You can't...I won't...I won't let you be frightened of me!"

"No," I said in a whisper as I backed away from him further.

"I...I...can't, NO, I won't! I won't live without you. Please Keira, I didn't mean to frighten you. I had to do that. I had to show them that you couldn't be touched. They had to fear it! They had to fear me and the very idea of it! Don't you understand, I'm trying to keep you safe and keep you in my world at the same time but it is difficult. There are so many dangers, so many things to fear...but...but me? To think it was me all along that I had to protect you from, the way I am." I cringed back as I had had a taste of justice and hated its bitter acidic after-burn. I shook my head and he shouted back.

"YES! Yes it is and don't try and deny me your true feelings. I frighten you, who am I to strike fear into the very heart that I am trying desperately to claim? Where is my hope? What is there for me to do? What can be done when you see me this way...? A Hell's Beast in love with Heaven's beauty." He ducked his head again and the pain was rippling from him as if it was erupting from his core. And I felt as though I was the one murdering him.

It was as though my heart had cracked under pressure and I knew only one man that could heal me. My God this was tearing me apart! How could I ever have thought so badly of him, been so scared of him? That man that had shown himself... was this the same man in front of me on his knees declaring his love. If I had nothing then this moment, only this moment in my life to last me until eternity, his words... his voice telling me that he loved me would be enough and I needed to hold on to that, I had to!

'I have to go,' I wanted to say, knowing that I had to put space from this night. I needed this time to get past this. I had to see things without Draven around. To face the facts and clear my head from the visions of the King, the Judge and the Executioner!

I cried out again as another flash of tonight's nightmare stole my concentration. It was Draven's hand choking the life from another being. I mean yes, I had seen Draven fighting but that was always different, that was in self-defence or from protecting me from death or kidnapping. Those men had truly wanted to hurt me so didn't that make it ok?

These were the things I needed to clear. To find clarity and make my decisions based on them, not on guilt at seeing Draven's pain or the intense love he had for me. I had to be smart. I had to leave. So I muttered the words aloud, the ones I knew would hurt the most.

"I have to go," I said, letting fresh droplets of myself fall from my eyes and disappear into the snow. He raised himself up in one liquid motion and in two strides he was in front of me, so close that if I was to see his face, I would have to strain my neck back so far that I would be looking straight up to the winter moon.

"No!" was all he said, and I tried to hold on to my resolve as I stared at his chest expanding with each stammered exhale.

"I have to," I repeated but his breath hitched and held for the longest time.

"Don't go!" He poured everything he had into those two little words and more tears gathered and overflowed. His voice was so silky smooth it felt like being placed in a deep, cool lagoon on a blazing hot day. I closed my eyes before the next stage came. I knew it was on its way because I knew what my answer was going to be. And as if he knew also he raised his finger to my lips to stop me from speaking.

He hesitated only a second before touching me but when I didn't take a step back he placed one warm finger on my frozen mouth. I closed my eyes and let another current of tears overflow, spilling down to his fingers.

"Please Keira... don't leave me," he whispered and it felt as though my heart had stopped beating as it too, waited for my answer. I looked away, moving from under his fingers, feeling like I had taken his place as the judge.

"Draven it's too late, I have to leave now, or I will just end up saying more things I will regret later on and I'm so tired of feeling a guilt that is enough for me to drown in."

"No, stay and punish me, you have not said enough to me and I deserve more. Shout at me, hit me and beat me down until I'm nothing more than a shell but please, just don't leave me!" He was begging and there was not one ounce of pleasure in it at all, but I knew I couldn't make it stop. It was too late for that wish.

"Then I will ask you, Dominic…please let me go." This time I did look up at him and when I saw the tears in his eyes for the very first time a sob broke free from my trembling lips.

"I am sorry, but I cannot do that, Catherine." He spoke like he was truly sorry for not giving me what I needed. I broke down completely then and fell into his arms and cried until I felt empty.

His strong hold wrapped around my torso and one hand held my head against his chest.

"Ssshh now, my little sweetheart." He smoothed back my hair and the gesture was making it harder for me to find control over my feelings. It was only when he took my hand in his and said the next words that I pulled myself back to our desperate situation.

"Come Keira, come with me." He pulled gently on my hand but I pulled back.

"No, I can't...I…"

"Keira you're exhausted and freezing. You need rest and warmth. Let me give you that at the very least. Let me take care of you." He was trying so hard to lead me away with him, back to the place I still couldn't go. It would have been so easy, like breathing, to just let him take me away to his tower. It was so tempting, knowing he would lay me down and encase me in his warm arms until sleep took over my mind, letting me escape this turmoil. But I couldn't do it. I wrenched my hand free and almost stumbled backwards.

"NO!" I shouted holding my hands up at him, like you would have to an approaching wild animal.

"Okay...okay, look we can stay out here a little longer but..." I didn't let him finish and he noticed me walking backwards.

"I'm leaving and you're not going to stop me."

"The Hell I'm not!" he said angrily but also certain.

"Draven, I want you to do something for me." I was still moving backwards but now he was moving forward, as though at any minute he would scoop me up and carry me to his room whether I resisted or not.

"Go on," he nodded cautiously.

"Prove to me how you feel," I said in a flurry of emotion and before he could speak, I had to say one last thing. I had to get it out before he gave me no option. I was taking quicker steps now and he was about to reach out to me.

"Because, Draven, if you love me, you will let me GO!" I cried out the word 'go' causing his arms to drop to his sides and his face winced in pain. This was the last image I saw because I turned and started running as fast as my cold limbs would carry me. And I didn't look back. I couldn't give in to the need. I ran like never before, not even thinking about what was making me move so fast. The world around me became a dark blur. I just kept going until I was far along the main road and out of breath.

Thankfully the moon was full and was lighting my way, otherwise this getaway would have ended very abruptly. I bent over to catch my breath, holding my waist as if that would help the stitch that burned there. It took me a while to get past that and I realised why. I hadn't stopped running until I was halfway home. I wasn't the fittest person at the best of times, not having the muscle strength for more endurance but I couldn't believe it.

I started back up and continued at the dull pace of walking. Soon, after my body's energy was spent from running, I got very cold, very quickly. My pounding heart wasn't making my skin hot like it had done but now it beat so slowly it was as if I was asleep. All my body wanted to do was shut down, but my mind was punishing itself by keeping it moving. My muscles were now screaming in protest, my feet felt blistered and painful. But I had to keep going, only halfway to go.

I almost hoped Draven would ignore my proof of love and come flying in to get me. I was just so tired it hurt just keeping my eyes open. My body shook in vain at its feeble attempts at keeping itself warm. My fingers were numb and my toes little cubes of ice. My lips had been bouncing against one another as my teeth chattered uncontrollable and my thin, black cotton top clung to my skin as though it was trying to help. Even the bottoms of my trousers were dripping, and the damp was making its way up to my knees.

I was a cold and broken mess. But I kept moving. I kept moving with the only knowledge warming my heart was that Draven had proved his love. He had not stopped me from leaving, he had not even followed. He had just simply...

Let me go.

This was the one thing that kept my unsteady legs moving and my frozen heart beating. I couldn't even tell if I was crying anymore because my cheeks were numb to any feeling. But nothing mattered because Draven loved me. He had done the hardest thing in letting go of an eternity of control and given it to me.

And what had I done with it? I had left.

I had simply walked away and all for what? Just to find myself walking down this icy road of heartache and despair. Is this how far I would let fear negate my actions in life? Is this how weak I had become or was it strength? I knew one thing for certain that answered that question and that was leaving Draven was one of the hardest things I'd ever forced myself to do. So now, all that was left was for me to start praying it was for all the right reasons.

The sound of an engine behind me made me try to focus enough of my dwindling energy to turn. When I did, I was quickly blinded by high beamed headlights. I shielded myself using my arm over my face to hide the light. I moved over so I wouldn't get run over, at least I had enough mental power left over for that idea.

I felt my foot catch on some uneven surface beneath the snow and lifted my eyes just in time to see the world differently. I must have been flying because the icy wind whipped out my hair and cut into my face.

"Draven?" I asked just before my dream ended and I discovered that I wasn't flying at all. I was falling...

Then darkness invaded me.

CHAPTER FIFTY-FOUR

YES, IT COULD GET WORSE

"**K**eira!" A voice brought me to, and only then did I realize I had fallen down in the snow and passed out. Arms pulled my head up and the snow clung to the side of my face.

"Keira! Open your eyes, girl!" A male voice sounded so strained speaking over me. It was so angry and upset.

"Oh come on Kazzy, please...!" Now a female voice mixed with heavy breathing spoke from a distance. I forced my eyes to open, but they didn't want to focus on the figure now standing over me.

"Come on, Frank, just get her in the car and we will take her to hospital." At that point my eyes made the distinction between shapes and faces.

Frank was stood over me and forcing his arms under me. He lifted me with care and hitched me up a few times to get better grip. It felt strange to be carried by someone other than Draven and the differences between the two were easy to distinguish. It had always seemed effortless to Draven and now that was not the same case with Frank. Although he was strong, he struggled at being graceful about it. At that moment I missed Draven so much it was like having a jagged edge ripped down my chest that allowed for my heart to coming spilling out.

"My God, she's like fucking ice!" Frank complained getting closer to my sister who was stood anxiously by the car door, holding it wide open, ready for Frank to place me.

"We need to hurry and get her to the ER." My sister's voice told me she was giving way to panic, and I needed to put a stop to it before I ended up strapped to a hospital bed with a familiar beeping next to my head for the night. I knew how this worked. I had been there and didn't wish to ever go back. Besides, I knew there was nothing really wrong with me that a hot bath and a good night's sleep couldn't cure. And some food wouldn't have gone amiss, I was starving.

"Li..Lib..by I'mm...ooo..kk" I couldn't speak for my teeth chattering that sounded like pebbles rolling around in a tin can.

"NO, you're not!" She sounded angry and who could really blame her. I grabbed her hand as Frank put me in the car and she screamed at the icy touch.

"Jesus! You're freezing, Kaz! What the Hell were you thinking?" She was shouting at me now and as crazy as it sounds, I felt like laughing. It was just the absurdity of it all. If only she actually knew what I had been thinking! What horrors lay there for her to find. She would have run a long time ago and I would have her now scolding me for not running faster, further and a whole lot sooner!

"Pleeaase nno hosspiiital" I stammered out and her eyes filled with tears. The last thing I saw before she slammed the door closed was her shaking her head. I must have closed my eyes for a few seconds because they flew open when we hit a bump in the road. Can you really do that? Sleep for seconds and have it feel like a small lifetime. My eyes just made out the crossroads that we had stopped at, the red light making me squint in the darkness of the backseat.

"Well, which is it Libs, home or hospital?" Frank asked flashing me a look in his rear-view mirror, catching my deathly white face pleading.

"Please Libs, take me home," I whispered without a hiccup

thanks to the heating in the car bringing some life back to my numb lips.

"It's just one night." She looked down, avoiding my painful memories.

"Olivia, I'm begging you, please don't take me there. They will see my scars, they will ask questions...they will see me as a suicide case and think that's what I was trying to do again. I can't...I can't answer their questions...I won't!" It felt like my night for begging but if that was what it would take then I would face Hell's fire to avoid those memories! I was afraid I would never make it through it all again, I couldn't relive it all and survive. Thankfully, I didn't have to wait to find out.

Frank turned left and started driving towards home without waiting for Libby's response. It was the nicest thing Frank had ever done for me and I would forever be eternally grateful for a gesture I doubt he knew the full meaning of. It had been a lifeline and I mentally thanked God for him. Neither of us said another word.

By the time we pulled up outside the house, my strength had come back to me and my body had started to thaw. Frank opened my side door and reached inside for me. I was about to protest when he abruptly spoke. Which coming from Frank sounded unnatural.

"Don't!" I let it go as I knew that emotion well enough. He was worried, upset and pained at seeing someone he considered as a sister in this situation. The brotherly love I felt from him was staggering.

All the time through my breakdown he had been the one to remain the same. There was no putting on a soft voice and handling me with velvet gloves. There had been no fake smiles and whispered concerns behind my back. No wincing at the sight of my bloody bandages and broken body. He had just been him. The only one who had remained the same. And one look at a man like Frank made you realize that no matter what evil lived among us, no matter what pain they inflicted and no matter what nightmares they created, there was still good in the world because men like Frank simply existed.

And so I let him put his arms under me and carry me in the house as though I was something dear to him, because I was…

His sister.

Libby ran me a bath without a sound. She helped me shed my wet clothes and waited with me until I sank into the comforting, most glorious feeling ever. She got up and left me to soak myself in the warmth of the water until I felt my skin wrinkle. Well, at least, I was a healthier colour.

I would have smiled if I didn't feel so lost and empty inside. I was sat up, chin to my knees and holding myself so tight I felt if I were to let go, I would break into pieces. I looked down the curve of my knees and watched little beads of liquid flow down them into the murky water that once held soapy bubbles on the surface. I didn't think it possible for me to have any tears left to cry but there they were, flowing down my body and escaping in the face of my grievous situation.

Finally, I made my head move, my legs straighten, and my arms heave myself out of the bath like I was some dead weight. I found a steaming mug of tea outside the door and thought I would start crying again. I picked up the mug with one hand and held on to my towel with the other but as I made my way along the hall the sound of Frank's voice made me stop. I made the decision to make myself listen to this and took a few steps down before sitting on one of the steps.

"No, no, like I said, she seems to be alright." It wasn't his usual friendly, easy-going tone. No, this was his serious voice that only came out when 'Pissed off Frank' rarely showed himself. I could tell he was on the phone to someone and I could tell by his manner, thankfully, it wasn't my Mother.

"Dom, I'm telling you she's fine! But what on earth did you do to her? And why the fuck would you let her walk home in this weather?" Frank was losing his cool and my mouth dropped at the sound of it being with Draven. I wished I had supernatural hearing at that point because Frank was only making a few acknowledged responses which gave very little away.

"Oh… Oh right, I see, No, no, I don't think you had any other choice. She's damn stubborn for sure." He seemed a lot calmer now which made me wonder what had Draven told him?

"No, just halfway until we found her and of course she refused to go to the hospital." This was so frustrating only hearing one side and having it keep stopping for the questions I couldn't hear.

"I couldn't make her, Dom, I'm not her Father and you should know that by now, the girl has a will of iron! Besides, I didn't want to add to her...her... well, her misery by bringing up shit with her past!"

"I don't think that's a good idea, she doesn't want to see anyone at the moment, let alone any doctors! Look, me and Libs will keep an eye on her tonight...yes, yes, we will keep checking for that, but do you really think she will go that far? She's not going to just get up and leave without saying anything to us." So Draven thought that I was going to cut and run. I wouldn't be surprised if I looked out of the window and saw it surrounded with guards! I would put money on Ragnar being out there at the very least.

"We will lock the doors and hide the keys if you really think it's an issue but to be honest, Dom, the girl is exhausted and just needs rest. I think you will find once she's had some sleep, she will see things differently in the morning." I was in two minds to go down there and ask him outright what Draven had told them because in no way could it have been the truth.

"No, you did the right thing calling us. I think you're right about her reactions to involving your family and like you said, I think you coming to get her would have just made it worse." So Draven had called them. Not only had he done as I asked by letting me go, he had also had a backup plan of seeing to my safety.

"Okay, we will do and yes, I won't forget, I will tell her now, before she goes to bed, I think she is still in the bath..."

"NO, Dom she isn't a child, she wouldn't fall asleep in the bath... Jesus! Okay, okay, we will go and check on her, but honestly man, stop worrying!" Frank was muttering the next bit and when I heard the phone being placed back in its charger, I gathered the muttering had been a goodbye.

"So, what did he say?" I heard Libby ask.

"He did nothing wrong, Libs, this was Keira's choice." Frank answered in a neutral tone. Nothing wrong! I don't bloody think so. I wanted to march right down there and put them right but after a nanoseconds thought, I knew that wouldn't be very productive. For starters, it wasn't like he could have told them the truth but come on, making it out like it was all me! Man, it was infuriating but what could I do?

So after a second's thought I did the only thing I could. I got up and went into my temporary room to hide myself away. I quickly changed into some old sweatpants, a black vest and my Dad's old college sweater for added comfort. It was huge on me, but I liked that. I also loved that no matter how many times it had been washed it seemed to smell like my Dad.

I brushed my hair with a lot more force than necessary, which was probably causing a year's full of split ends. It was only when it started to squeak that I plaited it still damp and flung it back over my shoulder to hang down my back like a rope to nowhere.

My activities must have been heard downstairs as soon enough I heard a light tapping at my door. The mood I was in just wanted to be left alone but I gathered my sister had hit her limit on being kept in the dark.

"Come in," I whispered half hoping she wouldn't hear and think I was asleep already. That didn't happen but neither did my sister as it was Frank.

"Hey...do you feel better?" He looked awkward stood in the doorway, like it was too narrow for his large frame, but he looked unsure about coming in further, as if I was catatonic or something.

"Yeah, I do...well, warmer at least." I tried to smile, not from wanting but more like needing, I didn't want Frank to feel uncomfortable.

"Come in, Frank," I said quietly and for a second I thought he was going to say no and flee the room thanks to his sullen expression. Instead he ducked once and came over to sit opposite me on the bed. We sat facing each other without speaking for a few moments and Frank looked deep in thought as though trying to find the right words. I decided to kick start this or he would be waking me up by the time he found them.

"Look Frank, I want to apologise. I am sorry that you both got dragged out to get me in the middle of the night and I'm more sorry that you were both worried." Frank frowned at this, which wasn't the reaction I was hoping for.

"Aren't you tired of saying sorry, Keira?" His question caught me off guard and I shook my head lightly in confusion.

"People don't think I take much notice because I stand on the side-lines and keep quiet, but I find that is the best place to see things clearly. Libs likes to get more involved, like your folks, but I realised from the start that all you needed was time to figure things out for yourself. I could see how exhausting it was for you, always having to put on that act, like you were fine all the time. Like you would be shitting fine after what you had just been through!" He clenched his fists at the memory and my tears misted at his confession of feelings that had obviously been on his mind for quite some time.

"But you did it, not very convincingly I might add, but you still did it! You put every single person before yourself and said sorry for something you didn't need to ever be sorry for. I would see you trying desperately to make your Mum and Libs feel better, which I appreciated more than you could ever know, 'cause trust me, in my life, the only thing that brings me pain is seeing your sister cry. I love her that damn much! But kid, you gotta know that I love you too." He reached out and squeezed my shoulder momentarily before carrying on,

"You will always be a sister to me, and I want you to know that I think you are one of the most selfless people I have ever known." After he finished I couldn't help my reaction. I threw myself into his arms and hugged onto him like any crying sister would. He made an 'Umff' sound as I hit into his chest but after a moment he wrapped his big arms around me and rubbed my back soothingly.

"It's alright, come on now, Ssshh." I was crying into his shoulder and when I moved my head back there were two wet patches on his soft, checked shirt.

"Man, if I knew I was going to bring on the waterworks I would have just said goodnight," he joked making me laugh as I let him go.

"Sorry, I guess it's just nice to know that I didn't have to fool everyone. You really are a great guy, Frank and I'm so happy to call you brother." At this he beamed a smile at me and gave me a wink.

"I know I'm great aren't I? But hey, do you think you could tell Libs that some time 'cause her hormones have been riding me hard," he joked some more.

"Yeah, you wish!"

"At the minute my only secret weapon is chocolate, seriously you would think she was on crack and I was her dealer...seriously addicted!" I laughed some more and the feeling was like being pumped with a cure for a numb state.

"Anyway, talking about great guys..." And here it was...the man talk. I raised an eyebrow and he winced.

"Okay, I know this is none of my business, but I spoke to Dom. He's really worried about you...I mean like crazy man worried! The man is obsessed, if you ask me, but hey, as long as he's good to you then I'm cool with the dude, but tell me truthfully...did he hurt you?"

"NO! Sorry but no, nothing like that." He looked relieved and continued.

"Then he's a good guy?" He knew the answer, but he just wanted to hear me say it. I didn't but I couldn't help but nodding.

"Then why did you run, girl?" I took a deep breath and looked down. What could I say?

"What did he tell you?" I said, deciding that was the smarter way to go.

"That basically some asshole pushed you and Dom pretty much nearly killed him because of it and it terrified the shit out of you. So you ran and he couldn't stop you." O...Kay...So maybe I was wrong. He had pretty much told him the truth and it was obvious which side Frank was on.

"You think it was the wrong thing to do, me running away don't you?"

"Yes!" Well, at least he was honest, if not a little blunt.

"Look honey, I get it. I understand how shit like that isn't easy for girls to see, especially after all you have been through the last couple of years. But let me tell you now, if that had been me and some guy with a death wish pushed down my Libs, then that man would not be breathing through anything but a damn tube!" He cracked his knuckles at just the thought.

"It's maybe a guy thing, I don't know, but if you're a real man then you don't just stand back and let someone hurt your woman. Dom's a big guy and I can't imagine he let him get away with it lightly, so I understand you being frightened an' all but just because he does that to a guy, who clearly deserved it, that doesn't mean you have anything to fear." And that was it in a nutshell. Fear.

I must have looked as deep in thought as I was because I only looked up when I felt the bed move. Frank patted me on the head twice and moved towards the door.

"Get some rest and think about what I said. Think about if you had seen some girl hitting Dom over the head with a pipe...what would you have done to that girl? Not the same thing, but still, the principle remains the same." The answer to that hit me without thinking. I would have probably killed her!

"How did you get so smart, Frank?" I said smiling at him in the doorway.

"I watched sports, brushed my teeth and got into my fair share of mischief but one thing I will always recommend...always listen to your Mother." He laughed at himself heartily and opened my door, but then something made him stop. He turned his head and met me with serious eyes.

"What is it?" I asked.

"Dom made me promise to tell you something before you go to sleep." He looked uncertain about telling me.

"He told me to tell you..." He looked down as if still deciding with himself before continuing…

"He hopes you finally have your proof."

CHAPTER FIFTY-FIVE

FORGIVE ME, FORGIVE ME NOT

That night I went to bed feeling completely lost in myself. I had thought about what Frank had said and it made so much sense in the world of men. But then again, I guess if the roles were reversed would I have acted the same?

The part that had hurt me the most was the begging for a life, begging was a sore spot for me, which made me think...was this just all about me and my stupid pride? Was it just another defect on my part caused by my unmoveable past? Morgan may be dead but what he did to me, what he put me through and how he had changed me was still very much alive in its own way.

I was damaged from it, I knew that, but would I really let it win? Was I going to allow it to make me weak when I needed to be all that much stronger or would I let it pull me under into the darkness where it still existed? One thing that night had certainly proved and that was that my choices were my own. Draven had been right...I had found my proof.

My body was now crying out for the rest my mind wouldn't allow. I had put the light out and tossed and turned in my bed like a fish on the bottom of a boat for over an hour. In the end, I sat up and looked about the dark room full of shadows I wasn't yet used to.

I had only slept in this room twice because I was always with Draven. I tried to blame the irritation I felt on the bed being too hard, or the pillows being too lumpy, but I knew the truth. Every time I had stretched out my arm it had found air instead of skin and flesh. Every time I had rolled over, I found an edge instead of a warm body to lean against, then my mind would flashback to me making this terrible choice. I had got so used to spending my nights next to Draven that it felt wrong on so many levels being alone. I hated it!

I got up and wrapped a blanket that lay at the bottom of the bed around my shoulders. I walked over to the window where a high-backed chair sat waiting for me to fill it. I slumped down and pulled my knees up to wrap the knitted wool around them. I then looked out of the window to an unfamiliar view of the back of the house.

This side backed onto the forest that surrounded both sides of the house and instead of my usual panoramic view of the national park and rolling green mountains, I was faced with a wall of dark trees stretching out ready to claim me. I shuddered at the irrational fear creeping up inside my fragile mind. It was because I was used to sleeping in the complete ease of Draven's protecting arms, but now I was alone and left wide open to the dark elements I knew existed.

Then something caught my eye. Something in the shadows of the trees, half-hidden by thick branches and snow-covered leaves. The moon glistened on every natural surface and provided enough light to see the black shadow. I could see the light in its eyes staring in my window like a lighthouse in the storm.

I raised my hand to the glass and placed my palm out against the window. My actions caused reactions. The shadow moved suddenly, and I let out my held breath at the sight of Ava stretch out her impressive wingspan before taking off to the skies. I watched her until out of sight, which wasn't for long given her speed. My heart seemed to ache more when she was gone and I curled up tighter into a ball and held myself with my head leaning against the side of the chair. It wasn't comfy but with the back having little sides it was easy enough for me to use as a pillow and I soon found myself asleep.

The next thing I knew I seemed to be floating. I was in that state somewhere between sleep and awareness. I had been dreaming about being outside Afterlife and I was running away from something. I kept looking behind me as I ran and every time I did, my eyes met nothing but more black forest I was leaving behind. I was in the thick of the forest and the only light was what the moon's rays could penetrate. I had been running towards some kind of clearing and I only knew this thanks to the light that seemed to be brighter up ahead.

It was when I had reached that clearing that it happened. I was stood on the edge of the cliff face looking out towards the deep valley floor when something hit me. I had been staring off into the distant sky and focusing on something moving towards me at some speed. At first, I thought it was Ava and even said her name aloud but as it came closer, I could see it was far too big to be her, although it too had wings. Then, before my eyes could take it all in at the speed it flew, it hit into me and grabbed a hold of my body.

I opened my eyes to find I was being carried off somewhere and the strong hands that had hold of me pulled me in closer to a hard chest. Then I was laid down on something soft and comforting. The darkness around me was too empty to make out any visual attempt at what was going on or who had gently placed me down as though I was a treasured gift.

A hand smoothed back my hair from my face and it felt cool on my sticky hot skin. I must have murmured something, because I felt my lips moving and the air flowing over my tongue that made a word. I know which word it would have been... no wait...not a word, more like a name.

"Draven," I whimpered his name again, hearing my own voice in a dream was a bit like catching a glimpse of yourself reflecting from a window in a passing car. One second you were there as someone else and the next you were gone like a distant memory. It

was getting harder to follow which me I was playing out but I knew one thing, no matter which one of us it was, for the first time tonight I felt comfort in the arms that had held me...if only for a short while.

The daylight glaring through my window was what woke me from my slumber. I threw an arm over my eyes and rolled over to lie on my back until my sleepiness subsided. I started to replay my night like a flicker book of events. It was hard to imagine waking up from a day like that and still finding out the truth was it had actually happened. It was when I got to the end of my private story of events that a memory made me bolt upright. It was last night, when I was dreaming while awake. I remember falling asleep on the chair by the window. I remember seeing Ava, calling out Draven's name, feeling as though I was floating but there was something else. I had actually woken a few times in the night to see a figure standing over me, watching me...guarding me.

Had it been Draven? Had he really come to me? I couldn't be sure but who else? So many questions with no way to get to the answers. I wanted it to be him and if that was the case then what did it mean? Had I put the night behind me so easily? I shook my head as if that would help sort out all the jumbled thoughts inside my mind. Of course, it didn't but that's when I felt something. Something soft and velvety. I looked down to discover my caller had left me a gift.

A beautiful gift.

A blood-red rose.

One tied halfway down the thornless stem with a deep purple ribbon. I picked it up and placed it under my nose to inhale its sweet scent deeply. It was from Draven. My first flower from my first true love. I turned it around in my fingers and took in every curve of its beauty.

It was perfect in every way, every petal tucked in at just the right point, whereas others spread out around the bud as if loving the show. To anyone else it would just have been a flower, but to me it was a symbol and that symbol was forgiveness. At that point I wanted to get up and race to his side like an invisible cord was tugging at my ribs. But then that dream went crashing out of the window when my cousin knocked on my door, firmly putting an end to my romantic reuniting fantasy.

"Can I come in?" Hilary asked me, which in itself was astonishing. She had only opened the door a fraction of an inch and when I didn't answer she opened it further to gauge my reaction. I nodded instead of throwing a shoe at her head like I wanted to. I wasn't in the mood to go through all this shit again but when I could actually see her face, I was shocked. She didn't look angry, aggravated or aggressive, quite the opposite...she looked sad. I must have been frowning because the first thing out of her mouth was her reason for being here.

"Look, I know that the last thing you want right now is to see me, but I couldn't wait anymore. I mean, I thought you would never wake up." Although this sounded like she was having a dig at me it wasn't the case.

"Why, what time is it?" I asked trying to take my eyes off her black eye, cut nose and split lip. Man, I had really done a number on her last night. I bet she was wondering why there wasn't a mark on me. Well, if she was, then she was hiding the fact.

"It's getting on for half four," she said after taking out her mobile to check. It was then that I noticed what she was wearing. It was the most casual I had seen her in yet, a pair of loose fitted jeans and a baggy, grey jogging sweater. She even had her hair pulled back in a high ponytail and no makeup.

If you asked me, it was the most attractive she had looked since she had been here. I mean my cousin wasn't ugly, just an over baked cake as my gran would have put it. Sometimes less was more and even though she had the clear signs of a beating she still looked good.

"Jack called, of course he wouldn't talk to me, but he did leave a message for you. He will be round here about sixish." She didn't even sound bitter when she said this, and I was starting to think I had woken up in the Twilight Zone.

"I have to ask, why are you here talking to me like last night never happened...actually scrap that, more like the last sixteen years never happened?"

"Oh, don't get me wrong, last night I hated you more than I think I ever have but someone came round here this morning and gave me something." Her eyes burned into mine at the point of remembering last night but where I thought they would retain the heat, they fizzled out. Now she just looked full of regret and forgiveness.

"What? A personality transplant, new soul or let me guess, a defrosted heart?" I said sarcastically which I regretted after seeing her wince.

"I guess I deserve that." Damn straight, but that didn't make me feel any better for it.

"Yes, you do, but that doesn't make it right, please go on."

"Dominic came round to see me this morning." I don't think I could have looked more shocked.

"WHAT?!" I shouted feeling the jealous rage bubbling up inside me like a bouncing kettle on the stove. No wonder she was being nice, this was all a ploy, it had to be.

"Keira please, calm down and let me finish...please." She held her hand out for me to sit back down as I had jumped out of bed and was storming around the room.

"He wasn't nice to me, Keira, actually he was a bit scary to be honest and if you ask me, he definitely has anger issues, but what he had to say worked. Hell, I would have been terrified not to do what he asked."

"What did he ask?"

"He said that I needed to look at some facts and realise some home truths before harbouring onto a hate that was very misplaced. He really does sound kind of old fashioned sometimes doesn't he?" Wow but she had no idea! My mind reeled at this new information. Draven had come here and didn't come up to see me, well that stung!

"He asked about you, I told him you were still sleeping, and he didn't want to disturb you, so he left after giving me the folder."

"Folder?" I asked but I remembered the answer to it before she replied. Last night I had asked Draven for it back to help Hilary realise the truth. So that's what this was all about...great! Nice Hilary will be lasting all of ten minutes in that case.

"Yeah, the police folder, I don't know how the Hell he got it, but he told me to look at it. At first, I didn't want to because I didn't want to feel anything for you but hate. He made me swear I would and he's a hard man to say no to. So, this morning I took a walk and read it."

"I don't need your pity, Hilary, so you can save it for someone who gives..."

"I don't pity you! I...I actually admire you. I had no idea what had happened, well, I mean not the details. Mum had told me only half of it as she thought it would have upset me. She still likes to believe we're friends. But I had no idea what you actually went through, yet here you are still breathing, still fighting!" She touched her face and smirked.

"You always did have a hidden wild streak." And then she laughed, making it sound weird without its falseness coating it.

"It actually got me angry to know what he did to you and I couldn't understand why I would feel that way. I mean I have hated you for so long it felt wrong to feel anything else. I'm going to be honest, the only reason I came here was to see how broken and miserable you were." Well, those were my theories confirmed.

"Of course, when I saw how happy you looked and then that ridiculously gorgeous boyfriend of yours showed up, I couldn't stand it. I wanted to take it from you, to destroy all that happiness, like you did to me." I started to shake my head, but she got up and threw her hands up like I was blind.

"I don't understand, what the Hell did I ever do to you?" I asked making her face flush red with a hint of anger she was trying to control.

"Do you know that when we were kids you were my best friend?" I had known this. I mean I still had a friendship bracelet in my childhood memory box at home. I had even gotten it out a few times ready to burn but found myself just stuffing it back in the bottom of the box with frustration.

"And you were mine, but all I know is that one day we were attached at the hip and then the next, you hated my guts and made fun of me in front of all our friends. Then you and your Mum moved away. When you came back a few years later, you made it your mission to make my life miserable and to this day I have no idea, no single clue as to why!" She actually laughed, but it was so lacking in humour that it sent a chill down my spine.

"I didn't think you did. You were the reason my Father left," she said with her arms folded, staring at me as though she had a lifetime's worth of blame in those eyes. Eyes that started to well up with pain and a relentless hatred.

"WHAT?!" I shouted not allowing myself to believe a word.

"It's true, you told your Mum that you had seen my Dad kissing another woman and because of THAT, my Mother kicked him out when he had nowhere else to go! She wouldn't even let him come to see me. YOU ruined my life! You broke up my family and all the while you still got to keep yours! Why was that fair? WHY?!" She was losing it now and I had tears in my eyes at all the years lost because of such a misunderstanding.

"Oh my God! Hilary, is that the only reason you have hated me all these years?"

"The only reason? What would be a better reason, Kaz?! You ruined my life, isn't that enough?" She stormed back over to me to shout in my face, but I got off the other side of the bed so that I wasn't beneath her. I held up my hands in an 'I come in peace' kind of way.

"Hilary, that wasn't me!" At this her eyes spilled over with tears that landed on the carpet.

"Yeah right, of course you would say that!"

"Hilary, has your Mum not talked to you about this, I mean, told you what really happened?" She looked both angry and confused which made her forehead wrinkle and I can imagine it was painful given her bruised face and cut nose.

"Look Hilary, I think you need to talk to your Mum, 'cause it wasn't me that told anyone anything. I didn't even know anything about your Dad leaving until you guys moved away. My mum just kept telling me he was away on business because she didn't want to upset me. She knew I was fond of my Uncle." I was trying to reason with her, and my voice found a very gentle, low volume.

"NO! You're lying! You must be lying...I ...I can't be wrong. Are you telling the truth because, so help me God if you're not, Kaz then I wouldn't be able to hold myself back!" She looked so past furious I was getting ready for an attack which I didn't have the heart for. Now I knew why it didn't matter about the past she had put me through, like letting open a window for it all to blow away with the wind. I didn't want to fight anymore, for she wasn't the only one exhausted.

"Ring your Mum, Hilary, demand the truth and if she refuses then ring my Mum and I will make her tell you what you deserve to know. You have a right!"

"Yes...Yes I will, I will ring her now, I don't care what time it is." And with that she left my room in a desperate state.

I got into the shower without really knowing what I was doing. It was as if I was operating on autopilot. I just couldn't believe all these years she had thought that I had been the reason for the greatest loss in her life. She idolised her father, always had but when he left it was as though he had taken a bit of her with him. She came back not quite fully whole but the part of her had filled with bitterness and rebellion.

I knew for a fact that her father had been caught having an affair, but only years later and well after the fact. It had never really been explained to me why he had left, and I remember feeling very vulnerable, wondering if a lot of Dads did this and praying my Dad never would. I think I did all the washing up for a whole year just in case.

Of course, I didn't know exactly what Hilary was going to hear from her Mum, but if it was the truth then she would have a new person to hate and I was pretty sure that someone was going to be my Mother. I didn't want to be the one to say, because it wasn't my place and I was extremely angry at my Auntie for not telling her daughter sooner.

I found out a few years ago when looking through some old family photos with my Mum. The conversation came up and my poor, teary Mother confessed to being the one to have to tell her own sister that she had seen her husband kissing a lady that worked at the local newsagents not far from our house. Of course, as it turned out, it wasn't just a few pecks on the cheek for a cheaper 'News of the world'. It had been a full-blown affair resulting in love. He soon left my Auntie for this other woman and went to live with her and her three kids.

So instead of letting Hilary be a part of her Father's life with this other family on the side, she moved them both away. She only came back when she was certain her ex-husband didn't live in the area anymore. The last my Mum had heard they were living in Carmarthenshire in Wales. I had no clue that Hilary didn't know any of this and now understood why my mother always told us 'be nice to her, she's had it hard.' That had been my Mother's excuse for everything and now I knew why...her guilt had been speaking every time.

I got out of the shower not recalling if I had even washed my hair, my mind was in a backlog of childhood memories. Every nasty word, every cruel gesture and every painful thing she'd ever done to me now made sense. Why wouldn't she hate me? I mean, if it had been the other way round then how would I have reacted? If she had succeeded in getting Draven from me, then what would I have done? I had gone pretty far last night and that was only at the hint of it.

After getting dry and dressed I walked back into my room to find Hilary sat on my bed. Her head was buried in her hands and she was shaking. At that moment, all hate we had felt for each other melted away just like a heatwave had swept through the room.

She heard my footsteps and she looked up. The sight made my heart break. It looked as though she had been sobbing nonstop since she left my room. Her face was red and blotchy, making her blue eyes stand out like they were dotted with broken blood vessels underneath the skin around them. Her lips were quivering, and the noise of air being sucked in so that she could cry louder was enough to set me off.

I ran to her on the bed and she fell into my arms which forced us both onto the floor. I was kneeling with her head cradled on my shoulder and she was slumped to the side soaking my top with an unending stream of tears. I smoothed back her hair and rubbed her back until she was spent.

"Ssshh, it's ok, you're not alone," I whispered making her release one more outburst of spluttered sobs. After a time she finally found some control to pull back to look at me in awe.

"Why are you being so nice to me, you should hate me?" Again another hitched breath and a cry came thick after her question.

"I don't hate you, I just never understood why you hated me, but now I understand."

"I spoke to my Mum and she told me everything, I yelled at her and said some pretty horrible things. Man, I want to hate her for lying to me!"

"I think you have lived with hate for too long, Hilary. That type of thing will destroy you if you let it...trust me on this. After what happened I really knew what it was to hate...I hated everything! I hated it for being sunny, I hated watching people smile and laugh at things I couldn't see the glory in. I even hated people being nice to me, their fake talk and happy eyes. But one day I realised, it wasn't all these things I hated...It was myself. I hated who I had become and who he had made me!" Okay, so now we were both crying and we really hugged each other for the first time in sixteen years. It felt like a friend I had lost and just stumbled across in passing, totally unexpected but utterly welcome.

We sat together for the longest time and when Libby came back from work and found us both giggling and gossiping like kids, with Hilary all bruised up, she nearly dropped dead from shock. It must have been the last thing she expected to get home from work to find.

Well, it was odd to say the least, but it felt so right at the same time. We both explained the past and after what happened last night, how we had come to this point. Of course, Libby asked the one obvious question I hadn't even thought of.

"But why the Hell did your Mum tell you it was Keira that told her?" Man, but that was a good question!

"Ah, well, this is the irony. She told me it was Keira because she knew what good friends we were, she thought that if I knew it had come from her that I wouldn't even question it. She knew I trusted you and she didn't want me thinking badly of your Mum, I guess she was protecting her sister the way your Mum protected her by telling on my Dad." She said this last part to me and I just shook my head at how one little lie had caused so many years of damage. It made no sense in my world but then again...what did? Why should I be surprised, wasn't my life riddled with crazy, unrelenting events that changed every course I walked down?

Time that day quickly turned into a time for everyone else. Once I had spent some time with Hilary, Jack turned up all worried and armed with an endless amount of apologies. He told me what she had told him and no surprises, how she had played the victim. He admitted it didn't take him long to realize the holes in her stories, but by then he felt so ashamed of himself for believing it, he didn't know what to say to me. He told me how every time he tried to be alone to talk to me, I would avoid him. It was true, I had been avoiding him but for all the wrong reasons.

After convincing him finally that I had forgiven him, he left after pulling me in for a bear hug. By this time it was dark outside and close to eight. I had wanted to go back to Afterlife ages ago, but after what had happened with my cousin and me, I knew I would have to wait. But now my time had come. I was going to see Draven and there was no stopping me.

That was until I got a phone call from the man himself. I hadn't answered it but a message was waiting for me by the phone written in Libby's hand. She hadn't wanted to tell me herself and only when reading the message did I understand why.

Keira,
Please don't come to me tonight,

THE TWO KINGS

I need time alone to think.
And I fear seeing you will only cloud my judgement.
I will come to you when I am ready.
Wait for me.
Dominic.

This was why he hadn't wanted to see me this morning...

He didn't want to see me at all.

CHAPTER FIFTY-SIX

SOMEONE'S SOUL IS ON FIRE

I t felt as though I had a dagger protruding from my chest and Draven had been the one who put it there. I picked up the phone three times before admitting defeat and slamming it back down on the receiver before it even had chance to ring. I wanted to speak to him, to hear the words for myself, but I was also afraid. What if this was the end? What if this time there was no going back? Could I really let this go, just go on without looking behind me? NO! I couldn't do that, and I wouldn't!

I was in the kitchen with a large glass of some spirit I found in the cupboard. It tasted like paint thinner as it burned down my throat but that was a good thing. I wanted that burn. I wanted to feel anything just as long as it wasn't nothing. I could deal with anything but numbness. I heard a voice being cleared and turned my head to see Libby with a worried frown on her face.

"I don't understand… why doesn't he want to see me?" I asked her facing back to the sink and swirling the liquid around in my glass.

"I think when he said to give him time, I think he really meant you," she answered sympathetically.

"I don't want bloody time! What I want is to go over there and demand him to speak to me!"

"Then why don't you?" It sounded simple enough, but Libby didn't know the consequences of that action.

"Because last night I asked him to do something very hard...I asked him to let me go and he did. And now he asks the same of me, how can I say no? How can I do anything but wait?" Libby had been nodding in agreement, which hadn't been the response I had wanted. I wanted her to tell me something, anything that would have made the excuse to go over there acceptable.

"He really scared you last night, didn't he?" Of course, Frank had told her, there was nothing he wouldn't have, so I wasn't surprised or angry.

"Yes he did, but after talking to Frank last night, I kind of understood it better. I don't condone what he did, not at all, but if the situation was reversed then I can't imagine I would have taken it well either."

"Men eh?" This was her answer for everything and we both laughed at how barbaric and caveman they could act. Of course, for Draven this was multiplied by about a thousand because not only was he half Angel, half Demon, he was also King of the hidden world of the supernatural. So granted, he had a lot of pressure to deal with and I gathered having to deal with a hysterical human girlfriend was something of a pain in the ass. Maybe that's why he didn't want to see me tonight? Maybe he just wanted me to take time to cool down before having to deal with it again. Some Demon/Angel quiet time...surely, I could give him that, right? Ok, so it didn't have to mean that he wanted to split up with me, I could just be feeling a little paranoid.

Ok, so after a few more glasses of whatever alcohol I was consuming, I started to feel better. I mean, for all I knew it could have been cooking sherry but it did the job so that was all I cared about. I was feeling quite merry and looking on the brighter side of life. I had made up with my cousin after a sixteen-year feud. I was friends with Jack again and I'd had one of the best heart to hearts with Frank, one that I would never forget. So life was looking good, all I needed now was to be allowed to see Draven and have wild, mad passionate makeup sex and all would be good in the world. Not too much to ask for...*right?*

It wasn't surprising when I looked at the clock and saw it was close to midnight. I had been moping about ever since Jack left and when Libby had started bringing me up cups of tea around ten, I knew she was worried about me being in my room drunk, crying and listening to Celine Dion's 'All by myself'.

She found, thankfully I hadn't been doing any of those things, apart from the drinking, but thanks to four mugs of tea in a row I was pretty well past the drunken stage. In fact, I had been painting, something I hadn't done in a while.

I took a step back to study what I had created. It was of a pulsating heart, like the ones you find in hallmark cards, not the blood pumping muscle…'cause, eeew on the second one!

The background was of the dark forest and the heart was amongst the shadowed trees looming around it. I tried to enhance it in a way that seemed as if it was glowing in the night by adding a light reflecting off the surfaces around it.

The most significant part was the huge, jagged lightning bolt that came from above and struck the heart's core, splitting it in two. One side gaped more to the side than the other and I did this to symbolise the distinction between mine and Draven's sides, as he was clearly the stronger of us both. I knew I was being overly dramatic by painting this but mixed with alcohol and feeling hopelessly sorry for myself this is what my mind had wanted to paint.

After Libby had come to say goodnight along with Hilary, which was still hard to get used to but nice, I decided to call it a night. I also couldn't help but hope for better things to come tomorrow. I even smiled at the thought of waking up to Draven by my bedside. It was a long shot, I grant you, but not an impossible dream.

I plaited my hair, so it hung like a rope down my back and got dressed into some light grey pyjama bottoms and a vest top to match. After brushing my teeth and washing my face, I put my painting against the wall to dry after laying down an old towel so as not to get paint on the carpeted floor.

Once in bed, my mind started to drift quickly into a world of

Draven Dreams. I strangely found myself transported back to a past and looking in on a Draven of a different time.

He wasn't wearing clothes as such, more like layers of cloth draped over his impressive shoulders with a solid brass coloured breastplate covering his chest. This then tied at the waist with leather wound round and round, all of which held symbols in some kind of metal.

I swallowed down the lump as my eyes travelled the length of him finding a huge sword hanging by his thigh, which was almost the length of his leg. His wrists were cuffed with thick, studded leather and one arm was bound in strapping right up and straining over his bicep. His hair was much longer but tied back with black cord giving him a harsher appearance.

He looked like a brutal warrior stood upon the base of a throne made of carved stone. He had his arms crossed over his chest making his muscles bulge and the leather stretch even further to accommodate them. Damn, he looked so powerful I had the insane impulse to both orgasm from the sight and run away in fear!

I looked about the room and saw I was in some sort of throne room. It reminded me of the Temple, but it was longer like a great hall. Stone pillars the width of thousand-year-old trees spread evenly down the room and all were points for a heavily armed guard to be positioned.

The ornate ceiling loomed miles above me making me feel like an insect fallen into a pit of snakes. My eyes scanned my new situation and thankfully I realised no one could see me. I was cloaked head to toe and hidden in a dark alcove away from all the people in the room, who were centred around Draven. He had never looked more like the King he was than at that moment.

"Let him come forth!" Draven's deep voice boomed out the command making everyone in the room twitch with fear.

"Yes, my Lord," said a servant who bowed deeply before him. I arched my neck to see around the people that hid my view of the great doors at the end. They were the size of a two-storey building and were made from dark mahogany. Great golden bars crossed over each other that looked to be a locking mechanism. The servant walked back towards them and slowly they began to open.

I waited along with everyone else as to what those open doors would reveal and at some point I was losing the knowledge of this being an actual dream. It felt too real. I could even smell the sandstone floor, feel the sweat beading down my forehead and taste the salt in the air. It felt like I was near the sea and I had the greatest urge to run for the doors and find out. But then a tall dark figure emerged in the opening, casting the longest shadow along the floor and that urge quickly turned into finding out who this man was. The firelight was too bright behind him to make out any features yet, so like everyone else I had to wait.

He walked with his head held high as though he was on the same level as Draven and when the King spoke, I knew this was likely so.

"My friend, I welcome you. I was told of your coming and hope our alliance will strengthen throughout the centuries to come," Draven said looking pleased at the sight coming closer to his throne.

"That is a likely prospect indeed, my King. You have my loyalty as I am sure I will gain yours," said a voice that I was surely mistaking. It couldn't be...could it? He got closer now and his long-hooded cloak floated around him like black liquid.

I had started to move through the crowd unconsciously and gave up all chances at being unseen. I, and the figure before Draven were the only ones who had their hoods concealing their identities and I wondered who would be the first to reveal themselves? I just didn't care now, as I pushed past bodies in my way getting to the front of the crowd. Murmurs and frowns were left behind me in my mission to get closer. I finally came to the front and saw just how close I was to both the men who now stood facing each other.

I made it there just in time to see the hooded figure raise the cloth from over his head. The man's face was now in full view and I couldn't prevent the scream that erupted from deep within me. It was a noise of sheer terror that echoed off the great walls and amplified it tenfold.

"NO!" I screamed out as I saw both Draven and Lucius turn to source the outburst in the crowd. I was very aware of the people around me moving back so as not to be associated with me. Draven looked furious as he stormed over to me shouting a command I didn't understand. It didn't take long to guess what it had been when I was seized by both arms. I looked to my sides and found two huge guards dressed in thick armour holding me securely.

"How dare anyone display such insolence in my presence!" he roared in my direction and at that moment I wondered if the theory was true, that if you die in your dream, did you really die in real life? Was this the end? Was I going to die at the hands of the man I loved before he even knew me?

My heart beat wildly in my chest and I thought it might pop out and hit the floor before he even reached me. I started to struggle in a feeble attempt to free myself but the pain that shot through my arms quickly put a stop to that motion.

Draven was at me in seconds and was now looking down at me as an enemy not as a lover, with his size seeming twice as big. He looked ready to crush me and one of his hands was at the hilt of his sword ready to unleash it. By this time, I was shaking with fear.

His face was more tanned than I was used to, and he wore a lot more facial hair, covering his flexing jaw and tight mouth with a black shadow. His deep-set eyes were onyx black, edged with their powerful purple ring. His eyebrows knitted together in a frown, one I was very used to, making him look as hard as granite. I gulped down a hard lump when he spoke again.

"Show yourself!" I jumped slightly when his face shot forward only inches from mine. He was trying to see underneath my hood that covered my face down to my lips but got frustrated, so without a further thought my hood was ripped back and my identity was revealed. This time it was Draven's turn to jump slightly and he took a few steps back.

"It can't be! Impossible!" he said, almost panicked. I looked up slowly watching my own eyelashes lift as I met his eyes. He looked as though I had struck his heart with a knife and took a step forward to plunge it in further.

"What manner of power is this?" he demanded to the room as if waiting for someone to own up to the prank. I tried to move once more, hoping to run away and wake up with my neck still in one piece, all the while Draven was turning to scan the room for answers. The guards gripped my arms tighter and when I let out a yelp in protest, Draven turned back his attention to me shouting once more.

"Let her go and don't ever touch her again!" he ordered his guards, who didn't need telling twice. They dropped their hold and stepped back like the others in the room.

"Do you speak?" His question was abrupt and rude, but I wasn't about to argue on etiquette. I didn't know what to say or if to say anything at all. Maybe playing dumb was the best course of action, although I'm not sure Draven was going to accept this.

"Let me put it another way for you, little one, if you refuse to speak then there are other means to loosen one's tongue, so I will ask only once more...Do you speak?" He had leant his head down so his words only entered my ears and it was enough to make me respond. I nodded five times in quick succession, which brought a scary amusement to his lips.

"Good, now you will answer my questions. Who are you?"

"I...I am..." I was just about to say my name when Lucius interrupted us.

"My Lord, might you let me deal with this one, I believe she has been spying in on a time which is not her own." The sight of him made me move backwards. He now stood next to Draven and the differences in the two were like Yin and Yang. Draven was the bigger out of the two but not by much. Lucius looked as I would have imagined him to look as the person he was first known as...He looked like Judas.

His hair was much longer with a full beard that was the colour of straw blonde, highlighted streaks made by the sun. His eyes knew me and I shuddered as they burned into me.

"You know of this girl?" Draven asked as he ignored my moving slowly further back.

"I have foreseen this one and she will cause you great pain, my Lord, you must have her destroyed at once." His words penetrated me like an electrical current. I came alive with hatred filling my veins and flooding my senses.

"He lies! You cannot trust him! He will betray you, Draven! He wants me to hurt you and he will kill me in order to achieve it!" I shouted out making Lucius hiss and Draven growl.

"And how exactly will killing you hurt me...unless Lucius, you know something I do not?" He turned to look Lucius in the face and was met by a dark grin. I decided then to risk everything and say the only words I knew he might listen to.

"If you kill me as he wants you to, you will be killing someone whom you yourself has named to be the Electus." I said the word meaning 'Chosen' in Latin hoping it would still have meaning in this time. Draven's gaze left Lucius to stare at me as though I had said the words he'd longed for all his lifetimes.

"Then it is true, my time is now, and I shall finally have her!" Draven reached out to grab me but the arm he touched started to simply fade away. The most painful sight was watching the horror on Draven's desperate face as he realised what was happening. Lucius placed a hand on Draven's outstretched arm and spoke too softly for a Demon from the pits of Hell.

"No, my friend, I am afraid the time is not now. The time has come to put an end to this historical play of mine and claim her for myself."

Draven pushed Lucius back and rushed to me to take the remaining part of my body in his arms. It was a strange sensation. Like being washed away with the tide, I was trying desperately to stay afloat. Draven's face looked down at mine as though my eyes were the last thing to vanish. His last word was the last thing I heard before I woke, mirroring the events of the night before...

"Please...Stay."

"Draven!" I shouted as I bolted upright in bed. I looked around the room for any signs of the dream, any sight of the warrior King but my room looked just as I had left it. Everything that was apart from the dark figure that stood watching me from the corner behind my door. I froze like small prey at the sight of the ultimate hunter.

"I am afraid not, my dear Keira." That voice! The voice from so many of my nightmares was here now, in my room! This couldn't be real...I had woken up, hadn't I?

"Lucius," I said without asking.

"Of course, who else would go to such lengths but I to obtain such a prize." He moved from the shadows and I half expected to see the same Lucius from my dream. I was wrong. He wasn't wearing a long cloak now hiding his body. In fact, it was strange to see him looking so casual. But what was I expecting, combat gear to go kidnapping?

He wore dark trousers, a dark red t-shirt and a long black jacket that went to the floor. It split in three around his legs to allow for the movement that brought him closer to the bed. He looked well-groomed with hair slicked back by fingers and a clean shave to reveal smooth pale skin. He had sharp handsome features, a high nose and square jaw with staggeringly beautiful eyes. It pained me to accept these facts as I hated him more than I could muster up the words.

"If you were hoping for someone else then that hope is wasted, he is not going to come and save you as you may think. Tell me Keira, did you like my little trip down memory lane? I think that day would have been far more interesting with you in it." He sat down on my bed as if we were old friends having a chat instead of playing cat and mouse.

"How did you..?" I started to ask on a whisper. However, his smile cut off that question as he seemed to be enjoying the level of control he had gained over me.

"It wasn't without its difficulties I can assure you, but I had to gain access into your mind somehow. You have a mind like I have never known, even Dominic's mind I can control but so far that has been the hardest...well, that was up until you that is. You have certainly been a challenge, but I knew I would eventually break you." He trailed one cold, white finger down the length of my cheek, and I shuddered when his Demon side spoke the last two words.

"Break me?" I asked not knowing if I wanted the answer.

"I have had a lot of years to master patience. And you were so

763

worth the wait. I knew your dreams were the key and with the added touch of alcohol in your system it made it barely a challenge. Of course, Dominic was right to keep you firmly within his grasp. I thought I would never catch you alone. And after all of Dom's hard work at keeping such impenetrable guard over your mind while you slept. But tonight I knew my chance had come. So, now you are going to do everything that I say and in return, I will not hurt you." At this point my panic fluttered up into a whole new level and I could feel my pulse beating in my neck. Lucius also noticed. He caught the column of my neck in one large palm and my breath caught on a squeeze.

"I want to hear you say it," he leant into me to look directly into my frightened eyes.

"Say it!" His voice lost that smooth edge and he commanded this of me.

"Say…what? I don't know what you want me to say?" I stated bravely only just being able to get the words out around his hold.

"I want you to say you are mine and under my control… NOW!" he shouted and squeezed his grasp tighter just so I understood the full extreme of my position. I closed my eyes and a stream of liquid came running down my cheeks from the corners.

He was still allowing me to breathe but I didn't know for how long. Then he shifted his body weight so that he was straddling me. He had each one of his knees at either side of me and with his free hand he whipped out his jacket to allow for space. It flew out like a black cloud and for a second I was in the dark.

I felt the desperation of my situation and knew that if I didn't agree, he would most likely kill me, but if I did what of me then? Wouldn't that be a fate worse than death? I would be under his control and there would be no going back. I couldn't take that chance!

"Never," I said barely moving my lips. His eyes narrowed as his anger grew but after seeing the certainty in my face he actually smiled.

"Very well, your choice has been made, one you will soon regret. It is time for you to learn the full extent of my powers." His face went very hard before placing each palm of his hands on either side of my head. At first, it looked as though he was going crush my skull in his hands and I actually braced myself for the end.

"Remember Keira, keep breathing or this will kill you." That was the only warning I received before a great and tremendous pain shot through my brain as though I was receiving shock therapy on full power! I tried to scream, cry out and yell but nothing came. It felt like my mind was a front door to a house that held an endless stream of vital information. I wanted to guard it with my life, but Lucius was kicking in that door trying to hack my system.

Every new wave he sent crashing through me, I felt myself getting weaker and weaker. The door was splitting and soon he would be in. I had never felt pain like it before and on top of it all I was running out of air. My chest felt constricted and ached for oxygen. I remembered his warning and took in a lung full of air that tasted bitter, like breathing through a blood mist that was surrounding him.

"Let go... just let yourself go and be mine, then it will all be over." Lucius whispered in a smooth voice. However, this had the opposite effect. I clung on tighter, I fought harder and I held on to what was left of that mental barrier as if my life depended on it. But after another wave of excruciating pain I was screaming inside to just do as he asked of me and let go of it all. I felt as though my head would explode, splitting at the invisible seams and then there would be nothing left for him to take. I was so close...just so close to ending it all but then one image flashed through my mind like a lifeline in this hurricane of agony.

Draven.

All of a sudden, I didn't only want to fight but I now wanted to destroy! I wanted to take his hold on my mind and turn it against him. Hate swam through my body and buzzed along my veins like a poison I was calling for. In fact, if I had any control over my body then I would have kicked and scratched, punched and screamed at anyone doing this to me, no matter if they were stronger or not!

So now I had to think, even with this drilling pain infecting my mind. I had to be smart and use what I knew I had. Lucius had said that my mind had been the hardest to control, so what if right now he was using all of his strength to get to me? But more importantly what if I wasn't using all of mine. My mind was clearly different, so I needed to try...to push back...to fight with my mind and turn the tables. I needed to find his door and kick it wide open, spilling all his secrets!

I heard him growl as he witnessed my resistance grow. This gave me hope and this time it wasn't wasted. I decided to push as I never had before and in doing so I brought out all the information I needed. He was Judas and he was now reborn as the Vampire King. He sucked the lives from his victims and drew strength from their fears, but what of his fears. With that single thought combined with my brutal assault on his own mind, I suddenly knew what he feared the most...what anyone would fear the most...

The day they died.

As soon as I thought it he let go of my head and sat back to really look at me.

"How...? It's not possible...! It can't be... Just what the fuck are you?!" He stared at me in disbelief as my mind started to form his greatest fear, bringing it back from just a memory, making it a reality.

"NO...what are you doing? You can't do that...you...!" He didn't finish, as the blazing sun erupted in the room scorching everything around us. I ripped my way back to his memories and stripped away his power, forcing it back on himself. He hadn't expected me to use his control back against him and his face screamed out this fact. It was raw terror and the need to regain his power once again, all of which was useless now. I had come too far to let go. So I dug even deeper, ignoring the pain it was causing me. I went back to that day he hung from a tree, the day his brothers in belief had murdered him. The day his flesh had burnt away and begun to fall in flakes of charred skin, floating to the heated ground as he was left there to hang.

The sun got brighter and stronger until it became a fire in the sky. It scorched the earth and bit at his feet like snakes in the grass, the stings just as deadly. Each flame like the fangs he had acquired from the Hell in which he was cast. This was his damnation. His punishment and his betrayal from both sides. This memory was his Hell and now I had cast it again for him to relive.

This time he would not survive my dreams!

"NO!" He screamed one more time and he grabbed at my arms in a useless attempt at stopping me, but the world around us just grew brighter still, like we had transported inside the sun itself.

His grip became so painful it forced me to open my eyes and I was met by Lucius' body alight in an explosion of fire. Nothing else was burning but his form and of course the hands that still held me. The smell of burning flesh was that of my own as Lucius was still here in my mind, not in body or in soul.

With one last scream, he burst into a figure of black ash and only when I moved did it disperse and float away out into the night like a swarm of flies. I got up and slammed my window shut making the frame and glass shudder. I was shaking and slumped down to the floor in a fit of tears, brought on from both pain and relief.

I had done it! I had beaten my nightmares but at what price? My arms started to burn greater now and my tears weren't just down to the stinging on my skin. I got up and turned on the light to find the cause, hoping it was still all in my mind. It wasn't. There, on both my elbows, were red raw handprints burning into my skin. I touched one of the finger marks and winced at the pain it caused. Oh great, more war wounds for Draven to fix!

Draven...I had to go to him! I had to tell him what happened tonight or if he still didn't want to see me then I could find Vincent. Yes, that is what I needed to do. Vincent would help me and hopefully heal me. Because the burning was growing, getting deeper and clinging on like his flaming hands were still there latched on to my skin.

So that is exactly what I did. I quickly put on a pair of jogging bottoms and after carefully putting on a bra and a loose zip-up hoodie I grabbed my car keys. By this time my arms ached like tonne weights had been strapped to them.

Driving was not going to be easy, but I knew I could make it, as long as I broke one of my golden rules...

Speeding.

CHAPTER FIFTY-SEVEN

TOUCHED BY JUDAS

I pulled my truck into the parking lot at Afterlife and at three in the morning I was the only soul around. I was glad of this because by this point I was a hopeless mess of tears and sweat. The burning on my arms was considerably worse than before and now, instead of a slight burn, it felt as though my skin was melting from my bones. I ran to the side door by the bins as I knew the front door would be securely locked like last time. I punched in the number on the security pad a few times after getting it wrong more than once. I put this down to watery vision and a pain-induced mental breakdown.

Once inside, I ran the length of the club and mounted the main staircase taking two at a time. The VIP was empty of all but one. Karmun was still behind the bar cleaning and re-stocking, ready for the next night. I guess he didn't sleep much. He heard me coming and put down a crate of Absinthe.

"Hey, Honey, but wait... what are you doing here?" He sounded panicked at seeing me and I didn't care why. Immense pain kind of reprioritises all logic in your mind and I think if a giraffe had been playing checkers with a gazelle in the corner, I wouldn't have batted an eye!

"Sorry but I need to speak to Vincent, where is he?" Karmun looked dazzled for a moment while he thought about what to do.

"Can't it wait until morning? I mean he's most likely asleep, Keira." This is when I lost my cool.

"NO, it can't bloody wait! Look, I'm sorry but this is an emergency and I don't want to involve you but if you could help me and point me in the right direction, then that would be more than great." This came out in an out of breath jumble, but he got the picture at least.

"Come on, I'll show you." He motioned for me to follow him and I was glad I didn't have to do any more convincing than that 'cause I think the next stage would have been screaming. We walked the way I usually came in and through the opposite door to the VIP, making it the second time in two days that I walked along the open hallway.

The night air cut into my clothes but was oddly soothing on my imprinted burns. Karmun didn't say another word and every now and again, I saw a great sadness sweep across his features. Maybe he was tired and now he had to escort me without reason to his master's brother's room. He must be wondering why.

We didn't need to walk very far but it was in a part of Afterlife I had never been before. The open hallway veered off to the left and the Temple's domed roof could be seen below from a different angle. We were now directly opposite where I had been standing with Vincent the night before. I was staring at the point when Karmun cleared his throat to get my attention. I looked back at him and saw that he held open a door for me.

"I can't go any further but turn right down the hall and his room is the door at the end. Be warned he might not be alone. I'm sorry," he added before walking away, leaving me to wonder what he was sorry for, or was it for something to come? Maybe Vincent wouldn't be happy with me for disturbing him, but what choice did I have. Draven didn't want to see me, Sophia would tell her brother instantly and it's not like I could go to hospital over this.

I did as I was told and soon was at his door gearing myself ready to knock. I tried to think of what I was going to say but the pain decided for me. The time was now, and I couldn't waste it. I winced as I bent my arm up to knock. I didn't do it very loud, but it seemed I didn't need to as Vincent's voice was clearly awake and said a very distinctive,

"Enter!" So that is what I did. I opened the door slowly and entered a low-lit space where all the candlelight was concentrated around the middle of the room. Of course, this was where I found Vincent and no...

He wasn't alone.

One look and I wanted to turn and run away from the level of shame that doubled my pain. Vincent's room was all centred around a huge round white bed that was raised only slightly from the ground. The bed was surrounded by a line of pillar church candles, all flickering as the air came in with me. Vincent lay on his back naked with only a white sheet covering the manly parts of his anatomy.

I gulped at the sight of milky white skin covering a mass of muscles that flexed when they saw me. Of course, the two beauties that lay on either side of him weren't paying me any attention whatsoever. One was too busy kissing every inch of him and the other was sucking on his neck, legs draped across half his body. Oh yes and did I mention they too were both very, very naked!

"Keira?!" Vincent's voice sounded a mix of strained, shocked and mortified. If I could have formed words, I think mine would have sounded the same. I decided this was one of the worst ideas I had ever had and bolted for the door with shame flooding an already emotional state. I started to run back the way I came but couldn't find the door Karmun had led me to. I was feeling along the walls in hopes of finding a handle or anything that led me far, far away.

"Keira! Where are you?" Vincent's voice filled the hallway and I knew he would soon walk around the corner and see me. This thought filled me with dread. Of course, I gave up and sank to the floor to lean back against the doorless wall.

"There you are...Keira...? What's wrong, what's happened?" He ran towards me and dropped to his knees opposite me. He grabbed my arms to shake me and I screamed causing him to freeze. I was sobbing now at the unrelenting throbbing that set every nerve in my arms alight. He was speaking but I couldn't make out the words because I could hear nothing over my cries. He didn't touch me on my body again, but just smoothed back my hair that had plastered to my head from sweat. I had slumped forward and rested my head on his shoulders to finish my sobbing.

"Ssshh, you're safe now, no one can hurt you here." This was what he had been telling me over and over and only now I could hear it as my breathing steadied and my tears ceased for the time being.

"Do you think you can tell me what happened...Keira?" When I didn't respond he called my name again.

"Keira, who did this to you?" He sounded so concerned and also controlled. He had anger bubbling up within him I could tell. He had fisted his hands and his lips were set in a firm line, mirroring his frown. I started shaking my head and was soon crying again.

"Alright...It's alright sweetheart, you're safe now, let's get you to Dominic."

"No, I will be alright. I just came here to see if you could heal me...you know, *like before...?"* He looked taken aback a moment, confused with my response.

"You still don't want to see Dom?"

"It's your brother that doesn't want to see me and I don't need to disturb him if you can heal me...he doesn't have to know about this." Vincent looked truly shocked.

"I know for a fact you're wrong and I have no idea where you would get an idea like that from. Dom's been an anxious wreck since you left him. He was getting prepared to let you go, so I don't know why you would think this. And besides, I would never keep something like this from my brother." I looked down like I was a child being told off by a parent. But then my head shot up just as quick.

"Wait! He wants to see me?" I couldn't understand how my sister would have got the message so wrong.

"But of course, in fact, I believe the word "desperate" would be a good way to describe it." He gave me a smile and when I lowered my head in disbelief, he raised it back up with his finger.

"You don't believe me? Do you really think an Angel would lie to you?" He laughed with his words and through the pain I managed a smile.

"Come," he said rising to his feet and offering me his hand. He noted the way my face creased as I lifted my arm through the torment.

We made our way through his home like ghosts creeping through the night. I half expected Vincent to walk through a wall and assume I would follow him through it.

It didn't take any time at all and we were back to being on the familiar stone floor I knew so well. We came to Draven's door from a different angle. Vincent knocked on the side door, instead of the main door that was situated at the end of the great hallway leading directly from the VIP.

My pulse quickened in anticipation of seeing Draven. Would he be angry I was here or pleased? Well, given the circumstances he didn't have much choice in the matter and besides I really did have bigger problems at this current moment. Like the blinding torture that was inflicting every cell up my arms.

Vincent knocked strong and hard three times, all the while looking down at me. I held my breath until I heard the familiar voice echoing through the iron-studded, wooden door.

"Enter!" I was surprised when it sounded so awake...didn't he sleep when I wasn't around? Vincent went in first, while I decided to remain around the corner of the door frame out of sight. I wanted to judge his reactions first before committing myself to these actions, although I had little choice in anything else.

"Vin? What's wrong?" Draven sounded concerned for his brother and his voice was smooth velvet without one ounce of indifference towards his kin.

"Dom, I knew you would still be awake."

"Yes and I am surprised you are here and not entertaining beautiful, twin angelic raptures...were they not to your liking brother or have you grown tired through old age? Too much for you, were they?" Draven laughed at his jesting and I was so surprised to hear this brotherly banter it made me smile through my dark situation.

"Not at all Dom but trying to enjoy myself knowing you would be sat here, yet again feeling sorry for yourself, well let's just say I felt it my brotherly duty to change that." Vincent sounded full of amusement as he knew something his brother didn't.

"Then if I were you, I would go back to your chamber and enjoy their Heavenly pleasures for you are wasting your time on me...Go and leave me to my figureless shadows." I had never heard Draven sound so small and fragile before and my breath caught in the back of my throat.

"Why would I do that when I have a gift for you?" Vincent sounded so smug I could hear the smile I couldn't see. Before Draven had time to ask he took two steps back and nodded for me to come in.

"Look what I found, Brother," he said as he moved to the side allowing me to be seen. Draven was on his feet before I could inhale a breath.

"Keira!" He was beaming at the sight of me. How could I have ever thought he wouldn't have been happy to see me? He was stood there dumbstruck for a few moments, staring at me as though I was a dream or a cruel joke from his brother and if he took a step closer, I would simply fade away. That thought took me back to my dream and I shuddered. Then someone broke the spell and he was at me in the blink of an eye. I looked up to him and smiled but it didn't last long on my lips before extreme pain killed all happiness, unknowingly caused by Draven.

He had grabbed me to him by the arms and I crumpled before him, screaming out at the unbearable burn that ran to the bone. Draven instantly let me go and through the tears I could just make out the horror on his face.

"Keira, what happened? You are hurt?!" I couldn't answer him. That was soon made apparent by the sobbing noises that consumed my vocal abilities.

"I should have mentioned that first, it seems she has somehow injured her arms, but she wouldn't tell me how." Vincent was adding as Draven scooped me up into his arms and was carrying me to his bed. He was so careful with every piece of me that I was amazed he could even hold on to me enough without me merely slipping away from him. I felt him lay me down and he allowed me time to catch my breath and cease my erratic crying before asking me once again.

"Keira, you need to tell me what happened? Did someone do this to you?" This question came through gritted teeth and a strained anger desperate to be allowed to bubble to the surface. All I needed to do was nod and I heard something in the room smash.

"Dom, focus! Now is not the time to lose it! Fix her and then we will reap our justice." Vincent's voice of reason could just be heard over my weeping. I looked up to see Draven above me with eyes closed and two hands clasped behind his head as if trying to pull forward the right actions needed in a mind clouded with rage, revenge and wrath.

He gripped on to himself but the pain in his face was too clear to be denied...it was fear. This startled me to a point that made me shiver. Draven was never afraid, so something in my situation had snapped that illusion. Something so bad even the impenetrable man I loved looked terrified. Suddenly my pain had a friend to join in my suffering...the very same fear.

"We need to see, take off her jacket." Vincent seemed to be taking charge where Draven was unable.

"DOM! Snap out of it! ta vajab sind" ('She needs you' In Estonian) He sounded angry, which was unusual for Vincent but one look at his face told me it too was laced with worry. My situation wasn't looking as clear cut for the healing I was used to.

Panic was slowly setting in but my brain was so overwhelmed by other sensations it was hard to focus for long. It was like being very, very drunk. Sometimes your mind would wander through the motions like autopilot, getting you here and there, like the journey I had taken back to Afterlife but now it was fogged by the burning throb that replaced alcohol.

Through this mist I felt my zip being pulled down and two sets of hands, trying in vain to remove my sleeves painlessly. I screamed so loud I used every shred of air left in my lungs. I thought the hands would stop but they couldn't, not now, I knew that. My mind still functioning at half its normal rate told me this. They had already caused the hurt, why stop now and prolong it. Like ripping off a band-aid, like they say here in America.

In the UK we would have said plaster. I wondered which was right? I lived here now, so shouldn't I accept the new terminology, or do I remain true to my roots? It was a strange argument to be having with myself at the mouth of Hell, but no one ever said turning insane was logical.

"Tanrının eliyle! Who did this!?" ("By the hand of God" In Turkish). Vincent spoke words I didn't know yet again, but it made me open my eyes. The first thing I saw was Draven's eyes glowing red like blood had been injected there and then lit by the Devil himself. His face was a hard mass of lines and the utter rage that presented itself was just as painful to witness as the pain in my arms.

I winced back into the soft bed wishing it could swallow me whole and put an end to all this misery. I looked away only to find Vincent staring down at my arms with a violent disgust painted on his perfect features. Then, my next mistake cleared the way for another onslaught of hysterics. I looked down at where their gaze was focused...my arms.

The red handprints were no longer, but instead lay bloody flesh beyond all repair. It looked as though I had been butchered! I screamed again and again, shaking my head to try and get the horrific picture from my mind.

Flesh that had bubbled and burnt down until it looked like stretched red plastic over bone. The edges were black and scorched around where each finger had been. Deep lacerations spread along the inside where the lifeline on his palms would have been. My veins had turned black down the rest of my arms, all the way to my fingertips, like an infection was spreading. The skin by my elbow looked to have caved in on itself leaving me with misshapen arms and blood pooled on the sheets beneath me. I could no longer use my arms and I'm not sure at this point that I ever would again.

"We have to heal her...NOW! It has already started to spread, and we need to reach it before it gets to her heart." Vincent's words seem to pull Draven from his private place in Hell and his head snapped up to look at him for what seemed like the first time.

"But the pain?!" Draven said in whispered panic.

"Dom, she is already in a great deal of pain as it is, we must act quickly!" I admitted to myself I was glad they were concerned for me, but I couldn't help wishing they would get a bloody move on, whatever it was they were planning!

"She needs something...think of the pain, Vincent...! Morphine or..." Draven was abruptly cut off by his brother's stern tone.

"There is no time! The essence of the touch will not accept drugs, look how it spreads. You must get her to open her mind to you...that is the only way, but we must hurry, or it will be too late!"

"Keira...my sweetheart, you have to listen to me." Draven was speaking so softly it was hard to picture the words coming from the same man whose eyes were consumed by such fury.

"It... hurts...ppplllease...make it...stop." I strangled out through screams, moans and cries. He smoothed back my hair from my forehead and kissed my salty skin.

"I will, my love, but you must be brave for me. I want you to do as I ask and let me in, open your mind as much as you can, so that I can take that pain away...otherwise the pain will be too much." He tried so hard to keep his voice level and void of the panic rising in him.

He wanted to remain strong for both of us I could tell, but the pain they talked about was terrifying me to a point where functioning beyond my reactions was a difficult task. I just wanted my mind to pop open and let Draven in but it was firmly closed. It had shut down thanks to Lucius' influence and now it was on lockdown, not allowing any other intruders in. I tried to concentrate, to break down the walls I myself had put there but it was too hard. The mixture of pain and fear had made it near to impossible to think about anything else.

"Dominic NOW!" Vincent screamed out at his brother who was obviously hesitating.

"She isn't letting me in!" he shouted back.

"There is no time! Do it now or we all LOSE HER!" So this was my answer...the root of their fears. My life and death hung on the scales, each side weighing the same.

One tip, one wrong move and my life would be no more. My

life, only without pain, without worry, without the traumatic past... but then I stopped breathing as the worst thought seeped through me in a purple coloured blur.

A life without…

Dominic Draven.

CHAPTER FIFTY-EIGHT

BREAKING DOWN WALLS

NO! I wanted to live! I wanted to feel the sun on my skin, hear the sound of new life entering this world but most of all to taste Draven's lips upon mine. I was NOT going to die! I would fight! I would not let fear take me over to the other side, they couldn't have me! I belonged to another!

"Restrain her!" Draven snapped out at his brother. Through my mental torture they had turned me around so that my head was now at the bottom of the bed. Vincent was stood at the end and had grabbed my arms to spread them up above my head. He held onto my wrists like live shackles. His fingers had circled around bone as if he was ready for the fight in me. I looked up to see his face upside down nod at his brother. My watery gaze travelled back to Draven to find him straddling me, keeping his weight from barely crushing me. He was on his knees at either side of my waist and was looking down at me with guilt riddled lines invading his stern face.

I took a deep breath as I waited for Hell's fire to touch me. Draven gave no warning, which I guess was better for me. I sucked in a quick breath at the moment he slashed open his own hands and placed them down on where Lucius had touched me. Suddenly I felt like dying!

I couldn't hear anything but my own ear-piercing screams of pure excruciating pain. Every type you could imagine! It was like a lifetime of pain, from stubbing your toe, to breaking your arm, all wrapped up into one moment. Years and years of accidents, illness, self-inflicted and Morgan induced body mutilation could not compare to this single moment in time where my body was being pushed so far past the limit, it felt as though I was dying over and over.

"She can't take much more! Damn it Keira, FUCKING LET ME IN!" Draven screamed down at me. He was now using all his body weight to hold me down as I was using every last surge of energy to thrash around the bed. Draven's hands were tight around the area that was minus all skin and he let his blood flow out from his body into me.

I was trying to focus on his words, his actions, anything but the room spinning around so fast I felt sick. It was like being on a Waltzer ride at the fairground, while smacked up on the worst kind of drugs. I was trying to get a clear picture of what was happening, but the world was no longer the same. I felt like a slashed-up Alice falling down the rabbit hole, only one where the Mad Hatter was the Devil and Wonderland was actually Hell!

"LET ME IN DAMN YOU, KEIRA!" Draven roared at me from his Demon side in reaction to feeling me fall further from his grasp. I just wanted it to end! I wanted peace after what felt like a lifetime of suffering. Didn't he understand...I just wanted to be numb.

"Gods, Keira! Then let me help you! Open yourself to me! I will not lose you! You are not allowed to fucking leave me, DO YOU HEAR!" Draven was still bellowing out at me, pleading with me and for the first time ever, he was crying freely. I felt his tears falling onto my face and the effect was like acid to my skin. The tears of a Demon and the tears of an Angel mixed, made for a powerful antidote to my suffering.

It felt like freedom.

I found my mind and the walls surrounding it. Walls that went up so high I could not see the top which was caked in cloud. I was a smaller version of myself in my mind, stood at the bottom trying to claw it down with tiny hands. Draven's voice still boomed overhead for me to let him in, like Zeus commanding the skies ...but how? I needed to think, to find a way of destroying what I myself had put there!

Then the most amazing thing happened. I started to feel Draven's tears roll down my skin once more and leave a burning path behind them. I lifted my hand to my face in my mind and caught a tear that was not my own in my hand.

I looked down as it glistened like a pearl and diamond combined. Then it started to glow like the orb I had dreamed of my first night at my sisters. It got bigger and bigger until I could no longer carry it so I threw it at the wall with both hands. The wall cracked on impact and caused a split to run up until out of sight. I heard it thunder above me and the Heavens opened up for the flood. The rain in my mind fell down in giant droplets that soaked on impact and as soon as the first one hit me I woke from my mental imprisonment gasping.

I looked up to see Draven smiling at me with hands still locked firmly in place. For a split second I thought I was dead and the Angel above me was leading the way for I now felt no pain. Nothing! It was just blissful numbness making my body feel as if it weighed the Earth and was sinking into the bed.

"Good girl. You did it Keira... You let me in and now you will suffer no more. Now just sleep...*Just sleep now...sleep...*" His words flowed over me like a warm blanket covering me from head to toe. I felt my lids growing heavy and being pulled down by no doing of my own. Then the world of Hell, fire and pain grew black and peaceful...

I lost myself to its beautiful simplicity of nothing but peace.

"It was Lucius!" Draven spoke in my lucid dream. He sounded angry although I could tell he was trying to keep his voice low and unheard.

"You are certain?" Now his brother was there and soon the image became as clear as their voices. They were both sat down on opposite couches in Draven's living space. Draven had his head in his hands and Vincent was shaking his head causing his halo of blonde curls to dance around.

"I felt his pain. I don't know how but she beat him, Vincent. She fucking beat him! She forced him back and denied him access to her mind. How is that even possible…how did she become so strong?" Draven's voice ached through exhaustion and a mass of horrendous events.

"It is impossible, Dom, Lucius is the strongest we know of for mind control…No human would stand a chance. You must be wrong, brother."

"But that is the thing, for I know I am not! Once she let me in, I saw everything. First her dream…what he showed her of our past but twisted it so that she became a part of it. It was when we first met Lucius, when we were comrades."

"But, Dom it's not poss…" Vincent started to say but Draven quickly interrupted his Brother, standing suddenly as his emotions got the better of him.

"She saw him, Vincent! She saw, Lucius… she called out to me and tried to warn me of his intent, but the dream ended before I could react. He took her away from me and it was a message. He wanted me to know." Draven was now standing tall and firm on his knowledge.

"But how do you know this?" Vincent asked innocently enough but his shock was clear.

"Because she did the only thing she knew how to do. The only thing to beat him and that was to access his mind. I don't know how she did it as I have never seen anything like it in all my years, but I saw for myself."

"What do you mean?"

"Her dream…while she was dreaming, she wasn't the only one Lucius was trying to control but as I had not slept since she left me, he could do little but focus all his attention elsewhere. If I had only slept, then I could have gotten to her quicker, I could have…"

"No! Dom, don't do that! Don't blame yourself for events unseen. If what you say is true and that was his plan, then it would have been a futile attempt at saving her from his actions. Which makes me wonder what was his gain in alerting you to his attack in the first place?"

"He wanted to send me a message."

"But what?" Draven's voice replied in stone-cold fear.

"He intends to take her from me."

"But that was before she beat him, which I still don't understand how?" Vincent sounded thick with disbelief.

"She was so, so clever. Sometimes I think I underestimate her. I told you she accessed his mind, but I didn't say what she did with it." Vincent didn't reply but just waited in silence as Draven once again took a seat. He let out a sigh and said,

"She showed him his fear, his only fear. She showed him the Sun." Draven sounded so proud, if I could have seen his features better, I believe he would be beaming.

"But that's…that's…"

"Impossible, yes… I know." Draven finished for him.

"How did she even know his fears?" Vincent asked clearly still astonished.

"I told her some while back of his history and she used this knowledge against him. I doubt very much that Lucius was ever expecting such power from my girl, but power is what he found and one a great deal more than his own." I even felt myself smile at this in my dream, thinking at least I wasn't as useless around the supernatural world as I once thought...I just hoped it was true, because let's face it, how freakin cool and kick-ass would that be!

"But she is human. Nothing on this Earth has that kind of power! We know this because we have looked for centuries." Vincent didn't sound so willing to believe it and I couldn't blame him.

"Brother, no one is more shocked than I, but I can only go by what I saw with my own eyes. The only way I can make sense of it is the more powerful the mind she gains access to, the more power she has to control. In our case, Lucius is the most powerful of our kind at manipulating the actions of others, then think of the supremacy she holds over all of us. She is after all, the 'Chosen'." I couldn't tell how Draven felt about this, but I needed to know...I needed answers. What did that mean exactly to be the 'Chosen' and what about this so-called 'Power' he was convinced I held. Was it true?

"So what are we to do? What did Pythia say on the matter?" My mind hunted around to pull that word from my memory and found her to be the Oracle, the one Draven had spoken of.

"Pythia told me of what I already knew the very first time I saw her. Keira is my Chosen, there is no doubt. She told me to protect her with my life and the Gods will do the same. She is too important to the prophecy for anything to be allowed to happen to her. Pythia told me of her power and I didn't believe it until now. This is the way the Gods have seen to her protection, but she must be taught how to use it"

"I'd say she's not doing too badly on her own with that one!" Vincent said sarcastically.

"Yes but look at the damage he was still able to inflict." Ok, so Draven had a bloody good point there! And there wasn't a cat in Hell's chance I was going to go through that shindig again!

"And how was he able to do that exactly...? I mean if she is so powerful then..." Once more Draven was interrupting his Brother.

"She is still in her infancy, Vincent. Like a child with a dangerous weapon. She doesn't know how to use it to its full advantage yet. Lucius knew this and used that power back against her, and he had little choice in doing so for she could have killed that Bastard! Next time I will teach her to do just that!" Draven erupted with this last statement.

"Sounds to me like she came very close in doing so." Draven just grunted at his brother's statement, then added his own views on the murder matter.

"Yes, but not close enough for my liking!"

"And your plans for revenge...what of them?" Vincent inquired. I could feel my head start to sink back under another level of exhaustion as I waited for Draven's response and it soon became the last thing I heard before I sank to the bottom...

"Death to one of the Kings."

I felt my head fall back after this dream had finished and I woke quickly wondering what had just happened? I was in a bed unlike the one I was used to in Draven's world. It was made up from layer upon layer of furs and cushions spread over the floor. I felt as though I was wrapped up in the softest silk and velvet combined. I stretched out and my hand grazed the rough sandstone floor in contrast to the covers I was entwined in. Then a voice broke through my sleepy state.

"My beauty awakes at last." Draven purred in my ear, making me jump. I whipped my head back around from staring at the floor and was faced with a very different Draven, one that I now knew from my dreams. I flinched back not knowing what else to do.

"Do not fear me, for I will not hurt you, child" His short cut beard tickled my arm as he lowered his head to kiss my bare shoulder.

"I am not a child," I said not knowing what else to say and after I said it I wondered why this of all things was what I went with? He raised his eyebrows at my little outburst, and he laughed once.

"Ah, your pride has been hurt but forgive me, my Queen." He lowered his head to me in a sign of respect before continuing with this new round of crazy.

"I merely meant that compared to my many years that is all. Fear not, your body is all woman and pleases me greatly." He was devouring me with his eyes running over every inch of my skin, which made me realize just how naked I was. I felt so exposed that I grabbed the cover and pulled it up to my chin making him laugh again.

"Your blush only enhances your beauty and makes your creamy skin glow. You must have come from somewhere cold for you to be so untouched by the sun... although your hair is the colour of pure gold and suits my tastes greatly...tell me, my beauty, where are you from?" He leant back to take me in better and wait for his answer. I bit my lip, not knowing what to say. I knew this was surely a dream, but I didn't think in dreams you could experience such real sensations.

"Where am I?" I ignored his question asking one of my own. Draven shifted his weight to lean on his arm that made his bicep bulge and the leather strap strain around it. He wore nothing on his torso and as the covers covered his lower half for all I knew he could be as naked as I was.

One thing was for certain and that was, if this was what Draven had looked like all those years ago then it was confirmed that he had always been breathtakingly handsome. He was simply stunning, and I was glad to be the one waiting for an answer because I couldn't speak for the beauty before me.

It was like a Greek God had dropped down to Earth for a quickie. His skin was touched with a sun-kissed glow and his hair was the night. Longer than I was used to, but tied down his back, braided in a leather thong, causing his features to be all the more striking. His bone structure looked to have been carved by a master of the arts, with a stone jaw and deep-set eyes that pierced through me, making my insides turn to mush.

"How is it you do not know or is it because Heaven dropped you at my feet for me to claim?" He was closing the space between us and I automatically put my hand out to stop him. My palm remained positioned flush against his hard chest and it moved to the beat of his heart. He seemed to react to my touch as his breathing became heavy and he closed his eyes.

"Please..." I started but he interrupted my spoken thoughts by letting a low growl surface, before suddenly grabbing my wrist at the hand that prevented him from coming closer. He pulled me roughly towards him and repositioned my arm around his shoulder as he shifted my weight backwards. He leant down and I now found myself under his huge frame that was hovering above me.

"You were saying please oh so beautifully...say it again for your King," he asked of me making me blush at the dark seduction in his voice. I quivered as he brushed his lips across my neck and down my collarbone.

I could smell the warm night air surrounding us from every angle. I could barely see over his impressive shoulders but what I could see was that the room we were in didn't have walls as such. No, instead it had huge richly ornate pillars arching up to the golden ceiling above. The room also held carved wooden chests and seats that were shaped like a half-moon on their sides.

Everything smelled so rich, even the lacquer that painted the wood its rich red colour and the blossoms from the gardens that must be below his open balcony. I could see the blanket of stars in the clearest night's sky just beyond the frame of muscle that still kept me caged.

I started to feel the covers moving down from my naked body and I grabbed at them with my hands, trying to clutch them back to covering me.

"Why do you keep such perfection from me? Are you really this selfish, my Goddess?" he teased making me swallow hard.

"I don't understand why I'm here...Is it Lucius doing this?" I asked this to both of us but when Draven expressed his displeasure in another growl I sunk back further.

"I will not allow you to speak another man's name in my bed! You are mine! You belong to me and only me, do you understand?!" I started to bite my bottom lip and nodded quickly in spite of his anger but thankfully this made his features soften before speaking once more,

"Now tell me, what is this Lucius' hold over you, my fearful one?" He was still trying to regain his calm, but I shook under him as he tensed his body above waiting for my answer.

"He doesn't! I mean...well...I don't know...why am I here and not with the 'you' from my time?" My question confused him as he frowned down at me, looking even more severe than usual.

"What time is it that you speak of?" He was now holding all his weight up on his arms and any normal man would have crumbled under the strain for so long. I couldn't think here...I needed to move, to create some distance from this muscle enclosure he held me under.

I decided my actions quickly and turned using all my weight to one side until I knocked his arm out and rolled off the bed. My sudden movements caught him off guard and he fell back on his side as I made my escape. I still had the sheet around me, and I got to my feet quickly pulling it tighter around my chest like I would have a towel.

"That was cruel, Princess," he said full of humour.

"Don't call me that, I am just a girl!" I said backing away from the bed where he still lay. He rolled on his back and laughed heartily up at the ceiling.

"Oh, but you are so much more than that! I am a King...did you know that? That will make you my Queen soon enough, but for now you will be known as my Princess. My Royal Goddess and no other man will be permitted to lay eyes on you! No other man will ever touch you and no other man will speak your name on their lips...but wait, for what is your name?" This question quickly prompted movement from him and before I knew what had happened, he was stood up and staring down at me.

He wasn't as naked as I thought as he had material draped around him like a long skirt tied to his waist by a thick leather belt studded in gold. His wide chest heaved, making his muscled six-pack tense as he closed the remaining space between us. He was backing me up against one of the pillars and I soon felt its carvings pressing into the curvature of my spine.

"This is just a dream," I said aloud to myself, making him cock his head to one side. He placed his arms either side of me to grip the column at my back and leant down to my ear.

"Then why not enjoy it?" he whispered seductively before kissing my neck. I moaned at the sensations it caused and when he felt my succumbing need, he wrapped an arm around my waist to pull me roughly into him.

I bent to him and moulded myself into his raptures. His lips searched out mine and he crushed them against me, forcing my mouth to open to him. It did...all too willingly. One strong hand worked its way up my neck, holding it there for a second in a demanding primal way, before travelling upwards to grasp a handful of my hair. Once there he steered my head to the side to gain better access to my lips. It was like being devoured by a passionate beast, his lips moving, grinding and sucking at my own until my legs turned to liquid. He was holding me up to him and I gripped onto his back, digging my nails down his skin under the erotic onslaught I was enduring.

He only released me when he knew of my desperate need for air. I was panting in his arms as he gently kissed my hairline.

"Such passion that flows through your veins, how responsive

you are to my touch...as if you have felt it before." He was looking back at me, taking in my face for his answers. It didn't take him long to find them.

"You are mine from a different time, aren't you?" I simply nodded.

"Then I do not have long to keep you," he said to himself. He nodded once before making up his mind and then took my hand in his.

"Then come, come and see the reason you are here." He turned towards the open walls that were so symbolic to my current situation. Was this why I was here? To see the walls I opened to Draven's mind. Was this still my sleep...my dream being controlled by another?

I let myself be walked to the edge of the balcony and I breathed in the warm air that made me feel so alive, as though it was pure energy. He pulled me to stand before him and held my shoulders from behind. I gasped at the sight before me.

"It is the most beautiful thing I have ever seen," I said on a gasp. My hands were at my face holding in my utter overwhelmed surprise. A golden city stretched out before me as the night sky slowly gave way to the coming dawn. The sand-coloured structures rolled down the hill from where we stood, all different shapes and sizes.

A large turquoise dome was in the centre surrounded by high walls of ornate stone carved into petal points at the tops of arches. It took me back to Draven's home and the Temple that lay at its core...at its heart. It was rimmed with gold and smaller domes were dotted around within its walls. These must have been the smaller buildings where ancient priests lived.

Its beauty was one thing but the feeling that I was somehow connected to this place was the confusing part. Was it that my thoughts were mixing with Draven's? Had my mind suddenly become an empty book, one where the pages could be filled by Draven's commands, his past and his own stories? Or was there something more to this place?

Draven's voice brought me back with a question.

"You like your new home, Princess?" he murmured in my ear

before tilting my neck to one side to kiss the skin more easily. I swallowed hard from the erotic feeling of his beard scratching my sensitized skin thanks to him sucking on my flesh.

"Is this...?" I didn't finish as his mouth released the words, over the skin he still held captive,

"This is Persia." He only ceased biting me when I gasped.

"What is wrong?" My mouth hung open and no power could make me close it and take all of this in. How was I seeing this as though from a perfect, flawless memory? He held me tighter waiting for my answer, one I couldn't find in this beautiful madness.

"I think I had better go home now," I said as though being able to stop a video that was playing.

"Then you have found enough peace in my time?" The question made me snap shut my gaping mouth and turn to face him. He ran a finger the length of my jaw and lifted my face up when he reached my chin.

"Perhaps another time, Princess." His lips tipped up in a smug smile when I bit my lip.

"Then grant me with a kiss before he takes you back." I closed my eyes as I let confusion seep over me. I felt his lips graze mine before lingering there long enough to allow a surge of lust to build. He suddenly crushed himself to me and I gasped in surprise. This was the opportunity he was looking for as I opened my mouth enough to let him surge in and fully taste me. He continued to kiss me until I felt as though floating in air. It was rough, it was commanding, and it was completely intoxicating.

The smell of his skin's musk started to change and the air around me grew a few degrees cooler. His touch became lighter and more soothing, like fingertips trailing along my skin.

"Keira...Keira...Time to wake, my Princess." Draven's voice echoed in the dark and I realized I was still living in the shadows of my mind. I called out his name as I opened my eyes to find I was lying down in bed. This time it was one I was very familiar with.

"I'm here Keira, no one will harm you." I felt like saying 'You said that before,' but thankfully didn't. After all it wasn't his fault

Lucius had come for me. If I hadn't been so stubborn then he would have never had the chance.

I saw Draven looking down at me, his face trying to mask the worry that lay there. I tried to sit up, but Draven held me still.

"You need to rest more. Your body is still weak from regenerating itself."

"But the dream! I dreamt of you...but it wasn't you...it...it was..." I was babbling and sitting up despite his warnings. I had to tell him, but he was making it difficult.

"Hush now, calm yourself. I know what you dreamt, Keira," he admitted, as though he was responsible, which hit me...

"You put it there?!" I accused shifting to see him better.

"I did," was all he gave me.

"But why...how?"

"Because you needed peace. I wanted to give that to you the only way I knew how. I took you back to that time with me and gave you something further than what Lucius showed you. A time when you would have been mine before his interference. I saw how you worried for me in your dream and I wanted to make it as if you had never disappeared from my arms. I wanted to share with you my home...my first home." Now I understood. Where Lucius had used the past to take hold of me to gain control...Draven had used it to ease my pain, to show me a part of his life before mine had begun. He wanted to share a part of himself with me to help me find the peace I had so desperately been searching for.

"Thank you." I said before throwing my arms around his neck and kissing him as though it had been an age since we had been together. He was certainly taken back but soon his surprise was replaced by eagerness.

"But wait!" I shouted half in his mouth, making him groan. I pulled back and whipped off the plain black top I had been dressed in. I even had a white cotton bra on, but I wasn't looking at that. No, I was searching my arms for new scars or pieces missing from my elbows. All I found were the old ones.

"They're fine?" I said as if it was another dream.

"Of course they are, I healed you Keira. The flesh and skin regenerated as though it never happened but the infection was harder to remove." He looked away briefly as though remembering the sight of me screaming in agony beneath him.

"What infection?"

"The Demon presence he left behind, but Keira I do not want you to think about it anymore. It is finished and I won't let anyone come that close again...ever. It. Is. Over," he said sternly as the last three words were ground through his teeth. I couldn't help it. I crossed my arms over my chest and stared at him.

"And how will you do that exactly, are you going to hide me away like Rapunzel?" Well I certainly had the hair for it.

"Rapunzel?" he questioned not looking at all offended.

"Yeah you know, long-haired gal, lives in a tower, sings a lot." he laughed at my description.

"Ah you mean 'رودابه', the beauty." He said the ancient words so swiftly like he spoke this language all the time.

"Excuse me?" I said causing him to smile at my understandable ignorance.

"It means Rūdāba. She is or was, where the brothers Grimm got their idea from I believe." He started to help me with my top as I was trying to pull it down over the mass of hair that went in every direction. I knew one thing...I wasn't looking forward to trying to brush out all the knots I had created. It looked like a chicken coop!

"Rapunzel was real?" I asked, fascinated.

"She was...of sorts anyhow. Let's see if I remember The Shahnameh's description correctly." He paused and looked up as though it was written on the bed's canopy.

"About her silvern shoulders two musky black tresses curl, encircling them with their ends as though they were links in a chain.
Her mouth resembles a pomegranate blossom, her lips are cherries and her silver bosom curves out into breasts like pomegranates.
Her eyes are like the narcissus in the garden and her lashes draw their blackness from the raven's wing.
Her eyebrows are modelled on the bows of Teraz powdered with fine bark and elegantly musk tinted.

THE TWO KINGS

*If you seek a brilliant moon, it is her face; if you long for the
perfume of musk, it lingers in her tresses
From top to toe she is Paradise gilded; all radiance, harmony and
delectation"*

Of course, he recited the poetry perfectly as though the one himself
to have written it.

"What was that? It was beautiful," I said lowering my lashes,
wishing for such beauty. Anyone would next to such a man as
Draven.

"It was from The Shahnameh, the book of Kings. It was written
by the Persian poet Ferdowsi around one thousand AD," he said
proudly and it seemed this was the day for learning a great deal
more about Draven's history.

"Yes and I will tell you one day who it is really about, but for
now you must sleep."

"No way! You can't tell me something like that and expect me
to sleep!" I moved out of his hold as he was trying to get me to lie
back down.

"Keira, you are being stubborn," he informed me but I didn't
care, I wanted to hear more.

"Alright, I will make you a deal... if you lie back, I will tell
you the story until you fall asleep." I suddenly felt about six years
old. It had been too many years to remember since I had been told
stories before bedtime. I nodded my agreement and shifted further
down to get comfy. I knew I was still fully clothed, but Draven
pulled the covers around me anyway, which felt nice and safe.

"There was a great Persian warrior named Zāl who was born
with white hair. He was Albino. Zāl was the son of Sām and the
grandson of Nariman, both of which were great heroes of ancient
Persia. However, because of his defect, Zāl was rejected by his
father. And therefore cast out as a child."

"That's terrible!" I shouted making him smile down at me.

"Yes it was. Anyway, so he roamed Persia, but it was only
when he was upon the mountain Damavand where the Gods heard

his cries. They sent down a bird so large it would block the sun and darken the skies when flying. Some say it was the holy Phoenix named Simurgh sent to guard the child blessed by God." I was nodding at him when he paused to take in my expression. He chuckled once at my enthusiasm and continued.

"The bird took him in until time passed, and he grew into a man, living on the land but never leaving the bird. Rumours of the silver man living in the mountains reached the ears of Sam, his father and he was soon found by the guilty man."

"Yeah, I'll say he's guilty alright!" I said frowning, once again making Draven smile.

"You are so very sweet, do you know that?"

"Draven," I said his name and blushed.

"Right...so where was I...Ah yes, so his guilty father could not reach him. So he prayed to the God's that had taken in his son and begged for forgiveness. Simurgh knew at once when the man's father would come for him and that their time together was at an end. She plucked three plumes from her breast and the heavenly voice spoke in her place. 'Burn this if ever you have need of me, and may your heart never forget your nurse, whose heart breaks for love of you,' she said adding that when in trouble she would appear as soon as the feathers were lit."

"So he left with his father? Poor Sim...ugh...you know what's her name," I said lamely causing Draven to take my face in his hands and kiss me gently on the lips.

"He did indeed return with his father, but his misfortunes were no longer. His father made every effort to redress his past wrongs and when he went off to wage war he was given his father's Kingdom."

"So what about Rapunzel, well I guess I mean...you know..." I still wasn't down yet with all the names and there was no way I was going to be able to say them with my accent!

"You mean Rūdāba. Well, she was the princess of Kabul, daughter of Mehrab Kaboli. Zāl had heard of her immense beauty and went in search of her to bed. But he became enraptured and fell deeply in love with her."

"Aww, I like this story"

"As I knew you would." He beamed as he smoothed back my hair before continuing,

"The story goes, Zāl came to the walls of Rūdāba 's palace where Rūdāba let down her tresses to Zāl as a rope for him to climb. Rūdāba seated Zāl on the roof and they both talked to each other for hours which was unacceptable in accordance with Persian tradition."

"But why?"

"Times have changed, my Love, getting to know one's wife usually came after the marriage bed," he said then burst out laughing at my face, which I could feel was my nose wrinkling in disgust.

"In the legend that followed, after being accepted by each of their fathers they married and when Rūdāba was giving birth to the unusually large baby, he soon realized his love was going to die. Near to giving up, Zāl remembered the feather of the Simurgh and followed the instructions which he'd been given that day."

"He used the feather!" I gasped.

"That he did. He placed the feather on the sacred fire causing the Simurgh to appear and instructed him upon how to perform a caesarean section, thus saving Rūdāba and the child." He finished the story as if he'd been telling it for years and I almost clapped at the ending. What a nice story, better even than the Brothers Grimm version. I was about to tell him so when he carried on.

"Of course, this is where the story that is written differs from the truth." He looked as though still not sure whether or not to tell me.

"How so?"

"What is written is not what happened. Zāl fell in love with Rūdāba, yes but she was a Demon that had possessed Rūdāba as a willing sacrifice. Don't look so horrified, Keira." He smirked at my scrunched-up face before continuing,

"You see, her past love and betrothed had been murdered in battle and she was so fraught with grief she gave herself to the Gods to be reborn. Of course, by the time Zāl came to find her she was not what she appeared." I placed my hands at my mouth and covered my shock.

"Oh no, what happened?" He smiled and pulled my hands away from my face and brushed the back of his hand down my cheek.

"When Zāl found out the truth, there was no other choice but to kill himself to be with her and it worked, as to this day they are still together. It was the only way for her to have him. She appealed to have his soul re-used once sold to Lucifer and he could see no reason against it." Draven was talking about this part like any businessman would about politics.

"They are still around? Like living together... after so long?" I could barely get my head around it.

"Yes Keira...and, well...you know them, quite well in fact." Ok, this was a bombshell! I was still shaking my head, thinking that I was sure I would remember something like that, when it hit me like thunder clapped overhead. I even jumped as if it had actually happened. I knew who they were...My God... could it really be?

"Sophia and Zagan!" I shouted making the bed vibrate.

"You are such a clever girl." Was Draven's only response before without warning my head hit the pillow and I quickly fell into a misty sleep hearing the last words from Draven's lips drift through my mind...

"Time for sleep, my princess."

CHAPTER FIFTY-NINE

MAKING PLANS

I woke up to hear Draven's voice and when I heard no reply, I knew he was on the phone. I was in his bed as I was before, and it felt a bit like Groundhog Day. I seemed to have had an entire night of waking from a series of dreams and I didn't know what to expect from one waking to the next.

I remembered my first dream and quickly shook it away as it included one face I never wished to see again! Then the next one came, and I savoured it for a while, even recalling the smell of the Persian sun on Draven's skin. I remembered his kiss and his strong desperate touch. It made my insides go gooey.

I rolled over and smiled into the pillow as I stretched out like a lazy pet. It was strange, as though all the pain I had endured was as if it had happened to somebody else and I had been the one looking down, watching it all. I knew what had happened alright but the pain...I'm sure it had been intense but it's hard to even compare it to anything when I had no memory of it to find. But I wasn't stupid as I knew something like that could leave more than just visible scars.

"Yes, I will tell her, no she's waking up now...alright Libby. Not to worry...Goodbye." I rolled around and was surprised to find Draven stood next to the bed staring down at me. From his voice it had sounded as though he was on the other side of the room. Well, certainly not anymore!

"Good morning," I said smiling and stretching once again until my toes curled.

"Well technically, it's the afternoon," he said smiling back.

"Draven! You let me sleep too late, I missed classes!" I sat up and realized I was now naked, as the covers rolled off me and rested around my waist. Draven's eyes flash purple once and then simmered down.

"Keira my dear, I hardly think today was going to be one of those days when you went to class!" He sounded exasperated at the idea.

"Why not?"

"You need rest, not a history lesson." He lifted the covers to my shoulders like a mother hen and I rolled my eyes.

"You gave me a history class this morning if I remember," I said teasingly causing him to be the one to roll his eyes.

"That was to help you sleep, so don't make me regret it. Besides, all you have been through lately, you need taking care of with some peace and quiet. Therefore, that is what you shall receive." He sounded happy on the matter, which had me worried. Dear God, what did he have planned...knitting and sounds of the ocean on repeat?

"I'm fi..." I stopped when he tilted his head and frowned at the word I was about to use.

"...I'm all good. I don't feel tired and I feel all fit and healthy." He wasn't looking convinced, so I tried a different route.

"I gather Libs rang and wanted to know where I was?"

"No, I rang her," he said before leaving the bedside to get me some water.

"Why?" I asked without leaving the concern out of my voice.

"Drink," he ordered and I gave up trying, so did as I was told. He wouldn't even let me hold the bloody glass!

"I rang her to explain why you left." He saw my face drop and hurried out the next bit.

"Don't worry, obviously I didn't tell her the truth. No, I merely said how you came to me in the night to give me what for and we quickly made up after that. I think she got the message. I also told her how we needed to spend some quality time together and that I was taking you away to make up for my behaviour." This was said very offhand, like the fact he was telling people I was going on a trip, when I clearly wasn't, was something normal. Well, I guess to him it was.

"Uhh...why did you do that? We both know I'm not going anywhere, well apart from home in a week's time but..." he cut me off by banging the glass down on the side table.

"Keira! Of course, I'm taking you away!" He was angry now and if this was his idea of peace and quiet then Hell must be a quiet place to live!

"Draven, listen to me when I say this...I am not leaving!" I said folding my arms across my chest like a child. He huffed and raised his arms above his head in a dramatic fashion.

"Stubborn like a mule!" he said angrily. Of course, I laughed which really didn't help the situation.

"Are you calling me an Ass?" He stopped and looked at me to find humour in that question.

"NO! Look Keira, I need to protect you. I cannot have that happen again. So you will just have to trust me and do as I say." Ok, that was so not happening!

"Draven, I will agree to stay here with you every night but I will not hide away from my life and I'm sorry, but you can't stop me." He was nearly vibrating at this point, with his fists held tight to his sides as if trying to regain just a shred of control. He looked damn close to shaking me!

"Why won't you listen to me, do you think I do this for my own gain? My only care is to keep you safe and if, as you say, keeping you locked in a tower achieves this then I will damn well do it, you can be sure of it!" Draven was trying to push me to the point of me agreeing but my will on this matter was beyond yielding.

"We both know that will not happen," I said calmly before continuing,

"Think what you are saying. I am not your prisoner and you

would never treat me so. I know you too well and I would bet my life on it."

"Not funny, Keira." Ok, so saying about betting my life was probably not the best way to put it but it was not intended to be funny.

"Look, I am not saying that I am about to do anything stupid. I know I still need Ragnar guarding me and I know never to spend a night away from you, not that I would want to anyway, but you have to meet me halfway."

"And where would this halfway be exactly, because no matter what I seem to do it is never enough!" At this point I really did feel sorry for him, he clearly was fighting a losing battle and with no glory in sight.

"Well, I guess halfway would be that we now know Lucius can't get in my defected mind! So glass half full on that one." I tried to joke but Draven was so not in the mood for Northern humour.

"Defected?" Trust him to pick up on my terminology.

"Well, yeah, there must be something wrong with my head...right?" At this he groaned and came to my side to grab both my hands in his.

"Keira, there is nothing wrong with your head!"

"Well, there must be something because according to you and your brother I am the only Being on earth that Lucius can't control." This statement sure got his attention.

"You heard that?"

"Umm, well yeah, but at first I thought I was dreaming, but now I know it must have been right after...the healing." I said this last part cautiously, not wanting to bring up what was obviously a painful memory for him. As expected, he winced at the flashback.

"To be honest, Keira, if you're expecting answers as to why, then I am afraid I don't have any for you. We both know you are different, but just how different is still left to be discovered." Oh great, so I was a freak without knowing why...bloody marvellous!

"Well, as long as I don't start shooting webs from my hands and glowing in the dark, I think we can class the inability of not being controlled as a plus." At this he finally laughed making my tensed shoulders relax at the sound.

"Maybe we should get you a stretchy spandex suit to wear if you are going to be a comic book superhero, that way I get to peel it off you." He winked at me and wore a crooked smile as his naughty thoughts came out to play. Now, I was laughing, and I playfully punched him.

"So, do we have an understanding on the whole me leaving thing?" His playfulness quickly diminished and was replaced by yet another broody frown.

"How do you expect me to protect you if you...?"

"Draven, please stop. We can take precautions, but I will not live a life of fear because of what might happen again. I am going home in a week and until then I have a mountain of course work to worry about...so near-death experiences are not even in the equation at the moment." I laughed again trying to lighten the mood but his was getting darker with every word out of my mouth. He didn't look at all happy but must have decided now was not the time to try and reason with me.

The rest of the day went by in blissful ignorance of last night's events and we were both happy to put it behind us and for the first time since knowing Draven, this was one night that the VIP went without its King. We spent the whole day and night hidden away in his room like we were a pair of love-struck teenagers. No one came, not even Vincent or Sophia, so I guessed this was at his orders.

Well, if that was the case then this was one order I was more than happy to comply with! Of course, the fact that I was a human with basic needs didn't go amiss as every time I returned from the bathroom there were drinks and a wide array of food waiting for me. It turned out to be one of the best days of my life and when the night crept in like an unwanted visitor, I found myself not wanting it to ever end.

"You know if you came away with me it could be like this

every day," he hummed in my ear as I leant against him on the couch. I sighed as the thought took me to my very own idea of Heaven, but I knew it was a false promise. Not that Draven wasn't a man of his word but for someone who controlled a world full of supernatural beings, I doubted this promise could be achieved for long. But I smiled at his tactics anyway without answering him the way I would have liked.

All throughout the day I hadn't been successful in getting him to take his kisses further, thanks to his belief that my body need time to relax and sex with Draven was definitely anything but relaxing... mind-blowing, orgasmic and truly breath-taking yes, but relaxing...uh that would be a no!

If you asked me, I think he was enjoying all my efforts more than he was letting on. I felt like some bloody leech trying to suck the life out of him! But alas, every time it started to get serious and I could feel him getting worked up...and I mean all the way up...he would groan and restrain me back so that he could regain his granite-like will. I was starting to feel like a sledgehammer going at it without even causing a dent.

When he convinced me it was time we got some sleep I told him to go lie down and I would be with him after I used the bathroom. Once there I brushed my hair until soft and falling in smooth waves down my back. I brushed my teeth until squeaky clean and minty fresh. I had already had a shower earlier that day and shaved my legs. This was embarrassingly under Draven's watchful eye. Especially more so when I nicked myself and Draven overreacted as if I'd slashed open a vein!

I checked myself in the mirror one last time and tied my kimono a little looser so that my cleavage was showing thanks to a black lacy pushup bra. I was also wearing a thong to match which made me walk a little funny back to the bed. Well, my seduction idea wasn't going to happen until I was on the bed, so it didn't matter if I was walking a little sideways.

As soon as he saw me coming, I smiled to myself as he turned his head to the other side. Oh, this was going to be so easy! I stepped up to the side and walked on the bed so that I was stood above him. I got a great view from up here, although I would have preferred a naked Draven to be below me.

He was still wearing a tight black vest showing off his perfectly sculpted arms that could crush every bone in my body. His long solid legs were encased in light coloured denim topped with a thick leather belt. This had a thick metal belt buckle with an Arabic symbol for "Strength" crudely hammered in the centre. I had asked him about it earlier and he explained it had been a gift from his brother.

It was a hard thing to imagine...Draven unwrapping gifts, as it was such a human thing to do. I had told him my thoughts, to which I had only received a shrug of the shoulders as my response.

He finally raised his eyes to me, and I saw his face tense as he held onto his last shreds of will. I smiled making it even harder for him.

"Come down here!" he forced out through gritted teeth. So, instead of sidestepping and joining him on one side, I simply fell to my knees and landed so that our sexes were knitted together. He groaned as the impact caused a reaction he was hoping to avoid. The silk robe fell from one shoulder and exposed one lace-covered breast that looked as though it would like nothing more than to pop out and be played with.

"What's wrong, Draven?" I asked as innocent as a child with their hand caught in the cookie jar. I let my hair fall forward and at this his eyes flashed purple. I knew that I had him!

He growled and grabbed the tie of my robe to use it to aid his control. He gripped it tight and pulled me until my lips met his. This action ignited the fire deep within my belly that was bubbling up and I tensed my body around him to get closer to the bulge that pressed painfully against his jeans. His hands pulled my hair up and twisted it to control my head.

I almost came right then! I, in turn, bit his lip causing his own fire to erupt to a new level. He spun me quickly and ripped the kimono from me in a brutal attack. I felt the seams unravel at every point and it made for the sexiest of sounds. I soon found myself to be a milky white body covered only in thin lace, quivering beneath him.

"You are an unstoppable Vixen that teases a man's will until it is destroyed at your feet. What have you to say in your defence?" He teased in a husky voice making me blush and beam at his compliment. He buried his head in my hair and inhaled me in as if stealing my essence.

"What can I say...I'm a girl with needs that only you can satisfy." This made him smile before he crushed his lips to mine and kissed me solidly while he took me from below. I ended up having all my orgasms screaming in his mouth, every time feeling him smile over my quivering lips.

At my last one he found his release as I bit into his shoulder not being able to control, understand or help myself. He arched back as one last thrust pounded into me as we came together. I could barely hear my own scream over his deep animal roar at the ceiling. It was as if I had just been ravished by a wild beast and now he was calling his pleasure to the moon.

Well, one thing I was wrong about, sex sure could be relaxing...well, that was the aftermath of six orgasms! I collapsed in a sticky mess of sweat dripping down every curve of my body and buried my head in his side under his arm. He held me closer to him and we both found sleep this way without uttering another word. A word that wasn't needed to end this perfect day.

The following week was a complete rat race. I spent every free minute doing an endless amount of studying for finals and handing in papers just barely before deadlines. Draven had kindly given me the week off work to make the time. The perks of dating your boss! Of course, nobody working there complained as Draven gave everyone a huge Christmas bonus for the first time.

I wouldn't accept mine, which was no surprise to Draven, although when checking my account there was a considerable amount greater there than there should have been. However, when I queried it, Draven simply shrugged his shoulders and played dumb, which we both knew he most certainly wasn't!

Mike seemed happy with the extra money over the holiday

season and could now afford to go skiing with his family for Christmas instead of letting his parent's fork out for it. He was such a good guy anyone else would have let his family pay and bought themselves a new snowboard. Okay, so I knew quite a lot of people here that wouldn't have done that, but you know what I mean.

No-one working at Afterlife really had anything to complain about as the wages Draven paid were the best around and people usually tipped the bar well. Of course, everyone put the new bonuses down to me and no one believed me when I said that I had nothing to do with it.

"I think keeping the boss this happy helps, Kaz," Mike had replied with a sly grin that forced me to flick water in his face after washing my hands.

It was my last shift before I travelled back to England the day after and one night that Draven let me work. It was the Christmas party and Afterlife knew how to hold one heck of a party! The entire place had been decorated in thick rich colours of green, red and gold. Wreaths and holly swags hung from the tall arched windows and doors.

A huge black Christmas tree dominated one corner of the room, which was covered with blood-red ribbon the width of a body cascading down to the floor. Massive gold baubles, the size of melons were decorated with the same blood-red drips in glossy paint.

There were also thousands of red twinkling fairy lights not only covering the tree but the whole club. It was like a gothic Christmas fairyland had replaced the usual Afterlife and I knew straight away one girl who was responsible for the transformation... none other than the sensational Sophia!

The first drinks of the night were on the house and at one point of the night the lights dimmed, and the music stopped for everyone to raise their glasses to the VIP and to a man they could barely see to thank. I wore a proud but hidden smile the rest of the night.

The night carried on in full swing and when my shift was over, I joined my friends in the party. We all danced in a group and I even let down my hair to whip around as the mixture of rock classics and dance music gripped me enough to dance until sweating. All my friends knew I was leaving for the holidays as a few of them were doing the same.

"So is Dreamy Draven going back with you for the holidays?" RJ asked me when we were both in the ladies trying to cool ourselves after our workout on the dance floor. I had been told not to tell anyone the plan me, Draven and his siblings had constructed, so I didn't know how to answer this one without lying. In the end I didn't need to as Lanie came in with streaming mascara down her face.

She was in floods of tears and between sobs told us how Drew had just broke up with her. I spent the next half hour rubbing her back and scowling at RJ every time she tactlessly mentioned how she was going to rip his head off! This just made Lanie give way to fresh new tears.

In the end Draven must have been worried at not seeing me in the club because he walked through the door in the body of a nineteen-year-old cyber Goth with electric blue and fuchsia pink hair. I only knew it was Draven when her eyes flashed purple and she winked at me. I tried so hard not to laugh at the situation but failed miserably. Both my friends shot me a shocked look at my tactless behaviour.

"Umm...sorry...I guess I don't handle crying in the right way," I said lamely whilst giving Draven evils as his female host left the bathroom.

"You've been doing fine up until now," RJ commented under her breath.

It only took us another ten minutes to clean Lanie up and convince her that Drew was a moron and therefore not worth her tears. It hadn't really worked as she was still sniffling, but it did get us out of the loo. After that things started to wind down and I soon found myself being crushed by Jack's embrace. I could almost hear Draven's growl in my head as no doubt he was watching.

After saying goodbye to all my friends in turn I decided to go and help Mike with the bar close down. I was acting on autopilot as my thoughts wandered to tomorrow. I had already packed that day and my black case with a smiley sticker on the side lay on my bed ready for the last few items before zipping it up and heading home for Christmas.

We had planned for Draven to follow shortly afterwards in his private jet but Ragnar was to guard me on the actual flight. At first Draven had wanted me to fly with him but I knew my mum would have been upset to know that the expensive ticket home wasn't going to get used.

Draven had wanted to keep my departure date a secret, with only my family and his knowing the ins and outs. Ragnar was going to be instructed on the day. He told me this was so no one's mind could betray them. I guess they knew mine wasn't an issue with that problem anymore. It had been a week since the last time I had heard Lucius' voice and my dreams were no longer being controlled or intruded on. It was becoming a distant memory, one Draven was happy for me to forget.

Draven had gone as far as not making any plans for England and I had told my family that as far as I knew his work was keeping him in the US for the holidays. My mum thought it a shame but was just happy to have us all home for Christmas, so she didn't make a big deal out of it. I was just glad to be turning my back on the past few weeks and hoping to come back to start a fresh new year...nightmare free.

My sister sent Frank up to get my suitcase and after saying a mental goodbye to the view I was going to miss, I met them all downstairs. It was hard to pretend to say goodbye to the waiting Draven at my doorstep. For him it too was hard, as he looked far too vulnerable to be the one in control.

Frank, Libby and Hilary had all wished him a Happy Christmas and said their goodbyes before quickly giving us some space. I walked around the side of the house to gaze at the sweeping valley and snow-covered national park. Draven wrapped his arms around me and pulled me into him for a tight embrace.

"We don't have to do this. You could change your mind and your family will understand after time. I could take you away with me? Anywhere you wish to go and somewhere only you and I know the whereabouts." I had heard these words all week. It was the same pleading voice and another twist on him hiding me away from the world.

"Draven, it will be fine. We have planned it so that nothing could go wrong. Even my family are convinced you won't be meeting me. No-one knows I'm spending Christmas in Liverpool and thinks that I am spending it at my Grandparents' place in Cornwall to be with the rest of my family." At this point he was looking deep into my eyes and caressing the side of my face in his palm. He looked so sad, as if it was the last time he might see me.

"I can't let anyone harm you...I can't let them take you, Keira...it would finish me," he said before burying his head into the top of mine.

"Nothing is going to take me, don't talk like that! Look at me, Draven." He didn't so I turned my head up so he had no choice. His face was riddled with pain and angst, it was the closest I came to giving into him and letting him take me wherever in the world he considered safe.

"We have a plan, you are going to ring Ragnar if there are any problems and he will do the same. If anyone is watching they will just think I am in the car with you and getting on your jet, not getting on a conventional flight with over a hundred other humans where they can do nothing. If anything, I am worried about Ragnar!" He grunted at this.

"No human eyes apart from yours can see him," he said, although I already knew this.

"I know, but that's not what worries me. I am just wondering how he is going to get his huge body into one of those tiny seats." At this he finally eased up and laughed.

We remained entwined until Draven loosened his hold and reluctantly said,

"It's time, they are waiting," at which point I found I really wasn't ready to let go. I turned into him and held him around the waist, making him wrap his arms around my body as though he could protect me from anything the Earth held against us. I knew this was silly of us both acting like this, as I knew he would be with me only hours after I landed but I couldn't help feeling the little nagging at the back of my mind...what if something did go wrong?

"Honey, sorry, but we're gonna have to leave now before we hit traffic." Libby's head popped around the corner and looked guilty as Hell for dragging me away. I just nodded in a sullen way before looking up to find Draven looking far off towards the mountains, as if this was where he would have liked to have hidden me. Well, it was too late now, I thought with a touch of regret. I looked back and saw Libby had gone to wait in the car and Frank had the engine started already to warm up. Another hint for me to hurry up, I thought bitterly.

"Ragnar will follow you in the black Range Rover behind and once you're at the airport he will board the plane. My jet won't be far behind and I should be knocking on your door tomorrow around noon, but Ragnar won't let you out of his sight until then." He had gone through this over and over but I just nodded as though it was the first time. I knew poor Ragnar wouldn't dare let me even go to the bathroom without guarding the door, not if his life depended on it!

"Ok...Hey, don't look so worried or is it the idea of meeting my parents for the first time that worries you?" I joked and it looked as though it took all the effort in the world for him to smile.

"You forget... if they don't like me I can just alter their minds so they think I'm the only man around they want dating their beautiful daughter." He winked and now I was laughing, just glad we were saying goodbye on a high note.

"I will miss you," I said reaching up to kiss him. He bent his head down and kissed me with all the passion of a love-starved man. I locked my arms around his neck and kissed him back with equal starvation. A shiver shot down my back when it ended as the nagging feeling sunk deeper to my core and I knew why.

It felt like...

A last kiss.

CHAPTER SIXTY

TARNISHED PERFECTION

B efore I knew it, I had waved goodbye to the owner of my heart and left feeling slightly empty inside. The nagging feeling was beginning to grow the further the car took me from Draven. I kept giving myself a mental shake, saying it was only for a day, two at the most. Everyone else around me was buzzing with excitement and even had Christmas songs playing through the car's stereo.

I found myself just moving my lips, trying to act as if I felt the same excitement but one look from Libby in the mirror and I knew I wasn't fooling anyone. Libby had felt for me when I told her that Draven couldn't join us for the holiday season. I then had felt even guiltier lying about it and receiving undeserved sympathy. But like Draven had said, it was for everyone's own good.

They had discovered that someone must be leaking information from somewhere inside the VIP and Draven suspected it was one of the new guests, as Lucius came to me not long after they had arrived. As far as Draven knew, this was his first encounter. I had tried in vain to tell him it wasn't, but I was met with the same problem as usual. Every time I opened my mouth to speak, I found blank words behind my lips. It was as though I was cast with some spell that wouldn't let me form the words, so as a result Draven left thinking this was the first incident.

One thing became clear though, whoever had made that phone call to Libby pretending to be Draven was surely the traitor. It didn't take me long to find out that Draven had never needed time alone and he was only waiting for me to forgive him.

I soon spotted the black four-wheel drive, two cars back and I felt my shoulders relax knowing my Viking beast of a Demon was back there keeping his guardian eyes on me. It was strange to think that it wasn't long ago that I had hated the idea of being 'guarded', but now I seemed to be relying on it for comfort. I was putting it down to all the bad things that had happened since.

Once at the airport, I had to play blind and dumb, not reacting to Ragnar right next to me, clung like a bodyguard to a celebrity. It was only when we reached the checkout desk when things started to get complicated.

"What do you mean, it's the wrong date?" I said staring at the lady in a smart red and navy airline suit.

"I am afraid this ticket is for the day after tomorrow," she said trying to be pleasant in telling someone their horrible news for the day.

"That can't be right," Libby said coming to my side. She grabbed the ticket from the lady whose name tag read 'Jean is happy to help'. Well, I didn't really care for the happy part, but the help was surely needed!

"I am afraid you booked the tickets for a separate day." Well, that sure wasn't helpful and I had to stop myself from saying, 'Well, no shit Sherlock!'

"Our mother booked the tickets...Oh No, look Kaz she did as well!" Horror filled my sister's eyes as she scanned the ticket over and over before letting me see the evidence for myself. She was damn right! My mother had only gone and booked my ticket for a different day!

"Well, can't we buy another ticket?" Libby and I both asked at the same time.

"Uh, I'm sorry, but that flight is fully booked, and the flight will be boarding soon, so those of you with tickets will have to hurry to the right departure gate." I felt sorry for 'Jean' at this point because Libby turned to scowl at her. I had to drag Libby over to where Frank and Hilary waited for us with anxious faces.

"Mum went and booked Kazzy on the wrong bloody date!" Libby screeched to Frank.

"Can't she swap the dates?" Frank added unhelpfully, bless him.

"I don't think it works like that Frank, the flight is fully booked," I said as Libby was muttering about our mother's incapability to use computers and all modern technology in general, while also blaming herself for not checking each ticket.

"Look it will be fine, I will just call Dominic and get him to pick me up and then fly out to you guys in two days...problem solved." Well, at least it seemed so for them but now I was wondering how this affected Draven's plans? Once I got these guys on their way, I could find a quiet place and ask Ragnar, who was still at my side frowning at our current situation.

"I can't let you fly out on your own!" Libby said, but Frank was nervously looking at his watch and the flight numbers on the checking board.

"Libs, I flew out here on my own remember? Look, if you guys don't go, you will miss the flight...is the spare key still hidden in that old jar in the shed?" Frank nodded before pulling me in for a hug.

"We will see you in a few days," he said making Libby curse under her breath.

"Libs, it will be fine, don't be too hard on mum and give everyone my love until I get there." I hugged her even though I could tell her mind was still running through every possibility. I hugged Hilary and waved them off until out of sight, watching my sister being pulled through security with Frank's strong arm around her shoulders. She looked like a lost sheep amongst the cattle of travellers.

"Well, what are we going to do now?" I said in a low whisper, trying not to gain too much attention, but when a passer-by stopped and stared I decided to get out my phone and pretend to be talking to someone on it.

"I will call my Lord, come with me." Ragnar held onto my arm and we walked through the crowded airport until we were outside one of the main terminals. It was still far too crowded to go unnoticed, but no-one could hear Ragnar let alone see him, so it was only me being paranoid for no good reason. He dug in his dark tan jacket and pulled out a phone that looked tiny in his hands. He pressed one button and began talking immediately.

"The mother made the mistake," he added after explaining our new situation. I wished I could hear the other side of this conversation, because Ragnar's head bobbing wasn't easing my irritation.

"Yes, I will. No, the car left after we did. I cannot detect any of our kind nearby. We will wait for the car and I will bring her back to Afterlife directly...Yes, my Lord, as always with my life," he said and passed the phone down to me, which must have looked mighty strange for anyone walking past, me taking a phone from thin air!

"Hi," I said very forlorn.

"Keira, are you alright?" Draven sounded concerned and hyped up as if he had been waiting phone in hand, ready for something to go wrong.

"Yeah, I'm fine, so what will happen now?" I asked, trying to sound a little less 'end of the world'.

"I am sending a car to pick you up and then we will decide when you get here. It will be alright, Keira, soon you will be safely in my arms once again." The thought made me smile and the nagging feeling I had all day seemed to evaporate.

"Good, I will see you soon then." I was about to hand it back when I heard Draven's words fill me to the core.

"Keira, I love you." I smiled and although he couldn't see me, I think he heard it in my reply.

"And I love you."

Ragnar had arranged for us to be picked up in a quieter part of the Airport, when his phone rang.

"My Lord?" He seemed surprised but nodded again and again as new orders were being given. Meanwhile, I was sat on my suitcase like a bored child.

"You want us to get to the jet?" Ragnar looked surprised, which brought my nagging fear rushing back to me in a heartbeat. He nodded a few more times and muttered acknowledgements down the phone, but his frown never left his harsh red face. The little potted scars seemed to stand out further when he looked this agitated and it automatically made me wonder what had gone wrong.

"But my Lord, that is not what we had planned...the girl she..." Ragnar shut up immediately once I heard shouting from the other end and we both flinched simultaneously.

"No, My Lord, I am sorry to question you... No, it will not happen again," he said after obviously being reprimanded, but still his frown remained. It was quite clear whatever Draven's changes, Ragnar did not approve.

"Yes, I will take her there now, you will meet us?" He waited for his answer and then nodded. Once he had received his new orders he snapped the phone shut and looked down at me with his dark red eyebrows closely knitted together and emitted a low growl.

"What is it...what's wrong?" I asked placing my hand on his arm, which felt a bit like comforting a tree trunk against the rain.

"My Lord wants me to take you to the hanger where one of his jets is being fuelled," he said looking around the airport as if he was scanning for enemies.

"But I thought it was only a minute ago he was sending a car for us?"

"It was, but now he has decided to change his plans." His usual husky voice had an uncertain edge to it that I needed to question.

"And you're not happy?" It was an obvious question.

"No, I don't like it because it is not like my Lord to be so unpredictable, but his word is law, so I do not question it. We have to move," he said, taking my suitcase in one hand and me in the other.

That was the end of our conversation, but I felt his tension flow through me like it was sticking to my skin in the form of a nervous sweat. I found myself being pulled along until Ragnar found what he was looking for. The next thing I knew I was being pulled into a taxi and sitting back while Ragnar took over the driver's mind. He sat back with a faded expression on his face as though he was listening to bird calls in the distance. It almost made me want to shake him, but I wouldn't have dared. So, I did all I could do...

I sat there and worried.

I had no idea how we got there but the one lot of security we did encounter, after a few words from the driver we passed without trouble. Soon we were driving towards a big aircraft hangar where the doors were opening to allow for the sleek black jet rolling out. That's when the brakes slammed on and thrust me forward, hitting into the back of the front seat. I made a noise as the air had been knocked out of me, but before I had time to complain, Ragnar had released his hold over the driver and forced him into a deep sleep.

"Something's wrong!" he said, in the worst tone to hear from a former Viking King and that was panic!

"Why?" I was almost too scared to ask but I gripped onto his arm as I waited for an answer, I was sure I didn't want to know. He was staring at the Jet as though he was waiting for it to blow up or something and when I jerked him for a response, he turned to stare at me so slowly I felt my skin prickle with fear.

"The King's jet is white." These were the last words I heard before all Hell broke loose.

I didn't even have time to scream as the car suddenly filled with a blinding light, as though someone had just released a flash bomb inside. I couldn't see a thing, but when the car's metal frame around us started to shake, I heard all the glass shattering outwards.

Ragnar's roar soon became a distant noise as an ear-splitting, high pitched hum filled the small space and made it near impossible to think of anything other than covering my ears and closing my eyes. It was only when I felt the cold air being inhaled, did I realize that it was so I could carry on screaming through the fog of disaster.

Then, far too quickly I felt myself being moved. First, I heard the rest of the window crash as the door was being opened on my side and then hands were on me dragging me from the car. I still couldn't see, and my hearing was playing on and off, as though someone was flipping a switch. The hands gripped onto my shoulders and yanked until my body slid out onto the tarmac, landing on my back with a painful thud. I was so scared I was shaking but I was trying desperately to hold on to whatever shred of emotional control I had left.

"KEIRA, RUN!" I heard Ragnar's thundering voice shouting through the craziness, but for me there was no going anywhere. Once I had fallen, I was quickly pulled roughly to my feet and held on either side by men towering above me. My eyes were still in blur mode, but I could just make out their shadows looming so close to me, holding onto me at the tops of my arms. I tried to squirm away, but it became too painful when their fingertips started to dig into my flesh, as if they were pointed at the ends.

"Enough!" A man's voice shouted without anger but held enough of an authoritative note to be obeyed. This was when my sight cleared, as though water had just been splashed in my eyes and my hearing was no longer consumed by the high-pitched hum that was causing my head to hurt. Of course, although all my senses were back, it only brought a new level to our dire situation into perspective.

Ragnar was fighting off a large group of men, all going at him from every angle. It also looked as though he had grown twice his size and all the figures around him looked like they could barely touch him. Ragnar was unstoppable and my hopes rose at the sight of three men being flung backwards like bowling pins.

Two behind him were approaching him with thick iron chains and I almost laughed at the idea of them holding this Viking beast captive. They sidestepped in sync and then ran for him at an incredible speed, but for the size of my giant protector, he was as swift as a hawk and as nimble as a jungle cat.

He spun on his heel and met them head-on. He quickly grabbed the chains before they hit him, and he wrapped them around his trunk arms a few times to get a grip. He began to run backwards, taking the two men with him, then whipped the chains out to the sides and back causing the two men to collide with each other in the middle, knocking them out with the force.

I almost started shouting in encouragement at the sight of him beating them down, but when the ones who had hold of me started to drag me backwards, my shouts turned into ones of desperation instead. Ragnar stopped after grabbing one by the neck and breaking it with one distinct snap.

"LET THE GIRL GO OR DIE!" Ragnar roared in his Demon voice, which sounded as though it could command Hell itself!

Meanwhile, the man whose voice shouted 'Enough' was making himself known as he emerged from the black Jet. Ragnar took one look at me before seeing him coming down the plane's steps...then his face crumpled in confusing defeat. I couldn't understand, he was just one man, but one thing I was sure of Ragnar definitely knew this man.

Everyone froze as if God himself had just popped down to state his claim in this, but considering I didn't know who he was, I was going to use this opportunity to run like Hell! I used my body weight to aid me and let my legs drop and then pushed back with all my strength. It wasn't a lot, but it was enough to take them off guard.

They lost their grip on me and I made my legs power forward over to Ragnar, thinking behind him would be my only hope at surviving this. The men behind me cursed, as they ran towards me, but I remained out of reach, and seeing what the other men had endured, they stopped before Ragnar was within reach to do the same to them.

He saw me coming and growled out at the men behind me in a warning they didn't need. He scooped me up with both arms and held me back like I was a frightened child he needed to prevent from witnessing this.

"Ragnar, the Viking King. It has been a long time since I have seen you. And now it seems you have a new charge to take care of. This is unfortunate, as now I will have to take her from you...unless you are willing to stand down." He was a tall thin man with silvery-white hair and had a handsome face with sharp features. A long, straight nose and a point to his chin made his high cheekbones seem all the higher. He didn't look like your typical bad guy, all dressed in a tailored beige suit and red tie...he even carried a briefcase for heaven's sake! Was he here to kidnap me or make me a business deal in buying real-estate?

"Carrick! Doing errands for Vampires now...? I would have thought that beneath you, Soul Collector?" Ragnar sneered and let me slide down to the ground. He moved to hold me back with one arm, hiding the rest of me with his colossal frame. I could see his muscular back tensed and ready for another fight, although something told me this next one he wouldn't find so easy.

There was something in Ragnar's voice that told me as much, like a respect he had to give this man and I knew he must be a big player in the Supernatural world. At Ragnar's words, he cocked his head to one side amused for a moment.

"It is not your concern why, but the will is. Hand the girl over to me and not only will I give you my word that she will not be harmed, but you too will walk away with your life...Although, I cannot vouch for your Master's wrath on the matter. I hear he is quite fond of this little human." He seemed intrigued with me as I arched my head round to see him at my mention.

"She is the 'Electus'!" Ragnar said and if he hoped to shock him into submission he failed. All he got was one raised white eyebrow.

"Is she now...? Ah, well that explains the circumstances, but unfortunately for you my friend, it does not change them. I am neutral in this fighting prophecy, but when commissioned I always fulfil my contract." Ragnar growled in response and pulled me further back behind him as his answer.

"The girl is still mine and I grow weary of discussing it with one of Dominic's servants, so I ask only once more...hand her over or face the consequences!" This Carrick said with a venomous bite, but Ragnar stood his ground. He widened his stance and braced himself for what looked to be his death.

"Ragnar, don't," I whispered, placing my hand on his arm, but he glared down at me and shook his head once.

"I have sworn to protect her with my life, and I am a man of my word!" he barked back, making Carrick roll his eyes as though bored.

"Very well Viking, then let your life be the price you pay for your loyalty. I hope you die with dignity, old soul, for it will not be lacking in courage." He said these words like a prayer, and they held respect, which I found surprising, considering he was the one that was going to take this life.

I made the decision that if I was going to be any help to him, I was going to have to really see what was going on. So, with this in mind I did something I rarely do...I dropped my guard and let the other sight take hold. I closed my eyes tight for seconds, until I was sure I had freed my gift, like letting loose the evil side of me.

I opened my eyes and the first thing I saw was Ragnar in his Demon form and seeing that this was the first for me, I couldn't stop my reaction. He knew in an instant what I had done.

He turned to look at me and I also couldn't help the frightened gasp that escaped. His face had no skin, just a fleshless bone skull with tiny holes pierced all over it. It was as though he had been locked in one of those medieval iron maidens that shut a person into a standing coffin full of nails.

His nose was just made of two elongated holes and his mouth was covered in what looked like metal cladding hammered in sections over his jawline to hold it in place. I felt the tears roll down my cheeks, as I looked into the hollows where his eyes had turned into small white dots. They sat in the middle of a dark mist that was flowing freely from his body. It could only be described as his energy that was making his body pulsate with anger.

I automatically stood back and saw two twisted horns break through his clothes and curl up around his exposed skull like a helmet. They had combined at the front, once they covered his face and met down at his chin to interlock like a bone beard. Now, to look at him, there was only twisted horn coming from either side of his exposed bloody spine to protect his entire head.

I kept taking steps back to give his growing body room, as his pulsating had reached its height. He then stood ready for the war against us. Ragnar was now the size of a Transit van, making me look like a toddler. Carrick's men pulled together and were ready to hit Ragnar with his first wave, but Carrick's hand went up to stop them. Maybe the sight of Ragnar looking like a Demon tank was enough to make him change his mind.

I soon received my answer.

The skies started to grow dark, like a storm was quickly taking hold and I felt an icy chill seep through every layer of my clothing. The clouds looked angry with us all, as they moved at such speeds. I could barely believe what my eyes were seeing. Clouds never moved like that, not even in a hurricane! Who was this man who could command the skies? There was only one man I knew with that kind of power...Draven.

"All in vain, Viking!" Carrick shouted shaking his head, causing me to really look at him for the first time. He was no longer a man but had now turned into Death itself!

That was the only way to describe him, he was Death! His suit had faded to a dark cloak that cut off at his chest. The hood was raised, hiding his face under a black plastic-looking material...or was it skin? It stretched across powerful, large shoulders and floated down stronger looking arms. This was different, as the man before was tall and of a slim build but not now...no, now he too was a warrior of a very different sort!

All of this was caught in a blink, compared to what my eyes were now fixated on. His torso was only half muscle and flesh, as it had been stripped away on most of his ribcage. There was left bloody ribs that encased a light glow behind, as if his own energy source was being protected by bone.

As I raked my sight further down, I saw that his waist didn't exist and only his dripping spine was holding him upright. The start of his pelvis was also on show, but then his cloak returned and flowed as though alive around the rest of his body. Literally, it looked as though a cloaked figure had had a section of his body removed and we were all looking at the result of only a remaining skeleton. If I thought Ragnar was frightening, then this guy took first prize for that award alright!

The Soul Collector, as Ragnar had called him, still had hold of his briefcase and this also had changed. Now he held a case which looked as though someone had filled it with blood, set the edges alight and dipped it in black tar. This was now being held back and made ready to throw.

It flew through the air and landed in between the two Demons that were ready for the fight. But I was wrong as there was no epic fight about to take place but only a sickeningly easy defeat. Ragnar didn't have a chance and the way his body reacted, told me this. He was actually moving backwards, away from the open black case.

At first, I couldn't see why, but once I stepped to the side, I saw the black wave coming towards him, like a black ocean coming crashing to the shore.

"Get back!" he ordered me in a Demonic voice that was so guttural it was all throat and no mouth! I stepped back again and again, not wanting to make any sudden movements, like sprinting into a run. As the wave got closer, I saw it wasn't mist or water. And it was no element of the Earth coming to claim us. No, this was made of the black souls that hadn't walked the Earth for only Carrick knew how many years.

They were scrabbling towards us like insects clawing their way across the space. It was as though, after centuries of being trapped, they had forgotten how to walk, talk or what it was to be human. Twisted, broken bodies barely made from anything but dust and fears, came closer to Ragnar. Black soulless eyes ringed with either a crystal blue or a deadly blood red-shifted around, searching out their prey. Their long thin bodies were within arm's reach, when they sniffed the air surrounding Ragnar and then they suddenly began to change and shift into other forms.

I screamed in vain, as I realised what forms they had chosen to torture my guardian and friend. It was his greatest fear... his only fear and now it was here to claim him, like his past had come back to once again finish the job!

Every black soul had turned into twenty snakes, each causing hundreds to go slithering up Ragnar's body, infesting themselves over every inch of him. He threw his head back and roared to the sky in his pain before falling to his knees in defeat. He curled up after a few pointless attempts at getting free, but soon the horrors of his past had him writhing around the ground in an unspeakable pain.

They had consumed him under their onslaught, and we had lost the fight.

I screamed over and over until I was out of breath. I ran over to him but as I got near, snakes lashed out at me in warning.

"STOP THIS!" I shouted towards Death himself. I couldn't

even tell if he could hear me or even see me, so I decided to put an end to my sight. It had only helped in seeing something I had absolutely no control over anyway!

I closed my eyes and listened to the chaos around me trying to find some last shred of my world to focus on. Then I heard her. She was calling in the night, flying around in the storm trying to find us.

"AVA!" I screamed out her name and everything went back to normal when I heard her replying call over the wind. I looked at Ragnar who was now back to the Viking I knew, apart from still being on the ground groaning in pain. Carrick had returned into the man in the beige suit and I had run towards him to beg for Ragnar's life.

"Please stop this! You don't have to kill him...Please! I will come with you!" I said sobbing, but still managing to find the words. Carrick cocked his head to look at me with a strange expression.

"You wish to give your life to save a... a Demon?" He was shocked and I gathered that didn't happen very often in his line of work.

"He's my friend and I don't want him to die!" I cried out again, turning around to see him barely moving on the floor and a scream erupted from me at the thought that he might be dead. Meanwhile, Ava came into view, circling above us and she seemed to be mirroring my fears with her own cries.

"How strange...A human girl, friends with the Demon Viking," he mused to himself, while stroking the lower half of his face.

"Very well, a deal is set, come now and save your friend, if you so wish it," he replied and he held out his hand for me to take in his. I cringed at the thought, but when I heard one last plea from Ragnar for me to run, I placed my hand in Death's, knowing Ragnar's fate was left with me. What choice did I have? I could not have him die, just to see me taken anyway. He grasped my shaky hand in his and gently pulled me back towards the plane.

"Come my dear, he will live...ah, but wait." He stopped and let go of my hand to go over to his open briefcase.

"Our deal," he said before uttering words I couldn't hear. Then

Ragnar's body went still and relaxed somewhat, almost as though he was sleeping peacefully. His suitcase closed of its own accord and he leant down to pick it up. He casually brushed the dirt off the leather and said,

"A true workman looks after his tools," and smiled at me, sending fear coursing down my back. He walked back over to me and picked up my hand without uttering another word. Some of the others had got into a white rusty van parked closer to the hanger and four others followed us into the plane.

The next minutes ticked by in a horror-struck blur. I was placed in a comfy, white leather seat next to a window and Carrick sat down opposite. He was quickly given a glass of water by a stewardess as if this was standard procedure. He then nodded towards me and then to the glass on the tray the girl held out to me. I just looked away, without answering. The window shade was up and I saw Ragnar still hadn't moved from his secure, curled foetal position.

"He will be alright, my dear, you saved his Demon soul through a selfless act. You should be happy at least about that," he said like a true businessman who had just received news on high stocks. The plane had begun to move ready to take off on the runway and I realised right up until this point I had been counting on Draven to come and save me. Even now, when my hope was useless and at the end of its thread...I still was expecting him to save me.

"I am being kidnapped so I don't really see the silver lining," I said bitterly, making him laugh.

"But you saved another in doing so. This is a noble act and a rare one at that."

"Are you going to let me go because of it?" I asked devoid of all emotion, but still had hold of a deep fear I was hiding.

"No, my dear, but I will praise you all the same. I am afraid my contract is life binding. No, I am sorry, but it is off to Lucius you must go." At this I finally broke down!

The mention of the very name I loathed, struck in me like a dagger protruding from my heart. It wouldn't let it pump my blood or beat my body into action, it had just stopped. I couldn't breathe for the sobbing flood of raw emotion bubbling up and erupting from me.

This was it!

This was my end...

And Lucius' beginning.

To be Continued...

ABOUT THE AUTHOR

Stephanie Hudson has dreamed of being a writer ever since her obsession with reading books at an early age. What first became a quest to overcome the boundaries set against her in the form of dyslexia has turned into a life's dream. She first started writing in the form of poetry and soon found a taste for horror and romance. Afterlife is her first book in the series of twelve, with the story of Keira and Draven becoming ever more complicated in a world that sets them miles apart.

When not writing, Stephanie enjoys spending time with her loving family and friends, chatting for hours with her biggest fan, her sister Cathy who is utterly obsessed with one gorgeous Dominic Draven. And of course, spending as much time with her supportive partner and personal muse, Blake who is there for her no matter what.

Author's words.

My love and devotion is to all my wonderful fans that keep me going into the wee hours of the night but foremost to my wonderful daughter Ava...who yes, is named after a cool, kick-ass, Demonic bird and my sons, Jack, who is a little hero and Baby Halen, who yes, keeps me up at night but it's okay because he is named after a Guitar legend!

Keep updated with all new release news & more on my website
www.afterlifesaga.com
Never miss out, sign up to the

mailing list at the website.

Also, please feel free to join myself and other Dravenites on my
Facebook group
Afterlife Saga Official Fan
Interact with me and other fans. Can't wait to see you there!

facebook.com/AfterlifeSaga

twitter.com/afterlifesaga

instagram.com/theafterlifesaga

ACKNOWLEDGEMENTS

Firstly, I would like to say huge thanks to all the readers out there that bought Afterlife and especially the ones who took the time to let me know they loved it. You're all brilliant and make my day!

A massive thanks goes to my family and friends for your endless amount of support and for always having faith in me, you really are a force to be reckoned with! I would like to thank my mum for her commitment to seeing that The Two Kings was read the way it always was meant to with her meticulous editing. Also to my sister who not only read the book many times but also made sure The Afterlife Saga looked the way it was always meant to with her fantastic and sexy front covers. They really are my biggest fans and as my sister often says,

"It's easy to Crave the Drave!"

Once again I would also like to thank bands like 30 Seconds to Mars, Shinedown, Foo fighters, Kings of Leon, Coldplay and so many others that helped me write the book of my dreams and inspired every word. If there was a song to listen to in this book it would be 30 Seconds To Mars, called L490 from the album This is War and I would recommend listening to it while reading the Chapter the Temple.

I would also like to mention my best mate in the world who made my school days bearable. To Rhian, what a truly wonderful friend you are and although we are miles apart, we're always right next to each other in our hearts.

I would also like to say a big shout out to my Dad who loves the saga and has remained a constant strength in my life. The other strength in my life is my fiancée Blake, who has made working each day a pleasure I wake up to. The support he gives me and the saga is immeasurable and mirrors my own enthusiasm when giving life to my stories. He is my anchor in the storm that is my imagination and keeps me floating along the waves of discovery.

I love you my rock.

When writing this book I gave birth to my wonderful daughter Ava.

Here is my dedication to my first-born Ava Jessica Hudson.

Flying on a Dream

I hold my breath,
>I take the pain,
>I see what's coming,
>It's the life we gain.

You look oh so beautiful,
>I can't help but cry,
>You're my baby girl,
>Happiness fills me so great, I could fly.

I hold you so close,
>I never want to let go,
>I touch your head,
>And let the love flow.

You are so tiny,
>A little bundle in my arms,
>A hand so small grabs for me,
>And a floodgate breaks the dam.

Now you drift off to sleep,

And I can't help but stare,
I gaze at beautiful blue eyes,
And skin so light and fair.

Dark hair frames an angelic face,
As dark and soft as the raven's wing,
I hold on to you so tightly,
As my heart soars and sings

You're my baby girl,
You're my Ava J,
You're my one and only,
On this forever Day.

I love you baby girl.

ALSO BY STEPHANIE HUDSON

Afterlife Saga

A Brooding King, A Girl running from her past. What happens when the two collide?

Transfusion Saga

What happens when an ordinary human girl comes face to face with the cruel Vampire King who dismissed her seven years ago?

Afterlife Chronicles: (Young Adult Series)

Stephanie Hudson and Blake Hudson

OTHER WORKS FROM HUDSON INDIE INK

Paranormal Romance/Urban Fantasy

Sloane Murphy

Xen Randell

C. L. Monaghan

Sci-fi/Fantasy

Brandon Ellis

Devin Hanson

Crime/Action

Blake Hudson

Mike Gomes

Contemporary Romance

Gemma Weir

Elodie Colt

Ann B. Harrison